# SPRING-HEELED JACK.

# SPRING-HEELED JACK,

## THE TERROR OF LONDON.

By the Author of "TURNPIKE DICK, the Star of the Road."

SPRING-HEELED JACK FINDS THE MURDERED BODY OF HERBERT LEIGH.

No. 1.

# SPRING-HEELED JACK,

## The Terror of London.

### CHAPTER I.

THE MURDER IN THE OLD MINT.

HE night was terrible, for a storm was raging over London. The wind was rushing with wild roars and shrieks along the streets, chimney pots were being hurled down upon the heads of the passers-by. On the river the shipping was being tossed and flung about, so that the vessels crashed against one another, and small boats were crushed into wreckage against the piers. The lightning flashed and the thunder boomed. But the roar of heaven's artillery did not drown the cries which rang out shrilly from a house in Wedge-street in the Mint.

The ominous deadly cries—

"Help!—help! Murder!"

People heard it as they were retiring to rest, and paused and listened and rushed to their windows to open them in spite of the storm. Pedestrians heard it and quickened their pace to a run, the constables heard it and sprung their rattles and dashed off in the direction of the sound.

"Help! murder! help!"

The landlord of the Three Mariners, what with the wind, and the lightning, and the thunder, and the terrible cry, dropped the shutter he was putting up, and nearly knocked over a tall man, wrapped in a long cloak, who had come upon him rapidly round the corner.

"The devil fly away with you for a clumsy brute!" cried the new-comer. "Ah! Simon Webster, is it you? You nearly smashed my toe."

The speaker was a man about forty, with a slouched hat and high riding boots, the rest of his attire being entirely concealed by his large cloak.

What could be seen of his face was dark and sinister, his eyes gleaming like coals of fire, and his black moustache hardly serving to conceal his wide and sensual mouth.

"Ah! is that you, Ned Wilmot?" said Simon. "I did not hear you coming. What with the rain, and the wind, and the thunder and lightning, and those terrible cries of murder, I was nigh dazed."

The man laughed hoarsely.

"Cries of murder in the Mint!" he said. "I should have thought that you'd got used to them. They're common enough here, I should have imagined. But let me enter. I'm wet to the skin, and shall be glad of something hot."

"You're welcome," said Simon, "though I'm not going to keep open long. Ah! there it is again. And see how the people are running—"

But before he could finish what he had to say the man whom he had addressed as Ned Wilmot had dived through the old-fashioned portal of the Three Mariners and entered the public room.

Public or not it was private enough now.

Those who had been seated round the dying fire had deserted it to have a last drink at the bar, and so, unobserved by anyone, the man walked straight to the fire-place and glanced into the dingy glass above it.

One glance and then all was forgotten; storm, and rushing crowds, and constables' rattles, and murder-cries.

All forgotten in the one stare he gave at a great splash on his face—the unmistakable splash of blood!

With a desperate oath he threw back his cloak so that one end resting on his left shoulder showed a well-fitting undercoat of a brownish-tinted cloth, and snatching a white handkerchief from his pocket he swiftly wiped from his features the hideous mark which the rain had kept damp upon them.

Then he flung the fine cambric upon the fire, where the lazy flames licked round it, and, all too slowly for the eager-eyed watcher, devoured it with a rush and a splutter just as Simon Webster entered.

It was as this worthy made his way towards the fire that Ned Wilmot saw that the bundle of papers he had carried in his left hand were splashed with blood also, and he hastily concealed them under his cloak.

"A dismal fire to welcome a traveller in such weather as this, Simon," he said. "Pile on some fuel and let's have some grog. I am frozen to the very marrow."

"It is too late to talk of making up the fire," said Simon, "I must close in a few moments."

"Nay, then, I need some supper and a bed," said Ned, "and what is more, I want a horse in the morning. I have to ride many miles before noon. Don't be surly, Simon, you know I always pay well."

With a kind of grumbling assent the landlord passed out.

Evidently he was in no good humour at the coming of his visitor.

And yet it seemed as if he dared not gainsay him.

Wilmot sat down and placed the tell-tale papers in his pocket.

"Confound that meddling fiend, whoever he may be," he muttered. "I was as nearly caught as a man could be. And that girl too. She saw my face. The Mint will be too warm for me now. What a clatter there is in the street to be sure. One would think none of them had heard a cry of murder here before."

The rush of people was indeed great.

It seemed more than it would have done—

mingled with the patter of rain and the roar of wind.

But it was enough, at any rate, to disconcert Ned Wilmot, and he rose from his seat again, pushed aside the red curtains, and peered out.

As he did so a vivid flash of lightning illumined the street, brightening up every dark and sullen-looking corner.

And for one instant he saw grinning at him a hideous face which was not that of a mortal.

A face with large eyes, with pointed eyebrows sticking out bristlingly, a peaky nose, and wide cavernous mouth.

This was all he could see now.

But he had seen the face and form too within the hour, and, with a cry of horror, he drew back.

Where he had seen it we shall know presently.

"That hideous fiend again," he said, shudderingly, as he drew back towards the fire. "Surely he is not going to haunt me! Death would be preferable to that."

As he spoke Simon Webster re entered with two steaming glasses of grog and some wood and coals to cheer up the fire.

He could not but observe how ghastly pale was the face of his guest.

But his thoughts were quickly diverted into a new channel.

Scarcely had Ned Wilmot drank off at a draught the contents of one of the glasses, when a thundering knock was heard at the door, and a loud, authoritative voice exclaiming—

"Open in the name of the law!"

Ned started up.

A wild, hunted look was upon his face.

"I mustn't be found here," he cried. "I know my way out by the back."

And without a word he rushed past the landlord and fled up the stairs.

In a moment Simon Webster had opened the door, and a number of constables entered.

"Let us come in and close your doors," said the leader of the body of constables. "We are in want of a murderer, and must search the house instantly."

"Come in at once, gentlemen," said Simon. "You may search wherever you please as long as you dont drag my wife out of bed."

He was like most of the inhabitants of the Mint —not very affectionately disposed towards the constables.

But he knew he must keep in favour with them for the sake of his living, and consequently he never placed any obstacles in their way.

The constables soon spread themselves over the house; cellars, bar parlour, bedrooms, all were searched; not excepting that of Mistress Webster, who treated them to some language far less polite than that of her husband; or that of the barmaid and servant, who cowered under the bedclothes to hide their fat little shoulders, but were inwardly laughing at the joke, as could be seen from the merry twinkle of their eyes.

At length, at the rear of the premises, they came upon an open window leading out to the leads.

Running along these a man could easily leave the premises and drop into the street.

"This is where the villain has escaped," cried Joe Bonsor, the head eonstable. "Let us go out and see where he has dropped."

But as he spoke a terrific flash of lightning seemed to rend the heavens, and cast a lurid gleam over the dreary, time-stained buildings at the rear of the Three Mariners, and a clap of thunder boomed forth enough to shake the place to its foundation.

And as they stood awe-stricken in that interval of light they beheld a terrible thing.

Leaping high in the air, springing over the summit of a stack of chimneys, was a form as of Satan, a bat-like body, in red tight-fitting garments, with wide wings, and a devil's face, sulphurous flame and smoke issuing from his mouth.

He leaped almost into the window where they stood spellbound.

But the light was gone then—darkness had fallen heavily, and they could only see his shadow form for an instant, before, with a Satanic laugh and a fresh emission of flame, he disappeared with a bound, which took him clear across the leads into the street.

By the time that the constables regained sufficient courage to emerge upon the flat roof and continue their search, the murderer, if such he was, had had time to escape, and their efforts were useless.

But who had been murdered, and where had the crime heen done?

## CHAPTER II.

DAISY LEIGH—WAITING AND WATCHING—THE ASSASSIN—THE CRY FOR HELP—SPRING-HEELED JACK TO THE RESCUE.

In order to explain the events in our first chapter we must ask our readers to accompany us to a house in a street not far from the Three Mariners.

This street was perhaps one of the worst in the Mint.

Over the whole place brooded the shadowy memory of Jack Sheppard and his days of crime.

Not a really respectable house was in the whole thoroughfare; dingy beerhouses, greasy chandlers' shops, nondescript places, with dingy bed curtains in palour windows flush with the street; dark courts and alleys leading into gloomy passages.

Such was the kind of place whence the cry of murder had proceeded.

In an upper room in a house, the door of which —mostly open—led to a staircase, the woodwork of which was like tinder, a young girl had been watching for a long, weary time.

The apartment was terribly poor and desolate.

A broken piece of iron served as a fender; the table had only three sound legs; there was only one chair and a stool.

In one corner lay a heap of straw covered with a few rags, and the window was patched with paper and other materials instead of glass.

Adjoining this place was a small ante-chamber—a cupboard—where a little bedstead made from rough pieces of wood had been constructed, on which was a palliasse and a few ragged coverings.

In the grate in the larger room a fire was struggling for existence, and before this crouched a girl.

She was about seventeen, and anyone looking at her beauty would have said what shame it was that she should be habited in such rags.

Her hair was dark and glossy, and arranged round her head in short, crisp curls.

Her eyes—large, brown, and brilliant—wore a sad and melancholy look, and a shadow of scorn marked her ripe, red lips.

Her dress consisted of a short skirt, ragged boots and stockings, and a low underbody, a shawl being drawn over her to hide the white and rounded shoulders and bosom, which matched the rare beauty of her face and the exquisite form, whose contours were lavishly shown by the thin, clinging garment.

Her only dress hung up in the little ante-chamber; she dare not risk wearing that in the squalid room, lest the chances of her going out would be destroyed.

The young girl, shivering before the miserable apology of a fire, shuddered more as she looked back upon the past.

She had memories of an infancy spent in a handsome house, and of tender faces and gentle voices round her.

Then came school-time at a pretty place by the sea—holidays spent at home with her father, Herbert Leigh, in a comparatively generously-kept and appointed house, and pleasant visitors, and plenty of life and fun.

Then came a sudden fall.

She was hurried home from school to meet a haggard, hunted-looking man, who took her instantly from home, and straight from luxury and happiness, to the hateful squalor of a third-rate lodging-house.

He could explain nothing.

He only said that terrible misfortune had fallen upon him—that he was accused of a deadly crime, was powerless to prove his innocence, and dared not show his face in any neighbourhood where he was known.

From this moment they went from bad to worse, until at last we see Daisy Leigh—pretty, dainty Daisy Leigh—crouched, cold and shuddering, by a dying fire in a wretched garret, waiting for her father's coming.

Presently, when her heart had become weary with watching, she heard a heavy foot upon the stairs.

She listened intently; the step came nearer—the door opened.

Yes, it was, indeed, her father, and in a moment her warm young arms were about his neck.

Then, as she drew him to the fire, she observed that his eyes were brighter than usual and a smile was on his lips, in spite of the wet state of his habiliments.

"Put on your dress, little one," he said; "don't shiver in the cold any more. I've brought you a better one to go out in, and better luck too. One more night in this wretched place and we can go to comfortable quarters."

"Oh! never mind me," said Daisy, drawing her shawl tighter round her bare shoulders. "Take off that wet overcoat, and I'll put the rest of the coals on the fire. If you have had good luck perhaps we can buy some more presently next door."

Herbert Leigh did as he desired, and then, while she was busy making up the fire, he opened a large bundle he had brought with him.

In this were a dress, a jacket, gloves, boots, and so forth, and in a separate bundle some food and a bottle of port wine.

"Drink some of that, Daisy," he said; "it will warm your blood, and then I will explain a little of what has happened.

"In the first place I am no longer compelled to hide my face," he continued, as Daisy drank some wine out of a broken tea-cup, "and in the second place I have discovered my enemy."

Daisy shuddered.

"Then pray let him rest," she said. "You have gone through enough danger. You do not want to use your perilous knowledge to bring fresh disaster on yourself."

As she spoke she started.

What was that sound?

Was it a creak of a footstep upon the stairs?

"Hush, father," she added. "I think I heard someone coming."

"Maybe James Winter going up to his room."

Daisy blushed.

"You forget," she said, "he left this place yesterday. I will go to the door and listen."

She went at once, but the sounds she had heard had ceased, whatever they were.

A furious wind blew up the stairs, and swept over her with a strange, death-like chill, the lightning flashed and illumined the dark landing and the darker stairs.

But she saw nothing.

There was a sound as of heavy breathing, but she set that down to the drunken snoring of Gadge Foote, the dwarf bagsman, who slept on the floor below, and closing the door she returned to her seat at her father's side.

"It was only fancy, I expect," she said; "the wind making the old stairs creep. Go on, father; I am all eagerness to know your story."

A shade crossed Herbert Leigh's brow.

"Ah! my child," he said, "I cannot tell you that now. It would be dangerous. But I have here, let me tell you, the papers which prove my right to wealth and name, usurped so long by the man who has been the cause of all my misery."

As he spoke, the door was flung open, the wind nearly extinguishing the candle, and a man's figure was seen standing—a dark shadow on a darker threshold.

"Whoever you are, enter," cried Herbert Leigh, rising and drawing back, with a strange, indefinable fear crawling to his heart. "I cannot talk to anyone whom I do not see, and the wind will put the light out if you do not close the door."

He had clutched the papers, which he had commenced opening on the table, and retreated behind the latter, pushing his daughter behind him as he spoke.

The new-comer uttered a low, guttural laugh, and entering, closed the door.

The flame of the candle became steady again, and, as he removed his hat, Herbert recognised him.

His face at first grew white and then swiftly flushed with anger.

"What do you want here, Ned Wilmot?" he cried. "Have I not had enough of misery and peril through you, that you need follow me here?"

"Don't talk like that, Mr. Leigh," returned Ned Wilmot, jeeringly. "You'll find it doesn't suit the situation at all. I'm here to demand from you the papers you have stolen."

"Stolen! What mean you, ruffian?" cried Leigh, indignantly. "The papers I have this night taken from Ashton Hall are my own; the papers which prove my birthright and my claims. It would be unpleasant if I called for aid, and had you arrested as the poacher, robber, and highwayman you are."

Ned Wilmot's evil face was distorted by an ominous scowl as these words were uttered.

"You'd better beware what you are saying," he said, savagely. "You'd find it difficult to get any aid here just now. I've taken special care that no one is in the house, and, as for anyone outside of it, you might shout and scream as loudly as you like. What with the wind, and the rain, and the thunder, you'd find no one to hear you."

Daisy trembled as she gazed at the man who spoke.

The expression of his face was truly awful.

But Herbert Leigh knew no fear.

He had obtained, after long years of waiting, of privations, and danger, the papers which could alone prove his innocence and his claims as next heir to Ashton Hall.

"Leave this room at once!" he cried, threateningly.

"Not without those papers!" cried Wilmot, fiercely, advancing a step nearer.

There was murder in his eyes, and Daisy's heart turned faint.

Her white bosom rose and fell in tremulous pulsations, and Ned Wilmot observing it, leered hideously.

"You'd best ask him to give them to me, Miss Daisy," he added, quickly. "Since you laughed at my love I've never felt very kindly towards you and yours; but, if he will give them to me, I promise never again to trouble you or him. If he doesn't give them to me willingly I'll have them by force, and you, too, before long."

There was that in his eyes which would have made many a girl less brave lose heart altogether.

But Daisy Leigh had a brave spirit in her plump, lithe form.

"Don't threaten me," she said; "I laugh at your menaces. But as for the papers I would rather my father gave them up than incur any danger. My love for him is greater than all my desire for wealth or position."

Ned Wilmot was about to reply, but Herbert Leigh interrupted him.

"Enough!" he said; "you have insulted both me and my child, and I refuse to say more to you to-night. I leave this place to morrow, and—"

"Give me those papers," said Ned Wilmot, interrupting threateningly.

"I refuse."

"Then I will take them."

With the words he sprang forward.

Herbert Leigh had anticipated this, and was ready for him.

Quickly passing the papers to Daisy, who clutched them in a brave, though tremulous, hand, he was just in time to avoid a blow aimed at him by his enemy.

Ned Wilmot was a strong man, and had been used to a rough and hardy life; but Herbert Leigh was by no means a contemptible antagonist.

He was in the prime of life—not, perhaps, more than forty-three years of age, and had seen a good deal of roughing it in his time.

The struggle was a deadly one.

The first blow being stopped, the two adversaries closed.

Chairs and table were overturned in the furious struggle, and Daisy, crouching in a corner, felt that some terrible crisis had come in the life of herself and father.

She could have escaped into her own room, but she would not desert him; and so, crouching there, pale, with tremulous bosom and palpitating heart, she sent forth again and again that awful cry which had rung out over the Mint through gusty wind and roaring thunder—

"Help—help—murder!"

But no help came.

At first, as Ned Wilmot had jeeringly declared, the voices of Nature had drowned the shrill cries.

And, so at length, when her father was thrown suddenly, and dashed his head against the iron of the fender, the only chance of aid for him was that of his brave child.

With desperate courage she sprang at the murderous villain.

But of what avail was her tender muscles against a brawny ruffian of this type?

Seeing at once her design, he struck her a blow as she approached him, which sent her, stunned and helpless, into a corner.

Then, as she lay there, unable to move, only able to collect her scattered senses sufficiently to know what the terrible scene meant, she beheld the final struggle.

Her father seemed to rouse himself for a last effort.

He used superhuman strength.

But in vain.

Ned Wilmot was not content with hands.

Just as Daisy hoped that her father had succeeded in obtaining a position where he could renew the battle, she saw something bright flash in Wilmot's hand.

Then there was an awful groan of pain and despair, and Herbert Leigh fell back dead, stabbed through the heart.

The sight of this seemed to infuse fresh strength into Daisy.

She roused herself, and, springing up, faced the assassin as he staggered to his feet.

She clutched in her left hand behind her the papers which had cost her father his life, and again her piercing cry resounded through the storm.

"Villain!" she exclaimed, with white lips. "I swear, by Heaven's mercy, to avenge this night's work. Be mine the task to hunt you to your doom. Ned Wilmot—"

"Cease your prating, wench!" said the man, advancing towards her with his face splashed with the blood of his victim. "Give me those papers!"

"Never, while life lasts!"

In an instant he sprang upon her.

But he had misjudged the power of those rounded limbs, now that their owner was roused to fierce energy by the spirit of revenge, despair, and her natural clinging to life.

Again and again he tried to fling her violently against the wall.

In vain.

Her muscles appeared to have resolved themselves into iron.

"I'll pay you out for this, my beauty," he said, in a voice of gasping rage, as he paused for a moment, holding her by both wrists.

Beauty!

That was indeed the word to express her appearance.

Her face was pale, with one spot of red on each cheek. In the struggle her shawl had been torn off, revealing the heaving roundness of her bosom, and the exquisite contour of her bare white shoulders.

Her eyes gleamed brightly; her lips were parted, showing the pearly teeth beneath.

In her left hand she still clutched the fatal papers.

By a sudden jerk, after a moment, Ned Wilmot endeavoured to throw her again; but as he did so an awful thing happened.

A loud and discordant laugh was heard without, and, in the midst of a terrific flash of lightning, there was a crashing of wood and glass, and an awful figure sprang into the room.

It was the form of Satan.

His body was attired in a red tight-fitting garment; his face was strange and horrible; his mouth wide, with fang-like teeth; horns grew from his forehead, and one foot was that of an animal with a cloven hoof.

As he gazed at the assassin with eyes which glowed like living coals, sulphurous flame and smoke was vomited from his mouth.

One glance was enough for Daisy.

She fell fainting on the floor.

As she did so the papers dropped from her nerveless grasp, and Ned Wilmot, with a wild cry, seized them, despite the presence of the fiend.

In an instant the Terrible Thing made a dash forward at him, but, with a cry like that of a lost spirit, the assassin leaped over the table and was gone.

The fiendish being who had caused the catastrophe glanced round the room for a moment, and, seeing pen and ink and paper, raised the table to its proper level, and, sitting down, wrote a few words.

"*Fear not, Daisy Leigh! He whom you saw this night is yonr friend. He arrived too late to save your father's life. But he will aid you to avenge his death. Use the gold he leaves and go to the address he gives, or you will hear no more of your friend* "SPRING-HEELED JACK."

The address was, "Mistress Barton, River Cottage, Edmonton;" and the purse was a silk one, through the meshes of which shone the gleam of many gold pieces.

Having left these on the table he securely fastened the door, and turned his attention to Daisy.

Raising her from the floor he gazed intently at her, and placed her on the bed of rags.

For a moment he feared that she, too, had sped away into the vast unknown—her lips were so pale and cold, her eyelids so blue, her face so cold, her form so rigid.

But when he placed his hand, or rather claw, under her left breast, he felt the heart beating feebly.

"She lives—she lives!" murmured the terrible-looking being. "She will yet avenge her father; and by this mark she will one day know who it was that befriended her."

Then with his sharp talons he scratched a double cross on her left shoulder, on the delicate white of which the blood quickly flowed.

Then he threw her shawl over her, poured a little wine between the lips which were already trembling with returning life, and, leaping through the shattered window through which he had come, disappeared ere she opened her eyes upon the scene of horror.

With bounds of wondrous and supernatural agility he sprang over the roofs of outhouses, over chimney pots and across leads; an awful form in the blue gleam of the lightning, until presently he reached the spot where Mr. Bonsor and the other constables were just preparing to emerge from the window.

Ned Wilmot's attempted capture is easily accounted for.

A man who had heard the shrill cries of "Help—help! murder!" had seen him emerge from the door of the old house, and fly like one demented along the street and round the corners.

He had pursued him, seen him enter the Three Mariners, and had at once hastened to give information to the constables.

By the time that Bonsor and his men, recovering from their terror of Spring-Heeled Jack, had crossed the leads and dropped into the street, Ned Wilmot had made his way along the dark and narrow thoroughfare, dashed down a narrow court, and made his way towards the river's side.

Here he had no difficulty in finding a boat.

He was not one to care who was owner of anything he desired to possess, and, accordingly, he leaped in, slipped the painter, and was soon rowing up stream.

At a little creek near Vauxhall Bridge he pulled the skiff ashore, jumped on the muddy, oozy pebbles, and, casting the boat adrift to follow the tide where it liked, he approached some steps, hastened up them, and, making his way along a narrow lane between dingy, lonely warehouses, reached presently a dirty-looking beershop.

It was long past the usual hours of closing, but three peculiar taps brought to the door a hangdog-looking harridan of about sixty years of age, who grinned in surprise as she saw him.

"What! you back again, Ned?" she cried, "come back like a bad shilling! You do look scared-like, too, just as if you'd seen a ghost."

"I've seen worse! I've seen the devil!" cried Ned Wilmot, with a forced laugh. "Let's have a bed-room, mother, and something to eat and drink. I think the nabs are after me, so put me in a room near the river's side, and I'll stop there on the quiet till to-morrow night."

And, while the assassin was calmly partaking of a good supper, the fiendish shape which had tried to thwart his designs on Daisy Leigh was darting across London in the now decreasing storm, leaping over the heads of the passers-by, flying over the hackney coaches, and creating such a panic in the minds of all that no one who saw him could sleep a wink that night.

And he, never caring about the terror he created, was speeding away towards Barnet on the first stage of his errand of vengeance.

---

## CHAPTER III.

ASHTON HALL — A STORMY INTERVIEW — A STOLEN MEETING—A SECOND MURDER.

IT was on the evening after the horrible murder in the Mint and the appearance of Spring-Heeled Jack, the mysterious unknown, that a man rode out from a little bye-alley near the Falcon Inn at Southgate, and made his way in the direction of Barnet.

The weather had now changed entirely.

Instead of rain and rushing wind, and the warring of lightning and thunder, there was only a light breeze, and the moon was shining brightly, while myriads of stars gemmed the sky.

The man was dressed in ordinary costume, looking as if he belonged to the farming class; but there was an air of satisfaction and snugness about him which seemed to tell that he had just had a slice of luck or was looking forward to the coming of some certain good fortune.

Though railways were then commencing to span the country they were only commencing, and had not yet done away with the footpad and the highwayman.

Consequently, the man carried in his holsters a goodly pair of pistols.

People had given up wearing swords, having

been compelled to do so by a "paternal government;" but things had not yet reached such a pitch that a man would be fined, perhaps imprisoned, for carrying a pistol to protect himself.

Metropolitan extensions had not in those days succeeded in joining Barnet to London.

Accordingly, it was not long before the man left the houses behind him, and started off on a wide, lonely road.

It was just the place to suit a dashing highwayman, and just the hour and the weather.

A crisp, hard road; on either side thickly-wooded land or high hedges; above a cloudless sky, and the moon and stars making a merry light.

Enough to give excuse for a high-spirited, daring fellow to turn out on the highway, and cry—

"Hurrah—hurrah! for the road!"

Even though it were only for fun and devilment.

So thought the man—Job Joskins, as he left the inhabited parts of the hamlet, and found himself alone on the silent highway.

Many a time, as he rode on, he turned to take a stealthy glance round him; and now and then he pulled up to listen, as if frightened at the echoes of his horse's footsteps.

But, at length, satisfied that his fears were groundless, he put spurs to his horse, anxious to reach as quickly as possible his destination, which was none other than Ashton Hall, the place mentioned by Herbert Leigh, the victim of the cold-blooded murder in the Mint.

This place was inhabited by, and supposed to belong to, Sir Roland Ashton, who had come into the property, it was said, in consequence of the failure of the other heirs.

Strange rumours, however, were spread in regard to him and his succession to the property.

Rumours that papers had been concealed or destroyed, and even that dark deeds had been done in order to secure him safe use of the golden revenues of the estate.

But as is always the case where people have command of money, Sir Roland Ashton was, if not liked, at any rate tolerated in the very best society.

In the neighbourhood he attended all the hunt meetings, balls, garden parties, and so forth, for he was only forty years of age, handsome, stalwart, with plenty of money, and was he not, therefore, lionised in such a manner that he knew himself to be regarded as one of the most eligible *partis* in the neighbourhood.

He was a well-looking man enough in his way, and could take a fence or a hedge with any man in England.

But there was a sinister gleam in his eyes at the best of times, and a cruel smile often hovered about his lips.

His household consisted of the usual servants necessary to a proper establishment, a middle-aged housekeeper, and a ward.

The former was a woman of no particular character showing outwardly.

The latter was a tall, elegant girl, evidently well ed, and yet having a shade of melancholy always n her face, even at the merriest meetings.

She was twenty-one on the day following the murder in the Mint, and her guardian had on that day promised to disclose to her the story of her life.

Otherwise she was a mysterious being.

She had entered Sir Roland's house some nine years before, and, coming straight from school, had been treated with uniform kindness by him, though his constant hints and inuendoes cast a painful shadow on her life.

In appearance she was of great beauty—tall, with long, sweeping limbs, broad, rounded shoulders, and an exquisitely-developed and voluptuous bust.

Her face corresponded with her form, and masses of golden hair crowned her well-formed head.

It was to the home of this girl—Constance Marfield and Sir Roland Ashton—that Job Joskins was hurrying along the Barnet-road, when, coming suddenly round a bend where the rest of the highway was hidden from view, he came upon a man whose appearance caused his heart to beat violently, and his brain to reel.

The man was riding a fine horse, and was attired in a guise which made him resemble almost in every particular, except the mask, those gentlemen of the road who used to frequent the lonely highways in the time of Tom King and his companions.

Job Joskins was almost abreast with the stranger ere he recognised what kind of traveller he had met.

"Stop, on your life!" cried the latter, "I want a word with you."

Job's hand made a slow and tremulous movement towards his holster.

"Hold!" cried the man again; "if you move I will shoot you through the head."

He presented a pistol ere he went on—

"You are Job Joskins, and you are going to Ashton Hall to tell Sir Roland Ashton how much money you will be able to collect for him at Rickworth to-morrow evening."

"You're the devil!" muttered Job, tremblingly.

"No, I'm not, though he is an acquaintance of mine," returned the highwayman; "but I happen to know that you have in your possession a goodly sum of money which you have already collected for your master."

Job Joskins did not reply.

In fact he was too terrified; but at this moment there happened something which took his thoughts in another direction with a vengeance.

There was a sudden loud peal of laughter—"Ha! ha! ha!"—then a whirring sound above the heads of both Job and the highwayman, and, glancing up, they saw the terrible apparition of Spring-Heeled Jack.

His cloak was spread out so as to resemble the wings of a bat, and sulphurous smoke and flame was issuing more than ever from his mouth.

Job Joskins was so terrified that he could not utter a sound, but his hair bristled on end so that his hat fell off; while the arm of the highwayman which held the pistol remained rigid and immovable.

The terrible being who had thus appeared—looming up between them and the moon—sped over their heads with the rapidity of a rocket, and disappeared behind the hedge on the side opposite to that where it had risen.

For a few seconds only the two men and their horses stood motionless—the riders seemed riveted to their saddles, the animals seemed turned to stone.

But after this momentary lull they broke away, one dashing in one direction, the other in the other—Job Joskins rushing away towards Barnet, and his quondam enemy making in all haste towards London, leaving the choice of road, fin act, to his horse's discretion.

They had scarcely gone when Spring-Heeled Jack made his appearance again, and, with a wild, unearthly laugh, glanced after the highwayman.

"Ha, ha!" he cried. "I knew you at once, Ned Wilmot. But you are not going to Ashton Hall before me. I am bound there to-night, to prowl round and discover all. We want no prying assassins there.

"As for Job Joskins," he added, as he glanced in the other direction along the road, where the "receiver" had just disappeared, "I have learned this night a secret which will be of use to me. It strikes me that there will be three people instead of two interested in the collection of money at Rickworth to-morrow night."

With many a leap and bound, over hedges, ditches, streams, and tree-tops, went the awful apparition, until it neared the site of an old ruin—the dilapidated remains of a house, which, a year or two before, had been burnt down, and which had never been rebuilt or even repaired.

He paused a moment ere he entered it, standing Satan-like behind a tree to think.

"I can hardly believe," he murmured aloud, "that I shall see again the body of Herbert Leigh in this strange spot. No doubt it was part of Ned Wilmot's bargain to bring the murdered man to this place, in order that Sir Roland should look upon it, and know that his hideous order was fulfilled. But how did he convey it hither when I have been on the watch?"

Overcoming his repugnance the weird being left his concealment, and, with a leap and a bound, had passed round the angle of the first ruined wall.

The moon was here shining in one gleaming belt of radiance, and in an instant Spring-Heeled Jack (since such was the name he had adopted) saw that the horrible thing was true.

Lying on its back, just where the moonlight fell upon its face, was the body of a man, and the features were those of Herbert Leigh.

"This is a strange mystery," said Spring-Heeled Jack, to himself. "Those who help me must be strangely remiss, or the body of this unfortunate could not have found its way to this spot. Ha! who comes here, I wonder. I will remain and see."

With his arms raised so as, by the aid of his cloak, to form the bat-like wings, he remained still, standing on the body, when, after a moment, a man came creeping round the angle of the wall.

This was Job Joskins.

The very last man whom Spring-Heeled Jack expected to see.

In an instant Job had recognised the weird form.

For one moment he was rooted to the spot in uncontrollable terror.

Then, with a wild yell, he turned to fly.

But Spring-Heeled Jack was too much for him.

In an instant he had bounded forward and seized the fugitive by the throat with his claw-like hands, then, with a twirl, flung him on his face.

"Ha! ha! ha!"

The demon laughter of the weird being resounded over the countryside as, kneeling down, he turned out all the pockets of the "collector."

Not a penny piece or a piece of paper escaped his notice, and, having transferred everything into a huge pocket, contained under his arm in the wing-like cloak, he proceeded to disrobe his victim.

"Oh! pray, Mr. Devil," cried Job Joskins, "pray leave me my clothes!"

"Not a bit of it," said Spring-Heeled Jack; "if you ride home naked your master will know you have not robbed him. Quick, or I shall put a bullet through your skull, or strangle you."

His long, claw-like fingers, clasped and unclasped before the eyes of the horrified man, and without further hesitation he began divesting himself of his clothes.

At every pause a grip of the terrible fingers was upon his neck, and at length he stood up as naked as he was born.

It was not a cold night, but still a man suddenly stripped of his warm clothes would naturally feel chilled, and he shuddered and trembled accordingly.

But while the luminous eyes of Spring-Heeled Jack were upon him he was powerless to move.

"Remember," said the apparition, in a solemn voice, "I know all. I know this murdered man. I know who killed him, and who urged him on to the deed. I know you, Job Joskins, and your dealings. Go home now and tell your master, Sir Roland Ashton, that Spring-Heeled Jack is on his track. Go home swiftly, without stopping, or I will follow and throttle the life out of you!"

And with these words the speaker gave a terrific bound over Job's head, and disappeared in a vapour of flame and sulphur emitted from his cavernous mouth.

Job Joskins gave one glance round furtively to see if his clothes were there; but they were all gone, even to his boots.

For an instant the hideous idea occurred to him of denuding the murdered man of his habiliments, and dressing himself in them, but hardly had the idea formed itself in his brain when the loud "Ha, ha, ha!" of the fiendish unknown was heard, and he fled towards the spot where he had left his horse.

On this he leaped, and, naked as he was, galloped down the road as hard as he could tear towards Ashton Hall.

Turning suddenly round a bend in the road leading towards the turnpike, he met a young girl coming from market, and, thinking he was the devil, she cowered down by the side of the road and shrieked loudly for help.

Her cries roused the attention of two constables on duty, and they hastened forward only to see Job on his horse pass like a flash, and the girl still sobbing and cowering by the roadside.

"Why, what is the matter, young woman?" cried one of them, in vain endeavouring to keep his voice steady.

"Oh! if you please, sir," said the girl, still afraid to move, "I saw the devil go by, naked, on a horse, and—"

"Ha! ha! ha!"

A demon yell of laughter resounded from behind a hedge, and, as the startled trio listened, horror-stricken at the awful tones, the unknown form of the mysterious leaper whizzed up from the ground into the air, and bounded over their heads.

The moon was still shining brightly in an unclouded sky, and all of them were able to note minutely his appearance—his scarlet body, his bat-wings, his sulphurous-breathing mouth; with a yell of horror the constables fled, leaving the unfortunate girl to shift for herself, which she did by rising, with a shuddering cry, and following them as best she could.

Spring-heeled Jack, with many a bound and

miraculous leap, followed, caught them up, and leaped over their heads, after which, with a loud laugh, he magically disappeared.

## CHAPTER IV.

### SIR ROLAND AT HOME—AN UNWELCOME VISITOR—A STOLEN MEETING.

SIR ROLAND ASHTON was in his library.

A queer old room, solidly and sombrely furnished, and full of dark, strange corners, but still a comfortable apartment.

Sir Roland had a puzzled, worried look upon his face, and yet not an expression that told of being absolutely displeased.

"To-morrow is the day when all must be divulged," he said to himself, as presently he paused in a troubled walk to and fro, and threw himself into a large arm-chair by the fire. "To-morrow all will be decided. I somehow fear that everything will not be as well as I could wish it; but I do not think there is anything to dread."

As he spoke there came an odd tapping, scratching at his window, and he started up.

Crossing the room quickly, in some surprise and perturbation, he drew aside the curtain and looked out.

But there was nothing near the window on the outside; only the tendrils and leaves of the vine, which crept nestlingly up the wall and stole upon the verandah.

He was just about to turn away impatiently when he gave utterance to an exclamation of bewilderment as he saw a naked rider dash across the grounds on a steed, which he seemed to recognise, though, in his present want of garb, he failed to distinguish the horseman.

As the mysterious apparition went by a thing like a huge bat rose from the ground and passed between him and the moon, leaping clean over the head of the naked rider and disappearing.

Sir Roland drew the curtains with a shudder, and walked back to his seat.

"Well," he said, "I do not believe in *diablerie*, or I should think that Satan and one of his attendant imps was paying me a visit. However, I suppose I shall know soon."

A quarter of an hour, however, passed before any one knocked at the door.

Then, in answer to his summons, Job Joskins appeared, his face still pale with fear and excitement.

Sir Roland, who had now drank himself into a jocular humour by frequent potations of old port, laughed loudly.

"Come in, Job," he cried. "Why, you look as if you had seen Old Nick himself."

"That's exactly what I have done," said the man, glancing over his shoulder and at every dark corner of the room.

"Drink a glass of wine, man, and don't be a fool," said Sir Roland, with some show of irritation; "do you know who it was who was riding just now naked through the grounds?"

"That was me, sir," said Job, with a grim smile, as he drank off the glass of wine; "and if you'll listen, sir, I'll explain everything."

"Go on ahead, then, Job," returned Sir Roland, with a yawn. "I daresay it's only a cock-and-a-bull story."

"I don't think you'll say so when you hear it," said Job, and, commencing from his start from Southgate, he narrated his adventures.

Sir Roland listened listlessly at first, and then eagerly, never once interrupting him.

When he had finished, he said—

"Are you certain that the man you saw lying dead was Herbert Leigh?"

"Quite certain. The moon was full on his face."

"That is well," muttered the baronet; "but it is strange that Ned Wilmot has not been here!"

"Ned Wilmot!" cried Job. "Ah! now I remember. He was dressed so strangely that I knew him not; but, now I think of it, it was he who stopped me on the road."

"But this mountebank—this dressed-up acrobat—what of him?"

Job shuddered.

"Nay, it was no acrobat—no mountebank!" he cried. "It was the devil himself, for he vomited forth sulphurous flames."

"Ha, ha, ha!" laughed a demoniacal voice outside.

Both started up, the baronet now as agitated as his man; but when they glanced out of the window all was still, save that a faint laugh seemed dying away in the distance.

"If these fellows come here playing their mountebank tricks," said the baronet, as he returned to the fire, "they will get more than they bargain for. I should think nothing of shooting them like dogs."

But though he talked in this strain he drank up greedily a tumblerful of wine.

"Don't get gabbling among my people, Job," said he, "about this. You don't know what mischief fools would make out of such a circumstance. But remember to-morrow night. I think it will be best for me to go with you to Rickworth."

"Very well, sir," said Job, much relieved.

"There is a coach which starts back at eleven from the White Posts," continued Sir Roland. "We can catch that, and be home at midnight. Go on, Job, and get yourself some supper; and tell the housekeeper to get mine ready in my bedroom, with a roaring fire. This place has a loneliness about it to-night that I cannot endure. Remember, Job, not a word; and if you should meet Ned Wilmot coming here to-night, let him not know that you recognised him!"

In another moment the baronet was alone.

Save for his awful thoughts.

But not for long was he suffered to be undisturbed.

This time there was a loud and decided knock at the window, and Sir Roland sprang up with an oath.

"Confound these mysterious visitors!" he cried. "Who, in the fiend's name, can it be who comes to the window instead of to the door?"

He hastened to the casement, and saw standing on the terrace outside a man so covered by a long cloak that it was quite impossible to scan his figure or his dress.

His features were entirely concealed by a broad-brimmed hat of felt.

"Who is it who comes like this to my window, instead of to my door, like a thief?" cried the baronet, furiously.

"No thief, Sir Roland; but one who has a right to enter, though he thinks it not safe to do so by the door."

The baronet staggered back.

"That voice!" he cried.

The new-comer laughed.

"Ah! no doubt you know me," he said, in a loud voice. "I am Ralph Ashton. Admit me at once."

There was no hesitation on the part of the baronet now.

He instantly opened the French windows and admitted the intruder, who, with a grim smile, entered and passed to the fire-place.

The baronet stepped out, glanced round him to see that there were no intruders, and then, re-entering, joined his unwelcome guest.

"May I ask the reason of this intrusion?" he said, furiously.

"Almost an unnecessary question, as if matters were not in a peculiar stage to-night," replied the one named Ralph Ashton.

He threw off his hat and cloak as he spoke, displaying an elegant costume, and coolly seated himself in a chair opposite to the baronet.

"Be quick and tell me the object of your mission," said Sir Roland. "I am in no humour to be interfered with to-night."

"I don't care one fig for your humour," said Ralph Ashton; "even if I came as usual to demand my rights, I should require a patient hearing, in spite of the cruel power over me which you have obtained through your villainy and falsehood; but I come on no common errand. I come to speak of the death of Herbert Leigh."

"I know of it," cried Sir Roland, who was, nevertheless, deeply impressed by the unexpected knowledge of his visitor.

"No doubt, since you ordered it."

"Have a care!" cried Sir Roland, extending his hand towards the bell-rope.

"Bah! I don't fear you," exclaimed Ralph. "I have a weapon with which I would shoot you like a cur, as you are, if you dared to ring."

He drew a tiny pistol from his pocket as he spoke, at which the baronet glanced, but made no reply.

"Yes," continued Ralph. "Herbert Leigh was murdered in the old Mint. I saw his dead body; and I know his murderer—Ned Wilmot."

"This is pure madness. I—"

"Spare your denials," said Ralph. "I am not in a position to show myself, in order to drag you to justice, but I will do so quickly, and risk all danger to myself, if you do not at once perform some tardy act of reparation."

"What mean you?"

"I mean that Herbert Leigh, who has been murdered by your order, has left a daughter."

The baronet recoiled.

"Ah!" he cried, "I knew not of this."

"No doubt," said Ralph; "but it is nevertheless true. Daisy Leigh lives in spite of her brutal assailant, and saw the murder of her father and knows his assassin."

"And whom do you say that she accuses?" said Sir Roland.

"Ned Wilmot, that ruffian, half-poacher, half-gamekeeper, who used to be in your employment, and who seems to be so still, although he is a highwayman and an assassin."

"Do you dare impute to me the incitement of Ned Wilmot to the murder of Herbert Leigh?" cried the baronet, fiercely.

"I say to your face that you are the most interested in Herbert Leigh's death, that I believe you ordered this man to procure you those papers at any cost, and that the reason why the body of the murdered man is even now lying not far hence, instead of peacefully in London, is because it was brought down here for you to identify."

Sir Roland was livid with rage.

He sprang up and seized the bell-rope.

"I will have you thrust from the door," he said. "I will listen to none of this. You have invented this story to frighten me and to extort money. There is no such person as Herbert Leigh. He died years ago, after hiding away from the consequences of his misconduct. Anybody, alive or dead, whom you produce as Leigh, will be an impostor. You cannot prove his identity."

"Daisy Leigh lives, and can prove all."

"She cannot prove anything, except that she is called Leigh. She cannot prove that her father was Herbert Leigh, for she knows not anything, save from his own lips, and that would go for nothing."

Ralph Ashton saw the difficulty.

"You have worked your villainy well indeed," he said; "but you shall not work in the same way with me. I am here once more to demand my papers."

"I have no papers."

"You may not have them, but you know where they are," replied Ralph. "You are afraid to let me have them, because you know that I could then prove my innocence of the vile charges brought against me, and boldly assert my rights."

The baronet had by this time recovered his equanimity somewhat.

The very mention of papers by Ralph had reminded him of his power.

"I refuse to hold converse with you. When you can prove your innocence you can return here, and I will do what I can for you. But I refuse to harbour in my place, a man over whose head the cloud of suspicion hangs. A forger is not a valuable acquisition to a family."

"You lie!" cried Ralph, fiercely, as he sprang to his feet. "You know I am innocent; you know you hold your title and your property by a fraud. I don't believe there is a drop of Ashton blood in your veins. But, beware; though at present I am compelled to visit you thus in the dead of the night it will not be for long. I will haunt you and yours in some way or another. I will force you to disgorge your ill-gotten spoil, and I swear never to rest until I bring you to justice as a thief and an assassin."

Sir Roland rang the bell violently.

"This is too much," he cried, "I cannot endure such insults in my own house. A prison cell will soon alter your feelings."

But Ralph was not to be caught thus.

Raising suddenly a glass which was half full of wine, he dashed it into the face of the baronet, and, rushing across the room, passed out upon the terrace.

Foaming with rage at the insult and the pain, the baronet rang more furiously still.

In a few moments two menservants appeared.

"Quick!" he said; "let the grounds be searched everywhere. That forging thief, who calls himself Ralph Ashton has been here, and has tried to take my life!"

The men waited for nothing more.

They fled through the window, calling on their way at the gardener's cottage to procure further assistance.

But it was all in vain.

Seek where they would they could find no one in the grounds.

At length, dispirited and tired, they were returning, expecting to receive savage abuse from their master for their failure, when a hollow sepulchral laugh sounded beside them.

Then a whirring, whizzing noise was heard, and they saw, leaping over heads, the awful form of Spring-Heeled Jack.

They noted well his diabolical attributes, his red body, his bat wings, his cloven foot, and saw the sulphurous smoke and flame issuing from his mouth.

For an instant they were paralysed with horror and dismay.

Then, as if unbound from the chain of fear, they fled with loud cries of alarm, nor stopped until they had all huddled into the baronet's room.

They expected a torrent of abuse.

They found him trembling and half-fainting in his chair.

He, too, had seen the awful visitation, which had stood at the French windows, and flapped its wings, and emitted its sulphurous smoke and flame, and uttered the words—

"Beware, Sir Roland Ashton, your time will soon come!"

He listened in bewilderment but no disbelief to the story told by the men.

He gulped down two glasses of wine, and gave the alarmed men some also.

"This is, of course, some vile trick," he said; "but it might frighten the women from the house. Say nothing of it below. I should not like it to reach the ears of Miss Marfield."

The men promised accordingly, and within half an hour the footman had told Emily, the lady's maid, the gardener had told his wife, and the butler had confided the news to the cook.

All, of course, under strict secresy!

Meanwhile, while Sir Roland slunk up into his bedroom and locked himself in, drawing the curtain closely, strange events were happening in another part of the house.

---

## CHAPTER V.

### CONSTANCE MARFIELD—A LOVE MEETING UNDER DIFFICULTIES.

CONSTANCE MARFIELD, full of thoughts of the morrow, when she was to hear the story of her life, and know her proper position in society, had retired to her room before Ralph Ashton's unexpected visit to Sir Roland.

She was not weary.

In fact, she had no desire for sleep; she only desired to be alone.

Her thoughts were anything but calm or pleasant ones.

For a long time she had been secretly betrothed to Ralph, whom she had met ere the hideous charge of forgery had been brought against him by Sir Roland.

They had been brought up together, in fact, and had loved at an earlier period than is generally the case.

Ralph was supposed, until the age of sixteen, to be the son of a poor relation of the baronet, whom he had adopted from charity. Constance was a ward left in his charge by a friend.

They were always together, and consequently the young girl became an adept in all kinds of boyish exercises, which in after years stood her in good stead.

Rowing, fishing, riding, cricket, birds' nesting, occupied the two, for they were very little interfered with by Sir Roland, and in those happy days of rough and ready play Ralph had abundant chances of observing the beauties of his sweet young companion.

Her face had already a womanly tenderness in it, her figure was well developed for a girl of fifteen, with firm shoulders, a budding bust, and lower limbs—displayed freely by her short skirts—which had been rounded and brought to perfection by constant exercise.

Ralph could not but feel the sweet influence of her presence, and, scarcely knowing what his feelings were, he was unhappy save in her presence.

It was an accident which proved to both their mental feelings.

They had been boating on the river, and, feeling flushed and tired, they drew their little skiff under the shadow of some trees, and, getting out, sat, or rather half reclined, on the soft green velvet of the bank.

Constance was then approaching sixteen, while Ralph was a little over that age.

The young girl was dressed in a white muslin dress, trimmed with blue, which set off her beauty to the best advantage, cut, as it was, square, so as to display a tempting view of the soft and delicately-rounded bosom.

With her head on his shoulder, and his arm clasping her lithe waist, they talked of the present and the future, and he saw how her eyes dimmed when he spoke of going abroad as a soldier in a marching regiment.

"Don't talk of going away," she said. "I should be so lonely without you."

He looked at her curiously.

"I am afraid I cannot idle my time away here very long," he said. "I am here, so I am told, merely on sufferance, and as I get older I must do something for my living."

The tears came into the girl's eyes, and she flung her arms round his neck.

"Don't talk about it any more," she said. "I can't bear the thought of it."

And then, with her troubled little form palpitating in his arms, he found himself raining kisses on her lips, while their hearts beat madly against each other.

This was first love, and both knew it.

"Darling—darling Constance!" said Ralph, "I may have to leave you, but it will not be for long. I must make a position, and get a good home, for you must be my wife, Constance."

And the girl, under the intoxicating influence of this first passion, shed tears of joy, and gave her promise.

After this unexpected episode the two were never happy apart.

They had been together nearly always before.

Now they were inseparable, but by a kind of tacit understanding Constance gave up most of her boyish enjoyments.

The young lovers mostly spent their time strolling through the woods, or lying side by side on the banks of the river, looking into each other's eyes, and, between their passionate kisses, planning sweet schemes for the future.

There was to be a cruel awakening, and it soon came.

One evening Sir Roland had gone to London, and the young people were left entirely to their own devices.

"Constance," said Ralph, "you have often wanted to have a look at the old west wing, which is never used. Let's go to-night. Sir Roland will

# SPRING-HEELED JACK,

## THE TERROR OF LONDON.

By the Author of "TURNPIKE DICK, the Star of the Road."

SPRING-HEELED JACK WHIZZED UP FROM THE GROUND AND BOUNDED OVER THEIR HEADS.

not be home until to-morrow; and if you meet me in the blue corridor after supper we can prowl all over the old place without being observed. I confess I am quite as curious as you are."

Directly after they had partaken of supper with the housekeeper they bade each other good-night and separated.

But as soon as all was quiet Ralph crept up to the blue corridor, tapped at the door of Constance's bedroom, and was soon joined by the young girl.

She was dressed in dark velvet, which, while it showed up the soft tinting of her skin, made her a less conspicuous object, and less likely to attract notice if anyone was watching.

We need not describe their wanderings about the old house.

They made no sound, for neither wore boots; and they had exhausted the old place, as they imagined, when they came suddenly upon a little door which had been left ajar.

All the rest of the building was dark and gloomy, and cobwebby and uncanny; but the room into which this door led was furnished in modern style, and was evidently used by Sir Roland as a kind of study, or counting-house.

There were papers littered about everywhere; and, indeed, no care seemed to have been made to conceal anything.

Nevertheless it appeared strange to Ralph that Sir Roland should choose such a place—far away across the uninhabited west wing—for a repository for his papers.

They were both going to retire and leave the place as they found it, when suddenly Ralph caught sight of his own name on a slip of paper.

Curiosity naturally caused him to examine the paper, and as he read a flush suffused his cheeks, and a bright light came into his eyes.

"Well," he muttered, presently, with clenched teeth, "I have been unable to warm towards Sir Roland, in spite of all he has done for me; but now I know him to be a villain."

Constance glanced at him as if she thought for the moment that he had taken leave of his senses.

"A villain? Oh! Ralph," she said, "Sir Roland may be stern and morose, and strange at times, but he is not a villain."

"Read this and see for yourself," said Ralph, with a laugh which was far from being musical.

The young girl took the paper and read.

We need not waste time in recapitulating it here; let it suffice to say that if the papers and certificates were true Ralph was the only son of Sir Guy Ashton, instead of the child of some distant poor relation.

"Now what do you think?" said Ralph, as Constance finished reading. "If this is true (and there can be no reason to doubt it), I am Sir Ralph Ashton, and proprietor of this place. If I can prove all this it will not be long before I am proprietor of something else, and that is yourself, dear Constance; for though we are both so young we are all the world to each other, and there can be no need to wait."

Hardly had the words left his lips when a loud and furious voice cried—

"What is the meaning of this? How dare you bring Miss Constance into the master's private study?"

It was the voice of Caleb Masters, the secretary and general factotum of the baronet.

He was a man of most unscrupulous mind, and, being deeply in the secrets of his master, he had often warned the baronet of the danger of leaving his private papers about.

"I am not aware that I have ever been ordered not to come into this room," said Ralph; "but what I have discovered now I am here makes me very thankful that I did come."

"And pray what have you discovered?" asked the secretary, concealing his alarm beneath a sneer.

"That I am Sir Ralph Ashton, only son of Sir Guy Ashton, and, consequently, master of this house," replied the daring youth. "While I hold in my hands these papers who can gainsay me?"

These words were fatal to his chance.

Caleb was a tall, wiry man, of great strength, and in an instant, before Ralph was aware of his intention, the secretary had leaped upon him.

Constance, thinking that murder was contemplated, filled the air with her shrieks.

But, finding that no one responded to her cries in that uninhabited wing, she cast aside all maidenly fear, and exerted all the power of her lithe young limbs to aid her lover.

In vain.

A cruel blow stretched Ralph on the floor, after he had made a brave resistance, and then Caleb turned savagely to Constance.

"You had better keep quiet, my young spitfire!" he said. "If you attack me again I shall make no difference because you are a girl. I shall serve you just the same as I have served him."

The girl saw that further resistance was impossible, or, at any rate, useless.

Her eyes were full of tears, and her bosom was heaving with emotion.

"You are a brute and a coward, Caleb Masters," she said; "and I don't believe that even Sir Roland will approve of what you have done. Help me to carry Master Ralph to his room."

"I don't want any help," cried Caleb, seizing the boy's insensible form, and carrying him as easily as if he had been a baby; "I'll take him to his bedroom, and you had better go to yours, or I shall have to take you. Ah! it's no use trying to look for the papers; I've got them safe enough. So come quickly."

Mostly for Ralph's sake Constance made no further resistance, and in a few moments the unfortunate boy was in his room, where Caleb roughly roused him to his senses, and locked him in.

This being done, and Constance having been secured also, Caleb saddled a horse and galloped away to London.

Next morning Sir Roland returned, and sent at once for Ralph.

The latter was furious at the discovery he had made, at Caleb's brutal blow, at the confinement in his room which had followed.

He confronted Sir Roland with flashing eyes.

"I am glad you have returned, Sir Roland," he said; "for, setting aside what I have discovered since you have been gone, I have been subjected to gross ill-treatment. When you know all you will, no doubt, turn Caleb Masters out of the house."

Sir Roland listened to what he had to say, and then said, calmly—

"I have heard all that has transpired since I left home, and I can only praise Mr. Masters for his courage and devotion to my service. In the first place those papers which you tried to steal are some old forgeries, which I keep by me in order to use if any of the old set try to annoy me. Sir

Guy never had a son. But as to that I have no more to say. What I wish you to know is that I have discovered your ungrateful forgery of my name."

Ralph reeled back in horror and astonishment.

"Forgery!" he cried. "I fail to understand what you mean."

"You remember that you bought a bracelet for Constance, my ward?"

"Yes."

"At the time I remarked upon its value, and expressed wonder at your being able to buy it."

"Well?" said Ralph, haughtily.

"I find now you told me a falsehood," said Sir Roland. "You said you had been saving up your pocket money, and I find that you forged a cheque upon my bank for twenty pounds, and sent Tom Smith, the blacksmith's son, to cash it for you."

Ralph pressed his hand to his brow.

What complicated piece of villainy was this?

"But this is all false," he said; "you know it is. I have never—"

"Spare your words," said Sir Roland. "I have quite made up my mind how to act. I am going to give you fifty pounds, and you must leave my house within the hour. If ever you show your face here again—"

"It will be as master," cried Ralph.

The baronet laughed dryly, though there was a certain nervousness in his manner.

"Don't worry your mind or other people's with that folly," he said. "Those forgeries are all destroyed. To make any such claim would only make things worse for you. So take this cheque and go."

"And if I refuse?"

"I will send for the constables, and they will take you to the lock-up."

Ralph was in a strange predicament.

If he dared the baronet to do his worst he might be convicted for the mere want of anyone to take his part, unless the necessary papers to prove his innocence and his identity were forthcoming.

"I will go," he said, "and I will take your money also, because it is mine; but I warn you that this is the worst day's work you have ever done. In a very short time I shall be able to prove the falsity of your words. You, in your black heart, know that they are false, and the day will come when you will regret that you so cruelly ill-treated and maligned one of your own kindred."

He turned on his heel as he spoke and quitted the room.

Sir Roland made no effort to call him back, and Ralph at once went in search of Constance.

But he could find no trace of her.

She had evidently been either spirited away or she had been confined in some secret room till he had departed.

At any rate, from the time that Ralph and Constance had entered the private room of Sir Roland they had never met.

They had corresponded by means of bribes to servants and so forth; and in their letters they had poured forth all the love which they could not explain by word of mouth.

Their hearts were still true.

But after the lapse of all these years Ralph was no nearer to proving his innocence.

He seemed, in fact, to be surrounded by such a network of villainy, that it was impossible to break through it.

On this evening—the eve of Constance's twenty-first birthday—she had received a letter which had caused her heart to leap with joy.

It was from Ralph, and said, merely—

"I am coming to see Sir Roland to-night. If all goes well, I shall demand to see you. I think that his villainy is overreaching itself."

But the hours had gone by, and he had not come; and Constance began to undress to go to bed.

She smiled sadly as she stood opposite the mirror when she had removed her dress.

"I am sorry that he has not come," she murmured. "I am sure that I should please him. He left me a raw, uncultured, immature girl, though with a true and faithful heart. He will find a woman, mature in judgment as in form, and still true. I am sure he will not think my looks have deteriorated."

Indeed, no.

She could not be insensible to her own beauty as she stood there gazing at the sweet, sad face, the masses of wavy hair, the large, round, creamy shoulders; the firm, voluptuous bust; the soft, enticing arms.

As she stood thus, admiring her beauty for his sake, a slight rustle startled her.

She listened eagerly.

Again the sound.

It seemed to come from outside the window.

A joyous feeling entered her bosom.

Could this be Ralph?

She went softly to the window, and peered through the glass.

At first she saw nothing, but after a moment she heard again the rustling sound among the ivy; and then a man's head appeared.

She could not recognise him in the strange, dim light; in fact, not having seen him for so many years, it was difficult for her to say how she would recognise him at all.

The stranger tapped at the window.

"Hist! Open, Constance," he whispered, with his mouth against the glass; "it is I—Ralph!"

She hastily threw a light shawl loosely over her gleaming shoulders to protect herself against the night-chill, and threw up the window.

"Is it you, really, Ralph?" she said, in low and tremulous accents.

"Yes, Constance. I am but little changed save in height and strength. May I enter?"

How could she hesitate? How, after five years of separation, could they allow a feeling of prudery to prevent their enjoying the delights of this stolen meeting?

"Yes, Ralph, come in," she said; "but you must speak low, for the house is full of spies; and if Sir Roland found you here, his fury would know no bounds."

There was very little said either low or loud for the next few minutes after Constance had closed the window, for Ralph had caught her to his heart and devoured her with hungry kisses.

Their lips met in long, passionate caresses, which seemed like an interchange of souls, and then, when they were a little calmer, he sat down in a large easy chair by the fire, and she, jumping on his lap, as in the happy days of old, nestled in his arms.

They were boy and girl again.

The lapse of years was forgotten.

In swift whispers he told her of the events which had occurred in the time which had elapsed since they last met.

"And you really believe that Sir Roland is a murderer?" she said.

"Yes. That is to say, the horrid crime was committed by his orders. No matter who did it, he was the murderer if he ordered it."

"And what do you propose to do?"

"I can do nothing in the way of punishing him yet," said Ralph. "I must wait and be patient. But for you, dearest Constance, I see no obstacle now to our speedy union. To-morrow you will be twenty-one, and your own mistress. No matter how, I am earning enough to offer you a good home, and, consequently, if you make delay it will be your own fault."

She nestled to him closely.

"Don't speak crossly, Ralph," she said. "I am sure I shall put no obstacle in the way of our marriage. I shall only be too glad to escape from this place, which is like a prison, where I am watched every hour. But how can it be carried out?"

"You must escape to me," said Ralph, "within a week from this time. I will be at this window with a rope ladder, and I will aid you to reach the grounds. I shall have horses ready, and we must fly at once to Baddington. There we can be married by special license, and we can defy all the Sir Rolands in the world."

"Within a week," she said.

They little knew what would happen in a week; little knew that at that very moment stealthy steps were approaching their chamber.

For a moment Constance gave herself up to the delicious thoughts roused in her mind by the words of her lover, who kissed and caressed her with a daring fervour which would at another time have brought blushes to her cheeks.

Then she roused herself.

"I fancy I hear sounds without," she said. "Let me go and listen."

She glided from his lap, and in a few moments was listening at the door.

As she did so Ralph also thought he could hear sounds as of creeping steps and whispering voices.

Of course it is easy to listen in the dark until you can fancy that you hear sounds.

And so at first they were not sure.

Both were loth to part so soon after such a long separation; but, as presently the noises came nearer, Constance glided across once more to her lover.

"Pray fly, Ralph!" she cried. "You will be seized and made a prisoner if they have suspected you and they find you here. Go, and if all goes well it shall be as you wish."

One more fervid kiss, and Ralph rapidly, but noiselessly, approached the window and threw it up. In a moment he was outside, rapidly descending, as he had ascended, by the ivy.

Scarcely had the casement been closed again than a loud knocking came at the door.

"Who is there?" cried Constance, in a sleepy voice.

"Sir Roland and Mrs. Levine."

This was the housekeeper.

"What is it you require at this hour?"

"Open the door! You have had that villain Ralph Ashton here, and we are seeking him."

"I refuse to open," said Constance; "there is no one here."

She did not for a moment suppose that Sir Roland would proceed to violence; but in an instant she found her mistake, for, with a rush of his powerful shoulders, he burst open the door.

He found Constance standing defiantly in the middle of the room in the beautiful *déshabille* in which Ralph had surprised her, and, furious as he was, Sir Roland's eyes could not avoid resting for a moment on the girl's superb form and gleaming shoulders.

"Where is Ralph?" he cried.

"I refuse to answer. Search the room," replied Constance, as she snatched up a shawl and drew it round her.

They did with no effect, as we know.

"He has escaped by the window, Mrs. Levine," said the baronet, presently. "You are certain you heard his voice?"

"Yes—certain," replied the housekeeper. "I heard them talking and kissing, and I heard something said about a speedy marriage."

Sir Roland laughed, though his eyes flashed vengefully.

"Ha, ha!" he cried, "there will, no doubt, be a speedy marriage—eh, Mrs. Levine? But of that to-morrow. Meanwhile, I am ashamed to find that you have received a lover in your bedroom. It is not wonderful, however, considering the stock you come from. In a few hours you will know all. And now to saddle my horse and capture that traitor and assassin."

If these words were intended to create any terror or despair in the mind of Constance they utterly failed.

She merely turned away with a contemptuous smile and walked to the window.

In a few moments the baronet had passed down the stairs and been met by Caleb Masters, who, though older, still looked just as powerful and just as crafty.

"Sir Roland," he whispered, "Ned Wilmot is here."

The baronet uttered an exclamation of astonishment yet half-pleasure.

"How imprudent!" he muttered; "yet he comes in the nick of time. Lead me to him. Where is he?"

"He is in your study. He says he comes to you on a matter of life or death, and no one has seen him save me."

In a few moments the baronet was in the presence of the dastardly assassin of the Mint.

"Excuse my intrusion at this hour," he began.

But Sir Roland interrupted him.

"Nay, this is no time for apology," he cried. "What I want you to understand as you are here is that Ralph Ashton has only just escaped from this house,. He cannot be gone far, follow him and kill him, for he knows our secret. Talk of nothing now, but follow on his track and never come back hither until you can tell me he is no longer living. Hasten—waste no time!"

Ned Wilmot made a wry face.

"You see, money—"

The baronet flung a purse well filled on the table.

"Take that for the present," he said, "and linger no longer."

The assassin pocketed the money with a grin, coolly lifted the wine bottle to his lips, and took a goodly draught, and then going to the French window, passed out.

"Fear not," said he as he went, "Master Ralph shall not trouble you long. I know his haunts, and it will be a puzzler to me if my knife doesn't divide his left ribs within a week!"

This settled, a few words were exchanged between Sir Roland and Caleb, and then the former once more sought his bed-chamber.

"By Jove! I never knew that Constance was such a lovely girl," he murmured to himself, as he got into bed. "I never before had such a good view of her charms. I must have her for myself. I might make a worse choice, and if I make up my mind I'll have her by fair means or foul.'

## CHAPTER VI.

DAISY LEIGH ONCE MORE—GEDGE FOOTE, THE DWARF BAGSMAN, TRAPPED.

GEDGE FOOTE, whom we mentioned in our first chapter, was almost the first one to enter the murder-room in the Mint after Ned Wilmot had escaped, and Spring-Heeled Jack had leaped out of the window.

He was a strange-looking being.

About four feet and a-half in height, he had a large head of a bullet shape, covered with shock red hair, massive shoulders, with scarcely any neck, long unshapely arms and bandy legs.

His hands were large and claw-like, and gave one the idea that one grip from them could squeeze the life out of a man were he ever so strong.

His face was such as might be expected from such a body, with small, cunning eyes, an upward turning nose and a big gash of a mouth.

He was a strange being, not only in his appearance but in his habits.

He was known as a bagsman, or "commercial traveller," but he was, in reality, a pedlar, who sold trinkets and so forth, and did odd strokes of business which were not consistent with strict notions of honesty.

In fact, he was supposed to be a receiver of stolen goods, and to take long journeys into distant parts of England for the purpose of disposing of things which had been appropriated by the thieves of the Mint.

Whatever he was, his movements were very mysterious, and he never gave the police the chance of catching him.

Well, on that dreadful evening, after Ned Wilmot had fled and the hue and cry after him was going on, Gedge Foote entered the room where the body of Herbert Leigh lay, with Daisy still on the couch of rags in the corner.

Those who had raised the alarm at first, when the cries of "Help—help—murder!" had ceased, had only seen the dead body, and had not observed the form of the girl in the half darkness.

But Gedge, who knew her well, and had often cast longing looks at the trim little figure in its shabby garments, and the neat little foot and ankle, was sure that the girl must be somewhere about; and re-lighting the candle, which had been overturned in the struggle, he sought for her and found her.

She was just recovering consciousness, her eyes were opening and gleaming round her as if to realise her position; her lips were pale—pale almost as the white breast which rose and fell in spasmodic throbs under Gedge's admiring gaze.

He knelt down and half-raised her, at the same time pouring a little brandy from his flask between the pouting lips.

"This is a terribly bad business, Miss Daisy," he said; "but you must try and bear up under it, if it's only for the sake of having revenge."

She shuddered as she looked at him.

He was so terribly ugly—uglier than ever when he tried to act the consoler.

But his kindness had given her life for the moment.

"If you will help me up I will go into my room and put on my things, so that I can see the people who will be sure to come," she said.

And she blushed even in the middle of her sorrow to think that he had caught her in such *déshabille.*

She had scarcely dressed when the heavy tramp of feet was heard, and presently two constables, an inspector, and a surgeon entered.

The girl gave her account of the affair as well as she could; but she was not pressed to say much.

The next day the enquiry would take place, and before then she would be able to collect her thoughts.

"But you can't stop here, my dear," said the surgeon, kindly. "This is no scene for you, and there really does not seem to be any accomodation for you."

"There's a person over the way—Mrs. Porter," said Gedge Foote, "who would gladly give the young lady a bed."

"Yes, Mrs. Porter, I know her," said the inspector, "very well. Come with me, and we will see that you are safe for the night at least."

All those three stout-hearted men felt compassion for poor little Daisy; she seemed so small and fragile a flower to blossom into life in such a terrible way as this.

On undressing that night in her strange room, she found the note which Spring-Heeled Jack had placed in her bosom, after he had felt her heart to see if she still lived.

She shuddered as she remembered the awful apparition which had saved her from Ned Wilmot, but yet she felt sure that he was a friend.

"Spirit or no spirit," she thought, "he saved my life, and, maybe, my honour, for I saw passions of every evil kind in that murderer's face. I know not the place he mentions, but I can find out. Gedge Foote, hideous as he is, seems kind, I will ask him."

Kind!

How little she knew of human nature when she could dream of trusting such a being.

But, then, how could she imagine that she had excited in the mind of this hideous dwarf a wild, mad passion, which could only be extinguished by death?

While Daisy was sleeping, in spite of her terrible trouble, and in consequence of a sly little something put in her warm drink by the worthy Mrs. Porter, strange things were going on over at the house where the murder had been committed.

The door of the room had been locked, everything had been left just as the police had found it; and a constable was located in the porch below to keep watch.

At first, of course, considerable excitement prevailed in the street; a motley crowd gathered round the door, and groups stood chatting at different points.

But people at last grew weary and went off to bed, the street regained its normal aspect, and the murder was left to be raked up again in the morning.

About an hour after the place had become quiet a strange thing happened.

A hackney coach came slowly and methodically round the corner.

It came from the direction of the Three Mariners, and on the box beside the driver was a man dressed in the garb of a policeman.

They drove down the street very quietly, and stopped at the door of the house of murder.

Then the door of the cab was opened, and two more men in the garb of policemen stepped out.

Their knock brought out the constable who had been left to watch in the parlour, and who, naturally imagining that the corpse would not be likely to run away, thought it no harm to doze awhile.

He looked at them in dubious amazement.

"Why, what's the matter?" he said.

"Hush! can't talk outside," replied the one who seemed in command of the new arrivals; and the whole party, including the one who had sat on the box with the driver, entered the house.

The constable looked still more disconcerted when he saw the new-comers in the light of the lamp.

There was not one familiar face.

"What is your business?" he asked.

"The body has to be removed."

"Where to?"

"The mortuary."

The man stared in bewilderment.

The proceeding, as he was well aware, was most unusual.

"By whose orders?" he asked.

"By those of the Chief Commissioner," said the head constable. "See, here is his order. Read for yourself."

The man was quite dazed by the wonderful quickness of the whole affair, but, in obedience to orders, he bent over the blue official-looking paper which the man produced.

That was all that was wanted.

In an instant one of the pretended constables drew from his pocket a handkerchief and thrust it into the face of the reading constable.

The effect was almost instantaneous.

He gave one reproachful look at the man in front of him, then his arms dropped helplessly by his side, his eyes closed, and he was a mere tool in their hands.

In an instant he was searched and the keys taken from him.

"Now then," said one of the men, "we must do all this very quickly. He won't be insensible more than a few minutes. You, Clarkson, stop here, and if he wants another sniff why give it to him."

Leaving one of the sham constables, whom they addressed as Clarkson, to watch the insensible man, they then ascended the stairs, and, without hesitation, entered the room where the tragedy had occurred.

They looked quite callously at the dead body, which already began to look awful in its pallor and rigidity, more especially when taken in conjunction with the horrible surroundings.

To them death was nothing.

In one way or another they had become careless of it.

Without a word they raised the body, and, dispensing with throwing anything over it, proceeded to carry it downstairs.

To cover it up would have disarranged their plans.

When they reached the basement story they did not pass out of the front door, but, opening a side one, which led out into a little court, they so held the murdered man that he looked as if he was incapably drunk, and was being assisted along by the policemen.

In this manner they helped him along until they reached the street.

No one was about.

The wonder-seekers were at rest for the moment.

So they had no difficulty in placing the body in the hackney-coach, and in doing everything unseen and unknown by anyone.

Then a light whistle brought out the man who had been left to mind the constable, and in a few moments all had quitted the neighbourhood.

This is how the body of Herbert Leigh had made its appearance in the vicinity of Ashton Hall.

The excitement at the disappearance of the body was very great—the "Mint" chuckled at the utter confusion of the police—the papers made a great thing of it.

But no clue was obtained.

Wherever Herbert Leigh's dead body had been spirited away there it remained, and poor Daisy felt doubly bereft.

Of what use were her unavailing declarations?

She knew who had murdered her father, she felt sure who had instigated the murder; but of what use would it be for her to make reckless and unsupported declarations?

It was best to bide her time.

Though she had been terrified out of all measure by the apparition of Spring-Heeled Jack, she felt that he was her friend.

She did not dare, as it were, to believe in the supernatural; but, of course, it was impossible to account in any other way for the strange appearance of the being who had rescued her.

She was content, therefore, to abide by what she had seen, and trust to the future to explain all.

She was without any protector now.

She could not look for protection to a being whom she knew not, and whom she could not call to her aid.

So in this predicament she turned to Gedge Foote.

She saw no wrong in this.

He had been kind to her; and, having lived in the same house as herself and her father, was comparatively acquainted with them.

She resolved to ask him, therefore, what best to do.

From all Gedge could derive from her words, Ned Wilmot, the man who had murdered her father, had made up his mind to possess her for himself, consequently anything which enabled her to keep out of the clutches of this fiend would be acceptable.

Loving her with an insane passion, which she had not the slightest conception of, he lost sight of the idea of his own repulsive ugliness, and only thought that incessant and patient waiting and never-ceasing attention would win her to himself.

If Daisy had had one notion of such a thing as this she would never have accepted his aid.

But, perfectly innocent of the fact that he could conceive such a mad idea, she confided to him the fact that she desired to quit the Mint, and proceed to the place mentioned by Spring-Heeled Jack, Mrs. Barton, of River Cottage, Edmonton.

She was perfectly ignorant of localities, and consequently she was quite unprepared to give Gedge any idea of the neighbourhood to which she desired to go.

However, Gedge knew.

"I could take you to the place blindfolded," he said, "but I don't think you'll like it."

"I must put up with it," replied Daisy, "since my father is dead, and his body has been spirited away. I have nothing to bind me to this spot, and I wish to quit it as quickly as possible. I fear every moment to see the hateful face of Ned Wilmot."

"You ought to wish that," said Gedge, "you could then give him into custody."

"No, no. It is useless. I could prove nothing," said the young girl. "Leave him to time and private vengeance. He will receive far greater punishment than he would at the hand of the law."

"It shall all be as you please," said Gedge; "but don't you think that your sudden disappearance, after the vanishing of your father's body, will give subject for suspicion by the police."

"I care not," said Daisy. "I will risk that and anything to get away from this place."

That evening Gedge Foote and his confiding companion quitted Mrs. Porter's, and taking a hackney coach in the next street, began riding quickly towards the vicinity of Battersea.

Although our story is a comparatively modern one, this neighbourhood had no resemblance to what it is at the present day.

It abounded in narrow dirty alleys and lanes, and long dreary stretches of swamp; at night it often happened that houses built on the edge of the water were entirely obscured by mist.

As the hackney coach rolled into one of these alleys, and then came out upon a dismal piece of marsh with not a house visible, and only here and there a bare looking tree, the girl's heart sank within her bosom.

What could her mysterious friend mean by asking her to immure herself in such a terrible spot of desolation?

Could it be possible that she was only escaping from one trap to fall into another?

However, it was too late now to retreat.

So she only made some commonplace remark about the dreariness of the surroundings.

"Yes, you're right," said Gedge Foote, "it's about the most dismal swamp that you can find round London. I expect your friend, however, had excellent reasons for advising this as a place of safety."

"No doubt!" said Daisy, as the horse drew up before a house, which looked only like a huge black barn in the lampless darkness. "I expect he thinks that no one will be likely to seek me here."

"Just so," said Gedge, "but even if he deserts you, remember, I know where you are, and that I will never betray your whereabouts."

And as he helped her to alight the dwarf bagsman squeezed her hand impressively.

The house, approached across a dismal garden, was apparently a small squarely-built one, and the door was soon opened by an elderly woman of nondescript appearance.

Of course Daisy was unaware of the fact that Gedge Foote had been there during the day, that instead of being Barton the woman's name was Foster, and that Spring-Heeled Jack (whatever that mysterious person might be) knew no more of this female and her place than the man in the moon.

But so it was.

Mrs. Foster was a friend of the dwarf, had assumed the name of Barton to oblige him, and Daisy Leigh was fairly trapped.

However, she made no enquiries. Young and simple as she was she had formed plans secretly.

She was told that her friend had paid in advance for her lodging and board for a month, and, thinking the woman meant the awful apparition who had so mysteriously befriended her, she accepted her position gratefully, and only wondered how long it would be before the mystery was explained.

It was late when they had had supper, and Gedge Foote was leaving.

They were alone as he rose to say good-bye.

"Good-bye, Daisy," he said. "I hope you will be comfortable here. But there's one thing I fancy your friend has forgotten."

"What is that?"

"I don't think you have any money."

The young girl flushed. She had never thought of this. The money left her by Spring-Heeled Jack had already been spent.

"Well," she stammered, "that is true; but I don't think I shall want any, at any rate, just yet. Everything has been paid for."

"Yes, yes," said Gedge; "but then you don't know what may happen, and you have no clothes with you."

They were in the little parlour alone, and he took her hand.

The light was very dim.

Only two candles were there to illuminate the room.

He felt her tremble, but she did not refuse.

He placed in her hand two sovereigns, which she held, reluctantly.

"You are very kind to me, Mr. Foote," she said. "I shall never be able to repay you."

"Will you not?" he said.

And then the impulse upon him proved too great—his passion overcame him.

In an instant his arm was round her waist, his lips glued to hers—her lithe body was held close up to his breast, so that he could feel the palpitation of her bosom and the rapid beating of her heart.

Then he released her without a word and fled.

Daisy fell into a chair—aghast, amazed, ashamed.

In an instant the whole truth was upon her.

This hideous dwarf loved her!

Herself was the reward he was going to claim for his protection.

She cried for very vexation, and spitefully wiped his kisses from her lips.

"Poor wretch!" she murmured; "perhaps he is not aware of his own hideous ugliness. But his wife! Heavens! that would be too terrible. I, who have been brought up, even through abject poverty, to be a lady in thought, and hope for a lady's career. Well, well! he has quickly put me on my guard. If he attempts to make love to me I must fly, no matter whither."

Poor little Daisy!

It was all very well for her to plan like this, but she knew not half the terrible wickedness of Gedge Foote's nature.

She was on the brink of an awful precipice!

---

## CHAPTER VII.

PURSUED BY AN ASSASSIN—CONSTANCE HEARS BAD NEWS—SIR ROLAND'S AND CALEB'S JOURNEY—SPRING-HEELED JACK TERRIFIES THE PEOPLE ON THE STAGE COACH, AND TAKES A RISE OUT OF THE BARONET.

NED WILMOT, although he had expected a far different reception by Sir Roland, and had hoped to be able at once to have explained his perilous position, lost no time in carrying out the murderous designs of his employer.

His plan was to follow the road which Ralph Ashton would be most like to take to reach London that night.

If he missed him he would disguise himself and haunt the neighbourhood day and night.

One thing was certain—

Sir Roland had made up his mind that Ralph Ashton must die.

And die he must.

The baronet had Ned Wilmot far too much in his power to allow of any denial.

So the man, whose character resembled nothing so much as that of an Italian bravo, rode off, whistling a song lowly to himself, and thinking how he should best get "the job" over quick and have time to enjoy himself.

Everything seemed very quiet.

The moon had come out suddenly and bathed all things in her silver glory.

Over park, and grounds, and lake, and road, the calm of an exquisite night had fallen.

Not a sound, save the vague and gentle sighing of the wind, was to be heard, and as Ned Wilmot's horse leaped the hedge and began to clatter along the high road, the noise of the horse's footsteps resounded far over the country side.

He had scarcely reached the bend in the road where the ruins stood, the spot where the dead body of Herbert Leigh had been found by Spring-Heeled Jack, when there was heard the loud and demoniacal laugh which had so terrified Ned Wilmot in the murder-room in the Mint and on the highway.

And then there came the ominous whirring as of wings, and, glancing up, the assassin saw the awful figure which had crashed through the window at the time of the murder.

There were the bat-like wings formed by his arms, and his great cloak, his red body, his terrible face, and the sulphurous smoke and flame rushing from his mouth.

Ned Wilmot had made many brave resolutions—the will of Sir Roland was to be carried out at all costs.

But his courage oozed out at his fingers' ends as he heard the well-known "Ha! ha! ha!" of the mysterious apparition, and saw his bat-like form hovering for that instant over his head between him and the moon.

With a yell of terror he put spurs to his horse and fled.

But of what use was it for him to fly?

What horse could keep up with the giant leaps, and rushes, and springs of Spring-Heeled Jack?

Over hedges, over the horseman's head, he leaped and gambolled.

Ned Wilmot, gasping with terror, lost him once, and with a feeling of relief he pushed on at a still greater speed to reach the bridge near the stream.

"He has disappeared for to-night," he muttered, "and so has my enterprise. I feel no nerve to attempt anything now. I must go to the Corner Pin and have a good draught of brandy. That accursed thing has driven all the life out of me."

But no!

He had not escaped.

There was Spring-Heeled Jack standing on the stone arch of the little bridge, and as Ned Wilmot came dashing up, at a rate which made it impossible to stop his horse, the strange being went leaping and laughing far ahead of him.

The blood seemed to curdle in Ned Wilmot's veins.

The apparition was certainly unaccountable.

But none the less was it terrible.

Little by little Ned Wilmot felt his nerves getting weaker, his head becoming dizzy, and his respiration difficult.

He felt certain that the end of it would be that he should fall from his horse, and then—

He scarcely dared think what the end of it would be with a being whose power and nature he could not fathom.

But, as if to save him, there came suddenly a burst of laughter, and a band of roysterers came rolling along from the Corner Pin.

This was a tavern standing some distance back from the high road, with a large pond in front, and green benches and tables round the open space.

These men had evidently been enjoying themselves to the top of their bent, and their voices rolled loudly and merrily over the country-side.

Nerved by the sound of companionship, Ned Wilmot struck his spurs into his horse's flanks, and, dashing round the corner, nearly plunging headlong into the pond, made for the door of the tavern.

With his usual diabolical "Ha, ha, ha!" Spring-Heeled Jack sprang high in the air, clean over the head of the rider, and alighted in front of the astonished merrymakers.

The latter were for a moment so horrified, so stupefied by the unaccountable apparition, that they could not utter a sound.

But as Spring-Heeled Jack, with a sudden bound, leaped clean over the pond, and disappeared among the trees in a cloud of sulphurous flame, they burst into a chorus of terrified yells and fled in all directions.

There was scarcely a cottage within ten miles that night where this terror was not discussed—a terror so new, so strange, so unaccountable.

Spring-Heeled Jack had only made his appearance a few days, but already his fame was spreading far and wide.

But, at any rate, he had stopped the pursuit after Ralph.

Sir Roland or no Sir Roland, nothing would have induced Ned Wilmot to move out of the Corner Pin that night.

He had escaped the awful apparition when he had feared that it would pursue him to his death, and so he passed into the public room and steeped his crime-stained soul in drink, to drive away the weird phantoms which were beginning to be his constant companions.

"I'll haunt the place to-morrow in the daylight," he muttered to himself, as he shuddered in his bed after supper, and drew the bedclothes over his head, "and look out for this Ralph Ashton, but, hang me! if I could do it to-night. That infernal thing has destroyed all my nerves. Man or devil, I'll have a shot at him the first time we meet again!"

A valiant resolve, truly!

But the assassin little knew what would be the result of the trial.

Meanwhile, leaving Ralph Ashton, and Spring-Heeled Jack, and the cowardly assassin of Herbert Leigh, we must return to Ashton Grange.

Constance Marfield, despite the scene in the bedroom on the night before, appeared in the breakfast-room at the usual hour in the morning.

Had she known the thoughts which occupied the

mind of Sir Roland she would probably not have attired herself as she did.

But she had only noticed the coarseness and rudeness of his bursting into her chamber the night before, and had not observed his look of admiration when his eyes had fallen unexpectedly on the glories of those rounded shoulders and the bare, voluptuous bosom.

As it was, the admiration of the sensual baronet—the man who placed his pleasures before everything; who spilled blood like water rather than suffer opposition—was heightened doubly by the ravishing picture she made on her birthday morning.

She was dressed in white muslin and blue ribbons; as on that day, long ago, when she and Ralph had first awakened to love's delicious thrill; her dress being really as low as for a ball, but a gauzy net veiling her creamy shoulders and superb bust, her bare arms gleaming also through the same material.

A beautiful colour was on her cheeks, an unusual sparkle in her eyes, her mouth seemed to pout more deliciously and to be wreathed by tremulous smiles.

How natural was it all?

For was she not to know love's sweet consummation within a week? Was not her longing love at length to be satisfied? Was not the patience of years to be rewarded, and was she not to be released from thraldom as Ralph Ashton's wife?

Alas! for her delicious hopes.

"You are looking quite charming on this your birthday morning," said Sir Roland, as she entered, and he advanced to meet her. "I think that as your guardian all these years I must claim a kiss."

She could scarcely refuse him this; and, in fact, he had often pressed her brow. So she raised her head for him to kiss, carrying out Ralph's suggestion that she was to allow him to suspect nothing.

But the kiss he gave her was not as usual.

He stooped and pressed his lips to hers greedily; not once, but twice and thrice, gliding his arm round her, and drawing her to him, and looking down into her astonished and half-frightened eyes.

"Really, this is a birthday to be remembered," he cried, as she contrived at last to release herself, blushing and afraid. "You seem to be younger and more girlish this morning than I have known you before. Sit down, my darling Constance; near me—so. I have very much to tell you. First, your own story, and then a great secret!"

Constance was unable to restrain a shudder.

Her guardian's manner had told her as plainly as it could what this secret would be.

She made no reply whatever, but as calmly as possible poured herself out a cup of coffee.

This seemed to produce an irritating effect upon the baronet, in spite of his love-sick mood.

His manner changed.

"By the way," he said, "I think I will tell you my secret first. From what happened last night I feel sure that you look upon Ralph Ashton as your lover still. This was all very well years ago, but since he has disgraced himself it is out of all reason."

"Nevertheless," replied Constance, recovering her equanimity and her speech in defence of her absent one, "I am going to be his wife. I have promised him, and I shall perform my promise. I am twenty-one to-day, and I can do as I please."

"In spite of his forgeries—in spite of the awful crime of murder which has now stained his soul?"

"I don't believe that he is guilty of anything of which you accuse him," said Constance, indignantly. "He is a good and true gentleman, and if the whole world is against him I will be hi wife."

Sir Roland smiled sarcastically.

"We shall see," he said. "For my part I doubt it much."

Constance made no reply.

The baronet also, without further remark, began to unfasten some blue papers and others, which he had before him, tied with a piece of red tape.

He noted with pleasure and evil triumph, as he stole a glance across the table, that Constance had observed what he was doing, though she kept her eyes resolutely on her breakfast, and that her white breast heaved under its gauzy black lace covering.

He knew her thoughts.

Knew that, in spite of her affected indifference, she was eagerly anxious to learn her history.

As I have before said, she was unaware of the real events of her youth.

But after what Sir Roland had done and said she was determined not to express any eagerness.

In fact, she would have rather remained in ignorance than ask him the slightest favour.

However, there was no need to indulge in these dogged fancies of hers.

Sir Roland drank off a cup of coffee nervously, cleared his throat, and said—

"Well, Constance, before we proceed to talk further of the matter we alluded to, and which is, I can tell you, so dear to my heart, I will explain your position here. You are my ward, as you know."

"Yes."

"I have been kind to you during my guardianship, have I not?"

"In your idea, perhaps. I consider I have been a prisoner."

"Only for your own good—only to protect you against the machinations of evil-doers."

She smiled ironically, but made no reply.

"Well," he said, "that may be your opinion, but it is not mine. In the first place, then, I must tell you that your name is not Marfield at all, but Harland."

"Why have I been here under false pretences?" she cried.

"For your father's sake."

"Does he live?"

"Yes."

The girl's colour heightened, and her bosom leaped joyfully.

"Oh! I am so glad," she cried. "How soon can I see him?"

"We will talk of that presently," he said, drily. "I must no longer beat about the bush, but tell you the whole story. Come closer to me, my dear—I don't want everyone to hear my words."

"Thank you!" said Constance, coldly. "I have excellent hearing, and would rather remain as I am."

She was in no humour to submit to any more of his daring caresses and rapturous kisses.

He pressed her no more, but continued—

"Your father was a man I met years and years ago on the Continent and took a fancy to, for he was about the same age as myself, and had apparently the same tastes.

"We had both plenty of money and spent it freely, and consequently you may imagine the hours flew by on golden wings.

"Tom Harland had a wife and daughter, much about your size, of charming appearance, and with her I very quickly fell in love.

"She was a being of passionate nature, and after a very few weeks of acquaintance, at a ball, where she had lain in my arms in many a dreamy waltz, we confessed our mutual wishes, and were married the very next morning by special license."

Constance did not like the style in which he told his story.

"Really, Sir Roland," she said, "your love affairs are far from interesting to me. I am anxious to hear my own story."

"I am telling it," said the baronet, in a voice of annoyance; "it is so bound up with my own that I cannot divide one from the other."

"Well, very soon after the marriage, an awful thing was discovered, which ruined three people's lives.

"It was found that Tom Harland, though received in and courted by society, was little better than a thief. He was a forger, a card-sharper; and, at last, to save himself from discovery and arrest, he committed the crime for which he was tried and sentenced.

"He murdered in cold blood the man whom he had basely robbed, and who had nearly effected his capture.

"He was arrested and tried (I forgot to say we were in England then), and was by some quibble of the law found guilty only of manslaughter.

"The judge, however, was of a different opinion to the jury, and sentenced him to penal servitude for life."

"And after all these years of terrible suffering he still lives?" said Constance, in tears.

"Yes; and, what is more, is free."

Constance uttered a joyful cry.

"Free? Oh! then I shall see him?"

"I am afraid," said the baronet, dryly, "that your ecstasy at the idea of clasping to your heart a thief and assassin, as you did last night, will be doomed to speedy disappointment. But listen patiently. The sorrow and excitement killed my wretched sister-in-law, and drove my wife mad. She was taken to a lunatic asylum, where she died not long after. You were about six months old at the time, and at Tom Harland's earnest entreaty, for the sake of our old friendship, I took you in my care, promising not to divulge your secret until you were twenty-one, when I was to tell you, and leave you to judge for yourself. But, unfortunately, something has happened to put a different complexion on matters entirely."

"What is that?" asked Constance, excitedly.

"Simply that your father has escaped from prison, and I know where he is."

"Well?"

Constance eyed him narrowly.

In her eagerness to hear all she had not observed that he had been gradually drawing his chair nearer and nearer to hers.

There was a malevolent look upon his face that somewhat alarmed her.

"It is far from well," he said. "I had not intended ever to tell you anything. I thought Tom Harland's idea of disclosing his shameful story to you the idea of a madman.

"I had intended to let you marry after you had attained the age of twenty-one, under the name of Marfield, and never tell you anything of the affair.

"That was when you were a little girl; but when you ripened into such glorious womanhood, my thoughts changed.

"In fact, Constance, I want you for my own wife."

"Ha! ha! ha!"

The demoniacal laugh of Spring-Heeled Jack resounded through the room, and a dark shadow crossed the window.

The baronet, leaping up with an oath, rushed to the French casement, opened it and hastened out on the terrace.

But in vain.

There was no sign of any being, human or otherwise.

With a much more subdued manner he returned to the room, and with an almost perceptible shudder closed the casement.

"Some absurd prank," he said, glancing at Constance, who was very pale. "I only hope that whoever has been mountebanking out there has not heard our conversation."

"No, indeed, for my father's sake."

"You would not like to see him recaptured, then?"

"You need not ask me the question."

"Well, then," said Sir Roland, resuming his seat, but keeping his eyes fixed upon the window, "I have made up my mind that I cannot do better than make you my wife. You understand my ways; we have lived so long together that we shall agree immensely well. I have grown to love you, and your charms of person are such that they have come upon me as a surprise now that I have noticed them more observantly. It is only for you to name the day, and you can sink your father's wretched story in the knowledge that you are Lady Ashton."

"I fancy," said Constance, smiling, "that I should have a better chance of being Lady Ashton if I married Ralph."

Sir Roland reddened with anger, but, suppressing it, said—

"My dear Constance, this is scarcely a joking matter. I offer you my hand, my heart, and my future. What is your reply?"

"I refuse unconditionally," she said, firmly.

"Will nothing move you?"

"Nothing."

"In that I fancy you are wrong," said Sir Roland; "if you refuse I shall, without a moment's hesitation, deliver your father over into the hands of justice. What he has suffered hitherto will be nothing to what he will suffer in the future."

"I pity my father; I am anxious to see him, that after all his trials I may forgive him," said Constance, with a wonderful calmness. "But I do not believe he desires to commit another crime."

"What crime?"

"To doom his child to marriage with an assassin, because he has himself been guilty, perhaps by accident, of a similar crime."

And with these words Constance rose defiantly from her chair, with flashing eyes and heaving bosom.

Sir Roland strove to approach her.

The interview had turned out badly—very differently indeed to what he had expected—and he resolved to endeavour to pacify her in a different way, by kind words and so forth.

But she guessed his intention, and thwarted him at once.

"To-day your influence over me ends," she cried. "I am now my own mistress, and I will no longer suffer your dictation. I shall quit this house to-day, and within a week I shall become the wife of Ralph Ashton."

The baronet, in spite of his rage, burst into a loud and discordant laugh.

"Ha, ha!" he cried. "Very good—very good! And, doubtless, as you will have to marry him in prison, you will be able to have your father to give you away. Ha, ha! a good joke, truly. See here."

He took from his pocket a piece of paper, printed with large characters, and handed it to her.

It ran as follows—

"£100 REWARD.—*This reward will be given to anyone who will give such information as shall lead to the apprehension of Ralph Ashton, accused of forgery and murder. A* FREE PARDON *will be given to any accomplice turning Queen's Evidence.—Apply to or address* MR. SUPERINTENDENT BUGGINS, *Police Station, Barnet.*"

A second paper ran as follows—

"£20 REWARD *will be given to anyone giving satisfactory information as to whereabouts of Thomas Harland, an escaped convict, who was sentenced nearly twenty-one years ago to transportation for life for robbery and murder, and who is known to have escaped to England. Believed to be in the neighbourhood of Barnet.—Information to be given to* MR. SUPERINTENDENT BUGGINS, *Police Station, Barnet; the* COMMISSIONERS OF POLICE, *Chief Office, London; or any Police Station in the United Kingdom.*"

"Poor Ralph!" murmured Constance, tearfully.

"And you would marry him in spite of this?" cried Sir Roland.

"Yes; for he is innocent," she cried; "and you, in spite of my father's public disgrace—a renewed disgrace—would marry me?"

"Yes; because I love you—because there need be no disgrace. Your real name need never be known, and as for your father, I will assist him to quit the country at once, and fly to some country where no one can find him."

"When can I see him?" said Constance.

"To-morrow night."

"Why not to-night?"

"Because I am going to Rickworth to-night with Caleb Masters to receive a large sum of money. I prefer taking him to going with Job Joskins, who came home here naked last night, and otherwise behaved himself like an idiot," returned the baronet; "besides, it will be necessary to be cautious in giving your father information of the rendezvous."

"Very well, then," said Constance, with cold calmness; "I will see him to-morrow night, and that interview will decide me. Till then, adieu!"

The baronet's face flushed and he advanced a step.

"You give me hope, then?" he cried.

Constance glanced at him with a look of derisive contempt from top to toe.

"Hope!" she cried; "yes, if you call that hope—a faint chance that you may be able to mate yourself with a woman who despises and hates you, and will always throughout her life regard you as lower than the most loathsome thing that crawls upon the face of the earth."

And with these words she suddenly swept from the room.

In spite of Sir Roland's words and the humiliating story she had heard, she had made up her mind, and it was by no means according to the notions of her guardian.

As soon as she had quitted the apartment Sir Roland opened the door and glanced after her.

He feared instant flight.

But that would not have suited Constance, for the simple reason that she would not have been able to communicate with her lover.

She passed straight up to her own room, and he heard her lock herself in.

Then he rang for Mrs. Levine.

The housekeeper, who had managed this strange household for so many years, was still comely, and hoped even now to be Lady Ashton when Sir Roland had sown his wild oats, hastened up.

She knew nothing of his matrimonial designs in regard to Constance.

"Mrs. Levine," he said, "I cannot quite explain to you my reasons, but I very much fear that Miss Marfield proposes to celebrate her majority by running away from home."

"Indeed!"

"And I must depend upon you to prevent this. When Miss Marfield comes down to dinner there must be some excuse for changing her room. Place her in the square chamber at the end of the gallery."

Mrs. Levine shuddered.

"That room, Sir Roland!"

The baronet frowned.

"Why not?" he cried. "What foolish fancies are you allowing to creep into your head? Have you been preaching to Miss Marfield, and infecting her with your idiotic reminiscences?"

This was not a very pleasant address to the woman who had prospective notions of marriage.

But she understood Sir Roland's moods.

"Certainly not," she said. "I will manage everything."

And so it came to pass that when Constance was going up to her room again that evening she was informed that she could not retire to her own room that night as the window had by some mysterious means fallen in, and been shattered to atoms.

Constance made little remark, because she suspected nothing.

But when she was once ensconced in her new chamber, which the housekeeper had endeavoured to render cosy by a bright fire, she knew the reason of the removal.

The windows were barred, and the door not only locked but secured by heavy bolts.

One glance she gave through the bars of her prison, at the moonlit landscape without, and then she flung herself on her knees beside the bed and burst into a passion of despairing tears.

---

## CHAPTER VIII.

### SPRING-HEELED JACK AND THE STAGE COACH

SIR ROLAND had decided, as we have said, to take Caleb Masters with him instead of Job Joskins, and accordingly, at eight that night the two worthies mounted their horses, and with pistols in their girdles, rode off to the Corner Pin

# SPRING-HEELED JACK,

## THE TERROR OF LONDON.

By the Author of "TURNPIKE DICK, the Star of the Road."

AS THE AWFUL APPARITION SAILED UP INTO THE AIR THEY FIRED POINT BLANK AT IT.

No. 3.

where the coach would take them to their detsination.

"I can't think what Ned Wilmot can be doing," said the baronet to Caleb, as they went on; "he has had plenty of time and opportunity to communicate with me."

"It's no use being impatient, sir," replied Caleb; "I think Ned's a wonderful man, and does the strangest tasks in the most wonderful way. I don't think he has had time to do much yet."

"Well, perhaps you are right," said Sir Roland; "but things are gathering round so strangely that, upon my honour, I begin to feel nervous."

"It's time you did," muttered Caleb.

"Eh! what's that?"

"I said there was nothing to feel nervous about," said Caleb, quickly. "He has had scarcely time to do anything yet, and, remember, he is always in danger of the hue and cry."

By this time they had reached the Corner Pin, and the baronet, alighting with his companion, passed into the bar.

The landlord at once bowed obsequiously, and turning to a shelf at the back of the bar, took from it a letter, which he handed to his guest.

The baronet eyed it unconcernedly, and ordering some warm brandy, opened the missive carelessly, and read it.

It was, as he expected, from Ned Wilmot, although the handwriting was disguised, and the name also.

It ran as follows—

"*The person whom you wished me to follow has evidently left the neighbourhood; but I will endeavour to trace him to London, and obtain the interview which you think so necessary. I was followed and impeded in my search again last night by that hideous apparition which has lately come into this neighbourhood. If he follows me everywhere I fear I shall have but a poor chance of doing as you wish.* "JOHN MAYNARD."

Ned Wilmot dared not sign his own name, and trusted to chance to enable the baronet to understand what it meant.

Sir Roland was not slow to comprehend.

He simply placed the note in his pocket, asked how soon the coach would be round, and ordered another glass for the landlord.

"Have you heard or seen anything of this strange appearance that has been going the rounds of the neighbourhood so much, Sir Roland?" asked Boniface.

"Yes; I have caught a glimpse of him," said the baronet; "and if I get near enough to him, and he plays his pranks on me, I will put a bullet through his head."

"That bain't no good, Sir Roland," put in a labourer, who was sitting over in a corner having a pint 'o' yale;' "cos big Tom Norris, the gamekeeper, saw 'un last night, and put the contents of his gun in 'un; and he only laughed 'Ha! ha! ha!' and jumped clean over his head."

"Bah! he missed his aim," said the baronet, derisively, though he felt very uncomfortable.

"Not he. He saw the light through the hole in his forehead, and he knows he shot him."

At this moment the awkward conversation was put a stop to by the arrival of the coach, and the entry of the driver and the guard.

"Got some extra pistols aboard for Spring-Heeled Jack?" cried the landlord.

The guard laughed, though there was very little merriment in the sound.

"Aye! that we have," he said. "Joe here's got his pistols and so have I, and my gun's about loaded up to the muzzle."

A kind of nervous laugh, more like a giggle than anything else, went through the little band of travellers who were waiting to take their places in the coach—The Express—which still went its rumbling way, in spite of the innovating railway.

The "iron horse" had not yet come into common use, and there were abundance of persons, as is well known, who clung to the old-fashioned style of conveyance long after the rails had made a network over all England.

Even in the present day there are plenty of people who delight in the Brighton or the St. Alban's coach.

The night on the present occasion was an exceptionally fine one.

The moon was bright, and the air balmy, and everything seemed to promise a good run.

But somehow or another the party seemed ill at ease.

The mention of Spring-Heeled Jack had cast damper on their spirits.

They might pretend to be brave.

But no one desired to see the portent.

However, they did not disclose their feelings to one another, and as no one liked to be more cowardly than his neighbour, they hastened to take their places.

All, however, including the baronet and Caleb Masters, were anxious—more so than they had ever been before—to reach their destination quickly.

They started at last, six outside and six in, two of the latter having come all the way from London, a widow and her daughter, who sat opposite one another, and were squeezed up in their corners by two male passengers of loud voice and large limbs, who professed to be quite at ease, but were, in reality, in a sad state of perturbation.

The road was hard and smooth, and the coach bowled on at a goodly pace.

But nothing happened.

As time went on and nothing appeared the travellers became more at ease, and even ventured to chaff each other, and peer curiously at little clumps of trees, where the shadows seemed to linger more than in others.

And indeed all passed off well.

Spring-Heeled Jack seemed to have given the high road a rest, and Sir Roland and Caleb, when they descended at the door of the Three Jolly Wheelers, at Rickworth, were among the loudest of the scoffers.

As they passed into the hamlet, however, after booking their return places in the coach, which went back to Barnet at eleven, a horseman darted out from a bye-way suddenly, and passed them with lightning speed.

As he went by a demoniacal "Ha! ha! ha!" burst from his lips, and a strange light glowed round his head.

The baronet staggered back, almost upsetting his companion.

"Confound that demon!" he muttered; "I thought we had avoided him to-night."

"Fear not, good master," said his companion; "I do not think that was the being they call Spring-Heeled Jack. He never rides, but leaps about on his own account."

"Nevertheless, he emitted fire from his mouth, and that was his accursed laugh," said the baronet.

"One thing I am resolved upon, when we return if he begins to play his accursed tricks I will fire at him, be he man or devil, and you, Caleb, must do so, likewise."

"That I swear," said Caleb.

Their further walk towards their destination was a silent one.

Both knew, or at any rate were afraid, that they would meet the mysterious presence on their road home.

But they expresed no opinion about it, and went on moodily towards the house where they were to receive the gold.

The man from whom they expected it was one who sometimes made a difficulty in payment, and, consequently, Sir Roland made it a rule to go there for payment himself; otherwise he would not have ventured out of the precincts of his own place while such a being as Spring-Heeled Jack was supposed to be in the neighbourhood.

It so happenened that on this occasion the debtor was most complacent.

He had had an unusually good run of luck, and the money was at once forthcoming.

So Sir Roland and Caleb were able to quit his house quickly, and return to the "Three Jolly Wheelers."

Here they entered the public room.

There were not many people present, but all knew the baronet, and he was greeted respectfully.

"Strange doings down here lately, squire," said one of the labourers.

"What doings?" asked Sir Roland.

"These ere murders and such like."

"Indeed! I wasn't aware there had been any murders down here," said the baronet, ironically.

The "yokel" was indignant.

What did it matter to him whether one murder had been committed in the Mint, in London, and the other somewhere else twenty years ago, so that the supposed perpetrators were said to be in the neighbourhood.

"Why ain't you seen the police bills, Sir Roland?" he cried. "There's one bill as has got the name of someone same as yourn—Ashton. Hundred pounds! I wish I'd be the one to catch him!"

"I wish you could catch him," said the baronet, "I'd give you fifty pounds more. He's a distant relation of the family, and I tried to do the best for him; but he's a bad egg, and the sooner he's brought to justice the better."

"Funny he should hide about Barnet, then," said another of the men.

"Yes," said the aforesaid yokel; "and then there's another one—Tom Harland, a man that's escaped from prison in Australia, he's hanging about here for something or other."

The baronet smiled.

"We're likely to have plenty of excitement then down in our neighbourhood," he said, "what with escaped murderers and Spring-Heeled Jacks."

The men were silent at this for a moment, and a shudder was observed to pass through their frames.

"Have you seen him," asked Caleb Masters, "that you are so dumbfounded?"

The first speaker shook his head.

"Aye," he said, "you may well say that. I've seen him, and, in fact, most of us have seen him. He's been a-jumping and a-leaping about this 'ere place like mad to-night, and I'm blest if I shan't be glad when he takes it into his head to be off."

"Aye! I don't want my missus and my youngsters skeered out o' their lives," said another; "and they do tell me that he was a-top o' the mission chapel to-night, a-sitting a-top of the little bell-tower, a-breathing out flame and smoke for all the world like a railway-engine."

Sir Roland laughed at this.

But nevertheless he looked askance at Caleb Masters to observe what effect the words had taken on him.

"Perhaps," said Caleb, "this diabolical apparition has something to do with the murders or the murderers."

A tall man who had been sitting in a corner rose up at this.

He had been sitting so far back in the shadow and was so surrounded by tobacco smoke that no one had been able to note his face much.

As he neared the door, the others could see that he was clad in rough garments, which did not seem to suit his style of figure.

His hair and beard were of grizzly hue, and his eyes were large and brilliant, with a hunted, frightened look in them.

"You're a meddlesome lot altogether," he said, as he looked savagely round at the assembled company, "and I expect this Spring-Heeled Jack that you talk about is the devil himself come to frighten out of ye the little wits you've got left."

And with this he went out, leaving the yokels sheepish and astonished, and Sir Roland white as death.

He leaned over towards Caleb, under pretence of taking a pipe-light to re-kindle his cigar.

"That was Tom Harland!" he whispered.

Low as were the words, they reached the ears of one of the men, who whispered to one of his companions.

Then both rose and left the room.

Sir Roland turned the conversation into other channels, waiting impatiently for the Barnet coach to arrive.

But in a few minutes there was a hullabaloo outside, the rush of feet, and the two countrymen who had gone out came helter skelter into the room, one without his hat and blood all over his face.

"Why, what's the matter, Bob?" was the chorus.

"The Devil!" groaned he of the gory nose, as he sank all of a heap on a bench.

"What was it, Bill?" said another, addressing the second one.

"Spring-Heeled Jack!" he gasped.

"Have ye seen him?"

"Aye, and felt him, too," said Bill; "I thought I heard Sir Roland say 'that's Tom Harland,' and so I whispers to Bob, and we both goes out to watch him so as to get the reward. But when we gets just by the pump, where he'd disappeared like, up came the Devil, up—up, into the air, with such a whirr and a whizz, with great wings all spread out, for all the world like a bat and such a 'Ha—ha-ing,' enough to make yer head spin."

"And did he strike your companion?" asked Sir Roland.

"No; the Devil he comes plump down aside o' Bob, a breathing out smoke and flame, and Bob, he screams out and runs right ag'in the pump, and smashes his nose in, by the looks of it. When he picks himself up from the ground, where he fell, the Devil was gone."

It was a few minutes to eleven now.

Sir Roland rose.

"Well," he said, "if this mysterious personage,

whoever he may be, sees that you always run away from him, why, you'll never get a chance of giving him a good leathering. For my part, if he comes near me to-night, I mean to put a bullet through him."

And with these words he took out his pistols and examined them in the light.

Then Caleb did the same, and with a good-night to the scared countrymen they went out.

"Sir Roland means business," said one of the men; "I could see it in his eye."

"Aye, that may be," said Bill; "but it's a main rum thing that he should a' known Tom Harland."

Meanwhile the baronet and his secretary strolling out saw the coach rumbling swiftly on.

It drew up presently at the door, and it was seen at once that no untoward accident had occurred on the road.

Everyone was jolly, and the guard and driver were in their usual spirits.

"Caleb," whispered Sir Roland, "we had better make no remark about this matter to any of the travellers. I fancy these yokels have been misled by some shadows of their own fancy, or by some one of their own companions, who has been frightening them."

"But you will keep a good look out?"

"Aye! that I will," said the baronet; "and for that reason I shall ride on the box-seat, where I shall be able to fire at this masquerading lunatic, whoever he may be."

Caleb made no reply.

He had serious doubts as to there being any masquerading in the matter.

But he did not wish to explain his feelings to Sir Roland.

Although he served him faithfully through everything, he did not respect or like him, and these bantering jokes he simply detested.

It so happened that two travellers on the box-seat descended at the Three Jolly Wheelers, and Sir Roland and his secretary were quickly accommodated.

In a few minutes the coach rolled off, and in the merry moonlight the horses trotted on swiftly towards Barnet.

For some little while all went well.

But presently, as they neared a part of the road where trees grew thickly on either side, loud shrill laughter resounded on all sides.

"Ha! ha! ha!"

It seemed to come from all points—behind, in front, on the left, and on the right; now loud and derisive, now shrill, now sonorous and defiant.

A dusky shadow of no particular shape seemed to flit from tree to tree, and mingle with the branches.

Then a strange form went leaping over the wide fields and gambolled in the moonlight.

An awe fell upon all.

Retreat it was useless to talk about.

They must go on, for, advance or retire, the fiendish unknown would follow.

Not a word was said.

The driver, alarmed as he was, nevertheless kept his team well in hand, so as to be ready if the horses took fright.

Sir Roland quickly drew a pistol from his breast pocket and waited.

Villain as he was he had abundant courage, and was resolved to put this matter to the test.

Presently, as the coach left the wooded part or the road behind, and came to a part where the hedges were high on either side, there was heard quite close at hand the demon laugh.

"Ha! ha! ha!"

And then, with a whirr and a whizz, Spring-Heeled Jack came leaping up towards the sky, clear above the heads of the terrified and astounded travellers, on the summit of the coach.

He looked an awful object, with his bat-like wings outspread, his mouth vomiting forth flame and smoke, his cloven foot showing plainly against the moonlit sky.

The horses, with discordant cries, huddled them selves together on their haunches. The guard, with a yell of terror, fell backwards from his seat, his blunderbus going off in the air as he fell.

Caleb cowered down affrightedly.

Not so Sir Roland.

As the awful apparition sailed up into the air, he rose from his seat, and, raising his pistol, fired point-blank at the figure.

An awful laugh broke from the lips of Spring-Heeled Jack.

Then, as he reached the ground again, he leaped once more over the coach, exclaiming, in his most sepulchural tones—

"Ha! ha! Sir Roland Ashton—murderer! You have failed."

This time he again alighted on the summit of the vehicle, where they could see his glaring eyes, his flaming mouth, his red, glossy body, his cloven hoof, and his long, talon-like hands.

Sir Roland, with a groan, fell fainting back upon the seat. The others, unable to look upon the awful being, cowered down and hid their faces.

"Caleb Masters," said the unknown, in a low voice, which sounded as if it were issuing from the tomb, "you have three hundred pounds in a bag in your pocket, belonging, as you think, to your master. Deliver that to me instantly or dread my vengeance. Refuse, and, at a word from me, the whole coach, with its occupants, will be consumed."

And, as he spoke, he breathed forth such a mass of flame and sulphurous smoke that his body was enveloped in vapour, and a suffocating odour pervaded the whole atmosphere.

Caleb raised his head mechanically, and glanced at the terrible apparition.

That glance seemed to fascinate him, and, as if obeying some order that he could not gainsay, he drew from his pocket the bag containing the bank-notes and gold, and handed it to Spring-Heeled Jack.

"Ha! ha! ha!" he laughed, as he placed it in a pocket in his wing-like cloak. "Tell Sir Roland I have come this time for some of his ill-gotten gains; next time I will come for his soul."

Then, in a cloud of vapour, which seemed suddenly to envelope him, he disappeared, no one seeing him quit the coach.

It was some minutes after his disappearance before anyone moved.

But as the demoniacal laugh sounded far away, as if it was gradually dying in the distance, the travellers and others roused themselves from their lethargy, and resumed their natural positions.

Sir Roland was with difficulty roused to life by the administration of some brandy. The guard, who had fallen so suddenly, was found to have seriously injured himself, having struck his head against a stone in the road.

However, all were able to proceed after a time, and Sir Roland was conveyed in a closed vehicle to the Hall, being unable to ride his horse from nervous weakness.

His evil heart, however, was by no means touched by the scene.

He recognised that some mysterious agency was at work against him, and that he had been robbed and threatened.

But he saw in all this nothing to cause him to amend his evil ways.

All the effect it had on him was to make him take additional vows of vengeance.

## CHAPTER IX.

### TWO FELLOW SUFFERERS—DAISY AND CONSTANCE—DAISY'S PERIL—A STRUGGLE FOR LIBERTY AND HONOUR.

POOR Daisy Leigh and Constance Marfield were now fellow sufferers.

And both through the same man.

In the first instance, at any rate, for the immediate cause of Daisy's peril was Gedge Foote.

For two or three days after her arrival at the pretended Mrs. Barton's (the real Mrs. Foster) she lived an excessively quiet existence.

It was a melancholy one enough, what with the hideously dismal surroundings and the terrible reminiscences of her father's death.

Mrs. Foster was not the best of companions, and, consequently, Daisy spent most of her time in her own room, where the bright sun of August only showed her wastes of ground stretching down to the water's edge, and a few cultivated fields and dreary-looking shanties, while the night generally swallowed up everything in misty darkness.

Mrs. Foster's was a mysterious life altogether.

She had, in fact, no visible means of subsistence.

Apparently she had plenty of money; she rarely ever went out, but the tradesmen called, and she paid them.

But she did nothing for her living.

Occasionally carts would draw up of a night at the door, and loud, rough voices would be heard laughing in uproarious chorus in the side yard, where there were all manner of rough sheds.

She said that her husband was a sea captain, and she had lost sight of him for some years.

At any rate, she had plenty of time on hand, and would often come of her own accord to gossip.

"What a strange thing it is!" said Daisy one evening, when Mrs. Foster had invited her into her cosy kitchen. "What a strange thing it is that the mysterious person who sent me here has never turned up."

"Mysterious person!" laughed Mrs. Foster. "Why, what on earth do you mean?"

"The person who gave me your address, and told me to come here. I have never seen him since the day of my father's murder, and I long to see him, to thank him, and to hear what plans he proposes to hunt up the assassin."

The woman laughed at her, as if she thought that she was taking leave of her senses.

"Why, what do ye mean?" she cried. "Why, I never! Say you ain't seen him, when he came the other night, and brought you here, and stayed to supper, and kissed you when he went away, and all that. Well, I never did!"

Daisy flushed, but still she could not help smiling, as she answered—

"Oh! I don't mean him, Mrs. Barton. He's nobody—that poor, ugly dwarf. He's very kind and lent me money, and showed me my way her and I think he did kiss me. But I forga him, because, perhaps, he'd had a drop to drin and was excited."

"Well, look here, Miss Leigh," said Mı Foster, emphatically, "there's some very stup mistake here. In the first place, my name ain Barton. It's Foster. Poor Mr. Foote! he forg my name when he told you, and when he came the afternoon afore you came he said, 'Bless me if I ain't told my sweetheart your name's so-an so. Don't be surprised, then, if she calls ye s If I tell her different, she's so timid, she'll g scared like.' And as for 'poor, ugly dwarf,' wonder how you can talk like that about a ch you're going to marry, and the banns up and all

This, considering the shuddering dread th words inspired, was a long speech for Daisy Leig to listen to.

But she suffered Mrs. Foster to proceed ar finish, and then broke into a loud, hysteric laugh.

"You are having a good joke at my expens Mrs. Foster," she said. "In the first place, have never had a sweetheart, as you call it, in n life. I never had a dozen words with Ged Foote before the day after my poor father's death and as for banns, of course, that is your fu though banns can be nothing to me for many long, long day. It was not Mr. Foote who bac me come here—it was a person whom I do n know (and she shuddered slightly). And so, sin I am in the wrong place, I must get back to th Mint as quickly as I can, or I shall lose my be friend."

She rose as she spoke.

She was resolved to proceed to her own room once, dress herself, and quit the house, using few shillings to enable her to reach the Mint, ar returning the rest to Gedge Foote at his ow place.

Mrs. Foster's laugh alarmed her.

"What is there to laugh at?" she cried.

"Very much, I think."

"What do you mean?"

"You talk of quitting this house?"

"Yes."

"Don't you know you can't?"

"Why not?"

"There isn't a window or a door through whicl you could escape if you were flying for your life, said Mrs. Foster, with a bland smile. "Once upc a time, ye see, this 'ere place was a mad-hous leastways a private asylum, kept by a doctor and lor' bless ye, the bolts and bars are that stron it 'ud take half-a-dozen strong men all their tim to get through."

"By what right can you detain me?" crie Daisy, drawing up her little body defiantly, he eyes flashing, and her bosom heaving.

"By the right given me by Mr. Foote," sai Mrs. Foster, flushing and losing her tempe "He brought you here and paid me well, and sai I was to take every care of you, and so on; and s you can't leave my house until Mr. Foote say you may."

Daisy had fallen into a trap.

She had suspected it before.

But now she was certain.

What was to be done?

Certainly nothing by being precipitate.

So she would be calm.

"When do you expect Mr. Foote?" she asked

"Either to-night or to-morrow night," said Mrs

Foster, "and then he isn't going away until the wedding."

"Your talk is absurd, and it annoys me," said Daisy. "You must know that in England a forced marriage is impossible if the girl only has courage."

"Ah! but if you persist in refusing him," said Mrs. Foster, "there is something worse. He will remain under this roof with you until you will be glad to marry him."

Daisy, even without the horrid leer in the woman's eyes, would have known what she meant, and a shuddering thrill passed through her frame.

She passed towards the door.

"I will go to my room now," she said, "and if Mr. Foote makes his insane proposals to me, he will find how I appreciate his madness."

"You had better speak more civilly to him than you do of him," said Mrs. Foster, "or you may find him dangerous. He knows he can do as he likes here."

"And that you would help him in his iniquity," said Daisy.

"Just so."

"I fear you not," said Daisy, defiantly; "no harm will come to me. Heaven will protect the innocent, much as you scoff at my resistance."

And she quitted the room.

As she did so she was in the passage, and with a sudden impulse she flew to the front door.

It was barred and bolted, both bolts and bars being on the inside; but a formidable lock was on the door, in which the key had been turned and removed.

There at any rate there was no escape.

She hurried then into her own room, where she felt certain she had never seen any signs of bars at the windows.

As may be imagined, she dashed impatiently towards the casement.

But there she gave vent to a little cry of dismay.

No one would have suspected the presence of bars.

But there, nevertheless, they were; artfully concealed by creeping plants, which on more than one occasion she had complained of as making the room so dark.

"At any rate I am safe here for a time," she murmured, as she bolted and locked her door.

But as she did so another click told her that by some machinery the room had been locked on the outside as well.

Tears stood in Daisy's eyes.

But her good little heart beat high with brave determination.

"The battle has begun," she said, "but I will never yield with my life. I know not what love is; but whatever it is I could not feel it for such a being as Gedge Foote."

On one thing she was determined.

She would remain on the watch all night, and as far possible would refrain from food.

She had a suspicion that if she did not take this precaution something might be surreptitiously administered to make her insensible, or, at any rate, to dull her intellect.

She could contrive somewhat to neutralise the effect of anything by only taking the tiniest quantities at a time.

And another thing, she would not undress herself, so as to be ready for flight at any moment.

She had not been in her room long before Mrs. Foster's voice was heard outside, and then a kind of wicket in the wall at the side of the door was pushed open.

"Here is your supper," said the woman.

A savoury smell assailed the girl's nostrils.

But she was reslolute.

"Thank you; I am not hungry," returned she.

The woman waited to hear no more, but slammed the little wicket to with a bang.

"All right," she muttered; "perhaps she won't be so cheeky when she's starved herself."

That night Daisy was undisturbed, and on the next likewise.

Loud voices and laughter were heard in the house.

But that was all.

She was used to strange noises in the place, and consequently this did not affect her.

She kept resolutely to her room all the time, and though Mrs. Foster unbolted the door, she never once took advantage of the permission.

Food she took in tiny quantities, just sufficient to keep body and soul together.

On the third night, however, just as she had removed her dress and her boots, to throw herself on her couch for a little rest, there was a knock at the front door, and presently someone entered.

Her room was not locked, and so springing noiselessly towards the door she opened it and listened.

"Quite a stranger," said Mrs. Foster to someone.

"Yes, quite. Couldn't get here before," said the familiar voice of Gedge Foote. "How's our young lady?"

"Hush! Don't speak loud. Don't speak here at all," said the woman. "She's turned rumbustious, and you'll have no end of trouble with her."

"I hope not," said Foote; "but let's go into the back parlour."

They were soon out of the passage, and, plucking up her courage, Daisy resolved to go down and listen.

Her bootless feet made little noise on the stairs, and it was not long before she stood in the front parlour, which was only divided from the back one by a folding door.

Here she cowered down, and, with eager ears, listened.

"I hope you've not been ill-using her," said Foote. "I didn't bring her here to be insulted, you know."

"Insulted! Who's insulted her I should like to know?" cried Mrs. Foster; "only I don't like these upstart wenches."

Gedge laughed.

"Well, you can't expect every girl to like to be treated in this way," he said; "and then I am not such a fool as to think I'm handsome."

"Oh! handsome is as handsome does," said Mrs. Foster. "Every girl can't expect to have her pick and choose, and she's as poor as poor can be—not got a farthing of her own, and you've been that generous to her."

"Well, never mind; tell us all that has happened."

The woman did so.

A brightly coloured story it was, too.

Evidently it did not increase Gedge Foote's good humour.

"It's no use her trying to escape me," he said. "I've had my eye on her ever since, a long time ago, I saw her trim little ankle tripping up the stairs on the Mint, and, hark ye, Mrs. Foster, it isn't only herself, though I'd be glad of her without a penny."

"What then?"

"Someday she'll be rich."

"How do you know?"

"That's my affair; but whoever marries her marries money. She won't be able to claim it yet, but she's bound to have it."

"Well, it's all easy enough if you only have pluck."

"How so?"

"Let me put a little sleeping stuff in her tea to-morrow evening; she'll go off into a fine slumber, and be as quiet as a lamb until morning. Then you can pay her a visit, and when she finds she can't help herself she'll go with you to church as ready as can be."

Daisy shuddered, and pressed her hands over her tremulous bosom.

Innocent of the world's ways as she was she had yet expected something of this kind; but she was not prepared for Gedge's answer.

"No, no! That won't do for me," he said; "it might do with some girls, but not for Daisy. She might marry me, but she'd hate me like poison ever after. And see how nice that would be when she got her money! No; I must tire her out, but I won't do as you say. Let's have a bit of supper now, and I'll think what's best to be done."

As Mrs. Foster kept her things in the front parlour Daisy thought it high time to go.

So she crept upstairs and into her room, where she locked herself in, and, throwing herself on the bed, indulged in a passion of tears.

This outburst and the quiet of the house, only disturbed by the dull murmur of voices, had their natural effect, and she fell presently into a heavy sleep.

How long she slept she knew not, but after a time she was awakened by a hot hand on her cold bare shoulder, shaking her to arouse her.

And, starting up, she saw Gedge Foote standing by the side of her bed.

His face wore a diabolical smile, and she could tell by the flush upon his hideous features that he had been drinking.

"I want to speak to you, Daisy," he said, in a thick voice.

"Why did you not send Mrs. Foster up, then, and I would have come down?" she said, striving to get away.

But this was not possible.

He had passed his arm round her waist, and was looking gloatingly upon her flushed face and her freely-displayed beauties—the white, dainty, girlish shoulders, and the budding bosom, now panting with angry excitement.

"Nay, I like you best thus, my pretty one," he said, bending down and kissing her pouting lips. "I shall not detain you long. Are you aware that your enemies are after you?"

"My enemies!" she cried. "Why should I have any?"

He laughed loudly.

"Why!" he cried. "You ask that? Was not your father murdered by your enemies because they feared he would prove his innocence and claim his property?"

"But my poor father is dead! Why should they persecute me?"

She was sitting quietly now, with her lovely head nearly resting on his chest, her white, dimpled shoulder touching his.

To resist him was, as she saw, utterly useless, and to cry out for help not only useless, but likely to bring upon her further disaster.

"Because you, as Herbert Leigh's daughter, are as dangerous as he was," said Gedge. "But I have sworn to protect you. You are poor and friendless. I will be your banker and your friend. I will make you my wife, and with my very life I will protect you against the world."

He could not but feel the shuddering thrill which invaded her form as he spoke, and it roused all his evil passions.

"Beware," he said, "how you insult me. I felt you tremble at my words."

"Can I help my feelings?" she said, meekly.

She thought it best to temporise.

"Nor can I help them," he said, and as if roused still more by her demure beauty he suddenly bent down and rained kisses on her lips, her neck, and her white, warm shoulders.

Strengthened by her shame she sprang up suddenly and wrenched herself from his clutches, with the exception of the grasp he had upon her arm with his left hand.

As she did so she gave vent to a long, piercing shriek.

This was followed by another and another, which rang through the old house, and went echoing out over the marshy land towards the river.

The effect upon Gedge was alarming.

His eyes glowed like coals of fire, his veins stood out like whipcord on his brow—his face was fairly distorted with passion.

"You've raised the devil in me now," he cried, as he rushed upon her and clasped her once more round the waist, "and you must take the consequences."

Again and again she shrieked.

And as she did so she exerted all the strength of her lithe, round limbs to throw him off.

The struggle—the contact with her lovely active frame—only served to inflame him the more, and as they both breathed hard in their struggles Daisy felt her strength rapidly giving way.

"Release me and I will listen to you quietly," she gasped.

He only laughed loudly, and kissed her.

And then, like an echo, came a terrible laugh from without.

"Ha! ha! ha!"

The demon laugh of the mysterious apparition was new to Gedge Foote.

But it was hailed with joy by Daisy.

Poor, shrinking, ill-used Daisy! She seemed to recognise the fact that the awful being who was the terror of London was in some way or another her friend.

The sound gave her renewed strength, and the muscles of her strong arms stood out as she held Gedge for a moment away from her.

"Gedge, you're mad to-night," she cried, gaspingly, trying to smile. "Let me be quiet, and I'll listen to all you say. Perhaps even I'll give you a kiss if you're very good. There's a good Gedge: let's sit down and discuss the future."

But the demon himself seemed to have possessed the dwarf.

His eyes were red, his features were more than ever distorted, and he laughed again aloud as she uttered her words breathlessly, for her bosom was rising and falling in tumultuous panting after her exertions.

"A kiss? Bah! you've defied me, and that won't satisfy me now. I'll have a dozen!"

Again the loud demon laughter—"Ha! ha! ha!" and then a strange sound was heard in the wide chimney.

Gedge was so mad with rage and passion that he heard nothing.

But Daisy did, and the thought that her protector was near gave her superhuman strength.

Her limbs writhed like those of a wrestler as Gedge struggled with her; but, though she felt sure that the combat would end at last in her discomfiture if no help was near, she seemed to be full of hope that she would be able to hold out if this was really a champion coming to the rescue.

Almost at the instant that, with white, set face and panting breast, she felt that she could resist no more, there was a heavy fall down the chimney, something rolled out upon the floor, and with a wild and sepulchral laugh and a burst of sulphurous flame and smoke, Spring-Heeled Jack stood before them.

Daisy in her present dilemma felt not the slightest fear of him.

But on Gedge the effect was electrical.

His hair seemed fairly to bristle on his head, his eyes appeared to start from their sockets, and his features worked convulsively.

He appeared as if striving to speak for a moment.

Then a wild, piercing shriek rent the air, and he fell prone on his face, striking his head violently against the fender.

As these strange cries and noises resounded through the house, it seemed wonderful that Mrs. Foster did not hurry up the stairs.

But she thought, of course, that the cries came from Daisy in her desperate struggles with Gedge Foote, and she purposely took no notice.

Daisy, meanwhile, trembling from head to foot, awed by the terrible aspect of the whole scene, afraid to look in the face the awful apparition which had twice saved her, knelt at its feet, her eyes downcast, the long, silken waves of her hair veiling her bosom as she bent forward.

"How can I thank you, mysterious friend?" she said, in a low, gentle, quavering voice; "twice have you rescued me, first from the hands of an assassin, this time from a fate worse than death. I know not how, but some day I may be able to reward you.'

There was no reply.

A strange stillness pervaded the room.

After a moment she looked up hurriedly, and a terrible faintness stole over her heart as she saw that the apparition had vanished.

A thick mist pervaded the room, a stifling sulphurous mist, which prevented her seeing much.

But, at any rate, she had heard and seen no movement, and she was alone with the senseless figure of Gedge Foote.

For a moment she stood leaning against the table in bewilderment.

The terrible scene which she had gone through, coupled with the apparition of Spring-Heeled Jack had for the time so shattered her nerves and bewildered her senses that she could not settle upon her course of action.

But with the first reawakening of her faculties she saw that unless something very miraculous occurred she was in no better position than before.

Gedge Foote would recover—he was only temporarily stunned—and after what had occurred he would be more desperate and furious than ever.

She could quit the room, but all the doors and windows below were bolted, and barred, and locked, and how, then, was she to escape?

Her first impulse, however, as soon as her strength began to return, was to put on her dress, hat, jacket, and boots.

Then, as she turned to the toilet table, she saw something which made her heart leap with joy.

It was a large bunch of keys.

Her eyes shone with pleasure, her bosom palpitated; for an instant she almost feared to clutch the keys for fear they should disappear before her eyes.

But at last she plucked up courage and seized them.

Then, with trembling limbs—more trembling because she saw that Gedge Foote showed signs of recovering—she made her way across the room, glided out, closed the door after her, locked it, and descended the stairs.

Where was Mrs. Foster?

Not a sound could she hear at first.

Then a loud snoring assailed her ears, and in order to be sure and prepared for any contingency she approached the back parlour and peered in.

The sight within would at any other time have excited her merriment.

Mrs. Foster was reclining in an arm-chair in a drunken sleep, her arms hanging helplessly by her side, her eyes only half shut, her face flushed, her mouth wide open, her toes cocked up helplessly.

But Daisy did not remain a moment.

Creeping out again she approached the front door, and as quickly as possible began to remove the bolts and bars.

Then she fitted a key to the lock, and, to her joy, opened it.

As she did so she heard a heavy stumbling noise upstairs, and Gedge Foote came heavily across the room, and began to try and force the lock.

He had recovered swiftly after she quitted the chamber; and now, finding himself in the dark and locked in, he began kicking and shouting to such an extent that he succeeded in awakening Mrs. Foster, who began to mumble vaguely and stumble about.

But by this time Daisy had succeeded in passing out.

Shutting the door as softly as she could she ran along the little garden, and without thinking which way she was going scaled the fence opposite, and hurried across the marsh land towards the river.

The only guide she had was a small trembling light, which she had often seen from her window, and which she therefore knew must be a fixture belonging to some riverside cottage or landing place.

The way she had come, however, was a rough and difficult one.

Fearful every moment of pursuit she endeavoured to rush quickly on, but the ground was full of holes and ruts, and every now and then she sank above her ankles in the cloddy soil.

As she toiled slowly on she became aware of sounds behind her, and, looking back, she saw someone pursuing her with a lantern.

It must be Gedge Foote.

The idea gave wings to Daisy's feet.

She had so lately escaped from desperate peril that her heart gave a great leap of annoyance and disgust at the very notion of being once more in his power, even or a moment.

Perilous and rugged as was the road, therefore, she hastened on.

Gedge, however, knew his way better than she did, and was able to make more rapid progress.

She soon saw this, and glanced round in every direction in search of some spot which would afford her temporary shelter.

But with the exception of a few stunted trees and so forth there was nothing.

She must go on trusting to her fleetness of foot and quickness of eye.

On, on she went, now falling on her hands, now going ankle deep in the slush and mud, cutting her palms and bruising her soft little knees against the hard stones.

But she was resolute.

Anything was better than falling again into the power of her pretended friend, the one who had so basely betrayed her.

She cared not for cuts and bruises as long as she was able to put a good distance between herself and pursuer.

The attempt, however, seemed vain.

Gedge Foote came on nearer and nearer.

As she was now not far from the river, she could see that the light she had before noticed was on a barge anchored close to the bank.

If she could but reach this!

Panting for breath, her heart beating rebelliously in her swelling bosom, she made one final effort.

The ground, however, became more rugged.

Gedge Foote was close behind her, she could hear his hard breathing; she seemed almost able to feel his clutching hands.

She knew now that wherever he caught her he would have no mercy.

And so, sick at heart at the prospect of losing home, and perhaps life itself, out on that desolate waste land, she gave one long shrill shriek for help, and made one more desperate struggle.

"Ha! ha! ha!"

What was that?

A loud demon laugh, a whirring sound of wings, a stump, stump, stump, as of some strange leaping animal.

And then a wild shriek from Gedge Foote, as the terrible apparition of Spring-Heeled Jack sprang between him and his victim.

To Daisy the awful sight was associated with safety.

And so, although she had no desire to pause in its presence, she made no exclamation of fear, but dashed away as quickly as possible towards the river.

Gedge Foote had fallen into a deep hole, and there for a few moments he remained crouching, with his hands over his eyes.

Then, as all seemed quiet, he ventured to remove his hands, and look up.

But Spring-Heeled Jack was not gone.

He was still near at hand, standing on a mound, a weird and spectral figure in the grey light, a strange vaporous cloud surrounding him, and smoke and flame issuing from his mouth.

"She has escaped me now by the devil's aid," he said; "but she shall not escape me always. Let her go now. I shall soon be on her track again."

The young girl meanwhile fled on towards the river bank, without once turning her head.

Now that Gedge Foote was not behind her, or rather was not pursuing her, she resolved not to trust herself on the barge.

She knew not what characters she might be trusting herself to.

Her late adventures had made her particularly careful.

And so she hastened along the towing-path, making her way naturally away from London.

Presently, arriving at a little rough-looking house, she saw several boats moored.

No one was near, and the idea occurred to her that she might pull herself across the river, and so make her way towards Barnet, where she might obtain some information in regard to Sir Roland Ashton, and learn perhaps the mystery which enveloped her father's death.

She was an imprudent little thing, but the thought occurred to her that if she was on the other side of the river she would at least have the broad Thames flowing between herself and her enemy.

So, without thinking of the peril to herself, she went down to the water's side, chose a light skiff, and entered it.

She had had very little experience with oars.

In fact, her trials had been confined to certain excursions she had taken with her father to places where she could pull a little boat over a still lake.

She had no conception of the force and current of the great river, and in a few moments, though exerting all her skill, she found herself being rapidly forced in the very direction she desired to avoid—towards London.

She had brought this peril on herself by her own act, and instead of screaming out, she tried all she could to make up for her rashness.

But it was a vain and weary struggle.

She still stuck to the oars, and contrived to keep the boat from coming broadside on to the current; but she could not properly guide it, and she saw that if she was not able soon to pause in her course she would be dashed against one of the stationary barges, or against some other obstacle, and flung headlong into the river.

Suddenly she saw on the left bank of the river a light which resembled the fire of a gipsy encampment, and as she neared it she observed with pleasure several figures gathered round it.

Instantly, without thinking who these people might be, feeling sure that Gedge Foote could not be there, or any of his crew, she uttered a loud cry for help.

As she did so, turning her head rashly towards the light, she did not see where she was going. The boat went with a crash against some black, ugly piles belonging to an old disused wharf or landing-stage, and in an instant the frail craft was upset.

There was one wild, despairing uplifting of her arms as she sprang up, a long shriek, one gleam of the white, dainty limbs, and the waters had closed over her!

---

## CHAPTER X.

### JOE DIMITY, THE SHOWMAN, AND HIS "MERRIE COMPANIE."

THE "Grand Imperial Circus and Royal Theatre," proprietor, Mr. Joseph Dimity, was on tour.

They had just reached the outskirts of the metropolis from the south coast, where they had done more or less successful business, and were now about to proceed to the north of England.

Nothing was farther from the thoughts of any one of them than the occurrence of any unusual thing to break the monotonous routine of their existence.

They were a kind of family party, in fact, and had dawdled on an existence of weary, dreary sameness for years.

Joe Dimity was a man of about fifty, with grizzly hair, a florid complexion, rather protuberant though kindly eyes, a big, wide mouth, and a podgy body.

He took the heavy father in the sensation dramas (lasting a quarter of an hour), which were acted by the company—characters in which he had to roll out his "r's" and talk of his "chee-ild," and so forth, and spread out grimy hands in benediction.

Mrs. Dimity was a tragedy-queen off and on the stage—a tall, bony woman, with a set colour, and black hair and eyes.

But she was the very reverse of what her appearance denoted, for she was the kindest-hearted woman that ever walked a stage, and was appealed to by everyone in the company when in trouble.

Then there was Miss Maria Hoskins, who united singing, dancing, and acting, and who was really wife to the Signor Bellini (alias Tom Bell), who was the dark-browed villain of the company, and who, off the stage, was the mildest fellow who ever emptied a pot of four-half in a village beer-house.

Maria was cruelly fair, with a roundish face, insipid blue eyes, and nose very much *retroussé;* but then her arms were a marvel, her shoulders well rounded, her bust superb, and everyone who had seen her dance in those very flimsy and very short skirts of hers, and those excessively pinked and glossy tights, declared that she possessed the finest pair of legs on the travelling stage.

There was Harry Banks, the clown, and Audley Harcourt (alias John Mullins), the walking gentleman and general lover, and Bob Lightley, the comedian, and others, all more or less clever, all contented, all happy in their way, and all very badly paid.

In fact, "treasury" was sometimes a pure fiction.

They clubbed together to procure their food, and often Joe Dimity and his wife would partake with much dignity of a piece of bread and cheese offered by one of his "company:" "With great pleasure, my boy. Don't feel hungry to-day, and 'twill save the missus cooking this hot day."

Poor Joe! Everyone knew the "house" had been an empty one the night before, but no one ventured to say so.

They lived in a gipsy kind of way, in fact, and had been together now so long, with the exception of two or three younger members, that they constituted quite a happy family.

On the evening when Daisy made her escape from Gedge Foote, Joe Dimity and his company had reached a wide piece of waste ground on the river-bank, where they resolved to camp out for the night.

They never put up at any place where they had to pay unless they were compelled to do so.

The caravans, three in number, carried the materials for stage and "auditorium" on their tops outside, and the company contrived to squeeze into the inside.

It was not altogether a very reputable or comfortable arrangement, but it saved money, and a week's lodging saved by all meant roast beef for dinner on Sunday.

So the married couples had half-a-caravan each—just room to stretch their legs—the batchelors had one caravan between them, and the spinsters the same.

The company had taken a considerable sum of money that day, and were enjoying a goodly *al-fresco* supper when poor Daisy's shrill cry for help resounded over the waters of the Thames and echoed along the gloomy banks.

It was not an unusual thing to hear the loud cry of some unfortunate creature plunging away "out of life's misery."

But there was something in the ring of Daisy's voice which seemed to tell that it was a young girl.

Harry Banks, the clown, and Bob Lightley, the comedian, both started to their feet.

"What's the matter?" cried Joe Dimity, almost dropping his spoon as he was devouring some fragrant pea-soup; for he was rather deaf.

"I heard a cry for help," said Lightley.

"Yes, and so did I," cried Harry Banks; "let's be off and see what it is."

Not to be outdone, the kindly showman and Audley Harcourt and the other male members of the company followed the clown and the comedian, who had already started off.

They were close to the river's bank, and in a few moments they were at the water's edge.

When they reached it, however, all was quiet.

But they remained perfectly still, listening.

Presently they heard another faint cry, and fancied they saw a white face drifting with the tide.

Harry Banks, the clown, was a powerful swimmer, as well as a brave man; and so he resolved to be the one to attempt the rescue.

"Look out for a boat, gentlemen," he said. "Now, then. Hullo! boys. Here we are again!"

And as he kicked off his boots (which were none too tight), he took a rush along one of the slippery beams which supported the piles, and plunged into the water.

The tide, as we have said, was running very strong, and Daisy, gradually becoming numbed in all her limbs, was being rapidly carried towards London.

She had only gone down once, and had come up without having swallowed much water, and so was able to cry out again for help.

Now, her clothes helping to keep her so, she was floating on top of the water, but her legs were rapidly losing all feeling, and, little as was the power of thought left in her, she knew that she was in momentary danger of the cramping chill stealing upwards to her body.

There were other things to fear also; she might be dashed against barges, and sucked beneath by the eddying water; her head might come in contact with piles or floating objects; or she might be left to suffocate amongst the river mud.

None of which was a pleasant prospect, and no doubt the very fear, which set her little heart beating so wildly, was the means of sending the warm blood rushing more warmly through her rapidly chilling body.

She saw even in the uncertain light the forms of the players dashing down to the side of the water.

She knew, therefore, that there were those not ar off who would try and save her.

This sent a thrill of pleasure through her frame, and kept her blood warm and her spirits up.

But she was drifting so rapidly!

Everything round her was so dark and gloomy.

Only far away the bright lights of the city.

All else black and sombre.

But what was that?

She heard a cheery voice; then a loud splash.

Some one had come to the rescue.

For an instant a wretched feeling came over her—a wretched question framed itself in her mind.

Could it be Gedge Foot?

But, no!

He could not have reached the spot in time.

"Oh! Heaven help me!" she said, "and give me strength. Only a few minutes more, and I shall be safe!"

Just as this idea came into her head with a pleasurable shock, she saw ahead of her some black beams standing up threateningly high out of the water.

A moment before she would have feared.

Now she welcomed it, and with a sudden access of strength thrust out her grasping hand to seize the woodwork.

Life is sweet, even to those who are in pain and misery, and consequently to Daisy Leigh her young and beautiful existence was a treasure she did not care to lose, with all its promises of future joy and happiness.

So with eager haste and unexpected power she seized the beam, and held on.

Still the bitter cold in her legs numbed them and made them useless, but her heart was beating hopefully, and her blood was beginning to course so rapidly through her veins that her head began to swim.

Oh! she prayed that her unknown rescuer might succeed.

And as if her prayer was answered, a dark object suddenly swam alongside of her. She saw something white which she knew to be a human face, and she felt that she was about to be saved.

Then came a reaction which might have been fatal.

The strain upon her nerves had been so great that now, when she felt rescue near, her strength gave way and she fainted.

However, Harry Banks was there, brave, good-looking, strong Harry, with his stout heart and iron resolution; the young girl was caught to his breast like a young baby, with his left arm, and with his right he struck out for the shore.

His companions had ran full speed along the shore, while he was swimming rapidly with the current, and as they saw the young girl fall senseless into his arms they were close upon them.

"Here! Harry—this way! By Jove! he's overweighted there," cried Audley Harcourt, and as there seemed some difficulty he too shook himself bootless, and plunged into the rushing stream.

Their united efforts soon brought the girl ashore.

"Now, then, for a good run," cried Harry Banks. "I don't wonder this poor little thing has frozen limbs. I'm like an icicle myself, and it's only autumn."

How much of this speech was heard by his friends we cannot say, for he had already started to run with his burden held to his breast like a baby.

He was immensely strong, as most men in his branch of the profession are, and Daisy Leigh was but a light weight.

More than this, he had caught a glimpse of her face before she had lost her senses, and he had recognised the fact that she was beautiful.

Harry Banks had need of a wife. At present there was not much accommodation for a fresh couple unless they slept on top of the caravans, but that he did not think of.

No one in the company pleased his fancy, except "Maria," and she was another person's property, and not for him. Thinking, therefore, he might have found a prize, "rescued from the deep," he hastened on with superhuman strength, towards the "camp."

Poor Harry Banks!

If he had only known to what peril he was bearing pretty Daisy Leigh, he would certainly have thought twice before he made such a rush with her to the caravan.

But it is not given to us to have fore-knowledge, and so on he went, followed by the rest of the company—the male members—until they reached the spot where the female strollers were dawdling over their suppers, and exchanging notes as to the cause of the excitement which had caused the desertion of all the male members of the show.

On learning the true reason of the defection, every one was ready at once to offer help.

"The poor dear!" "The pretty child!" and all manner of endearing epithets were applied to Daisy; but the most practical and beneficial thing was the taking her into the principal caravan by Maria and Mrs. Dimity, who stripped her, gave her hot drink, and rubbed her numbed little body all over with rough towels.

"She's a beautiful little thing," said Mrs. Joe, as they at last rested from their labours, and Daisy was re-dressed in night-things, and tucked comfortably in bed; "and there's nothing about her to show that she had any reason to commit suicide. It's been an accident or something."

"So I think," said Maria; "but let's examine her clothes, and see if they throw any light on the subject."

In another moment Mrs. Dimity had searched the scanty garments, which were Daisy's only possessions.

But they told no tales.

All the searchers found was a purse containing Gedge Foote's two sovereigns.

Maria smiled at this.

"She did not try to kill herself from poverty, then," she said.

"No, indeed," cried the "tragedy-queen." "Who knows? We may be on the brink of some strange discovery. Who can tell what mystery hangs about the life of this pretty child?"

"Well, she isn't exactly a child," said Maria. "She's quite seventeen by all I can see of her. However, she seems a lady, and I don't believe there's anything mysterious about her being in the water, except an accident."

Daisy, when at last she woke from the semi-sleep which followed her insensibility, tried to speak.

But Mrs. Dimity, curious as she was to know all, would not allow it.

She was conscious of the faet that a doctor ought, in the natural order of things, to have been called in.

But she was not a particular friend of the medical profession, and objected to strangers "spying about," and so, knowing she had applied the best remedies, she would not let Daisy spoil her chance by over-exciting herself.

"No, no, my dear," she whispered, kindly, as

# SPRING-HEELED JACK,

## THE TERROR OF LONDON.

By the Author of "TURNPIKE DICK, the Star of the Road."

SPRING-HEELED JACK SCENTS A HAWK IN THE DOVE'S NEST.

No. 4.

she bent over her pretty patient; "you must not excite yourself now. There will be plenty of time to-morrow."

"Only one thing," said Daisy, with a half-sob.

"Well, what is it?"

"You mustn't think I tried to commit suicide," said the poor girl. "I could not be so wicked. I was escaping from a cruel enemy, and I was upset from a boat."

"All right, my dear. We believe you," said Mrs. Joe; "but we won't listen to a word more until to-morrow."

And so Daisy was left to herself and her slumbers.

That night Maria slept with Daisy, and Signor Bellini—alias Tom Bell—had to accommodate himself with the comforts of the bachelors' caravan.

Next morning Daisy was delirious.

And she was still in the same condition, although a doctor had been called in, when the caravan once more set out towards Barnet, bearing the senseless girl towards the home of her deadliest foe—Sir Roland Ashton.

## CHAPTER XI.

### HOW CONSTANCE MARFIELD MET HER FATHER.

Sir Roland Ashton's terror at seeing Spring-Heeled Jack, and at the non-success of his attack upon that mysterious being, caused him a severe shock, and he was ill for several days.

But it had no effect on his malevolent spirit, except, in fact, to make him more brutal, and more eager for revenge.

During his illness he was attended by Caleb Masters.

The company of this vile parasite seemed to suit him.

They could plan over their evil schemes together, and this was just what kept the baronet pleased and amused.

At the end of the week he was quite recovered, and then his thoughts went back at once to the matters which, before his short illness, he had resolved upon performing.

And the principal matter was his marriage with Constance Marfield, or, as he now called her, Constance Harland.

She was still in her room; bolted and barred in, with barred windows, too, and seeing no one but the housekeeper, Mrs. Levine.

But her spirit was unbroken.

However much she might weep and mourn in secret, she was calm, bold, and defiant, when Mrs. Levine presented herself.

She expressed herself much delighted when she heard of Sir Roland's illness.

"It is a just punishment upon him," she said.

"And he loves you so," returned Mrs. Levine.

Now this sentiment was put on, and Constance knew it.

As we have said, the housekeeper had, in fact, been setting her cap for years at the master of the house, and was hoping that some day or another he would give up wooing elsewhere, and subside for comfort upon her very substantial bosom.

So she was in no way eager to aid him to the possession of Constance Marfield.

"He would make you a very good husband, Mrs. Levine," said Constance, somewhat contemptuously; "but he would not suit me. I know what a villain he is. I believe he is even worse than we really know."

"I do not believe it."

Mrs. Levine spoke positively.

It did not suit her to give credence to reports.

She was content to know that Sir Roland was only forty, wealthy, and handsome, and rich.

What more did she require in exchange for her own robust and mature charms?

"That is well, then," said Constance; "you are just the one for him. As for myself, I love Ralph Ashton (Sir Ralph he will be some day, as he ought to be now), and between him and Sir Roland there is rather a vast difference."

Mrs. Levine had evidently been thinking over a plan of her own.

"Yes; you are right," she said, musingly. "Can you keep a secret?"

Constance eagerly caught at this.

Evidently this woman had some plan in view which would benefit her.

"Yes; I swear to keep it, unless it is in regard to some crime, and in that case I do not wish to hear it."

Mrs. Levine laughed.

"No," she said; "it is no crime. It is a piece of fun which may benefit both you and me. Listen! I must whisper it to you, for even walls have ears, you know."

The housekeeper bent forward, and began talking rapidly and eagerly.

As Constance listened a smile passed over her lips, though a crimson blush spread from her cheeks up to the roots of her hair, and crept down pink and beautiful over the lovely bosom.

"Well," said Mrs. Levine, laughing, when she had confided her secret, "what do you think of my plan?"

"It is very clever," said Constance, still blushing; "but I cannot see how it would succeed."

"Oh! leave that to me," said Mrs. Levine; "I have been married once, and I'm no fool. I'll carry it through, and be glad of it. But there's no hurry. If you have to give in at all in regard to the marriage, plead illness and have it put off. Then have all manner of scruples, and you'll see when the time comes I'll make it all right."

On the day after the scene on the mail-coach Sir Roland Ashton received a mysterious missive.

This was from Tom Harland.

But the escaped convict was obliged to put off the promised interview for ten days.

At the end of that time Constance, still a prisoner, received a message in writing from Sir Roland that the time was come to see her father.

The young girl's heart gave a great leap.

She knew what her father had done, or, at any rate, been accused of and suffered for in the past.

But, nevertheless, she was so utterly destitute of friends that there was a wonderful pleasure in the idea that she was about to see one of her parents, one who had a right to protect her.

Alas! poor Constance.

She little knew the truth, little guessed the real character of the man with whom she was about to be brought face to face.

It was evening when for the first time for so many days she was permitted to leave her room.

Sir Roland, who had now quite recovered from the shock, and was looking his very best, awaited her in the drawing-room.

He had purposely taken excessive pains with his toilet, and looked younger even than he was.

No one looking into his easy, careless face would have imagined it possible that behind the handsome mask there lurked a soul as black as Satan.

"Good evening, Constance," he said, as calmly as if nothing extraordinary had happened in the household. "I hope you have not confided to any one the secret of your father's presence in the neighbourhood?"

Constance smiled derisively.

"I should have found it difficult to confide in any one," she said, "considering that I have been bolted and barred in my room. I have seen no one but Mrs. Levine, and my conversation with her has related to a very different matter."

She said this rather significantly, but Sir Roland did not observe her manner.

"True; but lovers can talk through bars," he said, lightly.

Constance made no reply.

Seing her mood, he thought it best not to irritate her further.

"I have to exact from you one promise," he said, "before you can see Mr. Harland."

"What is that?" she said. "I will not make you even a shadow of a promise unless I know beforehand what it is."

"Oh! it is very simple," said Sir Roland. "It is simply that you will promise to keep quiet while we go and see your father—that you will make not the slightest attempt at escape on this occasion, but return as you came."

"I promise," said Constance.

A short time before she would not have made this promise.

But since her conversation with Mrs. Levine affairs were altogether different.

"Very well," said Sir Roland; "pray go at once, and get ready for a walk. Do not delay, for your father is in great danger; he was seen at the inn the other night and recognised, in spite of his disguise, and the constables are after him everywhere."

Constance made no reply.

In a few minutes she and Sir Roland had set out.

Often afterwards she thought what an imprudent thing it was to have trusted herself alone on a dreary night with one possessing the desperate and villainous character of Sir Roland.

But, although such mystery and horror enveloped her father, her bosom was full of eagerness to see him; and, having given her promise to return quickly, she almost looked npon this as an implied assurance on the part of her companion that she was in no danger of being detained.

Passing across the grounds of the park, they made for a little gate which led out into a bye-lane.

At the other side of this lane was a kind of waste ground, with the ruins of some old buildings on it. People said that it had once been a training stable.

It was here that Tom Harland was to meet them.

Sir Roland did not at once cross the lane and enter the waste ground.

He passed up one way and Constance the other to see if they were watched, or if there were any one approaching either way who would be likely to notice where they were going.

No one was about.

"Let us lose no time now," said Sir Roland, "we are in luck's way. Come—quickly!"

He broke violently through the hedge.

As he did so a man's desperate voice said—

"Stop, or I fire!"

It was Harland who spoke.

"All right, Tom—it's a friend," said the baronet. "It is I—Roland Ashton, and I bring your daughter. Go into the ruin, and I will follow you."

The wretched man at once did as he was bid, and in a few moments Sir Roland and Constance had followed him into the ruined building.

An old crazy door closed the first portion of this, and having secured this, the escaped convict led the way in the dim light further into the stable.

Here he lit a lamp, and for the first time Constance Marfield, or Harland, stood face to face with her father.

Such a father!

He was a tall, broadly-built man, as we have already described him when we met him at the Three Jolly Wheelers, but his largeness was more the result of big bones than stoutness.

His clothes hung on him loosely, as if he had had all his flesh worn off him by hard labour and trouble.

His face was gaunt and coarse; it was white now with mingled dread and emotion, but you could see by the nose and the sensual mouth what manner of man he was when he had the chance of a debauch.

His eyes had an eager, hungry, hunted look, as of a wild beast.

Constance looked at him with a shudder.

But she tried as far as possible to disguise the appearance of disgust.

This man was, after all, her father, and it would scarcely do to betray to him at their first interview the feeling with which his first appearance had inspired her.

"This, then, is my father," she said.

"Yes," said Sir Roland. "Harland, this is your daughter."

The man had been quite surprised for a moment.

But he quickly recovered himself, and advancing, he put out his coarse hand to take her thin, slim one.

Constance, repressing the horror with which he inspired her, suffered him to grasp her palm.

"I am pleased to find you," said he, "more pleased than you can think. But I wish I could have met you under better and more pleasing circumstances."

"Yes, father. I wish we were not standing in the shadow of an old sorrow."

"That sorrow will always overshadow me while I am in England," said Harland, coming at once to the point. "What I want is to go away for ever from this country, and even from Europe, and when I can do that, you need not fear that any shame will ever fall upon your name or your father's. But while I am here, there is no limit to the disgrace which may overwhelm both you and me."

Constance, accustomed as she was to the trickeries of Sir Roland and all those round him, was not able to see through the shallow pretence of this man.

Father or no father, he was no gentleman, no man to be proud of, and, consequently, he would probably not be affected by any show of disrespect on her part.

But she felt that gentle sentiment towards him that she would never have dreamed of doing anything which would have made him seem little in his own eyes.

"Can I do anything to help you?" she said, softly.

"Yes," he said, "everything."

His manner was rudely eager.

But she ascribed this to her strange position, and, putting this together with his wild eyes and hunted look, she pitied him.

"Pray tell me how?" said Constance.

"In this way; in order to get away from England I must have money; in order to have money you must make me a promise. You are the only one who can—"

"Do not be evasive, dear father," said Constance. "Tell me plainly what you mean."

Tom Harland was incapable of understanding the bitter feelings of the young girl before him.

He came at once to the point.

"I mean this, then, Constance," he said. "I have no money, and there is only one man in England of whom I can get it. That man is Sir Roland Ashton."

"Well?"

"He is here, he will answer for himself," said Harland; "he is willing to advance me anything in reason to take me away to a foreign country, where I shall never be able to trouble anyone again."

"Yes."

"He makes one stipulation."

"Yes."

"And that is that you become his wife."

Constance turned deadly pale.

But she had the courage to speak out—

"And you—my father—surely you will not dream of such a sacrifice?"

"What am I to do?" he said; "this is my only chance. Do you know what is the terrible alternative?"

"No."

"Simply this—that, as my life is forfeited to the law, I shall be hanged!"

The girl shuddered.

But in a moment a thought occurred to her.

"You could only return to prison if they caught you," she said; "they could not take your life for a crime for which you were only sentenced to penal servitude."

Tom Harland langhed—a terrible, unmusical laugh.

"Ha! ha!" he cried, "you do not know all. For that old crime, which they chose to call murder, I was sentenced to transportation, but for the other crime I should swing."

"What crime?"

"The crime that gave me my freedom; for in order to obtain that I had to shoot one of the warders. That was, in my eyes, a necessary means of obtaining my freedom; but in the eyes of the law it is murder."

The girl, into whose bosom a ray of light had for a moment penetrated, shuddered with dread.

The toils were indeed closing round her.

How could she deliberately send this man to such a doom?

How could she consent to see this man hung—who, though a hardened criminal apparently, was yet her father?

"What am I to do?" she murmured.

The words were only addressed to herself, but Tom Harland replied to them.

"Your course is easy, my child," he said; "there is a handsome, rich man, in the prime of life, who wishes to make you his wife. What more easy than compliance? What hardship is there in that?"

"Every hardship," said Constance, melting into tears. "You do not understand; you cannot. Here, before the face of Sir Roland Ashton, I tell him plainly that I hate him. I shudder at his caresses, and were I to become his wife, my existence would be a living horror."

"Then you would prefer to devote me to a terrible and cruel death?"

He spoke bitterly.

But his manner was not quite that which was convincing to the young girl.

She wrung her hands.

"Oh!" she cried. "Oh! if I had only some one to advise me! Oh! Ralph, if only you were here to help me!"

As if in answer to her appeal for help a loud "Ha! ha! ha!" echoed in the night air.

Sir Roland started and turned pale, and seemed waiting for some horrid event.

But nothing came.

"You are not likely to obtain advice or help here," said he, after a pause; "you have simply to act upon your own responsibility."

"Let me speak to her alone," said Tom Harland; "retire a moment to the other end of the chamber. I may find an argument to change her stolid nature."

Sir Roland very reluctantly did as he was asked, and Tom Harland, coming close to Constance, passed his arm round her waist and pressed her to him.

As he did so he bent and kissed her, pressing his smoke-polluted lips to her tremulous ones.

Criminal as he was, she could hardly refuse to submit to this embrace, which was given in far from a fatherly manner; but when it was repeated again and again she repulsed him.

"Do not waste time, father," she said; "let me hear what you have to say. If you can find a way out of this terrible dilemma, pray help me!"

"I can, I think," said Harland, still keeping his arm round her lissom waist, and whispering in her ear. "Give your consent, so that I can get some money, and then, when I have made my escape, you can refuse to carry it out."

"I should be telling a lie."

"Nonsense! Only let me get the money and escape, and I shall write you a letter which will explain to you the means of evading the whole affair without uttering anything in the shape of a falsehood."

She could feel him breathing with eagerness as he pressed her to him.

It was an awful trial for him.

This, of course, she knew.

But what was her position—torn between parental duty and her loathing for the man who desired to force his love upon her?

"Tell me all, then," she said. "What am I to say to this man?"

"Say that to save me you will marry him in a month," replied Harland. "Say that, in order to prove all is right, he can give me half the money I want, and the rest after the ceremony. I will ask twice as much as I intended, and if he never sends me the other I shall not be hurt. So if you don't marry him I shall be no worse off."

"How much shall you ask?"

"In all, five hundred pounds."

He felt a sudden thrill pass through her form.

The light in her eyes showed it was one of pleasure.

"Listen!" she said, in a very low voice. "I have two hundred pounds saved up."

"You!"

"Yes; I have never spent half the money which he gave me as my allowance. Why—"

"You are a long time consulting," said Sir Roland, in an impatient voice.

"Not longer than is necessary," said Harland. "Proceed, Constance."

"Why he gave me so large a one, I could never understand," she continued; "at any rate, I have that sum in the Imperial Bank in London. If you come to my window in an hour or two's time I will give you an order to draw it all. You need not trouble yourself, therefore, about the second payment."

"But how am I to reach the window?" asked Tom Harland.

"You must do the same as Ralph Ashton did," she answered.

"And what was that?"

"Climb up by the ivy."

"Very well," said Harland, eagerly. "I will note carefully all the windows of the Hall to-night, and I will make my way to the one where I see two lights shown."

"Very well."

Harland released her now with evident reluctance.

"Sir Roland," he said, "I think I have arranged everything satisfactorily."

"She consents?"

"Yes. Ask her?"

For an instant the baronet seemed too overjoyed to speak.

His eyes beamed with delight, and his lips wreathed themselves into a smile.

He advanced quickly.

"You consent, then, my darling?" he said.

She looked at him contemptuously.

"Do not talk to me in that way," she said. "As I have told you, the word love as between us is worse than a farce. I loathe and detest you more than I should have thought it possible I could have done any human being; but I consent to yield to you simply to save my father from disgrace and death."

He took her hand.

"No matter; how I win you I care not?" he cried. "Were I to marry you by force I should be satisfied, because I know that you will love me afterwards. Loathing will turn to liking under my kindness and caresses."

She shuddered at this.

"Pray do not insult me," she said. "It is your caresses I dread. But, remember, I cannot be your wife for a month."

"Nay, I cannot agree to that," said Sir Roland. "All is ready. I have obtained a special license, and the ceremony will take place to-morrow night in the drawing-room."

Constance wrenched away her hand.

"Nay!" she said; "never will I consent to it. Not even to save my father's life could I agree to so swift a yielding up of all my hopes in life."

Harland here approached.

"Sir Roland," he said, "this is but fair. She has yielded solely to my persuasions. I have put everything before her in a straightforward way, and she has consented to become your wife. What more can you expect?"

"I do not expect shuffling."

"There is no shuffling," said Tom Harland. "You cannot expect Constance to be pleased at the prospect before her, or to wish to rush into matrimony against her will. In order that there shall be no doubt as to her intentions half the money I ask for can stand over until I reach America."

"What money is it you ask?"

"Five hundred pounds!"

"A cool demand," said the baronet; "but still dear Constance here is worth fifty times that amount. Be it so, then. I will give you three hundred pounds to-night, and the other shall be sent to you, wherever you are, the instant Constance becomes my wife."

"Which will be never," thought the young girl and Tom Harland as well.

"Very well; all is settled, then," said Constance. "Let us return to the house."

The baronet would fain have expressed his delight at her acquiescence.

But she drew away from him.

"There will be time enough for thanks another time," she said. "Let us return to the Hall."

"I will say good-bye, then, Constance," said Harland. "You have my eternal gratitude, if that is of any use to you, and gives you any satisfaction, and may you be more happy in the future than you now seem to hope."

She made no reply, and Tom Harland pressed her to his heart, and imprinted several kisses on her lips, much to the anger of Sir Roland, who throughout the interview had strangely resented the man's manner, and who now said—

"Come, Harland, you forget your danger. I and Constance will hasten back to the Hall now, and you had better remain here until we are out of reach. It will be safer for you not to remain with us too long."

"But the money? I wish to leave England to-morrow!"

"Very good. When all is quiet, make your way to the terrace beneath my study window, and knock three times. I will admit you then, and give you the money."

"How?"

"In gold or notes."

"That is well; I will be there," said Harland.

And then, as they prepared to go, he drew back into the shadow and concealed himself.

Sir Roland talked eagerly and freely to his companion as they made their way towards the Hall.

But he received no reply.

This dogged silence gave him a misgiving.

Constance and Harland had whispered together.

What if father and daughter had planned to deceive him?

He resolved at once to run no risks.

When, therefore, they reached the Hall, he called Mrs. Levine, and intimated that Constance was to be placed in the same bedroom as before.

The girl's heart sank at this.

She had hoped, either through Harland or Ralph, to escape before the forced marriage.

But now even that faint hope was taken from her.

As she entered her room after supper, being escorted to it by Sir Roland and Mrs. Levine, the former caught her in his arms and kissed her passionately.

"Ah!" he cried, as he held her resisting form tightly in his strong grasp. "Fate is, indeed, unkind to make you hate me, when my love for you is so great that the very touch of your lips thrills my whole form with ecstasy."

Her face was crimson with anger and shame.

But she made no reply.

Only when the door was closed, and she was

once more alone, she flung herself on her knees in tears.

"Never can I be his," she cried; "never, never! I could not submit to the humiliation and shame. I will die first—I will die first."

For hours she waited and waited for Tom Harland.

But he came not.

"I am deserted by all, even by Ralph," she murmured, as presently she undressed and retired to her bed; "but I will still hope on. Death must be preferable to being in the ignominious position of a slave to a man one hates."

## CHAPTER XII.

RALPH ASHTON ONCE MORE—IN THE OLD MILL—LAURA'S TREACHERY—RALPH CAPTURED.

When Ralph Ashton quitted Constance's bedroom on the night when Mrs. Levine had heard the two conversing, he made his way as swiftly as he could to the highway. After attending to a little business, and crossing over into a dense plantation, he found his horse, and leaping on its back, turned its head northwards and rode leisurely away.

He knew well that a reward had been offered for his capture.

He knew also that were he captured he would have great difficulty in proving his innocence.

But still he seemed quite careless of the necessity of disguise, and rode on as leisurely as if there was nothing to fear.

He had not proceeded very far, however, before he turned abruptly to the left and made his way in the direction of an old mill, which stood, deserted and weird-looking, on the margin of a stream.

Outside this he stood for a moment or so, and glanced round him to see if anyone might chance to be observing him.

Then he knelt down by the side of a tree, and groping about by the roots, got hold of a rope artfully concealed among the leaves and earth.

With this he gently pulled from the side of the mill a small ladder, which, it seemed, was the only means of entering the half-ruined edifice.

On reaching the little terrace, as it may be called, which ran round the mill, he opened a door which admitted him into the interior of the crazy old building.

He, of course, had first drawn up the ladder, and when he passed in he was in no hurry to strike a light.

Evidently he was well acquainted with the place.

He closed the door behind him, and then groping his way in the darkness, he grasped firmly the balustrade of the staircase, leading down to the basement.

Half way down this it was safe to light a lamp, and accordingly he carefully sought about for a niche where he had deposited some candles and an oil lamp.

They were gone!

He started in wonder and some fear.

Someone must have discovered his haunt.

For a long time he had made this spot one of his secret hiding places.

Who could have found him out?

Or was it only some other fugitive from justice, who had accidentally chosen the same place as himself?

The rats might have eaten the candles, but the disappearance of the lamp seemed to point with certainty to a human visitor.

The secret of the ladder had evidently not been discovered, but still it was with much doubt and trepidation that he struck a light and proceeded slowly down to the lower part of the casement.

As he went, he trod on something slippery, and looking down, he found it was a candle which someone had evidently dropped in his hurry.

He lit this as well as he could in its dilapidated state, and then, with a pistol in his right hand, he proceeded in his descent.

The days of which we write were, of course, comparatively modern.

Railways had commenced to spread their iron bands over England, and the old stage coach was beginning to retire before them.

But they were far from being extinct.

Years and years after the time when Spring-Heeled Jack began to frighten people in the suburbs of London the "Royal Mails" and "Expresses," and so forth, still ran over the dark highway road.

Very few were the cases, however, in which they were stopped by footpads.

Now and then the robbers became bold and defiant as of old, and great was the consternation about this time, when it became known in London that highwaymen had once more made their appearance.

They were not attired in the gay and jaunty dress which distinguished Tom King and Blueskin and so forth.

But the attire which they affected was sufficiently like the old style to cast terror and dismay into the hearts of any timid citizens who might come across them.

A tight-fitting, frogged frock-coat, a hat of a somewhat conical shape, a pair of high military boots, and a pair of pistols, recalled sufficiently well the memories of the days of Black Bess and Dick Turpin; and the blunderbuss, and so forth, were once more coming into fashion.

It was not, therefore, to be wondered at if Ralph Ashton, finding that his lamp was gone, suspected at once that his place of concealment had been discovered and utilised by some of the gentlemen of the road.

Cautiously he descended.

There was no light below—no sign, indeed, of life.

But he still clutched his pistol as he entered the vault, which on so many occasions lately had served as his resting-place.

For a few moments after he went in—the feeble light of his candle hardly serving to dispel the gloom—he could see nothing.

But presently he saw something lying in a corner.

He stood still and listened.

The silence was terrible.

Not a sound broke it, not even the breathing of a light sleeper.

What then was that "something" lying on the heap of straw, which until now had served him as a bed?

It certainly looked like a human form.

But could it be alive—so still, so breathless?

Summoning up all his courage, he approached, and bent down.

The form, whatever it was, was covered up with straw, and he drew some of it away.

There before him, sure enough, was a human body.

But it was dead.

The face was that of a man about forty years of age, dressed in a somewhat rough fashion, and with a somewhat rough-featured face.

His features were placid in death now, however, and pale as marble.

For a few moments Ralph Ashton could not discern how the unfortunate man had met his death.

But after awhile he saw a dagger sticking in his breast with a piece of parchment attached to it.

He knelt down and detached it, and on it were the words, "A victim of the vengeance of the Black Brotherhood!"

Strange words these in modern times!

"The Black Brotherhood!" repeated Ralph. "What can the words mean? It brings me back to times long, long ago. But whatever it may signify, it will not be safe to leave him here. Where shall I place the body?"

To leave him where he was would be to bring certain suspicion upon himself.

He resolved to search the pockets of the dead man in order to see whether there was any clue whatever to his identity.

But search as he would he could find nothing.

Conquering as well as he could his natural repugnance, he raised the dead body in his arms and began to reascend the stairs.

The lamp he had discovered on a little shelf in the vault, and by leaving the door open he was enabled to drag the body up without any fear of falling.

When he reached at last the terrace, which as I have before said, ran round the old mill, he dragged his hideous burden to that part which overhung the water.

The stream was very deep at this point, and rushed on with impetuosity, swollen with the late rains.

It was a deep stream, which at one time had been used to turn the big wheel of the mill.

Glancing round to see that he was not observed, he raised the body with all his strength, poised it for a moment over the wooden parapet, and let it fall with a great splash into the water.

It disappeared for a moment amid spray and foam, but presently as he watched he saw a dark object rise to the surface and go whirling away.

Ralph Ashton heaved a sigh of relief.

"There was no danger now," he thought, "of being accused of a crime which he never committed."

He would not, however, have been so easy in his mind if he had observed that at the very moment when he threw the body into the stream a man was watching him.

A man dressed from head to foot in black, with a black mask concealing his features.

He was standing concealed in the shadow of some trees on the other side of the stream, and he never uttered a word as the victim of the Black Brotherhood was dropped into the stream.

But as soon as Ralph Ashton had passed into the mill and closed himself in once more, the mysterious figure hurried along the bank of the river towards a wooden bridge which spanned the water at some distance.

Crossing this he came stealthily along the bank on which the old mill stood, and approaching it he swung himself with wonderous agility to the terrace.

Here he endeavoured to enter by the door, but found it closed on the inside.

He paused for a moment to think; and then, muttering, "I will keep watch elsewhere," he let himself down once more, and in a few moments was safely ensconced among the trees.

Meanwhile, Ralph, having once more descended to the bottom of the old structure, proceeded to a door at the back which opened out upon the level ground, and unfastening the rusty old chains and bolts, once more peered cautiously forth.

He might have taken the body out this way, but he would have had great difficulty in carrying it over the piles of rubbish and so forth which lay between the building and the stream.

Now, however, he passed out, proceeded to the spot where he had left his horse, and bringing him in, stabled him in the lower passage, and once more re-bolted the door.

Then returning to his room, if so it could be called, he removed the straw on which the dead body had been laid and placed it in an adjoining cellar.

Returning, he locked himself securely in, and going to a cupboard took out the materials for a fire.

Having lit this he brought out some food and a bottle of wine.

"The Black Brotherhood weren't hungry or thirsty, at any rate," he thought, with a smile, as he sat down before the pleasant blaze; "but I must find myself some new quarters. I can't make a dead house of my lodgings for anyone; neither can I share it with the Black Avengers."

His attempt to be cheerful was a very poor one. He had enough, indeed, to disturb his mind—the danger of Constance, the reward for his own apprehension, and the deadly enmity of Sir Roland.

He saw no chance whatever, in case of arrest, of being able to prove his innocence, and it was necessary therefore to conceal himself until by some miraculous means he discovered, and was able publicly to denounce the guilty party.

It was a wretched existence.

But there were mysterious circumstances connected with his secret life that broke the monotony.

Of these we shall know more hereafter.

At present we cannot raise the veil. Little dreaming of the watcher so near—of the new peril hanging over him—Ralph, in spite of all, passed presently into a heavy slumber, wrapped in his large cloak before the fire.

The corner where the dead man lay he carefully eschewed.

Nothing occurred during the night.

Ralph slept as if he was reclining upon the downiest of feather beds, and dreamed soft dreams of success and happiness.

The enemy, or whoever he was who kept watch without, made no sign.

And accordingly when he awoke in the morning, and found himself refreshed and invigorated, and his lamp burning low, Ralph almost for a moment forgot the terrible danger which was threatening him.

He arose quickly, roused the fire into a healthy blaze, and proceeded at once to get himself some breakfast.

A dismal commencement to a day this, cooped up in a dark and noisome cellar, cooking by the aid of a single lamp, while outside the sun was revelling amid the woodlands and glinting on the voiceful stream.

But it meant safety.

And this to Ralph Ashton was everything now in his unfortunate position.

He had very little prospect of success or happiness at present.

All he hoped for and worked for was the discovery of the guilt of Sir Roland, and the papers which would prove the falseness and treachery of the villain who reigned at the Hall.

To do this he must remain in England, and near to his old home.

Otherwise he would most certainly have cast everything to the winds, and endeavoured with Constance to have quitted England never to return.

One thing was very certain.

The old mill must no longer be his resting-place; at any rate for some time to come.

He had imagined himself quite at home and free from all intrusion in this deserted spot; but the discovery of the dead body had convinced him that he was not alone in the selection of the mill as a place of concealment, and he resolved to abandon it.

But whither was he to go?

Suddenly he gave vent to a smothered exclamation as a wild and daring scheme entered his mind.

At first he almost laughed at the wild romance of the idea.

But the more he dwelt upon it, the more feasible it became, until at length his thoughts had so far fixed themselves upon it, that he resolved at all events to try it.

It was a wild and daring project, but what it was we must reserve at present.

Its precise nature, and the extraordinary adventures to which it led, must be explained as our story unfolds.

Once this idea had settled itself on his brain it seemed to give elasticity to his frame and spirits.

He ate his breakfast with relish, and as soon as he had done so, he made his way to the stables and saddled his horse.

He had intended to remain where he was until night had covered the earth.

But he altered his plan now.

He would be off and away as swiftly as he could, and having paid a visit to Edmonton, would return as quickly as possible to put his plan into execution.

No one seemed anywhere near as he led his steed out into the open air.

Leaping into the saddle, he at once threaded his way through the dense plantation, and was soon in the highway galloping along in the fresh crisp breeze of the morning.

He had not been gone many minutes before another horseman emerged from the wood and followed him.

This was the man who had been watching him all night; but since the time when Ralph had disposed of the body by flinging it into the river, he had altered his appearance, and was no longer masked or attired all in black.

A brown, light-fitting surtout covered him, and his appearance now was very much like that of an ordinary traveller.

Edmonton was some distance from Barnet, and evening was already coming on when Ralph reached the town.

He made his way when he reached it to a little narrow thoroughfare leading from its centre to the open country.

Here he paused at the door of a small cottage and knocked.

The door was opened by an elderly female, who glanced at him in some astonishment, combined, however, with evident pleasure—

"Well, Mr. Ashton," she said, "this is, indeed, a surprise."

"I hope a pleasant one," he said, as he vaulted from the saddle.

"Indeed so, Mr. Ashton," she answered. "I thought it would be a long time before we should see you again, seeing what they're saying in those horrid police bills about you."

"Ah! well, they say a good many untruths," said Ashton, "and the worst of it is when the police get hold of anything there is no use in contradicting them. Once they get an idea in their heads it would take a regiment of drummers to beat it out again. But, come, I will take my horse round, and then—"

"No, no," she said, hurriedly, "you pop in. There have been a good many suspicious folks round here lately, and I don't think it's safe to show yourself too much."

"Perhaps you're right, Mrs. Barton," he said. "Is Laura at home?"

"Oh! yes."

"But where is the horse going?"

"I shall just take him through our passage and out into the back yard. You won't be stopping long, may be, and no one will notice it there."

"Very well," said Ralph, and knowing that her advice was the best, he hastened into the front parlour of the cottage, where a young girl was sitting, apparently unconscious of all that was going on around her.

She was about eighteen years of age, and was attired in somewhat dark and sombre garments, but they fitted her to such perfection as to show to advantage her rounded shoulders and her firm, solid bust.

She was far from *petite*, and her form and limbs were of the substantial order, though delicately moulded.

Her face was not by any means beautiful, but there was a pleasant look upon her features, and her eyes had a *piquante* expression in them which was very enticing.

She jumped up with an exclamation of pleasure as she saw Ralph.

"Oh! Mr. Ashton," she cried, "I am so pleased to see you again."

Ralph had lived in the house, and had been on friendly terms with mother and daughter.

But he was not prepared for the very enthusiastic nature of his reception, or for the way in which Laura's breast heaved and fell at greeting him.

"And so am I pleased to see you," said Ralph, as he took her hand. "I had not thought it possible to come and see you for many a long day."

"How was that?"

"Because I have been so hunted about for no fault of my own."

Laura turned slightly pale, and coming nearer to him placed her hand upon his arm and looked up into his face.

"Is it then really true?" she said.

"What?"

"That you are accused of murder."

"Yes. But accusation is neither guilt nor conviction," said Ralph, as he pressed her hand and sat down. "I know I am innocent, and feel sure that I shall prove it."

"Indeed, I hope so," said Laura, with what was to him unexpected and unnecessary fervour. "I should indeed be unhappy if I thought that you were in such peril."

Ralph began to feel uncomfortable.

He had never imagined that he had roused in Laura's breast anything more than mere brotherly feelings; and this intense susceptibility on account of his danger was anything but pleasing.

His heart was still true to Constance, his first love.

And, if not, Laura's grand and ample charms were by no means those which appealed to him in her stead.

"I am most gratified by your words," he said, somewhat uncomfortably; "and I only hope, therefore, that you will congratulate me upon the escape which I hope I shall be able to make."

"Soon?" asked Laura, anxiously.

"Yes; within a month," he said.

"And where do you propose to go to?"

"To America. But before I go I shall be united to the dear one of my heart."

He gave her no encouragement by his look to dream that she was the chosen one.

But perhaps at the idea of being united to Constance his face lighted up with pleasure.

At any rate, she uttered what was apparently a cry of gladness, and with ready blushes threw herself upon his breast, twining her large round arms round his neck, so that he could feel the throbbing of her heart and the warmth of her bosom against his.

This was more than he bargained for.

It put him in an awkward position.

What was he to do?

"Laura," he said, "I fear you are making a great mistake."

"How so?"

"I swear that I never in my life gave you any right to believe that I was your lover."

The girl drew herself up proudly.

He could feel a cold shudder pass through her frame as she withdrew herself from the position which she had taken up on his breast.

"You lie, Ralph Ashton," she said. "I have always looked upon you as my future husband. It was to me you told all your troubles, to me you explained everything, and spoke of the happy future; and now you think to fool me by talking of your love for another girl."

"I have never loved but one," said Ralph, calmly, though his heart misgave him as to the results of this interview—"Constance Marfield, who has been my betrothed almost from childhood."

"Then what meant all your kind words to me?" she cried, fiercely. "What all the whispered nothings with which you cowards deceive weak women? What meant you by your actions, by all your behaviour to me?"

"I meant nothing," cried Ralph, earnestly. "I swear I did not. You and your mother acted kindly to me; that was all, and I thought myself bound to be kind also to you. I try to act kindly to all, and yet I could not marry all those to whom I do so."

The girl's great brown eyes glared fiercely at him as he said this.

She seemed to imagine that he was jeering her, and this idea made her bosom swell with indignation.

One moment she sat still.

Then slowly she rose.

"I have made a mistake," she said.

And she quitted the room.

As she did so Mrs. Barton entered.

She was too hospitably eager to notice Laura.

The troubled look on Ralph's face she set down to general worry.

"I've seen to the horse," she said; "and I think I may say that only me and Laura know anything about your being here. It's safely housed now, however, and there needn't be any bother about hurrying off."

As she was speaking she was setting out on the table requisites for a good meal.

"You are very kind, Mrs. Barton," he said; "but I mustn't stop. In fact, I have only run down just to see you, and say good-bye, pay what I owe, and take away the few papers I left behind."

Mrs. Barton looked somewhat dubious at this.

"Ah! just so," she said.

Then, as if one thing was suggested by the other, she added, quickly—

"Why, where's Laura gone to?"

"I don't know," replied Ralph, as unconcernedly as possible. "I fancy Laura took offence at something I said."

"Ah! you young people," cried Mrs. Barton, "you're always a-quarrelling, and a-going on. Been making her jealous, I expect!"

"No, indeed," said Ralph, wishing sincerely that he was well out of the difficulty; "I have never led Laura to believe that I looked upon her as a sweetheart. I have been betrothed ever since I was a boy to Miss Constance Marfield, and I hope that in the course of a month I shall be her husband, and go with her to America."

Mrs. Barton looked sad.

But she was by no means of the same temperament as her daughter.

She was sorry for Laura.

Sorry, because she knew her wild, ungovernable spirit.

But she had never made up her mind as Laura had done.

Apart from his money, about which she had never as yet taken pains to enquire, she had regarded him as a very suitable husband for the girl, but she had never gone so far as to say that he had ever made love to her.

She would have looked more sad still if she had observed the figure crouching to listen outside the door—the figure of Laura, with wild, distended eyes, burning too much to admit of tears, her hands clenched, and her bosom heaving tumultuously.

"He means it, then," she muttered, "the cold-hearted villain! And he will go away to this other girl and leave me without even a sigh at my distress. But I will have my revenge. If I do not have him no one else shall."

Meanwhile, Ralph Ashton, rather relieved than otherwise by the absence of Laura Barton, ate his meal in peace, chatting meanwhile with Mrs. Barton.

"You quite make me forget my troubles," he said, after awhile. "I shall begin to imagine my danger is over."

"I wish it could be so," said the woman; "but if I were in your shoes I should never feel myself safe until I was out of England. Murder is a very ticklish thing to be accused of."

"You are right," said Ralph, "and in this case I should find it very difficult to prove that I was in the right."

As if in answer to these words the door of the room was flung suddenly and violently open.

Two men in the garb of police officers entered and closed the door behind them.

Ralph sprang up, and naturally glanced towards the window.

But one of the officers, coming forward, said—

"Mr. Ashton, let me beg of you not to make a scene. The window is guarded outside by several constables. I knew you, Mr. Ralph, when you were a boy, and if I could do you a service I would; but in this case I can do nothing. It is my duty to arrest you on a charge of murder."

"May I ask the name of the supposed victim?" asked Ralph, trying hard to be calm.

"Herbert Leigh."

"Then I am not far wrong in saying that the informant is my kind and virtuous relative, Sir Roland Ashton?"

"In the first place, yes," replied the man; "in the present case, however, information as to your whereabouts was brought by Miss Barton."

Ralph staggered back in horror.

Mrs. Barton turned deadly pale and caught hold of a chair-back for support.

"Great Heavens!" she cried; "rash, headstrong girl! what has she done?"

"She has had her revenge," said a voice as the door opened, and Laura stood on the threshold, pale and ghastly, with blazing eyes.

"Fiend!" said Ralph, with a contemptuous smile. "Constables, I am ready."

Within half-an-hour Ralph Ashton was an inmate of a prison cell charged with the wilful murder of Herbert Leigh.

## CHAPTER XIII.

JOE DIMITY'S CIRCUS ONCE MORE—DAISY IN CHARACTER—A HAWK IN THE DOVE'S NEST.

BARNET is by no means a lively place at any time.

But when we write about it, before the railway had roused it up a bit, it was a most barren looking spot.

However, a few days after the arrest of Ralph Ashton it seemed as if it had taken a new lease of life.

And no wonder.

There was a show.

Joe Dimity's Circus and Theatre Royal had arrived, and great was the excitement of all, young and old.

Daisy by this time had quite recovered from the effects of her impromptu bath.

And having nothing better to do, she had resolved to throw in her lot with the "strollers."

By doing so, she would escape all peril from Gedge Foote, at any rate, for a time.

And she would be able to earn her living honestly, if in what Banks the clown called "a rough and tumble fashion."

She was somewhat timid when for the first time she donned her theatrical dress and tights, exhibiting as it did, to a daring degree, her white shoulders and girlish breasts, and all the soft contours of her lower limbs.

Mrs. Dimity had been the one to suggest to her husband the propriety of retaining Daisy in the company.

She and "Maria" had had an excellent opportunity, when recovering her from the effects of her bath in the Thames, of observing the exquisite roundness of her form, and the softness and beauty of her limbs.

"Maria" was by no means jealous.

Her first thoughts were "professional."

"Wouldn't she look well in tights, Mrs. D.?" was her remark as she surveyed the half senseless girl critically.

"Yes; and perhaps she'll wear 'em the first time on the boards of the Theatre Royal," said the kind-hearted tragedy queen, suggestively.

"I daresay she'd be glad," said Maria; "I shouldn't fancy she's got many friends, although there's no doubt she's respectable."

And so when poor Daisy came to herself, after her long, delirious sleep, and found herself surrounded by kindly faces, and heard gentle voices speaking to her, she almost made up her mind to ask them to permit her to remain with them for a time, even before genial Maria suggested it.

When the latter first spoke of it she was attired ready for the performance of a court page—not of the usual type, but more of the character of a bayadeer, with plumed hat, excessively low dress, and trunk hose not much larger or more covering than a pair of bathing drawers.

The display of charms, consequently, were excessively lavish, and little Daisy blushed at the possibility of having to appear in similar costume.

Maria laughed at her scruples.

"My dear," she said, "you mustn't be squeamish. You would look ever so much better than I do in this dress because you're younger and smaller. I should be glad to give over this *rôle* to you. You have a charming little figure, and will look quite dainty and tempting in trunk hose and tights."

"But where am I to get any to fit me?" she said.

The words were uttered so demurely that Maria went into an ecstasy of laughter.

"Well, I don't pretend that mine will do for you, my dear!" she cried, shaking all over as she put a last finishing touch to her face with the hare's-foot, and then powdering her fat shoulders. "You would look as if you had just put on the clothes of Dimity's giantess, lately deceased. I'll get you a good set of tights at the next town, and as for the trunk hose and velvet bodice, and all that, we can soon make something up for you that will send the audience into ecstasies."

Daisy—modest as she was—was not foolish enough to worry her newly-found friends by indulging in prudery.

So, after a very little persuasion, she consented to join the company and to take "pages' parts," and others which would display her figure to advantage, until she had got rid of her "stage fright," and was able to take talking *rôles*.

The first time she was arrayed in her new and unusual finery she was the admiration of all the company, and Harry Banks fell head over ears in love with her.

Even before the strollers it was bad enough for timid Daisy to stand in that daring state of undress.

But when she went on the boards, and heard the buzz of voices, and saw the sea of heads, she felt dizzy and confused, and was hardly able to stand.

Harry Banks's jolly, genial voice was there, however, to cheer and encourage her.

"Keep up, little 'un!" he cried, *sotto voce*; "I'm here. If you fall I'll catch you."

But apart from this there was another thing which gave her courage.

This was the undisguised admiration of the audience.

Loud clapping of hands resounded through the wood and canvas theatre, mingled with all kinds of exclamations.

"Isn't she a stunner?"

"What a lovely figure!"

"What a pretty, innocent face!"

And then, to crown all—

"If she only learns to act that figure will carry her on to the London boards."

This reception roused Daisy to do her best, and in a very short time she had learned to go off and on the stage without feeling as if she was weak in her knees, and her legs trembling as if with ague.

Before the night was over Daisy Leigh (or Lottie Day as she was called in her new vocation) was the talk of the audience, though Maria's massive charms and really good idea of acting called forth the usual rounds of applause.

It was evident that Barnet was going to be a golden spot for Joe Dimity.

He absolutely kissed Daisy's forehead after the performance, which, far from making the "tragedy queen" jealous, caused her to laugh immoderately.

"My dear," he said, "you're a success. When you can learn to say a few words you'll get along famously."

"I'm glad you're pleased," she said, smiling round upon the genial company gathered on the stage after the audience had departed. "It is some little return for the kindness you have shown me. If it hadn't been for Mr. Banks I should have been drowned; and if it hadn't been for Mrs. Dimity and Maria I should have never got through my illness."

An explosion of merriment followed this speech, which somewhat disconcerted Daisy, who had so innocently called the leading actress "Maria," as if they had been bosom friends for years.

But that worthy lady soon put matters right.

"It's a shame to laugh," she cried, laughing herself all the time. "She's a dear, grateful, loving thing. There!"

And she threw her plump, warm arms round Daisy's white, rounded shoulders, and kissed her three times with such genuine vigour that Harry Banks, the clown, forgetting that for the nonce he was attired as a "swell of the period," threw a somersault, and came up before the two ladies with his toes together, and his forefinger in his mouth, crying—

"Here we are again! Holler boys! Oh! my, ain't it nice?"

Whereat Maria boxed his ears.

"Order in the gallery!" cried Joe Dimity. "To your dressing-rooms, ladies and gentlemen! and when you've made yourselves presentable, we'll have some supper at the Black Lion."

That night when Daisy went to rest in the little room at the inn, which was to be shared by Agnes Dymot, one of the strollers, about her own age, the latter, who had been detained on the stairs by Joe Dimity as she was hastening up, brought the orphan girl two packages.

The first she opened was from Joe Dimity.

It contained the fifteen shillings which she had paid for her tights and boots at a second-hand warehouse recommended by "Maria," and these words were written on a piece of paper in which they were enclosed.

"*Thank you for buying necessaries out of the two pounds, which were your only property! I return it as a first mark of my esteem, and I will pay you every week all the salary I can possibly afford*"

Poor Joe!

He dare not promise more.

The second note was from Harry Banks, and in it was enclosed a rose.

He had bought this early in the evening, but had had no opportunity of giving it to her.

The note was a very daring one, considering that their acquaintance was so short.

"DEAREST DAISY,—*Accept this rose as an offering of my devotion. Sweets to the sweet, you know. I am your champion against all comers. If you're ever in danger only say the word, and you'll find Harry Banks ready. 'Here we are again' is my motto, and while I live you'll never want a friend.*"

Daisy kissed the rose, and placed it with Joe Dimity's fifteen shillings under her pillow.

This was wet with tears of gratitude that night, but there was no tender response in her heart to Harry Banks.

She liked him as a friend; she thanked him as the preserver of her life.

But as regarded tender affection, or an atom of love, it did not exist.

The treasures of that little heart were as yet hidden, ready to be bestowed upon the first person who roused the latent passions of her gentle bosom.

She would have laughed with real scorn had she been told that she had already met her fate.

But in very truth she had.

Not that she knew it.

She had never looked upon his face.

But, nevertheless, she had been in his presence, heard his voice, his hand had touched hers, his breath been warm upon her cheek.

And yet she did not even know his name.

Happy dreams visited her that night.

She forgot for a time the tragedy which had so suddenly clouded her life.

Everything seemed *couleur de rose*.

She saw again in her dreams the glare of footlights, the flickering lamps of the "Theatre Royal."

But they were magnified tenfold.

The glare was that of a London theatre.

The audience was numbered by thousands.

Sweet music and the perfume of flowers filled the air, then came the roar of applause, and a handsome youth knelt at her feet.

Again came a rapid change, the youth disappeared by magic, the huge theatre seemed to contract, the lights grew dimmer, and Harry Banks, the clown, came leaping up through a vampire trap, shouting, "Holler, boys! here we are again!" and bore her through clouds of vapoury mist just as he had borne her through the black turbid waters of old Father Thames.

She awoke to find herself in the little warm bed at the inn, and her companion, Agnes Dymot, lying with her arms firmly and fondly clasped round her.

"I wonder who that youth was?" thought Daisy, as she turned over to go to sleep again; "he was very handsome."

She little knew what was coming.

Little knew that the strollers were, by stopping at Barnet, leading her into the greatest danger of her life.

But they were doing so unconsciously.

It was a danger of which they little dreamed!

The swoop of the hawk into the dove's nest.

# SPRING-HEELED JACK, THE TERROR OF LONDON.

By the Author of "TURNPIKE DICK, the Star of the Road."

"WHAT WANT YOU WITH THIS LADY?" ASKED THE STRANGE BEING, SEPULCHRALLY.

## CHAPTER XIV.

### SIR ROLAND ASHTON IN A NEW CHARACTER—BEHIND THE SCENES.

THE news of Ralph Ashton's arrest was received by Sir Roland Ashton with mingled emotions.

He would have been glad if his enemy could have been hung out of his way without further to do.

He was quite indifferent as to what fate befell him.

But he had no wish to be involved in it.

The trial of Ralph for murder would bring up, undoubtedly, the most trying reminiscences, and would produce, perhaps, the most awkward revelations.

He had never bargained for Ralph's arrest.

When he had spread about the idea that Ralph was the murderer of Herbert Leigh, he had trusted to his good sense to keep out of the way and fly to another country.

He had never bargained for the determined spirit which would make him stick to his own home to unravel the terrible mystery which hung over his life.

"This arrest is very awkward, Caleb," said the baronet to his steward, when the latter brought the news; "something must be done to prevent the trial."

"Are you afraid he will be hung?" said the man, cynically.

"No, indeed; that would be a mercy for which I could not be too thankful," replied Sir Roland; "but I fear the revelations which may be made at the trial. You see, there is no direct evidence against him. How are we to draw the net round him without implicating ourselves."

"We must manufacture witnesses," said Caleb.

"But how?"

"We have one."

"Whom do you mean?"

"Job Joskins. He saw some one standing by the body of Herbert Leigh up at the ruins."

"That was Spring-Heeled Jack."

"Yes—yes; but he can swear that he saw Ralph Ashton there first, and that he was going to denounce him, only that he was frightened away by this demon."

"Well; but his evidence doesn't count for much," said Sir Roland. "Ralph might declare that he was passing by accidentally and came suddenly on the body. The murder was committed in London, so that Joskins could not prove much."

"No; but it is a link in the chain," said Caleb.

"No one can connect him with the murder in the Mint," replied the baronet.

"That is easily managed," said Caleb.

"How?"

"We must produce some one who will swear that he saw him enter the house on the night of the murder."

"Well, I must leave all to you," said Sir Roland, "it will not do for me to mix myself up too much in the affair. Get your witnesses together, prove him guilty, and a thousand pounds are yours."

"And as much more as I want afterwards," said Caleb Masters to himself.

But he said aloud—

"Many thanks, Sir Roland. I will do my best, and in order to do so I must go to London at once."

"That means that you will want money," said his master. "I will write you out a cheque. Don't be afraid to spend it; only see that you link the chain properly. Don't let us make mistakes, for that would bring disaster upon ourselves."

It was on the day after this conversation that Sir Roland, strolling through the town, saw the flaming posters announcing the arrival of the Joe Dimity Troupe, and giving portraits of "Maria" in her most ravishing undress.

Daisy Leigh had not yet attained to the honour of being on the bills.

Those on the walls were old ones.

But Joe had it in his mind to have new ones printed soon, on which Daisy was to figure in all the glories of her tights and trunk-hose and plumed hat.

However, "Maria" was quite sufficient attraction to Sir Roland.

Anything in the female line caught his sensual fancy.

And so he resolved, in spite of his position, to figure at the performance that evening.

That was the second night of performance.

He was not there, consequently, to see Daisy's triumphant first appearance.

Occupying a corner where he was as far as possible screened from observation, he sat, with one or two of the young bloods of the neighbourhood, who had come on a similar errand to himself, rather to quiz the play than enjoy it.

Of course it was a queer affair to those accustomed to the real theatre.

But there were good points in it.

Maria's dancing was really first rate.

And when she came leaping on in her short muslin skirts as *premiere danseuse*, making a liberal display of her superb lower limbs, there was a genuine burst of applause.

The baronet's mind was at once inflamed.

He was one of those cynical ignoramuses who scoff at the virtue of the stage.

He thought that because a woman does not mind coming on the boards in partial undress she must be ready to listen to his fulsome adulation and submit to his loathsome caresses.

In Maria's case he was most wofully mistaken —never so much so, in fact, in his whole life.

She was a clever woman.

She could show all kinds of trinkets, good and bad, which had been given her.

Maria was poor.

She accepted them because she might want them in some case of future necessity.

But the return she made for them was very scanty indeed.

A smile or a pressure of the hand.

There was a tradition in the Dimity Troupe of an unrehearsed dramatic performance which had occurred on one occasion, when a "swell," who had obtained access to the wings, and had presumed to embrace her, was sent flying on to the stage by a well-directed blow delivered straight from Maria's plump shoulder.

He flew against Harry Banks, the clown, cannoned against old Toppledown, the pantaloon, and fell over into the orchestra, where he subsided into the big drum head first.

For the moment the audience thought this a great joke, and applauded.

But when Joe Dimity explained matters—told them that the "swell" had insulted his "leading lady," and made him dub up the price of a new drum—the mingled hisses and cheers were tremendous.

And, of course, when Maria reappeared she received quite an ovation.

"Eyes on and hands off" was her motto.

But on the stage she was the most daring, rollicking soul that ever trod the boards.

Sir Roland and his set were in raptures.

They had never expected such a treat.

But presently there was a buzz of expectation.

Daisy's name was not on the bills.

But her fame had travelled.

Those who had seen her on the night before had talked.

So the audience waited eagerly.

The dancing was over.

The play began.

Joe Dimity and the tragedy queen, knowing there were "real nobs" among the audience, exerted themselves to the utmost.

But presently Daisy entered as the page, bearing a note for the "Baron de Montfort, of Montfort Grange."

Her nervousness had greatly subsided.

But she looked as ravishing as ever.

Her eyes were now turned more boldly towards the audience, disclosing their exquisite depth and clearness; her hair fell in soft ringlets on the dazzling bare shoulders, so dainty and delicate as to resemble a living statue; her form and limbs were perfect in unison and proportion.

For an instant the audience were spellbound with surprise.

Then came a sudden and spontaneous burst of applause on all sides.

"By Jove!" exclaimed Leicester Lambton, one of the baronet's companions, "she's simply lovely. Deuced shame to have such a superb girl in a strollers' booth!"

"You're right," said another; "she looks a perfect lady, and her figure's beautiful. Why, what the deuce is the matter, Ashton? You look as if you had seen a ghost."

No wonder he expressed surprise.

Sir Roland had turned deadly pale; his eyes had retreated into his head, leaving black rings round them, and he had grasped the rail of the orchestra for support.

"I think I have," he said; "her face reminds me of one I knew long—long ago. She has made me feel quite ill. I will go out into the open air for a moment."

He hastened away as he spoke.

"Queer fellow that Ashton," cried Lambton, as he went, "making a fool of himself over a little stage beauty."

"She's enough to turn any man's head, if that is what she's done," said the other. "She's a dream of beauty! but she doesn't look as if she would stand any nonsense."

Meanwhile Sir Roland strode out upon the common, where the "pitch" had been made.

His heart was in a flutter and his brain in a whirl.

"Who can this girl be?" he muttered, as he paced to and fro. "The same face—the same expression! She is the very ghost of Augusta Leigh!"

He glanced round him to see whether anyone was watching him.

But, seeing no one near, he walked rapidly towards a spot where a light seemed to indicate something in the shape of a stage door.

"Yes, the very ghost of Augusta Leigh," he said, as he went; "only more perfect, perhaps, in symmetry. I must and will see her. What joy—what triumph to enjoy the caresses of the daughter of the woman who despised me, and then to fling her away—crush her beneath my feet in triumph! For she must die! If she is the daughter of Herbert and Augusta Leigh, she must die—and soon!"

The hideous fiend who thus lived in the guise of a human being walked quickly and eagerly forward.

At the door a man was sitting on a chair, just inside the opening.

He rose on seeing a stranger.

"Are you the stage-door-keeper?" asked Sir Roland.

"Yes, sir."

As the man spoke the baronet seemed to recognise a loafer whom he had often seen prowling about the neighbourhood.

"Are you a member of the company, or are you only employed for the week?"

"Only for the week, sir. I live in Barnet, sir."

"Do you know me?"

"You're Sir Roland Ashton, what lives up at the Hall," said the man, readily. "My name's Tugwell—Bob Tugwell. You may often 'a seen me about."

"I have," said Sir Roland, significantly recalling to his mind a day when he saw this fellow leap through a hedge with a brace of rabbits in his hand; "but tell me, my good fellow, do you want to earn some money?"

The man grinned.

"Do I not?" he said, "you try me!"

"Very good, then," said Sir Roland, as he took out his purse and presented the man with a coin; "here's something to buy yourself a drink when the play's over. Now listen. I don't want to stop here talking, because it will look suspicious. Do you know the boathouse down by the river?"

"Yes, sir."

"Be there to-morrow evening then, an hour before you have to come here, and I'll tell you what I want you to do. It's nothing very bad, only what's done every day."

"I'll be there."

"At what time?"

"Five o'clock."

"Very well. But tell me first what's the name of that young girl that came on dressed as a page?"

"Lottie Day; she's a stunner, ain't she?"

"Lottie Day!" mused the baronet, sauntering away without answering the man's remark. "Ah! well, that makes no difference. It is an assumed name, of course."

And with his breast full of evil triumph he rejoined his companions.

And unsuspecting any calamity, knowing nothing of the cloud hanging over her, poor Daisy received the plaudits of the audience with radiant smiles.

She was happy for the time, and grateful for her success.

But the tempest was louring. The destroyer was at hand!

Her dishonour and her death were both planned by the same demon who had compassed the death of her father.

## CHAPTER XV.

### RALPH ASHTON IN PRISON—A DESPERATE RESOLVE—TIMMS' MISSION.

The feelings of Ralph Ashton, when he found himself a prisoner under lock and key, were terrible indeed.

He was not satisfied of the power of Sir Roland to prove his complicity in the murder of Herbert Leigh.

But there was the forgery.

He would inevitably bring that forward.

Of course, he was innocent of this, also.

But he was powerless to prove even that.

The net which Sir Roland had woven round him was such that it seemed impossible to escape from it.

Hopeless, indeed, was everything in the future.

But he did not despair.

Such a feeling was foreign to his nature.

Yet who could aid him?

This was the thought which filled his mind with unrest.

The only being to whom he could look in his trouble was Constance.

But how to send a letter to her?

The warder who guarded the corridor in the prison where he was stationed was a young man of pleasant but somewhat weak and crafty face.

Surely he could be bribed to take a letter to Constance?

Of course, Ralph knew nothing of the change that had been effected in the young girl's rooms.

But this was not to be thought of as an impediment to his scheme.

The man must find for himself some means of communicating with her.

He lost no time in putting his plan into execution.

When the warder brought in his dinner he at once commenced the attack.

"You must have a dull time of it here," he said.

"Yes; not very amusing."

"Do you have any holidays?"

"Yes; I'm off on one to-morrow."

Ralph's eyes glistened.

"Ah! that's the very thing," he exclaimed. "How long will you be gone for?"

"Two days."

"Which part of the world are you going to?"

The man laughed.

"You're very inquisitive to-day, sir?"

"Aye, I am," said Ralph; "but you'll be well rewarded for it. I can put ten pounds in your pocket easily."

The man shook his head.

"Ah!" he said, "all prisoners say that; and then they want such outlandish things done that it's waste o' time to listen."

"Oh! this is not at all outlandish," said Ralph. "All I wish is to get a letter to my sweetheart."

"If that's all I daresay I can do it," said the young man, eagerly.

"Well, then, if you come in towards night I'll have the letter ready."

"Where does the young lady live?"

"At Barnet."

"That'll do for my country trip, then," said Timms, the warder. "Get the letter ready and I will be here to time."

Ralph's letter to Constance took considerable time and trouble.

He had to explain to her particulars which anyone of weak mind would not have been able to grasp.

But he felt confidence in her in everything.

What he asked her to do he knew well she had power and will to perform.

The end of the letter was of the tenderest kind, and hopeful in every way.

It is not given to us to read the future, and it was fortunate for Ralph and Constance that they could not.

Timms was true to his word.

Though it was not his turn to visit Ralph in the evening he contrived to do so; and without loss of time the prisoner proceeded to explain exactly what was required of him.

"When you reach Barnet," he said, "you must inquire for Ashton Grange—that is where Sir Roland, my uncle, lives, who denies my being his nephew. I am in reality the baronet, Sir Ralph Ashton, son of Sir Guy Ashton; but he has suppressed the papers which prove this, and consequently I am powerless."

"If that is the case, it would be better to let the trial come on," said the warder.

"No. He has me too securely in his clutches," said Ralph. "I have not a human being or one single document to prove my innocence. If I were acquitted of the murder of Herbert Leigh I should be convicted of the forgery. There is not the slightest chance of my showing my guiltlessness of that. No; my only resource is escape, and," he added, seeing the scared look on the face of the warder, "that, of course, is impossible."

"Well, to say the least, it isn't very likely," said Timms, sententiously.

"No. Well, as I was saying, Miss Constance Marfield, to whom this letter is directed, is kept under lock and key by Sir Roland, for fear she should take it into her head to elope with me. He wants her, I believe, for himself."

"Yes, sir."

"The difficulty you will have to surmount is the placing the letter in her hands. If it falls into those of Sir Roland or any of his hirelings all is lost."

"I quite understand. But if she's locked up in a room, I don't see the use of my trying."

"Yes. There is a man called Job Joskins about the place—a foolish, loutish fellow, and about as big a coward as you could find in a day's march. You must ask to see him; use bribes, threats, what you will, but discover in what room Constance Marfield is confined. Then you must hang about till night-time, and climb up in some way to her window. I have done so over and over again by the ivy."

"In that case you can tell me in what part of the house her room is?"

"No, indeed, I cannot, because she may have been shifted to another apartment; but I can say this: when last I saw her she was in the third bedroom on the first floor on the left side of the portico which faces the grounds adjoining the high road. See here, I will sketch the place."

He did so roughly and rapidly.

The man was naturally crafty and ingenious, and his wits were sharpened by the prospect of money.

"I think I see it all correctly," he said. "I will to-morrow afternoon, and try and see this Job Joskins. What is he?"

"Well, he's a groom, a coachman, a spy, anything. A paid satellite of Sir Roland is the best name for him," said Ralph. "He'd do anything for his master—tell a lie, pick a pocket—cut a throat, if he had the pluck. Well, here are five pounds. When you bring me the answer of Constance Marfield I will give you five more. If through your aid I escape from the consequences of Sir Roland's persecution, you shall have fifty more."

"Good," said Timms; "I'll do my best."

He took the letter, concealed it in a waistcoat underneath his uniform, placed the five pounds in his trousers' pocket, and prepared to go.

"Beware of Sir Roland Ashton," said Ralph. "He is the fiend incarnate. If you come across him don't trust him with a word."

"Never fear," said Timms. "I'll be as sly as a fox. It's my interest to bring this thing through properly, for, if I do, I shall be able to marry my girl that I've been waiting to get spliced to for more'n a year."

"Then I hope, for my sake, you'll marry her soon," said Ralph, with a smile.

If Timms, the warder, had had any idea that he was aiding in an escape from prison he would never have attempted such a thing as he was now about to experiment upon.

He simply looked upon it as a desperate attempt upon the prisoner's part to obtain through Constance Marfield's agency the papers which he could not obtain elsewhere.

But the truth was far different.

Ralph meant simply to escape from gaol.

He saw plainly that once in a court he had no chance.

Out from those stone walls he must go no matter what happened.

Timms lost no time.

The next day at noon found him at Barnet.

Half-past found him at Ashton Hall.

He had been "in the force" two years before he became a warder.

Consequently he had a little of the detective instinct about him.

He knew that the yokel mind was not, as a rule, of a very high order.

He had in his time experienced the ease with which a man of this kind can be persuaded into remembering a thing that never happened, especially when he is made to see a personal advantage in it.

So he passed through the lodge-gate boldly, keeping his eye on the front of the house, and soon making out the whereabouts of the bedroom mentioned by Ralph.

Presently he saw a servant approaching.

He at once accosted him.

"Which is the way to the stable-yard?" he asked.

"Round there to the right," replied the man. "Whom may you be wanting?"

"Job Joskins."

"Oh! yes; he's round there. Shall I go with you, and fetch him?"

"If you please," said Timms, who, never having seen Job, naturally felt anxious about identifying him.

And so they hurried on.

At the Corner Pin Timms had discovered that Job was in the habit of frequenting that noble house of entertainment, and having a social glass in the parlour, accordingly he knew how to open the conversation.

They were soon in the stable-yard, and John Timms, *alias* for the moment Bob Wright, was presented to Job Joskins.

The latter touched his forelock, and looked sheepish.

"Day, sir," he said. "What do you please to want, sir?"

Timms slapped his leg and laughed loudly.

"Why, don't you know me?" he cried.

"No; I don't," reiterated Job.

"Well you are—but there, I won't insult ye," said Timms. "You've got no memory, Job. Often's the time we've been at the Corner Pin and drank till all's blue."

Job began to think that, whoever he was, this stranger wasn't a bad sort.

So it wasn't worth while to offend him.

"Well, I'm not a good one at remembering at any time," he said. "I daresay you're right and I'm wrong. What is it you want with me?"

"Nothing very particular," said the disguised warder. "I've come here on a holiday; got a good berth in London now, and have two days' off. I thought I'd like to see some one I knew, so I came here to hunt you up and ask ye to have a drink."

Job Joskins glanced doubtfully round at his companions.

"Oh! all right, go on, Job," said one of the others, with a laugh.

And thus adjured, the groom grinned and went.

The warder did not intend quitting the grounds so quickly, however.

"It's a fine place this of Sir Roland's," he said. "How do you find things? Much about the same as usual, I suppose?"

"Yes; no improvement at any rate," said Job. "The guv'nor is just as glumpy as ever, and now he's taken on with Caleb Masters things are worse."

"Ah! yes; I should think so," said Timms, meditatively.

He didn't know Caleb from Adam.

So he didn't venture much.

"But," he added, "how is the young lady you used to speak to me about so much—Miss Constance Marfield? That used to be her room. Many a time I've seen her looking out of that window, so melancholy like, on the meadows!"

Ah! Timms, you ought to have been a detective officer!

Job was quite taken in.

"Ah! that there isn't her room now," he said; "she's t'other side. But ye see the window's barred now, so she hasn't much chance o' seeing out."

"A barred window! that's a rum thing to have in a private house," said Timms; "show it us?"

Job Joskins meditated.

He hadn't had his drink and he was always thirsty.

But, then, what on earth could his old boon companion want to know about Constance and her barred window?

He look doubtfully at his companion.

"Well, you see," he said, "I should get into a fine bother if Sir Roland knew that I showed you anything about the house. If he thought I even spoke about it it would be bad enough."

"It won't do any harm," said Timms.

"No, I don't suppose it will," returned Job Joskins, "especially as he's away from home. So we'll take a turn round."

Timms laughed outright.

"Well," he said, "I don't see it's necessary to take me all over the place to see Miss Constance's bedroom window. But I wanted to look round the place and see what it's like, as I often have heard of it."

Job Joskins did not say anything, but quietly passed along the broad walk.

Timms glanced round him everywhere—admiring the place, and taking note of every point.

Presently they came upon an angle of the building where the windows looked out upon the wide, glassy lake with its stately swans.

He noted at once the casement which was barred. The ivy was growing densely round it.

"That'll be easy enough to climb up," thought Timms, with intense satisfaction.

"Ah! well, this is a nice old place enough," he said, aloud (after observing that the park led through a wide avenue of beeches towards the lodge gates); "but I don't think I'd go without my dinner for it. Let's go and have a snack at the Corner Pin."

Job Joskins was nothing loth.

He had seen all the beauties of Ashton Hall until he was sick of them, and so off he went down the high road as soon as they reached it, and led the way at a swinging pace.

Timms let him go on in advance.

He was well wrapped up in his own thoughts.

"If I can get a letter to Constance Marfield through those bars, what's to hinder me giving her the things to escape with?"

Such were his cogitations.

And when he reached the Corner Pin he became so full of his own ideas that Job Joskins voted him a bore.

However, the grog flowed freely, and Job, under its influence, became very communicative.

In an hour's time Timms learned more in regard to the arrangements of Ashton Hall than he had dreamed of.

Job Joskins knew not what he was saying.

But he did not disclose any of the real secrets of the prison house.

He was too much linked in with the interests of the house—too deeply in the circle of its crimes to divulge anything.

But Timms saw that there was a skeleton in the house.

"It 'ud be worth a man's while to skirmish about here a bit," he said to himself, when presently he saw Job relapse into a drunken sleep. "If Ralph Ashton escapes, I'm hanged if I don't offer to go partner with him in routing out the secrets of this old place. I shan't have much trouble, I'm thinking, in getting that letter into the hands of Lady Constance, and while I am doing that I'm a fool if I can't give her a little help otherwise."

"My friend Job seems in for a long sleep," said Timms, addressing the landlord. "While he's snoring off his whisky I'll take a stroll round."

And so off he went.

He knew very little about the locality, but he had observed that there were some shops near, and he at once made his way towards an ironmonger's.

Here he purchased a couple of excellent files, and a few other necessary articles, and, having done so, he turned to go back to the Corner Pin.

As he passed round the corner of the lane a man sauntered up to him.

"You're Job Joskins's pal, ain't you?"

Timms felt the detective instinct being awakened in him again.

"I am," he said, smiling.

"You're square?"

"Well, I ain't a rounder."

The man laughed.

"If you ain't, Job is," he said. "He's talking about that little affair he was in up at Johnson's Farm years ago, when the plate was nabbed, and if you don't take care you'll get into trouble."

"Hurrah!" was Timms's inward cheer.

"I'll go back at once," he said; "and I'll stand a drain or so. Here's half-a-crown for you, and mind you keep 'mum!'"

"Thank ye!" said the man, grinning; "it's no interest of mine to tell anything."

"Ye see," said Timms, reflectively, "he's been in a good many jobs before he got in favour with the squire—Sir Roland I mean. Do you mean the plate robbery up at Johnson's Farm?"

"Yes; I said so."

"Well, ye see," said Timms; "I wasn't in that job. I was in London. Tell us all about it."

"You must know," replied the man (who said it wasn't his interest to tell anything), "five years ago there was a ball going on at Johnson's Farm, top o' the hill like, leastwise as ye get nearly atop, and after supper, when the servants went down to clear away, every bit o' plate was gone."

"Yes; I remember. Well?"

"Job Joskins was seen a-running like mad across the grounds with another fellow—Bob Taylor."

"Yes."

"Well, they nabs Job, but they lets Bob off, for he went like a greyhound. Job got off 'cos there wasn't any evidence against him; but it was a case of touch-and-go with him, and if Bob Taylor had only been found, and split, Job 'ud a got five years."

"Yes—so he told me," said Timms, complacently. "But I hope you don't open yer mouth to everyone like this."

"Not I. Only you being a friend like—"

"Just so. Here's another half-a-crown," said Timms. "Run into the Corner Pin again, order two glasses of grog, and tell Job Joskins to 'stow his jawin' tackle,' as the sailors say, for I shall be back in a minute."

He turned and hastened back to the ironmonger's shop.

There he made a singular purchase—something like a horse's bit.

With this in his pocket he made his return to the Corner Pin, and found Job awake, very much the worse for his inebriety and his subsequent snooze.

He looked washed out and half-foolish.

"Drink up and come along o' me," said Timms, in a half-whisper. "You've been opening yer cussed mouth about that affair at Johnson's Farm."

"What affair?" asked Job, with feeble bluster.

"Nabbing the plate."

"Why, who the devil *are* you, then?" groaned Job Joskins, helplessly.

Timms laughed loudly.

"Ha, ha!" he cried. "I thought you didn't remember me properly!"

Then, bending forward, he said, in a low voice, in Job's ear—

"*I'm Bob Taylor!*"

---

## CHAPTER XVI.

TIMMS HAS A NEW ADVENTURE—CONSTANCE MARFIELD'S DARING ESCAPADE—RALPH ASHTON DISAPPEARS MYSTERIOUSLY—SPRING-HEELED JACK AGAIN COMES TO THE RESCUE.

The effect of Timms' words upon Job Joskins was positively electrical.

They sobered him, at any rate.

He drew himself back in his seat, and stared at his companion with glassy eyes and crimsoning cheeks.

"If you're not a-jokin'," he cried, "you're a ghost!"

"A very substantial one, then," said Timms, who was becoming jovial in anticipation of the success he was bent on achieving. "But I want to be off now. Come along—you've drank enough for to-day. Let's be going before you get queer again."

Job was like a lamb.

Whatever Timms proposed he would at this moment have consented to.

In a few moments they were in the road, once more on their way to Ashton Hall.

"Now then, Job," said Timms, when they were out of hearing of everybody, "let's come to business."

"Business!" growled Job. "I'm afraid I've done a bad stroke of business to-day."

"Strikes me you have, if you don't look out sharp," said Timms. "But, come, listen to me. I've a note in my pocket that I want delivered to Miss Constance Marfield."

"Well, I'll give it to her."

"I'm very much obliged to you," said Timms, "but I'd rather not. I'm going to deliver it to her myself at her bedroom window to-night. You've got to put a ladder ready for me this afternoon; hide it away among the shrubs and ivy, you know. To-night you must be under the window about midnight, and keep watch while I speak to her."

Job Joskins made a feeble attempt at a smile.

"Only I know you're joking," he said, "I'd think you were mad."

"Mad! Why?"

"Cos it 'ud be as much as my place was worth to dream o' helpin' you."

"You've got to do it though," said Timms, in a tone of authority; "so understand me at once, and don't waste time. If you refuse to help me I'll go straight to Sir Roland and tell him all."

"You'd get into trouble same as me," blustered Job Joskins; "everyone knows that Bob Taylor was in it."

"Oh! that's your game is it?" said Timms. "Then what do ye think o' this?"

And he suddenly bent forward. Then there was a slightly clicking sound, and Job Joskins found himself handcuffed.

His face grew deadly pale.

"Wha—t's th—is me—an?" he stammered.

"It means, my boy," said Timms, forcibly taking him by the arm as in his old policeman days, "it means that you are my prisoner, and anything you say will be used against you, so you'd better shut up and come along quietly"

"Oh! lor'—oh! lor'," groaned Job. "Bob Taylor turned bobby? What'll the world come to next?"

"Ye see that was a little playful deception of mine," said Timms. "I'm no more Bob Taylor than the man in the moon. I know all about that burglary up at Johnson's Farm; but if you'd only consented to do as I asked you, I'd have winked at it, and let you off. Now, of course, you must take the consequences."

"Where are you going to take me to?"

"Straight to Sir Roland Ashton," returned Timms; "he's a magistrate, and he'll give me the order for your committal to prison."

Job groaned. That was the very thing of all others that he dreaded.

If he could only go to the lockup he might get off without being exposed to Sir Roland at all.

"Oh! dear—oh! dear," he cried, "this is awful! Who'd a thought I should be such a fool as to be taken like this?"

"You should have looked after your own interest, and not refused to do what I asked," said Timms.

"Is it too late?"

Timms shook his head.

"Ah!" he said, "I don't know whether to trust you."

"You could tell Sir Roland if I deceived you."

"True; but then you might run off and leave me in the lurch."

"No; I've got too good a berth."

"Well, I'm inclined to give you a chance."

"I swear I'll do as you ask."

"Very good," said Timms; "I'll try you. But, remember, if I find you trying any of your games I'll round on ye in a minute."

"Never fear," said Job. "You won't have to round. I'll do anything you like."

For a moment Timms thought that he would ask him to let Constance out of her captivity through the house.

But then Job might blunder. Constance would be placed perhaps in another room, and then all their plans would be ruined.

This would not suit Timms.

He felt certain that if he successfully carried out this campaign he would be handsomely rewarded.

So he was willing to risk a good deal.

"All I want you to do is to bring round the ladder and hide it, and be there at twelve o'clock to-night ready for me."

"I'll be there like a shot," said Job, "only pray, Mr. Constable, do take off these irons. There's the farmer's boy at Johnson's coming up and—"

In an instant he was released.

Timms placed the irons in his pocket with a kind of warning jingle.

"Ye see there's a man's life depending on this," he said, "so if ye do play me false look out."

They parted at the lodge gates.

Job turned in, much pleased to have escaped.

Timms betook himself saunteringly to a little beershop not far off to rest and eat.

At length night came.

Constance, knowing that from some reason or another she had nothing to fear from Sir Roland for the next night or two, retired to bed early.

The secret which Mrs. Levine had confided to her had roused her spirits, and given her a kind of sense of security.

She slept on quietly until the midnight hour arrived.

When she was awakened by a slight sound at her window.

She started up.

Then she plainly heard it once more.

Tap, tap, tap!

She began to glide from the bed in the dim lamplight as Timms peered through the glass.

Timms gazed at the beautiful creature and was so entranced for a moment that he forgot his mission.

Never had he seen such creamy skin, such softness of outline, such abandon, and luxurious contours.

But, after a moment he pulled himself together and tapped again.

"Hist!" he said.

Constance, of course, imagined that her visitor was Ralph.

There was no necessity, therefore, to make any elaborate alterations of toilet, and, consequently, she rushed eagerly to the casement bare-necked as she was.

"Who is there?" she cried.

"A messenger from Ralph Ashton."

"How do I know that to be true?"

"I have a letter here from him."

Constance opened the window slightly.

The letter was pushed through.

Leaving the window still open, Constance hurried to the lamp, turned it up, and tore open the missive.

As she read, her eyes glowed with amazement, her cheeks flushed, and her breasts heaved tumultuously.

It ran as follows—

"DEAREST CONSTANCE,—*I do not suppose that you have heard of my danger. If you have, do not despair, for the innocent are not allowed to suffer for the guilty. I am in prison on a charge of murder—the murder of Herbert Leigh, of which you, more than anyone else, know me to be innocent. But there is no proof of my guiltlessness, and therefore I must abide by the consequences. The only one in this world whom I can trust is you, Constance. If you fail me, then I must die.*"

Constance paused, and pressed her hand over her heaving bosom.

"As if I should fail him?" she murmured.

And then she read on—

"*By the aid of my messenger you can escape. When you do so, do not take him with you, but ask him to wait for you at some inn. For him to know my secret or guess at it would be a disaster which I fear to contemplate. When you quit the Hall and leave Timms, I wish you to make your way towards the pile of old buildings known as East's Mill. This, as you know, is a ruin. Beneath it is a vault; and, going down the dilapidated staircase, on the right you will find a small cupboard with a brass knob. Press this, and within you will discover a small box. Bring that to me; trust no one else with it. This is the task which I demand of you, which it seems to me is so great, because I do not see how you can properly do it. The only way I can suggest is for you to adopt some disguise. How and where you are to adopt this, I cannot tell. Do not think me selfish; I feel bewildered. I can only hope that out of all this chaos, and confusion, and trouble, I may find a means of escape for you and me for ever.*"

The white bosom of the reader rose passionately at this.

"No," she said to herself, "no! You shall not lose name and honour through me. If you persevere I feel that you will succeed, and if you do not, it will not be from any fault of mine, my darling."

Then, for the first time, she remembered that there was someone present at this dainty rehearsal.

She simply threw something over the creamy shoulders, which had made the unfortunate Timms imagine himself in Mohammed's Paradise, and approached the casement.

"Are you Timms?" she asked.

"Yes."

"Where is Ralph now?"

"In prison, as he told you."

"But where?"

"In London."

"How am I to get out?"

"Here," said Timms—the warder, the guardian of the public safety, the ex-constable—"are two very fine files; if you will file that side of the bar—just there—I will file away on the other side—just here—and will have you out in a jiffy."

"I can't get through that little space."

"Oh! no. But I'll enlarge the hole. Never you fear, miss," said Timms; "once that first bar's away I'll wrench away the rest. Then down the ladder you go, and away to London."

"Not so!" thought Constance.

But she did not say this to Timms.

"Very well," she answered; "if you file the iron that side, I will this side. I only hope it won't be heard."

She lost no time in commencing.

But how about disguise?

This was the part of the play which worried her mind.

All the time that her little steel instrument was surely but slowly eating through the iron she was wondering how she should obtain a dress suitable for concealing her person.

At length an idea struck her.

The young groom's clothes would fit her exactly.

"Stay," she said to Timms; "one word!"

"Yes, miss," returned the enraptured constable.

"You must have a confederate in all this?"

"I have."

"Who is he?"

"Job Joskins."

"Where is he now?"

"Within earshot."

"Then tell him to go into the house to the room of Harry Lang, the groom, and by some means or another get his best suit of clothes. They will fit me, and I know if Harry only knew it was for me he would be glad."

"We mustn't wait to see if he's glad," said Timms.

And down the ladder he went.

He was absent some time, during which Constance was not idle.

Before he loomed up again through the darkness she had filed through the bar.

In his hand Timms held a bundle.

"There you are, miss," he said; "and while you're putting on the togs I'll just wrench out the rest of these bars."

Poor Constance!

How her breast was heaving with hope and fear.

Success meant so much.

A union with Ralph, for which she had never hoped, an escape, equally unexpected, from the clutches of Sir Roland Ashton.

And then a marriage with her lover, and happiness ever after—at any rate, through the long vista of human life.

In a very short time she was entirely metamorphosed.

From a lovely plump girl she was changed into a handsome young gentleman; for the groom in whose clothes she had dressed herself was "quite the gentleman," and was regarded as a "great swell" by the girls of the neighbourhood.

The warder Timms had scarcely completed his work when she was waiting at the window.

"Now then, Miss Constance," said he, "I'm ready to help you."

She cast one look round the room to see if there

was anything which she desired to take away with her.

Then she stood upon a chair, threw the window half-way up, and stepped out.

Timms, the quiet warder (now Timms the enthusiastic) held out his arms to receive her.

But there was no need.

Constance laughed lightly.

"I want no help," she said; "pass down and I will follow you."

Timms—no matter what his idea might be—knew that to earn the money he desired and hoped for he must do exactly as Ralph Ashton wished, and act also in such a manner as not to offend Constance Marfield.

So he went swiftly down the ladder.

He was followed quite as quickly by the brave young girl, and in a few moments they were making their way in company across the grounds.

Without taking any notice of Job Joskins be it said.

Timms said "Good-night" to him in a chuckling undertone, which Constance did not hear.

"I wonder," she said, "that Joskins was so pleasant."

Timms laughed.

"Ah! I'll explain to ye another time why he was so pleasant, Miss Constance. Come along; don't run the risk of anyone seeing us."

After this nothing more was said.

The two went on together.

Out across the grounds into the lane.

Then Constance took Timms by the arm.

"Ralph told me I could trust you," she said.

"You can."

"You will do just as I tell you?"

Timms thought of the lovely vision he had seen through the window—those gleaming shoulders, that delicious bust, those expansive limbs—and he thought that he could do anything under the sun to win her favour.

"Yes; need you ask?" he said.

"Well, that is settled," she continued. "You must go on to the Corner Pin."

"Yes."

"I am going to East's Mill."

"That is a lonely part."

"I know it; but I must go by myself," replied Constance. "You must get two horses ready at the inn, and when I reach it there must be no delay. We must dash off at once."

"I know you are right," said Timms. "I will make no delay. I know there is no time to lose."

Constance was far better acquainted with the neighbourhood than Timms, and when she left him she paused only for a moment, and then made her way across the fields in the direction of East's Farm.

The particular building to which she had to direct her steps was the old mill where Ralph Ashton had met with his adventure with the victim of the Black Brotherhood.

Advancing towards this, the brave girl showed no hesitation, and, only glancing round her to see if she was watched, she made straight for the building.

Appended to the letter, of which we have given a part, was a full description of the spot—so accurately given that she was able at once to discover the rope, and make her way into the place by the same way that Ralph was in the habit of entering.

It was a most uncanny place for a female to enter at such a time of night; and there was, of course, a tumultuous feeling of excitement in the bosom of Constance Marfield.

But she restrained it well, and repressing an inclination to cry out or else fly from the place, she at length made her way down to the exact spot where Ralph had told her the box was that he wanted.

Not a sound disturbed the stillness of the place.

And yet she was watched.

Could she have seen how she would have been terrified, perhaps, to death.

But, fortunately, so intent was she on the purpose of her visit to this dark and mysterious spot, that she did not allow her glances to roam far.

Had she done so, she would have seen lying in the corner of the cellar where Ralph's mysterious box was a strange and ghastly object.

A man with his head tied up in blood-stained bandages; his face white and apparently death-stricken; his eyes glassy.

A man who looked, in fact, as if he had risen from the dead; as if he had been the victim of the Brotherhood whom Ralph had flung into the stream, who had come suddenly to life.

He seemed too weak to be capable of speech, but he watched her every movement, not knowing, of course, that she was a woman.

In the darkness he could not observe the graceful voluptuousness of the form which would show itself even in manly garb.

He only regarded her as an intruder, and watched her accordingly.

She was not long there.

Ralph had explained to her exactly where she was to find the precious box whose contents were to work his way out of prison, and accordingly with far less trouble than she had imagined probably, she quitted the place, and began to make her way towards the spot where she was to meet Timms.

Her natural woman's curiosity made her anxious to know what was in the box.

But as evidently the matter was one of life and death to Ralph, she determined to forbear.

She was not long in reaching the rendezvous.

Her steps were hurried by the aspect of the surrounding country.

In the deep darkness which preceded the dawn she fancied that she saw all kinds of shadowy figures leaping round her and beckoning to her.

She had been so long a prisoner that the sense of freedom was in itself oppressive, and she possessed a wrought-up feeling which caused her imagination to run riot.

Again and again she experienced an inclination to hide away somewhere, and leave all idea of advance until morning.

But when she remembered Ralph's deadly peril, when she thought of him eating his heart out in prison, she braced up her courage once more, and pressed onward.

Timms was waiting impatiently.

If Constance Marfield failed in her adventure, whatever was its object, so would he fail.

So when he saw the dainty figure come tripping up in its manly attire he pressed forward with enthusiasm to meet it.

"Have you succeeded?" he asked.

"Yes."

"Would you like a rest before we start?"

"No; let us press on. Are the horses ready?"

"Yes; they can be here in a few minutes."

"Get them quickly, then," said the young girl. "I am all impatience to be off."

Within ten minutes they had mounted their steeds and started.

Constance felt very awkward at first.

She was a good rider on a side-saddle, but with her legs crossing the horse like a man she felt a strangely uneasy sensation.

However this wore off as she proceeded, and she, moreover, determined to preserve her male *incognito*.

At first she had intended to put on her female attire again as soon as she neared London.

But now she had matured a plan in her head in which her male garb would stand her in good stead.

Meanwhile, as his intended rescuers were hastening towards him, Ralph, as may be imagined, was in a high state of excitement.

He had had a long consultation with his lawyer.

But the result had been anything but satisfactory.

Mr. Fortescue, the solicitor, was a man of high standing in his profession, and his mind was capacious enough to admit even the smallest piece of evidence.

But he seemed to see no loophole of escape.

The evidence all tended to criminate Ralph.

"You see, false swearing will go a long way," he said. "As you have been leading what is termed a vagabond life, having no fixed habitation, but living here, there, and everywhere, while hiding from justice, you cannot very well plead an *alibi*."

"Indeed, I cannot," said Ralph. "Even on that night—the night of the murder—I was very close to the murdered man's dwelling, and if the prosecution only get hold of the right persons they could prove it."

"Let us hope they will not."

"And yet, you see, Mr. Fortescue, if I do not admit my presence near at hand I cannot bring the guilty man to justice. Ned Wilmot was the man who killed Herbert Leigh, but how can I prove it."

"Daisy Leigh, the daughter, could aid you in doing so."

"Yes; but how to find her?"

"We must advertise, I suppose," said the lawyer. "I will see that several papers have it in to-morrow. It is strange that she should not have turned up before to punish her father's assassin."

"She has most likely been spirited away," said Ralph; "that is the only solution of the mystery."

What a frail chance of life!

The finding of poor little Daisy, who, in the new life among the genial Bohemians of Dimity's show, never saw or thought of a newspaper.

However, even this was an off-chance, and poor Ralph clung to it.

"I do not see why you should lose hope," said the lawyer. "I can't see how they can hang you on such very circumstantial evidence. But they may. You see, juries are very fickle, and judges are apt to be biassed. But the forgery business is clear, and, taking one thing with another, you are sure to get it hot, if you are convicted."

"Never mind, where there is life there is hope," said Ralph; "save me from the scaffold, and I shall not fear."

Strangely enough the man of law left the presence of the prisoner only a few moments before Timms entered the cell.

He was not alone, however.

One of the other warders was with him.

But he was able, by a variety of signs, to intimate to the eager man that he had succeeded.

"I see you have Mr. Fortescue for your legal adviser," he said; "you couldn't have a better one."

"I think he is a very clever man," said Ralph; "but I don't imagine he will have much chance to get me off with all the false swearing that will be done."

"Don't despair," said Timms; "help will come to you when you least expect it."

This was said in such a manner as to intimate to Ralph that he had succeeded in his venture; and the heart of the captive beat so high with hope that the light of a renewed life came into his eyes.

But there was no chance of a private conversation.

The second warder, having seen to the cell and uncovered Ralph's dinner, and placed it before him, sat down while he partook of it.

Timms would not run the risk of saying more.

Only when the meal was over, and he and his comrade were about to leave the prisoner once more alone, he said—

"Mr. Fortescue's clerk is coming this evening with the notes of his speech, &c., and if you want to write down anything ready for him you can have pen, ink, and paper."

"I should be very grateful," said Ralph.

This was suggested by Timms in the hope that he would be able to bring the materials, and explain the result of his visit to Barnet.

But in this hope the friendly warder was destined to be disappointed, for another man was sent with the materials.

Ralph was again, therefore, doomed to endure suspense.

But he did not despair.

He saw by Timms's manner that he had achieved some kind of success, and even that was a solace to his mind.

At length the weary day passed.

Evening seemed never coming; but just as dusk set in there was the welcome sound of footsteps in the corridor.

Then the door opened, and Timms entered, escorting a young gentleman with a large blue bag.

There was only one long, searching look given by Ralph.

Then his arms were opened, and the lawyer's clerk was sobbing on his breast.

"A good job that Lumsden wasn't on duty instead of me, Mr. Ashton," said Timms, when Ralph had finished his kissing of the ripe, red lips. "However, I mustn't stop now. Compose yourself, Miss Marfield. I shan't be able to return to-night, and so a stranger will come to let you out. Be as quick as you can in whatever you want to do."

"I only want a few minutes' conversation with Miss Marfield," said Ralph Ashton, "and then all will be prepared for my escape, I hope. How am I to give notice when my lawyer's clerk has concluded his business?"

"Knock loudly at your cell door three times," said Timms; "when Miss Marfield has gone I may have a chance of coming to your cell for half an hour, and then I'll tell you how I got on with Job Joskins."

"What happiness this is!" cried Ralph, when Timms had gone, and the young girl had sat down upon his knee and yielded herself up to his passionate caresses; "not only is there a chance of my escape now, but you are free from the loathsome attentions of Sir Roland."

"Yes; for ever, I hope," she said.

"We will get married as soon as I am outside these walls," said Ralph, "and then I shall ask you to accompany me to America. It is of no use attempting to carry on this uneven contest any longer."

"That is right," said Constance, "I will willingly go. I see no other chance of escape from this vile persecution. We must trust in time to prove your innocence."

"You have brought the box?"

"Yes; it is in my bag."

"Let me have it quickly, then."

Ralph had soon possession of it, and tenderly lifting her off his knee he turned his back to her, opened it, and took out several small articles.

These he concealed in his bed, and returned the box to her.

"I shall soon be free, I feel sure of it," he said, with a radiant smile. "When you quit this place where will you go?"

"I know of no one in London to whose house I can go," she replied.

Ralph reflected a moment.

"I know of no one now," said Ralph; "there was a person at Weybridge who would have been just the sort of individual to go to. But now circumstances have altered, and we had better trust to strangers. Go to the Lion Hotel at Islington, it is at the corner of Broughton-street, and await me there. Have you any money?"

"No," said Constance, blushing, "I have not."

"I have not much more than I need," said Ralph, "though I know where to get more. But take this sovereign. It will last you until I join you."

"What about my dress; do you think I had better change it?"

"Well, in the glare of hotel lights, I am afraid you won't pass muster as a lad, you are far too pretty," said Ralph, fondly. "If you can find a chance I would put on good female attire again; but be sure to wear a veil. And, now, dear, for the first time in my life I am in a hurry to get rid of you."

"Why?"

"Because every moment lessens my chance of escape," said Ralph; "it will take me some little time to prepare my plans, and so good-bye, my own darling. Be careful, do not let the happiness of your freedom disarm your suspicions. I do not yet know what kind of disguise I shall adopt, but whoever asks for you by the name of Waters will be myself."

One more embrace (so fond and fervent that it seemed to be born of a presentiment of the terrible future), and then Ralph Ashton gave three wavering knocks at the door.

Within five minutes it was opened by one of the warders.

Constance had by this time recovered her composure.

She at once prepared to go.

"Do you want this pen and ink any more?" asked the man.

"If you please."

The warder looked Ralph straight in the face as he spoke, and was able afterwards to swear that he had noted his features well.

"All right! But in an hour it will be 'lights out.' Don't forget."

The man spoke very kindly.

He liked Ralph, as, in fact, did all the warders; and consequently he was always willing to oblige him.

"I won't forget," said Ralph, smiling. "I've a lot of business to get through, but I think there will be time."

Then with a careless nod to Constance, in her capacity of lawyer's clerk, he turned and resumed his seat at the table.

The door was closed.

Ralph listened to the footsteps dying away in the distance.

Then he rose and raised his eyes and clasped his hands as if murmuring a prayer.

In another moment he was at work.

What this work was will be seen on a future occasion.

Suffice it that it was a plan of escape.

About half an hour after the departure of Constance Marfield, a strange suffocating odour began to pervade the prison.

The warder's room was at the end of the corridor leading from Ralph's cell.

Here the odour crept in subtly, making them sneeze.

"What's up?" said one, who was making some toast.

"Smells like brimstone," replied a comrade. "I hope the prison isn't on fire!"

At these ominous words they all leaped up.

"We'd better go and see, at any rate," cried the head warder.

And so they hastened off in different directions.

Presently two of them reached the door of Ralph's cell.

Here the smell was overpowering.

"He's set fire to his bed clothes and suffocated himself," said one. "Open the door."

In an instant the order was obeyed, and a dense suffocating vapour rushed out.

The men fell back a moment, and then hurried in again.

"Where are you?" cried one

There was no reply.

The cell was in complete darkness, except for the dull red glow of flames leaping up from the bed and clothes of the prisoner.

"Quick—bring a light!" cried Timms, who was one of the party.

In a moment it was brought.

The whole party peered in.

The room was full of dense and choking smoke.

But there was no sign of any human being.

"Where are you, Mr. Ashton," cried Timms, in alarm.

"Ha! ha! ha!"

Such was the reply ringing out through the cell and the corridor.

"He's gone mad!" said one.

"I should think he's the devil if he has a voice like that."

Again there was a loud and deafening peal of merriment.

And then amid a mass of sulphurous flames they saw a hideous form.

The form of Spring-Heeled Jack attired in the most terrific of costumes; his mouth breathing forth flames, his eye-balls glaring, his bat-like wings extended.

"You talk of the devil and he is here," said a

# SPRING-HEELED JACK,

## THE TERROR OF LONDON.

By the Author of "TURNPIKE DICK, the Star of the Road."

OVER THE HEADS OF THE OFFICERS AND ON TO THE BRIDGE FLEW THE MONSTROSITY.

6.

voice which had nothing of human intonation in it. "What want you with me?"

With cries of horror the warders fell back.

The awful being pressed forward and they retreated more quickly.

And in the corridor, which was arched and lofty, he leaped with one bound over their heads.

But he made no effort to escape.

He seemed only too anxious to indulge in his demon antics.

He leaped backwards and forwards over them while they cowered down, until reaching the end of the stone passage he vaulted over the iron railing down into the principal entrance hall.

His appearance here was greeted with yells of horror.

The porter fled, leaving the keys on the hook.

In an instant Spring-Heeled Jack seized them, opened the door and bounded out into the courtyard.

The gate of this was a very lofty one.

But it presented no obstacle to Spring-Heeled Jack.

With one upward tremendous leap he was on the summit of the gate.

Then with a downward swoop he was in the street.

Now there was no difficulty in his way.

With bound after bound he was off and away.

Over groups of people, over cabs, and coaches, and carriages, and omnibuses he went, screams of terror following him as he went.

But no one endeavoured to bar his terrible passage.

Away, and away he went, until he reached the quiet streets of the north.

Here he selected a dark and gloomy court, near the Angel, known as Mercer's-alley, and diving down this he disappeared in a cloud of smoke and flame before the very eyes of a constable, who afterwards declared that he had seen Satan of a certainty.

When the excitement at the prison had somewhat subsided, it was found that under cover of the horror produced by the appearance of Spring-Heeled Jack, Ralph Ashton had, in some way, contrived to escape.

In his room was left only the charred wooden bedstead, a table, and two chairs.

The bedclothes, and the bed, and everything of the kind were burnt up to a cinder.

What it all meant it was rather difficult to determine.

The fact remained, however.

The prisoner charged with the murder of Herbert Leigh was gone.

About ten o'clock that night Ralph Ashton, disguised as an elderly gentleman, put in an appearance at the tavern which he had mentioned to Constance Marfield, and asked for her under the assumed name upon which they had agreed.

No such person as he named had been there.

Neither by name or description could he discover anything in regard to her.

He did not get alarmed at once.

He was of too sanguine a nature to give way to fear.

A hundred causes might delay her.

For one, she might not have been able to obtain the clothes of which she was in search.

But as the hours went by he began to get nervous.

At length the place closed.

He had engaged a bed, but he did not remain. Some untoward accident must have happened.

Nothing else would cause her to be untrue to her appointment, and he resolved to hang about the spot till daybreak.

He accosted a constable presently.

"I'm in a queer fix," he said, "perhaps you can help me."

He happened to be a jovial member of the force, and he laughed.

"Well, we often help those who are in a queer fix," he said; "tell me what is the matter, sir?"

"It is a curious case, and a very painful one for me," said Ralph, aping well the manner and talk of an elderly man. "You see I expected a young lady here to-night, at this hotel, and I know that she would not of her own accord have disappointed me. She has never arrived, and I'm getting fidgety."

"Just so," grinned the constable; "someone you're sweet on, I expect."

"That's right. She's my daughter you see, and she is going to be married this week; but she's got enemies about, and she might have got into trouble."

"Well," returned the constable, sobered in his manner by the word "daughter," spoken impressively by Ralph. "It may be that after all you've hit on the very right person to help ye."

"I hope so."

"It's this way. My mate, John Loftus, was brought into the station with a broken head, and to account for it he told a very queer story. He said that while on duty a couple of hours ago, he saw a young lady came round the corner of Leman-street very quickly, and just as she did so, a four-wheel coach came dashing up. Two men leaped out and seized her!"

"Great Heavens!" cried Ralph.

"Stay," cried the constable, "have patience. She seemed confused at first, struck all of a heap. But after a minute she gave a shriek, and hollered out 'Ralph! Help—help!' The constable made a dash forward to help her, but a blow on the head struck him down."

"Ah! then he saw no more?"

"Just as his senses left him he fancied he saw one of the men pass a handkerchief or something over her face. And then he knew no more until he came to at the station."

"It is she—it is she!" cried our hero, dejectedly; "the one whom she loves is named Ralph. I have lost her after all."

"Don't say that, sir," said the constable; "if you take my advice you will go round to the station at once and see the inspector."

"Yes, I will," said Ralph, mechanically.

Then he gave the man a piece of silver and went.

But not to the station.

He had no desire to show himself in that disguise in the bright light of a police station.

Accordingly he betook himself once more in the direction of Mercer's-lane.

This dismal alley was in the same state of gloom as it was when Spring-Heeled Jack had gone leaping into it.

It was a place which, as as a rule, was shunned by the police.

It was full of strange-looking shops, where very little show of goods was made, where customers seemed few and far between, but which seemed to be able to keep open.

One of these was a kind of "dolly shop," as it

is called, where second-hand goods of all kinds were to be found for sale.

This was kept by a Jew—one Moses Robarts—who, if he liked, could have told a fine tale in regard to the disguise assumed by gentlemen "known to the police."

To this shady den Ralph Ashton made his way when he left the constable.

His mind was full of anxious and wretched thoughts.

To have held Constance to his breast—to have felt her heart beat against his—to have feasted on her kisses, and then to lose her thus !

It was simply maddening.

But it had the effect of making him desperate.

"No America for me now," he cried. "I will devote my life to secure her happiness. Poor Conny ! What may be her fate now ?"

Ah ! what indeed.

Half an hour after Ralph's entrance into the shop of the old Jew there issued from it an old and white-haired man.

He was attired in an ancient kind of cloak, and walked with a bent and feeble gait.

Was this Ralph?

Whoever it was he passed swiftly away, and made haste towards Barnet.

---

## CHAPTER XVII.

SIR ROLAND ASHTON PURSUES HIS VILLAINOUS SCHEME—DAISY'S DANGER—SPRING-HEELED JACK'S WARNING—THE ABDUCTION DECIDED ON.

SIR ROLAND ASHTON was punctual to his appointment with Robert Tugwell.

Five o'clock found him down by the old boat house.

A queer old place.

A place, too, which is destined to figure in our story as the scene of a terrible tragedy.

It is as well, therefore, to describe it somewhat minutely.

It lay at the very extremity of the grounds, where they adjoined a wide and somewhat deep stream known as the Brent.

To reach it from the gardens you had to pass through a piece of heavily-timbered ground, which was left to tangle "at its own sweet will," and was scarcely ever entered by any one.

The ordinary way to the boat house was by a wide path along the river's side, which in its turn was reached through an avenue at the edge of the park.

On either side of the boat house grew some tall poplars, and on three sides the undergrowth had grown high as well as bushy.

There was very little boating done at the Hall.

It was too dull an amusement for Sir Roland Ashton.

His active and crime-haunted mind longed for other and more exciting things to wile away his time.

The boats lay neglected, therefore ; the house itself was green and uncleaned.

In this dull autumn weather it looked like a veritable murder hole ; and so thought Bob Tugwell as he shiveringly waited.

Not for long.

In such matters as those which had relation to the gratification of his own selfish desires it was rarely Sir Roland was late.

"Good evening, Sir Roland," said the man, with a grin, as his patron approached. "I'm here to time, ye see."

"Good ; but let us have a little less grinning," said Sir Roland ; "the matter is a serious one for me, I can tell you."

The man saw at once that he to deal with one who would not on any account allow himself to be treated as an equal.

"I beg pardon, sir ; I'm all attention," he said, touching his hat.

"Very well," continued Sir Roland, lowering his voice ; "I spoke to you in regard to that young lady—Lottie Day—at the show."

"Yes, sir."

"I want to speak to her to-night. Can it be managed ?"

"Well, it's a risky thing to try."

He put on a doubtful expression of face as he said this, and shook his head.

Like all people of his class he knew how to "put the pot on."

"Yes, yes—I know all that," said Sir Roland, testily ; "if it were not a risky job I should not meet you in secret, or, in fact, think of employing you at all. Here are a couple of sovereigns. Now you must let me pass through just as she is going on the stage or coming off. It doesn't matter which, so that I catch her in the stage dress."

"Very well," said Robert Tugwell ; "but if you take my advice you'll come the day after to-morrow. To-night there'll be a regular squeeze in the little passage ; but the night after to-morrow she's in a piece where all the people are on the stage for a long time, and she has to go off and on secret like. You'll catch her alone then."

"Agreed," said Sir Roland, though he by no means relished the idea of delay. "At what time shall I come ?"

"About nine."

"Good ; I will be there," said the baronet, "and in the event of her not listening to my words, as I wish her to listen, there is another job in prospect for you by which you may earn fifty pounds."

The man fairly gasped.

"Fifty pounds !" he cried.

"Aye ! that's the sum."

"And what am I to do to earn it ?"

"If I fail—which I hope I shall not—in persuading her to quit the show, I want you to find me a lonely cottage, some few miles distant, where no cries or disturbances can be heard."

"Yes, sir ; I can do that."

Do it !

What would not the ruffian have done for fifty sovereigns ?

"You must get some woman to become tenant of it ; and all the time you must keep the show in your eye. I don't want to risk anything down here. When the Dimity Troupe have disappeared from this neighbourhood I want this girl carried off to the cottage. When that is done, and she is in my power, you shall have the fifty."

How lavish was the villain with other's money !

The man could but stammer out his thanks.

"It'll be a fortune," he said.

"Yes, to you. Well, now all is arranged you had better be off. On the night after to-morrow I shall be at the stage door punctually at nine. Even if I fail I will meet you here at noon on the following day."

Why was there no listener ?

Why did not the dull breezes of that heavy autumn day waft the burden of this hideous conspiracy to other ears ?

Alas!

There was no one to learn the peril of poor doomed Daisy.

The hawk was about to swoop into the dove's nest.

There was no fowler near to strike it down.

After a few more words the two villains parted.

Sir Roland, having nothing better to do, strolled down to the booth at opening time, to feast his eyes on the lavish charms of Maria and the gentle graces of his intended victim.

When he returned home he was slightly the worse for wine, and retired to rest at once.

The morning brought him news of the flight of Constance.

That was a black letter day in the household at Ashton Hall.

Never had the servants or Mrs. Levine known Sir Roland in such a terrible passion as he was on this day.

He had a double reason for being disgusted and put out by the disappearance of Constance.

There was a family cause which induced him to desire a union with her by marriage.

And also he had become so inflamed by her beauty that he wished to unite pleasure with business.

Every effort was, of course, made to discover her whereabouts.

Searching parties were sent out in all directions.

Heavy bribes were offered to everyone on the estate if they found her whereabouts.

But up to the time when he went once more to the stroller's booth no tidings had been received.

At length the night came when he was, by the aid of Bob Tugwell—the villainous door-keeper—to have his private interview with Daisy Leigh, or Lottie Day, as she was now called.

Still Constance was not forthcoming.

Job Joskins had held his peace.

For his own sake he dared not disclose one word.

He lived in constant dread of the mysterious man with so many *aliases*, who had pounced upon him, and caused him to divulge his secrets.

There were no flashings of telegraph wires from one police office to another in those days, and consequently no intelligence had yet reached Barnet of the escape of Ralph.

News of this would, of course, have redoubled his fury.

But his passion evaporated as he approached the spot where he was to meet Daisy.

His plan in regard to her was just such as would suit his hard and cruel heart.

He was utterly bewildered by her beauty and grace.

And he resolved to make her his own.

He felt a vengeful and terrible joy at the notion of enjoying her caresses for a time, and then devoting her to death.

There would be a month or so of love and delight in the lonely cottage.

And then a beauteous form would be found rigid and voiceless, and the awful mystery would never be divulged.

We shall see presently how his plans succeeded.

At present they promised well.

On reaching the booth he found Bob Tugwell at his post.

No one else was near.

"It's all right," he said, in a whisper whose hoarseness proclaimed that some of the golden bribe had gone in ardent spirits. "You've come in the nick of time. They're all on the stage now, and Lottie Day 'll be out in a minute."

"Which way shall I go in?" asked the eager baronet.

"This way," cried Bob Tugwell. "You see that curtain?"

"Yes."

"Well, stand against that and she'll come out right against you."

Sir Roland lost no time.

He pushed by the door-keeper, and in a few moments he was posted near the old faded curtain, which served as the means of exit from the stage.

He had not long to wait.

Presently there was a round of applause, and Daisy came out flushed and excited with pleasure.

She started in amazement and fear as she saw the form of a stranger.

A thrill of dread seemed to invade her frame.

Why she knew not.

She had never seen Sir Roland Ashton, or heard his voice.

And yet there was that in his appearance which seemed to tell her that he was an enemy.

"Be not alarmed," he said; "I am only here to ask you a few questions, and tell you something which, perhaps, may rejoice your heart."

He smiled at her in a way which he intended to be reassuring.

But she could not help, innocent as she was, observing the bold looks of admiration which he cast upon her bare white shoulders, her bosom tremulous with the excitement of the stage, her lower limbs exhibited in all their superb contours by the tights of her bayadeer costume.

"Who are you, sir?" she asked.

"It is of no use," he said, "to tell you who I am until I know whom I am addressing. I have my suspicions, but I cannot say if I am correct. Have you a few minutes to spare for me?"

"Ten minutes only."

"That will be abundance," said Sir Roland, as he took her hand and raised it to his lips. "I saw you from among the audience, and I at once recognised in you a likeness to an old and dear friend of mine."

"Indeed!' cried Daisy, opening wide her sparkling blue eyes, and scanning his features more curiously than before.

"Yes; your name is Lottie Day."

"Such is my stage name."

"Shall I tell you your real name."

"If you can."

"It is Leigh."

Daisy recoiled in some dread now.

Who could this be who had penetrated her disguise only by scanning her features?

"Ah! I am right," he cried, triumphantly.

"I have told you," she said, impatiently, "that my name is Lottie Day."

"Yes; you have told me so," cried Sir Roland; "but that is no reason why I am to believe you. I am sure that your name is Leigh, as mine is."

"Yours?"

"Yes," he said, as he repossessed himself of her soft little hand, and pressed it warmly. "If, as I believe you are, Miss Leigh—Daisy Leigh, daughter of the Herbert Leigh who was so cruelly murdered not long since, then I am your cousin, George Leigh."

A look of hope for a moment overspread her face, and took the place of an expression of incredulity.

"Can it be possible?" she murmured.

"Yes," he said, coming nearer and passing his arm round her waist. "I am your cousin George, and we have the same interests and the same enemies. We must love one another, and work together, and all will go well."

And then, before she could prevent him, or, indeed, know what was his intention, he had bent and rifled a kiss from her cherry lips.

She blushed brightly, all over her cheeks, neck, and bosom, and drew back.

"How dare you?" she cried, with flashing eyes and heaving breast.

"Do not be angry!" he cried. "I knew I had a cousin, but I had no conception that I had such a pretty one; for that you are my cousin I feel quite convinced."

Daisy could scarcely tell how to act in this emergency.

She had not the remotest conception whether this man was telling her the truth or not.

That he was Sir Roland, of course, she could not guess.

In fact, except the fact that he lived at Barnet, she had no reason to fancy that she was within the range of his power.

At any rate, she was resolved not to allow embraces and caresses from this suddenly discovered cousin until she was satisfied as to his identity.

"It is almost time that I returned to the stage now," she said, with as much hauteur as she could assume. "After the performance you can come and see me again, and tell me and Mr. Dimity all about it."

He could have uttered a curse at this.

It was by no means what he had bargained for.

As he gazed at her he could almost have wished for the moment that she was not Daisy Leigh.

Her beauty inflamed him—with her dainty bust and softly sculptured shoulders and rounded limbs.

If she were not Daisy Leigh then his title and his money might cast a glamour over her.

But he felt sure in his own mind that she was the girl he had stated her to be.

If so, as George Leigh, her cousin, he could pretend to aid her against her enemies; could work upon her innocent heart, and by gradually winning her confidence succeed in ruining her.

Surely never did arch-demon hatch so foul a plot.

He restrained his malediction.

To win her he must be calm and self-contained.

"Very well," he said, "it shall be as you wish. But as I am watched by one who is our mutual enemy, I will quit the place now. If I am not able to return to-night I will leave a note at the stage-door with the door-keeper. Good-bye."

Again he bent suddenly and kissed her, and clasped her lithe form to his breast.

As he did so there was a loud burst of applause in the little theatre, and mingling with it an ominous Satanic peal of laughter.

He started and turned pale.

That laugh was one well known to him.

Often and often he had heard it of late.

The weird terrible laugh of Spring-Heeled Jack.

"Ha! ha! ha!"

Still convulsively clutching the hand of the young girl, whom he hoped would soon fall into his toils, he drew aside the curtain which separated them from the stage, and peered into the auditorium.

As he did so, a fearful form leapt with one bound up the few steps from the stage-door, and came noiselessly to Daisy's side.

It was Spring-Heeled Jack!

The young girl trembled, and glanced at him in terror and amazement.

But she had seen the strange apparition before—it had befriended her; it had saved her life and her honour; and so, though her heart beat with increased swiftness in her bosom, she did not scream or cry out.

The weird being raised one hand warningly, and with the other he clutched her white and rounded arm.

"Beware!" he whispered, in such low tones that none but herself could hear. "That is your worst foe—Sir Roland Ashton."

All this occupied but a moment.

With a muttered curse Sir Roland dropped his hold upon the curtain, and again turned towards Daisy.

"The devil's in it—" he began.

And then, as he saw the hideous apparition before him, he gave a smothered shriek and fell.

It seemed as if his words had acted like an incantation.

Daisy was in a dilemma.

It was her turn in another moment to make her reappearance on the stage.

How could she leave this man here alone?

When he had fallen, Spring-Heeled Jack had disappeared as he had come, in a cloud of vapour.

She rushed to the head of the stairs and called out—

"Mr. Tugwell—quick!"

She was a brave and sensible little girl.

Although her bosom was panting with fear as she saw Sir Roland lying in a dead faint on the floor, she knew that to scream out near the curtain would disconcert every one on the stage and cause a panic throughout the establishment.

But there came no reply.

"Mr. Tugwell!" she called out more loudly, and in spite of the cold wind, which made a shiver run through her bare shoulders and scantily draped limbs, she crept down the steps.

No wonder there had been no reply.

Bob Tugwell was in much the same condition as Sir Roland.

He had—as we have said—been imbibing very freely with the baronet's hush money, and when he saw Spring-Heeled Jack his excited imagination had caused him to exaggerate its terrable aspect.

The horrible apparition was bad enough as it was in all conscience.

But magnified by the fumes of whisky and brandy, Spring-Heeled Jack was a creature of terrific size as well as terrible shape.

What was to be done?

Her tender little heart was all in a flutter.

But she had the sense to see that Tugwell would be very much the worse for any more liqour, while a small drop would, perhaps, revive Sir Roland.

Seeing a bottle of spirits standing, with a glass beside it, on Bob Tugwell's rickety table, she poured some out, and, running upstairs, knelt down by the side of her arch-enemy and poured a little between his lips.

Foolish Daisy!

Why did she not leave him to his fate?

Why did she not permit the evil life to pass out of existence—the life which would strive so persistently to ruin hers?

As he opened his eyes the look he gave her when her dazzling beauty revealed itself again to him as she bent her creamy shoulders over him ought to have warned her.

But she saw it not.

The "cue" was given on the stage.

"Ah! our page returns. Now the mystery will be solved."

And in an instant, pale and flurried, yet still exquisitely beautiful, she was on the stage.

Almost at the same moment Sir Roland recovered his senses and staggered to his feet.

"My plan has failed," he muttered; "I must quit this place at once. But she must be mine. Her beauty dazzles me, and, though she is an enemy, I feel as if I could be tender to her in spite of all. But to remain here would be madness. I know not how much that arch-fiend has told her."

He crept down cautiously.

He expected, of course, to find Bob Tugwell at his post.

He found him, on the contrary, still senseless on the floor.

A shiver ran through his frame.

"Then it was not a vision!" he cried. "This wretched creature has seen it also. Curses light on the fiend, whoever he is!"

And he strode out into the darkness.

He liked not very much the idea of his solitary walk across the moor, and along the lane leading to Ashton Hall.

But he had no inclination now to return to the booth, even to enjoy afresh the beauties of Daisy and Maria.

He wished to be at home to think.

On the way towards the Hall, however, he was haunted by the strange presence.

Every now and then a whirring sound was heard near him, and he saw a huge creature, like an exaggerated bat, leap over his head and disappear behind a hedge or a clump of trees.

He could hear the "Ha! ha! ha!" echoing wildly afar off, and a chuckling close to him.

He could smell the vaporous air, he could see the glaring eyeballs, and the phosphorescent light everywhere.

At length, overcome by accumulating horrors, he took to his heels and ran—still pursued by the demon-laughter and the demon-presence—nor stopped until he reached the porch of his own domicile.

As it was opened in answer to his violent summons, Job Joskins met him.

"Miss Constance has returned," he said.

But his words fell on unhearing ears.

At any other time he would have smiled with fiendish glee. Now he made no reply.

"Give me that light. I feel ill, and must go to my room. Bring me up some wine as soon as possible.

The wine having been brought he bade Job retire at once, refusing to listen to the story of Constance Marfield's return.

"It is enough that she is here," he said; "I am too ill to listen to more."

Left to himself he poured out a large bumper of wine, drank it, and set his fiendish mind to work to hatch fresh plots of mischief.

## CHAPTER XVIII.

### SHADOWS OF THE NIGHT—A STRANGE BURGLARY.

THAT night strange things had happened and were happening at Ashton Hall.

All the evening Caleb Masters had been "on the fidget," as Mrs. Levine expressed it.

In the morning he had received a letter from London, which had flustered him considerably.

He had turned colour and given vent to an oath as he read it, and had straightway betaken himself to the out premises to avoid everyone.

Evidently something had gone very wrong with him.

Again and again it seemed as if he were about to confide his sorrows to Sir Roland.

Once he went so far as to approach Sir Roland, when he met him near the stables, but then he wheeled round and walked off before a word was spoken.

When Constance Marfield was brought home in a state of half-insensibility to the Hall the hubbub and wonder created by her reappearance turned the tide of curiosity, and Caleb was left to his own devices.

He sat in his own room writing till very late, and, indeed, till some time after Sir Roland returned.

Then, when all was quiet, he rose, went to his door, and listened.

All was quiet.

"Just the night for my enterprise," he said, with a grim smile, and, reclosing the door, he proceeded to light a small lantern which he took from the cupboard.

This done, he went out into the passage once more, and cautiously crept up the stairs.

He made his way in the direction of that part of the building which had once been visited by Ralph Ashton in search of papers.

This was, as we know, in a part of the building which was seldom used or frequented.

The great diamond-paned windows looked out upon a part of the grounds which seemed in grim accord with that portion of the house, with long dreary terraces, green with age and neglect, and with tall poplars nodding their heads along their edges.

To-night the house was wrapped in utter silence.

Caleb's footsteps—in his stockinged feet—fell but lightly on the polished floor of the corridor.

At length he reached the part of the building furthest from the inhabited portion.

Here he produced a bunch of keys and let himself into a large room, at the end of which, opposite the window, was a high, old-fashioned bureau.

He smiled grimly as he entered and closed the door.

"How long I have waited and expected this hour!" he muttered; "but I did not know that it would come so suddenly. Two thousand pounds, or dishonour and gaol! Of what use would it be to ask Sir Roland? He would laugh at me. No—what I want I must take. It is of no use to dream of anything else. He will never suspect me."

Sitting down before the ancient bureau, he began manipulating the lock.

He did not know what key it was that opened it, and he had to try key after key.

But at length the bureau yielded to his pressure, and as the lid of the lower drawer flew open he beheld rolls of notes and gold.

The sight made his eyes glisten and his fingers clutch nervously.

He had come there to rob his master of a certain sum.

But the greed of gold was upon him.

"What will it matter?" he thought. "There's

an old proverb and a true one—'You may as well be hung for a sheep as a lamb.' If I take the lot there can be no more row than if I took only what I came for."

His greedy eyes were devouring the glittering treasure, his eager hands were already clutching the gold, when a terrific crash behind him caused him to start back on his chair and utter a smothered cry of terror.

As he turned round he saw an awful apparition, which seemed to freeze his blood and his speech.

For there behind him stood the form of Spring-Heeled Jack, just as he had crashed through the window.

One glance the wretched man fixed upon the spectre.

Then, with a gasping cry, he fell headlong to the floor.

Spring-Heeled Jack emitted a low, chuckling cry—

"Ha! ha! ha!"

But the man did not hear it.

His senses had left him.

Spring-Heeled Jack went to the door and cautiously opened it.

Then he listened intently.

All was still.

The household was evidently slumbering profoundly, and the sounds in this far-off wing did not reach them.

He reclosed the door, and locked it on the inside.

Then he approached the bureau, and took from it the gold and notes which had so overcome the senses of Caleb Masters.

These he placed in a strange-looking kind of wallet, and then he calmly commenced opening the other drawers.

One after another the contents were examined.

But they were quickly cast aside.

Evidently what he required was not there.

Presently, with a grunt of disappointment, the strange being rose, and once more approached the shattered window.

Through this in another moment he leaped.

Alighting on the broad terrace without, he at one more leap reached the ground below, and disappeared among the trees.

It was some time before Caleb Masters awoke.

The fresh air on his face, however, at length revived him, and he sat up, glaring round him in terror.

The awful apparition had photographed itself on his brain.

But all was still.

He had expected to hear the fiendish laugh, and to see the glaring eyeballs and the sulphurous flames of the strange being as it bent over him.

But it was gone. The room was empty.

The lantern burned with a dim light on the table.

The bureau was open; the window was shattered to atoms.

But the author of the mischief was gone.

And so was the money.

Caleb, even in his state of terror, crawled to the bureau to look for this.

His heart seemed to stand still with terrible disappointment as he saw the loss.

But he had no time for much reflection.

He must quit the room at once.

To be found there would be to be accused of the robbery, and of having an accomplice who carried off the booty.

So with what little strength he had left he crawled to the door, to make his return as quickly as possible to his room.

But it was, as we know, locked.

With a sickening presentiment of coming evil he turned to search for the keys.

But they were gone.

Spring-Heeled Jack had taken them with him.

A cold sweat broke out on the body of the would-be thief.

Here he was—locked in, with the evidences of robbery.

What was to be done?

He strove with all his might to force the door open.

In vain.

It was of strong massive oak, and the lock was in accordance with it.

"What can I do?" he muttered. "Accursed wretch that I am!"

Then the thought occurred to him that if he kicked and shouted loudly he should rouse someone in the household, and he could pretend that he had been assaulted by the thieves, and locked in.

With renewed vigour, therefore, he began battering at the door.

The sound went echoing along the corridor, and out into the night.

But with no result.

The inmates of the hall, even if they had not been fast asleep, would not have been aroused by a sound so far away.

With a feeling of despair he turned to the broken window and looked out.

If Spring-Heeled Jack had quitted the building in that way, surely he could!

Not so.

Below lay the terrace, dark and gloomy—far, far below.

Caleb Masters shuddered.

"It is of no use to attempt it," he muttered. "I should be dashed to atoms. Life, even in my desperate state, is too sweet for me to take the risk. I must remain here till morning, and trust to chance."

Morning!

Who would hear him in the morning more than then?

The part of the grounds overlooked by the shattered window was very rarely frequented, and the domestics whose sleeping apartments were nearest to the disused wing would be dispersed in the lower rooms, further off still.

It gradually dawned upon him that he might remain there and be starved to death.

He knew that Sir Roland had plenty of loose money about him, and therefore there would be no occasion for him to visit the room.

These thoughts came crushingly into the mind of the villain.

Hope began to desert him.

The more he considered over the matter the more the terrible thought resolved itself into certainty.

He would be starved to death!

Again he battered at the door.

He threw himself against it and shouted.

All in vain.

The echoes went mockingly along the corridor.

But no answer came, and Caleb, overcome with his terror, swooned again.

Next morning, Sir Roland Ashton, when he sat down to breakfast in the pleasant sitting-room opening out upon the front gardens, observed by the side of his cup a little packet neatly done up and addressed.

On opening it he found the bunch of keys and a note, which said—

"*You will find Caleb Masters in your private room in the west wing, which he visited last night for the purpose of robbing you. As I wanted the money myself I took it.*

"SPRING-HEELED JACK."

Sir Roland sprang from his chair with a terrific oath and rang the bell.

Mrs. Levine appeared, bland and genial, as usual.

"Send Job Joskins here!" roared Sir Roland.

Mrs. Levine was astonished.

She had never yet seen him in such a furious passion.

She had been a witness to some of his rages; but now his face was livid, his eyes sunken, and burning like coals of fire, while foam flecked his lips as he spoke.

"Is anything the matter?" she asked.

"Matter enough!" he cried, "when I have been robbed by the very people whom I have trusted. Read this."

And he handed to her the letter he had received from Spring-Heeled Jack.

"It is some mistake, no doubt," she said, when she had perused it; "or it is some ruffian who has robbed you and is striving to put the blame on the shoulders of Caleb Masters. Let us go at once and see into it. To let Job Joskins have anything to do with the matter would be to spread the news all over the neighbourhood."

This was common sense, and Sir Roland yielded.

"Follow me, then," he cried, and, seizing the keys, he strode from the room.

It is needless to say what they found.

Caleb had recovered from his swoon, but he was pale and shivering, and half-stunned.

He staggered to his feet as the baronet entered, however.

"Ah! master," he cried, in his hypocritical whine, "I am, indeed, glad to see you. I have been nearly murdered, and have had to see you robbed before my very eyes."

"You expect me to believe this?"

"It is the solemn truth, sir."

"And who is the thief?"

"That fellow whom you have seen prowling about; the impostor whom the people call Spring-Heeled Jack," said Caleb. "I was just crossing the end of the corridor, when I heard a strange noise, and wondering who could be in this part of the building, I came along the passage, and seeing a dim light and the door open, I entered this room."

"The door open," said Sir Roland. "Where were the keys?"

"In my pocket."

"And yet the door was open?"

"Yes, sir. I could see no one in the room at first, but the bureau was open, and all your notes and gold exposed to view. Just as I sat down to fasten it up again, there was a frightful crash, and Spring-Heeled Jack sprang into the room. His appearance alarmed me so that I fell into a swoon. When I awoke I found that I was locked in and the money gone."

"A very likely story," sneered Sir Roland; "very likely, indeed. I suppose this Spring-Heeled Jack tale is to deceive me. You have had some confederate here, stolen my money, and invented this to deceive me. You'll find yourself mistaken, my man. I shall have you instantly arrested."

For this Caleb cared not a rap.

Although guilty in intent, although he had gone to the spot for the purpose of committing a robbery, he had not absolutely taken one farthing.

There was not, therefore, anything to fix the guilt on him.

Accordingly he spoke boldly, and, without the slightest hesitation, declared his innocence.

Sir Roland began to doubt.

"The affair must and shall be sifted to the bottom," he said. "I shall send for the head constable and put the matter entirely into his hands. I will be guided by him."

"Very well, Sir Roland," said Caleb; "and as you evidently suspect me, I think the best thing I can do is to let someone else hold my position until my innocence is proved."

"Quite so. Take the keys, Mrs. Levine," said Sir Roland. "You had better remain on the premises, however, Masters. If you attempt to escape I shall have you seized at once and kept until the police come."

"No fear of my escaping," said Caleb; "I want it all proved and cleared up as much as you do."

And so he waited sullenly while the baronet delivered up the keys to Mrs. Levine and stalked out of the room.

When Sir Roland reached the breakfast-room again he found a constable awaiting him on the terrace with the news of Ralph Ashton's escape from prison.

"Troubles do not come alone," he muttered, gnashing his teeth; "but there is one thing to rejoice at—Constance is once more in my power. She shall be my wife before a fortnight is over her head. First to dispose of pretty Daisy, and then, by fair means or foul, Constance shall be Lady Ashton."

The constable had arrived very opportunely.

He was taken at once to the scene of the robbery.

But no evidence of any kind was found to connect Caleb Masters with the robbery except the uncorroborated word of Spring-Heeled Jack.

Mrs. Levine was invited to partake of breakfast with Sir Roland when the constable had gone.

"This seems a most mysterious affair," she said. "This Spring-Heeled Jack has so alarmed people that even the police are frightened of him."

"No wonder, if he can break through prison bars and release prisoners, as he has done," said Sir Roland. "It was he who gave freedom to Ralph Ashton."

"He seems to direct all his energies against this house and its inmates," said Mrs. Levine.

"Yes," said Sir Roland; "whether he is mortal or not, he is my enemy."

Mrs. Levine laughed incredulously.

"I am not so superstitious as you, Sir Roland;" she said. "I don't believe in ghosts, and supernatural beings, and so on."

"I fired right through him and did not hurt him," said the baronet. "Human or not, he bears a charmed life, and I fear that I shall yet be the victim of his vengeance."

"You are becoming morbid and ill, Sir Roland," said the housekeeper, thinking it a good opportunity to broach the one idea that was nearest to her heart. "You want some one to be more of a companion than I, as housekeeper can be—to be with you in your lonely hours and comfort you with her love."

She was sitting very close to him, and her plump white hand stole into his consolingly.

"You are quite right, Mrs. Levine," he said, pressing the hand, "quite right. I was about to speak to you on the very subject."

"Indeed!" said the widow, brightening up, though a deep sigh escaped from her ample bosom. "I am pleased, indeed, to hear that."

"Yes; I was about to say that I wished you to speak to-day to Constance," he replied, "to tell her that my wishes must be carried out at once. I will no longer put up with delays and subterfuges. Her flight proves that she does not possess much affection for the one whom she professed to desire to save; and, consequently, if she refuses to do as I wish, the person whom she desired to save shall be handed over to the authorities."

He felt Mrs. Levine's hand tremble with emotion as he spoke.

He was not blind.

He had long seen her preference for him though he refused to countenance it.

But in order to afford her no chance of making a scene, he rose to his feet, after squeezing her little hand confidentially.

"Yes," he said, finding she did not speak; "yes, tell her within a fortnight she must be my wife."

Mrs. Levine had risen too, now.

"Do you think that you are acting rightly," she said, in a broken voice, "in marrying a young girl who has no affection for you—who, in fact, does not even like you, who speaks of you in terms of loathing—when there is one who dotes on you, who would study your every whim, whose love would make you happy and contented?"

"Really," cried Sir Roland, somewhat embarrassed, "you bewilder me."

"You pretend not to understand?"

"Indeed, madam, I protest—"

His words were in vain; the next moment she was weeping on his breast, her arms around him, her voluptuous bust panting beneath the lace covering, which veiled but did not conceal her emotion.

"Really, Mrs. Levine, this is madness," he stammered; "it is something of which I never thought. You must forget this scene. I must have Constance for my wife. It is a happiness of which I have dreamed for years. Pray accept my kindest wishes for your welfare, and the hope that our friendship will last long and unbroken. But be assured that my scheme in regard to Constance cannot be altered."

Mrs. Levine had cards to play of which he knew nothing whatever.

In fact he could not have believed it possible for her to indulge in so wild and extravagant a plot.

He was surprised somewhat, therefore, when she suddenly drew back, saying—

"You are right, Sir Roland. We must both forget this little scene. I will do my best to insure your happiness in the way you wish, though I had hoped it would have been otherwise."

And so she quitted the room.

Though discomfited for a time she was not conquered.

In her inmost heart she nourished a feeling of anger against Sir Roland.

Yet still she resolved she would achieve her end.

"Constance shall never be your wife if I can help it," she murmured, as she went. "She will aid me."

Aye! so it might be.

But she little dreamed of the terrible cloud of disaster which was hovering over her, and which she was doing her best to hasten.

A cloud of treachery and murder foreign even to the fated house of the Ashtons.

Sir Roland smiled to himself when she quitted him.

"Bless me!" he murmured. "I had no idea that Mrs. L. was so lovesick. By Jove! she's a fine woman too! Hang me if a good many men would not prefer her to Constance! She has a splendid figure, and—but I must forget both her and Constance for a time. Daisy—pretty little Daisy Leigh—must be my care first. What a pity it seems that she must die; but she must!"

---

## CHAPTER XIX.

### THE SCENE ON THE HIGH ROAD—THE BLACK BROTHERHOOD AGAIN—SPRING-HEELED JACK IN A NEW CHARACTER.

THE consternation in Joe Dimity's Troupe when they heard of the swoop of the hawk upon the dove's nest was great indeed.

Maria hugged and kissed Daisy till further orders, so Harry Banks expressed it.

"To think you were so near us, and in such danger too," said Maria, "and were too brave to cry out and spoil the performance! It was all through the fault of that fellow Tugwell."

Tugwell, of course, had to bear the brunt of it to a certain extent.

But, fortunately for him, and, unfortunately for poor Daisy, there was nothing to connect him with Sir Roland.

He pleaded that he had been indulging in some extra drink, and that Sir Roland must have drugged him.

As for the appearance of Spring-Heeled Jack, he denied it altogether.

To acknowledge that he had seen the apparition would have been to confess that he had admitted the baronet to the booth, as Jack's appearance was long after the entrance of the former.

"We had better get out of this neighbourhood as soon as we can," said Joe Dimity.

"Oh! pray," cried Daisy, "do not quit the place for me. Do not let me be the means of your losing money."

"I should lose more money by losing you, my dear," he said; and indeed the showman would not for the world have dreamed of parting with her trim little figure from the show. "We've made a pretty tidy thing out of Barnet, and I think we can afford to look for another pitch after to-morrow."

Daisy was, of course, well pleased.

She feared Sir Roland.

She had heard enough of him from her father.

And now she had seen him, had observed the looks he had cast upon her form, had proved his falsehood even at a first interview, she felt eager to be out of his reach.

What object he had in view in telling her that he was her cousin, George Leigh, she could not conceive.

But whatever it was it could be nothing but evil.

She had, of course, only the word of Spring-Heeled Jack to prove he was Sir Roland.

But to her that was enough.

She could not forget how this mysterious being had before rescued her from Ned Wilmot, and she never questioned his truth.

During the day she received a letter, brought to the booth by a boy.

It was from Sir Roland, but signed "George Leigh."

He had not heard, of course, the warning words which Jack had whispered to Daisy, and consequently the treatment he had received from Daisy at the end of the interview had had little effect upon him.

The note ran thus—

"DEAR DAISY,—*I write to you thus because I know you are Daisy Leigh, in spite of your being called Lottie Day on the bills. I am not able to come to the booth to-night because I am being watched by the mutual enemy of whom I spoke. But before I go from this neighbourhood I wish to see you, in order to mature a plan for the restitution of our rights. Send me a letter addressed 'G. L.,' to the Corner Pin tavern, saying when and where you will meet me, as I want to go to London to-morrow or the next day. If I can venture near the booth I will, but that mountebank fellow of yours, dressed in the garb of Satan, has been haunting me ever since.*"

Of course, it is needless to say that this letter was written, not for the purpose of obtaining an interview, but of putting Daisy off the scent.

"Don't send any answer," said Joe Dimity, when Daisy told him. "Let him think what he likes."

"I'll take the reply myself," said Harry Banks. "I'll go to Ashton Hall and confront the villain!"

"My occupation's gone!" cried Audley Harcourt. "Banks has gone in for tragedy."

"Perhaps I might go in for manslaughter," said the clown, "if he comes hanging round here any more. But the difficulty is how to identify the rascal."

Then, as it occurred to him that he might "kill two birds with one stone"—that is, find out the author of her trouble and have her to himself also for an hour or so—he said—

"Come for a walk with me to-day, Miss Lottie, and I will see if we can't find this rascal out."

Daisy at once assented.

With stalwart Harry Banks by her side she was in no fear of anything.

And so out they went for a stroll.

There was a delicious sense of Bohemian freedom in that walk.

For Daisy, at least.

When with her unfortunate father she had resided in London, she had always been hiding away in back slums.

It was a new sensation, therefore, to find herself out in the lanes and green fields on this frosty, bright day, in the exhilarating air, which made a brisk walk a new joy.

Harry was in ecstasies.

He had completely lost his heart.

Every time he had to help her over a rough piece of road, or a stile, or a rustic bridge, the contact of her little hand sent a thrill through his very being.

Her eyes seemed to him the sweetest and softest in the world.

Her trim little figure, as it trotted jauntily along, appeared moulded with the grace of the angels.

Poor Harry!

Poor brave heart beneath the motley cloak!

He did not know what misery he was heaping up for himself by indulging in these love dreams.

On reaching Ashton Hall, Harry boldly turned in through the open gates.

He had made up his mind what to do.

If he met Sir Roland Ashton, and he proved not to be the man who had called himself "George Leigh," he would apologise for the intrusion, and say that they were mere strangers, and that they thought the park was open to the public.

If, on the other hand, he proved to be the man, he would beard the lion in his den, and boldly accuse him of his villainy.

He was saved from much trouble.

As they passed through the gates, unseen by the lodge-keeper, a gentleman on horseback swept by them.

He gazed in some astonishment at Daisy and her companion, but did not pause.

The lodge-keeper, roused by the sound of the galloping horse, came out and touched his hat.

"That is the one who said he was George Leigh," cried Daisy, whose heart began to beat high now with a dread conviction.

Harry Banks, without replying, stepped politely up to the lodge-keeper.

"Who is that gentleman?" he asked.

"That is my master—Sir Roland Ashton."

"The villain!" muttered the clown audibly.

Then, turning to Daisy, he added—

"Let us be going, Miss Day. These grounds are private, after all."

Daisy said nothing, but turned slightly pale.

She did not, in fact, speak or show any sign of emotion until they had got some distance from the Hall, and had reached a stile, leading the nearest way to the common where the booth was pitched.

Here she fairly broke down, and, leaning her arms on the top of the stile, burst into tears.

This was too much for Harry Banks' susceptible heart.

He gathered up the lithe form in his arms, holding her closely to him till he could feel the pulsation of her bosom against his breast, and kissed her again and again.

For a moment she did not repulse him.

It was pleasant to feel his strong, protecting arms around her.

And so, as their lips met, she yielded to the intoxication of the instant, and said nothing.

Harry Banks, poor fellow, took this for consent, and he redoubled his caresses.

"My darling—my own Daisy!" he murmured, between his kisses.

This recalled her to herself.

She drew gently away.

"Don't, Mr. Banks," she said; "please let us return to the booth.

"Not for a moment, Daisy," he cried; "let me tell you now what I may not have another chance of telling you. I love you, Daisy, with all my heart and soul. I loved you from the moment I held you in my arms that night when I saved you from the river. I know I am not well off, but I feel I have bright chances before me, and I know that you have brilliant talents. Between us we can make a stir in the world. Be my wife, Daisy;

give me the right to protect you, and not all the villains in the world shall have a chance of molesting you."

Daisy drew herself away still further.

"I am sorry to give you pain, Mr. Banks," she said, in a gentle voice; "but I had no idea of this, believe me. I thought you only looked upon me as a friend. It must be so. I cannot give you my love. I do not seem to have any to give. I know not, indeed, what the feeling can be like. Forgive me if I seem unkind, but—"

"Say no more," said the clown, gently, though his heart was torn with emotion.

He saw that she was in earnest, and he resolved not to distress her.

He pressed her little hand, and raised it to his lips.

"Is there no hope for the future?" he asked. "Must I think that I am doomed all my life to be without your love?"

"Pray—pray, do not speak to me of this any more," cried Daisy. "There will never be any hope. I am sure I shall never be able to love you as a wife should love her husband. I will always love you as a sister, but no more. Pray, let us return now."

Harry Banks said no more.

He helped her over the stile, and took her in the direction of the Corner Pin.

Arrived there, he entered, and brought her out a glass of port wine, which he insisted upon her drinking, and then, asking her to wait a moment, he re-entered, called for a pen and ink, and indited an epistle to "G. L."

It ran as follows—

"SIR ROLAND ASHTON, *alias* GEORGE LEIGH,—*Your little game is found out. If you want a good horsewhipping, call at the stage-door of Joe Dimity's booth on the common, and ask for*
*—Yours truly,* "HARRY BANKS."

He wrote this with the utmost equanimity, and handed it politely to the landlord.

"I expect someone will call for this," he said.

"Oh! yes; 'G. L.,' that's quite right," smiled Boniface.

And so Harry Banks, well pleased, went out once more, and meeting Daisy with a pleasant smile, as if his very heart-strings were not being wrung, proceeded to escort her home.

"I've left a letter for 'G. L.,'" he said, "that will do him ever so much good. He won't come to the booth any more."

And Daisy, glancing up shyly at his handsome face and stalwart form, almost wished that she could find it in her heart to love him.

But she knew it would be impossible.

Her love-dream was yet to come.

That night the roads round Barnet were dark and gloomy, and queer characters began to show themselves about as the dark hours came on.

As I have before said, the days of mounted highwaymen, with swords and so forth, had passed away at the period of our story.

But highwaymen of a sort were still to be found in the bye-lanes, and so on, armed with pistols and bludgeons.

The coaches which still ran on the road were armed in the old-fashioned manner, and often had to be defended in the old-fashioned way.

On the night when Harry Banks had walked home with his unwilling sweetheart, whose form as he saw it on the stage was his waking and sleeping dream, there were many persons going to and fro from a large ball in the neighbourhood given by Lord Eustace Elmore.

One carriage in particular contained a young lady and her mother returning after an evening spent in delightful enjoyment.

The old lady, wrapped in shawls, snoozed in one corner and dreamed of conquests in the olden time.

The young lady in the other corner was awake, thinking of the pleasures of that night.

She was, with the exception of a cloak, attired as she had been in the drawing-room.

Her dress was very low, with merely bands for sleeves, so that not only her large and rounded arms, but her breasts and shoulders were left bare.

Her face was very lovely; her hair dark, and worn in wavy curls, which fell upon her neck and caressed the fair white bosom as it rose and fell.

Her complexion was dazzling, her eyes deep blue, her lips rosy red, and her form altogether delicately moulded.

She had enjoyed herself to the "top of her bent," and was now conning her conquests over again, when there was a sudden stoppage, and the horses were thrown nearly on their haunches.

The old lady leaped up with a "Bless me, what's that?" and the young girl was about to look out, in spite of her bare shoulders, to see what was the matter, when the door was opened, and they saw before them four men attired in black from head to foot, and wearing black masks.

The girl seemed quite stupefied.

She had often read about highwaymen, and now she had met them face to face with a vengeance.

"Excuse me, ladies," said one of them, advancing closer, and talking in a tone of excessive politeness, "but I must trouble you to step out a moment."

"Oh! dear me," cried the old lady, "how dreadful! We shall catch our death of cold."

"Very sorry," said the man; "very sorry. We will not detain you long, however. Pray step out."

The young girl, upon whose bare shoulders the chill air of the wintry night struck keenly, recognised in the man's voice and manner an authoritativeness which would not be gainsayed.

She, therefore, tripped lightly out of the carriage. "What is your pleasure, sir?"

"Your money and your jewels," said the man.

She placed her hand in her pocket and drew forth a tiny purse.

Then she handed him two rings.

"Thank you, fair lady," said the man, as he placed the cash and jewels in a safe receptacle, "and now I will trouble you for that necklace."

She started away from him.

"No—no!" she cried, "not that. It is a present from one I love, and I cannot part with that. Anything but that."

"I cannot think of lovers," said the man, rudely; "give it to me, or I shall take it."

As he spoke he made a grasp, as if to snatch it from her neck.

She cowered down, holding both hands up as if to protect her diamonds, and at the same time she uttered a long, piercing scream.

As she did so there was a loud peal of laughter.

Laughter well known to many now.

The "Ha! ha! ha!" of Spring-Heeled Jack.

The leader of the Black Highwaymen drew back in dismay, and even the young girl, to whose aid

# SPRING-HEELED JACK,

## THE TERROR OF LONDON.

By the Author of "TURNPIKE DICK, the Star of the Road."

"I AM YOUR FATE—YOUR AVENGING DEMON!" REPLIED THE APPARITION.

No. 7.

the apparition had come, cowered still more with a cry of horror.

"What want you with this lady?" asked the strange being, in his deep, sepulchral voice.

But there was no reply.

The man, with a wild cry, had fled through the hedge.

"Fear not, fair lady," said Spring-Heeled Jack, "I am here for no harm. Tell me only who you are, and I will see that your jewels are restored to you."

But he was speaking to empty air.

The young girl had fainted.

Spring-Heeled Jack lost no time, but, dashing forward, he caught her up in his arms, and bore her swiftly towards the carriage.

The two man-servants were kneeling down in abject fear: the old lady, stripped of her jewels and her money, was insensible within the vehicle.

Spring-Heeled Jack searched in her pocket and in that of the young girl to try and discover a smelling-salts bottle. But in vain.

He, therefore, placed her gently on the widest seat, and with his claw-like fingers made a slight scratch on the fair bosom, now chilled with the night air, and scarcely moving with her scanty breathing.

Quitting the carriage, then he turned to the two man-servants.

"Your enemies have gone," he said; "mount your box quickly, and hasten to the nearest house or doctor's. Both your mistresses have fainted."

The other three highwaymen had not seen the apparition until it had caught up the young girl in its arms and approached the carriage.

They had then, with yells of horror, sprang towards their horses, mounted, and ridden off.

As soon as he had spoken to the two domestics, Spring-Heeled Jack turned towards the trembling steed which had been left behind by the leader of the highwaymen in his alarm, and, approaching it, leaped upon its back, and dashed off at furious speed in pursuit of the other robbers.

A strange and weird and terrible object he looked as he fled along thus on horseback.

It was the first time that he had ever been seen on a horse, and the few persons who caught sight of him uttered involuntary screams of terror and fled.

He looked, in fact, far more weird and terrible than he did when on foot, with the strange, phosphorescent light gleaming from his eyeballs, the vaporous smoke issuing from his mouth, his bat-like covering fluttering in the wind.

The horse, as if he knew that he had some strange being on his back, seemed to go at increased speed.

It appeared to fly along, scarcely touching the earth as it went, and this, added to its black colour, caused it to be partially invisible to those whom it did not approach nearly.

But the Black Brothers had obtained a long start, and when Spring-Heeled Jack at length drew rein, some miles along the high road, he had not obtained a glimpse of them.

---

## CHAPTER XX.

NED WILMOT — THE ATTEMPTED MURDER — RALPH ASHTON JOINS THE BLACK HIGHWAYMEN.

Two days after the attack on the carriage, which caused such dismay on the country side, and yet had gained for Spring-Heeled Jack a far better reputation than he had yet attained, a traveller, mounted on a black steed, made his way out of the wood known as Barlow's Coppice, and rode slowly along in the direction of Weybridge.

This was none other than Ralph Ashton.

He was not, however, so daring as to appear in public without disguise.

A large beard partially concealed his face, while a kind of soft felt hat was pulled low down over a bushy head of ruddy-coloured hair, which was most unlike his own chestnut locks.

Notwithstanding his last reception at Mrs. Barton's, he was about to venture there again (to the house to which she had hastily removed) in order to obtain from her some papers, which were of the utmost importance to him.

He had in his mind, too, a plan, by which he hoped to punish Laura in some measure for the cruel and brutal revenge which she had taken upon him.

Passing along the somewhat desolate road—not, perhaps, so desolate looking to him as it appeared to those who were unaccustomed to night adventures—he became conscious that he was being watched, or, at any rate, that someone was moving along in concert with him.

The moonlight was bright at times, though at others the silver goddess was obscured behind banks of clouds.

But when any light showed itself he could see a form flitting along on horseback among the trees or rushing along behind hedgerows.

Who it was he could not guess.

His adventure at the Mill, the avenging dagger and the scroll, signed by the chief of the Black Brotherhood, told him that the days of mysterious associations were not past, and that there was still danger lurking on the roads for those who had secret enemies.

He was well armed.

In spite of all changes in social manners, he never went out without his pistols, and his hand naturally clutched the butt-end of one of these as he transferred his heavy riding whip to his left hand.

Presently, as he reached the old-fashioned rugged bridge which spanned the river, the trees became few and far between, and the hedges gave place to palings.

There was nothing to conceal a horseman here, and, consequently, if the rider wished to cross the bridge, he would have to do so openly.

"I think the fellow is a highwayman," said Ralph, to himself, as he put spurs to his horse. "I expect when we pass these few cottages he will show his teeth."

Between this point and Weybridge there were two good miles without a sign of any human habitation.

It was for this lonely tract of country that Ralph knew he must prepare, if any danger lurked in the mysterious actions of the unknown traveller.

So he rode very swiftly, and kept his pistol ready.

Scarcely, however, had he crossed the bridge when there was a loud clattering of hoofs, and a man, mounted on a tall, grey horse, came dashing after him.

He put his horse on its mettle, but the stranger seemed to possess the better steed, for he surely gained on him.

At length Ralph suddenly pulled up.

The stranger thus shot past him; but, after a moment, he also reined in his horse.

"Am I going right for Weybridge?" he cried, in a loud voice.

Ralph Ashton knew the tones full well.

They were those of Ned Wilmot.

"What a strange meeting!" thought Ralph. "Is it a coincidence, or has he followed me for some fell purpose?"

"Yes," he said; "go straight on."

He had hardly spoken when he saw the right arm of the stranger raised, and a flash of light was followed by a report.

A stinging pain in Ralph's left shoulder told him that he was wounded.

"Ha! ha!" laughed Ned Wilmot. "I have guessed all along the road that it was you, Ralph Ashton, in spite of your disguise; when I heard your voice I was sure."

He fired again as he spoke.

But by this time Ralph had recovered his presence of mind.

He had felt dazed for a moment by the shock of the wound, and had failed to retaliate.

But now his pistol was raised, and he fired point-blank at his foe.

The darkness, however, was such that he was prevented from taking good aim, and, with a loud laugh, Ned Wilmot fired again.

Ralph made a side rush, however, at the moment, and was upon his adversary before he could attempt another shot.

"Cowardly murderer, you shall repent this!" said Ralph, as he raised his heavy riding-whip and aimed a tremendous blow at Wilmot's head.

Wilmot saw the blow coming, and caused his horse to swerve.

But, nevertheless, the butt-end of the whip caught him on the side of the head, and he staggered in the saddle.

Now came Ralph's opportunity.

Raising his weapon once more, before Wilmot could recover himself, he slashed him again and again across the face, leaning forward, seizing his bridle by the left hand, while he dealt rapid blows with the right.

Ned Wilmot was surprised, dismayed, bewildered.

But he was not daunted.

In his evil and bloodthirsty heart there was an abundance of real courage, and he strove hard to recover his position.

But Ralph did not give him a chance.

His arm went like a piece of machinery, while Ned could only make a feeble resistance.

Suddenly, however, he remembered himself, and drew from his belt a long knife like a bowie-knife.

He raised this aloft swiftly.

Ralph Ashton's head was close to him.

In another instant it would have crashed through skull and brain.

But our hero's time had not yet come.

There was a sudden rush, a leap of some dark form, and a pistol shot struck the murderous blade from the hand of the would-be assassin.

In the excitement caused by this strange and unexpected interruption Ralph let go the reins of Ned Wilmot's horse, and the murderer of Herbert Leigh, sticking spurs into his horse, fled.

Ralph did not attempt to follow him.

He could not dare under present circumstances to give Wilmot into custody.

And so he must wait until he could meet him under conditions which would be favourable to an act of retribution.

As Ned Wilmot disappeared along the dark road Ralph Ashton saw who it was who had befriended him.

It was one of the Black Highwaymen.

One of the Brotherhood whose mysterious doings had been revealed to him that night at the old mill.

"That was a close shave, my friend," said the masked man. "Was he a highwayman fighting in that strange fashion, or do we claim you as one of our fraternity?"

Ralph laughed.

"No," he said; "I am not one of the gentlemen of the road, nor is the man who assailed me. He is an assassin. I know him as the murderer of Herbert Leigh, whose fate you may have learned through the printed placards of the police."

"I have," said the man; "but if so, why do you not denounce him to the police?"

"I dare not, because I am accused of the crime myself," returned our hero.

"Are you Ralph Ashton, then—the one who escaped the other night from a London gaol, when they said that the devil helped you?"

"The same."

"Then follow me. We will give you protection."

"Many thanks," said Ralph; "but I desired to visit Weybridge to-night on important business."

"I warn you not to go, then," said the masked man, "for the place is swarming with constables. There has been a great robbery there, and the police are everywhere."

Ralph hesitated.

Yet one night would not make such a very great difference.

"Are you in the neighbourhood?" he asked.

"Yes; close by."

"Then lead on."

The man turned, and at the same spot that he had appeared took a flying leap over the hedge crying—

"Follow me!"

Ralph Ashton did not hesitate.

He knew not to what scene he was about to be introduced.

But he was exhilarated by the freshness of the scene, excited by the *rencontre* with Ned Wilmot, and, altogether, curious to learn the nature of the company to whom he was about to be introduced.

The horse he bestrode was not one to which he had been accustomed, and he was naturally doubtful whether or not he could trust it for a high jump.

But he did, and the powerful brute carried him over beautifully.

The man in the mask still silently led the way through a wood, until presently they reached an old building which looked like a deserted farmhouse.

It was white, or, rather, had been white, for wind and weather had now discoloured it; and there were great patches here and there which made it seem as if it was never used for human habitation.

There were the usual out-buildings.

But these, with the exception of the stables, were untenanted.

In the latter were a number of horses.

"We will put up our animals here," said the masked man, as he led the way towards the stables; "and then we will go into the house. I don't know whether anyone will be there except you and me, or we all went different ways to-night."

The door being opened, the horse which Ralph bestrode walked in as naturally as if she had been there all her life.

"Peggy knows her way, doesn't she?" said the highwayman, laughing.

Ralph glanced at him inquiringly.

"Do you know this horse, then?"

"I do well. It is mine."

"Yours?" cried Ralph, incredulously.

"Aye. I lost it one night when we attacked a lady's carriage, and the devil himself or one of his imps appeared on the scene, and spoiled all our fun."

"Ah!" said Ralph. "Well, I found her standing by the hedge; and as I am not in a position to go about horse-dealing at present, I took it."

The man laughed.

"I thought the devil had flown away with it," he said.

And then they passed out and entered the farm-house.

The place within was almost as dilapidated-looking as it was on the outside.

Warmth was obtained by immense fires lit through the building, but the paper was hanging from the walls and the ceilings, which had given way here and there, and had never been repaired.

When they entered the front room, however, there were two things which struck Ralph strangely.

The one was the extraordinary incongruity of everything in it.

The floor was sanded.

The chairs and tables were of common wood.

But on the walls were many oil-paintings of singular merit, and here and there were sketches which seemed to Ralph very familiar.

"These diggings of yours are odd enough," he said. "Have you been here long?"

"Yes. We have."

"It seems deserted except for you."

"You are right. After the awful things which have happened here, we don't run much risk of being disturbed," replied the highwayman. "It just suits us, for we pay no rent."

"How about the landlord, then?"

"Oh! he wouldn't come near here," said the other; "he was too frightened the last time he came."

"You speak mysteriously," said Ralph. "You may as well inform me what the story is."

"I will," said the highwayman, "it is a story which you ought to know. But before we begin let us call Elsie, and have something to eat and drink."

To this Ralph made no objection.

In the first place he didn't know who Elsie was, in the second place he was hungry and thirsty, and in the third place he was eager to hear the story of the house whose pictures seemed so oddly familiar to him.

In answer to the bell which the highwayman rang an old woman entered the room, a strange old woman, whose hair was not white but a kind of dappled grey.

She was bent with age and infirmity, and her eyes were so hidden beneath the heavy lids, so watery and bleared that she could not see well, and, indeed, she seemed scarcely to know whether there was one person or more in the room.

The name of Elsie had raised in Ralph's mind a vision of some beautiful girl, queen of the highwaymen, and he was utterly astonished and amused when he saw the old hag.

However he said nothing.

He had no desire to annoy his companion.

In some way or another he felt that this house had some mysterious connection with him, as if it would play an important part in his future life.

"Bring us some supper and some grog, Elsie," said the highwayman, "and be as quick as you can, for I want to talk business with Mr. Ashton before the others return."

The old woman stood as if petrified.

For an instant she appeared as if she had lost the use of her tongue. Then she mumbled out—

"Ashton! Ashton; that name's accursed. I hope there's no Ashton here!"

The highwayman winked at Ralph.

"No—no!" cried he, "it's only my fun. This is Mr. Jones, from London."

The old woman, only half satisfied, hobbled her way out.

But in a very short time she returned and brought with her some fine cold roast beef, bread, and the *et cæteras*, with a bottle of brandy, which she soon supplemented with the necessary sugar and hot water.

"That'll do now, Elsie," said the highwayman, "take this toothful, old girl, and then leave us to ourselves. If you hear our friends coming, give us notice."

Both Ralph and his companion were very hungry, and they attacked the solids first with good zest.

But after they had satisfied their hunger they drew their chairs up to the fire, and filled their grog glasses.

"Now, Sir Unknown," said Ralph, "will you be kind enough to tell me the story you promised? I am all impatience."

"Very well, you shall be impatient no longer," said the highwayman; "and as for being unknown, my name is Paul Pender. They call me Paul Jones sometimes, and say I'm a land pirate. But that is my name, and until I joined the Black Brotherhood I don't believe anyone could have said a word against it.

"But I'm not going to say a word more about myself.

"You want to know the story about this house, and you're not far wrong in doing so.

"To tell it you rightly, I must take you down to the Cornish coast one stormy night.

"That was a night, if I am to believe those who told me.

"A night when sea and sky were as black as ink, when a wild wind was raging round the coast, when fisherfolk trembled for their kindred at sea, and wreckers rejoiced at the prospect of plunderous murder.

"At this time a family of the name of Vernon lived at this farmhouse.

"They had a good many friends in America, and among them was a family of the name of Leigh.

"Nay, now, Mr. Ralph, don't jump up and get inquisitive too soon.

"These Leighs wrote over from America to say that they were coming home—coming home to seek a fortune to which they were entitled, or, at any rate, part of it; and as they were strangers to this part of England they asked the Vernons to meet them at Penwreath.

"At the proper time the father and his eldest son went there, leaving at home Mrs. Vernon and a daughter, Ada, and the servant, Elsie.

"While they were absent the women folk were visited by a gentleman and a kind of groom, who asked innumerable questions, said he was a relation of the Leighs, and promised to come down and see them all again when the American importations arrived.

"The gentleman dined and teaed in this farmhouse, and went away amazingly good friends with every one.

"But in the morning Mrs. Vernon and her daughter Ada were found dead in their beds, and a medical examination proved that they had died of poison.

"Elsie was like a mad woman.

"She loved her mistress and her child, and knew not how to express her grief at the loss she had sustained.

"When Mr. Vernon and Tom Vernon returned they were stupefied with horror, as were also their friends from America.

"It was all the more horrible because no clue could be discovered in any way to the murderers and their motives.

"However, this tragedy was nothing.

"Elsie was accused, but instantly acquitted.

"But in the course of one week the blood-stained chronicle of this house began anew.

"One wild and stormy night four men, armed to the teeth, arrived at the door of this house, and demanded admittance.

"They were all masked.

"Their noisy summons roused all the inmates—George Leigh, his wife, and son, as well as Mr. Vernon and Tom, but when they came down to learn what was the cause of the unseemly intrusion they were shot down without an answer.

"Not one of them survived.

"Old Elsie saw it all, and was found in a corner of the hall next day by the constables half insensible and idiotic.

"Nothing definite could be extracted from her.

"Only the few words—

"'Ashton knows. I heard them say "Come on, Ashton!"'

"Not one of the victims was even breathing when the constables arrived.

"The men had been shot dead as they came down the stairs, while George Leigh's wife was found with her throat cut in the bedroom.

"As if it was to be, Elsie was spared on both occasions.

"Some day she may yet tell tales, but her intellect is terribly clouded now; and, though she often mumbles the name of Ashton and talks of hidden papers, and so forth, none of us can make much out of her."

Paul Pender paused.

"Is that all?" asked Ralph.

"Well, it is to a great extent all," replied the highwayman. "It is all the story connected with the house, except that the landlord was so horrified by the succession of awful events that he has never once entered the house since they occurred. Elsie was given sole charge, and the place left to go to decay, until we found it in one of our forays, and decided on making it our headquarters."

"Did not Elsie object?"

"Not at all. She was persuaded that we were sent by the landlord, and that was enough. Do you not see how you are interested in all this?"

"I should be a fool if I did not," said Ralph.

"When you know more of my story, you will see that this is one of the links which will form the chain that will gibbet Sir Roland Ashton."

At this moment a strange shrill whistle was heard without.

Paul started up.

"Here they are!" he cried. "Now I can introduce you."

"You know little of me."

"More than you think."

"To my knowledge we have never met before."

"There you are wrong. We met at the Old Mill," said Paul, "where you found a dead body in the cellar, with a dagger in its breast, and flung it into the river. But of that anon."

And he ran to the door and opened it just as some horsemen, dressed all in black, as Paul was, dismounted from their coal-black steeds.

Old Elsie had tottered to the door also.

To her they delivered over their horses, telling her to take them to the stables, and then strode into the front room, their spurs jingling, their pistol-butts gleaming, their hangers concealed beneath their cloaks, clanking against every obstacle.

It was a scene fitted for the olden times—the times of Tom King, and Blueskin, and Jack Sheppard.

"Whom have we here?" cried the leader in a gruff voice.

"Ralph Ashton," said Paul Pender.

"He who is accused of murder?"

"The same."

"He is welcome, then. But does he know our rules?"

"I have told him nothing yet."

"That is well. I see that you are wounded, Mr. Ashton."

He pointed as he spoke to Ralph's left shoulder, which had been bound up by Paul.

"Yes; I was nearly murdered on my way hither," said Ralph, "else I should not have been here at all."

Paul quickly narrated the incident.

"You have done well by taking our friend Paul's advice," said the leader, "in not going to Weybridge. The place is alive with constables. There has been a burglary up at Newstead Hall, and there's the devil to pay all over the place."

"I am grateful I did not go there, then," said Ralph; "more especially as it has been the means of bringing me into such generous company."

"Good!" cried the leader, significantly. "Since you cannot quit our place without an oath of secresy, we will unmask. We are all both hungry and thirsty after our adventures, and, consequently, they would interfere with our comforts."

They all at once unmasked.

There was the usual dissimilarity of feature.

But there was one likeness among them.

Everyone had black hair and a black moustache.

The one who was evidently recognised as leader had a sword-cut right across his forehead.

A cut which nothing but a bandage could have hidden.

By this Ralph could always have sworn to him.

An hour passed in merry-making, and then the chief, addressing Ralph, said—

"When my comrades have retired, Mr. Ashton, I should like to have a private chat with you."

"With pleasuse; I was about to suggest it to you," replied Ralph.

When, therefore, the Black Highwaymen had

eaten, and drank, and sung to their heart's content, they retired to their rooms, and the "private chat" took place between Ralph and the leader, whose name was Josh Lorimer.

Whatever it was, it proved eminently satisfactory to both sides.

It resulted in a great access of wealth to the highwaymen—in an oath to be taken by all to use no violence on the road, and to molest no women.

Next day, when Ralph rode out towards Weybridge, he had on his left arm a black cross.

He was enrolled for the future as one of the Black Highwaymen!

## CHAPTER XXI.

JOE DIMITY'S TROUPE TAKES ITS DEPARTURE FROM BARNET—THE HAWK ON THE WATCH.

IF Joe Dimity had intended to remain for any length of time in Barnet what had occurred in relation to Daisy would have determined him to change his mind.

He had taken a wondrous fancy to the new member of his troupe.

He was making money freely.

But when Harry Banks' experience at the Hall had proved the truth of Spring-Heeled Jack's words, he resolved to go.

Maria and Mrs. Dimity concurred.

"If once the poor dear gets into the clutches of that villain," said Mrs. Dimity, "I know what will happen."

"I know," said the clown.

"What?" asked Joe.

"There'll be a special and unrehearsed performance in the public streets by one of the Dimity Troupe when I horsewhip Sir Roland if he annoys her, and send a pistol-shot through his head if he injures her!"

"And if your arm gets tired I'll go on with the performance," said Aubrey Harcourt.

It was all very well for the kind-hearted people of Dimity's Troupe to speak thus and to look forward, almost with pleasure, to the chance of chastising the man who was persecuting Daisy.

But they did not know the depth of his villainy, never guessed how diabolical a plot was being hatched against her.

Sir Roland Ashton had due notice of the intended removal of the people of the booth, and was informed by Robert Tugwell of the fact that the route was Weybridge.

It was strange, indeed, that by some unaccountable coincidence Daisy was once more to follow in the footsteps of Ralph Ashton.

Were they destined to be all in all to each other after all?

These two, who had never yet met face to face or exchanged words of love!

At any rate, fate was weaving a strange web round Daisy Leigh.

Robert Tugwell, acting under instructions from Sir Roland, asked permission to join the troupe as door-keeper and general help.

"Wages are no object," he said, when Joe Dimity mentioned the slender state of the exchequer; "all I want is to get away from this 'ere place. It's too hot to hold me. I've got a lot o' enemies about here, and if I can only pick up a bit of bread and cheese, and such like, I shall be quite satisfied."

Except that drinking bout, which had been the result of Sir Roland's bribe, Joe Dimity had had nothing to complain of in anything that Tugwell had done.

He had not the slightest conception that he was a traitor.

So Robert Tugwell was tacked on to the Dimity establishment, and when at length they began to move towards Weybridge, Sir Roland was duly informed of it.

"Nothing could have heen better for my plans," muttered the baronet when he heard this. "I have a secret mission to perform there, and I can kill two birds with one stone."

## CHAPTER XXII.

LAURA BARTON STILL PURSUES THE PATH OF TREACHEHY—SIR ROLAND'S VISIT TO THE COTTAGE—SPRING-HEELED JACK SECURES THE PAPERS.

LAURA BARTON, when she found that Ralph Ashton had escaped, was enraged beyond measure. Her nature was one of those fiendish and desperate ones which soften at nothing.

To her love had never been a soft and tender passion.

It was a fierce, all-devouring flame, scorching up her better feelings, and rendering her oblivious of reason and conscience.

She had allowed herself to be overcome by her desire for union to Ralph to such an extent that when she found that he was indifferent to her her senses seemed to become deranged.

From loving she hated.

Not with a quiet, slumberous hatred, but with a hatred which would devote life to the accomplishment of revenge.

Well known is the truth of the old poet's words—

"*Hell holds no fury like a woman scorned.*"

Such, truly, was the case with Laura, and her anger at his escape was furious.

Her mother could not comprehend her feelings.

She had always liked Ralph Ashton, and was, moreover, convinced of his innocence; and the vindictive feeling which induced her daughter to endeavour to hatch up some fresh treachery against him was beyond her comprehension.

Laura, however, was about to have helpers in her diabolical schemes whom she little guessed at.

Sir Roland Ashton had learned from the constables, and from the reports, too, of the capture, that it had been effected at the house of Mrs. Barton.

He at once, therefore, placed himself in communication with Laura, who was publicly spoken of as the one who denounced the prisoner; and, in reply to his letter, he received one which brightened his hopes greatly.

She informed him of the fact that Ralph Ashton had left in her mother's care a quantity of papers concealed in an old chest, and that on a certain night he was coming to the cottage to claim them.

"*You know best what to do,*" she said; "*he has wronged and insulted me, and I wish to see him recaptured. I will aid you in any way I can.*"

On receipt of this Caleb Masters was at once despatched to have an interview with the beautiful demon who was to be Ralph's betrayer.

Caleb was by no means delighted at his errand.

His affection for his master was of the very smallest, although he could not help feeling somewhat grateful to him for the fact that he had not given him into custody over the robbery discovered and rendered abortive by Spring-Heeled Jack.

But still, in the face of everything, he could not refuse.

When he saw Laura, he could scarcely conceive it possible that she could be guilty of the terrible cruelty she contemplated.

But when he beheld her smile he was satisfied.

It was the smile of a demon!

"When can Sir Roland come?" she asked, when Caleb had made known his identity.

"To-morrow night."

"That will do well. My mother, I know, expects him then," returned the girl.

"We will be down here early, then," said Caleb, "for two things—the box, and the capture of the escaped prisoner!"

"Just so!"

"But could we not arrange to secure the box at once?" said Caleb, insinuatingly; "my master would be willing to pay a good sum for it."

The young girl laughed.

"No; I could not make any such arrangement," she said. "I want my revenge as well as Sir Roland. I wish you to come for the papers at the the same time as Ralph Ashton. You can then take them from the box, while the constables arrest him."

"Very well," said Caleb, "at what time are we to be here?"

"At nine o'clock," said Laura. "That is the hour when Ralph is expected."

"And who will admit us?"

"I will. My mother will be asleep. I will see to that."

And she laughed maliciously.

She accompanied Caleb Masters to the door, and there they arranged a few further preliminaries.

They were evidently very particular, for they talked so earnestly that they did not observe a dark form glide up from beside the shrubbery, and plant himself close to where they stood near the gate.

He was enveloped in a cloak, so that no one could recognise him, and, indeed, so covered up was he that as he stood near the thickly-growing trees he could not be distinguished from the heavy shadows.

He listened patiently to all that was being said, never moving from his position, never seeming to be instinct with life.

Every word spoken by Caleb and Laura was heard by him.

He waited until the former had gone; then he moved forward, as if to accost Laura.

But as he did so two other forms appeared, creeping, crawling towards him.

Two constables, armed to the teeth!

Ralph, for it was he, was perfectly unconscious of their presence.

He had come down, as he had intended, on the evening before, when he was attacked by Ned Wilmot.

The next night was that on which he had told Mrs. Barton he would reach her cottage.

But circumstances had arisen which had made it better for him to come this evening.

Laura, as she leaned over the wicket-gate and glanced at the retreating form of Caleb Masters, saw not the figure approaching her, or the stealthy forms of those who were crawling up behind him.

Suddenly, however, a voice recalled her to herself.

"Laura!"

The well-known voice startled her.

"Ralph!" she cried, starting back, and almost gasping for breath as her heart leaped in her bosom.

"Aye! Ralph, whom you betrayed to his enemies, though you knew him to be innocent!" cried our hero. "But never mind. Your conscience will punish you best. I desire to utter no reproaches. Is your mother at home?"

"No."

"Can I enter?"

"No—that is to say, with my permission!" cried Laura, holding the gate desperately.

"There is no hurry. I can come again," said Ralph.

"To-morrow night, at nine."

"Ah! yes," thought Ralph, "to meet Caleb and Sir Roland. Fear not," he said, aloud—"I shall be here!"

The men's forms were coming nearer and nearer.

The ominous rattle of the handcuffs was heard faintly.

One came gliding up on one side, one on the other.

Laura, retreating towards the house, suddenly saw the two men, and, though astounded, was sufficiently self-possessed to relieve herself by a gasping sigh, and still keep retreating to the house.

The men were within arm's length when Ralph suddenly turned.

He saw the situation directly.

"Ha, ha!" he laughed, as he struck one of the constables a sudden blow in the face; "I am betrayed before the time."

The blow was delivered so swiftly and surely that the man staggered back.

But Ralph was not to escape so easily.

Both the men were, as I said, well armed, and the second at once drew a hanger and made a blow at Ralph's head.

Dead or alive the arrest was to be made; the reward was to be the same.

They were not yokels, but London constables—resolute and clear-headed men—who, besides fighting for a good reward, considered themselves to be doing their duty.

But they were unprepared to find such a determined resistance.

They knew Ralph to be a brave man, and, in fact, they had only come down to reconnoitre.

But when they found that he was there alone they had resolved to risk all and endeavour to make a capture.

The evil heart of Laura Barton beat with a joyous triumph as she saw the struggle.

Had she had physical courage equal to her mental she would have dashed in and joined in the affray; but, as it was, she stood leaning against a tree, gazing at the men engaged in their deadly struggle.

Did no compunction enter her heart?

Did no tender feeling invade her bosom?

No.

She was proof against all.

There was no womanly doubt or softness in Laura Barton; she had been wronged, as she thought, and her revenge made her stubborn and unyielding.

The blow which the man aimed at Ralph missed

its aim, or our hero would have ceased to figure in this story.

He contrived to avoid it, and then taking from beneath his coat a short, stout bludgeon, he proceeded to wield it with such goodwill that the man had to act on the defensive.

The one who had received the blow on the face had quickly recovered, and returned to the attack.

But a well-directed crack on the head sent him sprawling after a moment, and left Ralph to deal with his companion alone.

The latter was a stout, broad-shouldered man, and quite up to his work.

But Ralph seemed possessed of unnatural agility, and though the man made constant cuts and blows, our hero remained scot free.

Laura, with despair in her black heart, saw the officer suddenly struck down at the side of his companion.

And then Ralph came up to the wicket-gate.

"Traitress!" he exclaimed, "you are foiled again. Heaven protects the innocent, and will not permit a wretch like you to triumph."

With these words, and waiting for no reply, he bounded into the dark lane and disappeared.

"I hope he heard nothing to put him on his guard," she said, as she reluctantly took her way into the house. "To-morrow he shall be caught in a different way."

Eagerly she looked forward to the hour when Sir Roland and Caleb would arrive, and she determined to put in practice a cowardly and cruel *ruse*.

She knew that her mother not only believed in Ralph's innocence, but would do all she could to help him.

Accordingly, on the morning following the scene with the officers, she took her way after breakfast towards London.

She had always been a mysterious girl, and had had acquaintances of which her mother knew nothing.

Proceeding, therefore, to the north of the metropolis, she took her way to a street of dingy and doubtful aspect, which was composed of small houses, flush with the street, and shops full of odds and ends, that appeared as if useless to any one, but where, nevertheless, a good trade was done.

Entering one of these as if she was quite familiar with it, she found herself in the presence of an old woman whose appearance was as dingy and doubtful as the street itself.

She had a thin face, but a large red nose, which, with her bleared eyes, gave the idea that she was a friend to the bottle.

Her eyes had a shifty, cunning expression, and as she raised them to look at her visitor, she seemed as if looking her through and through.

One look was enough, although Laura was veiled.

"Ha! Miss Barton," she said; "glad to see you. Anything I can do for you to-day?"

"Yes, Mrs. Corcoran," replied the girl, unblushingly. "I want two sleeping draughts—strong ones, that have no taste, and are safe, too."

"A sleeping draught!" exclaimed the woman, in surprise; and laughingly, "won't your conscience let you sleep."

"Don't waste time in talking nonsense, Mrs. Corcoran," said the girl. "One of the draughts is for my mother, and the other for a man—a friend of hers, whom I want to give into the hands of the police. He's a double-dyed villain, and has quite imposed upon her, though the constables are after him for awful crimes. I want to stop the visits to our place if I can."

"Very well, miss," said the woman; "you needn't explain what you want it for."

Mrs. Corcoran was not many minutes absent, and returned with two small bottles of colourless liquid.

"Am I to give the whole of one of these to one person?" asked Laura, eagerly.

"Yes, the whole," said the woman; "but be careful not to give more, as it might send the person off into a sleep from which he would never wake again."

For an instant the breast of Laura beat high with excitement.

Would it not be a great revenge to give Ralph Ashton the two bottles, and have the pleasure of telling him to his face that she had destroyed all his hopes in life—that she knew him to be innocent—that she had given him a poison to which there was no antidote?

For such a potion as Mrs. Corcoran had given her would, if taken in too great quantities, work so subtly into the system as to render all antidotes of no avail.

The mad impulse to do murder, however, quickly passed away, and she saw it in all its folly.

She must be patient.

If she only bided her time she would be sure of her revenge.

"I will be careful, Mrs. Corcoran," she said, "never fear. If I gave an overdose, I should be a fool, for I should spoil my own game."

She paid the exorbitant price demanded by the woman, and then with an eager heart she took her departure.

Ralph little knew his danger.

The woman of all others in the world who was his deadly enemy had got him in her power, to the best of her belief.

She had in her possession the means of sending him into a deep sleep, or of destroying him.

At any moment her evil heart might change, and she might prefer a swift revenge.

She knew well that at her mother's house she would be able to administer the sleeping draught to Ralph if he came, for he and Mrs. Barton invariably had a cup of tea together, and at times something stronger.

How eagerly the wretched girl waited that evening!

But Ralph did not put in an appearance.

The time passed on.

Mrs. Barton in a disappointed way bade Laura bring in the tea.

The drug must now, at any rate, be administered to her, in order that Sir Roland Ashton and Caleb Masters should be able to enter the house.

The unsuspecting woman, therefore, partook of the tea, and by nine o'clock was sleeping profoundly in her arm-chair, in a slumber which would bind her for hours.

Precisely at the time named a timid knock was heard at the door.

The new arrival was Caleb Masters.

Much as he desired to aid his employer in receiving the box of papers, and, perhaps, also the person of Ralph Ashton, he had no wish to meet the latter suddenly.

It was quite on the *tapis* that the door of the cottage might be opened by the latter himself, and that would be a consummation most devoutly not to be wished.

He kept slightly aloof from the door, therefore, and waited until it was opened, in readiness for flight.

But when he saw the treacherous face of Laura, brilliant in its demoniacal beauty, he advanced reassured.

"Is all well?" he said. "Is it safe for my master and I to enter?"

"Yes, most certainly," returned Laura. "No one is here save myself and my mother, and she is sleeping. I have drugged her so that she will not wake until midnight at least."

"And Ralph Ashton?"

"He is not here."

Caleb wasted no more time in questions, but turning in the direction of the garden gate, beckoned eagerly.

Evidently Sir Roland had been hiding behind some of the thick clumps of trees, for he appeared at once, and, advancing, entered the house.

"This way," said Laura. "Follow me."

She led the way up the stairs into the room where Ralph's box was.

It was a little apartment on the second storey; a bedroom neatly furnished and clean as a new pin.

Laura drew the box from beneath the bed and gave Sir Roland the key, which she had previously stolen from her mother's pocket.

"I will keep watch," she said.

Sir Roland was too eagerly occupied in what was going on to take much notice of Laura, or his evil heart might have felt something congenial in the beauty of this soulless girl, whose vengeful feelings had so completely taken possession of her.

She looked specially beautiful on this night in her demoniacal way. Her face pale and stony, but her eyes blazing with a light which was almost supernatural.

The dress she wore fitted her like a glove, and being cut square, revealed just a tempting glance of her delicate bosom.

But Sir Roland cared for nothing of all this.

His mind was fixed only on the possession of Ralph's papers, and, perhaps, the capture of Ralph himself.

He placed his lamp on a shelf where it would cast a bright light over that part of the room where Caleb Masters was about to commence his dishonest work, and then the man, kneeling down, opened the box.

It was filled with clothes and papers; but there was also a bag of money.

The latter Caleb at once spotted.

"I'll have that while I'm handing him the papers," he thought; and when he gave his master the first bundle he quietly transferred the treasure to his pocket.

Sir Roland opened the documents as Caleb gave them to him, and as he did so he indulged in a running commentary—

"Ah! a copy of the very document which I thought I only possessed. What's this? George Leigh alive! Ha, ha! George Leigh, the miser! What wondrous fortune is this? If Constance only knew! We must unearth him. Let me see his address—Lone Farm, Berkhampstead! What a good name! Now, Caleb, some more; I have exhausted these things!"

Caleb at once handed up to his master another set of papers; and he was grabbing them with the same eagerness, when there was a sudden crash, a wild and unearthly peal of laughter, and, before Sir Roland could well realise what had happened, the papers were snatched from his hand.

"Ha! ha! ha!"

The weird and unnatural laughter rang through the place, and echoed out through the open window.

Caleb, glancing up from the spot where he knelt, by the side of the box, saw his master standing speechless, and Spring-Heeled Jack near him, holding in his hand the papers.

The man was as paralysed as his master, and knelt, still glancing up at the terrible apparition, with open mouth and glassy eyes.

For quite a minute both of them stood thus, while Spring-Heeled Jack seized upon all the other papers which the box contained.

Sir Roland at length reeled back from the position where he had stood so fixed and stone-like.

He rested his right arm against the head of the bedstead.

"Strange being!" he cried, in a hoarse voice, "who are you who are thus ever on my track? What want you with me? Who are you that you follow me wherever I go?"

"Your fate—your avenging demon!" returned the apparition, in so strange and hollow a voice that it chilled them to listen to it. "Until the hour when you die a shameful death I shall follow you. I am a spirit who is not to be appeased until vengeance is secured for all the wrongs you have committed. I cannot appear against you before a human tribunal, for they would not listen to me; but I will so work that the evidence I procure will be forthcoming before such a tribunal, and then your day is over."

Without waiting for a reply, the apparition leaped across the room towards the open door.

Laura was waiting in the hall below, listening, and looking out upon the night.

She had heard a crash, but she had no conception what it could be, until she heard a terrible laugh, and saw a figure descending the stairs, such as curdled her very blood.

She also stood for awhile transfixed with horror.

"Ha, ha, ha!" cried Spring-Heeled Jack. "Demon! traitress! you fear me now! How will you fear me when your great day of reckoning comes? Betrayer, cruel-hearted fiend, beware! Thus do I mark you as my own for ever!"

He sprang towards her.

The girl was powerless to resist him.

She leaned, panting and breathless, against the wall.

His sulphurous breath nearly choked her; his glaring eyes were so close that it seemed as if she could almost see into their fiery depths. As her hand was put out it touched his body—smooth, hot, panting.

"Ha! ha! you shrink. Murderess, for such you are in heart," cried Spring-Heeled Jack, as he clutched her round the waist with one arm, thus then I mark you with the brand of Cain."

And raising his right claw-like hand he made the mark of the cross on her forehead, tearing the white flesh as he did so.

Then he flung her from him, and she fell fainting on the floor.

In an instant he had opened the door ready for escape.

But he could not resist returning to the room where he had left Caleb and Sir Roland.

He leaped up the stairs again, therefore, and found Sir Roland kneeling near Caleb, who was lying in a dead faint.

With one clutch he was at the back of the baronet's neck, and had seized him and flung him across the room.

He gave a gasping cry and sunk into insensibility.

Then Spring-Heeled Jack bent for a moment over Caleb Masters; and, turning, sprang again down the stairs.

He leaped with one long powerful spring across the garden.

Then he was about to pause, when a shot came whizzing by his head.

"Ha! ha! ha!"

The laugh re-echoed weirdly over the landscape, and the terrible apparition sprang over the gate.

Then he darted along the lane.

But the place was alive with foes.

Again and again the shots of enemies rang out over the landscape.

Spring-Heeled Jack paused.

This was an unusual experience.

Who could be these suddenly-roused foes?

He turned and leaped towards the cottage. But there again he was intercepted.

As he neared the cottage a shot came so near to his face that it scorched him.

The mysterious being, however, though he evidently did not like the annoyance of this attack upon him, was not distressed about it.

He leaped and sprang from side to side, over hedges, across the lane, in and out the trees, as if to draw out his enemies.

After awhile he took to the open fields, and there began a series of gambols and outrageous antics which must have been intensely annoying to those who were attacking him so seriously.

In a few moments his *ruse* had its effect.

From different parts of the hedges around the open meadow came Bow-street Runners.

They had been sent down to prowl about for the purpose of arresting Ralph Ashton; but finding that they could not effect this, they resolved to endeavour to make another capture, which would redound quite as much to their credit.

The capture of Spring-Heeled Jack.

Already his name had become a bugbear.

Already it had become the terror of London.

Nursemaids used it as the nursemaids of thirty years before used the name of Napoleon, "the Corsican ogre," to frighten the children.

In various parts of the metropolis he had been really seen.

But where he had not been seen the brisk imagination of servant girls had manufactured him.

In fact, "Jack" was an excuse for a great many things which would have surprised him.

At any rate, quite a little cloud of London constables came out from the hedgerows, and disposed themselves about the field as if they were suddenly resolved to play a game of cricket by moonlight.

Spring-Heeled Jack was certainly in an awkward predicament, if, indeed, he was of such a nature that earthly troubles affected him.

But he was in no way discomfited.

He leaped about in the most extraordinary manner, perfectly puzzling to his would-be captors.

But it was a tiring game even to a being who was able to leap continually over the heads of his tormentors.

Had he had a mind he could, no doubt, have sprang away like some supernatural kangaroo, and distanced them all.

But evidently he was waiting for someone or something.

Suddenly, when another volley of bullets came whistling uncomfortably round his head, he gave a loud sepulchral laugh, followed by a strange, shrill cry, and in a moment afterwards the whole scene was changed.

From two sides of the meadow came a rush of horsemen, who leaped the hedges and charged down upon the Bow-street runners.

They were masked, and were dressed in black from top to toe.

They were none other, in fact, than a band of the Black Brothers.

The constables recognised in a moment that they had a difficult foe to deal with, and, consequently, they directed their attention more to the new comers than to Spring-Heeled Jack.

And well they might.

The Black Highwaymen swept all before them.

The constables, as we have seen, were by no means devoid of courage.

But the charge was like that of heavy cavalry, and it came, moreover, on two flanks.

They made an attempt to withstand their new enemies.

But in vain.

They were cut down, or ridden down, and in the midst of it all, Spring-Heeled Jack, with a loud "Ha! ha! ha!' made his escape.

The Black Highwaymen did not stop to follow up their victory.

They were contented at seeing their opponents dispersed in all directions, flying as if for their lives.

With loud laughter they affected to pursue them.

But as soon as they had seen that the constables were fairly beaten, and had entirely given up all hope of capturing their victim, they rode off in various directions, apparently with the notion of making a night of it on the road.

Three of the constables—resolved to make the best of their way back to London, and attempt, moreover, no make arrests of any kind that night—hastened towards the banks of the Brent, with the idea of crossing over to the other side, to the Eagle and Hound, a tavern where they could not only obtain some refreshment but a seat in the coach for London.

They had crossed over in a boat, and had left it by the bank.

Towards this they now made their way.

"That's a rum go about this Spring-Heeled Jack, George," said one of them, addressing his companion. "Can you make anything of him?"

"He's the devil, I should think," said the man addressed.

"I kept firing at him again and again," put in the other man; "but you might as well fire at the moon for all the effect it takes on him."

"I fired, too," said the one addressed as George; "but it's no use."

"It can't be a mortal man," said the other. "Oh! Lord preserve us!"

No wonder was it that he gave vent to this exclamation.

For as he spoke a cloud seemed to come between them and the moonlight, and Spring-Heeled Jack allghted in front of them.

"Ha! ha! ha!"

The terrible laugh echoed dismally and weirdly over the landscape.

It was a blood-curdling laugh, and the men, with trembling limbs and chattering teeth, were preparing to fly back in the direction they had come, with what little strength they had left in their legs.

But the apparition went flying on far in front of them, and in a few moments disappeared.

Not one of those men was there who did not wish himself safe in the neighbourhood of Bow-street.

"Ugh! I shall dream of this for months," said George, "and I shall feel a funny feeling, I don't know what, creeping up behind me!"

"Don't doubt ye! I know I shall," said the other.

The third was hurrying on ahead to secure the boat.

It was not long before they reached the river.

The boat was there and they eagerly re-entered it, congratulating themselves that they had seen the last of Spring-Heeled Jack, at any rate, for the night.

Alas! for the futility of human hopes.

They had scarcely left the shore when again there came a small cloud between them and the moon.

And with a crash, which threatened to destroy the boat, or, at any rate, to upset and immerse them all in the water, Spring-Heeled Jack bounded into it.

They were about to leap up.

But a loud and deep sepulchral voice restrained them.

"Hold! Be not mad! Sit still and row on towards the bridge! Ha! ha! ha! You ought to row quickly now, for you have the devil's luck with ye!"

The men mechanically seated themselves at the oars.

They seemed possessed of superhuman strength.

The boat appeared to rush through the water as if by magic.

The sensation was a pleasant one.

But it made their hearts beat terribly.

It was altogether uncanny.

The swiftness with which they sped along was, perhaps, imaginary.

Their feelings at their strange position were, doubtless, to be blamed for any unusual exultation.

A strange position in very truth.

Rowing in a boat along that silent river, with the very being whom they had tried to arrest—a being whose eyes glowed above them like lamps, whose mouth vomited flames, and about whose form a sulphurous vapour hung.

A being who had defied their bullets and fled from them, and then came voluntarily back to keep them company.

They said nothing — only plied their oars mechanically in the direction of a rudely-constructed bridge, which spanned the river some distance above the water.

The courage of the Bow-street runners had begun to creep back.

With safety came a desperate resolve.

They saw people moving about on the bank.

What if Spring-Heeled Jack was only an impostor, hiding away from some one; and what if they asked these people to aid them in catching him?

As they neared the bridge it seemed as if the monstrosity who had so long defied their efforts had divined their thoughts.

He gave vent suddenly to a loud—

"Ha! ha! ha!" and, with one spring, which shook the boat, he went flying through the air, chuckling as he went, and alighting on the rustic balustrading of the bridge.

The constables (one of whom, in the excitement consequent upon the hope of capture, had already grasped his staff of office like a club), looked up aghast as the extraordinary being sailed above their heads.

Then, as he alighted on the bridge, and went leaping away with his usual terrible laugh, they figuratively took to their heels.

They would have done so had they been on dry land.

But, as they were in the boat, they pressed on as swiftly as possible towards their destination, after arriving at which they lost no time in making their way to London.

Their courage, as regarded Spring-Heeled Jack, had evaporated.

"Never no more, George!" was the expressive observation made by one of them as they found themselves once more in safety.

And that sentence, incomplete as it was, expressed the ideas of all.

Spring-Heeled Jack had certainly impressed his enemies that night with a forcible idea of his power.

He had scored three victories.

He had routed ignominiously the myrmidons of the law.

He had proved to the enemies of Ralph Ashton (for whom he had so mysteriously taken up the cudgels) how he could defend him.

And he had left an impression upon the minds of Caleb Masters, Sir Roland Ashton, and Laura Barton that would never be effaced.

When Sir Roland and his worthy servitor had recovered from the deadly stupor into which the sight of Spring-Heeled Jack and his words had thrown them, they crept downstairs in the hope of obtaining some refreshment in the way of spirits to give them, at least, "pot-courage."

Their lamp had, fortunately for them, not been extinguished, but its light revealed to them at first a sight which was far from refreshing or likely to revive their spirits.

In the hall, where Spring-Heeled Jack had left her, was Laura Barton, still in a dead swoon.

The blood was pouring still from the wound in her forehead, where the claw-like hands of the strange apparition had marked the cross.

It had stained her face hideously, and trickled down upon the white breast, whose faint pulsation alone spoke of the presence of life.

"This must indeed be the devil!" muttered Caleb Masters; "it can be no man that thus defies every law, and laughs to scorn the endeavours of everyone to catch him."

"No, he is not the devil," said Sir Roland; "he is some mysterious being who has some dealings with those who understand the black art. There must be necromancers in these days, in spite of all they tell us."

And the baronet, laden as he was with crime, shuddered at the thought.

Caleb said no more, but moved towards the parlor, where a light was gleaming faintly.

Here they found Mrs. Barton in a profound slumber, as her daughter had said.

A bunch of keys lay on the table, and seizing these, the steward, who had been followed quickly by his master, searched in the cupboards and found a bottle of brandy.

It was like "manna in the wilderness" to those two men, who had lost all courage, and almost all

# SPRING-HEELED JACK,

## THE TERROR OF LONDON.

By the Author of "TURNPIKE DICK, the Star of the Road."

"CONSTANCE MARFIELD! CONSENT NOT TO THIS UNHOLY SERVICE!" SAID SPRING-HEELED JACK.

physical strength through the apparition of Spring-Heeled Jack.

They poured two cups full and drank them off at a gulp.

Then Sir Roland bethought himself of Laura.

"Come, Caleb," he said, "show a light. We must see to the girl. We don't want to run the risk of being mixed up in such an affair as this."

Passing into the hall, the baronet raised the senseless form of Laura from the floor and bore her into the parlor.

Here he tore open her dress, and placed his hand upon her breast to see if the fluttering of life still existed.

Only faintly.

But as the air came to her, and a little brandy was poured down her throat, her eyes slightly opened.

She glanced somewhat vacantly around her, and her magnificent bust rose and fell for a moment tumultuously.

The baronet raised her to a sitting posture.

"What means this wound on your forehead?" he asked, as he handed her a small drop of brandy.

"It is the mark of that accursed thing which haunts this neighbourhood," said Laura, drinking her brandy, but unable, nevertheless, to repress a shudder. "I only hope that some means or another may be found to stop his strange antics, or he will cause the death of more than one of us."

"Aye!" said Sir Roland, with a shudder, having time now to view well this beautiful traitress, and see how handsome she was; "aye! I know that twice running he has nearly killed me."

"What believe you he is?" said Laura, eyeing the door timidly.

"The devil, I should think," cried Caleb.

"Certainly he seems to bear a charmed life," said Sir Roland. "I have fired point blank at him only a few yards off, and the ball has taken no effect. But we must be going, Caleb. Miss Barton, what reward can I offer you for your attempt to-night to do me a signal service?"

"I need no reward, Sir Roland," said Laura, "more especially as we have so miserably failed."

"Nay, we have not failed altogether," said the baronet. "I have obtained a clue to something which will be of wonderful service to me. If I find that this clue leads to anything, you shall be rewarded handsomely. In the meantime accept this ring as some small recompense for all the trouble you have gone through this night for me."

He drew a handsome ring off his finger as he spoke, and, taking Laura's hand, placed it on its engaged finger.

Of course this was purely accidental, and Laura knew it to be so.

But it assumed the proportions of a strange coincidence in her mind.

"It would be by no means a bad thing to be Lady Ashton," she thought.

She knew him to be bad, cruel, selfish, unscrupulous.

But what mattered that?

Was she not the same?

So when he placed the ring on her finger she smiled sweetly at him.

Caleb had gone to get the horses ready, and so Sir Roland was at liberty to exercise at will his fascinations over this beautiful demon.

And beautiful, indeed, she looked, in spite of her wounded brow, with her dark hair falling in masses over her shoulders, her large eyes flashing, her pouting lips red with renewed life, her splendid bust revealed still by the *deshabille* which had been necessary to recover her from her faint.

The sparkle in her eyes emboldened him.

He raised her left hand with his right, intending to salute it; but a sudden impulse made him forget himself, and, slipping his arm round her waist, he drew her to him, and kissed her ripe lips.

One long, clinging kiss it was, and then she started away.

"Forgive me, Miss Barton!" said Sir Roland, who was almost as nervous at his act as herself, for, knowing her character, he could scarcely tell how she would construe it.

She smiled sweetly up in his face.

"Of course I forgive," she said, forgetting her *deshabille*, and wondering at his looks of admiration. "I put everything down to the strange and exciting events of the evening. But pray go now. My mother, as you see, shows signs of waking. She must know nothing of your visit. All the upset in the house can be put down to the visit of Spring-Heeled Jack."

Sir Roland, in spite of the false position he was putting himself into, looked very much as if he would like to rifle another kiss from that cherry mouth.

But Laura drew prudently away.

She was not the one to make herself too cheap, and Caleb's heavy tread, too, was heard approaching.

So with a smile he took her hand, pressed it warmly, and saying—

"Good-night, Miss Barton. Keep that ring, and if you are in any trouble, come to me and you will not find me forgetful."

Within five minutes after the baronet and his servant were riding away in the direction of Barnet.

As they neared the adjacent village, they resolved to pause and partake of some refreshments, fluid and solid; and ascertain if anything had been bruited about in the neighbourhood in regard to the doings that night of Spring-Heeled Jack.

The tavern was that to which the constables had gone when they had fled from the river's side after their row with Spring-Heeled Jack, the Eagle and Hound.

But it was certainly no constable's voice which was now roaring forth the refrain of a boisterous song.

As they neared the place the words of the ditty were heard plainly, and they paused in utter astonishment.

"You hear, Caleb?" said the baronet; "it is about Spring-Heeled Jack, as they call him—that hideous monstrosity which haunts our path everywhere. Listen! It is encored. Let us hear it out."

In response to loud shouts of applause and laughter, and banging of pewter pots on tables, the man with the stentorian voice once more sang out the words to a quaint, rude melody:—

"*The constables boast of their valorous hearts,*
*And their merry deeds under the moon;*
*But there's a sly dog among them just now—*
*That scatters them off pretty soon!*

"*We'll take him in charge for a rascally knave—*
*Come on lads—come, no holding back!*
*Ha—ha! in a crack,*
*Comes Jack—Spring-Heeled Jack,*
*And away goes the curs in a pack!*

"*There's many a lass and many a lad*
*Gets robbed on the dark highway;*
*But there's never a one, living under the sun,*
*Can call Jack a thief, anyway.*

"*The thieves, like the constables, boast of their pluck,*
*How they'll lay him right soon on his back!*
*Ha—ha! in a crack,*
*Comes Jack—Spring-Heeled Jack,*
*And away go the curs in a pack!"*

"Curse that fellow!" said Sir Roland, as he dismounted and prepared to enter the inn with Caleb. "He's getting too much for us. I'd give a thousand pounds if I could find a man to destroy him or fathom that mystery."

Ah! there were many who thought the same, Sir Roland Ashton.

But who succeeded?

"I'm afraid all the thousands in the world will never find out the mystery," said Caleb, with a growl; "and if people are going to sing about him, and make him popular, his pranks and antics will become worse than ever.

They had intended to go into the room for refreshment.

But one glance around determined them not to do so.

Within were such a rough crowd that the place was nearly crammed full; while near the fire were two men, dressed all in black, one of whom had been roaring out the rude ditty we have given above.

These, though they were not masked, were evidently members of the Black Brotherhood.

"I don't like the look of that crew," said Sir Roland, as they paused an instant at the door. "We'll have something warm at the bar, and then we'll ride home as fast as we can. Over supper I have something of importance to tell you."

And so, in a few moments, master and man were riding off again, full of their villainous schemes.

---

## CHAPTER XXIII.

DAISY AND HER ENEMIES—THE LONE FARM AT BERKHAMPSTEAD—THE MURDER.

BEFORE a roaring fire and an ample supper at Ashton Hall the ruffian baronet and his associate forgot for a time the terrible adventures of the night.

That is to say, they forgot the awful part of it—the tendency which it had to utterly unsettle their future.

"Caleb," said Sir Roland, "I'm almost obliged to believe that you know something about the disappearance of that money from my room in the west wing."

Caleb was silent.

"Well," he thought to himself, "perhaps it would be as well to tell him; and yet if I do he may send me flying."

He glanced up at his master's face resolutely.

"I wonder what he means?" he thought, as he saw the enquiring look that met his.

"Come on, Caleb," said Sir Roland, with a strange laugh; "speak out. Don't be afraid."

"I am not afraid of anything," said Caleb; "but may I tell my story in my own way?"

"Yes."

"Very well, then, sir," returned the steward; "you see since I've been in your service you've spoiled me, and made me more used to good things, and so on, than I ever expected to be. Well, I got extravagant, and—"

His master interrupted him.

"Ah!" he said; "just so. Don't make a long song about it. You've got into trouble, and you owe a lot of money. Don't be afraid to say how much."

"I'm almost ashamed to say how much," said Caleb, beginning to look very sheepish.

"I will tell you, then," said the baronet, calmly refilling the two glasses; "two thousand pounds! Nay, hear me out! What you found in the west wing was three thousand—a thousand more than you required to pay back the amount of that forgery. However, you failed over that; a more artful thief than yourself stole the cash, and you are now as penniless and as much in want as you were before you crept up to the west wing in the darkness when you thought I was asleep."

"I may as well confess that this is all true," said Caleb.

"Well, what would you do if I were to cancel all this—forget that you ever tried to rob me—and give you a cheque for two thousand pounds as well?"

Caleb raised his glass and drained its contents.

"I should think you the most generous of masters," he said; "but I can't say any more, for you might ask me to cut my own throat, and then I shouldn't be able to enjoy my life or your money either."

"No, I shan't do that," said Sir Roland. "I merely wish you to sign a paper saying that you did rob me, and then I will sign a cheque now for the two thousand you want, and tell you how you can earn a thousand more to set you going."

"Pray tell me, then, master," said Caleb.

"Replenish your glass and listen," said Sir Roland. "I am going to tell you a secret which I would not tell to everyone, and which I certainly would not divulge to you if I did not know that I had you pretty well in my power.

"George Leigh, of Lone Farm, Berkhampstead, is a perilous relation of mine.

"He is more perilous to me than Ralph Ashton, for the simple reason that were everything to turn up wrong between me and Ralph, he could only claim the title, for the fortune is nearly exhausted.

"Were I a coward I should say that I had only enough to enjoy myself for a time, and then blow my brains out.

"George Leigh is the one of all the family who has plenty of money, and from him are all our hopes of fortune.

"And, you see, Caleb, his money can be got at without lawyer's fees."

He paused, knocked the ashes off his cigar unconsciously, and continued, seeing that his companion and associate in villainy did not quite comprehend him—

"I have been trying for years to find out where he lived, so our chance visit to Mrs. Barton's hasn't turned out badly. I've found out now. There's no use in beating about the bush any more. Three nights hence I want to go down to the Lone Farm, and I want George Leigh's money. Do you get at my meaning now?"

"I think I do. You want me to assist you in ransacking the miser's place?" said Caleb, feeling ten thousand times more at his ease.

"I do, for the papers he holds, combined with what I have now discovered at Mrs. Barton's, proves that once George Leigh was dead—"

Caleb recoiled a little.

He had no desire for deliberate murder.

"Dead!" he said.

Sir Roland was "full of wine" now.

He did not care who heard him.

"Ha, ha!" he cried, "are you becoming squeamish? That is truly funny. Do you think we can enter the Lone Farm and obtain George Leigh's wealth without sending him to his eternal rest? Confound me, sir, are you a fool?" roared the baronet, who was warming to his work. "Do you think there is any other way to get at George Leigh's coffers except by a knife through his heart. Do you understand me now?"

"I do."

"Then drink and understand me again!" said Sir Roland. "At the time I have named we make our way towards Berkhampstead. I will endeavour to work my way into the old miser's house gently and coaxingly. If I fail then the bullet or the bludgeon must settle it. I am in desperate straits, I can tell you, Caleb, or I should not trust in you."

Caleb had done his inward reckoning now.

"Very well, Sir Roland, I will do my best to help you," he said; "but I know one thing you will have to see to first."

"What is that?"

"Your marriage with Miss Constance."

"What know you about it?"

"I know this, Sir Roland, and I hope you will not be offended," said Caleb. "That Tom Harland, the supposed father of Constance Marfield, is about the place again. That he boasts of the fact that he has you in his power, but that he will not betray you, which I think about tells his own story—he can't."

"Just so."

Sir Roland said these two words inquiringly and doubtingly.

He was beginning to feel uncomfortable.

"Well, you see," continued Caleb, "in one way or another I've picked up a few facts about things, and those facts tell me that if Miss Constance Marfield ain't another of the big family—ain't Miss Constance Leigh, for instance—I'm a Dutchman."

"You're about right, Caleb," said Sir Roland; "and so my plan is this. First we go down to the Lone Farm."

"Yes. That's the miser's."

"Then we settle his business and collar his coin," (the baronet was now getting drunk, and did not choose his English well) "and after that the great object of my life is to be achieved."

Caleb did not say that that would never be achieved.

He dared not.

He thought the more though, as he replied—

"I do not understand, sir, what that is."

"My marriage with Constance. That is the crowning point. Once Ralph Ashton is out of my way, and Constance my wife, every farthing of the Leigh and Ashton money is mine. For we will see that George Leigh makes no will, will we not, after to-morrow, at any rate, eh, Caleb?"

"Quite right, Sir Roland," said the man, with an ugly grin.

"With the money we take at the Lone Farm," continued his master, "I shall be able to put myself right, and give you enough to get yourself out of your difficulties."

"Thank you, sir," said Caleb, "and I can assure you that you will not find me squeamish."

"Very good," said Sir Roland. "Then to-morrow afternoon we will start for Berkhampstead. That business over we must hurry over my marriage with Constance. She shall marry me now whether she likes it or not."

"Let me suggest that there is one thing which will simplify matters most wonderfully," said Caleb.

"And what is that?"

"Let me obtain a drug—a narcotic, which will deaden her faculties without rendering her unable to speak or move. She will go about then like an automaton."

"A good notion," said the baronet, smiling.

The idea just suited him.

There was something delightful in the notion of having her entirely in his power—in marrying her while she was unable to offer any resistance—at the notion that she would wake up in the morning to the fact that she was his wife irrevocably."

"Then I will go to London on the day before that fixed for the ceremony, and procure the necessary drug," said his accomplice. "I know exactly where to obtain it."

"Here's to our success, then," said the baronet, as he refilled their glases.

The two villains accordingly pledged each other in bumpers, and then separated for the night.

On the next day, at the appointed hour, they took the coach, and were soon *en route* for Berkhampstead.

They did not go straight to their destination, however.

That would have been wilfully placing themselves in peril.

They quitted the coach at Houghton, and, after showing themselves at the Sun there, doubled back on the London road, and then began to cross the fields.

It was, of course, by far the longest way, and they knew that it would be early morning before they reached the old place.

But for this they did not care.

They were well aware that such an adventure as that on which they were about to start could not be carried out all at once in a rush.

They must have time to reconnoitre, and so forth.

On reaching the town and entering, which they did considerably after midnight, they made some alterations in their attire and general appearance.

Both Caleb and Sir Roland put on false beards and round caps, and hid their overcoats in a clump of trees by the roadside, showing underneath clothes of a far rougher material.

In the pockets of these coats were pistols and a couple of bowie knives.

"I think we've put the people off the scent," said Sir Roland, as they took their way along the lane which led to the Lone Farm. "If anyone was watching us anywhere, we have entirely altered our looks."

"The devil himself would not know us now," said Caleb.

Sir Roland shuddered, and looked round.

"Pray do not invoke his satanic majesty," he said, "or we shall have his imp, or substitute, Spring-Heeled Jack, appearing to us.

"Ugh! I hope not," grunted Caleb. "But

here we are; keep your stick handy for fear of dogs and prowlers."

In another moment they had broken through the hedge and were making their way to the house.

The Lone Farm well deserved its name.

It stood on the top of a wind-swept hill, with tall trees surrounding it—great poplars, that bent, and moaned, and swayed in the breeze.

It was a tall, gaunt, stuccoed building, that had once been white.

But now the wet and moss of years had made it green and stained everywhere.

Its flat face resembled nothing so much as a lunatic asylum.

Near it were red-tiled farm buildings, where the tiles were broken here and there, leaving great gaps for the water to come through.

A long narrow lane ran between these and the house, and a broad side ditch went stagnantly by, which had once been a trout stream.

Here and there in the house itself the windows were broken and the roof dilapidated.

Within, all was indicative of decay.

The house had at one time been full of splendid furniture; it had been upholstered, in fact, by a London firm once, regardless of expense.

That was when George Leigh had determined to take to himself a wife and to retire altogether from the grip of the rapacious relations who would have wrung every farthing from him and made his life a misery if they had known he was about to marry.

George had made heaps of money abroad, which, added to his paternal acres, made him a very wealthy man. But no one dreamed that George was a marrying man.

He was tall and gaunt, and ungainly, with an odd-looking face, though he had large earnest dark eyes.

Everyone, however, who thought him incapable of love was wrong.

George Leigh had his love-dream, like all others.

Only it came to him in a peculiar way.

He had gone down to a little country place, a mite of a seaside village, and he had taken lodgings at a house of a worthy couple, who had a daughter scarcely sixteen years of age.

She was a bonnie wee lass, a miniature little woman.

At first he took her for very much less in age than she was.

He treated her as a child.

He used to kiss her, and nurse her on his lap, and wonder at the depth of her great childish eyes.

But the idea of love never once occurred to him.

So things went on.

Everyone trusted him with Lily.

He used to take her out for walks on the cliffs, and out for rows in his boat.

At last came a summons for George Leigh to go to London.

It was only when this came that he knew how dear Lily Mayford had become to him.

They were sitting on a bench at the extremity of the garden when the letter was brought to him.

His arm was round her waist, and her head on his shoulder, and he was showing her some pictures.

She felt him thrill and his grasp tighten round her as he read.

This surprised and alarmed her, and she said, quickly—

"What is the matter, Mr. Leigh? Any bad news?"

He turned his head from the paper he was reading, and glanced down into her face.

In that face he read the fact that she was not a child.

And in his own heart he knew that he loved her.

"Well, it is bad news, little one," he said. "I am going away."

"Going away?"

The words to her young heart were expressive of great sorrow, and, without thinking how her action might be construed, she clung to him.

"Oh! don't say that," she said; "pray, don't say that."

"Would it be so bad for you, then, my little one?" he whispered.

"Yes—yes!"

"Do you love me, then?"

And he gathered her up in his arms.

"Yes; I do love you," she cried. "Do not leave me."

And then their lips met in long passionate kisses, and their hearts beat madly in unison.

When they were calmer George Leigh told her what had happened.

A dear friend of his to whom he had made a vow that he would come to him any distance if he were dying had written to claim his promise.

He must start for Paris without delay.

"But I shall not be long absent from my little darling," he said. "Only be true to me—be true to me!"

And out there, amid the sweet-scented flowers, they had exchanged vows of everlasting love and truth.

The departure of George Leigh was too hurried to admit of any explanation to the father or mother.

They saw when the two said good-bye that they were more than common friends; but they made no remark.

In their own minds they had long ago settled it that George Leigh and Lily were to be man and wife, and, though quite content that it should be so, they made no effort to find out how the land lay.

For some reason best known to herself Lily Mayford said nothing.

She preferred, perhaps, to keep her little love story to herself.

At any rate she said nothing, and George Leigh went off to Paris.

He was detained there far longer than he had intended. His friend was a long time dying, and during the whole time he received no news of Lily.

He had not asked her to write.

He had only asked her to be true to him, to wait for his return; and he was quite content to dream of her, to think of her delicate beauty, and to realise in imagination the delights which would be his when she was really his own.

At length he was free to return.

The friend who had claimed his presence died at last, and George eagerly returned to the village which held his treasure.

What did he meet with there?

Not the reception which he expected.

The Mayfords were there.

But where was Lily?

He knew there was something wrong directly he saw their faces.

But what was it?

"Was Lily dead?" he asked.

Alas! it would have been good for him if she had been.

It was not she but her heart that was dead to him; for three months after he had left her she had fled with a winning young cousin of hers, who had only brought his handsome face and fascinating manners into her company for the first time a few weeks after the lovers' parting.

To describe George Leigh's grief would be almost impossible.

He had such a strange way of showing it.

He grew deadly pale, his features became stony and rigid.

Scarcely a word crossed his lips, but what did pass was terribly expressive.

"With her then be accursed all womankind," he cried.

Then he at once set his plans in motion.

He knew that his relations were eager for his death, in order that they might clutch the wealth which he could not alienate from them.

Accordingly, looking upon them with as much hate as he did Lily, he resolved to beat them.

He accordingly sold off and let all he could, and through his lawyers he contrived to amass together a large sum of gold.

He had bought the Lone Farm when he had first felt his love for Lily Mayford, and had had it furnished in the very tip top of fashion; and had pictured to himself the joy of taking home his bride to the old place.

That was years—long, long years—before the time when Sir Roland Ashton and Caleb Masters made their way across the fields with murder in their hearts.

Ever since then George Leigh had lived in the old house alone, save for an old serving man.

He refused to see any neighbour, and, save for two rooms, he used the old place in no way.

No horses stood in the stables, no pigs filled the styes, no cows were in the sheds, no poultry made the farmyard lively.

It was the very picture of utter desolation and ruin.

The rooms were now mouldy and musty-smelling, the furniture was falling to pieces, and the whole house was as if it had been given up to ghosts.

For years and years George Leigh had never looked upon the face of a human being, save John Dobbs, his servant.

This faithful old domestic, was a tall, stalwart man, gaunt like his master, and of such fierce and furious aspect that when he was put out by any of the neighbours who presumed to be too inquisitive they went off alarmed.

He was just the one to guard such an abode of mystery as Lone Farm.

And seeing his fidelity and determination, and finding him in every way true and obedient, George Leigh began to be absolutely fond of him.

Of course it was useless to deny the fact that George was a miser.

He seemed to take a delight in keeping himself without creature comforts.

He never spent a penny which he was not compelled to spend, and, of course, he expected John Dobbs to be of the same mind.

And so Dobbs was.

Only when his master was reading his quaint, old books, and dreaming away his life, he made a little money for himself, so that when the master of Lone Farm was dining off dry bread and a herring, his man could afford a steak not paid for by his master's money.

Three nights before the arrival of the two murderous ruffians in the neighbourhood of Lone Farm George Leigh called John Dobbs into his private room.

It was a dingy room, with scarce a handful of coke fire in the grate, and two flickering candles giving their unpleasant light.

The furniture was massive and good, as was all furniture in the house, but it was discoloured and dirty.

The apartment looked, as indeed was the truth, as if it had never been cleaned for twenty years or more.

"Dobbs," he said, motioning him to a chair, "those letters you brought me last night were very important."

"Indeed, sir," returned Dobbs.

"Aye! the one told me of the death abroad of Lily Mayford. She died abroad—not very happy—and sent me a line to ask my forgiveness. Ah! well, she ruined my life, but I cannot keep back my pardon on the brink of the grave."

"No, sir," said John Dobbs.

He was used to his master's strange fits of melancholy.

"The other letter," continued the owner of Lone Farm, "was from Mr. Fortescue, the solictor, who had in hand the case of Ralph Ashton. There seems to me, from what he tells me, there is not the remotest doubt of his innocence. And there appears no doubt, moreover, that he is the son of Sir Guy Ashton, and consequently the heir to the baronetcy and the estates."

"From what you have told me, I have always thought so," said Dobbs.

"So you see, Dobbs," continued George Leigh, "I want to make my will."

Dobbs looked scared.

His master smiled.

"Don't be alarmed, Dobbs," he said, "in my will you will be well remembered. Get out a piece of foolscap and a quill, and write to my dictation. To-morrow you can go to Berkhampstead and bring me Lawyer Smith, and the whole thing can be done at once.

The old man reluctantly obeyed.

He knew, in fact, that it was useless to rebel.

But with many others he held the superstition that the making of a will was a preparation for death.

In concise terms George Leigh made his will.

There was no bungling or doubtfulness about it.

With the exception of five hundred pounds to John Dobbs, it left the whole of the property to Ralph Ashton.

Dobbs was more than satisfied.

He was an honest and trustworthy servant, and he could, had he been so disposed, have helped himself often to some gold.

But he had never felt the temptation, and the wish of his master to place him above want for the rest of his life brought tears into his eyes.

"Don't be foolish, my good man," said the master of Lone Farm, with a smile. "You have deserved that and more, but I know you do not covet more. It will do to keep you from want for the rest of your life."

The next day John Dobbs went in search of the lawyer.

He was away.

"He will not return for several days," said Dobbs, when his master asked him anxiously.

"It matters not," said George Leigh; "now that it is off my mind I am quite contented."

On the fourth night the wind blowed "great guns."

The trees in the plantations began to sway to and fro, and howls swept over the whole country-side, like the wailings of lost spirits.

It seemed as if there were some wild and supernatural beings at work.

Though every window and every crevice in the Lone Farm was closed up, a searching wind penetrated into the house.

Icy particles were driven by the wild wind against the windows, where they rattled like the tapping of skeleton figures.

"A wild night this, Dobbs," said George Leigh, as, in a fit of sudden extravagance, he placed a small lump of coal on the fire to rouse it up. "I think we will both have a small glass of spirits to keep out the cold—a very small glass, Dobbs, because too much spirits, you know, are bad."

And so he doled out a small drop of brandy to John Dobbs, who accepted it with becoming gratitude and solemnity, though he was looking forward to a good stiff "nightcap" in his own room.

Left alone, George Leigh poked the fire, and leaning his head on his right hand, gazed into the embers.

As the wind roared round the house, and swept down the wide chimney, something seemed to remind him of days gone by.

He called to mind a wild and stormy night by the seaside, when he and Lily Mayford had crept down to the shore, and watched the tossing ships at sea and listened to the shrieking and moaning of the wind among the jagged rocks.

He could hear her voice again, he could see her face, he could feel the touch of her warm little hand.

Little did he imagine that at that moment there were creeping towards him across the grounds two ruffians who sought his life.

Such an idea would have been the very last in his mind.

He had lived so long free from anything of this kind that the idea of robbery never entered his head.

"Poor Lily! she's dead!" he murmured, almost fancying he could see her face in the glowing embers. "I wonder how long I shall be before I follow her? Forgive her! How could she doubt it? I have wrestled with my hate and anger long since."

As he spoke the wind lulled slightly.

And, as he naturally paused to listen, he fancied that he detected a strange, clicking sound.

What could it be?

At present certainly it was not in the house.

He rose and approached the window.

The sound apparently came from beneath this, so opening it, in spite of the chill wind, he leaned out and listened.

All was still.

Save for the voices of nature.

So he drew back, and was about to close the casement again, when once more his ears were assailed by the strange sound.

His ears were very sharp.

All who have been travellers, used to sleeping in strange places, have acute hearing, and are ever on the alert.

"Thieves, by Jove!" was his inward comment.

He made no outcry.

He knew, in fact, that it would be useless, for the Lone Farm stood such a distance from the high road, that it was not possible for any one to hear any alarm, unless he rang the long disused bell in the turrets.

And besides, the place was looked upon as so uncanny, that no one cared to have much to do with it.

He closed the window, therefore, as noiselessly as he could, and proceeding calmly to the bureau he took out a pair of pistols.

Then, quitting his own room, he walked towards the chamber occupied by John Dobbs.

The wind seemed to make the place haunted that night to George Leigh.

He expected his servant to be awake and ready to receive to him.

He was a selfish man, and, having always lived within himself, he could not understand well the feelings of other people.

John Dobbs had, on the other hand, been his servant so long that he was used to his ways, and if, perhaps, he had heard a cry in the night, he would not have made an effort to see what it meant.

There had always been strange cries since George Leigh had returned from his love adventure.

He had heard him calling out for his "lost darling," and had rushed to his room, only to be told to go back and mind his own business.

So he had got into the habit of mugging himself up with a little "extra drop" of a night, and retiring, quite confident that he would hear no more of the master.

He was wrong in this.

His good old heart had no idea of the heart-burnings through which his master had to pass.

He never saw his sleepless nights, his tremulous views of daylight in the morning, when he viewed again the terrible loneliness of the next few hours.

It had become, then, an habitual thing that when poor George Leigh — poor, lonely George Leigh—retired to his own apartment, John Dobbs said "Good-bye!" to him, and never much troubled himself as to what the morning was to bring forth.

The servant looked upon the master as a slip-shod, weary man.

When George Leigh tapped at the door, and finding no answer, entered, John Dobbs was astounded.

He saw before him a man, calm, resolute, and determined.

"Master!" he cried. "What is the matter?"

"Thieves," said George Leigh. "At last the scent of my riches has gone abroad, and I have to fight them on my own ground. Here are my pistols. Come, John Dobbs, let us show them that we are not afraid."

Dobbs rose at once.

He also had had disturbed dreams.

He had heard strange noises in and about the old house.

In a few moments he was ready to follow and accompany his master anywhere.

As soon as John Dobbs had indued himself into as many things as he thought absolutely necessary, he descended the stairs with his master.

They went down in the dark.

Neither Dobbs or George Leigh had a spark of cowardice in them, and they were walking about in a house which was well-known to them, with no boots or slippers on.

It was better for both of them if they could only drop upon their enemies unawares.

By the time they had glided down to the big hall—the grand old central hall—which seemed as if it contained a special ghost in each shadow, the interlopers had become more venturesome.

They could hear plainly the work of the thieves (for Sir Roland and Caleb were no better), as they endeavoured to work their way hither.

Dobbs glanced at his master.

He knew, like an old soldier, that his commanding officer was right under any circumstances, and no matter what were his inward thoughts, he had sufficient confidence to know that if he followed his master he was not going far wrong.

"What are we to do, Mr. Leigh?" he said, as they placed themselves in the darkness opposite the place where a chink of light told them the robbers were at work.

"Take this pistol, Dobbs," whispered Leigh, "and when I fire, you fire also."

George Leigh then advanced to the door.

"Who is there?" he cried.

No answer.

"I ask you once more—Who is there?"

Still no reply.

"By Heaven! if you do not answer, I will fire through the door. We are early people here, and do not like strangers in the middle of the night. If they cannot account for the business which brings them here, we generally conclude they have no business at all, and we treat them accordingly."

A rude and boisterous laugh greeted these words.

But no answer was vouchsafed.

In an instant George Leigh was as good as his word.

He made no further remark, but aiming straight at the point of attack, fired point blank.

There was no cry of pain.

Only a hoarse laugh.

Then a furious bashing at the door, the timber gave way, and George Leigh was face to face with his enemies.

Sir Roland Ashton and Caleb Masters.

For even as a boy Caleb had proved himself a scorpion.

Of course, as we are aware, the baronet and his accomplice were in disguise.

But something seemed to tell George Leigh that they were familiar with him and his surroundings.

As the two villains sprang into the hall the master of the Lone Farm challenged them.

"Who are you?" he cried, "and what do you want that you burst into a man's house thus in the night? If it is money you seek you are wrong."

Sir Roland Ashton laughed hoarsely.

"Money! Aye! we do come for money, and before we go we will have it, too!" cried he. "Send off that scarecrow servant of yours, and then we can talk together."

"Who are you?" asked George Leigh.

A coarse laugh was the first answer.

"I think, as you and your man are the only persons in the house, that I can safely tell you my name. I am Sir Roland Ashton."

George Leigh drew himself back with a convulsive start, and John Dobbs was also similarly affected.

But the two men took the news in a very different way.

Dobbs saw the intrusion only in the light of an intrusion.

His master knew well that it was an attack, not only upon his property, but his life.

"If you are Sir Roland Ashton," he said, "you are the greatest enemy I have in the wide world, and I cannot see why you are here, except it be to rob me or take my life."

"I will do both, old man, unless you comply with my wishes."

"And those are—what?"

"Dismiss your man and I will dismiss mine," said Sir Roland Ashton.

"Very well. John Dobbs, keep this man company awhile," said George Leigh, "and see that he does not move from his place here. After what I have suffered I have no faith in anybody."

With an evil smile, which Caleb Masters quite understood and was prepared to act upon, Sir Roland Ashton made his way to the library with George Leigh.

"Do you suppose," he said, when the door was shut, "that I am going to stand any more of your hypocrisy?"

"I am at a loss to understand you," Leigh said. "I can't understand what it is you are aggrieved at. My money and my property are my own to do with as I choose. You are evidently excited, and it would, consequently, be better for you to leave my house and return at another date. You see I don't like intrusion. I have kept myself aloof for a long time, and I am resolved never to unbend to a coward, a villain, and an alien, as I believe, like yourself. Leave my house, Sir Roland!"

The words were bravely spoken.

The baronet knew that they were, and felt the full force of them.

He rose from his seat and listened.

The hour had come.

He must choose now, once and for ever.

"Is this your final answer?"

"Yes."

There was no further reply in words.

Sir Roland took one leap and gripped the unsuspecting man by the throat.

"Villain! murderer!" gasped Leigh.

He struggled violently.

But his strength was as nothing compared with the desperate iron-muscled adversary with whom he had to deal.

Poor John Dobbs—even had he been within hail—would have been useless.

As it was he had been left in charge of a wretch quite as ruthless as the master of Ashton Hall.

Caleb Masters, knowing the great stake at issue, and inspired by the desperate, murderous spirit of his master, attacked John Dobbs, hoping to silence him at the same moment that Sir Roland silenced the long-suffering George Leigh.

Leigh had his pistols ready, as we have before seen.

But the spring of his enemy was so sudden that it was impossible to use them.

As he endeavoured to fire at his foe, the weapon went off, burying itself in the old wainscoting.

Sir Roland made no remark.

A deep sigh of relief escaped his breast.

Relief that he had been fortunate enough to be saved from such a sure shot.

And without a cessation of his exertions, he still continued bearing his enemy to the floor.

At length by a sudden jerk he did so.

"Coward and villain!" cried George Leigh,

whose white face showed how the terrible struggle was playing upon his disabled body; "what want you?"

"Your life!" cried Sir Roland.

The grip of the baronet tightened round his throat. Then his hand sought his belt, and his long knife was produced.

It gleamed a moment, then descended, and was buried deep, deep in the miser's heart.

It was scarcely a sigh of satisfaction with which Sir Roland Ashton withdrew the reeking blade.

The struggle had been a desperate one, and he had succeeded in his hideous purpose.

But, nevertheless, he had committed another awful and deliberate murder, and he could not but feel how the crimes were accumulating surely and heavily on his soul.

But there was relief in his heart at the thought that there had been no interruption; that they had not been discovered in their awful villainy.

At the very moment that this idea crossed his brain a cry of agony awoke the stillness of the old house. Turning to see what it was, he saw Caleb Masters stagger and fall.

He had reckoned without his host.

John Dobbs had proved his master, and at the very moment that Caleb had imagined that he had won the day, and that the wretched man was at his mercy, he drew a small poignard from his pocket and thrust it into Caleb's throat.

The wound was instantly fatal.

Masters fell with a sudden thud, but Sir Roland, with his bowie knife still smothered with the blood of his foe was upon the serving man.

Against this red-hot assassin John Dobbs had no resource.

After a fearful struggle he succumbed.

Sir Roland was alone with three dead men.

But his villainous heart was too full of joy to allow him to act the coward.

Glad almost of being rid of a man like Caleb, who knew so much of his affairs, he began at once to ransack the place.

Money and papers in quantities soon filled his pockets.

But he was unable to take all he wanted, and so the sickening task devolved on him of disposing of the bodies. A tedious and horrid duty.

One by one the slain men were dragged down the stairs of the house, every crack of the boards causing the assassin to start and tremble.

At length the ghastly work was over, the signs of murder obliterated, and George Leigh's will destroyed.

But the wealth for which all this blood had been shed had not yet been discovered.

He must close up the old house, as it often was closed up for weeks together, and return after awhile to reap the blood-stained harvest.

He locked the place up carefully, and glided out through a window at the back.

"When I come next," he said, "there'll be a flare in the sky, and the mystery of the murder will be hidden for ever!"

## CHAPTER XXIV.

THE FORCED MARRIAGE—SPRING-HEELED JACK AND THE CLERGYMAN—THE WEDDING NIGHT—THE MORNING AFTER—A SURPRISE WITH A VENGEANCE.

NO one who saw Sir Roland Ashton at the Hall, after the cruel crime which had been committed by him and Caleb Masters at the Lone Farm, would ever have suspected that he had such a terrible thing upon his conscience.

He was just as gay and light-hearted as ever; and he went about with such a smile upon his face that the servants declared it to be quite a treat.

The change was especially grateful to Mrs. Levine.

She had quite matured now the plan which she had so long been thinking out, and the confession of which to Constance had caused the blushes to mantle in the young girl's cheek.

The baronet was especially gracious to her.

There was no wonder in this, because Mrs. Levine was absolutely indispensable to his plans.

Now that his monetary affairs were somewhat more settled there seemed no necessity any longer to delay the marriage with Constance.

Apart from the fact that her money was necessary to him he had an eager desire for this union.

Her personal charms—full, large, and voluptuous—were just such as suited him, and he resolved to put the matter off no longer.

The plan suggested by Caleb Masters was the one decided on; a special licence and an opiate would set all things to rights.

There was no longer any need for the Tom Harland farce.

No necessity to ask her to wed him to save a father from the scaffold.

It would all be carried out while she was in a state of semi-unconsciousness, from which she would not awake until the morning told her that her fate was irrevocably sealed.

On the third evening after the shocking occurrence at the Lone Farm, Mrs. Levine entered Constance's room.

"My dear," she said, "the crisis has arrived. The wedding is to take place to-morrow night."

Constance's face became rosy red, and her bosom rose and fell in one tumultuous heave, and then fluttered tremulously.

"Are you sure that all will be well?" she said; "that you will he able to succeed?"

"Oh! yes, my dear," cried the housekeeper, with a smile. "I shall succeed right enough. There is no fear of that. You may depend upon that. I shall do my best, for it is my heart's dearest wish to do as I have told you."

"I only hope that all will be well," said the young girl. "What a terrible scene there will be when he knows he has been deceived!"

Mrs. Levine laughed.

"Oh! I will chance all that," said she. "I will risk everything for such a consummation. I have thought it all over, and know what danger I run in doing what I am going to do. But I care not. I am determined to save you and please myself at the same time."

"And what part do you wish me to take in this farce," said Constance.

"You must dress yourself as a bride, and prepare apparently to carry out the programme as Sir Roland wishes it. Appear to consent thoroughly. Let nothing in your manner let him suspect that all is not as he wishes it."

"But he will wonder at my being so willing, after all."

"You must not appear too willing," said the wily Mrs. Levine. "You must appear to give way reluctantly at the last moment."

"And are you sure that all the arrangements can be carried out as you wish? It all seems so impossible and mysterious."

"The mystery will all be over the day after to-morrow," said Mrs. Levine, with a laugh. "I know the risk is a great one, but I do not mind that."

On the following day Sir Roland let Mrs. Levine into the secret of the sleeping-draught, and gave her strict injunctions how it should be used.

"Will she be able to walk about when she has taken it?" she asked.

"Yes, just as before, except that she may be somewhat mechanical in her movements," replied Sir Roland.

"But how will she give the responses?"

"Easily. That will be all right."

"And when will the effect of the opiate go off?"

"Not until to-morrow morning."

"She will be completely in your power then."

"Completely."

"And how soon before the ceremony do you desire the draught to be given?"

"About half an hour."

"Very well," said Mrs. Levine; "all shall be arranged satisfactorily. The marriage, you say, is to take place at eight. The drug shall be administered at half-past seven in a cup of tea."

"Do as you like," said Sir Roland; "arrange all things properly, and you may depend upon it you shall be rewarded."

"I hope so," said Mrs. Levine, with a smile—a smile so significant that it was as well he did not see it.

About half-past seven, just before the clergyman arrived, she brought into her master's room a couple of glasses and a bottle of port.

"Shall I pour you out a glass, sir," she said, "or will you wait until the clergyman comes?"

"Oh! pour one out now," said the unsuspecting baronet, "and one for yourself. Let us drink to the bride's health!"

With her back turned slightly towards her master, Mrs. Levine did as she was directed.

"Here's the health of Constance, soon to be Lady Ashton!" cried the baronet, as he drank his wine off at a draught.

"Here's the bride's health with all my heart!" cried Mrs. Levine, with another queer smile.

And she drank her wine off also.

At eight o'clock precisely Sir Roland, feeling very strange and confused, and yet excited, passed with the parson and his clerk into the room where the marriage was to be solemnised.

It was a square room on the first floor, the window of which opened out upon a terrace.

Already the bride was there with the witnesses—the housemaid, and Job Joskins, and Mrs. Levine.

Constance looked pale and unhappy, but still wonderfully lovely.

She wore a plain dress, and also a bridal veil.

Mrs. Levine, on the contrary, was attired in a dark-green velvet, cut low, and affording a lavish display of her large and well-formed bust.

The ceremony began.

Sir Roland seemed dazed and bewildered.

"Been drinking, I expect," thought the parson.

But the fees were good, and he didn't marry a baronet every day, and so he held his tongue.

Anyone entering the room would have imagined that it was Mrs. Levine who was being united to Sir Roland.

Constance appeared utterly afraid, and the housekeeper accordingly had to support her.

In doing so her hand took that of Sir Roland, and it looked as if he were about to place the fatal circlet upon her finger when a strange and terrible incident occurred.

There was a loud outcry of demoniacal laughter without.

The wild discordant laughter of Spring-Heeled Jack.

Then there came a terrific crash, the window was smashed in, and the awful apparition, which had so often alarmed Sir Roland and his associates, stood by the clergyman.

Both the latter and his clerk stood speechless and appalled at the unexpected phenomenon.

No one in the room, in fact, seemed able to utter a sound.

He advanced grimly, with outstretched talons, towards the baronet.

As he did so the flapping wings knocked against the table, on which the wax candles stood, and overset them.

The room was now in complete darkness, save for the feeble radiance of a wax-taper on the mantelpiece and the sulphurous flame emitted by the lips of Spring-Heeled Jack.

"Beware! Sir Roland Ashton," he said; "if you carry out this nefarious plot, your raoe will be run quicker than if you paused awhile to consider. Constance Marfield, beware how you consent to go through with this unholy service; and as for you, Mrs. Levine, vengeance will find you out when you least expect it."

"You," he added, turning to the parson and his clerk, "had better go away at once. Close your sacred books and leave this den of infamy."

No one answered.

Job Joskins and the housemaid were locked in each other's arms, and hiding their faces as if for mutual protection.

Mrs. Levine alone seemed as if unawed and unalarmed by the aspect of the awful being.

Constance clung to her, gaspingly.

"Beware, all of you!" cried Spring-Heeled Jack, once more in his solemn and terrible voice. "If you persist in going on, retribution will surely overtake you. My vengeance will fall swift and sure."

Then with a leap and a spring he passed through the broken window and disappeared.

"Go on—go on!" cried Sir Roland, in a hoarse, unnatural voice, "we have a taper's light. The Devil himself shall not step between me and my bride!"

"Really, Sir Roland," stammered the clergyman, "matters have taken such a strange turn that—"

The baronet rapped out an awful oath.

"Proceed," he said, "or I'll horsewhip you, and if that will not bring you to your senses, I'll blow your brains out."

The baronet seemed truly beside himself.

His face was deathly pale.

His features worked convulsively.

"Pray continue," said Mrs. Levine, in a low voice. "Pray continue!"

The priest accordingly went on, and in a few moments all was over.

Sir Roland advanced staggeringly to salute Constance.

But Mrs. Levine restrained him.

"Not now," she said, in a whisper. "You are upset—the wine and the excitement have overcome you. Let us sign the register and then retire to the drawing-room."

The register was soon signed, the certificate

given to Mrs. Levine, and then the party, with the exception of Job Joskins and the housemaid, retired.

The parson received his fees, drank a glass of wine and departed.

The baronet was by this time dazed and idiotic, but he chucklingly expressed his satisfaction at all that happened.

Mrs. Levine sat down beside him, and he at once placed his arm round her waist and kissed her.

He was too far gone now with the strange drug to know who she was.

At a sign from Mrs. Levine they took away all the lights save one little lamp at the extremity of the room.

The master of the Hall and his housekeeper sat n front of the blazing fire.

The drug, whatever it was, had quite dulled his perception.

Otherwise he would certainly have been astonished at the warmth with which his kisses were returned, and the quietude with which his somewhat daring caresses were received.

He felt intoxicated with delight.

"My darling Constance," he cried, as he again pressed his lips to the responsive mouth, "now that you are my bride, I feel contented. Life will be joyous for me where it was blank and lonely before."

"I will do the best to make you happy," said Mrs. Levine, in a low, tender tone, as she drew his head down upon her ample bosom.

She knew that he would soon be asleep if she could only coax him into it.

The warmth of his new resting-place had apparently a soothing effect upon him.

In a few minutes he was in a sound and heavy slumber.

As soon as by speaking to him and shaking him she had ascertained that he was safe and sure, she gently placed his head upon a pillow, and glided from the room.

She hastened at once to that of Constance Marfield.

The young girl was already dressed for a journey.

"Come quickly," said Mrs. Levine. "I have left him fast asleep. He is not likely to wake now until the middle of the night; but still I shall feel more satisfied when all is over and you are gone."

Tears ot joy stood in the face of Constance Marfield.

"You cannot be as eager for my going as I am to go," she said. "I am quite ready."

"Have you sufficient money?"

"Yes, thank you."

"And you are decided as to where you are going?"

"Yes."

"Then let us lose no time," said Mrs. Levine. "I shall see you as far as the Corner Pin and into the coach. As this is Sir Roland's wedding night," she added, wi h a laugh, "no one will think of disturbing him. So we will pass through the drawing-room where he slumbers, and go through the French windows on to the terrace. By these means no one will see us go out, and no one will even suspect our absence."

"Lead on. I am entirely in your hands," said Constance. "I am only anxious to be away."

Mrs. Levine said no more, but eagerly, though cautiously, passed out of the room.

They descended the stairs noiselessly, and, passing through the room where Sir Roland slept still soundly, went out on the terrace.

No one was about.

The moon was shining brightly, and they could see around them an immense distance.

But to all appearance not a living being was anywhere to be found.

The two women eagerly descended the steps, crossed the broad gravel path, and hurried across the grounds in the direction of the Lodge, where Harry Banks and Daisy Leigh had seen Sir Roland Ashton ride by.

They did not pass the little house, however.

Even at this hour they dreaded discovery if they attempted to open the gates with Mrs. Levine's duplicate key.

So they swerved slightly to the left, and making their way through some shrubbery they found a gap in the hedge and passed into the high road.

Still all was quiet and lonely.

The distance to the Corner Pin Tavern was not great, and at length they reached it in time to see the coach come swinging up for its ten minutes' stoppage, ere it dashed off again on its last stage.

The task of booking a seat was an easy one, and Mrs. Levine bade Constance adieu.

"I dread your going back," said the young girl, kindly, to the woman who had been so cruel to her, save at the last moment, and then only changed from motives of self interest.

"Why?"

"Because I am sure harm will come of it."

Mrs. Levine laughed.

"There is some danger, I admit," she said; "but then it is worth some risk to be Lady Ashton."

And after kissing the girl, who was going away alone into the wide—wide world, she hastened away.

Scarcely had she passed a few hundred yards along the lane when the now well-known laugh was heard—

"Ha! ha! ha!"

The woman heard it, glanced back, and saw Spring-Heeled Jack come leaping over the hedge.

She uttered a shrill cry of fear and cowered down in the road.

But it was not to her that Spring-Heeled Jack devoted his attentions.

He went leaping and springing towards the stage-coach, on arriving near which he was greeted by a loud scream of terror.

Those on the top doubled themselves up in as small a compass as possible and hid their faces; those within, consisting only of two ladies besides Constance Marfield, fainted clean away as the awful apparition came to the door.

Constance herself felt a terrible sinking of the heart and an inclination to contract herself into the smallest possible space.

But, nevertheless, she did not lose her senses.

"Constance Marfield," said Spring-Heeled Jack, as he stood there, with his glaring eyeballs and sulphurous-breathing mouth, "fear not! I mean you no harm. You have taken my advice and fled from that house of iniquity before it is too late. If you desire to see Ralph Ashton, be at the Queen's Arms, near Sadler's Wells, to-morrow night at eight. Ask for John Gray and you will have good tidings. Meanwhile, be brave and patient, and be sure that Spring-Heeled Jack is watching over you."

The young girl made no reply.

# SPRING-HEELED JACK,

## THE TERROR OF LONDON.

UP WENT SPRING-HEELED JACK INTO THE AIR AND THEN PERCHED BEHIND JACOB.

Although she felt sure that this mysterious being was friendly, that he meant to do her good, she could not avoid feeling an awe in his presence—an awe which prevented her from speaking.

She was pleased, in spite of the glad tidings that he brought, when he took a step backwards, leaped over the steaming, snorting horses, and disappeared.

All this had taken but a moment.

But it was some time before the spectators of the scene were sufficiently recovered to pursue their ordinary avocations.

At length, however, by the administration of stimulants, the two ladies within the vehicle were aroused to consciousness.

The driver and the guard were restored to something like common sense, and the travellers on the roof felt brave enough once more to glance around them.

A general rush was then made to the bar of the inn by the male part of the company, where sundry cups of strong waters were partaken of amid disjointed exclamations and wondering comments upon the astounding apparition they had witnessed.

At length, however, the driver and guard mustered up courage again to make another start, and presently, the travellers having been mustered together, the mail coach was swinging away towards London.

Meanwhile Mrs. Levine hastened back with all speed in the direction of the Hall.

Her heart was in a strange flutter of mingled triumph and fear.

She had played a bold and desperate game.

And—for the moment—she had succeeded.

But would the result be what she anticipated?

Everything appeared to favour her.

Not a human being had, to all appearance, seen her departure and return, and Sir Roland Ashton was still sleeping heavily, just as she had left him.

A smile of triumph wreathed itself over her lips.

"All goes well," she said, to herself; "my plot has succeeded so far. But when he wakes and finds who is really his bride, how will he take it? What storm of passion shall I not have to endure?"

She passed gently from the room and dismissed the servants to bed, telling them that she would take Sir Roland's supper into his room.

When the baronet awoke in his bedroom in the grey of the morning, after a sleep full of strange visions, he saw that he was not alone.

Lying beside him, fast asleep, was the form of his bride.

But what did it mean?

Had he suddenly gone mad?

Where were the fair tresses of Constance?

Those dark, waving locks belonged surely to another.

The sleeper's back was turned towards him, and, raising himself on his elbow, he leaned over and took a glance at the sleeper's face.

He drew back in dismay.

It was that of Mrs. Levine.

"What mad thing is this?" he muttered, lying back on his pillow.

Then, as he lay still, trying to recall the events of the previous evening, he saw a paper pinned to the curtain of the bed near the watch pocket.

He seized this eagerly, turned up the lamp and read it.

It was a marriage certificate between Sir Roland Ashton and Constance Ruth Levine, widow.

A demoniacal smile overspread the features of the baronet.

"She has tricked me somehow," he said; "but I will trick her in return. She shall think that I accept my fate; but the day will come when she will regret this hour. She has courted death by this fatal victory of hers. However, I will dissemble. I will meet her craft with cunning as deep. She shall have her own way. She shall reign as mistress of the Hall for a brief space of time, and then, swiftly and surely, the blow will fall. Constance Marfield shall be mine yet."

At first the idea of marriage with his ward had only occurred to him as the means of securing to himself the property.

Since then the idea had developed itself in a different way.

He had noted her charms of person, and his wish to make her his wife was now founded on a double feeling of interest and passion.

Never, perhaps, in her life, had Constance Marfield been in greater danger, as regarded Sir Roland's plans and desires, than at this moment, when he awoke to find Mrs. Levine lying by his side, installed by her clever and mysterious ruse as Lady Ashton.

## CHAPTER XXV.

### DAISY LEIGH ONCE MORE—THE HAUNTED COTTAGE.

JOE DIMITY'S next "pitch," after leaving Barnet, was at Weybridge.

This was not taking Daisy very far out of danger, it is true.

"But," as he was fond of quoting, because, he said, it so exactly suited his case always, "needs must when the devil drives."

"And he's always driving me," he would say, with a queer little comical smile.

The old posters were now all used up, and the fresh ones flaunted on the caravan and the walls of the village, announcing the new "star," Lottie Day.

This was perilous work, since the baronet knew that this was her assumed name for stage purposes.

But the whole company was on guard.

Little Daisy had become the pet of the troupe, and every one in the caravan was one of her body-guard.

She seemed to grow prettier every day.

The sorrow at the loss of her father was wearing off now, as such sorrows will.

Her eyes were lighter and more unclouded, while the exercise of dancing, which Maria was teaching her, was giving grace and firmness to her lower limbs.

Her appearance on the stage always created a good first impression, and she always went off amid a perfect roar of applause.

"That girl's worth her weight in gold," Joe Dimity would say.

And Harry Banks would sigh like a furnace, and think what a foolish girl she was not to accept him as a husband, so that they could go to London and try their fate on the legitimate boards.

Poor Harry!

He knew she was not for him.

But he couldn't help loving her, and would have protected her with his life.

She had good need of protection.

Robert Tugwell, though outwardly a friend to all in the show, and a most diligent servant, was a never-failing spy.

Every little incident was faithfully reported to Sir Roland.

His letters were in some cases exaggerated, just, as he expressed it, "to keep up the game."

But he told every word which seemed to suggest a change of ground; and Sir Roland was able to shape his plans accordingly.

Sir Roland had no wish to be in a hurry.

He preferred maturing his plans.

He had fallen in with his fate, apparently, with cool nonchalance.

In fact, except in one sense, matters were little altered at the hall.

Mrs. Levine was now no longer housekeeper.

She was Lady Ashton, and his wife.

So, for a time, he accepted her as a companion, until he could mature his other plans, in spite of the confession she had made that she had drugged his wine, and forged a letter to the parson, getting the name altered in the special license he brought in his pocket.

She took to her position well.

By caresses and endearments she endeavoured to coax him out of his secrets.

But it was useless.

He treated her in every way as a wife, but his black heart was a sealed book.

His plans, as regarded Constance Marfield and Daisy Leigh, were kept hidden in his own heart.

He was well aware that his wife would not be the one to aid him in anything which would tend to lessen her own power.

To ask Mrs. Levine (or as we must now continue to call her Lady Ashton) to assist him in any scheme having regard to Constance or Daisy Leigh would be ridiculous.

Accordingly he made no sign.

Certainly he had no fault to find with the new Lady Ashton in many ways.

She was good-looking, possessed a splendid figure, which, in her new style of dress, showed to its best advantage, and altogether behaved herself in the household as one upon whom her new dignity sat well.

So, yielding to the influence outwardly, and pretending to accord her all the respect which was due to her, he was secretly plotting against her; arranging so that she should serve his purpose for a time, and then be flung aside swiftly as soon as it suited him.

His fury at the escape of Constance Marfield was intense.

But even this he kept under.

He secretly sent messengers in every direction to discover her whereabouts.

In vain.

Wherever she was she was so well concealed that it was out of all question that he would be able to find her.

In regard to Daisy he was kept well informed, as we have said, by Robert Tugwell.

She could wait.

He always knew exactly in what place she was, and, consequently, there was no need to precipitate matters.

Yet it turned out in the contrary way.

Robert Tugwell had spent all his ready money, and was longing for more.

So one morning by the first post there arrived a letter for Sir Roland.

It was very brief, but to the purpose—

"RESPECTED SIR,—*The Dimity lot are talkin about going abroad. We shan't stay long at Wey bridge. I haven't had time to take the place yo asked me to look out for, but I have seen a place ju like what you wanted. It's an old cottage just i the middle of a wood. It's called Lilac Lodge, an it's supposed to be haunted. If you want the j done it had better be done at once, for I don't kno where we may be in a week.*

"*Your obedient servant,*

"ROBERT TUGWELL.

"*P.S.—A little money would be acceptable, as have run quite short.*"

The baronet smiled at the last words.

"Run short, eh?" he thought; "why, I don' suppose the fellow ever had so much money fo spending purposes in all his life before. But it' no use grumbling. If you deal with such peopl you must expect to pay through the nose."

The reply went down at once—

"*I will be down to-morrow night. I enclose fiver. Try and arrange about the cottage.*"

On the following day Sir Roland went out for ride alone.

He said he only intended to ride over to South gate on business, and return for lunch.

But, of course, this was pretence.

As soon as he had got well out of range o Ashton Hall he turned his horse's head, and, put ting spurs to his steed, he dashed off furiously.

The way to his destination was not very long.

But he was eager and impatient.

He was eager to see Daisy, even if he was un able to compass her destruction yet.

His passion for Constance Marfield was mingled with a mercenary feeling—a feeling that he would by securing her, secure also a certainty of th property, without any possible rivals springing u to oust him from his post.

The housekeeper who had forced herself int the position of Lady Ashton had no hold upon him whatever—not even her life was safe in his hands.

But towards Daisy he experienced a different feeling altogether.

Her gentle grace, her childish beauty, her bud ding charms, had roused in him a mad passion, which was not dulled or in any way affected by the knowledge that she was to be devoted to certain death.

Ralph Ashton he regarded as an obstacle which would soon be got rid of by the ordinary course of law. Constance could be secured by marriage.

But poor little Daisy, heiress to wealth which she knew not of, was a far more dangerous opponent.

All these things coursed through his brain as he rode swiftly along towards Weybridge.

There was another thought that occurred to his mind, and that was a most disquieting one.

Where was Spring-Heeled Jack, and would he, as before, interfere just at the moment when he was in the presence of the one for whom he had such a mad passion?

As he rode along swiftly through lanes and highways he kept glancing round him to see if any signs of the mysterious being was to be observed.

But no.

Spring-Heeled Jack seemed for the moment to have given up his wild gambols in the vicinity.

The country-side, in fact, was strangely still, and when presently he crossed a wide expanse without tree or building he felt convinced that, at any rate, his *bête noir* was not on his track.

Reaching the Weybridge Arms, a tavern not far from the spot where the Joe Dimity Troupe had made their pitch, he put up his horse, and, having partaken of some refreshment, he at once made his way towards the booth.

Tugwell was at the door.

That fact Sir Roland observed in a moment, though the spy did not recognise his master.

On his way across the common the baronet had placed on a wig and a false beard, and, with a slight assumed stoop, he was not recognisable as the bold, resolute villain, Sir Roland Ashton.

Pleased with this proof of the value of his disguise, Sir Roland did not at once reveal his identity to his accomplice, but, paying his entrance fee, strolled into the auditorium.

The play was at its height, and presently Daisy entered.

She was received with thunders of applause.

Evidently the audience had already begun to appreciate her value.

She was lookingly ravishingly beautiful.

She had on her page dress, as when Sir Roland had first seen her; her attire was more elegant, but still as daring—displaying the firm, small, budding bust and the rounded lower limbs to their full extent.

"She is distractingly lovely!" thought the insatiate villain, as he gazed upon her. "What would I not give if I could have her for my wife? But the law says 'No,' and, as she cannot be Lady Ashton, and is a perilous obstacle in my path, she must die. Poor girl—how beautiful! I will keep her alive as long as it is safe, and that will be very long if she can only be retained in security. In this lone and haunted cottage of which Tugwell speaks there would be very little chance of her communicating with the outer world."

Having feasted his eyes on Daisy's beauty as long as she was on the stage, he took his way from the auditorum and passed round to the door where Robert Tugwell was seated.

"Good evening, Tugwell," he said, in his own voice.

The man started and looked up.

But, though the tones were familiar, he did not recognise him.

"Good evening, sir," he said, constrainedly.

There was an abundance of rabbits on his conscience, and he had a wholesome fear of the constabulary.

The baronet laughed.

"Well," he said, "since you do not know me my disguise must be good. I am Sir Roland Ashton."

Tugwell jumped up with a ready apology.

Sir Roland was by no means pleased at this.

"You are a very bad accomplice," he said, in a low voice, which, however, was full of anger. "If you cannot keep our mutual secret, of what use is it to attempt to work together?"

Tugwell, who had responded so eagerly because he already scented some more gold, made abundant apologies and sat down.

"How soon will the performance be over?" Sir Roland asked.

"In an hour."

"Come then to The Weybridge—not the Weybridge Arms; my horse is put up at the latter place and I might be recognised. Be as quick as you possibly can after all is over."

"If I can," said Tugwell, hesitatingly, anxious to enhance his services.

But he was wrong in his estimate of the baronet.

"Can!" cried Sir Roland, with an oath. "If you can't do what I require there are plenty who can. So make no favour of it, but say at once. Are you going to help me or not?"

Tugwell saw that his line wouldn't do.

"I beg your pardon, sir," he said. "I didn't mean no offence, only I might be kep', and then if you was waiting long you might think I wasn't coming."

"No—no! I'll wait for you," replied his villainous employer. "I'm not going to return to Barnet until this affair is over now."

"Do you mean her?" said the man, jerking his right thumb over his right shoulder.

"Yes; Lottie Day, as you call her. I wish no further delay in the matter. I'm certainly not going to let her slip through my fingers by going away. Don't fail."

And, hearing a sound of someone coming, Sir Roland hastened off.

The Weybridge, which he had noticed on his way to the booth, was a large inn, a square modern building, with stone steps running up to the door of the private bar, all kinds of indiscriminate buildings at the back, and a long row of livery stables running at right angles with it, though not connected with the general structure.

He entered in his disguise, and in a few moments had got into conversation with a respectable specimen of the "oldest inhabitant" class, who could give him minute descriptions of nearly every place in the neighbourhood.

"I have never been in this place before," said Sir Roland, "and I don't know, therefore, if there is anything worth seeing."

"Oh! well, the place isn't without attractions," said the other. "It has its lunatic asylum, its haunted house, and many other things worthy of notice."

Lunatic asylum!

Why did those two words strike him so forcibly?

Was it that they spoke of an easy way to rid himself of little Daisy, or was it Mrs. Levine, now Lady Ashton, that presented herself to his mind in this way?

Whatever it was he pursued his enquires.

"Can anyone look at this asylum, and this haunted house?" he asked.

The man laughed.

"Well," he said, "you can look at the asylum from the outside; but I don't think that unless you had a very special introduction you would obtain an entrance. Dr. Catchem is a very particular man, and I don't fancy he likes people prying about."

"Then I won't go there," said Sir Roland, "on any account; I don't like prying of any kind. But tell me about this haunted house; where is it? That I suppose has only a few ghosts to defend it, and so I should have a better chance to pry."

"Oh! the house is easily got at," said the oldest inhabitant; "it is in the woods. Only a little place, but with a big story to it. They say that an awful murder was committed there some time since, and that the spirit of the murdered woman walks round it by night, dressed in white, with a gaping wound in her breast, from which the blood stains trickled on her muslin garments."

Sir Roland laughed.

"A real old woman's story," he said. "Who lives in the place?"

"No one."

"It is to let then?"

"Yes."

"Then, by George, I'll rent it if I can!" said Sir Roland; "I'm fond of all kinds of mysteries, and if I could only bowl out these ghosts and prove them impostors, I should be in the seventh heaven of delight.

The oldest inhabitant was highly amused at this.

"You won't have any difficulty about that," he said, "I can assure you. The agent, Mr. Parker, of Gracechurch-street, will only be too glad to let it to you. The only question which will be raised will be the length of the term for which you will take it. Plenty of tenants have taken it, but a week of it has generally settled them."

"Thank you for all this information," said Sir Roland; "of course, you mustn't take all I say as *au serieux*. Perhaps I may never think of this foolhardy idea again. But at any rate I thank you for your kind information."

Then they drank together and otherwise fraternised until at length Robert Tugwell appeared.

He entered the bar somewhat confused, for he had met certain persons on the road whom he suspected of being on the watch, and he had had to go out of his road somewhat to avoid them

Two men, dressed entirely in black, whose faces were hidden by black masks, and who looked more like a couple of old-fashioned highwaymen than modern denizens of the world.

They had followed him nearly all the way from the booth, and he had only escaped them by dodging through a hedge and lying *perdu* in a ditch until they had ridden by.

"Good evening, sir—hope I see you well?" said he, as he met Sir Roland.

He gave expression to no name because Sir Roland had not suggested one.

"Oh! Barnes, I am glad to see you," said the baronet, airily. "Didn't think you'd know me after all this time!"

"Oh! yes, I should have know you anywhere, Mr. Crawford," replied Tugwell, hazarding the first name that came uppermost in his mine.

"Well, then, have something to drink," said Sir Roland, "and then, if you have time, I want you to show me the way to High-street, Weybridge."

"All right, sir," said Tugwell.

He knew he was expected to do what he was told, or, at any rate, what was hinted at, and consequently he guessed it was proper to say, "Yes."

The "old inhabitant" laughed.

"You don't mean that you're so struck with the appearance of the place that you mean taking it offhand?" he cried.

Sir Roland joined in the merriment.

"No; not quite as bad as that," he said; "but I am so fond of anything in the ghost line, that I feel as if I mustn't let the opportunity slip. So I shall see this Mr. Parker at once, and learn all particulars. I should not think of taking a place without knowing what it was like."

They took leave of the man soon after, and in a few minutes the two accomplices in guilt were hastening towards the High-street.

It is needless to say that Sir Roland Ashton did not go to Mr. Parker's that night.

He had only made that an excuse in order to get away with Robert Tugwell.

The information given him by the old man had been useful to him.

But before he dreamed of making use of it, he was resolved to wait until morning and have a good view of the place, to see if it was suited to his deadly purpose.

"I have heard some particulars of your haunted cottage, Tugwell," said Sir Roland, as soon as he and his accomplice were beyond ear-shot of anyone.

"Indeed, sir, if you think anything of it I can take you straight to it—if you ain't afraid of the woods."

"What should I fear in the woods?" demanded Sir Roland.

"Nothing, Sir Roland; only they do say Spring-Heeled Jack—"

Tugwell paused and glanced nervously round.

He seemed to dread even the mention of that name.

"Tut! I do not fear him, even if he be the fiend he pretends to be; but it is my belief he is the greatest thief unhung. It shall go hard if I do not unmask him and bring him to justice."

This speech, instead of encouraging Robert Tugwell, seemed, in spite of its boldness, to have just the opposite effect.

He kept much closer to Sir Roland's side, and started at the slightest sound.

Sir Roland noticed this, but deemed it wise not to mention it.

They had now entered a lonely road which passed through a wood.

It was pitch dark, and the wind moaned through the trees in a most melancholy manner, so that Tugwell fancied that he heard weird voices and demoniac laughter.

Even Sir Roland paused sometimes to listen, and seemed half-inclined to turn back; but, uttering a scornful exclamation, and making an impatient gesture, as if ashamed at faltering, even for a moment, he then pushed on at greater speed.

At last they came to the cottage, a miserable place, which had at one time, without doubt, been used as a hunting lodge.

But the days of its glory had vanished, and it looked ghastly.

Well could anyone believe that ghosts and goblins haunted the dreary place.

The windows were mostly boarded up. Those which were not so were broken, and all of them were as dark as midnight, or the proverbial wolf-throats.

It was an awful place, fit for murders and all kinds of crimes, and, if report spoke truly, such had been its history of terror.

"It is a fearful place," said Tugwell, in a trembling voice.

"But one, Master Tugwell, just suited to my purpose," replied Sir Roland, with a fiendish laugh. "Come, Master Tugwell, be more of a man, and cast aside these fears. Those who would serve me must be bold and resolute. I pay well, but my service is of some danger."

"Of a truth, Sir Roland, you do pay well, and with drink a man may defy the devil. I will serve you."

The baronet gave one glance of scorn at his companion, and said—

"You have pleased me much in this matter. But, how are we to enter the house?"

"By a window at the back of the premises. I made that all right."

"Good! Have you the means of procuring a light?"

"I never travel without that, because of my

pipe. Come, Sir Roland, and let me introduce you to this ghostly residence."

Cautiously they crept round the house, and were soon standing beneath a low window.

"Jump on my back, Sir Roland; from thence you can climb on to the window-sill. The window opens inward. Push it, and the catch will give way."

"And how do you intend to follow me?" demanded Sir Roland, suspiciously.

"I can scramble up by this old piece of pipe, and you can give me a help into the window. My clothes are so bad that a tear or two more will not hurt them."

"Serve me faithfully, and you shall not want for clothes or for money to spend on your favourite drink. Now help me up."

Tugwell bent down, and, placing his head against the wall, made what is generally known as a "back."

On this extemporised platform the baronet leaped, and was soon in the window.

"Now then, there," he whispered, "come on up. I will help you in. Come!"

Tugwell did not pause an instant, but scrambled up the old piping, and was soon standing by Sir Roland's side.

"Now for a light; but stay. We must first close this window."

"And better cover it over in some way. It is not very likely that anyone will be passing, but it's best to be on the safe side. Who knows? Some poachers might be about, and carry some story down to the village that lights had been seen in the haunted house, and then all kinds of inquiries would be raised."

"True. I had forgotten that, and in these cases one cannot be too careful. See, here is an old screen here. We can place that before the window, and then think what is to be done."

The screen was soon placed so as to conceal the light—that is, when it was struck, and then Tugwell produced flint and steel, tinder, and a dark lantern.

"There! that is all right," said he, when he had lit the lamp. "It is not so brilliant a light as old Dimity's in his 'Halls of Dazzling Delight,' but it suits us, and is better for our purpose."

"After all, I do not suppose that it would matter much if people saw the light," replied Sir Roland. "The ignorant bumpkins would put it all down to ghosts."

"They would, Sir Roland, and would not come near the place for a hundred pounds. But, then, suppose these men should not be ignorant country bumpkins, but quite the reverse; that would be rather awkward. I mean people who are only a little, if anything, less knowing than Spring-Heeled Jack himself. What then?"

"I do not understand you. You must speak out plainly to me."

"Why, sir, they do say that there is a band of men about here, half-highwaymen, half-political offenders, who have a strange power of knowing everything that passes. Have you heard about them?"

"Yes. They are called the Black Band, I believe."

"Just so; and I have seen some of them in this wood."

"Say you so?" If that be the case, we had better search this old house. Who knows if we may not have fallen in o a nest of theirs?"

"No, Sir Roland; I do not think that. I think even they would not venture too much in this old house."

"Light the way—we must search at once," said Sir Roland, impatiently.

Tugwell did as he was commanded, but his heart was full of terror.

Sir Roland drew his sword, and, holding his pistol ready, advanced boldly.

If the outside had been dreary, the inside was forty times more so.

The furniture had not been removed; but it had been left to decay away, or become the spoil of the rats.

The curtains, which were of the richest damask, were covered with dust, and festooned with cobwebs.

There hung bloated spiders where once were festoons of flowers.

The hideous beetle slowly crept into corners, and there remained at ease.

They had lost all fear of their natural enemy—man.

Now and then a startled rat would dash away at full speed; but once having gained his hole in the wainscot he would turn and take an indignant survey of the intruders, much like an old landed proprietor might view a poacher.

"S'death! I think we are safe enough here, Tugwell," said Sir Roland.

"Do you think so, Sir Roland? Well, I am glad to hear it; only—"

"Only what? By Heaven! you croak like a raven. No fit companion for such a place as this. Speak out, and tell me what you mean."

"I mean that it is scarcely a fit place to take a young and beautiful girl to. I fancy she will scarcely like her lodgings."

"True! In thinking of my companion I had forgotten her feelings. Tut! I know not why I should consider them. What room is that yonder?"

"I know not, Sir Roland. Shall we enter and see?"

"Do so."

They found the room door bolted, but Sir Roland and his followers soon forced the bolts back, rusty as they were.

The door creaked upon its hinges and opened with some difficulty.

All the rooms had been dark, damp, and and musty, but this one was fearful.

The windows had been barricaded up, the very chimney stopped.

The furniture had been overturned; the chairs and mirrors broken.

The lamp, and table upon which it had no doubt stood, were overthrown, and there were patches in the carpet where the flaming oil must have burned large places before it could be stamped out.

Everything gave proof of a most desperate struggle—one of life and death.

Could any further proofs be wanted they were not hard to discover.

Here on the wall were large and horrible plashes, the deep colour of which told their nature.

The place smelt like a charnel-house, and, as if to tell the terrible history of the room still further, here lay a small white satin shoe, over there a piece of blue ribbon, and further off a small, delicate glove.

"Let us leave this room," said Sir Roland, with a shudder; "some awful crime must have been perpetrated here. Phew! how close the air is; I cannot breathe."

He hurried from the room, plucking at his throat as if he really were choking.

"Bolt the door after you, and follow me," he cried.

"It strikes me that will soon come to be the only haunted apartment in this house!" muttered Robert Tugwell, as he hurried after Sir Roland.

Sir Roland entered the apartment by the window of which he had gained admittance to the house, and, throwing himself on a chair, wiped the perspiration from his forehead.

"You don't seem well, Sir Roland," said Tugwell. "Will you do me the honour of drinking a little of this?"

And here the fellow produced a large flask bottle of whisky from his pocket.

The bottle being half empty sufficiently showed Sir Roland where the man's courage had come from. However, he made no reply, but drank deeply of the spirit.

"That puts fresh fire in a man," he cried. "I feel now able to face the devil. We must to work at once. To-morrow, in the name of Crawford, I will take this house. I know a woman who will come down from London and set things in some kind of order, and keep Daisy company."

"Will that be safe?"

"Fear not, Mrs. Corcoran is in my power. She dare not disobey."

"Good! I understand. Only women are not always to be trusted."

"She is," said Sir Roland, who suddenly began to notice that Tugwell was becoming very familiar, and wished to keep him in his place.

Fool! were they not bound by the common tie of crime, a bond which knows no distinction? The titled profligate is no better than the lowest scoundrel of Seven Dials.

"All right, your honour. I meant no offence. Only in these things—and in this, you see, I am somewhat interested—I like to be on the safe side."

"Fear not, I will make all right. I will hire the coach to carry the girl off, and will have trustworthy servants down from London to carry out my plans. Let us leave this place. When I come here again I will have it made more cheerful. Curse it! What was that?"

The two men had started to their feet, and gazed at each other with horror.

From the room—the dreadful room which they had just left—a terrible scream arose, followed by cries for mercy.

Then the furniture seemed hurled about, and the two awe-struck men knew in their trembling hearts that the terrible tragedy, whatever it might be, was being rehearsed.

Ah! how often had it been rehearsed?

How often had those vain cries for mercy echoed from that blood-stained room and rung through the house? Was it doomed that the terrific tragedy should be enacted nightly until the Day of Judgment?

Even Sir Roland, bold villain as he was, turned pale at the thought.

As for Tugwell, he had gathered so much false courage from the bottle of whisky that he had become positively defiant.

"I will solve this mystery," cried Sir Roland, "let the danger be what it may. Follow me, and hold the lamp steady."

The last two orders were not the easiest to carry out by Tugwell.

Follow he did, but the lamp was certainly not steady, neither was the bearer.

The door was reached, the bolts drawn back, and the two men stood upon the threshold peering into the room, unwilling to enter it.

Had they seen the phantom of the victim and the murderer they would not have been so horrified with surprise as they were.

The room was empty—just as they had left it—not a particle of furniture had been touched. No one was there, and all was quiet.

"Tut!" said Sir Roland, as he banged the door too. "Some deception of the senses, and—but what is this?"

As he spoke he held out his hand in horror.

It appeared really and truly to be stained with blood!

At first both men stood aghast and then Sir Roland, seizing the lamp, examined the door.

"Tush! look here Tugwell, and see how easily men can be fooled if they have not courage to look into things. Do you see that patch of what appears to be white?"

"I see it, your honour, and see that blood appears to be running from it."

"That is a kind of cochineal, the little insects in which gives forth this crimson fluid which so much resembles blood. Had we time, I doubt not that we should be able to explain the strange noises we have heard as easily as we have done this."

"I think it would take a precious long time!" said Tugwell, to himself.

"But I have no time to spare, just now," said Sir Roland, as he wiped the stain from his hand with his handkerchief, taking care to cast the latter from him and not to replace it in his pocket. I have now formed all my plans, and we need remain here no longer."

Tugwell was not sorry to hear this, and prepared with alacrity to depart.

The lights were all extinguished, the screen moved from the window, and both men, although they would not say so, breathed much freer in the open air then they did in the stifling atmosphere of the haunted house.

---

## CHAPTER XXVI.

### THE WARNING IN THE WOOD.

"PAH! that place leaves a nasty taste in the mouth," said Sir Roland, as he spat on the ground. "But old Mother Corcoran is used to such things, and in a few hours will make the place look as cheerful as need be."

"I think, your honour, that it would have been almost better not to have taken that house. I don't think Miss Lottie Day will like it."

"That matters but little," laughed Sir Roland. "She will not stay there long. I doubt not that I shall tire of her caprices before a month is out."

"And then?"

"How should I know what she will do? I know as little as I care."

This cruel speech made even Tugwell look surprised.

"Oh! it's nothing to do with me, sir. Only as I am so well-known at the theatre, don't you think that it would be better if I did not appear to have any hand in the abduction?"

Sir Roland looked rather suspiciously at his henchman.

But, being satisfied that the fellow was faithful, he said—

"Perhaps it would be as well that you should keep in the dark."

"I think so, too; until I leave the theatre to enter your service."

"My friend, do not make a mistake. For some time you will not leave the theatre, although you will be in my service. You must remain at the theatre and be one of the chief ones to mourn the young lady's disappearance."

"Ah! I am to play a double character?"

"Just so. You must play the spy and keep me well informed as to what may be going on, so that I may be able to prevent any rescue, and throw all suspicion from myself. Do you understand?"

"I understand, your honour, and will carry out your orders to the letter."

"I shall send at once for my secretary, and it will have to be through him that you communicate. Again, do you understand?"

"I do, and it shall be done."

"To-morrow you shall hear my plans for carrying the lady off. At present we will keep all secret. I will not venture to breathe these plans, even in this lone place. This time I'll prove myself equal to Spring-Heeled Jack."

"Ha! ha! ha!" rang that sepulchral laugh through the woods. "Ha! ha! ha! Who dares defy Spring-Heeled Jack?"

The baronet and his henchman started back in greatest amazement. They gazed all around but could not see anyone.

"Mysterious being," cried Sir Roland, "whoever thou art, tell me why thus you thwart my schemes; who, with some diabolic purpose, crosses my path to fustrate my purpose. Who art thou?"

"Who I am matters not. At the present it pleases me, Roland Ashton, to keep the matter secret. What I am, and who I am, you shall one day know."

"Tut! think not to frighten me with these juggling tricks. I am no ignorant peasant or timid boy to be frightened by such pranks. Tell me who you are, and what you want, and then leave and trouble me no more?"

"Ha! ha! ha!" rang the fiendish laugh through the wood. "Think you that I am to be commanded by such as you, Roland Ashton? You do not believe in me, yet you dread me. Beware, Roland Ashton, your career of crime and folly draws near an end. Repent whilst there is still time."

Again the woods rang with laughter, but this time it was Sir Roland who laughed.

"Be warned by you? Why, if you are what you appear to be, you are the fiend himself, and advice from you would be dangerous to take. Nay! you are but a cowardly impostor after all, and dare not show yourself, but by fits and starts, to take people by surprise. Begone, lest I should discover your whereabouts and treat you as a mountebank deserves."

"Look!" replied a deep, stern voice.

A small blue light, no bigger than that given by a glowworm, appeared upon one of the highest branches of a tree.

This grew stronger and brighter, until it was some seven feet high and four feet broad.

Then, as if appearing from a luminous cloud, the horrible figure of Spring-Heeled Jack was seen, his arms raised above his head, and his bat-like wings spread out to their full extent.

Instantly Sir Roland, who had been watching for this opportunity, drew forth a pistol and fired point-blank at the supposed fiend.

For a moment Spring-Heeled Jack remained still glaring down upon them.

Then, with a deafening yell, he plunged forward and seemed as if he would have descended upon their very heads.

But he passed over them and disappeared in the darkness.

"By Heaven! I have wounded him," cried Sir Roland, triumphantly.

"Ha! ha! ha! Roland Ashton, you did not even touch me!" came the terrible voice of Jack out of the darkness, seeming almost at the baronet's elbow. "Ha! ha! ha! You have done that to-night for which you will be sorry. Do what you will. Remember! you are watched. Every sin which you commit will be registered against you—a fearful list of blackness of heart, but for every one of which you shall pay the utmost farthing. You are lost—lost, and for ever!"

For a moment the baronet seemed stricken with fear, unable to speak.

Then he plucked up courage, and in a bold voice made answer—

"Be it as you will. If I am condemned for ever, no worse fate can befall. Therefore I will not repent, but will have a short life and a merry one. He who has forfeited hope must find relief in despair. So, farewell, good Master Devil—if devil you be. Henceforth we are foes, and I promise you that I will try the bullet-proof of your skin each time we meet."

"Farewell, Roland Ashton. We shall meet again, and that speedily. Injure not the daughter of Herbert Leigh, the man whom you caused to be murdered. Keep that sin from off your head, or vengeance will follow quicker than is now intended. Farewell!"

Another eldritch shriek and the deep laugh, then the whole wood seemed alive with fearful sounds.

These only lasted a few moments, and then died away until the same dread stillness prevailed.

"Sir Roland," whispered Tugwell, "do you still hold to your fell purpose?"

"Firmer than ever," cried the baronet, as he stamped his foot in rage.

"You are a determined man, Sir Roland. But be not rash—be careful."

"Away with all thought and care," cried Sir Roland. "If, as this fiend says, all hope hath gone, then let me meet my fate with the bold defiance which becomes a man. No more words. To-morrow Jacob Butler" (a worthy successor to the defunct Caleb Masters, who had expiated his sins at the Lone Farm in the moment of triumph) "will be here, and you shall receive an earnest of your future reward, if you are true to me. If you are false, your life shall answer it."

## CHAPTER XXVII.

### THE THREE JOLLY ANGLERS—"NEEDS MUST WHEN—"

"WELL, I can't make it out, Giles. That a gentleman should go for to shut himself up in a place like that when he's got lots of money fogs me."

"I 'gree with you, Luke; but then, these gentlefolks have all kinds of whims and fancies, they takes a liking to all sorts of queer things."

"They never took a liking to me," said Giles, scratching his head.

"Nor me, either," replied Luke; "but I heard that this Mr. Crawford was what the world calls a hypocrite—a fellow as loves solitude and melancholy.

"You mean a hypocondriac," said a tall, dark man, who was seated at a little distance from the speakers.

"Maybe I do, sir. I never was no wise particular as to the language I use, so long as I makes myself understood."

A murmur of assent ran round the company, who evidently agreed with Luke's noble sentiments.

The conversation just related took place in the snug little taproom of the Three Jolly Anglers, and the people conversing were men of the agricultural class—good honest fellows, but somewhat rough in their way, and much given to beer and tobacco.

The time was evening, when the grey twilight was quickly deepening into night.

The lamps had not been lighted yet—or we ought to have said candles, for lamps were luxuries for the rich, not for the poor, from whom in those days the very light of day was shut out by Mr. Pitt's window tax, whereby every window had to pay a certain duty. The bowls of the men's pipes with their charges of burning tobacco gleamed like red fiery eyes in the darkness.

"I spoke in no ill-will, friend," said the dark man, quietly. "But could you tell me who this Mr. Crawford is, and where he is about to reside?"

The men saw that the tall dark man was evidently a gentleman.

Now, "gentleman" is a very vague term, especially as some people use it. Money has nothing to do with it—manners and absence of false pride everything. In a word, it means the man who is gentle to his fellow-creatures; and so these rough working-men at once perceived the stranger to be, and therefore at once took a fancy to him.

"Well, you see, sir, we don't rightly know who Mr. Crawford is. He came down here all of a hurry. A nice kind of free-and-easy gentleman, as it seems, only somewhat glossy. Well, he takes the Lone—or Lilac—Lodge in the woods."

"For what purpose?"

"How should I know?" said the man, almost indignantly. "Gentlemen with a heap of money, like Mr. Crawford, do not give reasons for their actions."

"True! I hear this Mr. Crawford is very rich?"

"I should think so!" replied the man, with that strange admiration which many poor people have for rich ones. "He has untold wealth—millions!"

In his admiration of such boundless wealth, the man threw out his arms, and in doing so managed to knock over his jug of ale.

Not only was the ale spilt but the mug was broken.

"Dang my buttons!" said the poor fellow, scratching his head. "I'm in for it now. Well, it can't be helped. I must pay for it."

"Stay—stay, my good fellow!" said the stranger. "You met with this accident in doing me a service. Let me settle for this and supply you with some more. Ho! there, landlord; bring hither a couple of mugs of ale for these honest fellows, and take also for this mug which has been broken."

The astonishment of the men was only equalled by their gratitude.

They seemed to think that a gentleman so lavish with his money must be as rich as Mr. Crawford.

They now became as communicative as at first they had appeared to wish to preserve silence.

Indeed, so communicative were they, that a great deal of fiction became mingled with their story.

"Was the lodge really haunted?" demanded the stranger.

"Haunted? I should think it was," cried one. "Why there are nothing but ghosts in the whole place, as well it may be so, seeing the numbers of murders which have been committed there."

Here followed a number of blood-curdling stories that made one shudder, and if a tenth part of them were true the lodge must have been the scene of bloodshed from the time it was built to the time at which our story takes place.

"You indeed horrify me," said the stranger, while his lips curled with a sneer. "And so Mr. Crawford has taken this terrible house?"

"Who speaks of Mr. Crawford?" demanded a man, as he turned into the room. "If you fellows will be warned by me you will keep your tongues between your teeth. My master, sir—I mean Mr. Crawford—is not to be trifled with, I can tell you, and you had as well offend the devil as offend him."

No sooner had this man, who was no other than Caleb Masters' successor, Jacob Butler, entered the room, than the stranger pulled his hat firmly over his brow, and drew back into the darkest part of the room.

"We ask your honour's pardon," said the poor men, humbly. "We only ventured to answer this gentleman a few questions, and I hope there is no offence done."

"Egad! I am not so sure of that. Men in the position of Mr. Crawford do not like to have their business discussed in a common alehouse by labourers over their vulgar pots of beer."

The men began making a humble apology again, when the stranger spoke.

"Surely there is no harm in men talking of their neighbours? If there were, conversation would soon be very small indeed."

"Neighbours! Do you class these men with Sir—I mean Mr. Crawford—that you call them his neighbours?"

"Why not? Are they not his neighbours? They live in his neighbourhood, and therefore must be his neighbours."

"And who are you that you dare to speak thus of—of a gentleman?"

"A man, and not a slave. Why should not these honest fellows speak of a new comer to the neighbourhood—especially one who comes in such a mysterious manner."

"Mysterious manner? I do not understand you. Mr. Crawford does not believe in ghosts. He is rich, hears of this house, and, to please his fancy, determines to take it. Is there anything wonderful in that?"

"No; but something more than strange. Does he mean to call up the spirits from the vasty deep?"

"Perhaps he does, and perhaps he does not. That is his business, and not yours or mine. All I know is, that finding the house was so cheap, for none of the people hereabouts would have anything to do with it, he bought it."

"Bought it!" exclaimed the stranger in astonishment.

"Aye! have you anything to wonder at or complain about that?"

"Not I; but he must have a very queer taste

The house, as I have heard, is in ruins, and although furnished, the furniture is in such a fearful state that no one could use it."

"Phew! What of that? What cannot money do?" and here he slapped a heavy wallet which hung by his side, and winked—"and there is plenty of it here."

"Mr. Crawford is fortunate in possessing so much wealth, and so careful a man of business, who will not let his master's affairs be talked about," sneered the stranger. "I wish you good-evening."

Bowing low he strode from the room.

Mr. Jacob Butler saw that he had made a fool of himself,

But what could he do to mend matters?

Nothing.

The thing was done and could not be undone again.

Drinking off his liquor, he hastened out of the house, called for his horse, and having inquired his way to Lilac Lodge, galloped off in that direction.

We have described the way to the lodge as very lonely, but the path which the ostler had directed Jacob to take was far more lonely.

It led down between two large embankments, in fact, was a cutting to save a steep hill to the river, then Jacob was directed to turn to the right, cross over a meadow by a bridle-path, and so find his way to the wood, in the middle of which stood the lodge.

Although Jacob was no coward, he would scarcely have ventured on that road if he had heard the other's muttered speech as he left the inn yard.

"A curse on you as a mean, swaggering hunks! Not a sixpence, although I touched my hat to him as if he were a gentleman. Well, I have had my revenge. I've told you the worst and the longest road, and I hope you will meet Spring-Heeled Jack on your way."

But Jacob heard not the fellow's grumbling, and galloped serenely on his way, communing with his own thoughts.

"I wonder what devil's work Sir Roland is up to now," he mused. "No good, I'll be bound. He has been a hard master to me, although I have served him well. Never mind, I think I have my plans laid to catch Sir Roland, and when I do I'll have revenge for all the insults he has laid upon me. I'll swoop down upon him like—"

"Ha! ha! ha!"

The sepulchral laughter rang in the air. A blaze of light shot upwards, and discovered to the awestruck Jacob the horrid form of Spring-Heeled Jack.

Jacob cowered down upon his horse's neck, and tried to urge the animal on.

But the horse reared and shied so as nearly to unhorse its rider.

The next moment, with his awful laugh, Jack made a high bound into the air, and then, descending on the horse just behind Jacob, seized the reins from the now terrified man.

The horse was now entirely in Jack's hands, and he urged the animal on at a fearful pace, at the same time shrieking into Jacob's ear—

"Ride, Jacob Butler, ride! You needs must when the devil is the driver. Ho! ho! ho! Your master expects you. Sir Roland is all impatience for the arrival of his faithful secretary. Ha! ha! ha!"

"Mercy! mercy!" groaned Jacob, who really believed he was in the clutches of the devil. "Mercy! mercy! In serving Sir Roland I must have served you at the same time."

"True; but I expect more from my servants than anyone else."

"Ask me what you like and I will do it," groaned Jacob.

"Obey me, then, and I will spare your life a little longer."

"What would you have me do? Tell me, and I'll do it. Only let me go."

"Give me that leather wallet."

"But you can't want gold and notes, Mr. Devil, and my master will almost murder me if I do not take him the money in safety."

"What care I for that? Let him—it will be the first good action he has ever done. Ha! ha! ha!" roared Jack, at this joke, the fun of which, we need scarcely say, Jacob failed to see.

"I must not part with the wallet," he said, sulkily; "I cannot."

"Then part with your life. Look before you. That is the river to which we are dashing with such headlong speed. Refuse to do as I order and I will wring your neck and throw you into the stream."

This was said with such determination that Jacob had no room to doubt that the horrible phantom, or monster, would carry it out.

"Take the wallet," he said. "I would sooner be murdered by Sir Roland than you. Now go, and leave me."

"No, no, Jacob Butler; we part not like that. You must be punished."

Jacob remonstrated, but in vain.

The river drew fearfully near, and, as he saw the dark rolling waters, his heart fell within him.

On—on—on they sped, until they reached a high embankment, overlooking the river.

Then Spring-Heeled Jack gave one of his fearful screams, and leaped from the horse's back to the ground.

But the horse, with Jacob on his back, plunged forward over the steep embankment, and both horse and rider were soon swimming in the river.

"Ha! ha! ha!" laughed Jack, as he waved the wallet aloft. "Go, seek your master, Sir Roland, or Mr. Crawford, as he now chooses to be called. Tell him that Spring-Heeled Jack is on his track, and will never rest until he has hunted him down and brought him to justice. Hold to your horse, he will save you. Go with the stream, you will find a bank lower down, where you can land. Ho! ho! ho!"

And with a wild yell the horrible creature dashed away.

"Curse me, if I don't think he is the devil after all!" muttered Jacob. "Devil or not I will be equal with him yet, and have my revenge."

---

## CHAPTER XXVIII.

HOW JACOB REACHED THE LODGE, AND HIS ADVENTURES ON THE WAY—SIR ROLAND'S RESOLVE.

JACOB BUTLER scrambled out of the water by the side of his horse, for he had found that it would be safer to get off the animal's back and partially swim whilst he clung to its neck, than to weigh it down with his weight.

But Jacob's troubles of the night were not yet at an end.

No sooner had he reached the shore than he began wringing the water out of his clothes.

Taking advantage of being thus liberated, the still frightened horse dashed quickly away, leaving Jacob alone and disconsolate, standing on the banks of the river wherein he had been so perfectly drenched, and had lost his hat and whip.

"Now confound the beast! I do believe that he must be in league with the fiend also. To think of serving me such a scurvy trick as this!"

He looked ruefully at the dark, rolling waters, and began to think what he should do.

"Well, I have made a pretty night's work of it, and no mistake. Over a thousand golden guineas gone, my clothes spoiled, my hat lost, and gold-mounted whip gone. Then there's the horse—that has bolted. I shall have to pay for that out of my own pocket—Sir Roland will not."

Presently a broad smile came over his face as he said, with a wink—

"Won't he? It shall go hard if I do not make him. I have the key of his money chest, and also of his conscience, and if I do not make him dub up the expenses of this night it will be my own fault."

He turned round and glanced about him.

All dark and desolate—not a light to be seen in all the country.

"Confound it!" he muttered. "I think I must have been misled by that fiend into the wilderness. Surely this place must have some habitations near, and I would give something to dry my clothes and have something hot."

Well might he wish to do both, for the wind began to blow icily off the Thames, and Jacob shivered again.

"Well, it's no use standing here; I shall be chilled to death."

He climbed up the embankment, and once more gazed around him.

In the distance he saw a streak of light, which he guessed to be some town, but far too distant for him to reach on foot.

Then, to the left, he made out a thick wood.

"That must be the place," he growled; "and I had better make my way there. I hope Sir Roland will not show his temper to-night, for I am in no humour to stand it."

So, growling, he began plodding over the fields, which he had the pleasure of finding covered with mud.

Shivering with cold and gasping with rage, he at length reached the wood—scarcely a place a man would like to pass through at any time, but after such an experience as Jacob had, not at all inviting.

But Jacob had no choice. So he made a virtue of necessity, and entered the wood, humming a song as loudly as he could to show he had no fear.

He had passed on some way when he saw a glimmering light among the trees, and stopped to examine it.

"Surely that comes from some house. It may be the lodge or a farm. I don't care what it may be. Whatever it is, I shall make my way to it, and demand hospitality. I could not go much further; my limbs are completely numbed."

So he turned out of the narrow path he had been pursuing, and struck across the wood.

No easy matter this to do, for not only was the night dark, but, once off the path, Jacob Butler found himself floundering into ditches, fighting with brambles, which tore his clothes, and tripping over briers, which made him stumble forward and fall on his face.

"May all the curses of Egypt alight on Si Roland's head for this!" he said, as he picke himself up from a heavy fall. "I think he has supe natural powers, and knows that I have lost hi money, and so has bewitched me. But wh is this? Surely the light is now further to the left

He paused and looked anxiously around hi and then at the light.

"Pish! this night's work has unhinged m brain and set my nerves dancing. The light much nearer. If I hallo now I have no dou they will hear me."

Suiting the action to the word, he put hi hands to his mouth and sent up a loud cry f help.

Again and again he repeated it, and at last faint "Hullo! there" came from the direction the light.

"Is there any path that will lead me to you house?" cried Jacob.

"What do you ask for?" returned the voic "We care not for strangers in these parts."

"I have lost my way. I seek one, Mr. Craw ford, who has taken up his abode at Lilac Lodg If you cannot direct me to the lodge I pray y give me shelter."

There was a pause for a moment or two, as if th man was consulting some one, and then the voi cried again—

"I cannot direct you to the lodge. So com here. You will find a break in the hedge a littl to your right. Pass through it and advanc boldly."

Jacob Butler at once followed the fellow advice, but had not advanced far when he foun himself sinking into a swamp.

"Help! help!" he cried, "I am sinking i a swamp. Help! I have lost my way. Help m to find it and you shall be well rewarded!"

"Ha! ha! ha!" burst forth the terrible laug and high overhead Jacob Butler beheld Spring Heeled Jack leaping from tree to tree, his eye gleaming with a lurid light as he glared dow upon the secretary.

"Ho! ho! ho! Jacob Butler," he cried, "wh do you not hasten on your journey? Your maste awaits your coming with impatience. Fly to hi and tell him how well you have carried out hi orders Ha! ha! ha! he wants the money. Ho ho! ho!"

Although this strange being seemed so delighte at the miseries of the secretary, he seemed to hove near him, as if unwilling that he should encounte any actual danger. In that case in all probabili Jack would have assisted him.

But Jacob was able to crawl out, and then th monster, with another fearful shriek, disappeare as suddenly as he had appeared.

Swearing and vowing vengeance, Jacob, afte much trouble, managed to find the road agai and staggering on he succeeded at last in discover ing the lodge.

No sooner did he announce himself than he foun Mrs. Corcoran, who was already installed as house keeper, awaiting his arrival anxiously.

The two had met on several occasions before and knew each other's business thoroughly, s that no compliments passed between them.

"Well; so you have come at last. A pretty state Sir Roland's in, and you are in a pretty state also. Why, how in the name of evil did you ge into that plight?"

"I have no time to gossip now. Get me some brandy, you hag."

# SPRING-HEELED JACK,

## THE TERROR OF LONDON.

SPRING-HEELED JACK EFFECTUALLY PREVENTS THE CONSPIRACY.

No. 10.

"You would not have time to drink it if the hag did get it for you," sneered the old woman. "There goes Sir Roland's bell again. He has not ceased ringing it for the last two hours every five minutes. I would not be in your shoes for something."

"I must wash some of this mud off before I go into the presence of Sir Roland," cried Jacob.

"I know nothing of that," chuckled the woman. "I shall go and tell him you are here. Then you can settle the matter between you, and I shall not be to blame."

With that she hobbled away and entered the room which Sir Roland was pacing.

No sooner did Sir Roland hear of his secretary's arrival than he thundered forth an oath, and commanded that Jacob should instantly appear before him.

"Now, for impudence and courage to defend me!" thought Jacob, as he walked boldly into the room.

"Well?" cried Sir Roland, angrily. Then, pausing in surprise, he said—"What is the meaning of this appearance?"

"Wait!" said Jacob, quietly, and, walking to the table, he filled himself from a decanter which stood thereon a bumper of brandy, and tossed it off at a draught.

"What is the meaning of this insolence? Are you drunk?"

"No!"

And he filled himself another glass, and drank as before.

"Mad?"

"Almost. You would be quite so, if you had seen and heard what I have to-night."

"Where is the money?" demanded Sir Roland, who began to think that his secretary must be overcome with drink.

"I don't know."

"Don't know? Have you not procured it, as I directed?"

"Oh! yes. I procured it all right; but it is now in the hands of Spring-Heeled Jack. Be patient, Sir Roland, and I'll tell you all. Besides, I have a message—a terrible message to you."

"Be brief, then, for I have but little patience to hear you out."

Then Jacob Butler commenced a history which did more credit to his imagination than to his truthfulness.

Never had Spring-Heeled Jack appeared half so hideous, terrible as he was, than as he appeared to Jacob, and never had he done such astounding tricks.

He had by a wave of his hand made the secretary powerless. Then he had taken away the money. After which by another wave of the hand he had rendered the horse mad, so that Jacob was thrown into the Thames.

Not content with this, Spring-Heeled Jack had sat himself upon the waters, and floated down the river by his side, laughing and jeering at him.

"Can this be possible?" exclaimed Sir Roland, in surprise.

"Perfectly, I assure you, Sir Roland. I do not ask you to believe it, for I think I should almost doubt it myself, even if my own father had told me, and he was a man who always stuck to the truth."

"And this message that this impostor sent me?" stammered Sir Roland.

For a moment Jacob looked down, and seemed unable to reply.

"Why do you hesitate?" demanded Sir Roland, suspiciously; "you have not completed your story?"

"I fear your anger, Sir Roland, if I repeat the fiend's very words."

"Fear not; I have met the fellow, and we have come to a bargain."

"A bargain! You don't mean to say that you have sold yourself to the devil right out?"

"And if I had, sirrah, what would that matter to you? I can look after my own affairs."

"Well, Sir Roland, I mean no offence; but, if that be the case, after what I have seen to-night and heard to-night, I wish you would look after your own affairs. I reckon I am a match even for lawyers, but I am not in it when it comes to the devil."

The earnestness with which the artful villain said this made an impression even upon Sir Roland Ashton.

"Nonsense—nonsense! Jacob, you must know that I would not do that."

"Well, I must own, Sir Roland, he did not speak in a friendly way about you—in fact, he was so uncomplimentary that I scarcely like to repeat what he did say."

"Fear not; I shall not blame you for what he said. Take some brandy and proceed."

Jacob did take some brandy, and, as he drunk it, began to consider what he should say.

Then the time came, and he plunged into the matter at once.

"'Tell Sir Roland,' cried this fiend, 'that I know that he has no right to the title and the estates he holds; that he caused the murder of Herbert Leigh—aye! and many others too. Tell him that Harland hath summoned me to his aid, and we have sworn never to let him have rest until he is stretched cold and dead, as many of his victims have been. Warn him that his only chance is repentance and reparation, if not his doom is fixed, and no hand can stay it.' Then the terrible fiend disappeared, and the numbness of my limbs ceasing, I swam ashore, and made my way on foot here. I trust I may never pass so fearful a night again."

Sir Roland, although he attempted to conceal the fact, was greatly moved by the story he had heard from Jacob Butler.

He paced up and down the room several times, muttering curses to himself.

At last he paused at the table, and having drank off a glass of brandy, laughed—

"This Spring-Heeled Jack, in one way, is a fool. Does he think to terrify me by his threats and absurd pranks. If so he is mistaken. My mind is made up and my plans formed, and nothing, no, not even the devil himself, shall turn me aside."

"Out of the great respect and affection I have for you," whined Jacob, "I would implore you to consider before you make any rash step, sir."

"Silence, hound! Do you think that I have the same cur-like spirit as you have? No; I defy those who threaten me, and by fair means or foul I will carry my own way—aye! and have my revenge."

"Another insult," thought Jacob. "You shall not be the only one, Sir Roland, who will have his own way AND REVENGE."

"I have already defied this fellow, but cannot bring him to book. Now he has robbed me twice, and I will set the runners on to him. To-morrow see that five hundred pounds reward is offered for him dead or alive. Fear not, I will arrange matters with the Government."

"You had better let me communicate with the Home Office first, Sir Roland. A reward for the capture of a man who has robbed you. To capture him alive is nothing—a reward for his death means murder."

"Well, well, Jacob, do as you please; but I doubt not that my vote in the House of Parliament would outweigh the death of a fellow who has proved himself a dread and nuisance to all London. But do it your own way, only let it be done quickly."

"It shall be done, Sir Roland, as you order. Of a truth, being so threatened, you need the greatest protection. Shall I date my letter from here, Sir Roland?"

"Are you mad? No. From Ashton Hall. My presence here must be kept a profound secret. Nobody must know it."

"One does."

"What do you mean? Here I am thought to be Mr. Crawford. No one knows—"

"Yes; one—Spring-Heeled Jack."

"Confusion! is this fellow ever to dog my path? I tell you, Jacob, that come what will I will carry out my purpose. My plans you shall hear afterwards. I must—I will succeed."

"I trust your worship may. You must have spent a fortune here."

"Aye!" cried Sir Roland, as he waved his hand towards the handsome fittings of the rooms. "I came here, and I found this place a hovel. See what I have made it—a palace—a perfect palace! Truly your modern magician's wand is made of gold."

"In truth it is wonderful," said Jacob, as he glanced round in envy and admiration. "It must have cost a fortune."

"Tut! what of that? It may bring me one. Take that lamp and lead the way, and I will show you what I have made of this house."

Jacob did so, and his master led him through a suite of elegant rooms.

"There, Jacob, and when I came here spiders hung and built in the curtains, beetles crept on the floors, the damask of the furniture was eaten by the moth, whilst the rats ran rampant round the rooms."

"It is amazing, Sir Roland, truly amazing, and all this done in a few weeks?"

"You might almost say in a few hours. But more. When I came here I found the windows broken, and all are now repaired with coloured glass. Then the place hath the rich services fit for a countess."

"Wonderful! and what are the wonders in that other room, which is so closely barred and bolted?" demanded Jacob, as he pointed to the door of the haunted chamber.

A cloud passed over Sir Roland's brow.

"There is a mystery about that chamber, and therefore I propose to keep it closed."

"Haunted?"

"The idle gossips of the place say so—but then they say all the house is. Suffice it that I do not care to have that door opened. See that my orders are obeyed."

"Your will is law, Sir Roland, to your humble dependent, Jacob Butler."

"'Tis well. You see I have had strong oaken shutters put here to keep out thieves and ghosts. I think now that I can defy, in this stronghold, even Spring-Heeled Jack."

"Ha! ha! ha!" came the dreadful laugh from the haunted chamber, making both men start back in alarm.

"Keep out Spring-Heeled Jack!" came the dreadful voice. "Only the walls of the tomb shall do that, even if they succeed. Ha! ha! ha!"

Sir Roland drew his sword, and quickly unbolting the door, rushed in, to find the room empty and just as he had left it.

Staggering from the place, he closed the door and fastened it.

"Not a word of this to anyone," he whispered. "Do not breathe it to yourself."

"And do you mean still to follow up this—this—I know not what to call him."

"Most assuredly. The letter shall be written to-night to the Home Secretary and the police. I doubt not that in less than twenty-four hours Spring-Heeled Jack will be in Newgate."

Whether the baronet's belief came true our story will show.

---

## CHAPTER XXIX.

### THE ABDUCTION—SPRING-HEELED JACK'S WARNING.

THE night had come when Daisy, or Lottie Day, as she was now called, was to be carried off.

Sir Roland Ashton had taken every precaution to prevent failure.

Everything was suited to his plan, and the men whom he had engaged were hardened, unfeeling wretches, ready for any crime.

These men had been ordered to attend the theatre and having stationed themselves at different parts of the house, to be ready at a given signal to leap on to the stage and seize Lottie Day, and bear her off to a carriage, which was to be kept in waiting ready at the corner of the street.

Sir Roland Ashton had taken his seat in the stalls, and watched the performance with the greatest interest, so that he might discover the most opportune moment for the dastardly action.

Daisy appeared on the stage with a light bound.

The audience gave a roar of applause as Daisy entered, and as the Fairy-queen sang a topical song, full of meaning and hits at the aristocracy, and in praise of the working classes.

A song by no means truthful, but it told with the gallery and pit, who applauded to their uttermost.

It was near the time when the baronet had determined to give the signal, and he glanced round to see that all his people were in readiness.

When Daisy had finished her song, she stamped upon the stage and cried—

*"Spirit of the lonely brake,*
*Where there hides the venomed snake,*
*Bounded though the atmosphere,*
*Obey my call. Appear—appear!"*

Scarcely had she said the words when the other trap flew open, and a yell of horror arose from the audience, for the demon that appeared was not the fantastic and picturesque one which usually shot up before the audience, but Spring-Heeled Jack!

The ladies of the ballet fled in fear, leaving Daisy alone with the demon on the stage.

Almost swooning she crouched at his feet, gazing up at his terrible face.

"Daisy Leigh!" he cried in stern tones, "I have already warned you of the danger which surrounds you. Beware! for to-night the danger has come to a climax. There sits the villain who would ruin you for life. He calls himself plain Mr. Crawford, but he is Sir Roland Ashton."

"'Tis false !" cried Sir Roland, as he sprang to his feet. "Seize that mad impostor. There is a reward of five hundred pounds out for his capture, and I will double that amount to anyone who will take him dead or alive !"

"Ha ! ha ! ha !" roared Jack. "Let them who value their lives keep from my path. And you, Sir Roland, know from me that the day of your doom rapidly approaches. When it comes expect no mercy at my hands, for your sins have been so many and fearful, that to lighten the punishment for them one iota would be a crime. Your fate is sealed."

Uttering a sepulchral laugh, Spring-Heeled Jack bounded into the air, flew over the heads of the startled and terrified audience, reached the gallery, and turned round and faced the people as if he would have addressed them.

But he either altered his mind or perceived that they were too much afraid to listen to him.

With another fearful laugh he bounded through an open window and disappeared.

Before the actors or audience could recover from their terror Sir Roland sprang upon the stage, and, seizing the fainting Daisy, lifted her in his strong arms. Calling upon his retainers to follow him, and prevent any attempt at a rescue which might be made, he dashed off the stage with his lovely burden.

The cry aroused the actors and the audience to a sense of the crime which they had seen committed before their eyes.

They rose to attempt to rescue the poor girl.

But Sir Roland's men had been well selected, and were proficients in the noble art of self-defence.

The low comedian, Harry Banks, made a desperate rush after the baronet, but was received with a fearful blow from one of the pugilists that sent him flying into the orchestra.

And now the fight became general.

Blows were dealt right and left, many of them landing on the faces of those for whom they were least intended.

Women shrieked and fainted, men cursed and swore.

Never was there a scene of greater confusion inside a theatre, and, to make things worse, Robert Tugwell had, by the direction of Sir Roland, turned out the gas when the confusion was at the highest.

Luckily Joe Dimity preserved his coolness in the midst of all this confusion.

He had the gas turned on again and speedily re-lit. Then, placing himself in the centre of the stage, he cried—

"Ladies and gentlemen, I pray you to resume your seats. I can see that this is a plot to ruin me. Or, perhaps, the person who has done it considers that it is only a joke. If so, when I have brought this cruel night's work home to him, I can assure you that he shall find it no joke, for I'll have him punished if he be peer or peasant. A—"

He paused, for at that moment Harry Banks hurried on the stage, pale and trembling with excitement and rage.

"She's gone, guv'nor !" he cried. "The villains have carried her off. Old Tugwell declares that he was collared and held while some of the rascals bore her away."

"Who has gone ?" demanded Dimity, who, in the confusion, had thought Daisy had escaped with the rest of the ladies.

"Lottie Day !" almost screamed the infuriated actor. "The best and prettiest woman on the stage. She has been carried off by that scoundrel the baronet; but I'll find him out and then let him look to himself."

"Do you hear that, ladies and gentlemen ? There has been an outrage in my theatre. You have all been witnesses to it."

"And a pretty set of witnesses they are ?" said a voice in the gallery.

This remark, in spite of the terrible scene which had just happened, caused some laughter, as well it might, for black eyes were very popular; torn dresses and tresses seemed suddenly to have come into fashion; indeed, respectable as the audience really were, they had not that appearance.

"Don't laugh !" cried Mr. Dimity, angrily. "A young and beautiful girl has been ruthlessly dragged from my charge by villains. What may be her fate I know not. She may be the heiress of a large fortune, for a mystery overhangs her birth. Be that as it may, I here swear that I will not leave a stone unturned until I have found her, and punished the cowardly rascal who has caused this outrage to be committed."

Applause of the loudest kind met this announcement.

"I am not a rich man, by no means, but by hard and honest work I have managed to make some money. Now some of you may come across traces of this girl. Let them come to me at once, and let me know them. If these traces should lead to her discovery, I will present the person—man, woman, or child—with twenty pounds, and old Joe Dimity cannot say fairer than that."

"Three cheers for honest old Joe Dimity," cried Harry Banks.

After he had embraced the kind-hearted manager, and the audience having responded most lustily to the call, then slowly they arose and departed.

Gloom reigned over the company of Joe Dimity's theatre, for Daisy was loved by everyone.

The male part of the company hurried about, making inquiries at the inns and hotels, but to no purpose.

All they could learn was that a carriage had been heard driven away at a furious pace in the direction of London.

Then all clue ended, and, meanwhile, Daisy Leigh was in the power of her cruel oppressor.

She was thrust into the carriage, the baronet jumped in by her to support her with his arms; the door closed with a loud bang, and the coachman lashed the horses into full speed.

Away they dashed, and soon reached the wood.

No sooner had they entered its gloomy depths than Spring-Heeled Jack's demoniacal laughter could be heard—now from the right, now from the left, now in front, and now behind.

At length, with a terrific bound, he plumped down on the top of the carriage.

The coachman, in his fear, would have checked the horses.

But Sir Roland shouted from the inside of the carriage—

"Drive on—drive on ! or, by Heaven ! I will put a brace of bullets through you."

"Aye ! drive on as if the devil was behind you. Ha ! ha ! ha ! who knows but what he is—who knows ? How are you, Sir Roland ?"

And now Spring-Heeled Jack leaned over the top of the carriage and glared spitefully at the baronet through the right-hand window.

Sir Roland drew forth a pistol to fire, but Spring-Heeled Jack had disappeared before he had time to carry out his purpose.

"Ha! ha! ha!" yelled Spring-Heeled Jack, looking in at the left-hand window. "Ha! ha! ha! I see you have procured your lovely prize. But it shall never be yours."

"Who dare say so? I have her in my power and will keep her."

"I say so. Spring-Heeled Jack tells you that she shall never be yours."

"Fiend, I defy you!" cried Sir Roland; "and thus I prove it!"

As he spoke he discharged the pistol right in Spring-Heeled Jack's face.

The smoke cleared off and the malignant face still grinned on.

"Ha! ha! ha! Sir Roland. If that is the way you mean to defy me I think you had better try another plan. I will tell you good news. The constables have arrived and are on the search for me. Let them look out. Perchance they may meet me when they least expect it. For to-night, farewell."

With one of those wild supernatural yells which had in a great measure made his appearance and disappearance so terrible, he made a sudden leap, seized a branch of a tree which hung some distance above his head, swung himself up in it, and was gone.

"What am I to do, Sir Roland?" asked the terrified coachman.

"Drive on, you coward, or this girl may die. I will soon have this fellow in the bilboes; that will soon put an end to the lightness of his heels."

The carriage dashed on at full speed and soon arrived at Lilac Lodge.

Here they were received by Mrs. Corcoran.

"Ha—ha! Sir Roland," laughed the woman, right merrily, "so you have returned at last, and successful, I see."

"Yes," replied Sir Roland, somewhat sharply. "Don't stand there chuckling and crowing like an old hen, but lead the way to the room intended for this lady as she has swooned."

"Or pretended to do so; I understand all about it. This way, Sir Roland—this way. A bold heart commands success, and it deserves to do so."

"Ah, me! I have seen the time when—"

"Silence, woman," said Sir Roland, sharply, as he placed the still fainting Daisy on a sofa. "Silence, and get some wine to restore this lady."

Sir Roland, had he seen the scowl upon Mrs. Corcoran's face, would have doubted if he had done a wise thing to insult her.

She poured out a glass of wine, and throwing back the cloak which still enveloped Daisy, grumbled to herself.

"A nice lady, certainly—a common ballet girl! But she is beautiful, I must confess. Well, well, well! handsome is what handsome does—we shall see what this does."

The old woman, having relieved herself of these jeers at Daisy, set to work to bring her round.

The wine warmed her heart and made it beat with more activity.

The colour came back to her cheeks and lips, and, after having one or two deep sighs, she opened her beautiful eyes and gazed wonderingly around.

"She has come to herself, Sir Roland," whispered Mrs. Corcoran. "Shall I go and leave you alone with your charmer?"

"No, I will not speak to her to-night," said Sir Roland, hurriedly, in a whisper. "See that she has the finest raiment and the richest fare. Do not tell her who I am, but state that I love her dearly and will marry her."

The old woman looked up and gave a peculiar smile.

She had heard all about the strange marriage of Mrs. Levine.

"Ah! I know what you want," she said; "it shall be done. I agree with you that it is better that you should not be seen here alone on this night. The violence that has been used to capture her will make her less inclined to believe your protestations or to listen to your suit; it will be so fresh upon her mind."

"Do you think that she will ever forget it?" demanded Sir Roland, as he admired her secretly from a distance.

"Pish! of course she will. Is she not a woman? Give her fine clothes, dainty food, warm wines, and plenty of amusement, and she will forget everything."

"I trust in you," said Sir Roland, as he stole from the room. "See, she is awake."

No sooner was the door closed than Mrs. Corcoran hurried up to the couch where Daisy reclined.

"So, so, my pretty darling," she began, "you have recovered yourself at last? Upon my honour I thought I should have to send for the surgeon at one time. But you are better now. Your cheeks and lips, which had lost their tone, are now firm as in the fulness of health. Take this to drink."

Daisy, who was naturally thirsty from the excitement she had passed through, drank the contents of the glass which was offered her.

It was wine, and naturally increased her vitality.

"Come now, that is better. You will soon be as right as ninepence, and we shall be so jolly together. Have another glass. It will do you good."

Daisy waved the glass away and turned her weary head on the pillow.

"Well—well, perhaps you had better not at first take too much; but you will soon grow to like it. But good wine should never go a-begging, so I'll drink this."

And in one gulp the good wine had disappeared.

"Where am I?" demanded Daisy. "Who brought me here?"

"Ah! that's tellings," chuckled the old woman. "Don't you be alarmed, dearie. You are with them who will take good care of you."

"But why should I not know who I am with?" demanded Daisy.

"Because his lordship forbids it, miss—that is all I know."

"His lordship?" exclaimed the girl, in surprise.

"Lah! to think that I should have been so foolish as to let that slip out. But there—there, I know that you, who are a dear, good girl, Daisy, will not get a poor old woman into trouble for the slip of the tongue."

"I have no wish to get anyone in trouble," replied Daisy. "But why have I been brought here?"

"Because his lordship loves you, and would make you his lady."

With eyes flashing fire Daisy leaped from her couch and faced Mrs. Corcoran.

"Do you think that I would be forced into marriage with a man I do not love—nay, a man I do not know? Never!"

"Think, dearie, think! He is a fine gentleman—immensely rich—a nobleman! Look at that! Why, you ought to be thankful that he has carried you away from those disreputable strolling actors you were with."

"Thankful! Whoever he may be, I hate him for it. What right had he to take me away against my will? They were honest and good people, who, out of kindheartedness, did their best to help me, a poor, ill-used stranger. Let me go back to them. I remember all now. Let me go back to them."

"If so be that you are really foolish enough to prefer a mummer to a lord all I can say is I truly pity you," replied Corcoran.

"You pity me? Then you will be my friend—you will help me to leave this hateful place?" pleaded Daisy, misunderstanding the other's words.

"Nay, child; I dare not do that. You do not know the power his lordship has. Why, my head would not be safe on my shoulders two minutes if I did that. Great men like he fear no crime. They are tried by their peers, and their peers forgive them."

"Then what am I to do?" cried Daisy, imploringly. "I will not stop here."

"Hush! hush!" said Mrs. Corcoran, seeing the advantage she had gained over Daisy by saying that she was sorry for her. "Do as I tell you and all will be well. I have great influence with his lordship."

"You?"

"Yes; I am his foster-mother. Do you see? I will tell him that you do not love him—that you wish to rejoin your friends. Oh! he is a good-hearted gentleman, and will do much for me. Then your pretty pleading ways and sweet tearful face must move him to compassion. But you must not cross him."

"Must not cross him? I know not what you mean."

"Tut, child! Are you a schoolgirl? To-morrow his lordship will come to pay you his respects. Receive him kindly with smiles—"

"Never! The man who so ruthlessly tore me from my friends can only receive scorn from me."

"You little fool!" cried Mrs. Corcoran, stamping with rage she could scarcely help showing. "You little fool! will you not be guided by me? If not, look to yourself. I wash my hands of the whole matter."

Daisy feared that she might in her indignation have lost a good friend, and therefore hastened to ask what she should do to win the favour of the old lady.

"Why, dearie, there is not much to do," said the old woman, coaxingly, to the trembling girl. "His lordship, I tell you, wishes to make you his lady. Well, he don't like those theatrical things, and wishes you to put on these fine clothes and jewels, which he has had prepared for you. No great hardship in that, I should think."

"Perhaps you would not, but I should prefer my humble garments," replied Daisy.

The old woman looked snarlingly at the girl, as she answered—

"But his lordship would not. Do you think the tinsel gewgaws can give pleasure to a nobleman? No; I tell you it must be done to win his favour."

"Why should I try to win his favour?" demanded Daisy.

"In that you may please yourself, but I warn you not to gain his anger. He is a man who never forgives—a man whose love is a fierce passion, and whose hatred is a rage. Beware! Will you wear the clothes? They cannot hurt you. The jewels are handsome."

"I care not for them."

"Would they were mine."

"I would they were. You are welcome to them for my part."

"Ha! that is all very well, but what would his lordship say?"

Mrs. Corcoran continued to speak of his lordship; for, although she knew Sir Roland had no right to that title, yet she fondly imagined that it would make some impression on Daisy.

"Well, well—what next?" demanded the girl.

"That you will partake of these splendid viands and wines," said Mrs. Corcoran, as she indicated with her hand a small table on which meats, fruits, and wines were spread. "That is all. Surely you cannot object to that. Now, shall I help you to change your clothes?"

"No," said Daisy, quickly; "leave me a little while alone so that I may think the matter over and determine how to act. My head aches."

This request was so reasonable that Mrs. Corcoran would have injured her own cause by complaining at it.

She therefore put on the best grace she could, and bidding Daisy to rest awhile and think, for she would not return for an hour or more to hear her decision, she left the room, closing the door after her.

Daisy waited some few moments listening attentively.

Being satisfied that she was not being watched, she crept to the window and looked out.

Nothing to be seen but the dark branches of the trees as they tapped with twig-like skeleton fingers against the panes.

She then tried the sill, but found that shut and securely fastened—she could not tell how, for there was no sign of bolt or bar.

Still it was so fastened that she could by no means shake it, let alone open it.

She next turned her attention to the door.

That appeared bolted on the other side and unopenable.

She knew that she was a prisoner, and throwing herself upon her couch gave way to grief.

After a time her grief subsided, and, girl-like, she began to admire the jewels and dresses.

They were, indeed, of the richest and finest kind, and moved the young heart to longing.

In the midst of this occupation she was startled by a strange voice.

She started up and gazed around.

In the corner of the room was a handsome, old-fashioned screen, and from behind this she felt the strange voice must come.

"Who are you and what do you want with Daisy Leigh?" she demanded. "Speak, and do not fill my heart with dread!"

"Fear not, Daisy Leigh, I am a friend of yours, as I was to your father, and will serve you as I would have done him had I been nearer. May I approach you?"

"First tell me your name!" cried Daisy, who, after having gone through so many dangers, was naturally afraid of new enemies.

"Hush! speak not so loudly," replied the voice. "My name at present I dare not tell, but men know me by the title of Spring-Heeled Jack."

Daisy's first idea was to rush to the door and scream for help. Then she remembered that whatever the character of the strange creature was, to her he had always proved a true friend.

For all that it was not without some little trepidation that she bade him approach.

Then from behind the scene the gaunt figure of Spring-Heeled Jack appeared, but his face wore not that hideous aspect which it generally did, it was calm, and no phosphorescent light played round the mouth or eyes,

"Fear not, maiden," he said, in a calm voice, "believe me, I am your friend."

"I do believe it. Why should I do otherwise? Have you not proved yourself so?"

"I have tried to, but not always succeeded," he said, with clouded brow.

"Ah! you failed at the theatre, to-night," said Daisy, sadly.

"Not altogether, Daisy Leigh," he replied. "I had wished to save you and spare one for a little further time, but, perhaps, now that it has happened, it is all for the best. Fear not but that I will protect you here. I have a power over this man which he cannot shake off, and dare not defy. Know you who this man is?"

"No; but I have heard that he is a lord, a noble."

"He is no true noble. He is a scoundrel who has raised himself by every class of villainy a man could practice. Be warned, Daisy Leigh, wear not those dresses, touch not the wine and fruit!"

"If I refuse, the good woman here who has promised to protect me may cease to be my friend."

"Good woman! there is no good woman here except yourself."

"How?" cried Daisy, in the greatest alarm. "I understand you not."

"This woman, whom you call good, is by profession a poisoner."

"Great Heavens! then I am indeed lost," exclaimed Daisy.

"Not so. Avoid what they give you to eat or drink; refuse boldly to wear their clothes, and all will be well."

"The food indeed may be poisoned, but the clothes and jewels?"

"Are stained with blood!"

"Blood?"

"Aye! your father's blood! This man, who calls himself Sir Roland Ashton, was the cause of your father's murder. Although he himself did not strike the blow he directed the hand that did so. But fear not; your father's death shall be fully avenged. Be firm. Refuse all that they offer you, and all will be well. Each morning and night a store of provisions shall be placed behind that screen, to which you can help yourself, and fitting clothes shall also be placed there for your use. Will you obey me?"

"I will."

"Till then, sweet girl, adieu! When the hour of trial comes I shall be near to save you."

With remarkable grace he waved her a kiss and disappeared behind the screen.

She waited some moments and then peeped behind the screen.

Spring-Heeled Jack had gone. Gone, but how she could not tell.

But he had already kept his word, for there was a basket of provisions, wine, and some simple but good female attire placed ready for her use.

Of the latter she quickly availed herself; and feeling sure that she had true friends near her, threw herself upon the couch, when she wondered over the mystery until, worn out with fatigue, she fell asleep.

---

## CHAPTER XXX.

### THE CAPTORS CAPTURED—OR, THE CONSTABLES IN A TRAP.

"DICK CATCHPOLE, I tell you that we are going the wrong way."

"And I tell you, Elias Grabham, that we are making our way to the inn, as straight as we can go. Look there, Grabham; there is the light. Now what do you say?"

"Well I certainly admit that there is a light, which nobody can deny, but I don't think that it is the light we want."

"You are so stubborn."

"And you are so obstinate."

"Come, come, Grabham, it won't do for you and I to quarrel. When we came down here we agreed that we would go shares over this matter of Spring-Heeled Jack, and I am willing enough to stick to my word; and I'm sure, as an old pal and brother officer, you are to stick by yours. If we have lost a day looking for the fellow it can't be helped, and if we share the reward, five hundred pounds, that is two fifty for each of us, I do not think we should grumble."

"Right you are, Dick Catchpole, and there's my hand upon it. But you will pardon me for saying that I don't think this is the right way to the inn."

"Then you're a fool," replied Grabham, forgetting his peaceful intentions.

Dick Catchpole was about to make a somewhat sharp answer to this speech, which was certainly more true than polite, when a tall figure, dressed in a very long black cloak and slouched hat, stepped from a side-path and addressed them politely—

"I beg your pardon, gentlemen, but I heard—at least I fancy I did—some dispute about yonder light. As I am a native about this part of the country, perhaps I can tell you what it is and settle the dispute."

"I say it is the inn," said one.

"And I say it is not," said the other. "When we left it we came the other way."

"You are both right, gentlemen—both right—only when you left the inn you must have left it by the front door."

"In course we did."

"Well, that light comes from the back entrance, so you are both right, one declaring it was the light from the inn, and the other that it was not the light from the entrance where you left. So, at least, I understood you. Therefore you are both quite right."

"Dash my buttons if I ever thought of that!" said Catchpole.

"By the Lord Harry, but you are a sharp one," said Grabham; "you would make a first-class constable."

"Oh! no; do not flatter me. I could never hope to be so clever as those gentlemen are. Am

I mistaken in thinking that you gentlemen belong to that noble body of men?"

"You've hit it again," said Mr. Catchpole. "We hail from Bow-street."

"Ah! I thought so. May I ask the nature of the business which has brought you down here?"

"Not if I know it," said Mr. Grabham, placing his forefinger to his nose.

"Oh! I only asked, not out of curiosity, I can assure you, but because I fancied that I might know something of the matter, and so put you on the right track of the person for whom you are seeking."

"Well, I don't know, but perhaps you might. But who do you think we want?"

"A fellow who has wondrous agility, and is called Spring-Heeled Jack."

"By Jove! governor, what a fellow you are! You know everything."

"Not quite, but I do know something of this fellow. He will be very difficult for you to catch."

"Bah! Once let us get our claws on him, and he shall not escape, I warrant you. You country folk know very little of what we town-bred men can do. Let me once get hold of Spring-Heeled Jack—a firm grip, you know—and I warrant that he will not leap out of my clutches."

"Neither will he out of mine," laughed Catchpole. "Sir Roland Ashton has put too much on his capture for that. I only wish I had him now."

"Your hands, my good fellows. I see you are men of courage."

"We have to be, seeing the work we have to do," replied the men as they shook hands with the stranger.

"And would you really seize upon this desperate character, man or fiend, Spring-Heeled Jack, and capture him?"

"Only give us the chance. Don't I tell you that he shall not escape if once we get hold of him? You seem a good-hearted fellow. Come and show us the way to the inn, and over a glass of grog tell us what you know about this remarkable fellow."

"I cannot spare the time to-night. Besides, I have nothing much to tell that the whole of England does not know; only I know that he is in this wood to-night."

"Are you sure of that?"

"As certain as I am here. I saw him not long ago, bounding over these hedges and ditches more like a kangaroo than a man."

"And were you not frightened?" demanded Catchpole.

"Not I. As far as I have heard Spring-Heeled Jack never did any harm to anyone who did not propose to do harm to him. Therefore, I do not fear him. But you—"

"Well, what of us?" demanded Grabham, quickly. "What of us?"

"Why, if you have come down to seize him at the instigation of Sir Roland Ashton I do not think that he is likely to treat you with much respect, for he has—or at least it is supposed that he has—a bitter grudge against that person. Whether it be right or wrong I will not pretend to say."

"Right or wrong we don't care. We have nothing to do with the justice of the case. We have our orders to lock him up, and we will, too."

"Aye! that we will. We care nothing about the prisoners' guilt or innocence. All we have to do is to get them into prison, and then the judges can hang or pardon them as they think fit. We get our reward, and that is all we care about. Ain't it, Dick?"

"I should think so, Elias," laughed Dick; "and now we know that our man is so near us we will make our way down to the inn, and if our friend here will accompany us to drink to our success why he is welcome. That is all I have to say about it."

"I thank you kindly for your offer, but must at the present refuse. Perhaps I may join you later on. Tell them I wish you all the success your high merits deserve. This road takes you straight to the inn—you cannot miss it. I shall most likely meet you again. Until then I must bid you adieu."

The stranger bowed slightly, pulled his cloak further round him, and strode away.

"A strange fellow that!" muttered Dick Catchpole, uneasily.

"What's strange about him? I don't see anything strange in him. You are always so precious suspicious."

"And you are always so stupidly trustful. I don't like that man."

"I do," retorted Elias Grabham. "He was a thorough gentleman, for did he not refuse to drink at our expense, and yet warned us about this Spring-Heeled Jack?"

"That's just what I don't like. No honest man ever refuses a drink, especially at somebody else's expense."

Now, these two men, Dick Catchpole and Elias Grabham, were sworn friends, and really and truly loved each other like brothers.

They hunted up thieves together; they shared the rewards they gained, and when in London lodged in the same house.

Yet for all this they never missed wrangling and jangling with each other.

Nay, they very frequently sulked with each other for days.

They even went so far as to come to blows, but they very soon afterwards shook hands, and were as thick as it is said those gentlemen are whom it was their duty to capture—namely, thieves.

Marching along the road to the inn Mr. Catchpole managed to make himself particularly disagreeable, and consequently Mr. Grabham had retaliated with more than his ordinary insults.

On this occasion the sulks set in, and that to a very unusual degree even for these fellows.

Hands thrust in their pockets, heads bent sullenly down, they walked on in silence, when suddenly Mr. Grabham's foot kicked against something.

He muttered an oath and kicked what he considered a stone into a ditch.

Now Mr. Catchpole's sharp ears had caught the chink of gold; so he walked quietly to the ditch and picked up that which his comrade had so carelessly and angrily kicked away.

He thrust it in his pocket, for it was a bag of gold, and humming a tune walked on his way.

Grabham's curiosity was aroused, but the sulks would not let him speak.

As they reached the inn, however, curiosity overcame temper, and he asked—still in a surly tone though—

"What was that you picked up just now, Dick Catchpole?"

"What is that to you, Elias Grabham?"

"Well, I know it is something of value, or you would not have stooped to pick it up."

"May be it is—may be it is not," growled Dick. "At all events, it is mine."

"I cry shares," said Grabham, now convinced it was of value.

"Too late," replied Catchpole; "you should have called 'halves' when I picked it up."

With that he walked chuckling into the parlour of the inn.

Now, as the reader will perceive, neither Dick Catchpole or his comrade were pleasant men, or affable ones; but for all that we must own they were honest, at least, to each other.

Catchpole had not the slightest intention of disputing his old friend's claim to shares; but Elias had put him out, and he enjoyed putting Elias out.

The tap room was empty, so seating himself at a table, Catchpole called for a bottle of rum and two glasses. That being brought, he filled the glasses, and with a triumphant smile playing round his lips he pushed one glass over to his friend and invited him to drink.

"I don't want your rum," growled the other. "I want my share of what you found."

"Oh! if you won't drink you must leave it alone," replied the other. "I like my liquor too well to quarrel with it."

And he tossed off another bumper of neat spirits, and then another.

The temptation was too much for Grabham to withstand.

In the most absent manner possible he drew the glass towards him.

Then he let it remain for a little while untouched.

Then he raised it to his lips, and drank off the contents, and filled again.

"That's better. Now we will finish the bottle, and say no more about my find."

"Your find! Come, I like that. Wasn't it as much my find as yours?"

"Most certainly not. Did I not pick it up?"

"Yes; but then I was walking with you. We agreed to share over this job as we have done over lots of others."

"We agreed to share over the capture of Spring-Heeled Jack, I admit, but this has nothing to do with him."

"How do you know that? I want my share;" this in a bullying tone.

Both men had been drinking freely, and became heated.

"Then you won't get it. Besides, you kicked it away."

"Then it is as I suspected. I did find it first. At least show it to me."

Catchpole could not refuse this, and drew forth what proved to be a good-sized bag of gold.

How Elias Grabham's eyes glittered when he beheld this!

He was now more determined than ever to have a share of it.

"Come, Catchpole," he said, "this is too good a find for you to keep all to yourself. I must have my share."

"Not a guinea. Ha, ha! don't be in such a hurry to kick things out of your path another time. Lor'! this will be a standing joke against you as long as you live."

"Look here, Catchpole!" cried Elias, now fairly mad with passion at his loss, "you know, as well as I do, that you have no more right to that gold than I have. It ought to be returned to its lawful owner. Now, finding it don't make it yours."

"Don't it? Possession is nine points of the law, and I mean to keep it."

"Now, if you don't share half-and-half with me, I will give notice to the authorities of the find, and also to the lord of the manor, and we shall soon see where you are then."

"You will, will you? Do your worst; I defy you. Go and round on me, old pal."

"You are a nice one to call yourself a pal," sneered Elias Grabham; "you, who will not go fair shares with him."

"Not a guinea! I ain't one to give way before threats, I can tell you."

As he spoke he reached forward to take the bag, in order that he might replace it in his pocket.

This was more than Elias could stand, and he seized the bag also.

A struggle instantly ensued.

Both men were broad built, strong fellows, and with hasty tempers.

The bag of gold was dropped upon the table, and they grappled together.

Backwards and forwards they pulled each other, now one seeming to have the mastery and now the other.

At last, from wrestling they came to blows, and fought manfully.

Who was the better man it was hard to tell, for they fought until they were quite exhausted, and, separating, paused to take breath.

At that moment the window flew open, and Spring-Heeled Jack bounded into the room.

Seizing the collar of Catchpole's coat in one hand and that of Grabham in the other, he swung them round with wonderful strength—such was his tremendous power—and dashed their heads together as if they had been boys instead of grown-up men.

"Ha! ha! ha!" he roared. "What think you now of Spring-Heeled Jack? Is he to be so easily caught? Do you think that you will have the reward? Ha! ha! ha!"

And at each question he dashed their heads together.

"Mercy! help!" gasped Catchpole, who now was bleeding fast.

Elias Grabham said nothing, for he could not speak on account of his teeth being knocked down his throat.

"Mercy! Oh! you ask for mercy, do you? You, who never granted it to any one whom you seized—you, who are thieves yourselves."

"No, no, Mr. Spring-Heeled Jack; we are not thieves, but good, honest men, whose duty it is to protect all worthy citizens from criminals."

"Nice protectors, truly. Call you Sir Roland Ashton an honest man? And you would do his bidding, let it be what it might!"

"No, no, sir. Oh! do let us go, and we promise never to take you."

"Promise never to take me. Ha! ha! ha! Why you could not do it."

"Oh! if we once get away from you we will never cross your path again—we swear it."

"If I thought you would do otherwise I would take one under each arm and fly away with you."

"No, no; think of our wives and children, good Mr. Devil," implored Catchpole.

"That money on the table is mine; I placed it there for you to find. I knew you could not withstand the bait of gold. Gold, which is a blessing or curse to man, as he uses it."

"You may have the gold, sir. We do not want it!"

"Ha! ha! ha! You are generous with that which does not belong to you. Listen to me, and obey my orders, or worse will come of it."

"We will—we will! We'll do anything for you. Only leave us."

"Seek out Sir Roland Ashton; you will find him at the house in the wood. Tell him what has happened; refuse the pursuit of me."

"Oh! that we will," cried Catchpole, eagerly.

"You had better, for this is little to what shall happen to you if you dare disobey me; and now, farewell."

Hurling the men on one side, he seized the bag of gold and leaped out of window.

"He's the devil himself," groaned the affrighted Catchpole.

## CHAPTER XXXI.

### ROGUES IN COUNCIL.

SIR ROLAND was surprised when the two constables called upon him at Lilac Lodge, but hearing their business from Jacob Butler, who had at first declared only Mr. Crawford lived there, he at once admitted them to his presence.

Two more unfortunate-looking creatures than these luckless men could not well be imagined.

They had bruised themselves pretty considerably in their fight; but that had been nothing to the contusions which Spring-Heeled Jack had showered upon them, or, rather, had caused them to give each other.

Blackened eyes, swollen noses, cheeks bearing what the gentlemen of "the science" are pleased to call "mice," were among the number.

To add to this their clothes were stained with blood, and their linen collars and shirt fronts had the appearance of having been mangled in a very improper way.

The baronet looked at them with considerable surprise.

"Well, gentlemen," he said, at last, "you have found me out."

"Yes, Sir Roland—if you are Sir Roland," said Catchpole.

"I am Sir Roland. Now, my men, to your business quickly."

"All right, your honour; only we have a message for Sir Roland's ear alone, and when we came here we were told that only a Mr. Crawford lived here."

"Mr. Crawford and Sir Roland Ashton are one. It is a name I take when I wish to be in perfect privacy. Doubt not that I have reasons for it. But who has pierced my secret and told you that I am here?"

The two men looked at each other as well as their blackened eyes would let them, and then glanced nervously round the room.

"What ails the fellows?" cried Sir Roland, who had watched their movements with surprise and anger. "What do you fear? Speak out!"

"The creature that sent us," said Catchpole, "was no other than Spring-Heeled Jack."

"Ha! but you can tell him from me that I will have no dealings with him."

"I would not do it for a thousand pounds," replied Catchpole.

"Bah! you need not fear him. I have two constables from London who will soon have him in prison."

The two men shook their heads and sighed sadly.

"Those two constables will never place hands on Spring-Heeled Jack."

"What do you mean, fellow? Do you doubt my word or the force of the law?"

"Neither, Sir Roland. Constables may be found who can arrest this Spring-Heeled Jack, but not the two who came down here. *We are the two constables!*"

"You!"

"Yes."

"Then what is the meaning of this disgraceful appearance? I ordered—and was told my orders had been obeyed—two of the smartest men in the force."

"And as such we are reckoned. Truth to tell, I don't think any two men in all the body of constables in Great Britain smart more than we do at this precious minute. Do you, Elias?"

Elias groaned and shook his head sadly, then groaned again.

"What has happened to you? Why does not that fellow speak?"

"Because he can't. He hasn't a tooth in his head."

"What has he done with them?"

"Swallowed them. Couldn't help it, poor fellow. They went against his stomach, but he was compelled to do it."

"Compelled! and who by?"

"Spring-Heeled Jack!"

Every time this name was mentioned the men glanced nervously round, as if they expected to see the dread phantom behind them.

"Confusion!" cried the baronet. "Is this fellow always to cross my path?"

"He says he will," says Catchpole, and then he delivered Spring-Heeled Jack's message.

"We shall see to that," said Sir Roland, with a hollow laugh. "Perchance I may be more than a match for him. Return to your duty, my brave fellows; catch this man, dead or alive, and I will double or even treble the reward. And, hark you, my men, if you can manage to kill him by accident you know I would give you another hundred pounds each. Do you hear?"

"Very much obliged for myself and partner, Sir Roland, but it cannot be done."

"Not be done! Why, what do you mean?"

"I mean that I don't think there is a chance of killing this fellow. He is not a man, but a demon from the deepest depths of the bottomless pit."

"What can this man be who changes you from brave men—and such I heard you to be from your officers—into cowards?"

"A devil!"

"A devil! Well, devil or not, I will face him and conquer him yet. Would that he were here now."

Scarcely had he said the words than something darkened the window of the apartment.

The constables crouched down, and in silent horror pointed to the window, where there appeared the terrible form of Spring-Heeled Jack.

"Ha! ha! ha!" yelled the creature, as he spread out his long, bony arms. "Ha! ha! ha! Sir Roland, am I not kind in granting your wish? You desired to see Spring-Heeled Jack, and he is here to oblige you."

For a moment the baronet seemed overtaken with fear.

Quickly recovering himself, however, he rushed to the table and caught up a pistol.

He presented it with a rapid and good aim, and then fired.

The glass was smashed by the bullet, but as the smoke caused by the discharge cleared away Spring-Heeled Jack was still at the window.

He gave one of his horrible laughs and cried—

"Farewell for a time, Sir Roland—we soon shall meet again!" and with a bound disappeared from the window.

Sir Roland and the men hurried to the window and gazed out. They could not believe Spring-Heeled Jack was unhurt.

But they were mistaken. There he was, gamboling through the woods as merrily as ever; now and then glancing up at the window with a diabolical grin, as if he could see his foe and enjoyed his discomfort.

"The fiend is in him," muttered Sir Roland, loud enough to be heard.

"It's my belief that he is the fiend, Sir Roland," said Catchpole.

"And mine," mumbled Elias Grabham.

Sir Roland walked to a buffet, and taking therefrom a decanter of brandy and some glasses, filled one for himself and pointed to the men to do the same.

The two men eagerly accepted the offer, but when Grabham had taken his into his mouth he hastily spit it out, curled up, and writhed about, making the most hideous faces one could imagine.

"Why, what is the matter with the man?" demanded Sir Roland, angrily.

"Don't be angry with him, Sir Roland," said Catchpole. "It's the brandy has burned his gums. That's what it is. Take another glass of the spirit and toss it over your gums, down your throat. It will warm your heart and do it good."

"Aye! warm your heart; you need have something to warm your hearts if you are cowards enough to put up with the insults and injuries which you have received from that monster."

"Ah, the fiend!" said Catchpole, who since the money had gone had quite returned to the love of his old friend. "That fellow is the fiend, and no mistake. It's no good trying anything against him."

"Cowards! By your own confession you have been trapped, and that in a way which I do confess does more credit to his brain than yours. Be more cautious another time—assume disguises, and you may not only have your revenge, but become rich for life."

"Ah! it's all very fine to say get rid of your foe like that, but how are you to do it? I candidly confess that I don't see my way clear to manage it. I wish I could."

"Take some more brandy," said Sir Roland, who quickly perceived that he had made some impression upon the men. "Take some more brandy, and then draw near the table, and I will place before you a scheme which I have formed, and one which I think will be successful."

The men drank deep bumpers of brandy, and then drew up to the table.

"This is my scheme. This Spring-Heeled Jack has ordered you to London?"

"Yes, and in no very polite language either," said Catchpole.

"And you mean to go?"

"The moment I leave here, Sir Roland, I take the road to London."

"And you will do quite right," replied Sir Roland, quietly.

Messrs. Grabham and Catchpole were evidently much relieved by the baronet's approval of that movement, and, to show they were so, took advantage of his pushing the bottle towards them to drink a deep draught again.

"Yes; you must go. This fellow is evidently a very artful one."

"A good deal too artful for us," groaned Mr. Catchpole, sadly.

"Ah! you were duped. The stranger whom you met in the wood—he who directed you to the inn—he was Spring-Heeled Jack, and planned all this."

"Impossible! He did not look a bit like him," cried Catchpole.

Elias tried to make some remark, but, after a few gutteral sounds, he clapped his hands to his mouth, and became mute with agony.

"Lord love you, Sir Roland, I know what my pal would say."

"Indeed! You must be very quick of understanding then."

"Ah! but I have known him for years. We always agree to disagree."

"A very agreeable arrangement I should say," sneered Sir Roland.

"Well, I don't know that; but it works well. You see by that means we get to look at both sides of the question. He goes on one side, and I go on the other, and so between the two we knock out a happy medium, and very often nab the right man."

"And very often the wrong one," thought Sir Roland, but he did not say it.

"Ah! perhaps that is not such a bad idea after all, although I should be liable to find it a little bit confusing. But, then, I know nothing compared to you."

"I should think not," chuckled Mr. Catchpole, delighted at the compliment.

"Just so. Now, what I was going to suggest is this. You should return to London at once, report your failure and ill-usage to your superiors, and then retire on the sick-list; you need it."

"We do, we do. Nobody needs it more than we do. Curse the fellow!"

"Ah! he has done me much less injury than he has done you. But I swear I will have the deadliest revenge that wealth and power can command. Now, listen to me attentively."

"We are listening, Sir Roland."

"Good. When on the sick list I will allow you five pounds a week each."

"Five pounds a week each!" exclaimed Catchpole, and Elias clasped his hands in delight.

"Yes—on conditions. This Jack of the light heels goes about in all kinds of disguises. You must do the same. I am convinced that he is connected with some band of thieves or spies, who carry the information to him which he appears to gain by supernatural means, and help him in his cruel pranks. For all I know there may be two Spring-Heeled Jacks, and that is how he appears to travel so fast."

"By the Lord Harry, I never thought of that," cried Catchpole, smacking his leg. "You've hit it, and you have given me fresh life again."

"Then you agree to do as I order? Examine all the thieves' dens in London—in diguise, mind—and trace out this fellow. Do you agree?"

# SPRING-HEELED JACK,

## THE TERROR OF LONDON.

THE INTERVIEW BETWEEN SIR ROLAND ASHTON AND DAISY LEIGH.

"For myself and partner I do," said Catchpole.

"Good. Now go. Your remaining here longer would look suspicious, and we must keep this fellow in the dark."

"We'll have him yet," cried Catchpole, who had grown valiant over the brandy. "We will pay him out for his treatment of us."

"Remember, the reward holds good either dead or alive."

"I sha'n't forget the extra two hundred if he be shot in a scrimmage."

"Ah! it would be sad; but I should not regret it, I must confess."

Mr. Catchpole winked violently, and chuckled.

"Here is a week's salary for each, in advance," he continued, smiling.

"Thank your honour's honour kindly," cried Catchpole, as he and his componion took up the notes the baronet had placed upon the table. "Don't you fear, we'll put Master Jack in a box soon—a long black one—out of which he won't jump for a long time. Ho! ho! ho!"

Was that an echo, or was the laughter dimly repeated down below their feet?

Sir Roland saw the men waver.

He gave them more brandy, and then made them go.

"I will have revenge on this fellow," he said, when he was alone. "But I must smooth my features, as I must now visit my pretty little Daisy."

## CHAPTER XXXII.

SIR ROLAND TRIES TO TEMPT DAISY—HE MEETS SPRING-HEELED JACK FACE TO FACE, AND HAS REASON TO REPENT IT.

Daisy had been left undisturbed in her handsome apartments, but kept a close prisoner.

She soon found that Spring-Heeled Jack had been true to his promise.

He had not deserted her, but had kept her well supplied with provisions and wine as he had promised, all of which had been placed behind the screen in the mysterious manner in which the first had been placed, but she had never seen him again.

Mrs. Corcoran had expressed much astonishment as to where Daisy had obtained her new clothes, which she knew she had never supplied to her.

But as the girl simply said she had found them in the room, and, as far as Mrs. Corcoran could see, she had no other means of procuring them, she had to be content.

But there was the food and the wine; why was that not touched?

That was a greater mystery to Mrs. Corcoran than the clothes.

Not even one of the beautiful peaches had been tasted, and she felt certain that not a stopper had been removed out of one of the decanters. She was sure of this, for she examined them herself so often; and yet Daisy looked as fresh and well as ever.

The knowledge of a true friend being near had given her courage, besides which, in one of the baskets of provisions which Spring-Heeled Jack had left for her, she had found a small Spanish dagger, on which was tied a label bearing the words, "Strike and fear not."

This she had carefully concealed in the fold of her dress, taking the greatest care that the handle should be kept near to her hand, so that she might be able to draw it forth at the slightest show o' danger.

Now and then she could hear the weird laughter of Spring-Heeled Jack as he played his pranks and gambols through the woods.

She liked to hear it. She had long since ceased to fear it, and knew that sometimes it was given to show that a friend was near.

So matters had gone on for two or three days and nothing had happened.

Mrs. Corcoran came in now and then to visit Daisy, and although she could not conceal her ill-humour at the girl's refusal to don the apparel placed for her, or to eat of the different viands, yet she always spoke kindly and encouragingly to her captive.

On the evening of the day on which the constables had called upon Sir Roland, the old woman—who had persuaded Sir Roland not to visit the girl until she was better prepared—entered the room, and with a winning smile, said—

"Why, Daisy dear, how pale you look! Come, come, you must not fret. I tell you you will be at liberty soon. Ha! ha! that has brought the roses to your cheeks. Now you look your own beautiful self again."

"Mrs. Corcoran, how often have I told you that I cannot bear these compliments?"

"Compliments, forsooth! It is no compliment to tell a pretty girl she is pretty."

"It were better left alone," replied Daisy, with a wan smile. "Trust me, when a girl is pretty she will soon find it out for herself without any-one having to tell her."

"I'faith, you are right there, and such praise sounds fitter for a fine gentleman's lips than from those of an old woman like me. Am I not right?"

"If you mean it would sound well from the lips of the man who so foully tore me from my friends, I at once declare that it would not. I would sooner a hundred times hear him curse me. I hate him!"

With such vehemence and dramatic effect did Daisy say this that the old hag was startled.

"Nonsense, Daisy," she cried; "you must not speak like that. Remember, this fault, if it was a fault, was done out of love to you."

"Love to me!" exclaimed Daisy, in the greatest scorn. "Do not desecrate the word love by applying it to a man who could stoop to such an action. Do you think if I loved a bird that I should keep it in a cage if I saw it beating its wings and crying for liberty? No, it should go free, and if it loved me so little that it would not come back to my call, I should let it go and pray that it might be happy."

"You are a fool!" cried the old woman, startled at this outburst, and annoyed at finding that her pretended kindness had not had the effect she had hoped it would have. "Would you go back to those wretched strollers, and live a life of hardship when you might have one of luxury? Think! To be called 'my lady,' how delightful that would be—to be courted wherever you go—to have enough to spend on silks and satins, to—"

"Hold!" cried Daisy, in horror. "Are you also false? Can I trust no one in this horrible place? Am I alone? No; I defy his lordship's power, for I know there is one who will save me."

This speech gave the old woman no little amount of alarm.

In the first place, Daisy had placed a very strong emphasis on his "lordship."

Could she have found out that Sir Roland was not a lord?

If so, how had she done it?

She had been a captive, and yet knew who her captor was.

She had believed that he was a lord when she—Mrs. Corcoran—had first said so.

How, then, had she so suddenly changed?

Then, who was this one on whom she relied so much for protection?

Who could protect her in that solitary house, let alone save her?

No one.

The old woman felt sure of this, and banishing her fears, replied, curtly—

"I did but speak for your good; but as they say wilful men will have their way, what are you to expect from a woman? They are always more wilful than the men."

And here she burst into a loud laugh, and hurrying to the side table she poured out some wine into a tumbler.

Then with a quick action she drew from her bosom a small vial and poured into the wine a few drops of reddish fluid, after which she filled another glass of wine.

All this was done most carefully, so that Daisy should not see what she did.

"Come, dearie," she said, in the kindest tones she could assume, "come, we must not quarrel, you know, we must be friends. You know, dearie, that I would do anything to help you. Come, drink a glass of wine with me."

And she handed the doctored glass to Daisy, who took it almost in thoughtlessness.

"There's a good girl," chuckled Mrs. Corcoran. "Now we will drink together."

Daisy looked at her in a firm manner, but the old woman was so convinced that she had conquered that she did not notice this.

"Now let us drink good fortune to each other!" cried Mrs. Corcoran.

"Stay!" cried Daisy, as the old woman raised the glass to drink. "You have taken white wine and given me red."

"It's better for you, dearie," replied the old woman, with a smile on her lips and a scowl on her brow. "It is more strengthening, and will do you good."

"If that be true, good mother," said Daisy, who now suspected the old woman's truthfulness, "you should take the red wine and I the white."

"Nonsense, child, nonsense," said the old woman, quickly. "You are fretting, and need keeping up. Although I am old—and I would I were not—I need but little stimulant. A glass of the lightest wine would be quite enough for me."

"And me," replied Daisy, quietly; "I need no stimulant at all. My wrongs support me. So, my good Mrs. Corcoran, we will exchange glasses if you please, and then I will drink with you; but not until then."

"Now a plague seize upon her heart," thought old Mrs. Corcoran.

But she did not say so aloud, trying to laugh the girl into drinking.

It was no good.

Daisy was firm and refused all temptation.

"Have it your own way, miss," cried the old woman at last. "Do not drink with me if that be the return of all my kindness. I am sure I do not know why I should have plagued his lordship so about you. I had better have let him do just what he liked and closed my eyes to all your prayers and entreaties—all of which I believe to have been quite false. Now you may take care of yourself."

With that the old hag snatched the glass from Daisy's hand and placed it on the table.

Then she emptied her own glass, put that on one side, and hurried from the room, slamming the door after her—the door which closed with a secret spring and kept Daisy a prisoner.

Daisy rose from her couch and smelt the glass of wine.

There seemed to be nothing the matter with it. Could she be mistaken?

So lonely was she that she almost hoped that she had wronged the old woman and that she would forgive her.

"Perhaps if I drink the wine," she thought, "when she returns in a little time, which she is sure to do to wish me good-night, it may please her. Yes, I will drink it and tell her I did but joke to try her, that was all."

She raised the glass to her mouth to drink, but scarcely had the rim touched her lips when a stern voice—which came from where she knew not—uttered a warning.

"Daisy Leigh! Daisy Leigh!—beware. Did I not warn thee never to touch the food or drink supplied thee by thy most deadly foe? Disobey me and you shall perish. Obey me and you will be saved."

Daisy placed the glass down and turned quickly round to discover where the speaker was.

The room appeared to be empty, and yet the voice seemed to come from close behind her.

"Generous man, spirit or whatever thou art," she said, "I thank thee for thy warning. Tell me, is this woman treacherous also? Am I to trust no one?"

No answer came to this eager question.

A dead calm seemed to hang over the room almost as a funeral pall.

"Could I have imagined this?" she thought, as she tottered back to the couch.

Again the silence was disturbed by a softly-breathed sentence.

"No, Daisy Leigh, you have not imagined this. The hour is come, the enemy approaches, but the rescuer is near; be courageous, fear nothing, and all will be well."

"Am I mad?" exclaimed Daisy, as she sprang from her couch. "Am I dreaming that I hear this strange voice? At least I will show that I have courage."

With that she seized the lamp, and drawing forth her dagger carefully searched the room.

No signs of anyone there, not even behind the screen.

Indeed, her usual basket of provisions was not there, a thing which gave her some uneasiness, for she knew that if the hour of danger were not nigh, Spring-Heeled Jack would never have forgotten that.

Scarcely had she returned to her couch when the door opened and Sir Roland Ashton entered the room.

Daisy pretended to be asleep, but she grasped the hilt of her dagger.

"It is well," said Sir Roland to himself, "she sleeps. Then she must have drank the wine. How beautiful she is."

He stooped down and kissed her cheek softly.

Daisy's heart beat violently, but she never spoke, appearing to sleep still.

Presently, supposing her to be under the influence of the drug, he placed his arm around her waist.

In a moment the indignant girl had thrown him off and stood up boldly facing him.

"What means this intrusion?" she demanded, her eyes flashing fire.

"Intrusion! May I not visit my charming guest?" said Sir Roland, softly.

"Your guest! You mean your prisoner. Do not try to deceive me, Sir Roland Ashton. I know all."

"Sir Roland Ashton!" said Sir Roland, surprised and somewhat alarmed that his true character should be known. "You mistake, fair one, I am not Sir Roland; I bear a higher title."

"Conferred upon you by your housekeeper," said Daisy, scornfully.

"Confusion! can she have betrayed me?" cried Sir Roland, furiously.

"Oh! no. She has been true to her trust. In good truth, so plausible was the old wretch that I think I should have been deceived by her had it not been for the timely warning of a friend."

"The timely warning of a friend," cried Sir Roland; "impossible!"

"Impossible it may seem, yet it is true, Sir Roland," replied Daisy.

"Who is this friend?" demanded Sir Roland, passionately. "I insist on knowing."

"And I refuse to answer," replied Daisy, as passionately and as haughtily.

"This must be seen into," cried Sir Roland, and he hurried to the window. "No, the fastenings are all safe. Nothing touched. She must have guessed it."

Consoling himself with this idea, Sir Roland returned to Daisy.

"I know not, sweet one, what has put this wild thought into your head, but believe me it is false. Why should I deceive you?"

"I know not; but that it is for some bad purpose I am sure."

"Nay; you are too hard upon me. What harm have I done you? I took you from low companions not fit to breathe the same air as you—a life of privation and one which must have ended in misery. To what have I brought you? Look round and view this beautiful furniture. Are not these meats and wines of the best and rarest? Do not these diamonds almost dazzle one with their brightness? What more then can I do?"

"Let me leave this place at once. Restore me to my friends. Think you that the wild bird loves its cage because it is golden? No. I ask no reparation for the wrong you have done me, but let me go."

"Nay, sweet one, that must not be. As well might you ask a miser to give up his treasures as me to give up you, who are my treasure. Ask me to bring forth my heart, and I will do it as readily as give up you, for you are my heart. A man cannot live without his heart. You are my life, my love, my soul! Oh! sweetest Daisy, the flower of love, why are you so cold to me?"

As he spoke he moved towards the girl, who stood erect and defiant.

"Keep off," cried Daisy, as she snatched forth her dagger, "or I will kill you."

Sir Roland started back, for he had little expected such a fury.

"Daisy!" he cried, sternly, "be reasonable. These stage airs must be forgotten when you become my lady. Know that I have made up my mind that you shall be mine, and that on which I have set my mind must and shall be carried out. Tempt me not too far. I would love you and be gentle, if not—"

"You would show your true character, and prove the brute you are. I know you, Sir Roland, and fear you not. You see I am armed. Place one finger on me and I will strike."

"Nonsense, girl. Give me that dagger, it is no toy for women."

"Approach, and you shall find it no toy," replied Daisy, sternly.

"I do not fear it. I have parried many a blow in my time given by more practised hands than yours, fair one. Death at your hands would be sweet. Strike, and you will be so cruel."

With this he boldly advanced towards her, but she assumed so determined an air that he paused a few paces from where she stood.

"Daisy," he cried, "at least tell me why you shrink even from my touch."

"Because your hands are stained with blood," replied the girl.

"With blood! I understand you not. To what crime do you refer?"

"Are there so many that you are doubtful to which I allude?"

This remark was said so scornfully that Sir Roland was stung to the quick.

"Have a care!" he cried. "I am but little given to bear such taunts from one whom I have honoured with my love."

"Honoured with your love! Love from such as you means dishonour. Stand back, I say, or I will strike you to the heart."

"But should you fail, my pretty Daisy, what then? Would it not be better to have my love than my hate? No man has yet been able to brook my hatred—how, then, will a young girl do it? Can you tell me that, sweet Daisy?"

"I would dare your hatred sooner than be touched by my father's murderer."

"Your father's murderer! What mean you by that?" exclaimed Sir Roland, turning pale and starting back. "Who could have told you that?"

"So you admit it?"

"I? No. I knew Herbert Leigh, and have heard of his death; but mine was not the hand which struck the blow."

"But yours was the mind which directed it," exclaimed Daisy, passionately.

"Not so. Hear me. By Heaven I swear—"

"Silence!" exclaimed Daisy, drawing herself up to her full height. "Have you no reverence for aught that is pure and holy, that you swear by the Heaven you have outraged? Think you that the angels are deaf to the cries of your victims, that they close their ears to their curses or prayers for punishment on he who has so brutally used them? No! Water sinks into the earth, but blood flies upwards and bedews the Heavens. Repent while there is time. Go and sin no more."

This was said with such deep feeling and intention that even the hardened villain, Sir Roland Ashton, appeared touched.

"Daisy!" he cried, "no woman has ever touched my heart as you have done. You and you alone can save me from despair. Be mine, and—"

"Think you that I will permit you to wed me—you, my father's murderer—sooner a thousand deaths than that. I stand here alone with you, disgraced even by your presence, this dagger my only protection. Still, I fear you not. Such is my hatred for you that death would be preferred to one touch of your hand."

"Be it so," said Sir Roland, purple with passion. "I have tried all means to win you by love—they have failed, and now I care not what I do."

With a quick spring he dashed at Daisy, who made a blow at him with her dagger.

But Sir Roland was on his guard.

He parried the blow, seized her wrist, and in a few seconds had wrenched the weapon from her grasp.

Then with all his strength he forced her back on the couch.

She struggled hard, but what was her girlish strength against his?

The room seemed to spin round her, a dark shadow came over her eyes.

The brain whirled, all thought had gone, and she sank back insensible.

"Mine! mine, at last," cried Sir Roland, as he bent over the senseless girl.

"Never!" cried a stern voice, and Spring-Heeled Jack, who had been watching this scene from behind the screen, bounded over it and stood with outstretched arms over the fainting girl.

Sir Roland started back in horror.

How had the fiend come here?

The place had been securely closed — the windows fastened and the doors bolted and barred.

Still, there was this fearful creature, again baulking Sir Roland.

"Stand back, Sir Roland Ashton—to approach may mean death!" cried Spring-Heeled Jack. "Remember, I have no mercy for you. You, who would ruin the innocent; you, whose hands are stained with blood."

Sir Roland, as we have said, was no coward.

He sprang forward and cried aloud—

"Man or devil—I care not which—you shall not make the heart of Sir Roland Ashton tremble. Thus do I seize thee!"

But Spring-Heeled Jack had noticed his design, and frustrated it in the following manner.

With one bound he flew up to the ceiling, and descended with all his weight and force upon Sir Roland's breast, bearing him to the ground.

The baronet fell with a crash, and Spring-Heeled Jack grasped him by the throat with his claw-like hands, the nails embedding themselves in his throat.

"Now I have thee, Sir Roland!" laughed Spring-Heeled Jack, as he dashed the baronet's head upon the floor. "Now I have thee. If it were my pleasure I would wring the black heart out of your bosom. But, no, I will spare you at present—live on, sin more, and make your punishment here and hereafter more severe. Ha! ha! ha!"

At each of his fiendish laughs, Spring-Heeled Jack dashed the head of Sir Roland upon the ground, and fairly stunned him.

Then with a final blow, a bumper at parting, he sprang off the baronet.

Sir Roland was some minutes before he recovered himself.

When he did he staggered to his feet and gazed vacantly round.

"The fiend has gone!" he muttered. "Can this creature really be a devil sent to plague me? Impossible! I will not believe it. He is some maniac whose madness adds to his strength. I will match him yet, and, once in my power, I will crush him."

"Ha! ha! ha!" came in hollow, sepulchral tones from the cellar.

"Can this man—madman, or whatever he may be—pass through these substantial walls as easily as he seems to pass through the air? Let him do what he likes, I still will defy him. I have defied the devil often enough, and of a truth I shall not draw back from defying Spring-Heeled Jack. And now for my pretty little Daisy," he continued, turning to the couch.

He started back in angry surprise, for the couch was vacant.

"Gone!" he exclaimed; "impossible. Even if this demon should be able to pass through walls, ceiling, or floor, she could not; and yet she has gone."

He dashed behind the screen.

No one was there.

He hurried to the window.

It was fastened, and not a pane of glass broken.

The door bolted and fastened as securely as he had left it.

Then he staggered back to the table, and, seizing a glass of wine he found there, drank it off.

No sooner had he done so than a strange dizziness seized on him.

He tried to cry for help, but his tongue clove to the roof of his mouth.

He staggered hither and thither, trying to resist the drug, for he had drunk the wine which Mrs. Corcoran had drugged for Daisy.

A chill like that of death seized on his heart, and then he fell senseless on the floor.

---

## CHAPTER XXXIII.

### THE HAUNTED CHAMBER.

SIR ROLAND ASHTON, when he came to himself, was furious with rage.

Not only was he dazed by the drug, but his body was bruised all over.

What could he do? He summoned Mrs. Corcoran and Jacob Butler.

The old woman and the man were thunderstruck.

They had heard no noise—indeed, by Sir Roland's orders they had kept out of the way. No one had passed the door; that they were ready to swear.

Where then could Spring-Heeled Jack and the girl have gone?

That was the question they all asked, and that was the question which no one could answer.

"Follow me. I will have the place searched!" cried Sir Roland.

Having armed themselves the three started on their search.

Room after room was ransacked but without any result.

The rooms only echoed back their footsteps and whispers, for even Sir Roland spoke with bated breath, as one who walks in a churchyard at night.

Softly they stole along, almost seeming like the ghosts which were said to haunt the rooms.

At length they came to the room which led to the haunted one.

Sir Roland examined the door of the ghostly chamber carefully.

It was securely fastened, and appeared to be untouched.

"The search is useless, quite useless," he muttered.

"This fiend has managed to baulk me even in this; but I will be equal to him yet."

He was about to turn from the door of the haunted apartment when a strain of sweet melody filled the room.

From whom could it come?

As far as Sir Roland knew, there was not a musical instrument in the place; and yet now the air which floated around seemed filled with soft, dreamy music, like that of a harp when gently touched.

"What new wonder is this?" exclaimed Sir Roland, sharply.

"In good truth I cannot tell, and I like it not," said Mrs. Corcoran.

"Neither do I," grumbled Jacob. "I am not frightened of any man; but devils!—who can fight against them? Only saints, and we are not of that order."

Certainly Jacob Butler had never said a truer word in his life.

"Tut!" cried Sir Roland. "I do not believe in devils."

"Humph!" said Mrs. Corcoran, "I am not so sure about that."

"Are you afraid?" demanded Sir Roland, sharply.

"Not I. I have long since made up my mind to my fate, and fear it not."

"What a pleasant old lady!" thought Jacob; but he deemed it as well to be quiet, lest she should cast some spell upon him.

Mrs. Corcoran had an idea of her own about casting spells.

Certainly not a very poetic one, but one which was very effectual.

"Bah!" said Sir Roland, with a bitter laugh, "there is evil enough in this world without having it in the next. I will not believe in it."

Suddenly a low wail sounded, and then became louder and louder.

Then a sweet voice was heard as from a distance, which faintly sang—

*"Why should mortals fear grim death?*
*Tell me why—tell me why?*
*'Tis but a gasp of fleeting breath;*
*All must die—all must die.*
*The flesh to earth we must return;*
*A painful tribute all must give—*
*From worldly hopes and pride we turn,*
*The soul shall live—the soul shall live."*

Sir Roland stood entranced as he listened to this song.

Never had he heard anything so wildly plaintive and beautiful.

But far more than the beauty of the voice was, to his ears, the fact that it was Daisy's.

Yes; he could not mistake her sweet tones, and his heart bounded with triumph as he heard them, for he believed he should now recapture her.

"Unbar that door, Jacob!" he cried, in exultation. "If Spring-Heeled Jack thought to keep his *protégée* safe because he has hidden her in what is called the haunted chamber he is mistaken. Throw open the door and we will unearth this songstress."

It was not without some little trepidation that Jacob obeyed his master.

However, it was at length done, and the door thrown open.

Seated at the dressing-table, clad in bridal dress, sat Daisy.

Her face was turned away, and the bridal veil was down.

She sat as if in the deepest melancholy, with bent down head.

"So—so, mistress," cried Sir Roland, with a merry laugh, "you have not escaped us yet? By my faith, it shall go hard if I permit you to do so a second time, now I have you."

As he spoke he advanced boldly, and threw his arm round her lovely form.

Judge his horror when it collapsed, and a mouldy dust filled the air.

The veil fell off and exposed a grinning skull, which, snapping at the nape of the neck, rolled upon the floor.

A skeleton!

Nothing but a hideous skeleton, the very touch of which was horrid.

Sir Roland uttered a cry of horror, and started back from the fearful thing.

Even Mrs. Corcoran seemed somewhat upset, whilst Mr. Butler did not take any trouble to disguise his feelings, but bolted from the room.

"What can be the meaning of this?" cried Sir Roland, with a shudder.

"How should I know?" replied Mrs. Corcoran. "There is mischief brewing."

"Mischief brewing? What do you mean, you hag of midnight?"

"I mean," replied the old woman, turning fiercely on the baronet, and glaring at him, "I mean that vengeance is near at hand. The sword of justice is near, and only a strong arm and powerful will can thrust it on one side."

"How know you that?"

"Can you look at that," here she pointed at the skeleton, "and ask me?"

"I do not understand you. What have these musty bones to do with me?"

"Aye! there you ask too much. How should I know family secrets?"

"Family secrets! Dream you that this woman was one of my family?"

This was said so haughtily that the old crone burst into a laugh.

"In good truth, Sir Roland, I know not much about your family. I only know that death comes to all, and pays no respect to persons."

"Death?"

"Aye! death. Look at those bones. Can you forget that warning?"

"What mean you? I am strong and full of health—passion—I—"

"Stand on the brink of the grave. Be warned, Sir Roland, and pursue this girl no further. She is protected by those who have more power than you, and they must conquer."

"Be my fate what it may I will not retreat!"

"Do as you will; I have spoken," said Mrs. Corcoran. "I say no more."

The words had scarcely been said when a loud laugh sounded through the room, and Spring-Heeled Jack appeared by the fire-place.

"What!" he cried, "does Sir Roland tremble at death? Does he think that he can escape the immortal fate? Fool, your fate will be most terrible! Death and dishonour. Woe, woe! to you, Sir Roland! Look at that fearful reminder of death, and know that before long you shall be even as that is!"

"Fiend! Devil! Whate'er thou art—thus I defy ye!"

Sir Roland sprang forward to seize Spring-Heeled Jack.

But a well-directed blow felled him to the earth, and then, with his usual wild laugh, Jack disappeared.

Jacob Butler and Mrs. Corcoran hastened to Sir Roland's aid.

He was insensible, and bleeding from the mouth.

"This is a nice affair," grumbled Jacob Butler. "After all, I think honesty is the best policy."

"Did you ever try it?" chuckled Mrs. Corcoran, with a leer.

"Well, I can't say I have. Honesty hasn't been much in my way. But I've had serious thoughts of looking into the matter."

"And what keeps you from doing so?" demanded the crone.

"I ain't certain whether it would pay, and one might as well be dead as be poor."

"Better—far better," said Mrs. Corcoran; "but I have made a good long purse, and know how to keep it. Aye! and will, too. That is, until I am married, and then how I shall pet my husband. The late Corcoran—poor dear—had a happy life of it."

"Did he?" said Jacob, simply. "Well, I should not have thought it."

Scarcely politic; but although Mrs. Corcoran looked as if she could have killed Jacob, she answered in as sweet tones as she could assume—

"Ah! indeed he did; and a happy life he led. Nothing but pipes and beer all day."

Jacob opened his eyes and licked his lips.

He suddenly appeared to find charms in the withered old woman he had not seen before.

"Oh! he was a happy man. Never did a day's work in his life."

"Hum! You—you are a good woman, Mrs. Corcoran," said Jacob.

"I have tried to be, Jacob Butler, but the world is so censorious."

"Let it be; as long as we do our duty and look after ourselves, what does it matter?"

"What you think—I think. Oh! Jacob, don't look at me like that."

"I wasn't a-looking at you, that I know," replied Jacob. "I was thinking of a debt I owe."

"A debt! Gracious goodness! you are not in debt, Jacob Butler?"

"Well, it's only a little affair, and I can square it with him."

Here he pointed to Sir Roland and gave the old woman a queer glance.

The deed was done.

Jacob had fallen into the trap, and nothing could save him.

Mrs. Corcoran was the octopus which threw her deadly arms around him.

Unlucky man—miserable Jacob!

His fate was sealed, and the old harpy Corcoran knew it.

"Jacob—" she whispered to him, "Jacob, would you like to be rich?"

Jacob scratched his head and declared that he rather should.

"Then," whispered the old woman, "you can become so in a little time."

"Can I—tell me how?"

"Marry me."

"The devil!"

"No me."

"Well, it's much about the same thing," growled Jacob Butler.

"You are very complimentary, certainly. But I forgive you."

"You are very kind—very; but I have said nothing of marriage."

"But I have. Now listen, Jacob Butler. I know a great deal about you."

"No harm, I hope, Mistress Corcoran," said Jacob, quickly.

"No, not much; only enough to hang you," replied Mrs. Corcoran.

"To—to hang me! You don't mean to say that?" cried Jacob.

"I do; and not only do I say so but I will do it," grinned Mrs. Corcoran.

"Who—who could have told you?" gasped Jacob Butler.

"He did—he who lies there. Jacob Butler, I tell you that his day is nearly over. Join me and we will rule all. Who knows but that we may be the master and mistress of Ashton Hall. Do you consent?"

Jacob looked at the hag and felt inclined to murder her.

But there was that about the old woman's face he did not like—a firmness and sharp determination he could not understand.

"In a few days," she continued, "I shall have that man under my thumb. I know what he means. Now, will you marry me or not?"

Mr. Jacob Butler felt that he was pretty well under the lady's thumb, at any rate.

His spirit groaned within him; but the old witch had fixed him with her eyes, and he dared not refuse.

"Come," she said, "I have taken a fancy to you, Jacob, and I mean to marry you. Sooner or later you must give in, and it will be much better for you to accept at once. Marry me, and you shall be better than the master of Ashton Hall!"

"I suppose I must," groaned Jacob.

"Then that's agreed. Now, to prove how much I love you, Jacob, I will let you into a few of my secrets. Lean over to me, Jacob dear, and I will tell you my plans."

Jacob leant over and listened intently to what the old woman said.

It was a terrible tale—a fearful plot of the darkest crime.

Jacob Butler was not a particular man—very far from it.

But even his hair stood on end "like quills on the fretful porcupine."

"Gadzooks! you are a wonder. It isn't a five-barred gate that would stop your wild career. Why, Mazeppa would not be in the race with you!"

"I should think not. Mark me! to get on in this world you must get rid of all scruples of conscience. Now, Jacob dear, do you agree with me?"

"I'll agree with you in anything, so long as you find me in plenty of money."

"That's right, Jacob—perfectly right. But, see, Sir Roland is recovering."

"Not a word to him of this," said Jacob, eagerly. "It might spoil all."

"Never fear! I can keep my counsel, and—ha! ha! ha! he shall find you money."

"Ha! ha! ha!" roared the terrible laugh of Spring-Heeled Jack. "Do your devil's work, and fear not that you shall be rewarded. Ha! ha! ha!"

The two conspirators glanced round in fear, but no one was to be seen.

Sir Roland raised himself upon his elbows, and passed his hand over his forehead.

He gazed around as if thoroughly dazed, and murmured out—

"Where am I? Who has done this deed? Jacob, where are you? Come here!"

"I am here, your honour, and wish I wasn't! I don't like it."

"What has been the matter, Jacob?" demanded Sir Roland.

"Why, you have been knocked down with a blow from Spring-Heeled Jack."

"Ever to be crossed by that man! Jacob, to the stable, have out the carriage and the horses. We will start to-night for Ashton Hall. If Daisy has rejoined the company Tugwell will keep me well informed as to her movements. Jacob, come here."

"Jacob, go to your master," said Mrs. Corcoran, "and attend to him."

"Are you there?" growled Sir Roland. "Bah! the blow is shaking my brain."

"Do you not think that you had better go to bed, Sir Roland?" said Jacob.

"No! I will leave this house in an hour. You two shall accompany me."

"Hoity-toity! You speak finely," cried Mrs. Corcoran, flaring up. "Do you think nobody has a right in the world but yourself. I would have you to know differently. Those people who stoop to crime cannot be choosers of their friends. Crime, I have heard the parsons say, is the same as death. Death makes all men equal; so does crime, and you, Sir Roland, have steeped yourself well in that. We are equal by crime, if not by birth—equal, Sir Roland! What think you of that?"

Sir Roland looked at the man and woman with amazement.

"What means this change?" he cried, as he started to his feet.

"It means, Sir Roland, that we are masters of the situation," said Mrs. Corcoran.

"You?"

"Yes—Jacob and I. We have come to terms. Jacob is going to make me Mrs. Butler, and we are going down to live at the Hall."

"Live at the Hall? Impossible! What would Lady Ashton say?"

"What care I what Lady Ashton says? Besides, if I carry out your orders, Sir Roland, Lady Ashton will not have much to say in the matter. We settle these things by a way which is much quicker than argument."

And here the crone gave a shrill laugh, which was positively fiendish.

Sir Roland Ashton poured himself out a glass of wine and drank it off.

"And you, Jacob Butler," he said, "you mean to marry this woman?"

"I beg your honour's pardon, but it strikes me that the boot is on the other leg, and she means to marry me."

"Fools! You will live to repent this," muttered Sir Roland.

"Most people who marry do live to repent it," laughed Mrs. Corcoran.

"You speak from experience, I suppose?" snarled Sir Roland.

"Yes; my own and other people's. Poor Corcoran passed away in peace. His last few hours were the most peaceful ones he had after he married me."

"That I can believe," said Sir Roland, dryly, while he cast a quick look at Jacob Butler. "I only hope, for Jacob's sake, that he may have as peaceful an end. Do what you like; so long as you please me, I do not mind. But mark this, both of you. Serve me, and serve me faithfully, then I will be a kind master to you; let me see one sign of treachery, and I will dash you to pieces like I do this glass."

Taking the glass from the table he hurled it on the floor, shivering it into a thousand pieces.

Jacob turned pale as death, and even Mrs. Corcoran shivered at the baronet's fearful energy.

"Enough now!" he cried; "to-morrow we will leave here and start for the Hall. Be faithful, and you will not repent having served me. Swear that you will be faithful to me!"

"Swear! Ha! ha! ha! ha!" came the sepulchral voice of Spring-Heeled Jack.

"Heed not that impostor!" cried Sir Roland. "Swear!"

Mrs. Corcoran and Jacob swore upon their honour.

Could they have sworn on anything less substantial?

"Enough, Jacob; see that all is prepared for our journey. To-morrow we start for the Hall."

"And I go, too," came the voice of Spring-Heeled Jack. "Ha! ha! ha!"

## CHAPTER XXXIV.

### HUSBAND AND WIFE.

Lady Ashton, formerly Mrs. Levine, reclined upon her sofa in the drawing-room of Ashton Hall.

She had quite changed from the soft-spoken Mrs. Levine.

She had now become haughty and tyrannical, so that all the servants hated her.

Nothing was good enough for her ladyship.

Indeed, had she been born the heiress to millions she would not have been so exacting.

Dinners had to be cooked in the most *recherché* style.

As for diamonds and dress no lady in the county could equal her.

Her maids dressed as ladies, and waited upon her hand and foot.

She had been a servant herself once, had felt the sharp taunt and scorn of a master's tongue; but instead of teaching her a lesson of humility, it had made her more imperious than ever. If she ruled the servants with a rod of iron when she was housekeeper, one may fancy what she did now she was mistress.

As we said before, Lady Ashton reclined upon her drawing-room sofa. She was reading a novel, and placed it languidly on one side as Sir Roland entered the room.

"So, Sir Roland," she said, quietly, "you have returned home at last?"

"Yes. I do not suppose you have felt my absence very much."

"No," yawned the lady; "I have amused myself with my monkey, Coco."

"Whom you love better than your husband. Ours was a pretty love match!"

"Love match! who could have put that into your head?"

"You loved me when you married me, I suppose?" said Sir Roland.

"Ha! ha! ha! ha! Who could have put that foolish thought into your head?"

"You did; you declared you did the morning after we were married."

"Ah! those were the early days. You would not have a woman speak her mind during the honeymoon! No—no, Sir Roland, that comes afterwards."

Sir Roland uttered something which was certainly not a compliment to his wife.

But it was his interest not to quarrel with her, and so he answered kindly—

"Come, come, my dear. If business called me away from you so soon after our marriage, it was not my fault."

"Business! Sir Roland," said Lady Ashton, raising her eyebrows. "Are you sure it was not pleasure?"

"Pleasure, my dear. What pleasure can I have away from you?"

Lady Ashton made no reply, but throwing her arms above her head burst out into a loud fit of laughter.

"How now, Lady Ashton?" crie l Sir Roland "What means this most unseemly mirth?"

"It means this," Sir Roland. "That you cannot and shall not hoodwink me. I am not blind; you hate me, and your death would not cause me a moment's sorrow. But since we are husband and wife, our interests are the same, and that being the case, I will work with you. But let us understand each other. If our interests were not the same I should work against you."

"Candid, at all events," muttered Sir Roland.

"I meant it to be. Now, Roland, look here; I know what your object in life is. If you do as I wish, I will help you; if not—now mark my words—I will spoil every plan you have. If I benefit, well and good; if I do not, look to yourself!"

Sir Roland ground his teeth but could make no reply.

He knew too well that this woman had a fearful will of her own, and that, fight against it as he would, he was subservient to it.

"Be it as you will. Now we understand each other we can talk openly."

"Oh! certainly," replied the lady. "And to begin with, read that letter!"

Here Lady Ashton threw over a note to Sir Roland.

Sir Roland picked it up, opened and read it.

It was an exact account of what had happened between Sir Roland and Daisy.

This note was signed by Spring-Heeled Jack.

"Has that cursed villain been here?" demanded Sir Roland.

"I have not seen him," replied the lady, carelessly; "but I have written to him, and, as you see, he has written to me."

"You have written to him? And may I ask where you have written to?"

"A man named Lorimer brought the letter and carried back the answer."

"And what was the answer?"

"I do not know that I shall tell you, if you are going to poison me."

"It seems to me that you have some strange ideas," said Sir Roland, but turning pale.

"The strange ideas have come through a very good authority."

"What authority?"

"Spring-Heeled Jack!"

"What! has the scoundrel dared accuse me of such a purpose?"

"Aye! and proved it also. Mrs. Corcoran is a skilful woman, but she will have a great deal of trouble to match me."

"So you think that I would be guilty of murder?"

"I know you have been," was the calm reply; "and it shall be my purpose to prevent your being so again. I have no wish to be a heroine at the expense of my life."

"You know that?"

"Yes, Sir Roland; I do know that, and a great deal more. I advise you to be careful. You will find me a better friend than foe. Dear me! do you think I am ignorant of all your plans? No! I know them all."

Sir Roland bit his lip and glared with rage.

Here were all his plans upset by his arch enemy, Spring-Heeled Jack.

How could he have done it? With what swiftness he must have travelled!

"You wrong me, said Sir Roland. "I had no more intention of wronging you than—"

"Marrying me," laughed the lady; "but having done the one I will take care that you do not do the other. I have told you that if you are subservient to me I will aid you in your plans. Try to upset me and I will hang you."

Sir Roland looked at this woman, and in spite of himself admired her.

She was handsome, strong, clever, and determined.

Might she not be the one who could overthrow the power of Spring-Heeled Jack?

At all events he determined to try it, and made answer—

"I will not disguise from you the truth. Our marriage, as you know, was not intended by me."

"Far from it," said the lady, quietly. "I intended it, and had my own way, and mean to have it. You understand me?"

"Perfectly," said Sir Roland; but his cheeks grew purple with passion.

"And you will obey me. That Mrs. Corcoran must leave the house!"

"Let it be so. Do you think that I want the old woman here? No, let her go."

Scarcely had he said the words than he saw one of the curtains which were drawn over the windows move, and the hideous face of Mrs. Corcoran appear.

Mrs. Corcoran was always hideous, but now she appeared more so than ever.

Placing one skinny finger on her blue lips, to warn Sir Roland to silence, she pointed with the other to Lady Ashton, and then grasped her hands with a terrible motion, as if she clutched someone's throat.

There was no mistaking the sign.

It asked as plainly as words could have done,

"Shall I strangle her?"

Taking advantage of his wife having glanced on one side, Sir Roland nodded his head, and the old hag Corcoran glided softly from behind the curtain.

"The next thing that I must insist upon," said Lady Ashton, "is the dismissal of Jacob Butler. He knows too much of the family matters, and must be silenced."

"Be it as your ladyship wills," said Sir Roland; "I care not for the fellow."

"I am glad to find you so obliging, Sir Roland," smiled her ladyship.

"Yet, my lady, I would have you think for a moment," said Sir Roland. "Jacob has been a good and faithful servant to me, and has never divulged my secrets."

"True, but your secrets would be safer when he was dead."

"Ah! madam, talk not so lightly of death. It is often nearest to us when we think it furthest away. It would be better to be more charitable."

Lady Ashton opened her eyes in wonder; then burst into laughter.

"Why, Sir Roland, something dreadful is surely about to happen! I have heard that the devil can quote Scripture to suit his own purpose; but that Sir Roland Ashton should moralise is more than I could have believed. Wonders will never cease."

Meanwhile the old hag had crept nearer and nearer to Lady Ashton.

In one hand she held a napkin and in the other a bottle, from which she poured a colourless fluid on to the napkin.

Whether Lady Ashton noticed something peculiar in her husband's eyes, or whether she heard the creeping step behind her, no one can tell, but certain it is that she turned suddenly round and faced the murderess.

She sprang to her feet and cried aloud for help and mercy.

Help! mercy! When had these virtues ever entered the heart of Sir Roland?

Mrs. Corcoran sprang upon her, and thrust the napkin in her face.

There was a horrible stifling sensation—a faint, sweet smell, a dizziness, and Lady Ashton fell back insensible.

Then the old hag pressed the napkin over her ladyship's mouth and nostrils so firmly that to breathe was impossible.

A few faint struggles for life and then her limbs were stretched out in death.

"There," said Mrs. Corcoran, as she removed the napkin and gazed down at the horrible work she had done. "There; she won't trouble you again, Sir Roland. Ha, ha! my lady, you would have me turned from the house! Poor old Mother Corcoran was to go forth homeless! Ah! you were a kind, merciful lady—you were! But I was more so; I have found you a home from which you will never rise until the end of the world—the grave. Ha! ha! ha!"

"Have you no feeling—no remorse for the cruel deed which you have just now committed?" cried Sir Roland, as he gazed down at the livid face—now fast becoming rigid.

"Remorse! Ho! ho! ho! I like that! Have you no remorse? Who ordered me to kill her? You. You talk to me of remorse, and I reply that while such men as you are to be found, such women as I am will always be ready at hand to carry out your plans. Who is the worst? The head that plans the deed, or the hand which carries it out?"

"Silence, woman!"

"I will not be silent, Sir Roland," cried the old woman. "Henceforth I would have you to know that I am your equal. I have heard it said that in some eastern country, many—many years ago, that if a man murdered his wife the body was chained to the murderer, who had to drag it about with him, until the loathsome thing caused him to die with terror, or gave him some pestilence from which he died. You will bury this body, but you will drag about with you the ghost—the true corpse—remorse!"

Sir Roland paced up and down the room in the wildest agitation.

"Woman! fiend! devil!" he cried at last, "have you no remorse?"

"No. I was born poor, and learned in the school of privation that conscience was a luxury the poor could not afford, if they wanted to get on in the world. I have obeyed my orders. Yours be the blame—not mine."

The woman spoke so calmly and coolly that Sir Roland could not answer.

He felt that he was in her power, and bowed before her will.

"Be it as you like," he muttered; "he who once ventures on the path of sin must continue to the end. Step by step he sinks lower and lower into the quicksand of crime, until, powerless to move, the tide of time overwhelms him, and he sinks never to rise again."

"Ah! you have found that out, have you?" laughed the old woman.

"Alas! yes, and you have no feeling?"

"None! I have seen too much of life for remorse. But what is to be done with this pretty piece of death. Shall we not rouse the house and declare that her ladyship died suddenly? It would be as well to send post haste for a doctor. I have certain drugs which I can use to remove all odour of the drug I used. Trust to me, Sir Roland, I have had too many cases like this on hand to make any mistake about it. None will find us out."

"Ha! ha! ha!" rang a sepulchral laugh through the room.

The two guilty wretches turned round and gazed with horror at the window from whence the sound came, and there they beheld the horrible features of Spring-Heeled Jack.

"Ha! ha! ha! Sir Roland," roared Spring Heeled Jack. "Do you think that this crime will go unpunished? No! Murder will out, and although you escape for a time at last your meed of punishment will come; then you shall know who Spring-Heeled Jack is. Ha! ha! ha!"

And with a yell of laughter the horrible creature bounded away.

"Will this fiend ever haunt me?" cried Sir Roland.

"I suppose so," remarked Mrs. Corcoran; "but what harm does he do you? Be a man, Sir Roland, and defy the devil himself. Shake off this trembling cowardice, and knowing that you have little to hope for in the world to come, make the best of this. Now call up the servants."

Sir Roland knew the old crone was right and acted on her advice.

He seized the bell-rope and rang with all his might as he shouted—

"Help—help—help! Her ladyship is in a fit! Help—help—help!"

The sounds of hurrying feet—the confused murmer of voices.

Then Mrs. Corcoran flung herself down at the side of the couch, and began rubbing the hands of the dead woman, while Sir Roland bent over her as if in the most abject grief.

In rushed the servants, Jacob Butler at their head.

"What is all this?" cried Jacob, as he gazed in horror at the dead.

"I know not, Jacob. Your mistress was talking to me when she was taken with a sudden faintness, and—and became insensible, and—"

"She is dead!" said Jacob, as he placed his hand over his mistress's heart.

"Dead—impossible!" cried Mrs. Corcoran, putting on a look of the greatest surprise.

"Dead—my darling dead!" exclaimed Sir Roland. "I cannot believe it!"

Jacob looked uneasily at the servants as he made answer.

"I don't know about its being impossible, all I know is that it is true."

Sir Roland cast himself upon the body and kissed it passionately.

Far more passionately than he had ever done in her lifetime.

"Fly, Jacob, fly!" he cried, apparently overpowered with grief. "Seek a doctor at once. My darling—my darling! She cannot be dead."

"She's a precious good imitation of it," said Jacob, as he left the room.

"Don't overdo it," whispered Mrs. Corcoran, to the baronet, "or they will suspect something."

Then, in plaintive tones, she continued, aloud—

"Moderate your grief, Sir Roland. The poor dear angel has gone. All the tears in the world will not bring her back to life again. Ah! this is a wicked world, and in the midst of life we are in death."

"Who can know my grief? Who can fill her vacant place?"

Mrs. Corcoran felt inclined to say that she could, but prudence forbade her, and yet the old crone had some idea that she might throw over the servant and take the master.

But that, she thought, had better be left for the future.

The doctor came—a pompous country practitioner, who would have done anything to oblige Sir Roland Ashton.

So everything was arranged to the liking of Sir Roland Ashton and Mrs. Corcoran.

"This is a nice thing you have done," whispered Jacob to Mrs. Corcoran, as she and he left the room together.

"Yes; I think it is, Jacob," said the old woman, complacently. "I told you that you should soon be as good as the master of Ashton Hall—marry me and you will be, for I have him under my thumb."

---

## CHAPTER XXXV.

### THE BULL IN TOP BOOTS.

Down in the Borough there is, or rather was, a noted public-house with the somewhat mysterious sign of The Bull in Top Boots.

Whether it had been originally intended for John Bull in the usual top boots in which he is so constantly represented, history says not; but the sign showed a good, big bull, with long horns, curly pate, and fiery eyes, pawing the air with his front hoofs, whilst his hinder ones are encased in huge top boots—a particle of dress which, to say the least of it, must be rather inconvenient to the bovine animal, seeing that he has no feet to keep them on.

However, there was the sign and there the house, and a most disreputable one it was.

Gentlemen in flash clothes, who rode blood mares, and whose business took them out mostly at nights, and who had a horror of Bow-street, lounged about the place all day, drinking, smoking, and diceing.

Then there were a much rougher set of fellows. Men who did not seem to have washed or shaved for weeks.

These men appeared to have a kind of veneration for the men who kept the blood mares, and called them all "captains," although not one of them could claim to have been in their country's service; indeed, the only service they could do this country would be to hang themselves, and so save the country expense and the sheriffs trouble.

In a word, the house was a resort of highwayman, thieves, and the worst of characters, and it is to this place we must conduct our readers.

It was a dark, stormy night; the wind blew cold and chilly up the Thames. The rain fell in fitful showers, and the distant thunder told that a storm was not far off.

On such a night a crowd of men and women of the character we have described were seated in a long room of the Bull in Top Boots, rejoicing in their usual pastimes.

Two men were away from the rest, and as they drank their grog and smoked they watched the others keenly.

These two men were no others than Dick Catchpole and Elias Grabham.

They were carrying out Sir Roland's orders, and were ever on the watch.

"By the powers, Bill Blarney!" cried a tall Irishman, dressed in a lace coat, doeskin breeches, and top boots almost as high as the prancing bull wore. "By the powers, Bill Blarney; but that was a rare song that you gave us just now."

"Hold your whist, Pat Kelly; I'm not in the mood for singing."

"Now, Bill, I want a song," said a blooming lady of some thirty summers, with a complexion like a Dutch doll, and rolling eyes, which she used freely. "So tip us a tune, or maybe I shall take another lover."

"Arrah! Judy," replied Bill, "if you make me jealous, you beauty, it's meself that will murder the man who dare come between us!"

"Then sing me a song at once," said Judy.

Like most women, Judy knew how to get the best of her lover.

Bill Blarney submitted to the will of his charmer, and said—

"Shure, Judy, you know that I would never displease you. Only, maybe some of the company may not care about a song," and here he cast a quick glance towards Messrs. Catchpole and Grabham.

"If anyone objects to your singing, Bill, let them speak to me," said Judy, putting her arms akimbo and glancing fiercely round.

No one did object; in fact, every one seemed anxious to hear the song.

"Which one shall I sing, Judy, 'The White Boy's Lament,' or 'Bad Luck to the Devil?'"

"Give us 'Bad Luck to the Devil;' that always appears to me a kind of religious song," said Judy.

Thus urged, Bill Blarney struck up the following beautiful ditty—

### Bad Luck to the Devil.

"*Oh! bad luck to the Devil, he's dead!*
*He gained but a sad notoriety;*
*But his very worst foes never said*
*He ever gave way to sobriety.*
*He liked both to drink and to dice,*
*Loved lasses whose eyes brightly shone;*
*'Tis true he had many a vice,*
*But pity him now he has gone.*"

# SPRING-HEELED JACK,

## THE TERROR OF LONDON.

"DAISY LEIGH IS THE LASS I LOVE BEST, SIR ROLAND!" CRIED GEDGE.

"Chorus, gentlemen!" roared Judy; and amidst the rattle of pewter pots, the clinking of glasses, and stamping of feet, the chorus was roared out—

"*Oh! bad luck to the Devil, he's dead!*
*He gained but a sad notoriety;*
*But his very worst foes never said*
*He ever gave way to sobriety.*"

Encouraged by the success of the first verse, Bill continued.

"*Oh! bad luck to the Devil, he's dead!*
*He always went in for variety;*
*He is missed—at least, so 'tis said—*
*In the highest and lowest society.*
*But what they will do with his soul,*
*I'm sure I really don't know—*
*Above he'd break all control,*
*And be quite at home down below.*"

"Chorus, gentlemen!"

"*Oh! bad luck to the devil, he's dead,*
*He gained but a sad notoriety;*
*But his very worst foes never said*
*That he ever gave way to sobriety.*"

"I'm not sure that the devil be dead," said Catchpole, breaking into the conversation directly the applause had ceased. "I've heard people speak about a kind of devil that goes leaping about frightening people out of their wits."

"You mean Spring-Heeled Jack?" said Grabham. "I've heard of him."

"And it's meself that has seen him," said Bill Blarney.

"You have seen him! Where?" cried the rest of the company.

"Well, I was riding, but it don't matter where or for what purpose," said Mr. Blarney, suddenly remembering that his midnight frolics might be dangerous to repeat. "Anyway, I was having a canter over the country on my mare, quite at my my ease like—"

"That's more than any gentlefolk would have been if you had met them," laughed Judy.

"Hold your whist, Judy!" said Blarney. "Sure and you are not the girl to peach upon a lover?"

"I should think not. And let me catch the man who dares to peach upon my sweetheart—I'd precious soon wring his neck! But go on with your story."

"Well, the moon was sailing up aloft, and I was cantering over the heath, just humming a stave to myself, and wondering if Providence would kindly put some piece of good fortune in my way, when I heard the wheels of a carriage.

"In luck, Bill, my boy!" laughed Pat Kelly. "You always were a lucky dog."

"I don't so much know about that," said Bill Blarney; "but I did believe that I was, and that's the truth of the matter. Well, I puts my tit into a gallop, and away we went over the heath. A carriage came in view, and as I presented one of my pistols I invited the coachman to stop, which he did in double quick time."

"Quite polite and gentlemanly," laughed Pat Kelly—"a true Irish boy."

"But, oh! such a screaming and a squalling was set up that you never did hear."

"Women?" said one of the men, laconically.

"Ladies," replied Bill Blarney, in a tone which might lead one to think that he thought women and ladies two very different kinds of animals. "Ladies as highly born as any of us here."

Some people might not have thought this a great amount of praise.

But it seemed to meet with the approval of the company, and Bill, being applauded, looked round with the greatest satisfaction.

"Yes, gentlemen, they were ladies, and I fancy that ladies are rather partial to me."

Here the Hibernian highwayman coughed and pretended to be modest.

A thing he quite failed in, and set Pat Kelly off into shrieks of laughter.

"Be they women or ladies," said Mistress Judy, "they had better not let me catch them at any of their flirtations with my boy. However, go on."

"Well, I rode up to the carriage window, and, taking off my hat, said, after making the most graceful bow that I could—

"'I ask pardon, lady, or ladies, as the case may be, but I have a very painful duty to perform. It is suspected that a load of jewels are being carried over the country to help the Pretender, and I must examine you to see if you have any about you. Loyalty, and only loyalty, compels me to make this demand. Do not think that I would be so rude as to interfere with ladies, if it were not for the king and for the country. Perish the thought! It's meself as would scorn the action. But I have my duty to perform, and must do it. So please hand over your jewels, my pretty dears, and we will see what your purses contain!'"

"I warrant me you made a good haul?" laughed Judy.

"There you are wrong, Judy. The women flopped down on their knees, the coachman squealed like a stuck pig, and rolled off the box.

"I had them quite at my mercy, and was about to remove some articles of value which looked somewhat suspicious, when a dark cloud seemed to overshadow the moon.

"I gazed upward, and there, leaping down on the top of the coach, was that infernal imp of his chief, Spring-Heeled Jack."

"Did you seize him?" cried Judy, eagerly.

"No," replied Bill Blarney, somewhat ruefully. "On the contrary, he seized me."

"But you grappled with him?" demanded the warlike Judy.

"Well, I can't exactly say I did, for no sooner had he bounded on to the top of the coach than he bounded off that on to my back. Planting his knees firmly into my back, whilst he grasped me by the throat, he forced me down on to my face, where he held me firmly."

"And you did not kill the fellow?" said the fiery Judy, her eyes flashing.

"No, I did not. I should have liked to do so, but somehow he had the best of it."

"Had the best of it! What do you mean?' demanded Judy.

"Well, my jewel, he had me face downwards on the ground, and he held on with the power of a giant. I can't say he was too gentle, for I had reason to remember that there were stones upon that heath."

"You mean that he beat your thick head upon the ground?" cried Judy, indignantly.

"Well, Judy, darling, it must have been something like it, or I had a most powerful dream. But the next morning I found my head all bumps, and a cruel sensation of cramp down my back, as if someone had been kneeling on me and kneading me with their knees."

"In other words, you were jolly well whopped," said Judy, indignantly.

"Sure that was my opinion of the matter, my darling, but I did not care about mentioning it at once, and before company. Those things are best kept to one's-self. Sure, Judy, darling, you would not blame me because I could not fight the devil?"

"I would fight the devil and all his imps, if he came across me!" said the valiant Judy.

"Be gorrah! Judy. You have the courage of the devil, but you never met Spring-Heeled Jack. I wish he were here now, to let you know the fiend he is."

"Whatever he was, I should not be frightened. Well, what did you do?"

"Well, Jack held me down, and battered my face on the ground."

"And did you do nothing?"

"Oh! yes; I bellowed like a bull; but I soon found that the more I bellowed the more he bumped, and so I thought discretion was the better part of valour, and then I heard the monster cry—

"'On your box, coward, and drive for your life, or Spring-Heeled Jack will serve you as he has done this ruf—gentleman, I mean.'"

"Ruffian, you mean!" said a stern voice from a dark corner of the room.

The men turned round and glanced eagerly at each other.

Not a soul was there, and yet all had heard the voice.

As if to make the idea more ghostly the rain came down in fearful storms.

Then the lightning flashed through the windows, and the deep-voiced thunder rolled.

"Phsaw! who was that who spoke?" demanded Bill Blarney, as he wiped the perspiration from his forehead. "Surely Spring-Heeled Jack is not amongst us?"

This idea seemed almost to terrify the valiant Judy, but she was too much of a woman to show it.

No; sooner than give way, Judy Bulgrudery resolved to defy anyone.

"To think that you men should fear a fellow of that sort!" she said.

But as she spoke she glanced nervously over her shoulder.

"And do you not fear him, mistress?" asked Dick Catchpole.

"Me afraid of him? I would he was here now that I might tell him my idea of his high pranks. Bah! had I been a man he would have been in prison long ago."

Crash! bang! A livid flash of light and then the deep war of heaven's artillery sent forth its fearful fire!

Every one in the room was nearly blinded and even the courageous Judy seemed overcome, for covering her face with her hands she bent her head down and screamed.

The very air seemed impregnated with sulphur, and the glasses were shaken by the heavy thunder clap.

All were blinded for a time with the flash, but when they had recovered from the shock they looked up, and to their horror beheld a tall dark man, dressed in a riding cloak, which hid his figure from his neck to his feet.

He wore a hat slouched over his face, his hair was long, and his moustache turned up in the Mephistophelian style.

"I hope I do not disturb you, ladies and gentlemen, but, the weather being somewhat stormy, I thought I would take shelter here. Madam, your glass is empty—permit me to fill it?"

And with the greatest coolness possible the stranger drew from his pocket a black-cased bottle, with which he replenished Judy's glass.

The people all looked in horror at the man.

And yet, so far as they could see, the man was a handsome one.

Judy at first seemed inclined to refuse the drink; but the smell of it was too tempting, and she drank it off with great gusto.

"It's nectar!" she cried. "It's drink for the gods!"

"I am glad you like it, madam. You shall have some more anon."

"Who the devil are you?" demanded Bill Blarney, in amaze.

"Exactly so. My dear sir, in a society like this I am careful about giving my name."

There was nothing which one could call positively unpleasant in the man's manner, and yet there was a way about it which offended, because it appeared to claim authority.

"Men who will not give their name are to be suspected," growled Bill.

"Suspect as much as you like," replied the stranger, quietly. "It cannot hurt me."

There was no boastfulness in all this. It was done quietly and firmly.

"You speak boldly," said Bill, "Do you know who me and my pals are?"

"Yes—vagabonds—rogues—thieves! You may be worse; I don't know," replied the stranger.

"By the Lord Harry! I will not stand that," cried Bill Blarney, as he jumped up. "I'll teach you to respect the company you are in."

With that he sprung towards the stranger, making a clutch at his throat.

But, stretching forth a pair of muscular arms as he threw the cloak on one side, the stranger grasped him with a power which was fearful to witness.

The man's very bones seemed to crack beneath his grip.

Holding the man in his arms he lifted him up as easily as if he were a child.

"So," he cried, "you would attempt to rule me! Learn that I am above you all. Oh! you may call for help," he continued, as the men started up to rescue their companion from his grasp, "but I tell you, if anyone dares to place one finger on me, I will strangle this fellow first and his friend afterwards.

The people drew back in alarm, and Bill Blarney called aloud for mercy.

"Mercy!" cried the stranger. "What mercy do you deserve? But go! Too long have I defiled my hands with you."

With that he dashed the man across the room, throwing him on a table that was filled with bottles and glasses.

Loud was the crash he made in his descent, and louder still the cry Judy made at the overthrow of her lover.

Bully him herself she would to any extent, but would not permit anyone else to do the same.

With hands like claws and outstretched arms she flew at the stranger.

But he caught her easily in an embrace, and waltzed with her round the room.

So lightly, so deftly, and gracefully did he lift the woman that the people appeared surprised.

It was the dance of a demon.

Now they were pirouetting on the floor, now they were making the most extraordinary bounds into the air.

Judy was breathless, and could not speak, although she would have fain asked the stranger to desist.

Up and down, here and there, he danced all over the place.

The "Devil's Fantasia" would have been the fitting music to have played to it, for never was such a horrible impish dance.

It was now here we go up, up, up; here we go down, down, down.

Judy Bulgrudery gasped for breath and sighed for mercy.

But the stranger would not cease. He seemed endowed with special strength.

He whirled her about as if she had been a fairy, whilst his long legs were thrown up so high that the people started back, so as not to have their hats knocked off.

At last Judy did indeed grow faint, which no sooner did the stranger perceive than with the greatest kindness he placed her on a chair, and handed her a glass of punch, which, much exhausted as the lady seemed to be, she drank with the greatest eagerness.

"Now, gentlemen," said the stranger, as he bowed lowly, "and especially you, Catchpole and Grabham, I trust you will have a good remembrance of Spring-Heeled Jack."

"Then you are—" cried Catchpole, jumping forward.

"Spring-Heeled Jack!"

And with a loud laugh the stranger bounded over their heads and disappeared through the door.

---

## CHAPTER XXXVI.

### CATCHPOLE AND GRABHAM HAVE REASON TO REPENT THEIR VISIT TO THE BULL IN TOP BOOTS.

THE company at the Bull in Top Boots could scarcely speak. They were not men or women given to much fear or superstition.

But here, before their very eyes, had come a fantastic fiend whose nature they could not make out.

Even the redoubtable Judy Bulgrudery seemed scared.

"It's the fiend himself," she gasped, directly she could recover her breath. "Never did I have such a devil's dance, and may the saints protect me from such another. Although I do confess he behaved like a gentleman to me."

"Faith! he knew I was present, and thought he had better behave himself."

"What are you talking like that for, Bill Blarney?" cried the woman. "Don't you know he would just have treated you as a terrier would treat a rat—give you a good shaking and throw you over his shoulder."

Bill Blarney did not like this speech for two reasons. In the first place he had been the cock of the walk at the Bull in Top Boots, the admired of all, and now his comb had been cut. Secondly, Judy's speech seemed to partake more of admiration than horror at the grim goblin, and as he really did like Judy he was naturally somewhat jealous.

"Faith! and you need not be so proud of your dance with the devil, Judy."

"I don't see that. He can shake as pretty a leg in the dance as ever I saw," replied Judy, who saw Bill Blarney's jealousy, and was determined to make the most of it, woman-like, "and I don't see that he is so ugly."

"Hold your whist, Judy," said Pat Kelly, who would always stand up for his leader, be he right or wrong. "What's the good of annoying Blarney? Sure, no man can fight the devil, although some women can get over him. Faith! I've heard it said that most women are more than a match for him."

"So much the better for the women," laughed Judy; "but those two gentlemen over there seemed to know more about him than anyone."

It was a most skilfully-timed remark of Mistress Judy.

She liked Bill Blarney, and certainly had no desire to quarrel.

So having, as it were, established her supremacy, she turned on the unfortunate constables.

"We? We know nothing of this fellow!" stammered Dick Catchpole.

"Less than nothing," put in Grabham. "We are honest folk."

"Ha! ha! ha!" came the fearful laugh of Spring-Heeled Jack, sounding as if it came from the very roof tree of the inn. "Honest men! Ha! ha! ha! Two constables—two spies in the pay of Sir Roland Ashton. Honest men! Ha! ha! ha!"

The hint had been given and was soon taken by such a company.

"Hillo!" cried Bill Blarney, as he started up and glared fiercely at the constables, who were now as pale as death. "Is this true?"

"Of course it is," cried Judy. "Look at their faces. The white-livered cowards dare not deny it. Now, lads, let us show them our metal!"

"Stand back!" cried Dick Catchpole, as he sprang up and produced his staff of office—a little round piece of wood, much like an office ruler with a brass crown at the top. "Stand back! I am a sworn-in constable, and I claim the protection of the laws."

"Laws!" cried Blarney; "who cares for the laws? Hillo! lads, listen here."

The men who frequented the highly respectable establishment of the Bull in Top Boots crowded round Blarney, so that Messrs. Catchpole and Grabham found themselves prisoners.

"Beware!" cried Grabham, producing his truncheon; "this is felony."

"Oh! is it. Well, I think we have been pretty used to that. Eh, boys?"

"I should think so. Let us give 'em their quietus," growled one brawny fellow.

"Take care—take care! The first one who places a finger on me I shall arrest."

This useless threat caused the people to burst into loud fits of laughter.

Among the merriment could be heard the wild shriek of Spring-Heeled Jack.

"No, no, lads," cried Judy; "we had better not do that. Let us give them a lesson which will teach them better manners, and cause us some amusement. What do you say to tossing in a blanket?"

The suggestion was met with shouts of applause from everybody in the room save the two most interested—namely, Messrs. Catchpole and Grabham, who somehow did not seem quite to view the matter in the same comic manner as the others.

"Ladies, gentlemen!" urged Catchpole, as a

number of horny, but far from honest, hands were laid upon him; "you do me a wrong and yourself an injury. The law should be respected by everyone but lawyers. I do not wish to threaten you, but as one of the lower members of the law—"

"Shut up!" said a sturdy fellow, giving the constable a severe shaking.

"I protest, I—I— Let us go, gentlemen, and we will depart in peace."

"No!" thundered Bill Blarney; "that we will not do; but as one day we may be nabbed and compelled to take our trial we will give you the same fair chance as we shall have. Bring the prisoners forward and bind their arms."

Vainly did Messrs. Catchpole and Grabham try to escape and implore for mercy.

They were dragged ruthlessly forward and bound.

Bound, and that not in the gentlest manner, for it must be admitted that these gentlemen of the road and light-fingered people were not given to tenderness at the best of times, and when the men to be tormented were constables they looked upon the matter as a duty combined with pleasure."

"So, gentlemen, you are come here as spies," said Blarney, who had seated himself at the end of the room, and had put Judy by his side, as if she had been his queen. "Do you think that we will have spies at the Bull in Top Boots? No!"

"Mercy! kind sir," said Catchpole, as he dropped down on his knees.

"Mercy!" cried Grabham, doing the same; "we did not come here to spy upon you, but to see what we could find out about that horrible monster Spring-Heeled Jack, whom folks call the Terror of London."

"By my faith! but you have found out something about him," said Judy, laughing. "You see, he can appear like a gentleman, and not like a devil, which I hold that it is more than you can do, you spalpeens."

"You are right, Judy, my darling," said Blarney; "as you always are."

"Besides, may not this Spring-Heeled Jack be one of us?" continued the lady, being thus encouraged. "I have heard that he can make pretty free with other people's gold. In fact, I believe him to be a regular romany" (gipsy), "and a swell high-toly man" (highwayman), "who just puts on this disguise to frighten the constables. At all events, if the constables hate him he must be a pal of ours."

"Bravo—bravo!" cried the men. "Spring-Heeled Jack is a friend of ours!" shouted the men. "Whoever heard of his doing a poor man an injury? Long live Spring-Heeled Jack!"

"That's right, boys!" cried Judy Bulgrudery, as she seized up a glass from a table and filled it with neat spirits—"that's right! and whatever be our faults—and I don't pretend to say that we have not some—forgetfulness or treachery to our friends is not amongst them. So join me, lads, in drinking to Spring-Heeled Jack."

This was not quite what Mr. Blarney had reckoned on.

But what was he to do? The toast was received with such loud cheers that he felt even with the power he had over the men, he would not be able to stop them.

So, like the cunning fellow he was, he pretended to join in the cheers.

In fact, no one drank the health of Spring Heeled Jack as loudly as he.

In the first place, he greatly doubted if Spring-heeled Jack was a thief.

In the second, he came to the conclusion that if Spring-Heeled Jack really was a thief he would soon get the command over the others, and in that case it would be as well to keep friendly with him, so that he might be his lieutenant.

"Better be captain than lieutenant," he argued; "but better be lieutenant than nothing."

And so he became suddenly the most complimentary of all to Jack.

"Jack is a giant!" he cried; "but, although he did me a little injury just now, I bear him no grudge, and so I'll drink his health again and again."

And so he did, and so did the rest of the company, much as they would have drunk the health of the devil himself, if only for the drinking sake, for the customers of the Bull in Top Boots were thirsty souls, as the landlord well knew to his profit.

"Ha! ha! ha!" came the stern laughter of Spring-Heeled Jack, as if he held them all in contempt.

They glanced nervously round, but no sign of Jack was to be seen.

"Leave Jack alone and let us turn our kind attention to these gentlemen."

So spoke Judy Bulgrudery, and the two miserable constables cast looks of pleading towards her, for they saw plainly that she ruled and their fate was in her hands.

But there was no pity in the Amazon's face or manner.

She was as cold and stern as a statue. Pity! She enjoyed their pain.

"Oh! do have some mercy, ladies and gentlemen?" groaned Catchpole. "Consider that we are married men, and if you have no pity for us, think of our wives and have pity for them!" exclaimed Grabham.

"Wives! You are nice men to talk about wives. Do you pity the wives of the poor fellows you take up and have sent to Tyburn?"

The constables had a very good answer to this most unfair charge.

They might have said they only did their duty and obeyed orders, and the thieves did not.

But they dared not speak out boldly. Besides, there was a horrible practice at that time which made the constables hated even by honest, respectable men. I mean the fearful custom of giving blood-money!

This was managed in the following way—

A man started as highwayman, cracksman, or some other illegal profession.

The constables knew where to lay their hands upon him at any moment.

But, no.

They considered their own interests and not those of the public.

Of course a reward was offered for the arrest of the culprit.

But it was not enough.

More crimes were committed—more money was offered for his arrest.

At last the amount offered came to a large sum, and then the constables, who had treated the man almost like a friend before, swooped down upon their victim and carried him off.

They had all the evidence cut and dried, and escape was impossible.

So off in a cart, seated on a coffin, with his back to the horses, went Dare-Devil Dick, or Jolly Jack of Blackheath, and many others, who seemed to think it rather a noble thing, instead of a most degrading one.

Ladies wept and threw them nosegays. Noble lords, who were not a bit more virtuous or decorous than they are now-a-days—in fact, it seems to be the privilege of the aristocracy to remain like stagnant water, so still that it stinks; noble lords sent them cambric shirts to be hanged in, and laughed and chaffed the miserable wretches as they went to their doom.

Of course the clergyman was there to pray. But who listened to him?

Not even the doomed man who stood on the threshold of eternity.

How could he pay any attention amidst the cheering, yelling, laughing crowd, formed of the scum of the people and the ordinary run of the senseless, heartless aristocracy—the so-called nobles who have for so many centuries degraded England?

The fatal noose was tied and—well, we draw a veil over the last scene.

There hangs a man who a little time back was full of life and hope.

Wicked, we do not deny; but were the gay ladies and his noble patrons less so?

Worse—far worse. They were rich, and yet they had all the desires to act as amateur hangmen, even as a titled brute did the other day.

Then the constable pocketed his blood-money and went home to rejoice.

What wonder the people looked with hatred upon the constable, who far more encouraged crime than prevented it!

And so it was that not one look of compassion came in the face of man or woman when Catchpole and Grabham pleaded for mercy.

"No! we will have no mercy upon you," cried Judy, her eyes flashing. "Did not you, or some of you fellows, hang my poor husband for the blood money?"

"Hang them—hang them!" shouted the excited crowd. "They deserve it."

"No; we will not hang them, because I am not sure they are the men who led my husband on, and then seized and sold him to the gallows."

Catchpole and Grabham were delighted to hear this, for they now recognised the virago and knew that they had been the very constables who had sold her husband, and a pretty pull they had made out of it.

"No; we will not hang them. Bill Blarney, order in two bowls of punch as hot as the people can make it."

Catchpole and his companion seemed greatly relieved at this order, as they thought that all they would have to do would be to "pay their footing," as it is commonly called—that is, pay for the two bowls of punch, and then be permitted to depart in peace.

Unhappy men! How little did they know what was in store for them!

The punch was brought, and then Judy Bulgrudery, who had become suddenly as imperious as the Empress Theodora, ordered two of the strongest men in the company to take the bowls and compel the unfortunate constables to drink them—one each.

Vainly they implored to be spared, declaring that the punch was so hot that it scalded their mouths.

Their prayers were not listened to, or perhaps it would be better to say, were only derided.

They were compelled to drink not only the health of Spring-Heeled Jack, but of the whole company.

Resistance was useless, and with many a gulp they drunk off the punch.

The liquid being potent as well as very hot, soon had the desired effect upon the constables.

They staggered to their feet and began singing all kinds of songs.

"Now bring in the book and swear them in members of the Black Highwaymen."

This proposition seemed to sober the constables a little.

"Stop—stop" they cried; "to do what you wish would make us liable to be hanged.

"That is just what we know," replied Judy, with a laugh; "and just what we want."

The company roared at this piece of pleasantry, and called on them to sign.

But here the men were obstinate.

Their necks might depend on it, and they would not do so.

"Well, then," said Judy, with a laugh, "since you will not do that you shall join the merry company of Moonrakers."

"Any company sooner than that dreadful Black Band."

"Let it be so. Take them away, lads, and we will soon instruct them."

The miserable wretches were seized and dragged out into the porch of the inn.

Here they were placed back to back, at the mercy of the storm, which now raged fiercely, whilst the others took shelter in the doorways of the hostelry and the stables, all laughing with delight; and even the landlord came forth, pipe in one hand and a foaming tankard of brimming ale in the other, to witness what he was pleased to call the fun.

Presently a large blanket was produced, and six men seized it.

One of these stalwart fellows stood at each corner, and the other two took up their position one on each side.

Each grasped the blanket firmly with both hands, and then two others, lifting Mr. Catchpole up, threw him into the centre of the blanket.

Then the men who held the blanket ran all together, paused a moment, and sprung back suddenly, so that the blanket was stretched to its fullest extent, the consequence being that the miserable Catchpole was jerked some dozen feet in the air, from whence he fell back into the blanket.

Up he was thrown again, and this was repeated at least twenty times, until the unhappy wretch was so dazed with his flight through the air and the effects of the punch that he could do nothing but sigh and yawn.

The sport thus began to lose much of its excitement.

When he had been able to beg for mercy and yell as he sped upwards, the laughter had been uproarious, but now it was over.

Over for Catchpole, but not for his comrade, Elias Grabham.

Catchpole was removed from the blanket and Grabham forced to take his place.

Up he went, and being a somewhat lighter man than his companion, he flew up higher and came down much lighter, so that he lasted longer and the inhuman merriment was again resumed whilst Judy and some of the other viragos clapped their hands, and sang in chorus something like this—

> "*There he goes, up! up! up!*
> *There he goes, down! down! down!*
> *There he goes, head over heels,*
> *And falls on his feet or crown.*"

Surely never were two men so fearfully tormented as these two!

Mr. Grabham lasted out so well that the pleasure he gave them seemed inexhaustible.

But pleasure is fleeting, and after cursing, imploring, and shouting, he become as silent as his companion.

But the fun had become so fascinating that it was not to be easily relinquished.

Catchpole had somewhat recovered, and a cry arose that he should be put back and receive another dose.

Then somebody more fiendlike than the rest suggested that the pair of them should be put in and tossed in the blanket together.

With a yell of delight the proposition was accepted by the crowd.

Catchpole, pale and trembling, was lifted up and thrown with but little ceremony upon the body of his panting companion.

The additional weight needed additional strength, but for such work as this hands are never needed.

A dozen volunteers sprang forward, and up shot the luckless wights high in the air.

But now the so-called fun was redoubled, for the two constables knocked against each other as they flew up in the air or fell in the blanket.

There they bit, kicked, and scratched each other as well as they could, considering that their arms were bound.

Then Judy led off the chorus as before, singing—

> "*There they go up! up! up!*
> *There they go down! down! down! &c.*"

The chorus had been sung once through, and the repetition had come to the "Down! down! down!" when the words became prophetic, for Catchpole and Grabham came down clinging together.

The weight was too much for the blanket.

It split, and the two constables rolled through with a crash to the ground.

Amidst sneers and laughter they were lifted up and conducted back to the parlour of the Bull in Top Boots.

Here they were once more ordered to take the oath and sign the book of the Black Band.

They no longer hesitated, but signed at once.

"Now, mark what I have to say," said Bill Blarney, who had dictated the oath and witnessed the signature. "If you break that oath, or in any way, by word or deed—by writing or hinting—you try to betray the band, you will be dead men before twenty hours have passed over your heads. You, knowing this, still swear to be true to your comrades, and acknowledge me your captain?"

The constables gulped down the curses which rose to their lips, but made no attempt to utter them, only stammering out a weak, tremulous—

"Yes."

"Boys!" cried Blarney, "you have heard what they have sworn, and can bear witness to it?"

"We can!" shouted the men.

"And if they break their oath in the slightest degree the penalty is—"

"Death!" replied the stern chorus.

"We—we will be true to our word!" cried the trembling men.

"Ha! ha! ha!" came as the fellows said this, and a vivid flash of lightning showed the terrible figure clinging batlike to the window, glaring in with demoniacal pleasure at the scene.

Then came a loud burst of thunder, and when the people had recovered from their horror and astonishment the fiendlike figure had disappeared.

"By the horns of the devil! it is a terrible night," said Blarney, with a shudder. "I think, lads and lasses, we had better separate."

Blarney did not care to own the truth of the matter, but the fact was that he did not like the constant appearance of Spring-Heeled Jack.

Judy by this time had drunk so much that she would have faced the devil, as far as courage went; but the drink had deprived her of all powers of movement, and she leaned back in her chair snoring loudly.

So, as the rest of the company prepared to depart, Blarney made her as comfortable as he could on a settle, placing some old clothes, which he borrowed from the landlord, over her to keep her warm, and a sack rolled up by way of a pillow beneath her head.

In this comfortable position Captain Blarney left his charmer to sleep off the drink.

Then, pulling his coat tightly around him, he bade the landlord good-night, and having given some orders as to Judy's care and comfort, ventured out into the night.

The night was indeed a rough one.

The wind howled amongst the chimney pots—the rain came down in heavy showers, the lightning flashed through the dark, heavy sky, and the thunder roared and rattled like a battery of artillery.

Blarney made his way to Blackfriars Bridge, when the storm increased so in violence that he took shelter under one of the dark arches, little dreaming what adventures this would lead to.

---

## CHAPTER XXXVII.

### THE MEETING BENEATH THE ARCH—THE ROW DOWN THE RIVER.

As Blarney stood beneath the dark arch of the bridge, and glanced down the river, the sight he beheld was grand in the extreme, but terrible and wild.

The sky was as black as ink, only being lit up by the vivid flashes of the forked lightning.

The wind rushed along in fierce gusts, which it was hard to stand up against.

It howled through the arches, screaming like so many fiends, invisible to the eye, but palpable to touch and hearing.

A night on which witches and warlocks would hold their revels.

At his feet rolled the dark, swollen river, moaning and groaning as it hurried on to the sea.

Blarney believed himself alone, but, to his astonishment, a flash of lightning more brilliant than those which had gone before showed him a tall man, masked, and clad in a long cloak.

On his head was a slouched hat, and his legs and feet were clad in heavy riding-boots, the rest of his dress being hidden by his cloak.

There was something supernatural in the fellow's look that Blarney did not like, and he drew a little on one side whilst he eyed the dim outline of the stranger with the greatest suspicion.

"You need not fear me, Captain Blarney," said the stranger, in deep tones.

"By the powers! But he knows my name. Who are you?"

"One who has employed you more than once," replied the other.

"If that is the case, who are you—friend or foe?"

"A friend, and one who will reward you well if you serve me faithfully."

"Sure, the faithfulness of most services depends upon the pay."

"Of the payment you need not doubt. That shall be certain and good."

"Wurrah! but that's the kind of thing which suits Bill Blarney."

"The services I require will not be performed without some danger."

"What! now, and is it a coward you take me for? What would an adventure be unless it had a spice of the devil in it?"

As he said these words a fearful flash of lightning illuminated the scene, and Blarney again saw the stranger perfectly, and it must be confessed that he did not like his looks.

"But stop!" he cried. "Maybe you are the devil himself? I know Father O'Flaherty used to declare that I served him more than anyone else, and, be jabers! I believe his reverence was right."

"I can fully believe that," replied the stranger, with a bitter laugh.

"True for you, sir; but at the same time there's a difference between serving his Satanic Majesty directly and indirectly. The last you may do by accident, but the other—well, maybe it would be awkward."

"Fear not; I have not the honour to be his Satanic Majesty, or even one of his imps as yet. But I have no time to waste. Here are ten pieces of gold. Say that you will obey my commands and they are yours."

The temptation of the gold almost overcame all scruples on the Irishman's score.

But still he hesitated, and men, like women, when once hesitating, are lost.

"Well, your honour," he began, "I am sure I would do all I could to oblige you, but times are hard, and the ten pieces of gold would go only a little way."

"Do as I bid you, and when to-night's work is done the ten shall be doubled."

"Shure! and what a coaxing way you have," said Blarney, in the tones his name implies.

"Enough of that. Is it a bargain, or is it not?" cried the stranger, impatiently.

"Yes, sir, I'm on. Now what am I to do before I touch the shiners?"

"There are the ten I promised you. You see I keep my promise."

"And by the piper who played before Moses I'll keep mine."

"See that you do, or it will be the worse for you. I was at the Bull in Top Boots to-night."

"The deuce you were! I did not see you there," cried Blarney.

"I had no intention that you should. But I saw all the treatment that the two constables received, and their having to take the oath to the Black Band."

"Then you saw as pretty a little bit of sport as you ever did see or will again."

"And I saw Mistress Judy's pretty dance with Spring-Heeled Jack."

Blarney scratched his head, but said nothing to this.

"That does not seem to have pleased you quite as much?"

"Curse the fellow—no!" cried Blarney, quickly. "It's my belief that he is the devil himself. He has cast a spell upon Judy, and that's sure. I never saw her go on so before."

"He is no devil, but a man. I have often met him, and know what I say is true. One day, if it suits his purpose, he will carry your dear lady off, as—as he has done some others. I know the brute's character."

"If he dare lay a hand upon Judy Bulgrudery I'll have his life."

"I applaud your sentiment, Captain Blarney. I, too, have sworn to kill this monster whenever I get the chance. In that, at least, we agree."

"May your shadow never be less for those words," said Blarney.

"And now to business. You know the Thames-wall?"

"No one knows it better. I have had too many jobs on it not to."

"Good! And you can manage a boat well?"

"Divil a Thames waterman better, above or below bridge."

"Good again. You also know one Gedge Foote, a deformed scoundrel?"

"What man who has been on the road does not know Gedge?"

"Ah! I thought so. He is is a 'fence'—in other words, a receiver of stolen goods?"

"You seem to know him almost as well as I do," replied Blarney.

"Yes, I know him and what he is; but the business I have with him is very different from yours. You know his house?"

"What the old one down by the Mint? I should think I do."

"I must go there immediately," said the stranger.

"It's a jolly long walk," replied Blarney; "and such a night, too!"

"But I want to go the quickest way, and that is by water."

"Impossible! The river is far too rough for that—the boat might be swamped."

"I am aware of that, and have provided myself with a boat so broad in the beam that she will be safe even in this fearful night. You must take one oar, and I will pull the other."

"And when we have arrived there what are we to do?"

"You will have to ground the boat whilst I visit Gedge Foote."

"And after that—what then?"

"We must pull to some place of safety, where I will pay you the return money."

"It's dangerous work, but it shall be done. Where is the boat?"

"Here—moored close by the side of this pier," replied the stranger.

"Stay one moment. How did you know that I was here?" asked Blarney.

"Why I followed you from the Bull in Top Boots."

"Yes, yes, I know that; but about the boat—how did that come here? You had not time to get it since we left the tavern."

"Certainly not, most suspicious of men. That was placed there before nightfall. I had made up my mind to visit old Gedge Foote, but wanted someone to guide me."

"Why did you not go in the daytime, and by land?"

"For two very good reasons. In the first place, I do not wish to seen. You can understand that?"

"Yes; I have been placed in the same circumstances myself."

"I can well believe that. The other reason is that Gedge Foote does not care for visitors before this time of the night. He has reasons for that."

"I know he has," laughed Blarney. "Well, the pay is good, and I have often risked my life for less money, and so, sir, I am on with you. We had better start at once, as the tide will turn shortly, then the work we shall have before us will be almost more than we can manage."

The two men entered the boat, the painter was cast off, and the boat swirled out into the tide.

"Keep her head straight, your honour—keep her head straight, as if she gets broadside on to the tide we shall be lost. Curse it! what is that?"

The last exclamation was caused by a sudden thump on the bow of the boat, which made it nearly dip under water.

Neither of the men dared leave off rowing because of the rush of the water, and therefore they could only glance over their shoulders.

Not a thing was to be seen, and the boat now sped through the water.

"Bah! it's nothing," said the stranger; "pull on as quickly as you can."

They pulled with all their might and main, but both men seemed to think that there was something wrong with the boat.

"I should think this a bad boat to pull against tide," growled Blarney.

"It should not be; the man from whom I bought it declared it a splendid one for pulling. But we must be close on the house now, and in a few minutes shall once more be in safety. Give way, my lad!"

They did pull with might and main, and were soon under old Gedge Foote's house.

This house was one of those old buildings which had once been a mansion—almost a palace—but had long fallen into decay, and had become as miserable looking and as low as the neighbourhood had become in which it was situated.

The basement wall was only two feet from the river, and the balcony above overhung the stream.

The windows, save the one which was by the balcony that overhung the stream, were all securely barred and bolted, in such a manner that they seemed as if they would defy the most expert burglar.

One light, and that a dim one, was alone to be seen, and that shone from the window in front of which the balcony ran.

"The miserly wretch is at home," said the stranger. "Ship your oars and make the boat fast."

Bang!

And once more down went the bows of the boat; but this time they could see the cause.

Bounding from the boat on to the stone quay, Spring-Heeled Jack flew into the air, and then turning round, cried—

"Ha! ha! ha! I thank you for my row, Sir Roland. One day I will make you and your servants suffer for this wickedness. Would it were that I was at liberty to denounce you now! but I cannot. No thought of mercy should hold me back. I would strike and spare not. So go on your wicked way; but, remember, the day of reckoning is growing nearer and nearer."

"Fiend!" cried Sir Roland, as he drew a pistol, "thus will I—"

But before he could level the pistol Spring-Heeled Jack had disappeared.

"Aid me to land," said the stranger, who was none other than Sir Roland, "and wait for me here. Fear not! I will not keep you long."

Sir Roland leaped ashore, and hurried down a narrow lane, so as to reach the front of the house.

---

## CHAPTER XXXVIII.

### SIR ROLAND'S BUSINESS WITH GEDGE FOOTE IS SOMEWHAT INTERRUPTED.

OLD Gedge Foote sat in deep meditation in his own room, scanning some books of accounts by the aid of a single dip candle.

Three times did he go over one column of figures, and at last cast down his pen in despair.

"Confusion seize the girl!" he exclaimed, as he rose from his chair and paced up and down the room. "Confusion seize the girl! Has she bewitched me? She must have done, or I, Gedge Foote, who has laughed at the tears of beauty when pleading for mercy, either for themselves or for those they loved—not only laughed, but enjoyed it—would not now be so overthrown that I cannot pay attention to my dear books. I must be bewitched."

Throwing himself back into the chair he made another attempt, but without success.

Once more dashing down his pen, he sprung up, and was about to resume his march, when he was startled by a loud knocking at the door.

"Who can this be?" he muttered. "I expected no one, and few call on me who have not made an appointment."

He glanced hastily round the room to see that there were no valuables left about.

Then he carefully put away his books, and taking a brace of pistols from the wall, candle in hand, left the apartment.

No sooner had he done so than the catch of the window was forced back, and Spring-Heeled Jack entered the room.

Wrapping the cloak—which being bound to his arms and legs gave him the bat-like look which he had when he leaped through the air—round his body, he crouched down in a corner and waited to see what would happen.

He had carefully closed the window, but not fastened it, before this.

Meanwhile, Gedge Foote had crept down to the front door, and opening a small trap, not more than an inch and a-half in diameter, which was placed in the centre of the door, thrust forth the barrel of his pistol, at the same time exclaiming—

"Who are you, and what want you here at this time of night?"

"A friend! Open, Gedge Foote, and you will not repent it," said the voice.

"I open to no man who does not give me his name," said Gedge.

"Are you as particular with all your customers?" sneered Sir Roland; for it was he.

"Not all; but then, I know their voices—I do not know yours."

A muttered oath was all that this remark called forth.

"Begone!" said Gedge, sternly. "Begone, or I fire. My pistol never misses."

"Wait, and I will put my name under the door."

This seemed to satisfy Gedge Foote, who watched for the slip of paper.

But as he did so he took care not to withdraw his pistol.

The paper appeared, and Gedge Foote, having removed his pistol, quickly closed the catch and then picked up the scrip.

"Sir Roland Ashton!" he exclaimed. "What can he want with me?"

Once more the knocking sounded at the door.

"He once was a good customer of mine, and I must not refuse him admittance."

"Confound it, man!" cried Sir Roland; "am I to be kept here all night in the rain?"

"Patience—patience, Sir Roland, and I will unbar the door."

"There is no need to publish my name all over the Mint," said Sir Roland, as he walked in and shook the rain-drops from his cloak.

"It would not be the first time it has been heard there, or in Alsatia either."

"Bar the door. I would speak to you in private," said Sir Roland, not noticing this last speech.

"As you will, worshipful sir. I am at your commands."

Saying which, Gedge Foote closed and barred the door carefully.

"This way, Sir Roland—this way. It is a terrible night, and the business ought indeed to be urgent that has brought you out in it. This room I use as my office."

And with that the old miser lighted the way into the room where we first discovered him.

"Be seated, Sir Roland—be seated," said Gedge Foote, as he motioned towards a chair opposite his own by the table. "It is many years since we did business together. What is it now?"

"The cry that is made by most men, and which I had never let out of my mouth when I was young—"

"And that cry, Sir Roland?" demanded Gedge Foote, suspiciously.

"Money—the universal want. I want and must have a large sum of money."

"What! you the rich Sir Roland Ashton in want of money? Impossible!"

"It may seem so to you; but it is not so in fact. I have drawn largely on my estates. For all the money that is paid my agents is stolen."

"Stolen!—how? Do you think, Sir Roland, that I have had anything to do in this matter?"

"Far be it from me to think so," replied Sir Roland, "although I know, at one time, Gedge Foote knew as much about the gentlemen of the Mint as most men."

"Ah! that was when you were one of the captains of the Black Band."

"Hush! the least said of that the better," exclaimed Sir Roland, hastily.

"And the least said about my past affairs the better, Sir Roland," said Gedge.

"Well, let that be agreed; and now about the money?"

"Impossible! I have no money to lend," cried Gedge Foote.

"Tut! do not tell me that; I know you are wealthy, very wealthy."

"You mistake, my dear Sir Roland; "I have lost all my money."

"And how did you lose all your money?" demanded Sir Roland.

"The same way as you did," replied Gedge, taken off his guard.

"And may I ask how that was?" returned Sir Roland, sharply.

"Stolen!" grinned Mr. Gedge Foote, with a look of triumph, as much as to say, "I have matched you there, my fine fellow—one lie for another."

"Do not think to do me, Gedge Foote," said Sir Roland. "Remember, I know the history of the sunken pit, or well, or whatever you call it. What I want is gold, and that I mean to have. But mark you this, Gedge, you shall have twenty-five per cent. interest, and that safe, upon it."

"With security?" demanded Gedge, rather puzzled.

"Aye! with security. You know the Meadow Farm? Well, I will place all the deeds of ownership in your hands as security. Will that not suit you, you old Shylock?"

"Humph! How much do you want?" growled Gedge Foote.

"Two thousand pounds."

"Two thousand pounds! Are you mad?"

"The farm is worth five thousand pounds at least."

"Then there is the interest on my money."

"Which is more than covered. Come, Gedge, let us go and fetch the money, and then we will have one of your old bottles of Burgundy."

"You mean honourably to me?" replied Gedge, doubtfully.

"Of course I do. Why should I not?"

"True! Well, come with me. I know you know the secret of this house."

"I ought to. Was it not in my family for years? Aye! built for them, I believe."

"Then," hissed Gedge Foote, "why did they make that well?"

"I don't know," said Sir Roland, calmly, but his face showed that he was much annoyed; "to cool their wines, I suppose."

"Or drown their wives!"

"Silence, hound!" cried Sir Roland, passionately; "one word more and I quit this house."

"Do, and I'll keep my money. Good-night, Sir Roland—good-night!"

"Don't be a fool, Gedge. You know very well I don't mean that. Come, let me have the money, and then for the wine.

*Jolly old wine—jolly old wine!*
*The ruddy juice which flows from the vine."*

Followed by Sir Roland, old Gedge Foote, candle in hand, led the way down to the cellars of the house.

With a massive key he opened one.

A deep, dark, dank cellar, in the middle of which there appeared a pit.

They knew the pit, or well, but they did not know that Spring-Heeled Jack was close behind them—stealthily watching all their movements.

A looped rope over a pulley, which was fixed to the roof, hung over this well, and taking the candle-stick in his teeth, old Gedge descended into the well.

It was with difficulty that Spring-Heeled Jack could keep himself from springing on Sir Roland and hurling him down the pit.

However, he did; and, presently, by means of the double rope, the miser hauled himself up again to the top, with two heavy bags of gold slung round his neck and a well-crusted bottle in his pocket.

He was evidently used to the double rope, and landed himself safely without assistance.

No sooner did Jack see them reappear, than he lightly bounded up the stairs and hid himself behind a partition.

"There is the money, Sir Roland; now the title deeds of the Meadow Farm."

"Here!" cried Sir Roland, as he smacked them down. "Now, my dear fellow, let us drink to the lasses we love best—yours, Gedge?"

"Daisy Leigh!" cried Gedge, throwing himself back in his chair and raising his glass.

"Daisy Leigh!" cried Sir Roland, in horror. "You dare not say to my face that you have presumed to raise your eyes to a lady of my family?"

Before Gedge could answer, the sepulchral laughter of Spring-Heeled Jack rang through the room and he leaped upon the table, leaving them all in the dark.

## CHAPTER XXXIX.

### SIR ROLAND PLANS A DEED OF ROBBERY.

SIR ROLAND and Gedge Foote staggered to their feet in astonishment, and were just in time to see Spring-Heeled Jack throw open the window and rush on to the balcony.

Sir Roland dashed after the monster, and Spring-Heeled Jack leaped upon the balustrade, and turned as if to defy them.

"Ha! ha! ha!" he roared, as he shook the money-bags which he had snatched up in Sir Roland's very face. "This gold shall go to the poor. It shall not be used for the vile purposes to which you would put it."

Sir Roland's hands had nearly clasped him when, with another yell of demoniacal laughter, Jack leaped into the air, and with an aim and precision that was perfectly marvellous dashed down into the boat, staving it in.

Blarney yelled for help, while Spring-Heeled Jack leaped ashore, laughing loudly at the mischief he had created.

"The fiend has escaped!" cried Sir Roland, mad with rage.

"Yes," groaned Gedge Foote; "and he has taken all the money with him."

"Help! help! help! The boat is sinking and I shall be drowned!" roared Blarney.

"Never mind the gold, Foote," said Sir Roland, making for the door. "My man is in danger, and for reasons I cannot explain I would not have him killed for twice the gold."

"Would you? For reasons I need not explain, I'd rather save the money than the man," said Gedge Foote, mournfully; but nevertheless he hurried after Sir Roland and unbarred the door for him.

"I'll stand here, Sir Roland, and wait your return," he said. "Remember, three slight taps on the door will be enough to call me to re-open."

Sir Roland nodded assent and hurried away to rescue Blarney Bill.

No sooner had he gone than old Gedge, ever suspicious, began to think if he had done right in letting the baronet depart so easily.

"May this not have been a trick to do me?" he muttered. "May not this so-called fiend be in the pay of this Sir Roland—a servant, a friend?"

Gedge shook with rage when he thought of this, and at last gasped out—

"If I thought so I'd—I'd murder him; I would, indeed! He would not be the first one whom I have throttled."

And he held forth his long, bony hand, and cleaved the air as if he had someone's throat in his grip.

A more horribly fiendish-looking fellow could not be imagined.

"He talks about his family. Well, it was a good one. But who disgraced it? Sir Roland Ashton—the man with the iron will and no conscience. Ho! ho! ho! Sir Roland Ashton, I know enough of your past history to make you dread me—deformed old miser that I am. Ha! ha! ha!"

"Ha! ha! ha!"

Gedge Foote turned round in affright.

Surely he had not imagined that he had heard the laugh of the fiend!

And was it only fear which made him think that he saw a dark form like a huge bat bound lightly up the stairs?

But the light given out by the dim candle, which he had taken the precaution to relight before he followed Sir Roland, did not show him anything distinctly enough to convince him.

Then the laugh had been so subdued that it might really have only been an echo of his own.

"I am nervous—the loss of the money has made me so. But Sir Roland shall pay it me back. It was through him that I lost it, and he is answerable for it."

And so Gedge Foote consoled himself. Even fear giving place to the love of money.

Meanwhile, Sir Roland had hurried down to the river-side.

The boat had sunk, but Blarney had managed to catch hold of an iron ring in the stone wall, where he clung with desperation.

"S'death, Blarney, what a night we are in for!" laughed Sir Roland.

"Don't stand there laughing at me!" roared Blarney. "I wish I had never seen your dirty face. Here are my legs floating about up to my knees in the water, and the saints alone know how much deeper I shall sink if I leave go my hold. Pull me out or I must go down. My hands are as cold as ice."

"Give me your hand and I will pull you out," said Sir Roland, laughing.

"It's meself that will do that, and I never grasped the hand of a friend with greater eagerness. Sure, my top boots, which Judy admired so, have become nothing but leather 'Black Jacks,' full of water. Oh! that thief of the world—that Spring-Heeled Jack—to serve me a trick like this. What harm have I done him? But I'll have my revenge on the ruffian—be he man or be he devil."

By this time Sir Roland had pulled the fellow out of the water, and he stood shivering on the bank.

Certainly up to the knees he was soaking, and his top boots were wet through and thoroughly filled with water.

"Come," said Sir Roland Ashton, "I will put you in a way to gain that which will repay you for all that you have suffered."

"Do you think now that what you have promised me will repay the trouble, not to say the disgrace, I have been through? Devil a bit of it, Sir Roland! I like your pay better than your

# SPRING-HEELED JACK,

## THE TERROR OF LONDON.

SIR ROLAND SEVERED THE ROPE AND THE UNHAPPY WRETCH DISAPPEARED.

No. 13.

service, and you must either increase the former or decrease the latter. Here, stay a moment. I feel as if I was walking in Biddy Malone's washing tub. Boots ! they are buckets."

He paused a few moments, and, in spite of Sir Roland's impatient protests, pulled his boots off, and poured the water out of them, and even the baronet had to confess that they were full of water.

"Oh ! be jabers. Now I have got them off I cannot get them on again," groaned Blarney, as, seating himself on a projecting stone, he made desperate attempts to pull them on.

"Then throw them away," cried Sir Roland, impatiently. "We have no time to lose."

"What ! throw them away. The boots Judy admired so ? Go in my stocking feet ?"

"Take your stockings off will be the wisest plan," replied Sir Roland.

"Och ! and I think you are right, for it is penance I should do to be with you."

"Silence, fool ! I tell you that if you obey me to-night, not only shall you have money enough to buy fifty pairs of boots, but a full-blood mare, a pair of snappers, fine clothing—aye ! even finer than most gentlemen wear."

"You can? That can't be done on thirty shiners—you must know that, Sir Roland !"

"I know that perfectly well. But it can be done on a thousand !"

"A—a what ?" cried Bill Blarney, who seemed struck all of a heap at the sum.

"Upon ten hundred pounds and my especial favour," said the baronet.

Mr. Blarney made no further reply than flinging his boots—the boots which Judy had so loved—into the Thames.

Then pulling off his stockings he rose up and quietly observed—

"Show me the way to do that, governor, and I'm with you. It is not every day that a fellow gets such a chance, and I'm not the boy to give it up."

"I knew you would not. Now be careful and listen to me."

Here Sir Roland whispered something in Blarney's ear, which made even that hardened villain turn round and look queer.

"Do you mean it ?" he asked, in a hoarse whisper. "Can't it be done without—"

"Are you mad? Would you have him wake up the Mint ?"

"Well, I should not mind that with most men ; but Gedge Foote is a power in himself. Even the Master of the Mint is under obligation to him."

"True ; and, therefore, we must run no risks. You understand ?"

"Yes ; but Gedge Foote knows me too well to trust me in his cellar with him."

"Well, it must be done, and I have a way of doing it. Do not doubt, he will not suspect—and —well, I have the means of making him trust to my word. Come."

"There is only one thing I fear," said Bill Blarney, and he shrank a little back, as if wishing to withdraw from the arrangement.

"And what is that ?"

"The devil, or otherwise Jack o' the Spring Heels."

"Tut—nonsense ! I will do the deed ; you must get the gold."

Bill Blarney thought for a moment, and then said—

"I'm on, Sir Roland—I'll do it. The price is too much for anyone to refuse. I'll stick to you until all's blue."

"Then keep quiet. Gedge Foote is here, and we must go into his place unless he suspects something. Be sure to play your part well, and we must succeed."

## CHAPTER XL.

### THE MURDER IN THE MINT.

GEDGE FOOTE was pleased to see Sir Roland return, but he eyed Blarney somewhat suspiciously.

"What ! don't you know me, Gedge ?" cried Blarney, as he slapped the old man on the shoulder.

"No—stay a moment. It's Bill Blarney, or Blarney Bill !" he cried.

"That's right, old cock-of-the-walk, and it's many a good bargain I've brought to you."

"Aye, aye ! but let bygones be bygones. I have given all that up now."

This Gedge Foote said as he fastened the door securely.

"Given that up ? Why, you will never do that until you are in the grave, and then, if they bury you near a family vault, I believe you would steal all the coffin plates and handles, if they were silver."

"Then the coffins would not belong to any of your family," growled Gedge. "They were all buried in the prison precincts, I believe. Ho ! ho ! ho ! I had you there."

"If you do not keep a polite tongue between your teeth I'll pull it out."

"Come, come, no quarrelling. I will not have that," said Sir Roland.

"Then let him look to himself," replied Bill Blarney ; "I'm in no mood to jest."

"Neither am I," said Gedge, with a grim smile. "I don't jest, as a rule, and I think I am a match in strength for Bully Blarney."

And here the deformed wretch stretched forth his long arms so as to show their muscles.

There was no mistake about it ; they were im mensely powerful.

"Tut, tut, Gedge Foote," said Sir Roland ; "we all know your courage and strength. What man in the Mint could doubt it? Did you not wrestle and overpower the Giant Blacksmith, as people called him ? I remember it as well as if it were only yesterday, although I was only a lad then."

"Ah ! but I was a much younger man then. Not that I think I have lost much of my strength or skill," and here he glanced longingly at Bill Blarney, as if he should like to have another turn with him. "I think I could break a man's neck in a fall, as I did the Giant Blacksmith's, even now."

"To be sure you could—to be sure you could !" said Sir Roland ; "so one would not like to try jokes on you. But come upstairs and let us be jolly. I wish to settle about this money and speak to you about dainty Daisy."

Overcome by the praise which he received, and also anxious to hear what he could about Daisy, Gedge Foote led the way upstairs into the room we have before described, and placing the candle on the table motioned the others to be seated.

"Why, how is this, Blarney ?" he said, with a chuckle, "Where are your boots ?"

"By the powers ! how should I know ? They are floating away somewhere down the Thames. Shure ! that thief of the world, Spring-Heeled

Jack, treated me with a ducking up to the knees, and a pretty state I should have been in walking about with my boots full of water. So that I should not spoil your illegant carpet, I just took them off and threw them away."

"You are very considerate, Bully Blarney, I am sure," sneered Gedge Foote.

"Come—come! no more compliments," said Sir Roland, who was secretly enjoying this sparring. "Give him a pair of boots, Gedge Foote, for as we have lost our boat we shall have to spend a night in the Mint."

"Not the first time you have done that, Sir Roland Ashton," laughed Gedge.

"Nor will it be the last, I daresay," replied Sir Roland, carelessly.

"'Sdeath! I should think not. But if I give Bully Blarney boots, who is to pay for them?"

"To the devil with you, you spalpeen! Do you think that I want any one to pay for my boots?" cried Blarney. "There's a guinea for you," and he threw a guinea on the table.

"Not enough by half," said Gedge, coolly, as he thrust back the guinea.

"Oh! the thief of the world," cried Blarney, "to take advantage of a man's necessity. Shure! then, you are worse than a heathen Jew down Petticoat-lane."

"Make hay while the sun shines, you know," laughed Gedge Foote.

"But devil a bit of sun is there shining. Come, Gedge, out with the boots and a pair of warm stockings, and I'll spring another half guinea."

But Gedge Foote, the miser, was not to be done by Blarney.

It was not until another guinea had been advanced that the articles of clothing were produced and Bill Blarney made comfortable.

Then, Sir Roland having promised to pay all expenses, a large stone jar of brandy was produced, and the trio set to work to make a jovial night of it.

At least Gedge Foote imagined so. Little did he think how the night would end!

"See that that window is securely fastened, Gedge Foote," he said, as he poured out a bumper of brandy. "I have no taste for any further intrusion on the part of Spring-Heeled Jack. Even Bill Blarney has had enough of him."

"I should think I had. If I never see the devil again I shall not be sorry."

"If I see him again I'll have my arms round his throat," said Gedge.

"And do you think he would stand still and let you?" demanded Blarney.

"I should not ask him," replied Gedge Foote, with a chuckle, as he fastened the window securely, taking the greatest care to place a heavy piece of furniture in front of it, in doing which he was assisted by Sir Roland and Bill Blarney. "Once my hands are round a man's throat I don't think he has much chance of escape. What think you, Sir Roland?"

"I think that a fellow might as well try to get out of the pulley as your grasp."

"Ha! ha! ha! You have seen my handiwork, Sir Roland?"

Sir Roland shuddered, for he had seen Gedge Foote's performance, and a ghastly piece of work it was. But he deemed it wise not to say anything, and so passed it off with a laugh.

"We will not talk of these matters now," said Sir Roland, laughing; "but now let us have a jolly night."

Pipes were lit and glasses filled, and then many a tale was told—stories of such a nature that we certainly shall not write them down here, but which were received by the company with words of applause.

"Come, Gedge!" cried Sir Roland; "you used to sing a good song. Now let us have one."

"Nay, Sir Roland," laughed Gedge Foote, who had taken a great deal more drink than was good for him; "my singing days are over. I have no ear for music."

"Tut! man; let me see—this is how that song used to run in the jolly days of the Mint?"

And Sir Roland trolled out—

"THE MARQUIS AND PAIR.

"*I had just drank a cup and kissed the barmaid,*
*And of lies I had told her a few, I'm afraid;*
*When William, the ost er, says—'Here, Captain Dick,*
*I think if you ride to the heath, and ride quick,*
*With a couple of snappers, you may do the trick*
*On a marquis, who rides in his carriage and pair!'*"

"Hurrah!" cried Gedge Foote, who had now drank deeply of the spirits; "chorus—

'*On a marquis who rides in his carriage and pair!*'"

Then Sir Roland, who had thrown himself entirely into the party, sang—

"*So I mounted my mare, and I galloped along,*
*Just humming the tune of an old drinking song;*
*And beneath the dark tree used by old Turpin Dick,*
*I managed to do that neat little trick—*
*For the gold of the marquis I quickly did nick,*
*Then left him alone in his carriage and pair.*"

"Bravo!" cried Gedge Foote. "But how about that brandy? Who's to pay me for that?"

Gedge Foote had been drinking freely and felt quarrelsome.

"I will; don't think you shall lose by it. If you doubt me, here is my note of hand for it."

And, tearing a leaf out of his pocket-book, he wrote out an I O U.

Gedge Foote took it up, examined it carefully, and then placed it on a side-table.

"Will that satisfy you, Gedge?"

"Yes; that will do. But mark this—if it is not paid in time I shall be down at Ashton Hall with the bailiffs in no time."

"And we will give you as merry a meeting as you have given us in the Mint," laughed Sir Roland. "Now let us fill up our glasses, and Gedge shall sing us a song."

"It's many years since I sang a song," said Gedge, who was in that peculiar state of drink that he had left off being quarrelsome and had become morose.

"Nonsense, man. Have you forgotten the song that poor devil of an author, who had to seek the precincts of the Mint, wrote about you? Let me see, what was its name?"

"I know," cried Bill Blarney; "it was called 'My Character.'"

"Ah! that was it," cried Sir Roland. "No song was better known in the Mint than that, and no man sang it better than Gedge himself, or enjoyed the humour more."

Gedge Foote was tickled by this—his vanity was pleased and he did not fail to show it.

"Ha! ha! ha! I was a wild dog in those days. Ho! ho! ho! ho! Ugly as I am, the girls did not dislike old Gedge Foote. He used to win them."

"Buy them," whispered Blarney to Sir Roland, who nodded assent.

"Ha! ha! there was many a dainty little chit there; but none so dainty as little Daisy. Come, let us drink the health of dear little Daisy. Daisy, gentlemen, drink!"

Sir Roland's face turned red with passion, but he drank the toast.

"And now for the song," cried Blarney, and Gedge, who had drunk deeply, sang—

"GEDGE FOOTE'S HISTORY AND CHARACTER.

"*In childhood's hours, called sunny,*
*I never could delight*
*In jokes some folks called funny,*
*But dearly I loved spite.*
*My grandma's nice, soft cushions,*
*I stuffed quite full of pins;*
*With bruises and contusions,*
*I filled my brother's shins.*

"*For, oh! I'm a character—oh! I'm a character,*
*The like of which no one saw before;*
*Oh! yes, I'm a character—yes, I'm a character,*
*That people all do call a bore.*"

"*One day I got a blister,*
*And in the dead of night;*
*I wrapped it round my sister,*
*It drew her out of sight.*
*I've been a money lende r—*
*I ve kept a gambling den;*
*Paid dividends most slender,*
*And ruined many men.*

"*For, oh! I'm a character—oh! I'm a character,*
*A thing which no one can deny.*
*Yes, I'm a character—yes, I'm a character,*
*Who does deny it tells a lie.*"

"Bravo! bravo!"

Gedge bowed his thanks to the gentlemen who had so kindly praised him, and drank off his glass of spirits and water.

"Look here, Roland Ashton," he said, with sudden tipsy gravity, as he filled up another jorum of grog, "I'm not going to be gulled by you. I must have that money returned."

"So you shall, Gedge," replied Sir Roland, "have I not told you so?"

This was said in the most conciliatory manner, but there was a nasty twinkle in his eye Gedge Foot did not fail to notice.

"Told me so, yes—you have told me so; but I know what faith to put in your word. Bah! man, I never would trust anybody's word, and least of all would I trust that of Sir Roland Ashton."

"I know not why you should doubt me," replied Sir Roland, sharply.

"Pish! you are a bad man, Sir Roland; and bad men never care about their words."

"You ought to be a judge in such a case!" sneered Sir Roland Ashton.

He appeared to be very calm, but his eyes flashed fire.

Bill Blarney looked at Gedge Foote and opened a large clasp-knife beneath the table.

"I am a judge in such cases," said Gedge Foote, shaking his head.

"I should think very few good people had any dealings with you, Gedge Foote," laughed Blarney.

"So much the better, Bully Blarney, or I should not have you here."

Gedge Foote little thought how fast he was building up his own fate.

Then he cried, in a boastful tone, "I don't want the money—I have heaps of money—money I keep in a safe place, as you know, Sir Roland. Gad's life! I believe I could buy up Ashton Hall an l all the estates belonging to the family and not feel the poorer for it."

"And where do you keep all this vast amount of wealth?" asked Blarney.

"That's my secret, Bully Blarney," laughed Gedge Foote.

"We all know you are rich, Gedge," said Sir Roland, "and so you should be, considering the self-denying life you have led. Living all alone like a rat in a hole, how could you spend your money?"

"Ha! ha! ha! I've not been quite such a dull dog as you think."

"Indeed. I never heard that you were given to any gaiety, save now and then indulging in a social glass, as we have done this evening."

"Oh! I have had my fun," cried Gedge Foote, "only I was not such a fool as to let other people know it. Ask old Mrs. Foster, and she will tell you that Gedge Foote loves a girl's lips as much as most men. Ha! ha! ha! It was from her house that my dainty little Daisy gave me the slip. Pretty, dainty, little Daisy!"

Sir Roland bit his lip when he heard this hideous monster speak so of the charming girl allied to him by ties of blood-relationship.

But he made no remark, and bent his eyes down on the table, so that Gedge should not see their angry expression.

"Now look here, Sir Roland," continued Gedge, who kept on drinking freely, and who grew more impertinent as he drank; "you owe me two thousand pounds!"

"You seem to forget that I never had the money," said Sir Roland.

"What of that?" cried Gedge. "I have the acknowledgement of it safe enough, and, better still, I have one or two of your secrets, Sir Roland."

This was a dangerous thing for Gedge to have said, but he had drank too much to notice that.

"Ha! ha! Sir Roland. The lads of the Mint love old Gedge Foote, and would resent any injury done him. Be sure of that, and you, too, Bully Blarney. I'm not only free of the Mint, but I am one of the chief rulers. Ha! ha! ha!"

Sir Roland and Blarney exchanged glances with each other.

"I tell you, Sir Roland, that if I were to give the signal I could call up a number of men who would come to the rescue."

"I do not doubt it. I know that the rules of the Mint are very stringent," replied Sir Roland; but Bill Blarney noticed that he drew forth a sharp dagger made to cut as well as thrust—more like a hunting knife, in fact.

"Well, Sir Roland, I'll tell you what I will do. I'll not only forgive you that money, but I will advance you as much again, on one condition."

"Gedge, you are a prince of good fellows. Let me know the condition. It will be hard indeed if I cannot comply with them for such a sum."

"The thing is easy enough," replied Gedge. "Your cousin, Daisy Leigh, must become my wife!"

"Your wife! Are you mad? Have I not told you the thing is impossible?"

"Tut! Sir Roland. Do you think I care for what you say? I have an argument that will overcome all your scruples."

"And what is that argument?" asked Sir Roland, breathing heavily.

"The argument that moves all the world—money."

"You speak like a book," said Bully Blarney. "Money rules all."

"True," replied Sir Roland; "and as far as I am concerned, I should not care who married Daisy Leigh—whether it be our good friend, Gedge Foote, or anyone else. But I do not know where she is."

"That won't suit me, Sir Roland," said Gedge, as he lolled back in his chair. "You don't think that I was such a fool when I had once taken a fancy to the pretty little Daisy to lose sight of her?"

Sir Roland ground his teeth with rage, but answered, lightly—

"You speak to me in riddles, Gedge Foote; I do not understand you."

"Ho! ho! ho! None so hard of understanding as those who will not understand," roared Gedge Foote with a burst of coarse laughter, and he tossed off another bumper of neat spirits "Ho! ho! ho! That's a good one, that is. Do you think that I did not set my people to work? Of couse I did, and they precious soon ferreted something out. They knew all about her being at old Dimity's Theatre, and how she was carried off by you to the lone house in the wood, where, I suppose, she is now."

"So far I must admit that you have gained true information," said Sir Roland, quietly. "But you have not heard all the rest."

"The girl has not come to a violent death?" demanded Gedge, savagely.

"Not that I am aware of. I know not what has become of her."

"Don't humbug me. I'll not believe it. You carried her off."

"I do not deny it. I carried her off with the most virtuous designs in the world. I wished to save her from marrying a rascal so much beneath her—one Harry Banks, a clown."

"You protect her! A pretty protector you are, Sir Roland. Ha! ha! ha! Sir Roland Ashton setting up for a protector of innocence. That is rather too good a thing. No, no, Sir Roland—that will not do for us. We know a thing worth two of that."

"You may be remarkably knowing, Mr. Gedge Foote," said Sir Roland, calmly, "but I can assure you that such was my purpose. Not only did I do this at great expense to myself, but even whilst I was expostulating with the maiden in her folly, that fiend, Spring-Heeled Jack, bounded in at the window and carried her off, even as he did your money-bags."

"It's a lie!" roared Gedge Foote, who now, mad with drink, sprung from his chair. He leaned over the table, his blood-shot eyes glaring with rage, and his tongue hanging out of his mouth like a dog with hydrophobia. "It's a lie! Don't think to put me off with such stories, because I will not believe them."

"They are not stories!" thundered back Sir Roland Ashton.

"Oh! don't bully me. I am not to be bullied, I can tell you," retorted Gedge Foote. "A pretty thing, indeed, to try to make me believe this story. I suppose soon you will try to make me believe that Spring-Heeled Jack will come and bear me away?"

"I wish to Heaven he would!" cried Sir Roland, springing to his feet.

The gesture was not a threatening one, but Gedge Foote seemed to think so.

He likewise sprang to his feet and the two men grappled.

Sir Roland was a powerful man, but Gedge was much more so.

He twined his bony fingers round Sir Roland's neck and pressed him back.

"Blarney! Blarney!" cried Sir Roland; "strike this fiend down, or I am strangled."

Blarney, whom, truth to tell, had little reason to love Gedge, as few men of his class had—for they knew that the deformed dwarf would sell them to justice as soon as they were of no further use to him—sprung up, and swinging his chair round brought it down on the head of Gedge with such force that the blood spurted out.

Gedge Foote reeled back and gazed with horror around.

Yes; he saw it all now—the two villains were prepared for murder.

He had seen too many terrible cases in his time to doubt that.

The looks of the two men were like leaves from the Book of Fate, which he was doomed to read and find unalterable.

One quick gaze at the two and then he turned and fled.

Fled, shrieking and yelling for help, and pursued by Sir Roland Ashton.

Bully Blarney attempted to follow; but he had drank so much of the spirits that his foot catching against the table he fell flat on the floor.

Gedge flew out of the room like mad.

Sir Roland followed him as quickly as he could.

Away flew Gedge Foote through the place, yelling and crying for help. Up the stairs he flew and at last caught a bell rope.

"Dong, dong, dong!" the bell tolled out, and Gedge shouted in glee—

"The alarm bell is rang and the people of the Mint are aroused."

"Curse you!" cried Sir Roland. "You, at least, shall never live to tell the story."

Away—away! The chase of death, the victim first, the murderer following, and behind them retribution.

Sir Roland bounded up the stairs and Gedge Foote flew before him.

The house, as we have said before, was an old and handsome one, and, like most of these old-fashioned mansions, it had two staircases—one for the owner and his friends, and the other for the servants.

Gedge dashed down the back staircase, and was closely followed by Sir Roland, whilst Blarney took the other staircase, so as to cut off the miser's retreat.

But Gedge Foote saw through this movement, and darted off in another direction.

As if by a natural instinct he made for the cellar where he kept his gold.

Sir Roland was close upon his track, but fear lent Gedge Foote wings.

He reached the cellar, and at once seized the rope which hung over the well.

With this he swung himself over the yawning gulf, and began to descend the well.

"Saved! saved! saved!" he cried, in triumphant glee.

"Confusion! You shall not escape me!" cried Sir Roland.

As he spoke he made a dash with his knife at the rope.

At the same time he caught the other end of the rope, which passed over a pulley, and prevented it descending.

The strands of the rope were half cut through, and the miserable miser hung over the abyss, screaming and crying for mercy.

Sir Roland chuckled with delight as he beheld the fellow's agonies.

"Sir Roland—Sir Roland Ashton, spare me—spare me!"

"Not I, my dear Gedge Foote. I told you that I would pay you back the money, and I will. Ha! ha! ha! Egad! they say that there is truth at the bottom of a well. When you go there it will be the reverse. Lies—lies; nothing but lies!"

"Mercy, Sir Roland! Let the rope a little lower down, and then I can reach the secret passage where I keep my money."

"I thank you for having given me the information, Gedge. Would you not like to leave a lock of hair for your dainty little Daisy?"

"Sir Roland—Sir Roland!" he cried, "have mercy upon me. I will do all you wish; I will give you half my money."

"What care I for half your money? I will have all. Ha! ha! ha!"

"Take it all, but spare my life. I am not fit to die!"

"I don't know whether you are fit to die, but I do know that you are not fit to live," laughed Sir Roland. "I shall be your heir and spend your money on pretty little Daisy."

At this moment Spring-Heeled Jack glided into the cellar.

He was about to spring forwards to the rescue, when Sir Roland severed the rope and with a despairing shriek the miser plunged into the well.

Then Sir Roland turned and fled, calling on Blarney.

But as he fled the wild laughter of Spring-Heeled Jack sounded through the house.

Scarcely had he gone when Spring-Heeled Jack sprang to the well and lowered himself down by the remainder of the rope.

Down, down, down, he went; but at last he touched the water.

Clinging with one hand to the rope, Spring-Heeled Jack felt about until he grasped the miser.

Then using the double rope, he hauled himself and Gedge up.

He reached the brink of the well and swung himself over it.

It had taken all his herculean strength to drag Gedge up, but he had done it, and stood panting with exhaustion at the top of the well.

No sooner had he recovered himself than he turned his attention to the miser.

"He is dead!" he muttered. "The world has one villain less, but for all that I wish I had been in time to save him. But I hear the murderers approaching, and they must not see me at present."

With that he propped the dead body of Gedge—hideous in life, but far more so in death—up against the wall, and then hid himself behind some lumber.

"This way—this way," said Sir Roland, as he guided Blarney. "Now we can grasp the miser's gold. Half-way down this well there is a landing which leads to a secret passage. There you will find the gold."

"Begging your pardon, Sir Roland, since you know the place so well, do you not think that you had better go down and get the money?"

"No, no," said Sir Roland, quickly. "I do not care to go down there."

"In point of fact, neither do I," said Blarney, coolly. "It's not inviting."

"What have you to fear? Nothing. I will stand by this double rope and lower you down. I murdered Gedge Foote and I dare not go down that place."

"Well, I [illegible]n't like the looks of it," said Blarney. "A[illegible]ou sure the gold is there?"

"Positive. [illegible] not tell you that Gedge Foote brought up two [illegible]sand pounds from that place?"

"Two thousa[illegible] pounds! Perhaps that was all he had," said B[illegible]ney.

"I tell you that Gedge Foote was a miser—a money-lender; rich—very rich."

"Well, he ought to be. He's been one of the meanest old fences in London"

"And one of the most successful. [illegible] tell you that there is a fortune below?"

"You are sure of that? Now look here, Sir Roland Ashton!"

"Well, what is it?" asked Sir Roland, impatiently. "We lose time."

"Do you mean fair by me? I mean fair by you. Indeed, as long as I live I mean to stick to you. You are the sort of man I like, and I am the sort of man who will suit you. Now, are we agreed?"

"Yes," said Sir Roland, giving the vagabond his hand in apparent friendship.

"Good!" cried Blarney, as he wrung the baronet's hand in the warmest manner.

Sir Roland shrank from the familiarity, but had to return the grasp.

"Now, Sir Roland. Just you look well to that rope. Remember, one slip may send me to keep company with old Gedge. Bad enough it was to keep company with him when he was alive, but now he is dead it would be fearful."

"Tut! man, what hast thou to fear? You did not kill the old rascal. If ghosts really appeared I should be frightened, but I am not. Gedge Foote rests at the bottom of that well, and there he will remain until the Day of Judgment."

## CHAPTER XLI.

### WHAT THE ALARM BELL BROUGHT—SIR ROLAND AND BILL BLARNEY FIND THE MINT TOO HOT TO HOLD THEM.

It will be remembered that Gedge Foote in his frenzied flight had sounded the alarm bell.

Neither Sir Roland Ashton nor his villainous accomplice had thought of the consequences of the act of the man so cruelly murdered.

In the excitement of the moment, and in their greed for gold, they had given heed to nothing.

And yet those loud sounding notes had told their story of alarm only too well. Strange-looking men of the roughest description poured from the houses of evil repute—hurried shouts rent the air.

Torches were lit, and flashed on bare knives and pistol barrels.

"Gedge Foote has rung the alarm bell!" shouted

one gigantic fellow, who took the lead. "This way—this way!"

The mob increased every moment.

Their hoarse cries rent the air.

On they came yelling, cursing, and making the night hideous.

Let us now turn to Sir Roland Ashton and Bill Blarney.

At the very moment that they were about to descend into the well in search of the miser's treasure Bill Blarney started back and held up his hand.

"What is that?" he cried. "Don't you hear?"

"Hear what?" Sir Roland Ashton demanded. "Fool! do you want to make a coward of me as well as yourself?"

"I thought I heard a murmur as of a crowd of angry people."

"Bah!"

"Sneer away," said Bill Blarney. "You are too clever. Have you forgotten what Gedge Foote said about being on friendly terms with the people in the Mint? Have you forgotten that he rang the alarm bell?"

Sir Roland Ashton turned pale and trembled in spite of himself.

"Hush!" he said; "you may be right. Let us listen."

At this moment a hoarse roar came to their ears.

Then came a banging at the outer door, and a hundred voices demanded admittance.

"What are we to do?" Bill Blarney whined. "If we stay here we shall be killed to a certainty. What are we to do?"

"Hold your tongue!" Sir Roland hissed. "Let me think the matter out. I have been in a worse fix than this and yet have laughed at my enemies in the end."

Bang! Crash—crash!

"They are getting impatient," said Bill Blarney, alluding to the men who were thundering at the door.

"Let them," Sir Roland replied. "The bolts and locks will hold yet for some time. Keep quiet, and if I do not find a way out of this muddle never trust me again."

For some moments he paced up and down.

Bill Blarney watched him, wondering whether his meditations would ever come to an end.

Meanwhile the noise at the door became deafening, but Sir Roland paid no more attention to it than if the street was silent.

"We had better go upstairs again," he said at last. "I must confess that this place is just a little too warm for us at present."

"But what is the use of going upstairs?" Bill Blarney groaned. "That will be worse than staying down here. They will surely search the upper rooms first, and we shall be as helpless as a couple of caged rats."

"You idiot!" Sir Roland replied. "Has not this house a roof? And is there no hope in that direction? Stay where you are, if you like, I am going."

So saying he dashed up the back staircase.

Bill Blarney followed after a moment's hesitation.

As they reached the ground floor they heard a crash.

"Be jabers!" Blarney gasped; "they have knocked in the upper panels."

"Gedge Foote—Gedge Foote!" roared a voice; "where are you?"

"Here!" Sir Richard cried, imitating the miser's voice as well as possible.

"What did you ring the bell for?"

"I was wondering whether it would act well in a case of emergency."

"Open the door, then," shouted the first speaker. "You will have to stand something handsome for bringing us out at this time of night."

"All right," Sir Roland replied. "Wait a minute. Don't be in such an infernal hurry."

"That is not Foote's voice," cried another man. "Down with the door, I say—batter it down! There has been foul play at work."

Sir Roland waited to hear no more, but bounded up the stairs.

Bill Blarney was in the act of following, when his foot slipped.

His head came in violent contact with the edge of one of the stones, and he lay stunned and motionless.

"So much the better," Sir Roland said, as he continued his upward flight. "Foote's friends will put him out of the way, and rid me of a troublesome fellow. Ha! ha! ha! Knock away. I suppose you will be satisfied with one capture?"

At this moment the door gave way with a crash, and a number of men poured into the house.

Bill Blarney was correct in his notion that the upper rooms would be searched first.

"Hold!" cried the leader of the gang, raising the torch he held above his head, "hold! Here is the body of a stranger."

He had come to Bill Blarney's inanimate form, and in a moment a crowd gathered round it.

"Kill him—stab him!" shouted a dozen of the men.

"No, no," said their leader. "He is only stunned, and may be able to give some information. We will bring him round and settle accounts with him afterwards."

Two of the strongest raised Bill Blarney up and began to chafe his hands and rub his ears in no gentle manner.

Suddenly Bill Blarney opened his eyes.

He closed them again immediately, and his heart grew sick with fear.

"Now, then," said the leader of the men, "no shamming. Here, Rolley, just give him a tap over the head with your hammer, just to show him that we are in earnest."

"No—no!" Bill Blarney howled. "Don't do that, good gentlemen. I am sure that you would not like to hurt an inoffensive man."

There was a roar of hoarse laughter at this.

"Where is Gedge Foote?" demanded the leader.

Through all the gloom of apprehension Bill Blarney saw a ray of light.

"He has been drinking?" he replied. "He rang the bell, and when I told him how stupid he was he knocked me over the head."

"Well?"

"And then he ran into the cellar."

"That's a very likely story," the man said "but as there may be some truth in it we will go and see for ourselves. Light fresh torches there, and bring this rascal along."

"I'm afraid I shall have to leave you, kind gentlemen," Blarney said, in his most persuasive manner. "I have a very particular appointment on London-bridge, which I must keep."

"That's not bad," said the leader. "It's just

likely that you will have to keep an appointment in the river below London-bridge, if you don't keep a still tongue in your head and do as you are told. Pass a cord round his wrists and hold him tight. Forward, there!"

If ever a man felt inclined to shrink into his boots that man was Bill Blarney.

As his wrists were tightly bound, and as the men dragged him along, he gave up all hope.

A dull red mist gathered before his eyes and his lips became flecked with foam.

Death stared him in the face and mocked him.

The man who did not scruple to shed blood like water was an arrant coward at heart.

Down the stairs they went, a motley crew, and at last reached the cellar.

"See here," shouted the leader in a stentorian tone of voice, "one of the ropes has been cut."

"Mercy—mercy!" Bill Blarney screamed, falling upon his knees. "I will tell all if you will spare my life."

"We make no promises," the leader said, sternly; "but if you do not speak, and that instantly, you will never have another chance on earth."

"Sir Roland Ashton—"

These were all the words that came from his lips, for a long gleaming knife flashed before his eyes.

Speech failed him.

His tongue clove to the roof of his mouth, and, falling back upon his captors, he swooned away, and lay like a log of wood in their arms.

Just at this time Sir Roland was making his escape good.

He contrived to reach the roof—but how was he to find his way to the ground?

This was a question which puzzled his brain.

As he looked down the height made him giddy, and he clutched at an old iron rod supporting a stack of curiously-twisted chimneys.

One false step, one slight mistake, and he would be dashed to pieces.

Below he could hear the voices of the avenging crowd.

He knew that Bill Blarney had fallen into their hands, and, moreover, that they were dragging him down to the cellar.

Though he chuckled to himself over this the suspense was awful.

Bill Blarney might turn informer as to his whereabouts, and then men, thirsting for his blood, would rush upon the roof.

Sir Roland fell upon his hands and knees, and, crawling along to the edge of the coping, looked down.

The flickering oil-lamps, shedding feeble jets of ghostly light, seemed to blink mockingly at him.

What was he to do?

In this direction there were no possible means of escape.

Suddenly a thought occurred to him.

Why not hide himself in the chimney?

By pressing his back and knees against the brickwork he could lower and raise himself at will.

No sooner did the idea flash into his brain than he commenced to put it into action.

Trusting his weight to the iron rod, he climbed up it, and was soon seated on top of the stack.

What was his dismay to find that the aperture of each flue was too wide for him to support himself in the manner he had decided upon.

Back he went, and standing upon the roof pressed his hands to his throbbing brow.

Something must be done.

There was not a moment to lose.

He carried his life in his hands.

"I must try the other side," he said. "There may be a pipe or something by which I can lower myself. All still below—I wonder what can have happened?"

He looked down through the open trap-door by which he had gained the roof and listened for a moment.

Then he crept cautiously along the roof until he had reached the other side.

It was dark, fearfully dark.

The lowering sky frowned upon him, and London at his feet looked like a yawning pit ready to receive him.

As he felt along the coping his hand suddenly came in contact with something.

It was the top of a gutter down which the rain poured from the roof.

"Saved!" Sir Roland murmured, triumphantly. "I defy you all. An Ashton was never beaten, and the day is far off when I shall succumb to my foes."

Grasping still lower down with his hands, Sir Roland Ashton clutched the piping.

It was old and crazy.

It creaked and groaned under the very pressure of his hands, and Sir Roland uttered a curse as he thought it might give way beneath his weight.

What would follow?

He shuddered as he pictured himself a mangled corpse on the rough jagged stones below.

But there was no time for reflection.

Escape meant life, freedom, and the fulfilment of his plans.

To remain there would be courting certain death.

Keeping a firm hold on the rusty piping, he swung his legs gently over the coping, and then thrust his knees against the wall.

He went down hand over hand, expecting each moment to be his last.

How that pipe cracked and groaned!

Some of the holdfasts came out, and went jingling and rattling below.

But as the distance between Sir Roland and the ground decreased, he gained courage.

A mocking laugh rose to his lips as his feet touched the earth.

"Hurrah!" he hissed, "I am free. Where is all your cunning now, Spring-Heeled Jack? Where are all your plans of vengeance? Ha! ha! ha!"

He checked his ill-timed mirth, and looked about him.

"Which way shall I go?" he said, under his breath. "Ha! I cannot do better than take to the river. Once on the Surrey-side, I know a house in Southwark which will give me safe shelter, good food, and a warm bed."

So saying, he ran towards the river, where the tide was roaring and rushing, as if battling with a pack of fiends.

Down courts and alleys Sir Roland fled, never stopping to look back, or to take breath.

His way was fraught with danger, for at any moment he might be stopped and asked to give an account of himself.

Grim, and gruesome, and evil-smelling was the old Mint. It's very atmosphere seemed to reek with the blood of the betrayed and murdered!

Soon Sir Roland heard the churning and roaring of the foaming river.

Then he halted.

"It will be a great chance it I find a boatman hereabouts," he mused, "and if I do, he may perchance be an evil customer who would not scruple to rob me and give me a dip in the water afterwards."

As he reached the river bank he paced it to and fro.

All was still.

The night had grown so black that he could not see his fingers by holding them close to his face.

Suddenly he heard the sound of approaching footsteps.

Sir Roland stepped back and hid himself behind a pile of rotten timber.

The footsteps came on.

Sir Roland's heart beat almost audibly.

Was the stranger a man or a woman?

If a man, would he prove a friend or a foe?

## CHAPTER XLII.

HOW BILL BLARNEY WAS HANGED—SIR ROLAND AT SOUTHWARK—THE BLUE ROOM, AND WHAT OCCURRED IN IT.

THE leader of the gang, known by the name of Luke Spry, regarded Bill Blarney with a look of disgust and contempt.

"I did think that he would prove a little more game," he said. "Bah! I have a good mind to order him to be pitched head first down the well; and I'd do it, only I want information from him. Wake him up!"

"That's all very well," laughed one of the men who held Blarney; "but how is it to be done? He's as heavy as lead, and, to all appearances, as dead as a door-nail."

Luke Spry cast his eyes around.

He detected a bucket in a corner.

It was half full of water.

"I think this will do the trick," he said, swinging the bucket in the air. "Put him on his back and stand aside; I'll treat him to a bath."

Swish went the water over Bill Blarney's face.

"Help!" he murmured, feebly.

"Oh! yes, I'll help you," said Luke Spry. "Here, fill this bucket again, somebody!"

"No, no," Blarney pleaded, sitting up. "I don't want any more. Where am I? Who are you?"

"Come, come," said Luke Spry, "this sort of game won't do for us, you know. It's all very well with a woman, but it won't wash with you. Get up!"

Luke Spry accompanied these words with a kick that lifted Bill Blarney an inch or two in the air.

Spry's men laughed, but it was no laughing matter for the unhappy victim, who, bound as he was, ran to the other end of the cellar, and crouched down in a corner.

"Mercy!" he gasped. "Don't ill-treat a man who is in your power."

"Listen to me," Luke Spry said, drawing a pistol from his belt, and cocking it. "You may see at a glance that I am not the sort of man to be trifled with."

Bill Blarney did see it, and said so with a groan that came from the depths of his throat.

"Well, then," said Spry, pointing the pistol at Blarney's head, "listen to me a moment. Just before you fainted away, like a squeamish girl, you mentioned some man's name. Repeat it."

Bill Blarney's lower jaw fell.

He seemed to be pondering on the wisdom of such a course, but a glance at the muzzle of the pistol told him that unless he made a clean breast of all he knew that in all probability his brains would be scattered against the wall.

"I came here with Sir Roland Ashton," he whined. "I am only his servant—his miserable, wretched servant."

"I will take that for granted," Luke Spry said. "Go on, and don't keep me waiting, for when I grow impatient I am likely to pull the trigger."

"He owed Gedge Foote some money, and—"

"He murdered him?"

Bill Blarney nodded his head.

"Where is the body?" Luke Spry demanded. "Tell me, you dog, or make up your mind that your last moment has come."

Bill Blarney pointed to the well.

"Oh! down there," said Luke Spry. "Very clever, I dare say. Well, where is your master—this Sir Roland Ashton?"

"I don't know."

"You lie."

"I speak the truth," Bill Blarney avowed. "I would swear it with my last breath."

"Then," said Luke Spry, "he must be in the house."

"Unless you left the door open."

Luke Spry uttered a furious oath.

"What fools we were not to guard it!" he said. "But at any rate we have you to deal with. Bring him here."

The command was made to some of the men, who immediately proceeded to obey.

The strength died out of Bill Blarney's legs, and the men dragged him forward, grovelling abjectly on his knees.

His head had fallen upon his breast; his hands shook as if smitten with the palsy.

In truth, no more pitiful spectacle ever presented itself on earth than the wretch who but one short hour ago had been so bold and boastful.

"What shall be done to this man?" Luke Spry demanded, turning to the men "What does he deserve?"

"Death! death!" they shouted.

"You hear that?" Spry said, laying a heavy hand upon Bill Blarney's shoulder. "What have you to say against the sentence? Is it not a just one?"

"Not according to law!" Bill Blarney shrieked. "I demand to be tried before a judge and jury of my country."

This seemed to tickle the men of the Mint immensely.

Luke Spry alone remained grave and stern of feature.

"The law likes us not, and we like not the law," he said, with bitter sarcasm.

"But don't kill me without a fair trial," Blarney moaned; "some of you might fall into the same trap, and then how would you like to be served like this? I ask you how would you like it?"

"About the same as you," Spry returned. "But enough; we have wasted too much time already."

Again he turned to the men.

They were a strangely composed body, and the light of the torches lent almost fiendish expressions to their countenances.

"Comrades" Spry said, folding his arms, and

drawing himself up to his full height, "you have most justly condemned this miscreant to death. He is in your hands; it is for you to decide how he shall die."

"By the rope!" shouted a dozen voices.

"Over the well where Gedge Foote lies a murdered man," added one of the crowd.

"No—no; anything but that!" Bill Blarney howled. "If I must die, shoot me through the head and put me out of the world that way."

"No—no!" roared the angry crowd. "The rope—the rope! Hang the cowardly, murderous dog!"

"Your doom is sealed," Luke Spry said, addressing the unhappy wretch. "If you have anything more to say we will give you just one more minute, and no longer."

As a drowning man clutches at straws so did Bill Blarney faintly hope that help, in some shape or other, would come before that short space of time came to an end.

He counted and begrudged the moments.

How quickly they went by!

Surely time never flew so swiftly before.

When the last came he begged and prayed for more time.

"Only a moment," he said; "I have something to say. I can reveal things such as you never heard or dreamt of. I know a hundred secrets which will be useful to men like you. I know where treasure can be had for the asking, and—"

"Cease your prating," Luke Spry said. "Your tongue has wagged too long in this world already. It must now be silenced for ever. Come, let it be said of you that you died like a man, and not like a cur."

Bill Blarney raised his eyes to the roof of the cellar.

Could it be that he would never see the sunlight again?

Was he mad or dreaming?

The iron grip on his shoulders convinced him of the dread reality of his position.

He uttered an agonised cry and clasped his bound hands.

"Only a moment! Only one short, fleeting moment!" he cried. "Give me a drink of water. You can't find it in your hearts, hardened as they be against my appeals, to refuse me that!"

Luke Spry made a motion with his hand.

"Put a handkerchief over his eyes, and let there be an end to this scene," he said.

"I'll not die in the dark," Bill Blarney howled.

He struggled, but ineffectually.

In the hands of the men who held him he was as helpless as a child.

He was blindfolded and the rope passed round his neck.

Then hot blood rushed into his brain.

Every innocent scene of his youth and every darker one of his mis-spent life seemed to rise before him.

In the one short moment as he hovered between this life and eternity he lived an age—an age of awful terror and excruciating agony.

"Let him go!"

He heard these words.

They seemed to linger upon his ears for a long period, and then—

"It is all over with him," Luke Spry said. "Halloa! what is this? See, the rope is dangling loose. It must have shifted from his neck."

"I heard no splash," said one of the men.

"Nor I," said another. "Is there anything that he could catch his feet against?"

"No."

"Then the very deuce must have had a hand in this."

Luke Spry took the rope in his hand, and, drawing it from the well, examined it.

"As I live," said he, "it has been cut! Confusion! What on earth can this mean?"

"Why, that Gedge Foote is not dead yet, and— Oh! horror, what is this?"

One and all started back as Spring-Heeled Jack appeared.

He bounded from the well as if he had been shot from the mouth of a cannon.

"Back!" he cried. "Leave this house. You are not wanted here. Leave me to deal with that man."

The men glared at him in terror-stricken silence, but made no answer.

"Gedge Foote is dead," he said. "Let that suffice. The money shall be placed in proper hands. Go! I am master here."

The men retreated before him as he advanced with long, elastic strides.

"Man or fiend," said Luke Spry, "I will speak to you, though I fall dead at your feet. Tell me who you are."

"Spring-Heeled Jack."

This was enough.

Most of the men of the Mint turned pale at the mention of that awful name and retreated towards the staircase.

Luke Spry still lingered.

Instinctively he laid his hand upon a pistol, but in an instant the weapon went hurtling up to the ceiling.

"Do as I tell you," Spring-Heeled Jack whispered. "Don't tempt me to do you an injury. Leave everything in my hands and all will be well."

As he spoke he rose, as if by magic, and disappeared down the yawning mouth of the well.

"Mercy on us!" Luke Spry cried; "this is no mortal. It is a fiend who has the keeping of Gedge Foote."

With these words he followed the rest of the men.

Darkness and gloom now reigned in the cellar, as it did upon the river bank, where Sir Roland Ashton stood hidden behind the pile of timber.

As the footsteps increased in sound he saw a dull flash of light.

It came from a lantern with horn windows, such as may be found even at the present time in old-fashioned farmhouses.

Then Sir Roland heard a voice.

The man was singing, and in such a jovial tone that he must have been a light-hearted fellow to give vent to melody on so bad a night.

"This is no night-prowler or robber," Sir Roland said. "I'll hail him. Hullo, there!"

The man halted and broke off in the middle of a verse.

"Who calls?" he demanded, holding the lantern above his head. "Is that you, Bill?"

"Hang Bill and all his family!" Sir Roland thought.

He then walked out of his hiding-place.

"My friend," he said, "I am desirous of crossing the river. Can you assist me?"

He spoke in the direction of the light, for he could not see the man, from the fact that he was now holding the lantern before his face.

"Why?" said the man. "What does a gentleman like you do down in these parts?"

"I am a stranger to London and have lost my way," Sir Roland replied.

"Then you may think yourself lucky that you are not knocked on the head, and floating down towards Gravesend by this time."

"Indeed!" said Sir Roland, with an air of innocence. "Is this, then, a dangerous locality?"

"Not to those who live in it and know it well," was the reply. "But, my lord, or duke—for I see that you are one or the other—that diamond brooch glittering in your cravat would tempt many a half-starved wretch picking up his living by the water-side."

"You shall have it if you will row me across the river."

"What?"

"I mean exactly what I say, and no more or less, my friend!"

"Oh! I see," said the man, lowering the lantern. "You want to get across the river very particularly. How am I to know what game you have been up to? It strikes me very forcibly that you are not such a stranger to these parts as you pretend to be."

"Tush! man," said Sir Roland Ashton, impatiently. "The simple question is this, will you row me over or will you not? If you say 'No,' why there is an end of the matter."

The man was tall, and roughly clad, wearing a fur cap upon his head and a spotted handkerchief about his neck.

He grinned and rubbed his chin thoughtfully, as he stared at Sir Roland, who winced under the steady, suspicious eyes.

"Well," said the man, "if I don't row you across I know that nobody else will."

"Then why do you hesitate?"

"Because I might get into trouble if I tried to get rid of that brooch," the man replied. "I might be asked how such a fellow as me became possessed of diamonds."

"You prefer gold?"

"I do."

Sir Roland took his purse from his pocket, emptying the greater part of its contents into the palm of his hand.

"Here are ten guineas," he said; "I have left myself only five, so you see—"

"Oh! yes, I see," the man interposed; "but there happens to be a little difficulty in the way."

"What difficulty?"

"I have no boat."

Sir Roland Ashton muttered an oath under his breath.

"What is to be done, then?" he asked; "I cannot stay out here in the open all night, and I certainly should not think of trusting myself in one of these houses."

"I have it," said the man; "I will show you the way through the Mint."

"That will not do."

"Why not?"

"Because it will not," Sir Roland said; "and let that suffice. I had horrors enough getting here, without wishing to go back by the same road."

"Then," the man replied, "I suppose I may say that I am ten guineas out of pocket?"

He made a movement as if to walk away, but Sir Roland called him back.

"You seem to be an honest fellow!" he said. "Can you think of no way of getting me out of my difficulty?"

The man shook his head and became thoughtful again.

"No," he said, "I cannot. But stay. Why should I not borrow a boat? There are plenty here swinging idly on the tide. Who would be the wiser, eh?"

"Who, indeed!" said Sir Roland, delighted beyond measure at the idea.

"I wonder I did not think of it before."

"Never mind," said Sir Roland, jingling the gold in the palm of his hand, "fetch the boat, man. There is not a moment to lose—I mean that I shall be only too thankful when I am on the opposite shore."

"Right you are," the man replied. "Stay where you are. I shall not be long. Would you like to have the lantern? I can find my way very well in the dark."

"No," Sir Roland returned, with a shuddering glance at the distant houses. "Take it with you. Do be quick, there's a good fellow. I am as cold as an eel, and miserable to boot."

The man went away swinging the lantern before him.

Sir Roland watched the rays as they flitted too and fro with wistful eyes and deep-drawn breath.

As he had said, there was not a single moment to lose.

The men of the Mint might arrive at any moment.

Sir Roland fully knew what amount of mercy to expect at their hands, and he thought of what the stranger had said, and repeated the words.

"'You may think yourself lucky that you are not knocked on the head, and floating towards Gravesend by this time.'"

"Most truly," Sir Roland said, "I do think myself lucky. My curse on the fellow, how he lags! If he had been through what I have he would make better use of his limbs."

Sir Roland could not see the light of the lantern now, for the man had gone down to the water-edge, and was making his way through lanes of stranded mooring-piles and a chaos of all sorts of river craft.

He waited and waited until it seemed to him that hours had passed.

More than once a shout rose in his throat, for he thought he heard the hum of many men's voices in the distance.

Was it fancy or conscious guilt?

Remembering a simple but effective way to hear the approach of vehicles or footsteps, he stooped down and placed his ear close to the ground.

Nothing was stirring, save the wind, which sighed and moaned as if in grief that the night should hide so much wickedness.

Sir Roland rose to his feet, and as he shaded his eyes with his hand, he was gratified with the sight of the lantern.

"This way!" shouted the man. "Keep straight on, and fear nothing. Hallo! What's up now? The beacon in the old Mint is alight."

"The beacon!" Sir Roland gasped.

"Yes; look there!"

Sir Roland turned his head, and saw some rubbish mingled with tarred logs burning fiercely in a brazier fixed to the top of one of the houses.

"What does that portend?"

"That something is wrong," was the startling reply. "Possibly it means that a stranger who has found his way into the Mint is wanted."

# SPRING-HEELED JACK,

## THE TERROR OF LONDON.

SLOWLY THE BLACK SHADOW CREPT ACROSS THE FLOOR.

No. 14.

"Ha! ha! ha! That sounds like a joke."

"It may to you, perhaps," the man said; "but it wouldn't be to me if you happened to be the stranger in so great request. I am afraid, sir, that I cannot row you across the river."

"You cannot? Give me your reason."

"Because I dare not," the man replied.

Sir Roland Ashton tore his hair and ground his teeth in an impotent fury.

"See here," he said. "Take all—money—brooch—everything. I will confide in you. I got into trouble to-night, and it is just possible—"

"That the beacon is burning for you?"

"Yes."

"Then there is an end to the bargain. It is as much as my life is worth to have you in my company."

"Stay—stay, for mercy's sake!" Sir Roland said. "Surely you would not see an innocent man murdered before your eyes?"

"No; I will not wait to see."

As he spoke he scampered away as fast as his legs could carry him, and no sooner had the sound of his hurrying footsteps died away than there came another borne on the wings of the wind.

Sir Roland Ashton glanced up at the beacon and then at the flowing river.

"I suppose I must row myself across," he said, groping wildly and blindly about for the boat. "What shall I do—oh! mercy, what shall I do?"

He tried to utter the word "Heaven," but it stuck fast in his base throat.

"The boat at last!" he cried, joyfully.

He dragged at the chain mooring the frail craft, but it held fast.

Meanwhile the beacon burned brightly, and other lights were approaching the water's edge.

He heard his own name shouted by a number of voices.

The men of the Mint yelled to him to surrender.

"Not while I have an ounce of strength left in my muscles," he thought. "Curse the chain! how is it to be undone?"

It gave way unexpectedly, and he fell headlong into the boat.

Bruised and bleeding he sprang to his feet, seized the sculls, and settled himself to work.

The murkiness of the night did him a good turn.

It hid his form from the sight of his pursuers.

A yell of execration burst from their lips as they heard the click—click of the sculls in the rowlocks.

Sir Roland was pulling for his life, and if life was ever dear to him it was now.

On he went with long, sweeping strokes, little caring where he landed so that it was on the opposite shore.

"Boats! boats!" he heard his foes shouting. "This way. Murder! The villain must not, shall not escape!"

By this time Sir Roland was fairly in the middle of the stream.

Strong as he was, the tide forced the boat along out of its course, and it suddenly occurred to Sir Roland that if he rested on the sculls a few moments and allowed the boat to float as it chose, he might baffle his pursuers much easier than by attempting to reach the Surrey shore at once.

So feasible did this notion appear that he adopted it, and with such success that he heard Luke Spry and his men cursing with rage.

Suddenly several reports rent the air.

The men of the Mint were firing at random.

Sir Roland Ashton felt inclined to give a shout of defiance, but he checked it upon his lips.

It was well for him that he did so.

Luke Spry and three other men had taken to a boat.

Two of them pulled, one steered, and the fourth, standing in the bows, whirled a torch above his head.

Sir Roland Ashton saw the lurid light falling in flashes upon the dark, troubled waters, but it did not reach him.

He sat perfectly still and the boat floated on, now whirling as an eddy caught it, and now dashing along with the racing tide.

Something blacker than the night loomed before Sir Roland's eyes.

He knew that it was the hull of a ship, and grasped the skulls frantically, and only just in time to save his life.

In spite of himself he uttered a cry of terror, and a man watching on board the vessel leaned over the side and tried to pierce the pall-like gloom.

Burning lights from other vessels were seen to twinkle and gleam, and Sir Roland, having made sure that he had eluded pursuit, began to think of landing.

Pulling vigorously he succeeded in running the boat aground and stepped out ankle-deep in mud.

But to a man in such a predicament a little discomfort was nothing, and he breathed a sigh of relief as he clambered up what appeared to be a ship yard.

Here, again, caution was necessary.

There might be a watchman about the place or a dog, which would be a still more unpleasant customer to tackle in the dark.

But the wharf was deserted and as silent as the grave.

Sir Roland came to the conclusion that he had floated about a mile down the stream.

He was about right in his conjecture, but it took him some time to reach Southwark.

He made his way towards an ancient house over which hung an enormous sign, representing the figure of a wounded hart, and by such name was the inn known.

There was not a single light in any of the windows, and Sir Roland stared about him in perplexity.

"It is just like my luck," he said. "If I had not come Witchardson would have set up half the night drinking and playing cards. However, I must have him out of bed if he snores like the seven sleepers rolled into one."

He struck heavily at the door several times with his fist, and then waited for a response.

Was it the moaning of the wind or a warning whisper that caused him to start as he stood beneath the old-fashioned porch?

It might have been either, but he thought it was the latter, and stared up and down, as if expecting to see his inveterate enemy, Spring-Heeled Jack, appear at his feet.

"Accursed apparition!" he hissed, "I will find means to silence you yet."

Then he listened for the mocking, weird, unearthly laugh, but he listened in vain, and then he renewed his attack upon the door.

Crash! crash!—bang! bang!

He struck at it with wild fury and until blood spurted from beneath his finger-nails.

A terrible sensation came over him.

He compared himself to a hunted animal, but in reality he was more like a malefactor escaping from the sword of justice.

Suddenly one of the upper windows opened and a nightcapped head appeared.

"Hullo!" roared an angry voice, "what's the meaning of this row?"

"I want to come in," Sir Roland said, breathlessly.

"I daresay you do," responded the wrathful voice, "but perhaps you'll oblige me by keeping out. Go away you scoundrel, or I'll give you the contents of this blunderbuss."

Sir Roland crept closer to the wall as he saw the bell-shaped muzzle of the ponderous weapon, a terrible one in close quarters, for it was capable of belching forth half a pound of lead.

"Witchardson—Dick Witchardson," he said, in a concilatory tone, "don't you know me? Surely you have heard my voice often enough to recognise it now?"

"Why, bless my heart, it is Sir Roland Ashton!"

"The same."

"I beg your honour's pardon, I will be down in less than a minute."

Back went the nightcapped head and down went the window.

Sir Roland's fears increased every minute.

He knew that Luke Spry and his men were prowling about not far away, and, moreover, he was perfectly aware that they would not give up the search until all hope of finding him had fled.

A smile of exultation played on his lips as he heard the rattling of locks and bolts.

"Thank you, Witchardson," he said, as he passed through the open door. "You look surprised to see me."

"Well, Sir Roland," the landlord replied, "I'd just as soon have thought of seeing the—well never mind who. Come into the parlour; the fire is not out, and a drop of something warm will do you good. You are as pale as a ghost. I hope you haven't seen one."

"No, no," Sir Roland said, laughingly. "I want you to let me have the blue-room. I don't care about going to bed, as I have something particular to think about."

"Certainly, your honour," Witchardson said, "I'll see to it myself. But won't you—"

"No," Sir Roland interposed, "I don't care to stay down here. You need not ask questions, for I have my own reasons, and you know I prefer a silent man to one with a long tongue."

The landlord, who was a short, stumpy, and rather a jolly-looking little man, eyed Sir Roland Ashton curiously.

"Of course you know best," he said, as he led the way up a fine old staircase. "It is not for me to argue that point with my superiors, but I am afraid that your honour will find the blue-room just a trifle damp."

"The fire will soon put that all right," Sir Roland replied; "and, Witchardson?"

"Yes, your honour."

"Have you a brace of pistols that you can lend me?"

A troubled expression spread over the little innkeeper's face.

"I have, your honour," he replied; "but don't you see—well as you are not likely to require such things, why—"

"Do you think that I want to blow my brains out?" Sir Roland interposed. "Nay, my friend, I am too fond of life to make such an ass of myself. I never care to be alone without some weapon of defence. We live in troublesome times, you know."

"We do," Witchardson said, turning back and stopping half-way up the staircase. "They say that Prince Charles Edward will establish his right to the throne of England yet. Do you think so?"

"How should I know?"

"Oh!" said Dick Witchardson, staring up at the ceiling, "I thought you gave me a sign that's all."

"What sort of a sign?"

"To keep my tongue between my teeth," Dick Witchardson replied.

Sir Roland Ashton laughed again, and the discussion dropped as the blue-room was reached.

It was a handsome, stately apartment, and had sheltered many a distinguished personage.

Here cavaliers, true to the cause of King Charles, had plotted and sang and drank, making fun of Cromwell's followers, who so very soon turned the tables by making fun of them; and, so at least the legend ran, Bluff King Hal had quaffed a measure of sack in the room and complimented the landlord on the quality of the liquor.

The furniture was almost as old as itself, but, though faded and tarnished, it was still strong and capable of doing its duty well.

The fire, composed of logs resting on steel dogs, was soon ablaze, and Dick Witchardson, setting the lamp down upon the table, stood before his guest and rubbed his hands softly.

"Can I bring your honour up anything?" he asked.

"Yes," Sir Roland replied, "a bottle of your best wine. Then you can leave me for the night, as I shall do very well."

The wine and pistols were brought up, Witchardson withdrew, and Sir Roland Ashton, left alone to his reflections, pressed one hand to his brow and stretched out the other towards the fire.

"So," he muttered, "I have given them the slip at last. I am safe, for who would dream of coming here? Ugh! the dying glare from Gedge Foote's eyes haunts me, and it will be many a day before I forget them."

Rising, he advanced to the table, and, pouring out a glass of wine, swallowed it with the gusto of a man parched with thirst.

"Ha!" he said, "I feel better now. Wine warms a man's heart and braces up his nerves. I feel another man now, and could face almost anything."

He drank another glass of wine and then returned to the chair at the fireside.

A deadly stillness had fallen upon the night—the street was silent, and the only sound that Sir Roland heard was the rustle of the dying embers as they fell upon the hearth.

"I must end this," he said. "I must hasten back to Lilac Lodge, and once Daisy is in my power again she must never quit it. We will go abroad, where Spring-Heeled Jack cannot follow us. Ha, ha, ha!"

"Ha, ha, ha!"

The laugh was so much like the echo of his own that he glanced round the room in astonishment.

"How strange," he said.

"Strange," the echo repeated.

Sir Roland sat still and watchful.

The brace of pistols lent to him by Dick Witchardson were in his pocket, but there seemed no necessity whatever to draw them.

The door was closed and locked, the windows were guarded with shutters and curtains—might not somebody be lurking behind them?

Sir Roland made sure that such was not the case, and then sat down to think out his plans for the future.

"I must not give way to idle fancies or idle fears," he said. "I have been a fool to stay so long in the field of danger. Daisy, pretty Daisy, you shall be mine in spite of yourself."

"You lie!"

Sir Roland could not have been more startled had a thunderbolt fallen at his feet.

In that moment of terror he never gave Spring-Heeled Jack a thought.

"Who speaks?" he asked, in a whisper.

"Your foe!" was the reply. "I, who would have been your friend."

As these words were uttered Sir Roland Ashton saw a shadow creep slowly along the floor.

It was so dark and so sharply-defined a shadow that it seemed as if it might be palpable to the touch.

Onward it came, and Sir Roland Ashton's hair bristled as he recognised in it the shape of Spring-Heeled Jack.

The guilty man had passed through many horrors in his time, but he had never seen anything like this.

If Spring-Heeled Jack, who was for ever treading upon his heels, had appeared in the form of flesh and blood, Sir Roland would have done his best to put a bullet through the strange creature's brain.

But he could not grapple or fight with a hideous black shadow.

There it lay, almost at his feet, and he felt his blood turn as cold as ice, and then course madly through his veins with the heat of molten lead.

"Accursed fiend!" he yelled, "show yourself. I am prepared for you."

"I am here," said the voice of Spring-Heeled Jack. "This is one of the forms I am permitted to take. Do your worst."

Sir Roland almost swooned.

He stretched out his hand to grasp the bell-rope, and then the shadow vanished amid a peal of wild, mocking laughter.

Sir Roland's hands fell to his side.

"What horrible witchery is this?" he gasped. "Am I never to be free? Surely Spring-Heeled Jack could not enter this room? Am I going mad?"

His flesh crept upon his bones as he heard a strange, ghostly, rustling sound.

Glancing over his shoulder he saw that one of the white window blinds was fluttering.

The shutter had been thrown back and the window was wide open.

"How is this?" Sir Roland cried, starting to his feet. "Am I to have no rest?"

Drawing a pistol from his pocket he advanced towards the window.

"If I can only get a shot at the fiend," he said, grinding his teeth with fury, "I'll see if cold lead can penetrate his unholy body."

"Unholy! Ha, ha, ha!"

It was the voice of Spring-Heeled Jack, but he was nowhere to be seen.

With his finger on the trigger Sir Roland passed out on to an old wooden balcony that overlooked the street.

There was not a creature in sight.

The clouds had rolled away and the moon shone clear and bright.

"It is impossible that all this should be imagination," Sir Roland said. "When I entered the room all the windows were safe and—"

A gigantic bat-like form hovered over him for a moment and then, descending with the swiftness of a thunderbolt, struck Sir Roland down.

As he fell, uttering a cry of dismay, the pistol exploded harmlessly in the air, and Sir Roland Ashton lay stunned and motionless upon the balcony.

The report startled the echoes of the night, and Dick Witchardson started from his bed.

Pale and trembling with horror he hurried on his clothes.

"Mercy on me!" he gasped. "What a fool I was to give Sir Roland the pistols; he has committed suicide!"

"Help—help!"

The ostler, the boots, and the chamber-maids were running all over the house like scared rabbits.

"Keep quiet, will you!" Witchardson roared, as he opened the door of his bed-chamber. "Silence, you fools! Silence, you hussies!"

"Help—watch! we shall be murdered in our beds," screamed the fat cook.

"How the devil should that be, when you are all up?" Witchardson bellowed, almost beside himself. "Where's Tom?"

"Here I am, sir," the ostler replied. "Lor! a-mussy, what's the meaning of all this 'ere?"

"Come with me," Witchardson said, grasping the blunderbuss. "Get back to your rooms, you women."

"We won't—we can't—we shan't—oh!" shrieked the bevy of beauty, who were all of a heap on the landing.

"Then stay where you are and I hope you'll catch your deaths of cold," the landlord said, adding anything but a blessing on the heads of the ladies. "This way, Tom. Something has happened in the blue-room. Where's that coward, Bill the waiter?"

"Here I be," Bill squeaked; "but I ain't a coward."

"Then go in front with the lamp and show us the way upstairs."

Bill was a thin, musty gentleman, with weak knees and large sprawling feet, which were constantly getting in each other's way.

He did not seem to appreciate the idea of going in advance, but it so happened that Dick Witchardson, whether by accident or design, presented the blunderbuss at him, and the unhappy waiter skipped up the stairs, shedding oil and sparks as he went.

Suddenly Tom the ostler uttered a howl.

"What's the matter now?" Witchardson demanded.

"Hot fat," Tom gasped. "I've got about a quarter of a pint down my neck."

"I'll kick the lot of you into the Thames if you can't keep quiet," Witchardson growled. "Now then, here's the blue-room."

He knocked at the door as he spoke, but of course there was no response.

"What are we to do?" he said. "The lock is strong enough for a prison."

"I think," said Bill the waiter, every tooth in

his head chattering with fear, "that we ought to call the watch."

"Call the devil, you mean," Witchardson replied. "We shall have the Charlies here quick enough, never fear. We must break down the panels."

Witchardson was a strong man, but the panels were stronger.

They defied his efforts for some time, though he rained blows upon them powerful enough to have felled an ox.

"Sir Roland must be dead or dying," he groaned, as he desisted in his efforts. "Tom, run downstairs and fetch a crowbar. We must get into the room somehow."

The ostler did as he was told, and soon the sturdy panels succumbed with a crash.

All three rushed into the room, and then they stood gazing at each other in blank astonishment and dismay.

Sir Roland Ashton was nowhere to be seen.

The windows were closed and fastened, and nothing in the room had been changed.

On the table lay the pistol which Sir Roland had fired, and under it a scrap of paper.

"What's this?" Witchardson said, as he picked up the latter. "Hang it, I told you to send for the devil, and it strikes me that he must have been here."

"Eh!" the waiter said. "Oh! lor', you don't say so, sir?"

"Listen to this," Witchardson said, as he held the scrap of paper at arm's length.

The document had been written with a red liquid that looked like blood, and ran as follows:—

"Trouble yourself no more about that villain, Sir Roland Ashton. His arch-enemy, Spring-Heeled Jack, will take good care of him. Beware! Shelter him no more, or dire trouble will fall upon your house."

"Well, I never," Bill the waiter said, dodging behind Tom. "Don't you smell something like sulphur?"

"I do," Tom the ostler assented. "I'm a sinner—an awful sinner."

"So we all are," Witchardson said; "but we have done no harm. Where on earth has this mysterious being who calls himself Spring-Heeled Jack carried Sir Roland to?"

"To an earthly purgatory," said a voice behind him.

The landlord of the Wounded Hart started and grasped his hair with both hands, as if afraid that it would fly off his head.

"We can do no good here," he said. "Ha! I hear voices. The Charlies have arrived at last. Let them in, Tom, for this is a case for the law to inquire into."

"I wouldn't go down them blessed stairs alone for a thousand pounds," Tom declared.

"I begs to give warning," the waiter said, faintly. "Show me a man and I'll fight him if he be big as a house, but I can't battle with hobgoblins, and—"

At this moment Bill thought he felt the pressure of an icy hand on the back of his neck, and dropped the lamp.

The room was instantly plunged in darkness, and a general stampede took place.

Dick Witchardson discharged the blunderbuss, and made a hole in the celling as big as the crown of a man's hat.

Tom the ostler laid hold of Bill's ears, and rolled comfortably down a flight of stairs with him. The women screamed, a dog in the yard barked and howled furiously, and outside the watch hammered at the door, and demanded entrance in the name of the king!

At last something like order was restored. The front door was opened, and several old men, armed with staves, carrying lanterns, pushed forward to enter the house.

The first person they encountered was Bill the waiter, who was in such a mortal hurry to leave the place that he forgot everything except a strong desire to make himself safe.

But a rap over the head with a club about as thick as a broomstick checked his progress.

He retired into a corner, and having sat down in a violent hurry, gazed up at the ceiling and smiled in a sickly kind of fashion.

"Witchardson," croaked one of the old men of the watch, "someboby has been discharging fire-arms in your house. What does it mean? Is it a duel, a murder, or a suicide?"

"I know no more than the man in the moon," the landlord replied. "Sir Roland Ashton came here about two hours ago and took the blue-room, but he has been walked away by a spirit, or a—a—"

"Corpse—candle," Bill the waiter suggested, feebly. "I can see lots of 'em flitting about now."

He was looking in a dazed kind of manner at the lantern, and that accounted for the delusion.

"Hold your idle tongue," Witchardson said. "Gentlemen of the watch, I invite the fullest inquiry, for this matter has disturbed my mind more than you can think."

"It is a likely story to begin with," said the Charlie who acted as spokesman. "I suppose Sir Roland Ashton didn't come here with a well-filled purse?"

"What do you mean?'

"Why that he must be found," the watchman replied. "It's all nonsense about his being spirited away."

"Well, then, perhaps you will find him," the innkeeper said; "and when you do I hope you'll keep him, so that he does not trouble me again. Make what use you like of the house. It is entirely at your service."

"Give 'em something to drink," Bill suggested, sitting up, and rubbing his smitten cranium. "I could do a drop o' something warm myself."

This was not a bad idea, and the watchmen seemed to agree with it.

They refreshed themselves to a considerable extent, and then went upstairs to the blue-room, and came back just as wise.

"Well," said Witchardson, "what do you make of it? Nothing, I suppose? But now I have something to show you. Just glance at this slip of paper."

The watchmen gathered round and inspected the document, and having read it thought that it was time to go.

They had all heard of Spring-Heeled Jack, and the fact that he had been in the house and might be there still was more than a sufficient reason to give them a sudden dislike to the Wounded Hart and its vicinity.

"This," said the leader, "is a case for the Bow-street runners. We must go back to our duty. Disperse, men, to your stations; and if you should see this Spring-Heeled Jack, why, of course, you will take him into custody."

Of course they said they would, but every man made up his mind to shut himself up in his box and keep there until the sun rose and awoke the world to activity

## CHAPTER XLIII.

THE PRISONERS—GOLD MERE DROSS—THE WELL BEGINS TO OVERFLOW—RATS! RATS!—SPRING-HEELED JACK SOFTENS HIS HEART.

THE reader will remember that Spring-Heeled Jack brought the body of Gedge Foote from the well and propped it against the cellar wall.

The ghastly object was deposited in a corner of the gruesome place, where pall-like shadows lurked.

Thus it was that Bill Blarney, ignorant of what had been done with the body, pointed to the well when questioned by the men of the Mint.

He thought that the remains of Gedge Foote were still in the well, and his captors were too much excited to search the cellar; but at the time when Bill Blarney was being examined by the lawless tribunal and prepared for execution the sightless eyes of the murdered man were directed at him as they had been in life.

When Blarney was hurled into the well with the rope about his neck he felt the jerk and all the horrors of strangulation.

He experienced a sensation as if wheels of crushing weight and fitted with red hot tyres had passed over his neck.

Jagged flashes of vivid light danced before his eyes, his tongue enlarged and filled his mouth, and his heart and brain seemed to take fire and burns fiercely.

If he had lived an age as he stood on the brink of the well, he was suffering an eternity of awe now.

His senses reeled, a thousand mocking, devilish voices rang in his ears, and then he became plunged into a boisterous sea of molten metal, which rolled over him in furious waves.

All was over at last.

Oblivion came to the wretched man's rescue. Suddenly he experienced the sensation of returning life.

And life was now a hideous reality to him, for as his blood began to circulate, it set his veins tingling with icy coldness and then with burning heat.

Bill Blarney passed his hands up to his neck.

A piece of rope still encircled it, and the agonised wretch groaned and writhed like a cut worm, with an agony that has no name.

"Is this perdition?" he moaned. "Have I finished my earthly career to suffer torture for ever and for ever? Oh! no, no! Mercy!"

A sound he had heard often before fell upon his ears.

It was the drip, drip of the water of the well.

"I am not dead," Bill Blarney said; "I am in Gedge Foote's secret haunt. How did I escape? What miracle saved me? Hush, hush! I must not speak, or my enemies above will—"

"Your enemy is here," a stern voice interposed.

A light flashed up, and Bill Blarney gathered up his aching limbs in horror as he saw Spring-Heeled Jack bending over him.

The strange being held an old-fashioned oil lamp in his hand, and its light fell upon Gedge Foote's secret hoard.

What was the miser's gold to him now?

His lifeless hands could not bathe in it as they had been wont to do.

His eyes could not gloat over the shining metal, and no longer was its ring music to his greedy ears.

"So," said Spring-Heeled Jack, "you have your wish at last, Bill Blarney. Here is a king's ransom. Help yourself."

Bill Blarney only groaned and rolled over on his side.

"What?" said Spring-Heeled Jack. "You will not speak? This is poor gratitude to me for saving your life."

"Give me a cupful of water," Bill Blarney pleaded.

"There is plenty in the well."

The prisoner shuddered.

"Coward and murderer!" Spring-Heeled Jack cried, in a voice of thunder. "Your hapless victim has gone to his last account, but his body shall keep you company. Ha! ha!"

"Spare me that!" Blarney cried, clasping his hands. "Bring it not here. I shall go mad if you do—I shall go mad!"

"And would not that be a just punishment for your crimes?" Spring-Heeled Jack demanded. "It is said that when a wicked man goes mad that they live their horrible lives over again, for them there is no present, no future, no hope."

"Being of mystery," Bill Blarney said, in a despairing tone of voice, "if you took the trouble to save my life you will have mercy upon me now?"

He clasped his hands above his head and grovelled abjectly on the ground.

"No, no!" Spring-Heeled Jack replied. "You have brought this upon yourself. What mercy can you expect of me? You are my prisoner now, but soon you will be the prisoner of the dead. Ha, ha!"

Bill Blarney's blood ran cold with horror, and it seemed, in his over-wrought imagination, that Spring-Heeled Jack's form enlarged, and that flashes of lurid light came from his eyes.

Suddenly Spring-Heeled Jack extinguished the lamp and left the secret passage.

In a frenzy of fear Bill Blarney attempted to follow, but ere he was half across the damp, reeking floor a pair of arms, iron-like in their grasp, hurled him back.

Bill Blarney, thus thwarted, and, indeed, more dead than alive, gave up all notion of attempting to escape, and lay still and moaning as he thought of his hideous fate.

To have the body of the murdered man with him would be too awful.

It could not be true.

He was mad—the drink had maddened him, and he would awake presently and find that he had been dreaming.

So Bill Blarney endeavoured to persuade himself, and so he tried to hope, but the sudden creaking of a pulley put an end to all such ideas.

Spring-Heeled Jack, bearing the body of Gedge Foote in his arms, entered the secret passage.

"There is your companion," he said, placing the lamp upon the floor. "I will leave you the light, for the best of company cannot be jovial in the dark."

Bill Blarney pressed his hand to his eyes to shut out the awful sight.

Spring-Heeled Jack's mocking laughter rang in

his ears, and the wretch crouched like a hound under the lash.

"I have another companion for you, and I will bring him soon," Spring-Heeled Jack said.

"You are going then?" Bill Blarney said, removing his hands and casting a wistful glance at the demoniacal figure.

"Yes, but not before I have taken precautions to prevent you running away."

The prisoner's heart sunk as heavy as lead as Spring-Heeled Jack produced a strong cord.

"You hurt me," Blarney whined, as he was being bound, "the cords cut into my flesh."

Spring-Heeled Jack only grinned, which gave his face so horrible an expression that Bill Blarney almost fainted.

"Now," said the uncouth creature, "you may escape if you can, and I wish you joy."

"Don't go?" Blarney gasped. "Don't leave me here alone with the corpse. Kill me if you like, but don't—don't. Oh! mercy! Stay another moment?"

But Spring-Heeled Jack was already away, and the prisoner, bound and helpless, managed to crawl to the mouth of the secret passage.

Gazing below he could just see the water of the well.

A flickering ray from the lamp fell upon it and lent a ghastly hue to its black surface.

Bill Blarney thought of suicide.

He had only to crawl along a few more feet and then his miseries would be at an end.

He had heard that death by drowning was an easy one; but, sick at heart, he turned away, only to see the eyes of the corpse staring blindly at him.

Oh! it was awful.

Those eyes followed him everywhere, and when he closed his own matters became worse.

The body moved; it advanced, stretching out its stiffened joints.

The under jaw wagged mockingly, and Bill Blarney, unable to bear this pressure of terror, gave vent to a prolonged shriek and fainted.

. . . . . . . .

The dawn of day was slowly creeping over London.

Night had hidden its secret sins and crimes, and the broad, glorious sun would soon rise and cleanse away pollution with a flood of golden light.

A heavy mist hung over the river.

Few craft were moving about, but from the decks came the sound of preparation, for sailors are early risers.

A man leaning over the side of a vessel saw a boat emerge from the gloom like a shadow, and disappear silently and swiftly.

The man put his hand to his ear, and listened for the sound of the sculls, but he could hear nothing save the plashing of the water against the hull of the ship.

The tide was running up, and in another hour it would reach high-water mark.

The boat was going against the stream—a fact that caused the sailor to rub his nose thoughtfully, and speculate as to what sort of thing it could be that could go at such a rate against wind and tide.

All sailors are more or less superstitious, and this particular son of Neptune did not feel at all comfortable.

"What on earth was that lying at the stem?" he said. "It looks like the body of a man made ready to be shot overboard. Hang me if I don't speak to the captain about this!"

He did and was called a lubber for his pains.

The captain was all the more wrathful because his vessel was outward bound and ready to sail as soon as the sun came up.

"Do you think I am going to muddle my brains about who comes and who goes on the river?" he said. "You're a fool, Tarline!"

"Thank 'ee!" Tarline said, scratching his head.

"Don't you give me any of your insolence!" the captain roared. "Go about your duty and think yourself lucky that I don't report you to the owners."

Tarline went forward, grumbling under his breath.

"Well," he said, "I daresay I am a fool, but I can believe my own eyes, and if it wasn't old Nick in that boat it must have been his first cousin. Mark me, something will happen to this 'ere wessel afore it returns to England, if ever it does."

Consoling himself with this rather mournful reflection, Tarline went about his work, but the memory of the spectral boat haunted him, and if he saw it in his mind's eye once during the day he saw it a hundred times.

The boat which had so alarmed the old salt contained Spring-Heeled Jack and Sir Roland Ashton.

A heavy cloak enclosed the baronet's form, and he was unconscious of his journey upon the river, and of everything until he was roused by hearing a peculiar chaunting sound, which ceased as sense and feeling revived.

Sir Roland opened his eyes and stared about him in wonder.

He was in the very room in which he had met Gedge Foote on the previous night.

There was the table, the empty brandy bottles, and the dirty glasses, still reeking with the fumes of the fiery liquid.

Sir Roland rubbed his eyes and shrugged his shoulders.

He was chilly, shivering, and feverish.

"Let me think it out," he said. "Have I been in a trance? Is it possible that Gedge Foote drugged me, and that I have—no, no! It is all real. That fearful row across the river—the blue-room—the appearance of that fiend—"

"Who appears before you again?" Spring-Heeled Jack cried, entering by the door. "Sir Roland, I bring you back to old quarters. Have you no word of thanks?"

Sir Roland Ashton was dumbfounded.

He could not speak, but only sit and stare at the weird form towering exultingly over him.

He noticed that Spring-Heeled Jack carried a long cord in his hand, which trailed upon the floor like a serpent.

"What new devil's prank is this?" he contrived to gasp out.

"If I am a devil," Spring-Heeled Jack replied, "it is you who have raised me. But I have no time to waste words. The hours fly, and I must away."

Sir Roland's face paled as a thought flashed into his brain.

"I know where you go," he said.

"Yes; to Lilac Lodge."

"My bitterest curse upon you?"

"Of what avail are curses or blessings from such a man as you," Spring-Heeled Jack said, sternly. "If I followed my own inclination my hands would be at your throat, but—bah! I have no more words for you. Come!"

Whirling the cord above his head in a series of loops, he encircled Sir Roland and drew him upon his knees.

A few hastily-tied knots, and the baronet presented a rather ridiculous appearance.

He looked like a trussed fowl, and his struggles to get free only added to the security of his bonds.

"Wretch — uncouth wretch!" Sir Roland yelled, "my hour is yet to come!"

"It has," Spring-Heeled Jack assented. "Look well to it. Search your heart and ask yourself what you are. Uncouth, forsooth! Ha, ha, ha! You have travelled the long lane of debauchery, deceit, and murder, but retribution is at hand. Come with me and I will give you gold. You shall eat of it, you shall drink of it. To the well —to the well!"

Sir Roland Ashton felt his heart grow cold as he heard these words.

His features assumed a livid hue, and he made a supreme effort to burst his bonds.

His struggles were fearful to behold.

His eyes protruded from his head, and the veins upon his forehead stood out like bosses of whip-cord.

Spring-Heeled Jack raised his prisoner as easily as he would have picked up a child from the floor, and leaped from the room at a single bound.

His feet, if they touched the winding staircase, made no noise.

He seemed to be treading upon air, and Sir Roland became giddy as he was made a party to a fiendish waltz over balustrades, through archways, and in and out of rooms.

But at last the mad journey ended.

Dazed and bewildered he discovered that Spring-Heeled Jack had planted him upon the very brink of the well, so near the brink that one touch would have sent him headlong into the black abyss.

But such were not Spring-Heeled Jack's intentions.

Seizing the rope with one hand, Spring-Heeled Jack clutched Sir Roland with the other, and began to descend.

To Sir Roland the journey was filled with as many vague terrors as if he were crossing the river Styx in company with the ghostly ferryman, Charon.

"Hah!" cried Spring-Heeled Jack, as he sent his prisoner flying into the passage half way down; "here we are."

"Oh! the devil!" cried Bill Blarney. "Is it yourself, Sir Roland? It's much obliged that I ought to be to you for leaving me to take care of myself."

Sir Roland Ashton made no reply.

His hair bristled, his knees knocked together, and the marrow of his bones congealed.

"Gedge Foote—Gedge Foote—Gedge Foote!" he shrieked.

"Yes; to bear you two company," Spring-Heeled Jack said, mockingly. "What, do you not like the look of him now? He can make no more bargains. See, here is the gold that he loved to call his own. It is yours now. I, the trustee, make you a present of it. Now you can take Daisy Leigh abroad. What is there to hinder you?"

The next instant the prisoners were left alone.

"Your company is better than none, Sir Roland," Bill Blarney said; "but I would do my best to get out of it if my hands were at liberty."

"I am in no mood to talk over what has taken place," Sir Roland replied, sulkily. "I wonder what fate is in store for us?"

"By thirst while water is near you, and starvation with wealth within your grasp," cried the voice of Spring-Heeled Jack.

"He cannot mean it," Bill Blarney whined. "It would be too cruel, Sir Roland."

"Well?"

"Let us try to get rid of that body."

"How is it to be done?"

"By pitching it into the well."

"My hands are bound behind my back."

"Be jabers! I didn't notice that before," Bill Blarney said. "Spring-Heeled Jack has been more merciful to me than you. But we must get rid of the body somehow."

"I would not touch it," Sir Roland said, shuddering. "What is that?"

It was a low, gurgling sound, followed by the plash of water.

"Perdition!" Sir Roland cried. "The well is rising. We must perish."

Bill Blarney threw himself down upon his face, and began to howl dismally.

"Listen!" Sir Roland exclaimed. "It must be as I said. Do you not hear—do you not hear?"

"Yes," Bill Blarney yelled. "Will these horrors never pass away?"

The water was bubbling up furiously, and would soon reach the secret passage.

Presently a number of sewer rats, driven from their haunt, appeared, their red eyes gleaming fiercely.

They came in swarms, scampering about and squeaking, to the terror of the prisoners, who huddled into a corner and expected each moment to be their last.

"It is all over!" Sir Roland groaned. "If we are not drowned we shall be devoured. Oh! for one more hour of freedom."

The water was now running into the secret passage, and soon Sir Roland Ashton and Bill Blarney were ankle deep.

"Oh! for one more hour of freedom," the baronet repeated. "Is there no hope?"

"Yes, if you will promise to lead a better life," said the voice of Spring-Heeled Jack.

"I will," Sir Roland panted. "I will do anything you ask!"

"Swear?"

"I swear by all that is holy."

As Sir Roland breathed the last word, he felt his bonds cut through with a sharp instrument of some sort.

The severed cords fell at his feet, and wading through the fast rising waters, he seized the dangling ends of the rope, and began hauling himself up.

Breathless and drenched to the skin he reached the cellar, and was presently joined by Bill Blarney.

"So," said the baronet, "you are free, too, are you?"

"Why, yes," said Blarney. "Do you think that yours is the only life worth saving? But I am not going to stay here to talk, or Spring-Heeled Jack may repent of being so merciful, and make short work of us. Good-bye, Sir Roland, and when you want more dirty work done you must seek a meeker pupil than me."

## CHAPTER XLIV.

THE VALUE OF A BAD MAN'S OATH—SIR ROLAND BEGINS TO PLOT AGAIN—A PLAN TO CATCH SPRING-HEELED JACK.

It was a beautiful morning.

The sun shone gloriously, and the air was fresh and bracing.

The aspect of the landscape from Lilac Lodge was lovely in the extreme, but Jacob Butler had no eyes for it.

He was as miserable as a man could be, and the prospect of becoming the husband of such a hag as Mrs. Corcoran did not help to lighten the gloom, but quite the reverse.

"Ugh!" he said, shudderingly, "I wish I had nothing to do with this place or Sir Roland. I wonder where he can be? Four days have passed away and he is still absent. Well, for my part, it would be a relief to my mind if I heard that he had broken his neck."

He was standing with his back to the door and did not hear it open, and was unconscious of the fact that Mrs. Corcoran was stealing upon him, and listening to every word he said.

"If I marry that old wretch I am sure I shall poison her or myself," he said.

"Yourself, if you like, Jacob dear, after a month or two, but not me," said the hag.

Jacob Butler started, and his hair moved as if disturbed by a sudden current of air.

"Ha, ha! I was only joking," he said, forcing a feeble laugh. "Of course, I knew that you were behind me."

"Of course you didn't, you contemptible liar!"

The old hag's eyes flashed green with fury, and Jacob Butler could not help thinking that if she had lived in the time of James the First she would have been denounced as a witch and met death by burning or drowning.

"Hard words won't do any good, lovey," he said.

The last word nearly choked him, and it cost him an effort to get it through his lips.

"So you will poison me?" said Mrs. Corcoran. "Ho, ho! Well, your chance will soon come. To-morrow we shall be man and wife."

Jacob Butler turned livid, and looked at the window as if he contemplated hurling himself out of it, and thus avert his impending fate.

"Listen, you fool!" Mrs. Corcoran said. "I care as little for you as you care for me. We hate each other, but as we both have the same secrets in keeping it is necessary that we should make ourselves safe."

"Just so," Jacob gasped. "For my own part, I wish I had done it before. Lor'! how limp I do feel about the knees."

"We have Sir Roland under our thumbs," Mrs. Corcoran went on, casting a sidelong glance of contempt at her future husband. "He must and shall find money. Listen! that girl is singing again."

"I hear her," said Jacob Butler, "but where is she? We never see her in the day time, and yet at night I hear her walking about the house."

"Or the ghost of Lady Ashton?"

"Don't," Jacob groaned; "I can't bear to hear you talk about such horrible things. Do you believe that there are such things as ghosts?"

"I am sure of it."

"Have you ever seen one?"

"I have."

Jacob Butler pressed his hand to his waistcoat, and brought his chin down almost to his knees.

He was fated, not only to marry the ugliest old woman on the face of the earth, but a ghost-seer to boot.

"Whose ghost was it that you saw?" he contrived to ask.

"The spirit of the woman you hear prowling about this house at night," the hag replied. "You think it is Daisy Leigh, but it is not."

"Are you sure of it?" said Jacob, quaking in such a style that he could not keep a single joint still.

"I am sure of it. Listen!"

Jacob's mouth and eyes were open to their utmost limits, and his ears drank in every word the hag uttered.

"Two nights ago," she croaked, "I was sitting up late. I got it into my head that Sir Roland would return, and I did not care to be roused out of my bed, so I thought that I would wait and get him such refreshment as he might require."

"You always were a thoughtful creature," Jacob said, in a piping tone of voice.

"Peace, fool, and let me finish my story."

"Oh! it's only a story, then," said Jacob, much relieved. "When I was young I used to like fairy tales and—"

Mrs. Corcoran hooked one of her claw-like hands upon his ear and gave it such a wrench that Jacob Butler howled with pain.

"That's the way I have when I am playful," she said, grinning. "Now then, just be quiet, or I will turn my attention to the other side of your head."

"I'll be as dumb as a drum with a hole in it," Jacob promised.

"Well," said the hag, "I was telling you that I was waiting for Sir Roland. I was reading a beautiful book, full of such nice pictures. Ha, ha! Would you like to know the name of it? You may speak."

"Yes."

"It was De Foe's 'History of the Devil.'"

"Oh!" Jacob moaned. "I don't think I should care about reading that after dark."

"I did, because it interested me," Mrs. Corcoran said, with a hollow laugh. "As I sat glancing through the pages I thought the lamp began to burn dimly, and then I heard something that sounded like the rustle of a silk dress on the staircase."

Jacob Butler turned a sickly green, and he hung on to his waistcoat as if he felt very bad indeed.

"Hah! thought I," the crone continued, "that girl Daisy is about. Now is the time to catch her. I took the lamp in my hand and opened the door, and right in front of me stood the spectre of Lady Ashton."

As she spoke the rumbling of thunder came from a distant cloud, and Jacob Butler looked as if he was going to have a fit.

"I challenged the ghost to speak," Mrs. Corcoran continued; "but it remained speechless and motionless. It's eyes were fixed upon me—they fascinated me and held me powerless—but I did not lose nerve."

"You never do?" Jacob said; "you are all nerve."

"I could see right through the apparition," the hag resumed, taking a hideous delight in every word she uttered, "or I should have thought it was some trick to frighten me. Suddenly the ghost spoke."

In spite of all warning Jacob Butler could not keep his tongue still.

He felt that he must either speak or shriek like a maniac.

"What did it say?" he asked. "Make haste to tell me. The storm is coming, and you know that thunder and lightning makes me feel dreadfully bad."

"Woman!" said the ghost, "if you repent of the share that you had in my untimely end, you must turn your thoughts to vengeance, and Jacob Butler must help you."

"It was very kind of the ghost," said the wretched Jacob, "but I'd rather—oh! dear—oh! dear! I wish I was dead. I wish I may die if I don't."

At this moment the sky darkened.

Clouds of inky hue were rolling up from the westward and soon the storm burst in all its fury.

Jacob Butler grovelled on the floor and hid his face in his arms.

"The house will be struck!" he cried. "We shall be burnt to cinders. Was there ever such a place as this? It must be next door to the infernal regions."

Mrs. Corcoran looked at him contemptuously as he kicked spasmodically and wriggled about like an eel on a fish-hook.

The hag cared nothing for the storm, but seemed to delight in it, and clapped her hands as the jagged lightning rent the murky clouds asunder.

"She'll fly up the chimney on a broomstick presently," Jacob muttered; "I wish the devil would come and rid me of her!"

As he gave expression to this amiable wish a thunder-bolt fell with such a terrific explosion that Lilac Lodge rocked upon its foundation.

A dreadful smell of sulphur pervaded the apartment, and as Jacob Butler skipped to his feet, with the intention of taking refuge in the coal cellar, there came a furious knocking at the outer door.

"Who is that?" Jacob replied, starting back aghast, and almost swooning.

"Sir Roland Ashton," the hag replied. "You might have seen him riding through the rain and lightning if you had not covered your cowardly eyes. Let him in. We will bid him welcome. Ho! ho!"

Half dead with terror, Jacob Butler took his tottering limbs down the staircase.

He opened the door, and slipped aside to allow Sir Roland Ashton to pass.

The baronet paid no attention to Jacob, but passed along the hall like a man in a dream.

Sir Roland's face was deadly white, and his eyes fixed, as if he were walking in his sleep.

On he strode, up the staircase, and then shut himself up in a room.

"He's mad," Jacob said. "Everybody is mad here. Oh! murder, what a flash. If this storm goes on the house must fall."

He was making a dash towards that haven of refuge, the cellar, when a bell rang violently.

"That's Sir Roland," said Jacob; "I wonder what he wants? He came stalking in like a ghost, and now he kicks up a row. Let that old beast of a woman answer the bell; I won't."

"Yes, you will," she said; "Sir Roland wants to see you particularly, and me, too."

Jacob Butler felt inclined to sink into his boots, as he saw that Mrs. Corcoran was looking over his shoulder.

"Very well," he said; "but this will be the death of me, and then you can't marry me. So much the better."

The hag took him by the shoulders and twisted him round.

"If I hear another word of complaint from you," she said, thrusting her face close to his, "I'll weave a spell about you that will fill you with such pain that you will wish yourself dead a hundred times an hour."

"I knew it," Jacob groaned, under his breath; "she is a witch and in league with the devil."

Limp and damp with cold, clammy perspiration he followed his betrothed up the creaking staircase and entered the room into which Sir Roland had previously taken himself.

The baronet sat at a table with his face to the window.

"Sit down," he said; "this storm is in keeping with my feelings. Since I went away I have suffered the tortures of perdition. But enough! we will talk of that anon. Where is the girl?"

"Ask the booming thunder and the quivering lightning, for I know not," Mrs. Corcoran replied. "She may be in the house for all I know, or she may be a thousand miles away."

"Them's my sentiments," Jacob said, mildly.

He would have liked to add—

"And I wish I was a thousand miles away, too."

But he checked himself, for the hag's watchful eyes were upon him.

Before Sir Roland had time to speak again Daisy's voice was heard.

The dulcet notes rose clear and sweet, and seemed to lull the storm, for the clouds parted, and began to roll away.

"She is here!" Sir Roland cried, exultantly, "and she shall yet be mine! Daisy, my darling—Daisy, my love!"

"Beware!" said a voice, proceeding apparently from the massive wall. "Remember your oath!"

"I will remember nothing!" Sir Roland hissed. "An hour hence the house will be surrounded, and nobody will pass in or out of it without my permission. Ha! ha! I triumph at last."

Mrs. Corcoran rubbed her skinny knees, and Jacob Butler gave vent to a feeble chuckle, because he thought it was required of him.

It was a great relief to his mind that other people were coming to Lilac Lodge, as he saw some hope that his marriage with Mrs. Corcoran might be postponed, and thus give him a chance of escape.

"I left two officers in a hut in the wood," Sir Roland continued. "They will be followed by soldiers, and this fox who calls himself Spring-Heeled Jack will be unearthed and killed."

"Ha! ha! ha!"

"Laugh on," Sir Roland cried. "My hour of triumph is at hand and I will repay you with torture for torture."

"This is a most uncomfortable state of affairs," Jacob Butler said, glancing nervously at the wall. "There always was something wrong where women are concerned since the world began."

"Hold your tongue, idiot!" the hag hissed. "If you have nothing more sensible to say, keep your tongue between your teeth."

"Certainly, my dear," said Jacob, looking as if strangling her would have given him an appetite. "I will make no more remarks. Hah! another knock. More visitors."

"The officers," Sir Roland said. "Admit them at once. I will see them alone."

"In this room?"

"No; in the library," Sir Roland replied. "When I have been there this haunting fiend has never troubled me."

Jacob Butler ran joyfully downstairs and admitted Catchpole and Elias Grabham.

"You're a a rum object to look at," Grabham said. "What do you call yourself?"

"I don't call myself anything," Jacob returned, wrathfully. "I leave that to other people and I expect them to be civil."

"I s'pose you know who we are?" said Grabham, drawing himself up to his full height.

"You are police officers?"

"Right you are! And you had better mind how you behave while we are here."

"Oh! indeed," said Jacob Butler.

"Yes, indeed," Catchpole chimed in. "Me and my mate don't take sauce kindly. Now, then, take us into a room and get us something to drink, for we are as wet and cold as frogs."

"I hate the country!" said Elias Grabham, as he and his brother officer followed Jacob Butler. "The houses leak, and the roads are like sponge. Only think of that blessed place we had to put our heads into! Give me London and its mud and fog, I say, to all the trees as ever was growed!"

"And the fields full of spiders and grass-whoppers!" sneered Catchpole; "likewise the wopses and the bumble-bees—ugh!"

"There you are!" said Jacob Butler, flinging open the library door. "You'll find a decanter and glasses on the table. Leave a drop for Sir Roland. He will be down presently."

"And so will you—on the floor, if you don't behave better to your superiors," Grabham said, loftily. "Come along, Catchpole, my boy, and we will make ourselves comfortable while we may."

They had not much time to carouse, but they made the most of it, and drank a great deal before Sir Roland had time to get down.

The baronet put on a smiling face and a bland demeanour before the officers.

"We have had our troubles, gentlemen," he said, "but the reward in store for us will make the memory of them sweet."

"I ain't so sure of that," Catchpole said, shaking his head. "I'd willingly forget all about that 'ere Spring-Heeled Jack."

"So would I," assented Elias Grabham, glancing over his shoulder. "You are quite sure that he can't see or hear us?"

"Quite," Sir Roland replied; "I have had the walls examined and the chimney bricked up. This room seems to be the only one which he has no power to enter. You may speak freely."

"But," said Catchpole, with a knowing air, "it will be just as well not to talk too loud; we don't want to holler, you know."

"Quite so," said Sir Roland. "You have come down here to catch Spring-Heeled Jack, and the first question I have to ask you is whether you have hit upon any plan likely to be successful?"

"We have," Grabham replied. "The only thing we can think of is that it must be done with nets."

"With what?" Sir Roland demanded, in astonishment. "Did you say nets?"

"I did say nets and I means nets," Grabham replied.

"In fact," Catchpole remarked, "we both means nets, and I am sure, Sir Roland, that you will give us credit for a clever dodge when you have heard all about it."

"Well—well," said Sir Roland, "I am willing to listen to anything you have to say. Unfold your scheme as quickly as possible."

"It is this," said Grabham. "We mean to catch this skip-jack of a fellow in a novel sort of way. He goes flying in and out among the trees like a bat, doesn't he?"

"Yes."

"Well," Grabham continued, "supposing we stretched nets across from tree to tree, don't you think he might bounce into one and get nicely trapped?"

"Perhaps so," Sir Roland said; "but for the life of me I don't see where the nets are to come from unless you have brought them with you!"

"There you have hit the right nail on the head, your honour," said Catchpole, grinning, "and that is just what we have done."

"Where are they?"

"At the inn; we will go for them as soon as the sun goes down."

"Capital—capital!" exclaimed Sir Roland, rubbing his hands. "My influence at Court has enabled me to obtain the services of a detachment of soldiers, who, I hope, will be here before nightfall, and then every inch of the house will be well guarded."

"I think we could have managed the business without the help of the sogers," Elias Grabham said, looking down his nose. "Howsomever, I shan't grumble if we are well paid."

"I will see to that," Sir Roland said. "Fill your glasses again and join me in drinking confusion to that fiend on earth—Spring-Heeled Jack!"

"I'd like to have him under lock and key," Catchpole growled, as he drained his glass to the dregs. "I'd make it pretty warm for him, as hot, if not hotter, as— What's the matter with you, Grabham?"

"I thought I saw a shadow creeping along the wall," Grabham replied, as he held on to the arms of his chair.

"Which wall?" the baronet demanded.

"The one behind you, Sir Roland," Grabham answered. "Let it pass, for it might have been nothing more than my fancy."

"It was your fancy and nothing else," Catchpole grunted. "You are always seeing something or other which turns out to be nothing at all."

"I think that our interview is at an end," Sir Roland said. "We will meet here again and make merry when you have captured Spring-Heeled Jack. In the meantime, you will now make your preparations."

"Certainly—certainly," Grabham said. "The nets are rather heavy, and we should like your man to help us to carry them."

"Jacob Butler shall go with you," Sir Roland Ashton said.

The baronet touched a bell, and, in about a minute, Mrs. Corcoran appeared.

"Send Jacob to me at once," Sir Roland said.

The hag disappeared, and presently her voice was heard calling for her beloved.

She called in vain.

Jacob was either hiding or had given her the slip in spite of all her vigilance.

The old woman raved and tore the air with her hooked fingers like a maniac.

"Oh! my dear Jacob, my own manly Jacob,"

# SPRING-HEELED JACK,

## THE TERROR OF LONDON.

SPRING-HEELED JACK SHOUTED TO THE HORSES AND URGED THEM ON.

No. 15.

she cried. "How fondly will I embrace you when we meet again. I'll give you such a hug, my pet!"

Sir Roland did not seem much disturbed when he heard that Jacob Butler could not be found, and dismissed the officers.

Mrs. Corcoran stayed behind to have a few words with Sir Roland.

"I tell you," she said, "that this runaway idiot must be found, and at once. There is no telling what he may say or do to make himself safe. The fool thinks that his neck is in danger, and he will blab."

"Say you so," Sir Roland returned, frowning fiercely. "If such an idea had entered my head I would have found means to silence him. What is to be done? Who can we send in pursuit?"

"I will go myself."

"That, I think, will be the very best course to pursue."

"And remember," said the hag, "when I do catch him, I will not be interfered with in my treatment of him. Oh! I'll physic him—I'll physic him."

---

## CHAPTER XLV.

### WHAT BECAME OF JACOB BUTLER—OUT OF THE FRYING-PAN INTO THE FIRE.

As soon as Jacob Butler had shown the officers into the library the thought flashed into his brain that if he was ever to escape from the fate he dreaded then or never was the time.

He felt almost certain that as soon as Sir Roland went to interview Catchpole and Grabham that Mrs. Corcoran would not be far away from the keyhole of the library door, and he made up his mind to cut and run if it cost him his life.

Passing the hag on his way upstairs, he pretended to be hilarious, and hummed a tune.

"You are fond of music, deary?" Mrs. Corcoran said; "I am glad of that, for you will be able to sing to me when the winter evenings are long."

Jacob nodded and went his way, and Mrs. Corcoran, suspecting nothing, went hers.

After waiting about five minutes Jacob Butler made preparations for flight.

He sneaked like a thief down the stairs, starting and trembling as they creaked under his weight, and expecting every moment to be grabbed by the neck and hauled back to his dreadful captivity.

But fortune favoured Jacob Butler, and he got free of the house.

As soon as he reached the open air he took to his heels and ran at the top of his speed for a mile or so, and then paused to take breath.

"Thank goodness!" he gasped, "I will never be taken alive now. I have done with Sir Roland; and as for that old witch—ugh! I shouldn't wonder if she were to turn herself into a black cat or something as nasty and follow me."

The thought set Jacob Butler going again.

Leaving the highway, he plunged into a wood, plashing through pools of rain-water, and scratching his hands and legs with the trailing brambles.

But a little pain and discomfort was nothing to Jacob now.

All he thought of was how to put distance between himself and Lilac Lodge.

He had not the least notion in the world of what he was going to do, but poverty, starvation—anything, in fact—was better than being forced into a marriage with that wicked old woman, Mrs. Corcoran.

But at last the fugitive grew so tired that he could scarcely stand upon his feet, yet he was afraid to rest or close his eyes for a moment.

It suddenly occurred to him that if he could climb a tree and hide himself among the foliage that he would be comparatively safe.

Selecting an oak for this purpose, he commenced the ascent by grasping one of the lower limbs and hauling himself up.

Jacob Butler was no athlete, and by the time that he had settled himself in a forked branch he was fairly overcome.

"Now for a good long sleep!" he said. "I'm another King Charles. Ha! ha! I wonder what that bag of skin and bones will say when she finds that I have given her the slip? It would be as good as a play to see her dance about like a cat on hot bricks, and hear her swear like a trooper."

Jacob Butler closed his eyes and began to snore.

He was secure enough in his leafy perch, but his slumbers were disturbed by uncomfortable dreams.

He could not get rid of Mrs. Corcoran.

She travelled with him through that misty land of dreams, and refused to part company with him.

Jacob Butler groaned and wriggled in his slumbers, and when he awoke it was in consequence of a firm belief that Mrs. Corcoran had embraced him round the neck with a pair of red-hot arms.

"Hang it!" he said, as he rubbed his eyes. "How real that dream seemed to be! Hallo! what's that?"

A stone came hurtling through the branches and missed Jacob's head by about a quarter of an inch.

Then came another and another.

Jacob Butler dodged and bobbed about until he over-balanced himself and went down heels over head.

The branches broke his fall or the earth would have broken his neck.

He fell flat upon his back and lay staring idiotically at the sky.

"Don't, lovey—don't!" he murmured, feebly. "I wasn't running away, but only taking a little gentle exercise."

He fully expected to see Mrs. Corcoran and feel her sharp nails about his neck; and when somebody jerked him to his feet he howled with terror and fell upon his knees.

"What's the matter with you, you spalpeen?" grumbled a man's voice. "You're a curious sort of oak-apple to come rolling down. Be jabers! if you had fallen upon me there would have been some bones to mend."

Jacob gazed with fishy eyes at the speaker, and found that he was in the hands of a rather rough-looking customer.

But he was so relieved to discover that Mrs. Corcoran was not present that he burst out laughing.

"I certainly had a narrow escape," he said; "but, I say, what did you throw stones at me for?"

"At you?" said the man. "How the divil was I to know that you were up there. I was pelting birds to while away the time."

"Oh! that's it," said Jacob. "Well, as there is not much harm done, it is not worth while making a fuss about it. You seem to have been in trouble my man?"

"Trouble!" cried Bill Blarney, for he it was. "Trouble! No word in the English language or any other will describe what I have gone through lately. Look at me; I have been half-drowned, bound, beaten, cut with stones, torn with thorns, stormed at with lightning—but here I am, scarcely able to believe that I am alive!"

"Lor'! you don't mean to say so?" said Jacob, opening his capacious mouth. "Well, I have had a little taste of the same kind of thing. It strikes me very forcibly that you are escaping from somebody."

"You'll be struck still more forcibly if you talk nonsense!" Bill Blarney growled. "Well, well, goodness knows that I have no cause to be uncivil. Did you ever happen to hear of Spring-Heeled Jack?"

Jacob Butler's eyes stood out of his head like hat-pegs.

"Hear of him!" he said, in a hushed tone of voice. "I should think I have, and seen him too."

"Then you're the very man I want," said Bill Blarney.

"What for?" Jacob Butler demanded, starting back in alarm. "I've done no harm to you, and I'll thank you to leave me alone."

"You need not be afraid of me," Bill Blarney said. "I want to ask you a few questions. This part of the country is a favourite haunt of Spring-Heeled Jack's, is it not?"

"It is."

"When was he seen last?"

"Oh! not for nearly a week."

"Good!" said Bill Blarney, rubbing his hands. "Now, the next question I have to ask is—who are you?"

Jacob Butler hesitated.

If he told a lie his face might show it; but if he spoke the truth the man might be a friend to him in the hour of need.

"Sit down," he said, "and I will tell you all about it."

He did so, and Bill Blarney listened with an expression of face plainly telling that the story interested him keenly.

"It's strange that I should meet you here in this fashion," he said; "for it so happens that I am going to Lilac Lodge."

"You are?"

"Yes; and you are going with me."

"No, no!"

"But I say yes, yes!"

"I tell you I won't," Jacob Butler avowed. "I wouldn't go back again to that house for all the gold that lies buried under the sea."

"Just listen to me," Bill Blarney said. "I have cause to hate Sir Roland Ashton. He left me like a coward when I lay stunned and helpless after doing his dirty work."

"I hate him too," said Jacob, wagging his head; "and that is all the more reason why I don't want to go back to Lilac Lodge."

"Wait," said Bill Blarney. "What would you give to get rid of the old woman who is the torment of your life?"

"Everything I possess."

Bill Blarney took a brace of pistols from his pocket.

"I went down to the Bull in Top Boots," he said, "and the boys lent me these barkers and a few shiners to get along with."

"Very kind of them, I'm sure," said Jacob. "Well, sir, I think I will bid you good-bye."

"If you move until I tell you I'll blow your brains out!" Bill Blarney growled. "You know every inch of Lilac Lodge, and you'll have to come with me to-night and show me how I can steal upon Sir Roland unawares."

"But Mrs. Corcoran will scent me out and murder me."

"I'll put a stopper on her first," Bill Blarney said, flourishing one of the pistols. "What a treat it will be for you to know that she can never worry you again!"

"Ah! if I could only believe it I would go through fire and water."

"But it shall be an accomplished fact, I tell you," said Bill, flourishing one of the pistols.

Jacob Butler shook his head dismally.

"You've no idea of what sort of woman you have to deal with," he said. "She ain't a woman, in fact—she's a witch—a she-devil, and takes a delight in reading and talking about her master with the hoofs and tail."

"So much the better," Blarney said. "If I can get an interview with her I'll pitch a tale that I know where you are, and when I get her in a good humour—bang! over she goes, just as you fell out of the tree. Ha! ha! ha!"

Jacob Butler laughed too, but it was rather a dismal kind of a laugh.

"I have the cold shivers whenever I think of her," he said, "and I get the jumps when I walk about, for I seem to see her everywhere. Just now I could have sworn that I saw her peeping from behind that tree."

"I should like to catch sight of her," said Bill Blarney. "I have rather taken to you, Jacob Butler."

"Thank'ee, I'm much obliged to you."

"Because," Bill Blarney continued, "I should think that you would be the right sort of a pal in a row."

"Do you really think so?"

"I do, indeed."

Jacob Butler tried to look bold, but it was the old story of the ass in the lion's skin, and his true nature came out when the bushes rustled a little louder than usual.

"Here she comes!" he gasped—"here she comes! Hide me or I'm a dead man!"

Bill Blarney opened his mouth and roared with laughter.

"What!" he cried, "a warrior like you afraid of a woman? But this is only your good nature. You are considerate to the fair sex. Let me give you a word of advice, my friend."

"What is it?"

"Not to try to imitate Spring-Heeled Jack by skipping about like a parched pea."

"I can't help it—indeed I can't!" Jacob whined. "You'd be the same if you had suffered what I have."

Bill Blarney touched one of Jacob's ears with the muzzle of a pistol.

"I don't want to kill more people than I can help," Blarney said; "but if you don't do just as I tell you, and keep quiet into the bargain, you certainly will put me to the painful necessity of letting daylight through your head."

"Was there ever such a miserable man as I?" Jacob Butler moaned. "I must have been born under an unlucky star. Why didn't they smother me at my birth?"

"Well," said Bill Blarney, as he restored the

pistol to his belt, "your mother must have been very fond of children to have brought you up."

Jacob Butler made no comment on this rather doubtful compliment, but kept a wary eye upon Bill Blarney and his actions.

"Here's a flask full of brandy," Blarney said, suddenly. "Take a pull at it; the stuff is good and will steady your nerves."

Jacob certainly needed some kind of stimulant, for his teeth were chattering in his head and his face was as green as an unripe gooseberry.

"How do you feel now?" Bill Blarney asked, as he applied the flask to his own lips.

"A little better. Ah-h-h! The brandy went like fire through my veins."

"Which showed that you needed it," Blarney said, throwing himself down at full length upon the grass. "What a long day this has been! It seems to me that the sun has made up its mind never to go down again."

"I've lived a hundred years of mortal agony since this morning," Jacob declared. "You are quite sure that you will not let me go?"

"Quite so."

"Then I suppose I must resign myself to my miserable fate?"

"That is the most sensible speech I have heard you make," Bill Blarney said. "We shall not have long to wait now. The sky is growing red, and it will soon be dusk."

"The night is at hand," Jacob Butler muttered to himself. "Shall I ever see the light of day again?"

---

## CHAPTER XLVI.

### HOW THE PLOT TO CATCH SPRING-HEELED JACK SUCCEEDED.

THE sun was sinking below the beautiful landscape when those valiant officers, Catchpole and Elias Grabham, arrived at the inn at which they had left the nets.

These were enclosed in a curiously-shaped bundle, and had so excited the curiosity of the customers who had called to refresh themselves with good old ale, that when the constables arrived to claim their property they found it surrounded by quite a dozen grinning yokels.

Both the minions of the law had had quite enough to drink—in point of fact, they were half-seas over, and consequently high minded and lofty.

Stealing up behind one of the spectators, Elias Grabham dealt the man such a crack over the head with the crown-tipped official staff that he saw cartloads of stars, and shot like a rocket into the fender.

This little episode was more than sufficient to leave the way clear, for the yokels, ever in mortal fear of anything in the shape of a policeman, made tracks to the other side of the room.

But even the humblest of rustics have feelings, and when violently banged about the cranium may resent it in a similar manner.

Such was the case with the man who floated so suddenly into the fender.

As he rose to his feet he picked up the poker and threw it at Elias Grabham.

The aim was good.

The knob of the poker took the constable in that region known to pugilists as "below the belt," and laid him out as flat as a pancake on the floor.

"I'm a dead 'un!" he groaned, curling up. "Catchpole, see that that man is charged with my murder."

Mr. Grabham certainly did look uncommon queer, but all notions of his leaving this vale of tears vanished when his brother officer laughed.

"Catchpole," said Grabham, sitting up and hugging his knees, "you're a hass—a braying ass, that's what you are, and I'm jiggered if you mayn't carry the bundle yourself."

This only made Catchpole laugh all the more.

There was something very funny in seeing a man doubled up with a poker, according to his ideas, and he roared and rolled about until his sides ached and tears rolled down his face.

The rustics thought that they, too, might laugh now without offending the majesty of the law, and they took up the chorus until the rafters rang again.

"There—there!" said Catchpole. "Get up, Grabham, and don't look so sour. You brought it on yourself, you know, and we haven't time to stop to kick up a row. Let us have just one more glass, and then go about our business."

Grabham got up surlily enough, and seating himself at a table, made a remark to the effect that if he had a little more wind in his body that there would be an inquest held upon somebody.

A huge jug of ale was brought in by the landlord, and it proved so good that the constables ordered another.

They quaffed and made merry until Grabham manifested strong inclination to sing and dance; but Catchpole, becoming suddenly aware that dark ness had set in, whispered in Grabham's ear that it was time to go.

"Pull yourself together," he said; "you forget that we must see Sir Roland again."

"Who cares for Sir Roland?" Elias Grabham hiccuped. "I don't. Let him catch—"

"Hush! you fool."

"Who's a fool?"

"You are."

Elias Grabham closed one eye and tried to look angry out of the other.

The attempt proved a failure, and after reeling about all over the place for some time he clutched one end of the bundle and hauled it towards the door.

As soon as he got outside he went down, spreading himself out like a turtle, and Catchpole went flying over him, grazing his nose on the ground.

"Oh! dash it!" he said, as tears of agony rushed from his eyes. "Here's a mess! I shall have the gravel-rash for the rest of my life. Grabham, if you don't get up and act like a man I'll kick you in the ribs."

Grabham made no reply, but a sound came from his throat very much like the winding up of an eight-day clock.

"He's broken something," Catchpole gasped. "Cuss this place and everything in it! Grabham—Grabham, what's the matter?"

"Everything's the matter," Grabham howled. "I'm smothered in my own gore."

"Think of the time we are wasting—think of the money we are losing."

This speech seemed to rouse Elias Grabham to a sense of his position.

"Right you are," he said. "I'll pull myself together directly."

After a few minutes he got up, shrugged his shoulders, stretched out his arms, and announced that he was ready to proceed.

"Good!" said Catchpole. "We shall be in

time yet. Sir Roland will be pleased with us, and we'll make him shell out handsomely."

It was pitch dark now.

The moon was hidden by dark clouds, and every now and then a flash of sheet lightning quivered in the air.

Catchpole was anything but steady on his feet, but Grabham was much the worst of the two.

He tripped over every obstacle, bumped his head against trees, and suddenly disappeared altogether.

"Where are you?" roared Catchpole, groping blindly about. "What have you done with yourself?"

"I'm in an infernal ditch!" Grabham spluttered. "Lend a hand, can't you?"

"I will when I can see you."

The wretched and unfortunate Grabham was at last extricated and came out smothered in mud and weeds.

"It seems to me that somebody gave me a shove behind," he said. "Was it you?"

"Was it me?" Catchpole cried. "That's a nice sort of question to ask of a friend."

"Well, then, we are being followed."

"Nonsense! Here, catch hold of this bundle. It will be midnight before we get into the park."

It was all very well to say catch hold of the bundle, but where was it?

The officers felt about, and swore as they stumbled and jolted against each other, but no bundle could they find.

It had vanished as cleanly as if the earth had opened and swallowed it up.

"Here's a go!" said Catchpole. "Here's a nice state of things!"

"Nice—nice!—I call it—oh!"

"What's the matter now?"

"I'm caught—I'm fixed!" Grabham yelled. "I'm in one of them confounded nets"

Before Catchpole could say a word or give expression to his astonishment at this announcement in any way he felt something sweep over him, and in an instant he was in a similar predicament as his companion.

The constables kicked and roared lustily, but all to no purpose.

The more they struggled the tighter they were fixed, and at last got so mixed up with the meshes that they could move neither hand nor foot.

"Murder!" Grabham gasped, as he felt that he was being drawn along the ground. "Oh! please don't! I'm the father of a large wife and a family—I mean a wife and a large family. Help—help!"

"Ha! ha!" laughed a mocking voice, "I'll show you how to catch Spring-Heeled Jack!"

"Mercy—it's him!" Catchpole yelled, as he was bumped over the ground at a furious rate. "Farewell to everybody—farewell to everything!"

Onward they went in spite of themselves.

Over brake and bramble, dragged through gaps in hedges, turned heels over head in ditches, until the bewildered men began to think that they must have become mixed up in some intricate machine.

At last a halt was made.

But the officers could no longer ask for the help they were in so much need of.

The breath had been jolted out of their bodies, and they we e nly just conscious of the unpleasant fact that they were being strung up side by side on the stout branch of a tree.

"You will pass the night here," Spring-Heeled Jack said, now appearing before them; "and you may think yourselves lucky that I have let you off so easily. When you are free return to London and think no more of capturing me, and, above all, shun Sir Roland Ashton as you would an adder in your path."

"This is all a delusion," said Elias Grabham "My head is spinning round and round like a whirligig. Catchpole, we didn't ought to have had that last mug of beer. I'm quite satisfied that this is all a mockery."

"It are," Catchpole said, dismally. "It's such a delusion that we are both caught in our own trap."

"Ha! ha! ha!" laughed Spring-Heeled Jack. "Adieu, my friends. The night promises to be a wet one, but I daresay that you will be able to make yourselves comfortable. Sing him a song, Grabham—sing him a song of warlike deeds and glory."

At this moment the strange creature vanished as if by magic, and the constables, left to themselves, began to rub their aching joints and smooth their rumpled hair.

"Of all the pickles I was ever in this is the worst one," Grabham moaned. "Won't the people laugh when they find us bagged like a couple of hares!"

"I don't care how they laugh so long as I get my feet on the ground again," Catchpole said. "Hush! there's somebody coming."

The footsteps were light ones, but the night was so still that sound travelled far.

Bill Blarney and Jacob Butler were approaching—Jacob, of course, being in the rear, and as limp as a damp-rag.

"Lift your feet up," Blarney said, threateningly. "Shure you hop about like an old washerwoman on pattens."

"I wish I was a washerwoman," Jacob replied, with a smile. "I wish I was anybody or anything than myself."

"You'll be nothing at all soon, I can plainly see," Bill Blarney replied, clicking the lock of the pistol he held in his hand.

"I wish you would put that horrible thing away," Jacob said. "The very sight of it is enough to frighten me into fits."

"It is more likely to frighten you out of the world," Blarney returned, grimly. "Let me see. Where are we now, you white-livered, green-eyed, snivelling slab of misery?"

"Go it!" Jacob gasped. "Call me names. I don't care. You're like old mother Corcoran, she calls me 'Deary' one moment and pitches into me the next. It's a way women have of showing their affection, I suppose—drat 'em!"

"Hold your tongue," said Bill Blarney. "We must be getting near to Lilac Lodge now, but I see no signs of it. Don't they ever burn a light?"

"Yes," Jacob Butler replied; "but they take jolly good care to close the shutters?"

"Ah! that accounts for the darkness, then. Why could you not say so before, you tottering-limbed, green-faced caterpillar?"

"I s'pose I shall be a cabbage soon," Jacob said, meekly. "We are in the park now. I know these trees. Bless my heart! what's this?"

His head had come in collision with the toes of Elias Grabham's heavy boots.

Jacob Butler put out his hands, and as they came in contact with the net he gave vent to a prolonged howl and started back.

"It's alive!" he panted.

"What is?"

"The thing hanging on the trees."

Bill Blarney cocked the pistol again and stood on guard, ready for any emergency.

"Don't fire!" moaned the netted officer. "If you're a man and a brother you'll help me out. Me and my mate have been hung up here by Spring-Heeled Jack. We were going to set nets to catch him, but he caught us."

"He did," Catchpole assented, with a kick and a wriggle, "and very neatly, too."

"Spring-Heeled Jack!" Bill Blarney cried. "Curse the demon! he is ever on my track."

"Spring-Heeled Jack!" Jacob Butler squeaked. "Oh! lor'! Didn't I tell you it would be a foolish thing to go back to Lilac Lodge? It's as much as our lives are worth to attempt it now."

"But we shall, even though a worse death than Spring-Heeled Jack can deal stares me in the face," Bill Blarney said. "I am resolved to be revenged upon that scoundrel, Sir Roland."

"And shoot that virago?"

"Yes, if you act like a sensible man and help me."

"But, I say," said Elias Grabham, "won't you help us—a couple of poor fellows in distress?"

"Who are you?"

"Two constables, who—"

"That's enough," said Bill Blarney, laughing hoarsely. "You will hang there for a month of Sundays if it is left to me to take you down. I only wish that each of you had a rope round your neck. Remember your oath, dear boys, and don't forget that you belong to the band of Black Highwaymen."

"It's Bill Blarney," Catchpole roared.

"Yes," Blarney said, "I thought I would look you up, as I don't like to desert old pals."

Even Jacob Butler rose a little from the depths of his misery and laughed faintly at this small joke.

Had he known what was in store for him no ghost of a smile would have played on his lips.

"We will leave these two gentlemen," Bill Blarney said; "and if we are lucky we will pay them another visit as we come back."

So saying, he dragged Jacob Butler along, accelerating his movements every now and then by touching him on the bridge of the nose with the ice-cold barrel of the pistol.

"If ever I get out of this," Jacob said, "I'll lead a changed life; I'll be a changed man, and go to—"

"The devil!"

Bill Blarney ejaculated these words as a huge red light flared up before him.

It seemed to rush from the ground with the speed of a meteor, and went hissing upwards into the air, and tinged the clouds with red as it vanished.

"I never saw the like of that before," Bill Blarney said. "What was it—what can it mean?"

"That Spring-Heeled Jack is abroad again!" said a deep-sounding voice.

"Then here's my answer to him!" Bill Blarney roared.

Bang went the pistol, and Jacob Butler, overcome with fright, fell flat on his back, and kicked up his heels like an obstreperous donkey.

"Fool!" cried Spring-Heeled Jack, "your bullet has found a billet in the air. Let me see if I can take a better aim."

Bill Blarney caught Jacob Butler up and held him before him.

"Here! I say," Jacob cried, kicking and twisting furiously, "don't make a target of me; it ain't fair."

"You are safe, poor fellow," Spring-Heeled Jack replied. "I will not harm you. Had you placed yourself in my hands you would not have suffered so much misery."

"I will place myself in the hands of any man who will get rid of Mrs. Corcoran," Jacob said. "Let go, will you?"

This was to Bill Blarney, who did not intend to do anything of the kind.

Neither of them could see Spring-Heeled Jack.

He was invisible to them, but they could hear him as he took terrific leaps.

Jacob's faint heart throbbed and beat like the spring of a watch.

He had borne much, but could bear no more.

Squealing like a guinea-pig, he doubled up and sank fainting at Bill Blarney's feet.

"A thousand curses!" the ruffian hissed. "I am once more in the power of Spring-Heeled Jack."

"Go!" cried the voice of the mysterious creature. "I have better things to do than to waste time or words with such a scoundrel."

Bill Blarney felt grateful to hear this, and set about restoring Jacob Butler to consciousness.

This was not an easy task, but at last he accomplished it, and planted him against a tree.

"I saved a little brandy for myself, but you shall have it," Blarney said. "Drink it up, and we will get along again."

"Spare me—spare me!" Jacob pleaded. "I have suffered enough horrors for one night."

"It will soon be over," Blarney said, persuasively; "and then you will be a free man to do as you choose."

While this conversation was going on, Sir Roland sat within Lilac Lodge.

He drummed his fingers impatiently upon the table, and listened for any sound that might denote the coming of the constables.

At last, unable to bear the suspense, he rose and paced the floor like a wild beast that suddenly finds itself behind the strong iron bars of a cage

"Will they never come?" he said, clenching his hands. "Have their designs been thwarted—has that accursed fiend, Spring-Heeled Jack, upset their calculations?"

Just then Mrs. Corcoran glided into the room.

"Sir Roland," she said, "the hour grows late. Where are your hirelings—where are the soldiers that were to come to guard the house?"

"Something must have delayed them upon the road," he said; "but I cannot understand the conduct of those constables."

"I can."

"Explain it, then."

"It is as likely as not that they have deceived you," said the crone.

"Nonsense! I would trust them with my life, because it answers their purpose to be faithful to me."

"You have lived long enough in the world to trust to no man," the hag said, with a hollow laugh. "There is but one I mourn the loss of, or rather two—the husband who is gone and the man who was to have taken his place. Ah! Jacob—Jacob! how I should like to have you here for a few minutes!"

"It would go hard with him, I'm thinking," Sir Roland said, smiling grimly. "Hark! what is that?"

"The wind," Mrs. Corcoran said. "The night is dark and promises to be stormy."

A clock on the mantel-shelf struck.

"Nine o'clock and no news yet," Sir Roland said; "but I suppose I must be patient. Leave me, for I wish to be alone. When do you intend to start in search of Jacob?"

"At midnight."

"A strange, unearthly hour."

"It suits me well," the hag replied; "I shall find him huddled up somewhere, and then I will bring him back and set him on the stool of repentance."

"Poor devil!" Sir Roland muttered.

"In whose hands can he be better than in mine?" Mrs. Corcoran demanded. "Remember, Sir Roland, that he has a long tongue, which for your sake must be kept silent."

"And for yours."

Mrs. Corcoran snapped her fingers.

"When I fall who falls with me?" she asked.

Sir Roland Ashton bit his under lip.

"Enough!" he said. "This is not the time to discuss such questions. Did you not hear? I wish to be alone."

"And what if I choose to stay?"

"What!" Sir Roland cried.

"Do you want me to repeat my words?"

"Yes."

"Then what will you say if I choose to stay in the room?"

"But I order you to leave it."

"And I refuse!"

"Woman, beware how you trifle with me!" Sir Roland said. "I am in no mood to have my commands disobeyed, and if you do so it will be at your own peril."

"Peril! Ha, ha, ha! The man standing on the brink of a volcano talks to another of peril!"

"Go! or you will raise all the bad blood in my heart," Sir Roland said.

"I refuse to go, because if you are master of this place I consider that I am mistress of it."

"You are mad."

"There is a method in that madness," Mrs. Corcoran said, contemptuously. "But now, that I have told you my mind, I will go."

She banged the door behind her so furiously that the windows rattled.

Sir Roland examined the fastenings of the shutters before he went back to the table.

"That obstinate old woman must be got rid of," he mused. "She talks of long tongues. What a disturbance she could make if she were to unbridle hers! Yes; I have made up my mind. She must be got rid of. Why should I not do it myself?"

He asked himself this question a hundred times, and a devilish light gathered in his eyes.

Unlocking and opening a drawer in the table, he took out a dagger, enclosed in a morocco sheath inlaid with a filagree of gold.

The weapon was as sharp as a razor and as bright as a burnished mirror.

"One thrust with this," he said, running his thumb along the edge; "only one thrust with this, and all will be over."

But then he began to think of Jacob Butler.

He might repent of his run-away excursion and return.

If so, the first question he would ask would be about Mrs. Corcoran.

"Not to-night," he said, returning the weapon to the drawer. "I must wait the course of events. The constables must leave before I attempt to settle accounts with Mrs. Corcoran."

He sat thinking over the past until he became weary with the suspense and delay.

"Something must have happened," he said, leaning his head upon his hand. "Fate is against me. Mystery of mysteries! how is it that I can hear Daisy's voice, and yet not see her face?"

As he spoke he thought he heard a low, grating sound coming from the direction of the window.

Turning round, he saw the glinting of a piece of fine steel.

It had pierced the shutter, and was moving swiftly to and fro.

"So," said Sir Roland, "there is foul play at work! Perhaps Mrs. Corcoran is at the bottom of this. She may have anticipated the fate I have promised her. And yet she would not set an assassin to work so openly. It must be somebody who expects to catch me napping."

Sir Roland turned down the lamp to a faint glimmer, and then took a pistol, ready loaded and primed, from his pocket.

"I will give my visitor a warm reception," he said, dropping on his knees behind the table. "How busy he is! I almost envy him his employment!"

The file, for such the instrument was, kept on.

Its teeth soon cut through the iron bars.

The severed pieces fell with a clang.

Then came a pause.

It was evident that the burglar or burglars outside were startled by the sound.

Sir Roland kept silent and motionless.

He held his breath until his face grew hot and flushed.

Presently the shutters began to move.

They opened slowly, and then the head of Bill Blarney apeared.

"The scoundrel!" Sir Roland muttered under his breath.

"How is this, Jacob?" Blarney said. "There is a lamp on the table."

"Is it alight?" came Jacob's voice from below.

"Yes."

"Then I can't make it out," Jacob replied. "I have never known Sir Roland to use this room save in the day time. Hadn't we better bolt?"

"No, fool. There is not a creature in the room, so it is all right, and if there was I have got my barkers ready."

"So have I," Sir Roland thought.

After taking another and a still more careful survey of the room, Bill Blarney stepped from the window-sill and approached the table.

"Somebody was here not long ago," he said. "Perhaps Sir Roland himself. He may return; I will wait for him."

A blinding flash of light and a stunning report caused him to throw up his arms.

Bill Blarney fell back with blood gushing from his shoulder, and a terrible oath escaped his lips as Sir Roland Ashton rose from his place of concealment.

Blarney, filled with anguish, took aim at Sir Roland and fired.

The aim was nervous and badly taken, and Sir Roland had the satisfaction of hearing the bullet strike the wall with a thud.

"Villain!" the baronet cried, advancing with great strides.

"Villain in your teeth!" Bill Blarney replied, snatching up a chair and brandishing it over his head. "The world is not large enough to hold us both."

"I agree with you," Sir Roland replied, coolly. "You came here to take my life and yours shall pay the forfeit of your folly."

Seeing that Blarney held a dangerous weapon in his hands, Sir Roland stepped back to the table and secured the dagger.

The gleam of steel caught Bill Blarney's eyes, and, poising the chair, he hurled it with all his remaining strength at Sir Roland.

Again Bill Blarney missed his aim.

The chair smashed into pieces, and at the same moment strange sounds came through the open window.

Mrs. Corcoran had secured the hapless Jacob, and was dragging him into the house.

This seemed to attract Sir Roland's attention for a moment, and gave Bill Blarney the opportunity he desired.

Leaping backwards, he hurled himself bodily through the window, and fell with a crash to the ground.

"Confusion!" Sir Roland shouted. "He shall not escape me. I thought those idiots of constables were dragging Spring-Heeled Jack along."

Rushing to the window, he gazed below.

Bill Blarney had escaped, and the night was of such pitchy blackness that to have followed would have been an act of madness.

"I will seek him out, and cold steel shall be his reward," Sir Roland said, as he closed the shutters.

They flew open again instantly, and the head and shoulders of Spring-Heeled Jack appeared.

"Ha! ha! Sir Roland," said he, "you are making merry to-night. May I not be also one of your guests?"

Sir Roland hurled the dagger at the ghastly form of his foe, and then retreated back into the room.

Spring-Heeled Jack uttered a cry of exultation and vanished.

## CHAPTER XLVII.

### JACOB BUTLER HAS A HARD TIME OF IT.

Yes, Mrs. Corcoran had caught Jacob Butler.

He was in the act of taking to his heels when the hag caught him.

Fixing her talon-like nails on the collar of his coat, she dragged him along with a strength wonderful for a woman of her age.

But there was no need for so much fuss and violence.

If Jacob Butler had ever possessed strength or pluck he lost both the moment the struggle began.

"Don't!" he gasped. "Surely you never thought I would run away from the woman I promised to marry?"

"Of course you wouldn't think of such a thing," Mrs. Corcoran said, giving Jacob a twist in the neck that nearly broke it. "Of course you wouldn't, deary. If my poor first husband could look out of his grave, what a sight this would be for him!"

She bundled Jacob heels over head into the house and closed the door.

Jacob lay exactly where he had been thrown, and seemed to be in no immediate hurry to get up.

"Now then, this way," Mrs. Corcoran said, opening a door that led to the cellar.

"What?" Jacob gasped. "You don't mean to say that you are going to put me into such a hole as that?"

"But I do mean it. I will call you early in the morning so as to give you plenty of time to dress for the wedding."

Jacob Butler pulled a face as long as a fiddle.

"Look here," he said, "I will make a bargain with you."

"Well, speak out."

"If you don't keep me under lock and key, I will promise not to run away again."

"How kind you are, deary!" said the hag; "but I don't forget that promises, like pie-crusts, are made to be broken."

"But I'll take my oath, if you like."

"You may swear to your heart's content when you are in the cellar," Mrs. Corcoran said, maliciously. "I will put my ear to the keyhole and listen to you."

Jacob Butler gave up discussing the subject.

He found that it would be mere waste of breath to continue it, for he got nothing but mockery for his pains.

"Well," he said, "if I must go I must. If I refuse, I suppose I shall be murdered."

"And buried under the flag-stones in the cellar, instead of being allowed to walk about there like a gentleman."

"When a man is married his wife is bound to obey him," Jacob said, with a spark of defiance. "I'll alter all this sort of thing then."

"You shall have all your own way, my prince," Mrs. Corcoran said, sneeringly. "I'll cook your food, mend your clothes, and give you money to spend in the public-house, and when you come home drunk and silly I'll take your boots off and put you to bed."

Jacob did not relish these entrancing prospects of matrimonial bliss.

On the contrary, they made him look as if he had accidentally swallowed a tooth.

He crawled rather than walked towards the cellar door, and as it closed upon him he gave vent to his wrath in a torrent of abuse.

"You yellow-skinned harridan—you she-dragon—you monster in dirty stockings—you rattling dice-box of mischief in petticoats!" he howled. "I'd go to your funeral with the greatest of pleasure, and take good care not to be late. If I saw you dead at my feet I'd wear a white favour and set the bells ringing."

"You shall wear a white favour and the bells shall ring, too, to-morrow, deary," Mrs. Corcoran said, through the door. "What a happy pair we shall make to be sure!"

"I dread the hour as I dread the thought of seeing the devil," Jacob shouted back. "I won't marry you. I tell you I won't. Give me a rope and I'll hang myself."

"No, no," said the hag; "I can't afford to part with you yet. Life is too short to be always squabbling, so I will leave you."

"I wish you would, and for good and all," Jacob groaned.

"You are only joking. I know how fond you are of me, as you ought to be."

"You lie, you mildewed cat!"

Jacob kicked viciously at the door, but finding that performance brought him no consolation, but hurt his toes, he gave it up and went shudderingly down the damp staircase.

The cellar was certainly not a nice place to be imprisoned in.

In one corner there was a heap of litter and rubbish, the collection of years.

Large flabby masses of fungi grew upon the wall, and two or three red-eyed rats peeped at Jacob as he ran about as if the floor had turned red-hot under his feet.

"I don't want to die, but I'm hanged if I want to live!" Jacob muttered, as he ground his teeth with rage and misery. "Am I a man or a—a monkey? I'm treated worse than a harmless dog. I'm kicked about like a child's play-ball, and then—dash it—it's monstrous I am to be dragged up before a parson and made to swear to love and cherish a beast I loathe and detest."

Jacob Butler kicked his foot against the heap of rubbish and thought he heard something ring.

It was like the sound of glass, and Jacob, being glad to find something to do, determined to investigate the matter.

After pulling away some of the rubbish, he saw something shining, and, pulling it out, discovered it to be a bottle of rare old wine.

"Ha! ha!" he laughed. "I shan't be so bad off after all. I wonder if there are any more bottles?"

Further investigation proved that there were, and Jacob Butler now had it in his power to make a second Bacchus of himself.

Knocking the neck off one of the bottles, he took a long drink.

The ruby liquid was rich and delicious.

It was fit nectar for the gods, and Jacob felt as if a new lease of life had been given to him as he drank.

"I wonder who put that here," he said, aloud. "Whoever it was has my thanks."

"I did!" said a voice, which seemed to proceed from the floor.

Jacob started so violently that the bottle almost fell from his hands.

"Who spoke?" he asked, in quavering accents.

"Your master's much-feared foe."

Jacob Butler knew now that Spring-Heeled Jack was speaking, and he shook in his shoes.

"Sir Roland is no master of mine," he said. "I have done with him for ever."

"If you are in earnest I will find the means to set you free."

Jacob clasped his hands, and a thrill of delight went to his very heart.

"If you do I will bless your name as long as I live!" he said.

A light flashed into the cellar, and Spring-Heeled Jack stood facing the prisoner.

The appearance was so sudden that Jacob Butler had not the slightest notion of where the weird form had come from, but he did not trouble his mind on that score.

"Being of marvel and mystery!" Jacob Butler cried, falling on his knees, "have pity on me! Earn the thanks of a wretched, persecuted man!"

"I require no thanks," Spring-Heeled Jack replied. "I know your history and the fate in store for you. Choose between me and that."

"I—I don't know what you mean," Jacob stammered.

"Will you serve me?"

"Yes—oh! yes."

"Well and faithfully?"

"As I value my life here and hereafter I will," Jacob said.

"That oath has paid the price of your freedom," Spring-Heeled Jack replied. "Now listen to me, and mark every word I say."

"They shall be printed on my heart and brain," Jacob declared.

"As soon as I show you the way into the open air," Spring-Heeled Jack said, "make your way across the park, and so along until you come to four cross-roads. Do you follow me?"

"Yes; I understand every word."

"When you get there," said Spring-Heeled Jack, holding up a silver whistle in his hand, "you will sound a call upon this, and you will be answered by a green light which will flash thrice in the air."

"Yes," said Jacob, who in his excitement to get away did not exactly know whether he was standing on his head or his heels.

"Then wait," Spring-Heeled Jack continued, "and you will hear the sound of wheels. A carriage drawn by a pair of powerful horses will come up. A man wearing a slouch hat will be on his box, and as he comes within hearing you must utter this single word to him—'Lucifer!'"

"Oh! Lucifer?" Jacob said; "that's another name for Old Nick, isn't it?"

"Never mind what it is another name for," Spring-Heeled Jack observed. "All you have to do is to utter the word. Can you drive?"

"As well as a first-class coachman."

"Then you will change hats and coats with the coachman, and bring the carriage back to the park."

"What, must I come back again?" Jacob asked, dismally.

"Yes; because my man is more powerful and determined than you," Spring-Heeled Jack replied. "I want him to watch the road. What do you say—will you do all this?"

"Yes," Jacob replied, in a rather shaky tone of voice.

"If you fail me," Spring-Heeled Jack said, sternly, "I will increase your miseries tenfold; but if you serve me well you shall not go unrewarded."

"I only want my freedom."

Spring-Heeled Jack smiled.

"So men say when they are laid by the heels," he said; "but they soon alter their opinion. The greed for gold is born in the hearts of mortals. Men will do anything and stop at nothing to possess it. Wars have raged, good men have been murdered, innocent children have perished, and great kingdoms have been raised and overthrown for the love of the glittering metal."

"Yes, yes," Jacob said; "but isn't it time I was on my way across the park?"

"Not until I give you the word to go," Spring-Heeled Jack replied. "See here!"

He touched a portion of the masonry of the wall, and one of the huge slabs of stone slid back as lightly as if it had been a mere wooden panel.

"That is the way out," Spring-Heeled Jack said.

"That!" Jacob Butler echoed. "Where on earth does it lead to?"

"To the base of a hollow tree, in which there is a ladder by which you can mount to the top."

"Bless me!" said Jacob, startled into an expression of astonishment. "Whoever would have dreamed of such things?"

"I did, and made them a reality," Spring-Heeled Jack said. "You may go now. Stay! I have one more word to say."

"Yes; I am all attention."

"You will find a portion of the passage alight,

and will pass through a part arranged like a room, and furnished," Spring-Heeled Jack said. "It is just possible that you may see a fair-haired lad there. If you do, take no notice of him."

Jacob Butler nodded his head to signify that he understood what was said, and, leaping into the passage, breathed his thanks as he passed Spring-Heeled Jack.

Indeed, Jacob had to exercise great control over himself to prevent a shout of joy escaping his lips.

On he went, finding his way through the underground tunnel without much difficulty, for the floor was as smooth and level as a lawn.

Suddenly he saw a glimmer of light in the distance.

He stopped, for at the same instant he heard the sweet silvery tones which had so often floated through Lilac Lodge.

"What would Sir Roland give to be down here?" Jacob said, grinning. "He little thinks that I, the despised and persecuted, have become the trusted friend of Spring-Heeled Jack."

He went on again, but with a feeling of shame gnawing at his heart.

If he happened to encounter pretty little Daisy Leigh what would she say to him?

She might be armed with a pistol or dagger, and thinking that Jacob had no right in her hiding-place take such measures as would prevent him escaping after all.

Jacob did not feel quite so happy as when he started on the journey.

"Ahem!" he coughed aloud. "Ahem!"

The singing ceased, and Jacob thought he saw a figure flit from one side of the passage to the other.

"That's her," said Jacob. "What a good thing she didn't stop to ask questions? I am sure I shouldn't have the courage to look her in the face."

It was very generous of Jacob Butler to remember his past iniquities, but it may be supposed that he believed in the adage that "it is never too late to mend."

"Yes," he said. "As I told that murdering thief, Bill Blarney, if I ever got a chance I would turn over a new leaf and become a changed man. And so I will; so help me Heaven!"

Presently the passage widened, and he came to the room Spring-Heeled Jack had spoken of.

It was beautifully and luxuriously furnished.

On one side there was an elegant couch, replete with laced pillows and cushions, and on the other was a magnificent harpischord.

How such things had come there was a mystery to Jacob Butler, and all he could do was to open his mouth and stare in astonishment at everything that met his astonished gaze.

"It's wonderful—it's marvellous!" he said. "Why, it's like the 'Arabian Nights' Entertainment' I have heard about. It beats Sindbad the Sailor and his valley of diamonds. Hullo! here comes somebody else."

A tall, fair-haired boy of slender form walked into the apartment and sat down upon a chair, the framework of which was carved ivory.

He took not the slightest notice of Jacob, who, remembering the injunctions he had received, thought it better not to speak.

Jacob felt that he was treading upon air as he left this scene of wealth and luxury and once more entered the passage.

It narrowed again, but was dark no longer.

Richly-coloured lamps hung here and there, and the soft glow fell upon walls, which had been built and decorated by a master hand.

"Well, I'm blessed," Jacob thought as he went on, "I wonder what I shall meet next? Perhaps it will be an army of blacks, carrying vases filled with jewels on their heads? Nothing would astonish me now."

But something did, for suddenly Jacob felt cool air blowing upon his face, and, raising his eyes, he saw that he stood beneath the hollow tree.

"How am I to reach the ladder?" he asked himself.

"Stand still and firm, and you will see," said a voice.

The floor began to rise, and Jacob, thinking that this was some new trick to ensure his destruction, uttered a cry of alarm.

"I sink! I fall!" he called out.

"Keep your footing and fear nothing," said the voice. "If you have no faith in me you shall complete your lodging in the cellar."

Jacob said no more, but, closing his eyes, resolved to take matters as they came.

Suddenly his hand came in contact with the ladder, and he clutched at it as a drowning man clutches at a straw.

He mounted with all possible speed, and was soon in such a position that he could look down upon the ground.

Lowering himself from branch to branch of the withered oak, he sped away at the top of his speed.

He drank in the fresh, cool air, and it gave him additional vigour.

As he reached the four cross roads he halted to take breath, and then blew the whistle.

Instantly the promised green light flashed in the air.

Once!

Twice!

Thrice!

Then Jacob Butler stooped down and listened.

The sound of wheels soon came to his ears, and presently a carriage drawn by two horses appeared so close to him that he had to step out of the way to prevent being run over.

"Lucifer!" Jacob Butler said, faintly.

"What? Speak louder!"

"Lucifer!"

"Right; but who are you, my friend?"

"Spring-Heeled Jack's servant!"

"A new one, at any rate," said the man on the box-seat. "Show me that whistle."

Jacob Butler passed it up without a moment's hesitation, and it was presently returned to him with an expression of approval.

"I am to change clothes and places with you," Jacob said.

"My master said he might send somebody," the man replied, taking off his hat and coat. "You see I am pretty well aware of what is required. Now, then, jump up, and make all haste you can."

"What?"

"Don't ask questions, but do exactly as you are told, and no more."

Jacob Butler took the hint, and climbed on to the box as soon as the man had descended to the ground.

The horses were well trained, and, full of fiery metal, dashed away, and the park was soon reached.

"Halt!"

The horses seemed to know Spring-Heeled

Jack's voice, and came to a standstill without any effort on Jacob's part.

"Step in," Spring-Heeled Jack said, holding open the door and bowing low.

The fair-haired lad entered the carriage.

"I wonder who on earth he is?" Jacob meditated. "Perhaps he is some young lord or a prince."

"Get down, and I will take the reins," Spring-Heeled Jack said; "get down, but if you care for a lift on the road you may jump up behind."

"May I be so bold as to ask you where you are going?" said Jacob.

"To London."

"Then I will go with you."

"As you will. Mount quick, for we must be away. Ha! ha! ha! I leave you, Sir Roland, free and welcome to Lilac Lodge and all its contents."

He reached the box-seat in a single bound, and grasped the reins in his powerful hands.

He shouted to the horses and urged them on.

They broke into a gallop so headlong and furious that the occupant of the interior of the carriage thrust out his head, and cried out in a tone of alarm.

"There is nothing to fear," Spring-Heeled Jack cried. "Ha! ha! ha! This is glorious."

The wheels whirled round, striking showers of sparks as they passed over the hard flints.

Jacob hung on with his eyes starting out of his head, and expecting that the carriage would be overturned every moment.

It swerved and skidded to a fearful extent round corners, and yet Spring-Heeled Jack kept up the pace.

It might have been a race for life or death, and the horses never tiring swept along over mile after mile.

And all the time Jacob Butler was asking himself the question—

"Who was the fair-haired boy, and why was Spring-Heeled Jack in such a hurry to get him to London?"

## CHAPTER XLVIII.

### MRS. CORCORAN MEETS WITH A SAD DISAPPOINTMENT AND A SADDER END.

"JACOB, deary."

It was the gentle, dove-like voice of Mrs. Corcoran calling to her love.

"Jacob, deary," she said again, "are you asleep or awake? Your breakfast is ready, and so is a nice new suit of clothes for you to put on."

As there was no reply to this endearing summons Mrs. Corcoran opened the cellar door and peeped down the staircase.

"Oh!" said she; "you are obstinate, are you? I'll soon show you the way to find your tongue, young man."

As there happened to be a broomstick handy, she armed herself with it and stalked down the stairs with ghost-like strides.

"Now then," she said, rattling the stick on the flagstones, "wake up, or you'll go before the parson with an aching head."

It was so dark that she could distinguish no object clearly.

"Drat the man!" she said. "He has taken quite a new fit in his head, but I'll knock all that out as soon as the ring is on my finger."

Mrs. Corcoran, failing to see Jacob, or to get a word from him, began so feel about for him with the broomstick.

If Jacob had been there it must have come in contact with some portion of his anatomy, but as he was not Mrs. Corcoran got nothing for her pains, and lost her temper.

Suddenly she came upon the empty wine-bottle, and, picking it up, stared at it in unmitigated astonishment.

"Why," she cried, "he must have had company down here! Here—here! Confound him! he is no longer here. But how could he have got away? The cellar door was locked and fast, and these walls are as safe as a prison."

The more the old hag thought over the matter the more she was bewildered.

It puzzled and bothered her brains how Jacob could have got out of the cellar, unless he had become possessed of a supernatural gift.

"There wasn't much of him, but he was no ghost," she said, savagely. "At all events, he is gone, and I shall not be married to-day."

But she found it hard to drag herself out of the place where she had thought that her beloved was in such safe keeping.

At last she went upstairs, and just then Sir Roland had left his sleeping apartment, and was coming down.

"Is my breakfast ready?" he asked, in a surly tone of voice.

"No; and not likely to be for some time," Mrs. Corcoran said. "I have been dreadfully upset this morning."

"What about?"

"I put Jacob in the cellar last night, but he is no longer there."

"Good riddance to him," Sir Roland said. "I am tired of all this nonsense. The fellow is too much of a coward to open his mouth about us, and if he does we can face the matter out and have him sent to prison for slander."

"But," said Mrs. Corcoran, "you must forget that I was to have been married this morning!"

"I know nothing about that arrangement, and don't want to," Sir Roland said. "If Jacob comes back, I wish you both joy; but, if he doesn't, he may keep away and go to perdition for all I care."

"You are out of sorts this morning, Sir Roland."

"I am master of my own temper, and shall use it as I please," came the sharp reply.

"But I want you to look pleased and smiling," Mrs. Corcoran said. "Do you believe that dreams ever come true?"

"If they did," Sir Roland Ashton said, frowning, "I should not be here."

"Where would you be, then?"

"I would rather keep that to myself," Sir Roland replied. "At all events, I do not believe in such rubbish as dreams, so there is an end of that matter. Let me pass, woman, and see to my wants as quickly as possible."

Mrs. Corcoran stuck herself up against the wall like an eight-day clock, and grinned hideously as the baronet strode by.

"Ho, ho!" she croaked; "his nose and chin are in the air this morning. So he cares nothing for me, and Jacob may go to the devil. It strikes me he will have to follow you, Sir Roland, much as I hate him."

This thought seemed to give her much satisfaction.

# SPRING-HEELED JACK,

## THE TERROR OF LONDON.

THE HAG WAS MOUTHING AND MOCKING AT SIR ROLAND.

No. 12

She rubbed her skinny hands and then shook a bony fist in the direction Sir Roland had taken.

"So," she said, "I am only a puppet in your estimation. Pull the string and the figure will dance. The performance is just going to begin. True, Sir Roland—true, but it is the beginning of the end."

Then she began a horrible, witch-like dance and croaked the snatch of a song.

"Why should I not be merry in the face of all my disappointments?" she said. "Why not? Yes, I will; for Jacob will not forsake me. No, no; I'll take good care of that. A little patience and I shall have him back again, and then I must not leave him for a single moment."

"Curse you!" Sir Roland cried, flinging a door open. "What devilish scheme are you plotting now? Are you talking to your broomstick sisterhood. Come down, you witch, and cease that prating."

Mrs. Corcoran's red and rat-like eyes flashed fire as she heard these words from Sir Roland.

"Miserable wretch that he is!" she muttered. "He is foiled and disappointed at every step, and finds no better solace to his feelings than in bullying and cursing."

Presently she began to hobble downstairs, and having set Sir Roland's breakfast before him withdrew.

"Bah!" said the baronet, pushing his cup and plate aside. "What a farce this is, my trying to eat; my nerves require something stronger than coffee."

He rang the bell and Mrs. Corcoran appeared.

"What now?" she demanded, brusquely. "Am I never to have a moment's peace?"

"Take these things away," he said, gloomily, "and bring me a bottle of brandy."

"You had best beware how you swallow that liquid fire," the hag said. "Men in drink do things past recalling. If you would accomplish the object you have in view, you need a clear head and a steady hand."

"I care not," Sir Roland replied, imperatively. "Do as I tell you. Bring me the brandy."

Mrs. Corcoran croaked out something from the depths of her throat, and hobbled out of the room.

Presently she reappeared with a bottle half full of brandy.

"I suppose you haven't put anything into this?" Sir Roland said, holding the bottle up to the light.

Mrs. Corcoran laughed.

"What put such a notion into your head?"

"Because no notion is too bad to come out of yours."

Mrs. Corcoran laughed again, and this time her voice sounded as if it came from a vault.

"You are complimentary," she said. "What would you say if I told you that I suspected you of similar designs?"

"Bah!" sneered Sir Roland Ashton. "We have had more than enough of this prating. Bring two glasses, and sit down a few minutes."

"I do not wish to drink."

"But you shall."

"Well, if I must I must, and so there is an end of the matter," the hag replied. "Fool that you are to think that I should wish to destroy your life when you are so useful to me!"

As she spoke she placed the glasses on the table, and Sir Roland filled them.

"Drink first," said the baronet, "and drink down to the very dregs."

The old hag did so.

"You do not follow my example," she said. "What is the reason?"

"Because I wish to see what effect the liquor has on you," he replied. "If you had brought me a full bottle, uncorked and sealed, you would have saved yourself all this trouble."

"This is something new, Sir Roland," Mrs. Corcoran said. "What have I done to deserve it? Have I not proved myself trustworthy?"

"Henceforth I trust neither man nor woman," Sir Roland responded, fiercely. "Well, I think I may drink now, for the brandy seems to have no effect on you."

He raised the glass to his lips, but set it down immediately.

There was a great knocking and uproar at the door.

"What now?" he gasped. "Has that villain, Jacob Butler, betrayed us?"

"It may be so," Mrs. Corcoran said, starting to her feet. "Sir Roland, I call you to witness that I am your servant, your slave; I have acted under your instructions, and—"

"Peace, virago," Sir Roland said, interrupting her.

His face grew purple with fury, and he raised his clenched hands as if to strike the old woman.

But he refrained from doing this, for the knocking, kicking, and general confusion was going on with unabated vigour.

"I will sell my liberty as dearly as I would sell my life," Sir Roland said, as he advanced to the window.

Looking out he beheld a number of yokels, who mingled groans with roars of laughter.

At first Sir Roland Ashton could not comprehend the cause of this extraordinary scene, but presently he saw that the centre of this boisterous crowd was occupied by two of the most dejected-looking men he had ever set eyes on.

The individuals were Catchpole and Grabham.

The unfortunate officers had spent a most miserable night in the wind and rain.

Their shouts and cries for help had passed unheeded, and now that they were released they were nothing more than objects of mirth and ridicule.

Strips of netting clung to their uniforms, and their noses, absolutely blue with cold, gave them so comical an appearance that Sir Roland, angry and perplexed as he was, could not refrain from smiling grimly.

"I suppose I had better see this thick-headed pair of fools," he said. "Mrs. Corcoran, let them in, and tell the rest that if they do not take themselves off they will incur my displeasure."

Much relieved at finding that she was not to be arrested and dragged to durance vile, Mrs. Corcoran departed gladly on her errand.

Indeed, so overjoyed was she, that on her way to the door she armed herself with the identical broomstick which she had threatened Jacob Butler with.

Throwing open the door, she laid about her with such hearty goodwill that the yokels changed their bursts of laughter to yells of dismay.

The conflict was of short duration, but the execution was most satisfactory from Mrs. Corcoran's point of view.

At least half-a-dozen rustics scampered away

with heads to mend, and the hag chuckled as she gazed at her handiwork.

"I don't think you will come here again in a hurry," she said.

Then she turned her attention to Catchpole and Grabham, who stood trembling and eyeing the broomstick as if they expected a taste of it themselves.

"Come in, you two, if you want to see Sir Roland," she said, flashing her eyes upon them.

"Want to see him?" Grabham retorted, hoarsely. "I should just think we did. I shall never get rid of this 'ere cold. It will be the death of me."

"So it will of me," Catchpole asserted. "Ugh! Oh! dear."

He coughed, making a sound like a trombone out of tune.

"Well, I know nothing about it, and don't want," said Mrs. Corcoran. "Come, or I will bang the door in your faces."

Thus invited, the two crestfallen officers sidled into the house.

"Where is Sir Roland?" Grabham asked.

"You will find him where you left him last night."

"In the library?"

"Yes."

"How now?" said Sir Roland, as the constables entered the room. "What is the meaning of this?"

"It means that instead of us catching Spring-Heeled Jack he caught us," Grabham replied.

"So I should presume, judging by your appearance," Sir Roland returned. "Sit down and tell me how it happened?"

Catchpole and Grabham cast greedy eyes on the brandy-bottle, and Sir Roland, taking pity on them, passed it.

"Now," said the baronet, when both had drunk deeply, "let me have your story, and make it as short as possible."

Still acting as spokesman, Grabham told the story of the capture, and Sir Roland felt amused at it in spite of himself.

"You are a precious pair of noodles to employ," he said. "But what else could I expect? I have only to blame myself for trusting you with such work."

"Wait a minute, Sir Roland," Catchpole said. "I fancy that we have a bit more news which may interest you."

"Well?"

"As we were hollering and roaring in the blessed nets we see a carriage and pair drive into the park."

"Ha!"

"You may well start, your honour," Catchpole continued. "Just as it came near us the clouds shifted, and we could see by the moon who was driving."

"Who was it?" Sir Roland demanded, anxiously.

"The man who ought to have helped us to bring the nets away from the inn."

"Not Jacob Butler?"

"That is the man's name."

Sir Roland drummed his fingers upon the table and looked thoroughly bewildered.

"How in the name of wonder did he become possessed of a carriage and a pair of horses?" he said, musingly; "and more mysterious still, what was he going to do with them?"

"Be patient," said Catchpole, "give me time to tell all. Slung up as we were we could see a long way when the moon shone. All at once Jacob Butler changed places with Spring-Heeled Jack and away went horses and carriage at a speed fast enough to frighten Old Nick."

"Is this true?" Sir Roland Ashton asked, in astonishment, as he turned to Grabham.

"Every word, your honour."

"Look here, Sir Roland," said Catchpole, with an air of injured innocence, "I am not in the habit of telling lies, and—"

"Tut, tut! I meant no harm," Sir Roland said, interrupting him. "Did you see anybody else?"

"No, your honour."

Sir Roland Ashton swept his hand across his brow.

"I fancy I know what has taken place," he said, "and, therefore, I wish you to keep what you saw a secret."

Grabham nudged his companion in the ribs with his elbow, and Catchpole grinned.

"Certainly, your honour," said Grabham. "We know our dooty to our superiors, but—"

"You want to be paid for it?"

"Exactly."

"And you shall be," Sir Roland said, opening his pocket-book. "I am rather short of money, but as we are likely to meet again you must be contented with five pounds apiece for the present."

"It ain't much, considering how we have passed the night," Grabham growled. "When the moon went down it came on to rain like fury."

"And the wind seemed to blow holes in me," Catchpole groaned, as he was reminded forcibly of his recent sufferings. "Make it ten pounds apiece, your honour, and we won't grumble."

"I cannot just now," Sir Roland replied. "My expenses are enormously heavy, but all will be well in time. Trust to me, and I will—well, perhaps make both of you rich men."

"How?" both the officers demanded in a breath, with their mouths wide open.

Sir Roland cast a glance round the room.

"They say that walls have ears," he said, "and my experience gives me cause to credit the assertion. Listen! Lean forward over the table that I may whisper to you."

The constables did so, laying their heads closely together.

"What would you risk to share an immense treasure with me?" Sir Roland asked.

"Anything—anything!"

"Your lives? Another meeting with Spring-Heeled Jack?"

"Yes."

"Then you shall have the chance," Sir Roland replied. "Do you know Gedge Foote's house in the old Mint."

"Know it?" said Catchpole. "Rather! and the old fence too."

"The old fence, as you call him, is not likely to trouble anybody again," Sir Roland said. "He met with an accident—that is, he fell into his own well and was drowned!"

The constables glanced at each other and then at Sir Roland, but they deemed it prudent to say nothing.

"I will tell you how it happened," Sir Roland began, when Grabham interrupted him with—

"I s'pose your honour was present at the time?"

"It matters not to you where I was,' Sir Roland retorted, angrily.

"Oh! I beg pardon."

"That's right," said Catchpole, "and mind you don't put your spoke in again. Sir Roland, don't pay no attention to him."

"Gedge Foote hid his treasure in a secret passage half-way down the well," Sir Roland continued, "and he was in the habit of lowering himself into this snug hiding-place by means of a rope. Like the pitcher of old, he went too often—missed his grip on the rope and fell."

"And a good job too," said Grabham. "So there's money there, is there?"

"Yes," Sir Roland replied, "thousands of pounds—hundreds of thousands of pounds, perhaps. Gedge Foote told me—well never mind what he told me. Will you join me in the enterprise?"

"We will!" said Catchpole and Grabham, tragically.

"So far so good," Sir Roland said. "I will leave here for London to-morrow—perchance to-night, and you may make your own appointment where to meet me."

"What do you say to the West-end, your honour?" Grabham asked.

"Anywhere," the baronet replied. "I have no choice whatever in the matter."

"I mentioned the West-end because it is out of the way, and we are not likely to meet anybody we know," the constable said.

"Good!"

"Then say twelve o'clock at noon the day after to-morrow at Hatchard's."

"I will be there," Sir Roland said. "You may depend on me."

Soon after the constables took their leave, and a little later on Sir Roland learned that the detachment of soldiers promised from town had arrived.

He had no use for their services now, and, having seen them well-cared for, dismissed them.

"So," said the baronet, when he was again alone, "the miscreant, Jacob Butler, has betrayed me after all, and gone over to the service of my enemy, Spring-Heeled Jack. I know now what the arrival and departure of the carriage means—Daisy Leigh is no longer here; but I will follow and secure her, though the foul fiend stood in my path."

He spoke thus as he stood at the window watching the shades of night as they gathered on the landscape.

"At least," he said, closing the shutters and drawing the curtains close, "I shall be left in peace for a few hours. Oh! for one night's rest. Oh! for the sweet repose that belongs to me as a reward for labour."

Returning to the table he dropped his head upon it, and as he did so his hand came in contact with a piece of paper protruding from a drawer.

He had not noticed it before, and drew it out with a feeling of curiosity.

It was a note to him, and the writing was blood-red.

His first impulse was to fling the paper aside, but remembering that he would know no rest until he had perused its contents, he burst the seal and read—

"Your intended victim is no longer here. Sir Roland, you have been in my power a hundred times, but I have refrained from slaying you. I have given you opportunities to repent, but do not tempt me too far. Daisy Leigh will be safe and in good hands by the time you read this. Once more be warned, and be warned in time, or swift will come the hour of retribution and vengeance sure. "SPRING-HEELED JACK."

Sir Roland crushed the paper in his hand, and was in the act of hurling it down at his feet when he heard a strange sound behind him.

Turning his head, he saw that most horrible of old women, Mrs. Corcoran.

She was mouthing and mocking at him hideously.

One hand pointed at him and the other clutched a dagger.

Sir Roland uttered a fearful oath, and, springing to his feet, overturned the chair.

"So," he hissed, "you thought to steal upon me unawares! Woman, if such you be, give me that dagger!"

"I came here," Mrs. Corcoran replied, defiantly, "not to steal upon you unawares nor to take your life, as you may think."

"Why, then, are you armed?"

"To defend myself against a desperate man who has been foiled in all his undertakings."

"Wretch—witch! I believe not one word," Sir Roland cried. "Give me that dagger!"

With a quick movement he seized her wrist and pinned it against the wall.

In another instant he had possessed himself of the dagger.

Then all his evil blood boiled in his veins, and its reflection shone from his eyes.

"When you said that I am a desperate man and stop at nothing," he hissed, "you spoke the truth. Ah! you may twist, struggle, and turn, Mrs. Corcoran, but I have you now, and had you the strength of a giant I could hold you."

The hag felt this to be the truth, and her cheeks grew ashy grey.

"You will not harm me," she said, "for I meant none. Let me go, and I will trouble you no more. I have a little money of my own, and—"

"Yes, I know," Sir Roland interposed; "and you will use it in the cause of my destruction now that you discover I have found you out. I will not give you the least chance; I—"

"Would you murder me?" Mrs. Corcoran cried.

"It would be no murder to rid the world of such a wretch as you," Sir Roland replied.

As he spoke he tightened his grasp, and the hag groaned with pain.

"No—no—no!" she said, feebly. "You do but jest with me. Think of how I have served you! Think, if I die now, what sins I carry with me to the grave!"

"No grave would hold you," Sir Roland said. "Some ghoul would tear you from the earth and bring you back again. You shall burn! You witch, you shall burn!"

"Burn?"

"Aye, burn," Sir Roland repeated. "When you are dead I will fire this place. There will be a red glare in the sky to-night, and your ashes shall mingle with the sparks and burning fragments."

"Have mercy!" Mrs. Corcoran gasped. "Let me implore you on my knees to have mercy. You are only trying to frighten me. It must be so—say it is so!"

"It is not so. You must die."

Death now stared her in the face.

The white and always grim horseman that knocks alike at the door of the palaces of the rich and hovels of the poor, stopped before her, and bade her mount and ride across the shadowy border that lies between this earth and eternity.

Death was so horrible—horrible to her because she, guilty creature, had so many reasons to cling to life.

With a quick movement she struck at Sir Roland with her left hand and buried her nails in his cheek.

A yell scarcely human burst from his foam-flecked lips.

The dagger rose.

It flashed in the air and then descended.

Mrs. Corcoran uttered a gasping cry and fell.

"Oh! I am stabbed," she shrieked. "I am wounded to death. Wretch—villain—murderer—I will haunt you."

She raised herself on her elbow, but he struck at her and knocked her down.

"Seek the spirits of those you have sent before you," he cried, as her eyes dimmed and her limbs stiffened.

"Oh! murder—cold, cruel, heartless murder," the dying woman muttered, faintly. "The Heaven I have defied and wronged so long will avenge this."

These were the last words that passed her lips, and Sir Roland, throwing down the dagger, gazed at her body for some minutes in silence.

"Fool, to tempt me to dye my hands deeper in blood," he said. "Had you served me well, you might have lived out the remainder of your days, but I can have no obstruction in my path. Pah! what a wretched atmosphere is this I breathe. I gasp—I choke."

He placed his hands to his throat and wrenched his cravat off.

"Now to destroy the evidence of this crime," he said, hoarsely. "The fire will purge all. Ha! I must be quick. I will show myself to the villagers and help them to put out the blaze; but before they arrive the flames will be flying in seething wreaths about Lilac Lodge."

Piling some chairs against the wainscotting, he placed the lamp beneath them, and hastily left the room.

When Sir Roland Ashton passed outside Lilac Lodge, he stopped for a moment and looked back.

He thought he heard his name called by the woman he had so cruelly slain.

Sir Roland's face paled, his parted lips sent forth a steam-like vapour, and his knees knocked together.

"What now!" he gasped. "Is she not dead?"

"Sir Roland!"

He heard the voice now above him, and borne on the wings of the soughing wind.

The baronet clutched his hands and fled across the park.

As he reached the road, and saw lights twinkling from cottage windows, he felt more at ease.

Then he turned again and looked towards Lilac Lodge.

"Where is the red light in the sky?" he said. "Surely the overturned lamp has done its work by this time? If the glare does not appear presently, I must go back at all risk. But first to show myself to the people."

Walking hastily towards the inn at which Grabham and Catchpole had so distinguished themselves, Sir Roland entered and sat down.

There was a general movement among the customers to make room for the distinguished visitor, and the landlord dashed into the back parlour to smooth his hair, and to put on a snow white apron.

"Will your honour be pleased to walk into a private room?" he said, as he returned, and bowing low.

"No," Sir Roland replied. "I shall do very well where I am. Put some wine on the table, and let these honest fellows drink to my health."

"Your honour is too kind and condescending."

Sir Roland Ashton waved his hand in a manner implying that he required no thanks.

"I have had a long walk," he said, "and require a little rest and company. I get little of either at Lilac Lodge," he added, under his breath.

The company was made up of labourers, farmers, and village politicians.

They remained silent in Sir Roland Ashton's presence and held aloof from him.

The wine remained untouched upon the table.

"What have I done that you should keep away from me?" he asked, angrily. "Do you think that my presence will breed a pestilence among you? I wish to be merry to-night. When I came in here somebody was singing. Let the song continue."

The vocalist made an attempt to start again, but it ended in dismal failure.

No applause followed, and the men shuffled their feet uneasily.

It was evident that they resented Sir Roland's presence as an intrusion, and the landlord looked sheepish and ill at ease as he poured out the wine.

"Here's to a better understanding between us!" Sir Roland said, raising his glass to his lips.

The next instant it lay smashed to atoms on the floor.

A man with frightened eyes and distraught appearance had dashed into the room.

"Lilac Lodge is on fire!" he roared.

"What!" Sir Roland cried, starting to his feet, "the lodge on fire? Impossible!"

"Come and see for yourself," the man said.

The room became empty in less time than it takes to record the fact.

"This way!" Sir Roland shouted. "Follow me, men! Human life is in danger. Oh! my poor old housekeeper, she may not be able to escape."

His wrung his hands despairingly, and played his part so well that the men who had mistrusted him gave him their pity and help.

The red glow in the sky was fierce and angry.

Huge tongues of flame leaped and roared, as if with joy at the destruction they were creating.

Myriads of sparks danced and hovered over the burning building, and before the men, headed by Sir Roland, were half-way across the park, the roof fell in.

"It is useless—we can do nothing now," Sir Roland said. "The fire must have its own way."

This was so evident that no attempt was made to save any part of Lilac Lodge or anything it contained; but the crowd, augmented by troops of men, women, and children, remained until day dawned, and the sun shone upon the charred and blackened walls.

A search was then made among the rubbish, but no remains of Mrs. Corcoran could be found.

This seemed mysterious to Sir Roland Ashton, and he bit his under lip.

"Surely she was dead when I left her?" he said. "Yes; the flames have done their work only too well, and left no trace of the old hag behind."

## CHAPTER XLIX.

CONSTANCE MARFIELD MEETS DAISY LEIGH—JACOB BUTLER IS SENT ON A PERILOUS ERRAND—MYSTIFICATION OF ALL PARTIES.

It will be remembered that when Constance Marfield made her way to London, she did so with certain instructions from Spring-Heeled Jack.

He told her to go to the Queen's Head, Sadler's Wells, and on arriving there she was received by the landlord as if he expected her.

"It is all right, miss," he said; "you need not offer any explanations why you are here. I know all about it, but I am afraid you will have to wait a few days before your friend arrives."

"Indeed!" said Constance. "What course am I to pursue?"

"Remain here, and make yourself comfortable. You shall have every attention, and the best that the house can give is at your service."

"All this is very strange, and it seems to me more like a dream than reality," Constance replied. "I cannot make out why this weird creature, known as Spring-Heeled Jack, should take such an interest in me."

The landlord smiled.

"That you may find out sooner than you expect," he said. "At all events, I have received commands to see that you are well cared for."

Constance hesitated no longer.

She banished all fears and doubts from her mind, and made herself as much at home as possible.

Some days passed away, but no message came.

Spring-Heeled Jack remained absent, and Constance Marfield began to think that something must have happened to him.

Early one morning she was roused from her slumber by the rumbling of wheels and the voices of men.

Rising hastily, and looking out of the window, she saw a carriage, from which a dainty-looking lad was stepping.

A tall, handsome gentleman was handing him out, and then an individual, yawning and rubbing his eyes, dragged his legs down the steps, and looked vacantly about him.

Constance Marfield's heart beat audibly, and a wild cry of joy escaped her lips.

In the handsome gentleman who was paying such attention to the lad she recognised Ralph Ashton.

"Ralph! Ralph! dear Ralph!" she exclaimed, throwing the window open, "do I indeed see you again?"

Ralph Ashton kissed his hand gallantly.

"Yes," he said. "Come down as soon as you can. My heart is bursting to hold you in my arms again."

Constance Marfield dressed herself as quickly as possible, and was soon in her lover's embrace.

"Ralph," she said, "tell me what this means. I was sent hither by Spring-Heeled Jack, and now you are here. Who are these people?"

"You must have patience, darling, and I will tell you all," Ralph replied. "As strange as it may seem to you, Spring-Heeled Jack has everything to do with my being here."

"But this man and boy?" said Constance. "Who are you?"

"If you please," said a sweet voice, "I am not a boy, but a girl. I am Daisy Leigh."

"And I am Jacob Butler, or at least I think so," said another voice, which was not sweet, but cracked and harsh. "I never had such a journey in my life. How I got inside the carriage, or how Spring-Heeled Jack contrived to change places with Mr. Ashton, would puzzle that broomstick-witch, Mrs. Corcoran."

"Well, well," said Ralph Ashton, "to put an end to that matter, let us say we are all fairly puzzled. For my own part I have only a confused notion of what took place. At all events, here we are, and safe and sound. Daisy Leigh has escaped from that scoundrel, Sir Roland, and you, Constance, are once more at the side of the man who loves you dearer than his life."

At this moment the landlord's wife, a plump, buxom, comfortable-looking woman, entered the room with a tray laden with all sorts of good things for breakfast.

Jacob Butler was accommodated with a small table near the window, but he was so overcome with astonishment that he could eat but little.

If Mrs. Corcoran had bounced through the window, or had floated down the chimney, he would have taken her appearance as a matter of course.

Meanwhile, the three at the table were chatting on gaily, as if nothing had occurred to disturb their lives, and this helped to reduce Jacob to a state of semi-idiotcy.

He stared blankly, rumpled his hair all over his head until it looked like new-mown hay, and listened like a man in a dream.

"We must wait here until we hear from Spring-Heeled Jack," Ralph Ashton said; "that may be in a few hours hence, or days may pass before he tells us what course to take."

"How do you know this?" Constance asked.

"I have Spring-Heeled Jack's word for it."

As Daisy Leigh required rest she went to an apartment prepared for her soon after breakfast, and Jacob Butler, thinking wisely that he was in the way, went below to chat with the landlord and to bother him with a thousand questions.

These the landlord fenced cleverly, and compounded Jacob Butler potations of such extraordinary strength, that Jacob sank lower down into the depths of bewilderment, and finally, stretching himself at full length on the bench, went to sleep.

When he awoke he discovered that he had been put to bed.

Heavy plush curtains hid the room from view, and Jacob, drawing them aside, saw that night had come.

"Is it possible that I have slept the whole day through?" he said, sitting up. "What a fool I must have been to get drunk. I shall get into trouble to a certainty. What account could I give of myself if Spring-Heeled Jack were to appear and question me?"

The last word had scarcely left his lips when the curtains on the other side of the bed parted, and Spring-Heeled Jack thrust his face so close to Jacob that he uttered a yell and rolled himself on the floor.

"Ha, ha!" laughed Spring-Heeled Jack. "So this is the way you do my bidding. Get into bed again, fool, and listen to what I have to say to you."

"I am sure I am very sorry," Jacob Butler replied; "but really the landlord is more to blame."

"Peace," Spring-Heeled Jack said. "What you have done cannot be helped or recalled now. Listen."

"Yes, sir. I am all attention."

"When you rise in the morning you will find that your own clothes have been removed and replaced with others," Spring-Heeled Jack said. "Breakfast early, and as you value your life drink nothing stronger than coffee. Do you follow me?"

"Oh! yes. Oh! lor'."

"I am very angry with you," Spring-Heeled Jack continued; "but at present you have nothing to fear. Trifle with me again, or disregard my instructions, and I will throttle you as sure as you are a sinner."

Jacob Butler gave a wriggle and a spasmodic bounce in the bed, for Spring-Heeled Jack extended one of his long muscular arms and touched him on the neck.

"Don't—please don't," Jacob pleaded; "I will do anything you wish—indeed, I will."

"Good," said Spring-Heeled Jack. "I hope you will do so for your own sake. Now then, to finish my instructions. When you have put on the suit of clothes and other things placed for you, you will find yourself disguised as a farmer. Go then to Charing-cross and wait until you see Sir Roland Ashton in conversation with Catchpole and Grabham."

Jacob Butler groaned.

"How now!" cried Spring-Heeled Jack, "what is the matter?"

"Nothing—nothing," Jacob replied, hastily. "I have spasms sometimes, and they make me feel awfully queer."

"You had better dispense with them for a day or two," Spring-Heeled Jack said, grimly, "or you may have one you will not get over in a hurry."

Jacob made no reply, but he hung on to the side of the bed to keep himself from wriggling like an eel.

"The task before you is not a dangerous one," Spring-Heeled Jack continued, "and if you play your part well there will be no risk. Follow Sir Roland and the officers, and when you have seen them to their destination come back to this room, strike thrice with your fist on the panel over the fireplace, and I will come to you."

"I understand," Jacob Butler replied.

The curtains closed again and he was alone.

"Bless me!" Jacob gasped, "this is more awful and confusing than ever. I wonder what I shall be expected to do next?"

"Silence!" said Spring-Heeled Jack's voice.

Jacob Butler buried his head beneath the bed clothes, and kept it there until streams of perspiration poured down his face.

At last he came to the surface and breathing more freely fell asleep again.

When he awoke he found that Spring-Heeled Jack had been as good as his word.

On the chair nearest the bed was a suit of clothes, such as might be worn by a gentleman from the country, and a false beard.

Jacob put the latter on first, and stared at his altered visage in the looking-glass.

"Ha! ha!" he laughed; "I don't believe that even Mrs. Corcoran, clever as she is, would know me now."

This was such consolation to his mind that he cut a few capers, expressive of delight, about the room.

As he proceeded to dress himself his astonishment increased.

"Why," said he, "somebody must have taken my measure when I was asleep. These things fit me perfectly. Ah! well, it is no use wondering about such matters, or I shall lose my head altogether."

In a repentant state of mind Jacob Butler went downstairs.

The first person he met was Ralph Ashton, who eyed him keenly, but said nothing.

"I have seen Spring-Heeled Jack," Jacob faltered.

"I have seen him, too," Ralph replied. "If I had not, I should have made some remark as to your altered appearance. Do your duty, and say nothing more to anybody."

Jacob scratched his head and then shook it.

"We live in a strange world, sir," he said. "Who would believe that less than two days ago I was at Lilac Lodge, and now I am here with a mission?"

"Listen to me," said Ralph Ashton, interrupting him. "You will do well by keeping whatever Spring-Heeled Jack has said to you to yourself. A still tongue makes a wise head."

Jacob Butler rubbed the top of his cranium as if to satisfy himself whether there was any wisdom left in it.

"Well, sir," he said, "I will only say this. Spring-Heeled Jack saved me from a fate which I feared worse than death, and I will do my best to fulfil the task which he has set me."

"Well said," Ralph Ashton replied. "You will find breakfast ready for you in the room on the left."

So saying he turned upon his heel, and Jacob Butler proceeded to refresh himself.

His appetite had now returned and he made a hearty meal.

Suddenly the door opened and the landlord entered.

"Have a drop of brandy, my boy?" he said.

"No, thank you," Jacob replied.

"Just one."

"Not for worlds," Jacob replied; "and I will trouble you to leave me alone. I suppose I am not the only man who has got drunk in your house?"

"Don't lose your temper," the landlord said, grinning. "I thought I was doing you a kind action by asking you. You look all the better for your long sleep."

"If I look it I feel it," Jacob replied.

"I suppose you were not disturbed during the night?"

"Oh! dear no—not at all."

The landlord laughed in a peculiar manner, and closed the door.

"He didn't seem to believe what I said," Jacob Butler mused. "I—I wonder if he has ever seen Spring-Heeled Jack? If he hasn't I should like to see his face when he does. I'd bet anything that all the beefy colour would fly out of his face and leave him as pale as a turnip."

Having finished his breakfast Jacob left the inn and made his way through the salubrious localities of Clerkenwell and Smithfield.

He had seen nothing that morning of Constance

Marfield or Daisy Leigh, and he was wondering whether he should find them at the inn on his return, when he suddenly ran against a man.

It was Bill Blarney, and Jacob Butler, filled with terror, turned cold from the soles of his feet to the crown of his head.

"I beg your pardon," Bill Blarney said.

Jacob made no reply, for fear that his voice might betray him.

"Are you dumb?" Bill Blarney asked.

Jacob took a hint from this remark, and nodded his head.

"There is no man so dumb as he who chooses to keep his tongue between his teeth," Bill Blarney said.

Jacob Butler pretended not to hear and walked away.

Bill Blarney followed and placed his hand on Jacob's shoulder.

"You are just a little too clever," he said. "It so happens that I have been watching Sadler's Wells, and saw where you came from."

Jacob Butler felt inclined to shrink into his boots.

What he was to do now he had not the slightest notion in the world.

Suddenly an idea flashed into his brain.

"Since you have found me out," he said, "I may as well tell you the true facts of the case. That little affair got me into trouble, so I thought it better to bolt."

"It got me into trouble, too," Bill Blarney said, pointing to the shoulder which had been wounded. "But what a liar you are."

"Eh?" said Jacob, feebly. "That's rather strong language, you know."

"I repeat that you are a liar, and a contemptible one," Bill Blarney replied. "Look me straight in the face, and tell me who are the people you have been staying with?"

"If you want to know you had better go and ask them," Jacob said, sullenly. "You pressed me into your service, but I want nothing further of you. Leave me to myself or I will call for assistance and denounce you in your true character."

"You had better not."

"I will unless you take yourself off."

Bill Blarney eyed Jacob as if he could have stabbed him with all the pleasure in the world.

"This is neither the time nor the opportunity for me to settle accounts with you," he said; "but we shall meet again, Jacob, my boy."

"I'll take care to be prepared for you."

"In what manner?"

"With a brace of pistols."

Bill Blarney placed his hands on his hips and laughed uproariously.

"Why, you would only shoot yourself you fool," he said; "but perhaps that would be the better way of settling the difficulty."

As he finished speaking two constables turned a corner of the street.

Bill Blarney dived down a court and was lost to view in an instant.

"He is a coward at heart with all his bounce," Jacob said, as he moved away. "I wish I had not seen him—I don't feel quite so comfortable as I did. Hang him and everybody! The very air is full of mystery."

He took the longest route towards Charing-cross, knowing no other.

Passing along Fleet-street he entered the Strand, and then he began to proceed with more caution.

At any moment he might encounter Sir Roland Ashton, and he cast his eyes from one side of the street to the other, with some vague notion that the baronet might recognise him in spite of his disguise, and pounce upon him unawares.

In the days of which we are writing, the West-end of London presented a vastly different appearance to what it does at the present period.

There were but few houses in the Strand, and these were scattered about and standing mostly near the river, in their own grounds, and had fine gardens sloping down to the water.

Charing-cross was little more than a village, and had its fields, lanes, and green hedgerows, until the Mall was reached, and then, as now, fine buildings and handsomely-dressed people stamped the locality as one of wealth and luxury.

Jacob Butler wandered about for hours, but his eyes were not regaled with the sight of Sir Roland, or of the constables.

Jacob did not know whether to go back or not, but at last he decided upon putting up somewhere for the night.

But where?

This was a question that sorely puzzled Jacob Butler.

The sun went down and what promised to be a gloomy night began to set in.

At last Jacob made up his mind to take his way up St. Martin's-lane and enter the first house likely to provide entertainment, for he was not only hungry, but dreadfully thirsty.

"Nobody can say that I have not stuck to my post," he murmured, as he went along. "Hullo! This is a rather queer sort of neighbourhood, but I suppose it is none the worse for that."

Pushing open a door half covered with a red blind, he found himself at a public bar, presided over by a stalwart, beetle-browed man.

"Can I have a bed here?" Jacob asked.

"Yes, if you have the money to pay for it," was the reply.

"How much?"

"Two shillings, or three if you want any supper."

"That is just what I do require," Jacob replied. "I am half dead with hunger. Give me some cold meat and pickles, or anything you may have handy."

"Mary!" shouted the landlord.

"Yes, sir," said a slovenly-looking girl, appearing at the end of the bar.

"Show this gentleman into the parlour and lay the supper cloth."

As the landlord was speaking the door by which Jacob had entered creaked on its hinges.

Catchpole and Grabham entered.

They wore disguises, but of so flimsy a nature that Jacob Butler recognised them at once.

They looked at Jacob, and he stared back at them with compound interest.

"Beg pardon, sir," said Grabham, "but I fancy I have seen you before."

Now was the time for Jacob Butler to distinguish himself.

For all he knew Spring-Heeled Jack's eyes might be upon him at that moment.

"If you have," he said, "you must have a better memory than I possess. Where was it?—in London?"

"No; in the country."

Jacob Butler winced a little.

"Is not that a rather vague place to talk about?"

"So it is—so it is," Catchpole assented. "Here, I'll put the question straight—"

"Your supper is ready, sir," said the girl. "This way, if you please."

"And I am ready for it," Jacob replied.

It suddenly occurred to him that he had better take the bull by the horns, as the saying goes, and turning, he addressed the officers.

"You can easily see by my attire that I come from the country," he said. "I am going to sup in the parlour, and if you care to drink a glass or break a crust with me, I shall be glad of your company."

Grabham and Catchpole saw a chance of being well treated for nothing, and winked at each other.

They required nothing to eat, but in point of fluids they seemed incapable of pouring enough down their throats.

Then they began to boast and lie.

It was in their nature to do so and they could not have helped it had their lives been at stake.

Jacob listened and chuckled to himself.

He contrived to question them with such success as to discover not only the fact that they were going to sleep in the house, but also the number of the double-bedded room they had taken.

Jacob Butler thought it wise to pay for no more drink.

If the constables took much more they would be too sleepy to talk, and Jacob had made up his mind to listen to their conversation, when they thought they were snug and alone in the room.

This was not a bad notion on the part of Jacob Butler, and how it succeeded we shall presently see.

Neither Grabham nor Catchpole offered to pay for anything, and when they found that their patron had closed his purse-strings, they took themselves away to the upper regions of the house.

Jacob Butler followed in about five minutes.

In the first place he went to his own room, and divested his feet of the thick, heavy boots he had been wearing all day.

Then he peeped out of the door, and looked up and down the long, dark corridor.

It cost him an effort to screw up his courage, but remembering that he would be visited with condign punishment unless he did his duty well, he crept along as stealthily and noiselessly as a cat.

When the boards creaked Jacob started, and there was something unpleasant about the atmosphere of the place.

At last he reached the door hiding the constables from view, and Jacob Butler proceeded to place his ear close to the keyhole.

But woe to him!

His foot slipped and his head came in contact with one of the panels.

Jacob Butler picked himself up and ran for his life.

Tearing madly into his room he slipped off his clothes, and rolling into bed hauled the clothes about his ears, and then began to imitate a prodigious snore.

Presently he heard the sound of approaching footsteps.

They stopped at his door, and then somebody's knuckles began to tap.

Jacob Butler snored louder than ever, and what between fear and chagrin at his failure, he made the most horrible noises in his nose and throat.

Tap, tap, tap!

"Who—who's there?" he demanded, in a muffled tone of voice.

"I say," demanded Grabham, "have you been paying us a visit?"

"Why the devil should I do such a thing as that?" Jacob retorted, wrathfully.

"Well, the devil, or Spring-Heeled Jack, may have something to do with it," Grabham returned. "We were in bed when something rushed against the door and busted in one of the panels."

"It strikes me," said Jacob, as he gained sufficient courage to speak coherently, "that you have both been dreaming. Go to bed again and leave me to sleep in peace."

"We only came to ask you to get up if you hear any more noise?" Catchpole chimed in.

"I'll do that," Jacob replied. "Good-night. You wouldn't hang about there if you knew how sleepy I am."

"There ain't much sleep left for us, I'm thinking," Grabham growled. "Catchpole, why didn't you seize your pistols, and fire them, when you got out of bed? If you had banged away at the door, you must have hit something on the other side of it!"

"Grabham, my friend," said Catchpole, solemnly, "I followed your example, and kept still."

Mr. Grabham muttered something Jacob Butler could not hear, and then, after a few lively remarks of mutual recrimination, the officers swore to stand by each other until they perished, and sneaked back to their room, trembling every inch of the way.

They were up betimes in the morning, but not so early as Jacob Butler.

He was down and on the alert before they appeared.

Again Jacob took himself to Charing-cross and wandered about for more than three hours.

At last he saw a well-known figure approaching.

It was Sir Roland Ashton, and Jacob Butler dodged behind a broken down wooden fence, and watched with the keenness of a ferret.

Sir Roland looked carelessly about, and evinced neither surprise nor gratification when he was joined by Catchpole and Grabham.

They went away in company, and after giving them a couple of hundred yards' start, Jacob Butler followed, keeping close to the wall, and almost dodging his way from doorway to doorway.

In these days he would have been locked up on suspicion to a certainty, but constables, even in the most frequented parts, were rare articles then, and nobody seemed to take much interest in Jacob's movements.

Sir Roland and the officers reached Essex-street and suddenly turned to the right.

They descended the stairs and, hailing a boatman, floated away in the direction of the Tower.

So far all had gone well with Jacob Butler.

Up to that moment his presence had not been dreamed of by the conspirators.

He also hailed a waterman and looked sharply at him.

"Do you want a job?" Jacob asked.

"If I didn't I shouldn't be here," the man replied.

"Well, then, follow that boat at a distance," Jacob said.

"I understand," said the waterman, grinning. "I suppose this is some secret bit of business?"

"Whatever it is you will be well paid for it," Jacob replied, as he stepped into the boat. "Keep away, so that none of those men can recognise me, but pull ashore the moment they land."

The journey down the river was of short duration, as a swift ebb-tide was flowing.

Sir Roland, Grabham, and Catchpole soon stepped ashore; but before they were out of sight Jacob Butler was on their track.

He saw them enter the old Mint.

He followed them until he beheld them standing before the door of the house once occupied by Gedge Foote, and then he retraced his footsteps towards the river.

Now that his work was done all his old fear and horror of Sir Roland Ashton returned.

His face grew ghastly pale, and his legs tottered under him.

"Back again," he said, hoarsely, as he staggered into the boat. "Phew! I am hotter than a furnace."

"That's curious now, for you are as white as a snowdrift and look as cold as one," the waterman observed. "I hope you haven't brought a fever or any catching complaint into my boat."

Jacob Butler did not feel easy until he had landed at Blackfriars-stairs, and not quite safe until he had reached the inn.

It was still broad daylight when Jacob rushed up into the room in which he had seen Spring-Heeled Jack.

As he struck the panel above the mantel-shelf with his fist he felt something moist fall upon his face.

A mist gathered before his eyes and he reeled into a chair.

"Well," said the voice of Spring-Heeled Jack; "have you succeeded—have you seen Sir Roland?"

"Yes," Jacob replied. "But what is this? Your voice seems to come to me as in a dream. My head swims. I am sinking. Where am I going? Oh—help!"

"Fear nothing," said Spring-Heeled Jack, "but answer my questions and then you shall rest."

"Did Sir Roland meet the constables?"

"He did."

"And you followed them?"

"Yes."

"Where to?"

"To a house in the old Mint."

"That is well," Spring-Heeled Jack replied; "and now I will leave you in peace. Do you hear what I say?"

"Yes, I hear you, but I cannot see you."

"And yet I am very near you," Spring-Heeled Jack replied. "For the present, farewell."

Jacob Butler wrestled with the sensation of drowsiness that overpowered his senses.

Once he thought he caught sight of Ralph Ashton standing in the doorway, and then his head fell back and he sank into a long and dreamless slumber.

---

## CHAPTER L

### DEAD OR ALIVE.

What is that creeping painfully along the dark road so late at night?

The sky is red with leaping flames, and the wind howls a dirge to Lilac Lodge as it sinks under the destroying element.

Owls, bats, and other evil night-birds of prey leave their haunts and fill the air with shrill cries.

The sight is a strange one to them, and with leathery wings they flap and flip from tree-top to the crumbling buttress of the old church, and huddle together for company sake.

And as they crouch and squeak they seem to ask the same question—

"What is that creeping along the dark road so late at night?"

It is a lonely figure covered with tattered rags.

Now it stops as if fainting, and now it struggles along aimlessly until it reaches a pool of stagnant water, and then it stoops and drinks greedily.

It is impossible to say whether the figure is that of a man or a woman.

A wild cry of rage and agony bursts from its lips as the figure turns into a wood, and then all is still.

Tremble, Sir Roland Ashton! tremble, Jacob Butler! for Mrs. Corcoran, or her spirit, is abroad.

. . . . . .

Sir Roland, Catchpole, and Grabham, having entered the house in the old Mint, and, as they thought, unobserved, began to make preparations to carry out their scheme.

"This is a strange place," Catchpole said, shuddering and glancing nervously over his shoulder.

"Yes," Sir Roland replied, grimly, "and I have some strange recollections connected with it. You did not forget to come well armed I hope?"

"No, your honour," Catchpole replied; "both Grabham and I have a brace of pistols and plenty of ammunition. Why did you ask the question?"

"Because you may have reason to be glad of taking such precaution."

The constables glanced at each other as if they did not relish the job they had taken in hand.

"It ain't that I am afraid of mortal man," Grabham said, "but since that we are here I should like to know all about this place and what we are to expect."

"I had a narrow escape with the men of the Mint," Sir Roland replied. "They gave chase to me on the night that Gedge Foote met with his misfortune."

"It was an accident, I suppose?" Catchpole observed, a little dubiously.

Sir Roland paid no attention to this remark.

"I was thinking that this wild crew might think proper to come here again," he said, "and in that case it would be advisable to be prepared for them."

"They may have removed the treasure," Grabham suggested. "If so we have had all this trouble for nothing."

"Gedge Foote was no fool, and did not wag his tongue like some people I could mention," Sir Roland retorted, glancing at the constables.

"Then," said Catchpole, who began to wish himself outside of the old house, "I should like to know how you became possessed of his secret?"

"I was in difficulties and I came here to borrow money," Sir Roland said. "It was not the first time that Gedge Foote had obliged me, and I determined that he should do so again. We—"

"Who's we?" Catchpole interrupted.

"Well, if you must have it," said Sir Roland, "Bill Blarney was with me."

Both the constables started.

"Why didn't you tell us you were in league with that scoundrel?" Grabham said.

"Who said I was in league with him?" Sir Roland replied, with a scornful laugh. "I will be honest and speak out. I made use of him just in the same way that I am making use of you."

"Oh! that's the game, is it?" said Catchpole, who grew more sick at heart and uncomfortable every moment. "It strikes me rather forcibly that you know more about Gedge Foote's death than you care to tell."

"What if I do?" Sir Roland said, coolly. "I told you that I killed him, and that statement was one of simple fact. What course of action do you think you could pursue? Here are you two officers of the law met here with me to plunder a dead man's house!"

Catchpole rose to his feet.

"I wash my hands of this affair," he said. "No man in all the world is fonder of money than I am, but when I know that it is stained with the blood of a murdered man I—ugh!—turn away. Grabham, I think you will agree with me that we have had enough of this business?"

"Just so," Grabham replied. "I wish to Heaven that I had never moved a step towards this place."

"Gentlemen," said Sir Roland Ashton, with a sneering laugh, "I'll trouble you to remain where you are."

"What if we refuse?" Grabham demanded.

"Why, I shall help myself to the treasure, and when safe abroad with it take the trouble of putting the authorities in the way of letting them know what a brace of beauties are trusted with the care of life and property."

"You villain!" Grabham gasped.

"I am not aware that I have ever posed as a saint before you," Sir Roland returned. "Now, let us understand each other. It is you who threw out the suggestion that I killed Gedge Foote. I confess I did. Now, mark me! as sure as you are living men I will accuse you of being accomplices before and after the fact unless you do my bidding. Help me and you shall have your share, and I care not whether I ever see you or hear of you again."

Grabham and Catchpole staggered against the wall and looked helplessly at each other.

They were in a fix and could see no way of getting out of it.

"But why should we quarrel?" Sir Roland went on. "Here, almost within our reach, is money enough to make all of us rich and happy."

"Happy!" Catchpole groaned. "I have done many things in my life which I don't care to think about, but this is too horrible."

"This house is not calculated to inspire a man with pleasant thoughts," Sir Roland said, "and the sooner we are out of it the better. It will take us at least five or six hours to raise the treasure from the well to the cellar, so follow me and we will commence work at once."

"Catchpole," Grabham whispered, "what are we to do?"

"I don't know. Where's the use of asking me?"

"I took you to be a man of common sense," Grabham said, mournfully. "I'm in such a wretched state of mind myself that I don't know whether I am on my head or my heels."

"We must follow him through with it now," Catchpole remarked, in a whisper; "but wherever there is the stain of blood a curse follows—you can't wipe it out. It is the only thing the earth will not hide. It has a voice of its own—a voice that is heard in Heaven, and it cries aloud for vengeance."

"What lovely words!" Grabham said. "I feel better after them, Catchpole. Do you think that if we kept half our share of the money and gave the rest to some charity that—"

"Cease that prating and follow me," Sir Roland Ashton interrupted, turning in the doorway. "Ha!"

"What's the matter?" Catchpole demanded.

"I thought I heard a sound below," Sir Roland replied. "Give me a pistol. Good! Now it will be death to the man who crosses my path."

At this moment Catchpole shrieked, and Sir Roland turned fiercely upon him.

"What now?" he demanded.

"The shadow—the shadow!" was all Catchpole could utter.

"Shadow—shadow?" Sir Roland repeated. "Speak out, man. Use your tongue like a creature of sense and reason, or I will render it useless for ever."

"It was the shadow of that horrible old woman you had at Lilac Lodge," Catchpole blurted out.

The pistol fell from Sir Roland's hand, and he stared in blank dismay at the terrified constable.

"What fool's lie is this?" he cried, hoarsely.

"No lie at all," Catchpole replied. "If I was on my dying bed I would swear that I saw the shadow."

"It might have been your own."

"Am I like a witch?" Catchpole demanded. "Are my fingers hooked like a hawk's and my nails half-an-inch long? I tell you that the old woman is about somewhere."

"Impossible!" Sir Roland ejaculated. "How can that be, when she is—"

His utterance became choked, and a strange, rattling sound came from his throat.

He had seen the shadow himself.

It appeared for an instant on the opposite wall, and then vanished as if a sudden flash of light had been thrown upon it.

"What devil's work is this?" Sir Roland cried, as he recovered his speech.

"Your own!" said a hollow voice.

Grabham and Catchpole clutched each other by the arm and looked towards the door, which was blocked up by Sir Roland's form.

"I don't think it's any use staying here," Grabham said, feebly. "You'll agree with me, Sir Roland, that where there is a shadder there ought to be some cause for it."

Sir Roland did not speak, but passed his hand heavily across his brow.

The constables moved slowly towards the door, but the baronet waved them back.

"Cowards!" he said, "are you to be frightened like children by idle conjurings? This is the work of my enemy and yours. Mrs. Corcoran is dead, and if her spirit has been permitted to revisit the earth it cannot hurt us."

"It strikes me," Catchpole whined, "that everybody is either dead or dying. At all events, treasure or no treasure, I am out of this place as quick as my legs will carry me."

Sir Roland Ashton presented a pistol at his head.

"Hold up your hands!" he said.

# SPRING-HEELED JACK,

## THE TERROR OF LONDON.

"DIE! DOG—DIE!" SPRING-HEELED JACK HISSED.

No. 17.

Catchpole did so, and became so limp that he had to lean against the wall to support himself.

"Follow his example, Grabham," Sir Roland said. "Good! I am glad to find you so sensible and obedient. Now harken. I defy ghost and mortal, and will not leave this place until Gedge Foote's treasure is mine."

Grabham and Catchpole howled in chorus.

"If you do not swear to follow me to the bitter end I will blow your brains out against the wall!" Sir Roland continued. "Choose between death, and life and wealth. I am a desperate man, and nothing shall thwart me now!"

"To think I should come to this!" Grabham gasped. "Well, Sir Roland, agony can't be much greater than it is now, so I consent."

"I always go with you, Grabham," Catchpole remarked, "and so do I."

"Then come," said Sir Roland.

They descended the dark, dismal staircase, and trod almost silently on the thick carpet of dust which had accumulated there for ages.

Huge networks of cobwebs dangled from the filthy walls, and all kinds of hideous creeping things emerged from niche and cranny.

Sir Roland took a dark lantern from his pocket and flashed the disc of light to and fro over the heads of the constables.

He compelled them to go in advance for fear that they might play him some trick or bolt when his back was turned.

Down they went until they came to the cellar door.

A gust of wind from above caused it to sway gently.

Its creaking hinges sounded like the chains of a gibbet, and the constables, more dead than alive, came to a standstill.

"Go on!" Sir Roland said, sternly. "A few more paces and you will see the well yawning at your feet."

They reached the cellar at last, and stood in silence glancing round the fearful region.

Its walls ran with damp and slime, and every now and then a red-eyed rat dashed from one hole into another, squeaking in terror and rage at the appearance of the strangers.

There was the well, with its pulley and dangling ropes, just as Sir Roland had seen it on that awful night when Gedge Foote breathed his last.

Sir Roland advanced and examined the well by the light of the lantern.

A terrible oath escaped his lips.

"We are foiled," he said. "The water has risen above the secret passage and we cannot enter it. We must wait until it goes down."

"What! wait here?" Grabham demanded.

"Yes. We cannot be in a safer place."

Sir Roland took a cord from his pocket, and, attaching a coin to it, tested the depth of the well.

After a few minutes he repeated the experiment.

"The water is going down," he said. "We shall not be kept long in suspense. In less than two hours we shall be out of this accursed place, and each of us carrying enough gold to ransom a king."

To the terrified constables each minute was an age, but at last Sir Roland clutched the ropes and handed them to Catchpole.

"What am I to do with these here?" the constable demanded, starting back.

"Descend by the aid of them, unless you like to jump."

"No, no!" Catchpole [illegible] Roland, and show us the w[illegible]

"Psha!" said the baron[illegible] "it is easy enough. Lower [illegible] feet come in contact with a ledg[illegible] forward, and you will find yoursel[illegible] passage."

"If I don't find myself at the bott[illegible] well it won't be any fault of yours," C[illegible] howled. "Why don't you go first?"

"Because you would leave me like a brac[illegible] curs," Sir Roland replied; "and I don't mean [illegible] give you that chance. Quick! or you will fire my blood with anger, and then you may discover yourself making a sudden descent."

Catchpole, finding that there was no alternative but to obey, passed his trembling fingers round the rope and swung his legs over the well.

"Oh, lor'! oh, dear!" he yelled; "I am sinking! I shall fall and be drowned!"

"You would fall and be hanged if I had my way," Sir Roland replied. "Ass! idiot! Lower yourself hand over hand. How long are you going to keep us up here?"

Catchpole closed his eyes and went down, but so slowly that his arms became racked and filled with pain.

At last his feet came in contact with something, and he breathed a sigh of relief.

"I am all right," he said. "Lor'! how hollow my voice sounds here. Who is to come next?"

"Grabham!" Sir Roland replied. "Of course, our old friend, Grabham, is most impatient to join you."

"Am I?" Grabham replied. "That's all you know about it. But, here goes!"

Sir Roland lighted the constable on his way, and when a word told that he was safe the baronet descended himself.

"I never noticed that there was a door here," he said, as he stood at the entrance of the secret passage. "I suppose I must have overlooked it. See, here are some cords; attach them to the bags, and we will haul them up."

As he spoke the dark lantern was dashed from his hand, and the heavy door closed upon him with such force that it drove him against the shuddering constables.

All three rolled heavily upon the floor.

Sir Roland was first on his feet.

"Ho! ho! you are trapped again!" laughed the voice of Spring-Heeled Jack. "This time I will hold you safe. In six hours the water will rise again and flow over the lifeless bodies of three scoundrels!"

---

## CHAPTER LI.

THE ABDUCTION AT THE QUEEN'S HEAD—THE VAULT BENEATH THE CHURCH—TERROR OF CONSTANCE MARFIELD — APPEARANCE OF SPRING-HEELED JACK — FLIGHT OF BILL BLARNEY—THE STRUGGLE ON THE TOWER.

AT that good old inn, the Queen's Head, near Sadler's Wells, matters remained quiet.

Jacob Butler lay still sleeping out his well-earned rest, and Daisy Leigh and Constance Marfield sat chatting at a window overlooking a pleasant garden.

Fragrant roses and twining honeysuckle grew in the neighbourhood then, and people came from far and near—came to drink the waters of the celebrated well.

It was one of the most fashionable resorts of all London.

Gaily-dressed gallants took snuff from diamond-studded boxes and flirted with the ladies, who, adorned with patches, powder, hooped dresses, and enormous fans, presented odd spectacles.

The comparatively modern crinoline is but an infant when placed side by side with the dress worn by the feminine gender in the days when a monarch spoke the Dutch language from the English throne, and when starched coat-skirts were still in vogue with the male portion of the aristocracy.

From their place of 'vantage Daisy Leigh and Constance Marfield watched the gaily-dressed throng as it moved to and fro with the lazy yet elegant deportment taught in all schools.

The sight was a novel one to the girls, and amused them greatly.

At last they grew tired of the scene, and commenced chatting about themselves and their future prospects.

Ralph Ashton had gone out, giving no explanation as to where he was going or what time he might return.

"You must tell me all about it, dear," Constance Marfield said to her companion. "You have told me how this strange being, Spring-Heeled Jack, rescued you from Sir Roland and placed you in a secret passage running from Lilac Lodge to a hollow tree in the park; but the rest is still a mystery to me."

"And so it is to me, in honest truth," Daisy replied. "Well, I will tell you all I know.

"This secret passage was most elegantly furnished, and so hollowed out in places that a dozen people might have lived there in ease and comfort.

"I had a suite of apartments, if I may call them by such a name, and Spring-Heeled Jack seldom came near me.

"Everything was placed at my hand in the most mysterious way, but when Spring-Heeled Jack did approach me he treated me as if I were a princess.

"One morning when I rose from my bed I found a note pinned to my pillow.

"It told me to dress in a suit of boy's clothes, which I should find in a chest on the other side of the room, and that I was to make up my mind to leave that very night.

"I was not frightened.

"I knew that Spring-Heeled Jack had always acted as a true friend, and why should I fear him when he had rescued me from a fate worse than death?

"I did exactly as the note instructed me, and passed the day in reading, in playing the harpsichord, and singing.

"I was, in a manner of speaking, a prisoner, yet I was furnished with plenty of amusement, and in no instance did the time hang heavy on my hands.

"In the evening, when I was waiting and wondering what was to happen, and where I was to go to, the man who is here with us passed through the secret passage, and I saw him no more until Spring-Heeled Jack had placed me in the carriage.

"How I got there I cannot tell.

"I seemed to me that I was suddenly blindfolded, but I did not struggle, for Spring-Heeled Jack whispered in my ear—

"'Courage! courage! Trust me. I, who have protected you so long, will not desert or h... you now.'"

"What a strange yet noble creature he m... be!" Constance Marfield said.

"As soon as I was placed in the carriage I recovered myself," Daisy went on, "but the pace was too frightful to endure.

"The horses seemed to fly over the ground, and I expected every moment that the carriage would be dashed into a thousand pieces.

"After all I am but a weak and timid girl, and I cried out to Spring-Heeled Jack.

"He only laughed, saying that I was perfectly safe in his hands, so I withdrew my head and resigned myself to my fate, whatever it might be.

"I must have fallen asleep, for suddenly I became aware that I was not alone in the carriage.

"Jacob Butler, looking as if he had just awakened from a trance, sat opposite me.

"I questioned him as to how he came in the carriage; but he could give me no lucid answer.

"All he knew was that he had been lifted bodily down, and that it appeared to him that Ralph Ashton had taken the place of Spring-Heeled Jack on the box-seat.

"And then we came to London, as you see, Constance.

"My story is rather a vague one, and has perhaps left you in the dark as much as ever."

"I must confess that to be the case," Constance replied; "and, moreover, Ralph's conduct mystifies me. When I question him he only laughs, and says that I must seek a full explanation from Spring-Heeled Jack. It is not very likely that I shall do that. Shall we walk in the garden, Daisy?"

"Yes; the air is so fresh and beautiful that it will do us good."

The girls went downstairs, and Constance Marfield, stooping, picked up a tell-tale flower, and blowing lightly upon it, said—

"He loves me—he loves me not."

"Yes," cried Daisy; "he loves you, for see there is no more bloom left upon the stem."

She started as she saw the head and shoulders of a man protruding over the neatly-trimmed hedge.

The man wore a slouched hat, pulled low so as to partly conceal his features.

Daisy Leigh started back, but Constance faced the stranger boldly.

"What do you want?" she asked. "How dare you intrude yourself upon us?"

"A thousand pardons, fair lady," the man said. "I crave your charity. I am but a beggar in sore need of food and lodging. Bestow a silver coin upon me and I will pray Heaven to bless you."

Constance Marfield, thinking that the plea was a genuine one, advanced with a shilling in her dainty hand, and as the man took it he pressed her fingers lightly.

It might have been an accident, but it was not lost upon Constance.

"Daisy," she said, as she returned to her fair companion, "there is something about that man I do not like. I am glad he has gone away."

"He gave me a start," Daisy replied. "When I caught sight of his face I thought I had seen it before, but it must have been fancy. Shall we return to the house?"

"I think that would be the wisest course to pursue," Constance replied, "for we may be doing wrong by walking out without leave from

Ralph. I wish he would return. That man, beggar as he called himself, may be the agent of one of our enemies."

"Our fears may be groundless," Daisy said; "and yet we had better be cautious."

No sooner had the door closed behind the girls than the beggar-man peered over the hedge again.

Tossing the shilling contemptuously in the air, he chuckled and rubbed his hands as if he had discovered something to invoke his mirth.

"Now, by the bones of Saint Patrick!" he said, "I will fight Spring-Heeled Jack with his own weapons. The Bull in Top Boots shall see me to-night, and the Queen's Head shall lose a guest. Ha, ha!"

Bill Blarney, for he it was, laughed hoarsely.

"What a thing it will be to claim a ransom of this light-heeled gentleman!" he said. "With all his cleverness he never dreamed that I watched his movements, and saw— Never mind that! I know now that cold steel and dull lead will reach him, though he were the dullest of mortals, and and the time is not far distant when we shall try conclusions."

He turned away, keeping up the character he assumed by creeping and crouching, and begging of all the well-dressed people he met.

"Stand aside, you hound!" said a gentleman who was whispering soft nothings in a lady's ear.

"Hound!" Bill Blarney ejaculated.

"Yes, filthy hound! Get out of my path!"

Bill Blarney's hand went inside his coat as if to clutch some hidden weapon, but he withdrew it empty.

"Prince Charles Edward is not king yet," he said under his breath; "and there may be yet heads as noble as yours fall from the scaffold on Tower-hill."

The gentleman started, and his face grew ashy grey.

"What mean you by that?"

"That you are an arch-traitor and a conspirator against the peace and throne of King George."

"You know me, then?"

"Yes; almost as well as you know yourself."

"Come away," the lady whispered. "That man's looks and words frighten me."

"Aye, take him away," Bill Blarney said, scornfully. "He forgets the days when he was glad to clasp my hand."

"I clasp your hand!" the gentleman exclaimed, in astonishment. "You must be mad."

He laid his hand upon his sword as he spoke, but withdrew it as Bill Blarney snapped his fingers contemptuously.

"Yes—you, Herbert Stanfield," Blarney said. "Times have altered, and I daresay you find it convenient to forget the past. I never forget a face or a thing that has happened."

"I must speak to this fellow," Herbert Stanfield said, hurriedly.

"Fool!" he hissed in Blarney's ear, "could you not have made yourself known to me in a different fashion?"

"You gave the first offence," the ruffian replied. "So you have made it up with your friends?"

"Yes."

"And changed midnight rides on the highway for lolling about a drawing-room?"

"Hush! hush!"

"Well, well," said Bill Blarney, in a surly tone, "I don't want to harm you, but be careful how you tread on my corns. You know the old quarters, the Bull in Top Boots, in the Borough?"

"I am never likely to forget the den," Herbert Stanfield returned, with a nervous glance at the lady.

"Well, then, come down there any evening after this and stand treat to the boys," Bill Blarney said, in a whisper. "They will be glad to see you and give you a royal welcome. And now I will put matters right with your lady. You have good taste, Herbert, my boy."

Herbert Stanfield's face grew pale with passion, and his fingers itched to strike the scoundrel standing before him to the earth.

"Leave the explanation to me," he said. "Begone! You will see me ere long. I will bring sufficient money to pay my ransom, and then I hope that neither you or any of the band will ever trouble me again."

"Perhaps not."

"What did you say?"

"Nothing," Bill Blarney replied; "I only made a remark about a wound I have in my shoulder; the pain of it is enough to drive me mad."

Leaving Herbert Stanfield to stammer out some excuses to the lady, Bill Blarney slouched away, chuckling and grinning.

"What a stroke of luck to meet him after all these years!" he said. "His ransom will cost him something. I must keep my eyes wide open, and not let him slip through my grasp. Poor devil! he must feel uncomfortable now hat he is bowled out."

It was late in the day when Bill Blarney wended his way towards the Bull in Top-Boots.

A feeble oil-lamp was burning in one of the windows, shedding a sickly glare on the rough, uneven road beyond.

There was not a soul in sight, and Bill Blarney, after glancing furtively up and down the street, entered the house.

"Ha!" said the landlord greeting him with a smile. "So you have found your way back at last!"

"Yes; but winged like a sparrow," Blarney replied. "That was Sir Roland Ashton's work, and I owe him a grudge for it."

"What! Sir Roland?"

"Yes, but I have no time to tell a long story," Bill Blarney growled. "Are any of the boys here?"

"No; but I expect several presently," was the reply. "I suppose you are not in such a devil of a hurry that you can't wait a few minutes?"

"Time is no object to me just now," the scoundrel replied; "but I want a job done to-night. Ha! here comes Dick Sleuth!"

A short, stunted, evil-looking ruffian, with shoulders almost as broad as his body was long, entered the house, and was in the act of passing through to the rear of the premises when Bill Blarney stopped him.

"How fares it with you?" the latter asked.

"Rough."

"Short of money?"

"Yes, and short of temper into the bargain," Dick Sleuth replied, with an oath. "Let me pass, unless you are agreeable to wet a thirsty man's lips."

"Give it a name."

"Brandy."

"Put a bottle on the table," said Bill Blarney, winking at the landlord. "Dick is the best fellow in the world when you know how to treat him properly."

"That's so," the landlord returned, as he

reached down a black bottle and dusted it with his handkerchief. "Where is your bosom friend and pal?"

"What, Phil Tricker?"

"That's the boy I mean."

"I left him following an old gentleman with more rings and jewellery than he can possibly want; but I expect him here soon."

Dick Sleuth grinned as he made this explanation, as if he had said something comical.

The landlord of the Bull in Top Boots and Bill Blarney laughed in compliment to the speech, and Dick Sleuth's hardened face softened a little.

"I hope Phil will bring some swag back with him," he said. "If not, I will go on the lay with him outside Vauxhall; but people are getting so precious mean now."

"That is to say they take care of themselves."

"Bah!" Dick Sleuth growled; "they are so awfully suspicious, and have their chairs carried into the gardens instead of calling for them outside."

"I think I can put you in the way of a good thing, Dick," Bill Blarney said. "What do you say to running away with as pretty a young lady as ever you set eyes on?"

"That sort of game isn't in my line; I never tried it," Dick Sleuth replied.

"But will you say 'No' if I tell you that there is money to be had for the mere asking?"

"It's money I want, and money I must have," Dick Sleuth replied.

"Then let us sit down and talk the matter over," Bill Blarney said.

He led the way to the room where the band usually met to share the plunder and discuss future plans.

Dick Sleuth did not wait for a corkscrew.

He knocked the neck off the bottle with a blow of his fist, and poured half the contents into a long glass.

"Your health!" he said, taking a gulp which would have choked an ordinary man.

"And yours, my brave Dick!" responded Bill Blarney, sipping his liquor carefully. "Don't spare the brandy. There is plenty more where that came from."

"Leave that to me," Dick Sleuth said, as he took another pull at the fiery liquid. "Ah! this is good stuff. It warms the cockles of a man's heart, and saves him the trouble of eating."

Bill Blarney was a heavy drinker at times, but he could not refrain from gazing at his companion in horror and astonishment, for the brandy went down Dick Sleuth's throat like water.

It did not make him gasp, but a strange unnatural light came into his eyes.

"I—I don't think you had better have any more just now," Blarney said. "I want you to go with me to the Queen's Head, Sadler's Wells, after midnight, and help me to bring away a gal I have my eye on."

"You? Ha! ha!"

"If you think that I can love, you are vastly mistaken," Bill Blarney said. "I, like you, want money, but I want more—revenge—sweet revenge on Spring-Heeled Jack!"

This remark had the effect of sobering Dick Sleuth a little.

He shook his head and beat his hard, horny knuckles upon the table as if this was a phase in the promised adventure which he did not expect r entirely agree with.

"I never met anyone I was afraid of yet," he said; "but don't you think that will be a rather dangerous experiment to attempt?"

"Nothing risk, nothing have," Bill Blarney remarked.

"Just so," said Dick Sleuth. "But Spring-Heeled Jack is not like an ordinary man—if indeed he be man at all. He is here, there, and everywhere at once. His feet have wings, and he comes and goes from place to place at will."

"Then you give up the girl?"

"I did not say so. What is the figure? That is the most important question."

"Five pounds down, and ten more as soon as we get the girl under the vaults of St. Matthew's Church."

"Why do you intend taking her there?" asked Dick.

"Because it is a place only known to even a few members of the band."

"It's an awful place—a horrible place," Dick Sleuth said, with staring eyes. "I shall never forget the night I passed there alone. I heard such sounds and saw such sights as would turn the blood of the boldest man to ice."

"All the better," Bill Blarney returned.

"But the girl will go mad," Dick Sleuth said, "and if she do she will be no use to herself or to—"

"Enough of this!" cried Bill Blarney, interrupting him. "If you won't help me I must find somebody who will. The question I put to you is simple enough. Yes or No? Answer it one way or the other, and then I shall know what course to decide upon."

Before Dick Sleuth could reply the door opened and Phil Tricker entered the room.

He had the appearance of a man who had seen better days, and his tall, commanding figure contrasted strangely with that of Dick Sleuth, whose height was not more than five feet.

Tricker was evidently an assumed name, and as he walked across the room his gait had the bearing of a gentleman.

"Well," said Dick Sleuth, "what have you brought back?"

"Nothing."

"Nothing?" repeated Dick Sleuth, angrily. "What do you mean by nothing?"

"Just what I say," Phil Tricker replied. "When I came up to the old man and looked him in the face he reminded me of somebody I had known years ago. My heart failed me and I turned away."

"You're a nice sort of chicken to have for a pal," Dick Sleuth growled. "How do you think we are going to get along without money?"

"I don't know, and I scarcely care," Tricker said.

Something like a sigh escaped his lips, and his hands twitched nervously as he placed them on his knees.

"You don't care!" Dick Sleuth growled. "We'll see about that, curse you!"

"Come! come!" Bill Blarney interposed. "Leave your quarrelling to some other time. Tricker is a little odd at times, but when he really means business there is no better man to be found in the Bull in Top Boots. Dick, will you help me to-night?"

"Yes."

"Then tell Phil what is to be done, and ask him to join us."

"No," Dick Sleuth exclaimed, furiously. "You

and I can do the trick very well by ourselves. Let the white-livered—"

"Hold!" cried Bill Blarney. "I won't have this sort of thing. We don't want to start with a fight, which might, perhaps, cause us to end with failure."

"Let him say what he likes," Phil Tricker said, snapping his fingers contemptuously. "All the hard words in the world will break no bone of mine. I want to know nothing of your plans, and, to tell you the truth, I am sick at heart of the horrible business carried on here."

"Listen to the repentant sinner!" cried Dick Sleuth, with a laugh that might have come from the throat of a bear. "Perhaps the next thing he thinks of will be to peach on us."

"Not I," Phil Tricker replied. "You wrong me there, but I wish to Heaven that I could get back to the country and live and die there."

Other men walked into the room, and it soon began to fill.

"Perhaps it is just as well that Tricker is not in the job," Dick Sleuth whispered to Bill Blarney. "When I first knew him he was as bold and desperate as the rest of us, but he has greatly changed. Sometimes I think that he must be going mad."

"It would be awkward if he did so and roared out a few things he had seen here."

"It would," asserted Dick Sleuth, screwing up his features. "Ha! There goes eleven. Hadn't we better make a start?"

"There is time, for we are not going on foot."

"How then?"

"I have arranged for a horse and cart."

"Well," said Dick Sleuth, "of course we shall want something to bring the gal away in, but there is another thing to be considered. How are you going to prevent her from screaming?"

"With some wrappers, which will muffle her cries effectually."

"Right you are," Dick Sleuth replied. "I like to know all particulars before I start."

They partook of another glass and then walked out into the open air.

It was a dark, gloomy night.

The wind had hushed its voice, and the almost motionless clouds hung pall-like and heavy over the City of London.

Grim and gaunt were the shadows that lurked in dark entries, and strange and uncouth the people who stole from them.

As may be imagined, many of these night-prowlers were out for no good purpose, but among them were the poverty-stricken and the homeless.

Wretched, shivering beings, clad in tattered rags, crept through the darkness, houseless, miserable, and starving.

Bill Blarney and Dick Sleuth were used to such scenes and paid no heed to them.

A little distance from the Bull in Top Boots was a yard guarded by two high gates.

Here Bill Blarney stopped and whistled softly.

The signal was returned in a similar manner, and then the gates opened slowly.

"All ready?" Bill Blarney asked.

"Yes," a voice replied.

"Then come out and let us get on the road."

A man, shrouded from head to heel in a long coat, brought a horse and cart from the yard, and Bill Blarney signified his approval by placing some silver in the man's hand.

"You had better come with us," Blarney said; "for it may take two of us to get the girl out of the house. You haven't forgotten to bring your own pistols, I suppose?"

"No."

"Then all's well. Jump up and we'll get away."

Leaving the three conspirators to travel on their way towards the Queen's Head, we will return to the inn and ascertain what is passing there.

Nothing more transpired to alarm Daisy Leigh and Constance Marfield, but neither of the girls forgot the repulsive face of the beggar-man who had appeared before them so suddenly.

Ralph Ashton did not return, and, as the evening grew apace, Constance became uneasy, and her pale face told what was passing in her mind.

"Don't be alarmed," Daisy said. "A hundred things may have kept him away."

"True," Constance replied; "but, on the other hand, a hundred things may have happened to him."

"Isn't that looking on the dark side of the picture?" Daisy said. "Come, let us banish these vague fears and try to be cheerful. Hark! I hear footsteps."

"They are not Ralph's," Constance said.

Just then came a knock at the door.

"Come in," Daisy said.

Jacob Butler put his head into the door.

"A note for you, miss," he said, looking rather oddly at Constance Marfield.

She sprang to her feet, and, taking the paper from his hand, read—

"*You may not see Ralph Ashton for a few hours, but he is perfectly safe. Fear nothing and be surprised at nothing.*

"SPRING-HEELED JACK."

"Where did you get this?" Constance demanded.

"I found it, miss."

"Where?"

"Nailed to the door of my room."

"How strange!" Constance said, glancing a second time at the writing. "Thank Heaven that Ralph is safe!"

"Yes," Daisy returned; "I say 'Amen' to that. Now, dear, it is time that we were in bed. Shall I come with you to your room and chat for a few minutes?"

"No, thank you," Constance replied. "You must be quite as tired as I am, so let us say good-night. Light slumbers and pleasant dreams, Daisy."

The girls parted, and Constance Marfield, having reached her room, sat down on a chair by the bedside.

She locked the door, and then examined the fastenings of the windows, though scarcely knowing why.

And yet a nameless, undefined terror was upon her, and she was so impressed that she was not alone in the apartment that she peeped nervously into the cupboards and shook the curtains to make sure that nobody was lurking behind them.

"How silly of me!" she said, trying to laugh at her own fears. "I am as bad as a servant-girl after reading a ghost story."

Walking up to the mirror, she began to undress and to fold her garments neatly.

The bed was a cumbrous piece of machinery, fitted with four tall, carved posts, heavy velvet curtains, but comfortable withal.

It was a bed to woo the drowsy god, and Constance had no sooner composed her limbs and placed her head on the soft, yielding pillows than she fell asleep.

The room was on the first floor, and close to the window was a small outhouse with a sloping roof.

Constance had not been asleep many minutes when a church clock in the neighbourhood struck the hour of midnight.

The sound of the bell disturbed Constance for a moment.

She opened her eyes, but closed them again, and her gentle breathing told that she slumbered again.

A quarter of an hour passed away, and then the dark form of a man stole across the garden.

He was quickly followed by another, and as they met, they stood whispering for some moments.

"Give me a leg up," said Dick Sleuth, pointing to the outhouse. "I suppose you are sure of the room?"

"As sure as you and I are standing here," Bill Blarney replied. "Steady! Mind how you go. The tiles are old and a few of them may be loose. It would be a pretty business if they gave way and you came down with a run."

"Trust to me," Dick Sleuth said, as he ascended to the roof. "Now throw me that wrapper and stand below. I'll drop the girl into your arms and you can make off with her."

"Yes—yes!" Bill Blarney said, impatiently; "but don't stand there talking."

Dick Sleuth took a fine steel instrument from his pocket, and placing it between his teeth he began to crawl along the roof.

One or twice he stopped to glance at Constance Marfield's window to listen.

All was as still and as quiet as the grave.

Little dreaming of what was about to happen, poor Constance Marfield slept soundly.

With noiseless movements Dick Sleuth crawled along, and then with a cat-like spring he reached the window.

Throwing the wrapper round his neck he went to work at once.

Inserting the steel instrument at the side of the window he pulled it sideways, and the fastening slid back with so faint a click that it did not wake Constance.

But now Dick Sleuth had the most difficult portion of his task to perform.

How was he to open the window without making a noise and arousing the sleeper?

The window was one of small diamond-shaped panes set in lead, and opened outwards.

Its hinges might be rusty and creak at the slightest touch.

But Dick Sleuth, having gone so far, was not the man to stand upon trifles.

Opening the window an inch or two, he hooked his fingers over the top, and pressing it downwards, held it fast.

In a few moments he was standing in the room.

His feet, encased in list slippers, made no noise whatever.

Swiftly and silently he moved towards the bed, and drawing the curtains, gazed at Constance.

She had changed her position, and was now sleeping with her head pillowed on her arm.

Dick Sleuth unwound the heavy wrapper from his neck and shoulders and folded it double.

Then with a quick movement he threw it over Constance, and pressed it down over her face.

Constance awoke and tried to cry out, but a heavy hand was upon her mouth, and an arm as strong as an iron band was about her waist.

As the poor girl felt herself lifted up, and apparently thrown over a man's shoulder, she gave herself up for lost.

Suddenly she felt herself fall, and then, as she was caught, a voice hissed in her ear—

"Keep quiet, or I will murder you!"

Constance could not have uttered any sound now if she had been ever so much inclined.

All her breath had left her body, and her heart beat so audibly that she thought it must burst.

"Heaven help me!" she thought; "for I cannot help myself. Into whose hands have I fallen? Oh! Ralph—Ralph! it was an evil hour when you left me to endure such an outrage as this."

Bill Blarney, keeping Constance's head well covered, bore her away, and placing her in the cart threw a number of thick rugs over her.

He held her down, but there was no need for such violence, for Constance was so bewildered and terror-stricken that she lay as still as if death had suddenly overtaken her.

The cart jolted on its way, Dick Sleuth running after it and climbing in behind.

"I think I have done my work well and deserve my money," he said, breathlessly.

"You have, old fellow," Bill Blarney replied, "and you'll find me as good as my word."

"Do you really intend taking the girl to the vaults under St. Matthew's Church?"

"Yes. Why not?"

"Will she not catch her death of cold?"

"I can't help that," Bill Blarney replied, brutally. "She shall have the rugs and wrappers, and must make the best use of them."

The church alluded to has long since been pulled down.

It stood on the Surrey side of the Thames—so close to it that the shadow of its tower was reflected upon the water—and commanded a full view of London-bridge.

It did not take long for the cart to reach the church.

It was in a dreadfully dilapidated state even then, and no services had been held for some time.

"Steady!" Bill Blarney said, as he leaped from the cart. "We must make sure that we are not being watched. If you see anybody peering about use your barkers, Dick."

"Right you are," Dick Sleuth replied. "It's all right—there's nobody about. Out with the girl!"

"I'll carry her," said Bill Blarney. "Here, take the key and open the vault. You'll find a lantern if you pass your hand in on the left-hand side."

This was but the work of a few moments.

"Give me air," Constance groaned; "I am dying."

Bill Blarney removed the wrapper from the girl's face, and then a wild and piteous cry burst from her lips.

"Ralph, Ralph!" she shrieked. "Oh! come to my aid! Help, help!"

"Curse you!" said Bill Blarney. "Is this how you repay my kindness? Hold your tongue!"

But Constance redoubled her cries for help, and Blarney, brute and hound that he was, struck the girl's up-turned face with his fist.

With a bitter moan of agony she sank back in his arms and lay as still as death.

Blarney bore Constance to the mouth of the vault, and pointed to a flight of stairs.

"Down you go!" he said. "Quick, or I will hurry your movements with the butt-end of this pistol."

Constance knew that to disobey was to meet certain death.

"Have you no mercy?" she said, turning to him. "What wrong have I ever done you? For Heaven's sake let me go!"

"Down—down!" was all Bill Blarney could say.

Constance made no further appeal, but de scended the steps.

She almost fainted as the trap-door fell with a crash a few inches from her head; and, as she heard the key turn in the lock, she wrung her hands, and hot, scalding tears filled her eyes.

Bill Blarney had flung down some of the rugs after her, and collecting them, she wrapped them round her shivering form.

How cold, dark, damp, and horrible!

A dreadful smell pervaded the place, and Constance had to put great control upon herself to keep herself from going mad.

She shrank back when she thought that she was alone with the dead.

She dared not stretch out her hand for fear of touching some mouldering coffin; and at last she sank down upon the floor and gave herself up to despair.

Exulting in the capture of Constance Marfield, Bill Blarney and Dick Sleuth took themselves back to the Bull in Top Boots.

The house was open night and day for the convenience of its light-fingered customers, and the rascals, who had accomplished their villainous designs, called for more brandy and proceeded to pass the night in revelry.

But at last they tired of drinking and singing, and Dick Sleuth, finding that Bill Blarney had dropped his head upon the table and was snoring like a grampus, took himself away to his lodgings which were hard by.

Presently Bill Blarney felt a touch on the nape of the neck and opened his eyes.

They were heavy and bloodshot with drink, and for some moments he could not distinguish anything with clearness.

At last he fancied he saw something like a huge bird crouching in a corner of the room.

The figure moved and stood erect.

Bill Blarney remained speechless with terror when he saw Spring-Heeled Jack towering over him.

"Villain! unmitigated villain!" Spring-Heeled Jack said, in a deep, stern voice. "What have you to say for yourself? What excuse can you make for this night's work?"

Bill Blarney tried to speak, but his tongue clove to the roof of his mouth, and his teeth chattered in his head.

"Speak, I command you!" hissed Spring-Heeled Jack, "or this moment shall be your last."

"How did you get here?" Blarney contrived to articulate. "Who betrayed me? Who let you in?"

"That is my business and not yours," said Spring-Heeled Jack. "Let it suffice for you to know that every movement on your part was watched. Come, scoundrel that you are! I have determined to teach you a lesson such as you will never forget."

As he twined his long muscular arms around Bill Blarney the ruffian gave a gasping cry for help.

Spring-Heeled Jack silenced him with a blow between the eyes, and the room seemed filled with stars and jagged streaks of light.

"This is some of your own treatment," Spring-Heeled Jack said in his ear. "Poor, pitiful fool to think of thwarting Spring-Heeled Jack! I could have stopped that infernal cart a dozen times but I thought I would let you run to the end of your tether."

It struck Bill Blarney as Spring-Heeled Jack tossed him into the air and whirled him about until he was giddy that he had run a little bit over his tether.

Suddenly Spring-Heeled Jack stood him on his feet and glared into his face.

"Where is the girl—where is Constance Marfield?" he demanded. "Tell me what you have done with her!"

"I thought you knew all about her?" Bill Blarney stammered.

"Never mind what you think. Answer my question, you cowardly dog!"

"I don't know."

"Villain! you lie."

As he spoke he seized Blarney by the throat and forced him backwards.

"Help! mercy! help!" Blarney shrieked.

A door opened and footsteps approached.

"Ha! ha!" laughed Spring-Heeled Jack. "He who can catch me must be a clever man."

Raising Bill Blarney in his arms, the weird creature kicked against one of the panels in the wall.

It flew back, and Spring-Heeled Jack, carrying his burden as easily as if he had a child in his arms, darted through.

Click went the panel as it ran back into its place.

A passer-by in the street beheld a strange sight.

Something flew over his head and went bounding along with gigantic strides, now on the ground and sometimes in the air.

The man raised a cry of alarm and the inmates of the Bull in Top Boots, armed with all sorts of weapons, rushed into the street.

Too late!

Spring-Heeled Jack was away with his prisoner and had reached St. Matthew's Church while the bewildered miscreants at the inn were asking each other questions.

One of the church windows were open, and Spring-Heeled Jack, never relaxing his hold on Bill Blarney, sprang through.

Then Bill Blarney found himself lying flat upon his back on the cold stone flags.

"If your intention is to kill me," he gasped, "do so quickly, and put me out of pain."

"Kill you—yes!" Spring-Heeled Jack replied; "but why should I put you out of pain—you who scruple not to torture others? I will play with you as a cat plays with a mouse. You shall know what it is to feel agony of mind and body, and then—"

"Mercy!" Bill Blarney groaned. "I will tell you where Constance Marfield is. She—"

"Silence!" Spring-Heeled Jack interposed. If I did not know I could soon force the truth from your craven throat! Villain, I have a surprise for you. You shall see how London looks by night from the top of the church tower!"

"No—no!" Bill Blarney yelled.

He now saw through Spring-Heeled Jack's designs, and grovelled on the ground like a whipped cur.

"Anything but that!" he pleaded. "Spare me such torture as you hope to be forgiven your sins! Let me live a few more hours! You had mercy on me once!"

"And this," said Spring-Heeled Jack, planting his foot on the panting ruffian's breast, "this is your gratitude?"

"Give me one more chance," the wretch pleaded—"one—one!"

Spring-Heeled Jack laughed aloud, and dragging Bill Blarney after him, ascended the stairs of the tower.

That was an awful journey.

As Bill Blarney swung from side to side he was bruised and beaten almost out of his five senses.

He cursed, raved, prayed, and begged most piteously.

But all in vain.

The blood of his strange captor was up, and he paid no heed to any word uttered.

Bill Blarney closed his eyes when Spring-Heeled Jack stopped at last.

Cool, fresh air was blowing on his face and he felt revived.

He knew that he was on the top of the church tower, and that between him and the earth there was a space of fully a hundred feet.

What would happen next?

He dare not think or conjecture on his impending fate.

He felt his hair bristle and his blood run deadly cold.

At last Bill Blarney opened his eyes and saw that Spring-Heeled Jack was sitting down with his legs crossed and his hands on his hips.

"Poor fool!" Spring-Heeled Jack said. "You have brought this upon yourself. If you have anything to say, say it now."

"Is this to be my last hour?"

Spring-Heeled Jack leaned over the crumbling but still massive masonry and pointed downwards.

"Yes," he replied. "In a few minutes you will be lying crushed and mangled beyond recognition."

"Listen!" Blarney said, under his breath. "You will wrong yourself by destroying me. It will do no good."

"It will rid the world of a villain."

"Granted that I am all that you say," Bill Blarney continued; "there are others as bad, and if not worse. Sir Roland is your enemy. Spare me, and I will betray him to you."

Spring-Heeled Jack laughed again, and so loud that the air caught up the sound and rolled it away like rumbling thunder.

"So you think to bribe me?" he said. "No, no; I hold Sir Roland in my power, and can deal with him as I wish. You must die! If you wish to breathe a prayer or to make a confession I will give you five minutes to do so, but no more."

"Only five minutes?"

"Not a moment longer."

A sudden thought dawned into Bill Blarney's mind.

There was hope in it, though a faint one, but he clung to it as a drowning man clings to floating straws.

If he could but get a hold of Spring-Heeled Jack he would sell his life dearly.

"I thank you even for those minutes," he said, trying to look very repentant. "I have much to say and much to think of."

As he spoke he moved a little nearer to Spring-Heeled Jack and made a sudden grasp at him.

But Spring-Heeled Jack was on his guard.

He struck up Bill Blarney's wrist, and leaping to his feet, raised the ruffian aloft in his arms.

"Mercy! Oh! horror! Mercy!"

Spring-Heeled Jack brought him down with a thud upon the masonry.

"Die, dog—die!" he said. "Your last moment has come."

Bill Blarney struggled faintly; a gurgling cry of agony came from his throat, and he fell.

Down—down—down!

Spring-Heeled Jack turned his head aside and trembled.

The sight was too awful even for him.

Presently he heard a thud. All was over!

. . . . .

Constance Marfield had not moved.

She sat thinking and wondering whether her abductors would bring her food, or whether they had determined that she should die the fearful death of thirst and starvation.

What had she done to the villain that he should kidnap her just when her heart was filled with joy at seeing Ralph Ashton again?

She asked herself this question a thousand times, but could find no satisfactory answer to it.

"Oh! Ralph—Ralph," she moaned, "what will be your feelings when you return to the Queen's Head and find that I am no longer there? Oh! Daisy—pretty Daisy!—would that I had never left you for a single moment."

The darkness and horror of the vault were almost insupportable, and she passed her hand to her eyes and brow, thinking that she must be mad.

"Great Heaven!" she cried, "give me strength to bear this. Keep the balance of my brain clear and even. There must be some mistake; this dreadful man will find it out soon and set me free."

Suddenly she heard a sound proceeding from the top of the vault.

She strained her ears to listen, and her heart gave a great bound.

"Who's there? she called out.

"Your friend!" was the reply.

And Spring-Heeled Jack came leaping down the staircase.

"Heaven be praised for this!" Constance cried, joyously. "Oh! how can I thank you? How did you know that I was here?"

"It matters not, fair lady," he replied. "I came hither to save you, and here I am. I am aware that the scoundrels dragged you from your warm bed and so I have brought this cloak to protect you from the cold."

As he spoke he handed a long, handsome cloak to Constance.

It was richly lined with fur, and Constance was so grateful for it, that she could have thanked Spring-Heeled Jack on her knees.

She was advancing towards the steps when Spring-Heeled Jack confronted her and waved his hands before her face

Thrice he did so, and then Constance felt that she was sinking through the floor, and lost consciousness.

The song of birds and a flood of sunlight awoke her.

She was in bed, and in the room at the Queen's Head, too.

"Marvel of marvels!" she said, sitting up and rubbing her eyes. "What can this mean?"

She glanced keenly round the room, scarcely believing that anything she saw could be real.

"Have I been dreaming, then?" she said. "It is impossible. But how comes it that I am here?"

The curtains near her bed were open, and she glanced at the window.

It was fastened, and everything remained as she had left it overnight.

But suddenly her eyes fell upon a deep blue velvet cloak, lined with sable.

Constance Marfield started and turned pale.

"It was no dream," she said. "Spring-Heeled Jack rescued me from that horrible vault, and brought me here in some mysterious manner only known to himself."

Tap—tap—tap!

Somebody was knocking at the door.

"Who is there?" Constance demanded.

"Daisy Leigh!"

"Wait a moment, dear, and I will get up and let you in."

As Daisy ran into the room Constance clasped her round the neck.

"Oh! I have such strange things to tell you," she said; "sit down, and I will tell you as I dress."

Daisy Leigh opened her beautiful eyes wide as Constance narrated her wonderful adventures, and kept silence until she had finished.

"You take my breath away," she then said. "If I had not heard the story from your own lips I should have laughed at it as an idle one."

"Has Ralph Ashton returned?" Constance asked.

"Not that I am aware of," Daisy replied.

"I wish he had," Constance sighed, "I long to tell him what I have passed through. I wonder what can keep him abroad so long!"

## CHAPTER LII.

THE PRISONERS IN THE WELL—THE STORM—THE THUNDERBOLT—FALL OF THE HOUSE IN THE OLD MINT.

It was some time before Catchpole and Grabham could fully realise their position.

They stood and rubbed their bumped heads in fear and amazement, but at last the bitter truth dawned upon them in all its earnestness.

They were in a trap and there was no way out of it.

In spite of his rage Sir Roland Ashton never lost nerve.

He groped his way to the door and passed his hands over it.

There was no handle nor lock, so far as he could ascertain.

As he turned away, with a horrible oath on his lips, something chinked under his feet.

It was gold, but the sound was no longer music to his ears.

"Curse the demon!" he said. "Why does he not meet me openly? By all the fiends my sword should give a good account of itself."

"I s'pose we shall be let out of this crib soon," Catchpole whined. "No man with a heart in him could leave us to die here. It must be a lark."

"A lark be jiggered!" Grabham gasped. "There are three of us, and we must get the door open somehow, or we shall perish."

The place was so pitch dark that they could not see each other, but there was much comfort in talking.

Catchpole sat down, and hugging his knees rocked himself to and fro.

He began to babble and prate like a child, and talk of the scenes he had passed through.

"Hold that row!" Sir Roland said. "What the devil is the good of snivelling? Peace, or I will shatter your skull!"

"That's it," Catchpole moaned, "kick me while I am down. I am only a poor old sinner. I have always stood in my own light, or I should have held a good position before now. Sir Roland, you got us into this mess and you will have to get us out of it."

Sir Roland bit his lips in his rage, and paced the dismal place to and fro.

"Get you out of it!" he said. "I wish I could—and into the well."

"Hear him?" Catchpole returned. "He isn't satisfied with being the cause of all this misery, but would like to kill us into the bargain."

Just then a startled cry came from Grabham.

"What now?" Sir Roland demanded.

"There is a fourth party here," Grabham said, under his breath. I touched a face, and it was as cold as death."

"It is just possible that you have come across the dead body of Gedge Foote," Sir Roland said.

"Ugh!" cried Grabham, recoiling. "This is too horrible!"

Catchpole wriggled himself across the floor amid the damp and scattered gold, until he came in contact with Sir Roland.

The baronet struck furiously at the constable, but missed him.

He then drew a pistol, with the intention of putting Catchpole out of the world, when an unseen hand struck his arm up, and the weapon exploded harmlessly in the air.

"Coward!" hissed a voice in his ear, "coward to attempt to murder the miserable wretch you have lured here!"

Sir Roland turned his head sharply, and saw that Spring-Heeled Jack was looking over his shoulder.

"How now?" said the baronet. "Do you come here to taunt me?"

"No; I come to grant your wish," Spring-Heeled Jack said.

"I do not understand you."

"Think of the words you uttered just now," Spring-Heeled Jack replied. "Think of your boast. You wish to meet me openly—to try conclusions man to man. Your desire shall be gratified. The door is open, ascend to the cellar. I will follow you."

Grabham and Catchpole made a movement towards the opening, but Spring-Heeled Jack barred the way with his arms.

"Back!" he cried. "Do not attempt to leave. Your time will come quite soon enough."

"We are done for," Catchpole said, as the door closed with a bang.

"I don't think so," Grabham replied. "At the worst I don't think we shall get more than a kicking. Hark! there is a nice rumpus going on overhead."

As Sir Roland climbed hand-over-hand up the rope Spring-Heeled Jack followed him so closely that escape was impossible.

A lamp was hanging from the roof of the cellar, and shed its light upon the foes as they stood face to face.

Spring-Heeled Jack drew a rapier as lithe as a whip.

He bent it in his hands so that the point touched the hilt, and then let it spring out towards the baronet.

"Sir Roland," he said, "you wear a sword. Draw it, and defend yourself."

"You will fight me fairly?"

"Yes."

As Spring-Heeled Jack spoke there came a crash, and the old house was filled with rumbling echoes.

"Is this some new trick of yours to frighten me?" Sir Roland asked, glancing upwards.

"No," Spring-Heeled Jack replied. "A fearful storm is rolling overhead. Heaven is pouring down its wrath upon this wicked city."

Again the booming thunder shook the ruinous old tenement, and its very foundation trembled.

"Come, Sir Roland," Spring-Heeled Jack said. "You were all impatience just now. We need pay no heed to the storm down here, for the lightning, be it ever so blinding, cannot reach us."

"We are not on equal terms," Sir Roland said. "I must remove my coat. I suppose you will not take a mean advantage of me as I do so?"

"You measure my corn by your own bushel," said Sprind-Heeled Jack. "How often have I had the chance to end your wicked life and as often turned my hand aside, thinking that the hour must come when you would see the error of your ways? But enough! We meet at last. This world is too small to hold us both."

Sir Roland threw aside his coat and rolled up his shirt-sleeves to his shoulders.

He then drew his sword and advanced slowly upon Spring-Heeled Jack.

"You will do well to make your peace before we cross swords," Spring-Heeled Jack said, "for I shall kill you."

"You are too confident," Sir Roland replied. "The chances are on my side, unless you wear armour."

"I wear nothing of the kind," Spring-Heeled Jack said; "and base as you are, I would scorn to lend myself to unfairness. You are suspicious, Sir Roland, because you have acted the part of a villain so often."

"Then here's at you!" cried Sir Roland. "Living I have hated and detested you, and if the arch-fiend to whom you belong does not protect you, you shall die!"

He attacked Spring-Heeled Jack with such ferocity that sparks glinted from the rapier.

"Ha! ha!" laughed Spring-Heeled Jack. "Think not to break down my guard in that way. I see that I must give you a lesson in coolness."

"Devil that you are!" Sir Roland hissed, "I will rid the world of you!"

But to the baronet's astonishment his rapier went whirling up to the ceiling.

"Try again," said Spring-Heeled Jack. "Again you see I have your life in my hands. But I will not take it yet. I have promised myself this meeting for a long time, and I will enjoy it until I grow tired."

Sir Roland Ashton's face fell.

He confessed to himself that he had met more than his match, and as he took his sword again in his hand his face was pallid with fear and chagrin.

Meanwhile the thunder was cracking fearfully and the house rocked under the terrible force of the storm.

"I am in no hurry, unless you are," Spring-Heeled Jack said, sneeringly, as he saw that Sir Roland stood hesitating. "Will you attack or shall I? Do your best or worst all is over with you, and this night you shall be sent to answer for your long list of crimes."

As Spring-Heeled Jack finished speaking there came a fearful crash, like the springing of a mine.

Timber, brickwork, and masonry reeled and tottered.

"The saints preserve us!" Sir Roland shrieked. "The house is falling!"

Stunned by the awful visitation, he recoiled on his heels towards the wall, and as he did so he saw Spring-Heeled Jack vanish down the well.

Sir Roland crouched down and shrieked with terror as the walls fell like a house of cards.

The noise was deafening.

Crash succeeded crash.

Huge beams of wood, mingling with blocks of stone and jagged masses of brickwork, came thundering down in wild confusion.

Was it possible that a human being could escape being crushed under the *débris*?

Up to the present Sir Roland Ashton remained unscathed, for the terrible shower of death-dealing missiles had taken a slanting direction.

But the house was doomed.

It broke away piecemeal, as if a thousand men were at work upon it with pickaxes.

It was the dwelling of the wicked, the house of bloodshed and crime, and not one stone would remain upon another.

A thunderbolt had struck the roof, and the chimneys, crashing through, carried everything before them.

Sir Roland crouched closer and still closer to the projecting wall.

Presently he felt it moving and settling down upon him.

Then, with a cry scarcely human, he sprang to his feet and flung up his arms.

There was no hope of escape now.

The last ray fled from his heart as he cast his eyes upward and saw the massive wall parting and bulging out towards him.

The well was so blocked up with rubbish that he could not reach it, and Sir Roland, pressing his open hands upon his head as if to lessen the pang of the death-blow, swooned away and fell prone and senseless upon the floor.

## CHAPTER LIII.

### WHAT THE BARGEMEN FOUND.

DAY had scarcely dawned when Dick Sleuth made his way to the Bull in Top Boots.

Men who drink heavily overnight are very thirsty in the morning, and Dick Sleuth was no exception to the rule.

His tongue was parched and cracked, and his hands shook as if smitten with the palsy.

He was a horrible sight to gaze upon, and men on their way to honest labour shrunk out of his path and regarded him with loathing.

# SPRING-HEELED JACK,

## THE TERROR OF LONDON.

LOCKED IN A FIERCE EMBRACE THEY WENT HEADLONG OVER THE CLIFF.

No. 18.

"If you want to save my life, give me something to drink," he said to the landlord as he entered the inn. "I am as dry as a limekiln and as hot as a furnace."

"You look like it," the landlord replied. "I should think you poured a couple of pints of brandy down your throat last night!"

"And I feel equal to the task this morning," Dick Sleuth said, grinning. "Where's Bill Blarney?"

The landlord gazed at him in surprise.

"I forgot that you went away before he vanished."

"Vanished!"

"Yes—vanished like a ghost, and goodness only knows where he went to."

Dick Sleuth passed his fingers through his unkempt hair.

"I never was a good hand at guessing riddles," he said, "so perhaps you will tell me what you mean?"

"I mean exactly what I say," the landlord replied. "I looked into the back room about three o'clock and Bill Blarney was fast asleep. About a quarter of an hour after I heard his voice shouting for help, and when I ran back to the room he had gone."

"That's curious, to say the least."

"Curious! It is most mysterious and aggravating."

"Perhaps he dreamt that somebody was after him, and went—"

"Went where?" the landlord interposed. "The window is screwed down, and he couldn't fly up the chimney very well."

"That idea is against all common sense,'" Dick Sleuth said. "I see by your face that you have something else to tell me?"

"Well," said the landlord. "A fellow in the street created a disturbance, and swore that he saw the devil flying away with a man."

Dick Sleuth smote his forehead.

"I have it!" he cried, "Spring-Heeled Jack has got Bill Blarney!"

. . . . . . . .

For a short time we must turn aside from Sir Roland and give some attention to the man who had shared a portion of his career in crime.

This was Bill Blarney, hurled from the top of the church tower by Spring-Heeled Jack.

Down—down went the villain, yet strange to say he never lost his senses.

This made his punishment all the more horrible, and though the descent was but the work of a moment Bill Blarney seemed to pass through an age of horror.

In that one brief instant a thousand thoughts crowded into his mind as the earth seemed to leap up to meet him, and then came the crash.

A bargeman dragging laboriously at his long sweeping oars heard the thud and looked along the river bank.

At first he saw nothing, and thinking that some person had thrown something heavy from a window into the river he whistled and went on with his work.

Suddenly he rested on his oars and shaded his eyes with his hand.

He was looking at a queer-looking object sticking in the mud.

At first he could make nothing of it.

But whatever the thing was it was endowed with life, and the bargeman, filled with curiosity, pulled nearer to the bank.

"Why, dash it all!" he cried, suddenly, "it's a man sticking in the mud! I say, old fellow, how did you get there?"

This was rather an idle question to ask for several reasons, the principal one being that Bill Blarney having had all the wind knocked out of his body, and being shoulder-high in the thick, slimy mud, was not capable of going into any particulars.

"Well," said the bargeman, running his fingers through his hair, "I've seen a few funny things on land and water, but this beats the lot. I suppose I must have him out, dead or alive, or the tide will soon be over him."

The bargeman moored the lumbering craft he had been tugging at to a post, and, pitching a plank upon the mud, stepped gingerly along it, and took a critical survey of Bill Blarney's mud-bespattered features.

"The more I look at him the more I'm puzzled," he said. "Well, at any rate he looks like a dead 'un, and I suppose I shall get a trifle for his body."

But just then Bill Blarney put all such notions to flight by opening his eyes and glaring vacantly about him.

The villain's protruding eyes, and the dim baneful light that shone from them, startled the bargeman.

He was running to get on board his vessel when Bill Blarney called to him.

"Don't leave me here," he said, feebly, as he thrust one arm out of the mud. "Lend me a helping hand and I will pay you well."

But the bargeman did not seem to care to have anything to do with the job.

He kept at a respectable distance, as if convinced that there was something uncanny about Bill Blarney, and that he might be doing the world a good turn by knocking him on the head.

"Now, then," said Bill Blarney, "if you want to earn a guinea, you can do so by pulling me out and giving me a ride down the river."

"Wait a minute," the bargeman replied; "the first thing I should like to know is how you got there at all?"

Bill Blarney pointed to the church tower.

"Fell off?" queried the bargeman.

Blarney nodded his head.

"Well, then," said the bargeman, shuddering, "you have had a mighty narrow escape, that's all I can say. What a lucky thing for you that you didn't pitch on your head!"

"I shall think it a luckier thing when I am out of this altogether," Blarney growled, as he began to struggle frantically. "How would you like to be in such a position, you dunder-headed idiot?"

"Come—come," said the bargeman, "hard words will do no good. Here's my hand and you are welcome to it without payment."

As Bill Blarney crawled on to the plank he cast a furtive glance at the church tower and shook his fist.

"What are you up to now?" the bargeman asked.

"Nothing — nothing!" Blarney returned, hastily. "Let us get on board and pull away. What an escape I have had! You may land me at the next flight of stairs if you choose."

The bargeman was not loth to do this, as he did not like Bill Blarney's company and was glad to get rid of him.

Blarney tossed the man a guinea, but it was tossed back again.

"What!" cried the ruffian, "are you too proud to accept money?"

"No," replied the bargeman; "I am as poor as most people, but I would rather go without anything from you."

"Why?"

"Because you don't look as if you came honestly by it."

"Fool!" said Bill Blarney, as he went up the stone steps, "I should have thought that honesty or dishonesty made but very little difference to you."

The bargeman stared after the villain until he lost sight of him, and then he, returning to his work, meditated on the strangeness of the adventure.

Meanwhile Bill Blarney made his way towards the Bull in Top Boots.

He was stiff, sore, and aching in every limb, and his mud-covered clothes impeded his progress, so that he could scarcely drag one leg before the other.

People stared at him as he passed and made room for him.

Bill Blarney was certainly a queer-looking object, but he cared nothing for the eyes directed at him, or the remarks that passed from mouth to mouth.

At last he reached the Bull in Top Boots in a state of almost utter prostration.

Staggering into the house he fell upon his face, and the landlord could do nothing but stare at him in surprise.

"Dick Sleuth—Dick Sleuth!" he shouted.

The man came running up.

"What now?" he asked. "I thought by the sound of your voice that all the runners from Bow-street were round the house. Hullo! Who's this?"

"Lift his head and see for yourself."

"Bill Blarney! as I am a sinner," Dick Sleuth cried. "Pour some brandy down his throat. Something very odd must have happened to bring him back here in this state."

"So I should think," the landlord assented. "Pah! How his clothes smell! He has had enough of Thames mud to last him a lifetime."

Just then Bill Blarney rolled himself over on his side and groaned.

"No—no!" he gasped, "any death but that. Mercy—Mercy! Don't hurl me from the church tower."

"Hear that?" said Dick Sleuth, with an oath. "It strikes me very forcibly that poor Bill has had a very lively time of it."

"Spring-Heeled Jack must have had a hand in this business," the landlord said, shuddering.

The mention of that awful name acted as a restorative on Bill Blarney.

He opened his eyes and glared at those who were stooping over him.

"So," he murmured, "it was only a bad dream after all."

"Dream be hanged!" said Dick Sleuth. "You don't dream yourself wet through, battered like a mummy, and smothered with mud. What on earth have you been doing with yourself?"

Bill Blarney trembled from head to foot.

"Put me to bed," he said, "and I will tell you all about it. Don't leave me. Watch over me. Don't leave me for a moment."

"What do you fear?"

"Spring-Heeled Jack," Bill Blarney replied. "Ugh! shall I ever forget that fall?"

## CHAPTER LIV.

### JACOB BUTLER TAKES A WALK TO HAMPSTEAD HEATH AND FALLS IN WITH AN OLD ACQUAINTANCE.

THE series of passing events was more than sufficient to upset a man constituted like Jacob Butler.

His notions were hazy and he went about like a man in a dream.

Constance Marfield and Daisy Leigh seldom saw anything of him, for Jacob, when not asleep, resorted to the public portion of the town, and drank himself into a state bordering upon idiotcy.

It was during one of these bouts, when his head was throbbing with a splitting headache, that he wandered out of doors.

He was in that condition that he cared not where he went as long as he was out of the way of everybody, and chance took his wandering, erratic footsteps towards Hampstead Heath.

It was getting towards evening when Jacob Butler started on his journey.

"What a fool I am to carry on in this way!" he moaned, as he pressed his hands to his burning temples. "The landlord said I was to have what I liked, but I'll be hanged if it likes me. Ah! how beautiful and pure the air is! Curse the brandy! I wish every drop in the kingdom was turned into the sea."

When Jacob reached the heath he stood on the hill where the stately and ancient fir trees have reared their heads for twice a hundred years and looked in the direction of London.

The sun was going down like a huge ball of burnished copper, and as it sank behind a bank of purple clouds sailing up from the west the sound of distant thunder boomed through the air.

Our readers will remember that Jacob Butler had an innate horror of thunderstorms.

They filled him with a nameless terror even when under shelter.

"Bless my heart!" he gasped, "what am I to do?"

There was not a house of any description in sight, and the clouds were coming up too quickly to admit of him heading the storm and getting back to Sadler's Wells before it burst.

But there was one thing that Jacob Butler did not intend to do, and that was to remain under the trees and stand a chance of being struck by the electric fluid.

A second clap of thunder started him off like a rabbit that hears the sound of the sportsman's gun.

He tore madly down the slope, and taking the wrong road ran on towards Hendon.

It was a wild and desolate part in those days.

Dark woodlands flanked the rough roads, and farmers travelling that way took good care to keep their powder dry, for desperadoes lurked with evil intent under the overhanging trees.

Jacob Butler had no thought of being topped and robbed.

He had no money to speak of that he could call his own, but he dreaded the quivering lightning and booming thunder.

Onward he went, groaning, foaming, and perspiring.

Oh! for a house, or even a hut, where he could creep in until the storm had passed over.

Suddenly Jacob saw exactly what he desired.

It was a tumble-down, ramshackle sort of a building, standing in the middle of a field, and the belated fugitive made for it with hot haste.

Without stopping to knock at the door, or to ask whether his presence would be welcome or otherwise, he dashed in and found himself in profound darkness.

The hole in the wall serving for a window was blocked up with furze and bramble, but as Jacob's eyes became somewhat accustomed to the gloom he saw a few faggots smoking and smouldering in a corner.

"Is there anybody at home?" he asked, in weak, quavering accents. "I'm very sorry to come in so sudden, but there's a precious storm brewing."

No reply was vouchsafed to his remarks, and he, approaching the fire, crouched down before it.

There was no vestige of furniture in the place, and Jacob Butler had concluded that it was used by a shepherd as a watch-house at night when the door opened and somebody hobbled in.

At that moment a broad flash of lightning filled the hut with a lurid glare, and simultaneously a shriek of discovery came from Jacob Butler's lips.

Standing with her back to the doorway, and leaning on a gnarled stick torn roughly from a tree, was Mrs. Corcoran.

She looked so horrible and witch-like that Jacob Butler never for a moment believed her to be alive, and as she stalked with a gliding motion, horrible in itself, across the floor, the wretched man drew his knees up to his chin.

He thrust out his hands to ward off the old woman, but onward she came, and Jacob was soon made acquainted with the fact that there was nothing ghost-like about her.

Raising the stick with her skinny arms, she gave Jacob Butler the full benefit of it.

"Ho! ho!" she laughed, as he rolled on his back. "So we meet again, Jacob dear!"

Mrs. Corcoran's miserable victim was in no mood to reply.

His head had ached sufficiently beforehand, and now that he was treated to a vision of thousands of dancing stars he was not quite sure whether he was dead or alive.

"You thought that I was dead, did you?" said Mrs. Corcoran, with fiendish glee. "Ho! ho! You thought you had got rid of me for ever!"

"I never thought anything of the kind," Jacob replied, feebly. "I knew you would come back to me like a—a—a—"

"Like a what, deary?" Mrs. Corcoran queried, keeping the stick waving about a few inches over Jacob's cranium.

Mr. Jacob Butler was going to say like a devil, but he instituted the word angel, and tried to look as if he meant it.

"That's right, lovey," she said, making so hideous a grimace at him that he turned cold. "I am an angel—your angel, Jacob."

"Ugh!" Jacob ejaculated, rubbing his head.

"You won't rub that off in a hurry," Mrs. Corcoran said; "and if you are not careful I will give you another to keep it company."

"Don't!" Jacob pleaded—"don't! I'm confused and bumped enough already."

Mrs. Corcoran sat down, and, hugging her knees with her arms, rocked herself to and fro.

"I suppose you know that Lilac Lodge is burnt down?" she said.

"No!" Jacob replied, in astonishment. "Who set fire to it?"

Mrs. Corcoran pointed at him with a bony finger furnished with a hawk-like talon.

"You don't?" said she. "Then I will tell you the story. Listen!"

Jacob Butler crept up against the wall and leaned his aching head against it.

"Sir Roland stabbed me and left me for dead," Mrs. Corcoran continued; "then the coward set fire to the place, thinking that the flames would scatter my ashes to the winds."

"That was very wrong of him," Jacob Butler said.

"Do you really think so?"

"Ye—e—s."

"Then I don't believe you," said Mrs. Corcoran, grinning. "You'd give half your lifetime to know that I was buried twenty feet under the ground."

"Have it your own way," said Jacob, despairingly. "You are like the rest of women, and would have the last word if it choked you."

"What a dear, lovely dovey you are!" said Mrs. Corcoran, grinning more hideously than ever.

"Thank 'ee," Jacob replied, with the air of a man who has accidentally swallowed a tooth. "Never mind me. You were talking about Sir Roland and Lilac Lodge."

"So I was, my rose," Mrs. Corcoran replied. "Sir Roland's act saved my life. When the base coward stabbed me he set fire to the furniture, and it was the heat that brought me round."

"Oh!" said Jacob, thinking that he got a whiff of sulphur at that very moment. "I suppose that sort of thing agrees with you."

Mrs. Corcoran knew what he meant, and filled the hut with mocking laughter.

"At any rate, it saved my life," she said. "There is not much blood in my veins, so little could flow, and I dragged myself to the window. Ho—ho! how the flames chased me!"

"I wish they had caught you," Jacob muttered under his breath.

"But I cheated them," Mrs. Corcoran continued, "and when I stood free I hastened away, taking an oath, which I mean to keep."

"You always were a woman of your word."

"I swore to find you if you were above the earth, and never part with you again."

Jacob Butler's face fell, and he would have taken it as a compliment if the earth had opened and swallowed him up.

"And I swore to hound Sir Roland down and bring him upon his knees before me," Mrs. Corcoran continued.

"I have no doubt you will do it," said Jacob.

He found that he was in a trap, and, acting on the peace-at-any-price principle, tried to make himself agreeable.

"It is part of my plan to let Sir Roland believe that I am dead," Mrs. Corcoran said.

"What for?"

"To make the revenge I mean to take on him all the more sweet."

She looked so unearthly and devilish as she spoke that Jacob screwed his head into the mud-wall and groaned.

"And now, Jacob deary," said Mrs. Corcoran, "you must make up your mind to live a happy life with me. This is my place, and I am sure you will be able to make yourself comfortable in it."

"It might be a little—to put it mildly—a little better furnished," Jacob said. "But—but, I say, we ain't married, you know, and so you see it wouldn't be right for me to stay here."

Mrs. Corcoran became convulsed with laughter.

"Addle-pated fool!" she said, digging him in the ribs with the stick, "that is a matter which can be managed before another day is gone. Don't run away with the notion that I shall let you go out of my sight for a moment."

"But you must—hang it! you must," Jacob gasped.

"We shall see," said Mrs. Corcoran. "Jacob, come over here and kiss me."

Jocob Butler looked as if he could have bitten her, but he did as he was told, and looked as if he had feasted on early gooseberries.

"Now put your arm round my waist and tell me that you love me," said the hag.

"I can't," Jacob gasped. "I can't, I tell you—I can't. It's against human nature. Why do you torture me?"

"Because I know that you hate me," said Mrs. Corcoran.

"Before you came in my way," Jacob cried, wildly, "I was neither a coward nor a fool. But now I am both, and I feel that I am going mad. Hang it! I'll stand this no longer, for what are you but a woman after all, and an old and ugly one into the bargain."

Mrs. Corcoran smiled as she gave Jacob a side-long glance.

"Deary!" she said, "I suppose you don't want to be hung, do you?"

"Of course I don't. Who does?" he blurted out.

"Then you certainly will be unless you take my advice and marry me without any fuss," Mrs. Corcoran said. "I have you under my thumb, and a word from me would put the halter round your neck."

"But what about yourself?" he demanded.

"That's quite another matter, deary," the hag returned. "I want you because you will be useful to me."

"As your slave!" Jacob said, clasping his hands in anguish.

"The word was yours not mine, but it suits," Mrs. Corcoran said.

The storm having given free vent to its fury was now rolling, rumbling, and grumbling away in the far distance, and Jacob Butler cast a yearning glance at the door.

"I will make a dash at it when she is not looking at me," he said to himself.

But Mrs. Corcoran never removed her eyes from him.

She watched him as a cat that plays with a captured mouse, and there was something as helpless and terror-stricken as the inferior animal in Jacob Butler.

The gaunt, hideous hag revelled and gloated over the wretched man's misery, but all the time she plied him with endearing terms, which she knew were loathsome to him.

And all the time she kept the stick which had supported her tottering limbs ready for use, and Jacob knew full well what strength lay in her shrivelled arms, and that she could strike a blow of which a giant would not be ashamed.

"Come," said Mrs. Corcoran, "we must be merry. We will celebrate this joyful meeting with music. I heard you sing and saw you dance once, Jacob, and you shall do so now."

Driven to desperation, cold with terror at one moment and boiling over with rage the next, Jacob Butler hit upon an expedient he had never thought of before.

With a sudden nervous movement he shot out his arms with the intention of flooring Mrs. Corcoran and making his escape before she could recover herself, but she was too quick for him.

His fist rattled upon the ever-ready stick, which had parried the blow, and Jacob, recoiling back to his corner, thrust his injured knuckles into his mouth.

"Why, Jacob," cried Mrs. Corcoran, "I never thought that you could be so playful. I forgive you, deary, but don't try that game on again, or I shall be compelled to chastise you severely, and you wouldn't look well going to church with a couple of black eyes and a scratched face."

As she spoke the old crone hobbled about the floor and brandished the stick above his head in a manner that filled Jacob Butler with loathing and terror.

It was beyond human endurance to him now.

Regardless of all consequence she made a dash for the door.

Down came the stick, and Jacob Butler, flinging up his arms, fell prone and senseless upon the floor.

---

## CHAPTER LV.

### ON THE ROAD TO DOVER—THE MEETING ON THE CLIFF—THE WRESTLE—A SHRIEK FOR MERCY—THE FALL.

WICKED men are hard to kill.

What is called luck often favours them, and fate toys with them—buoys them up with hope until the meshes of retribution close finally and escape is impossible.

Such it would seem was the case with Sir Roland Ashton.

Ninety-nine men out of a hundred would have been killed when Gedge Foote's house came rattling down about the villain's ears, but a descending beam caught the wall as it came crushing down and broke the force of its fall.

Covered with bricks and rubbish, Sir Roland Ashton lay fully an hour before he returned to consciousness, and when he opened his eyes he could scarcely believe that he was still in the land of the living.

His brow had been severely cut, and a stream of blood was running down his face.

He put up his hand to stem it, and as he did so his hand came in contact with the beam which, falling in a slanting direction, had saved his life.

By degrees he dragged himself out of the heap of rubbish, but he could not stand upright.

Crouching down, he felt his way towards where he knew the staircase to be.

At first it seemed to be completely blocked up, but further investigation proved that such was not the case.

Using all his strength, Sir Roland Ashton pulled aside the *débris* until he could gain a firm footing.

Then he began to mount step by step on the wreck, until his eyes were rewarded with a beam of light.

It came from a lantern swayed to and fro by a man, who, amongst others, were surveying the wreck in amazement.

Sir Roland Ashton kept himself perfectly quiet. It took no great stretch of memory to remind him that his last meeting with the men of the Mint was the reverse from a pleasant one; so, ensconcing himself down behind a pile of joists and rotten floor-boards, he resolved to wait until such time as the coast would be clear.

He never gave Catchpole or Grabham a single thought.

Whether they were alive or dead was nothing to him.

The mission on which he had brought them to the place had ended in failure and ruin, and all Sir Roland troubled himself about was how to get out of it himself unobserved.

The men outside seemed to be searching for something very earnestly.

They prodded about the rubbish with sticks and iron bars, but did not approach Sir Roland, as he had taken the precaution to keep himself above the level of the ground.

It suddenly struck him that they were searching for treasure.

Gedge Foote, the miser, might have hidden money in all parts of the building, and the news of its fall brought hundreds of people to the spot.

At last they dropped away one by one, having found nothing to repay them for their trouble, and at last Sir Roland Ashton crept out of his hiding-place.

He was so covered with dust, soot, and cobwebs that he might have been well taken for one of the searchers, and he passed out of the Mint unobserved.

Making his way past the Tower of London, and giving a casual glance at the green on which so many unfortunate heads had fallen under the headsman's axe, he walked swiftly towards London Bridge.

Whither should he go?

Lilac Lodge was burnt down and Mrs. Corcoran was dead (so he thought), and that was some consolation.

At Ashton Hall there was no safety, for Spring-Heeled Jack—

Ah! was he dead, too?

"He must be," Sir Roland thought. "Both of us could not have escaped those walls. Ha! ha! ha! He is dead, and I am free of his accursed presence for ever."

Turning into an archway, he saw that a coach was being got ready for a journey, and glancing at the back of the vehicle, he saw that it was bound for Dover.

Why should he not go there too?

Anywhere was better than London, and he needed rest.

Give him time to mature his plans, and he would get Daisy within his power yet, for, if Spring-Heeled Jack was really dead, what other friend had she in the world to raise an arm in her protection?

Calling an ostler he borrowed a brush and removed a portion of the dust from his clothing, and after washing his face and hands in a tin pail, an operation which cost him a crown piece, he paid his fare and walked into the bar.

Here he found his fellow-passengers fortifying themselves for their long ride, and called for a glass of brandy.

As he was drinking it he saw a face look in at the door for an instant and then vanish.

To the majority of the people gathered round the bar there was nothing in this incident even to create a remark, but Sir Roland's visage changed.

He went to the door and looked out.

There was nobody in sight, and at last he returned and called for more brandy, drinking it neat.

"What a fool I am!" he muttered. "I start and tremble at everything. The fellow was some hanger-on, or, perhaps, some man looking for a friend."

"Time, ladies and gentlemen!—time!" sang out the guard, appearing with a long brass horn in his hand. "This way for the Dover coach, if you please."

Sir Roland had engaged an inside seat, and it was with great relief that he found himself the only passenger so situated.

The coach rattled away to the cheery notes of the horn, and soon after day dawned.

The sun came up bright and beautiful.

The heavy rain had laid the dust, and so refreshed all nature that the air was redolent with sweet perfume.

As London fell back in the rear so the spirits of Sir Roland Ashton rose.

He felt inclined to be merry, and chatted glibly with the guard and driver each time the coach stopped to change horses.

There was one of the passengers who never got down during the whole of the journey.

This was a man so wrapped up with capes, coats, and wrappers as to almost entirely conceal his face.

He had the appearance of an invalid, and this impression was increased when the coach reached Dover.

Sir Roland watched the silent man as he alighted slowly and painfully, and walked slowly away, disappearing down one of the bye-streets.

The baronet thought he could not do better than put up at the inn nearest to hand, and, having engaged a suite of apartments, he ordered a repast and sat down to enjoy it.

The table was near a window commanding a fine view of the sea rippling away until it became hazy and then relieved by the coast of France.

"Peace at last!" Sir Roland murmured. "Oh! how delightful all this is after what I have passed through."

As he spoke he held a glass of ruby wine to the light.

A hundred objects were reflected upon it in miniature, and Sir Roland startled the sleepy waiter into activity by dropping the glass and giving vent to a fierce oath.

"A thousand pardons!" said the waiter, who was a Frenchman. "Is not milor' well? Ah! you are faint."

"It is nothing," Sir Roland said. "The glass slipped through my fingers."

Yes; and on it Sir Roland had seen the face of Spring-Heeled Jack as plainly as ever he had seen it in his life.

What a strange and unaccountable fancy!

How could he account for it but that his brain was overwrought, and that his reason was giving way?

He pushed his plate away, and, leaning back in his chair, sat looking down at the scene before him.

Suddenly the man who had travelled from London to Dover, heavily wrapped and cloaked as before, passed the window.

Sir Roland gazed at him with eyes of suspicion.

There was something about the stranger that he could not make out.

The very way in which he had left the coach

and walked painfully away set the baronet thinking, and here was the man again under his very nose and apparently interested in the house.

"Shall I speak to him?" Sir Roland asked himself. "If I could see his face I should be satisfied. He may be some spy sent down to watch my movements."

It is probable that he might have put this notion into practice, but before he had a chance of doing so the man was gone.

"Curse the fellow!" said Sir Roland. "Why should I trouble my mind about him? Bah! I am like a child frightened by an ugly shadow on the wall. Who could possibly know that I am down here?—and, if such be the case, am I not armed and perfectly well able to take care of myself?"

Sir Roland smiled at his own folly, and more particularly that he had seen Spring-Heeled Jack's face mirrored on the wine glass, but the smile was a faint one, and flitting away left a frown upon his face.

The French waiter watched him, and wondered why he could eat none of the good things displayed so temptingly on the snow-white tablecloth, and he was still further perplexed when Sir Roland rose and announced his intention of going out.

"Milor' is not well pleased?" the waiter said, casting a deprecating glance at the table,

"Yes, very well pleased," Sir Roland replied; "but I have no appetite just at present. A word with you, my friend. I am no lord, but a plain, country gentleman, named Livock; but as I do not wish to be troubled with anybody, I shall never be in a mood to receive visitors. Do you understand me?"

"Ah! yes," the waiter replied. "Milor'—monseiur does not wish to be disturbed—Jules understand. He was valet to English gentleman years ago, and knows much."

"You seem to be a sharp sort of fellow," Sir Roland said.

Jules grinned, shrugged his shoulders, and rubbed his hands more vigorously than ever.

"Monsieur, pays me a compliment I do not deserve," he said.

"Nonsense!" Sir Roland returned. "How comes it that you are here after serving under an English gentleman."

"I will tell you," said the Frenchman, grinning. "I see by monsieur's face that I may repose confidence in him. I read faces, and I know—"

"You know what?" Sir Roland Ashton interposed.

"That you are no more Monsieur Livock than I am."

"You know me, then?"

"No," Jules replied, with another shrug of his shoulders; "you are wrong there, and yet you are right. I watched you as you sat at the table. Your eyes were fixed on the shores of my country, and I said to myself—'Monsieur has seen troublesome times—he flies from an enemy.' Hah! I see that I am right."

Sir Roland affected to laugh, but he betrayed the truth in the sound of his voice.

"We may become better acquainted," he said. "What other name are you known by besides Jules?"

"Carleon."

"Yes; and now, Jules Carleon, tell me about your late master, and why you left him."

"It is an odd story," Jules Carleon replied. "My master believed in a short life and a mer one. He could shuffle a pack of cards or throw set of dice—"

"Loaded ones?"

"Hah!" said Jules, laughing. "I see th monsieur has had some leetle experience in su matters. Well, yes. He was clever and w money, but, alas! he went too far. He made mistake, was caught, and shot dead by one of t party. Shall I ever forget that evening? N no, no!"

Jules Carleon shed tears, and Sir Roland ey him favourably, for he knew that he was standi before a villain and a hypocrite.

"You were present then?" said the baronet.

"Alas! yes."

"And what became of you?"

Jules Carleon's sallow face turned an oli green.

"I went out by the window."

"You were pitched out, I suppose?"

Jules Carleon's neck disappeared into h shoulders, and his mouth expanded into a broa grin.

"Monsieur has seen much of the world," h said.

"Are you tired of being here?"

"Oh! very. It's like a prison—so much to d and so little to get."

"I will talk to you anon," Sir Roland said "but in the meantime keep your own couns and a watchful eye upon any stranger who ma come to the house."

Jules Carleon bowed low.

"Monsieur's commands shall be obeyed," h said.

Sir Roland walked out of the room and into th open air.

He was haunted by the man who had travelle all the way from London in gloomy silence.

Sir Roland seemed to see the mysterious indi vidual at every turning, and lurking behind ever porch.

Leaving the grand old town Sir Roland ap proached the splendid line of cliffs.

He walked slowly and in an attitude of thought

He stopped on hearing footsteps behind him and looked round.

There was nobody within sight, and, as h could see for more than a mile each way, he pu the sound down to fancy.

And now he began to reflect what happines might have been his had he led a good and law abiding life.

But it was too late now.

He had travelled too far upon the road of si and wickedness to begin a new life.

So a demon whispered in his ear, and Si Roland listened to the persuasive voice.

"No—no," he muttered. "It is too late. Th course I have run must be finished, though it lead to perdition."

"To perdition!" repeated a voice.

Sir Roland Ashton stood transfixed as if a spel had suddenly fallen upon him.

"To perdition," said the voice again.

Sir Roland recoiled as Spring-Heeled Jacl appeared from behind a clump of bushes.

It seemed as if he had sprung from the ground and Sir Roland recoiled on his heels towards th edge of the cliff.

"Have a care, Sir Roland," Spring-Heele Jack said, pointing below. "The beach lies hundred feet down."

The guilty baronet passed his hand swiftly across his brow.

"You here!" he gasped.

"Yes. Why not?" Spring-Heeled Jack replied. "Like you, I came here for fresh air and peace."

"You followed me down?"

Spring-Heeled Jack smiled.

"Yes," he said, "I did. What then?"

"What then!" Sir Roland repeated in a fury. "I had a hope that you lay buried under the ruins of Gedge Foote's house. Curse you! How long will your hideous form cumber the earth?"

"A little longer than your handsome self, perchance," Spring-Heeled Jack replied, mockingly. "I escaped even easier than yourself, and I set your miserable dupes free."

"You mean Catchpole and Grabham?"

"Yes."

"What care I whether they live or die?" Sir Roland said.

As he spoke he put his hands carelessly in his pockets.

"You have pistols there!" Spring-Heeled Jack said, grasping him by the wrist. "Sir Roland, attempt no tricks with me, or, by Heaven! you shall rue it."

The baronet withdrew his hands, and with a quick movement threw his arms round Spring-Heeled Jack's waist.

"Now my time has come!" Sir Roland hissed. "Had you the strength of twenty men I would hold you now. My hour of triumph has come at last. Ha! ha!"

His grip was like a band of iron.

The light of fierce determination shone in his eyes.

"Rash fool!" Spring-Heeled Jack cried, "what would you do?"

"Hurl you over the cliff!"

"Well said," Spring-Heeled Jack returned. "We will go together!"

Sir Roland Ashton now felt that the tables were turned upon him.

Strong as his grasp was, it was but feeble in comparison to that which Spring-Heeled Jack now put into force.

"Come—come!" said the weird creature. "To travel down the cliff-side will be merry sport for me."

"I did but joke!" Sir Roland cried, as Spring-Heeled Jack dragged him closer and closer to the cliff. "Let go your hold and I will release mine!"

"Nay," said Spring-Heeled Jack, "it is useless! Come—come!"

Sir Roland shrieked and closed his eyes as he felt the earth leave his feet.

Then came a rush of strong air.

A sound like thunder dinned into his ears.

Earth and sky became mingled together as he and Spring-Heeled Jack went down.

Their whirling forms were followed by showers of dust and stones.

The startled birds wheeled and fluttered in fright.

All this happened in a moment, and then Sir Roland lost his senses.

## CHAPTER LVI.

### CATCHPOLE AND GRABHAM DISTINGUISH THEMSELVES AND MAKE AN IMPORTANT CAPTURE.

"MATE," said Catchpole, as he hobbled along at the side of Grabham, "I think I shall retire from this line of business."

Grabham rubbed his nose in a reflective sort of way.

"I should like to do it myself," he said, "but what can we do?"

"Anything is better than this life," Catchpole groaned. "I thought we were done for, shut up like ants in that infernal passage."

"Well," Grabham returned, "I must say that we ought to thank Spring-Heeled Jack for letting us out."

"Perhaps he left the door open by accident?"

Grabham shook his head.

"I don't think that," he said. "Perhaps he isn't a bad sort of fellow, after all."

"You can't expect much good from a devil," Catchpole said. "I can't think of him without trembling all over like a jelly, and I'll take jolly good care not to fall in his way again if I can help it."

"We are both agreed on that score," Grabham said. "What a sell for Sir Roland! I wonder if the house settled him?"

"If it didn't, it's a pity," Catchpole growled. "I'd give my last shilling to have the pleasure of putting a bullet through him."

These two worthies had only just got free from their perilous position in the Mint.

Just at the moment when both had made up their minds that they were doomed to perish by the hideous death of starvation they found the door of the secret passage open.

A quantity of rubbish had fallen into the lower portion of the well, almost blocking it up, and the constables, getting a good foothold, crept out and sneaked away like a brace of whipped hounds.

The hour was late, and they did not exactly know how to account for their absence at home or to their superiors.

To peach on Sir Roland would be to criminate themselves.

"I have it!" said Catchpole, suddenly.

"Have what?"

"A notion which I think will get us out of our trouble."

"Well, what is it?" Grabham demanded.

"We must swear that we have been following up the scent of the Black Highwaymen."

"Good!" Grabham cried, smiting his thigh. "I'll stand a drink for that, Catchpole, my boy. Where shall we go?"

"Into the first house we come to, for I am as dry as an oven."

A few yards further on they turned into an inn, and a tankard of ale was placed before them.

Catchpole drank first, and left so little for Grabham that he looked mournfully into the measure.

"I say, this ain't fair, you know," he said. "I thought we made an agreement to share alike in everything?"

"I couldn't help it," Catchpole replied. "I should have done the same had it been a large pailful."

"Well, then, perhaps you will—"

He said no more, for at that moment a horse came clattering up to the door, and a man, alighting in hot haste, ran into the house and called for a measure of wine.

He was in such a hurry to be served that he did not see the constables, who shrank back into the shadow and watched him narrowly.

"Bill Blarney!" Catchpole whispered, under his breath.

"Yes, sure enough," Grabham replied. "Now's our chance. Shall we collar him?"

"No; let him go, and then follow him."

"But he is on horseback."

"Well, we must get horses too. Hush! Hide your face—he is looking this way."

But Bill Blarney was perfectly unconscious of the constables' presence, and, having finished his wine, he asked the landlord where he could find a blacksmith.

"My horse has lost a shoe," he said, "and as I have a long journey before me, I am anxious to get on the road as soon as possible."

Catchpole glided out by the back door and Grabham followed him.

"We have him now right enough," said Grabham. "Run round to the Two-Necked Swan and get a couple of saddle horses. There's some precious game afloat, and we must see what it is. I'll stay here to keep an eye on Blarney."

Catchpole had scarcely left the yard when the landlord appeared.

"Jem!" he shouted.

"Hullo, there!" cried a voice from a hay loft.

"Just run to Naylor's and ask him to step over to shoe a horse," said the landlord. "Here's a shilling for you, and Naylor will get a crown for the job."

"Right you are, sir."

Jem, a shock-headed, thin-legged, wiry individual, put in an appearance and darted past Grabham.

"Here's a lark!" said the constable. "Here's a turning of the tables. Blarney will wish that he had never set eyes upon us. He's as good as on his way to Tyburn."

Some minutes elapsed, and then Catchpole returned, but on foot.

"The horses will be ready for us when we want them," he said; "but how are we to know which way Blarney is going?"

"If he goes north he means to take to the Barnet-road, but if south, Shooter's-hill will be his fancy," Grabham replied.

"You think so?"

"It's almost a certainty."

The smith came over and was soon at work, and in about a quarter of an hour Bill Blarney mounted and rode north.

"What did I tell you?" Grabham said, rubbing his hands with glee. "His game is to stop the coach, but we'll stop him with a vengeance. Let him have a good start, or we may come up with him, and then all the fat will be in the fire."

The constables took another drink to nerve themselves, and then walked round to the Two-Necked Swan, where, of course, they indulged in further potations. When they started heavy clouds obscured the moon, and half a gale of wind was blowing.

The night promised to be a blustering one, and people were hurrying homeward.

Catchpole and Grabham did not hurry their horses.

They knew that if Blarney had gone to the Barnet-road that he would have to wait fully an hour for the mail coach, and their idea was to take him red-handed.

When they had reached as far as Highgate they stopped and dismounted.

Catchpole dropped on his knees and placed his ear close to the ground.

"No sound of the coach as yet, but I can hear the cantering of hoofs."

"One or more horses?" Grabham asked.

"One."

"We are on the right track," Grabham said. "Blarney is congratulating himself that he is alone in this spree. How far do you think he is away?"

"A mile at least; perhaps more."

"Then we had better lessen the distance. Ha; there goes eleven. The coach should pass the Bald-faced Stag at half-past."

To follow a man is an exciting incident, but it pales a little when he has to be caught.

Catchpole did not feel quite as enthusiastic as Grabham.

He knew that Bill Blarney was a desperate man, and would sell his freedom dearly if not taken unawares.

Catchpole mentioned this to Grabham.

"What?" said he. "Are you going to turn funky? Think of the glory—think of the reward."

"It's all right to think about them," Catchpole said, dismally; "but supposing that Blarney gets the best of us."

"We are two to one," Grabham said, contemptuously. "You may go back if you like, and leave me to do the job alone. I must have money, and don't you see, you fool, that supposing that if we only scare Blarney away that every passenger on the coach will shell out handsomely to us?"

This was putting a new complexion on the matter, and Catchpole's spirits arose.

"You are always right, Grabby, my boy," he said. "I often think that it is a great pity that you didn't enter the army. What a fire-eater you would have made!"

Mr. Grabham put on a military air and gazed ahead of him.

"I fancy I see something," he said.

"Where?" cried Catchpole, reining in his steed. "Oh! lor!"

"You idiot!" Grabham growled. "You make enough noise to wake the dead."

The object descried by Mr. Grabham was nothing more ferocious than a scarecrow in the middle of a field.

The time was getting on, and the coach would soon be due.

The constables now drew their horses into a lane so unfrequented that it was completely overgrown with grass.

Soon the sound of a horn awakened the echoes of the night.

The coach, with its four spanking greys, was coming at last.

"Nothing alarming up to the present," Grabham said. "All's well. Can you see the lamps?"

Catchpole stood up in the stirrups and peered over the hedge.

"Yes," he said.

Grabham gave a grunt of disappointment.

"Bill Blarney must have got wind of us," he said. "It strikes me that he has sheered off, and left us nothing but a wild-goose chase."

Catchpole wished in his heart that such was the case, but kept it to himself.

On came the coach, the lights dancing and flashing, the horses going as if they had only just left the stable, and the passengers chatting merrily, glad enough to be so near London.

Suddenly a change came over the scene.

The report of a pistol startled the air.

The horses fell back upon their haunches, the

female passengers screamed and clung to the male ones, and the gentlemen turned white with fear.

Coachman and guard swore mighty oaths at this unexpected interruption, and a hasty search was made for an antiquated blunderbuss which ought to have been in the coach, but had been left behind as usual.

"Ladies and gentlemen," said Bill Blarney, "I am sorry to trouble you for your purses, but I must have them. Please to throw them down and save me the pain of discharging my stock of fire-arms. Coachman, keep your seat. I have my eyes on you, and if you move I will blow your brains out!"

The coachman and guard swore again.

To make matters worse, they could not see the highwayman, although they could hear him, and the chances were that he was not alone.

In point of fact, Bill Blarney had dismounted and was lying flat on the ground in such a position as to command a sure aim at any of the passengers he chose to shoot at.

But for once he had reckoned without his host.

As he was chuckling at his success and already counting the gains of his adventure he received a fearful blow on the head from a truncheon, and in another instant Catchpole and Grabham were on top of him.

"Hurrah!" Grabham cried. "We've got the scoundrel. Steady, coachman, with those horses, or they will be over us. We are constables."

"Constables!" cried the passengers, joyfully.

Then the ladies recovered from their fright and tittered, and the gentlemen all looked brave and said that if the officers of the law had not arrived that they would have tackled the highwayman and cut him into mincemeat.

Bill Blarney was completely stunned, and the constables bound him in such a manner as to make escape impossible when he returned to consciousness.

"There, he is a regular beauty," said Grabham, taking down one of the coach-lamps and flashing the light upon Blarney's face.

"Trussed like a fowl," Catchpole chimed in, with a chuckle.

As Grabham had predicted, the passengers were only too willing to pay for the rescue, coming as it did at a critical moment, and the constables' hats were half filled with guineas.

"The inside of the coach is empty," the guard said; "so you had better let us take you and your prisoner to London."

"That's all very well," said Grabham; "but what are we to do with our horses?"

"Leave them at the Bald-faced Stag."

"Right you are," Grabham returned. "Blarney's horse is not far away. Wait till we have found it, and then we'll all go home together."

The horse was found tethered to a tree and was soon stabled with the others.

Then the wretched Blarney was pitched into the coach as unceremoniously as if he had been a sack of sawdust, and the vehicle rolled away.

The man who had been the greatest coward of all sang a gallant song of love and war, and the ladies chatted glibly and flirted deliciously, for their hearts were filled with thankfulness that the terrible man who might have taken their lives was now as harmless as a child and beneath their very feet.

## CHAPTER LVII.

### THE SMUGGLERS' CAVE.

"HOLD! Who goes there?"

"A friend!"

"The countersign!"

"Nimrod!"

"Pass friend, and all's well!"

This conversation passed between two men at the mouth of a cave cleft by nature in a cliff.

One man, he who had put the questions, stood at the entrance with a carbine reclining gently on his arm, the other had toiled upwards with a huge bundle on his back, and, throwing it down as he passed the sentry, took a deep breath.

A little way below lay a boat rigged for rowing and fast sailing, and two men lying in easy attitudes glanced up at the sentry as if awaiting instructions.

When it was high tide the waves rose almost to the mouth of the cave, which for the first few yards was narrow, but widened into a spacious apartment.

Here lamps hung from the chalk ceiling, and the place was fitted with benches and tables.

Piles of barrels, full and empty, occupied the corners, and the walls were festooned with muskets, swords, and other weapons of war, some of which were of delicate foreign make.

This inner cave was occupied by about half-a-dozen men.

They were all of the seafaring type, for indeed they were smugglers.

They lounged about in the manner of men who had done their work well, and were now taking their rest.

There was a rich aroma of choice tobacco about the place, for all the men were smoking, and by certain coloured bottles and glasses placed handy it was evident that the smugglers appreciated the value of good wine.

At the end of this room, as it may be called, was a door with a grating fitted into it, and a stream of lamplight shone through the bars.

One of the men, a handsome, stalwart fellow, rose to his feet and went to the grating and gazed through.

"Still unconscious," he said, turning to his companion. "This is a wonderful thing, and how he escaped without being smashed to pieces is a mystery to me."

"The upper ledge broke his fall," said another. "Dick swears that when he looked up he saw something like a huge eagle clutching the man."

"Bah!" said he at the grating. "Dick has been taking too much French brandy of late. Eagles in these parts! Ha! ha! Well, at all events here the man is, and if he ever recovers he may tell us what he means by coming head downwards into our quarters. It looks like a case of suicide to me."

"Whatever it is, Fielder will be in a fearful rage when he comes back," growled one of the smugglers, emitting a wreath of smoke from his lips. "I pity the poor devil of a stranger who finds himself here."

"There is only one way out," laughed another. "It's a case of a bullet or a jump into the sea with a nine-pound shot for an ornament on his legs."

"Hush!" said the man at the grating. "Here comes Fielder at last."

The men rose to salute their chief.

He was a man of gigantic stature, black bearded, and muscular.

He flashed his keen eyes on the men, and, folding his arms, struck a commanding attitude.

"What is this I hear about a stranger?" he said, in a deep bass tone. "Tom Wary?"

"Aye, aye! sir."

"You have been here all day," Fielder said. "You may speak."

"All I know is that this man," here he pointed to the grated door, "come rattling down the cliff and fell at the mouth of the cave."

"Killed?" Fielder asked, carelessly.

"At first we thought he was," Tom Wary replied. "A shower of stones and earth followed him and covered him up, but when we dragged him out we found that he was still living."

"Why didn't you pitch him into the sea?" Fielder growled.

"We thought we had better consult you on that point, captain," Wary replied. "Of course it can be done now, if you wish it."

"I will have a look at him first," Fielder said. "Give me the key."

Striding across the cavern floor, he opened the door and gazed upon Sir Roland's upturned face.

"A gentleman, at all events," Fielder said, musingly. "There's precious little life left in him, and he would be none the wiser for a dip in the sea. The tide is running up, and—"

A heavy groan from Sir Roland checked the smuggler chief's utterance, and at the same moment the baronet opened his eyes.

"Bring me a flask of brandy," Fielder said.

As it was put into his hand he pressed it against Sir Roland's lips.

"Do you feel better?" Fielder asked.

Sir Roland groaned and closed his eyes again.

"Poor wretch!" Fielder said, and his heart was smitten with pity. "I haven't the heart to kill him now. Watch over him, and when he is able to speak call me."

In obedience to a motion of his hand a ladder was lowered from the ceiling, and Fielding, passing up it, raised a trap-door and disappeared.

Tom Wary dragged a bench to the door of the cell in which Sir Roland lay and sat down.

Whenever the baronet groaned or moved the smuggler plied him with brandy. It was the only medicine ever used in the cave, and the inmates had every faith in it to cure all the ills that flesh is heir to.

After an hour or so, Sir Roland revived somewhat.

"Where am I?" he asked, feebly.

Tom Wary shook his head.

"You must ask somebody else that question," he replied.

"Am I a prisoner?"

"You made yourself one."

Still confused and bewildered Sir Roland attempted to sit up, but he sank back moaning with pain.

"If you wish to see the captain I will call him," Tom Wary said.

"Captain?"

"Yes—my captain; the man I have followed for years."

"I am still at a loss to know what all this means," Sir Roland returned; "but I will see he captain, as you call him, when convenient."

Tom Wary took a whistle from his pocket and sounded a loud call.

The smuggler chief appeared almost instantly, and Wary retired.

"Do you know where you are?" Fielder demanded, sternly.

"That is the very question I was about to ask you," Sir Roland rejoined.

"Then I will tell you," Fielder said. "This place is mine, and the man who sets foot in it without my permission pays for the intrusion with his life. It seems to me that you were prying about, and met with a fall."

"Let me think," Sir Roland said. "Everything is vague and uncertain. I seem to have passed through a horrible dream. Ah! it comes back to me. Oh! this agony is almost insupportable!"

"Drink!" Fielder said, passing him the flask. "If I am a revengeful man by nature, I do not torture my prisoners."

Sir Roland gulped down the brandy as if it had been water, and then lay still, again endeavouring to collect his thoughts."

"I have no time to spare," Fielder said. "If you have anything to tell me—if your object was to seek me out and hand me over to what men call justice, as others have done, and paid the penalty for their folly, say so."

In spite of his sufferings Sir Roland Ashton smiled.

"No," he said. "I was hurled down the cliff."

"By whom?"

"A fiend known as Spring-Heeled Jack."

"I have heard rumour of him," Fielder said, "but I have no faith in his existence. You lie! This is but a ruse to throw me off my guard and give you an opportunity to escape."

"It is as true as the sky is above and the sea beneath us," Sir Roland replied. "He is the bane and curse of my life."

"Well, I will take your story for granted. Who are you?"

"Sir Roland Ashton, of Ashton Hall."

"The deuce you are!" said Fielder. "I have heard of you, too, from a man I have done considerable business with in London."

"His name?"

"Gedge Foote."

A cry of surprise and alarm burst from Sir Roland's lips.

"He spoke to you of me?" he said. "Well, he will never do so again."

"No! Why not?"

"Because he is dead, and the house he lived in is a heap of ruins."

"Murdered by Sir Roland Ashton!" said a voice so close to the smuggler that he started to his feet and dragged a pistol from his belt.

"Who spoke?" he demanded, hoarsely.

"Spring-Heeled Jack!"

Fielder dashed across the cavern, and entering the narrow portion, seized the sentry by the throat.

"Dog!" hissed the smuggler chief, "how dare you admit strangers here?"

"Strangers!" the man gasped. "What strangers? It is not true, captain. There must be some conspiracy against me."

"Can I not believe my own ears?" Fielder said, in a voice of thunder. "There is a man hidden in some part of the caves. I heard his voice, and—"

"You see him!"

Fielder turned sharply round and at the same instant Spring-Heeled Jack bounded over his head.

# SPRING-HEELED JACK,

## THE TERROR OF LONDON.

AS SPRING-HEELED JACK APPEARED A TERRIFIC EXPLOSION SHOOK THE BUILDING.

and taking an upward flight, seemed to vanish in thin air.

Smugglers, like all men that have anything to do with the sea, are superstitious.

Fielder staggered back, and bold and fearless as he was, he cried out in alarm.

The sentry discharged his musket aimlessly, and in a minute all the men were at the mouth of the cave.

A hundred questions were put and answered.

Some suggested that an immediate search should be made for Spring-Heeled Jack, but the chief shook his head.

"This is a mystery which I will endeavour to unravel," he said. "Let the prisoner receive every attention, for I begin to think that his appearance here was not by chance after all."

So saying, he walked away, leaving the men to talk of Spring-Heeled Jack, and to watch for him vain.

---

## CHAPTER LVIII.

### SHOWS HOW KIND MRS. CORCORAN WAS TO JACOB BUTLER.

"I SAY, you have tied my hands and legs," said Jacob Butler, ruefully. "What new indignity will you subject me to?"

"Yes, deary," Mrs. Corcoran replied; "I did that when you were having that nice little sleep."

"Sleep, be—"

"Now, don't swear," said the hag. "You must not use bad language before a lady."

"You brute—you beast!" Jacob Butler howled. "You knock me silly and senseless and call it sleep. Cut these cords or I'll—"

"Oh! yes," Mrs. Corcoran interposed, as she hobbled round him, "I daresay you will. No doubt you are game to do all sorts of wonderful things."

"Was ever a man in such a fix as this?" Jacob moaned.

"Many in a worse," said Mrs. Corcoran. "Better to have a rope round your ankles than round your neck."

"Oh! you she-devil—you vampire!"

"How nice of you!" said the hag, grinning maliciously. "Dear me, what a happy pair we shall make, to be sure! Come, deary, it is time that you had your breakfast, for morning has come. Let me feed you."

She approached Jacob Butler with a bowl and spoon in her hand.

He turned his head aside in disgust.

"Get away!" he said, with a spasmodic gasp. "I hate the sight of you. I'll not touch anything from your hands."

"Very well," Mrs. Corcoran returned; "if you won't eat it for your breakfast it must do for your dinner. Trust me, my dove, that you will return to your appetite before long."

"I won't," Jacob said; "I swear I won't. I'll starve myself, and think myself lucky to escape you in that way."

Mrs. Corcoran set the bowl down on the floor.

"I am going out," she said; "but I shan't be long."

"Where to?"

"To get the marriage license, my pet."

Butler's hair stood on end and his face went as white as a sheet.

"But look here," said Jacob, in dismay. "You are not going to leave me here, trussed up in this fashion?"

"Yes, I am, lovey; because you look so quiet and pretty. If I let you run loose you might get yourself into mischief, you know."

Jacob Butler opened his mouth to its utmost limits, and said certain things about Mrs. Corcoran and her attentions which it would be scarcely wise to repeat.

The old hag, after making sure that Jacob was perfectly secure, and adding a few more knots as an extra precaution, went out.

"I'm done for," Jacob groaned. "What a fool I was to leave the Queen's Head! What an ass I have made of myself!"

In his misery he rolled over with his face to th ground, and as he lay kicking and fuming h heard the heavy plodding footsteps of a man ap proaching the hut.

"Here! Hi! Help!" he roared.

The footsteps stopped, and it was evident the man outside was wondering where the voice came from.

Once more Jacob Butler lifted up his voice, with such effect that the stranger tried the door.

"It's locked!" Jacob cried, in a frenzy of excitement. "You can't get in that way. Pull the brushwood out of the window and then you can. Make haste if you want to save my life. That she-devil will be back soon, and she's more than a match for half-a-dozen men."

The man, who was a thorough rustic, and consequently as slow as a tortoise in his movements, did as he was told, and grinned hugely as he looked down upon Jacob.

"Quick! man, quick!" groaned the prisoner. "Out with your knife, and cut these cords."

But the man was in no hurry.

He had to ask himself whether he would be doing right, and Jacob's suspense became so agonising that he positively howled.

At last the rustic crept through the aperture and cut the cords.

"Free!" Jacob Butler cried. "Hurrah! My blessings on you, man, for this service. Here is all the money I have, but you are perfectly welcome to it. Ha! ha! ha!"

He was in such a hurry that as he emptied his pockets the coins flew all over the floor, and leaving the labourer to pick them up, he took a harlequin-like dive at the window, and raced away across the fields.

Jacob Butler felt just then that he could have handicapped himself against the very best man living.

Away he went like an antelope, until the breath left his body and his legs gave way under him.

As he fell sprawling a carrier's cart rumbled round a corner of the road, and the driver, thinking that Jacob had met with a serious accident, pulled up.

"Where—where are you going?" Jacob Butler gasped, as he staggered to his feet.

"To Islington."

"Then if you are a man with a grain of mercy in your heart, you will give me a lift."

"Willingly," said the carrier; "but you must tell me what you are running away from?"

"From a woman."

The carrier laughed.

"Well," he said, "I have seen a bigger and a bolder man than you do that. Jump up!"

The cart had no passengers, and as Jacob climbed in under the tilt he sank down exhausted.

At first he had some notion of regaling the

carrier's intellect with the story of his woes, but he abandoned the notion.

In the first place, the carrier might either disbelieve him, or call him a coward and kick him out of the cart; and, secondly, the man might fall in with Mrs. Corcoran and give her certain unpleasant information.

So Jacob concocted a story about a drunken, bad wife, who was hunting about for him with a poker, and the carrier laughed until tears ran down his face.

Mr. Butler got down at a convenient distance from the Queen's Head, and completed the rest of the journey on foot.

He sneaked into the inn as if he had just committed a theft, and the landlord hailed him with a roar of laughter, and followed that up with a dozen questions.

"Don't say anything to me." Jacob gasped. "All I want to do is to go to bed and try to forget what I have gone through."

"You're a nice sort of fellow to run away and leave the ladies," the landlord said.

"Ah! I forgot about them. How are they?"

"Well and hearty."

"That's good news. Has Mr. Ashton returned?"

The landlord shook his head, and bestowed a mysterious wink on Jacob.

"You had better ask Miss Marfield," he said.

"I can't talk to anybody until I have had a sleep," Jacob returned, "and so I am off. I say—"

"Well?"

"If anybody asks you about me take your oath I am not here."

So saying, Jacob Butler made a run for the staircase, and was seen no more that day.

---

## CHAPTER LIX.

### THE FALSE BEACON—THE STORM AT SEA—HOW JULES CARLEON CAME TO SIR ROLAND'S RESCUE.

DAVID FIELDER, the chief of the Dover smugglers, sat alone, with his feet resting on the trap-door that opened into the larger cave.

His own apartment was one which had been especially hollowed out for his use, and was furnished in a luxurious manner.

All kinds of things lay strewn about, and it was evident that Fielder had his hand in other things than smuggling tobacco and liquor.

The smuggler's face wore an expression of mingled gloom and bewilderment.

Sir Roland Ashton was in his power.

He had only to say a word, or to hold up a finger, and the baronet would tell no secrets.

But there was Spring-Heeled Jack to contend with.

Who was he, and how came he gifted with the marvellous power of motion?

David Fielder asked himself these questions so often that his brain grew weary, and at last, folding his arms upon the table, and sinking his head upon them, he fell asleep.

As he slumbered a change was taking place.

Heavy clouds shut out the blue sky and a thick, leaden-hued mist arose on all points of the horizon.

The men who watched at the mouth of the cave knew that a heavy storm was brewing.

Night might come before it would burst, but come it would.

The smugglers now became unusually active.

Some climbed the cliff-side and returned with bundles of brushwood, which was piled into a heap; and others prepared different coloured powders, sifting and handling them carefully.

Evening was coming on when David Fielder joined the men.

The wind was rising higher and higher every moment, and the foam-tipped waves tumbled over each other as if they were in haste to reach the shore and escape the doom threatened by the angry sky.

"Give me my telescope," Fielder said. "Ah!" he added, as he took a survey of the ocean, "we shall have some customers to-night. Is the beacon ready?"

"All ready to be fired," a man replied.

"That is well," Fielder said. "We share alike, boys, so the greater the haul the better. What do you make of yonder schooner?"

"She is a Spanish vessel."

"With a rich cargo, no doubt," Fielder said, smiling grimly. "The wind is dead against her, and it will take her from three to four hours to get into port. It will be dark by that time."

It was dark in much less, for the clouds gathered and mingled with the fog, and gloom soon fell upon land and sea.

Then it was that the real battle of the elements began.

A mighty gust of wind opened the conflict, and a reign of terror and confusion set in.

The waves, hurled against the cliffs in mad fury, sent up showers of white foam as it were in defiance to the clouds.

The scene was appalling.

Gust after gust of wind.

Crash after crash of thunder, and the lightning trailed and quivered along the leaping waves.

It was a night to strike terror into the boldest heart; but it was one suited to the smuggler's tastes, for, as we have hinted, David Fielder not only dealt in contraband goods, but was a wrecker into the bargain.

Suddenly a sound rose above the voice of the storm.

It was the report of a cannon fired at sea, and a plea for help to luckier people on shore.

"I thought as much," Fielder said. "The schooner could not get near enough to take a pilot on board. Light the beacon. But stay, we will show a light first."

Almost instantly a white light flared up, burning steadily.

It was as suddenly extinguished, and the smugglers waited the result in silence.

Another gun was fired from the ill-fated vessel.

The report was louder than the previous one, and it was evident that the ship was drifting on to the cliffs and destruction.

"Now light the beacon," said Fielder.

A man took a torch in his hand and walked towards the pile, but ere he reached it Spring-Heeled Jack stood in his path.

"Villain!" cried the mysterious being. "Murderer of innocent men and hapless women, your time has come!"

Clutching the man by the belt, and raising him aloft in his arms, he hurled him into the very midst of his companions.

The appearance of Spring-Heeled Jack and his action was so sudden that the wreckers could not step aside, and several were knocked heels over head down the cliff by the strange and weighty missile hurled at them.

David Fielder narrowly escaped sharing the fate of his followers, and he was so alarmed and enraged at what had taken place that he could do nothing but stand and glare at Spring-Heeled Jack.

But at last he recovered himself, and, setting his teeth, advanced with a cutlass in his hand.

But the chance of using it was denied him.

Spring-Heeled Jack kicked the unlighted pile of brushwood over the face of the cliff, and, uttering a loud, mocking laugh, vanished into the darkness.

"It's the very devil himself!" Fielder cried, aghast. "Confusion! we are despoiled of our prey. See, there go rockets from the harbour; and listen!—the schooner answers them."

Boom—boom! went the guns.

During this scene of confusion Sir Roland had not been idle.

He had been left alone in the inner cavern, and the craving to get away came strongly upon him.

Opening a large wooden chest he found that it contained articles of apparel such as the smugglers wore.

Exchanging his own garments for these he stood completely disguised.

"Now to run the gauntlet," he muttered. "It is worth risking, for death stares me in the face here."

The storm was at its heigth as he approached the mouth of the cave, and the smugglers were too intent on the murderous business they had in hand to notice him.

He crept out unobserved, and trusting himself to chance, grasped the bushes that grew on the cliff-side and lowered himself down.

He knew that there were steps hewn for the convenience of the smugglers, but he dare not approach them for fear of being seen.

Clinging, sliding, and slipping, with the spray dashing in his face, Sir Roland got a firm footing.

He stopped and peered through the awful gloom.

His heart beat almost audibly.

At any moment a flash of lightning might reveal his form, and what earthly power could save him then?

Steadying himself by placing his back against the cliff, he pondered on what he should do.

There might be a path down to the beach, but it was unknown to him.

A fatal step would hurl him into eternity, or leave him to battle for life in the raging sea.

Suddenly he felt a strange hand touch his arm, and he recoiled in horror.

"Courage, monsieur!" said a voice. "It is I—Jules Carleon—and I will lead you to safety."

"How did you find your way here?" Sir Roland demanded.

"It matters not," Jules Carleon replied. "It may be that I know more than David thinks or dreams of. Follow me, and I will put it out of his power to do you harm."

---

## CHAPTER LX.

SHARING THE GUINEAS—A LITTLE MISUNDERSTANDING—A PUGILISTIC ENCOUNTER PUT A STOP TO IN AN ODD SORT OF WAY.

For some days after the capture of Bill Blarney the triumphant officers, Catchpole and Grabham, did not meet.

This was not Catchpole's fault, for Grabham had kindly undertaken the charge of the money given by the passengers, and evinced, by his studied absence, a strong inclination to stick to the lot.

Catchpole dodged about the different inns used by Grabham, but he came not, and at last his disappointed colleague determined to seek him at his own home.

Mr. Grabham occupied a portion of a very old house in Cloth Fair, and the windows looked out upon the churchyard of ancient St. Bartholomew's Church.

The place had been tenanted once upon a time by some wealthy personage.

It had broad staircases, stained glass windows, and the wood-carver's art was prevalent on the oak panels, mantelpieces, and doorways.

Thither Catchpole wended his way, vowing vengeance on the man who had cheated him out of his due.

"What a fool I was to trust him!" he muttered, as he turned out of Smithfield-green and entered a dark, narrow street. "But wait until I have dug the fox out of his hole. I'll give him a bit of my mind, and a jolly good hiding into the bargain, if he isn't careful."

Mr. Catchpole looked very fierce, really as if he meant what he said.

"To be robbed like this!" he gasped. "To be robbed by the man I trusted! I have found you out now, Grabham, and hang me if I don't make you grin on the other side of your mouth!"

This little soliloquy brought Catchpole to an antiquated door, fitted with a knocker moulded in the shape of a dragon.

Catchpole laid hold of the monster and awoke the echoes of the house.

The noise was loud enough to startle a deaf man, but it had no effect on the inmates of the tumble-down mansion, so Catchpole repeated the operation, and with such vigour that he damaged the dragon's beauty and symmetry for ever.

A man living over the way came out with a stick thinking that some mischievous boy was giving full vent to his animal spirits, but on seeing that he had a real live constable to deal with he retired precipitately and hid his benighted head under his own roof.

Catchpole's second application produced the desired result, or rather it produced a one-eyed old woman with a visage as sour as vinegar and a head of hair that looked as if it had been tossed about by a rake.

"Is Mr. Grabham at home?" Catchpole asked, in a tone of voice that denoted that the name he had to utter almost choked him.

"How should I know?"

"Doesn't he live here?"

"Yes. But I have nothing to do with him. He lives on the top floor."

"Then how the devil am I to make him hear?" Catchpole demanded.

"Go round the back way and chuck some stones at his window."

Bang went the door in Catchpole's face, and he staggered back into the street just in time to prevent his cranium coming in contact with the iron dragon.

"That's the way with women—hang 'em!" he gasped. "There's no sense or reason about 'em. Chuck stones at the window! What next, I wonder?"

The gallant officer had no other alternative, however, so he marched himself round by St.

Bartholomew's churchyard, and, climbing the wall, felt about for a missile.

It was dark, and the gravestones looked so ghost-like that Catchpole felt anything but comfortable.

At last he secured a stone and hurled it up at a window behind which a light was shining, and cracked it.

Up flew the window-sash and out popped a head.

"Now, then," roared a voice, "what sort of a game do you call this?"

"That isn't Grabham's voice," Catchpole said, aghast. "I've gone and chucked the stone at the wrong window."

The constable dropped on his knees behind a huge tombstone, and kept his head well down, for fear that the irate proprietor of the cracked window might retaliate in a similar manner.

"I'll just step down and speak to Mr. Grabham, the constable, who lives next door," said the voice. "He will wake you up, young Jenkins. I know it's you, my lad, for I can see you."

Catchpole grinned.

This little event reminded him of his youth, when he broke windows and laid the blame on other boys' shoulders.

After a pause, during which the man above vowed that he would do all sorts of horrible things to the invisible Jenkins, he withdrew his head and returned to the delightful and aromatic art of making boots.

"Oh! Grabham lives next door, does he?" Catchpole said; "but which is next door. There's a house on each side, and I don't want to make another mistake, or I shall have the whole neighbourhood down on me."

This seemed so probable that the constable hesitated before he took another stone in his hand, and at last he made up his mind to watch for Grabham at the entrance of Cloth Fair.

This was the most sensible course to pursue, for if Grabham was at home his natural desire for stimulating liquors would bring him out-of-doors.

Catchpole had not long to wait.

He shrank back into a doorway as Grabham left his house, and touched him on the shoulder as he passed.

"What! my old friend?" cried Grabham, with a sickly smile.

"Your old friend, be jiggered!" said Catchpole. "You're a nice sort of party, certainly, to talk about friendship."

"Why shouldn't I?"

"Why shouldn't you?" Catchpole retorted, indignantly. "What do you mean by skulking away from me? Where's my share of the money?"

"What money?"

Catchpole was so overcome by this question that he spun round on his heels.

"Don't you give way to delusions," Grabham said. "There were certainly a few coppers—"

"Coppers!" Catchpole interposed, with a groan. "Guineas you mean!"

"There might have been a guinea among them," Grabham said, evasively. "Well, Catchpole, my boy, I want to do what is fair, so if you will walk round to a house I know we will settle the matter. I have been very queer during the last few days."

"Drunk you mean!" Catchpole said, wrathfully. "Drunk on my money!"

"Don't be hard on a man who has shared your joys and sorrows."

"Jigger my joys and sorrows. I want my money," Catchpole gasped. "There were a dozen passengers on the coach, and if they gave a penny they gave five guineas a piece."

"Then why didn't you count your share?"

"Because you took my hat away from me and shovelled the money into your own pocket."

"It was the action of a man and a brother," Grabham said, virtuously, "and to prove it I'll show you what we really got. When I returned home I tied the money up in a red handkerchief, and it hasn't been touched yet."

"Have you got it about you now?"

"Yes."

"Then come on and let me have my half, or there'll be a jolly row."

Grabham led the way through Smithfield and Clerkenwell, until Catchpole grew tired of walking.

"Where are you going to take me now?" he said.

"To the Queen's Head, Sadler's Wells."

"What for?"

"Because it is a quiet house, where we can talk without the fear of being disturbed," Grabham replied.

Little did he or his comrade think who were staying at the Inn towards which their footsteps were wending.

"Very well," Catchpole grumbled. "The house is kept by Ben Jordan, isn't it?"

"That's the very man, and a jolly good fellow he is."

"Is he?" Catchpole observed, dubiously. "I have heard that rather queer sort of people go to his house sometimes."

"So much the better for us. We may be able to pick up a bit of useful information."

"I've had enough information and work to last me a lifetime," Catchpole replied. "I want rest, and I think I shall go in for a road-side inn, with a bit of garden and a pig-stye at the back."

Mr. Catchpole rubbed his hands as he pictured this scene of bliss on his mind, and he dwelt upon it in silence until the Queen's Head came in view.

Opening a door that creaked warningly upon its hinges, and brought Ben Jordan, the landlord, suddenly out of a room, the constables entered and said "Good-evening" in a pleasant sort of manner.

Ben Jordan returned the salutation, and inquired his customers' pleasure.

"Well, you see," said Grabham, "we have a little business to transact, and so we thought we should like to have a private room for an hour or two."

"Certainly, gentlemen—certainly," said the landlord, smiling. "Anything to oblige you, I am sure. Follow me, sirs, and I will see that you are made comfortable."

"You may as well let us have something to drink."

"Wine, of course?"

"Yes; a bottle of the very best you have in the house."

"You honour me," said Jordan. "If I had such customers as you always in my house I should make a fortune in a few years."

He spoke with his tongue in his cheek, for he knew the officers well, and suspected that they had come there with no good intention to him or those in his house.

The room into which he showed Catchpole and Grabham was situated at the back of the house, and both the visitors expressed their satisfaction at the arrangements made for them.

Ben Jordan brought the wine and set it on the table.

"You will ring if you should require me again, gentlemen," he said. "The door sticks, and you may find some difficulty in getting it open."

"Ah! just so," said Grabham, winking at Catchpole. "Supposing you leave the key on our side, though?"

"Certainly," Jordan replied. "What object should I have in doing otherwise?"

"None—none!" Catchpole said, impatiently. "Thanks; but would you mind leaving? We wish to be alone."

Ben Jordan grinned as he left the room and heard the key turn in the lock.

"One good turn deserves another," he said, as he shot a small bolt. "Now we are equally secure, my friends. I don't want to know your business any more than I want you sneaking about my house."

"Now," said Catchpole, dropping into a chair, "out with that red handkercher, and let me hear what you have to say for yourself?"

Grabham shook his head, reproachfully.

"You wouldn't speak in that tone of voice if you knew how I have looked forward to this meeting," he said.

"Ah! I dare say. Well, never mind the meeting, but give your attention to the parting," Catchpole said. "I don't like the look of this place, somehow."

"What's the matter with it?"

"It looks as if it might be haunted by a ghost," Catchpole returned. "Now, then, are you going to produce that money or are you not?"

"Of course I am; but don't jump down my throat or I may bite you."

As he spoke he produced a piece of dirty, red-coloured rag, knotted and secured as carefully as if it contained the wealth of the Bank of England.

"There you are," he said, "and you'll find it all fair and square."

After struggling with the knots he opened the rag and emptied its contents upon the table.

Catchpole's eyes grew dim as he saw the coins displayed to his view.

Some of them were copper, a few silver, and one piece gold.

"How long have you been saving up these 'ere?" Catchpole said, with a grunt. "If you think to delude me with taking half this muck you're jolly well mistaken."

"If you don't like them don't have them," said Grabham, sweeping the coins back into his coat pocket.

No sooner had he done this than Catchpole threw himself into a fighting attitude.

"Come on," he said. "Stand up like a man. You have always looked upon me as a coward, but now I will prove that I am a braver man than you."

Mr. Grabham did not expect this sudden display of hostilities.

Indeed, it was the very last thing he did expect, and he was so upset, not only by the sight of Catchpole's clenched fists, but by the contortions of his face, that he staggered against the table.

"Do you really mean to say that you will strike me?" he said.

"Don't I!" Catchpole growled. "Of course I do. Come a little nearer, you low, mean thief!"

"Then I am afraid that I shall have to take you at your word," Grabham said, "and if you get a jolly good hiding don't blame me."

Now it so happened that the constables knew as much about pugilism as they did about the interior of the moon, and they did little more than hug each other.

A strange incident put an end to the encounter.

Whilst they were rolling and bumping about all over the room a terrific explosion took place.

It shook the house to its foundation, and above the flame and smoke the constables saw Spring-Heeled Jack hovering in the air.

Grabham, howling with terror, made for the window.

Catchpole dashed at the table, but Spring-Heeled Jack, alighting in the centre of the room, checked their progress.

"Stop!" he cried. "Stay where you are, or I'll leave no whole bone under your skins!"

"Oh! sir—please, sir, don't!" Catchpole whined.

"You came here to share money—where is it?" demanded Spring-Heeled Jack, grinning in such a ferocious manner that the constables almost fainted.

"I have it," Grabham said, feebly, "and I am sure that you are welcome to it, if you want it."

"Want it!" Spring-Heeled Jack said, contemptuously, "I want it! Ha, ha! What is money to me? Nothing! But there are the poor and starving—the desolate widow, the starving child crying for bread. They shall have it."

"Certainly!" Grabham said, as he produced a handful of coins. "I intended to give some of it away myself."

"Craven wretch, you lie!"

"Well, it isn't for the likes of sich as me to contradict you," Grabham said; "but I would be much obliged to you if you wouldn't look at me like that."

"This is not all," Spring-Heeled Jack said. "You tried to cheat your companion, but you cannot cheat me."

"It is every blessed farden," Grabham whined.

"Again you lie," Spring-Heeled Jack said. "Turn out your pockets, or I'll hurl you through the window you tried to crawl out of!"

With many a sigh and groan Grabham complied, and Spring-Heeled Jack left him nothing.

"I have nothing to say to you," he said, turning to Catchpole; "but be advised by me, and quit this house as soon as possible."

Catchpole was about to remark that he intended to do so, when a cloud of smoke arose, and Spring-Heeled Jack vanished in the midst of it.

Then the lights were extinguished by an unseen hand, and the constables, startled out of their senses, clung franticallly to each other.

They were afraid to move, lest they should fall into some trap set for them; but to remain there in darkness and suspense was horrible torture.

"Let us make for the door," Catchpole whispered, "I shall have a fit or die if I stay here any longer."

"He went through the floor," Grabham replied, in terrified accents, "and it is just possible that he may have left it open. We must creep round by the wall."

At length they reached the door, to their great joy, and burst it open.

A light was in the passage, and the constables hastened below.

Ben Jordan was at his work and smiled at them, but they gave him frowns in exchange.

"What's the matter, gentlemen?" the landlord asked. "I sincerely hope that you found the wine satisfactory?"

"It is not the wine that we grumble at, but the company you keep," Grabham said.

"Company—company?" Ben Jordan repeated, lifting his eyebrows. "I don't understand what you mean."

"Why, that Spring-Heeled Jack is in this house."

"In this house?" Jordan cried, falling back upon his seat. "Nonsense! You must be mad to make such an assertion."

"We ain't mad at all," Grabham replied. "The jumping scoundrel made me turn out my pockets, and took my money, and Catchpole's too."

"Is this really possible?"

"It is," Catchpole replied, with tears in his eyes. "He came through the floor as if he had been fired out of a cannon."

"I don't believe it—I can't believe it," said Ben Jordan. "I'm a law-abiding man, loyal to my king and true to my country, and I'll trouble you not to run my house down. What do you mean by coming here with a view to ruining me? Spring-Heeled Jack, indeed! Now, if Sir Roland Ashton had told me that—"

"Eh?" Grabham interposed, with a gasp.

"Oh! I happen to know something of your little games," Jordan replied, laughing. "I suppose you don't happen to know such a place as Lilac Lodge?"

The constables stared at each other in dismay.

"I think we had better be going," Grabham whispered, clutching Catchpole by the arm. "It strikes me that we have come to the wrong shop."

"Wait a minute," said Jordan. "It seems that you are afflicted with bad memory. You haven't paid for that bottle of wine yet."

"I haven't a farden to bless myself with."

"But your friend has, and I demand my due."

He walked round the bar, and closing the door that opened on to the street, planted his back against it.

"How much?" Catchpole asked, with a groan that came from the bottom of his heart.

"Five shillings."

The wretched constable produced the money as if he was parting with his life.

"Now you may go," Jordan said, as he opened the door, "and the sooner you are gone the better I shall like it."

"Come on," said Grabham, desperately. "Somebody will have to suffer for this. Come on, I say!"

## CHAPTER LXI.

### THE SHADOW ON THE BLIND.

Retaining Sir Roland's hand, Jules Carleon hurried the baronet along.

The Frenchman seemed to know the locality well, for his feet never once slipped, nor did he hesitate.

Sir Roland found that they were ascending, and that as they went the path improved, until it was almost as hard and wide as a public road.

"Steady now," Carleon said. "The smuggle have means of overlooking this portion of the wa and it's just possible that the lightning may revea our forms to them. If so, monsieur, they will sen quick messengers after us."

"Shoot us, you mean?"

"Yes; and they are excellent marksmen."

Sir Roland Ashton did not doubt this statemen for a moment.

His experience in the cave had convinced hi that the band of men were of no common mould and he saw signs in the faces of some that spoke o gentle rearing and good education.

How, then, had they drifted into such a style o life?

Men who have squandered fortunes in sin an debauchery must find the means of living, and ofte sink lower than becoming smugglers.

Sir Roland was fully aware of this, and, as h drew a mental picture of his own career, the colour were not very brilliant, though they might be calle startling.

"This path is filled with danger," he said, t Carleon. "You are not deceiving me? You ar not leading me into any worse trap than the one I have just escaped from?"

"Why should I do that, monsieur?" Jule Carleon returned. "Am I not your servant, now?"

"But how did you know that I was with th smugglers?"

"I did not," Jules replied. "I came upon you by accident. When storms rage one may pick up things worth having at times."

"You mean that you join the wreckers in their hellish work?"

"No," Jules Carleon replied; "I am too wise. I play the part of a jackal, and rest contented with such of the feast as the lions choose to leave."

"I see," said Sir Roland, who was crouching down behind a huge boulder. "Is the coast clear now? May we advance?"

"The lightning grows fainter and will soon cease altogether," Carleon replied. "Patience, monsieur. Is it your intention to return to the inn?"

"Where else am I to go to, in the name of common sense?"

"I will show you, if you will trust me," Jules replied. "I have a place of my own. It is what you English call cosy. Will you come?"

"Yes."

"And then?"

"I suppose I must think of returning to London."

"Not yet, monsieur," Jules Carleon whispered in his ear. "You and I—your servant—will go to a little village I know of. There you can take the rest you so much need. Do you consent?"

"Yes."

"And you trust me?"

"I do."

"It is well," Jules Carleon muttered.

Sir Roland thought he heard a sound like the closing of a knife, and kept a wary eye on the Frenchman.

"Now we may proceed," Carleon said, rising to his feet. "The wreckers have not done well to-night, and will sulk at home. They will miss you, monsieur."

Sir Roland now thought it better to tell the Frenchman his real name and circumstances.

He did so, and a cunning smile flitted over Carleon's face.

His moustache bristled and his eyes gleamed.

"Hah!" he ejaculated, "we live in a strange world, Sir Roland. I often wonder what the next is like. Shall we live, and love, and die, and so on, from sphere to sphere?"

"I am not inclined to argue the question," Sir Roland said. "My only desire just now is to get away from the danger that threatens me. Delay no longer, but take me where you will."

The Frenchman, ever polite and smiling, bowed low.

"This way," he said. "You have not far to go."

They went up the winding path, and crossing a broad open space, turned into a lane leading to some fields.

From this point Sir Roland could see the oil-lamps in the streets of Dover flashing and gleaming.

But it was not into the town that Jules Carleon led the baronet.

Suddenly striking off in an opposite direction, the Frenchman dived down a turning, so narrow and remote that the casual eye would not have noticed it, and Sir Roland found himself standing before a low-roofed, one-storied building, which might have done duty either for a warehouse or a stable.

"What place is this?" Sir Roland asked.

"My home."

Sir Roland glanced from the Frenchman to the house as if he mistrusted both.

"Pardon," said Jules Carleon, "but you hesitate?"

"Yes," said Sir Roland. "It may be that a long experience has made me cautious. I thought I saw a light flit across one of the blinds."

"You dream, Sir Roland," Jules said. "I am a bachelor, and nobody enters this house but myself. See, here is the key and here am I. If I have played you false I am unarmed and at your mercy."

Sir Roland, feeling somewhat reassured, opened the door, and Jules Carleon fetching down a lamp from a bracket held it above his head.

"I go before you," he said. "There are but four rooms, and, to satisfy you, we will examine them."

"I will take your word," Sir Roland said. "I daresay I am nervous and fanciful. Faith! it would not surprise me if I went mad and saw legions of ghosts."

Jules Carleon turned back upon him with so white a face that Sir Roland felt a thrill run through him.

"Ghosts—the shades of the departed!" the Frenchman said, under his breath. "Do you believe in such things?"

"I know not what to say."

"But if you saw with your own eyes?"

"Then I should believe."

Jules Carleon said no more; but his footsteps seemed to be unsteady as he led the way into a room.

It was oddly and uncomfortably furnished.

A pile of empty boxes covered with a red baize cloth did duty for a table, and a couple of rickety chairs completed the appointments.

"You do not go in for luxuries, I see," said Sir Roland.

"No," Jules Carleon replied. "Am I not a poor man? Am I not the humble waiter at an inn?"

He cast a side glance full of meaning at Sir Roland.

"Yes," the baronet replied; "but probably for your own purpose."

The Frenchman laughed as he produced a pack of cards.

"Will Sir Roland condescend to play with his humble servant?" he asked. "To-morrow we will change all this, but to-night, since I have done you so much service, I crave your leniency."

"I will not play to-night," Sir Roland said, wearily. "I wish to sleep."

Jules Carleon pointed to a door.

"There you will find your bed-chamber," he said.

"You expected me, then?"

"How you question me, Sir Roland. Perchance I keep a room for visitors. Why not?"

Sir Roland made no reply, but taking up the lamp stepped into the room.

He found this apartment better furnished than the other.

It contained a clean, white bed, an easy chair, and a few strips of good carpet.

Hastily removing the clothes he had borrowed from the smugglers' cave, Sir Roland threw himself upon the bed.

But he could not sleep.

Strange doubts and fears crept into his mind.

They kept him awake and on the alert.

He tried to convince himself that all was well, but in vain.

There was something sly and subtle about this man, Jules Carleon, who, passing at one moment as a humble waiter at an inn, suddenly changed his character into the man with a secret home, and a thorough knowledge of everything disreputable.

"It's a mystery to me how he knew me in my disguise," Sir Roland said to himself, "and now I begin to think that I must have been a fool to let out so much to him."

The house was very quiet.

Jules Carleon had said good-night as he passed the door, and had evidently gone to bed.

Why then could not Sir Roland Ashton take the rest he was in such urgent need of?

It was because he was so cowardly and base himself that he could trust no man.

Dim notions floated through his mind that Jules Carleon would suddenly enter the room and demand a ransom, and he twisted and turned these ideas into hundreds of shapes.

His eyes ached and burned with fatigue, and at last he fell into a fitful slumber.

There was no repose—no rest in it.

Sir Roland, like a fox, was, in a manner of speaking, sleeping with one eye open, for the slightest and most common sound in the room would have been more than sufficient to rouse him and set the blood tingling in his veins.

All was still outside.

The wind dropped, the storm clouds parted and dispersed, leaving the fair moon to reign undisputed in the sky.

The sea was still wild, as though it refused to be soothed after being lashed to fury.

All else in Nature lay sleeping.

Sir Roland Ashton had not closed his eyes more than half an hour before he opened them again, and started up in bed.

He had heard no sound.

Nothing had touched him. He had been but dreaming and he seemed to doubt whether he was still awake, for he rubbed his eyes and looked about him, as if to convince himself of the fact.

"Ah! it was but a dream," he said. "She is dead. Dead women, like dead men, tell no tales. And yet, what a curious dream it was. How vivid and realistic! I felt the pressure of her fingers upon my throat, and—"

Something, he scarcely knew what, attracted Sir Roland's eyes towards the window.

The moon was shining full upon the white blinds.

But Sir Roland was almost convinced that he had seen something flit across them.

It might be the shadow of a branch swaying about before the gentle breeze, or a hundred other trivial things might have accounted for it.

But Sir Roland was not satisfied.

He rose from his bed and examined the fastening of the window.

All was well there, and, cursing his folly and weakness, he was stepping across the floor when it became partially darkened by some object which had evidently taken its stand at the window.

Sir Roland looked round.

His arms went up with a convulsive movement.

His limbs became rigid and fixed.

If he had been a statue hewn from a block of solid marble he could not have been more motionless.

What was it that he saw at the window?

Only a shadow; but it was the shadow of Mrs. Corcoran

He could not speak.

He tried to shriek—to cry out; but his tongue refused to utter a sound.

At last the strength died out of his legs, and he fell with so loud a crash that Jules Carleon started from his sleep.

The Frenchman swore in his own language first, and then in English.

He loved his bed, and to be roused from it in the dead of the night was more than he could brook from even a baronet.

"*Parbleu!*" said Jules between his teeth. "Sir Roland must keep quiet while he is here. What a noise! Perhaps I had better go and see to him."

It was well for Sir Roland that this idea came into his head and that he acted upon it.

Jules Carleon found his new master lying upon his face, looking so white and ghastly that at first Jules thought he was dead.

To all appearances the foreigner was not a man of great strength, but he contrived to lift Sir Roland easily in his arms and place him on the bed.

"A strange creature this," Jules Carleon said, musingly. "Is it that he walks in his sleep? Hah! he looks at me! He speaks! Sir Roland, I am transported with joy to see you once more yourself."

"Take her away!" Sir Roland said, wildly. "Don't let her approach me! The sight of her is death!"

"Ah! there is a lady in the case," Jules observed, smiling. "A little *affaire du cœur*, I suppose, Sir Roland? But you are dreaming!"

"Dreaming!" said Sir Roland, pressing his hand to his brow; "no—no!"

"But I say yes—yes!" Jules said. "We are alone. Who else should be here?"

"I saw the witch!" Sir Roland hissed between his set teeth. "If flames will not consume her, if the earth refuses to bury her ashes, how am I t rid the world of her?"

Jules Carleon smiled to himself and made mental note of every word.

But he had heard enough, and thought it wis to put a stop to the baronet's ravings.

"Sir Roland," he said, gently, "you are no well. Be calm. Let me fetch you a glass of rar old wine. It will warm you to your very heart and do you good."

"Don't leave me," Sir Roland said, clutchin him by the arm. "No—no! I will not be lef alone. The spectre would haunt me and driv me mad."

"Well, then," said Jules, as he threw the be clothes over Sir Roland's icy cold form, "I wil not go. I will stay until day-light comes an disperses these idle fears."

"Not idle," the baronet said. "Do yo remember your own words? You asked m whether I believed in ghosts."

"I did, Sir Roland."

"I have seen one," the baronet replied. " have seen the spectre of a woman who died terrible death."

Jules Carleon twirled his black moustache an flashed a keen glance at Sir Roland.

"Was she young or old?" he said.

"Old—very old."

"How did she die?"

"By fire."

Jules Carleon uttered an ejaculation, but sa calm and still.

"You and the lady did not like each other?" h insinuated, after a pause.

"Ask me no more questions," Sir Roland said "How the night drags. Will it never end?"

Jules sat watching the baronet until the pale grey dawn of morning came creeping over th silent town, and Sir Roland, reassured, thanke the man and bade him depart.

Sir Roland was no sooner alone than, rolling over on his side, he fell into a deep slumber.

---

## CHAPTER LXII.

### HOW DICK SLEUTH WENT TO VISIT BLARNE IN NEWGATE—THE POWER OF GOLD.

WHILE these events were proceeding, Bill Blarney lay in Newgate.

Mentally and physically he was sore and distressed.

His head had been cracked, as recent bandages plainly showed, and his heart sunk at the though of dying a violent death at the hands of the hangman.

He knew that if such a fate was in store for him it was a deserved one, but he determined, very naturally, to escape it if he could.

To make matters worse, Grabham, in his zeal to do the thing properly, had emptied Bill Blarney's pockets of every farthing, and thus the captive was compelled to live on such fare as the prison authorities chose to provide.

This was neither tempting in appearance nor nice when tasted.

A small black loaf and a sickly mass of lumpy gruel was all Bill Blarney got each day.

He received no visitors, for the simple reason that nobody knew where he was.

He might have sent a note for assistance to Dick Sleuth or to some other comrade who fel inclined to help him.

But no warder would stir an inch without being

heavily bribed, and so Bill Blarney fretted and fumed in his cell and rattled his irons dismally.

His trial was coming on shortly.

In fact he might be called upon to plead at any moment, and what chance of escape would he have then?

Not the faintest.

Sentence once passed all would be over, save the short journey to Tyburn, with all its hideous ceremonies.

Bill Blarney groaned as these things recurred to his mind.

He was not at all smitten with pity for the misfortunes of other people, but he did not relish being strung up for a gaping crowd to stare at.

What a cowardly villain he was!

Give him liberty and a pistol, and he would as soon rob a helpless woman as eat his dinner.

But now that he was laid by the heels he whined and howled for mercy.

While he was thus engaged and grudging each moment as it flew by, there was consternation at the Bull in Top Boots.

The landlord was perplexed and alarmed at Bill Blarney's protracted absence, and so was Dick Sleuth.

All they knew was that Blarney had borrowed a horse and ridden out one night.

"This comes of being sly," said Dick Sleuth. "If he had said where he was going there would have been a clue to follow up, but now there is nothing—absolutely nothing."

"Well," said the landlord, "matters are getting serious, and by hook or by crook we must try and find out where Bill is. It strikes me that if you went to the Big Stone Jug you might hear something of him."

Dick Sleuth winced.

"That may be," he said; "but I hardly care to undertake the job."

"Why not?"

"Because when I went there," Dick Sleuth replied, "the warders seemed so precious fond of me that they wanted my company altogether."

"But that was years ago," the landlord urged. "I would go myself, but see the position it would place me in. Fancy the landlord of an inn going to see a highwayman."

"Well, then," said Dick Sleuth, "perhaps you will tell me the character that I am to play?"

"His mourning brother-in-law," the landlord replied. "Buy a good book, and present it before the chaplain's eyes, and after he is gone see what you can do with the warders."

This idea was feasible, but it had its objections.

Dick Sleuth shrank from going to Newgate, but at last he made up his mind to do so.

The landlord gave him a sum of money, and on the afternoon of a gloomy day he set out.

As he neared the prison he stopped and looked carefully up and down.

Little as he dreamed that Bill Blarney had been captured by Grabham and Catchpole, he knew these officers full well, and would have taken to his heels had he caught sight of them.

At last he ventured up the steps and knocked at a wicket.

"Now, then," growled a voice. "What now?"

Dick Sleuth pulled a long face, and squeezed a couple of grimy tears from his eyes.

"I am in great distress about a brother-in-law of mine," he said, "and I am afraid that he has got into trouble."

"What is his name?" the turnkey demanded, gruffly.

"Bill Blarney."

"Then you have come to the right shop, for his trial for highway robbery, among other things, will probably be on to-morrow."

"Oh! how dreadful," Sleuth cried, flinging up his hands. "What can I do? What would you advise me to do?"

"Shake hands with him, and say 'good-bye,' for he's booked."

As the warder spoke he whistled the air of a song he was learning to sing, and he rattled an accompaniment with a bunch of huge keys.

"Can—can I see the prisoner?" Dick Sleuth asked, overwhelmed with grief.

"Oh! yes, I daresay you can; but don't kick up that howling, for a man can only die once," the warder said. "Bill Blarney has had his fling, and I don't see what he has to grumble at, nor his friends either."

He threw open the door, and Dick Sleuth stole in.

There was something deathly in the very atmosphere of the prison, and Dick Sleuth, hardened to scenes of crime and misery as he was, shuddered and wished himself back again into the fresh, pure air.

He was received by another warder, who passed him on to yet another, and so on, until he was made acquainted with the fact that he was standing before the door of a cell which prevented Bill Blarney from following an exciting and often profitable mode of taking care of other people's money.

"Here's your dearly beloved brother-in-law come to see you," said the turnkey, who had brought Dick Sleuth to the spot. "Come, Blarney, don't look so down in the mouth. We all said that you would die game. Don't deceive us."

Bill Blarney stretched out his hand to Sleuth and forced a smile upon his lips.

"I suppose we can be left alone a few minutes?" he said.

"Yes; if your friend will satisfy me that he has nothing about him."

"What should I have about me?" demanded Sleuth, rolling up his eyes.

"Short, handy crowbars, files, screwdrivers, wrenches, and the like."

"Oh! I'll soon satisfy you on that score," said Dick Sleuth, throwing open his coat. "You may search me, if you choose."

The turnkey eyed him up and down, and, seeing that there was nothing bulky about his wearing apparel, walked out of the cell and locked the door behind him.

"Speak low," Bill Blarney said. "Thick as these walls are, there are ears which can hear through them."

"Well," Dick Sleuth returned, "I came here to learn how you got into this precious mess, and how you intend to get out of it."

Bill Blarney told how he had been caught, but as to escaping—that was quite another matter.

"I don't see how it is to be done!" he groaned. "Look at these irons—they drag me down, and a warder looks at them every hour to see that they are all right."

"Why didn't you let us know where you were?"

"Because I couldn't without money," Bill Blarney replied. "It costs a guinea down to get a warder to step over the road, and then the chances are that he would get drunk with your money and never deliver the message."

"Well," said Dick Sleuth, "our old friend at the Bull in Top-Boots has come down handsome. He has given me twenty guineas for your use. Now, the next question is, which is the best way to employ it?"

"I don't know," Bill Blarney groaned. "I don't see the good of it at all. All the counsel in the world couldn't get me off, for, you see, I was taken red-handed."

He whined out his words, and Dick Sleuth looked at him in disgust.

"Come, don't be a child," he said. "Money can do almost anything in the world. Can't you think of any idea?"

"No, I can't."

"Then I must for you."

"Do you think there is any hope?"

"There may be; but just listen to me."

Bill Blarney sat down, and as he did so the irons about his limbs clanked ominously.

"They ain't nice things to wear," Dick Sleuth said, "and I dare say you find them uncomfortable bed fellows."

"That's the worst part of it," Bill Blarney replied. "If they would take the beastly things off at night I shouldn't mind so much. But now for your idea. My brain is too confused to think of anything properly."

"Are you on friendly terms with your turnkey?" Dick Sleuth asked.

"Yes; or at least I think so."

"Well, then," Sleuth continued, "didn't you notice how he looked at me when he spoke about the crowbars and such like?"

"No."

"But I did, and I'll tell you what, Bill; that man would be your friend for a sum of money down and a bit more when you are free."

"Do you think so?"

"I am sure of it."

"But who is to put such a question to him?" said Bill Blarney. "Supposing he scorned the offer and blew the gaff? I should be done for, then, to a certainty."

"No doubt about it."

"Well, then, between two stools I am likely to fall to the ground."

Dick Sleuth made an attempt at a ghastly joke and seemed to enjoy it.

"No," he said; "I don't think you would fall so far, unless the rope broke."

Bill Blarney's countenance changed from white to green, and he shuddered as if he had been suddenly immersed in ice-cold water.

"I wish you wouldn't talk to me in that way," he said.

"I thought it would cheer you up a bit," Dick Sleuth replied, chuckling. "Well, well! we will say no more about it. How do you call the turnkey?"

"By kicking at the door."

"Then we'll have him in."

The turnkey answered the summons, and asked gruffly why he had been sent for.

"I wish to thank you for your great kindness to my unfortunate brother-in-law," Dick Sleuth said.

"Your brother-in law. Ha, ha!"

"Why do you laugh?"

"Because I know that you are nothing of the kind."

"Why don't you call me a liar at once and have done with it?"

"I will, if you like," the turnkey said. "If that is all you have to say to me it isn't much. Your time is up and you must come with me."

"Stop a moment," said Dick Sleuth. "Don't be in such a violent hurry."

"But I must, for I have other business to attend to."

Dick Sleuth paid no more heed to this remark than if it had never reached his ears.

He took a handful of guineas in one hand and began to count them into the other.

The turnkey was visibly affected.

His eyes sparkled and he brushed his hand across his mouth, as if the sight of the gleaming gold made it water.

"I not only wish to thank you," Dick Sleuth said, speaking plainly, and emphasising every word, "but to make you a present. Here are ten guineas for you, and there will be ten more if you do me a little favour."

"What is it?"

"Need you ask?" Dick Sleuth rejoined.

The turnkey tried to look innocent, but he looked hard at Blarney, and Blarney jangled the irons upon his legs.

"I think I understand," the turnkey said.

"Of course you do," said Dick Sleuth and Bill Blarney in a breath. "Will you do it?"

"Yes."

And I suppose I may go away and tell my friends that—"

"Tell them nothing," the turnkey interposed; "but you may tell me something. Where am I to come to fetch the rest of the money?"

"Do you know a house called the Bull in Top Boots, in the Borough?"

"Rather."

"Then that's exactly the place where the balance will be paid to you."

The turnkey said no more and Dick Sleuth went his way rejoicing at having succeeded in his mission and not a little proud of his own display of tact.

The sun was going down, and the shadow of the dismal prison was lengthened when the turnkey visited Bill Blarney again.

The prisoner was sitting crouched up in a corner of his cell, but he rose as the man entered.

"Go back to your place," the turnkey said, "and keep quiet."

Bill Blarney slunk back like a dog, and sat holding his breath, wondering what would happen next.

The turnkey had brought a lantern with him, which he set down on the floor and glanced round the cell.

"Blarney," he said, "if ever a man risked his life for another I am about to do so for you."

"I know it," Blarney began, "and—"

"Don't speak yet," the turnkey said, interrupting him, "and don't move after I am gone. When you hear St. Sepulchre's clock strike twelve, you may get up. Place your irons on the bench, and you will find the door open."

"What then?" Blarney said. "Will the coast be clear?"

"Yes," the turnkey replied. "It will be as clear as a bell as far as the yard. Go to the western corner, and you will find a rope dangling from the wall. I need not tell you what to do then."

# SPRING-HEELED JACK,

## THE TERROR OF LONDON.

"SILENCE, GIRL, OR YOU DIE!" SIR ROLAND CRIED.

No. 20

The turnkey opened the cell-door again, and, having made sure that there was nobody about, returned to Blarney, and so loosened his irons that, had he not held them, they would have fallen to the ground.

Now Bill Blarney seemed to live an age between hope and fear.

The hours which had passed so quickly now dragged themselves snail-like along.

It was scarcely nine o'clock and there were three more hours to wait.

The hands of the clock seemed to travel backwards instead of forwards, and when ten o'clock struck Blarney felt that he had lived through years of suspense.

He thought that some other warder might enter the cell, or that the governor might take it into his head to make a tour of inspection.

Though the cell was cold Bill Blarney's blood almost boiled, and profuse streams of perspiration poured down his face.

At last the time came for him to make a move. Gathering up the irons carefully, he placed them noiselessly on the bench.

Then, removing his boots, he crept noiselessly across the floor of the cell and placed his hand upon the door.

It yielded to his touch; but the hinges were old and rusty, and as they creaked, Bill Blarney started back in terror.

With bated breath he waited, fully expecting that two or more warders would spring upon him.

But nothing of the sort happened, and, after a long and painful pause, he opened the door and looked up and down the passage.

The coast was clear, and the only sound that came to his ears was a sigh or groan from some miserable prisoner.

With cat-like movements Bill Blarney reached the yard, and wending his way to the western corner, found the rope dangling from the top of the wall.

It was a stout piece of hemp, and knotted at intervals so as to make the ascent more easy.

Bill Blarney clutched the rope frantically, and went up hand over hand.

As he threw his legs astride the wall a deep-drawn sigh came from his lips.

He looked down into the street where the oil-lamps glimmered feebly, and was in the act of pulling the rope over, when he saw a man enter the yard.

Bill Blarney shut his eyes as he clutched the wall with his hands and prepared to drop.

The distance was great, and he might break a limb; but there was no time to waste in suppositions, and, letting go his hold, he descended, falling upon his feet.

At the same moment an alarm was given.

The man in the yard fired a pistol into the air, and a bell rang violently.

Though half-stunned and sickened by the concussion he had received in his fall Bill Blarney gathered himself up and took to his heels.

His only security lay in immediate flight, for death stared him in the face, and he ran as he had never ran before.

Twisting, turning, and doubling like a hare pursued by greyhounds, he turned out of Snow-hill, and found himself in a labyrinth of courts and alleys.

Dashing down a dark entry, he discovered that it had no thoroughfare, and hid himself half-fainting in the deep shadow of an old porch.

Presently he heard a footstep, and glancing at the door he saw that it was open, and that a man, bearing a lantern in his hand, was coming out.

---

## CHAPTER LXIII.

### JACOB BUTLER FALLS AGAIN.

WHILE these events were passing there were strange doings at the Queen's Head, near Sadler's-wells.

Constance Marfield and Daisy Leigh were on thorns about Ralph Ashton, and at the very moment that they thought something serious must have happened to him he arrived.

He came clad in a splendid suit of velvet, and mounted on a powerful roan horse.

The moment he appeared Ben Jordan, the landlord, ran out and whispered something in his ear.

Ralph only smiled and nodded, for he was all impatience to clasp Constance in his arms.

She met him with a wild cry of joy, and then almost fainted as she hid her pale face on his breast.

"Courage, my darling!' he whispered. "I regret that I have been so long away, but it was no fault of mine. There is yet danger and mischief abroad, and you must remain here."

"Danger! Mischief!" Constance repeated. "Oh! Ralph, those words mean that you must leave me again."

"I am afraid I must," Ralph Ashton said, sorrowfully; "but I shall triumph at last, and our reward will be peace and sweet happiness. Where is Daisy?"

"In the next room."

"And Jacob Butler?"

Constance Marfield laughed.

"I don't exactly know," she replied. "He is a strange man, but faithful, I believe. He has one failing, and that is taking too much drink."

Ralph Ashton frowned.

"That is a failing he must get over," he said, "unless he wishes to displease me. Daisy Leigh—Daisy Leigh!"

Daisy came running out of the adjoining room, and gave Ralph Ashton a hearty greeting.

"I did not like to disturb you," she said, archly. "Mr. Ashton, we have looked upon you as a wilful truant."

"And I am afraid that you will have to form that opinion again," he said, "for I must go away again to-night."

"To-night?" Constance Marfield repeated.

"Yes," Ralph returned. "Come, come! Constance, you must know that I am doing everything for the best. You trust me—do you not?"

"From my innermost heart," she replied; "but I can scarcely bear to part with you."

They sat down in the old-fashioned room, and Constance told Ralph of her abduction and marvellous escape.

"Yes," he said, "the story is not new to me."

"Not new to you!" Constance exclaimed. "Who could have told you?"

"The very man who has done me many a good service," Ralph Ashton replied, smiling quietly. "Spring-Heeled Jack."

At that moment a timid knock came at the door.

"Come in!" said Ralph Ashton.

Jacob Butler put his head and shoulders into the room, and his face wore an expression so woebegone, and yet so comical withal, that Ralph Ashton and the ladies could scarcely refrain from laughing outright.

"Well," said Ralph Ashton, "I hear that you have been in tribulation?"

"Tribulation isn't the word for it, sir," Jacob replied. "I have been through such things that now I wonder whether they really happened or not."

"The man who drinks heavily and makes a complete fool of himself is sure to get into trouble," Ralph Ashton said.

He eyed Jacob Butler keenly as he spoke, and Jacob hung his head and looked sheepish.

"Well," said Ralph Ashton, "as you seem to wish to speak to me, tell me what it is?"

"I want to know my position clearly," Jacob replied. "Am I to serve you or Spring-Heeled Jack?"

"You will serve me while I am here, and Spring-Heeled Jack when he calls on you to do so."

"Oh!" said Jacob, rubbing his head, and casting a vague glance at the ceiling. "That leaves me almost as wise as ever; but I suppose I must be satisfied with the answer."

"At all events, you will get no other," Ralph Ashton said; "and if you wish to preserve your peace of mind, you will pay attention to what I have said."

Jacob Butler, finding that his presence was not required any longer, withdrew himself from the room, and went below.

Ben Jordan was standing with folded arms and gazing through the open window into the roadway.

"Ha! ha!" he laughed. "Well?"

"Eh! What?" Jacob ejaculated. "What are you laughing at?"

"Oh! nothing," Jordan replied. "I thought you might have something to say, that's all."

"I'm losing the power of language as well as the power of thought," Jacob returned mournfully. "I feel sometimes that I could dash my thick head against the wall."

"Why don't you? It might do you good. Will you have a nip?"

Jacob shook his head, but the gleam in his eyes betrayed the wish which was in his heart.

"Well, only one," he said.

"Just so," said the landlord, passing a glass and bottle; "and then take a walk."

Jacob Butler shuddered and turned pale.

"I don't mean to Hampstead," the landlord said, laughing. "You needn't go quite so far."

"If you ever refer to that again," Jacob Butler gasped, "I'll—I'll throw something heavy at you!"

Ben Jordan placed his hands upon his hips and roared with laughter.

"I can picture you and that old woman," he said; "but what an odd story it was she told you."

"I wish she had never lived to tell it!" Jacob said, viciously. "How would you like such a fiend in petticoats to persecute you?"

"I think I should find some means of keeping out of her way," Ben Jordan said. "Ah! well, we won't talk any more about the matter, as I see it pains you. I suppose they are pretty happy upstairs—eh?"

"Happy!" Jacob cried, clasping his hands. "Oh! that such a fate was mine."

"Here is health, long life, and happiness to all three!" said the landlord. "Drink!"

Jacob Butler did so, and emptied his glass.

The liquor went down in such a hurry that he scarcely tested it, and when the landlord asked him to replenish his glass he did not say no.

"I say," Jacob exclaimed, "you have made this dose precious strong!"

"Yes, because it is the last."

It so happened that a masquerade was to be held at Sadler's Wells that evening, and as soon as dusk came a number of men set about lighting the coloured lamps, which might be counted by thousands.

Jacob Butler watched the scene as it grew in magnitude and beauty, and an irresistible longing came over him to go out and mingle with the gaily and strangely-attired people who now began to arrive.

As he was ruminating whether Mrs. Corcoran might not assume some disguise and attend the masquerade Ralph Ashton came downstairs.

"My horse," said he to the ostler. "I must away."

"So soon?" Jacob Butler ventured to remark.

"And why not, pray?" Ralph Ashton said, turning sharply upon him. "Am I to ask you when I am to come and go?"

"Bless me! no, sir," Jacob exclaimed, starting back in alarm. "I only thought—"

"Keep your thoughts to yourself," Ralph interposed, "and be still more secret in your thoughts and actions. Do you understand?"

"Yes, sir."

"Then take my advice."

So saying, Ralph Ashton disappeared out of the house, and in a few minutes was riding towards London.

"I've done something to offend him," Jacob Butler said, miserably, as he tugged at his hair. "I suppose I was born under an unlucky star. I never open my mouth without putting my foot in it."

Jacob had some thoughts of running away altogether; but where was he to go to?

He was only too well aware that Mrs. Corcoran would pursue him with all the energy of her witch-like nature, and that if he ever fell in her power again she would either put an end to his life or carry out her promise and marry him, which would be quite as bad, if not worse.

"I'm a miserable man," he moaned. "Nobody cares for me, and I wish I was dead."

"Don't make a fool of yourself," said Ben Jordan, who overheard the last remark. "Take a run out, and go to bed as soon as you come back."

At that moment a band of music commenced playing, and lured on by the soft, melodious strains, Jacob Butler sallied forth, and soon mingled with the vast crowd of masqueraders.

He had never seen such a sight in all his life, and Jacob soon forgot all his troubles in the novelty of the scene.

As he was watching a party of cavaliers, who seemed extremely attentive to an equal number of masked ladies, he felt himself touched on the shoulder.

Jacob turned and found himself confronted by a tall man, wearing a long coat down to his heels, and a conical hat.

The upper part of his face was masked, but the lower was sallow, and a well-waxed moustache bristled on his lip.

Jacob wondered who the man was and what he wanted with him.

"I think you have made a mistake," he said, feebly.

"No, *mon ami*—my friend," was the reply. "And yet, pardon. You wear no mask, and, thinking you might have lost it by accident, I called your attention—"

"I didn't come with a mask," said Jacob, interrupting him. "I happen to be staying in the neighbourhood, so I thought I would stroll in and see what was going on."

"Pardon—ten thousand pardons!" said the man, who, by his accent, proclaimed himself to be of foreign origin. "Will you drink?"

A sudden thought flashed into Jacob's brain, and he hesitated before replying.

He had been warned not to talk to strangers, and he cast a hasty glance over his shoulder to ascertain that he was not being watched by anybody from the Queen's Head.

"Well, you see," he said, "I should like to, but—"

"Oh! let us have no 'buts,'" said the stranger, taking him by the arm. "Life is too short to think twice about sharing a bottle of wine with a man. Let us be merry. Ah! this is a charming scene. It shall never be said in my presence that you English are a sad people."

He led Jacob away, half-resisting and half-consenting, and entered a tent erected at one end of the grounds.

Jacob Butler thought that he saw his companion make a sign to a man dressed like a monk, but he paid little heed to the circumstance, as it was none of his business.

The tent contained refreshments of the most luxurious description, and the foreigner, having called a waiter, ordered a bottle of rare old wine.

Jacob Butler now began to think that he had fallen into a good thing, and, raising his glass, he was about to pledge his hospitable friend when he was again tapped on the shoulder.

With some notion that he would find Spring-Heeled Jack at his side, and filled with terror at the thought, Jacob Butler turned his head slowly.

As he did so the foreigner sprinkled something in the glass of wine.

"I wonder who that was!"

"I saw nobody," said the foreigner.

"I—could swear that somebody touched me," Jacob stammered.

"Very likely. There is a great crowd here. It was an accident. Think no more of it, my friend. Come, let us drink!"

They did so, and as they set down their glasses empty, the foreigner removed his mask, and placed it on the table.

The face that Jacob now saw was that of Jules Carleon.

His bright eyes twinkled, and the end of his moustache went up as he refilled Jacob's glass.

"I like you," he said. "Let us be friends—at least, for the rest of the evening."

"It's very kind of you to say so," Jacob Butler replied. "But I can't think why you should choose to take so much notice of me."

He pressed his hand to his brow with a quick yet uncertain movement, and the Frenchman watched him keenly.

"Listen," he said, leaning across the table, and placing his hand upon Jacob's shoulder in a friendly fashion. "You are a poor man. Pardon—I do not wish to offend you."

"Oh! you don't offend me," Jacob replied. "I am poor—poor as a church mouse, and my master, for some reason best known to himself, keeps me very short of money."

"Who is your master?"

Jacob Butler shook his head.

"I can't tell you that," he said, beginning to stare vaguely about him. "I've been sworn to secrecy as to that, and wild horses couldn't drag it out of me."

"Well, well," Jules Carleon returned, "I will not press you, because it is a matter of no interest to me. But you said you were poor. Well, I am rich, and part of the mission of my life is to make other people happy."

"You must be a jolly good sort of fellow."

"You English have a hearty way of expressing yourselves," Jules Carleon said, as he took the wine-bottle in his hand. "Let me fill your glass again. No? Is not the wine good?"

"It is too good," replied Jacob, whose eyes were sparkling and dancing in his head. "It makes me feel so happy and yet so strange. Your voice comes to me as in a dream."

"Ah! said Jules Carleon. "How delicious! What would the world be without wine, love, and music? Did you say that Constance Marfield was pretty, and that Daisy Leigh was charming?"

Jacob Butler started and pressed his hands to his temples.

"What!" he exclaimed. "Did I mention their names?"

"Yes, my friend—yes."

"When?"

"Just now."

"Then I must be mad, or going mad," Jacob gasped. "Curse the wine! I wish that not a drop of it had passed my lips. Let me go—let me go, I say!"

He struggled to rise, but Jules Carleon's hand was upon his shoulder and detained him.

"Bah!" said the Frenchman. "What have I to do with these ladies, save that I love them one and all?"

Jacob's head fell forward, and he began to breathe heavily.

Then the man disguised as a monk advanced and stood at Jules Carleon's side.

"You have done the trick well," he said, in a low tone of voice.

"Yes," Jules Carleon replied. "He will answer any question I like to put to him now; but I must be quick or he will slumber too deeply. What shall I ask him?"

"Where he came from," said the monk, as he glared savagely at Jacob. "Call him by his name."

"My friend—Jacob Butler," said Jules Carleon, whispering softly in the drugged man's ear, "tell me where you are staying?"

"At the Queen's Head," Jacob replied.

"Good!" said the monk; "that is all I want to know. Come away."

"Jules Carleon laughed quietly as he rose from his chair, and, following the monk, they left the gay throng, and entering a carriage, were driven rapidly away.

A few minutes later on a waiter approached the table and gave Jacob Butler such a shaking up that his teeth chattered in his head.

"Now, then, timber lids," the waiter growled, "this table is wanted by other people, who are hungry and thirsty."

Jacob Butler only snored.

"He's as sound as a roach," the waiter said; "but surely half-a-bottle of wine can't account for the state he is in. Here! Hi! Wake up, will you! Open your peepers, and cut your stick, or

I'll hand you over to the tender mercies of a constable."

Jacob Butler opened a corner of one very fishy-looking eye, and closing it again, snored louder than ever.

"This is a pretty business," said the waiter, looking round. "Does anybody know who he is?"

Nobody knew and nobody seemed to care; but some young gentlemen bent on having as much fun as possible out of the evening, suggested that it would be an excellent thing to blacken Jacob's face and stand him on his head in a corner of the tent.

This probably would have been done had it not been for the appearance of two constables, and, unluckily for Jacob Butler, they happened to be our old friends, Catchpole and Grabham.

As they glared at the recumbent form of the man they had met at Lilac Lodge, the memory of their wrongs came back to them.

"All right," said Grabham, savagely, "we'll take of him. Stand back, ladies and gentlemen, if you please. This man is mad drunk, and there's no knowing what mischief he may do if he wakes suddenly!"

Lifting Jacob up in their arms in no gentle fashion they bore him away.

As soon as they got clear of the crowd Grabham vented his spleen on the unconscious fool by giving him half-a-dozen sound kicks.

"Now," said the constable, "we'll stow him away in the lock-up, and lead him a pretty life as soon as he comes to himself."

## CHAPTER LXIV.

### THE OLD WATER-MILL ON THE RIVER LEA.

It will be seen by what took place in the gardens adjoining Sadler's Wells that Sir Roland Ashton and Jules Carleon had returned to London.

This was at Sir Roland's express wish, for after having seen the shadow of Mrs. Corcoran on the blind, he made certain that the hag was either alive, or that her restless spirit had been sent from the grave to haunt him.

In vain did Jules Carleon urge that it was all fallacy on the baronet's part.

Sir Roland refused to listen to all arguments, and his one great desire being to leave the country, Jules Carleon consented to accompany him to town.

When they arrived the notice of the masquerade attracted Sir Roland's attention, and he determined to take Jules Carleon with him.

There it was that they fell in with Jacob Butler.

The moment that Sir Roland saw that most miserable of men he put Jules Carleon on the track, and with what result the reader already knows.

"So," said Sir Roland, as they were driven away, "Constance Marfield and Daisy Leigh are staying at the Queen's Head. Good! And now, how to trap them. I am convinced that Ralph Ashton cannot be far away."

"Undoubtedly!" assented Jules Carleon, who by this time had been made acquainted with all particulars up to date. "As you say, Sir Roland, Ralph Ashton is not far away, but he cannot always be at the Queen's Head. I will watch the place, and keep a sharp eye on Ralph Ashton's movements."

"What will be the good of that?" Sir Roland demanded, gloomily.

Jules Carleon laughed, and snapped his fingers contemptuously.

"You English have a saying that there is more than one way to kill a goose," he returned, "and I am going to show you the way to kill this particular goose."

"How?" Sir Roland demanded. "I do understand you."

"You know this Ralph Ashton well?"

"Only too well—curse him!"

"Have you any letters from him in yo possession?"

"Yes," said Sir Roland, bitterly. "What then? Still, I do not understand you."

"How dull you are!" Jules Carleon returned, abruptly. "What would be easier than to imitate Ralph Ashton's signature, and to send a pretty little note to one or both of the ladies? This very carriage could bring them to you. Ha! ha!"

"Your plan is a good one," Sir Roland said, meditatively; "but what if the forged letter fell into Ralph Ashton's hands?"

"I will see that such a thing does not take place," Jules Carleon replied. "Only give me *carte blanche* to do as I please, and success will follow."

"Agreed!" said Sir Roland.

On the following morning, as Ben Jordan, the landlord of the Queen's Head, was putting the bar to-rights, Jules Carleon entered, and called for a measure of wine.

Ben Jordan looked the Frenchman up and down with a critical eye.

There was something about him that Ben did not like, and he served him, took a guinea, and gave the change in silence.

"An old-fashioned place this," Jules Carleon said. "I had some difficulty in finding my way here."

"Had you," Ben Jordan rejoined. "I suppose you are a stranger? My ears tell me that you are a foreigner."

"But I have lived so long in this country that I consider myself an Englishman."

"You may consider yourself what you like," Ben Jordan observed, surlily. "Do what you will you can't turn a foreigner into an Englishman, or an Englishman into a foreigner. It's against nature and common sense."

Jules Carleon smiled as he raised his glass to his lips.

"True, my friend, true," he observed; "but when a man gets used to a country and the ways of its people, he is apt to forget that he belongs to any other sort."

"There you are right," Ben Jordan said. "I know that when a foreigner gets his nose in this country he is in no hurry to take it out again."

Jules Carleon's moustache bristled, and a flush of crimson suffused his face.

It was gone in a moment, however, and he laughed as he finished his wine and called for more.

"Will you drink with me?" he asked.

"No."

"And why not?"

"Because I only drink with my friends," Ben Jordan said.

"My new master told me that I should find you a silent, careful man," Jules Carleon returned. "You would not only drink with me, but shake me by the hand, if you knew from whom I came."

"And pray who may that be?"

Jules Carleon glanced over his shoulder and put on an air of mystery.

"Perhaps it will not be as well to say," he whispered. "But see here. Tell me whether you know this writing?"

As he spoke, he took a sealed packet from his pocket, and held it up before Ben Jordan's eyes.

The packet was addressed to Daisy Leigh, and as the landlord of the Queen's Head glanced at the writing a sudden and startling expression came over his face.

"How!" he exclaimed. "You come from Mr. Ralph Ashton?"

"Yes," Jules Carleon replied. "Last night my master met Jacob Butler, and pressed him into some service of which I do not know the nature, and sent me hither. I am to wait for an answer."

Ben Jordan had no alternative but to believe the villain's story.

There was Ralph's writing he had seen a hundred times, and moreover Jacob Butler had not returned on the previous night.

"Stay here," Jordan said; "I will take the letter up to the lady."

The moment that Ben Jordan turned his back Jules Carleon peered into the back parlour, and finding that it was empty he rubbed his hands, and chuckled under his breath.

Drawing a long gleaming dagger from under his cloak he slipped it into his belt.

"I must be careful, in case that the bait does not take," he muttered. "*Parbleu!* it would go hard with any man who attempted to stop my way to the door."

Ben Jordan went upstairs and knocked at the door of the sitting-room occupied by the ladies.

Daisy Leigh's voice answered him, and in another moment the sealed packet was in her hands.

"How strange!" she said. "Ralph said nothing about writing to me."

"Open it," Constance rejoined, impatiently. "I feel convinced that the communication must be of an important nature."

Daisy did as she was requested, and read aloud—

"DEAR DAISY,—*In the first place give my undying love to Constance, and tell her that I have at last found a place of safety for her and you. The bearer of this will bring you to me and then return for Constance. I have my own reasons for wishing you to come first, which I am sure you will not inquire into. As you have trusted me, so trust me now. I have heard from good authority that that villain, Sir Roland, is in London. Jacob Butler is with me, and I intend to keep him under my eye, for fear that he might make a fool of himself, as he has often done. Hesitate not, but come at once. The bearer will conduct you to a carriage which I have arranged shall wait for you and him near the Angel Inn.—Yours, with every kind wish,*

"RALPH ASHTON."

Constance Marfield took the letter in her hand, and read it through herself.

"There can be no mistake about this," she said; "but yet it is strange that Ralph does not say where you are to go to."

"Well," said Ben Jordan, who still lingered near the door, "if I might make a remark, it would be to the effect that Mr. Ashton thought his messenger might lose the letter, or be stopped on the road and robbed of it."

"Of course," said Daisy. "That is my own opinion, but would it not be better to see the messenger and put the question to him?"

"Certainly," said Ben Jordan. "I will fetch him up in an instant."

He found Jules Carleon standing in a listless attitude, such as a man waiting for a reply to letter might assume.

"Follow me," Ben Jordan said. "One of the ladies wishes to speak to you."

Jules Carleon did not hesitate for a moment, and as he stood before Constance and Daisy he removed his hat and bowed humbly.

"Where have you been instructed to take me?" Daisy asked.

The Frenchman shrugged his shoulders.

"That is a question I thought mademoiselle would ask," he rejoined, "but it is one that I cannot answer."

"What reason have you for refusing?"

"Because Mr. Ashton made me take an oath that I would not breathe it to a living soul," Jules Carleon replied.

"But I do not know you," Daisy said. "How am I to know that this letter is not a forgery, and that you have been sent to betray me into the hands of an enemy?"

No change came over the Frenchman's face.

He merely spread out his fingers, shrugged his shoulders, and inclined his head with a deprecating gesture.

"You do not speak?" Daisy said.

"Your words took me by surprise," Jules Carleon replied. "Your enemies! Ha! is it possible that one so young and beautiful can have enemies? I have done my duty, and if you mistrust me, mademoiselle, I must return alone, and leave Mr. Ashton to judge of your refusal."

As he spoke he bowed again, and walked towards the door.

"The man is honest," Constance whispered; "go with him."

"Stay," Daisy said; "I am sorry if I have hurt your feelings. I will get ready and be with you in a few minutes."

Jules Carleon did not seem surprised or pleased. It appeared to be a matter of perfect indifference to him whether Daisy Leigh went with him or stayed where she was, and he walked calmly back into the bar and finished his wine.

Thus thrown off her guard Daisy Leigh commenced dressing for the journey.

Constance Marfield assisted her, and, in a few minutes, she was ready.

"We shall not be apart for many hours," Daisy said, as she kissed her fair companion, "and yet even that short space of time will be too long. Good-bye. I shall count the moments until I see you again."

When she descended Jules Carleon held the door open, and followed a few paces in the rear.

He did not attempt to speak to her or walk at her side until the Angel, then an old-fashioned coaching inn, was reached.

A carriage with drawn blinds was standing under the archway, and Jules Carleon hailed the driver by holding up his hand.

Daisy Leigh had some slight misgivings as she entered the equipage; but she banished them, and as the horses started she drew up one of the blinds and, leaning back, looked out into the road.

Jules Carleon had shared the box seat with the the driver, and for more than an hour the horses trotted on in a leisurely way, as if instructions had been given not to hurry them.

The open country was soon reached, and the

day being deliciously fine, Daisy drank in the fresh, pure air, and felt extremely happy.

She loved the country with its fields and woods, and a new and brighter colour came into her cheeks.

Onward, still onward, the horses went, until they were brought to a standstill at a roadside inn.

Jules Carleon got down and held the door open.

"Mademoiselle will dine here and rest," he said.

"But I would rather go on," Daisy replied. "Our destination cannot be far distant?"

"We are half-way," the Frenchman replied; "and, mademoiselle, the horses must be fed and groomed."

Daisy said no more, but, alighting, permitted Jules Carleon to conduct her into a room, with a pretty window overlooking the river.

A sumptuous repast had been prepared, and Jules Carleon waited on Daisy at the table, passing the dishes and removing them with a trained hand.

He glided about like a shadow, and never spoke unless he was spoken to.

Daisy Leigh could not help being favourably impressed with the man's conduct, and she felt sorry that she had ever spoken sharply to him, or regarded him with a suspicious thought.

Two hours passed away, and the sun was going down when the carriage was brought round to the door.

Jules Carleon summoned Daisy with as much ceremony as if she had been a princess, and the journey was continued in the same quiet manner as it was commenced.

Now that Daisy had banished all fears and suspicions she began to look forward to meeting Ralph Ashton.

She was sure that he had some astonishing news to tell her, and was eager to hear it.

Sir Roland was in London, and perhaps he had discovered that she and Constance were sheltered under the roof of the Queen's Head, and if that was the case, Ralph's conduct could be easily accounted for.

The shades of night were falling as the carriage turned into a long, narrow lane, overhung with gloomy-looking trees.

Every now and then Daisy caught a glimpse of water through the foliage, and in spite of herself, the old misgivings forced themselves upon her mind.

She was wondering whether the journey would ever come to an end, when she heard a curious splashing noise, and looking out of the window saw that it was caused by the revolving of a water-wheel, over which towered an old wooden mill, overgrown with moss and creeping plants.

It was a gruesome looking place enough, and Daisy withdrew her head and shuddered.

As she did so the carriage came to a standstill, and in an instant Jules Carleon opened the door.

His lips were parted now with a triumphant smile, and his eyes gleamed and flashed like living coals.

"Mademoiselle," he said, hoarsely, "your journey is at an end, and that," he added, pointing to the mill, "will be your home until a better one is provided."

"That place!" Daisy cried, shrinking back in horror. "No—no! You must be mistaken."

"Indeed, I am not," Jules Carleon replied. "But come. I see Mr. Ashton approaching to meet us."

Daisy Leigh hesitated no longer.

She saw a man approaching and ran forward to meet him.

He caught her in his arms, and pushing aside the broad-brimmed hat which had hitherto concealed his features, revealed the face of Sir Roland Ashton.

"Oh! help! Mercy! Help!" the girl cried, struggling in the villain's embrace. "Oh! horror. This must be a dream! I am mad—mad!"

"Nay, my pretty birdie!" Sir Roland said. "Forgive me for thus caging you, but your cage shall be a golden one. One more kiss—only one more."

Daisy screamed her loudest and buffetted the baronet's face with her dainty hands, but he took no more notice of the blows than if they had been delivered with feathers.

"Help! help!" Daisy shrieked. "Is there no man of honour here to protect a helpless girl?"

"Sir Roland!" said Jules Carleon. "Her cries may be heard. To the mill with her."

"Help! help!"

"Silence!" Sir Roland hissed in Daisy's ear. "Silence, or you will find yourself in the water. It flows to the wheel, and the wheel crushes everything it comes in contact with."

"Would you murder me?" Daisy panted.

"Aye!" Sir Roland replied. "I am not the man to stand upon trifles. Silence, girl, or you cease to live."

Both he and Jules Carleon were holding her now, and Daisy's struggles had brought all three to the water's edge.

Again the terrified girl rent the air with her cries, and struggled with the strength of terror and despair.

"You die!" Sir Roland yelled. "Cease struggling, or you die."

At that moment there was a commotion in the water, and a white ghostly form shot under the surface.

It rose and leaped ashore, and Spring-Heeled Jack, reaching Sir Roland with one bound, felled him to the earth.

"Ha! ha! ha!" laughed the weird creature. "So I have arrived just in time. Fiend!" he shouted, turning on Jules Carleon, and seizing him by the throat. "Go to your well-deserved doom."

An unearthly cry went up as Carleon fell with a heavy splash into the water, and as he battled with the swift current Daisy Leigh fell fainting into the arms of Spring-Heeled Jack.

## CHAPTER LXV.

### JACOB BUTLER DISCOVERS THAT HE IS IN THE HANDS OF A PAIR OF TARTARS—THE LOCK-UP, AND WHAT HAPPENED IN IT.

JACOB BUTLER lay perfectly still when he awoke.

Where he was he had not the slightest notion, and the only thing that he was aware of was that he was lying upon his back, with something on his wrists that hampered their movements.

By degrees a confused train of thoughts dawned into his brain.

He remembered leaving the Queen's Head, of meeting with somebody who gave him wine, but that was all.

"Hang it!" he said. "What is this upon my wrists? Oh! lor', I'm handcuffed."

As this fact became palpable Jacob endeavoured

to stand upon his feet, but he found that they had also been secured.

"I must be in some dungeon," he groaned; "and here I shall be until I am murdered."

Then an awful thought occurred to him.

Mrs. Corcoran had perhaps caught him again, and manacled his limbs against all hope of escape!

"I'm done for now," he said. "I shall never recover from this shock, and the sooner I am dead the better."

A fresh pang of terror darted into his heart as he heard a key turn in the lock, and the door swing open.

Whoever the visitor was it was not Mrs. Corcoran, for though the hag's voice was rough and grating it was not one of such double-bass tones as Jacob Butler heard.

A light flashed upon his face, and simultaneously a heavy boot was applied to his ribs.

"How are you by this time?" said Grabham, staring down and grinning at his prisoner. "Ha! ha! ha! How are you now, eh?"

Jacob felt considerably relieved when he saw that it was only a constable.

"I don't know that I am any the better for seeing you," he replied, "and perhaps you'll keep your boots to yourself!"

Mr. Grabham gave Jacob another kick, which made him wriggle like an eel.

"Catchpole!" Grabham shouted, "he's come round and looks lovely. Come and have a look at him!"

Catchpole ran into the cell, and in the exuberance of his joy he took a good handful of Jacob's hair and tugged at it viciously.

"Oh! you brutes—you unmanly brutes!" Jacob gasped. "What have I ever done to you that you should treat me like this? Take these things off my hands and legs, or I'll report you to the authorities."

"You'll do what?"

"Report you to the authorities."

Grabham clenched his fist and pushed it with such violence against Jacob Butler's nose that tears of anguish rushed from his eyes.

"Oh! you hound—you devil!" Jacob gasped. "What am I to suffer next?"

Catchpole manifested a strong inclination to take possession of Jacob's hair again, but he refrained.

"Take them things off you!" Grabham said. "Oh! yes; that's likely, certainly. You're a dangerous character, and must be treated accordingly. I suppose you don't remember threatening our lives with a knife, which you picked off the table?"

"No; and I don't believe that I did," Jacob Butler moaned.

"If you contradict me I'll knock your two eyes into one," Grabham said, with an oath.

"That's right; let him have it," said Catchpole. "I'll swear to anything you like."

"Don't—don't!" Jacob pleaded. "You can't find it in your hearts to hurt a defenceless man."

"Can't we?" Grabham replied. "That's just where you make the mistake. We've got a long score to rub off with you, and we mean to do it now that we've got the chance!"

Jacob Butler gave a convulsive sigh, and, stretching out his legs, closed his eyes.

"He's been and gone and fainted," said Catchpole. "P'raps we've done a little too much?"

"Fainted be jiggered!" Grabham said. "Fetch me a pail of water, and I'll soon bring him round!"

At the mention of a pail of water, Jacob thought it better to open his eyes again.

"Not a pailful," he said. "Give me a drop to drink; my throat is parched."

"That comes of getting mad drink," Grabham replied. "My eye, how you did carry on! I can see the old gentleman who you knocked down with an empty wine-bottle. It's a great chance if he lives, and—"

"Eh! What?" Jacob cried, aghast.

"You nearly as possible killed him," Grabham continued, unblushingly, "and it took a dozen o us to hold you back."

"Lor' 'a mercy!" Jacob gasped. "I don't remember anything about it."

"Of course you don't," Grabham said, grinning, as he piled up the agony. "If the old gentleman dies you will be hung, as sure as eggs are eggs."

"And if he doesn't?" Jacob Butler queried, faintly.

"Why, then, you'll get transportation for life, and ought to think yourself lucky to get off so easy," Grabham replied.

Catchpole rubbed his hands gleefully as he watched the victim's contortions.

"And so," said Jacob, "that is why I am chained down like a madman?"

"Yes."

"Well," Jacob returned, "at all events, I shall have the consolation of saying something about you when I am tried."

"What do you mean?"

"Oh! nothing. Wait and see."

Grabham glanced at Catchpole, and that worthy's face fell until his chin descended to the top button of his waistcoat.

The constables drew aside, and held a consultation in whispers.

"See here, Butler," said Grabham; "if we consent to take the irons off, will you promise faithfully not to be violent?"

"I violent! Ha! ha!"

In spite of all his grief and pain Jacob could not help laughing.

Grabham removed the irons, and Jacob Butler sat up and rubbed his stiffened limbs.

"Now," said Catchpole, in a coaxing voice, "you can't say that we have been unfair to you. What would you say if we made things easy for you, and only took you before the magistrate on the charge of being drunk and disorderly?"

Jacob Butler had not much sense, but he had just enough to know that what he had said had taken effect on the constables, and he determined to improve the occasion.

"Oh! I don't know," he said. "You have told a lot of lies, and knocked me about. I haven't forgotten your visit to Lilac Lodge, what you came for, and what took place between you and Sir Roland. What a nice kettle of fish there would be to fry, if all the facts came out."

"Hush! hush!" said Grabham, placing his finger on his lips. "Men ain't saints, and if we did exceed our duty a little, why—"

"Oh! yes," Jacob said, interrupting him; "of course. If I had nothing against you, I should have been half killed, and then convicted on a false charge. Take me to a magistrate. I want to go before one now."

"Just listen to reason," Grabham said. "You are charged with nothing as yet, and if we like we can set you free."

"I don't want to be set free," Jacob replied, boldly. "I want the whole story to come out. My life is a misery with all these secrets hanging about it. I'll claim the protection of the law against that witch, Mrs. Corcoran, and Sir Roland."

The tables were now turned upon the constables with a vengeance.

They did not know what to say or do.

Catchpole, in a frenzy of mind, ran out and procured a bottle of ale, some cold meat and bread, which he sat before Jacob, and invited him to eat, and drink his fill.

"No," said Jacob. "I'll touch nothing from your hands. How am I to know that it is not poisoned?"

"Don't talk such nonsense," said Grabham, whose face had grown pale. "We were only having a lark with you. Catchpole, open the door. There, now! See how friendly we wish to be."

Jacob Butler smiled and shook his head dubiously.

"Oh! yes," he said; "I know your little games. You'll let me go because you are afraid of me, but you will save up your spite for another time."

"No, no," said Grabham. "On the honour of—"

"Oh! don't talk about honour," Jacob interrupted. "Well, if you wish to make terms with me you must fall in with my views."

"What are they?" Catchpole and Grabham demanded in a breath.

"You must catch Mrs. Corcoran and charge her with the murder of Lady Ashton," Jacob Butler replied. "I can't endure life while she is abroad."

"We'll do our best," Grabham replied; "but, you see, the old hag knew we paid visits to Sir Roland, and she might make matters ugly for us."

"Nobody would believe a word she uttered," Jacob Butler returned, contemptuously. "The sight of her will be enough to convict her."

"We agree," said Grabham. "Good-bye, Mr. Butler."

"There is another little matter which must be settled," Jacob said. "It happens that I have no money, so I'll borrow a couple of guineas of you."

Grabham and Catchpole groaned in chorus, but at last the coins were forthcoming, and Jacob Butler went his way rejoicing.

## CHAPTER LXVI.

### THE ESCAPE TO THE MILL—THE GOLD RETURNED.

HOLDING Daisy Leigh firmly, yet tenderly, Spring-Heeled Jack gazed upon Sir Roland.

The weird creature's gigantic form trembled with rage, and his eyes blazed like living coals, and he seemed about to leap upon the baronet.

But Daisy Leigh had fainted, and Jules Carleon rent the air with agonised cries as he battled with the stream.

The wheel seemed to revolve quicker, as if anxious to clutch him in its ponderous grasp, and the water toyed with him, now dragging him down, and then hurling him to the surface, and whirling him round and round.

The Frenchman's cries at last attracted the attention of some labourers, who were returning home from the fields.

As they came running down to the water's edge they saw a strange sight.

They beheld a huge white figure, bearing something in its arms, making its way with terrific leaps across the fields.

The spectacle was so strange and terrific that for a moment they forgot Jules Carleon, and would have taken to their heels had not Sir Roland Ashton staggered to his feet and hailed them.

"Stop!" he cried, wildly. "You must not let the man die! See! he is nearing the wheel. Ten guineas to the man who saves him!"

One of the men threw off his coat and plunged into the stream.

This example was followed by another, and they reached Jules Carleon just as he was sinking for the last time, and was within a few feet of the mill wheel.

Dragging Jules Carleon to the bank, they held him, almost between the jaws of death, until Sir Roland arrived.

Stooping down, the baronet lent his assistance, and in a few moments Jules Carleon lay upon the shore, motionless, and to all appearances bereft of life.

"I'm afraid he's gone, master," said one of the men. "We'll carry him to the mill, and try to bring him round, if you like?"

"Do so," said Sir Roland. "He is not dead—see! his eyelids quiver."

The mill itself was a short distance from the wheel, and the men made all haste to carry Jules Carleon to one of the upper chambers.

Sir Roland followed, pressing his hands to his bruised face.

The blow Spring-Heeled Jack had given him was a fearful one, and no sooner had the baronet reached the mill than he reeled, and fell half-swooning upon the floor.

"This is a nice business," said one of the men. "I think we ought to send for the constables—eh, Dick?"

"I was thinking so myself," Dick replied. "There has been foul play here. But what the deuce was that thing we saw dancing over the meadows like a will-o'-the-wisp?"

"Hanged if I know; but let us attend to this fellow or he will die."

Dragging off a portion of Jules Carleon's clothes, they set about rubbing him vigorously, and presently their efforts were rewarded with the desired result.

The Frenchman opened his eyes and sighed heavily.

"Where am I?" he asked. "Ah! me. Is this death?"

"You have been very near it," said one of the men. "How did you get into the water?"

Jules Carleon made no reply.

He thought it better to keep silence on the subject, and merely shook his head.

Just then Sir Roland Ashton recovered sufficiently to come to his side.

"My poor fellow," he said, "I told you how foolish it was to trust to the dangerous, slippery banks; but matters might have been worse. How do you feel?"

"Like a drowned rat."

"Well, well," Sir Roland said, "we have much to thank our good friends here for, and they shall receive the promised reward."

The men grinned at the sight of the shining

gold, and were about to leave, when Sir Roland called them back.

"I have paid you well," he said; "and now I want you to do me a favour. Keep your own counsel and say nothing about what you have seen, and it may be that I shall be able to put more money in your way."

The men nodded, and then Sir Roland let them go.

"I wonder if we can trust them?" Sir Roland said, musingly, as he watched their retreating forms.

"Oh! yes, so long as you supply them with money," Jules Carleon replied. "Now that we are here, tell me how you became possessed of the place?"

"I purchased it long ago, thinking that it would make a useful retreat."

Jules Carleon shrugged his shoulders.

"It seems to me that it is a place we had better leave as soon as possible," he said. "*Parbleu!* shall I ever forget my interview with Spring-Heeled Jack? No—no!"

"Curse him!" Sir Roland hissed, as he clenched his hands. "Whence comes the power that gives him the means of thwarting me at every turn? The girl has slipped through my fingers. Love has turned to hatred. She must die!"

"Good!" Jules Carleon said. "Such a revenge would be sweet indeed. Ah! how cold it is. Are there no means of procuring a fire?"

"Yes," Sir Roland said. "In the chamber under this you will find plenty of materials."

"We will go in company," Jules Carleon said, shuddering. "For the life of me I dare not go about this horrible place alone."

As he spoke a gust of wind shrieked and moaned about the mill like a restless spirit.

"Let us go," Jules Carleon said, as he hugged his bare shoulders. "I freeze—I perish of cold."

They went down the creaking staircase, and in a few moments some logs of wood were burning brightly.

"This is better—much better," Jules Carleon said.

He spread out his clothes to dry, and crouched before the blaze as if he could have devoured it.

"Do we stay here?" he asked, presently. "You are very silent, Sir Roland."

"We must remain here—at least, for to-night," the baronet replied. "Silent, did you say? My thoughts so madden me that I am afraid to speak. Jules Carleon, I tell you that Daisy Leigh dies, and then I care not what happens."

Sir Roland crossed the floor, and throwing open a cupboard, clutched a dark-coloured bottle and put it to his lips.

"Drink!" he said, passing the bottle to Carleon.

The Frenchman elevated his eyebrows.

"Why did you not tell me that you had such rare stuff here?"

"Because I had forgotten it."

Jules Carleon drank deeply, and then, covering himself up with a rug, rolled over on his side and went to sleep.

"Will this man grow tired of the undertaking, and betray me like the rest?" Sir Roland said. "If I thought so, I would make short work of him. Why not now? The mission I brought him to assist me in has failed—failed most miserably."

Sir Roland crept nearer to Jules Carleon and listened.

The Frenchman was breathing heavily and muttering in his sleep.

"He serves me but to serve his own ends," Sir Roland said. "I am in his power, and his one aim is to make profit by it."

The baronet took a knife from his pocket and glanced along the blade.

As he raised his arm he heard a heavy step upon the floor and the weapon fell with a clang from his hands.

Starting to his feet, Sir Roland saw that one of the labourers had returned.

"What do you want?" Sir Roland demanded, hoarsely.

"I have come back with your money, and here it is," the man replied.

"What!" the baronet exclaimed. "Are you so rich that you can afford to fling ten guineas away?"

"No," the man replied, nervously. "Heaven knows I am poor enough, but a strange thing happened to me and my mates as we were crossing the fields."

"A strange thing? I don't understand you."

"As we passed into the lanes," the man continued, "we were suddenly stopped by a ghostly figure. 'I am Spring-Heeled Jack,' it said. 'Return the money to the villain who gave it to you. His hands are stained with blood; he is a murderer, and every piece of gold will bring its curse.'"

"Bah!" Sir Roland said, contemptuously. "Are you so foolish as to be frightened by this scarecrow bogey? He is but a creature of flesh and blood, and will meet with his deserts like all criminals."

"I care not what you say," the man replied, "Take back your gold."

He flung it upon the floor as he spoke, and turned towards the door.

Sir Roland strode after him and laid his hand upon the man's shoulder.

"A word in your ear," he said. "Pick up the money. Fool that you are to tempt me! I see that you will go to the village inn and blurt out this story. If you do you will rue the day that you were born!"

"Nay," the man retorted; "Spring-Heeled Jack told us to keep the secret."

"And paid you for doing so?"

"Yes."

"That accounts for you coming back here with a virtuous speech and hurling the money in my teeth," said Sir Roland.

"You may think and say what you like," the man returned. "I wish to goodness that I had never seen you!"

As the man moved away his foot came in contact with something, and, looking down, he saw the knife which Sir Roland had dropped.

The labourer glanced at the sleeping Frenchman and then looked steadily into the baronet's eyes.

"It seems to me," said the man, "that my coming here disturbed you. Wake up, man—wake up! There is the scent of murder in this place!"

Jules Carleon started to his feet.

"Who calls?" he said, rubbing his eyes. "What has happened?"

"Nothing," Sir Roland replied, coolly. "I happened to drop a knife, and this idiot has got a notion into his head that I intended to use it for an unlawful purpose."

Jules Carleon turned pale and thrust his arms into his coat, which was now thoroughly dry.

"I do not trust you much," he said; "but I do not think you would play me such a trick as that."

Sir Roland laughed and snapped his fingers.

"No," he said. "I should be a fool to go against my own interests. But enough of this. I am sick of listening to such nonsense."

The labourer, growling something under his breath, slouched out of the mill, and Sir Roland, closing the door, placed his back against it.

"Which way shall we go?" he queried. "Whither shall we turn?"

"Anywhere out of this infernal place," Jules Carleon said. "In a short time the whole country will be up against us. Stay here, if you will, Sir Roland, but I go."

"Yes; it will be best," the baronet replied. "There is no safety here. What a fool I was to dismiss the carriage, for we must travel on foot. Pick up that gold, and follow me."

Sir Roland placed his hand upon the door, but it did not yield.

"S'death!" he yelled, "we are locked in."

"Ha! ha! ha!" laughed the voice of Spring-Heeled Jack. "Never words so true fell from Sir Roland Ashton's lips. You are locked in. Ha! ha! ha!"

## CHAPTER LXVII.

### BILL BLARNEY HAS AN INTERVIEW WITH MRS. CORCORAN.

When Bill Blarney saw the man at the door he felt his heart throb violently against his side and then stand still.

Blarney measured the man's strength against his own, and came to the conclusion that in a conflict success would be on his side; but a sudden cry or the sound of scuffling would rouse the inhabitants of the court.

"I must take the bull by the horns here," Blarney muttered, "and trust to this man's pity."

As he stepped out and the light flashed upon his face the man started back in alarm.

"Who are you?" he demanded. "And what are you doing here at such a time of night?"

Bill Blarney pointed to his bootless feet, which were cut and streaming with blood.

"I crave your mercy, sir," he said. "I have been attacked by robbers and beaten brutally."

The man who confronted Blarney was grizzled and hideous.

His ferrety eyes flashed suspiciously, and he put his hand to his breast, as if to make sure that some weapon he carried in case of emergency was there.

"Robbed!" he said. "Bah! who would steal your boots? It is you who come here to rob. Beware! I am old, but not feeble, and I am armed."

"Well, then, I will tell you the truth," Blarney replied. "I have just escaped from Newgate, and the bloodhounds are after me."

"You don't say so!" chuckled the old man. "What, have you slipped out of the great stone jug? Good. Ha! ha! Come in—come in; I like you for that."

Nothing loth, Bill Blarney accepted the invitation, and as he stepped into the house his strange host slammed the door and secured it with a ponderous chain.

"Now," he said, "speak out, and speak truthfully. Who are you?"

Bill Blarney gave a brief account of his history, and the old man chuckled hideously and cracked his fingers joints as he listened.

"Good—good!" he said. "You shall have shelter, and safe shelter, too, for nobody cares to disturb Rick Denton in his lair. Ho! ho! I have other guests."

He led the way up a long flight of stairs, and Bill Blarney presently found himself in a room furnished with stuffy chairs and a lop-sided table propped up against the wall.

Sitting before a smouldering fire was a woman rocking herself to and fro.

Her back was towards Bill Blarney, but something told him that he had seen her before.

"A friend of mine," Rick Denton said, nudging Blarney in the ribs. "Ah! my boy, this is a small world. Only think that you know Sir Roland Ashton and that she knows him, too."

"She knows him?" Bill Blarney exclaimed, starting.

"Who better than Mrs. Corcoran—the great, the clever Mrs. Corcoran?"

Blarney's brain reeled as this name was uttered.

"Impossible!" he said. "I heard that she was burnt at the fire at Lilac Lodge."

"Was she?" Denton replied. "Ho! ho! that's just where you make the mistake. She shall speak for herself. Mother, here is an old friend of yours come to see you."

Bill Blarney did not feel very comfortable as Mrs. Corcoran turned her ugly, wrinkled head.

The hag clapped her hands and hobbled up to the escaped ruffian.

"Where is he—where's Sir Roland?" she croaked. "Do you bring me news of him? Tell me where he is, that I may have my revenge?"

"I don't know," Blarney replied. "I wish he was where I have just come from."

Mrs. Corcoran looked disappointed.

"I traced him all the way to Dover," she said, "but he gave me the slip. Oh! to have him here! Oh! to watch him dying in agony at my feet! You, too, have suffered, Bill Blarney?"

"Yes," the ruffian responded; "and it will go hard with him when we meet."

"Give me your hand on that," Mrs. Corcoran said. "We have one object in view—his death! We will travel together and seek him out."

"I'd rather not just for the present," Bill Blarney said. "I must keep quiet until this affair has blown over."

"But you shall—you must—you shall!" the hag screamed, as she commenced to dance about in a frenzy of rage. "I have money and the means to get more. Jacob Butler has been faithless to me, but I will have him yet. Yes, yes! you shall take his place, Bill Blarney, and we will live for revenge."

Bad and wicked at heart as Bill Blarney was, he turned away in loathing from the witch-like old woman.

"We'll talk the affair over presently," he said as he sat down. "I'm weary to death. Denton, give me something to eat and drink. Ha! what is that?"

There was a noise in the court below, and Rick Denton held up his hand to enjoin silence.

"The hounds from Newgate have tracked you," he said.

Bill Blarney's face went livid.

"No—no," he said. "It must be a mistake."

# SPRING-HEELED JACK,

## THE TERROR OF LONDON.

JULES CARLEON TORE MADLY AT THE DOOR AS THE FLAMES AROSE.

"I wish I could say so, for your sake," Denton replied. "Hark! they are knocking at all the doors and demanding admission in the name of the King."

"What is to be done?" Bill Blarney said. "Tell me, is there no hiding place? Am I to be dragged back to that slaughter-house?"

Rick Denton seemed to enjoy Bill Blarney's terror, but presently he touched a spring in the wall and a panel flew back.

"You will find a staircase there," he said, "and it leads to the roof."

"A thousand thanks," Blarney returned, as he disappeared. "If I get clear away I'll not forget this."

As the panel returned to its place Rick Denton seized the lamp from the table and went below.

"Hullo!" he said, as he threw the door open wide. "What's all this fuss about? Ah! officers, I see. Good evening, gentlemen."

"You're mighty civil all at once," said one of the men. "Why didn't you come down before? We made noise enough to wake the dead."

"There's plenty of that in the court," Denton replied. "If I were to bother myself about every brawl I should find nothing else to do. Well, why have you come here?"

"A prisoner has escaped from Newgate, and we have traced him here."

"You don't say so?"

"Yes, we do say so," the officer returned, impatiently; "and if you use your eyes you will see that there are blood marks on your very door-step."

"Why, so there are," Denton replied. "How strange!"

"So strange that we mean to search your house."

"You are welcome to do that," Denton said, with an injured air; "but you will be wasting your time."

The officers did not think so; but finding no trace of Bill Blarney, they left the house and left the court.

As soon as Denton gave the signal that the coast was clear Bill Blarney returned to the room; but it seemed as if peace was to be denied him that night.

The clock was striking two when they were startled by hearing a loud knocking at the outer door.

Blarney started to his feet.

"Confusion!" he cried. "Who is that?"

"Hush!" said Denton in a low voice. "You need not be alarmed; you can hide yourself as you did before. Retire into the next room while I question the applicant."

Blarney returned no answer, but stepped into the room pointed out by Denton, and which being only divided from the other by a thin partition, he could readily hear all the conversation that passed.

The knocking was repeated, and Denton went to the casement, looked out, and demanded who was there.

"I am a traveller benighted on my way, and seeking a shelter from the storm. Can you accommodate me?"

"The hour is late," he said; "but are you alone?"

"I am," answered the man, "and am willing to put up with any sort of accommodation. I come to you quite by accident."

"Well," observed Denton, "I have but one bed unoccupied, but such as it is you are welcome to; so stay a moment, and I will admit you."

"Thanks!" returned the man; "I will not fail to reward you."

Denton made no reply to this, but moved towards the door, Bill Blarney waiting with impatience the entrance of the traveller, convinced that the tones of his voice were familiar to him.

The door was quickly unbolted, and the man entered.

"The fire is extinguished, you perceive," observed Denton, "and, therefore, as you are very wet, perhaps the sooner you retire to bed the better."

"Thank you," said the stranger. "I am very tired, so will do as you suggest, if you will be so good as to conduct me to the chamber. I wish to rise early in the morning."

"Very well, sir. Follow me, if you please," said Denton.

He took up a lamp and proceeded across the room, the man following him.

Blarney had silently opened the door of the room he was in just sufficient to enable him to peep out, and as the man passed by the door the light fell full upon his countenance, and it is needless to attempt to describe his mingled feelings of exultation and deadly malice when he recognised in an instant the features of Jacob Butler.

He could not without the greatest difficulty refrain from rushing out immediately from his place of concealment and seizing him by the throat; but he resisted the feeling as well as he could, and the unconscious Jacob walked on and ascended the stairs to which Denton conducted him.

When he had disappeared Bill Blarney rushed from the room and whispered in Mrs. Corcoran's ear—

"Jacob Butler—your Jacob Butler—is here!" he cried.

"It cannot be true!" the hag exclaimed.

"But it is," Blarney said. "It is true, for I saw his face."

At this moment Rick Denton entered the room.

"What brings this fool to me?" he said. "He tells me that he has lost his friends in a most mysterious manner. Why, mother, what is the matter with you?"

Mrs. Corcoran was capering about, flinging her arms above her head, and behaving in such an extraordinary style that both Denton and Blarney shrank from her.

"Into what room have you put him?" she demanded.

"In one of the rooms upstairs," Denton replied. "But what is the matter with you? Why are you so agitated?"

"Agitated!" the old woman shrieked. "I am delighted. Oh! I have rare reasons for being so."

"What do you mean?"

"I mean that he never leaves this house alive, unless he leaves it with me," Mrs. Corcoran replied.

"He looks to me as if he had very little life worth taking," Denton remarked.

"He has everything to me worth the taking," Mrs. Corcoran said. "How sweet to know that his dastard life is in my power! Oh! little did I think that kind fate would lead him to such a secret place as this. Let me see him—I must see him!"

"Wait till he sleeps," Denton said.

"No—no!" said Mrs. Corcoran. "Give me the light. I am too impatient to delay a moment."

"Well, then, since you will have it so," said Rick Denton, "I will go with you."

"Come now—come now!" the hag almost yelled.

Denton, without saying another word, took up the light and led the way.

When they reached the door of the room they stopped and listened.

Jacob Butler was breathing heavily.

"He sleeps!" said Mrs. Corcoran.

Rick Denton nodded his head.

Overcome with fatigue, Jacob Butler had stretched his weary limbs on the bed without undressing himself.

He slept soundly, little dreaming who was near him.

His countenance was pale and careworn, and it was evident that his mind laboured under some fear or anxiety.

"Ha! ha!" Mrs. Corcoran laughed. "'Tis he! Wake, you lovey-dovey traitor! Ho! ho! Wake, Jacob Butler, and meet the woman you have deceived so cruelly."

Roused by the old hag's voice, Jacob Butler did awake.

Starting up from the bed, he rubbed his eyes, and stared about him in stupefied amazement.

His face became ghastly, and his lips quivered as he caught sight of Mrs. Corcoran.

"Is this a dream?" he murmured. "It must be. It cannot be a reality."

"Oh! yes, it is, deary," said Mrs. Corcoran. "Consent to marry me, or this moment shall be your last!"

"Hear me!" Jacob Butler gasped. "I am defenceless—I am half mad! I have made a fool of myself. The people who would have been my friends have gone away. Back—back, you hag! Touch me not!"

"Will you swear never to leave me again?" Mrs. Corcoran hissed.

"No—no! I would rather die."

"Then die!" Mrs. Corcoran yelled.

As she snatched a knife from the folds of her dress Denton caught her by the wrist.

"No—no; not here," he said. "I will have no bloodshed in my place."

The hag struggled fiercely with him, but he held her as in a vice and forced her backwards towards the door.

"What madness is this?" Denton cried. "If you kill this man how can you dispose of his body? Listen to reason."

"I will listen to nothing!" Mrs. Corcoran yelled. "I will kill him, I tell you. Let me go!"

As they struggled, reeling to and fro about the room, Jacob Butler thought he saw an opportunity to escape.

More dead than alive, he made a dash for the door and rushed headlong down the stairs.

But his progress was suddenly checked by Bill Blarney.

"Not so fast, my fine fellow!" the ruffian said. "You must settle a little account with me before you go."

Jacob Butler gathered himself up for a supreme effort, and, hurling himself upon Bill Blarney, bore him down.

The action was so sudden that Bill Blarney was taken wholly unawares.

"Help!" he roared—"help! This wretch is choking me!"

Jacob Butler, driven to desperation, tightened his grip.

Blarney's eyes protruded from his head, his face turned purple, and foam gathered upon his lips.

His senses reeled, and had not Jacob heard footsteps descending the stairs it is probable that Bill Blarney would have ceased to live.

Relaxing his hold, Jacob Butler flew down to the basement of the house.

But another obstacle stood in his way.

The front door was locked, and Rick Denton had the key in his pocket!

---

## CHAPTER LXVIII.

### RALPH ASHTON REMOVES CONSTANCE MARFIELD FROM THE QUEEN'S HEAD—HOW JACOB BUTLER WAS DESERTED.

DAISY LEIGH remained unconscious for more than an hour.

When she returned to consciousness she found that she was lying within a tent, the folds of which were swaying to and fro in response to the cool night breeze.

Daisy was alone, and she looked about her with that bewilderment which comes upon a mortal awakening to sense and reason after a long illness.

Her head was pillowed by soft cushions, and a fur rug had been thrown across her.

"Where am I?" she murmured. "What has happened? Ah! I remember. Oh! Heaven be thanked that I am no longer in the power of that wicked man, Sir Roland."

As she sat up pressing her hands to her pale cheeks a woman entered.

She was strangely and quaintly dressed, wearing a short dress that scarcely descended to her knees.

Her dark hair was confined by a golden net of delicate texture, and about her waist was a golden zone, inlaid with sparkling gems.

Daisy Leigh did not speak.

She could only stare at the apparition in surprise.

The woman advanced, and kneeling down at Daisy's side, took her hand.

"I am called Lanoni," she said, in a soft, musical voice. "Do not be afraid of me. I will treat you kindly though you are a stranger and a house-dweller, as I see."

"A stranger—yes," Daisy replied. "But did not Spring-Heeled Jack bring me here?"

"Spring-Heeled Jack!" the gipsy replied. "Who is he?"

"The man who rescued me from Sir Roland."

Lanoni shook her head.

"I know nothing of what you are telling me," Lanoni replied. "One of my people found you where you are now. Close at your side was the paper containing gold. I will read the paper to you. 'Keep and protect this lady until I return. A goodly reward shall be yours.'"

"But how is it possible I could have been brought here unseen?" Daisy said.

"I am as much at a loss to know that as you," the gipsy replied. "However, you must make your mind easy. I am queen here, and my word is law. Not one hair of your head shall be harmed."

Daisy deemed it wise to say no more about Spring-Heeled Jack, and after partaking of some soup brought to her, she reclined again, and fell into a deep, refreshing sleep.

Curious eyes peered at her from time to time as she slumbered, and a stalwart man, armed with a musket, was placed near the tent by Lanoni.

"If a stranger approaches shoot him," she said. "This poor lady has gone through some terrible trial, and must be molested no more."

Leaving Daisy to the care of Nature's sweet nurse, we will ask the readers to return to the Queen's Head.

Day dawning found Constance Marfield still awake.

She had watched at the window for the messenger who was to convey her to Daisy until her brow throbbed and her heart grew sick with apprehension.

Her anxiety was shared by honest Ben Jordan, who, as the night advanced, began to think with Constance that some deep-laid plot had been hatched with success to entrap Daisy.

"It strikes me that that fellow Butler has played us false," he said. "By Heaven! if that be so, he had better keep out of the reach of my right arm."

Constance was too terrified to weep.

She could only moan and wring her hands.

When the dark pall of night lifted and rolled away before the bright sunbeams she sat staring with aching eyes into the street.

"Heaven help me!" she sighed. "What will become of me if matters turn out as I fear? What shall I say to Ralph? Oh! why is he not here to comfort and advise me?"

Scarcely had she breathed the last word when a horse galloped up to the inn door, and Ralph Ashton hurled himself from the saddle with such force that his spurs rang again.

His brow was dark and angry.

That he had ridden far was evident from the state of his riding-boots, which were splashed with mud and water.

Not a word did he say to Ben Jordan, who opened the door and stared at him with mingled terror and astonishment.

Constance ran to meet Ralph Ashton, but she stopped half-way, for he halted in the doorway of the room, and, folding his arms, gazed sternly at her.

"Where is Daisy Leigh?" he demanded. "Tell me quickly—where is Daisy Leigh?"

Constance Marfield sank down upon her knees.

"Oh! Ralph," she said, "was not the letter in your writing?"

"What letter—writing? I know not what you mean."

A bitter cry sprang from Constance Marfield's lips.

"You do not know?" she wailed. "Then all is lost. A man, whose voice had a foreign accent, came here, presumably from you, and produced a letter in your handwriting."

"In my handwriting?" Ralph Ashton said. "I have written nothing. Where is that letter?"

"Here!" said Constance. "Daisy gave it to me that I might read and read it again in the happy anticipation of meeting you and her."

"Pshaw!" Ralph Ashton said, as he ran his eyes over the paper, "this is a forgery, and who should the forger be but the basest of villains—Sir Roland Ashton!"

Constance Marfield fell forward in almost a fainting condition.

Ralph caught her in his arms.

"I am not angry with you, my child," he whispered, "for you alone have not been deceived. Courage! Daisy is safe."

"I fear the news is too good to be true," Constance cried. "Who told you so?"

"Spring-Heeled Jack."

Constance Marfield clasped her hands in a transport of joy.

"Ralph—dear Ralph," she said, "how much we have to thank that mysterious being for! He outwits our enemies even when they are in the zenith of their triumph."

"Yes," Ralph replied, dryly. "You shall see Daisy before many hours. Where is Jacob Butler?"

"He has disappeared. He went away the night before last and did not return."

Ralph Ashton's face grew dark again.

"If I thought he had any hand in this plot," he said, "I would send him to his reckoning without delay. Curse the meddling fool! He must have been tampered with by one of Sir Roland's agents, if not by Sir Roland himself."

Leading Constance to a couch Ralph Ashton paced the apartment with hasty strides.

"I have been much to blame," he said. "It was my duty to leave you better protected. Constance, prepare to come with me, for the roof of the Queen's Head is not strong enough to shelter you."

"I will go with you anywhere," she said. "I am all anxiety to get away. You are sure that Daisy is in safe hands?"

"Quite sure," Ralph replied. "He would be a stout-hearted man who would dare to approach her now."

"How are we to travel?" Constance asked, anxiously.

"On horseback," Ralph replied; "Jordan can accommodate us. We start in an hour."

Ralph went below shortly after, and though Ben Jordan was thankful to hear of Daisy's safety, he was in a terrible rage.

"To think that I should be taken in like this, and by a foreigner, too," he said, bringing his fist down upon the bar counter. "The forgery was well executed."

"It was," Ralph replied; "and only one man in the world could have done it. How cunning the villain is!"

"The Frenchman?"

"Yes; but he cannot hold a candle to his master, who is a devil in the form of a man."

"That I can readily believe," Jordan assented. "Will you not partake of some refreshment? You look worn out and weary."

"Yes," said Ralph. "Constance and I will breakfast together. Let us know the moment the horses are brought round to the door."

"Everything shall be as you wish," Jordan replied.

Late in the evening of the same day, as Ben Jordan was sitting alone in the back parlour and pondering on the strange events which had taken place under his roof, he heard the door open.

Thinking that it was some ordinary customer he rose slowly, placing his pipe carefully on the table.

"What can I have the pleasure of—"

He got no further.

Speech left him as he saw Jacob Butler standing at the other side of the counter.

"I've been in a precious nice fix," Jacob whined. "I was an idiot to take your advice and go to the masquerade."

Ben Jordan recovered his speech and strength of limbs.

Springing nimbly over the counter, he seized Jacob by the collar and shook him till his teeth rattled in his head.

"You blackguard—you graceless villain!" he said. "It strikes me very forcibly that you have been the cause of all this trouble."

"Troub—b—b—bubble!" gasped Jacob, whose head was flying from side to side. "Here, I say, don't shake the life out of me."

"I should like to," said Ben Jordan, "but I'll leave that job to hands more willing even than mine. What have you been doing with yourself, you contemptible scoundrel?"

Before Jacob Butler had time to reply Ben Jordan pitched him into a corner, where he lay huddled up and gasping for breath.

"Oh! lor'," he moaned, "haven't I been treated bad enough already?"

"Not half bad enough for my liking," Jordan said, towering over him in a threatening attitude. "Give an account of yourself, you white-livered hound!"

Jacob Butler did so as well as he was able, and Ben Jordan listened, smiling incredulously.

"And do you expect me to believe this cock-and-bull story?" he asked.

"I can't help it if you don't," Jacob replied. "Please don't ill-treat me any more. I am half worried to death now."

"The best thing you can do is to take yourself out of my house, and never come near it again," Jordan said. "Mr. Ashton has taken Miss Constance away with him, and I don't want you here."

"Very well," Jacob said. "I have no wish to stay where I am not wanted. I own that I have acted the part of a fool, but that I am guilty of anything else I flatly deny."

Ben Jordan pointed sternly to the door.

"I will listen to no more," he said. "Go!"

And Jacob Butler went, houseless and homeless. He dare not trust himself to the streets, and thus it was, after slinking about for hours, he, so fatigued that he could scarcely stand, found his way by chance to Rick Denton's house and into the presence of that most unpleasant female, Mrs. Corcoran.

---

## CHAPTER LXIX.

### THE MILL ON FIRE—MOMENTS OF TERROR—FALLING OF THE OLD STRUCTURE.

JULES CARLEON, white and trembling, started back as he heard Spring-Heeled Jack's voice.

"Mercy!" he cried. "That fiend will betray us!"

Again came the mocking laughter of Spring-Heeled Jack.

"Uncouth, misshapen wretch!" Sir Roland yelled, in a paroxysm. "Though it is given to you to thwart my desires, you can do me no harm!"

"How often have I spared your life?" Spring-Heeled Jack said, now appearing at a barred window. "Fain would I do so now if I thought you would commence a new life and sin no more. Miserable wretch, your life is in my hands, for this mill is on fire!"

"What!" Sir Roland cried, "the mill on fire! Then it was your dastard hand that did the deed!"

"You lie!" Spring-Heeled Jack cried. "But why should I parley with you? Listen!"

The sound of crackling wood came to the ears of the prisoners, and presently wreaths of smoke and tongues of flame began to rise through the floor.

"Help—help! For mercy's sake, help!" Jules Carleon cried, as he rushed to the door and shook it. "If you are a man take pity on us."

"Pity!" Spring-Heeled Jack echoed. "What pity have you ever shown your victims? What mercy would you have shown to an innocent helpless girl? Die, dogs—die, both of you!"

The smoke now became dense and suffocating. Sir Roland gasped for breath.

He stretched out his hands pleadingly, and his lips moved in supplication, but no sound came from them.

His throat swelled, and the water of anguish rushed from his eyes.

He reeled and fell face downwards upon the floor, leaving Jules Carleon to battle vainly with the heavy door.

Spring-Heeled Jack had removed his face from the window, but, moved to pity even for the heartless villains who so justly deserved death, he hurled the key through the bars.

Jules Carleon heard it fall, but could not see it. With the hot, lurid flames writhing snakelike on all sides of him, he grasped about for the key.

If he could only find it all would be well, for outside the mill ran a balcony with a bridge of planks attached to it, leading to the shore.

But all his efforts were still in vain.

The heat now became terrific.

He could scarcely breathe and had given up all hopes when his almost paralysed fingers grasped the key.

But now his strength was failing him, and it was with the greatest difficulty that he dragged his limbs to the door.

"The saints preserve me!" he cried. "One more chance—only one! Oh! what horrible agony is this? Must I die thus? No—no!"

He thrust the key into the lock, and, turning it, flung the door open.

"Sir Roland!" he cried; "Sir Roland!"

The baronet did not move, and Jules Carleon, rushing back, dragged him bodily along, and, regardless of consequences, hurled him into the quiet water beyond the door and plunged in after him.

This was scarcely accomplished when, with a mighty, roaring sound, the flames burst through the roof of the mill.

The old structure reeled and collapsed, its charred timbers and red-hot machinery hissing as they fell, a mere mass of *debris*, into the stream.

As this took place Spring-Heeled Jack appeared on the bank and peered right and left.

"I can see nothing of them," he muttered. "Well, the villains brought their blood upon their own heads. The world will not miss them."

And yet he turned sadly away, and went bounding across the meadows to avoid crowds of people who were now on their way to the mill, but too late to do any good.

. . . . .

Some days passed away, during which Constance and Daisy had been removed to a cottage near to the historic house in which the Rye House plot was concocted.

It was a pretty little place with a garden, and

Ralph Ashton remained long enough to satisfy himself that the retreat was likely to prove a snug and safe one.

Nothing had been heard of Sir Roland or Jules Carleon, but it seemed so certain that they must have been burned or drowned that the people, after hunting awhile for their bodies, came to the conclusion that they had floated away with the tide.

And now it seemed that happiness was almost within the reach of Ralph Ashton and Constance Marfield, and, indeed, the preparations for the wedding were commenced, and were almost complete, when Lanoni and her people took an affectionate leave of the ladies.

But the cottage was not left altogether unprotected.

A man, armed with sword and pistols, kept within hail during the day, and another patrolled it by night.

Business connected with family affairs had called Ralph Ashton to London, and the girls were sitting amusing themselves with needlework and chatting.

They could hear the footsteps of their guardian pacing the garden walk, and they felt security in the fact that he had only to discharge one of his pistols to bring the people of the neighbourhood down like a nest of hornets about the ears of any intruder.

Suddenly the footsteps stopped, and Constance, thinking that she heard a dull sound, went to the window and looked out.

The night was so dark that she could see nothing; but though she said nothing to Daisy, she felt alarmed until she heard the welcome footsteps return.

"Constance," Daisy said, "Ralph is later than he promised. I am getting alarmed again. The old feeling that something is about to happen has come again. You may call me weak and foolish if you like, but— Hark! What sound is that?"

"I heard no noise," replied Constance, whose white face betrayed her feelings.

"I could almost swear that I heard a footstep on the stairs."

"It could only have been the wind or the effect of your imagination. Come, come, take courage."

"There again," cried Daisy, her face becoming very pale and her lips trembling. "This time I am certain I was not mistaken. There is someone moving in the house."

"Probably the servant," returned Constance, who had herself heard the sounds. "I will go and ascertain the cause."

"No, no, no!" Daisy cried, detaining her by the arm; "do not stir, but—"

Before she could finish the sentence the door was hastily but silently thrown open, and Sir Roland and two or three other ruffians, masked, entered the room and advanced towards the terrified girls, who screamed aloud as they approached.

"Silence!" said Sir Roland, as he seized Daisy in his arms, and two or three of the other villains tried to secure Constance, who, however, was too active for them, and, flying past them, made towards the door, calling aloud for help.

"Curse her!" cried Sir Roland, "her screams will alarm the neighbourhood, and we may yet find some difficulty in completing the business. Secure her—do not suffer her to escape. This girl, at any rate, is mine, and I will away with my prize."

Daisy had fainted, and Sir Roland, raising her insensible form in his arms, rushed from the room and prepared to descend the stairs, while his companions went in pursuit of Constance; but her loud screams drove them off, for the neighbourhood was now alarmed, and men were approaching in all directions.

Sir Roland, fearful of the consequences of delay, made his way down the stairs with all speed, and supporting his unconscious burthen on his shoulder, darted across the garden, opened the gates, and hastened to the spot where the vehicle was in waiting to receive him.

Finding that their efforts were not likely to be crowned with success, his base associates followed him, and Sir Roland, having lifted his unfortunate victim into the carriage, followed quickly himself, and the other ruffians, mounting their horses, the whole were soon dashing away at a rapid rate far from the cottage and in the direction of London.

"At any rate, so far I triumph," cried Sir Roland. "I have been revenged, and Daisy is in my power, although Constance has escaped me for the present. But she shall not do so long. No; the time will come when she also shall be in my possession. Oh! this has been a brave night's work! Daisy, you are mine—you are mine, and cannot again escape me! How beautiful she looks, even in her paleness and terror! To obtain such a prize as this, was it not worth every risk? It was, and I glory in my success. She may heap upon me her scornful reproaches; I am fully prepared for them, and will heed them not. I said I would kill her. No, no; she is too young and beautiful to die."

As the villain thus spoke he once more fixed a look of admiration upon the girl, and then dared to pollute her lips with his kisses.

Poor Daisy! she was unconscious of the contamination, or her soul would have shrunk with horror and disgust.

---

## CHAPTER LXX.

### A DEN OF CRIME—SIR ROLAND'S TRIUMPH.

Nearly an hour had elapsed ere Daisy was restored to sensibility, and by that time the vehicle had proceeded quickly and was travelling through a lonely and unfrequented place without any danger of pursuit.

For some seconds she was not quite sensible of her situation or what had happened to her; but the motion of the carriage aroused her and recalled her to recollection, and fixing her eyes upon Sir Roland and Jules Carleón, who had also taken his place in the vehicle, she uttered a cry of horror and sank back motionless in her seat, covering her face with her hands and the blood turning chill in her veins.

Sir Roland attempted to take her hand, but she shrank from him appalled.

"Horror—horror!" she exclaimed. "Has villainy then succeeded, and am I indeed torn from those dear friends who have so long protected me and ran so many risks for my sake? Wretched, wretched girl that I am! When will my troubles cease? For what horrible fate am I still reserved? Oh! is there no human being at hand to help me and rescue me from the power of these miscreants?"

"Be calm," said Sir Roland, who still wore a mask; "for all your cries for assistance would be useless. Fortune has placed you in my power, and they must be keen and bold who can release you from it."

Daisy Leigh started at the sound of his voice.

"Ah! who are you that have dared to commit this cruel outrage?" she demanded.

"Behold!" answered Sir Roland, raising the mask which had hitherto concealed his features.

Daisy uttered a piercing shriek of the utmost alarm and despair when she recognised the well-known countenance of her persecutor.

"Sir Roland—villain—murderer!" she gasped. "Am I indeed in your power? Are, then, my forebodings thus terribly fulfilled? Then am I indeed lost! Heaven help me! for this is more than I can bear."

"Nay, lovely Daisy, but you must learn to bear it with calmness, fortitude, and resignation," returned the villain. "Yes, it is indeed Sir Roland, the dreaded Sir Roland, who has at length triumphed in the accomplishment of the wishes he has for so long a period entertained. Ere a week has passed away Daisy Leigh shall change her name!"

"Wretch!" cried Daisy, her bosom swelling with disgust and indignation. "Still will I set your power at defiance! Heaven will not suffer you thus to triumph in your atrocious designs. Tremble, for even now vengeance is impending over you, and will assuredly descend upon your guilty head in the midst of your iniquity!"

"Sweet Daisy," replied Sir Roland, "you may save yourself these threats, for I heed them not. My purpose, so far, is accomplished, and I will not fail to take advantage of it."

"Mercy—mercy!' exclaimed the terrified girl. "But I plead in vain; for well do I know that you are insensible to that feeling. Oh! help—help!"

"Forbear your cries, for there is no one here to listen to them," said Sir Roland. "We are now several miles from Hoddesdon, and travelling through a part of the country where we are not likely to be molested. My plot has succeeded, and you are mine beyond all chance of escape. And so you and the rest thought me dead? Ha! ha! ha!"

"Gracious Heaven!" Daisy cried, "interpose, I beseech you, to save me. Oh! Ralph, Constance, my dear friends, what has become of you?"

"You will probably never behold them again," returned the villain, "so you may as well make up your mind to the worst, and not indulge in useless regrets or lamentations."

"Alas—alas!" sighed Daisy, "and it is for a fate like this that I have been reserved! Would that death had long since ended my misery, for now, indeed, has life become a hateful burthen to me."

"Say not so, fair Daisy," said the miscreant, "for you may yet find that Sir Roland Ashton, the villain, as you would term me, knows how to appreciate charms such as you possess, and that he—"

"Hold, monster!" cried Daisy; "your words fill my soul with horror. Think not to triumph, for death will yet snatch me from the awful, the revolting fate to which you would consign me. But this must be all some terrible vision—it cannot be true. Oh! what have I done that I should be thus so severely punished?"

Her feelings completely overpowered her, and she sank back in her seat, unable to articulate another syllable.

She placed her hands across her eyes, for she dared not look in the countenances of the wretches with her, and she gave herself up entirely to the dreadful agony with which her heart and brain were filled.

Nothing could be imagined more horrible than Daisy's situation, and it was wonderful that her senses did not entirely leave her.

To find herself in the power of such a monster as Sir Roland, and entirely at his mercy, was dreadful enough, and the lateness of the hour, and the wild and dreary place they were travelling through, added greatly to her anguish.

From such a man she had everything to dread, and her very blood froze within her veins when she anticipated the sufferings that were in store for her.

But whither were the wretches conveying her?

Daring, indeed, must Sir Roland be to attempt the outrage he had committed when he was so vigilantly sought after by Spring-Heeled Jack. It showed, at any rate, that his power was not, as it had been imagined, destroyed, and that he would not fail to put his threat into execution, callous as he was to all sense of pity or humanity.

The climax of her fate, Daisy believed, was approaching, and she contemplated it with the most unbounded terror.

That Constance had not also fallen into the power of the wretches afforded the poor girl much consolation, and she wondered that Sir Roland had not taken care to secure her.

While she continued to indulge in these reflections the carriage proceeded at the same rapid rate, but she was suddenly aroused from them by hearing some observations that were made by Jules Carleon, and which immediately struck her and riveted every faculty in alarm.

"Your sword did you good service, Sir Roland," he said; "and I think the young gentleman will never trouble you again."

"Ah!" exclaimed Daisy, starting, and gazing intently in the ferocious countenance of the villain who spoke. "What do those words imply? Ralph Ashton? Speak! is it to him you allude? You surely have not—"

"He was fool enough to arrive at the same time I did and to attempt to obstruct me in my designs, and he has been justly rewarded for his trouble."

"Recall those dreadful words!" Daisy cried. "Oh! tell me that you have not murdered him."

"I merely ran him through the body," said Sir Roland, coolly; "but whether he is dead or not I cannot say."

Daisy could listen to no more.

She gave one piercing shriek, which resounded far around, and sank, senseless and inanimate, to the bottom of the carriage.

What afterwards occurred to her she had no knowledge of, but when she again recovered she found herself still in the vehicle, but Sir Roland and his companion had quitted it, and their places were occupied by two other ruffians.

Daisy Leigh passed her hand across her temples, and had at first only a confused recollection of what she had heard or where she was.

"Whither am I being conveyed?" she cried; "who are you that detain me here, and—ah! I remember now; they told me they had murdered him; they exulted in the monstrous deed.

"Fiends! was it not enough to tear me from his protection, but you must take his life?

"I see his blood still crimsons your hands—that blood cries aloud for vengeance, and it will overtake you. Yes, a most fearful retribution will descend upon your heads for this hideous deed.

"Ralph, noblest of men! and is it I who have been the innocent cause of bringing you to this dreadful, this untimely end?"

The men appeared not the least moved by Daisy's piteous observations, and quite overcome by the tumoult of agonising feelings that rushed upon her brain, she sank back in her seat and burst into a paroxysm of convulsive sobs that might have moved a heart of stone to pity.

"'Tis done—'tis done!" she at length ejaculated, in almost inarticulate accents; "misery can go no further; the final blow is struck; he has been foully butchered, and the utmost that villainy can invent cannot inflict upon me any greater torture. Death will soon release me from all my sufferings, and gladly will I welcome it in any form."

Once more the power of her emotions choked her utterance, and she sank into a lethargy of horror, in which every faculty, almost the sense of thinking, seemed for a time to be absorbed.

At length, as a wild feeling of frantic despair rushed across her brain, she once more started from her seat, and fixing upon the ruffians a look which even made them start, she exclaimed—

"Monsters! his blood be upon your heads! May his curses ring for ever in your ears, and writhe your coward, guilty souls with agony beyond all human endurance! Oh! he was good, he was amiable; but you—but where is he, the fiend in human shape—the heartless shedder of human blood? Let me behold him that I may ring my curses in his ears!"

"You may as well save yourself all this trouble and waste of breath, young lady!" cried one of the fellows, "for upon us it has no effect whatever. The man should not have been mad enough to attempt to oppose Sir Roland and then he might have escaped; but if people will be foolhardy and obstinate they must take the consequences."

"Oh! villains—villains!" groaned Daisy.

Ralph Ashton was murdered—murdered in defending hèr—and torture could go no further.

How long they had been travelling Daisy had no other means of judging than by seeing the dark shadows of night gradually dispersing before the appearance of morning, and she therefore felt convinced, from the rate at which the vehicle had proceeded, that they must have got a considerable distance from the neighbourhood in which she had been sheltered.

She peeped through the window of the carriage, and found that they were journeying through a wood.

Not a human being met her gaze, and therefore she could not entertain the least hope of obtaining any assistance.

The men were riding by the sides of the vehicle, but she could not perceive anything of Sir Roland, and she therefore concluded that he, not feeling inclined to listen to her reproaches, had hastened forward to the place of their destination.

At length the bitter, the almost insupportable, anguish of her bosom found some relief in a copious flood of tears, and she then sank, as it were, into a state of apathy, and was scarcely conscious of the situation she was placed in or what had happened.

But from this she was shortly aroused by the carriage stopping at what appeared to be the back of some building, before which several tall trees reared their heads, and almost concealed it from observation.

One of the ruffians who was riding by the side of the vehicle dismounted from his horse, and, breaking through the foliage, gave a signal at the concealed door, which was immediately opened.

A large cloak was thrown over Daisy's head, and she was lifted from the carriage and led towards the entrance.

"All right," said the man who admitted them; "thanks to my ingenuity, this business has been managed as successfully as could have been wished."

Daisy immediately recognised the voice of Sir Roland, and, unable any longer to support the terror of her mind, she uttered a faint scream and sank senseless in the arms of one of the ruffians.

Sir Roland took her from him, and advancing with her towards a staircase, one of his hirelings preceding him with a light.

"Send old Martha to me immediately, Sampson," Sir Roland said. "She will be able to do everything towards her recovery."

Sampson obeyed, and Sir Roland ascended the staircase with his insensible burthen, and entered an apartment at the top of the house, but situated in such a detached part of the building that not the least sound that proceeded from it could be heard by the persons who frequented the inn, for such the place was.

The door opened with a secret spring, and was formed so as to resemble the rest of the panelling.

The room was gloomy enough, and but indifferently furnished, and it opened into another of smaller dimensions.

Sir Roland placed the insensible form of Daisy in a chair and supported her until an old woman arrived.

She was a shrivelled old beldame, whose disposition well fitted her for the situation she filled and the many deeds of guilt she had seen committed since she had been an inmate of that house, a den of crime and infamy.

On entering the room and beholding Daisy she stood a few moments and gazed upon her, and her looks plainly showed that she viewed her with anything but feelings of pleasure and welcome.

"So, Sir Roland," she said, "you have thought proper to burthen yourself with this girl, who may cause us more trouble than enough."

"Hold your croaking, old she-cat," said Sir Roland, "and mind your own business. The girl will not cause you much trouble, I daresay; and as to my choosing to bring her hither that is my business."

"She-cat!" muttered the old woman, with a frightful look. "Old Martha has lived for something to be thus called. But—"

"Bah!" impatiently interrupted Sir Roland, "let's have no more of this, but attend to the girl, and see that she recovers. I shall expect you to relax a little of your sourness, if possible, for the girl will be under your charge, and must not be treated harshly. Mind this, or I will be the means of stopping your whisky for six months to come."

This threat seemed to have its due effect upon the old woman, for she looked very much alarmed, and somewhat softened the asperity of her tone.

"Well, well," she said, "if it must be so it must, but it is so many years since I did the amiable that I am terribly out of practice, and I am afraid that it will take me some time before I can become proficient in it again. However, I will do my best."

"That's enough," said Sir Roland, "and, mark me, you will lose nothing by doing so. I know how to reward those who render me any service."

"She is a fair thing enough," remarked old Martha, proceeding to use the proper remedies for Daisy's restoration.

"Ay!" Sir Roland returned, as he hung over the insensible girl; "she is beautiful—a fit wife for Sir Roland Ashton. But I will leave her to your care, and when she recovers beware how you answer any questions she may put to you."

"I will be careful," answered the woman; "old Martha knows how to manage her business well enough without receiving any instructions."

Sir Roland returned no answer, but once more gazing earnestly on the pale but lovely countenance of Daisy, he left the room, and hastened to rejoin his companions in a room where an ample store of refreshments was produced to recruit them after their journey, and to make merry after the success of their expedition.

"So you have returned safe, Sir Roland," said the landlord, who went by the name of Sneath.

"Yes," Sir Roland replied; "nothing could have been executed better than this plot, and I give you and the men you introduced me to all due credit for their services."

"They were sure not to fail in their efforts," observed Sneath.

"No; I was pretty certain of that," returned Sir Roland, "or I would not have trusted them."

"And you gained an easy access to the house?"

"Oh! yes. It was late before we attempted to do so, and we took them by surprise."

"But were they not alarmed?"

"They were," replied Sir Roland.

"And offered resistance?"

"Certainly; but of what use was it, opposed to these brave fellows?"

"No; I do not expect it was much," remarked Sneath.

"It would have been much better for Ralph Ashton had they not, for I am inclined to think that he has paid for it with his life."

"Ah!" ejaculated Sneath.

"Yes; I ran him through," returned the villain, "and left him bleeding and senseless on the ground. I hope the wound will prove effectual, for then I shall have gratified my revenge and got rid of my most bitter and hated enemy."

"But you have only succeeded in getting one of the girls in your power."

"No; I was rather unfortunate in that, but another opportunity may present itself, and I will not fail to avail myself of it."

"And which of the girls is it you have brought here?" asked Sneath.

"Daisy Leigh, you have so often heard me speak of," Sir Roland replied.

"Ah! her with whom you acknowledge yourself to be so much captivated?"

"The same."

"And will you persist in making her your wife?"

"Certainly," said Sir Roland, "or why should I take all the trouble and run all the risk I have done to gain possession of her? She is most beautiful."

"No doubt she will offer a firm resistance," said Sneath.

"And of what use will that be? Here she is perfectly secure, and there is no one who will assist her," Sir Roland replied. "We will call in a priest and he can make us one."

"True. But this affair will cause a great sensation in the country."

"That it is sure to do," Sir Roland returned; "but that matters little to us. They cannot possibly have any means of discovering your retreat, and we may therefore set them at defiance."

"We may. But now this affair is settled we must begin to turn our attention to more profitable business."

"Aye!" Sir Roland replied; "you will find me true to my word. You want money?"

"I do," Sneath said. "You have no cause to complain?"

"No," Sir Roland replied; "and should Ralph Ashton have received his death-blow it will be all but complete."

"You say that you have left the girl upstairs in an insensible state?" said Sneath.

"Yes."

"When she comes to know her situation her terrors will probably overcome her, and after all you may be disappointed in your prize, Sir Roland."

"Well, I must take my chance of that," said the baronet; "but I do not despair. I doubt not but that in time I shall be able to conquer her emotions with my usual skill. If Ralph Ashton recovers he will be mad with rage."

"Very true," remarked Sneath. "But he will leave no means untried to discover where the girl is concealed."

"I daresay not," replied Sir Roland; "but he might as well save himself the trouble, for his efforts will all prove unavailing. Daisy is as safe here as if she was concealed in the deepest cavern of the earth."

"She is."

"There is no chance of her escape?"

"None whatever."

"Then what have I to apprehend?"

"Nothing but the death of the girl through terror."

"Oh! I do not fear that," said Sir Roland. "She is not like one who has never experienced any troubles or dangers."

"Yes; no doubt the life she has experienced has not been the most agreeable," Sneath said. "But are you sure that you made your retreat from the house after the abduction of the girl without anyone following you?"

"To be sure I am," Sir Roland replied; "do you think that any person would have been mad enough to venture such a thing?"

"It certainly is not very likely. But the man from whom you procured the vehicle—are you certain that he may be depended upon?"

"Oh! there is no doubt of him; but Sampson will tell you more about that. He is not a man likely to be deceived."

"No, he is not," Sneath replied; "so I think we may rest pretty secure."

"Oh! yes; there is no fear of that. But let one of your comrades go and ascertain whether Daisy has recovered yet. Perhaps it may not be so well that she should see me at present."

"True," returned Sneath.

Addressing himself to one of the ruffians, he desired him to do as Sir Roland requested.

He quickly returned, saying that Daisy had recovered for a short interval, but immediately, on becoming conscious of her situation, she fell into a state bordering upon distraction, and was then raving in the most piteous manner, and it was as much as old Martha could do to attend to her.

She had succeeded, however, in getting her to bed, and was doing all she could towards her restoration.

"It is no more than I expected," said Sneath. "I begin to think, Sir Roland, that you will have much more trouble with her than you anticipated, and I do not see that you will be likely to derive much pleasure from having a mad wife. The prize, at any rate, will not be worth the trouble."

"Pshaw!" Sir Roland said, "you are meeting troubles half way. Of course it could not be expected that the girl would rest calm and contented all at once. She will be better by the morning, I have no doubt."

"And if she is not what can be done with her?" demanded Sneath. "She may require medical attendance, and we do not happen to have any doctors among our comrades."

"Old Martha is as good as a doctor," Sir Roland said, "and I have no doubt she will be able to attend to all her wants."

"And a most tender nurse and attendant, I daresay, she will prove."

"She will not dare to act otherwise after the caution I have given her," said Sir Roland. "But enough of this—let us wait till the morning, and mark my word that the result will be more favourable than you imagine."

"Well, I hope it may," said Sneath; "but I would advise you not to attempt to see her today."

"Certainly I shall not. I am too well aware of what the consequences would be likely to be. Come, push about the grog, and let us endeavour to be merry after the success of our plot."

The glasses were replenished, the ruffians drank freely, and soon all were engaged in riotous revelry, in which Sir Roland most heartily joined.

His spirits rose to a most exuberant pitch by the success his villainy had met with, and at the manner in which he had eluded the vigilance of those who kept watch over the cottage, and particularly Spring-Heeled Jack.

The old woman remained in constant attendance upon Daisy, who continued in the same state, raving incessantly in the most piteous manner, until at length, completely exhausted, she sank back in her bed in a state of apathy, and seemed to lose all recollection of what had happened to her or where she was.

The ruffians did not separate until a late hour, and when Sir Roland retired to the room prepared for him he sat down, and laughed secretly at the success of his unholy plot.

Presently a knock came at the door.

"Who is there?" Sir Roland demanded.

"Jules Carleon!"

"Come in, then."

The Frenchman glided into the room.

"So, Sir Roland," he said, with a cunning leer upon his face, "you are well satisfied, and safe at last."

"Yes; even from Spring-Heeled Jack," the baronet replied.

## CHAPTER LXXI.

### JACOB BUTLER FINDS THAT LOCKS AND BARS DO SOMETIMES A PRISON MAKE.

JACOB BUTLER'S agony was great in the extreme when he found the way to liberty barred.

His breast heaved convulsively, and streams of cold perspiration ran down his face.

He shook the door as a newly-caged wild animal shakes the iron bars of its cage, but finding that the result ended in nothing but vexation he looked about for some weapon to defend himself.

As chance would have it there was a heavy cudgel leaning in a corner, and Jacob, grasping it, stood on his guard.

He could hear Bill Blarney cursing, swearing, and choking, as he endeavoured to recover his breath, but, worse still, Mrs. Corcoran and Rick Denton were descending the stairs.

Denton had secured the knife, which only increased the old hag's fury, and well did Jacob Butler know what would happen if she once got her fingers fixed upon his throat.

"Back! Stand back!" he yelled, whirling the stick round his head. "I'll be the death of anybody who attempts to touch me."

Rick Denton stopped and so did Mrs. Corcoran, and the old man whispered something hastily in the hag's ear.

Mrs. Corcoran nodded, and sat down on the staircase as if thoroughly overcome with fatigue.

"Look here," said Denton, addressing Jacob Butler, "it's not a bit of use kicking up all this fuss. I don't want such noisy customers as you here, and if you'll stand quiet a moment I'll open the door."

This was exactly what Jacob Butler required, and a gleam of hope flashed into his eyes.

"I'll be peaceable if you let me go," he said. "I only want to get out of that old witch's reach. Why can't she leave me alone when she knows that I hate the very sight of her?"

Mrs. Corcoran screwed up her features and squinted horribly at Jacob, but she said nothing to him.

"Well," said Denton, "if you'll put down that stick I'll set you free, and think myself lucky to be rid of you so cheaply."

"How am I to know that you will not play me false?" Jacob demanded.

"Haven't I said that I want to see you clear of my premises?" Denton retorted.

"Yes; but that may be only a *ruse* to get me into another trap?"

"Bah! you fool," said Rick Denton, contemptuously, "I have had more than sufficient visitors here already, and I'll take good care that I don't open my door to another stranger."

"I'll do as you wish," Jacob Butler returned as he put down the stick. "Now keep your promise to me."

Rick Denton descended the remainder of the stairs leisurely.

"Stand aside, so that I can get at the keyhole," he said.

Jacob did so, but still keeping his face towards Mrs. Corcoran, for fear that she might suddenly pounce upon him.

Rick Denton made a great noise with the lock and bolts, and then, catching the luckless Jacob unawares, he tripped him up and laid him flat upon his back.

"Help! murder!" Jacob roared.

"Another cry, and it will be your last,"

Denton said, planting his hand over the prisoner's mouth.

Mrs. Corcoran came leaping down the staircase, and she was followed by Bill Blarney.

"I'll soon silence him," said the ruffian. "Raise yourself up a little, Denton, and I will stuff a gag into his mouth."

Jacob Butler closed his eyes and groaned dismally as this was done.

Denton then produced a strong cord, and tied him with such dexterity that showed he was an adept at such operations.

"There he is, Mrs. Corcoran," said the hoary-headed old rascal; "and we'll put him into a safe place until he comes to your way of thinking."

"What a blessing it is to see him like this!" said the old hag, with a burst of wild, shrill laughter. "It does my heart good. You may say good-bye to your wanderings, Jacob deary, for you and I shall never part again."

Jacob heard every word, and what he would have said may be well imagined.

"I'm strong enough to carry him now," Bill Blarney growled. "Where shall I take him to?"

"Into the little back room on the second floor," Denton replied. "It's a snug little place without a window, and if he gets out of it, I wish him luck."

Blarney tossed Jacob Butler over his shoulders with as much ease as if the wretched creature had been a bundle of feathers, and, running upstairs, laid him down with so little ceremony that Jacob felt every bone start in its socket.

Then the door was closed and locked, and he was left to his reflections.

The place was pitch dark and evil-smelling.

Jacob could hear the dripping of water in one corner of the room, and judged by the sound that there was a leaky tank or cistern in the room.

Sore in body and distressed in mind, the miserable man lay wishing that death might kindly put an end to his troubles.

He had no hunger, though he had eaten nothing for more than twenty-four hours, but a terrible thirst assailed him, drying up his throat and parching his tongue.

The gag in his mouth increased his agonies, and he twisted and turned, gurgling out incoherent prayers for a draught of water.

He felt that his senses were leaving him.

Strange visions floated before his eyes, and dismal sounds rang in his ears.

He tried to shriek, and hideous noises came from his throat.

His brain seemed to be bursting, and he strained at his bonds until they cut into his flesh.

And then he seemed to take the proportions of a giant, and his body enlarge until it filled the whole apartment.

Walls, floor, and ceiling pressed upon him with crushing force.

A fiery wheel bore down upon him, and then Jacob Butler fainted, and knew no more until he felt that water was being dashed over his face.

Looking up with eyes that were heavy as lead and felt like balls of fire, he saw Rick Denton bending over him.

The old villain removed the gag from Jacob's mouth, but some minutes elapsed before he could utter a sound.

"I don't know why you should persecute me," he said; "but since you seem to be in league with these wretches, I shall take it as a mercy if you will put me out of my misery. Anything will be better than the prospect of falling into that virago's power again."

Rick Denton grinned and shook his head.

"I have nothing to do with that," he said; "and as to making short work of you, why that would be a comfortable way of putting a rope round my neck."

"Then have mercy and set me free."

"No—no; I can't do that," Denton returned. "I am paid for what I am doing. You must take your chance."

"Where—where is Mrs. Corcoran?" Jacob gasped, faintly.

"Gone out."

"For what purpose?"

"I don't know exactly," Denton replied; "but I think that Bill Blarney has given her some information she intends to act upon."

"I wish it may lead her into a worse scrape than I am in now," Jacob said, earnestly. "I think I could give myself up to the hangman with pleasure if I only knew that she was dead. Give me some more water. Ah! what is this? You are trying to poison me!"

"Oh! dear no," said Denton; "I don't do things in that style—at least, not without orders. I have only given you a sleeping-draught to send you off nice and comfortable.

The draught soon had its effect upon Jacob.

He ceased to talk.

His lids closed over his eyes and his head fell back.

"Poor devil!" said Denton. "I could almost pity him. Marry Mrs. Corcoran! Ho! ho! ho! What a life of bliss is in store for him!"

At that moment Bill Blarney put his head and shoulders into the room.

"Well?" said Denton.

"It is not daylight yet," Blarney said, "and I was wondering whether it would be safe to make an attempt to reach the Borough."

"You are the best judge of that."

"I want to get there," Blarney said, "for Dick Sleuth and the boys will wonder what on earth has become of me."

"Well, wait a minute," said Denton. "I will go to the top of the road and see if the coast is clear."

## CHAPTER LXXII.

DAISY LEIGH IN THE HANDS OF A VILLAIN—A CHECK—THE SHOT THROUGH THE WINDOW.

When Daisy, by the constant perseverance of the old woman, was restored to consciousness, she looked around her, and beholding the frightful countenance of old Martha and the gloom in the apartment she started and trembled with surprise and alarm, and had no immediate recollection as to what had happened.

"Where am I?" she exclaimed. "What fearful place is this?"

"Be calm, young woman," answered Martha, "and do not give way to this nonsense. You are where it is useless for you to complain, and as for your friends, you are far enough away from them now, and where they will not find it very easy to discover you."

Daisy gazed at the repulsive-looking old woman with increased amazement, and then passed her hand across her temples to collect her thoughts.

# SPRING-HEELED JACK,

## THE TERROR OF LONDON.

"RELEASE THE BOY, OR YOU DIE!" SPRING-HEELED JACK CRIED.

No. 22.

"Ah! I see it all now," she moaned. "I remember all the dreadful particulars. I was snatched from my friends by that fearful man, Sir Roland, who slew my protector and friend. Oh! Heaven, I shall go mad. Even now I see him weltering in his blood—I hear his dying groans. Release me—let me hasten to him!"

"This frantic violence is useless," said the crone; "you cannot leave this place."

"Ah!" said Daisy Leigh, "dare you attempt to detain me? Are you a woman, and can you thus act to one of your own sex? Where is the murderer of Ralph Ashton? Where is the miscreant who tore me from my home? He dare not meet my reproaches; he dare not encounter the bitter maledictions I shall heap upon his head."

She burst into a violent paroxysm of convulsive sobs as she uttered these words, which having subsided, she again relapsed into the same state of distraction as before, while the old woman stood by and listened to her in silence, not knowing what to say or how to act.

"And but for me," resumed Daisy, "he might still have been living and happy. Yes; I have been the cause of all. I have ever brought misery upon those who have befriended me. There is a spell—a curse—attached to my destiny.

"But he may still be living! Yes; he calls upon my name! Woman, if such you are, stand aside, and dare not attempt to obstruct my way!"

As the poor girl said this she attempted to advance to the door, but was again prevented by old Martha; and overcome by her emotions, she once more sank in her chair and continued to rave.

The old woman, seeing that it was useless to expostulate with Daisy, did not offer to interrupt her agonised exclamations, until at length the poor girl was quite worn out, and sinking into a state of torpor, Martha was enabled to get her into bed, where she remained for some time in a state of utter unconsciousness.

The old woman could not but admire her extreme beauty, and something like a feeling of pity stole upon her insensible heart; but it was only for a moment, and she became as stern and callous as ever.

Throughout the day Daisy continued in the same state, raving frantically at intervals and then sinking again into apathy.

Towards night she was quite worn out, and fell into a deep slumber, which was a great relief to the old woman, who had not experienced so hard a day's work for many a year.

She had to watch her during the night, and she had, therefore, provided herself with a sufficient dose of her favourite beverage, to which she not unfrequently applied for consolation.

Daisy's sleep, however, was disturbed by frightful dreams, and in imagination she saw reacted all the horrors that had taken place.

Again she beheld Ralph Ashton sink bleeding to the earth; she beheld his ghastly looks; she heard him call upon her name in piteous accents, and at the moment when she was about to rush to his arms she was withheld by an herculean grasp, and looking up beheld herself in the power of the miscreant, Sir Roland, whose eyes gleamed with exultation as he pointed to the work of his cowardly hands.

The next moment she felt herself hurried along as by a whirlwind, and imagination became buried in obscurity.

The next morning she awoke just as the sun appeared in the east, and rubbing her eyes, she had but an indistinct recollection of what had happened until she beheld the old woman, who was seated by the fireside, half-dozing in her arm-chair, and then the whole dreadful truth recurred to her memory.

She started up in her bed and looked around.

The gloom of the apartment, which was only lighted by one small, grated window, and the general wretchedness of its aspect filled her mind with terror, and she trembled violently.

"Ah!" she exclaimed, "it is true—it was not a dream. Oh! Heaven, I am indeed a prisoner in an unknown place; torn from my friends, and in the power of such a hang-dog villain as Sir Roland."

The sound of her voice aroused old Martha, who started to her feet and hastily approached the bed.

"Where am I? Tell me, woman, I command you!" Daisy said, in a firmer tone of voice than she had before been able to assume. "For what purpose am I brought here? And who are you that is placed over me?"

"As to where you are," croaked forth the old woman, "it perhaps would not afford you much gratification to know. You are in the power of Sir Roland Ashton—of that you are aware. For what purpose you are brought here it is not for me to say. And as to who I am, they call me Martha, and that must suffice you."

"And what is the character of this house?" demanded Daisy.

"I cannot satisfy you, young woman," replied Martha, in her usual surly tones. "I am not here to answer questions, but no doubt you will find out what you wish to know in time."

"Oh! Heaven," Daisy exclaimed, "what will become of me? Is Sir Roland Ashton in this house now?"

"He is," answered Martha.

"You are a woman!"

"Indeed!"

"Have you no pity?"

"I am not allowed to deal in the commodity, and I must confess that I never felt much inclination to do so."

"Can you not feel for one of your own sex?"

"Aye! I might do so upon a pinch," replied the beldame. "But what would be the use of that?"

"Oh!" Daisy exclaimed, eagerly, "if you have one spark of pity within your breast, if you can indeed feel for a poor, deeply-injured, persecuted, broken-hearted girl, you will commiserate with my suffering—you will assist me to escape from the terrible fate with which I am threatened!"

"Assist you to escape?" repeated old Martha, with an ironical grin; "a very modest and reasonable request, truly. But, if you calculate upon that, you will find yourself very much mistaken, for indeed I shall do nothing of the kind."

"There is, then, no hope?" Daisy cried.

"None whatever, if you think to escape from this place," replied Martha.

"Surely," exclaimed Daisy, "surely you will not permit the villain, Sir Roland, the assassin, thus to triumph?"

"No doubt he fully expects to triumph, and for my own part I don't see that he has any reason to think otherwise."

Daisy turned from the old woman with a shudder of disgust and horror.

"The whole of it is," resumed Martha, "you may as well try to make yourself comfortable, young woman, and to submit without murmuring to your fate; for here there is no one to assist you, and Sir Roland is not the man to abandon any designs upon which he has fixed his mind. He has been at some trouble and risk to get possession of you, and, of course, he expects to reap his reward."

"And that should be the gallows," retorted Daisy.

Her fine eyes flashed indignation upon the old woman, who, however, was insensible to every feeling of shame, and took but little notice of what the poor girl said.

"The wretch may flatter himself in the success which has hitherto attended his diabolical stratagems," Daisy continued, "but there is a power that watches over all our actions, and will not fail to visit him with terrible retribution, even when he thinks that his triumph is most complete."

"I know nothing about that," returned Martha. "I never trouble my head with such matters, but I would advise you, young woman, to be a little more cautious in the language you use to Sir Roland, or—"

"What language do you expect me to use to one who has committed so daring and cruel an outrage against me?—to a wretch whom I know to have been guilty of every atrocious crime?" Daisy demanded.

"Well," said the beldame, "you can use your own discretion; but you may rest assured that whatever you may say will not prevent Sir Roland from putting his designs into execution."

"Heaven help me, then!"

"Well, I want not to listen to such stuff; so you may as well spare yourself the trouble of giving utterance to it."

"And can a woman possibly possess no more feeling towards one of her own sex?"

"I have before told you that I have nothing to do with feeling; I have heard of the word, but I can't say that I very clearly understand it."

Daisy looked at her for a moment, and could scarcely believe that such a hateful character could exist under the garb of one of her own sex; but the beldame was well schooled in vice and took no notice of her.

"I see," said Daisy, after a pause, "that it is useless to appeal to you, and I will say no more upon the subject. I will not yet despair; deplorable and alarming as my situation is, something will yet occur to rescue me from the power of the heartless miscreant who seeks to make my life miserable."

"Probably you may find that your sanguine hopes will be rather disappointed," observed Martha.

"Leave me," said Daisy. "I cannot look upon you with any other feelings than those of disgust."

"Indeed! I am obliged to you for the compliment," returned the old beldame, with a bitter sneer.

"Retire, I request of you," said Daisy. "I would be alone—left to the indulgence of my own thoughts."

"Very well," said the old woman, "I have no wish to keep you company. I suppose, however, by this time you will want some refreshment, as you have not broken your fast since you entered this place?"

"I need nothing," sighed Daisy; "there is not anything but liberty and peace of mind that I want."

"I do not undertake to supply you with them," replied Martha, as she quitted the room; "but I will bring you some provisions, and you can please yourself about eating them."

Daisy returned no answer to this brutal and unfeeling speech, and the old woman disappeared.

When she had gone the power of Daisy's feelings found some relief in a copious flood of tears, after which she arose and dressed herself.

Her brain was giddy, and she sank in a chair, for she could not support her trembling limbs.

All the horrors of what had happened and the situation in which she was placed rushed at once upon her imagination, and she was driven almost to the same state of distraction she had been in the day before.

The observations of old Martha convinced her, if she had even before entertained any doubt, that she had nothing whatever to hope, that there was no chance of her escape.

But could it be true that Ralph Ashton had indeed perished by the murderous hand of Sir Roland? The thought was almost too horrible to bear, but yet, after what she had heard, it was by far too probable for her to reject it.

Oh! the pangs that this maddened idea caused her. If Ralph had indeed met so dreadful and untimely a fate all hopes of protection would be at an end, and death would be a mercy to her.

And she had been the innocent means of sacrificing his life; but for her, had they never met, he might still have been living and happy.

Her agony was most indescribable, and her bosom heaved with convulsive sobs.

The poor girl wrung her hands in despair, and her heavy sobs for some time choked her utterance.

She at length arose from her seat and walked to the door of the apartment and examined it; but she found that it possessed neither lock nor bolt, but was perfectly secure.

She could not discover the secret spring by which it was opened, and indeed it was so nicely contrived that it might set detection at defiance.

She shuddered at the thought.

Here, then, she was entirely at the mercy of her cruel enemy, and could not protect herself against his intrusion at any hour he thought proper.

The dreariness of the rooms struck a deadly chill upon her heart, for they both only received light from a small iron-barred window, and which gave them indeed the aspect of the most dreary dungeons.

"Alas!" she sighed, "what dreadful crimes may not have been perpetrated within these walls!—how many poor suffering creatures like myself may have lingered out a life of misery and persecution in these very rooms, until the assassin's knife put a period to their wretched existence!"

She walked to one of the windows and looked from it, but the prospect that met her eyes was of the most gloomy description.

Clusters of tall trees, impervious almost to the light of day, alone met her gaze.

It was a place well adapted for the perpetration of any atrocious deed, and which plainly showed her the infamous character of the house in which she was confined from the loneliness of its situation.

There she could never hope to meet with any assistance, and, therefore, the horrors by which she was surrounded were made the more apparent.

The villain, Sir Roland, could not have fixed

upon a more fitting place for the execution of his diabolical plot, no place where he was more secure from interruption, and as Daisy contemplated it she gave herself up completely to despair.

How she trembled with terror when she thought of the cruel persecution to which she was sure to be subjected! With what horror did she look forward to the moment when she should again behold Sir Roland!

How could she look upon that guilty man, whose hands were stained with the blood of so many unfortunate victims, and, probably, Ralph Ashton amongst the number?

Surely the sight of him would drive her to madness.

She was interrupted in these reflections by the return of old Martha, who brought with her some provisions, and placed them on the table before her.

"There, young lady," she said, "is a repast fit for a princess, and, therefore, I should advise you to eat, for you must be hungry enough after fasting for so many hours. I never found sorrow weaken my appetite in the least, though certainly I have not experienced much of it in my time."

Daisy sighed deeply, but returned no answer to this ignorant and vulgar speech.

The old woman looked at her with a malicious expression of countenance for a moment or two.

"I suppose you do not require my attendance?" she observed; "for, no doubt, my company is not very agreeable to you; so I wish you Good-morning, and will leave you to yourself."

"Tell me, I beg of you," said Daisy, "whether I am to continue to be confined in this gloomy apartment?"

"For anything I know to the contrary, you are."

"And once more I ask you what is the character of the inmates of this lonely house?"

"Character?" repeated the old woman, "why, as for that matter, I believe they can none of them boast of possessing any other than a very bad one. They are jolly fellows, who live a life of freedom till they are caught, and make the public contribute liberally to their support."

"Thieves!" said Daisy, with a shudder.

"No," answered the old woman; "thief is the name only worthy of a paltry pickpocket; they are gentlemen of the road, and all of them accomplished cracksmen."

Daisy trembled violently, and looked at Martha with an expression of the utmost disgust.

"And can it be possible that a woman," she said, "an aged woman, can associate with such wretches?"

"Why," answered the beldame, "it is all a mere matter of taste, you know; I have done so for many years, and do not feel inclined to alter my situation, for I do not think that I could better myself."

"Wretched woman!" Daisy cried. "May Heaven pardon you for your sins, and bring you to repentance ere it is too late."

"Repentance!—bah! What have I to repent of? But I came not here to listen to a sermon; I have no taste for such matters, and therefore you had better keep your morality to yourself."

"I pity you," said Daisy.

"Pity! ha—ha—ha! I am much obliged to you, but I do not stand in need of it."

"Answer me one question."

"Well, what is it?"

"Will Sir Roland visit me to-day?"

"I believe he will not," answered Martha; "but you had better be prepared to meet him when he does, for it is not likely that he will delay his visit long."

"The villain!" exclaimed Daisy, warmly; "he cannot but expect that I shall receive him with my bitterest curses and reproaches."

"Which he will pass unheeded as he would the idle wind," remarked Martha.

"Never, by Heaven! will I be his wife," exclaimed Daisy; "sooner would I suffer death than that the monster should triumph. Weak, defenceless girl as I am, he shall yet find that I have the fortitude to resist him, and that I will suffer anything sooner than I will yield."

"Well," returned the old woman, "that is to be seen; but you will find that Sir Roland is a more determined and desperate man to oppose than you seem at present to imagine."

"Well do I know the villain's character," said Daisy; "but Heaven will give me strength, and even at the very time when he thinks his success secure he may be defeated and brought to that punishment his numerous and horrible crimes deserve."

"With that hope, then, I will leave you," observed Martha; "but I rather think you will be disappointed."

With these words the old woman quitted the room, and Daisy was once more left to herself.

The thoughts that rushed in rapid succession through her mind were of the most distracting description, and whichever way she directed them she could perceive no means of consolation.

The desperate character of the men by whom she was surrounded filled her bosom with the utmost alarm.

But how she shuddered at the idea of beholding Sir Roland!

She well knew his reckless and determined character, and that pity was a stranger to his breast, and therefore she had every reason to apprehend the worst.

The horrible character of the old woman also filled her with terror and rendered her situation doubly insupportable, since she had no person to whom she could confide her thoughts, and who would commiserate with her sufferings.

Miserably did that day pass away, but Daisy experienced no interruption, only at the times when Martha came to bring her her meals, and then she avoided entering into conversation with her, so revolting was her character to the girl, and so utterly destitute of pity or common humanity as she was convinced she was.

She judged that she was in a remote part of the building, for not the least sound met her ears, save the moaning of the wind among the branches of the trees that reared their tall heads far above the building.

The fate of Ralph Ashton constantly occupied her thoughts, and indescribable was the anguish that accompanied it.

Sometimes she dared to hope that he still lived, and that something might occur to make him acquainted with the place of her confinement; but that idea was too extravagant for her long to encourage it, and she quickly again relapsed into the most utter despair.

As night advanced her agony became almost insupportable; the dismal silence of all around chilled her heart, and yet she started with the greatest alarm whenever the least sound met her ears, fancying that someone was coming.

She feared to retire, for she had no means of securing herself against the intrusion of anyone in the night, and every description of horrible apprehension beset her mind.

Again she endeavoured to find the secret spring, but in vain.

After some time spent in this manner she again returned to the bedroom.

Her fears were aroused to the highest pitch, and when she reflected upon the cruel deeds that had probably been perpetrated in these very apartments she could almost imagine that she beheld the grim shades of the departed flitting past her in the chamber.

Frequently she started as she was almost convinced she heard dismal sepulchral cries in the pauses of the wind.

But she was soon satisfied that it was only the effect of her disordered imagination, and by degrees she became somewhat more calm.

"I have never injured those that are gone," she said, "and therefore what have I to fear? Ah! no, it is only the living I should dread."

A clock in the house now struck eleven, and suddenly Daisy felt so overpowered by sleep that she could not resist its influence although she endeavoured to do so, and having secured the door of the inner chamber as well as she could, she threw herself on the bed without undressing, and in a few moments a sound sleep stole over her senses.

It was not quite daylight when she awoke, but the grey mists were fast dispersing, and Daisy, not feeling inclined to go to sleep again, arose considerably refreshed.

She walked to the window and watched the sun as its first beams gradually penetrated between the thick foliage.

While she was thus occupied she perceived three men on horseback suddenly emerge from between a cluster of trees, and approach towards the house.

As they came nearer she was enabled to have a clearer view of their countenances.

She became convinced that they were some of the ruffians connected with the building, and she could not but tremble with dread when she reflected that she was in the power and at the mercy of such desperate villains.

They advanced immediately to the house, and she then lost sight of them, but she had no doubt that they had entered by a secret way.

Daisy quitted the window, and, resuming her seat, gave herself up to the dismal thoughts which all the painful circumstances in which she was placed and the anticipations in the future engendered.

Alas! what had she to anticipate, placed as she was among such heartless and lawless wretches, but the greatest cruelties?

And there was no hope, no chance of escaping from them!

Surely no sufferings could be greater than those to which she was exposed, and in vain she endeavoured to find the least consolation.

Martha visited her at the usual hour with the morning's repast, and was about to leave the room again without speaking, when our heroine prevented her by observing—

"I have a question to ask you, Martha."

"I have already told you that it is not my business to answer questions," returned the old woman, in her usual surly tones; "but what is it?"

"Simply to ask you whether Sir Roland is still in the house?" demanded Daisy.

"Certainly he is," said Martha. "You don't suppose that he would venture from it just yet when there is such a hue and cry after him?"

"And will he dare obtrude himself on my presence?" interrogated Daisy.

"That you may depend he will, young woman. He did not bring you here for the mere purpose of caging you up like a bird. No, no; he must have the pleasure of your society, and I have no doubt that you will see him before the day is out."

"Oh! Heaven," ejaculated Daisy, "I can never endure the presence of such a miscreant—such a monster!"

"No doubt that Sir Roland will convince you of your folly, and make you his wife in spite of your obstinate opposition."

Daisy Leigh fixed a look of mingled pity, horror, and reproach on the woman.

"And these remarks are made by one of my own sex!" she said. "But why do I speak to one lost to every sense of humanity? Your connection with the villains who use this dreadful den shows that you are inured to every vice."

"Thank you for the compliment," said old Martha, sneeringly. "However, I have no wish to speak to you, my pretty bird. I will leave Sir Roland to do that, so I wish you Good-morning and much joy. If I were younger, and in your place, I would jump at such a chance. There are not many girls who would scorn such an offer."

As the old woman left the room Daisy Leigh pressed her hands to her face and burst into tears.

"Great Heaven!" she exclaimed, "can nature have formed any human being so base and callous to shame or pity as this woman?"

Daisy rose to her feet and paced to and fro in a state of great agitation.

"Must I be tormented with this villain—Sir Roland?" she resumed. "Must I listen to his advances? His wife? No—no! Heaven spare me from such a fate!"

In her terror she struck her breast, and groaned in the agony of her despair. If Ralph Ashton had perished she had indirectly caused his death, and where had Daisy now to look for a friend, unless that mysterious being, Spring-Heeled Jack, came to her aid again?

Every sound that met her ears caused her to start violently, for she feared that it was Sir Roland approaching.

But several hours passed away, and Daisy was still alone, and the morning passed away without interruption.

But this state of things was not to last long.

Suddenly Daisy heard a door close, and immediately afterwards the sound of footsteps ascending the stairs.

Daisy Leigh felt a deadly faintness steal into her heart.

She trembled violently and sank into a chair, for now she was sure that Sir Roland was on his way to the room.

The next instant the door flew open and the object of her fears stood before her.

Daisy Leigh could not help giving utterance to a cry of horror as she beheld the villain.

She averted her head and moved to the other end of the room.

Sir Roland Ashton closed the door, and stood gazing in admiration and triumph at the beautiful girl.

He knew what was passing in her mind, he knew how she loathed him, but he cared nothing for that.

"Look up, Daisy," he said, advancing. "I have come to woo you. Tell me what I can do to prove my love?"

"Hold, monster!—villain!" Daisy cried. "Would that I had some weapon that I might rid the world of such a coward!"

"Nay!" said Sir Roland, "this is unkind. Villain, monster, as you call me, you will find that I can be kind and indulgent. I would bury the past, and whilst leading a new life forget it. Daisy, I love you—yes, love you dearly, insensible as you may imagine that such a heart as mine can be to the tender passion."

"What mockery!" Daisy replied. "You love! The word is polluted by such lips as yours. I will not hear you. Away—away!"

Sir Roland Ashton folded his arms and smiled scornfully.

"You must listen to me," he said, "and with patience and indulgence. I am not the man to be foiled in any determination I may have formed. Ralph Ashton is dead, and—"

"But," said Daisy Leigh, interrupting him, "there is yet another who will avenge my wrongs."

"And who may that be?"

"Spring-Heeled Jack."

"Let me whisper a word in your ear?" Sir Roland said.

As he spoke a few words in a low tone of voice Daisy Leigh started and trembled violently.

"Oh! base and cowardly miscreant!" she cried. "You boast of a triumph you have waded through blood to obtain. The curses of offended Heaven are hovering over your head for the crimes you have committed."

"Speak on! Rail on!" said Sir Roland; "your words fall idly on my ear, and yet it is happiness to listen to the music of your voice. You have called me a murderer, but I can justify my crimes, and—"

"Forbear—forbear!" Daisy exclaimed, shrinking still further away from the villain. "Your words shock my ears."

"And yet," Sir Roland said, "you must hear me out."

"Hold! Speak not," Daisy cried. "Do you not fear that your tongue may blister or shrivel? Such a thing has happened to bad men, I have heard."

"Bah!" said Sir Roland, contemptuously. "I heed not such idle cant."

"Heaven help me!" Daisy said, in faltering accents. "Must I listen to this man?"

"You must," said Sir Roland, "and it will be best for you to do so patiently."

Daisy Leigh sat down near the barred window, and lowered her head to her bosom.

"I repeat," said Sir Roland, "that I can justify the crimes of which you accuse me of."

"Oh! villain—villain!" Daisy ejaculated.

"Had it not been for Ralph Ashton," Sir Roland continued, paying no attention to the girl, "I should never have been guilty. He has always stood in my way, thwarted my designs, and made my life a bane and a curse. Now that he is dead he can foil me no longer. I know that his one great idea was to bring me to the gallows in the end, and I exult in the fact that I have forestalled him, and paid him in his own coin!"

Daisy Leigh raised her face and gazed at the villain. Her lips moved convulsively, but for some moments no sound came from them.

"Monster!" she cried at length, "fiend in human form, I despise you. Begone, and harrow my feelings no longer by your detestable presence."

"Humph!" Sir Roland returned. "You speak boldly, but you seem to forget that I am all-powerful here. I command you to consent to be my wife. You must obey. A priest is within hail to make us man and wife, and so we must become sooner or later."

"Never!" Daisy replied. "Never! by all my hopes of future happiness."

"Your obstinacy is but madness," Sir Roland said. "You are in my power, and to my will you must submit. You are mine, Daisy! You shall be my wife."

"Villain!" Daisy cried, "I would sooner face the burning stake, and suffer a frightful death."

"What madness is this?" Sir Roland said; "for you have not the means of braving the death you speak of."

"But Heaven will help me."

"Daisy," Sir Roland said, "I have risked too much to give you the chance of escaping again. You must and shall become my wife. I have the means to support us in comfort and in luxury, and if you will but forget with me the dreary past my future actions shall make ample atonement for the deeds I have committed."

Daisy Leigh stared at him aghast.

Was it possible that a wretch who had been guilty of such atrocious crimes could talk lightly of forgetting the past?

Did he dare to speak of love to her whom he had so cruelly wronged?

Sir Roland's villainy seemed to pass all the bounds of human baseness, and the longer Daisy gazed at her persecutor the more her horror and loathing intensified.

Sir Roland was not at all abashed by Daisy's demeanour, but fixed his eyes upon her countenance in a manner calculated to cause her the greatest alarm.

"Daisy," he said, sinking down at her feet, "here, on this knee, which has never before bent to mortal, I supplicate your forbearance. I plead for that love, which, if you do not entertain for me now, will come after marriage. I sue to you for forgiveness, and to be the means of reclaiming me."

"Help! help!" Daisy gasped. "Devil! your words are echoed by the curses breathed by the shades of your dead victims. They call for retribution on your guilty head, for your hands are scarcely dry of blood. Oh! Heaven—horror!"

"What idle mockery is this?" Sir Roland cried, starting to his feet. "Do you think that you speak to a child? Do you think I am to be scared from my purpose by such prattle? I have marked you for my own. I have struggled, fought—aye! even bled—to gain my purpose, and a few hours hence my triumph will be complete."

Daisy, overcome with terror, started back to the other end of the room.

All the horrors, the utter helplessness of her situation, rushed upon her mind, and despair took possession of her heart.

During all the trials she had suffered she had never experienced such a moment.

Sir Roland remained silent for a minute or two,

and seemed to watch the hapless girl's emotions with the greatest interest.

He approached her again and endeavoured to take her hand, but Daisy shrank from him as from the touch of a poisonous reptile.

"Oh! man—if man you are," Daisy said, pleadingly, "cruel as you are, you will abandon this design against my happiness. Let me go."

"Abandon this design!" Sir Roland replied. "Bah! I tell you, Daisy, that all my hopes are fixed on it. Your happiness or misery is in your own hands, for I am determined to hold you here until you consent to be mine for life."

"Never—never!" moaned Daisy, wringing her hands.

"But I will leave you now," Sir Roland continued. "I will give you a week to think over what I have said. Come, one kiss from those ruby lips, and I will be gone. That kiss shall seal my vows, which I have made in all sincerity."

Daisy screamed with terror and escaped from Sir Roland's outstretched arms.

"Heartless, guilty ruffian!" she exclaimed. "Oh! Heaven, why am I subjected to this disgrace and cruelty?"

"Fool!" Sir Roland hissed, "I ask but a kiss, and will not leave until your lips have touched mine. One kiss I say—only one. Ah!"

A ringing report rang through the room.

The window vanished beneath a cloud of smoke, and Sir Roland Ashton, flinging up his arms, fell with a crash at Daisy Leigh's feet.

---

## CHAPTER LXXIII.

### HOW A SECRET PASSAGE WAS DISCOVERED IN A MYSTERIOUS WAY.

We must turn aside from the events just recorded to see how Jacob Butler is getting on.

It was some relief to his wretched mind to know that Mrs. Corcoran was no longer in the house, and Jacob had some hopes that something might occur to prevent her returning.

Mrs. Corcoran seemed to have as many lives as a cat, which is said to have nine, and Jacob Butler, when left alone, began to count how many narrow escapes Mrs. Corcoran had passed through.

"Something must happen to rid me of her," he groaned. "No mortal was ever sent on this earth to be punished and tortured as I am. I wonder what the hag is up to now. There must be mischief in the wind or she would not leave me for a moment."

Rick Denton had relieved Jacob of his bonds, and the miserable man paced the darkened room like a caged Polar bear.

At present he could see no hope of escape, and as he thought of his position and the fate promised him he flew into a kind of frenzy, and after hammering at the door with his knuckles until they were sore, suddenly used his head as a kind of battering ram, and dashed it, regardless of all consequences, against the wall.

The operation proved somewhat painful, but it produced one good result.

To Jacob Butler's astonishment the concussion was not nearly so great as he had expected, and he went flying through an aperture down two or three steps thickly covered with dust.

Jacob had discovered a secret passage in the most peculiar manner possible. In point of fact, the top of his cranium had released the spring of a sliding panel, which, perhaps, might lead to the road of light and freedom.

Mr. Butler picked himself up and rubbed the injured portion of his anatomy ruefully. He found that he had succeeded in producing a lump about the size of a hen's egg, and, moreover, he was regaled with the vision of a large quantity of stars dancing about in violent commotion.

But these things were mere trifles in comparison to the unexpected discovery, and Jacob, as he picked himself up, could scarcely refrain from chuckling audibly.

The noise of his fall might have reached Rick Denton's ears, and Jacob Butler lay perfectly still, gasping like a fresh codfish.

All was still.

A deep, solemn silence reigned in the house, and Jacob Butler, satisfying himself that the noise caused by his tumble had not attracted attention, scrambled to his feet and walked back into the room.

His first act was to examine the panel and its spring.

After making himself acquainted with its mechanism he closed it, and removing the dust from his clothes, sat down and tried to look as if nothing had happened.

But this was not an easy task.

His head ached and throbbed as if it would fly off his shoulders, but he bore the pain for fear that if Rick Dentan entered the room suddenly his keen eyes would suspect that something was wrong.

It so happened that Jacob had decided to act wisely, for suddenly the door opened, and Rick Denton, bearing a basket in his hand, entered.

"Ha, ha!" he said. "I see that you occupy the same old corner. I hope you find it pretty comfortable."

"Not so much of that," Jacob returned; "but, like a beggar, I have no choice, and I suppose I must make the best of my position."

"Wisely spoken," said Rick Denton. "Well, you see we don't intend to starve you. I have brought you something to eat and drink, and you need not fear treachery. Mrs. Corcoran—ha, ha!—said that her lovey-dovey was to be kindly treated, and played no tricks with!"

"Hang her!" Jacob gasped.

"Of course. Just so. I have no objection," the old man said; "but she may have a few."

Jacob Butler was both hungry and thirsty, and he looked longingly at the basket.

"I suppose it is all right," he said. "I say, has she come back?"

"No; and I don't expect her for some time."

"Not to-day?"

"I can't tell," old Rick replied. "Eat, and don't bother me with a lot of questions."

"Oh!" cried Jacob Butler, with his mouth full, "I only wanted to say a few words to her."

"What about?"

"Well, you see," Jacob returned, "I have been thinking over this and that, and I am convinced at last that I have made a fool of myself. In short, I am willing to marry Mrs. Corcoran."

"She will be glad to hear that," Rick Denton chuckled. "You have soon made up your mind on the subject."

"Better that I should do so than lead the life of a dog."

"Just so; and I think you have taken the wisest course."

The old man grinned as he spoke, and glanced suspiciously at Jacob, who sat munching his food very much like a contented monkey.

"Ha!" said old Rick, "I suppose you think that because you tell me that your mind is made up that I shall let you out to ramble about the house?"

"The idea is yours—not mine."

"Of course you wouldn't try to get away or shout out of the first window you came to?" said Denton. "Oh! no. But I don't intend to give you the chance."

"And I didn't expect it," Jacob returned. "Haven't I told you that I intend to marry the old—Mrs. Corcoran, I mean. I wise she were in the house so that she might hear it from my own lips."

"She'll do that fast enough," Denton replied. "Don't eat so quick or you'll choke."

Jacob Butler had been stuffing his mouth as full as possible to keep down the feelings of exultation that filled his breast.

And yet it might be a question, after all, whether he had anything to crow about, for the secret passage might not lead to the open air, but to some cellar or den used for bad purposes by Rick Denton.

"I'll let Mrs. Corcoran know that you are so anxious to see her," Denton said, "and I have no doubt but that she will be overwhelmed with joy at your decision."

"Will she?" Jacob thought. "If she knew what was in my mind she would return quicker than she anticipated."

Rick Denton did not know exactly what to make of the sudden change in the prisoner's behaviour, but Jacob Butler appeared so earnest, and to enjoy the repast brought him so thoroughly, that the old man became convinced that Mrs. Corcoran had prevailed at last.

"So," he said, as he turned towards the door, "you accept your fate?"

"Yes," Jacob Butler replied. "I may as well do so cheerfully, as there seems to be no other alternative. I am tired of being trapped and caged. Hang it! man, you would do anything if you were in my place."

"Well, I don't know—perhaps I might," Denton said. "Mrs. Corcoran isn't a beauty, but beauty only lies skin deep, and I think she and you will make a well-matched pair. I wish you joy."

Jacob Butler dropped his face, for a heavy frown spread over his features, and he set his teeth to prevent himself saying something far from complimentary about Mrs. Corcoran and her chosen companions.

The fact that Jacob Butler relished his food seemed to annoy Rick Denton a little, and he turned, grumbling and scowling, towards the door.

When all was silent again Jacob Butler pocketed the remnants of the food, and then went to the door and listened.

The keyhole was a large one, and a glimmer of light shone through it.

Applying his eye at this draughty aperture, Jacob, having made sure that there was nobody upon the landing, stepped softly across the floor and applied his hand to the spring.

It yielded to his touch, and Jacob, descending the stairs on his feet this time instead of upon his head as before, began to look about him.

He thought it better to leave the panel partly open for fear that he might have to bolt back to the room at a moment's notice.

The secret staircase was very dark, but at last Jacob's eyes became accustomed to the gloom.

There were chinks in the wall here and there, and these enabled him to see where he was going.

Jacob descended the stairs until he came to a small room fitted up with antique furniture.

It was evident by the accumulation of dust and cobwebs that this apartment had not been used for some time.

As Jacob took a hasty survey of this place he noticed an old-fashioned rapier standing in a corner and secured it.

"Now," he muttered, valiantly, and striking a tragic attitude, "it will be death to the man who attempts to stop my way."

Crossing this chamber Jacob came to a door, which was luckily open, and, descending another flight of stairs, he reached the cellar.

The only way of egress was by a double trap-door, and Jacob Butler was convinced that it led to the court.

The next and most important question was how to get the trap-door open.

Mr. Butler, quaking from his head downwards to his shoes, gazed at the ponderous woodwork with his head on one side, and then noticing an old rusty bolt he stood on tip-toe and tried to wrench it back.

The bolt was old and rusty, and refused to move at first, but after a great deal of wriggling and perseverance on Jacob's part it began to creak and give way.

More than once Jacob thought he heard somebody moving about over his head, and streams of perspiration poured down his face as he wrestled with the obstinate bolt.

Suddenly it gave way.

The two flaps of the trap-door came thundering down, and Jacob, receiving one of them on his head, fell, floored like a nine-pin.

In another instant he was on his feet, and, springing through the aperture, darted up the court and into the street beyond.

Jacob Butler felt inclined to kick up his heels for very joy.

He scampered down one side of Snow-hill and up the other, but stopped for want of breath as he came in sight of Newgate prison.

As he did so he saw two constables approaching.

"Hi! you there!" he shouted. "Stop, Catchpole—Grabham! I have great news for you. I know where Bill Blarney and Mrs. Corcoran are."

## CHAPTER LXXIV.

### SPRING-HEELED JACK RESCUES A BOY, AND THIS INTRODUCES A NEW CHARACTER TO OUR STORY.

Daisy Leigh shrank back in silent terror as Sir Roland Ashton fell prone at her feet.

She saw blood flowing from his breast, and the shock was so sudden that she could not scream or articulate a word.

Before the smoke had cleared away she heard the bars being torn away from the window, and then she became aware that Spring-Heeled Jack was standing at her side.

Almost at the same instant the door flew open, and the old woman who had attended upon Daisy entered the room.

"Back, back, you hag!" Spring-Heeled Jack yelled. "If you would live to repent of your vile sins keep clear of me."

Old Martha started back at the sight of the strange weird figure towering above her.

Her face grew ashy grey, and, swooning, she fell across Sir Roland's body.

"Speak not!" Spring-Heeled Jack said to Daisy. "All danger is not at an end. Trust yourself to me, and all will be well. Ready!"

This word was addressed to someone outside the window, and immediately the masked face of a man appeared.

Daisy Leigh noticed that Spring-Heeled Jack raised her with his left arm, and that his right hung limp and apparently useless at his side.

The man outside received Daisy, and, throwing her lightly over his shoulder, descended a rope ladder.

In another instant Daisy found herself inside of a carriage, to which two spirited horses were attached.

They dashed away at a furious speed, whirling up clouds of dust, and rocking the carriage from side to side in a style that threatened to overturn it every moment.

All this added to Daisy Leigh's bewilderment, and she was beginning to think that her miraculous escape was but a dream after all, for she could see nothing whatever of Spring-Heeled Jack, when the carriage stopped suddenly.

Daisy Leigh shrunk back, thinking that Sir Roland's hirelings had overtaken the equipage, and then a cry of joy burst from her lips.

The door opened, and Ralph Ashton entered the carriage.

"Welcome, Miss Leigh!" he said. "I congratulate you. Excuse my left hand; I received a slight wound on the night that Sir Roland bore you away."

"Yes—yes, I know," Daisy replied, as soon as her delight would permit her to speak coherently. "How glad I am to see you! Sir Roland told me that you were dead."

"He did his best to make that an established fact," Ralph replied, smiling. "The coward stabbed me in the back, and I lost a quantity of blood."

His face was very pale, and it seemed as if he had gone through some great exertion recently.

"I am at a loss to account for these things," Daisy said. "How came you here? Was it not that wonderful being Spring-Heeled Jack who rescued me."

"Yes," Ralph replied; "and it was he who sent me hither."

Daisy passed her hand over her fair brow.

"He sent you hither?" she said. "Ah! I know now. You were with him. It was you who appeared at the window, and carried me away from that dreadful house."

"You make a mistake," Ralph replied; "but you must not ask me to tell secrets which I am sworn not to divulge. Sir Roland will not trouble us for some time, and we are going back to the self-same place you came from."

"Oh! how delightful to see dear Constance again," Daisy said, clasping her hands. "Ah! what horrors I have passed through!"

"But not unwatched or uncared for," Ralph Ashton replied. "Spring-Heeled Jack knew of Sir Roland's movements, and only waited to foil his designs when he thought his triumph complete."

"All this is so wonderful that it entirely passes my comprehension," Daisy said. "Who is this Spring-Heeled Jack? Is he mortal or—"

Ralph Ashton placed his forefinger on his lips.

"Hush!" he said. "Say no more respecting him, for he may be listening to us at this very moment."

"He seems to have been wounded like you?"

"Yes," Ralph replied. "But enough. I must insist upon silence. Forgive me, Miss Leigh, if I appear stern, but I have a method in what I say."

It was late in the evening when the carriage reached its destination, and Daisy Leigh and Constance Marfield were once more clasped in each other's arms.

They shed tears of joy over each other, and Ralph Ashton, after dining with them, left the girls to chat at will.

Ascending to his private room, Ralph Ashton threw off his coat.

"Lorrimer!" he said, softly.

"Yes, sir," replied a voice.

"Enter."

A smart-looking fellow entered the room.

"Attend to my shoulder, and help me to dress," Ralph said. "It is time that I was away."

"And should the ladies enquire for you?" Lorrimer asked.

"Say that I am writing letters and must not be disturbed for an hour or so. Now see to my shoulder; it is growing painful again."

. . . . .

The full moon was sailing in stately grandeur across the sky.

All nature lay basking in the light of the silvery beams, and the grand old woods were silent, for no breath of wind disturbed the stillness of the scene.

Here and there a party of frolicsome rabbits frisked about or a hare darted from her "form," and went scuttling away from cover to the open fields.

Here and there a bat wheeled and flitted about in its erratic flight, or a solemn, great-eyed owl floated down upon a trembling field-mouse, and committed a midnight tragedy.

Presently the air became disturbed by the sound of footsteps.

A man and a boy were wending their way through the path in the wood, easily discernible in the moonlight.

The man was of a half-caste gipsy type, brutal of feature, and surly of voice.

His companion was a pale-faced, fragile lad, and fatigue had so told upon him that he could scarcely drag one foot before the other.

"Let me rest," the boy said. "I can go no further."

"But you must and shall," the man replied. "We have only two more miles to go, and they must be done to-night, as sure as my name is Jem Basker and your name is Robin."

"Robin what?" the boy asked. "Why do you keep me in this suspense? Why don't you tell me where we are going to, and for what purpose?"

"Hold your chattering tongue," Jem Basker growled. "If you mind your own business and do as I tell you, we shall be friends; if you don't, why—"

"You will beat and illtreat me as you have done before," Robin said, interrupting him. "What a weary life is mine; I have only one consolation."

"And what is that?" Jem Basker asked, laughing hoarsely. "That you will die some day or other, I suppose?"

"We must all die," Robin replied, "but you

are wrong. My consolation is that you are not my father. You lied to me; you brought me up in that belief until I happened to meet Lanoni, the gipsy queen, and she told me—"

"Silence!" Jem Basker cried, in a voice of thunder, as he lifted his heavy hand, "Silence, you pale-faced whelp, or I'll not leave a whole bone in your skin."

"Ah! what a coward you are," Robin replied, fearlessly. "I know why Lanoni made you an outcast from her tribe; I know why she placed a ban on you, so that none of her people will converse with you."

"Silence—silence! I say," Jem Basker hissed. The light of fury came into his eyes, as he spoke.

"You tried to teach me to thieve," Robin continued. "You made out that men who were dishonest lived merry lives; but I know how miserable you are in spite of all your bluster and pretended indifference. Where are you dragging me to now? I will go no further. By the moon that is shining in the heavens I will not."

Jem Basker's face grew pale, and his lips worked convulsively, as the boy threw himself beneath a tree.

"Listen, boy," he said, at length. "You are going to a place where you will never know want again. I can make you rich for life, and so provide myself with money as to leave this accursed country for ever. Get up and follow me, or you will rue the hour that you angered me."

"It will not be the first time that you have left me bruised and senseless on the roadside," the lad said. "Before I move I will know more of your purpose. If you think to palm me off on somebody as a son, stolen in his infancy, I will be no party to the fraud."

Jem Basker recoiled a step or two and whirled a heavy cudgel he carried in his right hand in the air.

"Beware how you tempt me to-night," he said, hoarsely. "The man who sees gold before his eyes does not turn away from it because it is near the fire. The secret you crave to know will be divulged soon. Once more I bid you rise and follow me."

"You shall tell me the story with your own lips first," Robin said, "and I will then say whether I believe you or not."

Driven almost mad with passion, James Basker seized the boy by the collar and swung the cudgel above his head.

"Help!" the boy cried, despairingly.

"Help is near!"

The voice was so close to Jem Basker's ear that he turned with a terrified motion and recoiled before an awful apparition.

Hanging by his feet from the branch of a tree, with his arms and wings extended, was Spring-Heeled Jack.

The visitation was so sudden and terrific in appearance that Jem Basker could do nothing but stand and glare in speechless awe at the weird figure.

"Release your murderous hold!" said Spring-Heeled Jack. "I claim that boy."

With a quick and marvellous motion, Spring-Heeled Jack shook his feet from the tree and alighted upon them on the ground.

"Dog—cowardly dog!" he cried, clutching Jem Basker round the waist. "Thus do I repay such dastardly conduct as yours."

The ruffian went flying away as if fired from a cannon and lay stunned and bleeding from his face.

"My poor lad," said Spring-Heeled Jack, stooping down and taking Robin's hand, "have no fear of me. My appearance may be strange, and yet methinks I have as warm a heart as most men."

"I do not fear you," the boy replied; "but—but there is something unearthly in your appearance. Oh! sir, leave me to my fate! My punishment will be only the greater for your interference."

Spring-Heeled Jack gazed strangely at the boy. "So," he said, "I have protected you and saved you from savage blows for nothing?"

"Yes—yes, because—"

"Because you fear me?"

"I cannot help it," Robin replied.

"Well," said Spring-Heeled Jack, musingly, "that is not to be much wondered at. If this man will ill-treat you when he comes to his senses, why not trust yourself to my care. You will find that although uncouth in appearance I am not uncouth within. You have a secret?"

"Nay," Robin replied; "one is hidden from me."

"And I will unravel it, trust me," Spring-Heeled Jack said. "Come, follow me. If you do not like the place I take you to or the company you find there, breathe but a word and you shall be as free as the birds now slumbering in the trees above our heads."

"I fear you no longer," said Robin; "I will go with you."

"Spoken wisely," Spring-Heeled Jack said. "Leap upon my back. I am well able to carry your weight, and I must introduce you to one who is more like ordinary mortals than I am."

With the sense of the strangeness of his position upon him Robin did as he was requested.

A cry of a alarm came from his lips as Spring-Heeled Jack swept over the ground in a series of gigantic strides, and the boy nearly fainted from sudden fear.

"Hush—hush!" said Spring-Heeled Jack. "Be brave, and trust me as you would trust a friend."

While these events were passing, Constance Marfield and Daisy Leigh were enjoying each other's company.

"And so," Constance was saying, "Sir Roland is not dead?"

"No," Daisy replied. "His eye-lids were quivering as a sign of returning consciousness, as I was borne from the room. Oh! Constance—Constance, will there ever be an end to this mystery and misery? I feel that I should take my life if I thought I should ever fall into that villain's hands again."

"Hush! Daisy—hush!" Constance said. "We have noble protectors in my dear Ralph and Spring-Heeled Jack. We must be patient, for what can we, two weak, helpless girls, do by ourselves?"

Thus more than an hour passed away, and when a servant entered the room to prepare the table for supper he was followed by Ralph Ashton.

"I was afraid to acquaint you with the fact that I was going out, for fear that you might be nervous," he said, smiling, "but out I have been, and the strangest thing in the world is that I have brought somebody with me."

Constance Marfield and Daisy Leigh looked askance at him.

"Who is it, Ralph?" Constance asked. "Somebody I know?"

"No," Ralph replied, shaking his head; "and the odd part of it is that I don't know him myself."

"It is a man, then?"

"No, a boy. Come in, Robin."

As the pale-faced, care-worn lad entered the room, Constance and Daisy rose to greet him.

"I came upon this lad in a rather uncanny fashion," Ralph continued. "He was lying under a tree, where he said he had been placed by Spring-Heeled Jack."

"That is true, sir," Robin replied. "He told me to remain there until he sent somebody to me."

"And he sent you?" Constance said, looking earnestly at Ralph.

"Yes."

A silence fell upon the little assembly for some moments.

"It would appear," said Ralph, at last, "that there is some mystery about this youngster. He has been in bad hands, and we must take care of him. Indeed, we are commanded to do so, unless we wish to displease Spring-Heeled Jack, who has been so useful to us."

"We will be faithful to our trust," Constance said, as she stooped and kissed the boy on the cheek. "You must try to make yourself happy with us, my pretty little fellow."

"I could not be otherwise with you," Robin replied, with eyes sparkling with joy.

"Spoken like a young gentleman," Ralph Ashton said, heartily. "To-morrow I will see that Robin is better clothed, and then we will have a long talk, to see what is best to be done."

## CHAPTER LXXV.

### THE PEDLAR'S BOX.

THE moment that Catchpole and Grabham saw Jacob Butler, and heard his uplifted voice, they came to a standstill.

Then they manifested a strong inclination to bolt, but Jacob overtook them.

"Don't go!" he said, breathlessly; "I have had such a dreadful adventure."

"What's the matter now?" Grabham growled. "We're on special duty, and can't stop to chatter, so if you have anything to say, out with it at once."

"I suppose you know that Bill Blarney has escaped from Newgate?" Jacob said.

"Of course we do," Catchpole said. "Who should know it better than we?"

"Well," Jacob Butler continued, "I happen to know where he is."

"Oh! come now, that's too good a tale to be true," Grabham said. "You are trying to make fools of us, but it won't do, my fine fellow."

"It's a fact," Jacob gasped. "If you follow me I'll show you the house where he has taken refuge in, and Mrs. Corcoran, too."

"He's got Mrs. Corooran on the brain," Grabham said aside to Catchpole.

"Yes," that worthy assented.

"They're gone out together, but will return soon," Jacob Butler went on. "Follow me. The house is down a court—I don't know the name of it, because I found my way there by accident."

Grabham shook his head gravely, and tapped his forehead.

"I'm afeard that you have melted them two guineas in spirituous liquors, Jacob," he said; "but if so be that you are quite certain about what you say, why, of course, it will be our dooty to go with you."

"I am as certain of it as I am alive," Jacob Butler said; "as certain as that I have been near death."

Jacob Butler in his flight had so twisted and turned, that when he endeavoured to retrace his footsteps he discovered that he was completely muddled and mixed.

If he took the constables down one court he took them down twenty.

They knocked at doors without numbers and the curses of unoffending people were heaped upon their heads.

"Well," said Jacob Butler, after at least an hour of fruitless search, "if anybody had told me that I couldn't find the house I should have called that party a fool."

Grabham tilted his hat on one side and gazed pensively at the much-injured man.

"I'll have a few words privately with my mate," the constable observed; "so if you wouldn't mind standing aside, I should feel much obliged."

"Certainly," Jacob Butler said, and withdrew accordingly.

"What do you make of all this?" Grabham asked, in a whisper.

"Why, that he's gone wrong in the upper story," Catchpole replied. "Did you mark the glare in his eyes when he came running up to us?"

"I did," Grabham returned. "He looked like a wild beast just escaped from a cage. What are we to do?"

Mr. Catchpole took off his hat and ran his fingers through his hair.

"I've got an idea," he said, presently. "Grabham, my boy, he will be a source of trouble to us and must be got rid of."

"But how? You don't mean to say that—"

"I would put him out of the way by foul means," Catchpole interposed. "Bah—no! I had no such thing in my mind. But the law doesn't allow mad people to go prowling about."

"Ha!" Grabham ejaculated, "I understand you now. The idea is this: You and I collar Jacob Butler, we take him before a doctor and swear that he is a dangerous character, and bang he goes into a madhouse."

"That's the notion," Catchpole said. "Once we get him in he will be lucky if he gets out."

"Shall we take him now?"

"Yes," Catchpole replied; "but we must be careful how we collar him. He may kick or bite."

Smilingly the constables turned and walked slowly towards Jacob Butler.

"Jacob, my boy," said Grabham, "of course you are right about Blarney and Mrs. Corcoran, only you can't find the house where they are just now. You must have time to think over it, so take a little walk with us and get your head clear."

"My head is clear enough," said Jacob, backing slowly step by step.

There was something in the eyes of the constable and the way he approached that Jacob did not like.

"You are up to some game with me," he said. "Keep back—you mean treachery."

Grabham rolled up his eyes, and assumed the air of an injured man.

# SPRING-HEELED JACK,

## THE TERROR OF LONDON.

"IT IS POISON," MRS. CORCORAN SAID. "I WANT TO KILL TWO BIRDS WITH ONE STONE."

"This is hard after the way we treated you," he said. "We let you go free from the lock-up. We hail you as a brother, and follow you about on a wild-goose chase, and now you want to make out that we are deceiving you."

"I know it," said Jacob, still retreating backwards. "I am quite sure of it."

Grabham looked up and down the street.

There was no living creature in sight, save a ragged boy intent on making mud pies in the gutter.

"Catchpole," Grabham said, hoarsely, "now or never is our time. We must have him. Attack him in the rear, and if he gives us any trouble I'll give him a oner that will make him see a cart-load of stars."

Jacob Butler's countenance turned from white to red, and then green.

"Help! help!" he cried, feebly. "Murder! I won't be taken alive!"

But Catchpole was already upon him, and Grabham, true to his word, gave the luckless Jacob such a tap on the bridge of the nose that tears of anguish flowed down his cheeks.

"He's a dangerous customer, and we must put the darbies on him," said Grabham.

Click, click, went the handcuffs over Jacob's wrists and the unhappy man uttered a groan of despair.

"Now, Catchpole," Grabham said, "just run to the top of the street and fetch a coach. We must take him before Doctor Cuthem at once."

"Before who?" Jacob gasped.

"Before Doctor Cuthem," Grabham repeated.

"Why," Jacob demanded, "what on earth do I want to see a doctor for?"

"Be calm," Grabham returned, soothingly. "Only be quiet and no harm will come to you. You've had a bad shock to your nerves, and a little rest in a nice quiet place, where you will be taken care of, will do you a power of good."

Jacob Butler turned deadly pale.

He guessed the constable's meaning, and his lower jaw fell.

"Listen to me!" he said. "Only hear me. I—"

"I'll listen to nothing," Grabham interposed. "Catchpole, fetch the coach. We are wasting time by standing prating here."

Catchpole, rubbing his hands gleefully, bolted off, and presently returned with the coach.

"I call you to witness that this a vile, horrible plot against my liberty," Jacob Butler said to the driver.

"Don't heed him," Grabham said. "He's very bad. If we were to let him go goodness only knows what would happen. We found him standing on his head and talking all sorts of nonsense about the world being upside down."

"It's a lie—a base lie!" Jacob howled. "I'm as sane as the King of England!"

"Poor devil!" said the coachman, compassionately. "What did he say?"

"That he was the King of England," Catchpole replied.

Jacob Butler gave a gasp of horror and flung himself down on the ground.

"I won't go!" he roared. "I'm not mad! Help—help!"

"Lift him in," said Grabham. "Take care of his feet."

The warning came too late.

Jacob, overcome with feelings of rage and terror, let out with might and main.

One of his feet took effect in the centre of Catchpole's waistcoat, and the constable, after a wild backward flight, fell upon his back and lay gazing placidly at the sky.

"I'm afeard he's knocked all the wind out of my mate," Grabham said. "Get down, coachey, and lend me a hand. You'll have to go before the doctor and tell him of this."

"I don't care about these sort of jobs," the coachman replied; "but I see how the wind blows. It's a mercy that the poor fellow has not killed somebody."

Meanwhile Catchpole had somewhat recovered, and had risen to his feet.

Standing against a wall, with one foot raised and his hand pressed upon his waistcoat, he looked very much like a fat overgrown boy suffering from the consequences of a first dose of tobacco.

The constable was ill—very ill—and before he could take any part in the proceedings Jacob Butler had been dragged into the coach. Grabham was holding the wretched man by the throat, and the driver had taken his seat on the box.

"I'm mortal bad," Catchpole panted. "I'm afeard that I am wounded in a wital part. I haven't the strength of a child."

"If you can't hold him you can sit on him," Grabham returned. "I'm getting tired. Hang the fellow! I never dreamed that he was so strong."

Jacob Butler fought with his manacled hands, and exerted every muscle of his body in the struggle of despair.

But when Catchpole added his bulky weight, which he did by sitting upon the captive's knees and hugging him violently round the neck, Jacob Butler collapsed all of a sudden, and sank back moaning in a half-fainting condition.

"That's better," said Grabham. "He's all right now. Don't quite choke him, Catchpole. Let him have a little air, as we may have some way to go."

Leaving the coach to jolt and rumble on its journey we will take a peep into the interior of a similar vehicle which has just drawn up at the door of the Bull in Top Boots.

Mrs. Corcoran and Bill Blarney were the occupants of this coach, and the nice old lady was crooning and wagging her head from side to side in the most amiable fashion.

"I have heard of this place," she croaked; "but little did I ever think that I should come to it, and in such gallant company. I declare, Mr. Blarney, that if I did not love my Jacob so dearly that I could take quite a fancy to you."

"Could you?" Bill Blarney growled, under his breath, as he let down the window. "The wrinkled witch! you'd talk in another fashion if you knew what I have brought you here for."

Throwing open the door he walked towards the inn.

"Stop—stop!" Mrs. Corcoran cried.

"What's the matter now?" demanded Bill Blarney, swinging himself round on his heels.

"It is the duty of a gentleman to hand a lady from a coach," Mrs. Corcoran said, smirking.

"Ah! so it is," Bill Blarney returned. "Genteel society has been rather out of my line just lately, so you must put my conduct down to absent-mindedness. Come out!"

He jerked Mrs. Corcoran out of the coach in a rather unceremonious manner; but she only laughed.

"You will pay for the coach, deary," she said.

"Deary, be hanged!" said Bill Blarney, in a savage whisper. "Pay yourself. You don't suppose that the warders of Newgate left me much money. Haven't I come here to fetch some. Pay up, or that scarecrow on the box will think there is something wrong."

Blinking and gasping, Mrs. Corcoran dived her hand into the depths of a pocket, which seemed to end somewhere near her heels.

After producing an antique pair of scissors, a skein of thread, a pin-cushion, a reel of cotton, and a lump of dirty beeswax, she brought a greasy purse to light, and fished out half-a-crown, which looked as if it had passed most of its days underground.

"My fare is three-and-six," said the coachman, gazing in disgust at the hag. "It'll be four shillings if you keep me waiting here any longer."

Mrs. Corcoran screwed a malignant squint at the man.

"What thieves you fellows are," she said. "Three-and-six for riding in a mouldy coffin on wheels. Take another sixpence and think yourself well paid."

"I'll think myself lucky to get out of your sight at any price, you broomstick hag!" the coachman said. "I shouldn't wonder if money from your hands was red hot and smelt of brimstone."

"Wouldn't you, now?" replied Mrs. Corcoran, grinning. "Well, that's smart saying on your part, and I take it as a compliment."

The driver snatched the money, and, hissing out an oath, lashed his horses into a gallop and was soon out of sight.

"That man will remember you as long as he lives," Bill Blarney said. "Come into the house. Phew! I was afraid that he would drive away and fetch a constable."

The landlord of the Bull in Top Boots hailed Bill Blarney with delight, but looked rather queer and dubious as his eyes rested on Mrs. Corcoran.

"Who is she?" he demanded. "Where the deuce did you pick up that mummy?"

"Hush!" said Bill Blarney. "She's sharper than any needle and more cunning than any fox. I'll tell you why I have brought her here presently. Let me introduce you to her."

He did so, and Mrs. Corcoran, having partaken of a glass of brandy, addressed the landlord in such endearing terms that he looked inclined to strike her on the head with something heavy.

"Any news?" Bill Blarney asked.

"No," the landlord replied; "Dick Sleuth has been keeping himself quiet for fear that his movements might be watched after you got clear, but I expect him here presently."

"That's well," Bill Blarney replied. "I shall want his assistance, for Mrs. Corcoran can put us on a job that may help to fill our pockets."

"Good!" the landlord replied. "The boys are all hard up, and to tell you the truth my funds are running down like the tide."

Bill Blarney leaned forward and whispered in the landlord's ear.

"Put that old woman in one of the private rooms," he said, "the very sight of her makes me feel ill."

"I am with you there," the landlord replied, in disgust. "A hospital doctor wouldn't give five shillings for her carcase."

Perhaps Mrs. Corcoran overheard this pleasant remark, for she suddenly burst out laughing.

"Come with me," the landlord said, "and I will show you where you can rest."

Mouthing and grinning Mrs. Corcoran insisted upon taking his arm, and when the landlord returned to Blarney his face was pale and damp with cold perspiration.

"I wish you hadn't brought such a South Sea image to my place," he said, as he threw himself into a chair. "Bah! Pass the brandy bottle. I'd rather face all the traps in London than spend an an hour in her company."

"But she'll be useful to us," Bill Blarney said. "If I didn't know it, do you think that I should be such an idiot to tolerate her for an instant?"

"Well, well," said the landlord, "let us hope that she may bring us profit, and then—"

"I hope she will live to share it," Bill Blarney said, laughing.

Their eyes met, and then the landlord laughed too, as if his ruffianly companion had made an excellent joke.

"Now tell us all about yourself?" he said.

Bill Blarney did so, helping himself freely from the brandy bottle meanwhile.

"And now," said the landlord, when the story came to an end, "what wonderful story has this old woman to tell?"

"Not one story, but several," Bill Blarney replied. "In the first place she is satisfied that Sir Roland is in London, and, secondly, she is in possession of other information of a valuable character; but how the deuce she got it is more than I can tell."

"Nor can I, until you tell me what it is," said the landlord.

"You have heard of Mildendale Hall?"

"Yes."

"And something of the story connected with the place?"

"Well, yes," said the landlord; "but my memory is none of the best. Refresh it for me, if you can."

"I will," Bill Blarney replied, "and in as few words as possible."

Having gulped down another glass of brandy, he placed his hands upon his knees.

"Lord Robert Mildendale, the owner of the estate and Hall which bear his family name, married a gipsy girl as soon as he came of age.

"The match did not prove a happy one.

"The country people shunned Lord Robert and his beautiful dark-eyed wife, and for one whole year they remained shut up with scarcely a soul calling upon them.

"At Christmast-time a child was born.

"It proved to be a boy, and Lord Mildendale was delighted, for had he died without an heir the estate would pass to his cousin Charles—a man he hated bitterly.

"Lord Mildendale opened the hall, and gave a grand *fête*, but only the common people attended it, and his lordship in a fury swore an oath that he would train up his infant son to hate his race, and all men and women of his class.

"But Lord Mildendale never had the chance of carrying out his threat."

"The child died, I suppose," the landlord said.

"There you are wrong," Bill Blarney replied. "The boy was stolen."

"Stolen?"

"Yes," Blarney said; "but don't interrupt me, as I shall forget the story myself."

"Matters did not mend at Mildendale," he continued, after a pause. "Lord and lady led a miserable cat and dog life.

"One night—so it is said—his lordship, after

drinking heavily at dinner, struck his wife with a riding-whip.

"The blow descended about her bare shoulders and left a livid mark.

"She did not cry out or utter a word.

"Moving towards the door, she turned, and then her lips moved, as if silently invoking some curse upon his head.

"From that day to this she was never heard of.

"She fled from Mildendale Hall, and it was given out that she went back to her people.

"Strangely enough she left the child, and the boy grew apace for three years.

"One day he wandered from his nurse's side, and mysteriously disappeared."

"I suppose he fell into a pond, or something of that sort?" the landlord of the Bull in Top Boots said, indifferently.

"He did nothing of the kind," Bill Blarney replied. "The boy was stolen by a party of wandering gipsies, who had been waiting their opportunity for more than a year."

"How do you know that?"

"Have patience to listen to the end of the story," Bill Blarney said. "Lord Mildendale received an unsigned letter from Spain, saying that he might bid Good-bye for ever to his son."

"Humph! Well, I suppose his lordship took some little trouble to find the boy?"

"Yes; he spent some thousands of pounds."

"And never got a clue?"

"Not the slightest."

"Nor heard of his wife?"

"Yes; she died. A letter in the same handwriting as the first made him acquainted with that news."

The innkeeper passed his hand thoughtfully across his chin.

"Well," he said, "there is nothing very wonderful in the story, after all. It has been told and with truth in the world many and many a time. I see nothing very extraordinary in it."

"Listen," Bill Blarney said. "This bag of skin and bones, this withered skinflint of a woman, Mrs. Corcoran, declares that the boy was never sent to Spain, but sold to a man in England."

"It is all very well to say so, but can she prove it?"

"She says she can," Bill Blarney replied; "and she says more than that."

"That she knows where the boy is?"

"Yes."

"In that case," said the landlord, "I should imagine that there is a pretty good haul to be netted. What sort of a programme do you intend to follow out?"

"Why, to buy the boy back again, if possible, and then to make sound profit out of him," Bill Blarney replied.

"But supposing this man happens to be in possession of the secret?"

"Yes, but Mrs. Corcoran says he is not," the ruffian returned. "The fellow, it seems, is in trouble, and very likely would be only too glad to grab at a handful of guineas."

"I begin to see the drift of all this," the landlord said, after a short spell of silence. "You want me to advance the money."

Before Bill Blarney could make any kind of a reply, the front door opened with a creaking sound, and the landlord started to his feet.

"Hush!" he whispered; "it may be a visit from the Bow-street runners!"

Bill Blarney's face changed colour, and he grasped his throat with his hands in an uncomfortable sort of way.

As the landlord made his way to the bar he whistled unconcernedly, and still more so when he saw that the stranger was only a travelling pedlar.

"I have lost my way in this wilderness of streets," the pedlar said; "and, feeling tired, I thought I would come here. Can you board me to-day and let me have a bed to-night?"

"Good accommodation for man and beast," the landlord muttered.

"That is well," said the pedlar, removing a box from his back.

"You carry a heavy load?"

"Yes," the man replied; "I buy and sell jewellery—the real stuff and no sham-rubbish—so I shall feel obliged if you will let me keep the key of my room."

"Oh! certainly," the landlord responded, in his blandest tones. "But, sir, there are none here but honest people."

"Don't be offended," the pedlar replied. "He who carries two or three hundred pounds with him need be careful in these days."

"There you are right. You shall have the key, sir. Would you like to see your room now?"

"Yes; because I should like to rest an hour or two."

The landlord of the Bull in Top Boots turned his head aside for a moment.

He was wondering whether Bill Blarney had listened to what had taken place.

The pedlar went to a room, and when alone, and making sure that there was no other door or peephole through which his actions could be watched, he opened the box and gazed with greedy eyes at its glistening contents.

"A good lot and a fine bargain," he said. "What matters it to me where they came from! They are mine—mine, and will bring me a profit of more than a hundred per cent."

Closing the box, he locked it carefully, and placing it on the bed, passed his arm through the strap, and lay down beside it.

Meanwhile the landlord had gone back to Bill Blarney.

The ruffian received him with a grin.

"I suppose I stand in this?" Blarney said, pointing to the ceiling, and indicating that he alluded to the man upstairs.

"I don't know," the landlord replied. "So you heard what was said? Ah! I thought that you would take the trouble to listen."

"A man with a pair of ears in good order can't help listening, unless he stops them up."

"Which you would never take the trouble to do," the landlord said, laughing.

"Well, I can repay that compliment with interest," Bill Blarney replied. "See, here, I will make a bargain with you."

"Wait a minute," said the landlord. "This is a matter not to be in a hurry over. How are we to know that this is not a pitfall dug for us to fall into?"

"We must chance that," Bill Blarney returned.

Leaning forward he whispered something in his companion's ear.

"How do the terms suit you?"

"Well enough," the landlord replied. "I agree, providing that I have no hand in the matter."

"Then you may consider it done," said Blarney.

## CHAPTER LXXVI.

### THE HAUNTED TERRACE—LORD MILDENDALE SEES A GHOST, BUT NOT THE FAMILY ONE.

STANDING on a verdant eminence, shaded by fine old oaks and elms, the lofty turrets of Mildendale Hall rose in proud and bold relief against the deepening blue sky.

It was evening, and the sun, lingering amid a glory of crimson, purple, and gold, seemed loth to leave so grand a scene of its own creation.

But at last the orb sank below the horizon, and shadows of deep purple hue crept out from their hiding-places in the hill-sides, and chasing across the sky heralded the coming night.

Just as a few stars peeped out bashfully, and twinkled feebly, as if conscious that their light was not yet required, an old man, bent almost double, emerged from an avenue of trees and hobbled painfully towards the ancestral home of the Mildendales.

He leaned heavily upon a stick, and stopped every now and then to wheeze and catch his breath.

Shabbily attired—for he was in rags which fluttered in the wind—this decrepid old man posed in strange contrast to the noble house, ancient but stately, and filled with every luxury that money can buy and skill devise.

His way did not lay by the front entrance, but by a narrow path used by servants and trades-people, and which, as a matter of course, led to the rear of the building.

The mendicant, or at least he had all the appearances of one, seemed perfectly acquainted with the route, though it was so hard for him to travel, and hobbling on, he reached a small door, and knocked timorously at it.

He shrank back a little as he heard a burst of merry laughter.

"Ah!" he muttered. "Man and maid make merry to-day. It is his lordship's birthday. I wonder if there be any joy in his heart?"

Receiving no answer to his first summons, the old man knocked louder, and then the door flew open, and a gorgeously-clad footman appeared.

"What do you want?" he demanded.

"Charity, good sir, charity."

"You'll get nothing of that sort here," the flunkey replied, "and you may think yourself lucky that his lordship is away just now. He will be back presently, and mark my words, he will order me to set yonder mastiff free, should he happen to catch sight of you."

"Indeed!" the old man replied. "So he is no exception to his—I mean, the world. Because he knows not what poverty is, he deems it a crime."

"You had better go, indeed you had," the footman said. "If I had any change I would give you a penny. Bless me, man, why don't you go? Do you want to feel that dog's teeth meet in your shrivelled legs?"

For a moment the beggar raised his eyes, and a peculiar light shone from them.

"If you have no money," he said, "give me food and drink. I am only a poor old gipsy, and—"

The footman threw up his hands and started back in horror.

"Fly!" he cried—"fly while there is time! If Lord Mildendale knew that a man with Romany blood in his veins had been here he will leave no stone in the neighbourhood unturned until he has found him."

"And then," said the old man, coolly, "if his lordship found that man what would he do to him?"

The footman shuddered.

"Why don't you take my advice and go?" he blurted out. "Listen! I hear the sound of carriage-wheels. Go, I beseech you, or there will be more bloodshed in Mildendale!"

"Yes, I will go," the old gipsy replied, "but I and others will return. Tell Lord Mildendale that I, Namon Wallack, wish him and his son—ha! ha! ha!—many happy returns of this day!"

He turned and vanished from view so quickly that the footman stood motionless and dumbfoundered.

"An old man forsooth!" he said at length. "It strikes me that he must be young, hale, and hearty to be able to make his departure in such a fashion. Shall I mention this circumstance to my lord? No. He would only fly into a rage, and ask why I did not shoot the fellow down. I will let the matter rest where it is."

As Lord Mildendale entered the hall the sounds of merriment ceased, and the servants moved about with silent footsteps and grave faces.

His lordship was a middle-aged man, but the deep lines on his countenance, which showed that he laboured under no common sorrow, made him look much older.

He scarcely ever spoke, save to state his wants or to give an order to his valet, a staid, clean-shaven man, who seldom left his master's elbow from morn till night.

"Harmer," his lordship said, "give me a glass of wine and fetch me a book—any one will do."

He threw himself wearily into a chair as he spoke, and Harmer, gliding about like a ghost, obeyed his master's commands.

"I have a fancy to be alone," Lord Mildendale said, suddenly; and then he added to himself—"Forty years old to-day. Forty years of unrest and disappointment. Ah! well, I can employ my mind in looking back into the past."

Raising his eyes, he discovered that Harmer had already left the room.

The book fell from Lord Mildendale's hand, for a sound broke upon his ears.

It was the sound of footsteps upon the terrace walk, and he had often heard them when alone.

"Unreal mockery!" he said. "And yet, how they remind me of bye-gone days! They are but the echoes of the past. How often have I heard those footsteps as she paced to and fro with her baby boy in her arms! "Oh! my wife—my child—my child!"

Lord Mildendale dropped his face into his open hands, and a great sob of agony rose from his heart.

"I must go out!" he cried, suddenly. "I cannot breathe the atmosphere of this place; it chokes me. Would to Heaven that I had died long ago, and escaped this misery!"

Pushing open the French windows reaching from floor to ceiling, Lord Mildendale stepped out upon the terrace.

The full moon was shining brightly, and every object was as plain and distinct as at noon tide.

Lord Mildendale seemed to be watching for something.

He kept his eyes fixed on the further end of the terrace, as if he expected to see somebody there, and as he watched the ghostly footsteps went on.

"She will come again to night," he muttered. "This is the night in the year when she appears to remind me of the bitter past. Ah! At last!"

A faint, quivering light flashed up ahead of him, but the apparition he saw was not the one he had expected and had been waiting for with a fast-beating heart.

As in the reflection of a mirror he saw a strange, tall form of a man, weird and ghastly, who held a lad by one hand and pointed to him with the other.

"Heaven help me!" Lord Mildendale cried. "What may this mean? Fiend or mortal speak to me!"

But the mysterious form neither spoke nor moved.

Lord Mildendale tottered forward a few steps, and then the ghastly figure raised its hand.

"Beware!" it said. "To approach me is death!"

At that moment the boy turned his face and looked full into Lord Mildendale's eyes.

"My child—my son!" the nobleman cried. "Ah! he lives. Come to these arms and this heart which has yearned for you through many a weary year!"

As the vision had appeared so it vanished in an instant, and Lord Mildendale, gasping out a cry of terror, staggered back to the room and fell senseless upon the floor.

The noise of his fall brought Harmer to his side.

"He will die in one of these paroxysms," the valet said, as he raised his lordship and placed him in a chair. "Poor men envy the rich, but give me poverty to such a life as this man leads!"

## CHAPTER LXXVII.

### THE PEDLAR'S ROOM—MRS. CORCORAN HAS A TWINGE OF CONSCIENCE.

NIGHT had fallen gloomily upon London, and the great city lay hushed in slumber.

The sky was murky, promising both rain and thunder, and the river ran sullenly, as if lingering to join the coming storm.

All good people were in bed, but here and there bursts of uproarious drunken mirth came from the windows of houses of low repute, and made the night hideous.

For a wonder the Bull in Top Boots was comparatively quiet, and the front of the house showed no light.

This would have been quite sufficient to convince anybody acquainted with the habits and customs of the vile wretches who used the house that mischief was brewing.

Though the windows facing the street were plunged in darkness the back rooms were bright enough, and some score or more ruffians were drinking deeply and singing ribald songs.

"Come, come, boys," the landlord said, as he made his way into the room, where the merry-makers had assembled. "I must ask you to leave presently, for I am almost done to death. This makes the fourth night that I have been up, and if I try the experiment again the Bull in Top Boots will go into mourning for its landlord."

"Well," said Dick Sleuth, who sat at the head of the table, "bring in another bowl of punch and we will be satisfied."

The landlord grumbled out something under his breath as he turned towards the door.

Bill Blarney followed the innkeeper into the passage and tapped him on the shoulder.

"A word with you," he said.

"Well?"

"Make the punch weak, or some of those fellows will get so drunk that there will be no getting them out of the house at all."

"You may leave that to me," the landlord replied, grinning. "In half an hour we shall be alone."

"And then we must wait an hour or so," Bill Blarney replied. "It is very improbable that the pedlar can go to sleep with all this noise of singing under him."

"We must wait!" the landlord repeated, elevating his eyebrows. "What have I to do with it?"

"Well, it is all one and the same thing," said Bill Blarney, impatiently.

"There I can't agree with you," the landlord rejoined. "You make a proposition, and I agree to let you have your way to a certain extent; but that is all."

"You took good care to make terms with me," Bill Blarney said, sullenly.

The landlord swung himself sharply round on his heels and looked the ruffian steadily in the face.

"You owe your life and liberty to me," he said. "I have fed you, supplied you with money, and if I made terms with you it was only to get back what was due to me."

He snapped his fingers, and turning angrily away, walked into the bar.

The punch was soon brewed and consumed.

Then the company began to disperse, some reeling, others shouting and yelling, and a few quarrelling and declaring that they would settle their grievances at a more convenient opportunity.

Bill Blarney had kept out of the way, but no sooner was the door locked and bolted than he appeared again.

"Don't be angry," he said to the landlord, "I meant no harm. You have acted the part of a friend to me often I confess."

"Well, well, we will say no more about the matter."

"I thought it best to take Mrs. Corcoran into my confidence," Bill Blarney said.

"More fool you!"

"I don't think so," the ruffian returned. "She knows my character too well already, and my object is now to get her under my thumb, so as to make sure of her silence."

"In point of fact, I suppose you have asked her to help you?" the inn-keeper said.

"You have hit the right nail on the head," Bill Blarney replied. "The old hag possesses some potions, a few drops of which, sprinkled on the face of a sleeping man, prevents him waking, though a thunder-bolt fell at his feet."

"What a nice, pleasant old lady you have brought under my roof!" the landlord said, grinning. "I hope she will not try any of her experiments on me! Ah! here she comes."

Blinking like an old owl in the sunlight, Mrs. Corcoran came hobbling down the stairs.

"I have listened for his breathing," she said, "and he sleeps soundly."

Bill Blarney drew a deep breath and a death-like pallor stole across his face.

"This will not do," he said, striking his chest. "I have either drunk too much or not enough. Give me another glass of brandy and then I shall be ready for anything."

"Yes, yes," said Mrs. Corcoran. "Come at once. We must waste no time. He may wake suddenly. Strange dreams come to men in danger sometimes and put them on their guard."

The landlord's hand trembled as he supplied Bill Blarney with the fiery liquor, and as the ruffian and Mrs. Corcoran turned towards the staircase he went into the parlour behind the bar and closed the door.

The Bull in Top Boots had witnessed many a scene such as was about to be enacted under its evil roof.

Slowly and noiselessly Bill Blarney and the hag crept up the stairs, and they went on without stopping until they reached a spacious landing.

"That is his room," Mrs. Corcoran whispered, pointing to a door. "Are you sure that you have forgotten nothing?"

"Quite. And you?"

Mrs. Corcoran made a hideous grimace as she held up a phial filled with colourless liquid.

"Hush!" Bill Blarney said. "Now to open the door. The hinges are old; they may creak and wake him."

"In that case," Mrs. Corcoran croaked, "you must be quick and sure. He must utter no word or cry. Now!"

Bill Blarney took from his pocket a duplicate key, which the landlord had provided him with, and inserted it in the lock.

The ruffian listened intently as he turned it, but the pedlar still breathed heavily, and lay unconscious that his time on earth was drawing so swiftly to a close.

Slowly, inch by inch, Bill Blarney opened the door, and he and Mrs. Corcoran stole with cat-like movements towards the bed.

The pedlar, who was lying in an uneasy attitude upon his face, moved slightly as Bill Blarney stooped over him, but in an instant Mrs. Corcoran drew the stopper from the phial and sprinkled its contents over the slumbering man's mouth and nostrils.

He uttered one gasping, guttural cry and opened his eyes.

There was a horrible glare in them, as if he knew what was to happen and yet was aware of his helplessness.

The eyes closed again, but Bill Blarney stood hesitating and trembling in every limb.

"Fool!" said Mrs. Corcoran. "He has no more power than a log of wood. Give me the knife."

"No!" Bill Blarney said, hoarsely, as he raised the glistening blade. "Ah!"

The next instant he and Mrs. Corcoran were out of the room, and stood clutching each other, guilty wretches that they were; but the hag was not yet satisfied.

"I must go back," she said; "I must make sure that you struck home."

"No, no!" Blarney gasped; "let us go downstairs."

Mrs. Corcoran released herself from the ruffian's grasp and hastened into the room.

The next instant a shriek burst from her lips.

Bill Blarney's hair stood on end with terror, and he reeled heavily against the wall.

"What now?" he yelled, as he recovered his self-control and dashed into the room.

"Those eyes!" Mrs. Corcoran shrieked, as she sank upon her knees, "they opened again and fixed themselves upon me. Mercy! mercy!"

"Come away," Blarney said, seizing her by the shoulders, "come away, you witch! He is dead, I tell you."

"Yes, dead in body, but not in spirit," the hag moaned. "See there! See how he stalks towards me! He comes! He stands at my side! Oh! horror—horror!"

Maddened with rage and terror by the old woman's cries, Bill Blarney dragged her across the floor and forced her out of the room.

"Silence!" he shouted, "or there will be two deaths in this house to-night instead of one."

Just then the landlord appeared with a light in his hand at the foot of the stairs.

"Curse you!" he cried. "You make noise enough to wake the dead. Stop her tongue, Bill Blarney, or we shall have the night-watchmen surrounding the house."

As he spoke a loud knocking came at the door.

The landlord blew out the light, and simultaneously Bill Blarney seized Mrs. Corcoran by the throat and nearly throttled her.

"Do you know what you have done?" he hissed. "Listen to that knocking and ask yourself who is at the door. Witch! you shall not wait for the gallows."

But for once Bill Blarney had reckoned without his host.

With a quick movement Mrs. Corcoran struck up his hands, and, leaping to her feet, recoiled several paces from him.

"Not yet," she said. "I have had stronger and more desperate men than you to deal with. My feelings overcame me, but I am myself again."

Bill Blarney did not know what to do or which way to turn, and as he stood thus, undecided and cold with terror, the knocking at the door went on.

"Take that woman into the room on the left," the landlord called out. "I must quiet the barking of these bloodhounds!"

Fumbling with locks and bolts, the landlord of the Bull in Top Boots at last opened the door and peeped out.

To his astonishment he only saw Dick Sleuth standing before him.

"What the devil do you mean by this?" the innkeeper demanded. "Have you taken a sudden spite against me? Do you want to call the attention of every constable to my house?"

"Bah!" said Dick Sleuth. "I made sure that there were no traps about before I kicked up such a bobbery. I want to see Bill Blarney."

"He is not here," the landlord replied. "Dick, you are drunk. Go away, and come again when you are sober."

"I am sober enough to know that Bill Blarney is here, and that I must and will see him," Dick Sleuth replied.

"Humph!" said the landlord, as he admitted Sleuth. "You speak boldly. Such words as 'must' and 'will' don't suit me."

"Bah!" Dick Sleuth replied, "don't fly into a temper. Tell Bill Blarney that I have discovered Sir Roland Ashton's hiding-place."

## CHAPTER LXXVIII.

### SIR ROLAND RECEIVES A VISIT FROM OLD FRIENDS.

SIR ROLAND lay writhing with pain and rage.

He had left the den of infamy into which he had entrapped Daisy Leigh, and was now in apartments taken for him by the ever-watchful

Jules Carleon, who followed the baronet about like his shadow.

"Courage, Sir Roland!" Jules said. "All will be well now that the bullet is extracted. In a few days you will be able to go abroad."

"May the hand that fired the shot wither!" Sir Roland said, grinding his teeth furiously. "Just as I raised the cup of pleasure it was dashed from my lips by this foul fiend!"

"True," Jules Carleon said. "But have you not much to be thankful for? You still live, and, therefore, despair not."

"What else can I do?" Sir Roland demanded. "How am I to know that Spring-Heeled Jack is not in the house at this very moment? He seems to possess the power of entering and leaving any place at will."

Jules Carleon shrugged his shoulders.

"It is certainly mysterious," he said; "and yet I have a notion that I shall be able to pay him in his own coin before long. It is time that I went out to purchase the things you require, Sir Roland. You are not afraid of being left alone?"

"It matters little," Sir Roland replied, wearily. "Give me a glass of wine and then go. The pain has abated somewhat, and I will try to get a little sleep."

Jules Carleon left the room, closing the door softly behind him, and Sir Roland, posing his limbs as comfortably as possible, closed his eyes.

He was thoroughly worn out, and in a short time he began to breathe heavily.

He had not been asleep more than a quarter of an hour when a strange clicking sound came from the direction of the window.

Then the curtains parted, and Bill Blarney and Mrs. Corcoran stole across the thickly-carpeted floor.

"See!" Mrs. Corcoran said, "he sleeps."

"Never to wake again," Bill Blarney said, drawing a pistol from under his coat and holding it over the sleeping man. "Ha! what are you doing?"

Mrs. Corcoran was pouring something from a phial into a glass that stood on the table.

"I am killing two birds with one stone," the hag chuckled. "The man who finds Sir Roland's body will turn faint with fear. He will drink, and drink deeply."

Bill Blarney gazed ferociously down at the baronet.

Blarney's finger was on the trigger, but before the hammer could fall Sir Roland started from his sleep and sat up.

Mrs. Corcoran gave vent to a horrible yell, and Bill Blarney, hastily concealing the weapon, started back.

"Mrs. Corcoran! Bill Blarney!" Sir Roland cried. "Do I dream?"

"No," said the hag. "We have found you out, and thought that we would pay you a visit. You do not seem very glad to see us."

Sir Roland passed his hand over his brow.

"How did you get into this house?" he asked, "and what is your purpose in coming here?"

Passing his hand under the cushion he produced a brace of pistols.

"Bah!" said Bill Blarney. "If we had intended mischief we could have done it long ago. With regard to how we got here, we came through the window."

"You mean mischief," Sir Roland said, addressing Mrs. Corcoran. "I can see it in your eyes. Keep your distance, or I will blow your brains out."

"Sir Roland," the hag replied, "I have come here to tell you that I have forgiven and forgotten everything. It is absolutely necessary for your safety and mine that our friendship should be resumed."

"Just so," said Bill Blarney, "and they are exactly my sentiments. Are you alone in the house?"

"No," Sir Roland replied, startled at the question; "a sudden cry or a loud sound, such as firing a pistol, my friend, would bring assistance."

Sir Roland moved towards the table as he spoke, and poured wine into the poisoned glass.

"Drink," he said to Bill Blarney.

"No," the ruffian replied. "I have given that sort of thing up."

"And you?" Sir Roland said, turning to Mrs. Corcoran.

"After you," she said. "I should prefer a little brandy."

"It is there," he said, pointing to the bottle.

Sir Roland tossed the wine down his throat, and immediately a strange and awful expression came over his face.

He clutched his throat.

He uttered gasping cries and tried to speak, but speech failed him, and he reeled back upon the couch.

"Where is his boast about assistance now?" said Mrs. Corcoran. "Nothing can save him. In less than a quarter of an hour he will be a corpse."

Sir Roland still struggled feebly, but at last he became rigid, and a film gathered in his eyes.

"Poor devil!" said Bill Blarney; "he did not like dying at all. I suppose you are now satisfied?"

"Yes, for the present," said Mrs. Corcoran, coolly. "I have settled accounts with one of my enemies, at any rate, and I hope the time is not far distant when I shall have the opportunity of serving them all the same. This affair is over, and I suppose I must remain contented with it as one night's work."

The witch gazed at the ghastly body with fiendish delight.

"Aye!" said Bill Blarney; "and yet it was almost a pity to rob the gallows of its due."

"He was a coward and a villain," Mrs. Corcoran said, "and deserved his fate, even if it had been for that alone. The fool! What mercy could he have expected from me? He should have known me better."

"True; mercy is no ingredient of your nature."

"I never boast of it," said Mrs. Corcoran; "besides, had I spared his life he would doubtless have taken the first opportunity to have sacrificed mine, as he attempted to do before."

"To be sure, that is correct enough," said Bill Blarney, "and perhaps you have acted the wisest part."

"It was an extraordinary circumstance which brought him to this place," Mrs. Corcoran said.

"It was a fortunate one at any rate," said Blarney.

"There he lies," said Mrs. Corcoran; "and the longer I gaze at his odious corpse the more satisfaction do I feel at the vengeance I have obtained. He is gone to his last account, and a very pretty one, no doubt, he will be able to render."

"Come, come! we delay," said Bill Blarney, impatiently; "you have exulted enough over the deed, and the sooner we get away the better."

"Stop," said Mrs. Corcoran, approaching nearer to the body. "He may have something in his possession worth taking. It is not likely he would travel without money; I will search him."

She did so, and ransacking every pocket, turned out various sums of money.

"Come," she observed, "this, at any rate, will repay us for our trouble. A goodly sum this. Oh! Sir Roland, I know you were always a famous one to look after the exchequer. But what have we here? Some papers."

"We can peruse them by-and-bye," said Bill Blarney. "Come, come! let us go."

Bill Blarney and Mrs. Corcoran had scarcely made their escape when Jules Carleon returned.

As the Frenchman gazed at Sir Roland his face turned ashy-grey.

"Murdered in my absence!" he cried; "and yet I see no signs of violence."

Seizing the body of the inanimate man in his arms, Jules Carleon bore it to the window.

"Ha!" Carleon said, "the window is open. It is here that the assassins entered. *Parbleu!* it is all over with Sir Roland, I am afraid."

A faint smell came from the baronet's lips, and Jules Carleon guessed the cause at once.

"Poison!" he said. "He may not be dead yet."

Dashing out of the house, he ran to the nearest doctor, and returned with him in haste.

"The man is not dead," the doctor said. "His heart beats. Place him in bed and I will give him a drug which will destroy the effects of the poison."

The doctor's words were prophetic.

Sir Roland Ashton rallied, and when morning came had so far recovered as to eat a slight repast.

But not a word would he say regarding how the poison had found its way down his throat.

He kept his own counsel, and said nothing about Bill Blarney and Mrs. Corcoran.

"There is time yet," he muttered. "They are too clever! I will wait until I can take my revenge at leisure."

## CHAPTER LXXIX.

### THE FUNDS GROW LOW.

Sir Roland Ashton, having been relieved of the greater portion of his ready cash, found that the funds were getting too low to be pleasant.

He had a few notes left, but they would soon be gone, and he consulted Jules Carleon on the subject.

The Frenchman reflected with his head on one side and his eyes half closed.

"You must tempt fortune," he said. "Why not try the luck of the gaming-tables, Sir Roland?"

"A good idea that," the baronet replied. "It is a long time since I handled a card or shook a dice-box. We will pay our account, Carleon, and remove into a neighbourhood where we can win money, or—"

"Lose it," Jules Carleon interposed. "Fortune does not always treat her clients well at first. Sir Roland, how much money have you left?"

"About two hundred pounds."

"That is a small amount," Jules Carleon said, "but it may prove enough with care. Should that go, how then?"

"Oh! I must trust to chance," Sir Roland replied.

"The estates you spoke of to me are, then, valueless?" the Frenchman said.

"I can realise nothing from them at present," Sir Roland replied, bitterly. "If Ralph Ashton were dead—"

"Bah!" said Jules Carleon. "What is the use of waiting for dead men's shoes. Men must keep themselves. Try gaming, and if that fails—"

"Well?"

"You must do as others do—stop at nothing to get you own back with interest."

"You mean that I should turn a common thief?"

"Oh! no," Jules Carleon replied, laughing. "The swindler on a great scale is courted, but the pickpocket goes to prison. When a handsome highwayman is tried all the ladies run to see him and cry and sigh; but who cares for the hungry beggar who steals a loaf?"

"You reason well," Sir Roland said.

The next day saw a great change in the baronet's mode of living.

His time was now passed in one continued round of riot and debauchery, and he was very seldom sober.

But amidst it all, when the circling glass went merrily round, and the ribald jests of his companions made the room resound again with boisterous mirth, could he stifle the voice of conscience?

Could he bury in oblivion the dismal past?

Could he banish from his breast those dreadful apprehensions that rendered his life wretched?

The guilty know no peace.

Winning or losing he drank; he would stagger to his couch and try to sleep.

Sleep! there was none for him.

Frightful forms were continually flitting before his disordered imagination and ringing curses in his ears.

He would start from his bed and rush again to the scenes of wild dissipation, and there increase the torturing anguish of his mind.

Frequently was he upon the very verge of self-destruction.

He carried a loaded pistol with him, and sometimes put it to his head when more than usually despairing, but he shuddered at meeting such an end.

He clung to life in all its misery, for he did not dare to die.

"I am not doomed to perish thus," he would say. "There is another fate in store for me which I shudder to think upon, but which I feel is certain to overtake me. What would I not give were I now as innocent as in the days of my youth! Happy days! doomed never to return."

And then he would beat his breast and remain for some time in a state bordering upon distraction.

Most of the characters with whom Sir Roland had become acquainted were a set of sharpers and blacklegs, who freqented the various gambling-houses then so fashionable in London.

It was not long before Sir Roland was initiated into their arts, and they used him as a dupe and decoy to others.

He became infatuated with their proceedings; for some time they allowed him to be a sharer in the booty they obtained; and as his own pecuniary means were reduced to a mere phantom of what they formerly were, it offered to him a temptation which it cannot be supposed that a man in his desperate situation could resist.

But this the villains had determined should not last long.

They only watched an opportunity to beggar him altogether.

They formed a plan among themselves by which they should not only obtain the whole of his money, but the share in the plunder he had at different times received from them.

The fatal night arrived, and Sir Roland went as usual to the gambling-house, accompanied by two or three of his associates.

There was an unusual congregation of people there, and the play commenced with great spirit.

Sir Roland played and won.

Elated with success, he staked higher, and won again.

Higher still he staked, and then had to return all that he had won in the two previous games.

Still, nothing daunted, he played again, and once more fortune was against him.

He became somewhat nervous at this unusual bad luck, and looked towards his associates, from whose countenances and observations he could discover that they were bent on winning.

Once more he played for a high stake and was again a loser.

He could not help uttering a curse between his teeth; but desperation urged him on, and again and again he played and lost, until he found himself reduced to a very trifling sum.

The terrors of his situation were now fully presented to his imagination.

He paused for a moment, and scarcely knew how to act; but at length he excused himself to those with whom he had been playing, and going over to his associates, he drew one of them aside, and mentioning the terrible ill luck he had met with, requested the loan of a sufficient sum of money to try his luck again.

A positive refusal, accompanied by some sarcastic remarks, was all he received.

Sir Roland was astonished—confounded, and remonstrated; but an ironical laugh was his only reply, and the fatal truth now became evident to him.

"Villains!" he cried, and clasping his burning temples, he rushed from them.

He went to the table where he had been playing, but those who had plundered him were gone, and he saw the full extent of his misery.

"Duped—ruined! Oh! horror—horror!" he cried, as he darted like a madman from the fatal place and fled he scarcely knew whither.

Oh! the agony of that dreadful moment. He beat his breast and tore the hair from his head in the frenzy of his despair.

He reached the house in which he was living.

Jules Carleon met him and saw what had happened.

"You have lost?" he said.

"All!" Sir Roland gasped. "I am a beggar!"

"Then farewell!" Jules Carleon said. "I must see to my own interests. Bah! what a fool not to rob instead of being robbed."

The Frenchman passed out of the door, banging it behind him.

Sir Roland's brain whirled, his limbs refused to support him, and with one intense groan of anguish he sank upon the bed in a state of utter insensibility.

Had that utter insensibility have lasted for ever it would have been a mercy to him.

But he at length recovered to a full consciousness of his misery.

He looked around him.

His room was buried in profound darkness, but to his distempered imagination frightful objects seemed to flit before his eyes, and the mockery of demons rang in his ears.

He staggered to his feet; the perspiration rolled from his temples in torrents, and a raging fire seemed to burn his brain.

All the events of the evening rushed upon his recollection, and it is a wonder that his reason did not entirely leave him.

"Ruined—irretrievably ruined!" he groaned. "Oh! fool, worse than madman, that I have been to suffer myself to be thus duped by the wretches. And now what is to become of me? Whither can I flee? Where seek for assistance? Assistance! Despair—despair! Oh! I am now indeed fearfully punished for my crimes! And shall I still continue to drag on this life of horror? No; let me die, and at once end this career of crime and anguish!"

He snatched a pistol from the table as he spoke and raised it towards his head.

But again other thoughts rushed upon his brain, and he dropped the deadly weapon from his hand.

"No, no!" he cried. "I cannot, dare not, die. I dare not meet that terrible eternity where I must render up an account of all the manifold crimes of which I have been guilty. My soul shrinks appalled from the punishment that awaits me. Oh! horror—horror!"

Again the wretched man clasped his burning temples and traversed the room with hasty and disordered steps.

All the torments of perdition were raging in his breast, and he could perceive no ray of consolation, or hope by which to cling.

All was darkness, horror, and despair.

He had but a small sum left, which would only support him for a few days, and then he must become a wretched, wandering outcast upon the face of the earth, with no other resource but to plunge still deeper into crime or to perish of starvation.

The bare thought was enough to drive him to madness, and throwing himself once more upon his bed, the whole of that night he continued to rave in the most delirious manner.

For two days he was in a state of high fever and was unable to leave his room; but at length he recovered sufficiently to walk forth into the fresh air.

He would not visit his former associates, for he now entertained a horror and dread of them, and knew that he should meet with nothing but their scorn and derision.

He wandered from the city into the most secluded part, and where he could commune with his own harrowing thoughts without interruption.

Sir Roland shunned the haunts of man, and prayed that he could have shut himself out entirely from the light of day.

He felt the same bitter hatred for all mankind as he did for himself, and longed that he could flee to some place where he might perish unknown, and his name might be blotted for ever from the memory of all with whom he had been connected.

Here for hours he remained, and did not return to his lodging until the earth was veiled in the solemn darkness of night.

That shelter he must soon abandon, and become a shelterless wretch, unpitied and uncared for.

The time came.

The climax of his misery arrived—his last coin was expended, and he found himself entirely destitute.

No language can properly describe his agony at that time, and again the thought of self-destruction rushed upon his brain, and it was only the fear of dying that once more arrested his purpose.

He was compelled to leave his lodging, but he knew not where to direct his footsteps, and, indeed, all places were now alike to him.

There was nothing but starvation before his eyes, and at one time he thought of giving himself up to the officers of justice and of standing his chance as to the fate which might befall him; but then the idea of an ignominious death upon a public scaffold, amid the execrations and exultations of surrounding thousands, withheld him, and he determined to cling to liberty as long as he could.

The shades of evening had fallen before he prepared to quit his dwelling, and then, snatching up his pistols, and wrapping his cloak closely around him, he cast one glance round the room and quitted it, as he thought, for ever.

Sir Roland hurried through the city, fearful of being seen by anyone, and soon reached the outskirts, where he took the loneliest way he could find, and travelled on he knew not and cared not whither.

"How am I to live," he cried, "without money, without food? Why should I wander on when I know not where to go? And must I remain in this desperate condition until I breathe my last?"

His hand involuntarily grasped one of his pistols, and a fearful idea in a moment shot through his brain.

"Jules Carleon spoke words of wisdom," he said. "I have been robbed of all that I possessed, and why should I not retaliate? Am I to die a lingering death when there are those who have plenty? Have I not already sinned as far as I can go? Am I not a murderer? and why then should I hesitate to become a robber? Away with conscience! I must not, will not, starve."

In that moment the determination of the wretched man was taken.

He looked around him with the hope of beholding some traveller upon whom he might make his guilty attempt.

But not a human being met his view as far as his eyes could penetrate, and he walked on, still fixed and resolved in his purpose.

And now it became still darker than before, and a heavy peal of thunder announced a storm, which soon burst in all its fury.

This increased the misery of Sir Roland's situation, and added to the terrible determination which had taken possession of his mind.

He looked around him to endeavour to find a place of shelter, but nothing of the kind presented itself to his sight, and again he walked on, muttering curses to himself, and fully prepared, in the state of mind he was in, to commit any deed, however atrocious.

Sir Roland continued to travel in this manner for more than half an hour, completely drenched to the skin, and in a most miserable condition, when at last he came to an old shed which stood by the roadside, and gladly availed himself of the temporary shelter it afforded.

He seated himself on a block of wood, and muttered curses on the fate that had driven him to hide his head in such a place.

At length he was aroused by hearing footsteps, and looking out, he beheld a man enveloped in a cloak approaching the hut.

Presently he passed by the shed on the opposite side of the road, and Sir Roland saw that, although the man was travelling on foot, he was well dressed and probably possessed a well-filled purse.

Again he grasped the pistol, and watched the traveller with greedy eyes.

His arm was nerved.

He thought of his destitute condition.

There was probably the chance presented to him of replenishing his purse and saving himself from a lingering death.

Sir Roland could not resist the fatal temptation, but stealing out with stealthy and silent footsteps, he pursued the unconscious traveller. He came within a few paces of him, and then he paused.

A deathly sickness came over him, but it was only for a moment; he raised the hand which grasped firmly the fatal instrument of death and shot the stranger down.

His unfortunate victim gave but one frightful groan and then fell lifeless at the feet of his cowardly assassin.

For a moment the villain stood and gazed appalled at the work of his hands. All the horrors of his guilt rushed upon his mind, and even then he would have fled from the spot without seeking the object that had tempted him to the deed; but terror transfixed him to it, and he trembled in every limb.

The thunder rolled more heavily than before, as if in anger at the horrible crime, and the lightning flashed, imparting fresh horrors to the scene.

But the fear of someone approaching, and that he would be detected, at length aroused the murderer from the lethargy of horror into which he had fallen.

Stooping down, he turned the corpse of his unfortunate victim on its back.

The lightning flashed on his livid and blood-stained countenance, and again Sir Roland trembled violently and started aghast as he gazed upon it.

Distorted though the features were by the agonies of the violent death he had met with, Sir Roland could see that he was a handsome young man, apparently not more than four-and-twenty years of age, and the elegance of his apparel plainly showed that he was of no mean rank.

With trembling haste Sir Roland searched his pockets and secured a well-filled purse.

He waited for no more, but fled precipitately from the spot, he knew not whither, nor did he stop to ascertain until he had got to some distance from the scene of his dreadful crime, when he found he was returning towards the city.

Sir Roland paused and deliberated within himself how he should act, but at last he determined that he would return to his late lodging, the other inmates of the house not being aware that he had intended to leave it for ever, and, therefore, suspicion of his guilt, he thought, was less likely to be excited.

It would be impossible to describe the feelings of the assassin at that moment.

The fearful groan uttered by his victim still rang in his ears, and every sound that he heard he imagined was that of pursuit.

# SPRING-HEELED JACK,

## THE TERROR OF LONDON.

THE ROPE FELL CLEAN OVER JULES CARLEON'S NECK.

But the deed was done beyond recall, and there was nothing now left for him to do but to look to his own security.

The murder had been committed in the darkness of night in a lonely spot.

No one had witnessed its perpetration, and, therefore, what had he to fear, unless his own terrors and the tortures of his guilty conscience betrayed him?

No one could suspect that he had done the crime; or even supposing that they should, they had no proof by which to convict him, and, consequently, he was safe—safe from all but the vengeance of offended Heaven, which assuredly, sooner or later, would overtake him.

Fearing, however, that the body of his murdered victim might be discovered by some travellers and a pursuit commenced, he resumed his way with hurried steps, and reached the city without meeting with any individual on the road.

The storm had now entirely subsided, and Sir Roland slowly retraced his steps towards his lodging, which he entered without being observed, and, throwing himself on a seat for a few moments, was completely overwhelmed with remorse and terror.

"So, then," he muttered to himself, "I have again become a murderer; I have now stamped myself a monster of the blackest dye. Lost—lost! no penitence can now avail me, for what penitence can wash out the stain of the awful crimes of which I have been guilty? My days may be prolonged, but what will they be? Those of horror and unceasing torment. And must I not yet plunge still deeper into crime? Oh! yes, unless the avenging arm of Heaven stops me in my career and brings upon my head that retribution which I have so long feared."

He could proceed no further, but rocked his body to and fro in a state of the most inconceivable agony.

The silence of all around even added to his fears.

There was nothing whatever to interrupt the gloomy horror of his thoughts, but still he imagined at intervals that the dying groan of the murdered stranger rang in his ears, and at such moments he would start from his seat and gaze around him, trembling in every limb, and expecting to behold the dead man's ghastly shade standing before him.

At length he became a little more calm.

He opened the purse of which he had plundered the corpse of the unfortune gentleman and examined the contents.

There was a considerable sum, and Sir Roland wondered that the man had travelled unattended and on foot at that hour, and in so lonely a place, with so much property about him.

But he turned pale with horror at the sight of the glittering booty.

Sir Roland had long been hardened to crime, but now a reaction set in.

He had slain an unsuspecting and innocent man for the sake of his money, and each piece of gold seemed stained with the blood of the unfortunate victim.

It would be impossible to describe the tortures which Sir Roland endured on that dreadful night.

Sometimes he threw himself upon the bed and tried to go to sleep, but that was utterly impossible.

His over-wrought imagination pictured all kinds of awful horrors.

The murdered man was always near him.

The dimmed, glassy eyes followed him about, and the voice of vengeance rang in his ears.

At last day began to dawn.

The fitful light crept across the sky; but at last the bright, glorious sun rent the curtain of night asunder, and called upon the living world to be up and doing.

Pale and haggard to ghastliness, Sir Roland filled his hands with water, and dashed it upon his burning face.

Feeling somewhat refreshed, he walked to the window. Opening it, he looked out, and saw some men on their way to work.

How different were they to him?

They were poor, but cheerful.

He had squandered away a fortune in vice and debauchery, and had at last committed a fearful deed to recruit his funds.

But what was he to do when the ill-gotten gold was exhausted?

He could only return to his career of crime, and add to his list of atrocities.

"Miserable, guilty wretch that I am," he groaned; "the dying gasp of the murdered man will ever ring in my ears."

All day long he kept within the house, but as night closed in again his mind was so filled with horrors that he felt compelled to go out into the open air.

Suddenly a thought occurred to him.

Why not go back to the gaming-tables and try his luck once more?

He would now prove a match for the villains who had robbed him before, and he knew them too well to fear that they would ask how he became possessed of fresh funds.

As he made his appearance in the room he was greeted with frowns and jeers, but as he took a handful of gold from his pocket the demeanour of the gamblers changed.

"Why, Sir Roland," said a man, who went by the name of Pilkington, "have you been robbing the Mint, or have you been trying your luck on the road as a highwayman?"

Sir Roland Ashton winced, and went white to the lips.

"No matter," he said, hoarsely. "It is sufficient for you to know that the money is not yours. I am here to play, and not to talk."

"As for that matter," Pilkington replied, "I am perfectly willing to give you your revenge."

The same story was repeated over again.

Sir Roland lost, and saw with glaring eyes the gold swept into the pockets of the scoundrels who were too lazy to do an honest day's work, and lived by preying upon the foolish and weak-minded.

What chance had Sir Roland against such an army of knaves?

When all the money was gone, save a few guineas, he rose from the table and walked out of the room without saying a word.

A peal of mocking laughter followed Sir Roland, but he paid no attention to it beyond shrugging his shoulders and grinding his teeth.

He felt tempted to snatch the pistols from his pocket and put an end to at least one of the gamblers, but he abandoned the notion and strode into the street.

"I have been successful once in my new career," he said. "I must try again."

He paused and started.

A sepulchral voice murmured in his ears.

"Forbear!"

"Bah!" he said, looking round. "It was but my disordered imagination."

"The wages of sin is death," said the voice.

"Base, unreal mockery!" Sir Roland cried, snatching a pistol from his pocket. "Think not to deter me from my purpose. If the voice comes from that foul fiend, Spring-Heeled Jack, let him appear and try conclusions with a desperate man!"

The voice spoke no more, and as Sir Roland could not see a living creature, he walked on through the dark dismal streets until the houses became less.

He was walking in a southerly direction, and presently he came to a stream spanned by a rustic bridge.

Sir Roland stopped, and leaning his arms upon the rail looked down into the water.

"I will make my venture here," he said. "The night will not pass without somebody passing this way."

Even as he spoke he heard the sound of footsteps, and so near him that Sir Roland started violently.

Suddenly the form of a man loomed out of the darkness, and gazed at Sir Roland with astonishment, but with no expression of alarm.

"Ah! my friend," said the stranger, whose features were concealed by a broad-brimmed hat, "what are you doing here? Not contemplating suicide, I hope?"

Sir Roland grasped a pistol tightly and confronted the man.

"What!" the stranger cried. "Would you obstruct my way?"

The voice was familiar to him—or, at least, he thought so.

"I am a desperate man!" Sir Roland said, as he recovered himself. "I am armed with pistol and sword. I must have money. Give it to me, and pass on your way without injury."

"Daring ruffian!" the stranger returned. "If you think you will extort money from me by threats, you will find yourself vastly mistaken. Begone before I punish you!"

"I claim your money or your life," Sir Roland said. "Give me your purse, or take the consequences of your refusal?"

"Stand from my path, you villain," said the stranger, "or, by Heaven! this will be the worst night's work you undertook."

"Since you will not comply with my demands, I must use other means!" Sir Roland yelled.

He presented the pistol at the stranger; but in another instant the weapon exploded harmlessly in the air, and Sir Roland's wrist was held in a vice-like grip.

"Ah! curses on this mischance," Sir Roland cried. "You have gained the better of me. Your name?"

The stranger threw aside his hat and revealed the features of Ralph Ashton.

"Sir Roland," he said, "your career is at an end. I followed you, knowing your purpose."

"The torments of perdition seize you!" Sir Roland gasped. "Have I lived for you to triumph—to be defeated at last? Well, do your work, and do it quickly. My life is in your hands."

"I will not take it in the cowardly fashion you would have taken mine," Ralph replied, scornfully. "Dog as you are, I will fight you fairly. There is light enough for us; for, see, the moon has burst through the clouds. Draw your sword and defend yourself."

As Ralph Ashton uttered these words he flung Sir Roland from him with such force, that the baronet spun round and struck his shoulder heavily against the bridge.

"I thank you for this, Ralph Ashton," he said, as he recovered his balance. "I will fight you when and where you please, but not to-night—not to-night."

"Yes; here and now!" Ralph Ashton cried, stamping his foot passionately. "Do you think I will give you another chance to play the part of assassin? The long account between us must be settled at once."

"As you will," Sir Roland said. "I have hated you all my life, and if the fates decree that I must fall, my last breath will invoke a curse on you."

"Of what avail are curses or blessings from your vile lips?" Ralph Ashton returned, as he drew his sword. "Your intended victims are safe; all your plans have ended in failure; and the sharer of your villainy—Jules Carleon—will fall to-night."

"You lie!" Sir Roland hissed.

"Nay," Ralph Ashton replied, "I speak but the truth. He is aware of your last venture—oh! Heaven, that you could sink so low as to slay a defenceless man—and he is on your track. But another is close upon his heels, and he dies to-night."

"Another!" Sir Roland exclaimed. "I do not understand."

"His name is Lorrimer."

"I know him not."

"It is but an assumed name," Ralph replied. "He is better known as Harry Banks."

At this moment the moon shone out bright and clear, and its light fell full upon Sir Roland's distorted features.

Rage, fear, and every vile passion were depicted there.

"Harry Banks!" he hissed. "I give you the lie back in your teeth. He is playing his fool's part somewhere in the country, and is long-forgotten. My bitterest curse fall upon her—Daisy Leigh."

"So you have thought and hoped," Ralph Ashton replied, smiling; "but I have uttered no falsehood. But, come, draw your sword, for I swear that but one of us shall depart from hence."

"And thus I respond to your challenge," Sir Roland yelled; "and if the wound be not deeper and more effectual than the one I gave you before, I care not how soon I close my eyes upon the world."

The swords of the combatants met with such violence that sparks glinted from them.

Ralph Ashton was as cool as if he were taking or giving a fencing lesson, but Sir Roland was all impatience to end the fray.

Again and again he attempted to break through Ralph Ashton's guard, but each venture was attended by failure, and presently the baronet uttered a cry of pain.

"It was but a touch," Ralph said, lowering the point of his sword. "What! whine and cry like a child at the prick of a pin?"

Sir Roland, abandoning all discretion, rushed forward and lunged so furiously that he lost his balance, and Ralph's sword passed through his body.

"Ah!" the baronet gasped, "I am a dead man."

"One word," Ralph Ashton said, as their eyes met. "Let me hear you utter a word of repentance. Say 'Heaven forgive me!' and I shall be satisfied."

Sir Roland made no reply.

His eyes closed slowly, his arms fell helplessly to his sides, and he sank upon the ground, and after a few convulsive movements lay still.

"He brought his fate upon his own head," Ralph Ashton said, as he wiped his sword and flung the blood-stained cambric over the bridge. "Ugh! I would have spared him had it been possible to do so."

He turned sadly away, and huge clouds obscured the light of the moon as if to shut out the scene.

---

## CHAPTER LXXX.

### JACOB BUTLER GOES THROUGH MORE WOES.

THE hackney-coach which contained Jacob Butler and the two constables suddenly came to a standstill.

"Here we are," said Catchpole, thrusting his head out of the window. "Now then, driver, jump down and help us to carry a bundle of madness upstairs."

"I should like to know how much I am to have for this 'ere job," the coachman said, as he descended slowly from the box-seat. "It strikes me that there's more in this than appears on the surface."

"Look here," Grabham growled, as he alighted and rang the bell, "just you attend to your own business. We are constables of the law, and if we are so minded we need not pay you anything."

"Oh! that's the game, is it?" said the coachman. "Well, do your dirty work yourselves, for I'll be hanged if I take any hand in it."

Jacob Butler was still very weak, but a new hope grew into his heart as he listened to the altercation.

The coachman might be inclined to take his part, or better still, if the row went on, he might be able to escape.

Such an opportunity presently occurred.

Catchpole, anxious to take his colleague's part, rushed out of one door of the coach, while Jacob, gathering all his remaining strength, flew out of the other.

So quickly was this done that neither the coachman nor the constables had the slightest notion that Jacob Butler had decamped, and they continued to snarl and jangle at each other.

"If you don't do as you are told," Catchpole said, "I'll see that you get seven years."

"Seven years of what?"

"Of transportation," Catchpole returned; "and it is just possible that I could pile it up so that you got a taste of the cat-o'-nine-tails into the bargain."

This so roused the coachman's ire that as he alighted in the roadway, he shook a fist about the size of a shoulder of mutton under Catchpole's nose.

"I'll cat-o'-nine-tails you!" he said.

"Grabham," Catchpole squeaked, "come here! Don't you see that he's going to hit me?"

At that moment the hostilities were interrupted by the door being thrown open by a long, lean, half-starved looking man.

"Is the doctor at home?" Grabham demanded.

"He is," was the reply. "My master is at breakfast, and I wish I was. Lor'! how hungry I am."

"Joles," said Grabham, grinning. "It's my opinion that you were born hungry, and will die so. I wonder what amount of wittles would satisfy you?"

"I never went into that," Joles replied. "All I wish is that I could get enough."

He laid his hand tenderly upon his waistcoat, and groaned dismally.

"Well," he added, "what do you want? Since you come in a coach I suppose you are here on some important business."

"We are," Grabham replied, in a solemn voice that befitted the occasion. "We want the doctor to examine the mind of a poor chap."

"Where's the poor chap?" Joles demanded.

"A fainting in the coach," Grabham replied.

"Then all I can say that he has fainted himself under the seat," said Joles.

"Eh! what?" Catchpole and Grabham cried in a breath.

They made a dash towards the coach window and stood there aghast and overwhelmed with astonishment.

"Dash and jigger it!" Catchpole gasped. "Where is he?"

"Where is he?" Grabham repeated. "If you weren't a born fool you could see that he has got clear away and is chuckling in his sleeve by this time."

"Well," said Catchpole, rubbing his nose until it felt red hot, "I'm no more to blame than you. A nice journey we have had for nothing."

As if to relieve his feelings he seized the coachman by the shoulders and bumped his head against the door-post.

Nature had kindly furnished the man with a thick skull, but there is a limit to human endurance in all cases, and the afflicted one suddenly retaliated by hitting Catchpole a staggering blow between the eyes.

This was about the last thing the constable expected.

He who strikes an officer strikes at the law and braves the sword of justice, but the hackney-coachman neither thought nor cared for these things.

Before Catchpole had recovered from the effects of one blow he received another, which produced a pleasing vision of shooting stars, and then he sat down as if a cannon-ball had suddenly taken him in the waistcoat.

Grabham and Joles stood aghast and inactive at these proceedings, and it was not until Catchpole recovered his breath sufficiently to shriek for help that his brother officer drew his staff and attacked the coachman.

But Grabham had reckoned without his host.

He counted upon an easy victory and made a mistake.

Avoiding a blow from the staff, the hackney-coachman ducked his head and, running forward, caught Mr. Grabham in the abdomen and doubled him up like a hedge-hog.

Joles locked the door and bolted upstairs like a rocket.

"I'm a-dyin'!" Catchpole gasped.

"So am I," Grabham groaned. "I never felt so precious ill in my life."

"Well," observed the coachman, grinning, "you can die if you like, but I'll feel obliged if you'll put it off until after you have paid my fare."

"There's a warmint!" said Catchpole, as he staggered to his feet and leaned against a wall. "There's a double-dyed willin for you!"

"Oh!" said the coachman. "I don't mind you calling me names. Shell out—my fare is a crown—or I'll give you another dose of the same kind of physic."

As yet Mr. Grabham had not risen from the ground or made any effort to do so.

If he felt as queer as he looked he was certainly in a bad state.

"Catchpole," he said, panting for breath, "give him the money and let him go."

"But," Catchpole returned, "I haven't so much about me. Of course, I thought you would settle with him."

"Of course you thought I would do everything," Grabham snarled. "Settle! Dash it! he has almost settled me."

"And I'll do it right off if you keep me here any longer," the coachman declared. "My money, you pair of cowards, or I'll take it out in kicks. Five times twelve makes sixty, so there'll be thirty a-piece for you."

"You'll find the money in my weskut-pocket," Grabham said, looking at Catchpole. "I'm too weak to fish it out. Get rid of the willin; we are sure to drop upon him some other time."

The coachman examined the crown piece, and tested it with his teeth before he put it in his pocket.

Having done so at last, he climbed leisurely upon the box-seat, and took the reins.

"Kim up!" he said to the bony quadruped supposed to be a horse.

The animal responded by trying to fall down, but, having been forcibly reminded that such things as whips had not been as yet proclaimed illegal, the brute trotted away.

Grabham and Catchpole continued to stare at each other.

"I s'pose it ain't any use seeing the doctor now?" Catchpole said.

"Not a bit, you born idiot!" Grabham returned. "We've nothing to do but to go and save up our wengeance. Lend me your arm, for I'm as weak as a half-drowned kitten."

Leaving them to totter away, we will follow the flying footsteps of the ill-fated Jacob Butler.

Well was it for him that in those days the neighbourhood had but one broad street running from Holborn into the Oxford-road—a route so well accustomed to the jolting of the hangman's cart.

The rest of the locality was composed of tortuous, narrow ways, evil-smelling courts and alleys, leading goodness only knew where, but each and every one the hotbed of ignorance, vice, and infamy.

Jacob ran on until his legs refused to go any further, and he took refuge in a dirty little beershop.

A greasy, ill-clad fellow, smoking a pipe scarcely blacker than his own dirty visage, was unfixing an obstinate shutter from the door.

The man swore roundly as Jacob jostled up against him.

"Oh! I beg your pardon, I am sure," he said, breathlessly; "but I am in a dreadful hurry to find a friend, who I thought I saw come in here. Did he?"

"Did who?" the man demanded.

"A gentleman in a white hat, with a green patch over his eye," said Jacob.

Of course he expected to find no such individual as he described, but he felt that it was necessary to say something to account for his unseemly haste.

The landlord of the beershop looked him up and down with supreme contempt.

"Do you think you can catch such an old bird with that sort of chaff?" he asked.

"I—I don't understand your meaning!" Jacob Butler stammered.

"Oh! no; of course not," said the man, emitting a volume of smoke from his mouth. "You're precious innocent, ain't you? A man with a white hat and a green patch over one eye—ha! ha!"

Jacob Butler felt a little uneasy at the style in which the man treated him, but fearing that his ruthless pursuers might not be far away, he ventured to enter the inn.

"Not yet," said the landlord. "This is the Chequers, and you must give some account of yourself before you set a foot over the threshold."

"What," Jacob cried, in astonishment, "will you not serve me with refreshment? I have money to pay for it."

The greasy man laughed.

"I know which way the wind blows," he said. "The moment I set eyes on you racing down the street I said to myself, 'That cove's been and gone and prigged something, and he's coming to the Chequers to dispose of it.' There, now, haven't I hit the right nail on the head?"

"No," Jacob replied; "whatever I may be, I'm not a thief."

"Bless me! what a pity," said the landlord of the Chequers; "you are just the cut of one. However, I know that you are in some trouble or other, or you wouldn't be here."

"Well, I will own to that," Jacob Butler replied. "Only give me shelter, and I will pay you well out of my slender purse, and tell you the tale of my woes without a word of a lie."

"You'll be safe here, though the king's army were after you," the landlord said. "I, Ted Nickells, wasn't born and bred here without knowing my way about and how to baffle the two-legged traps. Follow me."

Gratefully enough Jacob Butler did so, and as soon as he and Ted Nickells were locked in a little room behind the bar, he told him the story of his wrongs.

Mr. Nickells did not appear to be much interested.

He smoked a great deal of bad tobacco and drank a large quantity of beer, which Jacob agreed, as a matter of course, to pay for, but he became more animated and genial when the fugitive took half-a-guinea and pressed it into his ready palm.

"Now that you really know how matters stand with me," Jacob said, "I should like to stay here for the rest of the day."

"And all night too, if you like," Nickells replied. "Hullo! Who's that knocking?"

Jacob Butler trembled from the top of his head down to his shoe-strings.

"Keep your teeth from chattering like marrow-bones and cleavers," Nickells said, savagely. "I daresay it is only one of my friends, after all. I'll go and see. At any rate, you have nothing to fear."

"I—I am not afraid," Jacob gasped; "I caught a bad cold once, and these fits will come on me sometimes, in spite of myself."

Ted Nickells made no reply to this explanation, but, tying on an apron, he assumed a business-like air, and walked into the bar.

"What! Jem Basker?" Jacob Butler heard him cry out. "Welcome! Come into the parlour, there's only—"

Mr. Butler could not catch the rest of the words which were uttered in a low and subdued tone.

Presently Jacob Butler was regaled with the sight of the new-comer, and the more he took stock of him the less he liked of him.

"You may speak out," Nickells said. "This chap is in a bit of a hobble, and come what may he is not likely to peach. How is it that you have come to London without the boy?"

Jem Basker spat on the ground and jerked out a furious oath from his lips.

"The boy is no longer with me," he said.

"Nonsense! bosh! But, stay," Ted Nickells added, "perhaps you have done the proper thing, and got your own price for him?"

"I have received nothing but a blow that very nearly knocked the life out of me," Jem Basker replied. "Look here!"

He removed his hat and showed a livid scar running in almost a straight line across his forehead.

"Who did that?" Nickells demanded.

"Spring-Heeled Jack."

Jacob Butler had been sitting on the extreme edge of a bench.

On hearing Spring-Heeled Jack's name mentioned so unexpectedly his legs shot out, and he came down so heavily that every article in the room jumped and rattled.

"What's the matter with him?" Jem Basker demanded.

"Did you—did—did—did you say Spring-Heeled Jack?" Jacob rejoined, as he picked himself up slowly.

"Yes," Jem Basker replied, eyeing the speaker suspiciously. "Do you happen to know anything about him?"

"Oh! no," Joseph replied, hurriedly. "How should I? But I have heard of him, and the very thought of the man—if man he be—gives me a dreadful start."

"Man!" said Jem Basker contemptuously; "what man can fly from tree to tree like a bird? Mercy! I can see him now, hanging by his feet from a branch. Ugh!"

"Yes—yes!" said Ted Nickells, impatiently; "all these fairy tales are very pretty, but what of the boy?"

"I suppose Spring-Heeled Jack has got him," Basker replied. "At all events, when I came to myself, and more than half-dead then from loss of blood, the boy was gone."

"So," said Ted Nickells, "you really think to palm that story off on me?"

"May I—"

The landlord of the Chequers held up his hand.

"Oh! I have heard you swear to this and that," he interposed. "That kind of swearing goes for nothing. Look me in the face, Jem Basker."

He did so, and steadily.

"Enough," said Ted Nickells. "You have spoken the truth."

"Why should I do otherwise?" Basker demanded. "Was it not here that I brought the boy when—"

"Never mind when," said Ted Nickells, interrupting him. "We will keep so much to ourselves, if you don't mind. Have you been to the hall which begins with an M?"

"Yes," Barker replied. "I disguised myself like an old man and went there; but the same story was told by a pampered overfed flunkey. 'Out upon all gipsies! Let the dogs on them! Shoot them down like vermin!'"

"Ah!" Nickells ejaculated, "then that fact alone almost proves that the boy has not found his way there."

"How should he," Basker demanded, "unless mere chance took him there?"

"Mere chance, as it is called, does wonderful things sometimes," Nickells observed, musingly. "Well, the matter stands thus. The boy has slipped through your fingers in an extraordinary way, and he must find his way back into them."

"Just so," Jem Basker assented, "and that is what I came to talk to you about. I—"

"Oh! I know what you are going to say before you speak. You are short of money?"

"You are a greater wizard than old Mother Corcoran, who used to be with Sir Roland Ashton, and was a witch."

Jacob Butler opened his mouth and gave vent to a startled cry.

"There's those spasms again," he gasped. "They always take me unawares."

"I wish you would keep them to yourself for awhile," Ted Nickells said, testily. "Your antics are enough to give a man the jumps."

"I'll walk into another room, if you like," said Jacob, who was cold all over with clammy perspiration.

"Do so," the landlord replied. "You will find the public kitchen at the end of the passage."

Jacob Butler walked, or rather tottered, out of the room.

"Is it possible?" he gasped, smiting his brow. "Can it be true? The old hag seems to be known by everybody. What does all this mean? Spring-Heeled Jack—a boy—Mrs. Corcoran. Ah! I begin to think that I had better stayed with Catchpole and Grabham, for if I am not mad now I shall be so soon."

"Where did you pick him up?" Jem Basker asked when he and the landlord were alone.

Ted Nickells explained, and gave a portion of Jacob's story briefly.

"He seems a likely sort of fellow, and may prove useful to us," Basker remarked. "There's something rather sneaky about him, and he would make a splendid spy. You must not be in a hurry to part with him, Nickells."

"You can't be too careful how you deal with a man like that," Ted Nickells replied. "He's all oil when he knows nothing and wants something, but he might turn to vinegar."

"I don't understand."

"Well," said Ted Nickells, "if we employed him to spy on other people, he might turn the tables, and spy on us."

"In that case," said Jem Basker, leaning across the table and speaking in a low tone of voice, "we should have to go to the expense of his funeral."

Ted Nickells laughed as if he had been listening to a good joke.

"I'll tell you what," said he; "there was something in our conversation that upset the fellow."

"So I thought."

"Then we must find it out," Ted Nickells rejoined. "I'll treat him well, and try to get on the right side of his affections."

"If it should transpire that he knows nothing about the Mildendale affair," Jem Basker said, "we can send him there with comparative safety."

"And what if he does?"

"Why, we must keep him under our thumbs, and take good care that he does not leave the Chequers until he has divulged all he knows."

"Right you are!" Ted Nickells returned. "Jem, my boy, your head is perfectly screwed on your shoulders. Who can tell but that this fellow coming here means a slice of luck for us?"

---

## CHAPTER LXXXI.

### WELL CAUGHT!

WE left Sir Roland lying upon the ground, prone, senseless, and to all appearances dead.

His sword lay at his side, and his hat close by.

One of the baronet's hands was pressed upon the wound he had received from Ralph Ashton, but there were no signs of returning life.

He lay there with his face upturned to the lowering sky, and when dawn came the solemn light stole across his features in a grim and ghastly manner.

Slowly the band of light expanded in the eastern heavens, and just as the breeze rose, scattering the clouds in all directions, Mrs. Corcoran, leaning upon a ragged branch, and looking like a witch who had lost her way, hobbled towards the spot where Sir Roland Ashton lay.

"Has Bill Blarney deceived me?" she mumbled. "Has he given me the slip? No—no, he would not be such a fool as that when he knows that I have it in my power to set the bloodhounds on his track at any moment. Something must have happened."

Suddenly the old hag came to a standstill.

She dropped the gnarled branch and flung up her arms.

Then a cry of mingled terror and savage triumph burst from her lips.

"Sir Roland!" she shrieked, as she stood glaring down at the body. "Ho! ho! It is he sure enough! Ah! there is blood upon his coat. My curse upon the man who has robbed me of my revenge!"

She fell upon her knees, and placed her hand upon the regions of Sir Roland's heart.

"Yes—yes!" she cried; "I am too late. He is dead sure enough. Ha! what is that?"

The sound of horses' hoofs caught her keen ears.

Mrs. Corcoran rose to her feet and strained every nerve to listen.

"Should it be Bill Blarney," she said, "he will help me to secure the body. It will be some consolation to know that my hands performed the last offices for Sir Roland."

Suddenly she heard a whistle, and answered it with a shrill cry, and Bill Blarney presently appeared.

"I could not help keeping you waiting," he said. "The traps have been playing a game of hide and seek with me, and—"

"Look there!" Mrs. Corcoran interposed.

She pointed at Sir Roland's body, and Bill Blarney, flinging himself from the saddle, rushed to her side.

"Is this your work?" he demanded, furiously.

"My work!" Mrs Corcoran returned; "my work! Do you think that I should let him die so easily. It was my desire to see him poor, starving, dying, maimed, and then to triumph over his miseries until life could hold out no longer!"

Bill Blarney took one of Sir Roland's hands in his, and then let it fall.

"It appears to me," he said, "that this has been done in fair fight. See, there is his sword, and he must have drawn it in self-defence."

"But is he dead?" Mrs. Corcoran gasped. "Tell me that he is not dead! There may—there must be some hope. The man who has led such a life as he has done does not die easily."

"At all events," Bill Blarney replied, "we had better remove the body. The light grows bolder, and people will pass this way before long. Raising Sir Roland's inanimate form in his arms, Bill Blarney placed it across the horse in as easy a posture as possible, and then, taking the rein, led the horse away.

Mrs. Corcoran brought up the rear, mouthing, mumbling, and shaking her head, as if there were something novel and delicious in the scene.

"If he be not dead," she said, "I will nurse him. Ah! how tenderly I will nurse him."

"Hold your brimstone tongue!" Bill Blarney said, turning his head. "I have met a good many queer characters in my time, but never one like you. I thought I had a conscience like gun-metal, but I'll be hanged if the sound of your voice doesn't make my blood run cold."

"Thank 'ee, deary," said Mrs. Corcoran; "but don't flatter me."

A savage frown crossed Bill Blarney's face.

"Keep your dearies for that white-livered hound, Jacob Butler!" he said, with an oath. "If you give me any more of that kind of rubbish I'll find the means of silencing you."

"Keep your temper," Mrs. Corcoran returned. "Keep your temper, Bill Blarney. Old as I am I have no more fear of you that the stick I hold in my hand."

As she spoke she cracked her thumb at him, and the ruffian quailed before the glitter of her bead-like eyes.

"Well, well," he said, "I don't want to quarrel with you. Why should I?"

"Because it would not answer your purpose," the hag replied, chuckling. "We ought to understand each other perfectly. If we don't it is time we did."

"Your words imply a threat," Bill Blarney said, fiercely.

"No, not a threat, but a caution," the crone returned. "But get along—get along, for I am anxious to know whether there be a spark of life left in Sir Roland."

They went on at a quicker pace now, and avoiding the main roads, took to the lanes and byeways, and at last Bill Blarney suddenly stopped the horse.

An evil-looking house peeping from behind some trees as if it were ashamed of itself was just visible, and into this building Bill Blarney and Mrs. Corcoran bore Sir Roland Ashton.

They placed him upon a dirty, frowsy bed in a back room.

Bill Blarney tore Sir Roland's coat open and examined the wound.

"He bleeds still," he said. "Give me that piece of looking-glass?"

"What for?" Mrs. Corcoran demanded. "Do you want to admire yourself?"

"Do as I tell you," Bill Blarney hissed. "You are enough to send a man mad with rage."

Mrs. Corcoran made a horrible grimace as she obeyed Bill Blarney's order.

He brushed the piece of looking-glass carefully with his coat-sleeve, and then held it close to Sir Roland's lips.

Suddenly Bill Blarney removed the glass and looked at it.

"See!" he cried; "the.e is breath upon it. Sir Roland lives."

"You are a most wonderful man, Bill Blarney," Mrs. Corcoran said, "and I feel that I should like to give you a kiss."

"Ugh!" said Bill Blarney, with a gasp of disgust. "Get out of my sight or I shall be tempted to do you a mischief."

. . . . . . .

Even as these things were transpiring, Jules Carleon, the Frenchman, was plodding along on foot.

He knitted his brows, and compressed his lips as he marched along.

"I was a fool to leave him," he said. "I never gave him credit for so much pluck. Little did I think that he would turn foot-pad, and how strange that I should be there to witness the scene!"

He stopped to look about him—now on the ground still sodden with rain-water, to see if he could find any traces of footsteps, and then across the meadows, which were occasionally illuminated by the light of the moon.

"Why did I not declare myself as he was robbing the body of the dead man?" he continued. "No! no! I was too clever to do that. Sir Roland might have paid the same kind attentions to me. And yet I have acted the part of a fool! I watched him return to the gaming-tables, I saw him stagger out again, a beggar, and then I might have confronted him with safety. It is a marvel how I lost him!"

Jules Carleon twisted his moustache savagely between his fingers.

"It was this way that he came," he added. "I marked his white face, and saw that he was determined to make another attempt to fill his empty purse."

As he finished speaking he stopped at the foot of a narrow bridge.

Jules Carleon's footsteps sounded hollow as he crossed to the other side.

Shading his eyes with his hands, he took a narrow survey of the country, and listened intently to every sound that came to his ears.

A faithful watch-dog was barking in the distance, the trees rustled and swayed gravely, as if whispering important secrets to each other, and the stream ran gurgling and murmuring on.

No other sounds disturbed the stillness of the early morning, and Jules Carleon shook his head dubiously.

"I am afraid that I have come on a fool's errand," he muttered between his set teeth. "Can it be that Sir Roland saw me, and hastened to make good his flight? Bah! No! Hullo! What's that?"

The sound of a galloping horse had been borne suddenly to his ears.

Turning quickly, he saw a man splendidly mounted on a steed full of mettle.

"Halt, there!" the rider cried. "Jules Carleon, I call upon you to surrender!"

"In whose name?" Jules Carleon shouted.

"In the name of Spring-Heeled Jack," the man replied.

The Frenchman started to run.

Terror lent wings to his heels, but something still more swift flew after him.

The man on horseback suddenly loosened a long rope from the saddle-bow, and, whirling it skilfully about his head, sent it whirling and writhing after the fugitive.

The looped end fell fairly over Jules Carleon's neck.

Then the rope tightened, and the Frenchman, uttering a yell of pain and terror, came to the ground with a crash.

## CHAPTER LXXXII

### LORD MILDENDALE RECEIVES A VISITOR.

When Lord Mildendale had recovered from the effects of the strange and unaccountable vision presented to him on the terrace, he summoned his valet.

The man was a well-trained servant, an individual who never spoke unless spoken to, and one who had made up his mind to be surprised at nothing.

"Harmer," said his lordship, "has anything happened to disturb the household?"

"Nothing, my lord."

"You are quite sure?"

"Quite, my lord."

Lord Mildendale swept his hand across his brow, and, leaning back in his chair, closed his eyes.

"I am not well," he said, speaking with an effort. "Pour a little brandy into a glass and hand it to me."

Harmer hesitated.

"Why don't you do as I tell you?" Lord Mildendale demanded, sharply.

"Pardon me, my lord," the valet returned. "This is the first time that I have kept you waiting for a moment, but—but, the doctor gave strict orders that you were to take nothing stronger than a little wine and water."

"Hang the doctor!" Lord Mildendale replied. "In future I will judge what is good for myself."

"Very good, my lord," the valet said, and passed the brandy.

Lord Mildendale conveyed the glass to his trembling lips, and then dashed it suddenly down upon the floor.

"No!" he said. "You are right, Harmer, and I am wrong. If I commence I shall go on until madness overtakes me again. Let me think. Has anybody called to-day?"

Harmer fidgeted about and pretended that he did not hear the question.

"I asked you whether anybody had called," Lord Mildendale said, sharply.

"No visitors, my lord."

"Visitors!" Lord Mildendale repeated. "Who worthy of that name have called upon me since? Harmer, you are keeping something from me—I read it in your face. Speak out, or fear my anger."

"Well, my lord," the valet replied, "a man did call at the servants' door; but, as he was of no consequence—merely a beggar, my lord—I thought you would not care to know."

"A beggar, and was he given alms?"

"No, my lord."

"And pray why not?"

"Because—because—"

"Well, because what?"

"Because he was a gipsy," the valet blurted out.

Lord Mildendale started to his feet.

"A gipsy!" he cried. "Why was I not told of this before? How is it that these vagabonds never appear only on this day, the day that brings back all the weary past? You have something more to tell me, Harmer?"

"I would have kept it from you," the valet replied, "for I know how these visits disturb your lordship's mind. The man who came here was apparently old and feeble, but—"

"Yes, yes—go on!" said Lord Mildendale. "Why do you falter and stammer? You drive me to desperation!"

"My lord," Harmer resumed, "I watched the man as he turned away, and suddenly all signs of age and feebleness left him. He stood erect, and, turning towards the hall, shook his fist."

"Ah!" gasped his lordship, "was it a spy in disguise, then?"

"Undoubtedly, my lord."

The nobleman sat silent for a few moments.

"I will go to bed now," he said, "and I shall not require your attendance any more to-night."

"Thank you, my lord."

His lordship sighed wearily as he left the room.

The moment the door had closed behind him the meek and staid demeanour of the valet changed.

Like the man he had described, he shook his fist.

"It is coming home to you now!" he hissed. "You treat your people worse than dogs, but the day of reckoning is at hand!"

Lord Mildendale retired to his sleeping apartment and examined it carefully.

He peeped behind the curtains, as if fearful that an assassin might start out from behind them.

His object, however, was not to go to bed.

Walking to the centre of the room, he stopped and folded his arms across his breast.

"So," he said, "I am to be denied a moment's peace. Those swarthy-skinned villains dog my footsteps and watch my house. I know what they mean—revenge! Ah! me, what is life to me, and why am I afraid to die?"

Suddenly he moved towards an old-fashioned bureau and touched a spring in its side.

A secret door flew open.

Lord Mildendale sat down, and, taking a bundle of papers in his hand, smoothed them out carefully, and even with tenderness.

In one of the folded sheets was a lock of hair, as dark and glossy as a raven's wing.

His lordship's eyes grew moist as he gazed at it.

"Oh! my wife," he cried. "Oh! cruel—cruel Fate."

Then a strange and determined expression came over his face.

He put the letters away. He did not close the bureau, but opened another door, from which he took a small bottle, filled with a dark-coloured liquid.

"I have kept this," he said, holding it up to the light of the lamp, "in case that I might be driven to extremities. Ugh!"

He shuddered as his fingers closed upon the phial.

"Why should I hesitate?" he continued. "What else is left? Deserted, friendless, and alone, I am far more miserable than the rag-clad vagabond who whines for bread from door to door. Oh! horror to perish by a murderer's knife, and yet that is my promised doom. I know full well what the vision of to-night meant. It was my death omen."

Walking slowly but firmly to his dressing-table, he poured the liquid into a crystal glass.

"I wonder," he said, as he stood gazing at the reflection of his haggard face in the mirror, "if a single creature will mourn my death or shed a tear over my grave? No—no!"

He raised the glass, and tilted it slightly.

The death-dealing fluid touched his lips, but there it stayed, for a hand of iron grasped his wrist.

Lord Mildendale turned cold, and it seemed to him that his heart had ceased to beat.

What new horror was this?

The hand upon his wrist was like ice.

Without the power to resist he gazed at it marking the blue veins and delicate hue of the skin; but his horror grew more intense, and he almost swooned as he saw that long, talon-like nails grew upon the fingers.

At last reaction set in.

Uttering a shriek of terror he tore himself free; and there, standing calmly before him, was the tall, ghostly white form, the horned head, the shaggy hair flowing over the broad muscular shoulders—the awful creature of his vision.

"Who are you?" Lord Mildendale gasped.

"I am called Spring-Heeled Jack," was the reply.

"Are you man or devil?"

"It is not for you to ask such a question," said Spring-Heeled Jack. "Let it suffice that I was sent to save you from a rash and foolish act."

As he spoke Spring-Heeled Jack dashed the glass containing the poison upon the floor, and trampled the atoms under his feet.

Lord Mildendale recoiled step by step from what he took to be an apparition from another world.

"Go!" he cried, wildly. "Torture me not."

"I bring you news," Spring-Heeled Jack said.

"From the region of torment?"

"Nay. News you will be glad to hear. Your son lives!"

Lord Mildendale started forward, but as he did so, Spring-Heeled Jack dashed something in his face, and the nobleman sank slowly upon the ground.

"Good!" said Spring-Heeled Jack. "Strange, indeed, that this man who owns this place knows but few of its secrets."

As he spoke he pressed his hand upon a panel in the wall.

A clicking sound followed, the panel revolved, and Spring-Heeled Jack vanished from the room.

---

## CHAPTER LXXXIII.

### SIR ROLAND IN THE HANDS OF HIS ENEMIES.

It was midnight.

A hundred clocks proclaimed the dismal hour.

Some jerked out the notes sharply, but the clock of St. Paul's boomed out each stroke slowly and sullenly, as if rejoicing in the murk and gloom that hung over the City of London.

Just at this time there came bumping and jolting along the Strand a huge, queer-looking vehicle.

At first sight it had the appearance of a hearse, and the sleepy watchmen stared at it stupidly, but made no attempt to approach it.

Those blink-eyed guardians over the public peace and safety were never in a hurry to run their heads into danger.

Indeed, all they ever did was to spring their rattles, wave their lanterns, and shout "Murder!"

The queer-looking thing upon wheels was nothing more terrible than a caravan, such as gipsies use when travelling from fair to fair.

A bony horse attached to it dragged its weary limbs over the uneven road, and it is more than probable that the poor animal would have fallen had not the constant application of a whip, wielded by a brutal man, reminded the beast that it would be as well to keep up.

Suddenly a little window opened, and Mrs. Corcoran thrust out her head.

"My lovey-dovey Billy Blarney," she said. "Wasn't it a good idea of mine?"

"What idea?" grumbled Bill Blarney, who was driving the worn-out quadruped.

"Why, hiring this conveyance. It holds Sir Roland nicely, doesn't it? Poor dear, he can lie down at full length, which he couldn't have done if we had hired a carriage."

"If he feels as easy as I do," said Bill Blarney, "his bones must be coming through his skin. I never had such a jolting and rocking in all my life."

"It will soon be over, my own," the hag returned. "Why have you made up your mind not to go to the Bull in Top Boots?"

"Because the boys would object."

"Object?"

"Yes. Sir Roland would be welcome enough if he had a pocketful of money," the ruffian replied; "but as he hasn't they would kick him into the street, and leave him to die in the gutter."

"Would they, now?" Mrs. Corcoran remarked. "How very unkind of them to be sure! Well, where are we going?"

"To the Chequers."

"Where's that?"

"A house in Smithfield just off Cloth Fair."

"Near our old quarters?"

"Yes," Bill Blarney replied; "but don't bother me with questions just now, or this blessed horse will go down on his knees."

"All right, my diddy-doddy."

Bill Blarney turned round with such a threatening gesture that Mrs. Corcoran withdrew her head precipitately.

"I'd give a few years out of my life to have the pleasure of choking her," Bill Blarney said, brutally. "Bah! the very sight of the old witch turns my heart."

The caravan rolled and jolted on until Blarney brought it to a standstill at the door of the Chequers.

Ted Nickells came running out.

"Why, Bill!" he said, starting at the sight of the ruffian, "who on earth would have thought of seeing you?"

"What, did you think I was dead?"

"The wicked live long," Ted Nickells replied, grinning. "You are a stranger indeed!"

"Am I welcome now?"

"Of course," the landlord replied. "But, I say, what is the meaning of this box on wheels? What is inside?"

"An old hag and a wounded man," Bill Blarney replied, in a whisper.

"Well," said Ted Nickells, "I'll ask no more questions, because I know what a strange fellow you are. Do you require any help?"

"Yes; to get Sir Roland out."

"Not the Sir Roland Ashton I have heard so much about?"

"The same."

Ted Nickells put two fingers into his mouth and whistled shrilly.

"This is a surprise," he said. "Hullo! here is the old lady. Bless me! what a nice old party to take a drive with. Well, well, Bill Blarney, you always were a good judge of beauty."

Mrs. Corcoran put her head on one side and looked waggishly at Mr. Nickells.

"You do not mean what you say," she said. "Ah! men were ever deceivers."

Bill Blarney growled out something under his breath to the effect that there would be no deception in him if he could get Mrs. Corcoran's throat between his fingers.

"Come—come," said he, "we waste time. Let us have Sir Roland out."

The wretched baronet only moaned as he was taken into the house.

They carried him upstairs and placed him on a couch.

"This is a bad case," Ted Nickells said.

"A bad case!" Mrs. Corcoran repeated. "Oh—oh! he is worth a dozen dead men yet. You should have seen him a few days ago. He is quite cheerful now. Aren't you, Sir Roland?"

The miserable, pain-stricken man turned a pleading look upon the hag.

"What have you brought me here for?" he asked, in a voice that was scarcely audible.

"To make you well, deary," Mrs. Corcoran replied.

"Let me die!" Sir Roland groaned. "I shall be much better out of the world. What have I to live for?"

"Lots of things," Mrs. Corcoran returned, encouragingly. "Die! Heyday! I don't intend you to die for many a long day."

"You torture me—you persecute me," Sir Roland said. "You have brought me here out of no kind motive. Why not do your work at once? I am wounded and helpless. Kill me, if you will, but do not increase my pain by taunts and jeers!"

"Hear him!" Mrs. Corcoran said, turning to Ted Nickells. "We found him dead to all appearances, we take him to a nice country house, and supply him with all sorts of nice things, we bring him here at an enormous expense for a change, and this—this is his gratitude."

Sir Roland Ashton rolled his head from side to side, as if the bodily pain and mental torture he suffered were too great to bear.

Even Nickells, hardened as he was to all sorts of sights, could not help feeling a pang of pity for the unhappy man.

"Let him be," he said to Mrs. Corcoran. "You can do no good by worrying him."

"Quite right," said Mrs. Corcoran, courtesying—"you are quite right, my dear sir. I am Sir Roland's nurse, and when he gets well I hope that he will have no occasion to find fault with my treatment. Ha! ha! ho! ho!"

"Get her out of the room," Nickells whispered to Bill Blarney. "She will kill the man."

"It is all very well to say get her out of the room," Bill Blarney returned, "but to get her to do it is quite another thing."

"Does she drink?"

"Like a fish."

"Then I'll give her a dose which will quiet her," Ted Nickells said.

The landlord of the Chequers proved as good as his word.

He went below, and presently returned with a decanter and three glasses.

Putting one into Mrs. Corcoran's hand, he filled it up with brandy.

"Good stuff, this!" said Mrs. Corcoran, smacking her skinny lips.

"Yes," Nickells replied; "and the best of it is the liquor never paid a penny duty. Have another nip."

Mrs. Corcoran did not say No, nor did she object to a third, and presently her cat-like eyes began to blink and grow dim.

Then her head took to nodding, and finally she fell asleep and snored like a litter of pigs.

"Now, then, we can talk with freedom," Nickells said. "I have much to tell you, but I will begin with what has happened lately."

"Fire away," said Bill Blarney. "I am all attention."

"Jem Basker is here."

"Jem Basker! What Jem Basker? The outcast gipsy?"

"Yes."

"Why, it was he who—'

Ted Nickells held up his hand.

"Don't talk so loud," he said. "You remember the old adage that walls have ears?"

"I stand corrected," Blarney replied, softening his voice. "So Basker is here, and I suppose he has brought the boy with him?"

"Nothing of the kind."

"Why not?"

"Because it happens that something or somebody named Spring-Heeled Jack took the boy from Jem Basker."

Bill Blarney uttered an exclamation of surprise and struck himself a heavy blow on the chest.

"Spring-Heeled Jack!" he gasped.

"Yes. Do you know him?"

"I should think I did," Bill Blarney replied. "Why, man alive, if I have had one adventure with that flying demon I have had a dozen."

"Who is he?" Ted Nickells asked.

"Sir Roland knows," Blarney replied, "or, at least, he says that he has more than a suspicion; but he will not impart the secret."

"Then he must be forced to do so."

"Leave that part of the business to Mrs. Corcoran," said Blarney, laughing. "If she can't screw the truth out of him nobody can."

"You think so?"

"I am sure of it."

"Well, then, we will leave him to her tender mercy," Nickells replied, grinning. "I have told you that Jem Basker is here, but I have said nothing about the other fellow."

"What other fellow?"

"Oh! a soft sort of cove, with frightened eyes, and who almost goes into fits at his own shadow."

"I suppose he has a name, and uses it sometimes?" Bill Blarney said. "What does he call himself?"

"Jacob Butler."

Bill Blarney burst into such a loud roar of laughter that Mrs. Corcoran woke up and started to her feet.

"What a noise!" she gasped. "I was just dreaming a pretty dream—that I saw you in the hangman's cart on your way to Tyburn. What were you laughing at?"

"At one of Ted Nickells' jokes," Blarney replied, cautiously, and winking at the same time at the landlord of the Chequers.

"May I hear it?" Mrs. Corcoran asked, glancing suspiciously from one to the other.

"Well, no," Nickells replied—"that is, you wouldn't care to hear it. It was about a man who came here and borrowed another man's property."

"Oh! that's nothing," said Mrs. Corcoran, "I should imagine that happens very often."

"Just so," said Ted Nickells.

Bill Blarney was now more anxious than ever to consult with Ted Nickells.

"We will run downstairs while you look after Sir Roland," he said, glancing at Mrs. Corcoran.

"Very well," she replied; "but I know you want to talk secrets."

As soon as they were below stairs Bill Blarney clutched Nickells by the arm.

"That old witch must not know that Jacob Butler is here," he said. "Keep him close, but keep him out of my sight."

"You seem to be very anxious about this man?"

"I am," Bill Blarney replied; "and I have particular reasons for being so."

Suddenly the door upstairs opened, and the sweet voice of Mrs. Corcoran was heard.

"My lovey-dovey Billy!" she screeched, "Sir Roland has told me something good, and I want you to share it."

The conversation between the hag and the ruffian was carried on in whispers, but it resulted in Bill Blarney making a hasty exit from the Chequers and riding a horse, lent him by Ted Nickells, at full speed towards the village of H[illegible]deston.

"If Sir Roland has not lied, or is not mad, this bold stroke means a fortune. Courage! Never say die! Here goes to live like a man or die like a mouse!"

---

## CHAPTER LXXXIV.

### THE FIRE—BILL BLARNEY'S TRIUMPH.

DARKNESS had fallen upon the landscape, and Daisy Leigh and Constance had just parted for the night when a man entered the garden.

Ralph Ashton was away from the cottage, [illegible] now—as he thought—that Sir Roland was dead [illegible] last there was little or no danger to apprehend.

The stranger approached the house cautiously, and, after fumbling in his pockets, placed something under the porch and retired.

From the substance a spark presently shone and grew fierce and red, when it suddenly burst into a flame.

Daisy was suddenly awakened by a loud, crackling noise, and starting up with terror and astonishment from the bed, found that the room was full of smoke, which almost suffocated her.

She screamed aloud, and Constance Mar[illegible] rushed from her room and discovered that the flames were leaping up the staircase.

"Good Heaven!" she cried, rushing into Daisy's arms, "the room is on fire. Oh! help, help, help!"

The flames now entered the room, and they found it impossible to escape by that way.

Destruction seemed inevitable.

Constance and Daisy screamed aloud and rushed about the apartment in the most frantic manner.

Suddenly the flames took a different direction, and the doorway was left free.

Constance darted on to the landing, dragging Daisy after her.

They staggered to the stairs, and had only just begun to descend them when they heard the loud

# SPRING-HEELED JACK,

## THE TERROR OF LONDON.

"HOLD!" CRIED SPRING-HEELED JACK, "THERE MUST BE NO BLOODSHED."

shouting of a man, and presently Daisy Leigh heard her name pronounced.

The next moment a man dashed through the smoke at all hazards.

He seized the girl in his arms and prepared to descend the stairs with her.

Daisy remembered no more, for her senses had entirely left her.

When she recovered she found herself in an old barn, through the apertures in which the moon shone brightly and revealed to her all the terrors of her situation.

She was supported in the arms of Bill Blarney, whose dress was disordered and his face blackened with the smoke.

"Oh! Heaven," she screamed, "for what am I reserved? Release me, and suffer me to depart."

"Silence, girl!" exclaimed Blarney, sternly. "Hold your complaints and reproaches; this is neither the time nor the place for them. I have saved your life at the risk of my own."

"Ah! I remember now," said Daisy. "Let me go, and Heaven will reward you."

"Psha!" interrupted Bill Blarney, passionately, and his eyes then wandered towards the door of the old barn, as if fearful every moment that someone would approach. "No preaching, girl, for I am not in the humour to listen to it. A spell is upon me; I came hither to kill, and now, strangely enough, I am in love."

"Wretch!" cried the horror-stricken girl, "dare not to speak to me in this strain."

"Not dare!" shouted the highwayman. "What is there that I will not dare to do?"

"You dare not brave the vengeance of Heaven!"

"Why talk to me thus, girl?" shouted the villain. "I scorn its power."

"Oh! monstrous — monstrous!" exclaimed Daisy. "Abandon your atrocious designs; leave me and go where you will, and even after all I have suffered from you I will forgive you, pray for your repentance, and—"

"Girl, I want not your prayers; I have hitherto braved the frowns of fate, and will still abide by the consequences of my daring."

"Wretched man!"

"Weak fool I should be, were I now to suffer myself to be subdued by the remonstrances and entreaties of an obstinate girl."

"Hear me—in pity hear me!"

"You plead in vain."

"Mercy—mercy!" supplicated Daisy. "Oh! think of my unprotected state, the misery to which I have been so cruelly subjected, and relent. What have I done that you should persecute me?"

"Everything," Bill Blarney replied; "your friends were my enemies, and thus I hated you; but hate as turned to love."

"Miscreant!"

"Sweet Daisy," Bill Blarney said, "you must come with me. We will go to London and live a merry life."

As he spoke Bill Blarney leered and attempted to place his arm round Daisy's waist.

"Heaven help me!" Daisy screamed, still struggling violently in the villain's odious embraces. "Unhand me, monster—miscreant! release me. Oh! help—help."

"Fool!" cried Bill Blarney, "your cries are in vain; they cannot reach the ears of anyone who can assist you."

"Mercy—mercy! Oh! Heaven," screamed Daisy. "Fiend in human shape, forbear! Let me die—let me die this instant; anything to release me from this monster's power!"

"Pretty Daisy!" the ruffian returned; "you are mine—mine! Listen, I will tell you a secret. Sir Roland has given you to me."

In the agony of despair Daisy struck him in the face, and, breaking from his hold, rushed screaming from the barn, and had already advanced some distance into the broad moonlight ere he overtook her.

"Girl!" he cried, "are you mad? Think you that I am to be alarmed by your screams and will suffer you to escape me?"

Daisy fell upon her knees and burst into tears.

"Once more, oh! man of guilt, I implore your mercy and forbearance. Mercy—mercy! as you hope for mercy when your career has run to a close."

"Mercy!—ha, ha!" laughed the hardened miscreant. "I seek it not—I mock, I scorn, it."

"Reflect—reflect!"

"Hang reflection!" shouted the highwayman. "What service will that be to me? Reflect—yes, and if I should what would it do? It would but recall the past, and strengthen my hatred and revenge against mankind. This very night you and I will speed for London, and to-morrow shall see us man and wife."

"Horror—horror!" Daisy groaned, starting to her feet and once more making towards the door.

But she was prevented by Bill Blarney, who seized her in his arms.

Daisy's piercing shrieks rent the air, but Bill Blarney heeded them not.

No feeling of pity could move him to relent in his diabolical purpose, and as his brutal determination increased, so did the strength of the poor girl diminish.

Still she struggled with all the power left in her, with more success than could have been expected.

But at last, completely exhausted, she gave utterance to one groan of agony and despair, and again sank insensible in the arms of her remorseless and brutal persecutor.

"Curses on her weakness!" exclaimed Blarney. "How is it that women always faint when they are in a little trouble? Oh! how beautiful she looks still in her anguish."

Alas! insensible, indeed, must his heart have been, or the melancholy innocence of that beauteous face would have moved him to pity.

But nothing could have the least effect upon that hardened and remorseless wretch, and his impatience increased every moment as he endeavoured to restore Daisy to life and consciousness.

Several minutes elapsed, but his efforts were all in vain, and again he cursed the misfortune that attended him, and listened breathlessly to the least sound, fearing pursuit, yet undecided how to act.

Should he abandon Daisy?

No—no; he could not do that, even though he should ultimately plunge into inevitable destruction.

He had ventured thus far to obtain possession of her, and he would be a coward and fool to pause now.

He still continued to support her in his arms, and he tried by every means in his power to recall her to sensibility.

But ineffectually, and he began to think that the power of her terrors had been too much for her—that nature was completely exhausted, and that her gentle spirit would no more return to consciousness or animation.

He placed his hand upon Daisy's heart.

It scarcely beat, and the fears of the ruffian increased.

"Cursed fool that I am!" he exclaimed. "I shall be defeated by my own impetuosity. How pale she looks! she scarcely breathes. What shall I do? I cannot leave her here, and have no means of reviving her."

While Bill Blarney stood over Daisy's inanimate form in the old barn, various were the conflicting thoughts that passed in his guilty mind.

He was startled by the least sound, and went to the door, not venturing to open it, but peeping through a crevice to ascertain whether there was any reason for his fears.

The shadows of the tall trees upon the moonlit earth was all he saw, and he returned again to the side of his hapless victim to gaze upon her and to ruminate what he should do.

He dare not venture forth in search of water lest Daisy should recover, and availing herself of his absence, make her escape.

"What!" he exclaimed, "after all the trouble I have taken, all the risks I have run to get her in my power, shall I now relinquish my prize?"

Daisy now breathed a deep sigh and presently afterwards opened her eyes, but her senses were still wandering and she looked vacantly around the wretched place, but as yet she did not recognise the villain Blarney.

"What place is this?" she asked, faintly. "Whither have my footsteps led me? I am cold—cold, and yet my brain burns to madness. Oh! I have had a most frightful dream."

Her eyes now fell upon the forbidding countenance of the ruffian, and with a scream of horror she started to her feet.

"Ah! that hated form — that fearful countenance!" she exclaimed. "Oh! heaven, then, indeed, it was no vision."

"Daisy!" said the ruffian.

"Away! miscreant—monster!" she cried, the very tones of his voice appearing to strike a deathly terror to her soul. "Repeat not my name—dare not to contaminate my ears with your hated voice. Oh! why had I not died rather than have awakened to this horror and misery?"

"Girl," observed Blarney, coolly, "these complaints, these reproaches are all unavailing."

"Brutal wretch—to call you a man would be a gross libel upon the sex—my piercing cries shall rend the air and call down upon you the vengeance of Heaven!"

"You have already found that your cries are useless," said Bill Blarney. "Come with me. It is time that we were upon the road. My horse is tethered near at hand and he is quite able to carry us both."

He advanced towards her with a determined air as he spoke.

Daisy bounded past him with the rapidity of lightning and made towards the door; but before she could open it he seized her in his arms and held her with the strength of a giant.

"Help, help, help! Save me from this monster!" screamed the frantic girl.

Louder she shrieked, making the very air resound again, but was answered only by the enraged maledictions of her terrible assailant.

"Mine, mine—you are mine!" Bill Blarney yelled.

It was a terrible moment of peril.

Daisy's fate hung upon a thread, but Heaven interposed to save her when all hope appeared to be at an end.

Suddenly the shouts of several voices were heard upon the air.

They reverberated on Bill Blarney's ears and struck into his soul like a death-knell.

He released his hold, and Daisy sank upon her knees with clasped hands and completely overpowered as Blarney staggered towards the door.

Again Daisy shrieked aloud for help.

"This way—this way!" exclaimed several voices.

The next moment the door was burst violently open and several men rushed into the barn.

Daisy uttered a cry of joy and gratitude.

"Secure the villain!" exclaimed one of the men.

He had scarcely given utterance to the words when Blarney, drawing forth a pistol, discharged its contents at him, and he fell wounded and bleeding to the earth.

The ruffian took advantage of the confusion which this occasioned, and darting from the place with the rapidity of a hunted hare, in a moment he was out of sight. Two or three of the men hastened in pursuit of him, and the rest remained behind to attend to Daisy and their wounded companion; but Bill Blarney had outstripped his pursuers, and all traces of him were lost.

---

## CHAPTER LXXXV.

### THE APPREHENSION OF BILL BLARNEY.

Bill Blarney plunged into the deepest recesses of a wood, muttering curses all the way he proceeded.

On he went at the top of his speed, and the shouts of his pursuers soon died away in the distance.

The first streak of morning was fast appearing in the eastern horizon, and Bill Blarney cursed its golden beam, for now the labourer would be hastening to his daily toil, and the danger of detection multiplied.

At length, breathless and panting, he paused, and, leaning against a tree, gave himself up to the dismal thoughts which the failure of his diabolical designs, and the misery and danger of his present situation, engendered.

"So, with all my boasting that I would take this girl back with me to London, the tables are turned on me," he soliloquised. "Bill Blarney is done at last."

Just then he thought he heard the sound of footsteps rustling among the grass, and, turning in a different direction, he quickly resumed his flight.

However, he thought it would not be advisable for him to venture out of the wood in the daylight, and, therefore, only determined to proceed until he could find some place in which he might conceal himself until the shades of evening should have fallen.

He penetrated into the thickest part of the wood, and he threw himself on the earth, and for some time abandoned the weary thoughts which had before oppressed and tormented him.

Blarney had been in this situation about an hour when he heard the tramping of horses' hoofs approaching near the spot where he was secreted, and his apprehensions returned.

He placed his pistols ready for action by his side, and then crouched himself into as small a compass as he could, and scarcely dared to breathe.

The horsemen were advancing at only a walking pace, and all was so still that he could distinctly hear everything they said as they came on.

"It is a fruitless task, Ned," said one of the men, "so we had better return and receive further instructions. I do not believe that he is anywhere concealed in this wood."

"Nor I," observed another; "but I should like to have the pleasure of taking him. It would be a mighty satisfaction to me."

"That it would," said the man who had been called Ned. "But come. We must increase our speed, and receive instructions how we are to proceed in this pursuit."

They now urged on their horses, and the next instant galloped past so near to the place where Bill Blarney was concealed that he grasped his pistols and trembled, fearing that they would see him.

They, however, went on without casting their eyes in that direetion, and were soon hidden among the trees from Blarney's sight.

He breathed again, and arose upon his feet.

"So," he said, "the dogs are all upon the alert for me; but I will yet give them some trouble to scent me out. Oh! no doubt, they would glory in seeing me swing, but I do not think my time has come yet."

He threw himself back, being tired with the exertions he had undergone during the night, and remained silent for a short time.

From the conversation that had passed between his pursuers, it appeared that they thought he was not anywhere concealed in the wood, consequently he considered that for the present he was quite safe.

Time wore on, and no sounds met the ruffian's ears calculated to create alarm, and he continued to reflect deeply upon his situation and the course it would be advisable for him to pursue.

He was greatly bewildered, and for a considerable time was unable to form any reasonable plan; but at length a sudden thought flashed upon his brain, which he wondered had not occurred to him before.

In one part of his guilty career Blarney had been in some way connected with smugglers at Dover.

They had rendered mutual assistance to each other in their lawless schemes, and they had sworn the usual oath of fidelity, under all and any circumstances.

He had not seen them for some years, but he knew that the captain was still living.

The only danger would be in travelling to their places of rendezvous while the pursuit was kept up after him.

But it was the only chance he had of present concealment, and he was therefore compelled to run the risk with whatever peril it might be fraught.

At length the dreary day passed away, and the shades of evening set in.

Blarney then sneaked out of his hiding-place and cautiously resumed his journey.

At length he emerged from the wood, and, avoiding the high road, entered the fields.

He had not proceeded far when he perceived a horse grazing in one of the pastures, and a sudden thought darted across his mind.

"This is fortunate!" he exclaimed; "you are mine, my noble steed. Exchange is no robbery, for no doubt my horse has found another owner by this time."

In a moment the ruffian leaped upon the animal's back, and off it started.

"Bravo!" cried Bill Blarney. "Bravo! Now, my fine fellows, catch me if you can! Before tomorrow's sun shall have risen I shall be far away, far out of your clutches. Let me but reach the smugglers' rocky cavern, and I shall be once more secure, and can arrange my plans. It is a wonder to me that I have not received a visit from Spring-Heeled Jack, but perchance his power has left him, or he may be dead."

He continued to travel on for about two hours with unabated speed, avoiding the villages on his way as much as possible, for the horse only having a halter round his neck, and, of course, being without saddle, it was likely to cause suspicion. However, at length, having proceeded many miles and being much fatigued, he thought he might venture to stop at the first inn he came to, and rest and refresh himself.

He had no sooner formed this resolution than he entered a small retired hamlet, where a house just of the description he wanted presented itself.

He made up to it, and stopping before the door, called aloud on the host, who quickly made his appearance.

"I am travelling to the market to dispose of this horse in the morning," Blarney said; "but as I have come some distance, and feel rather tired, I want refreshment and rest. Can you accommodate me?"

"Ah! that I can," replied the host; "walk in, and you will soon be able to test the quality of the accommodation I can afford you."

"All right," observed Bill Blarney; "just place my horse in the stable, and then bring me the best refreshment that your house can supply."

"It shall be done," said the man; and, calling to his ostler, he gave the horse in his charge, and invited Blarney to follow him into the house.

The highwayman was ushered into a comfortable room, and the landlord quickly placed provisions and a foaming tankard of his best ale before him.

"Ah!" remarked Bill Blarney, as he commenced operations, "this is very good fare, and I have no doubt I shall do ample justice to it, for I am devilish hungry. Will you take a glass of ale?"

"Aye, to be sure I will," the landlord replied; "here's towards your good health."

"Thank you."

"Do you intend to sleep here to-night?"

"Why, yes," said Blarney; "as I before said, I have travelled some miles, and I do not feel inclined to go any further till I have snatched an hour or two's sleep. Besides, I happen to have a considerable sum of money about me; and there have been so many daring robberies of late that it is not safe for a person to travel at night."

"Very true, sir," said the landlord; "there are some desperate fellows about the country, and never a night passes without some robbery taking place. A few of them have been taken and suffered the penalty of their crimes lately, but there are many of them still at large who seem to set detection at defiance. There is a gang called the Black Highwaymen, and the biggest villain of the whole lot is one Bill, or as he is sometimes called, Bully Blarney."

"I have heard of him," said the ruffian, without betraying the least confusion.

"Heard of him!" replied the landlord; "I should like to know who has not."

"He is a desperate rascal, I believe."

"A greater villain never mounted the gallows. There is scarcely a crime in the calendar which he has not committed; but, notwithstanding the search that for months has been made for him and the large reward offered for his apprehension, he still contrives to elude their vigilance, and I do not think they will ever take him."

"I do not think they will," said Blarney, with the same coolness as before; "but I should be inclined to think that he has left the country."

"Oh! no," replied the landlord. "It was thought so by most people, but two constables who called here, and were telling me about Blarney's escape from Newgate, were quite sure that he is still in England."

"My friends Catchpole and Grabham," thought the highwayman; and he then observed aloud—"Well, this man is certainly a determined fellow after all."

"He is a determined scoundrel."

"Undoubtedly he is."

"And I only hope that he may soon meet with his just reward."

"Aye."

"Times are hard enough, Heaven knows, and we hadn't need be pestered by such villains as he is."

"Very true," said Blarney; "but did the fellow ever do you any harm?"

"No," answered the host; "but that has nothing to do with it. He has been a general pest to society, and although I have not suffered from him yet, I do not know how soon my turn may come."

"Ah! that's right enough."

"Heaven send that he may never come near me."

"He is nearer than you imagine," thought Blarney, and he could scarcely forbear smiling as this thought occurred to him.

"Well, well," he observed, carelessly, "Providence keep us from all such rascals, say I. I think I acted a wise plan in putting up here to-night."

"You did, for it is a lonely way to Barnet Fair, and no doubt there are plenty of scoundrels on the look out for booty."

"Yes," replied the robber; "and it would have been the ruin of me if I had lost the property I have about me."

"I daresay it would; but I wonder you did not delay your journey from home till the morning."

"Why, it would have been better. But it's no matter; I am safe enough here, I daresay."

"Quite safe; and with good fare and a comfortable bed you cannot require anything else."

"Certainly not. However, I must start early in the morning."

"As soon as you like. You will not find me in bed, I daresay."

"Well, then," said Blarney, having finished his meal, "I will take another tankard of ale, and then I will get you to show me to my room."

"Very good," said the host.

"Ha! ha! ha!" laughed Bill Blarney, when the landlord had left the room. "You little think, my fine fellow, how near this notorious scoundrel, this desperate highwayman, is to you. Well, I have heard a very pretty character of myself, but I must acknowledge the faithfulness of the portrait. However, I think I am safe enough here, and after a few hours' rest I shall be in a better condition to resume my journey."

The landlord returned with the ale.

"Come," said Blarney, "you must help me to drink this."

"Well, you are very good," said the host, taking the proffered glass. "I like to meet with a friendly person like yourself. He is always welcome to the Wheatsheaf."

"No doubt of it," returned the highwayman. "And, since I have fared so well, I shall not forget to call again when I come this way."

"I am much obliged to you. Civility, good accommodation, and excellent fare you will always find to be Abel Gibson's motto."

"I believe you," said Blarney. "And now I will thank you to show me to my chamber."

"This way, sir," said the landlord, taking the lamp and proceeding towards the door.

Blarney followed him, and, after ascending a short flight of stairs, was ushered into a comfortable chamber.

"I will call you at an early hour in the morning if you are not awake," said the landlord.

"Thank you," said the scoundrel.

And the landlord quitted the room.

"So far, so good," Blarney mused. "I have managed to elude my pursuers hitherto, and I have no doubt that I shall be able to do so in the future. It is a fortunate job that I found the horse, or I might not have been able to manage my business so well. By this time to-morrow I hope to arrive at the end of my journey, and then I shall be in perfect safety, and may laugh the endeavours of my enemies to take me to scorn. Ha! ha! ha!"

He fastened the door, and threw himself upon the bed without undressing, so that he might be ready in case of any emergency, at the same time placing his pistols at his side.

He was so tired by the exertions he had undergone that he soon fell asleep.

How long he had slept he knew not, but he was suddenly aroused by hearing a loud knocking at the outer door of the inn.

Blarney started from the bed immediately, and, grasping his pistols, listened attentively, and a foreboding of something wrong crossed his mind.

The knocking was repeated with more violence than before, and then he heard a window thrown open, and a voice, which he recognised to be that of the landlord, demanded who was there and what they wanted.

"Open the door, in the name of the king!" commanded one of the persons outside in an authoritative tone.

"Confusion!" exclaimed Blarney. "They are officers! What devil's luck has brought them here just at the very moment when I was priding myself upon being so secure? What shall I do? How can I escape them? But let me be calm; after all, it may not be me they want."

"In the name of the king! Heaven bless me!" said the innkeeper, in accents of alarm. "What have I done to offend his majesty? This must be some mistake, gentlemen."

"No, no, it is not a mistake," returned the man who had before spoken; "but open the door, you have nothing to fear. It is not you we want."

"No; I knew it could not be," said the landlord; "but, pray, might I ask who it is you do want?"

"Have you any lodgers in your house?"

"One; who came here about two hours since."

"A tall man of dark complexion, prominent nose, black eyes and hair, dressed in a brown coat, light breeches and waistcoat, and high boots?"

"Why, goodness me!" exclaimed the landlord, "it is the very description. Who can my guest be?"

"If you say that the description I have given corresponds with his person," answered the officer, "we have no doubt that it is he of whom we are in search. From inquiries we have made, he was seen to pass through the village about two hours since."

"Dear—dear! Who is he, then?"

"Open the door, and then we will answer the question; don't keep us standing here all night!"

"In a moment, gentlemen—in a moment," said the astonished landlord; and the next instant Bill Blarney heard him descending the stairs.

"I am lost!" he cried, as he grasped his pistols. "Cursed fool that I was to venture to stop here! What will become of me? How can I escape?"

"Upstairs?" he heard one of the officers at that moment demand.

"This way—this way," replied the host; "no doubt he sleeps, and you will be able to take him easily, and without his having an opportunity of making any resistance."

"They are coming!" Bill Blarney gasped; "even these pistols may not avail me! Would that I could make my escape! Ah!—the window!"

He rushed to the window as he spoke, and, throwing it open, was in the act of placing his foot upon the sill, when the room door was burst open, and before he had time to offer any resistance he found himself secured by the officers, and struggled in vain to release himself from them.

"The game is up," he said; "I am grabbed at last."

"Yes, my fine fellow," returned one of the men, "the game is indeed up, and it is quite time that it was. You have carried on a very pretty career for years, and given us no end of trouble; but we have been too deep for you this time, and have got you safe enough now."

"Dogs!" cried Blarney, fiercely. "Oh! I could crush you all, and—"

"No doubt of it," interrupted one of the men; "but we are not going to let you, you may depend upon it."

"Goodness me!" ejaculated Abel Gibson, the landlord; "only to think that such a monster should seek shelter in my house, and that I should think him such a civil gentleman, and should even drink with him. But I hope to have the pleasure of seeing him hanged, and that will be some consolation to me for the manner in which I have been deceived."

"Croaking old hound!" said Blarney, in furious accents, which made the worthy host almost jump out of his shoes.

The officers had now secured Blarney by placing the handcuffs on him.

"Have you any place where we can secure him till the morning, when we will take him before the nearest magistrate?" asked one of the officers.

"Yes, there is the out-house," replied the host; "that is safe enough. I will defy him to escape from that."

"We will take good care of that," said the constable; "for we will guard the door during the night, and he must be even more clever than we take him to be if he contrives to slip through our fingers. Show the way. Come, Master Blarney, we will have the honour of escorting you to your new lodging."

"Stand off, reptiles!" exclaimed the ruffian, fiercely; "it is enough for you that you have secured me and will have the price of my blood. Attempt not to lay hold of me; I will follow you."

He frowned bitterly as he spoke, and the landlord preceding them with the light, the officers placed themselves on each side of him, and they moved towards the old out-house.

Having placed him in it, they fastened the door, and then took their seats outside, the host having brought a table and provided them with such refreshments as they required.

Bill Blarney paced the gloomy place for some time with disordered steps, and in a state of mind which may readily be imagined.

"Nailed at last—nailed at last!" he muttered, "all my hopes at once annihilated. Oh! curses, curses! Little did I expect this, and so soon, too. My career, indeed, is now fast drawing to a close, and I shall mount the scaffold amid the scoffs, revilings, and execrations of a gaping multitude. But I will not tremble. No; away with fear! I will at least die as I have lived—firm, daring, and reckless."

He paused for a few moments, and in spite of all his efforts the agony of his mind became almost insupportable, and he beat his breast and raved in the most violent manner.

"And must I then perish at last by the hands of the hangman?" he said. "Must the gallows indeed be embellished with my carcase? Yes, of course—I cannot expect anything else; I dare not imagine that they will show me any mercy."

He again paused and endeavoured to compose himself, but that was a task not very easy of accomplishment, and he gave it up in despair.

Completely worn out with thinking, he at length stretched himself upon some straw, and in a very short time he fell off into a sound sleep.

He was awakened in the morning by one of the officers shaking him by the arm.

"Come, come," said the man, "get up, you snoring scoundrel; it's well for you that you can sleep in this manner."

"It shows that I have a clear conscience," Bill Blarney returned, with a reckless and sarcastic grin. "Now, what do you want?"

"Why, the time is come when we must introduce you to the magistrates," answered the officer; "no doubt your reception by them will be of the most cordial description."

"I daresay it will," Blarney returned, with contempt. "But it is not the first time they have had the pleasure of seeing me. Lead on, I am ready!"

The officers conducted him to the outside of the house, where they had a cart in waiting, into which they lifted him, and then drove off to the place where the magistrates were assembled.

The news that Bill Blarney, the daring highwayman, was taken had spread like wildfire, and a large crowd of persons were assembled in front of the inn to see him.

They followed the cart as it proceeded on its way, shouting and pelting him, and giving utterance to the loudest execrations. Blarney stood erect in the cart, and viewed them with stern indifference, although in his heart he invoked the most terrible curses upon their heads.

It is unnecessary to enter into the particulars of his examination before the magistrates, which lasted a considerable time, when he was remanded for further evidence and removed to prison.

Notwithstanding his assumed firmness and indifference as to the fate which was likely to befall him, the villain, when he was left alone in his dismal cell, suffered the most intense anguish of mind, and paced backwards and forwards in the most disordered manner, cursing and lamenting by turns.

Not that he was tormented with the horrors of conscience.

No! his guilty soul, hardened as it was in crime, was insensible to such a feeling; but still he could not look upon the approaching termination of his career without being appalled.

"To die like a dog!" he soliloquised; "to be held up to the scorn and execration of a gaping multitude; to give my enemies an opportunity of exulting in my fate—oh! this is more than I can bear to think of. Would that I had the means of deceiving the hangman! But of what avail are my wishes? They will take good care that I have no such opportunity."

He bit his lips and frowned fearfully as these thoughts occurred to him.

Again he traversed his gloomy dungeon with hasty steps, and gazed with despair upon the blackened walls which enclosed them. The day to which he was remanded at length arrived, and the highwayman was once more taken before the magistrates, when to his chagrin he saw Ralph Ashton in court.

The examination lasted but a short time, and Blarney was, of course, committed to take his trial at the approaching assizes of the county.

"Ralph Ashton," said the villain, as he was about to be taken from the dock, "I suppose you think it is now your turn to triumph, and doubtless you have reasons enough to do so; but do not be too confident yet. Do not make too sure of happiness, although the gallows may rid you of an enemy. Sir Roland lives, and were he and I gone, there are others who seek your destruction."

"Shameless, hardened villain!" Ralph said. "Well indeed do you deserve the fate in store for you."

"That may be," Blarney said, defiantly; "and all that I regret is, that my plan was not more sure. With my last breath I will invoke curses upon your head and all those who are connected with you; may—"

Before the ruffian could finish the sentence the officers laid hold of him, dragged him from the dock, and forced him into his dreary dungeon.

## CHAPTER LXXXVI.

### A DUEL INTERRUPTED.

FOR some days after Spring-Heeled Jack's strange visit to Lord Mildendale the nobleman kept himself a close prisoner to his room.

Mental worry had done its work, and he looked as if he had passed through a long age of misery.

The lines on his face and brow grew deeper.

His eyes sunk into his head, his cheek bones protruded, and he was taken with occasional fits of trembling, which nothing could allay.

It seemed to him that death stared him in the face at every turn.

His life was a misery to him, for he knew that he was being watched by the strange roving people who had sworn to take his life.

Mysterious letters found their way into his house, and the very air seemed filled with uncanny sounds and whisperings.

The memory of Spring-Heeled Jack haunted Lord Mildendale day and night.

Asleep or awake he saw the gaunt, weird form, and heard the stern voice thundering in his ears.

He tried to think that Spring-Heeled Jack was but a creature of his imagination; but then he remembered the words, "Your son lives."

"If that be so, why is he kept from me?" Lord Mildendale groaned. "If I could but hold my boy in my arms I could die in peace. No, no! The fiend mocked me."

Weak and feeble, he walked to the window and gazed at the fair lands he was once proud to call his own.

Now wealth, luxury, and rank were nothing to him.

At last he began to rally, and accompanied by Harmer, who took care to be armed with pistols, walked out into the park one day.

As they proceeded Harmer, the valet, espied a stranger approaching, and called Lord Mildendale's attention to him.

Shading his eyes with his hands, his lordship gazed steadily at the man, who was young and handsome.

A sudden change came over Lord Mildendale's face.

"Harmer," he said, "I know this gentleman, and wish to have a few words in private with him."

"Certainly, my lord," the valet replied. "I will retire at once. Is it your wish that I should keep within sight?"

"No," Lord Mildendale replied. "I am in no danger. Go back to the Hall."

Harmer walked quickly away, and Lord Mildendale and the stranger met face to face.

"Richard Cranston!" Lord Mildendale said. "Many a day has passed away since I saw you. What brings you here now?"

Richard Cranston, who was the younger man of the two, gazed steadfastly at the nobleman.

"I will tell you presently," he said. "My lord, you are strangely altered."

"Yes. I have had much to alter me."

A rather awkward pause ensued.

"Lord Mildendale," Richard Cranston said at length. "We were friends once, or, at least, you gave me the pledge of friendship."

"Well—well!" said Lord Mildendale, impatiently. "Is that all you have come to tell me?"

"I beg that you will bear with me to the end," Cranston continued. "You are aware that I courted fortune in a foreign land, but I have just returned home. Can you not guess the reason?"

"No."

"Dare you say that to my face?" Richard Cranston demanded, as the hot blood flew to his face. "My father borrowed money of yours with the understanding that it should be returned by easy instalments. My father and yours were schoolfellows, as we were. Shall I finish the story, or—"

"I see what you are driving at," Lord Mildendale replied. "You come here to blame me for claiming my own. When my father died I called in all debts. I was in want of money, and got it by legitimate means. Tell me where you find the sin of that?"

"I charge you with playing a mean part," Cranston said. "I charge you with ruining a once happy home. You swooped down upon my father at a time when he could not pay; you ruined him—you sent him to his grave with a broken heart; you drove my helpless mother and sisters into the world. Lord Mildendale, you are a coward, and unworthy of the man from whom you took your name!"

"Beware!" Lord Mildendale hissed, placing his hand upon his sword. "The blood of a passionate race runs in my veins."

Richard Cranston snapped his fingers.

"If I feared you," he said, "do you think that I should be here? I have not done yet. In a foreign clime, where news travels slowly, I was left ignorant of what had happened. At last a letter came—a letter that told me that those I loved were starving, while I revelled in the lap of luxury. As swift as the wind could bear the ship along I returned. Lord Mildendale, you tell me to beware. It is you who had best do so."

"Do you threaten?"

"No, I act."

"Speak out," said Lord Mildendale. "I am not good at solving riddles."

"Since my return I have heard strange things concerning you," Cranston went on. "'Tis said that a curse has fallen upon you and your house. Well may that be so—"

"Hold!" Lord Mildendale cried, in a voice of thunder. "Remember where you are!"

"I do," Cranston replied, "and I have come here to make you the present of the contempt of an honest man."

As Lord Mildendale started back with an exclamation of rage on his lips he drew his sword.

"You shall pay for this insult with your life!" he said, hoarsely.

"Or claim yours for a long list of injuries perpetrated under the cloak of friendship!" Richard Cranston replied.

His rapier flashed from its sheath, and he stood so nobly and gracefully on his guard that Lord Mildendale could not help admiring him.

"Bah!" said his lordship, sneeringly. "Why should I condescend to cross my sword with you? Go back to the mother and sisters you speak of and live for their sakes."

"They would have scorned me if I had avoided this meeting," Cranston returned. "I came here for the purpose of obtaining satisfaction, and, by Heaven! I will seek it, though I fall dead at your feet."

"Then here's at you!" Lord Mildendale cried.

The two men attacked each other fiercely, but suddenly their swords were struck up, and they started back in horror at Spring-Heeled Jack, who had suddenly rushed between them.

"Hold!" he cried. "There must be no bloodshed. When the clouds that hover above the towers of Mildendale Hall have dispersed, then, and only then, may your swords be drawn."

"What fiend from the infernal regions are you?" Richard Cranston said. "What vile mummery and mockery is this? Back! or I will see whether cold steel can find its way through your uncouth frame!"

Spring-Heeled Jack laughed until the woods rang again with the sound.

"Spare your breath and stay your hand," he said. "Attempt not to approach or touch me, or you will rue the day that the light of Heaven first shone in your eyes. Lord Mildendale, back to your Hall. I will come anon to you. The time grows apace when each moment must be given to repentance. Away—away!"

Richard Cranston dropped his sword, for suddenly a spell seemed to seize him.

A strange, yet delicious, aroma filled the air, and he heard Spring-Heeled Jack's voice as in a dream.

His eyes closed, his arms fell helplessly at his sides, and he fell upon the green sward which, but for Spring-Heeled Jack's intervention, would have been stained with blood.

Lord Mildendale only stopped for a moment, and then, as the demoniac form of Spring-Heeled Jack seemed to tower higher and higher, he turned and fled in terror.

---

## CHAPTER LXXXVII.

RALPH ASHTON PAYS A VISIT TO BILL BLARNEY—SUDDEN APPEARANCE OF THE WITCH OF THE HEATH.

Ralph Ashton's country house lay in ashes, but its inmates had all escaped.

Daisy, after her terrible interview with Bill Blarney, was sheltered in a cottage, and Constance remained ever at her side.

For some reason of his own Ralph had removed the lad he had rescued from Jem Basker's clutches and said no more about him than that he was perfectly safe and happy.

Constance knew Ralph too well to put many questions to him, and yet she was sorry that Robin had left, for he was a bright and entertaining lad.

One day Ralph Ashton, after seeing that the ladies required nothing, and leaving an armed man to watch over their safety, announced his intention of paying a visit to Bill Blarney.

"The wretch will pay the penalty of his sins before long," he said, "and perchance he may be able to unravel the tangled skein in which he is so mixed up with Sir Roland."

Ralph walked slowly and thoughtfully towards the county gaol, and was admitted to Blarney's cell.

Ralph Ashton was shocked at the sight that met his eyes.

He found Bill Blarney rollicking upon a bench, singing a flash song, and accompanying himself with the rather discordant music of his fetters.

The ruffian grinned at Ralph Ashton, and then went on singing—

"*So jolly I'll be, even unto the last,*
*No care for the future, no thought of the past;*
*Though gossips predicted I'd meet with a noose,*
*I can kick away life, as I'll kick off my shoes.*

"*With a hey merry ho!*
*Hey merry ho!*
*We must live as we can;*
*When we can't, let us go!*"

Ralph stood for a moment and gazed at the reckless and hardened scoundrel with mingled feelings of surprise, pity, and disgust; but Blarney, having finished his song, looked up at him with a careless expression.

"Good day to you, Master Ashton. So you have come to pay your respects to the grateful individual whom the country has so kindly provided with board and lodging! Very friendly this, and you perceive I know how to appreciate it."

"Blarney," said Ralph, "I came here not to taunt you or to add to the misery of mind you must already be enduring. I—"

"Misery of mind!" repeated Blarney, with a scornful laugh. "Come, I like that; it's a good joke. Why I never was more happy in my life. You see that my spirits are not much depressed; you see I can sing at the prospects of dying upon a gallows. What are you here for? To tell me to turn over a new leaf and be good?"

"Blarney," Ralph said, "I came not here to talk to you upon that subject, but to offer you the chance of prolonging life."

"Indeed!" returned the prisoner; "but suppose I do not think proper to accept it upon the terms that might be offered me? I would rather receive my quietus in a dance upon the tree than the darbies for the few years longer I might chance to live. The only charms that life has for me are liberty of principles, the liberty of the highway—in short, the liberty to do as I please, the same as your great and titled thieves are allowed; deprive me of these, and you may have my life into the bargain."

"And is it possible that nothing can bring you to a sense of shame?"

"I do not think it is very likely."

"You can gain nothing by this obstinacy."

"And I have nothing to lose but my life, and that I have before told you I do not value a straw."

"But why to the last should you seek to injure those who never injured you?"

"Ha! ha! ha!" laughed the ruffian; "so you have come upon that suit? I thought as much; but you may as well save your breath. I hate you and all that belong to you. Let that suffice. I regret to hear that nobody perished in the flames."

"Hear me, Blarney," said Ralph, after a pause; "I promise to exert all my influence to serve you, upon one simple condition. In the first place, tell me where Sir Roland is."

"It shall never pass my lips."

"You cannot be decided."

"Once for all, I tell you I am."

"Hardened villain!"

"Ha! ha! ha! I am obliged to you for calling me by my proper name, but you shall never get a word out of me."

"This obstinacy may be conquered at last!"

"You will soon have the opportunity of trying the experiment," returned Blarney, with a sneer; "but I am rather inclined to think that you will find me in the same state of mind after my trial as you do now."

"Can no arguments move you?"

"There is only one."

"Name it."

"Liberty!"

"That I cannot promise you."

"Then I will accept of no other terms."

"Repentance and good conduct might afterwards procure you that," remarked Ralph.

"And those, in my turn, I cannot promise," returned Blarney.

"Then our meeting is at an end?"

"Whenever you please. I did not seek it," said the ruffian. "I wish you would leave me to my dungeon and my harmony, which you interrupted. Ha! ha! ha! You came here thinking to find me down in the mouth and chicken-hearted. You thought I should be only too pleased to tell you all I know about Sir Roland. Ha! ha! ha!"

Ralph Ashton looked at the villain for an instant with an expression of disgust, and then, without saying another word, he quitted the prison.

Constance and Daisy were anxiously awaiting his return, not that they expected any beneficial results from his interview, and, therefore, expressed no disappointment at what he told them.

"I knew it would be useless," Constance said. "From such a miscreant what could be expected? I am inclined to think that he does not possess any knowledge beyond that he has shared in Sir Roland's crimes in some measure."

"I am weary and tired," Ralph Ashton said. "No sooner is one difficulty got rid of than another crops up. Daisy, are you better?"

"Much, I thank you," she replied.

"Do you think you could undertake a journey?" Ralph asked.

"Oh! yes," Daisy said.

"Then prepare yourself for it to-morrow," Ralph replied. "We are going back to London. Blarney will be taken there to be tried, and I must be present."

Constance now thought that he would say something about Robin, but not a word fell from his lips.

Ralph Ashton's conduct now seemed very strange and mysterious.

Instead of ordering a carriage to be brought to the village, he announced that it would be in readiness at the next.

"You, Constance, will walk over with me first," he said, "and then I will return for Daisy."

The girls looked askance at each other, and Ralph, walking to the window, looked up at the sky.

"There will be a storm to-night," he said. "So much the better for our purpose; there will be nobody about to watch our movements."

"Unless it be Spring-Heeled Jack," said Constance.

As Ralph Ashton turned towards her there was a strange expression upon his face.

"That singular creature has left this neighbourhood—perhaps for ever," he said.

"Indeed!" Constance returned. "Who told you so?"

"Himself."

Before Constance or Daisy could say more Ralph Ashton quitted the room, and did not return until he came dressed and equipped for the journey.

Constance soon made herself ready to accompany him, and in a few minutes they were on their way, which lay through a wild and desolate part of the country.

The storm came quicker than even Ralph had expected.

The sky suddenly turned black as jet, and the elements broke into open rebellion.

The frequent peals of thunder and the vivid flashes of lightning were terrific, and Constance was very much alarmed.

Ralph, however, endeavoured to quiet her apprehensions.

They pursued their way as quickly as they could, until they reached an open heath, after crossing which they would enter the village; but the lightning increased in vividness, and just as they had reached an old tree an awful flash darted from the heavens and completely rent its noble trunk in twain.

At the moment that the lightning struck the tree, standing before them in its lurid glare, they beheld a form wild and horrible.

It was that of an old hag, with shrivelled features and fierce black eyes, that were fixed full upon their countenances and glared with a supernatural expression.

Her snake-like hair floated on the blast.

In one hand she carried a leafless branch of a tree, and the other was pointed in a menacing manner towards them.

Constance could not help giving utterance to a scream of terror at the sight of this strange and awful-looking object, which had seemed to rise from the earth.

Constance clung to Ralph, who was as much astonished as herself at the appearance of the hag and at such a moment.

He quickly recovered himself, and placing his arm round Constance's waist, he waited impatiently to hear what would be the result of this extraordinary meeting.

The woman stood for an instant or so with her eyes still fixed upon the faces of the lovers, and then she burst into a fearful laugh, and her countenance assumed a loathsome, malignant expression.

"Woman, if such you are," Ralph said, "what seek you with us?"

"To tell thee of the future—to reveal to thee the happiness in store for thee," replied the hag, in harsh and discordant tones.

"Bah!" Ralph cried. "Begone, then—your task is fruitless; think not that you have credulous fools to listen to you and to believe in your idle prophecies."

"But thou shalt listen to me, Ralph Ashton," said the hag; "and thou must—thou shalt believe me. The time is not far distant when another shall possess that heart thou now believest to be entirely devoted to thee, and when the blush of shame and ruined innocence shall mantle in the fair cheek of her who now hangs tremblingly on thine arm. Mark me, Ralph Ashton—mark me!"

"Oh! Heaven," groaned Constance, pale and horror stricken.

Had it not been for the support of Ralph's arm she must have fallen to the earth.

"Bold crone!" exclaimed Ralph, "think not thus to impose upon me. I treat your remarks with scorn."

"But thou dost not, Ralph Ashton," returned the witch-like creature; "thou canst not, however thou mayest boast. Even now thine heart trembles. The tempest now rages on high, but it is not half so severe as the one which is preparing for thy breast. There is blood upon thy name. It reeks upon the shield of the Ashtons. 'Tis the blood of murdered men, and crieth aloud for vengeance. Canst thou wipe it out?"

"Liar!" Ralph cried. "This hand of mine is unstained with innocent blood."

"But Sir Roland!" the witch screamed. "What of him—Sir Roland? Ho, ho!"

Once more the mysterious woman laughed in wild derision, and while the lovers were still transfixed to the spot in speechless amazement she again waved her hand menacingly, and, moving quickly from the place, was out of sight in an instant.

"Gracious Heaven!" exclaimed Constance, "to what a strange thing have we been listening to? The woman must have been mad."

Ralph Ashton remained silent.

His face was pale, and his head lowered upon his breast.

"Ralph—Ralph!" Constance said, tearfully. "That woman's words have made you unhappy. Never will I be faithless to you—for are you not all the world to me?"

He did not speak, but stooping, kissed her reassuringly, and in a few moments entered the village, and Constance found herself in a warm, and cosy inn.

Ralph retraced his footsteps towards Hoddesdon, and in about an hour's time returned with Daisy.

"The carriage!" Ralph said, addressing the landlord. "Time flies, and I have much to do even when I reach London."

## CHAPTER LXXXVIII.

### A STRANGE MEETING.

SOME weeks elapsed without the occurrence of anything worthy of recording in these pages.

Constance and Daisy now occupied a pleasant little house overlooking the River Thames.

They had found it perfectly ready and prettily furnished, while well-trained servants went about their business as if they had lived there all their lives.

One fine morning Constance and Daisy felt inclined to take a walk before breakfast.

They had rambled about for some time inhaling the fresh air, when, feeling rather tired, they walked towards a shady tree.

They had advanced to within a few paces of it, however, when they were surprised at hearing the noise as if of someone breathing heavily proceeding near it.

They paused for a moment and listened, but still the sound continued, and they began to feel somewhat alarmed.

The girls at length imagined that they must have suffered themselves to be deceived, and that it was only the breeze of the wind rustling the leaves.

They once more advanced, but suddenly they uttered a cry of astonishment, and started back aghast when they beheld the figure of Sir Roland Ashton reclining on a bench that ran round the tree.

Sir Roland's face was covered with his hands, so that they could not behold his features, but they knew his form.

Trembling with alarm, they were preparing to retreat from the spot when Sir Roland awoke, and, rubbing his eyes, started to his feet.

Sir Roland looked dreadfully ill, and he winced as he moved, as if he still suffered extreme pain.

"By all that is wonderful!" he at length exclaimed. "Constance! Daisy! But how is this? Where am I, and—"

The girls did not give him time to finish the sentence, but, having somewhat recovered themselves from the confusion into which they had been thrown by this sudden and unexpected appearance, they hastily retreated towards the house, as much terrified as if they had seen some frightful apparition.

"Ah!" cried Sir Roland, "you shall not escape me thus, desperate and dangerous though my condition be. We must have a word or two together. Stop—stop!"

Finding that Sir Roland was pursuing them, Daisy and her companion were ready to sink with terror, and called aloud for help.

Ralph Ashton, who had come to search for them, and had been alarmed by their cries, rushed to the spot.

It would be almost impossible to describe the scene which followed.

Both Ralph Ashton and Sir Roland were for a moment or two transfixed to the spot, and stood gazing at each other with mingled expressions of surprise, confusion, and hatred; but at length Sir Roland uttered a dreadful oath as a full sense of the danger of his position rushed upon him.

Ralph Ashton roused himself from the state of inaction into which he had by astonishment been thrown.

"Ah! villain—robber—murderer!" he exclaimed, as he drew his sword, "have we, then, met again? Wretch, for whom the gallows has long yearned, what has guided your footsteps hither?"

"Ralph Ashton," Sir Roland returned, "the hatred you bear towards me is mutual. I am unarmed, and still suffering from the wound you gave me. I am much better, and the day may come when you may have to plead mercy of me!"

"Daring miscreant!" exclaimed Ralph, as he rushed towards him, "this moment will I save the hangman his trouble! Thus do I send you to your final account, and avenge myself for the slur you have cast upon my name. Die, monster—die!"

Sir Roland folded his arms.

"Strike me, a wounded, helpless man!" he said. "Such a thrust would do your sword honour."

Ralph stopped half-way, and lowered the point of his rapier to the ground.

"No," he said; "I thought I had rid the world of you; but I will not harm you now. I will find other means. Your accomplice, Bill Blarney, is in prison, and you shall follow him. Sir Roland, you are my prisoner!"

"And I surrender," Sir Roland replied, calmly. "The world shall hear my story and yours. How proud then will you be of your name?"

Ralph bit his under lip until a thin streak of blood ran down his chin.

"What a villain you are!" he said. "Cowardly, cruel, and shameless!"

Sir Roland smiled.

"I sought you out," he said, "for I wish to make you an offer."

"An offer?"

"Yes; and one which I think you will accept," the baronet said. "I have no money, but money I must have. Give me some, and I will quit the country for ever."

"How can I trust you?" Ralph returned. "Gladly would I see your back on such terms; but I know that you would return to your scenes of vice when the last guinea had slipped from your fingers, and then the same story of crime would be repeated again."

"I am in earnest," Sir Roland replied; "indeed, I am dreadfully in earnest. I hate the sight of this country, and would fly to another; I care not which, so long as it was one where I can live unknown. Ralph Ashton, I have more bitter enemies even than yourself; I have but lately escaped from them."

"You have suffered much," Ralph said, lookin sternly at him.

"Suffered!" Sir Roland repeated, shruggin his shoulders. "The tortures of the Inquisitio pale before what I have gone through. Will yo grant my request?"

"No," Ralph replied. "Go your way, bu beware how you cross my path again."

Sir Roland turned aside; but as he did so h glanced at Constance and Daisy.

"The hour of my triumph may yet come," h said. "I do not despair, though I have scarcel a guinea in the world."

He walked slowly and painfully away.

Sir Roland wandered on for many hours, unti he was footsore and weary. He endeavoured t find some shelter for the night, but his efforts wer in vain.

Besides, it was now so late that he despaired o being able to meet with any accommodation i even he should come to an inn or other habitation and he was now so completely fatigued that h could not, without the greatest difficulty, drag o his dreary way at all.

At length, after walking for more than hour, he came to the end of the heath; but the prospect before him was little, if any, more cheering.

It was a long and dismal lane, overarched by tall trees, and whither it led Sir Roland had no means of forming any idea.

However, he traversed it as fast as he could, and endeavoured to put the best heart upon the business that was possible.

Little more than a quarter of an hour's walking brought him to the end of this lane, but still no village or town, or the least sign of a human dwelling met his gaze, and he paused for a moment or two and considered what to do.

"There is an infernal spell upon me," he ejaculated; "not a house, not a shelter, not a traveller. In what wild part of the country am I? I cannot proceed in this way much longer, for I am as tired as a dog, and yet how can I rest myself in the open fields with this wound still torturing me?"

He growled out a curse between his teeth on his misfortune, and proceeded along a narrow footpath across the fields now spread before him.

This was a task of no small difficulty, for night had come on and there was no moon.

The night was pitchy dark, and he could see nothing distinctly for more than a yard before him.

However, after he had walked across two or three fields he perceived a shadow of something that appeared like a building of some description before him at no great distance, and, inspired with fresh hope, he hurried towards it.

On coming up to it he was somewhat disappointed on finding it to be only a pile of ruins, of what appeared to have been formerly a farmhouse, and which did not offer the least chance of shelter; but walking round it he was more pleased on beholding attached to it at the back a modern building, and which proved to be an inn.

He requested a newspaper, if the landlord could accommodate him with one, and having brought it to him, the host observed—

"These are shocking times that we live in, sir. Nothing but crime. I wonder what the world is coming to."

"Ah!" said Sir Roland, ironically, and anxious to dispense with the company of his host, as his remarks were anything but in unison with his own thoughts at the time.

# SPRING-HEELED JACK,

## THE TERROR OF LONDON.

"DIE, DOG, DIE!" SPRING-HEELED JACK YELLED, SWINGING JULES CARLEON ALOFT.

. 26.

The man was, however, not to be so easily stopped.

"Nothing but murders and robberies in the papers, sir," he said. "Dreadful times—dreadful times! A person isn't safe a moment."

"No," returned Sir Roland, with his former brevity.

"I only wish they may catch them both, and all such villains," continued the landlord.

"To whom do you allude?" the baronet asked.

"Why, like Bill Blarney, who will be hung as sure as eggs are eggs."

Sir Roland could not help starting slightly.

"Oh! yes," he said. "Ah! I have heard of him before."

"It would be something very surprising if you had not."

"Why so?"

"Because he is one of the most desperate villains in the country," replied the landlord.

"Yes, yes. Have you ever seen him?"

"No," answered the landlord, with a shudder. "Heaven forbid that I should, unless it was upon the gallows. There was another dreadful murder some time ago, and it was said that it was committed by a nobleman."

"Who said so?" Sir Roland demanded.

"Why, there is some story going about that a Frenchman has offered to give evidence, and I believe there is a reward offered for the nobleman's apprehension."

"Well, I wish they may catch him," said Sir Roland, with a feeling of terror he could but ill conceal.

"And so must every honest, well-meaning person."

The landlord then retired from the room, and Sir Roland, being left to himself, took up the paper.

In almost the first paragraph he read the offer of a reward for his own apprehension and conviction.

"Very good," said Sir Roland; "but they shall not catch me quite so easily as they, perhaps, imagine. I am not known in this neighbourhood, and therefore I am safe."

When morning came he found himself suddenly so indisposed that he could not leave the place; and, vexed and somewhat alarmed lest his illness should prove serious, he was compelled to make arrangements with the landlord to remain there another night, resolving, if better, to start again at daybreak.

He awoke at any early hour in the morning, and felt so far recovered that he rose immediately, and, having dressed himself, determined to depart without delay.

He had scarcely come to this resolution, however, when he was attracted by a noise at the window, which looked upon the back-yard of the inn, and presently he saw the gate opened and the landlord enter, followed by two men, of whom he could not obtain a distinct view at first, but when he did so, to his surprise and consternation, he recognised them to be two officers.

He drew himself back, so that they might not observe him, but continued to watch their actions from a position where he could do so without being perceived in return.

The landlord pointed towards the window with a significant gesture, and then, motioning the men to follow him, they walked across the yard quickly and entered the house.

"Curse him!" Sir Roland muttered. "Am I betrayed? How is this? And by what means can the constables have traced my footsteps? Oh! Jules Carleon, how I wish I had you here now!"

These words were uttered in the space of a moment or two, and whilst he spoke he was looking for the means of getting from the house.

There was no other way than by the window, and that, now the officers were in the house, was almost hopeless.

Sir Roland, weak and ill as he was, was not the man to yield without a struggle, and he therefore leaped from the window on to the roof of a shed which happened to be immediately beneath it, and from thence, with very little difficulty, alighted in the yard.

He rushed into a stable, and, throwing himself on the ground, covered himself with some straw, and awaited the result in breathless anxiety.

He had not to wait long, and, fortunately for him, it turned out according to his best wishes.

In a moment he heard a noise in the house, and then several voices, apparently speaking from the window of the chamber he had just quitted.

"He has escaped," said one of them. "He must have seen us enter the yard and has gone by the backway; and see, the gate is open, which proves that I am right. He cannot have been gone many minutes, so quick! and he must fall into our power."

Sir Roland's heart throbbed violently against his side, and he scarcely dared to breathe.

It was a moment of life or death to him, but still the words he had heard the constable utter inspired him with some degree of hope, and when he heard the window closed, and knew that the men had retired into the house, that was his time for action.

There was no one to observe him, and hastening from the stable, he sprang like an affrighted hare from the entrance, and turning an angle of the building, took a contrary way to that which he was almost certain the officers would pursue.

He gained the top of the village in an instant, and met with no person in his way.

"So far, so good," he muttered to himself, wiping the perspiration from his forehead. "I have managed this affair pretty cleverly. I have deceived the blood-hounds, and they are pursuing me on the wrong track. Before they find out their mistake I shall probably be far away from them."

Having now recovered himself, Sir Roland pursued his way, anxiously wishing that he might meet with some means of conveyance; but that was not likely, as he avoided the high-road, and was fearful of entering a town or village in the daylight lest he should encounter the danger he so much apprehended.

In this manner he continued to travel, without having an opportunity of once breaking his fast throughout the day, and as the dusky shades of evening fell he entered a wood.

Feeling too tired to proceed any further, he stretched himself on the earth and gradually fell asleep.

How long he had been so he could not imagine, but he was suddenly aroused by hearing footsteps approaching.

He jumped up in an instant, and grasping a heavy stick he had broken from a hedge with one hand and a pistol in the other, he looked around him.

He had scarcely time, however, to do so, when there was a rustling sound among the foliage, and two men forced their way from between a thick cluster of trees, and having got into the more open space, the moon shone full upon their countenances.

Sir Roland's confusion may be readily conceived when he recognised their features as those of the constables from whom he had escaped in the morning.

It was mere accident that had brought them there, for they had given up the pursuit after several hours, considering it quite hopeless, and were returning on foot towards the place where they intended to put up for the night, when they encountered the very object of their search in the singular and almost miraculous manner that has just been described.

For an instant all parties were so taken by surprise that they were unable to move, but stood gazing at each other, apparently almost doubting the evidence of their senses; but at length Sir Roland put himself in an attitude of defence, and his looks and whole demeanour plainly showed that he was fully determined not to be taken easily.

"We have you now," said one of the constables, "and are resolved, after all the trouble you have given us, not to let you escape this time, at any rate. Come—come, this show of resistance is madness; you see we are armed."

"And so am I," returned Sir Roland; "and what is more, I am desperate. Fools! there are only two of you, and think you that I will suffer myself to be taken? Do not obstruct my way, or it will be worse for you."

"Rash man!" cried the constables, as they advanced towards him.

Sir Roland sprang upon them, seized both their arms, and the pistols they held in their hands exploded in the air.

He then immediately grasped his stick and and stood resolute.

The constables were completely astounded at his daring.

"You see how useless it is to oppose me," Sir Roland said. "Go home, and spare yourselves any further unnecessary trouble, and let me go about my business. I do not wish to harm you, but I will not be obstructed."

He made a motion to depart as he uttered these words, when the constables, having recovered themselves, once more rushed towards him, both of them having drawn their cutlasses.

Certainly the odds were greatly against Sir Roland, but, nothing daunted, he dealt about them such quick and heavy blows as completely disabled them for a time.

Sir Roland walked deliberately away from the spot before the constables had recovered from the surprise and confusion into which his cool and determined conduct, and the blows he had dealt them, had thrown them.

Sir Roland plunged into the thickest part of the wood, and then considered it prudent to quicken his speed, for he had no doubt the men would pursue him again and might obtain assistance, in which case his escape would be rendered almost impossible.

"Ha! ha! ha!" he laughed, as he proceeded; "I have taught these fellows a lesson, I think, they will not easily forget; and if they are wise they will make their way to the nearest town, where they may rest their bones after the drubbing I have given them instead of following me."

He paused for a moment to listen, but he heard not the sound of pursuit, and he therefore proceeded with more confidence.

## CHAPTER LXXXIX.

### DEATH OF JULES CARLEON.

As Jules Carleon fell half-strangled to the earth, the man who had captured him in so peculiar a manner loosened the rope and rode slowly up to the Frenchman.

"Now, my fine fellow," said the man called Lorrimer, or still better known as Harry Banks, "you must come with me. Don't roll your eyes about like that, for you are far more frightened than hurt."

Jules Carleon groaned and pressed his fingers between the rope and his throat.

"Oh! you need not fear that you are going to be hanged just at present, though you deserve it so richly," Harry Banks said, smiling. "My master will interview you and deal with you as he thinks proper."

"Your master!" Jules Carleon gasped; "why, who may he be?"

"Wait and see," Harry Banks rejoined, as he slipped a piece of cord round his captive's wrists. "There, now, you are all right and comfortable. Now then, my lad, I'll give you a lift into the saddle, and away we go!"

Jules Carleon turned white to the very lips, and trembled until his teeth chattered in his head.

"Listen to me," he faltered. "Let me go free, and I will tell you all I know concerning myself and Sir Roland."

"Your offer comes too late," Harry Banks replied. "Sir Roland is beset on all sides. His arch-enemy, Spring-Heeled Jack, is on his track, and the officers of the law are in search of him for cold-blooded, cruel murder and highway robbery."

"Then other eyes than mine saw the deed!" Jules Carleon hissed between his set teeth.

"Yes; but we lose time."

"No—no!" the Frenchman whined. "I know much more. Promise me my liberty, and—"

"I promise you nothing," Harry Banks said, interrupting him, sternly; "and under all circumstances you will do well to keep your tongue quiet for the present."

So saying, he lifted Jules Carleon into the saddle, and, climbing up behind him, took the reins and galloped away.

The horse was a powerful animal, and well able to bear the weight of both men.

For more than an hour the journey was continued, Harry Banks saying nothing to his prisoner, save to remind him by touching his ear with the barrel of a pistol that escape was impossible.

Jules Carleon had hoped to meet somebody on the way from whom he could implore protection, but Harry Banks chose unfrequented paths, now guiding the horse at a footpace through dark woods, and now along unfrequented lanes, so that not a human creature appeared.

The sun came up, gilding the tree-tops with golden light, but still the horse went on.

Suddenly it stopped, and Harry Banks, leaping from the saddle, clutched Jules Carleon by the collar.

"Mind how you get down," Banks said. "I have no wish that you should break your neck just yet."

Jules Carleon turned a malignant glance upon

the speaker, and showed his teeth like a wolf at bay.

"What now?" he demanded. "Where do you intend to take me? I see no house."

Harry Banks made no reply; but still retaining his hold on the Frenchman's collar, he lifted him clean out of the saddle and planted him on his feet in a rather unceremonious manner.

"I'll go no further," Jules Carleon declared, throwing himself down at full length. "You have no right to take the law into your own hands."

Harry Banks took a whistle from a side-pocket and blew a shrill call upon it.

This signal was answered in a similar manner, and presently two strong, stalwart men appeared.

Harry Banks merely pointed to the prisoner, and in an instant the men, stern of face and silent, hoisted the Frenchman upon their shoulders.

Jules Carleon knew now that resistance would avail him nothing, and that it would be waste of breath to cry out for assistance.

His captors bore him swiftly along for some minutes, and when they came to a standstill Jules Carleon discovered that they had arrived before the ruins of a once noble house.

The sometime neatly-tended garden was now choked with weeds and rank grass.

Damp moss, coarse litchen, and evil-looking fungi had taken possession of the terrace, and the walls and windows of the house were almost entirely hidden by huge masses of straggling ivy.

Jules Carleon could but stare at the strange-looking place in utter astonishment.

He had never seen the like of it before, nor dreamed of the existence of such a place near London.

He turned to put a question to Harry Banks, but that individual had disappeared, and as the other men refused to utter a word, and were deaf alike to entreaties and questions, the Frenchman shrugged his shoulders and resigned himself to his fate.

They marched him between them through a wide, spacious hall, so thick with the dust of ages that their footsteps produced no sound.

Turning sharply, they began to descend a flight of stairs, and then abject fear struck into the Frenchman's heart.

It flashed through his mind that he had been brought to this strange, weird house to be left to starve and die; and as his lower jaw fell great beads of perspiration gathered on his brow.

"Mercy!" he gasped. "You are men, and can feel compassion for a fellow-creature in misfortune."

Not a syllable was uttered by the men, who held him as in a vice.

Down—down they went, until their progress was obstructed by an oaken door studded with huge, flat-headed, iron nails.

One of the men struck thrice at the door.

It was opened almost instantly by Harry Banks, who carried a lantern in one hand and a bunch of keys in the other.

"I am ready. Bring the prisoner along," was all he said.

He led the way down a long, narrow passage as dark as midnight, and then, swinging open another door, pointed down into a dismal dungeon.

A grated window admitted a feeble ray of light into this dreary region, and Jules Carleon shuddered from head to foot as he caught sight of a grindstone, leaning against which was a headsman's axe.

He shrank back at the sight, and clawed the air frantically with his bound hands.

"No—no!" he wailed. "You will not leave me in such a place as that!"

Harry Banks made a motion with his hand to the two men, and in another instant Jules Carleon found himself thrust into the dungeon.

He heard the door close with a bang, and the rumbling echoes produced by the sound struck into his heart like a death-knell.

As a tiger dragged from its native jungle and newly caged, so the Frenchman paced his prison and glared round it.

He strove to break the bonds that held his wrists, but strove in vain.

He gnawed at them with his teeth, and in his frenzy bit into his flesh, but the cords held fast.

If he could only free his hands he could secure the axe—the very weapon which perchance was intended to sever his base head—and defend himself against all comers.

Again and again he endeavoured to release his hands with the strength of madness and despair, but all his efforts were useless, and at last he threw himself down and howled in a dog-like fashion.

For hours he was left alone.

Nobody came to him, and he heard no sound indicative of any human creature being near him.

At length he rose to his feet and began pacing the limits of the dungeon.

There was something awful in the manner in which he walked from wall to wall, turning slowly, and going over the same ground over and over again in a hopeless, hang-dog fashion.

Suddenly something in the structure of the floor attracted his attention.

It was a square trap-door, fitting so closely that it was a wonder that it did not escape his notice.

Jules Carleon stopped suddenly, and gazed at this new discovery with feelings better imagined than described.

There was evidently a chamber under the one he occupied.

But what manner of a place could it be?

The Frenchman knew that men in the olden times built queer hiding-places and dreadful dens, with the view of exquisite torture for their victims, and this dungeon under a dungeon might be full of nameless horrors.

Perchance it was filled with the bones of murdered men—men who had died slowly, shrieking for the help that never came, and perishing in such agony that to dream of it makes the blood run cold.

Jules Carleon pictured so many horrors, linking them with his impending fate, that he rushed to the wall with the intention of dashing his brains out.

Ere he could reach the other side of the dungeon a hand of iron grasped him by the back of the neck and swung him round.

Jules Carleon and Spring-Heeled Jack stood face to face.

For several moments neither spoke a word.

They glared at each other—Spring-Heeled Jack in mockery, and the Frenchman with eyes that protruded unnaturally from his head and his breath coming short and thick.

"I bid you welcome!" Spring-Heeled Jack said at length. "Jules Carleon, your new home does not seem to meet with your approval."

The Frenchman hung his head, and bit his under lip until it bore the marks of his teeth.

"You have nothing to say?" Spring-Heeled Jack continued. "No excuse to make for your career of villainy? Well, perhaps silence in your case may be golden."

"What should I say to you?" the Frenchman rejoined, hoarsely. "I am your prisoner, and at your mercy."

"Mercy!" Spring-Heeled Jack repeated. "Expect no such thing from me. I have erased the word from my heart for such men as you."

"And yet, methinks I could tell you things you would care to know," Jules Carleon said.

Spring-Heeled Jack held up his hand.

"Nay," he said. "I know all. You lent your villainous brain and hand to abduct an innocent girl to place her in the power of Sir Roland."

"I was his servant and acted under his instructions," Jules Carleon pleaded.

"I will ask you one question," Spring-Heeled Jack said. "Refuse to answer it and I will force the words from your throat. How came you to discover that Ralph Ashton and the ladies were staying at the Queen's Head, Saddlers' Wells?"

"I drugged Jacob Butler," Jules Carleon replied.

"Ha!" Spring-Heeled Jack cried.

A smile crossed his features for an instant.

"Poor fool! to be led into such a trap," he said. "So far, so good. Your statement has opened my eyes to something I did not know before."

"And you will set me free?" Jules Carleon pleaded. "You will give me time for repentance?"

"Not I!" Spring-Heeled Jack replied, scornfully. "You had the opportunity of abandoning your evil ways and heeded it not. Jules Carleon, villain that you are, your time has come!"

As the singular creature spoke he strode to the centre of the dungeon and opened the trap-door.

The wooden flap struck the floor with a hollow sound.

"That," said Spring-Heeled Jack, pointing to the black abyss below, "will be your abode until the end of your days. Nay, I will give you one more chance. If you survive four-and-twenty hours I will set you free."

"A thousand thanks!" the Frenchman murmured.

Spring-Heeled Jack replied with a hollow laugh.

"You will find that you owe me no thanks," he said. "Come, prepare! My time is precious."

Grasping the Frenchman with both hands Spring-Heeled Jack swung him aloft.

Jules Carleon closed his eyes and tried to breathe a prayer, for he thought that his last moment was at hand.

But the words stuck in his throat, and no other sound came from his lips save a gurgling cry of horror and despair.

He felt his body leave Spring-Heeled Jack's grasp, and then came the descent.

Although it was but of a moment's duration it seemed an age to the wretched man.

In that one short, swift instant he lived his life over again, and then—Jules Carleon fell upon a heap of straw, half dead with fright, but in no wise bodily injured.

The trap-door closed over his head wtth a crash, and he lay still for some time, scarcely believing that he had escaped death; but soon he raised himself and endeavoured to pierce the gloom with his eyes.

It was impossible to do so.

So pitchy was the blackness that he seemed to feel it, and though he held up his hands within an inch of his face they were invisible to him.

This enforced blindness was more terrible than anything he had undergone.

The straw beneath him was plentiful—indeed, it was so thick that as he groped about, moaning in the wild bitterness of his heart, he waded knee-deep in the bed prepared for him.

Now Jules Carleon began to rave and tear his hair.

He asked for mercy, he pleaded for a drink of water, he wailed for daylight; but his cries were unheeded.

Ghastly, weak, and half-maddened, he threw himself down and lay still.

Then it was that a strange and unaccountable sound came to his ears.

First it was but a mere rustling in the straw, which he might have caused himself by some involuntary movement; but Jules Carleon, reclining as motionless as a statue, knew that such was not the case.

Straining every nerve, he listened.

His heart rose into his mouth as the rustling increased and was followed by a scampering sound.

Then, as he heard a strange, sharp, squeaking, he leaped to his feet and recoiled in horror.

Hundreds of small, fiery-red sparks were glaring at him.

He knew that these bead-like jets were the eyes of famished rats, and Jules Carleon, throwing all his strength into one supreme effort, burst the cords which bound his hands.

"Help—help!" he yelled.

The rats, infuriated at the sound of his voice, leaped upon him.

There seemed to be thousands of them.

Jules Carleon beat them back with his hands and feet, but the blood-thirsty creatures were not to be denied.

Again and again Jules Carleon made the dungeon ring with his shrieks, but at last his voice and speech failed him.

Exhausted and swooning, he fell upon his face, and then he felt a sudden pang at his heart as if some fine, but intensely sharp, instrument had been thrust into it.

He uttered a gasping cry and closed his eyes.

Death had kindly saved the Frenchman the last horrors of existence, and the rats feasted upon his lifeless body until a white, fleshless skeleton testified to their voracity.

---

## CHAPTER XC.

### MRS. CORCORAN TAKES TO WANDERING ONCE TOO OFTEN.

Little dreaming that her beloved Jacob was an inmate of the Chequers, and that Bill Blarney was again in prison, Mrs. Corcoran become very unsettled in her mind.

It now behoves us to tell how Sir Roland escaped from the Chequers.

He had, as the reader already knows, been conveyed to one of the secret rooms of that most villainous inn, where he lay wounded and almost sick to death.

Cordials were administered to him by one of those doctors who in those days, but happily not in these, took their fees and asked no questions.

Sir Roland grew stronger hourly; but he kept the secret to himself, and watched for an opportunity to escape.

Mrs. Corcoran paid him every attention; but she was thrown off her guard, keen-sighted and cunning though she was, for Sir Roland still feigned being so utterly weak that he could move neither hand nor foot.

One day, whilst pretending to sleep soundly, Mrs. Corcoran left him.

Sir Roland opened his eyes and listened.

He could hear the sound of voices below, and knew that some important conversation was being carried on—and, indeed, it was over the furtherance of the plan by which Bill Blarney was to burn the cottage at Hoddesden, and thus wreak revenge upon Ralph Ashton and those he held dear.

Sir Roland heard Mrs. Corcoran's shrill voice, and knowing that when that amiable old lady started talking that she went on steadily for some time, he rose, and, hurrying on his clothes, went to the window.

It was barred, but the ironwork was so rusty and rotten that it required scarcely an effort to break it away.

Beneath the window was a shed with a sloping roof, and Sir Roland, after making his way through the window good, twisted a sheet into knots, and lowered himself silently and gently.

He dropped into a yard, and scaling a wooden gate, went racing through the wretched, squalid neighbourhood, and away, whither he knew not, until by accident he encountered Daisy Leigh and Constance Marfield.

The reader is acquainted with the scene which took place when Ralph Ashton opportunely appeared, and how the baronet fled into the country, only to find the officers of justice upon his heels.

In such a predicament we must leave him for the present, and turn our attention to other characters

Great was Mrs. Corcoran's rage when she discovered Sir Roland's flight, and without delay or staying to replenish her purse, she set out in search of him.

Now Mrs. Corcoran had an excellent constitution, and a marvellous one for her age; but it broke down at last.

She began to mumble as she wandered on and on, and the people who met her moved hurriedly from her path, fully believing that the old crone was mad.

How chance led her into the presence of Ralph Ashton will be presently seen, and also how Mrs. Corcoran played the part once attributed to a great personage, of whom it was once said—

"*When the devil was ill, the devil a saint would be;*
*When the devil grew well, the devil a saint was he!*"

It wanted now but a week to the trial of Bill Blarney, and as the time rapidly approached Daisy's emotion rather increased than abated, notwithstanding all the arguments and remonstrances of Ralph Ashton; for she could not think of encountering that guilty man again, and in such a fearful position, without feelings of horror.

But an event was about to take place to divert her attention, and which created the deepest surprise and interest in the breasts of all who were sheltered in the home provided by Ralph Ashton.

It was now drawing towards the close of autumn, and the weather was becoming cheerless and unsettled, but only a day or two previous to the time to which they all looked forward to with so much anxiety, fear, and repugnance.

It was more than usually gloomy, and the dark clouds that obscured the horizon gave certain warning that there would be a storm before long.

The day, however, passed away, and it was not till the darkness of night spread itself upon the earth that the tempest, which had so long threatened, commenced, and raged with fearful violence.

This storm continued with unabated fury till past ten o'clock, about which time several rustics who were returning from their labour approached an old shed or out-house, situate at no great distance from Ralph Ashton's river-side residence.

"Well," said one of the men, "the storm does seem likely to abate at last."

"Yes, Tom Giles," returned one of his companions, "now we are all wet to the skin; and so we have no occasion to thank it for its mercy. It certainly was a most fearful one."

"Aye! you may say that, Roger," said the first speaker, "and what must those poor creatures suffer who have no place to put their heads under? Now, we have got a comfortable cottage and a good cheerful fireside to retire to, and something to eat, and, therefore, we should not grumble when we reflect how many there are in the world who are so much worse off than ourselves. But, hark! What was that?"

"Did you not hear a cry?"

"Not I."

"There it is again."

"Ah! I heard it then, sure enough."

"It sounded like the cry of some poor creature in suffering," said another of the men.

"Yes, it did," observed Tom; "just like the moans of someone in their dying moments."

"Heaven bless me!" exclaimed Roger; "I hope no one has been waylaid and murdered."

"Murdered!" cried all the others in a breath, and with looks of consternation.

Again the dismal wailing sounds were repeated, and seemed to grow fainter and fainter.

"It is a woman's voice, I am certain of it," said Tom.

"And proceeded from the old barn yonder, or I am much mistaken," said one of his companions. "It is lucky we have a lantern with us. Let us hasten there and see what is the matter."

"But there might be danger," suggested one of the rustics.

"Danger!" repeated Tom Giles; "and shall we suffer that to prevent us from hastening to the rescue of an unfortunate fellow-creature? There are five of us, and therefore what have we to fear?"

"To be sure not," said Roger. "If we have rascals to contend with, I daresay they will find us a match for them. It is most likely some poor creature who has crept in there out of the storm, and may be dying. Come, my lads, come!"

Encouraged by the observations of honest Roger they followed him, and soon reached the barn, when the cries of the wretched sufferer were more audible, and they were now convinced that they came from a woman.

They listened for a moment or two to ascertain whether there were other persons in the miserable shed, and then, pushing open the broken door, they entered.

The man who carried the lantern held it up to get a better view.

An object met their observation, crouched down in one corner of the barn, which filled their hearts with pity and horror.

It was the emaciated form of an old woman of apparently more than seventy years of age, whose shivering body was only partially concealed by a ragged gown, the only semblance of a covering she possessed.

Her feet were almost bare, and her long, grey, and matted hair hung over her naked shoulders.

She was huddled up in one corner, her bony elbows resting on her knees, and her head reclining on her hands.

She seemed to be suffering great agony, and broken moans escaped her lips.

"Poor creature—poor creature!" said Tom Giles; "she is, indeed, in a sad plight—perishing, dying, I am afraid."

The wretched being raised her head from her hands at the sound of his voice, and fixed upon them a ghastly look of mingled surprise and terror.

Her cheeks were hollow and pale as those of a corpse, and altogether she presented a spectacle of misery and destitution, which was truly piteous to behold.

"Who are you?" she gasped. "What want you here? Am I not suffered to die even in this wretched place?"

"Die, my poor woman!" replied Tom Giles. "No, no; not if we can help it. Poor old creature—poor old creature!"

"Ah!" shrieked the woman, "words of pity—words of kindness—and addressed to a poor old wretch like me? Go—go, and leave me alone to die. You—you mock me!"

"Mock you, my good woman?" said Roger. "No, no; Heaven forbid that we should do anything of the kind. But who are you, and—"

"Who am I?" interrupted the old woman. "Who am I? Ask me not! Go—go! I am a wretched outcast, unworthy of a thought. But, oh! I am starving—starving! No food for these two days, and so cold—cold!"

"Unfortunate old soul!" said Tom Giles. "You look ill and miserable; but come, we will send you to where you shall find shelter and relief."

"Shelter—relief?" repeated the woman. "No, no; I deserve it not. I am a wretched woman who—but, oh! this anguish—this dreadful agony—I—"

"My good woman," said Roger, "there is not a moment to be lost; we should be worse than monsters did we suffer you to remain here to perish. Had we not better take her to Mr. Ashton's house? And we well know that she will be kindly received by its benevolent inmates."

"Mr. Ashton!—that name!" screamed the old woman. "No—no; not there—not there! I—I dare not meet his sight! He would drive me from his presence with disgust. He would consign me to a prison. He—"

She could not finish the sentence; her strength was completely exhausted, and with a dismal groan she sank insensible on the earth.

"She seems to know Mr. Ashton," said Roge "and is terrified at the mention of his name."

"Ah! poor old soul," returned Tom; "I fe that she is mad. But certainly she will be bett attended to there than at one of our homes, an therefore assist me, my lads, and we will at on convey her thither."

The man's companions instantly complied, an raising the emaciated form of the wretched o woman in their arms, they issued from the bar and proceeded towards Ralph Ashton's house wit out delay.

The inmates of the villa were seated in t drawing-room, when they were startled by hea ing a violent ringing at the gate, and the ne moment a servant entered the room and i formed them that some peasants had brought wretched creature whom they had found in t out-house close by, and requested that th would take her in and see to her wants, as s appeared to be dying.

"Dying!" repeated Daisy. "Oh! where she?"

"They have placed her by the fire in the hal miss," replied the servant; "but she is quite i sensible."

"Let us see to this," said Ralph; "it appea to be a case of great emergency."

He immediately quitted the room, followed b Daisy and Constance, and descended to the hal where the wretched old woman was still in state of insensibility, while the female servan used all the means that suggested themselves t them towards her recovery.

The miserable appearance of the unfortunat creature greatly shocked every beholder; but Con stance and Daisy had no sooner approached to wards her, and glanced at her pale and hagga countenance, than they uttered an exclamation o astonishment when they recognised in her featur those of Mrs. Corcoran.

"Gracious Heaven!" cried Daisy, "this i indeed, an extraordinary and unexpected even Miserable woman! what can have guided h footsteps to this neighbourhood? and how gre must have been her sufferings!"

"She appears to be dying," said Ralph Ashto who evinced no emotion whatever. "Let her b conveyed to a room; and hasten, one of you, addressing himself to the servants, "and call i medical attendance immediately."

"I fear it is too late to save her," Constanc said. "Oh! quick—quick! delay not a momen for how much may depend upon her recovery! Sh may be able, in some measure, to unravel the r markable mystery connected with the disappea ance of Lady Ashton."

One of the servants immediately hastened t the nearest doctor, and the female domestic carried Mrs. Corcoran and placed her in a war bed, while Daisy and Constance became more an more anxious every moment.

They watched Mrs. Corcoran with the greate impatience, but still she remained insensible, an she seemed so much exhausted that all chance o her restoration seemed to be at an end.

"Alas! she is, indeed, punished for her guilt, said Daisy. "Where can the miserable creatur have been all this time?"

"Be composed, Daisy," said Ralph Ashto "I feel convinced that something will arise ou of this circumstance. See, she breathes agai she will yet be restored to her senses, but I fe that the shock will be more than her strength ca support. You had better retire and let the intelligence be gradually imparted to her, when she may be inclined to make a confession of all she knows."

"Oh! I cannot bear the thought of leaving her," said Daisy.

"But it is absolutely necessary, Daisy," returned Ralph. "I will send for you as soon as the wretched woman is restored to sensibility and I have prepared her for the meeting. Come, let me prevail upon you!"

Daisy and Constance reluctantly complied, and, casting an anxious glance upon the ghastly features of the apparently dying woman, they quitted the room, Ralph remaining behind.

The medical man now arrived and proceeded to apply such remedies as the urgency of the case required; but, from her emaciated appearance, he gave it as his opinion that Mrs. Corcoran was too much reduced to be recovered entirely, and on no account would he suffer her to be disturbed, as he feared that the least excitement would be attended with fatal results.

In a short time Mrs. Corcoran breathed more freely, and the doctor having succeeded in administering to her a restorative, she opened her eyes and glared awfully and vacantly around her.

"Dying—dying of hunger!" she articulated in a faint and hollow voice. "Oh! I am justly punished for my crimes. But—but where am I? Who are you? What place is this? In bed, and attended with such kindness! Forbear—forbear! I deserve it not. I am a wretch unworthy of pity or assistance in my misery. I have committed crimes that should make human nature shudder. Let me die, and end this wretched existence; but not in prison—no—no; although a dungeon is the fitting place for me. Oh! conscience—conscience!"

"Unfortunate woman!" said Ralph Ashton, "sinner as I fear you have been, nevertheless, Heaven is merciful, and—"

"Ah!" shrieked the old woman, fixing her eyes with frenzied earnestness upon him, "what voice is that? It is familiar to my ears. Who are you? and why came you hither?"

"Wretched woman," said Ralph Ashton, "do you not know me?"

"Ah! I recollect you now—you are Ralph Ashton, the lover of Constance Marfield," cried Mrs. Corcoran, and her whole frame trembled violently with terror and remorse. "Then—then I am lost; retribution has at last overtaken me. But do not consign me to a prison. I—I am a wretched old woman, and I feel the hand of death upon me; but, mercy—mercy! let me not perish in a dungeon."

"Fear not, for every care shall be taken of you," said Ralph; "but endeavour to compose yourself, and, if you would hope for pardon from offended Heaven, ere the hand of death may seal your lips for ever, make some atonement for your past transgressions by confessing all that you know."

"Confess!" repeated the miserable old woman, "yes—yes, I will. Oh! I have been most guilty; I have connived at the most hideous crimes; blood—blood is upon my conscience; it will press me down to perdition. But I did not murder her; no—no, hardened as my heart was, I could not perform the bidding of the monster. I will tell the truth; it was I and Jem Basker who suffered her to escape. But that was years ago—years ago."

"To whom do you allude?" demanded Ralph Ashton, eagerly.

"Ah! you know her not," said Mrs. Corcoran. "It was Lord Mildendale's wife. Even Lord Mildendale, wretch as he was, had not the courage to commit the inhuman deed himself, and I undertook to administer poison to her during his absence from the Hall. He believed that she had perished; but I could not resist her piteous applications for mercy, and, after binding her by an oath—a terrible oath—to secrecy, I gave her her liberty. Thank Heaven that I did so—that, at any rate, I have not that dreadful crime upon my conscience."

Ralph Ashton started.

The old woman was saying something now that interested him keenly.

"Listen," he said. "Was it not given out to the world that Lady Mildendale fled from her husband in consequence of his ill-treatment?"

"Yes—yes! But that was a lie," Mrs. Corcoran said.

"Beware, old woman!" said Ralph Ashton, solemnly; "you are probably now on the verge of eternity. Have you then spoken the truth?"

"Do you doubt me? I tell you again that the villain was deceived. I preserved the life of his wife."

"And whither did she go?"

"I—I am faint. I have not strength to answer these questions. Spare me—spare me!"

"Nay; remember it is the only reparation you can make for the crimes you have committed by revealing the truth. What became of Lady Mildendale?"

"She went back to her own people, I believe."

"Ah!" said Ralph. "Then there may yet be hope?"

"Hope of what?"

"Of justice being done at last."

"Lady Mildendale had a son," Ralph Ashton continued. "What would you say if I brought him here to see you?"

"See me!" repeated the woman, with a look of terror. "See a guilty, miserable wretch like me? Oh! no, I dare not behold him. I cannot meet his reproaches for the injuries I have done him. Oh! why was I brought to this place? Oh! why was I not suffered to perish in the storm?"

"As your penitence is sincere, so will you meet with his forgiveness."

"Oh! I must not, dare not, hope for it," groaned the guilty woman. "But, oh! I have most severely suffered for the crimes I have committed. But all will soon be over now. Yes; I am dying—dying! But, oh! how shall my guilty soul enter upon that fearful eternity? See—see! my victims enter the room; they grin upon me and appal me with their fiery eyes. The fiends are waiting for their prey. Do not let them come near me. Keep them off, I say! Save me—save me—save me!"

Her emotions became most frightful.

As she thus spoke her eyes glared wildly round the room, and, exhausted with the strength of her sufferings, she sank back on her pillow, and again became insensible.

"She must not be disturbed, sir," said the doctor; "the excitement she has already undergone has been too much for her, and I fear that she cannot long survive. At any rate, I must advise you to suffer her to remain quiet for an hour or two, which is the only chance there is of restoring her."

"Well, be it as you say, sir," observed Ralph Ashton. "The guilty woman has not revealed what she knows in another quarter. Ugh! it makes me shudder to thing of this woman's career. She must see Daisy and Constance, and perhaps their presence may rouse her to tell all."

"It would not be safe for her to see them at present," returned the doctor; "the interview would be a greater shock to her feelings than she has strength to support. Besides, I think that she has really disclosed all she knows."

Ralph shook his head, and, desiring the doctor to exert his utmost skill to save the wretched old woman, and to give him immediate notice if any more dangerous symptoms made their appearance, he retired from the room and rejoined Daisy and Constance, who were most anxiously awaiting him, and eagerly enquired what had taken place.

"And does the doctor entertain any hopes of her recovery?" inquired Constance.

"Why," answered Ralph, "her frame is so debilitated with suffering that he is apprehensive it will ultimately be attended with a fatal result; but still he considers that it is not at all improbable she may linger for a day or two. It is very fortunate she was discovered by the peasants who brought her hither, or she must have perished before the morning."

Constance returned no answer, and she and Daisy then retired for the night.

The night passed away, and at an early hour on the following morning Ralph Ashton went to the room of the suffering woman, whom he found perfectly sensible, and although excessively weak, much more calm and resigned than she had been the night before.

"Oh! sir," she said; "a poor, guilty being like me merits not this kindness; you should rather view me with loathing and disgust."

"Heaven forbid that I should not extend a feeling of mercy towards the contrite sinner," replied Ralph; "but remember that you may shortly be summoned into eternity, and if you have anything more to reveal by which you can make some atonement to those whom you have injured, now is the time to do it, and to endeavour to make your peace."

A convulsive shuddering came over Mrs. Corcoran.

"Oh! I cannot, I dare not, look for mercy from Heaven, whose laws I have so greatly offended," she cried. "I feel that I am lost—lost for ever—and my wretched soul quails with terror at the thought of death. But I have not concealed anything from you—I solemnly swear by Heaven that I have not, and that I have stated nothing but truth, and yet—"

"Yet what?"

"You seek to know the fate of Lady Ashton?"

"Yes."

"I slew her with these hands," Mrs. Corcoran said. "Sir Roland stood by and saw the deed of his own instigation done."

"Great Heaven!" Ralph exclaimed; "this is too terrible!"

"Oh!" Mrs. Corcoran shrieked, "that pang! I grow very weak; give me something to moisten my lips, I implore you; a burning thirst consumes me. Alas! it is useless; my time is come, and nothing can save me! Oh! how heavily do my sins press upon me. What terrors shake my guilty soul and bid me despair!"

"Be comforted, unfortunate and misguided woman," Ralph said, "and pray to Heaven for mercy."

"I cannot—I dare not," gasped forth the wretched woman, with a shudder; "prayer would be blasphemy uttered by lips like mine. Lost—lost! I dare not ask for pardon."

Ralph Ashton administered a cordial to her which after a few minutes seemed to revive her but the significant looks of the doctor convinced him that he apprehended the worst, and that death was close at hand.

"Will you not see Constance and Daisy?" Ralph asked, "that you may be assured of their forgiveness for anything they may have suffered from you?"

"Oh! I dare not see them," cried the dying woman. "How can I encounter their reproaches? How shock their senses by the contemplation of the last sufferings of a miserable wretch like me?"

"They will not reproach you; pity alone will inhabit their breasts towards you."

"Pity!" she repeated. "I am unworthy of it. Horror and disgust is all that I can expect or deserve. But let them come! I will struggle with my feelings and behold them, so that they may witness the poor abject creature which guilt has made me."

Ralph again tried to soothe her, and then quitted the room and hastened to the apartment where Daisy and her companion were anxiously awaiting him.

"Come," he said; "the unfortunate woman has consented to see you; but let me beg of you to control your feelings as much as possible, for any violent excitement occasioned her might terminate fatally, and, even as it is, there do not appear to be any hopes of her recovery."

"Heaven pardon her!" said Daisy and Constance in a breath.

When they entered the room they found that Mrs. Corcoran had just sunk into a temporary doze, and the medical gentleman motioned them to be silent.

They approached nearer the couch, and as they gazed upon the emaciated, agonised, and careworn countenance of the guilty woman they shuddered with terror, while at the same time a feeling of the most fervent compassion filled their bosoms.

In a few minutes a convulsive movement thrilled through Mrs. Corcoran's frame.

She breathed a deep sigh, and, opening her eyes, fixed them with an expression of mingled terror and supplication upon the faces of the girls.

"Oh!" she groaned, "you have come then to witness the last moments of a poor guilty wretch like me. Oh! what terrors appal my soul! What bitter agonies does my conscience inflict as I gaze upon you and remember all that you suffered!"

"Be calm, my poor woman," said Daisy, in gentle and compassionate accents, "and rest assured, as your penitence is sincere, so do we pardon you."

"Oh! this is too good," said the suffering woman; "I do not deserve such words of kindness and pity, and from those too whom I have so greatly injured. But vengeance has overtaken me at last. Oh! yes; I am, indeed, severely punished."

"Say not so," returned Daisy. "Mercy may be extended even at the eleventh hour if the heart is sincere. But is there anything of which you have not disburdened your conscience?"

"No, no; I have confessed all. I have told Mr. Ashton everything. I have been connected with the most atrocious crimes, but I saved the life of one, long supposed to be dead. She may yet be living. Heaven send that she is! Mr. Ashton will tell you—at Mildendale—she—oh!"

She could say no more.

A violent paroxysm of pain seized her, and her reason fled.

The trembling girls could not contemplate her dreadful sufferings without experiencing feelings of the greatest horror, and they were at length prevailed upon by Ralph to leave the room, he remaining behind to watch the result, as the crisis of the old woman's fate seemed rapidly approaching.

## CHAPTER XCI.

### SIR ROLAND FINDS A NEW COMPANION.

SIR ROLAND ASHTON had passed through an extraordinary career, but tracing back through the long list of adventures in which he had been a principal actor, he could find nothing to compare with his present plight.

Without money, without a roof to shelter his benighted head, and without a friend, his position might have excited pity, but the villain deserved none.

An outcast he wandered on, with a woe-begone, hang-dog expression.

In less than a week the once well-dressed, gentlemanly-looking man became a ragged, shoeless, shuffling beggar.

It was almost impossible to recognise him.

Children clung closer to their mothers' gowns as he passed.

Watch-dogs howled and barked at him, and when he mustered up sufficient courage to hobble up to a cottage door and beg a crust of bread or a drink of water, it was given to him grudgingly.

The humble country folk shrank from Sir Roland.

There was something about him and his appearance they could not understand, for his rags were the rags of fine linen, and the torn coat, hanging in strips about his back, still bore the traces of rich and costly style.

The baronet was beset on all sides.

Ralph Ashton, Spring-Heeled Jack, and a dozen other men, independent of the officers of the law, were his enemies.

On the evening of the third day after his struggle with the constables, he stood upon a hill overlooking a village nestling in a pleasant valley.

The sun was going down in a glory of crimson, purple, and gold.

Soft shadows rose from the meadows, and the nightingales made the woods ring with exquisite music.

It was a sublime and touching scene, but Sir Roland had no eyes for it.

He was wondering where he should rest his head that night, and whether, when he awoke, it would not be by the hand of a constable or one of his enemies shaking him rudely by the shoulder.

"I have heard men joke and say that a mortal can die but once," he muttered; "but which among them would not cling to life as I cling to it? Life! It has lost all joys for me, and yet I fear to die, while I curse the very breath I breathe."

He wandered down the hillside, marking how the river that ran through the village darkened as the sun went down.

In the golden light it had been a pretty, laughing, silver stream, but now it reflected nothing but grim, odd-looking objects, which grew more and more uncouth as the darkness increased.

Sir Roland had acquired the habit of searching his pockets with some notion that he might find some hidden or forgotten coin.

He did so mechanically now, and passing his fingers along the binding of his waistcoat, he suddenly came upon something round and hard.

A short time back he would have paid no attention to such a circumstance, but now it was so full of importance to him that he stood still and held his breath.

A shilling—nay, the meanest coin turned out of the mint would be welcome.

Tearing the cloth aside with anxious and trembling fingers, something bright and flashing fell into the palm of his hand.

It was a guinea, and a cry of joy and exultation burst from Sir Roland's lips.

It would have made men who had known him in the days of old wonder to hear that cry.

He had squandered and wasted thousands of such coins, but now one was a fortune to him.

He regarded it with glistening eyes, and fingered it with almost affectionate tenderness.

"No damp road-side bed to-night," he said; "no sneaking under a haystack or into a barn, and up again before daylight for fear some churl of a labourer should discover me and drive me from the premises like a cur. Ha! ha! I'll eat and sleep royally to-night, and leave to-morrow to take care of itself."

And yet he almost feared to enter an inn.

His experiences of the last one he had put up at had left no kindly thoughts in his mind, and he hesitated and pondered on the best course to pursue.

As he did so a man brushed by him.

The stranger was a big, lumbering, broad-shouldered fellow, wearing a huge soft-felt hat, pulled so far down over his brow as to conceal the upper part of his features.

Sir Roland, remembering that it was the custom of country people to greet each other when they met, said—

"Good-night!"

"Oh! good-night," the man said. "You're no inhabitant of these parts, I'll swear."

"How do you know that, my friend?"

"Because you have the voice of a gentleman."

Sir Roland Ashton winced as if this reply did not agree with his feelings.

"Well," he said, forcing a laugh. "I'm poor enough, goodness knows. You would say so, if you could see my rags."

"I can't see them now because it is dark," the fellow replied; "but I had a good look at them while it was light. In point of fact, I've had my eye on you since seven o'clock."

Sir Roland felt his heart beat against his side.

"You have followed me?" he said, faintly. "What for?"

"Because you looked tired out, hungry, and hunted, as I have been myself many and many a time."

The baronet breathed more freely.

Perhaps he had fallen in with a friend in need, and if so, nothing could be better.

"Well," he said, "I'll own that I have had

rather a rough time of it. I was just wondering where I could sleep to-night."

"I suppose you have no money?" the other growled.

"No," Sir Roland replied, clenching the guinea in his hand and transferring it slowly to his pocket. "If I had I should not remain long in my present miserable state."

"Ah!" the fellow rejoined. "Well, you can follow me, if you like. I suppose you are not over and above particular where you sleep?"

"No," Sir Roland replied, laughing. "I have envied a dog in its kennel and a horse in its stable."

"And yet," said the stranger, "I'll be bound that you need not tax your memory much to go back to the days when you rested your head upon down—eh, Sir Roland?"

"You know me, then?" the baronet cried, starting suddenly and violently.

"Only by recognising you from a description issued by those troublesome fellows, the constables."

"In that case I may as well give myself up," Sir Roland gasped.

"Any fool can do that," the stranger said, laughing hoarsely; "but it takes a clever man to give the traps the slip and set them at defiance. Now, I take you to be a clever man, Sir Roland, and you won't do anything so silly as to open your arms to the constables' claws."

"But what chance have I of escaping from them if every man can recognise me?" Sir Roland demanded.

"Bah!" said the man; "not one in a hundred would do so. It is part of my business to look at everybody, for the simple reason that I often fancy everybody is looking at me. But, come, we lose time. Follow me, and I'll show you the way to a place of shelter, so secure that you will be able to laugh at the constables, though they were as thick as the dust under your feet."

Sir Roland Ashton hesitated and hung back.

Treacherous himself, he feared treachery.

"You will not deceive me?" he said.

"Why, man, you talk like a fool!" the man said. "If I were so willed, could I not take you prisoner myself, or bring these village people about your ears like a nest of hornets? I suppose that you have lived long enough to know that a cry of murder acts like magic on such people as these?"

"Yes," Sir Roland replied, shuddering.

"Then why doubt me?"

"Because I do not know who you are."

"Come a little nearer, and I will soon set your mind at ease on that point."

Seeing that Sir Roland still hesitated, the man advanced towards the baronet and whispered something in his ear.

"Ha!" the baronet replied, starting. "I have heard of the gang."

"Gentlemen, if you please."

"Gentlemen, if it suits you better," Sir Roland returned, with a touch of irony in his voice. "So your name is Joe Rollins?"

"So I am called, and that is quite as good as any other name for you to know me by."

"I do not wish to dispute that," Sir Roland replied; "but your communication still remains a mystery to me. In what way can I serve you, and —and the gentlemen?"

"You are a scholar?"

"Granted."

"Well, that is just what we require," Joe Rollins replied. "Come—come! Let us delay no longer."

"One word more," said Sir Roland. "How comes it that you have not taken up your quarters nearer London?"

"Because here we excite no suspicion."

Sir Roland hesitated no longer, but stepping to Joe Rollins' side kept pace with him.

"I must explain one thing to you," Rollins said, as they walked along. "I have been away for some time doing a stroke of business, so if by chance we should find a little difficulty in being admitted to Loddon's retreat don't be surprised, but leave all to me."

With these words Joe Rollins and the baronet once more hurried on their way, and soon gained the end of the village without meeting a single person on their road.

Mr. Loddon's house was situated in a secluded spot.

The place itself was comfortable in its external appearance, and not at all likely to excite any particular notice or suspicion.

The inmate, who had several men living with him dressed in the garb of servants, was supposed to be a person of some property, and who, having met with some early misfortunes in life, had been induced to take to this comparative life of seclusion.

He was constantly attired in the most sober style of dress, and the general seriousness of his aspect whenever he walked abroad excited a feeling of respect in all who beheld him.

Little, however, did anyone imagine that he was the author of some of the most daring robberies that had been committed in the neighbourhood, and that his house was the depository of stolen property.

Joe Rollins approached the house and looked up at the windows in front, but no light appeared in any of them.

He then walked round to the back, where he beheld the rays of a lamp glimmering in one of the windows.

"All right," he said to Sir Roland; "they have not all retired to rest, and I shall be able to obtain admittance in a minute or so."

He approached the bell-pull and rang a peal that reverberated through the house, and then waited impatiently for a reply.

The light immediately disappeared from the window, and all remained silent.

"Ah!" said Joe Rollins, "ever cautious. They do not expect friendly visitors at this time of the night, and, therefore, pretend not to hear the summons. But this will not do; I must compel them to answer me."

He again pulled the bell with greater violence than before.

The light once more appeared in the window, which was shortly afterwards cautiously opened, and a man protruded his head, demanding who was there and what he wanted.

"Admittance!" Rollins replied.

"Admittance!" repeated the man. "That is rather a strange request for a stranger, my master, and at this hour of the night. This is not a public inn, and, if you are a traveller, no doubt you may gain accommodation in the village."

"I am no stranger," Rollins returned. "Do you not know me?"

"Know you! How should I?"

"But I know you, Will Loddon, so come

# SPRING-HEELED JACK,

## THE TERROR OF LONDON.

"SIR ROLAND," SAID SPRING-HEELED JACK, "THIS IS A MERRY NIGHT FOR US TO MEET."

No. 27.

down, and do not keep me waiting here all night."

"Ah! who are you that knows my name?"

"Come down and see."

"Are you a friend or foe?"

"A friend!"

"The word, then?"

"Secrecy."

"Your name?"

"Joe Rollins."

"Ah! I know your voice now," said Loddon. "Wait but a moment, and I will open the door to you."

"All right."

The fellow retired from the window, after having extinguished the light and stretched out his head to ascertain whether it was indeed "all right," and the next instant Joe Rollins heard his footsteps descending the stairs.

Shortly afterwards the chain was removed from the inside of the door, which was opened by Loddon.

"Why, it is Joe Rollins, sure enough," he said; "but who is that with you?"

"Sir Roland Ashton," Rollins replied. "I am sure you will make him welcome, for the traps are as anxious to get hold of him as they are of me."

"Humph!" said Loddon, dubiously. "Well, I suppose he may enter."

"Where's Sam?" Rollins asked, as he and Sir Roland stepped over the threshold.

"In the snuggery."

"All right; lead us to him.

Loddon obeyed, without making use of any more observations.

The "snuggery," as Mr. Loddon had called it, was a rather large, and certainly not uncomfortably-furnished, underground apartment, which was approached by a secret passage, and afforded every facility for escape.

Here Loddon and his companions were wont to assemble at certain hours to exult in their lawless successes and the good things with which they took good care to be always amply supplied.

On the entrance of Joe Rollins and Sir Roland some men started up in amazement, as if they could scarcely believe the evidence of their eyes.

"Is it possible, Joe," one of them cried, "that I see you again?"

"Aye! Sam Clinker," answered the latter. "I daresay you never again expected to do so, unless it was to see me mount the scaffold."

"And have you never been out of the neighbourhood since your escape from Newgate?" asked Sam Clinker.

"No."

"It was rather a bold step of yours."

"Perhaps it was; but am I welcome here?"

"To be sure you are."

"You will afford me concealment?"

"You cannot doubt it; and right glad am I to see you safe. It is some time since we saw each other before."

"It is," returned Joe Rollins. "But I daresay we shall not part again in a hurry. Now let me introduce my friend, Sir Roland Ashton. I know you will give him shelter and food for a time, for he has promised to become one of us."

"He must take the oath," Sam Clinker growled.

"Of course," Loddon added.

Sir Roland bowed in acknowledgment of these remarks.

"I become one of you willingly," he said; "and I can only hope that the constables will not scent me out."

"I hope not, my boy," said Loddon, heartily pressing his hand. "The traps will not think of looking for you here, for you know that I am beyond suspicion. But, come—drink and refresh yourself, and then we will talk further of this business."

"Ah!" Sir Roland cried, taking a seat at the table, "I am in excellent condition to accept of your invitation, so here goes. Success to our future undertakings, and destruction to every sneaking cur!"

"Bravo!" cried Joe Rollins. "We all heartily respond to that toast. Ha! ha! ha! How little do the fools suspect the real character of the solemn and melancholy-looking gentleman, to whom they all bow in respect when he approaches them!"

Sir Roland laughed, though in his heart he felt very much ill at ease.

The men he was surrounded by were fierce, swarthy-looking fellows, whose eyes watched his every movement.

He drank deeply, and then, feeling compelled to say something more, he asked the name of the village he had wandered to.

"It is called Mildendale," Loddon replied. "You must have seen the Hall as you came along."

"I saw a fine and noble building at the end of a magnificent avenue of oaks," Sir Roland said.

"Then you saw Mildendale Hall."

A silence fell upon the men, their eyes moved restlessly from Sir Roland Ashton to Loddon, as if they wished to say something but feared to speak in the baronet's presence.

"Rollins," Loddon said, suddenly, "a word with you aside."

"A hundred if you like," Joe Rollins said.

The two men carried on an inaudible conversation at one end of the "snuggery" for some minutes, and then Loddon spoke aloud.

"What think you of the plan?" he asked.

"It is a most excellent one," Joe Rollins replied, "and Sir Roland is the very man to help us to carry it out."

"Then let him take the oath," Loddon said, "and he shall then hear all about it."

A fearful oath was administered to the baronet—so horrible, indeed, that it cannot be repeated—and at the end of the ceremony he was duly installed as one of Mr. James Loddon's followers.

"Now, Sir Roland," said the owner of the house, "I am going to show you how I can appreciate the services of a man true and useful to me. To-morrow shall see you as well clad as ever you were in your life. Money shall be no longer a stranger to your pockets, and, moreover, I promise that if you use the tact and judgment which should come natural to such a man as yourself, you shall move once more in good society."

Sir Roland made no verbal reply, but he opened his eyes wide and elevated his brows in mingled amazement, doubt, and bewilderment.

"These things come to my ears as fables," he said. "Pray tell me what I am to do to deserve all these favours?"

"That you shall know before many hours have passed over your head," James Loddon replied. "At present ask no more questions, but drink and make merry. There is no lack of good wine in the cellar, so let the glass go round."

It went round so frequently that soon Sir

Roland's senses began to reel, and yet it seemed strange to him that the liquor had no apparent effect on the rest of the men seated at the table.

At last, whilst in the act of raising a flagon to his lips, he slipped from his chair and fell beneath the table.

A mild burst of laughter followed this mishap, but James Loddon held up his hand.

"Silence!" he said. "I thought I would give him a soothing draught, but he may not be asleep. This man is as cunning as a fox and as slippery as an eel. Marked you not these things in his eyes?"

"Aye, that I did, before I brought him hither," Joe Rollins replied. "So much the better for us."

"Or so much the worse, perhaps," Sam Clinker growled. "I don't care for strangers. We might as well keep open house for every worn-out baronet, or for all the beggars in the land who happen to have aristocratic blood in their veins."

"Peace, fool—peace!" James Loddon replied. "You would cut a handsome figure and play a pretty part in the drama which will be presently acted. If Sir Roland turns white-livered he dies. If he behaves—ahem!—like a man he may count on jingling a thousand guineas. Bear him up to bed, lads, and see that he is made comfortable. To-morrow I will tell him what is required of him."

## CHAPTER XCII.

### JACOB BUTLER REFUSES TO DO JEM BASKER'S BIDDING—THE THREAT—THE BITER BIT.

JACOB BUTLER, we have left you far too long in the cold, and our apologies are due to you, considering the important part you are destined to play in our story.

Ted Nickells, the landlord, wary and weasel-like as he was, took care that Jacob should not fall in Mrs. Corcoran's way.

When the hag left in search of Sir Roland he felt somewhat relieved, for he was not particularly anxious for the company of either.

It was Jem Basker who was likely to bring him most profit, and, therefore, Sir Roland might "go hang" as the saying went, for all the landlord of the Chequers cared.

Jacob Butler occupied a little pokey room, and whenever he attempted to leave it Ted Nickells was sure to arrive with the news that constables were watching the house.

This intelligence acted like a talisman of evil on the unhappy Jacob, and threw him into a state of abject alarm.

"But look here," he said one morning; "I must get away somehow. I have only a few shillings left, and where I am to get more is a mystery to me."

"Don't trouble your head about money matters," Ted Nickells said, with the air of a man moved to pity. "We can make that all right one of these days. I wonder a smart fellow like you don't take a situation."

The "smart fellow" looked dubiously down at his thin legs.

"I am wasting away," he said, "and shall soon be nothing better than a walking skeleton."

"Bosh!" Ted Nickells replied, encouragingly. "Don't get such stupid notions into your head. Now, what would you say if I were to find a man who might—I don't say for certain that he would—take you for his servant, pay you well, feed you well, and treat you well as long as you were true and faithful to him?"

"I had a good master once," Jacob Butler replied, shaking his head sadly, "but I made a fool of myself."

"That's nothing uncommon to human nature," Nickells said. "'Once bitten, twice shy,' says the old adage. If you wish for a situation, I'll speak to the gentleman I have in my mind, and let you know in an hour or two."

Jacob Butler's heart was too full to utter his thanks in a straightforward manner, but he contrived to mutter them out in some kind of fashion; and when Ted Nickells left him Jacob covered his face with his hands and gave vent to a flow of grateful tears.

"Who," he murmured, "would expect to find so much kindness in a man of his appearance? Well, well, how often are we deceived! What joy it would be if he were to introduce me to a man who would take me away from these scenes of misery! Ah! how I would work. Wages? Bah! What care I for them, so that I breathe the pure air, and eat the bread of honest labour."

Poor Jacob!

Little did he know what was in store for him.

In the very midst of his hopes and enthusiasm Ted Nickells returned.

"I am very sorry to tell you," he said, gravely, "that those two confounded constables, Catchpole and Grabham, with a man I do not know, are dodging about my premises again, and they evidently suspect that you are hidden here."

Jacob Butler turned as white as a sheet and clasped his trembling hands.

"You will not give me up to them?" he gasped. "I would rather die than fall into their clutches again."

"You may trust me," Ted Nickells replied. "This is not the first scrape I have been in by many a one, and I always find a way out. Ha! ha! Well, Jacob, my boy, don't fluster yourself about such a trifle, for I am the bearer of good news, as well as that which appears to annoy you."

"And that is—" Jacob began, feebly.

"That is, I am going to introduce you to a—er—a gentleman, who requires to have a useful man," Ted Nickells interposed.

"And does he live far away?" Jacob Butler inquired, in accents of trembling anxiety.

"Miles away."

"Thank Heaven for that!"

"Ah!" said Ted Nickells, "I have noticed that London does not seem to agree with you."

"I hate it—I abominate it," Jacob cried. "I would rather occupy a mud hut on the summit of a mountain than live in the midst of this great city's so-called splendour."

"Of course," said Mr. Nickells, slowly and gravely, "you would like Mrs. Corcoran to share the hut with you?"

Jacob Butler nearly fainted.

"What was that you said?" he asked, as if he could not believe his ears.

"I repeat," said Ted Nickells, speaking slowly and distinctly, "that you would not care to live anywhere without the charming Mrs. Corcoran?"

"Where is she?" Jacob demanded, in a hoarse, startled whisper.

"Oh! never mind where she is now," replied the landlord of the Chequers, tapping the side of his nose with his forefinger. "I happen to know where to lay hands on her whenever I want her, so you must be contented with that."

Jacob Butler felt that his hair was rising slowly on end.

"Lor' a' mercy !" he gasped ; "I would rather perish on the rack than meet with that old woman again."

"Just so," Ted Nickells observed. "But you needn't scare yourself with the idea that I am going to bring Mrs. Corcoran to you, unless—"

"Unless what ?"

"You compel me to do so," Ted Nickells said, shaking his head waggishly.

"I—I—I don't understand what you mean," Jacob Butler stammered.

"How dull you are !" Ted Nickells returned. "You must be aware that, although I am one of the kindest-hearted men in the world, I don't board, lodge, and sleep people here for nothing, or almost next to nothing. No, Mr. Butler ; I am not quite such a fool. And with regard to yourself, I have found you a master who is, in a manner of speaking, in partnership with me."

"Eh ! what's that ?" Jacob Butler gasped. "In partnership with you ? Then he's a—"

"A what ?" Ted Nickells interposed. "Don't let your tongue run away with your discretion, friend Butler."

All Jacob's golden dreams melted away into mist in a moment.

Ted Nickells saw the change in his face and laughed.

"You have to choose between being bundled into the street and left at the mercy of Mrs. Corcoran or the constables," he said ; "or— Oh ! here is the very gentleman I was speaking to you about."

At that moment Jem Basker entered the room.

"I'm sick and tired of this idle life," he said, as he threw his furry cap upon the ground and himself on a bench. "Nickells, if I don't start again I shall get rusty and my bones will creak as I walk about."

"What a fellow you are, Jem !" said Ted Nickells. "Well, I don't want to detain you any longer at the Chequers than I can help ; but the great question is, have you found a man to travel with you ?"

"No," Jem Basker replied, surlily.

"Then," cried Ted Nickells, as he pointed exultingly at Jacob, "I have found one for you. There is the very article you want."

"Humph !" Jem Basker growled. "Can you recommend him ?"

"I can," Nickells replied. "He is a gentle-minded, obedient man ; but not the one to stick at trifles. He knows his way about the world, and a trick or two, I can tell you."

"I should like to know for what purpose I am to be employed," Jacob Butler said, eyeing Jem Basker with disgust. "It has just occurred to my mind that the situation might not suit me."

"Shall I tell him ?" Jem Basker asked, looking at the landlord of the Chequers.

"Yes."

"Now just you attend to me, and ask no questions," Basker said, shaking his brawny fist at Jacob Butler. "I suppose you know by this time that you are as good as a prisoner here ?"

"I know it now," Jacob faltered, "and it has dawned upon me that the stories about the constables watching the house have been hatched up to keep me in a perpetual state of fever."

"Ha !" cried Ted Nickells, thrusting his hand under his coat. "Would you dare to doubt my word ?"

"Leave him to me," Jem Basker said. "If he requires tickling under the ribs I am the man to do it. Now then, attend to me, my tulip. You are going to travel with me."

"If I think proper, I suppose ?"

"Don't interrupt or you will find yourself in my bad books," Jem Basker said. "We are going to Mildendale for the purpose of keeping watch over the Hall and to lay our feelers on a boy, if possible."

"I'll have nothing to do with such business," Jacob replied, stoutly. "Do your dirty work yourself, and let me go. I'll run the risk of being caught."

"Fool !—idiot !" Ted Nickells hissed. "You have sealed your own fate. Consent to Basker's terms, or—"

"Or what ?" Jacob Butler demanded.

"You die !" Jem Basker cried, in a voice of thunder.

As he leaped to his feet he drew a long knife from under his jacket and flashed its blade unpleasantly near Jacob's throat.

"What !" Jacob cried, starting back, "would you murder me ?'

"Aye ! as I would stick a pig or twist the neck of a pigeon," Basker replied. "I am not the man to dally with trifles. You either go with me and do my bidding or you go out of the world. The choice is yours, not mine."

This speech took Jacob Butler's breath away.

He now saw that he was in the hands of two desperate villains, who would stay at no point to gain their end.

Jacob felt a new nature growing within him.

With a sudden rush he darted forward and hurled himself upon Jem Basker.

The ruffian, thrown off his guard by this unexpected attack, slipped and fell heavily.

But Jem Basker retained his hold on the handle of the knife, and he struck furiously at Jacob Butler, who, however, contrived to ward off the blows and at last to secure the weapon.

"Nickells—Nickells !" Basker howled, "he is choking me. Help—help ! Strike him with something heavy. Knock him down, or I am done for ! Oh—oh ! I am stabbed !"

"Bear witness that he brought it on himself," Jacob cried, holding the blood-stained knife aloft. "What I did was in self-defence. Back—back ! out of my way, or I will serve you in the same manner."

Jem Basker rolled about the floor in an agony of pain, and Ted Nickells and Jacob Butler stood face to face, glaring at each other like a pair of rival tigers.

"I give you warning that I will run you through if you attempt to block my way to the door," Jacob Butler yelled. "Let me depart peacefully, or I will leave you a corpse."

Ted Nickells replied with a low, grating laugh.

Stepping hastily back against the wall he pressed his hand upon something near the window, and almost instantly afterwards the portion of the floor upon which Jacob Butler stood began to descend rapidly.

The wretched man dropped the knife, and, flinging up his arms, uttered a wild shriek of despair.

That cry was followed by a dull, thudding sound, and then Ted Nickells remained alone to attend to Jem Basker.

Ferocious triumph gleamed from the eyes of the landlord of the Chequers.

"Are you much hurt?" he asked, sinking down at Basker's side.

"No, no; it is only a flesh wound—so courage! I would have spared that white-livered dog, but nothing can save him now. He has brought his death on his own head."

## CHAPTER XCIII.

### SIR ROLAND LEARNS WHAT IS REQUIRED OF HIM.

WHEN Sir Roland Ashton opened his eyes he found that he was in a warm and comfortable bed.

"Ah! this is delicious," he said, as he stretched out his limbs. "This is a sweet reward for all that I have undergone."

A glance round the room showed him that it was handsomely and expensively furnished.

Many of the articles were of great value, and the walls were hung with pictures painted by the old masters.

"I wonder how Loddon became possessed of all these things," he mused. "Here wealth and luxury go hand in hand, and yet it would seem that Loddon and his associates are nothing better than common robbers."

His reflections were disturbed by a light footstep, and in another moment James Loddon entered the room.

"How fare you this morning, Sir Roland?" he asked, folding his arms. "The hour is late, but I let you sleep on, thinking that a long rest would do you good."

"And it has," the baronet replied. "Save that an old wound gives me an occasional twinge, I almost feel my old self again."

"That is good news," Loddon replied, wheeling a chair to the bedside and sitting down. "A few words with you, Sir Roland, and then I will leave you to dress. You will find breakfast prepared in the room in which you met my followers."

Sir Roland murmured his thanks, and then, posing himself in an easy attitude, announced that he was ready to listen to anything James Loddon had to say.

"You may remember that we spoke of Mildendale Hall?" he said.

"Yes," Sir Roland replied. "I remember that perfectly well, but I have but hazy notions of what followed."

"You must blame my good old wine for that," Loddon returned, smiling. "But now to business."

"Yes—yes," said Sir Roland, eagerly. "I am all attention."

"I am glad to hear that," James Loddon replied. "I admire the man who is willing and ready to risk even his life in doing a good stroke of work."

Sir Roland's face fell a little.

The last remark jarred a little upon his feelings, but not liking to show that it did so, he composed his features as quickly as possible.

"My principal reason for making this place my residence," said James Loddon, speaking slowly and distinctly, "was to make a raid on Mildendale Hall and to strip it of its treasure, which is reported to be immense.

"I have been put to much expense, but I can lay hold of no information which will be of service to me; in other words, I have failed to procure a plan of the Hall. This, among other things, you must get for me, Sir Roland."

"I fail to see my way to do that," the baronet said, shaking his head dubiously. "In the first place, how am I, an utter stranger to the neighbourhood and its inhabitants, to obtain admission to the Hall?"

"By strategy."

"By strategy!" Sir Roland Ashton repeated in amazement.

"Yes," James Loddon replied, calmly. "That is the only way. Lord Mildendale lives the life of a hermit, and almost invariably refuses to see anybody; but, Sir Roland, you who have moved in good society must be possessed of the tact and address which will remove the difficulty."

Sir Roland lay still, and thought the matter out for some moments.

"Of course I am willing to do my best," he said at length; "but what if the recluse refuses to see me?"

"You must persist in calling upon him until he does," James Loddon replied. "In less than an hour you will be provided with everything necessary for a man of rank; money, horses, servants will be at your disposal, and you have only to give the matter your entire consideration to make success certain."

"There must be some reason why Lord Mildendale keeps himself so close a prisoner," Sir Roland said. "Can you give me nothing to make a handle of—some information which would give me an excuse for introducing myself?"

"I was coming to that," James Loddon replied. "There is something, but you must be careful how you make use of it. Lord Mildendale grieves in solitude for two reasons. He drove his wife from the Hall, or got rid of her otherwise, and his child, a boy, was stolen in his infancy."

"Tell me the story, or, at least, all that you know of it from beginning to end," Sir Roland said.

James Loddon did so, and then a quiet smile stole over Sir Roland's face.

"The path grows a little clearer," he said. "Now let me speak."

"Yes; go on."

"I must not remain here."

"Not remain here?" James Loddon repeated, frowning. "Pray, why not, my friend?"

"Because it would be bad policy," Sir Roland replied.

"I do not see that."

"But I do," Sir Roland replied. "As I moved to and fro people would grow accustomed to seeing me. Lord Mildendale might suspect something and set his servants to watch me."

"That is true," James Loddon replied. "I never thought of that. Your head is screwed on the right way, Sir Roland."

The baronet smiled at this compliment, and then went on speaking.

"If a house was found for me a few miles away," he said, "I could suddenly appear as a gentleman lately returned from abroad and who desires to go into society. I could make my calls in the ordinary way—of course, using an assumed name—and let you know the result."

"Capital!" James Loddon said, rubbing his hands. "The only difficulty I see is to procure a house; but I daresay that can be got over with a little trouble. Ah! an idea strikes me."

"If it is a good one let me hear it," said Sir Roland.

"I don't think you will say it is a bad one," Loddon returned. "Not far from Dagenham there stands an old mansion which has remained uninhabited for many years, and consequently it needs repairing badly. The agent of the estate has attempted to let the house, but in vain—"

"Why?" Sir Roland interposed.

"Because foolish people declare that the mansion is haunted."

"Foolish people speak the truth sometimes," Sir Roland said.

"Surely you don't believe in ghosts?" James Loddon rejoined, laughing.

"I don't know," the baronet replied, shuddering in spite of himself. "That is a question I would rather not go into at present. Please proceed, for I am anxious to hear your plan throughout."

"It is simply this," James Loddon said. "The ruined mansion could be hired at a low rental, and once there you could proceed to carry out my instructions."

"I agree," Sir Roland said.

"Then you had better go and look over the place this very day," Loddon said. "I will leave you now, and everything shall be in readiness for your journey soon after noontide."

Loddon was walking slowly towards the door when Sir Roland called him back.

"What is the name of the man who will go with me?" he asked.

"You cannot have a better or bolder fellow than Joe Rollins."

"And what name shall I assume?"

"Oh! any name will serve," Loddon replied. "Suppose you call yourself Reginald Fernie?"

"Yes; that will do," Sir Roland said; "and now I will rise and prepare for the work before me."

When Sir Roland Ashton had breakfasted Loddon called him into another room, and showed him a superb suit of clothes, a rapier, silver-mounted pistols, and a purse well filled with gold.

"You may consider all these yours," Loddon said. "Make the best use of them, but don't be afraid of spending money. Whenever you run short send to me, and I will forward a fresh supply."

"Nothing could be better," Sir Roland said. "But," he added, pointing to the lace-trimmed tunic and other garments, "these things do not appear to be quite new."

James Loddon passed his hand to his chin as he turned towards the baronet and looked him steadily in the eyes.

"No, Sir Roland," he said, "they are not quite new. They belonged to—er—well, a friend of mine, who had the misfortune to die before his time."

"Indeed!"

"Yes, he was incautious, and disregarded all my warnings," Loddon said. "Poor, reckless fellow, it was his own fault entirely."

"You—you killed him?"

"Dear me!—no," Loddon said, in a tone of mild reproach. "I don't do things in that way unless absolutely driven to it by an act of treachery. My friend overstepped the mark of boldness, and was hanged for asking a rich farmer for his purse."

Sir Roland Ashton understood what James Loddon's words implied, and strange thoughts flashed through his brain.

How often had he overstepped the mark of boldness, and was woe to be the end?

Come it would, as he knew it must; but he drove it from his thoughts, and now that fortune seemed to smile on him again he was ready to go back to his old ways and sink still deeper into the pit of sin and crime.

Yet Sir Roland did not relish the idea of attiring himself in the clothes of a man who had been strangled like a dog; but he had no alternative left, and retired to make himself ready.

In about half an hour Joe Rollins appeared, mounted on a horse, and leading another by the bridle.

Rollins was dressed as a groom, and looked very neat and smart in his new character.

James Loddon, having given Sir Roland full instructions how to find his way to Dagenham, shook him heartily by the hand, and watched him until he turned a corner of the road and disappeared from view.

"If," said Loddon, as he turned into the house, "that he knew I have given Joe instructions to shoot him down should he attempt to slip away, Sir Roland would not feel so comfortable in his mind nor look so happy."

At the same moment Sir Roland Ashton was turning that very idea over in his mind.

"I must play my part well until I get enough money to escape the country," he said to himself. "With all Loddon's cunning I will make use of him in such a way he little dreams of."

Sir Roland had been furnished with a disguise for his face in the shape of a pair of whiskers, which he put on for fear of detection.

The journey to Dagenham was a long one, and when the horses grew tired their riders put up at an inn to rest and refresh.

They were astir early the next morning and reached Dagenham just as three o'clock was boomed out from an old church tower.

Sir Roland then went in search of the estate-agent.

Fain would he have gone alone, but Joe Rollins stuck to him like a leech, and it suddenly dawned upon the baronet's mind that the man never intended to leave him for a moment.

Reginald Fernie, as Sir Roland Ashton now called himself, lost no time in making himself known to the agent—a white-haired, business-like old gentleman named Stanley.

"I may as well tell you, Mr. Fernie," he said, smiling, "that an absurd notion has taken possession of the silly folks that the house is haunted, and no man, woman, or child will go near it after nightfall."

"So much the better," said Sir Roland, so eagerly that Mr. Stanley stared at him in astonishment. "That is—of course—I mean that, being a man of quiet habits, I do not care to be disturbed."

"Just so," said Stanley. "Well, Mr. Fernie, under the circumstances I can let the house and grounds for two hundred pounds per annum, and that sum includes the lake about a mile away, where, if you care for such sport, you will find excellent fishing and shooting."

"I am delighted with the prospect of taking up my residence in the neighbourhood," Sir Roland replied. "I consider the rental extremely low, and will at once see about having the necessary repairs and alterations attended to, and then my furniture can follow. Shall I pay you a deposit, Mr. Stanley?"

"Oh! dear no; that is not at all necessary," the agent replied, rubbing his hands with delight at finding so ready and amiable a tenant. "All I will ask you to do is to sign an agreement that you will take Cypress House for one year at least."

"Certainly, Mr. Stanley," Sir Roland replied. "A pen and a dip of ink, if you please."

As soon as the agreement was signed the agent produced a bottle of prime old port and two glasses.

"Your health, Mr. Fernie!" he said, holding the ruby-coloured fluid up to the light. "I hope to have the honour of your acquaintance for many years to come."

"That sentiment finds an echo in my heart," Sir Roland said, as the rim of the glass touched his lips. "You are a married man, Mr. Stanley?"

"Yes."

"Then I drink to you and your family," Sir Roland said. "May they live long, and be happy and prosperous!"

All this time Joe Rollins, rigid and motionless, had mounted guard on the other side of the door; and when Mr. Stanley bowed Sir Roland out, he noticed that the man's face wore a rather queer expression.

A cynical grin lurked under the corners of his mouth, and his eyes danced with mirth which he could not conceal.

"Aha!" said Mr. Stanley, good-humouredly; "I see which way the wind blows. I suppose you would like a glass of wine, my fine fellow?"

"A flagon of good old brown ale would suit me better," Joe Rollins replied. "Wine only tickles my throat and aggravates my stomach."

Mr. Stanley laughed as if he thought this was a good joke.

"You shall have it," he said, ringing a bell.

A servant appeared in answer to the summons.

"Mary," said the agent, "show Mr. Fernie's man the way to the kitchen, and let him have such refreshment as he requires."

"I would rather have it here or go without," said Joe Rollins, glancing at Sir Roland Ashton.

"My servant has queer ways, and I regret to say that I humour him in them," Sir Roland observed, as he marked Mr. Stanley's look of astonishment.

"An old and trusted servant, I suppose?" the agent said.

"Yes," Sir Roland replied. "He saved my life, and what else can I be otherwise than grateful to him?"

"Certainly not," said Mr. Stanley, grasping Joe Rollins' hand and pressing it warmly. "Mary, fetch some beer, and mind that it comes from the best barrel."

Joe Rollins winked at the girl so meaningly that she blushed up to the roots of her hair, and bounced indignantly away to do her master's bidding.

"Oh! by-the-way, Mr. Stanley," Sir Roland said, while Joe Rollins was pouring about half-a-gallon of ale down his capacious throat, "you have not provided me with the keys of Cypress House."

"I will do so at once," the agent replied, darting back into his office. "Here they are, my dear Mr. Fernie. I daresay you will find the locks a little rusty, but a little oil will soon put them all right."

The sun was going down when Sir Roland Ashton and Joe Rollins left the agent and made their way at a foot-pace in the direction of Cypress House.

They reached it in about a quarter of an hour, and, tethering their horses to a tree, ascended the dismantled terrace and stared long and steadily at the ghostly-looking house.

"A curious place this," said Joe Rollins. "I don't wonder that people swear it is haunted. It is old and ugly enough to be anything."

"You are right," said Sir Roland; "but I think we have stood here long enough. Let us have a look at the interior."

"Ha!" Joe Rollins ejaculated.

"What is the matter?" Sir Roland Ashton demanded in a tone of anger.

"I thought I saw a horrible face peering from yonder turret window," Rollins replied.

"A face!" Sir Roland gasped. "What kind of face was it?"

"To describe it baffles me," Rollins said. "I never saw anything like it in my life before."

"It must have been fancy," Sir Roland returned, speaking as if he did not mean what he said.

"It may have been," Rollins remarked. "Perchance it was a shadow caused by the sunlight dancing in and out of the ivy."

"Most likely," said Sir Roland. "At all events, if we find a stranger here we will give him notice to quit in a summary manner. Now, then, to open the door."

Selecting the largest key from the bunch, he inserted it in the lock.

It yielded easily, and a puzzled expression passed over Sir Roland's face.

"This is strange," he said; "the lock seems to have been repaired lately."

"Then somebody must have taken advantage of the ghost story and is living rent free," Joe Rollins said.

"Get your pistols ready," said Sir Roland, "for we may find an awkward customer to deal with. If you see a man, teach him a lesson he will not easily forget."

Joe Rollins turned towards Sir Roland with a smile.

"You seem inclined to leave all the glory to me," he said. "If there be a stranger here he may be some poor devil of a tramp, and to fire at such poor game would be waste of powder and shot."

Sir Roland Ashton muttered something under his breath which Joe Rollins did not hear.

The baronet was alarmed at the notion of a hideous face at the window and at the good condition the lock was in.

For the life of him Sir Roland could not get Spring-Heeled Jack out of his head, and yet that strange being had troubled him so little of late that it was scarcely probable that he had mysteriously found his way to Cypress House.

"Pooh—pooh!" Sir Roland muttered to himself. "I shall be afraid of my own shadow next."

With this he turned the key in the lock and threw the door open.

Rumbling echoes like distant thunder came up from the lower regions of the ancient house, and fully a minute passed away before Sir Roland Ashton and Joe Rollins crossed the threshold.

"Hullo!" Rollins exclaimed, "visitors have been here lately. Look at the footmarks in the dust."

Sir Roland did look, and was at once convinced that at least half-a-dozen men had crossed through the hall within the period of a week.

"Strange!" he said, looking askance at Joe Rollins.

"It's more than strange," Rollins returned, "it's deucedly ugly. These fellows may think of calling again when we don't want them."

"We must prepare against that," Sir Roland said. "Now to search the house. Keep your eyes open."

"Leave that to me," Rollins replied. "I am wide awake, and no mistake."

Deep and solemn were the shadows which fell upon the paneled rooms as the baronet and his so-called servant passed through them.

With noiseless footsteps they wandered hither and thither, peering into nook and cranny, glancing up winding staircases and down dark places, leading goodness only knew where.

At last they came to a small room built into the wall of one of the turrets.

This apartment was about nine feet square, and the daylight was only admitted by an aperture pierced into the wall, through which nothing larger than a rat could crawl.

Admittance was made by a solid oak door, fitted with an enormous lock and bolts, sufficiently strong to have defied the bodily strength of a regiment of soldiers.

"Ah!" said Sir Roland, with evident satisfaction. "I will make this my private study. It is quite large enough for me."

"But not large enough for us both," Joe Rollins observed, meaningly.

"You can choose another room, my best of friends."

"Sir Roland Ashton," Joe Rollins said, "I will be plain with you. James Loddon furnished me with such instructions as to make that arrangement impossible."

A heavy frown swept across Sir Roland's brow.

"So," he said, "I may take it that you were sent to spy upon my actions?"

"No," Joe Rollins returned. "I was told to take great care of you."

"It is one and the same thing," Sir Roland said, contemptuously.

"And if it be so, what then?"

Sir Roland Ashton remained silent.

"It is scarcely worth while you and I having words over the matter," he said at length. "When I come to turn matters over in my mind, I cannot but think that James Loddon is right. He knows little of me, and has trusted me with much."

"Just so, Sir Roland; that's the sensible way of looking at it."

"Well," the baronet continued, "we will endeavour to make room for us both, and so—"

He ceased speaking and started as a peal of thunder boomed across the landscape.

"Another storm," he said. "See how dark the air has grown!"

"We must look to the horses or they may be struck by lightning," Joe Rollins said. "Follow me quickly, or the chances are we shall be drenched to the skin."

Just then another peal of thunder, much louder and nearer than the first, rolled about the old house, and the heavy clouds, shutting out the last lingering rays of the sun, brought night upon their sable, storm-laden wings.

Joe Rollins, with the caution of a man ready for any emergency, had brought a small lantern and a flint and steel with him.

"Steady—steady!" he said, as he felt his way along with his hands in advance of his face. "Wait a moment, and I will get a light."

Sir Roland Ashton saw sparks fly as the steel struck with a sharp, clicking sound against the flint; but either the tinder was damp or insufficient, for no satisfactory result was obtained.

Joe Rollins began to curse and swear like one of the renowned troopers who fought at Flanders.

But suddenly he ceased to speak and the sparks ceased to fly.

Sir Roland could not make out what had now happened.

"How long are you going to keep me standing here?" he asked, angrily.

A flash of lightning gleamed upon the wall for an instant, and then the darkness was blacker than before.

Strangely enough, when the vivid lightning lit up the surroundings momentarily, Sir Roland saw no sign of his companion.

"Rollins—Rollins!" he called out. "Play me no trick, or you shall pay dearly for it."

No verbal response was vouchsafed to this threat, and Sir Roland, drawing a pistol from his belt, vowed that he would fire at random if Joe Rollins did not answer to his name.

All remained silent.

"I will call out three times," Sir Roland said, "and then, if you do not speak, look out for yourself."

"One! Two! Three!"

"Ha! ha! ha!" shrieked a horrible voice. "Most noble baronet, why don't you fire?"

Sir Roland Ashton uttered a cry of horror and started back. As he did so he felt a pair of long, wiry arms encircle his waist, and the next moment his head was dashed violently against the wall.

A thousand jagged lights, more brilliant than the lightning, flashed before Sir Roland's eyes, and as they became greater and died away he lost all consciousness and lapsed into oblivion.

It was impossible for him to tell how long he had remained in this state.

He heard the storm raging, knew that he was drenched to the skin and chilled to the marrow with cold; but his eyes were dim and hazy, and he could make out no object distinctly.

Suddenly it dawned upon his brain that he must have been removed by some mysterious means from Cypress House.

Slowly, but too surely, the events of the day came back to his tortured brain, until his thoughts ceased at the remembrance of Joe Rollins endeavouring to get a light.

Where was he?

Independent of the deluge falling from the sky, Sir Roland Ashton could hear a great rushing of water.

The baronet pressed his hand to his throbbing brow, rubbed his eyes, and moved his hands about.

Presently he became convinced that he was in a boat, and as his vision cleared a little he saw a peculiarly-shaped white object sitting opposite him.

Sir Roland with a great effort forced himself into a sitting posture.

Then what the baronet had dreaded had become a reality.

He was in a boat, which had been anchored by a pole in the middle of a lake.

The lightning flashed and the thunder rolled furiously overhead, and Heaven and earth seemed to have come together.

But it was not the storm or his position in the boat that terrified Sir Roland Ashton.

It was not danger from the conflicting elements

that caused him to yell out an exclamation of horror, to leap to his feet, and then to sink crouching like a wild animal at bay under the bows of the boat; for Spring-Heeled Jack, ghastly and mocking, sat in the stern, pointing with extended hands and arms at the baronet.

Squatting cross-legged, and seemingly finding enjoyment in the very fury of the storm, the weird being laughed until the sound of his voice rose above the crashing thunder.

Suddenly he ceased this wild and terrible mirth, but his attitude remained unchanged.

"Sir Roland," he said, "this is a merry night for us to meet."

The baronet could not speak.

His tongue clave to the roof of his mouth, and a strange feeling came over him, as it he were already numbered with the dead.

## CHAPTER XCIV.

### THE ROOM WITH THE MOVING WALLS.

WHEN Jacob Butler found the floor giving way under him, he thought that an earthquake or something of a similar nature had taken place.

He did not, indeed, seem to sink; but in the first moment of his fright it appeared as if the ceiling of the room had flown upward towards the sky.

But Jacob Butler knew better when the boards suddenly tilted and shot him upon his back in a cellar.

Before the unhappy man could rise he heard a whirring sound, and knew that the flooring had returned to its former place and shut him hopelessly in.

Jacob Butler lay perfectly still where he had been deposited with as little ceremony as if he had been a sack of coal or a bag of rubbish only fit for a lumber-room.

In point of fact, for some time he was too miserable and broken-hearted to get up, but at last he did so, and endeavoured to see what sort of place his new prison was.

A feeble ray of sickly light came from the roof, which only made the cellar more dismal and repulsive.

"Ah! woe is me," Jacob Butler groaned. "It is my fate to fall into bad hands. But this must be my last adventure. Surely I am cast down here to be murdered!"

Jacob groaned again, and as he moved forward with the notion of examining the cellar walls his foot struck against something.

It was the knife he had dropped, but which had luckily descended with him.

"This is better than nothing," Jacob said, as he stowed the weapon away in his pocket. "At least I shall have the satisfaction of defending my life again. Ha! ha!"

Jacob Butler had nothing to laugh about, and the sound that came from his lips was nothing better than an hysterical wail.

Like any other man in such a position, Jacob shouted in a loud voice to be let out, but he received no reply whatever.

Not a sound above or below indicated that he was being watched or listened to.

Jacob's mind would have been relieved even if his persecutors had rushed in and pounced upon him.

"No door and no window!" he moaned. "What will become of me? Do they mean to starve me? Is it their intention to drive me mad with thirst, and then taunt me with the result of their cruelty? Sinner as I am, I don't think I deserve this."

Jacob felt very much inclined to burst into tears, but he resolutely kept them back.

"No—no," he said, "I won't be a child. If my time has come I'll die like a man, and, perhaps, after all, death in any shape would come with a kindly hand, for, if I live, Heaven only knows what fresh miseries I shall have to endure!"

More than an hour passed away—it seemed an age to Jacob—and then a kind of wicket opened in one corner of the ceiling.

Down came a basket, covered with a white cloth.

"Food and drink!" said Jacob. "At any rate, he doesn't intend to starve me."

It suddenly occurred to Jacob that Ted Nickells might, however, intend to poison him.

"Well, I can't help it if he does," the prisoner said, in tones of desperation. "I'll eat and drink, and take the consequences, whatever they may be."

There was nothing peculiar in the taste of the food or light wine, but Jacob Butler had not got more than half through his meal when he began to feel very drowsy.

He felt no pain—no discomfort.

The sensation was rather pleasant than otherwise, and at last he fell slowly back, pillowing his head upon his arm.

The sleep into which Jacob Butler lapsed was sound and long.

When he awoke he could see by the fading light that the day was passing swiftly away, and that the cellar would be soon plunged in profound darkness.

Jacob stood upon his feet and shook himself very much in the fashion of a retriever dog after a plunge in the water.

He was cold and chilly.

His limbs were cramped, and to set his blood flowing afresh he began to pace to and fro.

It was now that a very odd notion got into his head and refused to leave it.

He seemed to think that the cellar had grown much smaller.

With a nameless terror at his heart he stared at the walls, up at the ceiling, and down on the floor.

Nothing came of these investigations but bewilderment. Jacob rubbed his eyes and stared again.

"Of course it must be all fancy," he said to himself; "but I could have sworn that there was a huge cobweb in that corner. Where can it have got to, unless somebody has been here and swept it down?"

It goes without telling that Jacob received no reply to this perplexing question.

"No," he said; "nothing has been disturbed. Here is the basket just as I left it when I fell asleep, and," he added, thrusting his hand hurriedly into his pocket, "I have not been searched, for here is the knife."

Jacob Butler took another and yet more narrow survey of the cellar.

He tapped the walls with his knuckles.

They were as sound and hard as any he had ever tested, and yet Jacob, in spite of all his mental remonstrances against himself, became convinced that those selfsame walls had moved.

The unhappy man returned to the middle of the floor and sat down again.

"Let me think this out," he said, dropping his head upon his open hands. "I must keep my senses about me, or all is indeed lost. Now it is impossible that these walls—"

A sound as of a chain running through a pulley attracted Jacob Butler's attention.

He ceased speaking, and glanced hurriedly and fearfully over his shoulder.

"Bah!" said he; "what next shall I think? I'll have some more wine; so here goes to drown my sorrows."

Jacob raised the bottle to his lips, but it got no further.

Just as he was in the act of drinking his eye happened to catch sight of the opposite wall.

To his horror he saw it move slowly towards him.

Jacob Butler dropped the bottle with a crash and started to his feet.

"Mercy on me!" he gasped. "Then I was not wrong. What can be the meaning of this?"

Appalled, and almost stupefied with terror, Jacob Butler stood staring at the now stationary wall.

He had heard and read of the old German tortures.

As swift as a flash of lightning the story of the Chamber with the Seven Windows rushed into his brain.

A man was placed in the room, and each morning he missed a window, until he stood in a kind of huge coffin, which suddenly closed in upon him and crushed him to death.

Could such things exist in England, the land of the brave and the free?

This hideous piece of mechanism so terrified Jacob Butler that he reeled to and fro like a reed blown before the wind.

"Murder—most horrible!" he shrieked. "It is impossible that there are such fiends to take life in this way. Oh! help—mercy! Help!"

There was no sound but of the masonry, as it was slowly moved again by some powerful agency.

Jacob Butler tore his hair.

He laughed, wept, pleaded, and threatened all in a breath.

Then his senses began to give way.

Loud sounds rang in his ears, strange, uncouth forms danced before his eyes.

In a moment of madness he rushed forward and dashed his shoulder against the wall.

But it defied his efforts.

It came on with that horrible gliding movement which turned Jacob Butler's blood to ice and drove him frantic.

"I am lost—lost!" he cried. "In a few moments my long career of suffering will be at an end."

## CHAPTER XCV.

### MRS. CORCORAN GETS A LITTLE BETTER.

When Mrs. Corcoran was very ill she thought herself the greatest of sinners, but no sooner did her iron constitution show signs of mending than she began to repent of saying what she had.

"I can't retract my words," she mumbled one day when left alone. "The very people I have wronged have been kind to me. What evil chance brought me to this place! I daresay I should have come round all right without their help."

Thus did the ungrateful old hag reason, and she determined to take a leaf out of Sir Roland Ashton's book and pretend to get no better, or at least, to be so ill as to only hobble feebly about the house and grounds.

Wretched, wicked, cruel as she was, a slight flush of shame rose to her sallow cheeks as she thought of practising this hypocrisy.

"I must get away," she argued. "Ralph Ashton will not be satisfied with what I have told him, but seek to know the whole history of my life. Ah! what a wonderful story that would make in a book."

This idea seemed to afford Mrs. Corcoran some consolation, for she grinned horribly, and then composed her features into an expression of mingled woe and repentance, for she heard, or thought she heard, the sound of a light footstep outside the door.

Mrs. Corcoran's quick ears did not deceive her.

She groaned deeply as the door opened and Daisy Leigh entered the room.

"Are you better this morning?" Daisy asked. "See here; I have brought you some nice fresh grapes from Mr. Ashton."

"Did he send them?" Mrs. Corcoran rejoined, wincing at the knowledge how little she merited the slightest act of kindness.

"Of course he did," Daisy replied, smiling.

Mrs. Corcoran pressed her hands before her eyes as if her feelings were too much for her; but she was looking through her fingers at the splendidly-moulded form of the pretty girl and wondering whether she would ever fall in her power again.

Daisy Leigh drew a chair up to the bedside and sat down.

"Now that I am here with you alone," she said, "I should like to ask you a few questions."

Mrs. Corcoran winced again, and gave vent to such a hollow groan that Daisy became alarmed and stretched out her hand towards one of the medicine bottles.

"It is not physic I require, my dear," she said, "but peace and ease of conscience."

"Both will come if you so shape your mind," Daisy said, kindly.

Mrs. Corcoran shook her head and sighed in the most dismal manner.

"I am afraid not," she said. "I am too far gone for that. Oh! dear, when I think of what I might have been and what I am my heart seems to stand still."

"Listen," said Daisy Leigh. "I wish to speak to you about the time that I was a prisoner at Lilac Lodge, and I hope you will tell—"

At this juncture Mrs. Corcoran became so ill that it appeared more than probable that she would succumb to the attack.

"Oh! don't—don't," she gasped. "Oh! for goodness' sake, don't ask me any questions about that dreadful place and that bad man, Sir Roland."

Mrs. Corcoran became quite hysterical, and Daisy Leigh turned her head aside with an expression of pity, but not unmingled with disgust, which she could not help feeling at the sight of the horrible old woman.

"Very well," Daisy said; "I will be the last to put you to pain. Perhaps after a little more sleep you will be in a calmer mood."

"I hope so," Mrs. Corcoran whined; "I hope so, indeed. Oh! dear, what a dreadful thing it is to be in such pain as I suffer!"

Daisy placed the grapes on a table at the bed-side and left the room.

"So," said the crone, "it seems that I am not to be left alone. I shall be cross-examined until I am half out of my mind, and then sent into the world with a good book and a sermon. Ho! ho! I must clear off before it is too late. Patience—patience! I must gull the girl into the belief that I have a wonderful story to tell her when I get up—yes, when I get up. Ha! ha!"

Ralph Ashton had not been near Mrs. Corcoran for two days, and this made the old hag very uncomfortable.

It was not his presence that she required, but the mere fact of his absence for so long a period was more than sufficient to raise the artful crone's suspicions.

She had asked the doctor about him, but received a mild rebuke to the effect that she was not to trouble herself about other people, but to get well as soon as possible.

Neither Daisy Leigh nor Constance Marfield had said a word about Ralph, and Mrs. Corcoran shuddered at the thought that he might have taken it into his head to go to Mildendale.

And yet he surely would not do so without asking her more questions; but, under any circumstances, Mrs. Corcoran had no other alternative but to await the course of events.

In about two hours' time Daisy Leigh returned.

She was accompanied this time by Constance Marfield.

Mrs. Corcoran fidgeted about as if she wished the girls at the other end of the world.

"We have not come to ask you any questions," Constance Marfield said, "but to tell you some news."

Mrs. Corcoran opened one eye and then the other, but so slowly that the operation took fully a minute.

"News, my dears!" she said, wearily. "What sort of news can you have to tell me?"

"We have kept it from you because you have been very ill," Constance Marfield continued; "but I think you are well enough to bear it now."

"Bear it!" Mrs. Corcoran thought. "Then I suppose there must be something the matter."

"Thank you, my dear," said she, aloud. "I shall be pleased to listen to anything you may have to say."

Constance seemed to hesitate, as if the subject she had come to speak upon was not a pleasant one.

"A man of the name of Bill Blarney has been seen in your society," she said at last.

"Ah!" Mrs. Corcoran gasped, "ah! yes; I am sorry to say that I have been so wicked as to be in his society on some occasions."

"You will never see him again," Constance said.

Mrs. Corcoran opened her eyes wide enough now

"Why not?" she demanded. "Why not, my dear young lady?"

"Because he is in prison, and will most assuredly be condemned to die a violent death."

Mrs. Corcoran sat bolt upright in bed.

"In prison? Condemned to die a violent death?" she repeated, hoarsely. "No—no! You must be joking with me?"

"I wish I could say I was," Constance replied. "The man has brought his own fate upon himself. In two days' time he will be tried before a judge and jury, and Daisy will give evidence against him."

Mrs. Corcoran clasped her hands.

There was no need for her to feign anything now.

She looked bad, and felt so into the bargain.

"I know the villain," she said at length. "He will tell all sorts of lies and say anything to get me into trouble; but you won't listen to him, will you?"

Daisy Leigh touched Constance lightly on the elbow.

"You fear what this man may say?" Constance resumed. "Tell me—did Sir Roland Ashton prompt Blarney to drag me from the Queen's Head?"

"I believe not. But how should I know?" Mrs. Corcoran replied. "He is villain enough to do anything to gain his own ends."

"But you must have heard him say something respecting me and Miss Leigh?"

"And of Ralph Ashton too," Daisy chimed in, softly.

"Let me rest to-day," said Mrs. Corcoran, groaning heavily, "and I will tell you all I know. I can't collect my thoughts while I lay still. It seems an odd thing to say, but it is the truth. My memory is bad, and things and circumstances of the past only come back when I am moving about."

"I suppose we must be content with that," said Constance, looking at Daisy.

"I suppose so," Daisy replied, with a rather anxious glance at the old hag; "but we certainly must not let her get up without the doctor's permission."

Just then the doctor was announced, and he pronounced Mrs. Corcoran's condition to be so favourable as to allow her to sit by the window, and even take a gentle walk in the garden on the morrow, providing she kept herself perfectly quiet during the rest of that day.

The news concerning the imprisonment of Bill Blarney had a most startling effect on the old hag.

He might at any time implicate her, and, for all that she knew, the officers of justice might be on their way to seize her even at that very moment.

Mrs. Corcoran had an innate horror of being locked up in a prison cell.

The thought that women were sometimes hanged as well as men would throw her into a profuse perspiration.

In the outside world she had played her wretched part with an amount of boldness bordering upon recklessness, but then she had always secured somebody on whose shoulders she could cast the blame.

But now Bill Blarney, with a hundred secrets locked up in his breast, was in prison, and, doubtless, brooding over the hour when he would be summoned to take that short but terrible ride to Tyburn; and she had confessed to murdering Lady Ashton!

"Oh! fool—weak fool that I have been!" she said, clawing at her scanty stock of hair. "If I am dragged to prison and sentenced to die a felon's death, who have I to blame but myself. Ah! Time flies, and I must be quick and sudden in what I determine to do. Have I the patience to wait until to-morrow? I think not. I fear I shall go mad, or do something very rash, if I remain here!"

# SPRING-HEELED JACK,

## THE TERROR OF LONDON.

SIR ROLAND WAS GAZING UPON THE REMAINS OF JULES CARLEON.

## CHAPTER XCVI.

### SIR ROLAND HAS TO SWIM FOR HIS LIFE.

It is said that before a man shakes off this mortal coil he experiences but one supreme moment of agony in his life.

It may have been thus with Sir Roland Ashton when he found himself in the presence of the demon-like figure of Spring-Heeled Jack.

The manner in which he had been spirited away from Cypress House, to an open boat on the lake, was so mysterious; the awful surroundings, the terrible storm rolling overhead, were so bewildering and hideous, that the wretched man fully believed that he had parted with this world for ever, and had been claimed by the arch-fiend.

"Ha! ha! ha!" laughed Spring-Heeled Jack. "Well met, Sir Roland. 'Tis a merry night for a revel. Ha! ha! ha!"

The sound of his wild mirth mingled with the booming thunder, and the quivering lightning seemed to dance upon the blackened water as in sport of Sir Roland's misery.

"For what purpose have you brought me here?" he gasped out.

"To punish you as you richly deserve," Spring-Heeled Jack replied, pointing down at the lake.

"To punish me?"

"Yes."

"My time has not come yet," Sir Roland said, plucking up courage. "With all your show of mummery you have no power to harm me. Once again, I defy you!"

"Beware!" Spring-Heeled Jack cried; "beware how you tempt me!"

At this moment the masses of louring clouds were rent asunder by a vivid, appalling flash of forked lightning, and followed by so stunning a crash of thunder that Sir Roland shrieked aloud in his terror.

It was like the crack of doom, and for fully a moment the baronet sat, huddled up, dazed, and blinded.

Suddenly he was roused by the sound of Spring-Heeled Jack's voice.

"So, Sir Roland," said the singular creature, "you have fallen into luck again? Take care? Have done at once with these men, who will make a dupe of you."

"What men?" Sir Roland demanded.

"Bah!" Spring-Heeled Jack rejoined. "Think not that prevarication or lying will serve you. Nothing is hidden from me. I know all. Step aside from this evil path; seek to earn an honest living, and repent of your sins."

The last flash of lightning seemed to have split the clouds into atoms, for the storm was now rolling away.

Sir Roland grew bolder.

"My sins!" he said, laughing hoarsely. "Forsooth! I should require the whole of my lifetime over again to repent of them."

"Wretched man!" Spring-Heeled Jack cried, leaping to his feet and drawing himself up to his full height. "Base, mean, bloodthirsty villain! those words have sealed your doom."

As he advanced from the stern to the bows of the boat, Sir Roland gathered himself up for the coming struggle.

Spring-Heeled Jack stopped mid-way in the boat.

"Master of ill-fated yonder house," he said, extending his arm in the direction of the dismantled mansion; "craven cur, and murderer, you are not fit to live, yet there is that within me that makes me too proud to take the life of a creature base as even you are. You are unarmed—"

"For that reason you bluster and threaten," Sir Roland interposed. "You come as a thief in the night, and as an assassin bent on doing murder in secret."

"Most noble speech!" Spring-Heeled Jack rejoined with another peal of hideous laughter. "Look into your own heart, Sir Roland. Have you never acted the part of a thief, have you never stricken down the unwary and defenceless?"

Sir Roland remained silent for some time.

"My bitterest curse fall upon you!" he said at last. "I might have been a different man, had you not dogged my footsteps and haunted me with your devilish form."

"And yet," said the singular creature, and there was some sadness in his voice, "how many chances have I given you?"

"You give me!" Sir Roland yelled. "Who are you to shower your favours? You, a fiend, born and cast forth from the lowest depths of perdition to blight the world!"

"Enough!" Spring-Heeled Jack cried. "I will listen to no more. You must leave this boat; it is mine. Away!"

Sir Roland peered through the gloom to the nearest shore, and Spring-Heeled Jack laughed again.

"Sir Roland," he said, "you must fall back upon your courage. If ever you return to Cypress House it must be by swimming across the lake. Away, or I will hurl you into the waters with these hands."

Sir Roland Ashton knew full well that Spring-Heeled Jack would keep his word.

The baronet took a hasty glance around, and then began to remove his coat.

"No," Spring-Heeled Jack said. "You must go as you are."

"I shall perish, assuredly," Sir Roland returned.

"I care not!" the weird creature replied; "the world will be well rid of you. Go!"

Again he advanced with out-stretched arms, and Sir Roland, hesitating no longer, leaped upon the edge of the boat, and plunged into the water.

As he rose to the surface and struck out for his life he turned his head.

He could see nothing of Spring-Heeled Jack or the boat, but he heard a rushing sound as of something being propelled swiftly along the surface of the lake.

The weight of his clothes bore Sir Roland down, and the waves which the storm had raised swept over his head again and again.

Sir Roland was an expert swimmer, and he battled for life with the strength of despair.

Now the wound he had received from Ralph Ashton began to trouble him.

It seemed to break open afresh, and the baronet, with a cry of dismay, threw himself upon his back.

"It is useless!" he cried. "There is no hope! I must die, and my lifeless body will be found when morning comes."

A drowning man clutches at a straw, and Sir Roland clung to life as long as his muscles possessed an ounce of strength.

He had no notion of where the nearest shore was, and for all he knew he might be drifting into the centre of the lake.

The water bubbled into his mouth and gurgled down his half-choked throat.

He spat it out and buffeted the waves, for as his strength failed so did his presence of mind leave him.

Once he sunk, and then all sorts of odd forms danced before his glaring eyes.

Voices a thousand times more horrible than Spring-Heeled Jack's shouted "Come—come!" into his ears, and then, as he rose to the surface, he gave vent to one frantic cry for help and mercy.

At the same moment something touched him.

He flung his arm round it, and it held him dangling before the very jaws of death.

The object that had saved Sir Roland's life was a log of wood, and the baronet, having realised this fact, held on until his breath and faculties returned.

He began to reason that wind and wave would drift the log ashore, but, oh! how icy-cold the water was.

It numbed his limbs and chilled the very marrow of his bones.

Weak, faint, and cold Sir Roland knew that he must perish ere long, even though the means of life were within his hands.

He raised up his head, but the darkness was so pitch-like that he could not see an inch before his nose.

Suddenly something grated against his feet.

It was the pebbly bed of the lake, and Sir Roland uttered a shout.

It was a shout of triumph, but had no tone of thanksgiving in it.

His life was saved, and that was all he cared for.

No thought of turning from his evil course entered his mind, and, as he waded towards the bank and fell exhausted upon it, he cursed those he called his foes, and swore a bitter oath of revenge.

The only thing he dreaded was another visit from Spring-Heeled Jack.

He lay still, and, listening, almost fancied that in the sighing of the wind, and the water lapping the shores of the lake, he heard the stealthy footstep of his foe.

But he was mistaken.

Spring-Heeled Jack did not return, and at last the baronet staggered to his feet, and turned his livid, distorted face towards Cypress House.

The journey was a short one, but it took him fully half an hour to accomplish.

His feet slipped and reeled on the terrace steps, and more dead than alive he reached the door.

It was open, but the hall beyond was buried in impenetrable darkness.

"Rollins! Rollins!" he called out, faintly.

Nought but the rumbling echoes of the old house answered his voice.

Sir Roland leaned against the wall for support.

Though his body was deadly cold his brain seemed to burn and flame like a raging furnace.

Again he shouted, and then, as the echo died away, he though he heard something creeping along towards him.

"Is that you, Rollins?" Sir Roland asked.

"It's all that is left of me," growled out a voice.

"Where is the light?" Sir Roland said. "Show light, I implore you!"

"It's all very well to say that," Rollins replied; "but deuce a bit can I do so. Where are you?"

"On the right hand side."

"I scarcely know my right hand from my left," Joe Rollins said, with an oath. "Keep still, and I will find you, if I can."

Presently Sir Roland felt a hand touch his own.

"Why, what is this?" Rollins said, shrinking back. "You are as wet and cold as a frog."

"So would you be if you had been where I came from."

"Where is that?"

"In the lake."

"The devil!" Rollins exclaimed. "How on earth did you find your way there?"

"Ask me no questions, but procure a light, for mercy's sake!" Sir Roland replied.

"I have my flint and steel here," Rollins replied; "and perhaps I can make a torch out of a piece of the old wainscoting."

"Why did you not do so before?"

"Because I have only just recovered my senses."

Click! click!

Joe Rollins was at work with the flint and steel.

Sparks began to fly, and presently the tinder took light.

Joe Rollins tore a piece of the rotten wainscoting from the wall, and soon a flame was obtained.

Sir Roland and the man sent with him by James Loddon stood glaring at each other in mute dismay and astonishment.

Rollins' brow bore a terrific bruise, and his face was stained with clotted blood.

"How came this?" Sir Roland demanded.

"Ask the man in the moon," Rollins replied. "All I know is that I was hurled down a flight of stairs in a violent hurry, and that I lay stunned for hours."

"You did not see who struck the blow?"

"No."

Sir Roland grasped his chin, and stood in a thoughtful attitude.

"Strange that you did not!" he said.

"I saw something, but could not make out what it was," Rollins returned. "It looked like a tall white object."

"Ah!" Sir Roland exclaimed.

Again he reflected.

Should he tell this man all he knew about Spring-Heeled Jack and what he had passed through?

No; for it was more than probable that Rollins would insist upon returning to Mildendale at once, and in that case Loddon might think proper to dispense with Sir Roland's services.

"You are silent," Rollins said. "There seems to be more than a mystery in this. How did you manage to tumble into the lake?"

Sir Roland Ashton was never at a loss for a lie as an excuse, and he promptly replied—

"When I missed you I thought you had left me for some reason of your own."

"A likely thing that," Rollins interposed.

"Hear me out," Sir Roland said. "I called your name out at least a dozen times, but receiving no answer, I groped my way down the stairs."

"You must have stepped over my body!"

"If so, I did not touch it," Sir Roland continued. "I went out into the open air, still calling out your name. Suddenly, I thought I saw a figure in advance of me, I ran forward to meet it and fell into the water."

"Do you expect me to believe this story?" Rollins demanded, contemptuously.

"Look at me," Sir Roland said. "Do you think I dived into the lake on such a night as this for my own amusement?"

"Well, no," Rollins returned, in a mollified tone of voice; "but my own opinion of the matter was that you pushed me down the stairs."

Sir Roland Ashton laughed in spite of himself.

"What nonsense!" he said. "That would have been a mad, objectless trick. Bah! Have you your pistols?"

"Yes, I have; and mean to keep them, too," Rollins replied, surlily.

"Let us get upstairs, then," Sir Roland said. "We must light a fire, and perchance, on our way up, we may find the lantern."

This turned out to be the case, and Sir Roland and Joe Rollins, having returned to the room in the turret, made up a roaring fire, and sat before it drinking brandy from a flask.

Joe Rollins had not forgotten to bring some food with him, which he shared with the baronet, and as time went on, and morning dawned, so did the courage of the men, who had met with so strange an adventure, return.

Sir Roland had dried his clothes by degrees, taking off one garment at a time, and when the sun came up and streamed through the turret window, he felt as if he had received a new lease of life.

"It is time that we were away," Joe Rollins said. "We must return to Loddon and tell him what has happened, and abide by the course he advises us to pursue."

"I almost fear that he will laugh at you for being frightened at what may have been nothing but a shadow," Sir Roland said, smiling.

"And I you, for wallowing about the lake like a porpoise," Joe Rollins growled. "However, I am anxious to get away from this infernal place, and if I ever return to it it must be properly furnished and guarded.

---

## CHAPTER XCVII.

### A TERRIBLE DISCOVERY.

JAMES LODDON, the cool, calculating, studied scoundrel, had listened to the story told by Sir Roland and Joe Rollins, and sat brooding over it.

"It passes my comprehension," Loddon said, after a pause; "but there is one thing more than extraordinary about it. Did not the agent tell you that people avowed the house to be haunted?"

"Yes," Sir Roland replied.

"Now," said Loddon, smiting the table with his fist, "it strikes me that Cypress House is haunted with mortals of flesh and blood like our own."

"I fail to follow you," Sir Roland Ashton said, raising his eyebrows.

"I will explain myself," Loddon returned. "It is nothing uncommon for a band of robbers or coiners to take possession of an old house, and keep up the ghost trick to scare the villagers away from the locality. It has been done a hundred times, and such may be the case in this instance."

Sir Roland knew better, but he made no remark.

"You will return within two days," Loddon said, "and you shall take a number of men with you to act in the capacity of servants. In the meantime a waggon-load or two of furniture will be on the way to make the place comfortable."

"It will take something to do that," Joe Rollins said, gloomily. "The place is as rambling as a dozen barns strung together. Bah! The thought of those old rooms makes me shudder."

"You have gone through enough not to shudder at anything," Loddon replied, leering across the table at his follower. "Bah! be a man. Ghosts or mortals, we will soon rout them out, or my name is not what it is."

For two days all remained quiet, and then a man arrived and announced that three rooms had been made ready at Cypress House.

Sir Roland Ashton at once prepared to depart, but with no light heart, though he knew that he would have armed men at his beck and call.

In the evening of that day he once more set foot across Cypress House.

The men had been busy, and one of the rooms presented a brilliant and almost splendid appearance.

"A strange man this Loddon," Sir Roland mused, as he divested himself of a long cloak and sat down. "Few could have fitted up this place with so much despatch. Well, here I am, and I will triumph yet, in spite of every obstacle thrown in my way."

Joe Rollins brought the baronet his dinner, and waited at his elbow while he ate it.

Sir Roland's appetite was not good, but he drank a quantity of wine, and the hot blood brought a flush to his cheek.

"Ah!" he said, "I feel better now, Rollins; our friend Loddon's words have been ringing in my ears all day long. We must ascertain whether his conjecture about the robbers or smugglers is right or wrong."

"Loddon seldom makes a mistake," Rollins replied. "When will you start on the voyage of discovery?"

"As soon as I have finished this bottle wine."

Joe Rollins grinned behind the baronet' chair.

"A beggar on horseback can never go fast enough," he said. "This mountebank with aristocratic blood in his veins would have given ten years of his life for a crust of bread and a drink of water a short time ago, and now he lingers over wine costing half-a-guinea a bottle. Wait; we shall see the outcome of all this."

Sir Roland Ashton sipped his wine at leisure, and as he did so he set his mind to work to plot and plan against those who might have offered the hand of friendship to him.

"I must be in no hurry to go away," he mused. "I must have revenge on Ralph Ashton. I will drag Constance Marfield from him. Loddon shall help me, and if he be so minded he shall take Daisy Leigh to his tender care. All goes well. There is no risk of funds, but I must play my cards well."

Then he turned smilingly to Joe Rollins.

"Fetch a lantern," he said, "and a supply of ammunition. I am determined to explore the house before going to rest."

"Shall I ask any of the other men to accompany us?" Rollins asked.

"No," the baronet replied; "I don't see the necessity of doing that."

"As you like," Rollins returned, sulkily; "but remember what occurred when we were here alone!"

"I don't think that we shall be troubled with a repetition of such an event," Sir Roland said.

"We must keep our eyes and ears open, and try what cold lead will do if we are disturbed."

Joe Rollins shrugged his shoulders, and left the room.

He soon returned, and Sir Roland, rising from the table, stretched his arms above his head.

"I feel ready for almost anything," he said. "Is all quiet below?"

"Yes."

"Then we will start at once."

Traversing several long passages, they began the descent into the lower part of the building.

The light of the lantern danced fantastically on the damp, slimy walls.

Hideous creeping things, long undisturbed, darted from their hiding-places and fled, startled, before the strange unaccustomed flare.

The dust lay as thick and soft as a velvet pile carpet, and silenced the tread of the two men as they moved swiftly forward.

Sir Roland carried the keys of the building in his belt, and he drew them out as he came to a heavy door.

"I am afraid we shall have some little trouble here," he said, as he glanced from the lock to the keys.

He tried half-a-dozen, but the lock remained fast, and Joe Rollins began to growl and grumble.

"I can see nothing in this," he said. "What can come of it but chilled bones and aching limbs?"

"My friend," Sir Roland said, "I cannot consent to live in a house until I know how it is constructed, or what it contains. Ha! this key fits; see, my patience is rewarded at last."

"And mine is almost spent," Joe Rollins muttered aloud.

Sir Roland paid no attention to the remark.

He then opened the door and peered into the darkness beyond.

"Hold up the lamp," he said. "High—higher! Above your head."

Joe Rollins complied, and the light fell upon the walls of a dungeon.

It was utterly devoid of anything like furniture, but there were heavy iron rings riveted to the wall, and a few pieces of rusty iron chain lying here and there upon the floor.

"Ah!" said Sir Roland. "If all the ghosts of the unhappy wretches who have from time to time been lodged in this place could revisit it, I wonder how many there would be?"

Joe Rollins shuddered from head to foot, and the lantern trembled in his hand.

He had had some experience of prison-cells, but they were palaces in comparison to this dismal region.

"I don't see the good of going into such subjects," he said. "There is nothing here. Let us go."

"Stay," Sir Roland returned, "there is a door on the other side. Let us see where it leads to."

Joe Rollins muttered a curse under his lips, and felt inclined to turn back and leave Sir Roland.

The door pointed out by Sir Roland opened upon a winding flight of stone steps.

Sir Roland led the way, and Joe Rollins had no alternative but to follow.

Presently they found themselves in the very dungeon into which Spring-Heeled Jack had conveyed Jules Carleon.

The headsman's block and axe had been removed, but there were footmarks upon the floor, and Sir Roland pointed them out.

"Get your pistols ready," he said. "Loddon was right, you see. Strangers have been here. Ghosts leave no trace behind them. We have to cope with mortals."

As Joe Rollins looked to the priming of his weapons Sir Roland's attention was attracted towards the trap-door.

He tried to raise it.

In vain!

It seemed to have been sealed down by some composition which had hardened between the chinks.

"We must return some other time and force this open," Sir Roland said. "It may be that our unwelcome guests are beneath our feet at this very instant."

He was about to leave the dungeon, when the light of the lantern fell upon what appeared to be a small wicket fixed in the wall.

"One moment," he said, as Joe Rollins was striding hastily towards the door. "Perchance we may find a way out here."

Rollins turned pale.

"This is madness!" he said. "If there are robbers or coiners here, we shall be outnumbered and murdered."

"We hold the key of the position," Sir Roland replied, "and are a match for more than a dozen men."

"As you like," Joe Rollins said; "but if anything happens, lay none of the blame on my shoulders."

Sir Roland's notion was to catch Spring-Heeled Jack napping and bring him down for good and all with a bullet.

The baronet had come to the conclusion that his singular foe had taken up his residence within the walls of Cypress House, and Sir Roland had determined to ascertain whether such was the case.

Advancing towards the wicket, he tried it with his hand.

It remained fast.

"It opens with a spring," Sir Roland said, as he pressed his fingers here and there. "Stand by, Rollins, while I smash the wicket with my fist. If a head appears let your aim be sure."

Joe Rollins did not relish the task appointed to him.

At the same time, he did not like to show the white feather.

Drawing a pistol from his belt, he pointed it in a line with the wicket.

"I am ready," he said, steadying his voice. "Step aside quickly after you have struck, Sir Roland, for, if there be occasion for me to fire, I might hit you."

"I will take care to follow your advice, my friend," Sir Roland said. "Now!"

Lunging out his right arm, he struck the wicket, and smashed it so completely that the fragments of wood and iron flew about in all directions.

There was no occasion for Joe Rollins to pull the trigger of the pistol.

After the noise of the fallen fragments had subsided all remained as still as the grave.

Sir Roland waited a few moments, and then peered through the aperture.

Passing his hand along its sides, he came to what seemed to be a knot of wood.

Pressing it with all his might, he saw a portion of the wall revolving as on a pivot, and soon there was sufficient room for a man of ordinary bulk to pass through.

"You see," he said, triumphantly, "our labour has not been in vain. Here is another staircase, and at the base we may discover something to astonish us."

"I shouldn't wonder," Joe Rollins remarked. "Nothing would astonish me just now."

"Are you afraid?" Sir Roland demanded, turning sharply on the man.

"No—no. Why should I be when I have so brave a man as you to back me up?"

"Then lead the way," said Sir Roland, "and take care that the light falls well ahead."

"I have no wish to take part in any of the glory of this expedition," Rollins returned. "I am your servant, and will follow."

"Bah!" Sir Roland Ashton said, with a contemptuous sneer. "Give me the lamp."

Joe Rollins did so gladly enough.

"What is that?" he said, suddenly, and coming to a standstill.

"Rats!" Sir Roland replied. "There seems to be hundreds of them, but armed with light and weapons they cannot hurt us."

"I would rather face five hundred soldiers than as many of the brutes," Joe Rollins said, wiping the beads of clammy perspiration from his brows.

"I am not partial to them," Sir Roland replied, with affected carelessness. "Follow! We have but a few more steps to go."

In a few moments they came to a door.

It stood ajar, and offered no obstacle to their progress.

The rusty hinges creaked and groaned as Sir Roland dragged it wider open, and stepped across the threshold.

Flashing the lamp to and fro, his eyes were attracted by something that made his blood run cold.

It was the body of a man whose flesh had been gnawed and torn from its bones.

As Sir Roland gazed at this frightful spectacle, a number of rats scurried away.

A cry of horror burst from Sir Roland's lips, for, in the torn and worried fragments of clothes which clung to the almost fleshless skeleton, he recognised those which had been worn by Jules Carleon.

Joe Rollins stepped back, sick at heart, and Sir Roland following quickly, lost his balance, and dropping the lamp, extinguished it.

At the same moment, he heard the door above close with a loud bang, and then a loud peal of mocking laughter rang out of the awful darkness.

## CHAPTER XCVIII.

### THE MOVING WALL STOPS AND COMES ON AGAIN.

Of all the horrible positions in which a man could be placed, Jacob Butler's position was perhaps the worst.

Picture his position if you can.

It may be realised in some baneful nightmare, but not, happily, in life, for civilisation, aided by the giant arm of the law, has long swept away all such dens as that over which Ted Nickells ruled.

Jacob Butler was as helpless and as hapless as an infant whose destruction is sought by a brutal ruffian.

The sheep knows nothing of death nor feels a single pang until the knife is at its throat; but the wretched prisoner at the Chequers had sense and reason.

In that one moment of unendurable agony he suffered a thousand tortures and a thousand deaths.

To die like a caged rat, to be crushed and mangled by the devilish piece of machinery was torture so exquisite in its agony that he flew from side to side, yelling for mercy, cursing and threatening in a breath.

"Cowards! Villains! Cowards!" he shrieked.

Again and again he hurled himself against the gliding walls in a maddened attempt to stay their progress; but he might as well have tried to stem a mountain torrent with a wisp of straw.

"Heaven help me!" he said, sinking down at last, and covering his eyes with his hands. "Little did I think that I was destined to die thus. I will try to be calm. I will endeavour to meet death as becomes a man."

He remained in the same attitude, expecting each moment to feel the fatal embrace.

Every incident in his life flashed through his brain with the swiftness of lightning.

He went back to the days of his childhood and wandered through leafy glades and along verdant banks.

He heard voices, which had been long hushed in the grave, calling to him in accents of love and endearment.

Familiar forms and faces drew near to him, and reproached or consoled him.

Death!

Why did it not come and put him out of this excruciating misery?

Let its ghastly hand fall ever so heavily now it would be welcome.

But the hand was stayed, for the gliding walls were still now.

How long Jacob Butler had remained on his knees he could not tell.

The period might have extended over but a few moments, but Jacob Butler seemed to have passed through an age longer than his past life.

If he had been suddenly dragged into the daylight, and had found his hair turned as white as driven snow, he would not have been surprised.

Removing his hands from his eyes he glared wildly and frantically round his fearful prison.

The dimensions of it were now so small that by stretching out his hands he could have touched the opposite walls.

But, strangely enough, a fresh basket of provisions had mysteriously found its way into the place.

"Oh! horror, my sufferings are not, then, at an end," Jacob Butler groaned. "The villains intend to torture me as a cat tortures a mouse. This may go on for days. I shall go mad—mad—mad."

He beat his breast and tore his hair.

He shouted out to Ted Nickells to finish his devilish work, but no kind of a reply whatever was vouchsafed to him.

If the villain had taunted and mocked at him, the unhappy man would have found some consolation even in the sound of that inhuman voice.

But silence, dead silence, in that den was worse than the voice of a demon.

Soon an unnatural calmness came over Jacob Butler.

He smoothed the terrified expression out of his cheeks, and the frightened glare died out of his eyes.

He rose and made an examination of the walls

as coolly as a mason sent to repair them might have done.

He could find nothing to account for the motive-power that set them in motion.

Then he sat down upon the floor, and began to eat and drink.

In a word, Jacob's faculties were numbed, and as the criminal for whom the black tree of death is ready partakes of a last meal, so he feasted with Death, gruesome and grizzly, for his guest.

Over that meal Death and Jacob Butler touched hands and rubbed shoulders.

They were becoming accustomed to each other now, and in a very short time their acquaintance-ship would be complete.

Jacob ate wolfishly, and, having finished the bottle of wine, lay down to sleep.

Perchance the pale horseman who bears his victims to the land of shades might carry him away while he was in a state of oblivion.

At all events, he slept with his head pillowed on his arm, and slept soundly.

What dreams came to him?

Dreams of freedom and happiness.

But the awakening?

It came at last, and Jacob Butler, forgetting where he was, stretched out his limbs and yawned.

His hands and feet came in contact with the walls of his prison, and then the bitter truth rushed into his brain.

While he had slumbered the walls had been set in motion.

They might be moving now.

He thrust out his hands to convince himself whether such was the case or not.

The walls were stationary.

Jacob Butler lay perfectly still.

He was beyond raving now.

He did not even think of death.

He had suffered too much in mind and body to care what happened, and yet—and he was surprised at the fact—the balance of his mind had not given way.

Presently he heard a curious, throbbing sound, such as people in these days are accustomed to when travelling on board a steam-vessel.

Then there came the clanking of chains, and a sharp clicking noise, as of cog-wheels whirling swiftly round.

The walls were closing.

They pressed upon Jacob Butler.

He felt their crushing force.

The hot blood surged upwards, and rushed into his brain.

Ah! bitter death.

How long was he to suffer?

"Quick! mercy! quick!" he screamed.

As his voice pealed through his stone-coffin, for coffin it was now, he heard the sound of voices.

Oaths, yells, and shouts mingled with each other in chaotic confusion.

The walls flew back with a crash, and Jacob Butler fainted, as something like a huge hammer struck the floor above his head.

## CHAPTER XCIX.

### A PLOT TO RESCUE BILL BLARNEY.

MRS CORCORAN, having risen from her bed, occupied her fertile mind as to how she could escape from Ralph Ashton's house.

That she was being closely watched she knew too well, and the question now was how could she elude this vigilance.

The hag called herself a fool over and over again for confessing what she had done, and if she had dared she would have unsaid every word.

But that was impossible, for she knew that Ralph Ashton had accepted her statements as truth, and believed fully in them.

Mrs. Corcoran, after hobbling about the house for some time, expressed a wish to go into the garden.

Daisy Leigh went there with her, much to the witch-like old woman's rage and chagrin.

One fact consoled her.

Daisy put no further questions to her, but Mrs. Corcoran was on thorns with regard to Bill Blarney and his impending fate.

The hag, finding that she was not to be allowed to walk out alone, became suddenly weak, and had to be assisted back into the house.

Her sham attack lasted until evening had closed in, and then for a time she was left alone.

Now or never was the time.

If she did not make an attempt to escape she might never have another chance.

Mrs. Corcoran went to the door and opened it noiselessly.

She crept along the landing, and, leaning over the balustrade, put her hand to her ear and listened.

A light was shining in the hall, and she could hear the servants bustling about in the kitchen.

Then a door opened and closed.

Swift as a hare, Mrs. Corcoran darted back to her room, and began to whine and groan most piteously.

Nobody came near her, and after a few minutes had gone by, she ventured out again.

Mrs. Corcoran heard the sound of voices.

Daisy Leigh and Constance Marfield were talking.

"I wish Ralph would return," Constance said, "for I feel convinced that this old woman upstairs is playing the part of a hypocrite."

"Thank you, my dear," the old crone muttered. "I shall not forget that in a hurry."

As Mrs. Corcoran mumbled out the words under her breath, she winked and blinked like an owl in the sunlight, and shook her fist.

"Do you really think so?" said Daisy Leigh, taking up the conversation. "She has appeared to be so repentant, and so grateful for all we have done for her."

"And yet," Constance Marfield returned, "I have noticed when she did not think that I was looking at her a baneful expression in her face. I shall not feel easy in my mind until Ralph comes back. His absences have grown more frequent, and I begin to fear that he must be in some trouble."

"We must leave all to him," Daisy replied. "He knows best, and rest assured that he weighs the consequence of all his actions before putting them into operation."

Constance Marfield sighed so deeply that even Mrs. Corcoran, in her elevated position, could hear it.

She waited to hear no more.

It was enough for her to know that Ralph Ashton was not at home.

Pacing slowly and stealthily towards the window the hag rolled up the window-blind with her hands, and looked out.

The night was dark.

The new born moon was hidden under heavy clouds, and not a star twinkled in the sky.

The window-sash was an old one, and might make a noise if anybody attempted to raise it.

But Mrs. Corcoran, artful and cunning, was at no loss for a method.

Placing one hand heavily upon the upper portion of the sash she proceeded to raise the lower so slowly that the movement was almost imperceptible.

The hag held her breath until she grew purple in the face.

At last the aperture was sufficiently large to admit of her passing through, and then she began to breathe more freely.

The distance between the room and the ground was fully twenty feet, and, for such an old woman as Mrs. Corcoran was, the task of dropping into the garden without meeting with some dire accident seemed next to an impossibility.

But Mrs. Corcoran was not the woman to halt at trifles, or even at difficulties when she had made up her mind to overcome them.

Twisting a pair of sheets into knots she secured them together, and having tied one end to the bedstead, she lowered the other quietly out of the window.

These proceedings took scarcely a minute to accomplish, and then Mrs. Corcoran began to descend.

It was a bold act, but she thought of nothing and cared for nothing so long as she could leave the house behind her back.

Down, down she went.

Her shrivelled fingers cracked and seemed to turn red hot. But she held on like grim death.

Her feet touched the ground at last, and she could scarcely suppress a cry of exultation.

"Ho! ho!" she croaked. "Free at last! Now, my fine gentlemen and finer ladies, we shall see how much good my confessions will do you. Fool that I was to open my mouth like a gaping idiot! You shall pay a heavy ransom for this, my dears."

Scudding across the garden, she reached the gate.

Her hand was upon it to push it open, when she heard the sound of approaching footsteps.

Mrs. Corcoran darted into the midst of a clump of laurel bushes and flung herself flat upon the earth.

The footsteps approached.

The gate opened, and a man with heavy, determined strides passed into the garden.

Mrs. Corcoran could not see who it was but she guessed that Ralph Ashton had returned.

In that case there would soon be a hue and cry after her.

As soon as the footsteps ceased to sound on the gravelled pathway Mrs. Corcoran rose and took to her aged heels.

If the arch-fiend had been behind her, and bent on taking her, she could not have gone faster.

Down roads and lanes she sped, until her strength gave way and she fell a huddled heap by the roadside.

A sharp cracking sound that rang through the air like a pistol shot brought Mrs. Corcoran to her feet again.

She heard the sound of heavy wheels and a man's voice urging a team of horses on.

"A waggon bound for London!" said Mrs. Corcoran. "What a slice of luck it will be if I can get a lift."

She had no money, but she argued that such a circumstance might be rather in her favour.

She was old and poor, and where was the man who would not pity her?"

The waggon came on, and then Mrs. Corcoran proceeded to act her part.

"Oh! please sir," she cried, shrilly, "will you give a poor woman, old enough to be your blessed mother, a lift on these dismal roads?"

"Whoa, there!" shouted the waggoner. "Who speaks?"

Mrs. Corcoran came forward as the horses, obedient to the well-known voice, brought the lumbersome vehicle to a standstill.

The night was so dark that the waggoner could not see how ugly Mrs. Corcoran was, or it is more than probable that, good-natured as he was, he would have left her to more tender mercies than his own.

"Oh! it's a woman," said the waggoner, with emphasis. "Well, what is the matter with you?"

A certain amount of suspicion lurked in the tone of his voice, for he had met more than one footpad disguised in female attire.

"Bless your dear heart!" Mrs. Corcoran whined; "I must have perished if I had not met you."

"Well, well," said the waggoner, impatiently. "What do you want?"

"A lift on the road to London, if you are going so far."

"That's exactly where I am going to," the waggoner replied. "I suppose you have no money—eh?"

"Not a farthing."

"Then don't tell me a long story about your poverty, because I am in a hurry," said the waggoner. "Jump up and make yourself as comfortable as possible. You'll find plenty of straw at the bottom of the waggon."

Straw! No clover could have been sweeter to Mrs. Corcoran's senses.

She burrowed in it like a mole, and was soon fast asleep.

When she awoke daylight had come, and the sun was high and shining gloriously bright.

The waggon still went on as if it were a piece of jolting, rumbling clockwork.

Mrs. Corcoran still kept herself concealed, for as yet there were no signs of London.

By peeping through the straw she could see the hedgerows on both sides of the road, but presently houses of town-type began to appear.

They grew greater in number and closer together, so Mrs. Corcoran began to argue that she could not be far away from her destination.

At last the waggon stopped, and the man in charge climbed up.

He looked rather surprised that he could see nothing of Mrs. Corcoran, but presently a rustling in the straw convinced him that she had not slipped away, or rolled out behind.

"Now then, mother," he said, "here we are at Camberwell-gate, and I go no further."

Mrs. Corcoran crept out, and her appearance so alarmed the waggoner that he vacated his position and jumped down into the road.

"What's the matter, deary?" the hag asked, as she descended. "Thank you, lovey, for the nice ride."

The waggoner said nothing, but he opened and shut his mouth like a fish out of water.

"You don't seem to be at all well, my pet?" said Mrs. Corcoran, grinning.

"Well," the waggoner blurted out, "you may think it well that I did not catch sight of you last night."

"And pray why?" demanded Mrs. Corcoran, curtseying.

"Because I would rather have been hung than had you in my waggon."

"You don't say so?"

"I do; and what's more, I mean it," the waggoner replied.

Mrs. Corcoran laughed like a hyena.

"Well, now, that's odd," said she. "I had a boy like you once, but he died before his time. Take care that the same thing does not happen to you."

"Out, out, witch!" said the waggoner, half in rage and half in terror. "Keep your evil eyes from mine, and take yourself off."

Mrs. Corcoran smirked and grinned as she turned her back upon the man who had done her such good service.

"Camberwell-gate," she muttered; "then I can't be very far away from the Borough. I'll look in at the Bull in Top Boots and find out all I can about Bill Blarney."

The distance was not more than two miles and a-half, but it took Mrs. Corcoran fully an hour to get over the ground.

The landlord of the Bull in Top Boots stood in his shirt sleeves at the door.

His attitude was a reflective one.

The expression of his face was sad, and his head had sunk between his shoulders, as if bowed down by no common sorrow.

He did not observe Mrs. Corcoran, and she crept up stealthily behind him.

"Poor fellow—poor Bill Blarney!" the landlord said, half aloud. "I little thought that you would come to such an end after all your troubles."

Mrs. Corcoran advanced with cat-like movements, and touched him lightly on the shoulder.

The landlord of the Bull in Top Boots turned sharply round, and staggered back at the sight of the hag.

"You didn't expect me?" said Mrs. Corcoran.

"No, I didn't; and if you want to know the truth, I—"

Mrs. Corcoran checked the rest of his speech by holding up her hand.

"The truth is all very well in its way," she said; "but it won't save Bill Blarney's neck, eh? Don't you think that if the truth be spoken, as it will be, unless something is done, that it will go a long way to stretch Blarney's neck?"

"I don't follow you," the inn-keeper said, with an expression of loathing and disgust upon his face.

"What fools men are!" Mrs. Corcoran said. "Women possess all the wit and wisdom. Listen to me. I have been staying with some of the witnesses for the prosecution."

"You—you have?"

"Yes; with Constance Marfield, Daisy Leigh, and Ralph Ashton."

"You are mad!" said the landlord of the Bull in Top Boots. "I don't believe a word you say."

"I can't help that," Mrs. Corcoran returned; "and if you persist in remaining pig-headed, the fault will be none of mine. What would you say if I told you that I have hit upon a plan to save Bill Blarney's life?"

"That you were a fool, and a liar into the bargain."

"Of course you would," Mrs. Corcoran said, in no wise put out by this amiable speech; "but such a plan I have, and could, with a little help, put it into successful operation."

"Come in," said the innkeeper, holding the door open. "Dick Sleuth is in the parlour, and crying his eyes out at the loss of his old pal."

"I never knew tears to do much good," said Mrs. Corcoran. "If I thought that I could have my way by snivelling I'd shed buckets full."

Having entered the inn Mrs. Corcoran requested to be served with refreshments.

She refused to say a word until she had eaten and drunk her fill, and then she seemed to be in no hurry to speak.

On the other side of the table sat Dick Sleuth in an attitude of dejection.

It was odd to see this brutal ruffian shedding grimy tears for the fate of a villain as bad, if not worse, than himself.

"And so," said Mrs. Corcoran, after fully half an hour had passed, "to-morrow Bill Blarney will be tried for his life."

"He will," Dick Sleuth responded, dismally, "and all the ruses we have tried to get into the prison have proved ineffectual."

"Ah!" said Mrs. Corcoran, "what else could you expect? Young man, you have something to learn yet."

"Come, come," said the landlord, impatiently, "we are not here to waste words. If you really have anything to say to the purpose out with it."

Mrs. Corcoran took another sip of brandy, and blinked so hideously over the top of the glass that both the landlord and Dick Sleuth felt inclined to throw something heavy at her.

"Now to talk sensibly," said Mrs. Corcoran. "Now to show you that I am really in earnest."

"Ah! that's the style," said the landlord.

"Is Bill Blarney's mother alive?"

This question seemed so far away from rescuing the scoundrel that Dick Sleuth and the landlord could only stare aghast at each other and in silence.

Mr. Corcoran repeated her question.

"How should I know?" Dick Sleuth rejoined. "I never heard him say that he had a mother at all."

"But he must have had," Mrs. Corcoran returned, "and the fact of his not mentioning her proves to me that she is dead."

"Well, what of it?" gasped the landlord. "What the devil has Bill Blarney's mother to do with getting him out of Newgate?"

"Everything."

"Bless my bones and shoe-buckles!" said the landlord; "why don't you speak out plainly and not keep us beating about the bush in this fashion?"

"I am coming to the point presently," said Mrs. Corcoran, calmly. "The more haste less speed, and experience has taught me never to do anything in a hurry."

The landlord made a gurgling sound in his throat and drummed his fingers impatiently upon the table.

"Well," he said, with a groan of resignation, "I'll say no more; but leave you to explain yourself as you think proper."

"That's right, deary," Mrs. Corcoran replied. "I am going to take the place of Bill Blarney's mother."

Dick Sleuth shot out his legs, and almost upset the heavy table.

"Yes," Mrs. Corcoran returned; "I am going to take the place of Bill Blarney's mother. I am not as yet known at Newgate, and if the warders' hearts be made of stone, they will listen to me."

A light suddenly dawned on the minds of Mrs. Corcoran's listeners.

The landlord of the Bull in Top Boots smote his thigh, and Dick Sleuth's face brightened up considerably.

"You begin to see that there is something in my plan after all?" Mrs. Corcoran said.

"I do," Dick Sleuth said; "but I am thirsting to know more. A close watch is kept on the warders, and they cannot be bribed."

"I they could, I would not give them a penny," Mrs. Corcoran rejoined. "I have a better idea than that. How many men can you muster here at any given time?"

"About twenty-five," the landlord replied.

"Strong, game, and willing to risk a little danger for the sake of an old friend like Bill Blarney?"

"Yes."

"Then bid them come," said Mrs Corcoran. "I will go to Bill Blarney and tell him that his friends will be in court and make a rush to get him out of the dock."

Dick Sleuth's face fell again, and the landlord looked extremely dubious.

"You have not calculated on how the court will be guarded," he said.

"Oh! yes I have," Mrs. Corcoran replied; "and the more officers present the better the chance of rescue, for the officers will only fall over each other, and hamper each others movements."

"There is something in this," said the landlord, glancing at Dick Sleuth.

"Yes," he replied, "and every time I think of it I like it better."

"Mrs. Corcoran, you are no beauty, but your head is screwed on the right way."

"I wish I could return the compliment," the hag returned, grimly. "Well, the next thing is, I must have funds. If the warders cannot be bribed to set Bill Blarney free, they will not be above taking a guinea or two from his poor old mother."

This seemed to tickle the landlord so that he roared with laughter as he drew out his purse.

"How much will you want?" he asked.

"Give me ten guineas, and send for a hackney coach."

The first part of the request was no sooner made than complied with.

The golden coins jingled musically on the table, and Mrs. Corcoran, gathering them up with her fish-hook-like fingers, stowed them away in some remote portion of her attire.

"When will you start?" the landlord asked.

"As soon as you like," Mrs. Corcoran replied. "The sooner the better."

"In an hour's time, then?"

"That will do."

---

## CHAPTER C.

### JOE ROLLINS TURNS UPON HIS MASTER.

The sudden extinguishing of the light, followed by the peal of mocking laughter, had such an effect upon Sir Roland Ashton and Joe Rollins, that strength of action and power of speech failed them.

The weird, unearthly laughter was not repeated, and Sir Roland, after groping helplessly about in the darkness, suddenly ran violently up against Joe Rollins, who turned swiftly and seized the baronet by the throat.

A deadly struggle took place.

Rollins was no more sure of who he had encountered than Sir Roland was into whose hands he had fallen.

Writhing and struggling they reeled hither and thither.

Now it was Sir Roland who was uppermost, and then Joe Rollins.

Both men had a grip of iron, and exerted their strength to the utmost.

At last Joe Rollins got Sir Roland down and pressed his thumbs into his throat.

"I am choking," the baronet gasped. "Help! Mercy! Help!"

Maddened with rage and fear as Rollins was, he recognised Sir Roland's voice, and relaxed his hold.

For some time Sir Roland lay perfectly still, and Joe Rollins thought he had killed him.

"Well, I don't suppose it matters much," Rollins thought. "No doubt Loddon will be able to find as good if not a better man to do the work at Mildendale Hall. But this is, nevertheless, unfortunate. How am I to explain it away?"

At that moment a hollow groan broke upon his ears.

Sir Roland Ashton was not dead, but he had been very near saying good-bye to this world.

"Come, come," said Joe Rollins, "there is not so much harm done after all. Let me raise you up, Sir Roland. I mistook you in the dark for an enemy."

Sir Roland raised himself upon his elbow, and placed his hand upon his throat, which still bore the indentations of Rollins' finger marks.

"You villain!" the baronet hissed. "You shall suffer for this!"

"I am truly sorry," was the answer; "but you cannot forget that you grappled with me. How was I to know that I was not struggling with—"

"Spring-Heeled Jack!" said a voice in his ear.

"Did you speak, Sir Roland?" Joe Rollins asked.

"No," the baronet replied.

"I could have sworn that I heard some other voice than your own," Joe Rollins said.

The baronet turned cold with fear.

He guessed who had spoken, and in the open air would not have been so much alarmed.

The darkness made a coward of him, and the very being whose life he sought might retaliate by taking his.

A silence ensued after this.

Joe Rollins fumbled about with the flint and steel which he never moved about without.

At last he procured a light and trimmed the lamp.

"Let us get away," he said, casting a hasty, shuddering glance into the dungeon where the skeleton lay. "I cannot breathe the atmosphere of this place."

Sir Roland was still weak from the effects of the struggle, but he, too, being anxious to leave the loathsome spot, followed as quickly as possible after Joe Rollins.

The last-named stopped and applied his hand to the door which divided two staircases.

The door did not yield to his touch.

It was locked and fast.

Joe Rollins turned his head slowly and looked askance at Sir Roland Ashton.

"It would seem that we are caught in another trap," Rollins said, hoarsely. "What hands but ours, or such as are bent on taking our lives, could have fastened this door?"

"I know not," Sir Roland replied. "There may be some mistake; try again."

Joe Rollins did so, and more vigorously than before, but the result was the same.

And now a new fear crept into Sir Roland Ashton's base and blackened heart.

He made sure that Spring-Heeled Jack was at the bottom of all the mischief; but could he tell Joe Rollins what he feared?

"Let me try," he said, frantically; "even if the door be fast, there must be some means of removing the lock."

"What other means have we?" Rollins asked. "You speak as a man who is hiding something from me. What is it?"

"Nothing—nothing!"

"I will not take that for an excuse," Rollins said. "You fear something. I have noticed you turn your head over your shoulder from time to time, as if you thought you were being followed."

"A mere idle fancy on your part," said Sir Roland Ashton."

He forced the words and a smile to his lips.

"Well, I care not, so long as we get out of this stone cage," Joe Rollins said. "Hark! Do you not hear those ravenous rats? They have glutted themselves on some poor wretch, and will serve us the same if we are not away."

An idea flashed into Sir Roland's brain.

He drew his rapier from its sheath, and removed the point by breaking it off under his foot.

"A novel screw-driver this," he said, "but it may serve. Stand aside, my friend, and I will see if I can get you and I out of this little difficulty."

"A little difficulty you call it!" Joe Rollins growled. "What more could a man wish to make him miserable? Death below, hungry-eyed and sharp-teethed rats on all sides, and an iron door between him and liberty."

"Talking is useless," Sir Roland said. "Hold the lantern in such a position that I can examine the lock."

"Bah! it is waste of time," Joe Rollins said. "Better trust to our voices in the hope of rousing somebody."

"We shall see," Sir Roland replied. "A farmer's wife knows that there is more ways than one to kill a goose, and the same saying must apply to a captive desirous of getting out of prison."

Joe Rollins shook his head, but Sir Roland, pushing him aside almost contemptuously, went to work with a will.

The screws in the lock were old and rusty, and refused to yield.

Sir Roland persevered, and presently one of the heads of the screws gave way.

"I should have thought of this before," he said. "I might have known that it would be impossible to turn the screws in their present state."

"You had better think of something definite, and act upon it," Joe Rollins growled. "The light will not hold out much longer."

Sir Roland Ashton made no reply; but again shortening his rapier by breaking it into two parts, he hacked away at the screws until they yielded one by one.

Then the lock came off easily enough, and soon Sir Roland, and Joe Rollins were in the inhabited portion of the house.

Sir Roland Ashton sat down to rest.

He pressed his hand to his throbbing brow and tried to think calmly.

In what manner had Jules Carleon, the Frenchman, met his awful fate?

How had he come to Cypress House, and for what purpose?

Sir Roland asked himself these questions again and again, but all was a mystery to him.

Presently he heard a commotion in the hall below, and, to his astonishment, James Loddon was ushered into his presence.

"What has happened?" Sir Roland cried, starting to his feet.

"Nothing," Loddon replied. "Don't alarm yourself. I thought I would come to see how you were getting on, and talk over our future prospects."

The cloud of anxiety which had gathered upon Sir Roland's face cleared away.

Joe Rollins did not move until James Loddon gave him a meaning glance, and then he withdrew.

"I have come to say that your visit to Lord Mildendale must be postponed for a few days," Loddon said.

"Why?"

"Because his lordship is very unwell," James Loddon replied. "Have you no other scheme yon can think of?"

In a moment Sir Roland's evil mind went back to Ralph Ashton, and the fair girls under his protection.

He told his sleek-faced, villainous patron of the story from beginning to end, and dwelt eloquently on the beauty of Constance Marfield and Daisy Leigh.

"It shall be done," Loddon said, when Sir Roland had ceased speaking. "I have more power than even you dream of. The girls shall be taken from Ralph Ashton, but for some time, at least, they must not be brought here."

"Where to, then?"

"Leave that to me," said James Loddon. "Fill up your glass, Sir Roland—or Mr. Fernie, as I suppose I must call you. Here's to our health, and may we triumph."

"One more word," said Sir Roland. "Will my services be required in removing the girls?"

"No," Loddon returned. "I will arrange everything in my own way."

---

## CHAPTER CI.

### THE MYSTERIOUS STRANGER.

It was Ralph Ashton who passed Mrs. Corcoran so closely.

He looked worn out and tired, but he nevertheless greeted Constance and Daisy with his old fervour.

"Well," he said, "and how is the patient progressing?"

"I was just saying that I wished you would come home," Constance said, as she nestled down at his side. "I have not liked the old woman's ways since you have been away."

"Ah!" Ralph exclaimed, "you mistrust her, then?"

"I do."

# SPRING-HEELED JACK,

## THE TERROR OF LONDON.

THE DOORS FLEW OPEN WITH A CRASH AND SPRING-HEELED JACK APPEARED.

"You think she is desirous of leaving us?" Ralph Ashton asked.

"That is exactly my idea," Constance replied. "She seems fidgety and ill at ease."

"At all events she must remain here until after that scoundrel Blarney's trial," Ralph said. "Daisy, run upstairs, and tell Mrs. Corcoran that I wish to speak to her."

Daisy rose at once and went upstairs.

Presently a scream from her lips startled Ralph Ashton and Constance Marfield.

Ralph rushed out into the hall and met Daisy, whose face was so pale that, for a moment, he was appalled.

"She is gone!" Daisy cried.

"Gone?" Ralph repeated. "Impossible! She must be hiding somewhere."

"No—no," Daisy replied, wildly. "The window is open, and she escaped from it, as the knotted sheets testify."

The idea of Mrs. Corcoran lowering herself out of the window was so odd that Ralph Ashton did not know whether to laugh or give vent to his anger.

"If she is really gone," he said, "there is an end of the matter for the present; but, fear not, I will find her before many hours have fled over our heads."

Ralph searched the house himself, but with no result; and then, closing the window, he went downstairs to supper.

In the morning one of the servants brought a note to Constance from Ralph.

He had departed again, but promised to return soon.

Constance looked a little sulky.

Her lover was so seldom at her side now.

But her face cleared when she remembered that she owed all to the man who had played so brave and noble a part.

Constance and Daisy spent the day together, and in the evening sat down in the window recess to work and chat.

They were suddenly stopped in their conversation by hearing a rustling sound amongst the foliage in the garden, and, looking towards the spot from whence it seemed to proceed, they beheld the form of a man suddenly emerge from one of the walks and advance towards the house.

They at first took but little notice of this circumstance, for they imagined that it might only be one of the servants who had been absent from home.

But when the man made a pause, and stood immediately beneath the window, raising his eyes towards the room, their curiosity and surprise were increased.

They hastily withdrew from the window, and they were both of them so much amazed that they could not speak for a minute or two.

"Oh! Constance," at length said Daisy, "this, at any rate, is sufficient to create our most serious apprehension and suspicion. Such conduct as this, and from a stranger, is most mysterious. He can have no good motive in coming to the house at such an hour."

"Nay, Daisy," said her companion. "We have nothing to fear, for he cannot obtain an entrance to the house, if such even should be his wish. Such singular behaviour as this looks like that of a madman."

"He must have been hiding and watching us for some time," said Daisy. "He may have companions at hand, and should he have any evil designs against us, unless we alarm the servants, they may labour under every disadvantage, and the consequences might be fatal."

"Do not disturb yourself, Daisy," Constance replied. "Should we see anything farther to strengthen our apprehensions we can instantly ring the alarm bell, and the plans of this mysterious intruder will be frustrated."

They now ventured again to glance from the window and beheld the mysterious stranger still standing there, in the same attitude as before.

They had a full view of his countenance by the light of the moon without his being able to observe them, and they saw that he was a remarkably handsome man about the middle age, but they had not the slightest recollection of his features.

However, he had all the appearance of a gentleman, and one who had travelled far, for his face was dark and swarthy, as if tanned with the sun.

"This is certainly most extraordinary," said Daisy. "Who can this stranger be, and what is it that prompts him to such suspicious and singular conduct?"

"I cannot conjecture," Constance replied; "but it certainly, as I said before, looks more like the behaviour of a madman than anything else."

"I repeat that he must have watched us, or obtained some information in the neighbourhood respecting us."

"And of what interest would that be to a stranger?" Constance asked.

"I am completely bewildered," Daisy said; "still, he appears to be alone."

They now once more looked from the window, and found that the object of their anxiety and curiosity was gone.

"He has probably only removed round to another part of the house," said Daisy. "It cannot be any good that has brought him here at this hour of the night."

"What designs can he possibly have?" said Constance. "He does not look like a robber; besides, no one could be so daring as to attempt any outrage alone. Compose yourself, Daisy, I do not believe that we have anything to fear."

A quarter of an hour elapsed in this manner, and they saw nothing more of the stranger.

They made up their minds that whatever might have been his intentions at first, he had abandoned them and departed, and they, therefore, became more easy in their minds.

All remained still in the house, and the fair girls at length sought their beds, and, notwithstanding the numerous thoughts this remarkable circumstance created in their breasts, they soon fell asleep, from which they did not awaken till the morning.

At the usual hour they were summoned to breakfast, and to their great delight found that Ralph Ashton was waiting to welcome them.

After the repast was concluded Constance related to her lover the adventure of the night before, Ralph Ashton listened to her with the most unbounded amazement.

"Can this be possible?" said Ralph; "or are you certain that you were not mistaken?"

"Oh! no," replied Constance; "that could not be. Daisy and myself were both sitting at the window when we saw him, and he remained in the same attitude for several minutes."

"Well," Ralph returned, "such behaviour as this, and from a perfect stranger, is to me perfectly unaccountable. I must endeavour to find him out and to demand an explanation. He may mean harm, and yet he cannot be one of our old foes, for I have good reason to know that they are far away. It is perfectly inexplicable. And you have no recollection of his features?"

"Not in the least," Constance replied.

"And he has not the appearance of a thief?" Ralph asked.

"Oh! no," said Daisy. "On the contrary, he has all the aspect and bearing of a gentleman. Constance has suggested that his intellects are deranged."

Ralph lost no time in making every inquiry in the neighbourhood, but without any success.

Nothing more, however, was seen or heard of the mysterious stranger, and when the day had passed by they began to think that there was no further ground for their alarm, although the singular visit of the gentleman to the garden still remained to them all a matter of the greatest astonishment.

Constance and Daisy had almost forgotten to think of it, and their minds were fully occupied with the affairs of more immediate interest to them.

But the troubles of Constance and Daisy were not yet at an end, notwithstanding their prospects now appeared so promising; fresh calamities were in store for them, and from a source which they could never have expected.

They had now been living at the riverside villa for some weeks, and since the appearance of the mysterious stranger nothing beyond the advent of Mrs. Corcoran and her escape had occurred to disturb them, and they therefore believed most confidently that all apprehensions of future danger were entirely at an end.

They frequently exchanged visits with the neighbouring gentry, and their society was sought after with avidity by all the most fashionable and honourable persons in the county.

Sometimes Ralph was called from home.

Daisy and Constance would take a ramble among the surrounding scenery alone, for they apprehended no danger, and felt confident that they were too much esteemed for any one to wish or attempt to molest them.

On such occasions they would seldom recur to the past, but form the most sanguine anticipations of the future, and look forward to the time when they should be united to those who possessed their undivided affections.

Ralph Ashton was called away by a message brought to him by a man on horseback, and in the afternoon the girls went for their accustomed walk.

They strayed rather farther than was their usual custom.

As it was peculiarly fine, they did not regret the circumstance.

Having rested themselves for a short time at the cottage of an honest old woman, whom they had greatly befriended, they once more turned their steps towards home.

Deeply engaged in conversation, they had proeeded some distance, when they were suddenly roused by hearing a hasty footstep behind them.

Looking round they beheld, to their terror, the mysterious stranger, who had before caused them so much alarm, approaching quickly towards them.

They were so overcome with confusion, amazement, and alarm, that they were unable to move, and their fears increased when they could perceive no other person near the spot to whom they might appeal for protection.

They clung to each other in consternation, and the object of their terror, uttering an exclamation of exultation, increased his speed, and soon came up to the two breathless and trembling girls.

"Thank my lucky stars!" he exclaimed; "the opportunity I have so long sighed for is at length granted me, and I am permitted to gaze upon the most lovely of Nature's works. You are no strangers to me, although I am unknown to you."

He addressed his observations more particularly to Daisy, and it was with difficulty that she could find words to make any reply to this bold and insolent speech.

But at last, in a voice in which which shame and indignation were blended, she spoke.

"Who are you, sir," she exclaimed, "that dare thus to insult two unprotected females? Begone! and let us pass unmolested on our way, or you may have cause to repent most bitterly the outrage you now attempt to commit upon our feelings."

"No, by all my hopes! I have longed too ardently for this meeting to suffer us to part so easily," returned the stranger, with increased boldness. "You must listen to me. I have watched my opportnnity, and I know that you are alone."

"Help—help!" Daisy screamed.

"Cease your cries!" said the stranger; "for sooner would I perish than inflict the slightest injury on you. But I must, I will, reveal the passion with which your superlative charms have inspired me, even though death should immediately follow my presumption. I am a gentleman, wealthy, honourable, and am ready to lay my heart and fortune at your feet. Again I swear to become your slave for ever, and—"

Again Daisy's screams and Constance's cries for help interrupted him.

At that moment an enraged voice was heard calling loudly upon the villain to desist, and Constance uttered a scream of delight when she beheld Ralph Ashton coming towards the spot.

The stranger saw him, and giving utterance to an exclamation of vexation and disappointment, he fled, and before Ralph could reach the spot, he was out of sight, and had effected his escape.

"Thank Heaven I have been enabled to return!" Ralph said, in a voice hoarse with rage and emotion. "Who was that man?"

"The stranger, Ralph," Constance replied; "the man who some time since so excited our fears and suspicions."

"Is it possible?" exclaimed Ralph; "and he has escaped!"

"He has dared to speak of love to Daisy," Constance said.

"The daring ruffian!" Ralph Ashton cried, his eyes flashing with resentment; "who can it be? But I will find him out and punish him for this outrage. Daisy, compose yourself. You are safe now."

"Oh! yes," said Daisy, who had now partially recovered from the terror; "with you, Mr. Ashton, I know I am. Oh! how have my feelings been outraged by this mysterious, this unknown man. I had hoped that all my troubles were at an end, and that there was no other individual left who would seek to annoy me. Why am I thus selected for constant persecution?"

"Come," said Ralph; "let us return home. Fear not, but I will devise some future means of discovering this stranger and bringing him to an account for his actions."

Daisy made no reply, and they moved towards the villa.

It would be useless to attempt to describe the

excitement which this adventure caused in the minds of Constance and Daisy; but they were unable to form the least conjecture as to who the stranger was, and all the endeavours of Ralph Ashton and the men he had set to watch were without effect.

Ralph Ashton was burning with rage, and was determined, should he discover the perpetrator of the outrage, to try conclusions with him by dint of cold steel.

It was strange, most strange, that no person in the neighbourhood had the least knowledge of having seen the man.

From all that Constance and Daisy had seen of him, he seemed, both from his manners and appearance, to be a person in a superior station of life, and that circumstance rendered him the more formidable enemy to contend with.

But Ralph determined not to relax in his endeavours until he had found him out and obtained satisfaction for the offence he had already committed, and to prevent the perpetration of any further outrage.

"It seems, dear Constance," Daisy said, when they were alone, "as if I were never destined to have a moment's peace."

"Fear not," Constance replied. "No one will now attempt to harm you; and this stranger, when he reflects upon their utter impracticability, will doubtless abandon his designs, and probably he has by this time left the neighbourhood altogether for fear of detection. He must be mad—he is mad."

"And yet I cannot divest my mind of the fears that have taken possession of it," Daisy returned.

"Try to do so, for I must hope that they are groundless."

"The boldness of his looks and words show him to be a determined man."

"But Ralph is on his guard against him, and any attempt that he might make must fail of success."

"After what I have already experienced, is it not enough to make me apprehensive?" said Daisy.

"True," Constance replied; "but this stranger can have no opportunity of putting any designs he may have formed into execution."

"Ah! Constance, we well know the artifices that suggest themselves to the minds of bad men. How much have we both suffered from them, when even every precaution was used to protect us?"

"Let us hope that such dangers will never occur to either of us again."

"Alas!" said Daisy, sighing; "if they should, I could never, I am convinced, again find fortitude to support them. Ours has been a strange life, Constance."

"It has," Constance returned; "but I must confess that I do not see anything in this recent circumstance to create such serious alarm."

"I would that I could make up my mind to think so," Daisy replied; "but I can never be sufficiently thankful to Ralph for my deliverance in such a critical moment of peril."

On the following morning Daisy and Constance would be on their way to London to give evidence against Bill Blarney.

Ralph Ashton, having left the house well guarded, suddenly disappeared, leaving Constance warning that neither she nor Daisy were to venture out-of-doors on any account.

About eight o'clock in the evening a servant brought word that a beggar in great distress was at the gate.

Ever alive to the feelings of humanity, and apprehending no danger, the girls asked to see him, and when the beggar was presented to them they beheld the aged form of a man leaning on a crutch, and to all appearance in the last stage of illness and destitution.

Their hearts were moved to the tenderest compassion at the sight of this pitiable object, especially when he lifted his head and revealed his countenance, pale and emaciated, evidently with want and misery.

"For the love of mercy! good, kind ladies," he said, in a faint voice, "bestow your benevolence upon a poor old soldier, who has fought hard in the service of his country, and has received no other reward but wounds and neglect."

"Poor man!" said Daisy, taking out her purse and presenting the man with a piece of gold.

"Oh! thanks—thanks, most benevolent lady," said the beggar. "But—but—oh! I am so faint. I have not tasted food for many hours—my poor limbs fail me—oh!"

As the miserable old man thus spoke he sank down upon the floor, apparently completely exhausted, and looked imploringly at Constance and Daisy.

"Unfortunate man," said Daisy, "wait but a moment, and we will procure you some refreshment."

"Oh! Heaven be thanked," he ejaculated, looking gratefully upon those around him. "Heaven be thanked for sending me such kind friends in the hour of my extreme misery. I have limped many a weary mile this day, and have not broken my fast for many hours, but your benevolence has saved my life."

The beggar was once more about to return his thanks, but Daisy waved her hand, and committed him to the care of the servants with strict injunctions to see to his comfort.

It was not long after this that the girls thought about retiring for the night.

"Why do you sigh so, Daisy, and appear so melancholy?" inquired Constance.

"I know not from what cause," Daisy replied; "but within the last few minutes an unconquerable sensation has come over me, as if something dreadful was about to happen. I wish it was morning."

"Most strange!" said Constance; "nothing has occurred to you to-day to occasion this, and you must endeavour to shake off the sad impression."

"I will try, Constance; but, alas! I fear that I shall not succeed. Last night, too, I had strange dreams, that have at intervals tormented my mind ever since."

"Nay, this is weakness."

"It may be so, but I cannot conquer it."

"Try—try. There is certainly no occasion for your sadness that I can perceive. There is no danger at hand."

"Heaven send that there may not be," said Daisy; "but again I wish that it were morning and that we were once more with Mr. Ashton."

"He is not far from us, and what should we have to dread?" demanded Constance.

"I know not; and yet something seems to whisper to me 'Beware!'"

"For goodness sake do not give way to these apprehensions."

"I know I must appear very ridiculous, Constance," Daisy returned; "but in spite of all the efforts of my better reason I cannot help it. Do not let us retire to rest yet, my dear Constance."

Constance looked at her with the utmost surprise, especially when she beheld that she was trembling violently, and knew not what answer to make.

"Well," she said at last, "I do not feel tired, and therefore have not the least objection to comply with your request. But it grieves me to see you in this melancholy mood. Let's talk on other subjects."

The house was now wrapped in the most profound silence, and the clock at that moment struck twelve.

"Hush! Hark!" Daisy said, holding up her hand and directing her eyes towards the door. "What was that?"

"What?"

"Did you not hear that noise?" Daisy asked, still looking towards the door.

"I heard nothing," Constance replied. "You have suffered your fears to get the better of you."

"No, no. I am almost certain I heard the closing of a door."

"And what of that?" Constance demanded. "Most likely it was one of the servants who has only just retired to rest."

"Ah! it seemed to come from the direction of their rooms," said Daisy.

"Come, indeed I do not see that you have any cause for alarm. Let us retire to rest."

"Not yet—not yet."

"Why, it is now midnight."

"True! but, oh!—hark again! Surely that was the front door which was cautiously opened."

"Ridiculous!" said Constance. "Who would open the front door at this hour?"

Daisy made no answer, but her face became paler, and she trembled excessively as she listened with breathless attention.

And now a strange noise also met Constance's ears, and she involuntarily clung to her companion in fearful amazement and expectation.

"Gracious Heaven!" exclaimed Daisy. "Do you not hear footsteps ascending the stairs towards this room? Some treachery is at work. Ah! the old beggar. Who—"

Before she could finish the sentence the room door was burst open, and several men, whose faces were concealed in black masks, entered the chamber and rushed upon them before they had time to utter a cry of alarm.

"Take her!" said one of the intruders, who appeared to be the leader, pointing to Daisy. "Seize her and away!"

The terrified girls now shrieked aloud, but immediately their mouths were gagged, and while two of the ruffians seized upon Daisy the others bound the distracted Constance, in spite of all her violent efforts to release herself from them.

A large mantle was now thrown over Daisy's head. She felt herself lifted in the arms of the men and borne from the apartment.

The horror of her feelings overcame her, and she fell insensible.

## CHAPTER CII.

### THE ANTIQUE WARDROBE.

The grey dawn of morning was stealing over the landscape when James Loddon galloped at a furious pace towards Dagenham.

On reaching Cypress House he threw the bridle-rein over his horse's neck and dismounted.

He was immediately admitted into the house by a man who had remained up all night to receive him.

"Where is Sir—Mr. Fernie?" Loddon asked, as he threw aside his cloak and wiped his heated brow.

"In bed."

"Conduct me to his room."

This was done at once, and James Loddon advancing to the bed, shook Sir Roland roughly by the shoulder.

The baronet started up and gave vent to a cry of alarm.

"Ha! ha! ha!" Loddon laughed. "Did you think that I was the old gentleman in black come to spirit you away?"

"I scarcely know what to think now," Sir Roland replied. "What on earth brings you here at such a time?"

"To tell you that my plan has succeeded."

"What!"

"Yes," Loddon cried, exultingly. "Daisy Leigh is in my power, and is by this time on the way to Reigate Caves. It will take a clever man to find her out now."

"But what of the other girl?" Sir Roland asked, when he had recovered from his surprise. "Did you not secure her also?"

"No," James Loddon replied; "I was afraid of having my hands too full. Have I not done enough, think you?"

"I have no reason to grumble," Sir Roland replied; "and yet—"

"Well," demanded James Loddon, finding that Sir Roland hesitated, "what else would you have had?"

"It would have pleased me better had I known that Ralph Ashton had been plunged into the very lowest depths of misery," Sir Roland replied.

"Let this console you," the other ruffian said. "I left the girl you call Constance bound, gagged, and senseless. If she recovers from the shock and fright it will be a wonder to me."

Sir Roland Ashton bit his under lip with an air of vexation.

"Fain would I have had an interview with her before she died," he said. "She deceived me—"

"Deceived you!" James Loddon interposed, with a roar of laughter. "Ha! ha! ha! That is not bad."

"Listen," Sir Roland said, as the hot blood of anger rushed into his face. "She underwent the ceremony of marriage with me, and—"

"Gave you the slip?"

"Yes."

"Then if she is your wife, why do you not claim her as such?" James Loddon asked.

"I scarcely know whether it would hold good in law," Sir Roland returned.

"Oh! I see," said Loddon. "It was one of those marriages where a friendly parson is called in in a hurry, and a woman is married to a man whether she cares for him or not?"

"I confess that you have struck the right nail on the head," Sir Roland said.

"Bah!" said James Loddon, with a contemptuous sneer. "If I were you I would say no more on that score. At all events, I am contented with my night's work. This Daisy Leigh is a little beauty, and no mistake. I am a jolly bachelor, and I will wed her. There shall be no mock marriage; I will tame her to my own will and then lead her to the altar."

"But she has a lover."

"His name?"

"Harry Banks."

"Ho! ho!" cried James Loddon. "Tell me where I can find this amorous gentleman."

"That is more than I can tell," Sir Roland replied.

"Harry Banks is my rival," said James Loddon, leering. "I will rob him of his bride. He shall wear a green willow round his hat for his lost love. Ha! ha!"

The villain spoke as if he had been drinking heavily.

"And now, my friend," he resumed, "you must begin to rehearse the part you have to play before Lord Mildendale. In yonder chest—here is the key—you will find plenty of fine clothes. And now, adieu!"

"You are going away?"

"Yes; to Reigate Caves."

"And when shall I have the pleasure of seeing you again?" Sir Roland asked.

"I know not," Loddon replied, as he moved towards the door.

The next instant the door had closed behind him, and Sir Roland Ashton leaped from the bed.

"Curse him!" he hissed. "What a fool I have been to tell him so much and to play into his hands! But wait—patience!"

"Patience!"

He heard the word repeated, but thinking that it was nothing but the echo of his own voice, paid no attention to it.

A man acting as sentry was pacing up and down outside the door.

Sir Roland called him in.

"I will break my fast in half an hour's time," the baronet said.

The man bowed and retired.

He communicated with somebody below, but did not desert his post.

"So," Sir Roland muttered, "I am suspected and watched. When Rollins—hang him!—leaves me another man takes his place. Very clever to clip my wings thus, but I will find means to fly before it is too late."

"Too late!"

Sir Roland Ashton turned his head and glanced suspiciously round the room.

"How now?" he said. "Am I not then alone?"

"Alone!"

Sir Roland became alarmed, all the more because the voice was so much like his own.

He threw open the cupboards, glanced into an old wardrobe, which as yet contained none of his personal effects, but he met with nothing to add to his fears.

A brace of pistols, inlaid with silver, lay upon the dressing-table.

He took them in his hand and examined them minutely.

The weapons were loaded and primed ready for use.

"Fool to be scared at the echo of my own voice!" he said. "Now to dress."

Sir Roland did so, and went down to breakfast.

No sooner had he entered the room in which the meal was prepared than Joe Rollins glided in and stood at his elbow.

Sir Roland did not greet him in the accustomed way.

"I hope you slept well," Rollins said.

"That is more than you can have done," Sir Roland replied, sulkily, "for you have been on guard all night."

"Oh!" Rollins replied, "I am one of those peculiar creatures who can sleep with one eye open."

Sir Roland made no reply, but went on with his breakfast.

When he had finished he took a walk, and spent the day in loitering about.

Evening was drawing near when James Loddon's injunctions suddenly occurred to him.

Repairing to his bedroom, he unlocked a chest and drew out a handsome court suit, and attired himself most carefully.

"Ha!" he said, as he gazed at his reflection in the mirror; "time and trouble have dealt easily with me after all. Curse that Rollins! There he goes, pacing up and down outside with the regularity of a pendulum. I am the same Sir Roland—"

"The same Sir Roland!" cried a voice.

The baronet did not move.

He had no need, for the mirror showed him every object in the room.

He heard the doors of the wardrobe open with a crash, and saw Spring-Heeled Jack standing between them in an imposing attitude.

"How handsome and noble is Sir Roland Ashton!" Spring-Heeled Jack said.

## CHAPTER CIII.

### MRS. CORCORAN GOES TO NEWGATE.

Mrs. Corcoran felt more than an ordinary amount of delight at the task she had set herself.

Her presence would quiet Bill Blarney.

It would keep his tongue still, and what was even more delicious to the old hag, she would be able to torment him without the fear of resentment.

Mrs. Corcoran did not look exactly like a lady who indulged in the luxury of a ride in a hackney-coach, and the driver mildly hinted that he would prefer seeing whether she could pay before he set the horses in motion.

The coachman, who had been blessed by nature with a face like a red-hot warming-pan, grinned from ear to ear when he saw a glittering guinea held temptingly between the hag's bony fingers, and actuated by the notion that he might get more than his legal fare, he whipped up his steed, and away went that wonderful machine on four wheels.

Mrs. Corcoran jolted from one side of the coach to the other, until what few teeth she still possessed chattered and rattled in her head.

She held on to whatever she could, and arrived at Newgate in almost a breathless state.

The coachman got down and touched his hat.

Mrs. Corcoran gibbered and grinned at him in so horrible a style that the man's bottle nose lost its beet-root hue, and he fell back a pace or two.

"Your fare," said Mrs. Corcoran, skipping at him sideways, "is two shillings. Oh! you villain, to treat an old woman like this."

"You said you wanted to do the journey quick, marm," the driver said.

"Quick!" Mrs. Corcoran screamed. "Did you think I wanted to be battered into a jelly? The wheels of your coach are all odd sizes, the window is cracked, and the straw on the floor as damp as ditch-water. Here's your money."

The coachman clutched at it, and climbed back to the box-seat with the utmost expedition.

"Witch—old witch!" he yelled, when he was at a safe distance; "where's your broomstick, you she-devil?"

Mrs. Corcoran paid no attention to the pleasant nick-names bestowed on her or to the amiable query.

She turned away, and walked up the steps leading to the warder's gate.

Then Mrs. Corcoran began to weep.

She positively howled as she applied her knuckles to the wicket, and became limp and faint as the face of a burly man appeared.

"Now, then," said the gaoler, with the gentle consideration of his class. "What are you kicking up all this shine about?"

"Oh! that I should live to see this day," Mrs. Corcoran moaned. "Oh! that the boy I have nursed in my arms should perish on the gibbet."

"What boy?" the warder demanded.

"My own Bill—my precious Bill."

"It strikes me that we have a good many Bills here," said the gaoler. "What's his other name?"

"Blarney!"

The head of the warder disappeared, and the wicket closed with a crash.

Mrs. Corcoran screwed up her lips and shut up one bleary eye.

She had not expected this kind of treatment, and the result of all her crocodile tears proved most disappointing to her.

"Ho! ho!" she muttered. "This is the game. Well, I will not despair, but go upon another tack."

Mrs. Corcoran took a guinea from her pocket, and slid it half-under the door.

She watched the coin with eagle eyes.

Presently it moved a little, and then disappeared as if the warder had suddenly discovered its presence and pounced upon it with the avidity of a hawk upon a sparrow.

Then Mrs. Corcoran knocked at the wicket again, and a little louder than before.

The aperture remained closed as if hermetically sealed.

"Odd—very odd!" the hag mumbled. "What on earth can the fellow mean? I suppose he is like a tiger who has tasted blood and wants more. Well, I'll try another, and if he keeps himself shut up I'll go to the governor and swear that he has accepted a bribe."

Mrs. Corcoran placed another guinea in exactly the same position as the first.

In like manner did it vanish.

Then came a faint clicking sound.

The wicket was ajar, and the warder was gazing at Mrs. Corcoran in mute astonishment.

"Please let me in?" Mrs. Corcoran whined. "What harm can a poor old creature like me do?"

"My orders are imperative," the warder replied. "Nobody is to see Bill Blarney before his sentence, which is as sure as you are on one side of the door and I on the other. Take your money back."

"No, no."

"But I say Yes."

"Listen to me a moment," Mrs. Corcoran pleaded. "I am Bill Blarney's mother—the only real friend he ever had. The poor lad fell into bad company, and if he suffers, others will have to answer for his murder. Let me see him, if only for a minute?"

When the warder had said "Take back your money," he stretched out his hand, but did not display the coins.

There is something magical in gold that keeps the palm of a man's hand closed, and Mrs. Corcoran knew this well.

She produced another guinea, and then a faint smile crept over the warder's face.

"You see," he said, in a mollified tone of voice, "by admitting you I should risk my situation. Why didn't you go to the justices of the peace and ask them for an order so that you can see your son?"

"They are so cruel — so dreadfully hard-hearted," Mrs. Corcoran moaned. "Are you a married man?"

"Yes."

"And you have children?"

"I have," the warder replied; "a reg'lar staircase of them, and the eldest, aged sixteen, is the top step."

"Then put yourself in my place," said Mrs. Corcoran, adding another guinea to the one she already held in her hand. "Think of what you would do and what you would risk to see your boy at such a time as this."

The gaoler could not help feeling pity for the old woman, ugly as she was.

"If I was the law, which I am not," he replied, "I should offer no objection, but—"

"You will let me in?' Mrs. Corcoran interposed. "If you don't I'll put the country to the expense of an inquest and the burial of my body."

Her grief was so frantic, and the addition of this threat to end her mortal career quite affected the gaoler.

He hesitated a moment and then opened the door by degrees, as if to make sure that Mrs. Corcoran was not accompanied by anybody.

"There can't be any harm done," he muttered to himself. "Bill Blarney is pinned like a cockchafer against the wall. Here," he added aloud, "go straight down the passage, and tell the first warder that you meet that David Dredger said you might have a few words with your son."

Mrs. Corcoran felt that she could dance for very joy.

But she moderated her transports, and kept up a woe-begone demeanour.

It was not long before she came within sight of the other warder.

He rose from a three-legged stool, took a pipe from his mouth, put a fragment of a month-old newspaper in his pocket, and challenged Mrs. Corcoran.

She gave him David Dredger's message, and added a guinea to it.

The second warder was not affected with many qualms of conscience as to the performance of his duties.

He put the guinea in his pocket and dragged a bunch of keys from his buff leather belt.

"This way," he said. "Blarney will be glad to see somebody. Just stand where you are while I see if he is comfortable and fit to receive visitors."

Mrs. Corcoran trembled and shook in her boots as she heard the warder speak to the criminal.

"Here's a nice old lady come to see you," said the gaoler.

Bill Blarney said something uncomplimentary to old ladies in general.

"I don't want to see her," he growled. "What's her name?"

"Why, it's your own mother!" the warder returned.

"My what?"

"Your mother."

Bill Blarney began to ruminate.

His own mother had died in a drunken fit long ago, and Bill Blarney had never dreamed that she would ever come to life again.

There was some mystery in this, and he began to think that it would be better to see his maternal substitute.

"Well, bring her in," he said; "but I wish she had kept away, for there will only be a scene."

In another instant Mrs. Corcoran in all her ugliness stood before him.

She placed one skinny forefinger upon her lips to enjoin silence, and remained silent herself until the warder had left the cell and paced some distance up the passage.

"Bill," she said—"Bill, don't you know me—me, the best friend you ever had?"

Bill Blarney was glaring at her, and in such a mighty rage that the fetters he wore jangled noisily.

"So," he gasped out at last, "you have come to torment me! Have a care. I thought to have died with every secret locked in my breast. Have a care, I say, for you know that I can tell some very ugly stories with respect to yourself."

"Fool!" Mrs. Corcoran hissed in his ear. "I have come to save you—to put you on your guard—to tell you that your pals at the Bull in Top Boots will risk their liberty and lives to rescue you."

"Are they here—here now?" Bill Blarney demanded, still staring at the hag in blank amazement.

"Here!" Mrs. Corcoran repeated. "No; I have come alone. The little journey has cost me five guineas, and this is my reward."

Bill Blarney raised one of his manacled hands and swept it across his brow.

"Can I believe you?" he said, hoarsely. "This is no trick to raise my hopes and then dash them to the ground?"

"No, lovey-dovey."

Blarney made a wry face and spat upon the ground.

"Once for all," he said, "free or helpless, dead or alive, don't talk to me like that. It freezes me to the very bones."

"Very well, dearie," the hag croaked; "you shall have all your own way."

"Come nearer and tell me all," Bill Blarney said, with eyes wide open with expectancy. "How do my pals think they can get me out of this hobble?"

"By making a dash for you when the court is sitting."

Bill Blarney groaned, and a sudden elongation of his face told how hopeless he thought the scheme was.

"Whose idea was that?" he asked.

"Mine."

"Yours?"

Bill Blarney felt in no mood for mirth, but he could scarcely refrain from laughing.

"And pray why not?" Mrs. Corcoran demanded, bridling up. "Don't you like it?"

"It's all very well in its way," Blarney replied, "but the next question is how is, it to be carried out?"

"That you will see," the hag returned. "Your share in the affair will be to hold yourself in readiness for anything, and to be surprised at nothing."

"I have lived in that condition of mind for years," Bill Blarney said. "Well, forgive me, if I have appeared ungrateful, but—hang me! I can't believe you are in earnest even now."

Mrs. Corcoran cracked her thumb at him contemptuously.

"Bah!" she said. "Is this all you have to say when I might have left you to die?"

"Well—well!" Bill Blarney returned; "if you were cooped up as I am, you would think and say all sorts of things."

"You certainly are penned up pretty well," Mrs. Corcoran said. "Well, never mind. I will send the warder for a bottle of wine, and we will drink success to our meeting outside these stone walls."

## CHAPTER CIV.

### DAISY LEIGH A PRISONER—THE PERILOUS ESCAPE.

How long Daisy had remained in a state of unconsciousness after her seizure she had no means of ascertaining.

On recovering her senses, she found herself in a carriage, which was being driven at a rapid rate, and placed between two men.

One of them, on seeing her revive, removed his mask, and her feelings of horror may be imagined when she recognised in him the mysterious stranger whom she had so much reason to dread.

She could not speak or utter any exclamation of alarm, for the gag prevented her.

Her bosom throbbed with horror and disgust.

The stranger fixed upon her a look of admiration and triumph, and then, in spite of all her efforts to resist him, took her hand and pressed it vehemently to his lips.

"Lovely girl!" he exclaimed, "kind fortune has smiled upon me, and you are mine."

"For the love of Heaven," Daisy cried, "oh! tell me what you intend to do with me? Whither are you taking me? Oh! spare me, and restore me to my friends."

"Restore you to your friends, after all the trouble it has cost me to obtain possession of you!" he replied. "Oh! no; I should be worse than a madman to do so."

"Villain!" Daisy cried. "Dare you, a stranger, and a man who can be guilty of such an atrocious outrage as this, talk to me thus? Release me, and suffer me to return to my friends, or the vengeance of Heaven will pursue you to destruction."

"Nay, my pretty flower," he coolly returned, "it is useless for you to talk to me thus, for I heed it not. I am not a man to be easily daunted in any designs upon which I have fixed my mind, and so well have I formed my plot that I defy detection. Before the morning we shall be far beyond the reach of any of your friends. You are mine, and no power on earth can deprive me of you."

"Oh! Heaven," Daisy exclaimed, "and is there no one who will fly to my assistance? Help—help!"

"Cease those cries," said the villain, who was no other than James Loddon, "or I shall be compelled to use violence to silence you. Besides, your cries here are useless; there is no one at hand who can hear them or come to your assistance. This part of the country is lonely and unfrequented, and at such an hour it is not likely that anyone is about."

"Heartless, fearful man!" Daisy said, and again became insensible.

When she again recovered, she found herself still in the carriage, which was pursuing its course with unabated speed.

Once more, with tears and supplications, she appealed to the ruffians, but in vain; and she gave herself up to the most abject despair, and saw that all her efforts to escape from her fate were useless.

As James Loddon had truly stated, it was a lonely and unfrequented part of the country they were travelling through, and Daisy had not the least recollection of it.

In this manner they proceeded for more than a couple of hours, and at length entered on a wild and barren moor, which having crossed, they stopped before a large and gloomy-looking house, which stood alone.

Daisy could not perceive the least signs of any other human habitation as far as her eyes could penetrate through the darkness.

"This is the place of our destination for the present," Loddon said; "and thanks to my lucky stars that have crowned my stratagem with such success. I must leave you soon to carry the news of my good fortune to a friend."

"Gracious Heaven!" exclaimed Daisy, "and is there no power to release me? Oh! mercy—mercy."

"Why should you entertain such fears of me?" he demanded. "My intentions are honourable, although—"

"Honourable!" Daisy said, interrupting him. "Bad, cruel man, have you no sense of shame? Can you thus recklessly add insult to your brutal outrage? Oh! forbear—forbear."

"This is not the time or the place to argue upon this subject," said James Loddon; "bad as the opinion you have formed of me may be—and I confess that, at present, appearances are against me—you will find that I know how to behave kindly to those whom I esteem."

"Oh! Heaven," Daisy cried, "are my ears to be thus shocked, and by one who is a complete stranger to me? Is there no pitying being at hand to rescue me from this misery?"

"No one, fair girl," said Loddon, with a look of triumph; "my plans have been too well matured to suffer that circumstance to take place."

"Help me, then, oh! Heaven," Daisy moaned.

She sank back on her seat in a state of utter despair.

Meanwhile one of the men had pulled the bell violently, and at length it was opened by an old woman of forbidding appearance, and who seemed as if she had been indulging in a sound sleep.

James Loddon now left the carriage, and, after talking for a few seconds to the old woman, he returned and assisted Daisy to alight.

She saw it was useless to resist, and, therefore, resigned herself to her fate, scarcely aware of what she was doing.

Loddon took a light from the old woman, and then led his trembling victim along a spacious hall, and, ascending a wide staircase, ushered her into an apartment which was furnished in an ancient manner, but had all the appearance of former elegance.

Daisy cast a hasty glance round the room, fixed upon James Loddon one look of reproach and supplication, and then, sinking in a chair, she covered her face with her hands and sobbed as if her heart would break.

James Loddon stood at a respectful distance from her, and gazed at her intently; but he did not attempt to interrupt her grief for some time.

It might be that a sentiment of pity found a place at that moment in his bosom.

James Loddon was a man now fast verging upon fifty, but his features were still what might be described as handsome, and his figure was noble and commanding in the extreme.

For several minutes Daisy sat in a state of the greatest mental agony and almost unconscious of what was passing around her, but at length she raised her tearful eyes, and, beholding her persecutor contemplating her, she was aroused to a full sense of the horrors of her situation.

"Tell me who you are," she cried, "and for what wicked purpose have you thus cruelly torn me from my friends and brought me hither? I know you not, and what can I, therefore, have done that you should thus inflict this cruel outrage upon me?"

"Listen!" Loddon replied, as he gazed with the most ardent affection upon her. "I know I shall receive your reproaches, and deeply do I regret that I should cause your heart one single pang of anguish; but love has urged me to this bold and dangerous step."

"Oh! Heaven," Daisy exclaimed, "am I indeed doomed to suffer this accumulated misery? Must I listen to language such as this, and from a man who is a complete stranger to me? As you hope for mercy, do not detain me, but restore me to my friends."

"You deem me cruel," Loddon returned; "but I am not so. I should indeed be a monster, hateful to myself, could I entertain one thought but of love and admiration towards you."

"Oh! villain—villain!" Daisy gasped; "but you will not dare to persist in keeping me a prisoner in this unknown place; you cannot be so insensible to pity as to turn a deaf ear to my agonised supplications."

"Would that I could restore you to liberty!" said Loddon; "in the assurance of your love, how happy should I be! But fear not, for here no harm shall come to you, but all the respect and attention be paid you that your situation demands."

"Will nothing move you to relent?" Daisy cried; and she burst into a violent paroxysm of tears.

"I will leave you for the present," said he.

"Cruel man!" said Daisy; "can you thus coolly talk after the misery you have inflicted upon me, and that with which you still threaten me? Forbear! If you have but a spark of humanity or honour left within your bosom, suffer me to leave this place."

"Nay," said Loddon, "what folly it is to talk to me in this manner, after all the trouble I have taken to bring you here! Think you I can so readily resign a treasure? No, beauteous damsel, sooner could I resign my own life; for now that I see how lovely you are that life would no longer be of any value to me."

"Wretch!" Daisy cried, as she started to her feet, "can you have the presumption to suppose that I can ever entertain any other feelings than those of detestation and disgust towards a man who has acted in the manner you have done towards me?"

"You make use of harsh language," said James Loddon; "such, indeed, as ill becomes your lips. But I bear it all with patience, and time will show you how little I merit it, notwithstanding the course to which I have been urged."

He pressed his hand upon his heart as he spoke, and moved towards the door.

"Again I implore you," said Daisy, "if you would not break my heart, to let me go."

"I cannot let you go," Loddon replied; "compose yourself, and fear not; for notwithstanding the apparent severity of my conduct, you shall ever find me most studious of your happiness."

"Determined villain!" Daisy exclaimed, her cheeks glowing with indignation, "think you that such base and daring conduct as this will be permitted to go unpunished?"

"I will leave that to chance," said Loddon. "Adieu! I do not despair of you yet viewing me with a more favourable eye."

He said no more, but stalked from the room and locked the door after him.

Daisy, overwhelmed with grief and consternation, sank on her knees and sobbed convulsively.

James Loddon had not left the room long before another man entered.

He was stately in his deportment, and stood bareheaded before Daisy, who regarded him with an expression of unmitigated horror.

"How dare you intrude upon me?" she said. "Is it not enough that I should be tormented with one wretch in human form?"

"Pardon me, Miss Leigh—" he began.

Daisy interrupted him with a cry of alarm.

"You know me, then?"

"The man I serve does nothing without making himself fully acquainted with its object," was the reply. "Miss Leigh, I must beg of you to accompany me."

"Whither?"

The man smiled as he stroked his moustache, which was as black and glossy as the raven's wing.

"I am not allowed to answer that question," he said. "Believe me that no harm will come to you. But—"

"You hesitate?" Daisy said.

"Yes; because I have a very delicate office to perform."

"What is it?"

"I must blindfold you."

"Blindfold me!" Daisy exclaimed. "Tell me the next indignity I am to be subjected to?"

"I only follow my instructions," the man replied. "If I were a free agent I might act in quite a different way."

Daisy Leigh took her purse from her pocket and held it out in her hand.

The man shook his head.

"It is not money I require, but your goodwill," he said, in a softened tone of voice.

"My goodwill!" she said. "How do you expect to earn that of any woman when you are in league with a villain?"

The man glanced over his shoulder towards the door, and a peculiar expression came over his face.

"My name is Henry Palmer," he said; "and if you will trust me, I will endeavour—"

"Stay!" Daisy interposed. "I trust no such men as you. I am helpless—I am in your power—and the empty triumph of torturing an innocent woman is yours."

Again the peculiar expression came over Henry Palmer's face.

"Well, then," he said, "I have nothing more to do but my duty."

"Your duty!" Daisy sneered. "Oh! for the help of one man of honour."

Palmer made no reply, but, taking a snow-white handkerchief from his pocket, he folded it carefully.

"Miss Leigh," he said, "you blame me, but the fault is none of mine."

Daisy advanced boldly with her arms to her sides.

"Blindfold me, brave man," she said, "and take me where you will. I know you now as the slave and hireling of a villain!"

Henry Palmer winced, and the handkerchief, slipping from his fingers, fell fluttering to the ground.

As he stooped to pick it up the hot blood of anger and shame rushed into his cheeks.

"Miserable, pitiful wretch that I am!" he muttered under his breath. "Oh! for one day, one hour, of freedom."

Then he looked steadily into Daisy's eyes.

"You reproach me, and not without cause," he said; "but the day may come when— Ah! well, it matters not."

He passed the handkerchief over Daisy's eyes kindly, but firmly.

Daisy lost courage and she almost fainted.

"This is most villainous," she said, feebly. "Heaven protect me now. I seem to be beyond all earthly succour."

Henry Palmer took her gently by the arm and led her towards the door.

"Fear nothing for the present," he said, "for now you are as safe as if you were with your friends."

Downstairs they went, and then Daisy heard a Babel of tongues.

In the midst of all the confusion she heard the word Reigate, and treasured it up in her mind.

Presently the sound of wheels grated harshly, and Daisy felt herself gently raised and lifted into some kind of luxurious vehicle.

She prayed silently and earnestly.

All hope seemed to be at an end, and gladly would she have courted death in any shape.

Presently the handkerchief was removed from her eyes.

It was daylight now, and the sudden rush of light almost blinded her and confused her senses.

After a time her vision cleared, and she saw Henry Palmer sitting on the opposite seat.

They were alone in the carriage.

In spite of all her repugnance, Daisy could not help acknowledging that the man who was in charge of her was handsome and gentle of face.

He remained silent, leaning his elbow upon his knee and his chin upon the palm of his hand.

Daisy was in no mood now to ask questions, and mile after mile went by without a word being exchanged.

At last the horses began to slacken their speed, and Daisy, peeping through the window, saw that she was in a most beautiful part of the country.

It seemed to be one vast garden, formed by the lavish and beautiful hand of Nature.

But what eyes could she have for so magnificent a sight?

Her heart was as heavy as lead, and her brain throbbed wildly.

"Is this our destination?" she asked.

Henry Palmer glanced carelessly at the country.

"Yes," he replied. "We have not very far to go. We are now descending into the valley."

"What valley?"

"Ah!" Palmer replied, "you are a true woman—you ask questions."

"You are a base man," Daisy rejoined. "How true it is that a man may smile and be a villain!"

"True," Henry Palmer replied. "I deserve that name, and any other you may choose to call me."

At this moment the carriage came to a standstill.

Daisy shrank back as the door was flung open by a man whose face was concealed beneath a hideous mask.

"We alight here," Henry Palmer said, with the air of a gentleman.

The scene had changed.

The surroundings were gloomy in the extreme.

What appeared to be chalk cliffs, covered with creeping plants, were on either side, and the carriage had been driven into a road which narrowed towards the end like the neck of a bottle.

Daisy was preparing to alight, when Henry Palmer checked her with a motion of his hand.

"I must repeat the ceremony," he said, as he produced the handkerchief. "You will see strange sights enough before long."

Daisy submitted to the operation of being blindfolded, and then, with a heavy sigh, she suffered herself to be led away.

Henry Palmer led her to a seat and whispered a word of encouragement in her ear.

Encouragement!

Daisy felt that she must go mad, for the place into which she had been taken was as still and silent as the grave.

Suddenly she heard the sound of laughter.

"Welcome to our new queen!" shouted a hoarse voice.

"Heaven defend me!" Daisy gasped. "Is that meant for me? Would that I had died before this day dawned!"

The handkerchief was still over Daisy's eyes, and she began to wonder whether she was doomed to remain in this region fraught with mystery and crime, when light again streamed into her eyes.

It was not the light of day, but that emitted by a number of lamps strung upon ropes suspended from a naturally-formed cave.

How the handkerchief had been removed from her eyes Daisy could not tell.

She was alone, quite alone, and though she could hear the sound of voices she could perceive nobody.

The couch on which she had been placed was of a most luxurious and expensive kind.

It was composed of red satin, fringed heavily with bullion.

By leaning forward Daisy could see the entrance of the cave, and it struck her that escape might be possible if she made a sudden dash for liberty.

That hope fell to the ground as she saw a man pass from one side to the other.

He carried a carbine on his arm, and his aspect was so ferocious that the fair prisoner trembled.

Another burst of laughter startled Daisy Leigh, and even while she trembled at the harsh, discordant noise Henry Palmer appeared.

He had a silver salver containing refreshments in his hand.

Daisy Leigh motioned him to stand back with an impatient wave of her hand.

"I can neither eat nor drink here," she said, her eyes flashing with indignation. "It is an insult to offer me wine which, for all I know, may be drugged."

"Upon my honour, no!"

"Your honour!" Daisy Leigh exclaimed, shrugging her shoulders. "You must set it at a great price."

"Yes; why not?"

"Why not?" Daisy Leigh replied, "because you are a villain and deserve the doom of a felon!"

Henry Palmer stood still for a few moments as if he did not know what to say or do.

"My instructions were to take you into the midst of our band," he said; "but as I have some power here I have spared you that."

"And for that you have my thanks," Daisy Leigh replied. "Pray accept them."

"It is not your thanks I require."

"What, then?"

"Your goodwill and confidence."

Daisy Leigh shrank from him as if she had been stung by a serpent.

"You are mad!" she said.

"Would to Heaven I was!" he replied. "If madness could blot out the bitter past, how gladly would I crave for its agonies! But enough! The day may come, Miss Leigh, when you will know me better."

There was something in the tone of the man's voice that made Daisy tremble.

For a moment she felt inclined to speak kindly to him, and ask what dire event had bound him to such a band of miscreants.

The next moment she abandoned the notion, and, holding down her head, remained silent.

Just then a rough-looking fellow swaggered into the cave.

He carried a sealed packet, which he put into Palmer's hand, and then, drawing himself up erect, saluted with a military air.

"Any answer?" he asked.

"Wait."

The man stepped back as Henry Palmer perused the document.

It seemed to puzzle him considerably, and more than once he swept his hand across his brow.

"Who gave you this?"

"A man on horseback."

"Did he give the pass-word?"

"Yes."

"And the countersign?"

"Again, yes."

"Describe him," said Henry Palmer, with a puzzled look on his face.

"He was tall and pale," the messenger replied. "His eyes were bright, he wore no moustache, his riding-costume was of costly material, and he carried a rapier at his side jewelled in the sheath."

Still Henry Palmer looked puzzled.

"Would you know him again?" he asked. "Your description is too vague to follow."

"I should know him among a million," the messenger replied; "but his face was of that peculiar type which defies language to depict."

"Where did you meet him?"

"Near the Fox-under-the-Hill, at Ringwood."

"Enough!" said Henry Palmer. "But stay. Why did you ask me whether there was any answer?"

"Because the man who accosted me said it was to be sent to Cypress House."

"To whom?"

"Spring-Heeled Jack."

Daisy Leigh started and turned pale, but she pressed her hands before her eyes and controlled her feelings.

"Spring-Heeled Jack!" she murmured. "Then I am saved!"

# SPRING-HEELED JACK,

## THE TERROR OF LONDON.

THE STARTLED ROBBER FIRED THE CARBINE INTO THE AIR.

No. 30.

## CHAPTER CV.

### HOW JACOB BUTLER GAINED HIS FREEDOM.

THE change in Jacob Butler's position was so startling and so sudden that he went nearly mad with joy.

The noise above his head increased, and he added to it by shouting for help at the top of his voice.

"We can hear you, but we can't see you," said a voice. "Where are you?"

"Under your feet," Jacob yelled. "Rip the flooring up. Quick!"

"Don't be in a hurry," said the voice. "You are all right."

Jacob Butler clasped his hands, and tears of gratitude streamed from his eyes.

"What has become of that villain Ted Nickells?" he asked.

"Oh! he is all right," said the man overhead. "We have him handcuffed, and trussed as neatly as a fowl."

A curse and a growl from Ted Nickell's lips confirmed this statement.

Then came a sound as if some instrument had been inserted between the flooring, and the next instant there was a crash, followed by a flash of light.

Jacob Butler looked up, and saw a face peering into his.

The visage belonged to Catchpole, and no sooner did he see who the prisoner was than he uttered a cry of exultation.

"Here's a go, Grabham!" he said, turning his head aside for a moment. "The man in this 'ere trap is no other than our old friend Butler."

"Nonsense!"

"Well, come and look for yourself."

Grabham now changed places with Catchpole.

"Yes; it's me right enough," said Jacob; "and when you've done staring I hope you'll lower something to enable me to crawl out of this awful hole."

"Who'd have thought it?" Grabham asked. "It's enough to take a man's breath away."

"If you had gone through what I have you would have no breath left to take away," said Jacob.

"I ain't quite sure," said Grabham, wagging his head from side to side in a dubious fashion, "that we ought to release you without taking proper advice at headquarters."

"Headquarters! Where do you mean?"

"Bow-street."

"Hang Bow-street!" Jacob almost yelled.

"So plenty of men have said," Grabham returned, grinning, "and these very men have been hung for their impudence. However, as you must come out one time or the other, I suppose you may as well do so now. Catchpole!"

"Yes."

"You'll find a short ladder in the back-yard. Fetch it up."

Mr. Catchpole went very leisurely on this errand, and Jacob Butler reflected during the constable's absence.

How the officers had come so opportunely to his assistance puzzled him.

He could make nothing out of it; but one thing was certain.

They had rendered him excellent assistance, and had saved him from a dreadful death.

Presently Catchpole came waddling along with the short ladder over his shoulder.

Grabham again made good use of an axe, and presently the ladder was lowered through a hole sufficiently large for Jacob Butler to crawl through.

"Now, then," said Grabham, "up you come; and don't forget, my boy, that we have a few words to say to you."

In spite of the fact that Jacob Butler felt like a man suddenly reprieved from the scaffold, he felt his heart sink within his breast.

It seemed to him that he had been rescued from one enemy to fall into the clutches of another.

"Well," he said, as he began to mount the ladder, "I hope there is an end of all little differences between us."

"Oh! just so," said Catchpole. "We'll talk about that presently."

As he spoke he laid hold of Jacob's hair and jerked him through the aperture with as little ceremony as if he had been a sack of shavings.

"Murder!" Butler shrieked. "Do you want to pull the top of my head off?"

"There's gratitude for you," said Catchpole as he tripped Jacob Butler up so suddenly that he fell flat on his back. "Grabham, don't we ought to be ashamed of ourselves for saving the warmint's life?"

"We do," Grabham replied. "I could shed tears of grief and shame when I think of it."

Jacob Butler picked himself up and stared in dismal dismay around him.

In one corner of the room he saw a number of ponderous wheels on which chains revolved by means of a huge crank.

He saw now by what infernal mechanism the walls below had been moved, and a sensation of rage took possession of his heart.

"Where is that scoundrel Nickells?" he demanded.

Catchpole pointed to the other end of the room, and then Jacob Butler not only saw the villain who had attempted to take his life in such a horrible fashion, but Jem Basker.

Ted Nickells and Jem Basker were handcuffed, and bound back to back with strong cords.

"You hound—you dog!" Jacob yelled, as he advanced towards Ted Nickells, and shook his fist. "When I was helpless you drove me nearly mad with terror! Why shouldn't I strike you, now that you have no power to retaliate?"

"That's a matter for you to consider about," Nickells returned, grimly. "I would think twice about it, if I were you, for we might meet again."

"I don't think there's much fear of that," Catchpole said, grinning. "However, I don't blame you for keeping up a good heart. I should do it myself, if I were in your place."

Jacob Butler now became conscious that there were other officers in the house besides Catchpole and Grabham, for just then a strange man put his head and shoulders in at the door.

"We have searched most of the rooms, but can't find anything worth taking away," he said.

"And never will," Ted Nickells said, triumphantly. "I should be a fool, indeed, to tell you where my little hoard is hidden."

At this moment Jem Basker began to groan in the most heart-rending fashion.

"What's the matter with you, my buck?" Grabham demanded.

"I think I must be dying!" Basker moaned. "It's cruel to bind a wounded man like me."

"Of course it is," Grabham returned, grimly. "If I were you I would make a complaint about it. Ah! wouldn't you like to get at me just now."

There seemed to be no manner of doubt about this.

The half-bred gipsy fellow favoured the constable with a glance full of hatred and bitterness, and then relapsed into moody silence.

"Just so," said Grabham, "I thought as much; but, my friend, I am not going to trust you an inch out of my sight, so you can make you mind easy on that matter. Mr. Butler, I daresay that you have some recollection of our last meeting?"

The individual thus questioned started violently.

"Why, yes," he said, in faltering accents, "and I am not likely to forget it in a hurry."

"There's a sensible speech for you," said Grabham, glancing at Catchpole. "It warms my heart to hear a man speak like that."

Catchpole gave vent to a low, grating, unmusical laugh, and eyed Jacob as if he could have swallowed him without the proverbial pinch of salt.

"That being the case," said Grabham, as he fumbled in his pockets, "I am afraid that we must ask Mr. Butler to adorn his wrists with a pair of handcuffs."

"No—no," Jacob cried, in accents of alarm; "I am not your prisoner."

"Ain't you?" Grabham responded. "We'll see about that, jolly quick. Now then, just stretch out them delicate hands of yours, and you'll see how pretty they look when I have done with them."

Jacob Butler cast a hurried glance around the room.

He saw that one of the windows was open, and he made up his mind in an instant what to do.

Pretending to comply with Grabham's request, he advanced slowly, and then, suddenly swerving round, he made a dash for the window with the agility of a harlequin.

"Stop him!" Catchpole and Grabham yelled in a breath.

The sound of their voices came too late to bring up assistance, for Jacob Butler was already through the window.

The distracted man who had made such a bold dash for freedom had not the slightest idea of the distance that lay between him and the ground, nor did he give such a thing a thought.

The only object he had in view was to get clear away, and he went down heels over head, until something brought him to a standstill with a jerk that knocked the breath out of his body.

Jacob Butler opened his mouth something after the fashion of a man about to make an impassioned speech, and then he closed it again, as if he had forgotten what he was going to say.

Though half-stunned and frantic with fear, he set his body in motion again, and went rolling down a sloping roof, ending in a gutter protected by a coping.

When Jacob Butler ended this part of his journey he found himself a fixture between the tiles and the stonework.

It so happened that when Jacob came to a full stop, which he did so suddenly that his very teeth chattered in his head, his arms were close at his sides.

Struggle as he would and did, he could not move them, and the wretched man, groaning with despair, lay still.

Uncomfortable as his attitude was, it saved him from observation; for when Catchpole and Grabham rushed to the window and looked out they could see nothing whatever of Jacob Butler.

"Well, I'm blessed!" said Catchpole. "He's vanished like a ghost."

Grabham said something very unpleasant relative to Jacob Butler.

"Well," he added, "I suppose we must be satisfied with the haul we have made. It's an odd thing that you and I should have been watching the Chequers so long, and come so strangely upon the man who has given us so much trouble?"

Catchpole assented with a grunt.

"And yet," he said, "I shall never feel at ease until we have settled him."

Jacob heard all that was passing, and shuddered.

"They mean to take my life at the first opportunity," he said to himself. "If I could only get clear away out of this predicament, I would give them some trouble to catch me."

He then heard Grabham say something to the prisoners within the house, and made another effort to release himself.

This time he was a little more fortunate, for he got one of his hands free, and by dint of much twisting and turning at last succeeded in scrambling to his knees.

Casting a hasty glance at the open window, Jacob Butler clutched the coping with both hands, and, lowering himself gently and noiselessly over it, dropped into a yard.

Luckily for him his feet alighted on some straw, so that the weight of his body produced no greater noise than a dull, heavy thud.

But the troubles of Jacob Butler were not yet over.

The yard was guarded by a high gate, which was not only locked, but was furnished at the top by a double row of formidable steel spikes as sharp as razors.

Jacob's agony and suspense were almost more than he could bear.

It seemed to him that he had been born to fall from one trap into another, and that his evil star was constantly hovering above his head.

When a man's position is desperate he does not stick at trifles, and Jacob Butler made up his mind to surmount the difficulty before him at any cost.

Waiting a moment to ascertain that he was not being watched, he clambered up the gate, and, grasping the spikes, attempted to throw himself clear over them.

Vain hope!

The spikes took a fancy to Jacob Butler's nether garments, and he hung midway between earth and air as helpless as an infant.

It would have been all over with him had either Catchpole or Grabham come to the window just then.

But they did not, and Jacob, almost black in the face with his late exertions and his inverted attitude, kicked and strived to get free.

Sudddenly he heard certain stitches giving way.

The sound was like music to his ears, and he redoubled his efforts.

Crick—crick—crack—crack!

"I shall be down with a vengeance in a minute," Jacob thought, "and it's a hundred to one that I shall pitch right on the top of my head."

Suddenly his garments gave way.

Jacob Butler set his teeth to prevent a cry escaping from his lips, and, closing his eyes, thrust out his hands.

This saved his cranium, and he suffered no more damage than falling upon his back, and producing a sound as if an empty sack had been flung out of a window.

In an instant Jacob was on his feet.

He heard the sound of voices.

He saw Catchpole and Grabham gesticulating violently at the window, and fled like a stag startled by the sound of the huntsman's horn.

As Jacob Butler had come into the neighbourhood so he left it.

He knew nothing whatever about the locality, and did not stop to ask the passers-by, who stared wonderingly at him speeding away as if for a wager.

At last the thoroughfares began to widen, and presently Newgate Prison came in view.

Jacob Butler now stopped to take breath.

If sheer exhaustion had not stopped him, the sight that met his eyes would have produced the effect.

As he heard the grating of locks and bolts the visitors' door opened, and an old woman hobbled into the open space, where, on Monday mornings, savage crowds came to see criminals die.

Jacob Butler recognised the old woman at a glance, and his heart went down like a deep-sea plummet.

It was Mrs. Corcoran.

She lingered for a moment to exchange a few words with the warder at the gate, and then, bowing her head as if overwhelmed with grief, began to limp slowly and mournfully in the direction of Giltspur-street.

Up to that moment she had not seen Jacob Butler.

He dodged into a doorway, and crouching down in the shadow, hid his face beneath his hands.

Mrs. Corcoran came on, her weeping and wailing changing to such a hideous chuckling, that Jacob felt his blood run cold.

Would she pass and leave him unobserved?

This was a most important question for Jacob, and it was presently answered to his dismay, when Mrs. Corcoran suddenly stopped and glared at him, with a wondering expression twinkling in her keen, grey eyes.

## CHAPTER CVI.

A FIGHT IN THE CAVE—HENRY PALMER WOUNDED—THE SENTRY RECEIVES A VISIT FROM SPRING-HEELED JACK.

HENRY PALMER noticed that a sudden change had come over Daisy Leigh at the mention of Spring-Heeled Jack.

He saw the careworn expression die out of her eyes, and a look of pleasure take its place.

"Perhaps," he said, "you can throw some light on this mystery?"

"I!" Daisy rejoined, feigning astonishment. "Indeed, how should I know what you are talking about."

"I will tell you," Henry Palmer rejoined. "I hold in my hand a most extraordinary document. It comes in a handwriting I do not recognise, and is unsigned."

"What has all this to do with me?" Daisy said. "I wish you would not bother me with such matters."

The shadow of disappointment clouded Henry Palmer's brow.

He made a hasty motion with his hand, and the man who had brought the message retired from the cave.

"Miss Leigh," he said, "I will read to you what is written on this paper."

"As you please," Daisy rejoined, with affected carelessness.

"It concerns you," Henry Palmer continued. "It contains but a few words, and each and every one is relative to you."

"Really!" said Daisy, elevating her eyebrows. "Well, I'm willing to listen to you."

Palmer unfolded the paper and held it out at arm's length.

"*Watchful eyes are upon you*," he read. "*Let the lady you have in charge free, or beware of the vengeance of one who fears no mortal.*"

"It is a strange document," Daisy said, "but how do you know that it concerns me?"

"Who else should it concern?"

Daisy Leigh remained silent.

"Miss Leigh," Palmer said, lowering the tone of his voice to a whisper, "this message came too late, for my mind was already made up. I asked you to trust me, but you refused to do so. I do not wonder at that; and yet in whatever light I may appear to you now, believe me that I was once a gentleman."

"I have been always given to understand that a gentleman can no more change his nature than the shape of his body," Daisy said.

"If that were so," Henry Palmer returned, "I should not be here now. There is no time for me to tell you my history. Let it suffice that drink, gambling, and riotous living have made me what I am."

"And you will always remain what you are?"

"I hope not," Palmer replied. "As a bird flutters its wings against its gilded cage, so my heart is ever aching for freedom."

"The world is before you," Daisy Leigh said. "Why do you not go before it is too late?"

"Yes, yes," he said, with sudden energy; "I will go, and you and I shall breathe the air of freedom at the same instant."

There was something so peculiar in the tone of the man's voice that Daisy Leigh glanced up at him.

"You have something more to say to me," she said. "I begin to trust you. Go on. You have my confidence now."

"May I hope—"

"What?" Daisy demanded, interrupting him sharply, and so suddenly that he recoiled a step from her.

"Great Heaven! what am I talking about?" Palmer said. "Well, since I have began I may as well finish the words which were trembling on my lips. I did the bidding of James Loddon, as I have done it before, may a time and oft, but little did I think what strange emotions it would cause me. Miss Leigh, don't turn from me; I—I love you."

Daisy could only stare at the man in blank amazement, for speech had left her.

"I had calculated upon your indignation. I knew what effect my words would have upon you," Henry Palmer resumed; "and yet—"

"You must be mad!" Daisy interposed. "Leave me. I will not listen to another word."

"Pardon me," Henry Palmer said. "It is with pain I tell you that your position is one which compels you to listen to me, and I hope you will do so patiently to the end."

"And this is the man who speaks of gentlemanly instincts," Daisy said. "The man who, whilst sighing over his misdeeds, does not scruple to insult a woman's ear with the protestations of his vulgar love."

"Yes," Palmer said, folding his arms; "you must and shall listen to me, but had you waited but a few moments the words which have passed your lips would never have been uttered."

"Enough," Daisy cried. "The very sound of your voice is poison to my ears."

"I love you, it is true," Henry Palmer said, letting Daisy's reproach pass unheeded; "but not as a man who loves a woman desiring to take her as his wife. My love springs from the remembrance that I once had a sister who suffered cruel wrongs at the hands of a base and designing villain."

Again Daisy looked at him, and she saw the light of truth and honesty flashing from his eyes.

"I do not think that I fully understand you," she said, faintly.

"The fault is mine, not yours," he replied. "I have played the part of a scoundrel in bringing you here, but I will set you free, even though my life pays for the risk. At dawn, when all is quiet, I will come to you. Trust me, you shall return unharmed to your friends, and the only reward I ask is that you will think of me sometimes."

Daisy Leigh made no reply, but she held out her hand.

Henry Palmer took it, and, touching it lightly with his lips, turned away.

For some time Daisy sat still, wondering what would happen next.

The circumstances surrounding her sudden abduction from Ralph Ashton's protecting arm, and the events which had followed closely upon the dastard deed were so dream-like that she could scarcely bring herself to believe in their reality.

She became so tired now that she could scarcely keep her eyes open, and at last she threw herself back upon the couch and fell into a profound slumber.

How long she had slept before she was roused by a light touch on her shoulder she had no means of telling.

On opening her eyes she beheld Henry Palmer standing before her, in the same attitude he had assumed when previously speaking to her.

"What has happened?" Daisy asked. "Why are you here? Why do you disturb me?"

"The time has come."

"What time?" Daisy said, sitting up and rubbing her eyes to convince herself that she was awake."

"Have you forgotten that I promised to set you free?" Henry Palmer rejoined. "I drugged the wine for the men in the inner cave and they are all fast asleep and will not wake for hours. I served the sentry in the same manner. See!"

He pointed to the mouth of the cave, and there lay the form of an inanimate man.

"Come!" Palmer said. "We must go; for if even one of the men should recover from his stupor all is lost."

Daisy rose to her feet and followed her guide.

"We must pass through the inner cave," he said, "for it is just possible that some messenger or other from James Loddon may appear."

Daisy shrank back.

"Why cannot we go out there?" she demanded, pointing to the main entrance.

"You must do as I tell you or do nothing," Henry Palmer replied. "If we should be caught certain death awaits both."

"So be it," Daisy said, sighing. "I am entirely in your hands."

"Hush! not a word now. Follow me, and take care that your dress does not trail upon the ground."

Daisy gathered up her skirts gently and her feet peeped in and out as she followed the man who had promised to guide her to the way to freedom.

Slowly, slowly, on they went until Henry Palmer came to a standstill before a pair of heavy, velvet curtains which divided the two caves.

Palmer parted these noiselessly with his arms, and then Daisy saw a sight which she never forgot.

About the floor lay a number of men in uncouth attitudes, and all breathing heavily.

Some were calm and placid, while the faces of others were distorted by hideous dreams.

Packs of cards lay strewn about, and on the walls hung coats, and hats, and wigs, ready to be put on by the rascals at a moment's notice.

Pistols, loaded and primed, mingled with empty flasks and wine bottles, showed that the men had drank deeply.

Such were the men, and such was the scene that Daisy Leigh gazed upon.

Henry Palmer pointed to the sleeping men, and whispered a word or two in Daisy's ear.

"You must step over their bodies," he said. "Do so boldly and carefully."

Daisy hesitated a moment, and then began her short but perilous journey.

Only too well she knew that she carried her life in her hand.

One false step, a light touch of her dress upon the upturned face of one of the men, and all hopes of escape would come to an end."

Steady! Steady, now!

Henry Palmer had removed his heavy boots and walked on, turning his head now and then to make sure that none of the men were stirring.

At last all obstacles were overcome in safety, and then reaction set in.

Daisy Leigh felt so faint that she could scarcely keep her feet, and Henry Palmer lent her his strong arm to lean upon.

"Courage—courage!" he whispered. "Do not give way at this critical moment."

Daisy Leigh could not trust herself to speak.

She had passed through so much danger that she felt inclined to scream in spite of herself.

At last she recovered her self-control, and signified with a motion of her hand that she was ready to proceed.

Nailed to the cavern wall was a short, strong ladder, which led to a trap-door cunningly fitted into the roof.

The crisis was at hand.

If Henry Palmer could remove the trap-door without rousing any of the robbers all would be well.

Silently and stealthily as a cat he crept step by step up the ladder.

When nearly at the top he turned and looked back.

The men were still sleeping, but some of them restlessly.

One swarthy scoundrel, whose neck and chin were completely hidden by a jet-black beard, made a gurgling sound in his throat, and rolled over upon his side.

Henry Palmer held his breath, as he drew a pistol from his belt.

Daisy, feeling more dead than alive, crouched in abject terror against the ladder.

But the man did not wake, though he mumbled in his sleep and cursed his ill-luck at cards.

Standing on the ladder, Henry Palmer opened his hands and placed them firmly against the trap-door.

At first it refused it yield, but it did so when more pressure was put upon it.

And then the woodwork began to creak and groan ominously.

"Heaven help me now!" Daisy thought. "It would be a cruel fate indeed to fall into the clutches of these villains after having come so far."

Great beads of perspiration rolled from Henry Palmer's brow.

At last his exertions were rewarded.

The trap-door yielded completely and slid back noiselessly into a kind of groove.

Then Daisy Leigh began to mount the ladder.

It was no easy matter for her, for it was perpendicular against the wall, and, careful as she was, she could not help her dress rustling as she ascended.

With a sudden movement Henry Palmer passed his arm round her waist and drew her through the trap-door, which he immediately slid into its original place.

"So far, so good," he said, exultantly; "we have but a little further to go, and then we shall breathe the fresh air."

They were now in a kind of passage which inclined in an upward direction.

"You may walk without fear of being heard now," Palmer said. "If the men were awake they could not hear you, and woe to him who shows his head and shoulders through the trap-door."

A little further on they came to a leafy screen, through which the sun was glinting and dancing with the fanciful shadows cast by the rich shadows.

Throwing aside this curtain formed by Nature, Henry Palmer took Daisy Leigh by the hand and led her into the open air.

The sudden rush of light dazed and bewildered Daisy, but the fresh, balmy breeze soon restored her.

She saw a magnificent landscape stretching away for miles at her feet, and the scene was so beautiful that, under any other circumstances, she would have lingered to ponder on its wonders.

Henry Palmer led the way into a kind of gulch, shaded by beech-trees.

He stopped, and pointing to a miniature cavern in the chalk, said—

"Miss Leigh, I must ask you to remain here a short time while I make the necessary preparations for your departure."

Before Daisy could reply, Palmer was on his way.

Daisy watched him as he climbed up the steep ascent with the agility of a goat, and her heart sank as she thought that something might occur to prevent his return.

What else but the love and reverence of a friend could she feel for him now.

He had been true to his word.

He had saved her from the power of an abominable villain, and perchance his life would pay the penalty of the act.

Daisy's eyes swam with tears as she thought of these things.

She blamed herself bitterly for having uttered cruel, harsh words to the man who thought lightly of his own existence when compared to hers.

"I have been taught a lesson," she said. "What can I give this noble-minded man but my gratitude? Stay! Ralph Ashton will hear my story, and he will help this hero to the means of getting a better living."

Leaving Daisy Leigh for a moment, it behoves us to follow Henry Palmer.

Above the portion of the gulch he ascended lay a narrow road, which gradually descended and passed the main entrance of the robber's cave.

Alone, Palmer argued with himself, he would not be challenged by the sentry, even supposing that the man was awake.

He was bent on going eastwards to the nearest village where he could procure a closed vehicle and a pair of fast horses to convey Daisy back to her friends.

When Palmer came in sight of the cave he stopped and looked about him.

The sentry was not in sight, and, concluding that the man was still in a state of slumber, Daisy's new-found friend stepped cautiously along.

Suddenly his foot slipped on a rolling-stone, and he fell, sending down a shower of loose earth.

Cursing his ill-luck, Henry Palmer scrambled to his feet, and, as he did so, he saw the sentry leap to his feet and snatch up his carbine.

"Halt! there," the man cried, as he rubbed his eyes. "Who goes there?"

"A friend."

"I know no friend at such a time and place," the sentry replied. "Ha! it is Palmer."

"Yes," was the reply; "you must have been drinking heavily not to recognise me."

"Drinking heavily!" the man repeated. "Nothing passed my lips more than what you gave me."

He reeled as he spoke, but recovered his balance with an effort.

"Ah!" he cried, pressing his hand to his brow, "there is something wrong. You traitor, you drugged me!"

As he spoke he glanced into the interior of the cavern, and then brought his carbine to his shoulder.

"You have betrayed our captain!" he said. "Where is the girl? Speak—and quickly, too—or I will blow out your brains!"

"What foolery is this?" Palmer cried. "Let me pass!"

"No—no!" the sentry replied. "You have played us false! What ho! there—help—help!"

"Let the man pass!" cried a voice of thunder in the sentry's ear. "Idiot, your lips have sealed your own doom!"

The sentry uttered a cry of horror as he beheld Spring-Heeled Jack standing before him.

The strange, weird creature seemed to have sprung from the earth.

"Avaunt, fiend!" the sentry yelled.

At the same moment his finger pressed upon the trigger, and the carbine exploded harmlessly in the air.

Fearful then was the expression on Spring-Heeled Jack's face.

Raising the sentry in his muscular arms, he hurled him into the ravine below, and watched him as he went headlong down the steep incline shrieking with terror and clutching at the roots and bushes protruding from the jagged masses of chalk.

"Back!" Spring-Heeled Jack shouted to

Palmer—"back—I know all! Leave the rest to me. If you value your life hide yourself!"

Before Henry Palmer had time to make any kind of a reply the robbers came tumbling helter-skelter over each other from the cave.

They had snatched up whatever weapons came to hand; and their hoarse cries of alarm, blended with curses and imprecations, rent the air.

Henry Palmer hurled himself bodily into a thick clump of bushes and lay still.

He could hear what the robbers said, and now that their alarm had somewhat subsided, they talked more calmly.

"I thought that we had been suddenly attacked," said one; "but I see nobody."

"Not even the sentry!" added another. "There must be something the matter, or Phil Eade would not have quitted his post."

"He has quitted it for ever, I fear," a third replied. "Look down straight beneath your feet, and tell me what you see."

Advancing to the edge of the narrow roadway, the robbers peered into the ravine below.

Bold and stony-hearted as most of them were, they could not forbear shuddering.

"There has been foul play here," said one of the men. "Poor Phil must have been taken by surprise. Here is the carbine which he fired, and the barrel is still warm."

The men looked at each other in speechless dismay.

"Palmer must know something of this," said a swarthy villain. "Ha! a thought strikes me. Where is the girl? I did not see her as we passed through the cave."

Several of the robbers ran back, and almost instantly returned.

"We have been betrayed!" they shouted. "The girl is gone, and who but Henry Palmer could have helped her to get away?"

"Who, indeed!" roared the rest. "Death—death to the traitor!"

## CHAPTER CVII.

### SIR ROLAND ASHTON PAYS A VISIT TO LORD MILDENDALE.

Sir Roland recoiled from the mirror as if he had been shot.

He laid his hand upon his sword, and drawing it turned to confront Spring-Heeled Jack, but he was no longer present.

More mysterious still, the doors of the wardrobe were closed, and Sir Roland stood glaring at them with the air of a man doubtful whether he is asleep or awake.

"Could I have been mistaken?" he said, as he walked backwards slowly. "No, my eyes did not deceive me. The fiend is here."

Sir Roland threw open the wardrobe.

It was empty, and though the baronet sounded the panels, he could find no clue that might lead to a solution of the mystery.

Sir Roland exerted his strength, and removed the wardrobe from the wall.

Here, as before, the result was just as unsatisfactory, for there was no apparent aperture in roof, wall, or ceiling by which any living creature could escape.

Sir Roland Ashton sat down in his fine clothes—the borrowed plumes in which he was to play so mean a part—and, leaning his elbow heavily on the table, grasped his chin

His almost bloodless lips quivered convulsively, and his fingers twitched.

"How much longer am I to endure these horrors?" he said, half aloud. "Patience—patience! I must dupe James Loddon into letting me have a large sum of money, and then I will take myself off to France or some country where this John-o'-dreams—this base mockery cannot follow me."

He thought he heard a low, mocking laugh in response to his words, and he laid his sword upon his knee ready for use.

Suddenly he heard the sound of heavy footsteps approaching the door.

Joe Rollins entered the room, bearing a sealed packet in his hand.

"A letter for you," he said.

Sir Roland grasped the packet, and, glancing at it, saw that it was directed to—

"*William Fernie, Esq., Cypress House.*"

"Ha!" he exclaimed, "I expect this comes from our friend Loddon."

As he burst the seal something round and heavy rolled out.

It was neatly enclosed in a piece of paper, and, unfolding it, Sir Roland saw that some words were written upon it.

Few as they were they brought a sudden flush of colour to Sir Roland Ashton's face, and then as quickly his features assumed a death-like hue.

"*Beware of the silver bullet,*" he read; "*its billet is intended for your brain unless you turn back while there is time, and there is yet time for repentance.*"

The bullet, smooth and exquisitely cast, lay at his feet.

He took it up in his hand and toyed with it in a mechanical fashion.

"Who brought this packet?" he said, with an air of assumed indifference as he turned to Rollins.

"Nobody here saw the messenger," Joe Rollins replied. "The packet was found thrust under the door."

Sir Roland Ashton bit his under lip and moved his feet about uneasily.

Then he burst out into a roar of unnatural laughter.

"I—I don't understand you," he said, in faltering accents. "Speak out. Tell me what all this mummery means."

"I will," Joe Rollings replied. "I will speak for myself."

Sir Roland started again, and his lower jaw fell, as if the man's words had given him a sudden shock of terror.

"Last night as I lay in bed," Rollins said, "and listening to the wind mingling with the mumbling of thunder in the distance, I thought I heard the rustling of some garment sweep against the wall. The moon was then unhidden by the advancing clouds, and shone so brightly that I could distinguish every object distinctly. The sound was repeated several times, and I raised myself on my elbow, but could see nothing to account for the noise."

"Which proves at once that you were in a state between sleeping and waking," Sir Roland said. "You were, in point of fact, dreaming. I have experienced the same thing myself over and over again."

"Hear me out," Rollings said, "for I think that my story will interest you."

"Why interest me in particular?"

"Because of all men in the world it concerns you most."

"Proceed," said Sir Roland, waving his hand. "I suppose I must hear the finish of this wonderful ghost story."

"I did not say that I had a ghost story to tell," Joe Rollins returned, angrily. "But listen. For some time I lay as fully awake as I am now, and quite as watchful. I saw nothing; but this is what I heard. Suddenly the room seemed to be filled with the flapping of wings, and then a voice spoke sharply in my ears."

For a moment Joe Rollins ceased speaking, and glanced at Sir Roland.

The baronet merely changed his attitude, and leaned a little forward as if to listen more attentively.

"Well!" he said, "what did the voice say?"

"It said that you murdered a man named Gedge Foote, a miser in the Old Mint," Joe Rollins replied, speaking slowly and impressively. "It said that you slew your own wife. It said—"

"Hold!" cried Sir Roland. "I will hear no more."

"My story does not seem to please you," Rollins returned. "Well, I can scarcely wonder at that; but you had better hear the end of it."

Sir Roland turned and paced the room with agitations in his features and movements.

"Go on," he said, shrugging his shoulders.

"Thank you!" said Rollins. "The voice told me to beware of you. It told me that you knew how to offer one hand in friendship and stab with the other. It told me more—that you purposed to make James Loddon your dupe, and that your only object now was to fly from the country, and laugh in your sleeve when you gained the shore of a foreign clime."

Sir Roland Ashton thrust his fingers into his ears.

"Enough—enough!" he cried. "This is either some idle story concocted to destroy my peace of mind, or, as I said before, you were dreaming."

"Nay, not dreaming," Rollins replied, sternly. "But whether I choose to believe what I heard is quite another thing."

"You know the value of a still tongue," Sir Roland said. "It would be bad policy to repeat the story."

"Bad for you, no doubt," Rollins said, sneeringly. "I know how to hold my peace, as I do to open my lips. I have been paid for doing both."

"Ha!" Sir Roland exclaimed. "I think I understand you now. You want your lips to be locked with a golden key."

"Just so," the man replied, coolly. "Loddon gave you money. How much?"

"Fifty guineas."

"Give me half," Rollins said, "and you may depend upon my secrecy until—"

"You have spent every coin?"

"No," Joe Rollins replied, laughing. "Until James Loddon gives you more, and then you and I will share it."

"What if I refuse?" Sir Roland Ashton demanded, hoarsely. "What if I tell James Loddon the story of your infamous attempt at extortion?"

"As you please," answered Rollins, coolly. "One tale is good until another one's told."

"What child's trick is this?" the baronet said. "What puerile plot is this to frighten me?"

As he spoke he hurled the silver bullet into the fire-place.

"Stay!" he said, as he crossed the room; "I may as well keep it in memory of a fool."

He searched in vain for the bullet, though he could have taken his oath that he saw where it had fallen.

"Strange, most strange," he muttered. "This house, like others I have been sheltered in, seems full of idle conjuring. I—"

He ceased speaking, and an icy thrill ran through his frame.

A cold, clammy hand touched the nape of his neck and was then withdrawn.

"Rollins," he said, "who or what touched me?"

"I saw nothing," the man replied, sarcastically. "Methinks that you are full of strange fancies to-night."

"It may be so," Sir Roland said, passing his hand before his eyes. "Yes, yes; I am not very well. Don't leave me. It—it is not that I am afraid of being alone, but—"

"I bring you two items of news," Joe Rollins said, interrupting him. "First and foremost, our leader has sent me a message to the effect that you are to visit Lord Mildendale to-morrow."

"Why did not the message come direct to me?" Sir Roland Ashton demanded.

"I know not," Rollins replied, curling his upper lip scornfully; "and if you seek to inquire you had better put the question to James Loddon himself."

"Well—well," Sir Roland said, in a calmer tone of voice, "we will say no more about the matter. Am I to go alone?"

"No."

"Who with, then?"

"With me."

Sir Roland endeavoured to conceal the expression of anger which gathered on his face at this announcement.

Joe Rollins did not fail to notice it, and smiled cynically as he folded his arms tightly across his breast.

"You have something more to tell me?" Sir Roland Ashton said, after a pause.

"You will take it as a mere trifle," Joe Rollins said, "but the men here are getting discontented."

"Why?"

"Because they swear that the house is haunted."

"Haunted?"

"Yes; and nothing can drive the notion from their heads."

There was another pause, during which Sir Roland Ashton glanced involuntarily at the mirror and then at the wardrobe.

"So," he said, almost breathlessly, "they have seen—"

"They have seen nothing, but have heard much," Rollins interposed. "They say that in the dead of night they are roused from their slumbers by shrieks and groans."

"Rubbish!" Sir Roland said. "Men who eat and drink heavily suffer from nightmare."

"One or two might," Joe Rollins returned; "but it would be strange indeed if the whole household were affected in a similar manner at the same time."

Sir Roland's attendant knew that the baronet was keeping something from him.

It needed no very keen eye or great amount of

perception to see this, and more than once Sir Roland had it on his lips to tell all he knew of the awful visitation he had received from Spring-Heeled Jack.

And yet he kept the secret locked up in his breast, hoping to find an opportunity of laying his mysterious foe low at his feet.

"You tell me that the men have seen nothing," he said. "What have they to fear? They forget that such an old house as this is naturally full of echoes, and strange noises."

"And voices?" Joe Rollins added.

"Voices!"

"Yes; voices—the voices of restless spirits, saying that their bodies were foully slain."

Sir Roland Ashton started and clutched at the back of a chair for support.

"What if I put him on his guard about you?" Rollins rejoined.

"You dare not."

"Why?"

"Because—"

Joe Rollins held up his hand and cracked his finger and thumb at the baronet.

"So much for your threats," he said. "I will be plain with you. I am your servant in one sense of the word, but your master in another. My instructions with regard to yourself are simple plans, but full of meaning."

"What are they?"

"That if I catch you tripping in any one particular I am to shoot or stab you to the heart, as I may choose."

Sir Roland recoiled on his heels and smote his brow with his open hand.

"A light dawns upon my brain," he said. "I have been brought here to serve a scoundrel, and when my work is done I am to be murdered."

"The words are yours, not mine," Rollins said. "If you are faithful you will be rewarded, but show the slightest sign of treachery, and your doom is sealed."

Sir Roland Ashton made no reply, but, walking to an escritoire, opened it, and drew out a bag, which he emptied, and began to count out a pile of glistening gold.

"There is your share," he said, pointing to one heap.

"And for the present you are safe," Rollins said, as he swept the coins into his pocket. "Sir Roland, you and I must now row in the same boat. We are necessary to each other. We must swim or sink together."

Sir Roland shuddered, for he felt that all his projects had now fallen to the ground.

There was no hope of escape now.

The man would watch him closer than ever cat watched a mouse, and hot tears of rage and bitterness gathered in the baronet's eyes.

"So let it be," he said. "You mean that death alone shall part us?"

"You have fathomed my meaning to a word, Sir Roland," Joe Rollins replied. "To-morrow we start. You, as the polished man of fortune, I—ha! ha!—as your very humble servant, and I am sure that in all our journeys and adventures we shall understand each other very well. Your health!"

Joe Rollins took a flask from his pocket, and having drunk deeply handed it to Sir Roland.

"No, no," the baronet said; "you go a little too far."

"But you must," Rollins insisted. "Are we friends or foes?"

"Friends."

"Then drink to the bargain, or I shall not believe that you are in earnest."

Seeing that he had no alternative but to comply, Sir Roland took the flask, and just touched his lips with it.

"Now are you satisfied?" he said, with loathing and disgust written upon every feature.

"Quite."

Sir Roland turned his head aside to conceal the half-maddened expression on his face.

"Your dinner is ready, sir," Rollins said, altering his insolent demeanour to one of abject submissiveness. "Allow me to conduct you to the dining-room."

"I can eat nothing," Sir Roland replied. "I am weary, and yet I fear that I cannot sleep."

"I will keep you company, to-night!" Rollins said. "The arm-chair will do very well for me. You need repose, Sir Roland. It will not be well to let Lord Mildendale see those haggard cheeks and blood-shot eyes to-morrow."

With a gesture of rage Sir Roland began to tear off his rich apparel, and then threw himself upon the bed.

Joe Rollins sat down, and, crossing one leg over the other, began to hum the tune of a song.

At last Sir Roland closed his eyes, and his heavy breathing told that he had fallen asleep.

"Poor fool!" Rollins muttered. "Weak wretch, who starts at his own shadow. His life is a bane to him; but I must hold him fast. Little does he think that I share his notion of saying good-bye to James Loddon and the whole crew. But it cannot be done yet—not yet."

Day was dawning bright and cloudless when Sir Roland Ashton awoke with a start.

The first object that met his eyes was his too constant attendant.

Rollins was seated in the chair, looking as if he had never changed his attitude, nor closed his eyes during the livelong night.

He nodded and smiled at Sir Roland in so familiar a style that the baronet ground his teeth with rage.

"As you had no dinner yesterday," Rollins said, "I suppose you feel inclined to make a hearty breakfast?"

"You may bring me up some chocolate and toast," Sir Roland replied.

"Bah! What a meal for a man with a ride of twenty miles before him!" the fellow said. "Nay—nay! you must have something more substantial."

"I will leave it to you," the baronet said, wearily. "When I have breakfasted you shall help me to dress."

"Certainly—certainly, your honour," Rollins replied, bowing. "The word 'dress' reminds me that a special hair-dresser has been retained for you. I will send him up immediately."

Sir Roland Ashton scrambled out of bed, the instant that Rollins had closed the door behind him.

A pair of pistols, inlaid with silver, lay upon the table, and the baronet took them up and examined them minutely.

"I thought as much!" he said, dashing the weapon down. "The scoundrel has drawn the charges I put in and substituted powder and paper. What a trap I have fallen into! Let me think it out, if I can. What am I to do? Which way am I to turn? Curses on this life; others shall answer for what I suffer."

At this moment a knock came at the door.

"Come in," said Sir Roland.

A lean, lank, ugly-looking fellow put his head in at the door.

"Who are you?" the baronet demanded.

"The hairdresser, may it please your honour."

The fellow did not seem to please Sir Roland, who eyed him with suspicion.

"I can dispense with your services if you will leave the materials of your trade with me," Sir Roland said.

"Very well, your honour," the man said, as he placed a box on the dressing-table; "you know best, but—"

"But what?"

"I had orders to shave you and dress your hair," the man replied. "Your honour's hair has grown long, and will show beneath the wig."

Sir Roland only waved his hand, and the fellow, after lingering for a moment, bowed almost to the floor, and then wriggled like an eel out of the room.

Soon after Joe Rollins appeared, bearing a tray in his hand.

Something seemed to have upset him, and he glared savagely at Sir Roland.

"What is the matter?" the baronet asked.

"You upset all my arrangements and your own at the same time," Rollins said. "Why on earth could you not let the hairdresser attend upon you?"

"Because I did not like the look of him."

"Bah!" said Rollins, sneeringly; "you know what this may lead to. Ripton—that's the hairdresser's name—will repeat this to Loddon, and he will be as savage as a bear with a sore head."

"Why?"

"Because you refuse to follow his injunctions."

Sir Roland drank a cup of chocolate, and trifled with the rest of the meal.

"When do we start for Mildendale Hall?" he asked, suddenly.

"At eleven o'clock," Rollins replied. "Your carriage will be brought to the door punctual to the moment.

Sir Roland glanced at the handsome watch which James Loddon had provided him with, and found that it was already ten o'clock.

He dressed himself with scrupulous care, aided by Rollins, and by the time that the sound of wheels rumbled up to the house, the baronet's appearance was one of wealth and magnificence.

The circumstances which now surrounded him reminded him of old days, and he went jauntily down the broad stair-case with his hat under his arm.

The jewelled hilt of his sword flashed and gleamed in the sunlight as he passed the windows.

Truly Sir Roland Ashton was still a handsome man, and Joe Rollins could not help admiring the ease and grace with which he made his way to the carriage.

The equipage was perfect.

The coachman was a blaze of crimson and gold, as were the two footmen, and the trappings of both horses and carriage were of a most elaborate description.

Joe Rollins was dressed in black, faced with silk cords, and looked every inch what he was intended to be—the confidential servant of a wealthy gentleman.

Nothing had been forgotten, even down to a gold case filled with visiting-cards, which Sir Roland toyed daintily with in his hand.

At last a start was made, and the horses being fresh, half the journey was soon accomplished.

The brightness of the day died out under heavy banks of clouds, and by the time that Mildendale Hall came in sight rain was falling.

A heavy gloom had settled upon earth and sky, and the wind sighed dismally among the trees of the grand old park.

One of Lord Mildendale's servants, watching from the window, wondered at seeing so magnificent an equipage approaching.

Such a thing had not occurred since the day that Lady Mildendale had vanished, and the man, seeing the carriage draw up and the footman get down, ran to the door.

Lord Mildendale was at home, he said, as he took the card, but he was not sure that he was inclined to receive visitors.

However, he would ascertain, if Mr. Fernie would condescend to step into a reception-room.

Sir Roland walked into the room, and Joe Rollins, who knew how to play his part well, took his station outside the door.

At the moment of Sir Roland's arrival Lord Mildendale sat in the library, poring over an old volume of family records.

The old expression of weariness was upon his face, and he merely looked up as the man entered.

The servant advanced with the card lying in the centre of a silver salver.

"Mr. Fernie," Lord Mildendale said, as he held the slip of enamelled pasteboard between his finger and thumb; "I have no recollection of his name. I will see nobody. Have I not said that this house is for ever closed against visitors?"

"Pardon me, my lord," the man said; "this gentleman comes as befits a prince. It may be that he has important business."

"Well, well," Lord Mildendale said, testily, "I suppose I must see him. Show him into the blue drawing-room, and I will come down directly."

In a few minutes Lord Mildendale and Sir Roland Ashton were face to face.

His lordship waved his hand courteously as an invitation for Sir Roland to resume his seat, and then sat down himself.

"I see so few people," Lord Mildendale said, smiling sadly, "that I am at a loss to find a reason for the honour of this visit."

"It simply amounts to this," Sir Roland said. "I have lived most of my life in foreign parts, and, having been fortunate enough to acquire wealth, I have returned to England to end my days in peace and enjoyment."

"In peace and enjoyment," Lord Mildendale repeated, moving his eyes restlessly to and fro. "Would that such a portion were mine!"

"And, having purchased a small estate in this neighbourhood—or rather in the same county," Sir Roland continued, "I thought I would do myself the honour of calling upon you."

"You are kind, Mr. Fernie," Lord Mildendale returned; "but you will find me poor in conversation and companionship. I have suffered much."

"Yes," Sir Roland replied; "I have heard something of your story."

Lord Mildendale's face assumed an earnest expression, and a new light flashed into his eyes as he leaned forward.

"You have heard my story?" he said, hoarsely. "Who told you—where—when? Answer me quickly, I beg!"

"It was not in this country," Sir Roland replied. "On my way home I passed through Spain, and happened to fall in, by accident, with a wandering tribe of gipsies."

As the last word was uttered Lord Mildendale started to his feet.

He paced restlessly up and down for a few moments and then returned to his chair.

"Mr. Fernie," he said, "you must think me very rude, but take no notice of me, I beg. If you have heard my story you must sympathise with me in my affliction."

"I do," said the arch-hypocrite, "and hence my principal reason for calling upon you."

"Tell me all you heard and all you know," Lord Mildendale said. "This is a new and unexpected phrase in my miserable history."

"The story is rather a long one," Sir Roland said, artfully; "and as it will take some time to tell, I had better call again when you are in a calmer mood to listen to me."

"No, no," Lord Mildendale returned. "You must be my guest. I will order a suite of apartments to be got ready for you."

While they were conversing the air had grown darker, and as Lord Mildendale finished speaking, a clap of thunder burst over the house and shook it to its foundation.

"This seems to be a season of storms," Sir Roland said, as his face changed colour. "Gale and tempest seem to follow me wherever I go."

"A tempest has been raging in my heart for years," Lord Mildendale said. "But why should I dilate on my troubles to you? Mr. Fernie, you will accept my invitation—you will be my guest?"

This is exactly what Sir Roland desired.

"With pleasure," he replied.

As Lord Mildendale walked across the room to ring a bell, in order that he might give instructions as to the disposal of Sir Roland's carriage and servants, he heard a strange voice whispering in his ear.

"Beware!" it said; "beware!"

"What have I to beware of?" he asked, turning towards Sir Roland Ashton.

"I did not speak," the baronet replied.

"No, no—of course you did not," Lord Mildendale returned. "This is but a repetition of what I have heard so often. Strange that awake and asleep I am so often warned against a man I have never seen! Sometimes I think that my senses must be leaving me."

"Battle with such idle notions," Sir Roland said. "Exercise your powers of will, and victory will be yours. All men are subjected to hallucinations at times. By-the-way, you speak of hearing the name of a man you have never seen?"

"Yes."

"What is the name?"

"Sir Roland Ashton."

The baronet's lips moved as if he would have spoken, but the entrance of a servant put an end to all further conversation.

## CHAPTER CVIII.

### THE PREPARATIONS TO RESCUE BILL BLARNEY—THE ATTEMPT.

Jacob Butler trembled in his shoes.

He kept his hands before his face, but his terror was awful, for he knew that Mrs. Corcoran was glaring at him with her weasel-like eyes.

Perhaps the old hag's thoughts were of such a nature as to cause her to heed but little the man's strange attitude, otherwise it is more than probable that Jacob Butler would have fallen into her clutches again.

"He's either drunk or ill; but it's nothing to me," she mumbled. "The best thing I can do is to make my way back to the Bull in Top Boots. Ho—ho! I chuckle and laugh, for an old woman has done what big, strong men would fear to attempt."

Hobbling down Newgate-street, she suddenly turned down one of the lanes leading southwards, and Jacob Butler was free again.

He drew a deep breath, but remained still, for power of motion had forsaken his body.

Sweeping away the great beads of perspiration which had gathered on his face and brow, he glanced to the right and left.

As far as he could see there was nobody in sight likely to molest him, and yet he thought that everybody eyed him with suspicion.

This was, of course, nothing more than a fancy, and at last he began to creep down Holborn-hill, until he reached the door of the Saracen's Head.

Jacob Butler, after fumbling about in his pocket, discovered a shilling with a hole in it, which he had kept about him for luck.

Luck!

What kind of luck had the miserable coin brought him?

It was worth just twelve pence and no more, and he determined to spend a portion of it in the purchase of a drink of brandy.

He stood much in need of stimulant, and as the liquor flowed down his throat he felt stronger and better.

As he drained the glass to its dregs and set it down he began to ponder on what he should pursue.

He had no money and no friends.

He knew that there were thousands of such forlorn wretches in the world, but that fact did not bring him any consolation.

"What—what am I to do?" he gasped, as he clutched his hair.

Just then he heard voices talking in a room.

"Hang it, Cranston!" said a man; "if your servant has been taken ill, you can easily find another."

"But where?" said the other. "I want to be off at once. I promised Lord Mildendale that I would pay him another visit before long."

"Bah!" said the first voice. "He has been sufficiently punished. Let him go—at least, for the present. And as for the servant, I will ask our friend the landlord if he happens to know of a likely man."

Jacob Butler pricked up his ears.

Here was a chance which might not occur again in a hurry, and he made up his mind to avail himself of it if possible.

Walking up to the half-open door, he looked into the room.

He saw two handsome young men sitting at a table with a bottle of wine between them.

"Pardon me, kind gentlemen," he said. "I could not help overhearing your conversation. If either of you want a servant, let me offer myself for the place."

"You look a likely man enough," Cranston said; "but before I take you into my service I must know something about you."

Jacob Butler's face fell, but he plucked up courage.

"The master I served so long is dead," he

# SPRING-HEELED JACK,

## THE TERROR OF LONDON.

"HELP! MURDER!" JAMES LODDON CRIED. "I AM A SLAIN MAN!"

No. 31.

said, "and, consequently, he can give me no character. Give me a trial, and you will find me faithful and honest."

"What do you think of him, Raymond?" Cranston asked. "I will leave it all to you."

"I rather like the look of the fellow," Raymond replied. "He looks as if he had knocked about the world a good deal."

If he had known the man's history he might have said that the world had knocked Jacob Butler about considerably, and said it with truth.

"Very well," said Cranston; "I will give you a week's trial. The coach starts in an hour's time, so you had better run to your home or lodgings and pack up your luggage."

This was no trifling obstacle for Jacob Butler to get over.

He had nothing in the world more than what he stood upright in, and a lonely sixpence in his pocket was all his fortune.

"I am sorry to say that I have been out of place a long time, and necessity has caused me to part with all my belongings," he said.

"Poor devil!" ejaculated the good-humoured Raymond. "Hang me, if I didn't think so the moment I looked at him! See here, my fine fellow—your present state of poverty ought to make you all the more grateful in falling in with such a slice of luck."

"It does," Jacob cried, clasping his hands. "I will work my fingers to the bone—I will do anything to show how grateful I am."

"Well, well," said Cranston, tossing a guinea across the table, "go and get yourself a change of linen, and if you serve me well I will fit you out better at some other time. Don't forget the coach. I will book a seat for you."

While Jacob Butler, with a bounding heart, went in search of a hosier's shop, Mrs. Corcoran was on her way towards the Bull in Top Boots.

She hired no hackney-coach now, but preferred to walk, so that she might chuckle and crone over her success.

And truly she had succeeded wonderfully well.

As she crossed London-bridge she sat down to rest, and began to wink and blink with her bleary eyes so hideously that passers-by stepped out of her path in disgust.

The sun was warm, and, as Mrs. Corcoran was in no hurry, she might as well indulge in a little doze to brighten up her faculties before she presented herself in triumph at the Bull in Top Boots.

Mrs. Corcoran had good reason for feeling weary, for she had undertaken a task full of risk, and there had been a great probability of her being retained in the same unpleasant establishment as that occupied by Bill Blarney.

The hag fell asleep, and slept on until she was suddenly roused by the sharp notes of a horn blown by the guard of a coach.

It seemed to Mrs. Corcoran that her repose had been of a somewhat protracted nature, for the sun, which had been over her head when she sat down, was now behind her.

On came the coach.

The team of spanking horses tossed their heads in answer to the cheery notes of the horn, and the ruddy coachman handled the reins skilfully, and cracked the long whip just for form's sake.

Mrs. Corcoran glanced at the outside passengers, and then her wizened face underwent a change.

Could she be mistaken?

Did her eyes deceive her?

No!

There sat her beloved Jacob Butler at the side of a smart young gentleman, and looking as if he had just received a new lease of life.

Yelling with rage, Mrs. Corcoran ran after the coach.

"Stop! stop!" she shrieked.

One of the passengers, taking her for a beggar, threw a penny into the road, and the hag's gratitude found vent in a curse.

"Stop!" she howled. "Murder—thieves!"

The coachman seemed inclined to stop, but it was not so with the guard.

"Drive on, Bill!" he said; "the old witch is either mad or drunk."

Off went the horses again, and Mrs. Corcoran, overcome with conflicting emotions, fell all of a heap into the road.

So maddened with rage was she, that when a man stopped to pick her up she scratched and bit at him like a wild cat.

"Lie there, you savage beast!" the man said, starting back; "and if I had my way I would drive a waggon over you."

A moment after Mrs. Corcoran got up of her own accord, and mumbling out all sorts of horrible expressions, crossed the bridge in a frenzied kind of dance.

In these days the amiable old lady would have been taken care of by the police; but at the period of which we are writing it was no uncommon thing to see lunatics at large.

The people soon forgot all about Mrs. Corcoran, and she reached the Bull in Top Boots in such a state of exhaustion and fury that she tumbled headlong into the doorway.

The landlord, who was drinking in the bar, was so startled that he jerked his glass violently against his teeth.

Swearing vengeance against the intruder, he dashed round the counter.

"What the devil is the meaning of this?" he demanded, as he hauled Mrs. Corcoran to her feet. "What sort of prank do you call this?"

"Prank!" Mrs. Corcoran gasped. "Oh! if I had him here only for one moment!"

"Had him here! Who?" the landlord demanded. "I always thought that you were a little wrong in your head, but now I know that you are mad in right down earnest!"

"Let me sit down," said the hag, panting for breath. "Ah! that's better; and now I can tell you all about it."

"Ah! do," said the landlord. "Have they tried and hung Bill Blarney before his time?"

"No, no; but I saw Jacob Butler on the top of a coach," Mrs. Corcoran replied. "The white-livered hound looked as proud as a lord."

The landlord of the Bull in Top Boots smote his thigh as he uttered a furious oath.

"What has he to do with us just now?" he demanded.

"But he has everything to do with me," said Mrs. Corcoran. "Ah! well, I suppose I must be content to know that he is alive. My time will come yet."

"Of course it will," the landlord said. "Have you been to Newgate?"

"Yes."

"Then go into the parlour. Dick Sleuth and a select assembly of the boys are waiting for you. I'll just bolt the door and then follow you."

But Mrs. Corcoran refused to move until she

had been provided with some refreshment, and she took such a quantity of it, that the landlord made a remark to the effect that he compared her to a walking distillery.

At last the virago limped into the parlour, where she was hailed with acclamations of delight.

"What news?" cried Dick Sleuth, making way for her at the table. "Have you seen Bill?"

"Yes."

"And how did you find him?"

"Pinned like a cockchafer against the wall," Mrs. Corcoran replied, as she sat down and again helped herself to something stronger than water.

Dick Sleuth groaned dismally and buried his dirty face in his no less dirty hands.

"So," he said, "they have made up their minds to hold him tight?"

"Of course they have," Mrs. Corcoran returned. "You didn't expect that they would bind him with cotton and leave all the doors and windows open, did you?"

"No," the ruffian replied; "but what chance have we to get him away if they march him into the dock with his irons on?"

"Just as much as if he had them off," Mrs. Corcoran replied. "There is sure to be a crowd in the street; and you know how fond such men who hang about are of the officers. You must have a cart filled with straw ready and bundle Bill Blarney into it while the fight is going on."

Dick Sleuth looked a little more hopeful.

"What do you think of the notion?" he asked, turning to a most villainous-looking rascal named Collyns.

"Oh! well enough," he replied. "The attack will be so unexpected that we ought to succeed without much trouble."

"You have something inside your head besides bone and water," Mrs. Corcoran said, wagging her own cranium admiringly at the ruffian. "Now for the next question. How many men have you ready for the job?"

"About five-and-twenty," Dick Sleuth replied.

"More than enough," said the hag. "Of course they will be armed?"

"Every man-jack of them."

"What with?"

"Knives and pistols."

"That's the style," Mrs. Corcoran chuckled. "It will be a strange thing to me if Bill Blarney is not among us to-morrow night."

At this moment the landlord, who had mounted guard over a sliding panel which did duty for a door, held up his hand.

"I fancy I can hear something outside," he said, in a hushed tone of voice. "Silence, all!"

Not another word was spoken, and the landlord, closing the panel, began to whistle a lively tune.

He made his way across the bar, and peered through the keyhole of the front door.

"Catchpole and Grabham by all that's unlucky!" he hissed. "Confusion take them! What do they want here?"

The landlord was not kept long in suspense.

Grabham applied his knuckles and feet at the door.

"House! House!" he cried. "Open in the name of the king. We are officers of the law, and demand admittance."

"My house is my castle," the landlord replied, "and I'll know what you want before I admit you."

Crash!

Mr. Grabham, exasperated by this speech, had hurled his full weight against the closed portal.

"Come on, Catchpole," he said. "If he won't open the door, we'll have it down about his ears precious quick."

---

## CHAPTER CIX.

### THE HUNTING-SPEAR THAT CAME THROUGH THE WINDOW.

Gloom and darkness had settled upon Cypress House.

Beyond the grounds, where the rank marshlands stretched away for miles and miles and ran parallel with the broad, flowing river until it widens to the ocean, the ghostly will-o'-the-wisp danced, and strange birds of prey held high revel.

The horned moon peered now and then from dense masses of murky clouds, and the night wind skrieked and moaned as if it bore upon its wings the lamentations of tortured spirits.

All else was silent save the tramp—tramp of the watchmen on the terrace and within the house.

It would seem that James Loddon's men were ever on the alert.

While some rested the others paced the gloomy house, and closely guarded it against surprise.

The sentry on the terrace yawned as he turned upon his heel and resumed his lonely march.

Nothing had disturbed him, but the awful silence had a voice in itself, and the man strained his eyes eastward to catch the first grey streak which would tell of day coming to roll back the curtain of night.

But as yet all was as black as pitch, and, resting his musket on his arm, the man went tramping on more like a machine than a human being.

Presently a strange sound caught his ears, and, bracing himself up, he brought the barrel of his musket forward.

The sound was nothing more than the rumbling of wheels in the distance.

It might be nothing more than some waggon jolting from village to village, or some farmer in his cart plodding his way along to the early London market.

But suddenly two red specks grew out of the darkness, and as they came flitting along, enlarging each moment, the sentry raised his voice—

"Somebody rides this way!" he cried.

Almost instantly he was joined by another man, who, shading his eyes with his hands, said—

"It is a carriage of some description or other. If I mistake not, James Loddon rides this way."

The flashing lights grew larger and larger, and the wheels rumbled louder.

Both men ran down the terrace-steps and approached the vehicle.

"Halt!" they cried in a breath. "Who goes there? Stand, or we fire!'

James Loddon answered the challenge by leaping from the carriage.

The men saluted him, and he returned the salutation in gloomy silence.

His followers knew that something was wrong, and they waited for him to speak.

"Where is Sir Roland—the man we call by the name of Fernie?" at last he demanded, in a husky tone of voice.

"He has departed to Mildendale Hall, in accordance with your instructions," one of the men replied.

"Curse him!" Loddon hissed between his teeth. "A nice trouble he has got us into. The girl has escaped from the caves, and our hiding-place will soon be as public as the highway."

Then came a pause.

The men did not know how to express themselves in return for these startling tidings, and they thought it best to let their furious leader explain himself without asking any questions.

"The man I so fully relied upon has betrayed me," James Loddon went on. "That is the worst cut of all. I could have trusted him with my life—"

"Surely you do not allude to Henry Palmer?" said one of the men, interrupting him.

"I do—the base traitor! But his life shall pay the penalty of his act!" Loddon replied, adding a terrible oath. "He shall rue the hour that led him to sell me—he shall curse the day he was born! Enough! I cannot trust myself to speak! Let me pass!"

He pushed his way past the astonished men.

They would have lingered to question the driver of the carriage, but James Loddon's stern voice bade them follow him to the house.

Once indoors and in the full glow of the lamp-light, they saw how terribly their leader had changed in a few hours.

His cheeks and eyes had fallen in, and his clothes seemed to fit him so badly that they hung about his frame in huge wrinkles.

As he walked to and fro, pressing his hands to his forehead and beating his breast with his clenched fists, those who watched him knew that he had something more to tell.

"Filby," he said, stopping, and turning his searching eyes on one of the men. "Has anything disturbed you here?"

"Nothing very particular."

"What do you mean by nothing in particular?" Loddon demanded, angrily. "Tell me at once all that has happened."

"We have heard strange noises," Filby replied; "but we have put them down to natural causes."

"You have seen nothing?"

"Nothing whatever."

"Then you have been lucky," Loddon replied. "When I went to the caves to interview the girl, I was pounced upon by a demon and nearly throttled."

Filby and the other men, who by this time had come upon the scene, stared at their leader as if they thought he had gone mad.

"I speak but the truth," Loddon continued. "As the fiend held me in his grip of iron, he thundered in my ears these words, 'I am Spring-Heeled Jack! Away for ever from your scenes of crime, for our next meeting means death to you!'"

The men began to murmur and glance over their shoulders.

"I have heard of a being called Spring-Heeled Jack, the terror of London," Filby said; "but I put it down to idle rumour."

"Idle rumour does not leave finger marks on a man's throat," Loddon replied. "See here!"

He pointed to his own throat, and the men saw several marks as red as blood.

"And what is more," said James Loddon, resuming his march up and down, "this demon seemed to know Sir Roland perfectly well."

"Ha!" Filby cried, starting back. "Is he then in league with him to destroy us?"

"Such does not appear to be the case," Loddon replied, "for it would seem that this Spring-Heeled Jack is his bitterest foe. I had the statement from the demon's own lips. Sir Roland—Sir Roland, you will have to explain why you have been so careful to hide this from me! Bolt, lock, and guard every door. Are my own rooms prepared for me?"

"Yes, sir," Filby replied; "everything is in readiness for your reception."

"Good! I will go upstairs."

Some of the men would have followed him, but he waved them back with an impatient gesture of his hand.

"I have lived too long and done too much to fear man or the devil," he said. "The fiend came upon me unawares, or I would have tried whether his body was invulnerable to cold steel."

He drew a long gleaming sword as he spoke, and began to mount the stairs.

In spite of his bold speech, fear as well as rage had taken possession of his evil heart, and it was not without a thrill of terror that he entered an apartment alone.

Fain would he have had company; but to have shown the white feather to his men would have lost him too much authority.

The room into which he strode with heavy steps was a handsomely-furnished one.

He examined the fastenings of the windows carefully, and every inch of the place to make sure that nobody was lurking about, and having satisfied himself on this score, he sat down.

"The night is here, and the night is coming," he said. "My stronghold gone, what may I expect but worry and pestering? That this demon, who seems to wear wings upon his feet and whose muscles are of steel, is mortal, I am sure. Curse him! and curse the hour that brought Sir Roland Ashton into my presence!"

He laid his sword and pistols close at hand, and, seeing that decanters and glasses had been placed ready for his use, he took a deep draught or wine.

It filled him with artificial courage, and the old fierce, determined light came back into his eyes.

"I must find means to put this matter straight," he said, as he leaned his chin upon his open hand. "Two things are certain. Sir Roland Ashton and Henry Palmer must die, and the sooner they are out of the way the better."

He took up his sword, and, balancing it, ran his eye along the blade from hilt to point.

"If I only had them here now," he said, "they would never give me more trouble. What a fool I was to worry myself about this girl! Well, what is done cannot be recalled, and I must make the best of a bad bargain."

There was one thing the room lacked.

Though the windows were fitted with curtains, there were no blinds, for Cypress House had been furnished in a hurry, and several things were yet needed to make the place complete.

James Loddon did not notice the omission, and if he had, probably he would have given no thought to it.

He still sat there, drinking deeply and talking to himself until one of the decanters was empty.

His hand was upon another, when he heard a slight sound outside.

It was nothing to alarm him.

Merely a rustle as if the wind had blown a spray of ivy against the window, and passed unheeded.

It would not have done so had he turned his head.

Spring-Heeled Jack was glaring at him with a

face so dreadful that a bold man's heart would have stood still with fright.

Those terrible eyes were upon him, and one long ghastly arm held something, which was hidden by the darkness of the night.

James Loddon swallowed glass after glass of wine, until it began to have its effect upon his senses.

His head fell heavily forward.

A gurgling sound came from his throat, and as his arms dropped helplessly to his sides, he slipped from the chair and fell in a dead sleep upon the oor.

Spring-Heeled Jack opened the window and alked into the room.

His gigantic form seemed to enlarge as he oured over the sleeping man.

"Why should I not slay the villain now that he unconscious?" he said. "No, no! That would be but poor punishment for such a villain. As he has inflicted so shall he feel."

The gaunt, awful-looking creature took a glance round the room, and then, squatting cross-legged upon the floor, watched James Loddon as he moaned, turned, and twisted in his drunken sleep.

The effect of wine soon leaves such a man as Loddon.

He was used to pouring it like water down his throat, and in about an hour he showed signs of recovering.

Then Spring-Heeled Jack rose, and once more vanished into the darkness.

"Ha!" said Loddon, drowsily, as he scrambled to his feet and sank into a chair. "The last glass was too much for me. Alone? Yes. Well, that's a comfort. It shows that I am not to be disturbed to-night."

Little did he think how he was reckoning without his host.

The avenger was on his track.

His doom was as surely sealed as if he had fallen upon his own sword.

"My throat burns," he said, "my lips are parched, and my tongue is swollen! I must have more drink! To-morrow will be the time to get sober!"

He rose and stretched out a trembling, uncertain hand to grasp one of the decanters.

As he did so he saw something at the window, and started back with a cry of alarm.

That cry was not repeated, for in another instant a hunting-spear came hurtling through the window.

The weapon came as straight as an arrow from a bow, and, passing through James Loddon's body, drove him backwards.

So sudden was the blow delivered that at first the wretched man felt only a numbing pain.

But then came the anguish, and as it darted through his body and seemed to set his heart on fire he saw the shadow of Spring-Heeled Jack.

"Help—murder! I am a slain man!" James Loddon shrieked.

And then he tottered backwards, and fell so heavily that the head of the spear pinned him to the ground.

The noise occasioned by his fall, added to his yell of agony, brought up Filby with at least a dozen men at his heels.

"Stand back!" Filby cried. "Give him air. Who in the name of that's horrible has done this?"

"Spring-Heeled Jack!" shouted a voice. "In such manner die all villains with murder and rapine in their hearts!"

The men fell back, appalled by the unearthly character of the voice.

Their faces turned from red to white as they glanced at each other.

They could see nothing but the glass lying in shivered fragments on the floor, and James Loddon terribly wounded, and perhaps to the very death, at their feet.

"I fear we can do but little here," Filby said. "We must now look for another leader. A curse is on this awful place. Lads, take my advice, and leave it before it is too late."

"But what," said one of the ruffians, pointing to Loddon's body, "are we to do with this?"

"He is dead, and let him rest," he said. "For my own part, I mean to make tracks for the old place. Follow me. We will lay hands on everything we can get, and make ourselves scarce without further trouble."

## CHAPTER CX.

RALPH ASHTON'S NEW SERVANT — DAISY'S LOVER PRESENTS HIMSELF—THE RIDE TO LONDON—STOPPED ON THE WAY.

CROUCHING in the recess formed by Nature in the chalk cliff, Daisy Leigh waited, with no small degree of impatience, for the return of Henry Palmer.

As time went on, and he did not put in an appearance, she came to the conclusion that something had happened.

As she heard the ringing report of fire-arms, fear got the better of her discretion, and leaving her hiding-place, she fled—she knew not whither.

Danger lurked in every step she took.

She fled up the gulch, leaping frantically over the huge stones that obstructed her path, and tearing away the briers and brambles which clung to her dress.

The horror of being retaken was so great that she would have welcomed death in any form.

But Daisy Leigh was fragile, and it was evident that this strain on her strength would be too much for her to bear.

Such soon proved to be the case, and the girl fell, striking her brow, and rendering herself unconscious.

She knew no more until she opened her eyes, and found that she was in bed in the room she had learned to love so well.

The breeze passing through the open windows fluttered the snow-white curtains, and fanned her face deliciously.

It was like waking from a horrible dream, or from a long, weary illness.

"Constance!" she cried. "If this be reality you must be near me."

In another instant a smooth, rounded arm was placed under her neck, and tears fell upon her face.

"Daisy—dear Daisy!" Constance said. "Thank Heaven you are safe now!"

"But how did I get here?" Daisy asked. "Have I been dreaming? Did a fever suddenly seize me?"

"Hush—hush!" Constance whispered. "You must not talk; indeed, I am disobeying orders in speaking to you. Ralph brought you back. Listen! That is his footstep upon the stairs. How glad he will be to see you so much better!"

The door opened gently, and Ralph Ashton stole silently across the floor.

"Constance," he said, "how fares it with poor Daisy? Has she shown any sign of returning consciousness?"

"See for yourself, Ralph," Constance replied, in joyous accents. "Daisy can answer that question herself now."

As Ralph Ashton reached the bedside Daisy took his hand and pressed it to her lips.

"What do I not owe you?" she said, sobbing in the fulness of her heart. "Everything—home—a brother's love. Aye! even my very life."

"If you talk to me in that strain I shall run away," Ralph replied. "You owe me nothing. Let us both thank Heaven that I found you at a most critical moment."

"But how came you to be there?" said Daisy Leigh.

"I was making my way towards home," Ralph replied. "You must let that explanation suffice for the present."

Daisy passed her hand across her brow, and looked from Ralph to Constance in a bewildered fashion.

"I can make nothing out distinctly yet," she said; "my brain seems to be whirling round and round. There was a man named—"

"Henry Palmer?" Ralph interposed, with a smile.

"Yes."

"He is here."

"Here?" Daisy repeated, raising her beautifully arched eyebrows. "Surely you must be joking with me?"

"Indeed I am not," said Ralph Ashton. "Strangely enough, I came upon him, too, and it was he who furnished me with the startling news regarding yourself."

"All this is like a tangled skein to me," Daisy said. "Henry Palmer! Ah! he was good to me, in spite of what I said to him."

"Yes," said Ralph; "and I have found him a new place."

"Where?"

"With me," Ralph replied. "Henceforth he is my servant."

"Can all this be possible?"

"Not only possible, but true," Ralph returned; "and, what is more, the robbers' haunt will be broken up in a few days. I have other news to tell you, but you are not strong enough to hear it now. Constance!"

Constance Marfield seemed to understand what was required of her.

She advanced with a glass containing a liquid in her hand, and held it to Daisy's lips.

"You must drink this," she said. "It will soothe you and do you good."

"Were it deadly poison I would not murmur if it came from your hands," Daisy said.

She swallowed the draught, and in a few minutes her eyes closed in peaceful slumber.

"Ralph," Constance said, placing her hand upon his arm, "I want you to make me a promise."

"I will if it be possible to perform it," he returned.

"Promise me that you will not leave us again—at least, for some time."

A grave, sad expression settled on Ralph Ashton's face.

"Constance," he said, "it is when I am at home that danger is rife and plots are laid against us. I cannot promise to stay at home for any lengthened period, for I am sure that I should break my word."

"What a strange life you lead!" Constance Marfield said, after a pause.

"Yes, it is a strange life," he assented, as he took her hand in his own. "A very strange life indeed."

"You will never let me know all its secrets, I suppose?" Constance said.

"You know its very best secret."

"And that is?"

"That I love you."

"Thus it is harder to be always parting with you," Constance said. "Your visits are short; you are here one minute and gone the next. Indeed, I think that you are beginning to grow very much like Spring-Heeled Jack."

Ralph Ashton laughed loudly at this idea, and then chided himself.

"I shall wake Daisy if I make that noise," he said. "Come, let us leave her. She will sleep on for several hours, and then wake with new strength and almost her old self again."

Constance Marfield kissed the sleeping girl, and then followed Ralph Ashton downstairs.

At the base of the staircase they encountered Henry Palmer.

The man drew himself on one side and saluted.

"I shall have a few words to say to you presently," Ralph said, as he opened a door and ushered Constance into one of the prettily-furnished rooms.

"Very well, sir," Palmer replied; "you will find me ready to execute your commands. Shall I remain where I am, sir?"

"Yes."

In a few minutes Ralph Ashton returned and beckoned to his new servant to follow him into the garden.

"We met in a strange way, and I have taken you into my service on a still stranger recommendation," Ralph Ashton said. "I think I told you that Spring-Heeled Jack stopped me on the way and told me what a plight you and Miss Leigh were in?"

"Yes," Henry Palmer said; "but I am yet bewildered. I see and hear things like a man in a dream. Who and what is this Spring-Heeled Jack—how comes it that he knows you?"

Ralph Ashton held up his hand.

"I might ask how it comes about that he knows you?" he said. "I know this much. It is Spring-Heeled Jack's mission to punish the bad and reward the good. His actions have proved that over and over again. But it is not of Spring-Heeled Jack, or of the manner in which you find yourself here, that I wish to speak to you entirely. I have something of greater importance—I have to exact a promise from you."

Henry Palmer turned his full, frank eyes upon Ralph Ashton's face.

"I fail to comprehend your meaning," he said.

"Oh! I will make myself perfectly comprehensible presently," Ralph Ashton said, smiling. "You must henceforth look upon Daisy Leigh as a stranger."

Palmer started, and for a moment his face turned deadly pale.

"You do not think—you would not accuse me of being such a villain as—"

"Don't jump at conclusions," said Ralph Ashton, interrupting him. "I know what the strength of a young man's love is, and how great a struggle it takes for him to overcome it."

Henry Palmer hung his head.

"What you say is quite true, sir," he said, in a low tone of voice.

"No [illegible] master of his own heart," Ralph said; "but [illegible] school and tone it if he be so willed. Palmer, [illegible] I have said is for the best. Daisy Leigh has no [illegible] to give; her heart is not her own."

"I had already made up my mind to hear that," Henry Palmer said. "But must we be absolute strangers?"

"Yes," [illegible] replied. "I think you would find such a [illegible]."

"I will abide [illegible] decision," Henry Palmer said; "[illegible] will be [illegible] most impossible to remain here, and no [illegible]"

"But you will [illegible] remain here," Ralph Ashton replied. "I have a small establishment in London, which is at present unknown to the occupants of this house. You will ride with me to town to-night."

"Willingly, sir—willingly," Henry Palmer said.

Soon after this conversation had come to an end Constance called to Ralph, telling him that Daisy was awake, and felt so much better that she desired to leave her bed.

"Let her do so if she wishes," Ralph said.

In a short time Daisy, leaning lightly on Constance Marfield's arm, walked into the garden.

An expression of pleasure played on Daisy's face as she saw Henry Palmer.

She advanced quickly to meet him, and held out her hand.

To her surprise the man turned his back abruptly upon her.

"What does this mean?" Daisy said, turning to Ralph Ashton. "Have I heaped more insults upon the head of the man who risked his life to save mine?"

"It means that he is obedient and faithful," Ralph said, as he led her away. "Let matters rest where they are, Daisy. The time may perhaps come when you will know each other better, and under different auspices. As matters now stand, Henry Palmer occupies the position of a servant, and must keep his place."

"Oh! you are cruel to him," Daisy cried. "No, I don't mean that—I mean—oh!—"

"I know exactly what you mean and what you would say," Ralph Ashton interposed. "Yes, Daisy, I am cruel; but it is out of kindness that I am so. But I will say no more. Run away to Constance, and in a few minutes we will dine, for I must be on the road to London before dark."

"To London?" Daisy faltered. "Must you go to that dreadful place again?"

"Yes," Ralph replied; "indeed I must."

"And you will leave us here?"

"So well guarded that I should have but few apprehensions if I heard that the house was attacked by a regiment of soldiers," Ralph said.

"But new foes seem to crop up," Daisy said.

"Yes; at the instigation of old ones," Ralph returned. "I will tell you something. The man who played a villain's part and dragged you from this house will never have it in his power to attempt such a thing again. He is dead."

"Are you sure—quite sure?"

"Yes. Spring-Heeled Jack tells no lies, and it was from him that I had the information."

"At whose hand did the villain die?"

"Spring-Heeled Jack's," Ralph Ashton replied. "You may take the news as a fact, Daisy."

"I do not doubt it," the girl replied. "Well, I have no pity for the scoundrel. Oh! Heaven be thanked for my timely rescue."

Night was closing in when Ralph Ashton ordered his horse, and one for Henry Palmer, to be brought round to the door.

He bade the ladies an affectionate farewell, and reminded them that one of his missions was to ask for a postponement of Bill Blarney's trial in consequence of Daisy's weak state of health.

Constance was reluctant to give any evidence at all, but Ralph Ashton had as firmly made up his mind that the scoundrel should swing as Mrs. Corcoran and a select party of light-fingered gentlemen had planned for Bill Blarney's escape.

The stars were shining faintly when Ralph and his new servant commenced their journey.

Ralph Ashton had another object in going to London.

He had determined to find Mrs. Corcoran, and either to bring her back to his house a voluntary prisoner, or to charge her on her own confession, and hand her over to the officers of justice.

Neither master nor servant spoke for some time, until a peculiar sound came borne on the wings of the wind.

It was like a Babel of tongues in the distance, and Ralph Ashton brought his horse to a standstill and listened intently.

"What do you make of it, Palmer?" he asked.

"Nothing very distinct," was the reply; "but it strikes me that we shall soon come on an encampment of gipsies, and find the people fighting among themselves."

"I like it not," Ralph Ashton said, "for there seems to be something ominous in the hum and buzz of human voices. However, we can do nothing but ride on."

Presently they saw lights twinkling in the distance.

Then the noise grew louder, and they could distinguish the angry barking of several dogs.

"It is as I thought," Henry Palmer said. "It is a faction fight among the gipsies, and if we wish to avoid hard blows we had better turn aside."

"Nay, I think you are wrong, after all," said Ralph. "See those torches yonder? The men seem to be searching for something."

At this moment they were espied by one of the gipsies.

A hoarse shout rent the air, and then the whole crowd of lawless gipsies moved towards the riders.

Ralph Ashton passed Henry Palmer a brace of pistols, and drew those with which his holsters were fitted.

"If they are not mad with rage," said Ralph Ashton, "you shall see how the utterance of a single word can quiet them."

On came the gipsies, flashing torches here and there, shouting, cursing, and yelling as if they had taken the word out of Ralph Ashton's mouth and gone mad indeed.

One gigantic man, whose face was the colour of walnut-juice, and whose hair flowed over his shoulders in tangled masses, advanced, brandishing a pike so close to Ralph Ashton that his horse reared and plunged violently.

"Hold, fellow!" Ralph cried.

"Fellow in your teeth!" the gipsy replied, grasping the handle of the pike tightly, and bringing its point on a level with Ralph's breast. "Nobody passes this way without giving a good account of themselves!"

"That we can do if you act like reasonable beings," Ralph replied. "Let us pass—we are peaceable men, and do not bark like dogs. When we bark we bite!"

"Dismount!" said the gipsy in a voice of thunder, as a number of others gathered round. "We suspect that you are on the way to Mildendale Hall, and, consequently, we must search you."

"Search us!" Ralph said, scornfully. "You know not to whom you speak."

"And care not."

"Zanoni!" Ralph said, as he leaned forward over the saddle.

The word acted like a magic spell on the gipsies. They fell back instantly, and Ralph Ashton smiled to see the impression he had made.

"You see," he said, "I do not come among you without a pass word," he said. "Where is your queen?'

"In yonder tent."

"Conduct me to her?" said Ralph. "She knows me very well."

All this was a mystery to Henry Palmer.

He said nothing, but sat still, staring in bewilderment at the strange scene.

"This way," said the gipsy, who bore the pike. "Sir, if we have given offence, you must pardon us! Zanoni, our queen, will tell you that we are perfectly justified in our action."

As if at a given signal the gipsies faced round, and the two horsemen followed in the direction of a snow-white tent, which stood apart from a number of others in the distance.

## CHAPTER CXI.

### CATCHPOLE AND GRABHAM FIND THE BULL IN TOP BOOTS A DANGEROUS ANIMAL.

THE landlord of the Bull in Top Boots finding that the constables were determined to force a way into the house, thought it better to open the door himself.

"What a pair of fools you are," he said, as he threw it open. "You make noise enough to wake the dead. What's your reason for coming here?"

"We were here once before," Grabham observed, as he tapped the side of his nose with his forefinger, "and we are not likely to forget it, are we, Catchpole?"

"Not if I live for a thousand years."

"You came here when you were drunk, and some men played pranks with you," the landlord said. "I remember the circumstances perfectly well. What is your business now?"

"I suppose you don't happen to know a man named Jacob Butler?" Grabham enquired.

"Never heard of him."

"Nor a nice old party named Mrs. Corcoran?"

"No," said the landlord, shaking his head. "Nice old ladies are not much in my way."

"Well," Grabham returned, "of course, we ain't bound to believe you, unless we like. I suppose you have heard of the Chequers, in Lower Smithfield?"

"I believe that there is such a house."

"The Chequers is bust up," Grabham cried, exultantly. "Me and Catchpole bust it up. We put up the shutters, and Ted Nickells and a pal are laid by the heels in Newgate."

These were interesting items to the landlord of the Bull in Top Boots, for he knew Ted Nickells very well, and had done a considerable amount of business with him.

He kept his countenance, however, and looked the constables straight in the eyes.

"Well," he said, after a pause, "what has this to do with me?"

"We thought that Jacob Butler, who we found shut up in a nice trap at the Chequers, and who gave us the slip after we had saved the beggar's life, might be here," said Grabham.

"Yes, yes; I daresay," the landlord gasped. "I ask you again what all this has to do with me? The man is not here, I tell you, and there's an end of the matter."

"There I begs to differ with you," Grabham returned, in an exasperating tone of voice. "We suspect that your house is something after the same character as the Chequers, so we have come just to have a look round it."

"Oh! come in," said the landlord of the Bull in Top Boots, as he threw the door open wide. "Don't study my feelings on any account. Worry me until I go mad. Turn my house upside down, and when you have done that, drink all the liquor you can find in the bar."

"Now that's kind of you," said Catchpole, grinning, "and we'll have a drink to start with, if you don't mind."

"Certainly," the landlord replied; "come round to the other side of the bar, and I'll make you as happy as a pair of donkeys in a clover field."

Neither of the constables resented this rather doubtful compliment.

Both were very thirsty, and full of officiousness.

"What is it to be?" said the landlord, as he led them on the other side of the counter.

"Brandy is our favourite weakness," said Grabham, grinning at Catchpole.

"Then brandy it is," said the landlord, pouring out two glasses of the liquor. "I suppose you don't care about the water?"

"We consider it a weakness," Catchpole replied. "The man who puts water with his liquor ought to be shot."

"Hear, hear!" said Grabham, as he placed his glass to his lips, and put it down empty. "Them's my sentiments, Catchpole, my boy."

"And so," said the landlord, as he pushed the brandy-bottle invitingly towards the constable, "you suspect that there is foul play going on in my house."

"What are we to think?"

"You are right, Mr. Grabham," said the landlord; "but how can I help it? All sorts of people will come to my house, you know."

"Just so," said Grabham, as he gulped down another glass of brandy. "You see it ain't us, but the law, as interferes with you."

"Granted!" the landlord said, as he sipped his own glass of brandy carefully; "but just attend to me for a moment. I suppose that you have a warrant, authorising you to search my house?"

"If we hadn't we shouldn't be here," Catchpole replied.

"I should like to see it very much," said the landlord, removing his hand from his chin.

"Oh!" Grabham chimed in, "this is the first time that we have ever been asked to do such a thing."

"That may be," the landlord of the Bull in Top Boots said; "but I happen to know something of the world as well as you. Show me your warrant, or out you go like a shot out of a gun!"

Messrs. Catchpole and Grabham rubbed their knees very hard, but said never a word in response to this challenge.

"You see," said the landlord, in continuation, "it is all very well for you to come blustering here, but you have a cool, calculating man to deal with. Here am I, a humble individual, paying rent, taxes, and licenses; I am loyal to my king, and hence I have as much right to be protected as a peer of the realm."

"Of course you have," said Grabham. "Who said you hadn't?"

"In that case," the landlord resumed, "you must produce your warrant before you search my house."

"Eh?"

"I mean exactly what I say, and no more and no less."

Both Grabham and Catchpole scratched their heads.

They looked at each other.

Catchpole snorted in a defiant manner.

Grabham gave vent to a kind of vengeful groan.

Suddenly an idea dawned upon his mind.

"You are right," he said; "but it so happens that we are empowered to take any person we suspect into custody; and we suspect you."

It was now the turn of the landlord of the Bull in Top Boots to show the white feather.

He turned colour as Grabham playfully displayed a pair of handcuffs.

"Come—come," he said, "this is all nonsense. If you wish to search my house, of course I have no objection. Where would you like to begin—the top or the bottom?"

"There's no hurry," said Catchpole, who was getting rather blinky about the eyes. "Of course we must do our dooty, unpleasant as it may be; but there's no reason why we should do it as if we wanted to break our necks."

The landlord of the Bull in Top Boots smiled.

He saw how matters were going, and was sufficiently wide awake to keep the gallant constables well supplied with the ardent spirit which was fast confusing their senses.

"Of course you know best," he said; "but I have my business to attend to. Supposing we have just one more nip, and then go in search of this mare's nest."

"Catchpole," said Grabham.

"Well, what's the matter with you?"

"You're drunk."

"You're a vile perverter of the truth," Catchpole said, hiccuping.

"That's another name for a liar," Grabham said, clenching his fists.

"You may call it what you like," Catchpole replied, staring at his companion with lack lustre eyes. "I know my business as well as you, if not better."

Grabham, who was not quite so drunk, saw which way the wind was blowing.

He upset Catchpole's glass, and that gentleman, thus deprived of his liquor, fell to swearing in a manner worthy of a trooper.

"You clumsy owl!" he said. "It's a waste of good brandy."

"But not a waste of common sense," Grabham retorted. "You can hardly stand on your legs!"

"What?"

"Don't try that game with me," said Grabham. "I know how much courage you possess; I can weigh it to an ounce."

Mr. Catchpole tried to look angry out of one eye, which, of course, was a dismal failure.

"Well," he said, with the air of a man who suddenly woke to the fact that he ought to do something. "I am in your hands. You are my superior officer and your word is law!"

This speech seemed to impress Mr. Grabham very favourably.

He rose to his feet, and, having expanded his chest to its utmost limit, blew out his cheeks and snorted like a grampus.

"Before we have another drop of drink," he said, "we will search the house."

"Good," said Catchpole. "I'm ready!"

By the way he staggered about when he left his chair would have convinced a looker-on that he was unready to do anything but go to sleep.

"Dash my buttons!" said Grabham; "if you wouldn't make a saint swear."

"Ha! ha!" Catchpole laughed, idiotically. "I know what I am up to. Lead the way."

The landlord of the Bull in Top Boots had watched all these proceedings with feelings of joy.

"You are trying my patience," he said. "How long do you expect me to dance an attendance upon you?"

Grabham seized Catchpole by the arm, and they passed the room, concealed from view by the sliding panel.

All would have gone well, had not Mrs. Corcoran sneezed, and so loudly, that Grabham stopped and held up his hand.

"What is that?" he demanded.

"Only my cat," the landlord said, as his face grew damp with perspiration.

"My cat!" Grabham repeated, contemptuously. "You tell that tale to your grandmother."

"I would I had one," the landlord replied, "but, poor dear, she has been dead and gone many a year."

The astute Mr. Grabham, struck the panel with his knuckles, and winked at his fellow constable.

"There's something wrong here," he said, "this sounds hollow-like."

"Most cupboards do," the landlord remarked. "There is nothing very extraordinary in that."

"Oh! no," said Grabham, "that's just my idea. Supposing you lend me an axe, and let us see what is inside this ere cupboard."

The landlord did not know what to do.

He felt a cold thrill run through his frame, and a feeling in his feet as if he had been suddenly lifted into the air.

"I have met a few men in my time," he said, "but you certainly are the most foolish. My house is open to you. Confound you! there is no room there, but there is one a little further on."

"Let's have a peep at it."

"This way."

Grabham rushed into the apartment, with Catchpole staggering close upon his heels.

Then they looked round for the landlord.

The door was closed, and he was nowhere to be seen.

"There is something wrong," said Grabham.

He dashed at the door.

It was securely locked, and both the constables, instead of taking prisoners, were in custody themselves.

"This—this is truly awful," said Grabham, mopping his brow with a huge red handkerchief.

"Oh! lor'!" Catchpole shrieked, "my feet are giving way under me. Help—help! Murder!"

"So are mine!" Grabham yelled.

Some piece of machinery was at work.

The floor descended at a violent rate.

Suddenly it stopped and tilted upwards.

Both constables shot forward and fell upon their hands and knees.

Then came a rushing sound and they saw the ceiling return to its original position.

It did not take long to convince Catchpole and Grabham that they were imprisoned beneath the house.

"This," said Catchpole, sitting down all of a heap upon the floor—"this is your fault."

"Mine?"

"Yes, yours."

"Say that again and I will punch your head."

"Do it."

No sooner said than done.

Grabham fetched the companion of his misfortunes such a crack on the side of his cranium that it rattled like a box of dice against the wall.

"There," said Grabham, "how do you like that? I hope you are satisfied now."

Catchpole was more than satisfied.

He grasped the side of his head as if suddenly seized with an attack of toothache.

"Grabham," he said, vaguely, "there was a time when you would have extended the hand of friendship rather than knuckles, which I may compare to the sting of a wiper. Don't you think that you would do better to try and see your way out o' this 'ere mess, rather than smiting me in a way as don't become a man and a brother?"

"Why, yes," said Grabham; "I should have exercised my intellects; only you exasperated me in a manner past human endurance."

"Never, never," Catchpole observed. "I wouldn't go for to do such a thing."

He was fast growing maudlin, and to Grabham's horror he suddenly manifested a strong inclination to sing.

"Dash it!" Grabham howled, clutching at his hair. "What is the matter with you now?"

Catchpole opened his mouth in such a manner as a boy does when he expects a cherry to be put into it.

But no sound came from his pursed-up lips.

"Catchpole! Catchpole!" said Grabham, shaking him violently by the shoulder, "don't you see the fix we are in? Rouse yourself—rouse yourself, I say!"

"I'm a miserable man, with sins enough for half-a-dozen," Catchpole moaned. "I'm a wicked wretch, and ought to be kicked from one end of the world to the other."

"Then kicked it is!" said Grabham.

He used his feet with such force that the unfortunate Catchpole flew from one side of the cellar to the other.

This stern kind of discipline seemed to revive him somewhat.

He picked himself up, and placed his back against the wall.

"I shall remember this," he said. "Grabham, my boy, a kick is a kick, and a blow is a blow, which, as the proverb says, 'A sarpint's child is more keen than a bad tooth.' No, I don't mean that. Hang me if I do know what I mean!"

"I don't think you do."

For the first time it occurred to Catchpole that he and his fellow constable were in danger.

As his senses grew clearer so the awkwardness of the position became impressed on him, and now he began to whine and sob like a schoolboy after a sound caning.

"We are done for at last," he said. "Grabham, my boy, give me your hand, for we are doomed to perish together."

Mr. Grabham did not see the matter at all in this light.

He had not the slightest wish to die just at present, and said so most emphatically.

Indeed, he went so far as to say that he wouldn't die, for the simple reason that he wished to live; but as for Catchpole, he could curl up like a door-mat and perish comfortably for all he, Mr. Grabham, cared.

"But ain't there a door?" Catchpole groaned. "Ain't there something we can crawl out of?"

"I don't see anything, but I can smell the sewers," "Grabham replied.

"So can I."

"A short spell of silence followed this unpleasant discovery.

"This is only to frighten us," Grabham said, at last. "All we have to do is to keep quiet for a time, and then the laugh will be on our side. That precious landlord shall swing for this little game, or I'm no sinner!"

"Don't talk so loud," Catchpole returned, in a hushed tone of voice. "He may be listening."

"Listeners never hear any good of themselves," Grabham observed, with an amount of boldness he did not feel in his heart. "I'll show him no mercy."

"But what annoys me most," said Catchpole, with another dismal whine, "is that Bill Blarney's trial commences to-morrow, and if we ain't there—"

"Hold!" Grabham said, "I smell a rat."

"Where?" Catchpole gasped, drawing up his legs.

"Not a real rat, but I have an idea that we are shoved down here to keep us away from the trial," said Grabham. "But wait a while; I'll just have a look round this place."

The cellar was dark and gruesome in the extreme.

It was the sort of place that no decent-minded man would have thrust a dog into.

The only furniture it contained consisted of an empty barrel, two or three planks, and a broken-down bench.

But as for a door, or anything approaching an outlet, Mr. Grabham could find none."

"This is awful!" he said, hauling out his handkerchief, and rubbing the end of his nose until it seemed to have turned red-hot. "I thought the landlord was having a sort of a kind joke with us, but now I know different. We are dished like eggs, Catchpole; and there's nothing for us but to make up our minds to die like men and Britons."

"Don't say that," Catchpole said, in accents of abject despair. "I can't think of it without a shudder. Just now you wouldn't have it that we were in a bad fix."

"But I think different now," Grabham replied.

At this moment the constables were startled by hearing a sharp clicking sound, and none the less astonished were they to see the landlord of the Bull in Top Boots advancing towards them, bearing a lantern in his hand.

## CHAPTER CXII.

### SIR ROLAND ASHTON RECEIVES A CHECK—JOE ROLLINS DETERMINES TO HAVE HIS SHARE OF THE PLUNDER.

"If," said Lord Mildendale, "your story be true, both my wife and child are alive?"

"So the woman who acted as leader of the

wandering tribe informed me," Sir Roland returned.

Lord Mildendale trifled with the handle of his delicate cocoa-cup, as he looked enquiringly across the table at his guest.

"But tell me," he added, after a pause, "what could have possessed this woman to have told you this story concerning myself? She had no idea that we should ever meet."

"It is said of these strange people that they can read the stars," Sir Roland replied; "and perhaps she had some mysterious means of knowing that we should become acquainted."

"Bah!" Lord Mildendale returned, contemptuously; "I will not give ear to such idle nonsense. You might just as well ask me to believe in witchcraft at once."

And yet, even while he spoke, his lordship's face was grave and sad.

He remembered the visit he had received from Spring-Heeled Jack, and his heart sank within him.

Sir Roland made no reply to the last speech, but drummed his fingers thoughtfully upon the table.

"You must think me rude and uncouth," Lord Mildendale said, "but, see here, Mr. Fernie. You fall in with a tribe of gipsies, whose whole aim is, of course, to get money out of you. At some time or another they have been in England, and picked up a scrap here and there of my sad story. What follows? They seize upon the first name for their pack of lies, and it happens to be mine."

"If you think so," Sir Roland replied, "nothing more need be said on the subject. For my own part, had I not taken a serious view of the affair I should not have intruded upon your privacy by calling here."

"Nay, nay," said Lord Mildendale. "You must not misunderstand me. Do not misconstrue my words, I beg. You do me honour by staying with a lonely and almost heart-broken man. Pray do not go to-day. Let me show you over this old place, and I think you will find that it contains a few things worth looking at."

Sir Roland Ashton's eyes glistened.

Matters were coming to a crisis.

The opportunity he desired and had fenced so cleverly for was almost within his grasp.

"Well," he said, "I must confess that you nettled me for a moment. But let it pass. You have, indeed, a splendid ancestral home, Lord Mildendale."

"Yes," his lordship replied. "And it contains as much wealth as any of the king's palaces in London."

"You astonish me."

"In the days of the struggle between the Cavaliers and Roundheads," his lordship continued, "hundreds of thousands of pounds worth of plate and other valuable property were concealed in the vaults below. It is impossible that the Lord Mildendale then living could have possessed the whole, or even half of it. However, it has never been claimed; there was never a clue as to its rightful owner, and so we came to look upon it as our own."

"Which was the most natural and profitable thing to do," Sir Roland said. "I shall be most delighted to explore this romantic region."

"It is a long time since I looked at the antique things," Lord Mildendale said; "for when—well, never mind, at a certain period of my life I lost all interest in them. It will be as much a treat for me as for you, Mr. Fernie."

Sir Roland Ashton's keen eyes twinkled, and he laughed in his sleeve.

"If he gave me the keys of the whole place and told me to help myself he could not do more," he thought.

"When will you conduct me over the Hall?" he asked, aloud.

"When you have sufficiently recovered from the fatigue of your long journey," Lord Mildendale replied.

"Then," said Sir Roland, "I am entirely in your hands, for I am so far from being tired that I feel a little exercise would do me good."

"Come, then," his lordship replied, "we will delay no longer if that is the case."

As he spoke he rang a bell, and a servant glided into the room.

"Liffy," said Lord Mildendale, "bring up a lighted lantern, with a good supply of candles."

The man looked surprised at the request.

He bowed and left the room, muttering half-audibly to himself.

"What new, mad idea has he got into his head?" Liffey growled. "Lantern—matches—candles! Perhaps he intends to set the house on fire, and burn us to death in our beds."

Liffey also noticed the queer way in which Sir Roland was looking at Lord Mildendale on his entrance, and the man's mind was troubled as he went downstairs to comply with his lordship's commands.

On returning to the room he found host and guest chatting most affably.

"You surprise me," Sir Roland was saying. "Only fancy, a coronet of diamonds worth half a million! Do you say that it has never seen daylight all these years?"

"As I am a living man, it is a fact," his lordship replied. "But you shall see it soon, and tell me whether it is not fit to grace the head of a princess!"

Sir Roland not only felt inclined to see the diamonds, but to handle them into the bargain.

Lord Mildendale rose, and taking the lantern in his hand, beckoned to Sir Roland to follow him.

They went down a flight of stairs, and as they did so Sir Roland stepped before a stained-glass window, on which was encrusted a coat of arms.

It was not the work of the heraldic artist that brought him to a standstill, but for a moment he could have sworn that he saw a face peering at him through the window.

But there was so much light and shadow about that he might easily have been mistaken.

And yet he turned pale and trembled.

Lord Mildendale did not notice his agitation; but taking a small key from his pocket, he opened a door leading to a small room, which at first sight appeared to be filled with all sorts of old lumber.

In the corners were trunks thickly covered with dust, old garments, broken swords, rusty pistols, and litter of almost every kind of description.

"Surely," Sir Roland Ashton thought, "there is nothing of a valuable nature to be seen here?"

He was mistaken.

Advancing to one of the chests, Lord Mildendale proceeded to open it.

The lock was so old, and in such a bad state of repair, that it repelled the key over and over again.

# SPRING-HEELED JACK,

## THE TERROR OF LONDON.

THE WINDOW SHIVERED AS SPRING-HEELED JACK LEAPED BODILY THROUGH IT.

No. 32.

"Let me try?" Sir Roland said. "I am accounted to be very strong in the wrist."

He took the key from Lord Mildendale's hand, and stooping down, commenced his task.

As he did so he felt a sharp touch on his shoulder.

"Yes?" he said, raising his head.

"I beg your pardon," Lord Mildendale rejoined. "Did you wish to speak to me?"

"I thought you called my attention to something," Sir Roland said.

"No, indeed."

Sir Roland glanced nervously round the room.

The light of the lantern fell upon its walls and floors, and though there were one or two ugly-looking shadows, there was nothing else to attract suspicion.

"The lock remains obstinate," Sir Roland said. "I cannot open it."

"Perchance there may be something in the key-hole," Lord Mildendale said. "Bring the lantern a little nearer so that we can see."

Sir Roland took up the light to comply, when it was dashed from his hand and hurled against the wall with such force that it flew into fragments.

"What in the name of wonder is the meaning of this?" Lord Mildendale demanded, aghast at the suddenness of the event.

"It means," whispered a voice in his ear, "that you had best beware of the villain who is here to dupe you."

"Ha!" Lord Mildendale cried. "Heard you that? Heaven have mercy upon us! Procure a light by some means."

"Heard I what?" Sir Roland yelled, drawing his sword and slashing right and left. "Death to the demon dog!"

Sir Roland's voice was so terrible that Lord Mildendale crouched against the wall.

"Put up your sword!" he cried. "Sheath your sword, I say, or you will do yourself or me a mischief!"

Sir Roland made no reply, and Lord Mildendale heard a heavy thud, as of a body falling upon the floor.

"Help—lights!" he cried, rushing to the door, and making his voice ring through the building.

His cries found a response in some of the men-servants, who soon gained the spot.

Ahead of them all was Joe Rollins, and his first notion was that Sir Roland had by some means betrayed himself to Lord Mildendale.

The baronet lay prone on his face, as if he had been struck down by a heavy club.

Joe Rollins, kneeling at Sir Roland's side and raising his head, discovered that blood was flowing from his mouth.

"My lord," said Joe Rollins, "I beg you tell me how my master came to this state?"

"I am at a loss to account for it," Lord Mildendale replied. "It seemed to me that Mr. Fernie was suddenly taken with a paroxysm of rage, for he hurled the lantern against the wall."

"Humph!" said Rollins. "Well, I can do no more now than put him to bed. Perhaps, when he wakes, he will be able to furnish me with a more satisfactory account of this mysterious affair."

## CHAPTER CXIII.

### THE BOAT ON THE RIVER.

The landlord of the Bull in Top Boots, swinging the lantern in his hand, came striding along as if nothing out of the ordinary course had happened.

Those brave constables, Catchpole and Grabham, hailed his appearance with feelings of delight, but for the time being they could do no more than stare at him in astonishment.

It seemed to them that he had sprung from the ground, and the suddenness of his appearance took away their breath and left them without the power of speech.

The landlord placed the lantern on the floor of the cellar, and folding his arms tightly across his breast, looked calmly at the two men he had so nicely trapped.

"Well," said he, "how did you find your way down here?"

"That's a good 'un," Catchpole contrived to gasp out. "Dash my buttons if that ain't the neatest thing I ever heard in my life!"

"It beats cock-fighting," Grabham chimed in, smiling feebly; "but perhaps our friend here has only been having a lark with us."

"A lark! What do you mean, you wooden-headed idiots?" the landlord demanded. "Do I look like a man given to playing larks? Do you think I pay rates and taxes to make a fool of myself and other people?"

"Oh! no," said the valiant Catchpole; "only I thought—"

"You think!" the landlord interposed. "Oh! lor', you think! A man must have brains to think."

Catchpole rubbed the top of his cranium, as if to convince the landlord that the brains were there.

"I tell you what it is," said the inn-keeper. "You came prying about into what does not concern you. You make yourselves drunk at my expense, and now that you have fallen heels over head into the cellar, you want to put the blame on my shoulders and get me into trouble."

"Don't be 'ard on us," Grabham groaned. "I don't deny the liquor, which was good and strong, but as to falling—"

"Hush!" said Catchpole interrupting him; "a soft answer is worth two in the bush, and a kind word is like a bird in the hand."

"Hold your tongue, you long-eared ass," Grabham gasped. "Why can't you let me speak?"

"The friend of my youth, the sharer of my official troubles, calls me an ass!" Catchpole moaned, dismally. "Oh! this is 'ard, too 'ard to bear without the shedding of manly tears."

"There is more brandy than water about your tears," the landlord of the Bull in Top Boots said. "Well, since you say I placed you here, here you shall remain while I send to Bow-street for one of your superior officers. He shall see the state you are in, and judge for himself."

"But," Grabham observed, in his most affable tone of voice, "you can't deny that you didn't put us here, can you. If we had come down of our own accord, of course it must have been by a staircase."

The landlord made no reply.

Taking up the lantern, he held it above his head.

"Well," he then said, "look at the right-hand side of the cellar, and tell me what you see!"

"Why, bless my 'art," Catchpole exclaimed, "if there ain't the staircase!"

"It wasn't there ten minutes ago," Grabham declared. "Didn't I crawl all round this place on my hands and knees?"

The landlord opened the lantern and blew the light out.

"Who's a hass now?" Catchpole shrieked. "Grabham, you born fool, what did you want to put your spoke in for?"

They heard the landlord running up the stairs, and made a dash forward to follow him.

The darkness was so pitch-like that they could not see where they were going, and coming into violent collision, the result was attended by most unpleasant consequences.

Catchpole shot forward and furrowed up the loose earth of the cellar-floor with his nose, and Grabham, shooting out in the opposite direction, bumped his head against the cellar wall, and produced a sound like a cracked basin.

For a moment all was still, and then the dismal place was filled with the sounds of grief and lamentation.

"I've busted in the top of my head," Grabham groaned.

"Don't talk to me!" Catchpole howled. "My nose is red hot, and there's no end of blue and yaller lights dancing afore my eyes."

"This way, gentlemen!" shouted the landlord, from the top of the staircase; "this way, if you please. I most earnestly hope that you have not stumbled over anything."

"Don't say a word in reply," Catchpole whispered, as he staggered to his feet. "There's no knowing what he mayn't do if we put him out of temper."

"I'd like to put him so much out as wouldn't leave him any temper to make use of," Grabham growled, under his breath. "Where's that staircase? It's gone again. It's like the ghost of a flight of steps."

"I've found it!" Catchpole sang out in triumph. "I've got it! Mind how you come, or you'll run foul of me again."

At this moment a ray of light fell upon their faces.

The landlord had re-lit the lantern, and was kindly showing them the way.

More dead than alive the constables crawled up, and would have made their way out by the front door, but they found that way locked and barred against them.

"No, my friends," said the landlord; "before you got too drunk to know what you were talking about or doing you accused me of harbouring bad characters, and I insist on you searching my house."

"Don't want to," Grabham said, surlily.

"But you shall," the landlord replied. "You have some idea what the lower part is like, and now you shall have a look at the top."

"My friend," said Catchpole, feeling his half-flayed nose tenderly, "show me the man who has never made a mistake, and I'll give in. We have seen quite enough, thank'ee."

"I don't like to part with you like this," the landlord said, grinning; "you are such excellent company. Well, if you must be going we will have a parting glass."

"Not being a man as bears malice, I sees no objection to that," Catchpole returned, removing his hand from his swollen nasal organ. "I'm as dry as a fish."

Grabham said nothing, but by the way that he opened his mouth it was evident that he was capable of drinking anything so long as it did not affect the contents of his pockets.

"You are right," said the landlord, winking knowingly at Catchpole. "The best man in the world may make a mistake, and I like the man who is sensible enough to own it."

As he spoke he filled up three glasses almost to the brims with neat spirits, and pledged the constables.

They responded heartily, but no sooner were their glasses empty than they began to sway about, and roll against each other in the most strange and unaccountable manner.

Grabham was the first to fall.

He went down with a flop, and lay as still as a dead cod fish.

Catchpole was not long before he followed suit.

Flinging his arms about wildly for a few moments, he fell headlong across Grabham's body.

"Done!" said the landlord, rubbing his hands exultantly. "That has settled them."

Walking backwards he touched the spring of the secret panel, and it flew back instantly.

Out came Mrs. Corcoran, and Dick Sleuth, with his fellow ruffians treading closely upon his heels.

"Ha! ha! ha!" yelled the hag, wildly. "Ho! ho! This is good—glorious!"

"Don't kick up that row, or you will rouse the neighbourhood!" said the landlord of the Bull in Top Boots.

"I can't help it—I really can't," Mrs. Corcoran screeched, as she hopped round and round the insensible constables. "Don't they look white and nice? What are you going to do with them?"

"You will see presently," the landlord said, as he stepped into the parlour. "Just keep your wagging tongue still, and you will see that we know how to have some fun here as well as serious business."

He presently returned with a quantity of soot in one hand and some red ochre in the other.

He mixed them up in a little water, and then bedaubed the features of Catchpole and Grabham in such a manner as to make them look perfectly horrible.

Mrs. Corcoran laughed until tears rained from her rheumy eyes.

"It's better than a play," she said. "I wouldn't have missed this for anything you could have made me a present of."

Now then, Dick, and the rest of you!" said the landlord. "Lend a hand here. We will give our friends a nice little treat. I hope they will know each other when they come to their senses!"

. . . . . . . .

It was a cold, blustering night on the Thames.

The tide ran strong, and its mournful voice joined in chorus with the roaring of the boisterous wind, which came sweeping along in angry gusts from the Essex marshes, the home of fog and gloom.

The wharves and landing-stages wore a miserable aspect.

Huge cranes became converted into monstrous, awful spectres, and where the ships lay at anchor their lights danced upon the water like corpse candles over the graves of the wicked.

Whirling round and round, bumping against slimy walls, and dashing against wooden piles, was an untended boat.

At first sight it appeared as if it had broken loose from its moorings.

Several mariners on watch saw the fragile craft as it dashed along on the top of the tide, but paid no heed to it.

There were no oars in the rowlocks, and such as caught a glimpse of the boat, as it darted along, came to the conclusion that it concerned them nothing.

Had it been daylight the watchful mariners' eyes would have been regaled with a strange and most uncommon sight.

There were two men in the boat—two men who lay snoring soundly in blissful ignorance of the fearful danger they were in.

The wind, battling with the tide, so lashed the river into fury that waves rose to a considerable height, and every now and then a quantity of water found its way into the boat.

Suddenly the boat, swinging round, struck its stern against a post with such violence as to almost throw one of the men out.

As it was, the concussion awoke him with a start, and, sitting up, he began to rub his eyes, as if they had offended him and he determined to get them out of his head as quickly as possible.

"This is a dream," he said. "As sure as my name's Grabham, it's a dream, and one of the most horrible I was ever troubled with."

As Mr. Grabham spoke he pinched his arms so painfully as to make himself squeak like a dying pig.

"No," he gasped, "I'm awake; but what's this—an old sack instead of my coat? A boat—the river? Lor' 'a mercy! I'm a dead man as sure as I'm a sinner."

Straining his terrified eyes, he thought he saw something in the bows of the boat, and kicked at the object with such earnestness that it sat up and howled.

"Is that you, Catchpole?" Grabham bellowed. "Tell me I ain't a dead man crossing the river Sticks—tell me I ain't a madman?"

"You kicked liked forty loonatics," Catchpole replied; "but — but — dash it! we're on the river."

"I know we are," Grabham yelled. "I know we are, Catchpole, but the question is, how did we get here?"

"Have you been pulling?" Catchpole asked, with child-like innocence.

"Have I been pulling!" Grabham gasped. "There ain't no oars to pull with."

"What?"

Catchpole sat bolt upright, and laid violent hands on his hair.

"There ain't no oars to pull with!" Grabham repeated. "There ain't nothing but sack-cloth and ashes—which, I mean to say, my coat is gone, and I've been thrust into a bit of sack-cloth."

"So have I," said Catchpole, as he made a hurried examination of his garments, "Here's a pretty state of things!"

"I don't call it nice at all," Grabham howled. "Here we are spinning round like a whirligig, and may be smashed up at any moment."

"Don't talk like that," Catchpole said, dismally, "it makes my blood run cold, and as if—"

He said no more, for just then a wave dashed over the bows of the boat, and not only soaked him to the skin, but poured about half a gallon of nauseous water down his throat.

Catchpole was very ill as soon as he could get his breath.

No landsman smitten with sea-sickness could have been worse.

"This is awful!" he groaned. "I'm dreadfully bad."

"I'm everything!" Grabham cried, wildly. "Can you swim?"

"No."

"Of course not," Grabham said; "what's the use of you. You can't do anything."

"Well," Catchpole returned, as the boat danced about like a cork in the middle of an eddy, "can you swim?"

"I was never fond enough of cold water to try."

"Then don't grumble about me," said Catchpole. "Oh! I say—oh! lor'!"

"What's the matter?"

"Look at this great thing bearing down on us."

It was the hull of a vessel, and the lights hanging at the masthead looked like vengeful eyes.

"We are saved!" Grabham cried, starting to his feet. "Ship a-hoy—help! Get out of our way—help!—you'll run us down. Murder!"

"Go to old Harry!" roared a voice, as the vessel passed within a couple of feet of the boat, and passed it.

"Oh! the cold-hearted willains to leave us to perish," Grabham groaned, as he sank down at the bottom of the boat. "Oh! the horrible wretches! Ah! Catchpole, I've got an idea."

"What is it?"

"We will tear up the floor boards and make oars of them."

"Grabham," said Catchpole, with emotion, "if I have ever said anything to offend you forgive me. That 'ere idea is a splendid one. We'll get ashore and—and—well, I don't know what we will do, for I'll be hanged if I can think where we come from."

"Nor I," Grabham replied, with a groan, which he jerked spasmodically from his throat; "but what does that matter now? We have our lives to think about, so up with the floor boards."

"It's all very well to say up with them," Catchpole gasped. "The bothering things are nailed fast down."

"Wrench 'em up!" Grabham cried. "Use all your strength, or we shall be drowned like blind kittens."

After a deal of wrenching and tugging the constables contrived to rend up two fragments of the flooring, and so energetic was Grabham that he contrived to spring a leak.

It was bad enough to have the water washing over them without having it pouring through the bottom of the boat.

"Pull away!" Grabham shrieked; "pull for the shore, or we shall be food for fishes in less than ten minutes."

"We are going against the wind," Catchpole roared. "Back water, and I'll turn the boat round."

Mr. Catchpole's intentions were perfectly good, but his ill-luck followed him even in the moment of extremity.

He caught what is called by aquatic gentlemen "a crab," and, shooting off the seat, fell flat upon his back.

The boat heeled over, and Grabham, in his terror, howled like a hungry hyæna.

But now the boat was fast drifting towards the shore, on which a red light gleamed faintly.

On closer examination the light was found to be glimmering through a crimson curtain, and Grabham uttered a cry of joy as he leaped ashore, or rather up to his knees in soft, spongy mud.

"Come along, Catchpole," he shouted; "our troubles are nearly at an end. This house is an inn, and we'll soon be warm and comfortable in bed."

"I've stuck fast," Catchpole yelled. "Don't leave a man to die in this horrible stuff."

"If I come back for you," said Grabham, "I shall be in the same muddle. You must get out of it the best way you can."

"Wait until you ask me to do you a turn," Catchpole groaned, as he flopped about like a stranded flounder; "only—oh! I'm down."

He was soon up again, however; and what with rolling over and over and crawling on his hands and knees, he contrived to get a firmer foothold and followed Grabham up to where the light was shining brightly.

A savage dog dashed out of a kennel, and took a strong fancy to one of Grabham's legs; but, not liking the taste of the mud with which the limb was covered, retired hastily, and barked out a loud warning to the people at the inn.

The crimson blind disappeared as the door opened, and a gaunt, hungry-looking man, holding a candle, sputtering and guttering in the wind, appeared.

"Hullo!" he cried, sharply. "Who comes here at such a time of night?"

"Two poor travellers, half murdered and half drowned," Grabham replied.

"I must have a look at you before you enter the Ship and Mackerel," the man said, in a tone of suspicion. "I am not used to such customers as you."

Shading the light with his hand, the gaunt man advanced slowly.

He stared hard at the constables for some moments, as if he could not tell what to make of them.

Then he burst out laughing.

"If I were not a man of strong nerves," he said, "I should have been frightened at the sight of you. What foolery have you been up to?"

"I—I don't know what you mean," Catchpole stammered. "Don't keep us standing here in the cold. If you know the meaning of the word mercy, let us in."

"We are officers of the law," Grabham said. "We have been badly treated, but when and how we don't know, because our thoughts are all muddled and mixed."

"Well, come in," the man said, pointing to the open door. "But stay; I must tell my wife to get out of the way for a few minutes while you wipe your faces. I never saw such a pair of horrible frights in my life."

When Grabham and Catchpole had entered a room, which seemed to be flavoured with mud, burnt straw, tallow, rum, and rank tobacco, they were shown a looking-glass.

The constables could scarcely recognise their own features, and as they glared at each other, the truth of what had happened began to dawn into their minds.

"We have to thank the Bull in Top Boots for all this," Grabham said, savagely. "That house is doomed."

"We'll have it down," Catchpole cried, striking a tragic attitude. "We'll not be satisfied until we see it a pile of ruins."

"Shake hands on that," said Grabham, "and then we'll go to bed. Landlord, we can pay for all we have. Call us two hours after the sun rises, and let us have some eggs and good rashers of bacon for breakfast."

"Right you are," said the gaunt man. "Did you happen to mention the Bull in Top Boots?"

"Yes."

"You mean a house in the Borough."

"Right my friend."

"Ah! I know it," the man returned. "There is a precious bad lot there. Follow me, and I will conduct you to a double-bedded room. Throw your clothes outside, and I will have them dried and brushed by the time you want to get up."

"You're a good fellow," Grabham said, with emotion; "and if you should ever want a helping hand in anything, just run round to Bow-street and ask for me."

---

## CHAPTER CXIV.

### IS A SHORT ONE, BUT FULL OF STRANGE THINGS.

The gipsies who had escorted Ralph Ashton and Henry Palmer halted as suddenly as they had made the attack.

Their leader then approached.

"You must dismount," he said, civilly but firmly. "Your horses will be well cared for, and if you are honest, as you say, no harm will be done to you."

Ralph Ashton merely smiled as he leaped from the saddle and motioned to Palmer to follow his example.

"I have some notion," Ralph said, "that your queen and I are not quite strangers. Conduct me to her. My man will remain with you."

So saying, Ralph Ashton strode into the tent without the slightest hesitation.

Lanoni was reclining in a graceful attitude upon a pile of velvet cushions.

She rose to greet Ralph Ashton, who bowed respectfully to the commanding woman who ruled over so strange a race of people.

"I heard a commotion," Lanoni said, in a sweet, musical voice, "and expected that a prisoner would be brought to me presently, but I had no notion of seeing you, Mr. Ashton."

"It matters not now that I am here," Ralph replied, smiling. "Your men take the law into their own hands strangely."

"They are bound to do so," Lanoni replied, with a slight toss of her head. "All their actions are sanctioned by me."

"And I do not question them," Ralph replied. "Well, since I am here, have you aught to say to me, or do you dismiss me?"

"You are welcome," Lanoni replied, "for I have much to say to you."

As the gipsy spoke she waved her hand towards a kind of camp-stool, and Ralph sat down.

A conversation then passed, the result of which will be made known to the reader as the story progresses.

When Ralph Ashton left the tent his face wore a bewildered expression, and he passed his hand across his brow as if he had heard something that had intensely astonished him.

The gipsies fell back and made a kind of lane for him to pass through.

Ralph Ashton said nothing as he remounted his horse, and kept silence for a long time as he and Henry Palmer rode side by side.

At length Ralph Ashton spoke.

"Since that I believe in your honesty," he said, "and am firmly convinced that you desire to lead a new life, I may have to repose a great amount of confidence in you."

"You honour me by those words," Palmer replied. "What other pledge than my oath can I give you of my sincerity?"

"I desire none," Ralph Ashton said. "You may see and hear strange things, but keep your own council, for it will be as well for yourself as me."

"You will remember," Ralph continued, "that I told the ladies that my object in going to London was to endeavour to procure a postponement of the trial of a scoundrel named Bill Blarney?"

"Yes," Henry Palmer replied.

"I have other missions on which I may call upon you to take a part," Ralph said. "Let nothing surprise you. Be continually on your guard; but if at any time I should leave you and remain absent for a lengthened period, have no fear for my safety. I have much—much to accomplish."

Ralph Ashton sighed as he spoke, and Henry Palmer stared at him in surprise.

"If the world knew my true story," Ralph resumed, "it would pity me. But no matter; I must rest content and wait with patience, hoping for a just reward after all my toil and trouble."

The conversation then dropped, and nothing more was said until Ralph Ashton extended his arm and pointed to the dome of St. Paul's, behind which the full moon was shining brightly.

"Our journey is almost at an end," he said. "You see yonder house?"

"Yes."

"It will shelter us for to-night."

The announcement was as sudden as it was mysterious; but Henry Palmer had been used to strange doings all his life, and he made no reply.

The house which Ralph Ashton had pointed out stood alone, with a garden fenced in with high hedges.

As they approached, Ralph took a silver whistle from his pocket and sounded it.

As if by magic the gates opened, without any apparent human aid.

Henry Palmer looked as if he wished to ask a questione in explanation of this, but he caught Ralph's ye looking into his and said nothing.

"At the rear of the house you will find a man who will lead our horses to the stable," Ralph said, as he dismounted. "If he should challenge you, as he may, wave your hands twice before your face."

"And then?"

"Remain still while he attends to the horses," Ralph Ashton said. "He will then return and show you to your quarters, which I hope you will find snug and comfortable."

"One word more," Henry Palmer said, as he laid his hand upon the bridle of Ralph's horse. "Do you travel further before daybreak?"

"It is out of my power to answer that question," Ralph Ashton replied. "If we do, I will let you know in good time. If not, rest content. Eat well, drink with moderation, and sleep until you are summoned."

In a few minutes the man who had looked to the horses returned.

"This way," he said, opening a door, beyond which a lamp was shining.

As the light flashed upon the man's face and form, Henry Palmer was struck by the strangeness of his appearance.

He was a medium height, but the immense width of his shoulders made him look shorter.

His head was as round as an apple, his hair cropped close to the scalp, while a pair of goggle eyes, which roved restlessly to and fro, did not improve his personal appearance.

The man's arms were so long that his hands hung below his knees, which were slightly inclined inwards, and one shoulder was higher than the other.

"Ah!" he said, returning Palmer's glance; "you must think me an oddity, but if you only knew—if you only knew."

"Knew what?" Palmer demanded.

"What I have suffered, and what I owe Mr. Ralph Ashton."

"He has been kind to you, then?"

"Kind?" the man echoed. "Who rescued me from the fangs of bloodhounds, set on me by a villain? Who raised me in his arms when I was all torn and bleeding, and gave me a home? It was Ralph Ashton, and I—Seth Redwell—would willingly die a hundred deaths for his sake. But come—follow me!"

As Palmer trod in Seth Redwell's footsteps he heard him repeat Ralph Ashton's name several times. At last the deformed man stopped and pointed to a door.

"That is your room," he said, "and in it you will find everything you require."

As he uttered the last word he turned and hobbled down the passage.

On opening the door, Henry Palmer found himself in a well-furnished apartment.

A substantial meal was ready, and the guest thus silently invited sat down and began to eat and drink.

"Well," said Palmer, half aloud, "wonders will never cease. I have stepped from robbers' cave, and serfdom worse than the basest slavery, to a gentleman's servant. I wonder what will happen next?"

Henry Palmer pushed his plate away, and, feeling weary, lay down upon a couch.

He had scarcely closed his eyes than he opened them again, for he made sure that he heard somebody moving about the room.

No.

He was alone, and yet he could have sworn that he heard the door open and footsteps treading lightly across the floor.

"I was but dreaming," he said. "I will rest, so as to be ready when my master calls me."

"Serve him well, and you will be rewarded," said a voice in his ear. "Betray him, and it were better that you never had been born."

"Who speaks?" Henry Palmer cried, as he started to his feet.

"Your best friend."

Henry Palmer rubbed his eyes, and stared about him in amazement.

He was still alone, as he could plainly see, for the glow of the lamp so filled the room that there was no shadow.

"What fancies are these?" Henry Palmer exclaimed, pressing his hand to his brow.

"No fancies," the voice replied.

"Who speaks? I ask again," Palmer cried. "Is it Mr. Ralph Ashton?"

"No."

"Who, then?"

Henry Palmer flung up his arms and uttered a cry of dismay as he saw a portion of the wall roll up like a scroll of paper.

In another instant Spring-Heeled Jack stood before Ralph Ashton's new servant.

For some moments Henry Palmer could not speak.

His tongue clove to the roof of his mouth, and he felt a deadly cold thrill pass through his frame.

"Mysterious being!" he cried, at last, "why do you visit me?"

"To tell you that your every action will be known to me," Spring-Heeled Jack replied. "I am the faithful watchman of the man you serve. Even now I go to protect him in the hour of danger."

"Then I must go too," Henry Palmer said.

"Stay!" Spring-Heeled Jack cried, extending his arm. "Remain where you are. It is my decree."

"I'll heed it not," Henry Palmer said, advancing hurriedly towards the door. "I must and will share the danger of the man who—who—"

A sudden faintness came over him.

He began to reel and totter, as if under the influence of some potent drug, and as he closed his eyes it seemed to him that he was replaced on the couch.

Then he knew no more until he was roused by Seth Redwell, who said—

"It is full daylight. Come with me, and we will exercise the horses. Mr. Ralph Ashton is away, and may not return until to-morrow."

"Why did he not send for me?" Palmer demanded.

"Because it was his wish to travel alone."

"He knows best, of course," Palmer returned. "I want to see him—I want to tell him—"

"What?" Seth Redwell interposed, in a peculiar tone of voice.

"That I have had a horrible visitation," said Henry Palmer.

"Ha!" Seth Redwell exclaimed. "Speak on. Tell me what it was, what passed, and what was said?"

"Beware!" said a voice, which seemed to come from under the floor. "Remember your oath!"

"Let us go," Henry Palmer said, in a bewildered tone of voice; "let us go—anywhere. I cannot breathe the atmosphere of this place."

## CHAPTER CXV.

### SIR ROLAND ASHTON FINDS THAT THE LONGEST LANE HAS A TURNING.

When Sir Roland Ashton returned to consciousness he discovered that he was in bed, and alone, in a spacious room.

The sun had risen, and was filling the chamber with a glare of ghastly yellow light, denoting that a storm was at hand.

For a long time the baronet could not make out what had happened, and he lay, tortured in mind and body, trying in vain to collect his thoughts.

From head to foot he was as sore as if he had been beaten with a heavy cudgel, and the slightest movement caused a groan of pain to burst from his lips.

"Why am I here alone?" he said, aloud. "Why has Rollins deserted me?"

Raising his eyes, he saw a bell-rope hanging close to the head of the bed, and, stretching out his hand, he seized it.

The silken rope gave way under the pressure, and fell, coiling and writhing like a serpent, on the floor.

Another glance showed Sir Roland that the bell-rope had been cut, and he uttered a cry of rage and dismay.

"I cannot bear this agonising suspense," he said. "I must get up and dress, though it costs me my life!"

It took him fully ten minutes to drag his aching limbs from the bed, and more than half an hour to huddle on his clothes.

Dashing some cold water over his face with his hands, he advanced to the door.

It was locked, and the key was on the outside.

"So," said Sir Roland, biting his under-lip, "I am a prisoner! Hah! It is possible that, whilst unconscious, I may have been removed from Mildendale Hall."

Bracing himself up, he went to the window, and flinging the curtains aside, looked out.

"No," he muttered; "I recognise everything, and yet—what has passed? Has the brain which has served me so well given way? Am I bordering on childishness? Oh! no. Horror of horrors! I would rather die than that should be."

The room was so high up from the ground that had Sir Roland been possessed of his usual strength escape would have been impossible.

Turning on his heel, he walked to and fro until his eyes were attracted by something on the dressing-table.

It was a bottle, round the neck of which a piece of paper was tied.

The bottle was half-full of brandy, and upon the paper some words were scribbled.

They swam before Sir Roland's eyes, and it was not until he had swallowed a copious draught of brandy that he could read them and bring their purport plainly to his brain.

"*I have bad news for you*," he read, repeating the words half-aloud. "*I shall be permitted to see you again, and then you must take your chance as before. You are a prisoner, but if you use your wit you may yet escape.* "J. R."

"This comes from Rollins," Sir Roland said, with an oath, as he dashed the paper down upon the floor. "But what does he mean?"

"He has bad news for me. I am a prisoner while he is free. Ah! I am warned in time."

Up to the present moment it had never occurred to him to look for his sword and pistols, but now that he did so, he found that they were conspicuous by their absence.

"Helpless, unarmed, and yet ignorant of what has happened," Sir Roland hissed, as he clutched his hair. "Fool—fool! to fall into this trap."

He rushed at the door, as if intending to hurl himself against it, but stopped half-way.

"Nay," he said; "that would be madness. How am I to know that I am not being watched at this very moment?"

He had scarcely time to throw himself into a chair, when he heard the sound of footsteps.

Then the key grated in the lock, and as the door opened slowly, Joe Rollins made his appearance.

Sir Roland started to his feet and ran forward to meet him.

"What has happened?" the baronet gasped. "Tell me in a word."

"Sit down," Rollins replied, coolly. "It will take a good many words to explain the meaning of my note."

"Well, then, be as brief as possible," Sir Roland said, as he fell back into his original attitude.

Joe Rollins walked deliberately up to the dressing-table and finished the small quantity of brandy left by Sir Roland.

"You seem to have been thirsty," Rollins said. "Well, I don't wonder at it. Ah! it is a pity that Lord Mildendale delayed showing you his family treasures until too late."

All that had passed now flashed into Sir Roland's brain with the swiftness of lightning.

"Curse him and the treasure too!" he said. "But how comes it that I am a prisoner here? Speak out, man, unless you wish to drive me mad!"

"Nay," Joe Rollins replied, slowly, as he crossed one leg over the other; "I would have you keep your senses, if you can."

"If I can!" Sir Roland rejoined. "There is some hidden meaning in your words."

"Well, I must confess there is," Rollins replied. "Now prepare yourself to listen to the worst, and to do your best to get out of a serious muddle."

The little colour left in Sir Roland's face faded away, and left him as white and ghastly as a corpse.

"Well," he said, hoarsely, "I am all attention, but you seemed determined to keep me in suspense."

"It is because I wish you to summon all your nerve and strength to listen calmly to what I have to say," Joe Rollins returned. "Are you quite prepared now?"

"Yes."

Joe Rollins leaned forward and placed his hands upon his knees.

"In the first place," he said, slowly, "our old friend, James Loddon, is dead."

"Dead!"

"As dead as a door nail," Rollins said.

He watched the effect his words had on Sir Roland, and it was most startling.

A clammy perspiration burst upon his brow, and his hands twitched convulsively.

"You mock me!" he cried. "Wretch that you are, you lie!"

"I wish I could bring myself to believe that I did so," Rollins said. "He came to Cypress House to tell us that the girl, Daisy Leigh, had escaped from Reigate Caves, and that the man who had rescued her was one of Loddon's own and most trusted followers."

"Confusion!" Sir Roland yelled. "Go on. Perdition! the night seems to be coming fast indeed. Who told you all this?"

"A man who was making good his escape lest he should meet with the same fate as James Loddon."

"I will try to listen calmly," Sir Roland said, as he clutched the arms of his chair. "What next?"

"I will tell you in as few words as possible," Rollins replied. "It seems that Loddon went up to a room prepared for him, and remained there drinking and sleeping in turns, as the men supposed, for some time. His absence did not excite suspicion until a loud crash was heard—"

"And then?"

"How you interrupt me!" Rollins said, impatiently. "The noise was so great that the men, fancying that something had happened to James Loddon, rushed up into his room. They found him lying upon the floor impaled with an old-fashioned hunting-spear!"

"Who did the deed?" Sir Roland demanded.

"You must not put such a question to me. That remains a mystery."

"But James Loddon," said Sir Roland, as the pupils of his eyes dilated; "said he nothing?"

"Not a word after the men rushed in; but some declare that they heard him shriek out that he was a dead man."

A short spell of silence followed these words, during which Sir Roland Ashton dropped his head heavily upon his open hands.

"And now for the rest," Joe Rollins said, in continuation. "Lord Mildendale has been made aware, by some mysterious means, of the conspiracy against him, and your position is now an extremely unpleasant one."

"Am I his prisoner?"

"Just so."

"And you?"

"Oh! as for myself," said Rollins, leering craftily out of the corner of his eyes, "I was taken prisoner too, so I thought that—"

Sir Roland leaped out of his chair.

"Dog!" he cried, "you have not dared to betray me?"

"There you go again, jumping at conclusions," said Rollins. "But let me tell you that I know the value of the bluster of a bully, and know how to deal with it. The plot discovered, I thought I might as well save my neck, and I did so by telling Lord Mildendale all I knew with regard to yourself."

"What a villain you are!" Sir Roland cried, furiously. "It is well for you that my weapons of defence have been removed."

"I should have been prepared to meet such an emergency," Rollins said, laughing. "However, I have said all I have to say, and I will leave you now."

"You shall not go!" Sir Roland shouted, as he placed his back against the door. "If I am in danger you shall share it. Remember, that you told me we should rise or fall together, and I will hold you good to your word."

"Stand aside," Rollins said. "Do not tempt me to do you an injury."

"What else have you done, villain and white-livered hound?"

"Take the words back to your teeth!" Joe Rollins returned, with a dreadful oath.

He lunged out one of his powerful, muscular arms; but Sir Roland caught the wrist, and held it as in a vice.

"My sufferings—my agony," he said, jerking out each word, "my rage—have now lent me the strength of twenty men. I would hold you in close keeping though the realms of darkness yawned at my feet. Ha! ha! Your word shall be your bond—we will sink or rise together."

"Unhand me, fool!" Joe Rollins hissed. "I am armed, and your life is in my hands."

"And yours in mine," Sir Roland yelled.

With a sudden movement he threw his arms round Rollins, and bore him with such a crash to the floor that the windows rattled.

Joe Rollins had not prepared himself for such an attack, and he lay still for a few moments, for the back of his head had sustained a severe blow.

Sir Roland never relaxed his grip for a moment, but, increasing it, contrived to fix one knee upon Rollins' chest.

"What would you do?" Rollins then gasped out. "Would you murder me?"

"Why not?" the baronet replied, as a baneful glance shot from his eyes. "What care you whether I die like a dog?"

Joe Rollins saw the deadly malice in Sir Roland's face, and knew that, unless he could do something either by sheer strength or stratagem, his last hour had come.

"Listen to me—" he began.

Sir Roland choked back all further utterance by clutching him by the throat.

Joe Rollins gasped, groaned, and writhed; but all in vain.

"I told you I had the strength of twenty men!" Sir Roland hissed. "You have brought this upon yourself. Had you been true to me we might both have escaped. Before I rise there will be one less traitor in the world. Die, dog—die!"

Joe Rollins' eyes rolled fearfully in his head.

His face turned purple and his tongue protruded from his mouth.

The faintness of death came over him, and, as the first agony passed away, it seemed to him that he was falling into a troubled sleep.

"Yes," Sir Roland yelled, as his victim became fainter and fainter; "I will kill you! I meant to do so some time or other, but the time has come quicker than I thought."

Sir Roland Ashton heard a crash as if the roof had fallen in.

Something icy cold and lead-like in its weight was dashed in his face, and as he recoiled with a cry of horror upon his lips, he heard a voice roar out—

"That man shall not perish by your blood-stained hands!"

As if by magic a darkness had come over the room, and when Sir Roland, howling like a wounded beast, scrambled to his feet he found that Rollins had been removed.

Then the baronet glared about him to discover the cause of the sudden darkness, and found that the curtains had been closed by an unseen hand.

All this was so hideously mysterious and so fearful that the baronet beat the air wildly with his outstretched arms, and cursed and raved with the vehemence of a madman.

At last nature could endure no more.

Froth, streaked with blood, gathered upon his lips, and he fell in a dead faint.

How long he had remained in this state he had no means of finding out; but he was fully aware of one thing, and that was somebody had been in the room, for he had been thrown, all huddled up and distorted, on the bed.

Night had come, and the room was plunged in pitchy darkness.

"Let death come now," he said. "I care not how soon I am wiped with all my misery from the face of the earth."

"Wretched man!" said a voice. "Have you no word of repentance, no plea for mercy ere you leave this world?"

"What will repentance avail me?" Sir Roland shouted back. "Mercy! I have shown none; how much can I expect?"

To his terror he saw a bluish light begin to burn in the middle of the room.

At first it flickered faintly, and then became stronger and brighter.

Sir Roland uttered neither sound nor word as he watched it, and yet he almost expected what was about to happen.

Out of the strange, uncanny light a form grew and absorbed it. It was the form of Spring-Heeled Jack, luminous and horrible.

"I have come for you," the awful being said. "I have come to claim my own."

Sir Roland Ashton offered no resistance, either by word or motion.

Speech and strength had left him, and he lay perfectly still.

"Come!" Spring-Heeled Jack said, in a voice of thunder.

He snatched Sir Roland up, and tossing him aloft in those arms like bars of steel, leaped bodily through the window.

Amid the crash of wood and glass they descended into the darkness of the night.

Down—down—down they went, as if into a bottomless pit, and as that awful journey was made, a streak of forked lightning rent the sky asunder, and a fearful peal of thunder startled the echoes of hill and dale.

## CHAPTER CXVI.

### MRS. CORCORAN PAYS ANOTHER VISIT TO NEWGATE.

THE inmates of the Bull in Top Boots were making merry.

One and all made sure that Catchpole and Grabham were drowned, and were floating down with the tide, out of which they would be picked by some chance watermen, who would, without troubling themselves about the formalities of the law, sell their bodies to the nearest surgeon.

Not far from the Bull in Top Boots was a wharf, along which the river ran, and it was to this place the unhappy constables had been conveyed and set afloat.

The painting of their faces was but a devilish idea to startle such as might come upon them.

"What a lovely wind there is to night!" said Dick Sleuth, rubbing his hands. "It does my heart good to hear it. The flood-tide is in full swing, and no boat without oars could live an hour in it."

"That's true," the landlord remarked, as he passed the bottle round; "but, somehow, I wish those fools had not come here."

"Why, deary?" Mrs. Corcoran asked.

"Because, you witch, I can't help feeling some amount of compassion for them."

Mrs. Corcoran leaned back in her chair and gave vent to a ghoulish chuckle.

"Compassion!" she echoed. "Ha! ha! Unwelcome guests here have to pay a high price for compassion, I'm thinking. Bah! they are best out of the way. Let them drown."

An ominous silence followed the hag's words.

"Well," said the landlord, at length, "as what is done cannot be recalled, it is folly to discuss the matter."

"Who wants to recall it?" Mrs. Corcoran demanded. "They were in our way. Fool that you are! has it not struck you that they cannot give evidence against Bill Blarney now?"

"True," said the landlord; "and it has also struck me that they may have been saved. If they should turn up, farewell to all our meetings at the Bull in Top Boots."

As he spoke the front door rattled violently.

"What was that?" Dick Sleuth exclaimed, as he clutched the edge of the table. "The wind?"

"No," said Mrs. Corcoran, placing her hand to her ear. "Somebody is trying to get in."

"Let them try!" the landlord said, trying to look unconcerned. "All the lights in the bar are out, and we are safe for the present."

"I can hear something else," one of the company remarked; "and it sounds like a whistle."

"Wait until this confounded gust of wind has passed over the house," Dick Sleuth growled, "and then, perhaps, we may be able to make out whether one of our friends is giving us the usual signal."

"We must be very careful," the landlord said, sweeping his hand across his brow. "It may be only a *ruse* to lure me out of doors."

The wind roared and rumbled in the chimney like a prolonged peal of thunder, but at last it died away, and then all listened.

Presently they heard a peculiar whistle.

It was repeated three times.

"All's well," the landlord said; "stay where you are. I will run round and open the door."

He was not away more than half-a-minute before he returned with a man who was out of breath, and looked as if he had undergone some kind of danger.

"Hullo! Crafty," Dick Sleuth cried, jumping up and seizing the man by the hand. "Who on earth would have thought of seeing you here to-night?"

"I never thought anything about it myself," Crafty replied. "A precious job I have had to get here. If I have spotted one officer on the look-out I have spotted a score, and here I have been dodging about ever since four o'clock this afternoon to bring you a bit of news. Pass a glass with something in it; my throat is as dry as a lime-kiln."

"Well, what's the news?" Dick Sleuth demanded, as Crafty set the glass down empty.

"I can give it in a few simple words, but you will say that they are full of meaning," Crafty replied. "Bill Blarney will not be tried to-morrow."

Mrs. Corcoran uttered a shriek of dismay, and flinging her arms open, upset a brandy bottle.

"Not tried to-morrow?" she exclaimed, paying no heed to the accident or the fact that the liquour was flowing down her gown. "Bah! what idle story is this?"

"It is not an idle story," Crafty replied; "and you can learn the truth of it yourself."

"Let the man speak, will you?" Dick Sleuth said, turning fiercely upon Mrs. Corcoran. "Go on, Crafty."

"It seems that some gentleman has made a representation to the clerk of arraigns, and that the trial will be put off to the next sessions."

"I wonder who this interfering fool can be?" the landlord said.

"Who but Ralph Ashton?" Mrs. Corcoran returned. "He, and no other man in all the wide world would have interested himself in the matter. You may take that as a fact from me."

"What is to be done?" Dick Sleuth demanded. "All our plans are upset, and we have taken all this trouble for nothing."

"Will it spoil like meat on a hot summer's day?" said Mrs. Corcoran, contemptuously. "This delay may prove an advantage, instead of a curse."

"You speak in riddles."

"Yes—to a post."

Dick Sleuth scratched his head, and looked a little savage.

"You are a strange old woman!" he said, bursting out laughing; "but I can't be angry with you more than a minute at a time. If you have more wisdom in your head than all the rest of us, tell us what you mean."

"I mean that our plans can be strengthened, and if they are weakened the fault will lie upon our shoulders," Mrs. Corcoran said. "I will go to Newgate again to-morrow, and comfort poor Bill with the assurance that we have not forgotten him."

"Bravo!" shouted a chorus of voices. "Bravo! Well said! Well done!"

Mrs. Corcoran received the burst of applause calmly.

"I'll go to bed now," she said, "for I shall want a clear head, and," she added with a meaning glance round the table, "money! Don't all empty your purses at once, but remember this—if I go empty-handed, I may come away from Newgate without having seen the prisoner."

Several guineas were placed in Mrs. Corcoran's hand.

She counted them carefully, and, having made sure that each was of sound and sterling metal, tied them up in a knot in a handkerchief which might have passed through the hands of a laundress with advantage.

Then she rose, and, bidding the company Good-night, made a sign to the landlord to release the spring of the secret panel.

He did so, and the hag instantly disappeared into the gloom beyond, as if she had melted into it.

Then silence fell upon the Bull in Top Boots, save when the ruffians snored, and twisted, and turned as they slumbered in uneasy attitudes upon the floor.

Mrs. Corcoran was up betimes in the morning.

Indeed, she was awake and hobbling about long before the sun had risen, and the old hag seemed to be chaunting some unholy incantation.

Had Matthew Hopkins, the witch-finder of Manningtree, been alive, he would have made no scruple about marking Mrs. Corcoran as a victim for the ducking-stool.

Always ugly, she looked perfectly hideous now.

Her rheumy eyes, half-closed, looked as if they belonged to some uncared-for pig, and her dirt-begrimed face was puckered up into—if the expression may be used—a hundred wrinkled grins.

Mrs. Corcoran was almost mad with thirst.

She felt that she could have drunk a bucketful of water; but as that was an almost unknown luxury at the Bull in Top Boots there was none in the room.

So the old hag had to be contented until she heard the landlord stumbling about downstairs, and cursing loudly.

"Don't swear, lovey-dovey," Mrs. Corcoran said, throwing her bedroom door open. "What has upset my pet?"

"Pet be hanged!" the landlord growled. "Why couldn't you keep quiet? You have roused every mother's son of us."

"You don't say so! I'm so sorry," said Mrs. Corcoran, in an exasperating tone of voice. "Really, now, I thought I was doing you a kindness."

Mrs. Corcoran danced downstairs as she spoke, and seemed to enjoy the landlord's discomfiture.

"Did I snore?" she asked, with her head on one side. "Did I make a noise in my sleep?"

"You did everything horrible and devilish!" the landlord grunted, under his breath. "I suppose," he added, aloud, "that you want something to drink?"

"Exactly so," Mrs. Corcoran said. "I think I'll try water for a change, but, if it isn't fit to drink, give me anything but brandy. I had more than enough last night, and my sleep was haunted with bad dreams."

Mrs. Corcoran shuddered and glanced over her

shoulder, as if she expected to behold a repetition of her vision.

He hands trembled as if smitten with the palsy, and she could scarcely convey the glass of liquor to her lips.

The landlord of the Bull in Top Boots watched her keenly.

"How do you feel now?" he demanded.

"Much better," Mrs. Corcoran replied, with a gasp. "But what was it that you gave me? I don't remember the taste of it."

"Oh! it is a concoction of my own," the innkeeper said—"an extract of sweet and bitter herbs."

Mrs. Corcoran shot a sharp glance at the landlord.

"So," said she, "you know something about mixing potions, eh?"

"Rather!"

Mrs. Corcoran stretched out her skinny arm and tapped the man on the shoulder.

"See here," she said, "don't make a mistake with me, or attempt to do so, for I might make it awkward for you, and every mother's son who comes here."

"I don't understand you," the landlord said.

"Pooh! nonsense! Oh! yes you do," Mrs. Corcoran returned. "I simply mean that you would do a stupid thing in trying to poison me, after all my work is done and I am no further use to you."

The landlord smote his brow heavily, and put on an air of injured innocence.

"Do you think that I could be so base?" he cried. "Well—well! What next will you get into your head?"

Just then some of the men, whose eyes were yet dull with sleep, and whose flesh was grimy with dirt, appeared, with almost the same words upon their lips.

They all wanted drink of some kind or the other.

Drink—drink—nothing but drink!

They had ruined their bodies with it, and would have bartered away their souls for it.

The landlord of the villainous den attended to the wants of his wretched customers as quickly as possible, and having taken a nip of something strong to steady himself, lit a fire, and suspended a huge copper kettle by the handle on an iron hook deeply encrusted with soot.

Some coffee was made, and drank with feverish haste, but little or no food was partaken of, and the men looked like a gathering of ogres, with a witch acting as president.

It was a grim and gruesome meal—if meal it could be called—and then Crafty, who looked as if he had slept among the coals all night, called for another stoop of brandy.

"No—no!" said the landlord, determinedly. "All liquor will be sealed until to-night. When Mrs. Corcoran returns from Newgate we'll have a jolly flare-up, but no more now, or I shall have you all dead drunk before noon."

When the sun had struggled through the murky mist, which hung like a pall in the sky, and the light grew stronger, Mrs. Corcoran thought of starting on her journey.

She was well provided with money, and she did not entertain the slightest doubt that she would be able to gain easy access to Bill Blarney's cell.

This time she preferred to walk, and reached Newgate just as shopkeepers were taking down their shutters and London was waking to activity and business.

The same warder was at the gate, and Mrs. Corcoran approached him boldly.

She went with money in her hand now, and the door was opened for her in an instant.

Another guinea admitted her into Bill Blarney's unpleasant quarters.

The wretched ruffian looked as if he had not moved since Mrs. Corcoran had visited him.

The moment he caught sight of her he began to moan and whine like a whipped cur.

"Hush!" said Mrs. Corcoran; "don't make a fool of yourself."

"I can't help it," Blarney groaned. "I have just heard that I am to be kept here in this horrible state for another fortnight, and it may be longer. I'd rather be hung out of hand than bear this awful suspense."

"Would you?" observed the hag, grinning. "I dare say that there are plenty of people here who will oblige you. You have only to say that you intend to plead guilty, and I have no doubt that the authorities will hasten the trial on."

"Curse you!" Bill Blarney howled. "If you have come here only to mock me go your way."

"If I did," said Mrs. Corcoran; "you would be in a bad plight. I have come to tell you that your pals at the Bull in Top Boots are as true to you as ever, that they know all, and— Hush! I thought I heard a footstep."

"So did I," Bill Blarney whispered back. "Some sneaking spy has his ear against the keyhole, and is listening to our conversation."

Mrs. Corcoran's eyes flashed with a greenish light, and she clenched her skinny hands so tightly that her finger-joints cracked.

"Ho! ho!" said she. "If that be so I will remember that man and mark him for my vengeance."

Forgetting that the warder had taken the precaution to lock the door, Mrs. Corcoran tried to open it.

"I must bide my time," she said. "Now, Blarney, dear, just listen to me and don't fly into a temper or catch a fever, for neither will be good for your constitution."

## CHAPTER CXVII.

### CATCHPOLE AND GRABHAM GET THE SACK, AND CLAIM COMPENSATION.

GRABHAM was the first to awake.

Strange dreams had haunted his visions, and so uncomfortably had he rested that he discovered he had kicked off the bed-clothes.

Cold and shivering, he drew them all huddled up over his half-frozen frame, and then feeling a little warmer, glanced at the other end of the room to see how his friend Catchpole was getting on.

It seemed that Mr. Catchpole had been also restless, for his feet were where his head ought to have been, and the top of his cranium was within a few inches of the floor.

"If he don't change that attitude he will choke," Grabham said. "Here! Hi! Wake up there, or there'll be an inquest at the Ship and Mackerel."

Catchpole replied with a terrific snort, and then seeing that he was upside down, reversed his position.

For some moments he lay flat on his back, staring placidly at the ceiling.

"Grabham," he said, at length, "I fear the

# SPRING-HEELED JACK,

## THE TERROR OF LONDON.

LORD MILDENDALE UTTERED A CRY OF ALARM AND CLUTCHED HIS RAPIER.

adventure of last night will be my last. I'm a dying man."

"Nonsense!" Grabham replied; "there's a lot of life in you yet. Don't you go for to get such rubbish in your head."

"I can't help it," Catchpole rejoined, with a choking sound in his throat. "I dreamt that I was in a coffin not half big enough for me, and that—"

"Ugh!" said Grabham, interrupting him; "don't talk in such a way—it makes my blood run cold. Get up and dress yourself; you'll feel better after breakfast."

"I don't want no breakfast," Catchpole said, as he wriggled his head painfully from side to side. "I shall never be better. I'm a dead man."

"I think," remarked Grabham, in an artful tone of voice, "that landlord said he would leave a flask of brandy on one of the chairs."

"Eh! what's that?" Catchpole demanded. "What did you say?"

He sat bolt upright, and brushed the back of his hand across his mouth.

"I thought I could make you sing another tune," Grabham said, smiling. "Here's the brandy, and here's to your health, my boy."

Catchpole scrambled out of bed in as much a hurry as if somebody had suddenly shouted "Fire!"

"You greedy wretch!" he yelled. "Don't gulp the lot down. None of your old tricks with me!"

Mr. Grabham waxing wrath, hurled the flask at Catchpole's head, and the vessel would have been smashed to atoms had it not fallen on the other bed.

As it was, most of the liquor escaped, but the remainder soon found its way down Catchpole's throat.

"I do believe that I feel a little better now," he said, smacking his lips, "and I think I'll put off dying just a little while."

"You are the most disappointing liar I ever met!" Grabham growled. "Well—well, it is no use kicking up a row. Let us have something to eat, and then we will talk over what is best to be done."

"There'll be a precious row at headquarters," Catchpole said, "as we went to the Bull in Top Boots on our own accord."

Before Grabham could reply the door opened, and a great heap of wearing apparel was thrown into the room.

The constables sorted out their garments, and as soon as they were dressed they made their appearance downstairs.

Breakfast was ready, but gloom and silence presided at the meal.

"We can't walk through London in a couple of old sacks," Catchpole said, as he pushed his plate away. "What are we to do?"

"Borrow some clothes of the landlord.'

"But supposing that he refuses?"

"He can't—he shan't!" Grabham said, mildly. "If he does I'll take him into custody."

"We have had enough of taking people into custody lately," Catchpole said. "I'm all on thorns to know what will be said to us at Bow-street."

"I've been thinking," said Grabham, "that it will be just as well to hold our tongues about the Bull in Top Boots."

"What in the name of wonder are we to say then?" Catchpole demanded.

"Oh! we must hatch up some story that we went down the river after some thieves who were getting away with some contraband goods," Grabham replied.

"I don't think that yarn would go down," Catchpole said; "besides, you forget that you told the landlord here where we had been to.'

Mr. Grabham scratched the top of his nose in a half-savage, half-thoughtful manner.

"That's right," said he, "so I did; but I don't suppose that he will think any more of the matter than he will of walking as far as Bow-street with us."

"I wish that we hadn't made such a pair of asses of ourselves!" said Catchpole, leaning his head upon his hand and groaning heavily. "I never felt worser in my life. Our new inspector, Nabbitt, is a tartar, and you won't get over him with any lies like we could old Slopes, who was half-blind and as deaf as a post."

"We must take our chance," Grabham said, crossing the room and ringing a bell. "The first thing is to see whether the landlord can fit us up with a couple of coats."

When the landlord was questioned on the subject he shook his head.

He was afraid that he had nothing likely to fit the constables, whose faces fell at this announcement.

"Then we must go in our shirt-sleeves," Grabham said. "Hold hard! Why, we must all be wool-gathering! Why can't we have a hackney coach?"

"You can have forty, if you are able to pay for them," the landlord replied. "In the first place, I want a crown-piece from each of you, and then you are free to depart, and do what you like."

"A crown-piece each?" Grabham gasped.

"Yes; and little enough, considering the trouble that you have given me," said the landlord.

"But what if we say that we won't be swindled in such a way?"

"Why, then," said the landlord, smiling and rubbing his hands, "you will compel me to follow you to Bow-street, and speak to your superior officers."

At this moment Grabham caught sight of a most extraordinary shadow on the wall.

It was the shadow of Catchpole's head with his hair on end.

"Pay—pay, for goodness' sake!" said the startled constable. "Don't let us have any nonsense about such a trifle. I'll come down with my share as soon as I get my week's wages."

"But," gasped Grabham, "if I pay ten shillings only two will be left in my purse!"

"And two shillings will take you handsomely to Bow-street in a hackney coach," said the landlord of the Ship and Mackerel.

Grabham parted with the money as reluctantly as if each coin was a drop of his heart's best blood.

"Thank you," said the landlord, as he pocketed the money. "Shall I call a coach for you? If I sent my man he would naturally look for sixpence."

"And he have to look for it until his eyes flew out of his head," Grabham said. "All right, my friend. We shall remember the Ship and Mackerel for many a long day."

"I hope you will," the landlord replied, pleasantly, "and that you will look in whenever you are passing."

A coach was soon brought to the door, which opened into a narrow, dingy street, and away went the constables, jolting over the stones, and bumping violently against each other.

It was a dreadful journey in more than one respect.

Catchpole and Grabham were in doubt as to the reception they would receive at Bow-street; but as to that matter they were not kept long in suspense.

Summoning up the air of a man who had done his duty, and done it nobly, Grabham rushed into the office, followed by Catchpole, who, for the life of him, could not keep his knees from knocking together.

Mr. Nabbitt was at his desk, and ready for them.

Before Grabham could open his mouth Nabbitt struck the desk with a heavy ruler, and the constables skipped as if pens had been inserted in the calves of their legs.

"Silence!" the inspector roared. "Do you hear me, you idle villains? Silence!"

A man on the top of St. Paul's might have heard him.

Grabham, with a cold feeling of horror running through his body, began to back slowly out of the office, for it suddenly occurred to him that he had forgotten to pay the hackney-coach driver.

"Come here!" Mr. Nabbitt thundered. "What the devil do you mean by these antics? Come here, you wooden-headed scoundrel, or I'll floor you with this ruler!"

"I—I want to go outside for a few moments," Grabham gasped.

"Then you won't do anything of the kind!" Nabbitt yelled, red with fury. "Tell me, you idle scoundrels, what you did with yourselves after taking Basker and Nickells to Newgate?"

Grabham and Catchpole nearly fainted as the hackney coachman sidled into the office.

"Come," said he, "if you don't want me any longer, pay my fare and let me go."

"Ah!" cried Mr. Nabbitt; "we shall get at the truth now. Where did you drive these men from?"

"Why, from the Ship and Mackerel, on the river-side, below Billingsgate," the coachman replied. "What's all this? A conspiracy to rob a poor man of his due, I suppose."

"Pay the man, and get rid of him," shrieked Mr. Nabbitt, as he leaped off his stool. "Pay him at once, you—you—well, I don't exactly know what to call you."

In another instant Grabham stood penniless in the world.

Mr. Nabbitt then seized him and bumped his head against the wall.

"There, that's for you," he said. "You are discharged. Get out of the office before I do you a serious mischief. As for you, Catchpole—"

Catchpole did not wait to hear more, but made himself scarce by bolting down the passage that led to the street.

In another instant he was joined by Grabham, who was clinging to his head with both hands, as if he was afraid that it would jump off his shoulders.

"I thought as much!" Catchpole gasped. "I had a presentiment that we should get the sack."

"I can't think of anything yet," Grabham groaned. "Hold on to me for a moment or I shall go down all of a heap."

Catchpole lent him a friendly arm, and in a short time Grabham so far recovered his self-control as to be able to look about him.

"And this," he said, in a dismal tone of voice, "this is what we get for doing of our dooty."

"It's the way of the world," Catchpole observed, soothingly.

"The world!" Grabham echoed. "We are chucked into it with a vengeance. The world! Ha! ha! Oh! my head. What in the world are we to do?"

"Go home and sleep," said Catchpole, sagely. "there's nothing like sleep for a bruised heart and a bumped head."

"No, no," replied Grabham. "I can't sleep with my tortured mind. My brain's on fire! I thirst for revenge and compensation! Let us go down to the Bull in Top Boots at once, and scare that landlord out of twenty guineas apiece. He did the best to drown us, and if we like we can charge him with attempted murder."

This idea seemed to meet with Catchpole's approval.

"Right you are," said he. "We will just run home and change our clothes, and then drop down like a couple of cannon-balls into the Borough."

"We will," Grabham cried, as he struck a tragic attitude, and his knuckles against a door-post at the same time. "This little freak shall make him shake in his boots. Oh! my head—my precious head. Why was I ever born to be banged about like a drum?"

As Catchpole could offer no explanation to this query, he thought the best thing he could do was to lead Grabham away, and did so, to the more peaceful clime of Covent-garden.

Then they parted, promising to meet in an hour's time, and both were punctual to the moment.

"Now then for wengeance!" said Grabham, doubling his fists. "I've brought a brace of pistols with me."

"So have I."

"And we'll use 'em, too," Grabham returned.

"Certainly," Catchpole returned, with a lengthened face.

"Then come on," said Grabham, "for I feel that if I don't do something desperate I shall bust."

Thus, spluttering with rage, they made their way to London-bridge, and crossed the river.

If they had been a little earlier they would have seen Mrs. Corcoran, which would have probably upset all notions of paying a visit to the Bull in Top Boots.

When within a few paces of the inn they halted.

"We must go in sudden like," said Grabham, "and give the landlord a shock before he has any time to hatch up a story. Old Harry ain't more artful than he, so we must fight him with his own weapons."

The landlord of the Bull in Top Boots little suspected what was about to happen.

He whistled and hummed a merry tune as he busied himself in washing up a trayful of dirty glasses and tankards, and yet he could not get the constables out of his mind.

"Of course they are dead," he said to himself, "and nobody will ever suspect how they came into the river. But I feel sorry for the fellows, because, idiots as they were, they may be missed by somebody."

The landlord had to drown his qualms of conscience by swallowing a bumper of brandy; but the liquor which had so often soothed him in times of trouble refused to do so now.

"Why did they want to come here meddling

with my business?" he said. "If they had been sensible men I should have greased their palms, and—"

Crash!

The door flew open and the landlord fell backwards, for there were the constables, the men whose bodies he thought were floating down the Thames, standing before him.

## CHAPTER CXVIII.

### AND YET ANOTHER PLOT.

The robbers who had escaped from Cypress House took themselves to one of their secret haunts, and Filby was elected captain.

Before doing so, they laid hands upon everything that had belonged to James Loddon, and, feeling themselves rich and secure, became bold, and talked of further projects.

Filby swaggered about, like all beggars on horseback do; and he, having been in James Loddon's confidence, it suddenly occurred to him to make a journey to Ralph Ashton's house, and, if possible, to see what Daisy Leigh was like.

Saying nothing to his men, he absented himself, and when he returned in the evening he was so changed that the men could not make out what had happened to him.

"Captain," said a ruffian named Jarris, "what has happened? Are you in love?"

"I can't deny it," Filby replied. "I have seen the fairest beauty on the face of the earth."

"Her name?"

"Daisy Leigh."

"What?" shouted a chorus of voices.

"You may be surprised that I have been fool enough to pay a visit to the locality in which Ralph Ashton lives, but such is the case. I saw Daisy Leigh walking in the garden."

"Better leave the girl alone and attend to business," Jarris growled. "I daresay she is very pretty, but—"

"By all my hopes," Filby exclaimed, "she is a perfect divinity, and such a being as I would sacrifice anything to obtain. "Oh! Jarris, it is impossible that any man could gaze upon that fair creature without loving her! My heart acknowledges her power, and nothing whatever can destroy the sentiments with which she has inspired me."

"Come, captain," said Jarris, with a smile, "you are talking a deal of nonsense."

"Nonsense!" repeated the captain; "you may call it so, if you please, but I have spoken as I sincerely feel, and would make any sacrifice to be able to obtain her love."

"Love, captain!" ejaculated Jarris. "Ah! you stand but little chance indeed in that respect. Consider that you have never once spoken to her, and that she is betrothed, as we have heard from Sir Roland, to a man named Harry Banks, who, for some reason best known, I suppose, to Ralph Ashton, is kept mysteriously out of the way."

"By Heaven! he shall never possess her," said Filby, vehemently.

"This is ridiculous, Filby—perfectly ridiculous, and I am surprised to hear you talk so," Jarris said. "Who, pray, is to prevent it?"

"I will."

"You?"

"Yes; I will, I say."

"Ha! ha! ha!"

"You may laugh, if you please," said the captain of the band of ruffians; "but I repeat that I will take good care that Harry Banks, nor any other man besides myself, shall not make her his wife."

"Well, this is a bold assertion, at any rate," observed Jarris.

"You may think so, but I will fulfil it."

"In what way?"

"Why, by bearing her from Ralph Ashton's house."

"Nonsense, captain," said Jarris; "that is utterly impracticable; and think of the danger you would run in making the attempt."

"You know well that I am not to be deterred from the accomplishment of any designs upon which I may have fixed my mind by the thought of danger. This girl must be mine!"

"Yours?"

"Yes; my wife."

"Your wife? Ha! ha! ha!" Jarris laughed. "A rare joke that! You have a mind to be facetious upon the subject."

"Indeed! I am not."

"Nonsense!"

"I tell you again that I love her."

"Then I pity your case," said Jarris, contemptuously.

"Why?"

"Because you can never expect that she will return your passion."

"I know not that."

"Well, there is nothing like having a good opinion of yourself," said Jarris, with a smile.

"You may think me mad, if you please," said Filby; "but I say that before many weeks, perhaps days, have elapsed I will have her in my power."

"It is impossible."

"But I say it is not."

"How do you make it appear?"

"You will see anon."

"Well, when I do I will believe it, and will acknowledge you to be a much more clever fellow than I even now take you to be."

"I am determined."

"But determination will not alone ensure you success."

"My plans are matured."

"What are they?"

"As I shall not ask you to assist them, I do not think it prudent to make you acquainted with them at present," Filby replied.

"Why, you do not think that I would betray you?" Jarris demanded, as a frown settled on his face.

"Far from it, my dear fellow; I know you too well."

"So I should think."

"I do," Filby replied; "and I trust you will excuse me for this reserve."

"Well—well, I will not press you upon the subject; but I would have you be cautious," Jarris said. "You have us to consider, as well as yourself. Have a care, captain."

"Oh! you need not tell me that."

"And yet it is a pity to disturb the happiness of the girl, after the many sufferings she has experienced," Jarris said. "I always thought that Loddon was a fool to interfere with her."

"I will not harm her."

"You design to tear her from the protection of her friends."

"True."

"Would not that be inflicting an injury upon her of the most serious description?"

"Well, I cannot help it, though I regret it; it is the strength of my love that goads me on."

"Psha! this is certainly a strange and unreasonable idea altogether."

"I do not consider it so."

"You may not, but I do. Besides, the girl can never love you, and do you think it likely that she will ever consent to become your wife—the wife of a robber, who sees the shadow of a dangling halter on every wall he passes?"

"My persuasions, my eloquence, may overcome her objections," said Filby.

"And what if they do not?"

"Why, then, although it would be much against my wish to do so, I must use force."

"And can you expect to derive any happiness from a forced and clandestine marriage? But, seriously speaking, you cannot intend to make her your wife, should you ever have the power to do so?"

"But I tell you again, that I do."

"I would advise you to deliberate coolly before you attempt anything rash."

"I have deliberated enough already," Filby replied.

"Think again."

"It is useless. Nothing can alter the resolution I have formed."

"Well, you are a remarkable man to a certainty," remarked Jarris, smiling.

"You may deem me so, but you will find me as good as my word."

"I do not doubt that you will make the attempt."

"The attempt!" repeated the captain.

"Yes," answered Jarris.

"Aye! that I will, and flatter myself that I shall be successful."

"Well, I hope that you will not be disappointed."

"I have seldom been disappointed in the accomplishment of anything upon which I have fixed my mind."

"But in this instance you may."

"If fortune does not forsake me, I shall not."

"Fortune is a fickle dame," said Jarris, winking at the other men.

"True; but I have hitherto generally experienced her smiles," Filby replied.

"Well, there is nothing like encouraging hope."

"Aye! what is the use of giving way to despair?"

"But, of course, you must have some assistants in your plot."

"I have already secured them," said Filby.

"Are you certain you may depend upon them?"

"I have no doubt of it."

"You know them, then?"

"They are here," Filby replied—"and you," he added, placing his hand upon Jarris's shoulder. "I was only joking with you when I said that I should not require your help."

"And you contemplate seizing upon the girl, and bearing her away?"

"I do."

"Where to?"

"The old Haunted Farmhouse.

"Ah! that is a place well adapted for concealment."

"It is."

"But I would have you remember—"

"What?"

"The consequences, should you be discovered."

"I have well considered them all, and am prepared to run every risk," Filby replied.

"To me it appears a wild and dangerous project," Jarris said, rubbing his chin thoughtfully.

"It may."

"It must indeed be a fine woman that would tempt me to run such a risk," said Jarris.

"I admit that she is very handsome; but it is the affections of beauty I seek," Filby said, laughing.

"You have not a very high opinion of yourself," said Jarris, "if you do not think you could not contrive to win the heart of her upon whom you have fixed your mind."

"That may be; but you are more experienced in these matters than I am."

"But I would have you abandon your designs in this instance."

"I should be an idiot if I did, now that I have proceeded so far."

"Think of the vigilance that will be used to discover you," Jarris urged. "Think of the hue and cry which will be all over the country."

"I have thought enough about it, and will take good care that they shall not detect me."

"I am fearful that you will find yourself mistaken."

"No, I shall not."

"Then you must leave the country."

"Well, perhaps I may do that. I have no particular attachment to the country. With Daisy Leigh safe in my possession I could be happy anywhere."

"I am inclined to think, captain, that she will never become yours," said Jarris.

"Psha! Jarris. What is the use of your attempting to dishearten me in this manner?"

"The chances are against you," Jarris said. "Daisy Leigh is secure under the protection of her friends, and may set your schemes at defiance."

"We shall see."

"True."

"My plans will be worked so secretly that they cannot have the least suspicion; and will, therefore, be unguarded."

"Why, of course, they do not know you, and, therefore, cannot be aware of their danger from you," said Jarris; "but mind you do not be too impetuous, and by that means betray yourself."

"Oh! leave me alone for that."

"It would be rather an awkward thing to be discovered.

"It would; but I do not fear that I shall be."

"And when do you intend to put your designs into execution?" Jarris asked.

"As soon as possible."

"That idea is a most dangerous one," observed Jarris.

"But, indeed, it is not so," Filby replied.

"How do you think you can ever accomplish such a desperate undertaking?"

"I shall be able to contrive some plot, never fear; or the inventive brain of the man we call Plotwell will be able to supply me with one. I will instantly see him upon the subject."

"After all, I am afraid that you will involve yourself in some alarming danger, Filby."

"I do not apprehend anything of the kind," returned the captain; "for I never act in any of those matters without the greatest caution."

Jarris saw that it was useless to argue with his leader any further, and he therefore said no more; and, shortly afterwards Filby left him, and sought out the man called Plotwell.

Plotwell was a crafty, shrewd villain, who was ready to lend his assistance to any infamous deed, and, therefore, his master found him a most useful instrument.

Had he followed the theatrical profession, Plotwell would have made a most excellent actor, for he could assume almost any character at will, and so disguise himself that he might defy detection or suspicion; and it was in consequence of that peculiar talent that he was almost invariably successful in any design he undertook.

"Fear not, captain," he observed, when Filby had made known to him his wishes. "Fear not but that, if you have set your mind on this young lady, she shall be yours—I will answer for that; and you know that my promise may be depended upon."

"True, my good Plotwell," said Filby. "I have every confidence in your zeal and fidelity; but only prove successful in this, and your fortune is made."

"It shall be done, sir," said Plotwell; "you may consider it as already accomplished."

"You raise my hopes, Plotwell; but how do you purpose to realise them?"

"You must allow me some short time to consider of that, sir; but I will not keep you long in suspense."

"Worthy Plotwell," said Filby, "you have made me the happiest man in existence. How can I ever express my thanks?"

"Oh! captain," answered the hypocritical villain, "you know I do not need them; I am always anxious to perform my duty."

"I know it. Both I and poor Loddon have had plenty of proofs of your sincerity. I am already greatly indebted to you for the services you have rendered me."

"Not at all, sir; I am only too happy to think I have been able to serve you. This girl will make you a most lovely wife. But the lady is not likely to give her consent to become your wife after you have forced her away from her home against her will."

"And how can she help herself when she is once in my power?"

"That's true, captain," said the villain, "at any rate; and it shall be no fault of mine if you are not equally successful on this occasion."

"Ah! I knew I could depend upon you, Plotwell; and for your praiseworthy exertions I shall owe you an everlasting debt of gratitude."

"Nay, sir," returned the scoundrel; "you quite overwhelm me with such unmerited compliments."

"You must devise some scheme, Plotwell—some scheme by which I may get her in my power," said Filby.

"I will, captain."

"And that without delay, my good fellow."

"With as little delay as possible. I will try to introduce myself to the house," said Plotwell.

"You, Plotwell?" said Filby.

"Yes," answered the ready and deep-designing knave. "I will hit upon some scheme to do so, depend upon it, and if I fail not our success is certain."

"That is well; I will leave everything to you, my faithful friend."

"That you may safely do, captain, for I shall use the same care and exertions as if I were more immediately interested in it. Before many weeks have elapsed I predict that Daisy Leigh will be in your power."

"Well done!" exclaimed Filby. "It has made me one of the happiest of human beings. Desperate as is the course, I am, under all circumstances, compelled to adopt it."

"I commend your determination, captain," said the villain Plotwell; "but, after all, you must expect that the young lady will be no easy conquest."

"True, Plotwell; but her virtue and her beauty make her a prize worth the trouble I have already gone through to obtain possession of her. I will not, however, desist until my plans are crowned with success."

"They cannot fail, captain," said Plotwell, "if common caution is but used, and you know you can depend upon me. The young lady, however, will not be well satisfied with the change."

"I do not anticipate that she will," replied Filby, grinning; "for I believe that she is most fondly attached to this play-acting fellow."

"Your wishes in all respects shall be faithfully attended to," said Plotwell. "At the Haunted Farmhouse, Rainham, she will be in your power."

"Yes," answered the captain of the robbers; "no one would think of searching for her there."

"You will make every arrangement there for her reception, I believe?" said Plotwell.

"I will," replied Filby; "and when I once have her within its walls, my triumph will be complete."

"I trust it will," said Plotwell. "But our plot must be managed with the greatest caution and ingenuity to prevent detection."

"I shall depend upon you for that, good Plotwell."

"And you will not find your confidence misplaced, captain."

"I know I shall not. But, pray, lose no time in inventing some scheme for the furtherance of our designs."

"I will lose not a moment," returned the rascal; "and I have no doubt that some ready plan will soon suggest itself to me. Rest your mind contented, sir, till you see the result of my deliberations."

"I will do so, Plotwell. But I acknowledge that in such matters as this I do not possess any superabundant stock of patience."

"Have they many servants—male servants, I mean—at the river-side villa?"

"I am not sure; but I believe not."

"Could I by any contrivance get admittance into the house," continued Plotwell, "the business might be easily managed. I could let in our colleagues in the stillness of night, and the girl might be borne away without any alarm being created."

"True. It is a good suggestion, Plotwell; but I do not think it is altogether easy of accomplishment."

"I have had much more difficult tasks to accomplish," returned Plotwell, "and never yet failed; and, therefore, I am most sanguine."

"I am glad to hear you say so, for I know you never make any assertion without you are fully confident of success."

"I do not. But you have revealed your thoughts to Jarris?"

"I have."

"And what says he?"

"He does not see the probability of the success of my wishes."

"Well, it matters not," observed Plotwell. "We can do without him. He is your follower now, captain, and therefore will not attempt anything to mar your plot?"

"Oh! no; I am certain of that," said Filby; "and if he did he would know very well what to expect."

"Well, that is satisfactory, captain," said Plotwell; "and so far we have nothing to fear if you do not allow your impatience to get the better of your prudence."

"I will be cautious, Plotwell," replied the captain of the ruffianly gang.

"No one knows you in this neighbourhood, and, therefore, suspicion cannot attach to you in this. I would advise you not to be seen any more than possible."

"That advice shall be attended to," Filby said. "But pray exert your energies, my good Plotwell, and give me the earliest notice of anything that may have occurred to you, which may seem at all calculated to strengthen my hopes."

"I will set my inventive faculties to work immediately, captain," replied the rogue; "and do not fear the results. Probably by to-morrow I may be in a condition to make known to you some reasonable plan."

"Oh! that you may, Plotwell. That would, indeed, set my mind at rest. This lovely girl is the constant subject of my thoughts, and you need not wonder that my suspense has become almost intolerable."

"It shall soon be dissipated, captain. Hope for the best, and fear not that you will be disappointed."

"I will not," answered Filby; "for I know full well that I can place the utmost reliance upon your desire to serve me."

"You do me no more than justice by that supposition, captain," said Plotwell.

And, after some few more observations, they parted.

"Oh! this is a crafty, useful rascal!" said Filby to himself, when Plotwell had quitted him. "Most fortunate am I in having such a ready instrument to aid me in my deep-laid schemes."

Such were the thoughts of Filby, and he awaited to hear the plans of his faithful servant, Plotwell, with the greatest impatience.

He did not study the danger of putting his villainous designs into effect.

His whole thoughts were engrossed by the idea of becoming the master of that beauteous girl who had so captivated his senses, and a feeling of vanity and self-confidence prompted him to believe that his success was certain.

That the inventive faculties of Plotwell would soon suggest some promising plan of operations he had not the least doubt, for he knew that in any act of villainy he felt quite at home.

The villain seemed to take a sort of malicious pleasure in witnessing the misery of others, especially when he was further incited to the perpetration of crime by the certainty of reward.

Since Filby had seen Daisy his desire to possess her had become more inflamed than before, and he could neither think, speak, or dream of anything else.

He made other visits to the riverside with the hope of beholding her again, and it was that anxious wish which tempted him, at all hazards, to scale the garden-wall, in order that he might reconnoitre the house, and ascertain whether there was any practicable part about the building, should it be found at last necessary to attempt a forcible entrance.

The light which burned in the room occupied by Daisy Leigh and Constance Marfield attracted his attention, and he paused and looked anxiously up at the window.

Although the interval was so short, and he was situated at such a distance from them, his eager eyes immediately distinguished the lovely features of Daisy and her companion, and he became completely rivetted to the spot, and insensible to the danger by which he might be surrounded.

What were his feelings at that moment?

We cannot describe them. His heart throbbed violently within his breast.

What would he not have given could he at that moment have thrown himself at her feet, and given expression to the love with which she had inspired him?

But an instant, however, and she was gone, and it then occurred to him that the fair girls must have seen him, and they might be induced to create an alarm.

Reason and personal safety dictated to him that he should immediately depart.

But still he lingered on the spot, with the hope of beholding the object of his admiration again.

The lateness of the hour, however, and the certainity of the utter uselessness of his remaining in that dangerous situation, at length warned him to depart, and after casting one more lingering look towards the window, he quitted the spot, and once more scaling the wall, slowly retraced his steps towards the secret retreat, and sat for a long time brooding over in his mind the adventure of the night.

"I have seen her again," he muttered, "and my fate urges me on to fresh exertions. I would not pause now in my determination even to purchase a diadem."

Sleep was that night a stranger to his pillow, and he tossed about in the utmost restlessness till the morning.

His thoughts were constantly occupied with visions of Daisy's face, and the more he reflected upon her, the more did his resolution to obtain possession of her gain strength.

In the morning he summoned Plotwell into his presence, and made him acquainted with the whole circumstance.

"Your pardon, sir," observed Plotwell; "but I cannot help thinking that you acted with much imprudence in venturing so near the house, especially at that time of the night."

"Why so, Plotwell?" inquired Filby.

"Why, sir," answered the dog in human form, "you might have been discovered, and then consider the dangerous position in which you would have been placed, and all our well-formed plans might, and would, no doubt, have been at once frustrated."

"True," said Filby. "I admit that it was wrong of me to do so; but, however, no harm has accrued to me in consequenee, and I will be more cautious in future."

"It is absolutely necessary, captain."

"But I have seen the object of my new-born love once more, and I am more anxious than ever to get her in my power. Every moment of delay is agony to me, and may be fraught with danger."

"Leave everything to me, sir," said Plotwell, "and you need not, I can assure you, fear the consequences. I am always pretty certain in the cards I play."

"I know you are, Plotwell," returned his master; "and I place every reliance in your perseverence and ability."

"And you have no reason to repent of your confidence, sir. But do you not think that Daisy Leigh or her companion must have beheld you in the garden?"

"I do not think it is likely that they did, or else they would have raised an alarm," said Filby.

"It is fortunate that they did not," said Plotwell, "or you might not have found it a very easy matter to escape."

"True; I might have incurred some danger," remarked Filby; "but tell me, Plotwell, has any idea suggested itself to your inventive faculties?"

"Yes."

"Ah! tell me what it is, that I may, at least, encourage some degree of hope."

"You may encourage every hope, sir," replied Plotwell, "if you will but strictly adhere to my advice."

"I will do anything—abide by anything you say, good Plotwell," said the villain; "but pray do not keep me in suspense. What is your design?"

"To become an inmate of the house."

"That you have told me before," said Filby, with a look of impatience and disappointment; "but how do you propose to accomplish that?"

"Why, sir," answered Plotwell, "you well know the skill I possess, I believe, in assuming any disguise that may answer my purpose, and under which it is possible for those who know me well to detect me?"

"Well—well," said Filby, impatiently, "I am fully aware of your ability in that respect, Plotwell, for I have often tried you. But what is it you now intend?"

"Why, captain, of course, as I have been so successful on former occasions, it is not too much to predict that I shall be so on this. I daresay I shall not find it any more difficult to impose upon the inmates of that house than any other individuals."

"True—true. Proceed."

"As an aged clergyman I should be almost certain to banish all suspicions, especially if I saw the ladies. I will solicit relief for a charity. It is not likely that they will refuse me a temporary hearing, and, once beneath the roof, our plot will be all but accomplished."

"Ah! by Jupiter," exclaimed Filby, "this is an excellent plot, and, well managed, cannot fail to succeed. Thanks—thanks! Let no time be lost in putting this ingenious design into execution."

"Your pardon, sir," said the villain, "but we must not be too hasty. It will require some days to mature our plot."

"More delay—more delay!" said Filby. "This is most torturing!"

"It cannot be helped, captain," said Plotwell. "It is always better to use the utmost precaution in such hazardous undertakings as these, or they may be easily rendered abortive. I, however, promise you that I will use all the promptitude I possibly can."

"I know you will, Plotwell; but you may guess how agonising it is to me to retard the accomplishment of my hopes."

"True, sir; but delay will only render the gratification of them the more certain. Before long, I again promise you, if you will only follow my counsel, that Daisy Leigh shall be in your power."

"That promise is sufficient to stimulate me to anything," returned Filby; "and I promise to obey you."

"That is enough, sir," said Plotwell. "Then I will immediately set about the accomplishment of the task I have imposed upon myself; and, in the meantime, I beg of you to wait with patience the issue, and upon no account to venture again to the villa, lest you should be observed, and some suspicion be excited."

"I will not," said Filby; and, after some farther conversation, Plotwell left him.

The scoundrel's hopes were now more excited than ever, and he did not for a moment doubt that that crafty rascal, Plotwell, would succeed in his nefarious design.

He had observed he had frequently experienced the consummate skill with which he had managed similar affairs before, and he, therefore, calculated upon his triumph being almost certain.

Plotwell absented himself during the day, and Filby was thus left to his reflections and the society of his followers; but he did not think it prudent to make them acquainted with the whole of his designs at present. Guilt is ever suspicious, and thus it was with Filby.

During the day, however, he reflected deeply upon all that Plotwell had said to him, and the longer he did so, the more he became convinced of the certainty of the success of the nefarious scheme which his ready myrmidon had laid down.

"Plotwell is an invaluable fellow," he said to himself, "and without him I should never have been able to carry many of my amatory intrigues into execution. He will succeed with his usual consummate skill. The risk I run is great, but what peril is it not worth to gain so inestimable a treasure?"

Filby, in addition to his other failings, possessed an ample share of vanity, and, indeed, it was that feeling which had emboldened and rendered him triumphant on many former occasions.

Numerous were the unfortunate victims who had fallen beneath his infamous arts, and yet he could with indifference, or a feeling of exultation, look back upon his crimes.

But now he really felt something like a sincere affection for Daisy Leigh.

Her extreme beauty and apparent innocence had made a powerful impression upon his heart.

He was so supreme in his own self-estimation that he imagined his success in that case would have been all but certain, and it was that impression that urged him to be more determined in his present designs.

"She shall never become the bride of any other man than myself," he said. "I have fixed my mind upon her, and nothing shall prevent my obtaining possession of her. Once mine my felicity will be complete, and my whole thoughts—m whole study—shall be devoted to her happiness."

Thus did the libertine soliloquise when he wa alone; but he deeply regretted the delay in th furtherance of his designs which Plotwell had suggested, although he could see plainly enough that it was absolutely necessary, as, if he was too hasty in putting them into execution, it might, in a great measure, if not altogether, prevent their success.

"And do you still persist in your designs against Daisy Leigh?" inquired Jarris, in the course of the day.

"Certainly," replied Filby. "What should induce me to abandon them? I have set my whole affections upon her, and cannot live without her."

"Well," observed Jarris, with a smile, "you are really most enthusiastic over this business, Filby. And do you, indeed, wish to make her your wife?"

"Such, alone, are my intentions," said Filby.

"Ha! ha! ha! You certainly entertain a very excellent opinion of yourself, Filby, to imagine that you can so readily estrange the affections of the girl from the man to whom she is affianced."

"You may treat my ideas with derision, Jarris, but you will find, notwithstanding, that I shall succeed," Filby said.

"Well, I hope you may not be disappointed."

"If I am, it will be the first time I have been upon anything on which I have set my mind."

"But again I ask you, my friend, have you seriously considered the consequences, should you fail?" Jarris demanded.

"I have; and am ready to brave them all. It is not a little that will daunt me, and especially in such a cause, I assure you."

"You are a bold man in these amatory affairs, I know," remarked Jarris, "and I only hope you may not get yourself into trouble on this occasion."

"Oh! I do not fear that," answered the captain. "I have got a clever abettor in the person of Plotwell."

"Aye! he is an arrant rascal."

"And, therefore, of the more service to me."

"You do not flatter yourself much," said Jarris, with a laugh.

"I seldom do," replied his companion.

"And has Plotwell yet hit upon any scheme which is likely to further your wishes?"

"He has; and I have not the least doubt of the success of what he has proposed."

"What is it?"

"Pardon me," observed Filby, "but, notwithstanding the friendship I know you entertain towards me, I would rather decline entering into an explanation at present."

"Well, I will not press you; but I must advise you to be cautious."

"Oh! you have no occasion to warn me. I am always pretty safe in these matters."

"Why, you have been fortunate hitherto; but you may not always be so."

"I do not apprehend any danger," replied Filby; "and my plans are so deeply laid that nothing, I am convinced, can frustrate them. Before many days have elapsed, Daisy Leigh shall be in my power."

"Consider the excitement the abduction of the girl will cause."

"I have considered everything; and so powerful are the sentiments with which she inspired me, that nothing whatever can daunt me in my proceedings."

"Time will show which of us is right," answered Captain Filby.

"It will; and I shall be most happy, should I find myself mistaken."

"You will do so, depend on it. When the girl finds that my sentiments are sincere, and that I intend to make her my wife, I do not fear but that she will yield to my importunities.

"You must entertain but an indifferent opinion of her, after all, to imagine so," said Jarris.

"Indeed I do not," returned Filby.

"Such a wife would not be worth the possessing, if you could so easily supplant her lover in her affections. But you cannot be serious, and, after all, will abandon these mad designs."

"You may call them mad, if you please, but, nevertheless, you will find that I will persevere," Filby said, casting an admiring look at himself in the mirror.

"Then it is useless for me to offer any argument against your intentions."

"True; although I know you do so from the best of motives."

"You only do me justice by believing so," Jarris said. "But may you not be deceived? Are you quite certain that you can depend upon Plotwell?"

"Quite certain," Filby replied. "What reason have I to doubt one from whom I have received so many services? Plotwell will undertake and accomplish anything for a master who, he knows, will so amply reward him."

"But even he may this time fail, notwithstanding his ability in these nefarious transactions."

"Were I to entertain these apprehensions, I might certainly calculate upon being defeated," replied the captain of the band; "but Plotwell is a crafty knave, and the plan he has suggested is so plain, yet subtle, that it must succeed."

"I am glad to see you so sanguine," said Jarris, "but would rather decline having anything to do with your plot."

"I do not ask you, for I know that I shall be able to accomplish it without your assistance, and I trust that I have your good wishes for my success?"

"You have."

"And nothing will ever transpire from you that might tend to frustrate my purpose?"

"Why should you ask the question, Filby? You ought to know me well enough by this time."

"Well—well, we will say no more about it. I am perfectly satisfied."

"You ought to be, for you have had plenty of opportunities of judging of the sincerity of my friendship."

"I have," replied Filby; "and I have never doubted it for a moment."

"In a few days, then, I suppose, you will attempt to put your plot into execution?"

"I have said so."

"And of course you will leave this neighbourhood?"

"Certainly, and perhaps before. Everything will be arranged at the Haunted Farmhouse for the reception of the damsel, and there I shall be entirely safe from detection."

"I hope you may; but I fancy that you will find it rather a difficult job to convey her there without her creating an alarm on the road."

"Oh! leave me alone. I will not fail to use every precaution to prevent that," said Filby. "The seizure will be made at midnight, and when there is no one about to obstruct us."

"At midnight!" repeated Jarris. "Do you then mean to attempt to make a forcible entrance of the house?"

"I do," Filby replied.

"How do you purpose to accomplish that?"

"That you will see hereafter," Filby replied. "You and the rest will have full instructions how to act."

"Have you reflected maturely upon the punishment which will be sure to follow such an outrage, should you be detected?" Jarris asked.

"I have frequently before told you that I have,"

replied the captain of the band; "but as for detection, I have not the slightest apprehension of it. Plotwell will be in the house previously to admit us when the family have retired to rest, and before any alarm can be created we shall be far from the spot."

"Plotwell in the house!" said Jarris, with amazement. "How did he contrive that?"

"I have before told you that he has hit upon a plan, which you will be made acquainted with by-and-bye."

"I am completely at a loss to understand you, and cannot place any confidence in the success of so wild and dangerous a stratagem."

"Had you been as used to similar stratagems as I have you would, though," observed Filby.

Jarris made no further observations, seeing that it was useless to do so; but, not being quite such a villain as Filby, he could not entirely approve of his designs, and he could not help hoping that something would occur to frustrate them, although he would have much regretted should his friend be detected, knowing the dangerous consequences which would be sure to result to him in such an event.

Filby now left him, and retired to his own apartment, where he reflected deeply upon his guilty designs, and awaited with impatience the return of Plotwell.

"No; Daisy Leigh," he ejaculated, "nothing can save you from me. No earthly power will I suffer to thwart me in my purpose.

"I would sooner perish than see you become the wife of another.

"Ralph Ashton, you little expected to meet so powerful a rival.

"To that crafty Plotwell how much am I indebted.

"Once let Daisy Leigh become my wife, I will then hasten to the Continent, where I may set discovery at defiance.

"True I am rather older than she, but I still think that with my experience in these affairs I shall be enabled to conquer any feelings of repugnance it is likely she will possess towards me, and do not despair of ultimately winning her affections."

He rubbed his hands and chuckled with glee as these thoughts occurred to him.

No feeling of compunction ever entered his mind.

He became every moment the more determined to pursue his unlawful plans, quite indifferent to all consequences that might follow.

Vanity was one of the principal ingredients of Filby's nature, and it was never more fully exemplified than on this occasion.

It even led him to imagine that it would be next to an utter impossibility that Daisy, notwithstanding her affections had been previously engaged, and the violent means he was using to gain possession of her, could long resist his importunities.

This idea emboldened him to proceed to the utmost limits, and to be totally regardless of the dangerous results to himself in the event of failure or discovery.

"She shall—she must—be mine, even if the consequences should be such as to cost me my life!"

He was interrupted in his cogitations by the entrance of Plotwell.

"What now, Plotwell?" demanded Filby. "You have been absent a long time."

"True," answered Plotwell; "but I have not been idle."

"I daresay you have not; but have you furthered the plot in any way?"

"I have."

"How?"

"I have seen our colleagues, and prepared them to be ready to act on the shortest notice."

"That is well; but you have not made them at present too well acquainted with your designs, have you?"

"No," returned Plotwell; "it is not at all likely that I should act with such imprudence. But there must be some delay in the execution of our plans."

"Delay!" repeated Filby. "That is most annoying!"

"It is, I admit; but it cannot be helped."

"Why so?" demanded the captain.

"Because some suspicion is excited in the mind of Ralph Ashton, and the house is being watched."

"How do you know that?"

"I heard it in the tavern. It will not be safe for you to be seen about, and I would therefore advise you to keep out of the way."

"Curses!" exclaimed the captain of the robbers, in a tone of vexation; "this is most unfortunate. But why should it retard the progress of the plot?"

"Because it is absolutely necessary that their excitement should have abated before we can venture to put our plans into execution with any chance of security. However, in the course of a few days we may be able to make the attempt, and, in the meantime, sir, you may rest satisfied that I will be successful."

"Every moment of delay to me seems fraught with danger," remarked Filby.

"Do not entertain any apprehensions, sir," said Plotwell. "If we only act with caution, I promise that all will be right. I have never deceived you yet."

"You have not, my worthy Plotwell."

"And you may depend upon it I will not do so on the present occasion if you will only put confidence in me."

"I do; but is this all that you have got to make me acquainted with?"

"It is, and I regret much that you ventured near the house."

"Why, I acknowledge that it was very imprudent of me to do so, but I did not expect that any harm would come of it."

"And there will not, if you will only act as I advise," said Plotwell.

"I will abide by all you counsel, however tiring it may be to my patience," Filby said. "Thi interruption to the completion of my hopes only renders me the more anxious to obtain possession of Daisy Leigh."

"You may safely reckon that she is yours, captain," replied the villain Plotwell. "I will give the fellows every instruction how they are to act when we shall require their services, and, no doubt, they will behave in a manner that must command success."

"I suppose I may trust them even in such an adventure as this?" Filby said.

"Certainly. What reason have you to doubt them when you have so often trusted them before?" Plotwell returned. "They will perform their task well and faithfully; to that I will pledge my word."

"That is enough," said Filby; "and if they do

so, they need not fear but that I will liberally reward them."

"They are confident of that, captain, and are therefore ready to do anything that you may require them. But are you still resolved to make the girl your wife?"

"I am," Filby replied. "In no other way can I secure her to myself; and so powerful is the affection I bear her, that I am willing to make any sacrifice to obtain possession of her."

"But the marriage must be a private and a forced one," said Plotwell, "for it is not likely that she will consent to become the wife of a man of whom she knows nothing, and whom she will be inclined to look upon with disgust and terror, after having been the perpetrator of such a daring outrage."

"Very true; but I have no doubt that I shall soon be able to conquer her repugnance."

"I sincerely hope you may, sir," said Plotwell; "but where will you get a minister to perform the ceremony?"

"Oh! I shall find no difficulty in that."

"No?"

"No. There is the Rev. Mr. Churley, who is under several weighty obligations to me. He will not object, I daresay, to stand my friend on this important occasion."

"Ah!" said Plotwell, "I did not think of him. He is not immaculate, I believe?"

"He is a sordid man, and will not fail to be tempted by the offer of reward," Filby replied. "I know I may confide in him, and will immediately communicate with him upon the subject."

"I would certainly do so without delay, sir," said Plotwell, "for it will be necessary to have all our plans properly matured before we attempt to put them into operation."

## CHAPTER CXIX.

THE PLOT FRUSTRATED—AWFUL APPEARANCE OF SPRING-HEELED JACK—THE FIRE—THE ROBBERS CAUGHT IN THEIR OWN TRAP.

NIGHT came, and the robbers fell to drinking and gambling as usual.

Filby, though his plot was delayed, was in high spirits, and, after partaking of goblet after goblet of wine, he wished them all good-night and retired to his room, ordering some more wine to be taken up.

"Fortunate man that I am," he muttered, throwing himself into a chair, "to possess so able an instrument as Plotwell! Had it not been for him, my chances of success would have been very doubtful."

"My triumph is now all but complete, and I do not fear but that I shall be able to persuade Daisy to yield to my will, and then what care I for the wrath of Ralph Ashton?

"He will find me an antagonist not easily to be coped with, and I will, therefore, set him at defiance.

"What will it avail him, when she is mine?

"I feel that I am unworthy of her, but did she only look upon me with favour, there is nothing that I would not do to render her happy."

Taking a goblet of wine, he drank it off as these thoughts occurred to him.

Vain, presumptuous fool that he was to suppose, even for an instant, that he could ever win the esteem, much less the love, of Daisy Leigh!

But the zeal and ingenuity which the scoundrel, Plotwell, had evinced, gave him the utmost satisfaction, and he had not the slightest doubt but that he might depend upon his secresy.

"No matter," he said, getting up from his seat and pacing the room; "I shall yet be able to conquer her feelings of dislike.

"Shall I now be foiled in one of the dearest projects upon which I have ever set my mind, and when I have the means in my power of accomplishing my wishes? Never!

"I should indeed consider myself weak and fallen if I did.

"If she still continues obdurate, force shall make her comply with my wishes, although I would rather that she became my bride by her own free consent.

"Curses light upon the moment when she first beheld Ralph Ashton!"

Thus Filby alternated between hope and fear, his self-vanity prevailing over every other feeling, and he was fully determined that, whatever might be the consequences, nothing whatever should ultimately frustrate him in the accomplishment of his plans.

After swallowing another goblet of wine he staggered to the bed and threw himself heavily on it, without removing his clothes.

Little reckoned he what was in store for him.

Little did he think that his vile plans would recoil on himself and the villains who were so eager to help him.

Before he fell into his drunken slumber he heard a clock in the neighbourhood strike twelve.

Then he rolled over on his side, and, pillowing his head on his arm, began to snore.

Plotwell, Jarris, and some few of the robbers still remained below carousing.

The wind roared and howled about the din of infamy, but they heard no warning or sound of danger in its awful voice.

"Come, one more bumper," said Plotwell. "Let us drink to the success of our new captain's enterprise."

"Hear! hear!" they all shouted.

"And to our brave little band," cried one of the robbers; for whenever you give the word you will find us ready. I believe we understand one another pretty well?"

"We do," said Plotwell.

"Yes; we are brave," said another, "and prepared to face anything; it is not often that we have suffered ourselves to be defeated, and I don't think you'll have any occasion to complain."

"I place every confidence in you," said Plotwell, "and I need not tell you tell you that I shall not fail to reward you according to your merits."

"And if you do that, my friend, you will consign us to the hands of the hangman," said another, with a coarse laugh, in which his comrades joined.

"Bah! Bob," said the man who had first spoken. "Jokes like that always make me feel a disagreeable sensation about the neck. We must not suffer the hangman to pay his respects to us just yet."

"How blue the lamps burn!" Jarris said. "Hang me! if they don't look as if some kind of powder had been thrown on them."

"That's true enough," said Jarris, with a burst of drunken laughter. "What of it? What if they went out altogether? I suppose we know our way about this place without a light—eh, boys?"

Just then all were startled by a terrific sound as if a door had been burst open.

# SPRING-HEELED JACK,

## THE TERROR OF LONDON.

"I'LL HAVE YOUR LIFE, YOU WITCH!" BILL BLARNEY HISSED.

The crash was followed by a noise like thunder.

It boomed through the house, awakening the echoes, and so startling Plotwell and his ruffianly companions that they huddled together in speechless terror.

The bold Plotwell's heart now sank as heavy as lead.

His face turned ashy grey, and, as he strove to speak, the blood fled from his lips, and left them a dull purple.

"What can this mean?" he contrived to gasp out at last, turning to one of the men. "Is it possible that the officers of justice have tracked us down?"

"They would not come in such a style," said the man addressed. "Hark! do you not hear that strange sound?"

There was no need for him to call attention to it.

It was a sound of a pair of huge leathery wings flapping, and, as it ceased, a wild yell of mocking laughter rent the air.

Nor was this all.

Before the robbers could rush to the door, a crackling and hissing sound told of the presence of fire.

Then came another yell of laughter, and an awful voice crying out—

"Doomed! doomed! doomed!"

Shrieking with terror, Plotwell rushed to the window, followed by some of his companions, the others made for the door.

They were foiled in both directions.

The window was guarded with stout iron bars, and a more formidable obstacle met them at the door.

A volume of smoke, filled with flickering tongues of flame, caused the villains to retire hastily.

"Help!" Plotwell shrieked. "Mercy! Help!"

"You call for help at a time when no help can come!" shouted a voice. "Villains, your plot has failed, and you must prepare to die!"

One man, bolder than the rest, essayed to reach the landing, in spite of the fire and smoke, but a pair of strong arms thrust him back.

Grovelling, whining, beseeching, and cursing in a breath, the robbers ran round and round like rats in a cage.

Suddenly Spring-Heeled Jack appeared in the very midst of the terror-stricken wretches.

Where he had come from, or how he had passed unscathed through the flames none could conjecture.

They saw that awful form towering above them with extended arms, and it seemed as if a demon had been sent to mock their agony.

"You must die," Spring-Heeled Jack cried. "No earthly power can save you. As your master perished by my hand, so you must die now."

Plotwell sank upon his knees and wrung his hands; but before he could speak Spring-Heeled Jack had vanished.

Smoke and flame increased every moment.

The floor grew hot beneath the villains' feet, and the paint upon the panels blistered and bubbled under the terrible heat.

"The window — the window!" Plotwell shrieked. "It is our only chance. Seize the bars and tear them away. Quick—quick! Oh! what agony is this?"

Half-a-dozen hands seized the bars, and it seemed for a moment that Plotwell's advice would have enabled the robbers to escape; but as the first piece of iron bent and broke a mighty wreath of flame, like an avenging serpent, rushed roaring into the room, carrying death and destruction before it.

There were a few stifled cries, a wild, prolonged yell, and then the floor gave way, carrying the charred bodies of Plotwell and his companions with it.

In spite of all this noise and confusion Filby slept soundly, and it is probable that he would have perished in his drunken slumber, had he not been roused to activity by the grip of a hand.

Starting from the bed on which he had thrown himself in his clothes, he saw that he was in the presence of Spring-Heeled Jack.

At first Filby thought that he must be dreaming, and that the terrible form before him was but the result of a hideous nightmare.

He rubbed his eyes and pressed his hands, and then slowly recoiled before Spring-Heeled Jack, who, advancing slowly, pointed in silence at the guilty man.

"Listen!" said the strange being. "Hear you not that roaring. It is fire. The scoundrels who would have followed you—who were willing to destroy the peace of an innocent girl—have gone to their doom. You must follow them."

"Doom—follow them?" Filby cried, smiting his brow as he started back. "I—I—I do not comprehend. Stand back, monster. Are you the arch-fiend himself?"

"No," Spring-Heeled Jack replied; "and neither am I one of his agents, with whom you should be very well acquainted. This accursed place took fire while you and your brother scoundrels were carousing. It was no hand of mine that set the place in a blaze. I would scorn the action, much as you deserve the fate in store for you."

At this moment a beam fell with a crash, a door crumbled up like a scroll of paper under the terrible element, and the room was filled with smoke.

Spring-Heeled Jack's form grew dim and melted away.

"I will not die like this!" Filby cried, hoarsely. "I cannot, I dare not die in such a way."

The volume of smoke almost choked him, and he fell upon his hands and knees, thinking to escape its suffocating influence; but the floor grew so hot that he could not bear the pain.

Staggering to his feet he groped blindly for the door.

Perchance he might be able to hurl himself down the staircase, and reach the cellars.

The villain was reckoning without his host.

There was no escape for him.

Death in its most awful form stared him in the face, and though he battled with the strength of despair against the destroying element, all hope had fled.

He reached the door and flung it open.

A wall of fire confronted him—a wall of lurid light in which frightful forms seemed to dance wildly, and uncouth faces grinned with gruesome hideousness at him.

The supreme moment of agony was at hand.

It was the moment in which Filby was destined to live a lifetime; when all the events of a misspent life singled themselves out and passed before his eyes in swift but vivid array.

Strangely enough he thought of Daisy Leigh.

It seemed to him that she was near him.

He called her by name, he asked her to forgive him, he asked her to pray for his wicked soul, and even when strength deserted him, and he fell forward upon his face, he murmured her name as if it brought him comfort and numbed the pain attending his awful end.

The roof fell in.

For miles around the glare in the sky was seen, and when morning came a crowd of white-faced men, searching the ruins, discovered the remains of the robbers—remains so horrible and inhuman in appearance that they fled as if from a plague-stricken spot.

## CHAPTER CXX.

### THE LANDLORD OF THE BULL IN TOP BOOTS COMES TO TERMS.

THE sudden and awkward, not to say startling, appearance of Messrs. Catchpole and Grabham at the Bull in Top Boots has been briefly described.

If a bomb-shell had fallen at the innkeeper's feet, or had a thunder-bolt found its way down the chimney, he could not have been more surprised.

But wary by nature, and trained in every degree of low cunning and artfulness, he soon recovered his self-possession.

"Bless me!" he said, forcing a smile upon his lips; "how you startled me. I wish you good morning, gentlemen."

"He wishes us good morning," said Grabham, who was red hot with fury to the tip of his very nose. "Did you ever hear the likes of that, Catchpole?"

"Never—no, never," Catchpole replied.

The landlord of the Bull in Top Boots happened to catch sight of something in Grabham's hand, and saw that the object was a pistol.

In a moment his whole demeanour changed.

Diving his hand under the counter, he produced a brace of splendidly finished pistols, loaded and primed, and which had evidently been kept handy in case of an emergency.

"If that is your game," he said, taking aim at both the constables' heads, you will find that two can play at it. By the Lord Harry, if you attempt to pull that trigger, I'll scatter your brains against the wall behind you!"

"Who said that I was going to pull the trigger?" Grabham demanded, in a feeble tone of voice that betrayed he had been caught in his own trap.

"Nobody," Catchpole said, answering for him. "We merely stopped down for an explanation," he added, turning to the landlord. "We want to know what you meant by setting us adrift in an open boat without oars?"

"Put that pistol away," said the landlord, turning to Grabham, and entirely ignoring Catchpole. "If you don't I shall let fly with these barkers, and you will find that they will bite uncommonly sharp."

Grabham complied with this request so hastily that it is a wonder that he did not explode the weapon by accident, and shoot himself in the leg.

The landlord's keen eyes detected something else.

He noticed that the constables were not in uniform, and the thought that something was wrong, flashed into his brain.

"You want an explanation," he said. "Well, so do I. Show me your warrants or authority for coming here, and I will obey you in the name of the law, even though it be to walk to Bow-street!"

This was a clincher.

Catchpole glared at Grabham, and Grabham rubbed his nose as he looked at his companion.

"We haven't come on official business," Grabham said, after a rather long pause, "and I may as well tell you we have been discharged from the force. It was you who did the trick for us, and if you are a man, you will give us some compensation."

The landlord of the Bull in Top Boots put down the pistols conveniently near him, and placing his hands on his hips, he laughed until tears ran down his cheeks.

"I have had to deal with a good many men in my time," he said; "but you are a pair of the funniest fellows I ever came across."

"There's nothing funny in trying to drown a couple of fellow creatures," said Grabham.

"No; that's true enough," said the innkeeper. "Who ever tried to do such a wicked thing?"

"You did."

"When?"

"Why last night," Grabham almost howled. "Come, now, you can't say that you didn't take a mean advantage of us when we were in liquor. Did you paint our faces? Did you clothe us in sackcloth and ashes, and shove us adrift on the river?"

The inn-keeper raised his eye-brows and stared mildly at the men, as if he wished to deal kindly and gently with them.

"I am afraid this is a case for the nearest mad-house," he said. "I don't know what you are talking about. You were not here last night, and, in point of fact, if my memory serves me well, I have not seen you for a month or more, until you came tumbling into my house this morning."

"Oh! there's a whopper for you," Catchpole cried.

"A whopper!" Grabham gasped. "I've heard some lies in my time, but this—"

"Wait just a moment," the landlord said, interrupting him. "It would be useless to argue with such a pair of out and out rascals as you, who would levy black mail on a workhouse child, if you thought you could get it; but, out of respect for myself, I'll call an unbiassed witness, who shall speak the truth before your very faces."

Turning his head, he roared out—

"Tom!" in such a stentorian tone that caused Catchpole and Grabham to skip as if they had been tickled with some sharp instrument.

"Hullo! there," replied a voice from the back of the premises. "Do you want me, guv'nor?"

"Yes, I do," the landlord shouted in return. "Come here at once."

A queer-looking individual shuffled into the bar.

At a first glance it would have been hard to tell whether he was a boy with an old looking face, or a man who had suddenly stopped in his growth.

"Here I be," he said, without deigning to look at the ex-constables. "What's the matter, guv'nor?"

"Nothing much," the landlord replied. "I only want to ask you one or two questions, Tom, and you'll be good enough to answer them in a straightforward fashion."

"Fire away!" said Tom, puckering up his features into a most extraordinary grin. "Is it about the bottle of brandy I broke a week ago? You said I drank it, but I'll swear that—"

"No, no!" the landlord interposed. "Bother the brandy! All the talking in the world won't bring it back. How long have you been in my service?"

"Ten years, next Christmas-day."

"Were you here last might?"

"Of course I was," Tom replied. "Where else should I be—eh?"

"Now," said the landlord of the Bull in Top Boots, beating time to his words with his forefinger. "Just tell these gentlemen if you saw them here last night."

"I'll take my oath I didn't," Tom replied.

"And you were here—in this bar."

"I never left it from noon till I shut up."

"What do you think of that?" asked the landlord, turning triumphantly to Catchpole and Grabham.

"Why that it's a pack of lies," Grabham said.

"Put it down that the gentleman called Tom is mistaken," said Catchpole, who felt that he was growing limp. "It ain't polite to call a man a liar, you know."

"Oh! jigger the politeness," Grabham roared. "Don't we know what happened? Why, dash it all, can't we prove what we know to be the truth?"

"You have come to the wrong shop to bluster," the landlord said. "Tom."

"Yes, guv'nor."

"Put on your hat, and find the nearest constable," the innkeeper said. "I'll have no more of this kind of thing. These fellows have lost their situations through getting drunk, and now they have come here with a cock-and-bull story, thinking that I am fool enough to pay them for lying."

"Chuck 'em out," said Tom. "Only say the word, and you'll see 'em floating across the road as elegantly as a pair of kites."

"No, no," the landlord returned. "Fetch a constable, I say. I'll have these fellows taken to Bow-street, and charged with attempting to extort money."

Grabham's face grew hot.

He mopped his manly brow with a handkerchief of immense dimensions, and turned a pair of bewildered eyes upon Catchpole, whose optics were as dull and lustreless as stale gooseberries.

"Wait a minute," said Grabham. "Just listen to me. Do you happen to know a house called the Ship and Mackerel?"

The landlord did not change colour; the expression of his face remained the same—but the question put by the gentleman who had been so lately kicked out of Bow-street had a magical effect on his nerves.

"Yes, Tom," he said, quietly; "I think you had better wait, if only to bear witness what these fellows have to say to me."

Then, turning to Grabham, he added—

"What was the name of the house you pleased to mention?"

"The Ship and Mackerel."

"I have heard of it," the landlord said. "It stands on the river-side about a mile below Billingsgate, if I am not mistaken."

"Of course it does," Grabham returned. Well, we managed to get ashore and crawl more dead than alive into the house."

"Tom," said the landlord of the Bull in Top Boots, "you may go about your work. I have a few words to say to these gentlemen. If I should require your services I can easily call you."

"Ain't there to be no chucking out?" Tom demanded, in a disappointed tone of voice.

"No, no; nothing of the sort."

"Nobody to be pitched into."

"No! Go about your work," said the innkeeper.

Tom shuffled off, grumbling and scowling, and Catchpole and Grabham felt quite relieved when he was gone.

"Since you mentioned the Ship and Mackerel," said the landlord, glancing over his shoulder and speaking in a whisper, "I may as well tell you something. You may think yourselves lucky that you got out of the place alive. Norreys, the landlord, is one of the most artful fences in all London, and he only keeps the house as a blind."

"Why, that's the very thing he said about you," Catchpole remarked.

"I don't wonder at it," said the landlord of the Bull in Top Boots; "but let it pass. So, you are in misfortune?"

"Quite down, and almost settled," Catchpole groaned.

"I am not the man to see a couple of fellow-creatures in distress without extending a helping hand," the landlord said, "and if you walk into my private parlour, I will see what I can spare out of my slender purse."

"No—no," Grabham exclaimed. "We shall do very well where we are. We don't threaten, and we don't come here to extort money. You have had your lark with us; you have been the means of us being kicked into the streets, and we have come to you to do something for us, until we can get something to do."

"That's a fair way of putting it," the landlord said. "Well, since your are afraid to walk into the parlour, I suppose I must let you remain here. Wait a minute, I will come to you presently."

The landlord dived into the room behind the bar, and presently returned with something that sounded rich and crisp in his hand.

"Mind you," he said, "I don't help you because I am compelled to do so, but because you are poor. I don't want to boast, but I believe that I have as good a heart as most men."

As he spoke he placed two five-pound notes on the counter, and the constables pounced down upon them with the avidity of hawks wheeling down upon a brace of half-fledged sparrows.

"Just one word," the landlord said. "This settles the question for once and for ever. Don't come here again or you will raise my dander to an extent which may end in serious mischief. I hope you fully understand and comprehend my meaning?"

"Certainly, sir," said Grabham politely, as he pocketed the bank note. "We are very much obliged to you. One last drink and then we will part for ever."

"No—no," said the landlord. "You and my house must be strangers from this moment. I have endeavoured to act like a man towards you, and now good-day."

Catchpole and Grabham having discovered that the landlord meant to be as good as his word, and that there was nothing more to be had at the Bull in Top Boots, removed themselves from the house as quickly as possible.

"Well," said Catchpole, when he and his companion had walked a hundred yards or so down the dark, grimy court; "matters haven't turned out so bad—eh?"

"We should have got double as much if we had stuck to him," the greedy Grabham remarked.

"I'm content for one," Catchpole replied. "I

feel quite relieved that we got out without any more bother. Lor', how thirsty I am! Let's go somewhere and have a drink on the quiet. Will you change your note first, or shall I change mine?"

"That's a nice question to ask me, considering that you owe me a crown!" Grabham growled.

"Very well, I'll pay you, and stand treat into the bargain," Catchpole said. "Where shall we go?"

"I know a nice quiet crib in Buckler's-rents," Grabham replied. "The stuff is good there, and I have heard say that every drop of it is smuggled."

"I don't see that it matters to us since we have left the force," Catchpole said. "We, like the rest of men, want quantity and quality for our money, so let us go to Buckler's-rents."

Acting as guide and pioneer, Grabham led the way.

He turned from the street into a bye-way so odoriferous that Catchpole instinctively laid hold of his nose and held it tight.

At the end of the passage was Buckler's-rents.

It was a huge yard or square, flanked with dilapidated houses, tumble-down and evil-looking.

The open space was filled with every kind of rubbish.

Heaps of refuse, dust, decaying cabbage leaves, and filth of an indescribable nature, lay neglected, rotting alike in the sun and the rain.

Catchpole began to think that Grabham had some evil intent in his mind, and came to a standstill.

"What beastly place is this you have brought me to?" he demanded, wrathfully. "I'll not budge another inch until I know what your little game is."

"My game is to go into that house," Grabham replied, pointing to a most villainous-looking building in one corner of the square. "What are you afraid of?"

"Of catching a fever or some sort of plague," Catchpole replied, with good reason in his speech.

"A glass of corn brandy will knock all that nonsense out of your head," Grabham replied. "Come on, and if Daddy Muckrum is at home, he will find us something to warm the very cockles of our hearts."

Catchpole offered no further opposition, but, still holding on to his nose, followed Grabham.

None of the doors of the houses in Buckler's-rents seemed to be blessed with handles or knockers, but stood invitingly on the jar, and emitted sundry flavours, varying from pork and fried onions to the bloater sputtering upon the gridiron.

Suddenly faces began to appear at the windows, or rather the apologies for such luxuries, for the frames contained more fragments of dirty rags than glass.

There were heads of matted hair, eyes hollow and ghoul-like, and cheeks which had long forgotten the healthy application of soap and water.

The poorest of the poor lived in Buckler's-rents, and it had its contingent of thieves, and even worse characters.

Grabham pushed open the door of the house occupied, or rather, partly occupied, by Daddy Muckrum, for the journey had not as yet come to an end.

There were several more flights of stairs to ascend, and as Catchpole, following gingerly after Grabham, slipped and stumbled up the crazy steps, he cursed Daddy Muckrum, the corn brandy, and the hour which had brought him to such a fearful place.

At last Grabham stopped, and without standing upon any kind of ceremony pushed open a door and entered a room.

What a room!

Its gloom, its aroma, vile in its intensity, gave Catchpole a thrill of horror, but he forgot all when something in the corner, like a bundle of rags, began to move, and Daddy Muckrum shuffled into the light.

Daddy was as ugly as the old woman in the nursery rhyme who

"*Lived upon lucifer matches and gin.*"

He was humpbacked, big-headed, shamble-kneed, splay-footed, and hare-lipped.

When he spoke his words came hoarse and horrible, and his very breath seemed to heat the atmosphere.

Faint and overcome Catchpole sat down upon a chair.

He did not notice that the article of furniture had lost a leg, and a howl of terror burst from his lips as he fell sprawling on the floor.

When Daddy Muckrum laughed he produced a sound like a cracked bell, and such was the sound that smote Catchpole's ears as he staggered to his feet and sat down upon a bench.

"I see nothing to grin like a goblin about," he said; "why the devil couldn't you tell me not to sit down upon that thing?"

Daddy Muckrum's grimy eyes flashed, and Grabham, anticipating something unpleasant, came to the rescue.

"Come—come," said he, "there is no harm done. Daddy, bring out a bottle of your best, and my friend shall pay for it. He is a good fellow at heart, but rather short-tempered."

"So am I," Daddy Muckrum remarked, meaningly. "This room isn't fitted up like a palace; but I like people to know that I am lord and master over it."

"Which nobody disputes," Catchpole said, hastily. "You seem to know Mister Grabham?"

"Oh! I know him," Daddy Muckrum replied, as he shuffled towards a cupboard; "he wouldn't peach on me. He knows better."

"Of course—of course!" said Grabham; "but there is no fear of anything of that sort now. I have left the force, and so has my friend here, Mister Catchpole, who ought to have been introduced to you long before this."

Daddy Muckrum turned round, and shaded his eyes with his hands.

"Left the force!" he said; "I suppose you mean that the force left you?"

"Well, it's one and the same thing," Grabham returned, laughing; "but out of it we are, and we must either strike into some new line of business or starve."

Holding a bottle in his shaky hand, Daddy Muckrum gazed intently at the ex-constables.

"This is no foolery, is it?" he queried. "This is no trap set to catch me? You know I have only to raise a finger, and all Buckler's would swarm down upon you like a flight of hornets."

"You must be an idiot to think that I would do such a thing," Grabham returned, gruffly.

"If I did think it," said Daddy Muckrum, "I would make this place a warm shop for you."

As he spoke he filled up the glasses, not forgetting one for himself.

Catchpole pronounced the liquor as the most excellent he had ever tasted, and handed Daddy Muckrum the five-pound note to be changed.

The old man passed his claw-like fingers carefully along the crisp piece of paper, and then went to the window, where he made himself more hideous than ever by putting on a pair of horn-rimmed spectacles.

All of a sudden he made a dash at the table and clutched the bottle.

"What's the matter?" Grabham demanded.

"The matter!" Daddy Muckrum growled; "the matter is this—the note is a bad one."

"A bad one!" Catchpole and Grabham shrieked in a breath.

"Yes, it is!" Daddy Muckrum roared; "and you knew it before you came here. You thought to palm it off on me, you thieving dogs."

Striking the window-frame with his fist, he dashed it open, and was about to make his voice heard in Buckler's-rents, when Grabham seized him by the collar and dragged him back into the centre of the room.

Catchpole, seeing that matters were assuming a serious aspect, made himself useful by clapping his hand over Daddy Muckrum's mouth.

"There's some mistake," Grabham hissed in the old man's ear. "We took the note for a good one at the Bull in Top Boots."

The old man wriggled and writhed like an eel. He heard what Grabham said to him, but he thought that it was but a ruse, and, exerting all his strength, he hurled the men from him, and rushing once more to the window, filled the air with his frantic cries for help.

## CHAPTER CXXI.

### "YOUR SON, MY LORD, YOUR SON."

It is now necessary that we should explain how Lord Mildendale was made acquainted with Sir Roland Ashton's villainous purpose.

After the astounding events which occurred when the nobleman was about to show the baronet the ancient treasure of Mildendale Hall, his lordship retired to his private room and doubly locked himself in.

The first idea that entered his brain was that an attack had been made on the Hall by his old enemies, the gipsies, but discovering this to be a mistake, he was at a loss to account, in any way, for what had happened.

There was something so uncanny and so unaccountable in the whole proceedings that his lordship's brain whirled while he tried to think it out.

His guest, the supposed Mr. Fernie, had been stricken down at his feet, and was now lying upon a bed of pain.

Lord Mildendale turned up the lamp, and unsheathing a sword which hung upon the wall, he held the weapon in such a manner as to be ready for any surprise.

"There must be more in this than I can grapple with at present," he said. "No harm was done to me, and evidently no harm was intended. But this man—this man who comes to me surrounded, as it were, with the wealth of a monarch, and in princely attire—can it be that there is some horrible mystery connected with him?"

"There is," said a voice.

Lord Mildendale raised the point of his sword, and stood on guard.

"Who speaks?" he cried out in trembling accents.

"One who desires to be your friend," was the reply.

Lord Mildendale glanced furtively round the room, which he had believed to be occupied by no other living creature than himself.

As he gazed to the right and left, he heard a slight rustling sound, and saw that a paper was being pushed under the door.

He did not attempt to see who had brought the mysterious missive, but snatching up the paper, he unfolded it, and ran his eyes over the clear, bold handwriting with which it was filled.

A mist gathered before his eyes as he read the following—

"FROM SPRING-HEELED JACK,—*The man under your roof passing in the name of Fernie is a murderer and a villain. He is no other than Sir Roland Ashton, who, having dragged an honourable name down into the very mire of degradation, is now in league with a band of thieves. Their leader is dead, and the doom of the rest is sealed. Sir Roland Ashton is but the poverty-stricken dupe sent here to spy upon you and your ancestral Hall, with the view of robbery. An attack has been arranged as soon as Sir Roland leaves, and your life will be sacrificed, if necessary. Keep the scoundrel a close prisoner until I remove him to safer quarters.*"

Lord Mildendale read the document again and again with increasing astonishment.

"This must be the truth," he said. "Ah! an idea strikes me. I will send for the man Rollins, and if he lies his life shall answer for it."

Lord Mildendale rang a bell, and a servant answered the summons almost instantly.

"Did you meet anybody on your way upstairs?" his lordship asked.

"Nobody, my lord."

"How is—is Mr. Fernie?"

"His valet reports him to be in a very bad plight, my lord," the man replied."

"His valet! You speak of Joseph Rollins?"

"Yes, my lord."

"I wish to speak to that man," Lord Mildendale said. "See that he is sent to me at once."

The servant left the room, and soon after Joe Rollins swaggered jauntily into the room.

Lord Mildendale at once taxed him with the truth, and Joe Rollins, finding that further concealment was useless, offered to tell all he knew, providing that he was pardoned, and allowed to go free.

This being granted, Joe Rollins made a clean breast of the affair, reserving himself the statement that he had acted merely under instructions, and that he was more to be pitied than blamed.

Lord Mildendale, overcome with disgust and astonishment, dismissed the wretch from his presence, but not before Rollins had exacted a reluctant permission for him to see Sir Roland before he left.

"Yes," said Lord Mildendale, "and you may tell him that he never did a worse thing than to enter my house under such pretences."

The reader knows what took place at the interview between Sir Roland and Rollins; what took place during the fearful struggle between the two men; and how Spring-Heeled Jack claimed the prisoner.

The crash of wood and glass startled Lord Mildendale and the whole of his household.

It seemed as if the shock of an earthquake had shaken the building, and for some time no man had the courage to go and see what had happened.

At last Lord Mildendale ran downstairs shouting to his men.

Pale-faced and affrighted they flocked to his side.

"Follow me!" he said. "That villain has either made good his escape or something terrible has happened to him."

At heart Lord Mildendale was no coward, but so mysterious and bewildering had been the events of the few days past that he had almost come to the conclusion that they had been caused by no mortal agency.

For a moment the men held back, but when his lordship spoke again they rallied.

Drawing his sword, Lord Mildendale rushed upstairs.

The men followed him.

On the landing, outside the door of the room in which Sir Roland had been imprisoned, they found Joe Rollins lying flat upon his face.

To all appearances there were no marks of violence on the man's body, but he was dead.

In his stiffening hand they found the key of the door, which, to the astonishment of all who had come upon the scene, was still locked.

Death had smitten Joe Rollins down so suddenly that he lay as if asleep.

It was an awful sight and the men could do nothing but stare aghast and in silence at each other.

Lord Mildendale's hand trembled as he removed the key from the dead man's grasp and applied it to the door-lock.

As the door opened he started back, as if fearful of encountering some awful scene or apparition.

But there was nothing to be seen but the smashed window and some overturned chairs, as if a violent but short struggle had taken place.

"The villain did not make his own escape," Lord Mildendale said; "and, indeed, if he did so he must be dashed to pieces on the terrace."

One of the men leaned out of the ruined casement and peered below.

"I see nothing," he said, as he turned his head.

"Then we are wasting time by staying here," Lord Mildendale said. "A strict watch must be kept outside the Hall to-night. Let all the fire-arms be loaded, and no man leave his post until dawn."

The men grumbled audibly, for not one among them cared for the task.

The night, however, passed quietly away, as also did the following day.

Park, field, and woodland were searched, but nothing of Sir Roland Ashton could be ascertained.

The news of his mysterious disappearance spread like wild fire among the country folk, and, superstitious and simple-minded, they gave out that the arch-fiend had flown away with the baronet, and consequently his earthly career had come to an end.

That evening, as the sun was going down in a glory of crimson purple and gold, Lord Mildendale strolled sadly and thoughtfully into the park.

His life was becoming unbearable.

Childless, wifeless, conspired against, and with foes on every side, what availed all his wealth?

What cared he for the luxuries that money could buy?

Gold to him was but yellow dross, and willingly would he have given all in his possession for the purchase of a few years' peace of mind and quiet happiness.

As the sun went down, and the mellow shades of twilight fell upon the landscape, the wind rose and the woods began to murmur.

The stately trees, bowing their leafy heads, seemed to be whispering secrets to each other—secrets of the Hall not far away, secrets locked up in the breast of the lonely man, who, with the deep lines of no common sorrow in his face, walked with ghost-like tread.

Lord Mildendale paid no attention to the increasing darkness, but he was disturbed from his reverie in a remarkable way.

More than once he thought he heard the sound of footsteps, and strange voices in the air.

He had become almost accustomed to such fancies, and paid but little heed to them.

Suddenly he heard himself called sternly and loudly by name.

There was no mistake about it this time.

"The voice rang out as clear and distinct as a bell.

Lord Mildendale halted.

Then he uttered a cry, and laid his hand upon his sword, for coming towards him was Spring-Heeled Jack leading a pretty boy by the hand.

"Your son, my lord, your son," Spring-Heeled Jack cried.

Lord Mildendale stepped forward, and then, he was alone amid the gathering gloom.

Spring-Heeled Jack and the boy had disappeared as suddenly as they had appeared, and Lord Mildendale was left standing aghast, half-mad between doubt and fear.

Nature had endured much, but it could endure no more.

He reeled, tottered, and fell groaning on the green sward.

---

## CHAPTER CXXII.

MRS. CORCORAN ROUSES BILL BLARNEY'S IRE—THE ATTEMPTED MURDER IN THE CELL—ARRIVAL OF THE WARDERS—MRS. CORCORAN LEAVES NEWGATE AND HAS TO RUN THE GAUNTLET.

MRS. CORCORAN listened at the keyhole of the cell door for some time, and peeped through it with the hope of catching a glimpse of the eaves-dropper.

But she could see nothing save the grim, grey, stone wall beyond.

"It was only a warder going his rounds," Bill Blarney growled. "Well, what more have you to say to me?"

"Ho! ho!" croaked the hag; "it would seem that you are in a hurry to get rid of me."

"To tell you the truth, I could wish for a more pleasant visitor," the ruffian said, snarlingly.

These words roused Mrs. Corcoran's wrath.

"What an ungrateful villain you are!" she hissed. "Bill Blarney—Bill Blarney, I am a dangerous woman when put out. Your life is in my hands, and I can undo all that has been done by a single word."

Bill Blarney remained silent, but his rage was so great that his face became hideously distorted.

"I came here to have a nice little chat with you," the crone said. "I have come to tell you that your friends are still true, and you reward me by heaping insults upon my head."

"Curse you and your nice little chats!" Bill Blarney returned. "You laugh in secret at my misery, you mock me; you have another method, beyond charity, in getting me out of prison. It is your plan that I shall remain under your thumb as long as I live."

"Quite right, my dear," said Mrs. Corcoran; "and I will tell you more. I dangle the halter over the necks of all your pals, and if they are not careful down it will come and strangle every mother's son of them."

Half-choking with rage, Bill Blarney, ironed and manacled as he was, threw himself upon the hag and seized her by the throat.

"If my pals are true to me they will come in spite of you," he said, hoarsely; "but your power over them shall end. Die! hateful wretch."

His fingers closed upon the old woman's throat with a vice-like grip, and she, with protruding eye-balls and blackened features, fell slowly back.

Mrs. Corcoran had not dreamed of being attacked in such a manner.

Thrown entirely off her guard, and finding herself as helpless as an infant in the ruffian's grasp, she could do nothing but pant, and gasp out inarticulate sounds, which she intended to be appeals for mercy.

She knew that unless assistance came, she would be a dead woman in less than a minute.

But no cry could she utter.

The cell was swimming round and round.

A blood-red mist gathered before her eyes, and sounds like peals of thunder crashed on her ears.

An awful rattling noise came from her throat, and the death hue gathered upon her face; but still Bill Blarney, the relentless villain, the cold-blooded murderer, held on to her throat.

He dragged her from one side of the cell to the other, seemingly with the intention of dashing her head against the wall; but just then the door opened, and a couple of warders rushed in.

One of the men, a stalwart fellow of gigantic proportions, threw his arm round Bill Blarney's neck, and forced him backwards.

Still Bill Blarney did not relinquish his grasp, and it is possible that Mrs. Corcoran would have breathed her last had not the other warder struck the would-be murderer over the wrist with a baton.

Bill Blarney was then thrown heavily upon his back, while Mrs. Corcoran, more dead than alive, writhed, quivering and groaning, to the further end of the cell.

"This is a nice business," said one of the warders, as he rapped Blarney's head smartly on the floor to remind him that no nonsense would be taken from him. "This is a nice business, Jack. Confound it! why did the authorities consent to postpone this rascal's trial? It would be much better to hang him out of the way."

"No doubt about that," replied the other warder. "Well, all we can do is to fix him up against the wall, and then see if the old woman is likely to recover."

Bill Blarney roared, fought with hands, teeth, and feet like a fiend.

"Let me get at her!" he yelled. "I care not what becomes of me. Let me get at her, I say!"

"Oh! yes, certainly," said the gigantic warder. "You shall have all your own way. Come along, my beauty; you shall have the wall to try your strength upon presently."

Riveted into the wall was a strong iron ring, to which was attached a couple of strong short chains, placed there to hold refractory prisoners.

Bill Blarney had made the acquaintance of this contrivance, and it filled him with horror.

"No—no!" he cried, with foam-flecked lips; "not that—anything but that! If I must die, put me out of the way, but don't torture me! Don't make every moment of my life a living death!"

"You should have thought of that before," said the warder, as he hauled him along. "You can't expect any mercy or consideration from us now."

Bill Blarney's strength was failing, but he still struggled like a wild beast.

All was in vain, and in a few minutes he was pinned against the wall.

Then, with a deep, hollow groan, he drooped his head upon his breast and began to sob like a child.

"I didn't mean to do it—indeed I didn't," he said. "She aggravated me in such a manner that no flesh and blood could bear."

"Hold your tongue!" said the warder. "You may think yourself lucky that we have not given you a taste of the press-room. Come, Jack; let us have a look at the old woman. It strikes me very forcibly that her light has been snuffed out."

It did indeed appear that Mrs. Corcoran had shaken off this mortal coil, and that she had left this world to account for her many crimes and sins in the next.

One of the warders passed his arm round her neck and raised her up.

"She ain't dead," he said, "and I think she will come round presently."

Mrs. Corcoran verified this statement by open ing one eye and sneezing.

The old hag had as many lives as a cat, and i was not long before she was able to speak.

"Only think," she said, "that my boy—my own son—should treat his poor old mother so."

The warders grinned, and winked at each other.

"You ought to be proud of him," said one. "But, Jupiter, he seemed to be very firmly attached to you when we came in."

"Ha! ha!" roared the other fellow. "That's not bad. Now, old lady, what do you mean to do?"

"Let me rest a few minutes," Mrs. Corcoran replied, "and then I shall be able to go. I don't want anything to be said about this little affair, and I am willing to buy your silence with a couple of guineas. The poor boy lost his temper for a minute—that's all. He is suffering from the sense of his wrongs, and they drive him mad."

The warders pocketed the money, and Mrs. Corcoran, after wheezing, panting, and moaning for a few minutes, suddenly announced her intention of leaving the cell.

She was still in a bad plight, and could hardly totter, but she made up her mind to get away as quickly as possible.

Half-way to the door she stopped and looked at the ruffian.

"Bill!" she said; "Bill, why don't you look up and speak to your old mother? You may never see her again, you know."

These words had a strange meaning for Bill Blarney.

"I can't help it," he said, sullenly. "I don't suppose you'll miss me very much."

Mrs. Corcoran said no more, but leaning heavily on one of the warder's arms, left the cell.

The passage she had to traverse was a long one, and it seemed as if it would never end.

Something told the old woman that there was danger abroad, and she increased her pace towards the turnkey, who was amusing himself by cracking nuts, and throwing the shells through the wicket at supplicants who had friends or relatives in durance vile.

The turnkey whistled a lively tune as he unlocked the ponderous door, and swung it slowly open.

As Mrs. Corcoran passed out a gentleman passed in.

He wore a cloak down to his heels, and a slouch hat that partly concealed his features.

The stranger turned round, and having looked sharply at Mrs. Corcoran, followed her into the street.

"Stop that woman !" he said.

As he spoke he tilted up his hat and revealed the features of Ralph Ashton.

Of all the men in the world that the old hag expected and least of all desired to see, Ralph Ashton was that man.

Mrs. Corcoran began to run.

When we say that she began to run, we mean that she took to her heels.

Clawing the air, she rushed through the people gathered about the prison gates.

They made way for her, not wishing perhaps to have their faces scored by her claw-like nails; and Mrs. Corcoran, once in the open space, fled towards the Fleet river, which in those days was almost overshadowed by the debtor's prison, and was flanked by a number of ruinous houses.

"Stop that woman !" Ralph Ashton said again. "Ten guineas to the man who catches her and brings her back to me."

The mention of so large a sum had a magical effect upon the crowd.

Among the loafers and loiterers were shoeless, starving wretches, to whom a full meal had been a stranger for many a day.

They took up the cry, and rushed after Mrs. Corcoran.

The hag had a good start, and made the very best use of it.

One of her shoes came off, but she did not stop to pick it up.

Then the other went flying into the air, and she ran bare-footed and bleeding over the stones, like a hunted hare with a pack of merciless hounds on her track.

Mrs. Corcoran made for the houses, and the first one she happened to reach appeared to be uninhabited.

The door swung upon one rusty hinge, which creaked out a remonstrance as Mrs. Corcoran dashed into a passage.

The flooring was rotten, and so full of holes that Mrs. Corcoran had to take flying leaps from point to point before she could reach the foot of the staircase.

It was an odd sight to see the witch-like old woman accomplish what proved a barrier to her pursuers.

The crowd of men and boys had now considerably increased, and, jostling, pushing, and fighting, they fell over each other in wild confusion.

Their progress thus impeded gave Mrs. Corcoran time to breathe.

But only for a moment did she stop.

Then she went up the stairs, three at a time, and, kicking open a door, found herself in an empty room, which, if possible, was in a more dilapidated condition than the passage.

The window of this unpleasant apartment looked down into a back-yard, which seemed to have long been used as the cemetery of left-off boots and dead cats.

The distance to the ground was not great, and Mrs. Corcoran determined to drop it.

Gathering up her skirts and holding her breath, she clutched the window-sill for a moment, and then went down, and lay, half-stunned, on a heap of rubbish.

Up again, Mrs. Corcoran ran across the back-yard, and made a wild leap at the top of the wall.

Her fingers touched it, but the greasy slime and moss covering the brickwork refused Mrs. Corcoran's clutch, and hurled her back.

At the same moment a man, risking life and limb, jumped bodily through the window, rushed towards Mrs. Corcoran, and, raising her in his arms, threw her, as lightly as if she had been a bag of feathers, over the wall.

That man was Dick Sleuth, and the moment after he had disposed of Mrs. Corcoran so unceremoniously, but effectually, he picked up a brick-bat and hurled it at a head which appeared just then at the window.

The head disappeared with marvellous alacrity, and then Dick Sleuth, mounting the wall with consummate ease, looked about for Mrs. Corcoran.

To his astonishment and dismay, he saw that she was floating swiftly, if not gracefully, down the Fleet river, and by the speed she was going, it looked more than probable that the Thames would claim her before help could come to her assistance.

"Well, let her go," Dick Sleuth said. "If she had been caught, mischief might have come of it. Living, she might have put us in an awkward predicament; but dead, she can tell no tales."

## CHAPTER CXXIII.

### SIR ROLAND'S NEW QUARTERS AND GAOLER.

THE way in which Sir Roland Ashton was removed from Mildendale Hall was, to say the least, remarkable.

That either he or Spring-Heeled Jack could have escaped death seemed impossible.

The rush of air drove the breath out of the baronet's body and he fainted.

Yet death was not to follow that faintness, for he recovered, and felt that something cold was being flung upon his face.

Swift as lightning all that had passed flashed into his brain.

For some time he dare not open his eyes for fear of encountering the baneful gaze of Spring-Heeled Jack.

But at last he felt compelled to do so, and was astonished to see Henry Palmer, who was seated at his side and bathing his temples with a sponge.

Sir Roland Ashton knew the man as having been one of James Loddon's band.

Had he been ill?

Was the past but an ugly dream?

The baronet asked himself these questions as he gazed at the man attending upon him in the capacity of a nurse.

"Henry Palmer," Sir Roland Ashton said, at last.

His voice was so feeble that it was scarcely audible.

Palmer made no reply, but, dropping the sponge into a basin, folded his arms and stood motionless.

"Why do you not answer me?" Sir Roland demanded. "Are you dumb?"

"No."

"Then tell me where I am and how I came here?"

"You were found."

"Found?"

"Yes; half-dead, on your face, in the middle of a field, and my master brought you hither," Henry Palmer replied.

"Your master?" Sir Roland returned. "Tell me whether I have been mad or dreaming? Is James Lodden alive, or is he dead?"

"He is dead."

"Then you have found a new master?"

"Yes."

"Who is he?"

"That you will see presently," Henry Palmer replied. "Ask me no more questions, for you will get no answer."

Something else then occurred to Sir Roland's mind, and he bit his tongue to keep back the words of rage that rose to his lips from his blackened heart.

He remembered now that it was Henry Palmer who had been chiefly instrumental in rescuing Daisy Leigh from the caves at Reigate.

On second thoughts he came to the conclusion that it would be better not to say a word about that matter.

"Come," he said, after a pause, "you need not treat me like a brute. Is your new master a kind and generous man?"

"Very," Henry Palmer replied, dryly.

"I am glad to hear that," Sir Roland said.

As he spoke he touched his pocket, and discovered, to his great relief, that his purse had not been removed.

"We ought to understand each other, Palmer," he said. "It is my wish that your master should know nothing of my past career, as, I have no doubt, you desire that your own should be kept secret."

"But it so happens that my master knows all about me and you too," Palmer replied. "Enough! Say no more, or you will put me to the painful necessity of gagging you."

"Gagging me?"

"Such is the command given to me, and I must obey it."

Sir Roland gazed under his eyes at the man.

The threat of gagging was evidently made in good faith, but the baronet could not have kept his tongue still even if his life had been at stake.

"At all events," he said, "give me the assurance that you have not taken service under a fiend in human form, named Spring-Heeled Jack?"

Henry Palmer rose, and taking a silken scarf from the table, twisted it round Sir Roland's mouth.

"If you attempt to remove that," Palmer said, "it will be at your own peril."

Sir Roland was too much astonished and overcome to do anything of the kind.

He lay still, glaring round the room, noticing that the furniture was antique, and the shutters were not only secured with heavy bars, but also lined with iron.

More than an hour passed away in this style.

Palmer sat with folded arms, and only moving when the lamp required trimming.

At last a bell rang, and he rose hastily as if he expected the summons.

Taking a curiously shaped key from his pocket, he unlocked the door, and secured it carefully behind him.

"In the name of wonder what will happen next?" Sir Roland thought. "What new tortures are in store for me?"

He did not dare to remove the gag from his mouth, for he could not tell who might be watching him, even though the room appeared to be unoccupied, save by his miserable self.

The suspense grew too awful to bear calmly, and at last Sir Roland dragged his aching limbs from the sofa.

Supporting himself by leaning heavily on the backs of the chairs, he approached the door and listened.

He thought he heard voices below, but the sound was so muffled and indistinct that it might be nothing more than the moaning of the wind.

The baronet thus worked his way round to the window, and stood staring at it.

He did not touch the fittings.

He feared to do so; for the icy-cold hand, the grip of which he knew so well, might be laid upon his throat at any moment.

"If I only knew where the window led to," he muttered, "I would wait with patience for an opportunity to escape."

His keen hearing, sharpened by a life of extraordinary adventure, heard the sound of a soft footfall beyond the door, and Sir Roland had scarcely time to hurry back to the sofa, and throw himself at full length upon it, when the door opened and Spring-Heeled Jack entered.

The strange being paid no heed to Sir Roland Ashton, but strode to the window.

Click! Click!

The shutters flew back, up went the sash, and Sir Roland saw by a rosy light in the sky that day had dawned.

Spring-Heeled Jack leaned out of the window, and seemed to be looking intently at something below.

He made no sound with his lips, but passed his hands to and fro as if practising a code of signals, and then, hey, presto! he was gone.

The window ran down, and the shutters closed after him with a crash.

The weird creature's strange entrance, his silence, and his magical exit filled Sir Roland with horror.

He felt that he had fallen into a trap, out of which there was but one way, and that led to the grave.

The imprisoned baronet's feelings were worked up to such a pitch, that had a weapon been left within his reach, it is probable that he would have laid violent hands upon himself.

As he tore his hair, he cursed and raved under the gag which he dared not remove.

While he was in this half-maddened state, Henry Palmer appeared, dressed and equipped as if for a long journey.

A kind of haversack hung at his belt, and the lash of a postilion's whip was twined round his hand.

Without speaking he removed the gag from Sir Roland's lips, and then broke the silence.

"Stand up!" he said.

"I suppose I must obey you," Sir Roland observed, shrugging his shoulders.

"It will go ill with you if you refuse," Henry Palmer said, unwinding the lash from his hand, and cracking it meaningly in the air.

Sir Roland Ashton's face grew dark with passion.

"Complete the catalogue of indignities you have to shower upon me!" he said. "What next?"

"Turn round, and stand with your face to the wall," Henry Palmer said.

"What!" Sir Roland almost screamed.

The lash whirled over Palmer's head, and the baronet shrank instinctively from it.

"Would you dare strike me? Would you beat me like a dog?" he demanded, hoarsely.

"Yes, if you are obstinate. Turn your face towards the wall, I say."

Boiling over with impotent rage Sir Roland obeyed, and as he did so a strong cord was slipped under his arms and drawn so tight that he gave vent to a cry of pain.

"Come, come," said Henry Palmer; "you are more frightened than hurt. You and I are to be companions for a short time, so we may as well, to use your own words, understand each other. I must obey orders, which I shall not abuse or budge from, and you will do well to obey me. March!"

He pushed Sir Roland lightly by the shoulder towards the door, and the baronet, overcome with shame and rage, felt ready to sink into the earth.

The staircase was but a short one, and ended in a broad passage, in which were several doors of strong workmanship, but without handles or any visible appliance for opening and closing.

At first Sir Roland thought that he was to be merely removed from one room to another, but he was mistaken in this notion.

Palmer led him to the further end of the passage, and then threw a kind of hood, made of heavy material, over his head.

"Ready?" said a voice.

"Yes," Palmer replied.

"Then go, and remain with him until I come."

The voice that Sir Roland heard was not that of Spring-Heeled Jack, but he fancied that he had heard it somewhere before.

It came to him like an indistinct memory; but no time was left for him to think, for in another instant he discovered that he was in a vehicle, and being driven at a rapid pace along a narrow road.

Opposite him sat Henry Palmer, cool, collected, and smiling, as if the trip was one of pleasure, but the hand that had held the whip was now occupied with a pistol, the polished barrel of which gleamed spitefully in the rays of sunshine gleaming brilliantly through the chinks in the curtains.

"Where are we bound for?" demanded Sir Roland, unable to suppress his speech any longer.

"Home."

"Home! What home?"

"Your last home," Henry Palmer replied, as calmly as if he were making an ordinary remark. "My answer does not surprise you, I suppose?"

Sir Roland felt the veins upon his forehead growing thick and hot.

"So," he said, "you are Spring-Heeled Jack's slave?"

"There you lie," Henry Palmer said, twirling his moustache.

"Then tell me the name of the man you serve?"

"I have permission to do so now," Palmer said. "The man whose servant I am is named Ralph Ashton."

"Ralph Ashton!" Sir Roland cried. "Impossible! You mock me."

"Nay, I do not," Palmer returned. "He has heard of your capture. It is he who sent me to bring you to his presence, and he expects me to do so before sundown."

Bound as he was, the baronet leaned forward, and made a snatch at the pistol; but Henry Palmer was too quick to be caught in such a way.

He merely laughed, as he shifted the weapon from one hand to the other.

"You really deserve to have your brains blown out, Sir Roland," he said; "and if you and I were at variance perhaps I should not scruple to do it. How foolish you are, for now you compel me to tie your hands."

This he did in less time than the words recording the action can be written, and Sir Roland, with a groan of dismay upon his lips, threw himself back, and maintained a sullen silence.

The carriage went on with unslackened speed for many a mile, but stopped once in the middle of a wood, through which a broad path ran.

Here the tired horses were changed for fresh ones, and the journey was continued until the sun began to sink beneath a bank of deep purple clouds.

And now it was that Henry Palmer began to show signs of anxiety.

He drew the curtain nearest to him aside, and peeped out, holding the check-string in his hand, so as to warn the driver when to stop at a moment's notice.

This he presently did, and the horses came to a standstill.

"Our journey has come to an end at last," Palmer said, touching Sir Roland on the shoulder. "You will be accommodated with comfortable quarters for an hour or so, and then I will hand you over to Mr. Ralph Ashton's tender mercies."

"Curse you for this!" Sir Roland said, grinding his teeth. "There is life in me yet, and we may meet again."

"It is more than probable, but I don't think that you will be conscious of the fact."

"What mean you?"

"That I may have to act the part of sexton!"

A cold thrill crept through Sir Roland's frame.

"I understand you now," he said. "I have been brought here to be murdered."

"Guilty men are prone to think ill of others," Palmer remarked. "You are measuring other people's corn by your own bushel, Sir Roland. But come, follow me. I have neither the time nor inclination to parley with you."

When Sir Roland left the carriage, he found himself standing before a small house, situated in a large square garden.

It was not Ralph Ashton's residence, and there was some consolation in that to the baronet's mind, for he had shrunk from the thought of being brought face to face with the girls he had attempted to injure so grievously.

How often he had wondered what he should say to Daisy Leigh and Constance Marfield if the time should ever come when he would be compelled to kneel at their feet and plead to them for mercy!

He knew their gentle natures—he knew how

# SPRING-HEELED JACK,

## THE TERROR OF LONDON.

THE ROPE DESCENDED NEARER AND NEARER TO SIR ROLAND ASHTON.

No. 35.

good and pure they were, and their very virtues made him hate them the more.

The house that met his gaze had an odd look about it.

All the blinds were drawn, as if the shadow of death lingered within the building.

No smoke, denoting good cheer, arose from the chimneys, and there were no signs of life save he, Henry Palmer, and the driver, who now wore a mask upon his face.

The very horses stood as motionless as statues, and the birds, ceasing from hopping among the trees, looked down in silence upon the strange scene.

And a strange scene it was.

Palmer led Sir Roland along the path to the rear of the house, and, stopping suddenly, pointed to a freshly-dug hole in the ground.

"Why do you call my attention to it?" Sir Roland demanded.

"Ask yourself the question."

The baronet's blood coursed hot and cold in turns through his veins.

The blood fled from his lips, and left them as white as his pallid features.

"I cannot," he said, hoarsely, "for I know not what it means."

"The earth that gives man the means of existence claims him in the end," Henry Palmer replied, solemnly. "The debt of nature must be paid."

"Yes, yes," Sir Roland said, trembling from head to foot. "I know that all men must die; but that—that—"

"Is your grave."

So saying, Henry Palmer hurried Sir Roland into the house, and closed the door after him with such a crash that the woods took up the sound and hurled it back in a discordant echo.

## CHAPTER CXXIV.

### DADDY MUCKRUM'S FRIENDS—THE CELLAR WITH THE BLACK BEAM.

DADDY MUCKRUM had scarcely raised his voice, when all Buckler's-rents was in a state of ferment and excitement.

Windows and doors flew open.

Men roared and bellowed like wild beasts waiting to be fed, women shrieked like Banshees howling at the door of a haunted house, and even little children, who could scarcely toddle, added to the din by piping a shrill chorus.

Every thief, low character, and wretched outcast knew the sound of Daddy Muckrum's voice.

Evidently something was wrong with the dirty, grimy old man, who was part and parcel of his filthy habitation; and to deem that he was in danger was more than sufficient to rouse every man, woman, and child in the horrible colony.

On they came, brandishing whatever weapons came uppermost.

Pikes, pistols, pokers, and even battered domestic utensils, formed out of iron, were carried by the motley throng, which, strangely enough, was followed by a few ill-fed, mangy curs, who seemed to enter into the spirit of the situation, and snarled and showed their teeth viciously.

"This way—this way!" Daddy Muckrum yelled. "Keep an eye on the door. Help—help!"

It must not be supposed that Catchpole and Grabham were silent or inactive while all this was going on.

With sinking hearts and trembling limbs they ran to and fro like rats in a cage, and howled "Murder!" at the top of their voices.

The crowd passed up the ricketty staircases in so solid a body, that it is a marvel the wretched structures did not give way, and bury the excited wretches beneath a heap of *debris*.

Onward they rushed into the room, and Daddy Muckrum meeting them, held up one arm as a signal to halt, and with the other pointed to the two trembling men who were now crouching in a corner.

"These fellows—" Daddy Muckrum gasped, jerking out each word with an effort, for rage and spite had almost taken his breath away—"These fellows come to me, they drink, they loll about my place, and then tender me a flash note in payment."

"Hang them!" said a burly fellow, stepping to the front. "Why, why—they are traps! I've seen them over and over again, though I forget their names just now."

Catchpole felt that he must say something, or die out of sheer fright.

"Which, I beg to differ from you, my kind, good sir," he said; "we were constables, but are so no longer. As for the note, only give us time and I will prove that the landlord of the Bull in Top Boots gave it to me, and my friend another, which he has in his pocket at this very moment."

This speech brought a roar of laughter from the throng.

"What liars they are," said Daddy Muckrum. "Who can believe them?"

The mob were not disposed to discuss the question.

Buckler's-rents disliked the arm of the law, and it unanimously voted that the best thing to be done was to hang Catchpole and Grabham out of hand.

But Daddy Muckrum had no wish to go to such extremes.

"No, no," he said; "since they had tried to be clever with me they shall stand treat all round, and hand over the flash flimsies. I daresay they can be made use of in some way—eh?"

The horrible old man burst into a roar of laughter as he finished speaking.

The ex-constables were in a most miserable pre dicament.

They had not a farthing in the world to bless themselves with, but they fumbled instinctively in their pockets.

Catchpole found two brass buttons, and Grabham's fingers encountered nothing more valuable than an old knife and a piece of string.

Suddenly a brilliant idea occurred to his fertile imagination.

"Ladies and gentlemen," he said, appealingly, "we must throw ourselves upon your mercy—that is, my friend, Mr. Catchpole, must for a short time—"

"Eh? What's that?" Catchpole demanded. "What do you mean by leaving yourself out of the question?"

"Why, I mean that I am going to leave you here while I fetch some money," Grabham replied.

"Oh! no, you ain't," said Catchpole, wagging his head from side to side. "I can imagine you getting away on such an excuse as that, but I can't imagine you coming back."

"You fool!" Grabham hissed; "you ass! you idiot! you have spoiled the only chance we had."

"I don't care a rap what you think or say," Catchpole moaned, as he wrung his hands. "I will not be left here alone a moment with this pack of fiends."

The lawless mob seemed to enjoy this scene immensely.

No over-fed cat torturing a terror-stricken mouse was more inclined to play with its victim than these men and women were to make sport of the wretched beings in their power.

It was a kind of excitement which for them had a pleasurable relish.

It was a holiday for them, and the outcast and ragged forgot their own woes in the greater misery experienced by the men at bay.

The burly ruffian who led the gang rejoiced in the name of Mike Slicer, and advancing with heavy strides upon Grabham, he dragged him out of the corner.

"Take him below," Slicer said; "Daddy and I will follow soon with the other joker."

Poor Catchpole did not look much like a joker.

No undertaker's mute ever looked more woebegone than he, and if a prize for a lugubrious countenance had been offered then and there, he would have surely taken it.

"Oh! lor'—oh! dear. Oh! dear—oh! lor'," he gasped, sinking on his knees. "Please don't be hard on me!"

"Hard on you, you sneaking thief!" yelled Mike Slicer, seizing the unhappy man by the throat, and shaking him until his teeth chattered in his head. "Shut up that snivelling row, or I'll put a stop to it with my fist."

"I can't," Catchpole groaned, cramming his knuckles into his eyes. "It's 'ard, very 'ard, that I should be brought to this through no fault of my own."

Meanwhile two ghoul-like men and a horrible woman had charge of Grabham, and were dragging him down the stairs, followed by an exulting mob.

Then came Catchpole's turn, and in spite of alternate cries for mercy, and threats of the direst kind, he was compelled to follow his companion in distress.

Mike Slicer fastened upon his collar with the ferocity of a bloodhound, while Daddy Muckrum, hopping about like a huge carrion crow, contented himself with digging the ex-constable in the ribs and kicking his legs whenever a chance occurred.

Down—down they went, the staircase creaking and groaning.

At last they reached a dark, dismal, dungeon-like place.

It was a kind of cellar, filthy beyond description, and all the more horrible because of a huge black beam that ran from wall to wall.

There was an aperture between this massive piece of timber and the ceiling, and Catchpole turned all sorts of colours when he noticed that a rope attached to an iron hook was dangling from it.

Grabham had not yet observed this.

He was too much occupied with wondering whether he was on his head or his heels, but when the beam and rope were pointed out to him he uttered a cry of terror, and collapsed into the arms of the woman, who at once proceeded to bring him to a proper sense of his position by pulling his ears and hair with the utmost vigour.

"Now, then," said Mike Slicer, still pointing to the beam, "you plainly see that we don't intend to stand any nonsense. If you haven't any money you must have something valuable, so out with it, or you swing, as sure as eggs are eggs!"

Catchpole and Grabham were not only damp with clammy perspiration, but as limp as rags.

"We have nothing — nothing whatever!" Grabham groaned.

"Then we'll settle with you first," said Mike Slicer, taking the end of the rope in his hand and twisting it into a noose.

Grabham thorght that his last moment had come indeed.

He closed his eyes and opened his mouth, but no sound save a gurgling noise came from his throat.

At last, even in his misery, he remembered that the buckles upon his shoes were silver.

But he could not say so, for he had lost the power of speech.

He could only point down at his shoes, while he rolled from side to side like a drunken man.

"Hold hard a minute," said Daddy Muckrum; "he wants to say something."

"Buckles—silver!" Grabham gasped.

"Kick off your shoes," Mike Slicer growled. "If you have told us a lie you can die as well with them off as on. Ah! they are the genuine article, so you may consider your neck saved for the present. Now then, perhaps, the gentleman with a face like a turnip can find something as good, if not better."

Catchpole was the gentleman with a face like a turnip, but he shook his head.

His shoe-buckles were of white metal, and he had nothing better to offer.

"Then shake hands with your pal, and say good-bye to him for ever," Mike Slicer growled. "You'll not be the first man by many a one who has danced from that beam. Hallo! what's that?"

It was a sound like the beating of a gong.

In a moment the scene was changed.

Men, women, and children—yes, the very children had come to witness the horrible sight—vanished from the cellar like uncanny spirits at the dawn of day.

The door went to with a crash, and Catchpole and Grabham were left to enjoy each other's company and to puzzle their almost shattered intellects how to get out of the infernal trap.

---

## CHAPTER CXXV.

### ONE HOUR TO LIVE.

Henry Palmer conducted Sir Roland Ashton into a small room, and there removed the bonds from his hands and wrists.

Sir Roland was delighted and astonished at this procedure, which he had never expected for a moment.

He was too artful to show by any expression in his face how pleased he was, and merely sat down upon a chair pointed out to him.

The room had no windows in the walls, but daylight was admitted by a small skylight in the roof.

Sir Roland glanced carelessly up at it, and Henry Palmer, pretending not to notice him, left the apartment without saying a word.

The moment he was gone Sir Roland scrutinised the room, but the skylight in particular.

By standing upon a chair, if drawn to the centre of the room, he felt convinced that he could touch the skylight; but hope fled from his breast again when he discovered that every article of furniture was screwed tightly down to the floor.

"I am baffled in every way," he hissed between his teeth; "but there may be yet time to devise some plan of escape, and turn the tables upon Ralph Ashton, clever as he is."

Sir Roland Ashton returned to the chair, and, leaning his chin upon his hand, began to reflect.

It seemed a marvel to him that he had been unbound and left alone, for there might be nothing between the door and liberty.

Stay!

A sentry, silent and motionless, might be outside the door—a sentry with firearms, who knew how to use them, and whose aim was sure.

Sir Roland wondered how long he was to be kept in suspense before Ralph Ashton appeared to take his revenge.

He had not long to wait.

A heavy footfall announced the fact that somebody was approaching, and that the time for him to brace up his nerves had come.

He turned his head as the key grated in the lock.

He expected to see Ralph Ashton enter with a darkened brow and every feature full of anger.

But he was disappointed.

There was more sorrow than anger in the young man's face as he confronted Sir Roland.

"I need not tell you," Ralph Ashton said, as he locked the door and placed the key in his pocket, "that you are my prisoner?"

"It is mockery to do so," Sir Roland rejoined. "Reflect! You, who boast of being a law-abiding man, have broken the greatest law of your country. You have deprived me by force of my liberty. The traitor who brought me here has treated me to a kind of ghastly mummery; but it is to you that I look for an explanation. I ask you by what right you have ordered me to be kidnapped and dragged hither like a slave who is sold in a market where flesh and blood are bartered away for gold?"

"Dare you ask me such a question?" Ralph Ashton cried. "Reflect! Think of the wrongs you have done me, and the still greater wrongs you have inflicted on those who are near and dear to me."

"What if I plead guilty to the impeachment?" Sir Roland replied. "Are you my judge? If I have offended the laws of society I demand a fair trial at the hands of my fellow-countrymen."

"Your fellow-countrymen!" said Ralph, with a curling lip. "Where are they? Give me proof that there are twelve such unholy wretches as you in all the world and I will set you free."

"You are sarcastic," Sir Roland said.

"There is truth in my sarcasm," Ralph returned. "But enough of this. You are here to answer to me for all the evil you have done. For once I take the law into my own hands. Not long ago we met, and I thought I had rid the world of you, but now I will make doubly sure that you shall blight the face of the earth no longer!"

Sir Roland's face was a study as these words were uttered slowly and impressively.

Rage, fear, and hatred mingled together and distorted his features.

"My life does not belong to you, and you have no right to claim it," he said, hoarsely. "Your man, this traitor, Henry Palmer, showed me a hole in the ground, which he said was to be my grave. So, Ralph Ashton, good and noble-minded, you have brought a defenceless man here to slay him!"

"I hurl the lie back in your teeth," Ralph Ashton replied. "It is you who have slain the defenceless; it is you who have wronged the weak and helpless; and yet, how many chances have you had to repent? Fain would I give you another if I thought you would make good use of it."

"Curse you!" Sir Roland exclaimed. "I require no favour at your hands. Would that I had some weapon here, I would make you alter your statement about bringing me to account!"

"The opportunity you desire will be soon given to you," Ralph Ashton said; "and now I will leave you with these words. You or I have but one hour to live!"

A hope sprang into Sir Roland's breast.

"You will fight me fairly?" he said.

"Yes."

"But if you fall your men will not allow me to escape?"

"They will," Ralph Ashton replied; "for I have given them orders which they will not fail to act upon."

"Stay!" Sir Roland cried, as Ralph Ashton was moving towards the door. "I have reason to believe—nay, I know, that you are in league with that fiend, Spring-Heeled Jack. If you fall, will he let me go free—will he cease to hunt me and dog my footsteps?"

Ralph Ashton smiled.

"I am in league with no fiend," he said. "Let this suffice you. If I fall Spring-Heeled Jack will never trouble you again."

"Will you give me the choice of weapons?" Sir Roland asked.

"No; we fight with swords."

"I am content," the baronet said. "You will find that my old nerve and skill have returned. Beware! Better let me go free than tempt fate!"

Ralph Ashton made no reply to this, but strode out of the door, banging it behind him.

With all his apparent bravado Sir Roland felt sick at heart, for he could not help acknowledging two things.

Ralph Ashton was not only a good swordsman, but he had right and justice on his side.

When the young man closed the door so violently behind him Sir Roland thought he heard the lock give out a peculiar clicking sound.

It seemed as if the bolt shut back again, and the baronet, after waiting for a few minutes, stole lightly across the floor, and touched the door lightly with his hand.

It yielded, and a grim smile stole over the baronet's face.

"So!" he muttered. "The fool told me that I had, perchance, but one hour to live. We shall see."

He did not open the door sufficiently wide to look out just then, but returned to the chair and sat down, as if unaware that the road to liberty lay open to him.

No sound disturbed the stillness of the house.

It was as quiet as the grave.

The sun was sinking fast, and the time was slipping away.

Sir Roland sat pondering whether he should brave out his position with a bold face or attempt to fly.

Yes; that would be the better course, though he might be caught and dragged back ignominiously to the house again.

Crossing the floor again, with the utmost caution he opened the door and looked out into the passage.

It was empty, as, perhaps, the entire house might be; but what had he to encounter outside?

Sir Roland looked round for some weapon, but could see nothing.

He stole along the passage until he came to the door which would admit him to the open air.

His sharp eyes told him at a glance that lock had not been turned; but the latch was a peculiar one, such as to require a lightness of touch to be raised without noise.

Desperate men accomplish extraordinary things.

Holding his breath, Sir Roland Ashton placed two fingers upon the latch and pressed it down by degrees.

It was a dangerous task, for Henry Palmer or some other man might suddenly appear and shoot him dead.

Presently the latch was released from the catch, and the door opened slowly.

Sir Roland leaped out into the open air, and taking a short run, cleared the hedge with a bound.

Then he heard a ringing report.

A bullet came crashing through the hedge, and whistled ominously over his head.

Sir Roland ran on, conscious that he was being pursued, for he could hear the sound of voices behind him.

But he never looked round or slackened his headlong pace until he felt that he was struggling against fearful odds.

He reached a game cover, and flinging himself down, burrowed under a huge heap of decayed leaves driven there by chance by the wind, and lay still.

---

## CHAPTER CXXVI.

### JACOB BUTLER LOSES THE COACH AND HIS WAY.

We are afraid that Jacob Butler has been left too long in the cold, but he has been pretty happy and comfortable since we saw him perched on the coach.

He saw Mrs. Corcoran on that memorable morning when she gave chase, shrieking and yelling, across London-bridge; and it was not until the four greys and the whirling wheels had taken him a considerable distance into the country, that he could breathe with anything like freedom.

There are many people in the world who would call him a coward for being afraid of an old woman, and it must be confessed that Jacob Butler's heart was not of that material which makes a brave man.

And yet some excuse can be made for him.

He had been badgered and buffetted about the world, kicked and knocked about like a football, and whirled about like a weather-cock in a gale of wind.

Mr. Cranston noticed the pallor of his new servant's cheeks, and was at a loss to understand its meaning.

He, however, made no remark on the subject until the coach stopped to allow the passengers time for refreshments, and then Jacob not only declined liquid stimulant, but refused to leave the vehicle.

"What's the matter with you?" Cranston demanded.

"I don't feel very well, sir," Jacob replied.

"All the more reason that you should take something," his master returned. "Take this shilling and get yourself a glass of brandy and water with it."

"I'd—I'd rather not if it's all the same to you," said Jacob. "I had something to drink before we started, and that will last me until we reach the end of the journey."

"I shall find you an economical servant if you go on in this way," Cranston said, laughing. "but new brooms sweep clean, they say."

Poor Jacob hung his head.

He was dying to tell Mr. Cranston that his life was made a misery by an old witch, who he firmly believed had the power of transporting herself to any place at a moment's notice, and, indeed, it would not have surprised him much had Mrs. Corcoran suddenly popped her head out of one of road-side inn windows and called him by name.

It was quite a relief to him when the guard and coachman came out of the house, brushing their coat-sleeves across their mouths.

The passengers climbed up, the fresh horses began to dance and neigh as the cloths were removed by the tight, thin-legged ostlers, and away went the coach again.

Heavy, louring clouds were rolling up in the westward.

The coachman pointed at them with his whip, and remarked to the nearest passenger that a heavy storm was approaching.

This was too evidently the case, for thunder began to roll and rumble heavily in the distance.

"We shall get a precious soaking unless we can reach the next stage before yonder clouds overtake us," the coachman said. "They are working against the wind, and we may just escape."

For the first time that day the driver of the team used his whip in earnest, and the horses, throwing back their ears in astonishment and indignation, broke into a gallop.

The coach rolled from side to side with such violence that several of the passengers started to their feet, and gave vent to cries of fear and expostulation.

"Keep your seats, gentlemen!" the guard shouted. "There is nothing to fear unless the storm overtakes us. One of the leaders is mortally afraid of lightning, and kicks like mad at the sound of thunder."

This announcement was not very consoling or encouraging to the passengers; but one and all having agreed to leave the issue to the coachman, they resumed their seats, and hoped for the best.

Then came a race between the impending storm and the almost flying coach.

The horses swept mile after mile from under their iron-shod hoofs, and the storm clouds shifted from point to point, as if dodging the coach, and determined to vent its fury upon its living freight.

The passengers plainly saw that the next stage could not be reached until a deluge of rain descended, and they were preparing for the worst when a sharp, cracking sound smote their ears.

One of the wheels had given way.

Over went the coach, its fall being fortunately broken by a hedge, and away flew the passengers—some this way, and some that.

When Jacob Butler picked himself up—which he did with the vague notion that his head had flown from his shoulders—he discovered that he had fallen into a freshly-ploughed field, and that his next-door neighbour, so to speak, was Mr. Cranston, who lay face downwards and with outspread arms as if the shock had killed him.

Jacob raised his master in his arms and rested his head upon his knee.

"Thanks—thanks!" Cranston said. "I don't think I am hurt much. There are no bones broken, I am sure. Leave me, and see if you can be of assistance to anybody else."

At this moment the storm thundered down its voice and fury of hail and rain upon the hapless assembly.

The horses kicked and plunged so violently that the partly-stunned guard and coachman cut the traces and let the affrighted animals go.

It was an awful scene.

Earth and sky grew almost as dark as midnight.

The passengers, groaning and binding up their wounds and bruises with scarves and handkerchiefs, huddled together like sheep, and as timorously, for the fierce, quivering lightning seemed to be bent upon their destruction.

Quiver—quiver! Crash—crash!

Heaven and earth seemed to be at variance, and had met together in mad battle.

"I have travelled this road for over twenty years," the coachman said, as he shaded his eyes to protect them from the blinding glare, "but I have never seen anything to equal this."

Nobody cared to discuss this subject, and scarcely a word was spoken, until one mighty band of lurid flame shattered the clouds, and drove them in different directions.

Then the storm was virtually over, and the passengers, forgetting their aches and pains, began to congratulate each other on what appeared an almost miraculous escape.

The coachman then began to think what had become of the horses.

"Will some gentleman walk up the road to the Rose and Thistle and tell the landlord what has happened?" he said. "The house is not more than a couple of miles away, and help will be sent immediately."

"My servant shall go," said Cranston, beckoning to Jacob Butler.

"Then let him take a near cut across the fields," said the guard. "He will save nearly a third of the journey that way."

Jacob Butler had an aching head, and every limb seemed to have been thrashed with a heavy stick, but he was so anxious to distinguish himself in his new master's eyes that he started off at a good pace.

We have said that the storm had been split up into fragments; indeed, the last terrible flash had sent many little thunder showers to wander about the country to boom and splutter out their lesser wrath.

One of these overtook Jacob Butler before he had gone half-a-mile, and though the conflict of the elements was nothing in comparison to what he had previously witnessed, the dashing rain blinded and bewildered him.

Jacob Butler wandered from the beaten track and lost his way.

How he had contrived to do such a thing he had no more idea than the man in the moon; but there was the painful fact, and the more he turned and the further he plodded, the greater pickle he found himself in.

He had got into a maze of lanes and byways sc intricate that, after tearing madly about for a quarter of an hour, he found himself exactly at the same spot he had started from.

"What will Mr. Cranston say," he gasped; "what excuse can I make for putting my foot in it like this? Oh! fool—fool! no sooner do I get out of the frying-pan than I fall into the fire."

At last it struck the bewildered man that he had better keep straight on at all risks.

He argued that if he did not reach the Rose and Thistle Inn, he would certainly come upon the overturned coach and the people who were expecting his return with help.

Jacob started and kept steadily on.

The rain had now ceased, and the sun was shining brilliahtly.

Mr. Butler mounted a bank and gazed to the right and the left of him.

Not a house could he see, nor a living creature, and as for the coach it seemed to have vanished completely.

Jacob Butler opened his mouth and gave vent to a wild halloa.

The woods and fields echoed back the sound, but no welcome response came from a human voice.

"Well I'm blest!" Jacob groaned, as he sat down, heedless of the fact that the grass was as wet as a ditch. "Well I'm blest! Was ever man in such a muddle as this? Here I am, I don't know where, and going it may be further afield every moment. I wish I was dead! Why didn't I die before I was old enough to know such misery?"

The idea suddenly occurred to him that he had been unconsciously making his way back to London, and the notion was so fraught with terror to him mind that he leaped to his feet, and trotted and hobbled along in the opposite direction.

If Jacob Butler had been a wise man he would have found his way to the fields by the prints of his own footsteps in the mud, but being a bit of a fool, and half worried out of his life into the bargain, he did nothing of the kind.

Onward, sometimes to the right, now to the left, hither and thither, he went, but all in vain.

At last, with a groan of despair, he flung himself down upon the damp earth.

Poor Jacob!

How all his hopes fled at that moment.

He had looked forward with some reason to a life of honest work and peace.

But now all his hopes were dashed down at his feet—the feet with which he kicked, as he lay, as if spurning his hard fate.

No man ever got to the end of a journey by lying or standing still, and Jacob, perhaps, feeling the truth of this, rose, and removed the stains of mud, occasioned by his voluntary fall, from his coat and breeches.

Then he planted his back against a tree, and tried to think.

But his brain was all of a whirl, and refused to allow any train of thoughts to work in its proper order.

"Ah! me," he sighed. "Would that the robins would cover me up with leaves, like they did the children in the wood!"

Jacob Butler was a rather full-sized child, and, had he reflected for a moment, he would have come to the conclusion that his personal appearance was not such a one as the robins would take a fancy to.

At length Jacob Butler made a move forward; but it was not long before he came to a standstill at the sound of voices.

Two or more men were talking loudly, and in tones of anger.

At first Jacob Butler could not make out where

they were; but suddenly a wreath of smoke curled up from behind a clump of bushes.

"Tramps or gipsies," thought Jacob. "I must be very careful. These sort of fellows have no scruples about turning a man's pockets inside out, and dropping him into a pond afterwards."

But how to get away without being seen or heard was the question.

"The job must be done quickly, if done at all," said one of the voices. "Lord Mildendale has been driven half out of his wits with one thing and another, and I don't think it will be a hard task to catch him napping. Young Cranston has come back, as you know; he has had one meeting with his lordship, and sworn vengeance against him."

Jacob Butler pricked up his ears at the mention of his master's name.

"I should like to have a peep at these men," he said under his breath. "There seems to be some conspiracy at work, and it may be that I have been sent here as the instrument to upset it."

"Well," said another voice, "our queen's instructions must be obeyed. So, when we catch his lordship, we are to take him to—"

"Hush!" the first speaker interposed. "I hear something."

Jacob Butler's foot had crushed a dry twig with a snapping sound, and, almost instantly, a swarthy head appeared over the clump of bushes.

From the back of this head flowed hugh masses of shaggy hair, which gave the man such a terrific appearance that Jacob Butler tilted on his heels and felt ready to faint.

"I beg your pardon," he stammered, "but can you direct me to a house known as the Rose and Thistle?"

The gipsy leaped over the bushes, and being joined by another man, they advanced upon Jacob Butler and took him by the arms.

"We can direct you anywhere," said the first man, who had espied Jacob; "even out of the world, if you have grown tired of your life. I hope, for your own sake, that you have not been listening to our conversation?"

"No—no," said Jacob; "of course not. I have quite enough to do to mind my own business."

The gipsies then exchanged some words in an unknown language, or kind of jargon, out of which the unhappy Jacob could make no meaning.

"We have only your word for that," said one of the Romanys, who went by the name of Jim Pinfold. "Tell us how you got here, and all about yourself? You will do well to tell us the truth, for we have the knack of knowing when a man is lying."

Jacob Butler told his story from beginning to end, and left nothing unsaid, save that he was in Mr. Cranston's service.

"It's an odd kind of tale," Jim Pinfold said; "but it is an easy thing for a stranger to lose his way in these parts. How far do you think you are from the Rose and Thistle?"

"I am sure I don't know; I wish I did!" Jacob Butler rejoined, dismally.

"Well, supposing you put it at six miles, and you won't be far out."

"What?" Jacob Butler almost shrieked. "Is it possible that I have wandered so far out of my way?"

"Not only possible, but true," Jim Pinfold replied. "What do you say, Ricketts?"

Mr. Ricketts, who looked as if he had been broiled in the sun from the day of his birth, nodded his head, and gave an assenting grunt.

"Which is the way, please?" Jacob Butler demanded, wringing his hands. "I must get there by hook or by crook."

"The nearest path is through the woods," Jim Pinfold said; "and as we are going that way we may as well have the pleasure of each other's company. What do you say to that?"

Jim Pinfold clapped Jacob Butler so heartily on the back that he winced and wriggled under the smart.

"Of course I have no objection," he said, hesitatingly; "why should I? I should like to stand treat when we reach the Rose and Thistle, but, unfortunately, I have no money."

"What?" Ricketts cried. "No money! A gentleman travelling from London on a coach without a well-filled purse! Bosh! Nonsense!"

"It's a mournful fact, nevertheless," said Jacob. "I'm not a gentleman, but a gentleman's servant."

"What's your master's name?" Jim Pinfold demanded.

Jacob Butler made no reply.

"Speak out!" Pinfold cried, fiercely.

"Well, you see, I—I—" Jacob gasped, jerking out his words as if they hurt him—"I am not quite at liberty to tell you who he is; but I assure you that he is one of the best and kindest-hearted of men."

That Jim Pinfold was determined not to accept this answer became evident by his startling and violent behaviour.

He seized hold of Jacob Butler's throat, and bumped that unfortunate man's head against a tree.

"Now, then," said he, "will you speak out, or will you compel me to increase the dose of physic?"

"His name is—is—is— Oh! lor', don't throttle a man."

"I will," Pinfold roared, savagely. "I'll make short work of you unless you out with the name. Quick! or you are a dead man."

"His—his name is Cranston, and he lives in the adjoining village to Mildendale."

Jim Pinfold's arms fell to his sides as if he had been suddenly electrified.

He glared at Ricketts and Jacob Butler in turns, and ran his sun-browned hands through his hair.

"Why did you not say so before?" he said. "You would have saved yourself both time and trouble."

"I don't see—see—that—that I am called upon to answer every question put to me by a stranger," Jacob Butler replied, with an effort at boldness.

"We are on friendly terms with Mr. Cranston," Pinfold said. "He has been kind to us and our people. Come, I apologise, and will now show you how to get to the Rose and Thistle in less than five minutes. Take this to your master; he will know what it means."

Jim Pinfold pulled an antique ring from his finger and pressed it into Jacob's hand.

"Be careful with that ring," Pinfold said; "for it is just possible that you will have to bring it back to me with some kind of message. Now follow me."

The gipsy was as good as his word, and in a very short space of time Jacob Butler had passed over the threshold of the Rose and Thistle.

He had come late, but it was a case of better late than never.

The landlord became all excitement in a moment.

He shouted to the ostlers and helpers, and up

they came running with straws in their mouths, like—we beg their pardon, but we cannot help the simile—pigs in windy weather.

Horses were dragged from the stables, and two being harnessed to a conveyance, raced down the road to the scene of the catastrophe.

Meanwhile, the drivers of the coach and the guard had succeeded in recapturing the horses, which had galloped away to some distant fields.

The coach was left for a wheelwright to attend to, and the passengers, somewhat forgetting their sorrows, crowded into the new conveyance and were driven to the Rose and Thistle.

"Where on earth have you been to all this time?" Cranston said, turning to his servant.

"I am sorry to say that I was overtaken by another storm, which so confused me that I lost my way," Jacob Butler replied.

In the excitement of the time he had forgotten all about the ring given him by Jim Pinfold, but remembering it now, he thrust his finger and thumb into one of his waistcoat pockets.

The ring was conspicuous by its absence, although Jacob Butler could have sworn that he put it there.

Jacob tried the other pocket, with the like result, and a feeling of horror stole over him.

"It—it must be somewhere!" he gasped, with his eyes standing out of his head in a most unnatural manner.

"What must be somewhere?" Cranston said. "Don't look at me in such a horrible style, man. Have you taken leave of your senses?"

"I'm looking for something I cannot find," Jacob replied, tearing away at his clothes. "Dash it all, what have I done with the ring? Oh! here it is."

Cranston held up his hand.

"Hush!" he said, as he took the ring. "I know what this means. Say no more."

Jacob Butler saw a strange expression come over his master's face.

It was an expression of satisfaction and exultation, mingled with suppressed fury.

"I suppose you know how to keep a still tongue in your head?" he said, as he pressed a guinea into Jacob's ready palm.

"Oh! yes, sir—of course, sir," Jacob replied. "I have secrets of my own. I mean to say—"

"Never mind what you mean to say," Cranston said, interrupting him. "Never say a word about meeting those men or about the ring, and I'll be a true friend to you. Betray me, and you will find that I can be a bitter foe."

"I'll be very careful," Jacob Butler replied. "Yes, sir; I think I will take a little brandy and water, for what with one thing and another, I feel quite upset."

## CHAPTER CXXVII.

### ALIVE OR DEAD?

The sound of the gong or drum which had so disturbed the inhabitants of Buckler's-rents had brought a still stranger sight to the place than the one which had been enacted in Daddy Muckrum's cellar.

A cart had driven up to the entry, and two men, jumping down from the box seat, began to haul away at the loose straw with which the lumbering vehicle seemed completely filled.

After digging and diving about with their hands they produced what appeared to be the lifeless body of a man.

It was the remains of a man who had suffered the penalties of the law that morning at Tyburn, and, after hanging the usual time, had been mercifully given up to his friends for burial.

But why bring it to Buckler's-rents to be interred?

We shall see.

The body was carried into the nearest house, and having been stripped to the waist, Mike Slicer began to rub the cold, blue hands with all his might.

Another man forced open the jaws of the seemingly lifeless man, and thrusting his fingers down his throat, drew out a silver pipe about two inches in length.

Mike Slicer's strength was giving way, and another man took his place and went on with the work of restoration.

Presently the body began to glow, and a minute later a hollow groan from the half-hanged wretch announced that Justice had been cheated of her lawful prey.

This man was no other than Ted Nickells, late of the Chequers, against whom was a variety of charges, and the judge and jury, without troubling themselves about the episode in which Jacob Butler had been so interested, determined to hang the villainous innkeeper out of hand.

It is just possible that Ted Nickells did not feel very thankful to his friends of Buckler's-rents for bringing him round to sense and reason.

As his blood renewed its circulation, and went coursing madly through his veins, the torture he underwent was agonising.

An awful weight seemed to oppress his chest, and a red-hot band of iron seemed to have fastened upon his throat.

"Let me die," he moaned—"let me sink and die! This pain is too great for mortal to bear!"

But the man went on rubbing and rasping the tortured man's flesh, paying no heed to his words, until Daddy Muckrum, who had watched the scene with intense interest, gave the word to desist.

"Now for a good stiff glass of brandy," said Daddy Muckrum. "Make him drink it down to the dregs, and then let him go to sleep as long as he likes."

Ted Nickells glared about him.

He had been snatched from the grave, and his burning brain was powerless of comprehension as yet.

His head sank back a moment after the brandy had been poured down his throat, and he fell into a heavy slumber.

"Bravo! Hurrah!" Daddy Muckrum cried, rubbing his hands. "This has turned out better than I expected. What shall we do now? Eh! my friends, what shall we do now to celebrate this joyful occasion?"

"Why, hang those curs in the cellar out of the way," Mike Slicer growled.

"No—no!" Daddy Muckrum chuckled. "We must not be quite so hard on them just now. What do you reckon that Grabham's silver buckles are worth?"

"About ten shillings."

"Then," said Daddy Muckrum, cracking his finger joints most hideously, "we will drink to his health, and Catchpole's—why not?"

"I don't care whose health I drink, so long as I get something between my lips," Slicer returned. "Hang me, if I thought that Nickells would come round at all, and I'm almost as sore as he,"

"But he's alive, that's one comfort," Daddy Muckrum replied. "Come one, come all, and I'll open a couple of bottles of the very best stuff I have in the house."

While the ragged, rascally lot were carousing, the conditions of the ex-constables was most deplorable.

They fumed and fretted in the loathsome place.

"This—this," Catchpole gasped, shudderingly, as he caught sight of the black beam and dangling rope again—"this comes of trusting to our fellow man."

"Our fellow man be blowed!" Grabham growled. "It comes of trusting to a low, cunning blackguard, you mean!"

"What's the upshot of it to be?" Catchpole howled. "These wretches mean to hang us, after all. They will never be satisfied with a pair of silver buckles."

"I don't suppose they will," Grabham returned. "If you had taken my advice, I could have got away and brought assistance; but as it is we are as helpless as a pair of babies."

Grabham on his way across the cellar knocked his head against the rope and set it swinging.

"Ugh!" he said; "the sight of this horrible thing makes my blood run cold."

"So it does mine."

"You deserve to be hanged," Grabham declared; "but I don't see why I should die because you have made a fool of yourself and me into the bargain."

Catchpole made no reply; but fell to groaning and moaning in the most heart-rending manner.

He could hear the noise and boisterous laughter going on upstairs, and more than once he called out to Grabham that the ruthless wretches were coming down.

But this was a mistake, and it was well for them that Daddy Muckrum's partisans did not put in an appearance.

They were enjoying themselves, in their way, too much to think of anything else.

One bottle after another was opened, and the fiery fluid flowed like water.

It was a wonder where the people—a people of rags and patches—got the money from.

Drink was their idol, and they worshipped it at the cost of the destruction of mind and body.

Hoarse-voiced men and blotched-faced women toasted each other in the damning glass, until some reeled and fell upon the dirty floor.

But Daddy Muckrum only grinned, and poured out the spirit with a lavish hand.

The sight was not an unusual one to him, and he exulted in it because it brought him profit.

Cursings, ravings, and awful blasphemy rent the air, but at last the horrible din sank down to guttural sounds.

Buckler's-rents was drunk, and even Ted Nickells was forgotten.

He had been left to sleep out his sleep of horror—to dream over again the scene at Tyburn, and when he awoke, with parched tongue and bloodless lips, he glared round the room and the miserable bed on which he had been thrown as if he had awakened to find himself in the world of punishment.

"No—no!" he gasped, struggling into a sitting position; "I am—not—not—there. The silver pipe did its work well. But why am I alone? Let me think. No—no, I cannot! My head is on fire, and my brain is fit to burst."

He rolled himself from the bed, and looked about for something to drink.

He knew Buckler's-rents well, for he and Daddy Muckrum had often done business together.

Nickells staggered towards the door, and reaching Muckrum's house halted and leaned heavily against the door-post.

Suddenly he heard a sound in the cellar.

"I suppose Daddy is down there," he muttered. "I'll go and see, for this awful thirst is killing me."

Little dreaming of what he was about to do, he reeled down the stone staircase and fell heavily against the door.

Then he tried it with his hand, and was astonished to find it locked though he could still hear voices from the inside.

"Hullo, there!" he cried, in a weakened tone of voice. "Are you there, Daddy?"

"Yes," said Grabham, answering for Muckrum.

"Then open the door."

"I can't—the lock has slipped," Grabham re-replied, in muffled tones. "I think I left the key outside."

"Yes."

"Then turn it."

Ted Nickells did so, and Catchpole and Grabham rushed out pell-mell, flooring Nickells, and trampling upon his body.

"Help! help!" he yelled.

"Don't stop!" Grabham roared. "Come along, Catchpole. Show the brutes a clean pair of heels. If ever I show my nose in this accursed place again may I be hanged, indeed!"

"And so may I," Catchpole replied. "If they try to stop me now I'll bellow like a mad bull."

It was quite evident that he meant to keep his word in this particular, and the way he used his legs did him credit, considering that they had to carry a bulky body, and a rather top-heavy head.

And into the so-called square they dashed, up the narrow entry, and then into the street.

Then they stopped to take breath.

"What—what shall we do?" Catchpole panted. "I suppose you ain't desirous of paying another visit to the Bull in Top Boots?"

"No, no," Grabham replied, shuddering; "anywhere but there. Let's get further away. I've got an idea."

"What is it?"

"To go back to Bow-street, and try if we can't be taken on again."

---

## CHAPTER CXXVIII.

### THE ABDUCTION — THE SHADOW AND THE REALITY — LANONI CALLS AT MILDENDALE HALL.

BAD, black-hearted, and mean as Sir Roland Ashton was, he could not help feeling ashamed at fleeing from Ralph as he had done.

It was like sneaking out of a fight, and now the young man would have more reason to despise him.

Sir Roland thought how ignominious was his position, and how he would be jeered at, if discovered hidden under a heap of dead leaves, like a frightened cur.

The sounds of pursuit died away, but it was quite dark before he dared venture out, and then, striking into a wood, he took the path the deepest in shadow.

The wretched man's conscience was haunted by all sorts of fancies.

He was being pursued.

He heard a sound as of a pack of hounds on his track.

A hundred times the form of Ralph Ashton rose up before him, mocking him, and calling him coward.

Sir Roland Ashton thought he must go mad.

The night was pitchy dark, and the solitude of the wood was so awful and death-like that he could scarcely endure it.

Every now and then the leathery wings of a bat, flapping close to his face, startled him, and brought a suppressed cry to his lips.

The dull yellow eyes of an owl glaring at him sent him back several paces.

To his imagination every gnarled tree became a spectre, and the sweat of a nameless agony gathered upon his brow.

He had no idea of the part of the country he was in.

It suddenly occurred to him that he might wander into the open again, and thus fall into the hands of his enemies.

He stopped, and sank down beneath a tree, and closing his eyes, tried to shut out the horrible visions that danced before them.

But he could not sleep.

He saw the newly-dug grave as plainly as if it lay at his feet, and more horrible still, he beheld a rope with a noose at the end of it, dangling before his eyes.

He grasped at it a hundred times, and cursed the visions with breath that came hot from his lips.

But was it a vision?

The rope was so plain that, dark as the night was, it stood out in bold relief, and sometimes seemed as if it would touch his face as it swung to and fro.

At last it vanished suddenly, and Sir Roland, thinking that his brain had become calmer, folded his arms, and again tried to sleep.

At last he did so, but little dreaming who and what was above his head.

What would have been his feelings had he known that Spring-Heeled Jack, stretched at full length on a branch above his head, had been watching him for hours.

It was almost daylight when Sir Roland Ashton opened his eyes.

For a moment he was confused and bewildered.

His thoughts were in a state of chaos, and for the life of him he could not think how he had got into the wood.

While he was rubbing his eyes, and endeavouring to bring back the events of the previous day, Spring-Heeled Jack watched him keenly.

A demoniac grin was on the strange being's face as he, uncoiling a rope from his arm, lowered it slowly and surely.

Nearer and nearer it went down towards Sir Roland.

Then the baronet saw the reality of what he had taken to be a shadow in the darkness.

He leaped to his feet, but was too late to escape the noose.

It fell over his shoulders, and then the rope was drawn tight.

"Help! mercy! help!" Sir Roland gasped.

. . . . . . . . .

Turning aside for a moment, we must ask the reader to accompany us back to Mildendale Hall.

His lordship was found by a keeper on his rounds, and quickly conveyed to bed.

In the evening he was sufficiently well to rise and sit in the library.

He had not been long there before a servant entered and informed his lordship that a lady wished to see him.

"A lady!" Lord Mildendale repeated. "Her name and business?"

"She will give neither, my lord."

"What is her appearance?"

"She is tall and commanding," the man replied. "She has dark hair and eyes, and has the look of a gipsy woman."

"Lanoni!" his lordship muttered. "She has kept her word, then; she told me that she would come when my troubles were greatest."

Then he turned and looked the man earnestly in the face.

"Can I trust you?" he asked.

"I hope so, my lord," the man replied.

"Then listen," said Lord Mildendale. "It is not my wish to see this woman, but she must be made to believe that I am busy at present and will give her an audience in an hour."

"Yes, my lord."

"Leave the rest to me," Lord Mildendale said, snatching up a pen with a trembling hand, and beginning to write. "Is Darkley in the house?"

"He is, my lord."

"Then send him up to me."

The servant left his lordship, who went on writing, stopping now and then as if he were penning instructions requiring thought and care.

The man, Darkley, entered the room and stood behind his lordship's chair.

He was well named, was this swarthy, powerful fellow; silent, morose, yet ready for any emergency.

"Darkley," Lord Mildendale said, "you know who is below. How came it that that woman crossed the fields unobserved?"

"I know not—nobody knows," Darkley replied.

"You know what errand she has come upon?"

"I can guess."

"She must be disposed of," Lord Mildendale said. "The opportunity is a good one, and—"

"Disposed of?" Darkley said, interrupting his lordship. "I don't quite follow your meaning."

"You will find all necessary instructions here," Lord Mildendale said, pointing to the paper. "You were this woman's lover once, I believe?"

"Yes."

"Before—before—"

"Before I betrayed my people," Darkley said. "Quite right, my lord. There is no need to mince words about it. I left them to join you."

Lanoni had been shown into a handsomely-furnished room.

She tossed her head scornfully at the gorgeous footman who eyed her quaint dress, and when left alone she paced the apartment with hurried footsteps.

"I have kept my word," she said. "I swore that I would come—and come alone. I am here. Now, my noble lord, you shall hear the truth from my lips. You shall know that the crime of years ago is no longer a secret, and that the gibbet shall take the place of your ancestral hall."

Half an hour passed away, and then the door was thrown violently open, and Darkley and two other men rushed in.

Laoni cluched at a knife which she carried in her girdle, but it was wrestea from her grasp and

In another instant a mantle was thrown over her head.

The gipsy queen had the strength of half-a-dozen ordinary women, and her struggles were of such a fierce and determined character that the men had to use every effort to prevent her to escape from their clutches.

"Villains — dogs — wretches !" the woman shrieked, frantically. "Would you murder me ?"

"Ah ! that I would if I had my way," Darkley replied.

Lanoni recognised his voice.

"You hound—you traitor !" she cried, and then sank back.

Her strength had failed her at last.

"I'm glad she's quiet," Darkley said, grinning. "Confusion seize her ! I thought she would have slipped through our fingers. Is the carriage at the door ?"

"Yes," one of the men replied.

"Then pitch her into it," Darkley said.

The brutal ruffian laughed hoarsely as the senseless form of the woman was dragged across the hall and placed in the vehicle.

"She'll want company," Darkley said; "so I'll ride inside, but I'll take care to bind her hands and feet. She'll be as wild as a hawk when she comes round and finds herself in the power of one of the men she hates most."

The journey was a long one, but Lanoni did not return to consciousness until near its completion.

"Well, my beauty," said Darkley, "I hope you are comfortable and happy. Why, hang me ! if this doesn't remind me of old times."

Lanoni fixed her beautiful eyes steadily on the ruffian's face.

"You shall be reminded of old times before you die," she said. "Where are you taking me to, you dog ?"

"Your pet dog, you mean," Darkley said, grinning from ear to ear. "That's right—call me some more nice names. I like 'em."

"Where are you taking me ?" Lanoni repeated.

"To a place where you will be able to rave and shriek to your heart's content," Darkley replied. "I hope your majesty will pardon me for sitting before you with my hat on, but the night is precious cold."

Gazing at the rascal with loathing and disgust, Lanoni sank back.

"The time will come when you and your cowardly master shall think bitterly of this hour," she said. "I laugh you and him to scorn ! Retribution will fall upon him and the cringing curs who fawn upon him for the sake of his money ! Dog that you are—cur !—he made a good choice when he engaged you !"

"So he has often said," Darkley replied. "He pays me well, and the life is better than wandering about the country."

As he spoke the carriage came to a standstill, and the door was opened by a man.

Lanoni heard the sound of rushing water, and she was not a little astonished to find that she had been brought to the sea coast.

"Now, your majesty !" said Darkley, "I suppose I must cut the cords which have held your pretty ankles so nicely."

He did so, and Lanoni, leaving the carriage, looked at the other men who had assisted in bringing her to the lonely spot.

"What is your purpose ?" she demanded, drawing herself up to her full height. "Is it murder ?"

"Well, not just at present," Darkley said; "but that will depend upon how you behave yourself."

"I did not speak to you, villain," Lanoni said.

"Well, then, you had better speak to the men," Darkley returned, in an aggravating tone of voice, "for not a word will you get out of the other fellows. But, come, our way lies down the cliff. Mind you don't slip, my charmer, for if you do you'll break your neck to a certainty. A lamp here ! What a devilish dark night it is."

It was indeed, and the lamp brought from the carriage only added to the gloom.

Darkley fixed a strong grasp upon Zanoni.

He knew her character too well to trust her.

If she had attempted to leap over the cliff and drag him with her he would not have been surprised.

But she was passive, and walked slowly down the roughly hewn path in silence.

Presently a light flashed up, and a man dressed in seafaring costume appeared.

"Is that you, Corder ?" Darkley demanded.

"Yes, it is," was the reply, "and it is lucky that you spoke, or you might have found a bullet in your brain. Why have you come at such a time ?"

"You'll find all your instructions in this paper," Darkley said, thrusting forward the document which Lord Mildendale had written. "Here's this nice lady, a real gipsy queen, come to stay with you."

"I wish his lordship had sent her somewhere else," Corder said, in a grumbling tone of voice. "How has she offended him ?"

"That is best known to himself," Darkley replied. "Lead the way, Corder, and if you have a keg of brandy or whisky in the cave I will help you to empty it."

"I don't doubt it," Corder replied, turning the slide of a dark lantern, and flashing the light on Lanoni. "What ! tie a woman's hands ? Isn't that going a little too far ?"

"If I hadn't," Darkley retorted, "she would have gone so far that we shouldn't have seen any more of her. You'll do well to keep her hands out of mischief, I can tell you."

"I'll find means to tame her," Corder growled.

So saying, he kicked some brushwood away with his foot, and disclosed a narrow flight of steps.

"Go down," Darkley said, sternly, to Lanoni.

The gipsy queen hesitated, for all was gloom and darkness beyond the stairs.

They seemed as if they led down to the very bowels of the earth, and she turned appealingly to Corder.

"If you have a spark of honour in your breast you will save me from these ruffians," she said.

"Don't speak to me about honour," Corder growled; "I did without that long ago. I found it didn't pay. Come, no nonsense; descend at once, or I shall have to assist you."

"It is hard to believe that there are such men in the world," Lanoni said. "The rich scoff at the poor, and hold them up to mockery; but the day shall come when the pampered dogs shall cringe—when the tables shall be turned upon the oppressor !"

She raised her eyes to the sky, and then, tossing her head contemptuously, descended the stairs at a swift pace.

# SPRING-HEELED JACK,

## THE TERROR OF LONDON.

SPRING-HEELED JACK PLUNGED HEADLONG TO RESCUE THE MAN HE MOST HATED.

At the bottom of the staircase a strange sight met Lanoni's eyes.

From the roof of a cavern, into which no ray of sunlight could penetrate, hung a lamp enclosed in a red shade.

A rich and ruddy glare fell upon the walls, and heightened the colour of the indignant gipsy woman's face.

"I think it is time for me to go," Darkley said. "I don't see that I can do any good by staying."

"Yes, go dog," Lanoni said. "I loathe your very presence. Beware how you retrace your steps. I read by the stars—"

"Ha! ha! ha!" laughed Darkley, interrupting her. "You must be a very clever woman to see the stars through the roof of this cave."

"Fool!" said Lanoni, "I leave you to rush upon your own fate."

"Yes," said Corder. "I think it is time that you were going, Darkley. You may tell his lordship that I will obey his instructions to the letter."

Darkley made Lanoni a polite bow, but she took no notice whatever of him.

"Now," said Corder, when he and Lanoni were alone, "you see this knife?"

"Yes; I see it. You need not flash it to and fro before my face."

"It all depends upon yourself whether I cut your bonds or run it into your body," Corder said.

"You are a brave man to speak thus to a defenceless woman."

"Oh! I know all about the defenceless woman," Corder returned, sneeringly. "I have heard of you before, and I know you to be possessed of the strength and passion of a tigress."

Lanoni laughed, and thrust out her wrists.

"You must promise to be quiet before I set you free," Corder said.

"Well, I promise."

"And you will keep your word?"

"I have never broken it yet," Lanoni replied.

"Then I will trust you so far."

As he cut the cords and they fell to the floor, Lanoni looked at her wrists, which bore the evidence of how cruelly she had been treated.

"What next?" she demanded. "Come! fulfil the programme, and fill your pockets with blood-money. Am I to die to night?"

"I said nothing about dying," Corder said, gloomily. "Sit down. I will go and fetch my daughter, who will wait on you."

"Your daughter!" Lanoni exclaimed. "How I pity the poor child! How she must love and respect her father! Ha! ha!"

The gipsy queen's laugh roused Corder's evil blood.

"You had better be quiet," he growled, as he trifled with the handle of the knife. "I am in no mood to be jested with."

"How can I help feeling merry?" Lanoni said. "Let me see the daughter of such a father."

Corder lifted his arm in a threatening style, but he dropped it to his side and turned away.

"You shall," he said, as something like a sigh escaped from his lips.

As he went away, Lanoni thought she heard him say—

"Poor Amy! Poor Amy!"

The cavern in which Lanoni stood was furnished with a table and chairs.

The floor was thickly carpeted, and the space was divided by a pair of rich velvet curtains which hung from ceiling to floor.

Lanoni walked to the curtains, and parting them, discovered a well-appointed sleeping apartment.

"I have seen many strange things, but none so strange as this," she said, musingly. "This place seems to have been kept in readiness for me, or it may be for another of Lord Mildendale's victims.

Hearing the sound of a light footstep she turned, and saw Amy Corder.

Lanoni started back as if one of the fairy folk had appeared before her.

Amy Corder was lovely in the extreme.

Her eyes were as blue as the summer's sky, and a wealth of golden hair neatly plaited about her head gleamed and flashed beneath the light of the lamp.

Her figure was lithe and graceful, and her rounded limbs were exquisitely formed.

"So," said Lanoni, when she had recovered from her astonishment at seeing so beautiful a vision in so strange a place, "you are my gaoler's daughter?"

Amy Corder nodded her head.

"Are you dumb, my poor child?" Lanoni demanded. "No; you sign to me that you are not. Why, then, do you not speak to me?"

The pretty little girl laid her two dainty fingers upon her ruby lips, as if to signify that she had been ordered not to speak.

"Ah!" Lanoni said, compassionately, "your father would beat you if you spoke to me. Poor child! Come! you must not be afraid of me. Let me kiss you?"

Amy Corder ran into the gipsy's arms, and clung affectionately to her.

"We shall know each other better soon," Lanoni said. "Perhaps you will have an oppor tunity of talking to me."

At this moment Corder, whose face was dark with passion, strode into the cell.

"What is this?" he demanded, fiercely.

"It is nothing to be alarmed at," Lanoni replied. "Your little girl—ah! how like a flower in the midst of a desert she is—seems to be surprised to find me here."

"I'll have none of this tomfoolery!" Corder said, fiercely. "She is here to wait upon you. When you require anything, name it to her, and she will bring it to you."

"May she not speak to me?"

"No."

"Why not?"

"That is my business."

As the ruffian replied to Lanoni's question, he tore Amy rudely from the gipsy queen's grasp and thrust her out of the door.

"You had better sleep now," he said, turning to Lanoni. "It may be that a long journey is in store for you."

"A journey through the dark valley of death?"

"You seem to dread it," Corder sneered.

"I am not afraid to die," Lanoni replied, haughtily; "but I confess that I fear to live in such company as yours."

## CHAPTER CXXIX.

### SIR ROLAND ASHTON HAS A NARROW ESCAPE—THE MISER AND HIS MONEY.

As the rope touched Sir Roland Ashton he looked up, and then an awful cry of horror burst from his lips.

The noose tightened about his neck.

He felt himself drawn to his feet and elevated in the air.

"Mercy !" he gasped, as the blood surged into his brain. "Mercy ! I am not fit to die."

"Neither are you fit to live," Spring-Heeled Jack cried, in a voice of thunder. "The fate is of your own seeking. You must perish. Ha ! ha ! Die, hound that you are, and become the food of carrion crows."

The agony of death came upon the wretched man.

He clutched at the rope convulsively; but it only tightened the more about his neck.

Even in that moment he was conscious that his toes were but a few inches from the ground, and he strove frantically to reach it.

But in vain.

The pain he suffered for some moments was awful.

Heart and brain seemed to take fire and rage like furnaces.

He could not speak or utter a sound now.

A dream-like torpor fell upon his senses, a thick, blurring mist gathered before his eyes, and then—then all was oblivion.

A loud, ringing laugh, hideous in its mocking triumph, awoke the echoes of the wood, as Spring-Heeled Jack, leaving the body of the baronet dangling in the wind, went bounding away.

Scarcely a minute later an old man, bent nearly double, and leaning heavily on two sticks, came crawling at a snail's pace through the wood.

On his back he bore a box such as are used by a pedlar to display his wares.

"Ha ! ha !" chuckled the old man, puckering up his wrinkled features. "This is just the place I have been looking for. No prying eyes here. No, no ! Ah ! well, I think I am safe in most places, for who would ever dream that I carried a thousand pounds in notes and gold in this old box. Ha ! ha ! Dick Slyme is a cunning old rascal."

This reflection seemed to afford the aged man much consolation.

Suddenly a change came over him.

Unslinging the box from his shoulders he placed it carefully on the ground, and then kicking the sticks away with an expression of contempt he stood erect and stretched his arms above his head.

"Good," he said, "I feel something like a man now. I must have a look at my precious hoard now. I must feast my eyes upon it. It does them good. But stay, I must make sure that none but the birds are watching me."

Richard, or Dicky Slyme, as he called himself, dodged about the trees, his keen eyes wandering restlessly, and whilst thus engaged he saw the body of Sir Roland Ashton.

Many a man would have taken to his heels at coming upon so horrible a sight, and certainly most men would have been filled with a sensation of terror.

But it was not so with Slyme.

"Why here's a gentleman who has grown tired of his life !" he said, with a hideous chuckle. "I wonder if he has any money about him, or anything that can be converted into coin."

Chuckling and clawing at the air with his hooked fingers, he moved forward.

"Why, he's quite warm !" he muttered. "Well-dressed, good-looking before he swung himself up, I daresay. Hah ! This comes of gambling, I suppose; or perhaps there is a woman in the case. What a fool a man must be to hurl himself out of the world because a pack of cards won't fill his pockets, or a doll of a girl refuses to listen to his lies about love. Love forsooth ! It is more fleeting than beauty."

Dicky Slyme dived his greedy hands into Sir Roland's pockets, and quickly emptied them.

"Not much," he said, with a disappointed growl. "Not much, but better than nothing. But he has a watch, and a valuable one. Dicky, you are in luck this morning. More money—more grist to the mill ! Well, well, it's an ill wind that blows nobody good."

He turned away, but stopped after walking a few paces.

"I'll cut him down," he muttered. "Yes, I had better do that. He may recover, and live to know now foolish he has been; and I am sure, if he is a gentleman, as he appears to be, he will not grumble at the slight reward I have taken for saving his life."

"Dicky Slyme hauled a huge knife out of his pocket, and severed the rope in twain.

"It's enough to make a man shudder to look at him," he said; "and perhaps I might if I had not seen death in all sorts of forms. Now to make myself scarce."

Having stowed away the plunder gained at so awful a price, the wretch once more burdened himself with the box, and, resuming his gait of a decrepid old man, hobbled painfully away.

He had not gone far before he heard something like a shower of small pebbles rattle on the lid of the box.

"What's that ?" he said, with a startled glance upward. "It can't be hailing, for there isn't a cloud in the sky."

"Stop !" cried a voice.

Dicky Slyme staggered forward, and nearly fell upon his face.

He thought that Sir Roland Ashton had recovered consciousness and was giving chase to him.

Flinging aside the sticks, he was about to take to his heels, when the voice checked his progress.

"Stop !" it cried again.

Dicky Slyme did stop, and stood trembling violently in every limb.

He could see nobody, and that fact filled him with more fear than if he had been confronted by half a dozen men.

"Put down that box and empty your pockets," said the voice; "put down that box, Richard Slyme."

The old man began to whine and snivel.

"I must be dreaming—I must be going mad !" he said. "Oh ! good sir, whoever you may be, I am sure you will not rob an old pedlar, who gains a wretched living by—"

"Robbing the poor and helpless," the voice interposed. "I know you, Richard Slyme."

"Then come on, whoever you are !" Slyme shrieked, opening the knife with his teeth and standing at bay. "I'll not be robbed ! I'll die first, and I'll sell my life dearly !"

The next instant the weapon slipped from his grasp, and he stood shaking as if suddenly smitten with the palsy.

He heard a crushing, as of some wild animal trampling down the bushes, and nearly fainted as Spring-Heeled Jack leaped at his feet and clutched his throat.

"The box—open the box, I say !" Spring-Heeled Jack hissed in the old rogue's ear. "I have watched you long, Richard Slyme, and the hoard you have piled up by fraud and usury must be returned to your starving victims!"

"No, no—I mean yes!" Dickey Slyme gasped; "only give me time and I'll do what you wish. Off, hideous wretch—off!"

Spring-Heeled Jack laughed and uttered a cry of triumph.

"I did not think to come across you so easily," he said. "Such men are a curse to the world! Did you see a body swinging from yonder tree?"

"No. Oh! no."

"You lie!"

"I meant to say yes," Slyme groaned; "but how can I say or do anything properly when you are holding me in that vice-like grip?"

"You robbed that body," Spring-Heeled Jack cried. "I saw you do it. I saw you cut it down, and I followed you. When you have disgorged your ill-gotten gains, you shall take its place upon the tree."

Dick Slyme fell upon his trembling knees, and clasped his hands frantically.

Great grimy tears welled into his eyes, and his brow grew damp and dewy with beads of icy cold perspiration.

"Don't kill me," he yelled; "I will do anything—give up everything. Let me live!"

As he spoke he threw down the box.

The lid flew open, and first of all a collection of trumpery articles came tumbling out.

"You see everything I possess," Slyme whined. "Take all and let me go my way in peace."

"Bah!" said Spring-Heeled Jack. "If you think to deceive me with such a lame story as that, you are vastly mistaken, my friend."

"Oh! yes—oh! lor'! I am listening to you."

"Isn't there a little contrivance called a false bottom to that box.

"If there is, I am not aware of it."

"Again you lie."

"Well?" Slyme groaned, as he rocked himself to and fro; "of course, there may be. I bought the box cheap of a man, who was found dead in a pond soon afterwards, and perhaps—"

"Silence!" Spring-Heeled Jack cried. "See here!"

Raising the box by the strap, he smashed the bottom in with one blow of his fist, and out flowed the glittering gold and bundles of crisp notes.

"What have you to say to this?" Spring-Heeled Jack demanded, sternly.

"Nothing—nothing!" Slyme gasped. "Don't take all! Don't leave me to starve in the world."

"You may rest assured of that," Spring-Heeled Jack replied. "No privations in the world shall trouble you, nor shall you trouble the world."

"Mysterious creature!" Richard Slyme moaned, "have mercy upon me. I know that I have done much wrong—that I have much to answer for. Let me live, and I will end my days in repentance."

"If I thought that you would keep your word I would grant your request," Spring-Heeled Jack said; "but you are too great a sinner to be in earnest. You have robbed the widow and orphan. When they have wept you have laughed with fiendish glee. When their hearts have bled with the wounds of pain inflicted by you, your own has rejoiced."

"I know—I know!" Slyme cried, in a voice of frantic pleading. "I see it all now. The curtain has risen and all my iniquities lie here before my eyes. Let me live—let me live!"

Spring-Heeled Jack passed his hand behind his back, and then dashed a colourless liquid in Slyme's face.

He started to his feet as if the potion had stung him, and then begun to totter.

A gurgling sound came from his throat, his knees bent, and his body collapsing, left him prone and senseless upon the sward.

When reason returned night had come.

The empty box lay beside him; but Spring-Heeled Jack and the treasure had gone.

"A curse on the thieving wretch!" he said, under his breath, as he staggered to his feet and leaned for support against a tree. "I will unmask him yet. I shall have the satisfaction of seeing him die the death he threatened me with. He thinks he robbed me of all; but I have another secret hoard, and I will use it in hunting him down."

The night air cooled his fevered brow, and he moved hastily forward, determined to get out of the wood as soon as possible.

He had not taken more than a hundred paces before he ran against some living object—the dead man restored to life!

Richard Slyme stood face to face with Sir Roland Ashton!

## CHAPTER CXXX.

### MRS. CORCORAN GOES THROUGH A NUMBER OF REMARKABLE ADVENTURES.

When we last parted with Mrs. Corcoran she was, to say the least, in a very damp state.

Dick Sleuth, in the excess of his zeal, had given her a kindly lift over the wall of the besieged house, but only to fling her into the Fleet River, which, though never a deep one, was plentifully supplied with thick oozing mud and weeds of the thickest and rankest kind.

Mrs. Corcoran had never learned to swim, yet she floated.

It may be that her clothes kept her up; but people who knew her and were cognisant of her witch-like propensities would have remembered an old adage which states that the devil takes care of his own.

And really it seemed so.

There had been heavy rains, and the Fleet River was in a high state of turbulation.

Its pea-soup-like waters gurgled and boiled against its filthy banks, and round and round went Mrs. Corcoran, part and parcel of a heap of rubbish, which swirled round her and clung affectionately to her.

Mrs. Corcoran did not cry out or shriek for help as a drowning woman would have done.

As long as she floated she did not care, for it occurred to her mind that sooner or later she must be swept against one of the banks, and avoid the fate of sundry dead cats and dogs which were accompanying her on her way to the River Thames.

Fast and furious flowed the tide, and at last Mrs. Corcoran began to feel alarmed.

She was making her way fast towards the common sewer, and as she beheld its entrance gaping at her like a huge devouring mouth, she opened her own and gave vent to a terrific shriek.

It was heard as far as Ludgate-hill, and business people stopped and, wondering what it meant, looked askance at each other.

Another screech drew a crowd down to the river bank, and boy—all boys have keen eyes—

espied the old woman, who was now spinning round and round like a whirligig.

"There she goes," said the youth! "If she ain't saved, she'll be in the sewer in less than a minute. Hi! stop her. Ain't there a man among you?"

This query caused several gallant gentlemen to take off their coats, but they put them on again, and felt quite relieved when a sturdy bargeman appeared on the scene, and pushing everybody aside, prepared to rescue the old hag.

He did not stop to divest himself of a single garment, but wading boldly in, breasted the tide, and catching hold of Mrs. Corcoran's dress, hauled her ashore.

Then how the gallant gentlemen who had taken off their coats cheered.

Of course, each and everyone of them meant to have done exactly the same thing, only they were prevented.

Who, indeed, has a soul so base that he would not risk his life in the cause of lovely woman?

When Mrs. Corcoran was brought ashore, and laid limp and drenched upon the bank, she was surrounded by a large concourse of people, principally of the sterner sex.

Some of the young swells had expected to see a pretty girl, and all were ready, to see that she wanted for nothing, and to convey her to a place of shelter and comfort at a moment's notice.

Indeed, at least half-a-dozen hackney-coaches had been called, and squabbling had already commenced respecting who had the right to take charge of the lovely one in distress; but when Mrs. Corcoran's walnut-hued visage became visible the hackney-coachmen were left fareless, and to swear, for the young swells took to their heels.

There was not much to wonder at in this, and even the boy who had espied Mrs. Corcoran in the first instance gazed at her with an expression of disgust on his youthful features.

The bargeman, too, did not look very pleased, for he had expected something for his trouble, and did not now see his way very plainly how to get it.

Each moment the crowd became thinner, so did the hope of reward.

Mrs. Corcoran looked as poor as a church mouse, and nobody seemed to care how she got home or what became of her.

"You're a nice lot, certainly," she snarled. "You saw me before—you know you did."

"Well," said the bargeman, running his fingers through his damp hair, "if I ever pull another she-devil out of the water may I be drowned!"

At this juncture somebody suggested that society would be benefited by Mrs. Corcoran's return to the water, whereat the old hag picked herself up and glared defiance at the crowd.

"You are a parcel of well-dressed curs!" she said. "There is only one man among you, and he shall not go unrewarded. See here!"

Mrs. Corcoran made a sudden grab in the direction of her pocket.

It was hard to get at, as the folds of her dress clung tenaciously together, but at last she managed to get her hand in.

"If she gives you a shilling," said a fat man, grinning, "mind it is a good one."

"You go and snarl at your underpaid clerks, and leave my business alone," Mrs. Corcoran retorted.

This sharp rap over the knuckles caused a roar of laughter, and the fat man's face assumed the hue of a red-hot warming-pan.

"If I had my mind," he said, "I would have you sent to Bridewell, and well thrashed by the beadle."

"If I had my mind," said Mrs. Corcoran, "I would have you boiled down and sold for cheap candles."

There was another roar of laughter, and the corpulent one bounced off like a cannon-ball.

The bargeman expected nothing more substantial than a silver coin; but when Mrs. Corcoran dropped a guinea into the palm of his hand, he stared from it to its donor in mute astonishment.

"Now," said she, "perhaps you can take me to a place where I can go to bed while my clothes are dried. I'm just a little chilly, you know."

The bargeman grinned, and could not help admiring Mrs. Corcoran's pluck.

"Yes," he said. "Come with me; we have not far to go."

The crowd melted away, and the bargeman, escorting Mrs. Corcoran into Fleet-street, turned suddenly into a narrow street on the left hand side.

It was then, as now, called Water-lane, but its character has vastly changed.

In those days no police officer dared show his nose in the locality, and there the worst of criminals held the high revel unmolested.

Mrs. Corcoran bestowed a wink on herself.

She was perfectly aware of what sort of place she was being taken to; but she kept her own council, and pretended to be profoundly ignorant.

"Funny sort of place this," she said.

"Very; but very snug," the hangman replied, dryly.

"Lots of courts and alleys to dodge up and down of," the old hag said. "Dear me, I wonder the people who live here don't lose their way!"

"Most of the people who live here were born here," the man returned, "and it's just possible that they will die here, unless—"

"Unless what?"

"Oh! nothing."

"I suppose you were going to say that they would die here unless they died somewhere else?"

"Just so."

"Well," said Mrs. Corcoran, "one thing is plain. A man can only die once, even it it be at Tyburn—eh?

The man came to a standstill and stared hard at the crone.

"You speak like a woman who knows something of the world," he said.

"I know one thing," Mrs. Corcoran observed.

"What is that?"

"That you no more get your living as a bargeman than I do."

"Oh! indeed."

"Yes, indeed,'" Mrs. Corcoran resumed. "This place used to be called Alsatia in the days when the Mohawks used to wait upon the young gallants reeling home to the Temple or down Fleet-street after dinner."

"That's right."

"Well, then, don't attempt to deceive me," Mrs. Corcoran said. "This court leads into Bouverie-lane—that into Hanging Sword-alley. Oh! I know all about it."

"So it seems," the man growled. "Well, since you seem to know so much, I may as well tell you the truth. I do get my living at the water-side, but not as a bargeman."

"It is nothing to me," said Mrs. Corcoran. "I

thought I had better let you know that I am no greenhorn. I'll be bound that you know the Bull in Top Boots, in the Borough?"

"Of course I do."

"I have seen you there."

"You have! When?"

"Only a few nights ago," Mrs. Corcoran replied, with as pleasant a smile as she could summon on her face. "And it so happens that I know a little more."

"You know what?"

"What you brought there to dispose of, and what price you received for it."

"Hush!" said the man, glancing fearfully over his shoulder. "Even here I dare not have such things talked of aloud."

"Oh! the surgeon came for it and took it away," Mrs. Corcoran observed. "He said it was a fine subject, but—"

"Hold your tongue, will you!" the man said, turning fiercely upon Mrs. Corcoran. "Keep your mouth closed, or I'll—"

"You'll do nothing rash or stupid, I am sure," Mrs. Corcoran replied. "Dick Sleuth parted with me less than an hour ago, and it is more than probable that he has taken the precaution to follow me here."

"Why didn't you tell me before that you knew this gang?" the man demanded.

"Because, Sam Snatcher—"

"Ah! you know my name?"

"Of course I do."

"I wish I had left you in the river."

"I daresay you do," Mrs. Corcoran observed. "But how foolish you would have been to have done that. Sam Snatcher, if you had done your very best to make your fortune, you could not have done so good a turn for yourself as when you fished me out. Is this the house we are to stay at?"

"Yes," Sam Snatcher replied.

"I can't say that its appearance would recommend it to a lady of title," Mrs. Corcoran said.

As she spoke she glanced up at as ugly a house as was ever conceived in the mind of an architect, or put together by means of brick, mortar, and timber by a builder.

It was propped up against a sturdier house over the way, which seemed to resent the intrusion by leaning sulkily in a contrary direction.

A more evil-looking dwelling-place could not be imagined.

It was as black as if it had been erected since the day that soot was invented, and its windows, small and oddly shaped, looked as if they had been formed for villainous eyes to peer out of.

This uninviting domicile had a porch, the door-post of which was scrawled all over with odd kinds of marks, each of which had its particular meaning, and were closely scrutinised by the inhabitants of the salubrious locality as they slunk by to pass in and out of their dens.

Sam Snatcher, as Mrs. Corcoran's guide called himself, opened the door, and led the way into a close, stuffy hall, so dark that he had to call attention to some objects lying about the floor.

Mrs. Corcoran skipped with agility over a wooden bucket and sundry discarded saucepans, and groped her way up a staircase.

"There," said Snatcher, pushing open a door, "you can go in there. Chuck your clothes out, and Harriet shall dry them for you."

"Who's Harriet?"

"My wife."

Mrs. Corcoran was soon in bed, or, rather, an apology for one in the form of a dirty straw mattress and a heap of rags.

Most people would have gone to sleep under the circumstances, but the hag was too wise to do anything of the kind.

Slip-shod footsteps, which ceased outside the door, convinced her that Sam Snatcher's wife had removed the clothes, odoriferous with the perfumes of the Fleet River, and then Mrs. Corcoran began to think what she should do in case of a bother.

She had taken the precaution to remove the rest of the money and place it under her head, but otherwise she was in the power of the occupants of the house.

After holding her breath and listening for some time she thought she heard the sound of voices.

Mrs. Corcoran wrapped the ragged counterpane round her bony frame, and crawled softly to the door.

"Ah!" she muttered, "I was right. They are talking about me."

Yes; Mr. and Mrs. Snatcher were conversing, and what they said did not come pleasantly to Mrs. Corcoran's ears.

"She wouldn't fetch much, you see," Snatcher was saying, "and it would be a dangerous experiment anyhow, for she seems to be well acquainted with Dick Sleuth and the whole of the gang who make the Bull in Top Boots their headquarters."

"That may be," replied his amiable wife; "but I think otherwise."

"Well, what do you think?"

"That they would be glad enough to get rid of the old woman."

"Would they?" Mrs. Corcoran snarled under her breath. "Ho! ho! This is the way the wind blows. But I must listen."

"She ain't a thing of beauty," Snatcher said, laughing hoarsely. "She's as much like a mummy as ever I saw anything in my life; but one thing is clear—she has money to spend, and it must have been given to her for some purpose. Go to her, Harriet, and see if you can worm out any of her secrets."

"I will after she has rested awhile," Mrs. Snatcher replied.

"You'll have to be a clever woman to do that," Mrs. Corcoran muttered under her breath. "So I'm like a mummy—I shouldn't fetch much! Ha! ha! Mr. Snatcher, if I don't turn the tables upon you presently, you may call me a fool for my pains."

With this Mrs. Corcoran slipped back into bed, and closing her eyes, pretended to snore most prodigiously.

Like the fox in the fable, she kept one eye open, and directed that towards the door, which after a time opened slowly and admitted Mrs. Snatcher.

Harriet, the wife of Sam, Snatcher by name and snatcher by nature, for the ruffian was nothing more nor less than a stealer of bodies, was a most miserable-looking woman.

It was not her poor threadbare gown that gave her this appearance.

It was her face, sallow, wrinkled, and woebegone.

She had acquired a nervous habit of jerking her head over her shoulder, as if she expected to find that she was being followed by somebody, and when she walked she lurched forward as if ready to run away at a moment's notice.

"She's asleep," she muttered, as she looked at

Mrs. Corcoran. "I wonder if I ought to wake her?"

"Oh! no, my dear, she isn't," Mrs. Corcoran said under her breath. "She's quite wide awake enough to upset any little plan you may have in your mind."

Then she yawned and opened her ghoulish eyes.

"Ah!" she said, as if surprised at not finding herself alone in the room, "Mrs. Snatcher, I suppose?"

"Yes; and I am come to know if I can do anything for you."

"Nothing, thank'ee, deary," Mrs. Corcoran said. "I'm almost as comfortable as if I was at home."

"I am glad to hear that," Mrs. Snatcher replied, as she sat down upon a rickety chair. "Dear me! my husband and I have been talking about the wonderful escape you had."

"To say the least, it wasn't very pleasant," Mrs. Corcoran replied.

"Did you fall into the Fleet River accidentally?"

"No," the old hag replied. "I was pitched in it in a friendly kind of way."

"In a friendly kind of way?"

"Well, you see," said Mrs. Corcoran, "there were certain troublesome people after me, and my friend, Dick Sleuth—your husband knows him very well, and what a demon he is when he makes up his mind to do anything—just gave me a lift over a wall, and splash I went into the river."

Mrs. Snatcher twitched her head over her shoulder for the fortieth time since she had entered the room.

"Bless me!" she exclaimed, holding up her hands. "How lucky it was that my husband happened to be about at the time. I came to thank you for giving him a guinea, it was so kind of you. Now ain't there anything I can do for you?"

"Yes."

"What is it?"

"Dry my clothes as quick as possible, for I want to be up and away," said Mrs. Corcoran.

These words were uttered more in the tone of a command than of a request.

Harriet Snatcher did not seem to appreciate the way in which they had been delivered.

"But you must feel very weak," she urged. "Won't you eat or drink something if I fetch it for you?"

"No," Mrs. Corcoran responded. "I have paid your husband well, and I will pay you too, if you do as I wish."

"Very well," Harriet Snatcher returned; "you shall have your clothes in a quarter of an hour."

A very long quarter of an hour passed away, and Mrs. Corcoran began to feel uneasy.

She had strong suspicions of foul play, and they increased as the minutes flew by and nobody came near her.

She entertained some notions of converting the ragged bed-clothes into apparel, but for once she was outwitted.

She could do nothing without her garments, and so she lay, fuming and fretting, until fully an hour had passed away.

At last she could bear the suspense no longer.

Wrapping herself in the counterpane, she went to the door, and flinging it open noisily, screeched down the staircase.

"How long are you going to keep me here?" she yelled. "If you attempt to play the fool with me, you'll live to rue it."

No answer came from the region below, and after bellowing until she was hoarse, Mrs. Corcoran came to the conclusion that she was alone in the house.

"Those devils are up to some mischief," she said, clenching her hands and setting her teeth. "A nice predicament I am in, certainly. What if Snatcher has gone in search of Dick Sleuth and found him? What if they have connived to put me out of the way? Sleuth knows that I can hang him and his pals whenever I choose, and he might not shed many tears if he heard that I was under the ground."

Mrs. Corcoran ceased speaking, thinking that she heard a noise as of somebody moving about in one of the lower rooms; but it was nothing more than an echo.

"Snatcher will not dare attempt any act of violence until he sees Sleuth," she resumed, "and it is merely a toss-up of a coin what he will say. What am I to do? Come—come; I must keep my head about me."

Glancing at the window, Mrs. Corcoran saw that the blind, yellow with age, was pinned to the roller.

Removing some of the pins, she used them to hold the counterpane close about her, and then moved towards the landing.

But another thought flashed into her brain, and she turned back.

She wanted some kind of weapon to defend herself with in case of sudden surprise or attack.

There was nothing, as far as she could see, likely to suit her purpose, save the rickety chair.

In a moment she had made up her mind what to do.

She broke off one of the legs of the chair as noiselessly as possible, and weighed it in her hand.

It was a heavy piece of old-fashioned, twisted mahogany, and if used with a steady hand, would knock the sense out of a man's head at a single blow.

The hag now felt that she could give blow for blow, and began to descend the staircase.

Light and skinny as she was, it creaked and groaned under her weight.

At last Mrs. Corcoran reached the hall and passed unmolested up to the door leading into the open air.

The door had been made fast, and defied all her efforts to open it.

"I thought as much," the crone said. "There's a nice consultation going on about me somewhere. I shouldn't wonder if Sam Snatcher and his precious wife have taken themselves to the Bull in Top Boots. If there's a way out of this murderous hole I'll find it."

Mrs. Corcoran then retraced her steps and tried door after door.

All were locked save one that led to the cellar, and this would have been so but for the simple fact that it boasted of no lock at all.

It was bolted at the top, and a slip of wood had been driven between the door and the woodwork to show whether it had been tampered with.

"Very clever, I daresay," Mrs. Corcoran chuckled; "but it so happens that I am wide awake to all tricks of this kind. I wonder what I shall find down here. A grating leading into the street, perhaps, or it is just likely that I may fall upon some of Sam Snatcher's secrets.

What Mrs. Corcoran saw and what she found must be reserved for another chapter, as other characters claim our attention just now.

---

## CHAPTER CXXXI.

### SIR ROLAND ASHTON GOES OUT TO SEA AND MEETS WITH AN ACCIDENT.

WHEN Richard Slyme and Sir Roland Ashton ran against each other in the wood it was so dark that recognition was impossible.

Both suspected that robbery was the other's object, and they clutched each other with the ferocity of desperate men.

Sir Roland had not long recovered sensibility, and he went under, Slyme falling heavily upon him.

The baronet heard a grating sound.

Richard Slyme was opening his knife with his teeth.

"Hold your hand!" Sir Roland cried. "Would you murder me?"

"Why not?" Slyme hissed. "I suspect it was your intention to rob me, and murder me into the bargain."

"No—no!" Sir Roland cried, in a despairing tone of voice; "you wrong me. I am a gentleman by birth—I am a baronet."

"Then," said Slyme, relaxing his hold, "I beg your honour's pardon. Oh! what I have suffered. I have been robbed and shamefully maltreated."

"By whom?"

"By a fiend," Slyme gasped. "A fiend in white, with wings, horns upon his head, and masses of tawny hair hanging about his shoulders. Ugh! the very thought of him makes me shudder."

"Listen, my friend," said Sir Roland. "This same fiend has tortured and robbed me. Overcome by fatigue, I fell into a doze under a tree. This wretch, the self-same devil haunting the earth, came suddenly upon me, half-strangled me with a rope, and then emptied my pockets."

Slyme winced a little when Sir Roland Ashton spoke of being robbed, but he spoke calmly.

"How did you escape?" he asked.

"I know not," Sir Roland replied. "I was either cut down or the rope broke. I must have lain for hours bereft of sense, and the agony of returning consciousness was far greater than the pain first inflicted."

"Well," said Slyme, after a pause, "what say you? We are brothers in distress. Shall we keep each other's company until we are out of this wood, at least?"

"I was about to put the same question to you," said Sir Roland.

"Then you agree?"

"Yes; with all my heart."

"I am a poor pedlar," Slyme said, in a whining tone of voice; "and before I was robbed by the fiend there was a tinder-box and steel in my pack."

"It may have been left," Sir Roland said; "but will it be safe to travel with a light?"

"It will be much safer than stumbling about in the dark," Slyme returned.

As he spoke he removed the pack from his back, and, falling on his knees, began fumbling about the much-lightened receptacle of his wares, which he carried as a blind to his real business.

"Here it is!" he said. "Gather up an armful of dry brushwood and twist it into a torch. I am as blind as a bat, and shall dash my head against a tree presently."

Sir Roland Ashton did as he was requested, and then Slyme went to work with flint and steel.

Presently the tinder caught, and in another moment the torch was alight.

Now both men looked at each other in silence.

"I have seen you somewhere," Slyme said.

"Very likely," Sir Roland replied. "I have travelled through most parts of the country."

"Yes—yes; but I mean in London," Slyme said, pressing his hand to his wrinkled brow, as if endeavouring to recall some circumstance. "Was it in the Old Mint? Yes, I am sure it was in the Old Mint. You are the man who used to have dealings with Gedge Foote."

"You make a mistake, my honest friend."

"Oh! no, I do not," said Richard Slyme, recoiling a few steps on his heels. "I know very well what I am talking about, and, what is more, I never forget a face after I have once looked into it steadily."

"Well," said Sir Roland, forcing a laugh to his lips, "if you have seen me in the Old Mint? Take it for granted that I have had dealings with a man named Gedge Foote—what then?"

"Gedge Foote was cruelly murdered."

"Ha! you surprise and alarm me."

"Do I?" said Slyme, with a touch of sarcasm in his voice. "There are many people who lay the deed to your charge."

"Most people are liars," Sir Roland said.

"I know that," Slyme returned. "Let a man be in want of money, what won't he say or do to get it? But about my friend, Gedge Foote?"

"I see that you are determined to make me angry," Sir Roland said. "The only way that I injured the man you speak of was to pay him thousands of pounds in interest."

"Did you, though?" Slyme said, smacking his lips. "Ah! such customers as you, Sir Roland, are very rare. Well—well, Gedge Foote is dead and gone, and I don't see that it matters much to me how he died. To say the best of him he was a hard, flinty-hearted man."

"So," said Sir Roland, anxious to change the subject, "you lend money?"

"I used to do a little in that way," Slyme replied, evasively.

"But you have given it up?"

"I didn't say that," Slyme said, with a hollow groan, which he fetched up from the depths of his chest. "But think how I have been robbed to-day—think how I have been robbed!"

Sir Roland Ashton slapped the old miser encouragingly on the shoulder.

"Cheer up," he said; "you must not think of it. Go to work and make more money."

"I would if I could, but I don't see my way clear to do so," Richard Slyme moaned. "A thousand pounds gone in a moment! Think of it if you can. Put yourself in my place, and—"

Mr. Slyme's feelings overcame him and he could say no more.

Only inarticulate groans and mutterings came from his lips, and Sir Roland deemed it wise to say no more at present with regard to the money-lending business.

But the conversation was resumed when they had passed out of the wood and entered a road white and plain, even in the darkness of the night.

"What you said has set me thinking," Sir Roland remarked, "I am a man of business, and

I am sure that you are one also. What would you say if I were to ask you to lend me five hundred pounds on my note of hand?"

"I should say No," Richard Slyme replied, with a most determined shake of the head.

"Well, that's honest, at all events," Sir Roland said, with another forced laugh. "But what if I could place good securities in your hands—would you say No then?"

"No."

"You mean that you would lend me the money?"

"Yes; if we could agree about terms."

"Oh!" said Sir Roland, "I don't think that terms would stand in the way. But I must be careful how I talk to you. Ha! ha! I remember that you said a man will say anything and do anything to get money."

"So he will," Slyme growled.

"Well, then," said Sir Roland, "I am going to prove an exception to the rule. Five hundred pounds I want, and if you don't care to lend me the money at the rate of twenty-five per cent. somebody else will jump at the chance, so there is an end of the matter."

"Just so," said Richard Slyme, in a meditative tone of voice. "Well, you needn't put yourself out of temper about the matter. Perhaps you wouldn't mind telling me the nature of the securities you wish to offer?"

"They relate to my family estates," Sir Roland replied.

"Humph!" Slyme grunted. "Have you got them about you?"

"Before I answer that question I must ask another," Sir Roland rejoined. "If the securities are satisfactory, are you in a position to lend me the money?"

"Well, yes."

"At once?"

"You are in a mighty hurry, Sir Roland."

"I don't mean to-night," Sir Roland said. "Supposing you take me home, and I showed you the deeds. Well, in case that you agreed to my terms, you could let me have the money when you found that everything was satisfactory—say within a week?"

"I don't suppose that my inquiries would extend over that period," Slyme returned, a little hesitatingly. "Well, I live at Climping. I don't keep any money there, you know—not a farthing—but we could arrange the business there just as well as anywhere else."

"Certainly," said Sir Roland. "Climping did you say? How far are we away from the place?"

"Not more than two miles if we cross the fields there by the road."

"I'll leave it all to you," Sir Roland said.

Not much more was spoken during the rest of the journey, which was completed within an hour, and Richard Slyme, pointing to a hut, said, with a chuckle—

"That's my country retreat."

"It is snug enough, at all events," Sir Roland said.

"Nobody would think—"

"Nobody would think what?" Sir Roland queried, finding that Slyme had ceased speaking and looked as if he had startled himself by speaking at all.

"That a man of business habits would care to live there," he said.

"Oh! that is your business," the baronet returned. "Come; let us get inside. The air is chilly, and the dew on the grass has made my feet damp."

Richard Slyme took a huge key from his pocket, but did not seem to be in any hurry to approach the door.

"What are you waiting for?" demanded Sir Roland, who had been trying to curb his temper, but was fast losing it. "If it is your idea to play the fool with me, I will wish you good-night."

"You are a gentleman by birth, and one of honour, I suppose," Slyme said. "I want you to make me a solemn promise and keep it?"

"If it is one that can be kept, you may trust me with confidence."

"Whether this transaction comes to anything, or whether it does not," said Richard Slyme, "swear to me on your word of honour that you will never tell a living soul that you have seen me to-night or been to my place."

"There are two promises, but they are easy ones to keep," Sir Roland said. "I swear."

"On your word of honour?"

"On my word of honour," Sir Roland said, placing his hand upon the region of his heart.

Richard Slyme then opened the door, and after fumbling about for some time took down a lantern which hung suspended on a hook.

"This way," he said; "here is my sitting-room. "You will not find it to your taste, I daresay, but it is good enough for me."

The apartment was such as a decent-minded man would not have thrust a pig into, but Sir Roland Ashton made no complaint.

It was not his policy to do so.

He was too much occupied with his thoughts to pay attention to trifles.

He drew a three-legged stool up to the table and sat down.

Richard Slyme, blearing and blinking cunningly, faced him.

"Now, Sir Roland," he said, "be good enough to let me look at the documents you spoke of."

"Presently," the baronet replied. "I am so tired that I would fain rest awhile."

"You can rest while I run my eye through them," Slyme said.

As he spoke he placed the lantern in the centre of the table.

It was an old-fashioned one, of heavy manufacture, with horn windows and an iron ring at the top.

Sir Roland, after a moment's pause, placed his hand in his breast-pocket, and drew out a number of papers.

"These are the ones, I think," he said, rising, and pulling the lantern closer to him.

As Richard Slyme stretched out his greedy fingers to clutch the papers, Sir Roland seized the edge of the table, and overturning it, hurled it upon the miser.

It was the work of a moment.

Before Slyme could leap to his feet or utter a cry for help, Sir Roland Ashton was upon him, his hands on the usurer's throat and his knee on his chest.

"This is my security," Sir Roland hissed. "I want money, and I will have it. You keep your hoard here, but I will not trouble to ask you where it is. I will find it for myself."

Slyme uttered a gasping cry, and struggled frantically to force back the murderous fingers which were throttling him.

In vain were his efforts.

Presently he lay still.

His limbs began to stiffen in death, and then Sir Roland rose and surveyed the body of his victim as well as the darkness of the place would allow him.

The dawn of day was stealing fitfully across the sky.

Sir Roland crossed the room, and threw back the window-shutters with a trembling hand.

Then once more he turned his blood-shot eyes on the remains of Richard Slyme.

"The light will soon strengthen," he muttered, "and then there will be light enough for me to see. Is he dead? I thought I saw his eyes open. Did he move? No! no! It was but fancy."

The curtain of night was rolling back fast, and then Sir Roland commenced his search in the awful presence of death.

He found nothing in the room marked by his crime, and rushed into the next.

Here, like the other, was dust, dirt, filth, and abomination.

Sir Roland threw the mattress from the bed, and ripped it open.

Something fell heavily upon the floor, and he pounced, hawk-like, upon the object.

It was a leather bag, carefully tied and sealed at the top.

"At last!" Sir Roland cried. "At last! But there must be more. I need not hurry, for who will suspect what has taken place in this den?"

Sir Roland shook the straw from the mattress, and then examined the covering.

"I thought as much," he said. "The cunning old fox took care to sew up the bank-notes. Here they are—so crisp, so musical! Richard Slyme, I fear those securities will not be of much use to you now."

Hastily stowing away the proceeds of his horrible crime, Sir Roland returned to the front room.

He did not look at the body now, but stood with his back towards it.

"I had better leave the shutter open," he said. "If it is closed passers-by will wonder at it, and perhaps come to ascertain what has happened. Ha! the key—I must have the key and lock the front door."

He had set himself an awful task.

To get at the key he was compelled to search the dead man; but he did it, and then, white and livid to the lips, hurried from the house.

Having locked the door and made sure that it was fast, he hurled the key into a pond, and then, walking down the road, struck into a bye-way until he came to a stile.

This he mounted, and, sitting on the top bar, began to reflect on the best course for him to pursue.

He would not go to London, for, large as the place was, every inch of it was fraught with danger for him.

What, then, should he do?

His blood-stained hands had possessed him of a considerable amount of wealth.

How much he did not know, for he did not dare to stop to count the miser's hoard.

"Why not go abroad while I have the chance?" he muttered. "I can make my way to the coast before Slyme's body is discovered and a hue and cry raised. Why not go abroad, and rid myself for ever of that fiend, Spring-Heeled Jack?"

The idea seemed so feasible that Sir Roland jumped down from the stile and struck across the footpaths leading through verdant meadows and cornfields.

The bright—the bright and glorious sun was rising grandly in the sky, chasing away the last lingering clouds of night.

The golden corn waved a welcome to the resplendent orb, the birds swelled their throats in joyous song, and all nature awoke to life and beauty.

What a contrast there was, even to the smallest insect crawling upon the leaf, to the dark-browed and darker-hearted man, who strode along with all his evil passions roused, and yet startled at the echo of his own footsteps!

How like a cur and coward he was!

What good could come of money gained as he had gained it?

The curse of Cain was upon his brow, the hand of every honest man was against his, and his against every man.

The footpaths came to an end, and then Sir Roland found himself upon a broad, straight road.

To the west lay London; to the east, the wild coast.

What cared he how wild and rugged it was, so that he reached the ocean, and found the means of crossing it?

He was as ignorant as a babe of the locality; but if he kept straight on—yes, if he kept straight on—his feet must take him to the sea-shore at last.

He had, however, not gone very far, when he heard the rumbling of wheels behind him.

Looking round, he saw an old-fashioned, tilted cart, such as travelled from village to village delivering goods and occasionally picking up a passenger.

Such lumbering, jolting vehicles may be seen even in these days; but the steam-horse, tearing on its iron road, and starting on fresh journeys nearly every day, will soon leave the carrier's cart, and its five-mile-an-hour steed, things of the past.

Sir Roland waited until the rickety, creaking thing on wheels came up to him, and then, assuming a cheery voice, he hailed the driver.

The man, who was fast asleep, and had left the road to his horse, woke up and rubbed his eyes.

He was not accustomed to be hailed at so early an hour in the morning, and Sir Roland's appearance startled him in no small degree.

At a first glance he took the baronet to be a highwayman, and swinging his whip round, shook the butt-end threateningly.

Sir Roland Ashton laughed.

"My friend," he said, "I am no footpad or common thief. Come, wake up thoroughly, and you will see that I don't look like one of the light-fingered gentry."

"Well, I s'pose I ought to beg your pardon, sir," the carrier said; "but a man on the road has to be very careful. He comes across some odd characters, I can tell you."

"I daresay he does," Sir Roland returned. "Where are you bound for?"

"Alburgh-on-Sea."

"Have you room for a passenger?"

"Plenty," the carrier replied, "for there's only me and my dog in the cart."

"Your dog?" said Sir Roland, smiling. "I hope he is not given to biting?"

"He never bites the people I call my friends."

the carrier replied, significantly. "Ponto, come here, lad."

A huge shaggy dog, with fragments of straw all over his coat, appeared, and growled as he caught sight of Sir Roland.

"What is he making that noise for?" the baronet demanded.

"That's only his playful way of telling people to mind what they are about," the carrier said, grinning. "He will be quiet enough when I tell him to lie down. Did you want a lift, sir?"

"Yes."

"Where to?"

"Why, strangely enough, I thought about making my way to Alburgh-on-Sea, where I expect to find a very old friend," Sir Roland replied. "I started at daybreak, hoping to meet the early coach."

"You must be a stranger not to know that no coach will pass this way before noon," said the carrier.

"Then I may as well travel with you," Sir Roland replied. "Come, I will make a bargain with you. If you reach Alburgh-on-Sea before the sun goes down I will give you a couple of guineas."

"It's a mighty long way, and I shall have to change horses three times, but I will do my best," the carrier replied. "I think I can do it, as I have very few parcels to deliver. Lie down, Ponto—lie down!"

But Ponto continued to growl, much to Sir Roland's disgust and rage.

Even when the baronet had climbed into the cart and taken up a place at the back part of it, the dog continued to snarl and show his teeth so viciously that the carrier found it necessary to quiet him with an application of the whip.

It would be tedious to follow Sir Roland all through the long, dreary journey.

The carrier was true to his word.

He drove into Alburgh-on-Sea ere the sun had gone to rest below the horizon, and Sir Roland, having paid the man even more liberally than he had promised, dismissed him, and turning a deaf ear to his thanks, walked swiftly away.

Few men knew how to make use of time better than Sir Roland Ashton, and he at once proceeded to carry out his idea of going abroad by walking into an inn used by sea-faring men and enquiring whether there was a sailing vessel in the harbour bound either for Holland or Belgium.

He was told that a brig lay in the river, but could not sail until the morning, as the tide would not serve.

Sir Roland said, smilingly, that he was not in so much a hurry to part with his native country, and throwing down a guinea, he asked the men assembled to drink.

"I will go and interview the captain of the brig at once," he said. "He may not be inclined to take me as a passenger, so in that case I should have to look out for another vessel."

He had passed out of the hostelry and walked a few paces when he heard heavy, lumbering footsteps coming after him.

Sir Roland thought it best to stop, and turning, he confronted a broad-shouldered, strapping fellow, who, pulling a greasy lock of hair, hitched up his trousers and kicked up his right heel in the fashion then in vogue with sailors.

"Begging your pardon, sir," the man said, "did I understand as you wanted to make *for* Holland?"

"Yes, you did, my friend."

"Well, sir," the man continued, "it struck me when you spoke that you would rather start to-night than in the morning."

"That may be, and is, the case, as I have very important business to transact abroad," Sir Roland replied.

"I s'pose you ain't particular as to what sort of vessel as you travels on board of?"

"Not the slightest."

"Then," said the sailor, extending his arm towards the ocean, "you see that vessel?"

"Yes."

"She's at anchor now," the man said; "but as soon as the moon rises she'll be off to the coast of Holland. Say the word and I'll put you on board. Give me what you like, and you can settle the rest with the captain. I know what things are, I do."

"Well," said Sir Roland, "I may as well tell you the truth. I am in danger of being arrested by sheriff's officers, and, as I do not see my way clear to pay just at present, I may as well take my ease on the Continent for a time."

"That's exactly what I thought," said the sailor, grinning. "I've met some few gentlemen like you in my time. Say the word and you'll be in Holland some time to-morrow, and no questions asked."

"Ha!" Sir Roland said. "I should imagine that yonder vessel knows the smell of schnapps—eh, my friend?"

"I should think she did," the sailor replied. "Well, shall I have my boat ready by nine o'clock? I've got a way of signalling to the captain, and I'll let him know that we are coming on board."

"Very well," said Sir Roland. "I'll trust my life and safety in your hands, and give you a guinea for your pains, as you say I can make terms with the captain."

"You'll find that he will not hurt you," the sailor said. "At nine o'clock, if you go down yonder flight of stairs, I shall be there waiting for you."

They then parted, Sir Roland wandering about, listening to the rush of the ebb tide and the hoarse roar of the waves as they dashed sullenly on the rocky shore.

On certain places the cliffs seemed to tower nearly to the sky, which was now growing dark under heavy banks of clouds.

"What a splendid haunt for smugglers!" Sir Roland said, as he surveyed the lonely scene. "Ah! sheet lightning in the distance. It promises to be a rough night. So much the better; our little vessel will escape observation all the easier."

He did not return to the inn for fear the men there should question him as to whether he had taken a berth on board the brig.

He lingered about, walking up and down in secluded places, marking how the sea rose angrily, and how the lightning increased in vividness.

At last the time drew near for his departure, and Sir Roland moved towards the flight of steps pointed out by the sailor.

It was terribly dark now, and he walked with caution, for fear of slipping down some unseen place.

Suddenly he saw a gleam of light and heard a voice.

"Keep straight on," it said; "the boat is ready for you."

# SPRING-HEELED JACK,

## THE TERROR OF LONDON.

"HOLD, MONSTERS IN THE FORM OF MEN!" SPRING-HEELED JACK CRIED.

No. 37.

At this moment the thunder began to roll and rumble in the distance, and Sir Roland, anxious to seek the shelter of the vessel, hastened to descend the stairs.

No sooner had he stepped into the boat than it shot out into the stream.

"Steady—steady!" he said.

There was no reply, and then Sir Roland Ashton found to his horror that he was alone.

"Treachery—treachery!" he cried out. "Help! A hundred guineas to the man who will take me ashore."

No welcome voice replied to his.

The tide had turned now, and a side current swept the boat along at a furious rate.

Sir Roland Ashton seized the oars, and pulled with the strength of despair and agony.

But the tide, battling fiercely with the storm-laden wind, drove him along at a furious pace, and soon he knew, by the violent motion of the frail craft, that he was out at sea.

The baronet knew it was useless to cry out or shriek for help now.

He also knew that nothing short of a miracle could save him, unless he could reach the vessel, whose black hull was sometimes made visible by the quivering lightning.

He kept the boat's prow headed to the waves; but the billows, breaking over him, drenched him to the skin, and filled his heart with a terror defying all description.

Billow after billow dashed over him.

And then, sick at heart, he pulled the boat round and made for the shore, heedless of the consequences.

The mighty waves swept him onwards to destruction.

The boat leaped and danced like a thing of life, and then suddenly collapsed and crushed up, like a nutshell under the hoof of a horse.

Sir Roland gave himself up for lost.

Buffeted, hurled hither and thither by the foamed-capped, vengeful waves, he, nevertheless, caught sight of the rocks and cliffs every now and then.

Drowning men will clutch at straws, and Sir Roland battled for life.

He was a good swimmer, but of what avail could be the strength of a single man in such a scene of commotion?

He knew it.

He knew he was doomed, and one great despairing cry rose to his lips.

Then came another, scarcely less horrible, when he saw the form of Spring-Heeled Jack emerge from the mouth of a cave and dash boldly into the surging, seething waters.

Sir Roland Ashton felt a hand of iron upon his collar, and became conscious that the creature he most hated had saved his life.

Then a volume of water rushed down his throat, and he knew no more.

## CHAPTER CXXXII.

### IN WHICH WE TAKE A PEEP AT OLD FRIENDS.

THERE is a ridiculous story told of an old woman who was tossed up in a blanket as high as the moon, but the author whose fertile imagination carried him and the old woman so far never ventured to give an account how his heroine got back to earth again.

Perhaps she slid down comfortably on a moonbeam, or it may be she married the man who gathered sticks on a Sunday, and is soothing the pains of his everlasting penance in a wifely fashion.

To a certain extent we may compare the woes of Catchpole and Grabham to this old lady.

They truly had been tossed high and low, and probably they would have been much relieved had they found their way into the orb which sails so grandly across the sky when the sun has deserted the earth.

Grabham's notion of going back to Bow-street was, to say the least, a bold and novel one.

He and Catchpole, the partner of his many sorrows and few joys, had been ignominiously dismissed the force for bad conduct and neglect of duty, and it was hardly to be expected that the superior officer, Mr. Nabbitt, would receive them with open arms.

Catchpole shook his head, and pumped up one of his far-famed groans.

"Nabbitt would only laugh, or chuck a pail of water over us," he said. "I don't see the good of making fools of ourselves."

"Then what are we to make of ourselves unless we get something to do?" Grabham gasped. "We can't live on grass and nettles, can we? We can't eat stones, can we?"

"I didn't say we could," Catchpole remarked, mildly. "I never went for to think such a thing."

"I wish you would think of something which would put a few shillings into our pockets," Grabham said, savagely. "Where's the use of shaking your head and groaning like a sign-board in a gale of wind? Haven't you got a grain of sense left in that fat head of yours?"

Mr Catchpole pressed his hands to his head, which was not only fat but hot now.

"I don't know," he said, feebly. "Everything seems to be upside down. The world ain't what it used to be, Grabby."

"Don't Grabby me, you idiot! I'm going straight to Bow-street, and you can do as you please."

So saying, Grabham turned in a huff upon his heel, and marched away with his button-shaped nose in the air.

"Stop! stop!" Catchpole cried, in a kind of shriek. "Don't leave me in this murderous neighbourhood. I'd rather have another up-and-downer with Spring-Heeled Jack than be left alone in this place for twenty minutes."

"I've done with you," Grabham replied, haughtily. "I've done with you for hever!"

Catchpole shed maudling tears.

"It's enough to break a man's 'art when the friend of his youth turns upon him," he said. "Fare thee well, Grabham! I daresay you'll be called at the inquest."

"What inquest?"

"The inquest on my body," Catchpole said, with a horrible light glaring out of his eyes. "What is life to me? Why should I wish to live when there ain't nothing to live for? Fare thee well, I say again, for in less than an hour I shall be as dead as a doornail.

Grabham scratched his head.

He did not know exactly what to make of this declaration on the part of Catchpole, who for once looked as if he really meant what he said.

"Then why don't you act like a reasonable man?" he grunted. "Why don't you be ruled by me? What harm can there be in seeing Nabbitt? He can't kill us, you know."

"But he knows how to kick mortally hard,"

Catchpole said. "It will be a long time before I forget—"

"Well, you hadn't much to grumble at," Grabham interposed. "It was I that got the force of his boot, and it lifted me a couple of feet into the air, I'll swear. Catchpole, much as you make me savage, I can't bear to see you miserable, so just take my arm, and we'll triumph yet."

Catchpole forced a smile to his lips, but there was no lightness in his heart.

"I'll take your advice," he said.

"There's a good fellow," Grabham returned.

It took them some long time to reach Bow-street, and when they did, they found the thoroughfare blocked up by an excited mob.

In the midst of the crowd was Nabbitt and a constable hanging on to a brutal-looking fellow, and endeavouring to force him into the office, an attempt which the prisoner's friends had determined to thwart.

Nabbitt's hat was off, his coat was torn, and one of his eyes wore the first signs of a promising black eye.

The constable was, if possible, in a worse plight, for a stone had struck him on the head, and the wound was bleeding profusely.

Grabham saw the very opportunity he desired in a moment.

"Come on, Catchpole," he shouted. "Now is our chance."

"Yes; a chance to get a broken head and a couple of black eyes," said Catchpole.

"You fool!" Grabham cried. "Don't you see if we help Nabbitt now he may be inclined to do us a good turn? Come on; use your fists and shoulders against these warmints, and we are as good as in the force again."

So saying, Grabham rushed boldly into the crowd.

He hit a man who was doing nothing more than looking on a staggering blow under the ear, and floored him so completely, that he went down like a ninepin, and was trampled on by half-a-dozen roughs.

Catchpole followed up this victory by knocking an old woman down, and elbowing a fat man in the waistcoat.

This new force in Nabbitt's favour turned the tide of the battle.

The mob hesitated, and then gave way.

Some fled, thinking that at least a dozen constables had arrived on the scene, and Nabbitt and the constables dragged their prisoner into the station, and bundled him into a cell with as little ceremony as they would have handled a sack of coals.

At first Nabbitt did not recognise the men who had rendered him such valuable help, but when Catchpole and Grabham presented themselves, his heart smote him.

Nabbitt was a man of violent temper, but he was just in many respects.

"So," he said, "you have come back?"

"We happened to be passing this way, sir," Grabham said, meekly; "and seeing as how you were hard pressed, we thought it our duty to lend you a hand."

"It is a pity that you forgot yourselves on a former occasion," Nabbitt said. "You might have become excellent members of the force."

"Men do forget themselves at times," Catchpole chimed in. "Take us back, Mr. Nabbitt. You can if you like."

"Well, well," muttered Nabbitt, thoughtfully; "I suppose that one good turn deserves another."

"We'll never offend again," Grabham said. "Please don't be hard on us!"

"I will look over your misconduct this time," the superior officer returned. "Go home and return in an hour's time. I'll send to the stores for new uniforms, and I hope that you will never disgrace them again."

Catchpole and Grabham could have danced for very joy.

"Thank you, sir; oh! thank you," Grabham exclaimed, clasping his hands. "We may have been foolish, but we have been very unfortunate. I suppose you couldn't see your way clear, sir, to lend us half-a-crown a-piece?"

Mr. Nabbitt pulled a long face as he thrust his finger and thumb into his waistcoat-pocket.

"Here's the money," he said, with a grunt; "but I suppose the only use you will make of it will be to get drunk."

"No, sir, no," Catchpole said. "What we want is wittles. If you only knew what we have been through with since we were here, you—"

Grabham silenced him with a dig in the ribs which knocked the breath out of his body.

"Go away now," said Nabbitt; "come here in an hour's time, as I said before, and then, when you are fitted for duty again, I will grant you leave for the rest of the day."

Catchpole and Grabham left Bow-street Police Office smiling all over their faces.

They had travelled down a long lane, but the turning had come at last.

"Catchpole, my boy," said Grabham, "we shall have our revenge yet. I gave you one in the ribs because I did not want you to say anything about Daddy Muckrum and the crew in Buckler's-rents. When we are fully established, we'll take some other men there, and bust up that crib."

"Yes," said Catchpole, growing suddenly valiant under the stroke of good fortune; "there's a heap of people we have to settle with. There's that lot at the Bull in Top Boots, Mrs. Corcoran, Jacob Butler, and Sir Roland Ashton, if we happen to fall across him."

"True," Grabham said, turning the half-crown he had borrowed between his finger and thumb. "What do you say to just one drink?"

"Not until we have made all right at Bow-street," Catchpole said. "One drink leads to another. It is the first drink that makes a man drunk."

"How do you make that out?"

"Because if he didn't take a first drink, he couldn't begin with a second, and, consequently, wouldn't get drunk at all."

"There's sound sense in that," Grabham said; "it's a sentiment as does you credit. Perhaps you are right. We will wait until we have got into our new uniforms, and then there won't be any harm in having a pint of nut brown ale or so."

"Not a bit," Catchpole replied. "The thought of it makes me thirsty; but I will sacrifice my feelings to the cause of duty."

Having delivered himself of this beautiful sentiment, Catchpole wrung Grabham's hand, and parted affectionately with him.

In less than an hour they met again, and Catchpole, who had kept his word and was as sober as a judge, noticed, to his grief and pain, that there was a wild expression in Grabham's eyes, and a tendency about his knees to give way under the weight of his body.

"This is sad—very sad," he said. "Oh!

Grabham, I am afraid that you have used that half-crown to base purposes."

"The man who bullies me," Grabham replied, shutting one eye, and trying to look angry out of the other, "will get his head punched. I wouldn't stand any cheek even from Nabbitt."

Catchpole, overcome with horror, started back aghast.

"You can't go to Bow-street in this awful state," he gasped.

"I'll go to Bow-street in any state I like," Grabham declared, lurching forward.

"Don't talk so stupidly," Catchpole groaned. "Here's a street pump; let me cool your head."

Something like a flash of reason dawned into Grabham's brain.

"Well," he said, "I confess I am a bit top-heavy. Pump away; but mind you don't wet my clothes, or there'll be a jolly row."

Mr. Grabham was certainly what sailors term "three sheets in the wind," and on endeavouring to fix himself in a convenient attitude under the spout of the pump his foot slipped, and he lay upon the grating for all the world like a great fat turtle.

Catchpole did not venture to raise him up, but seizing the pump-handle, worked away like a Briton engaged in a good cause.

The cold water not only splashed upon the back of Grabham's head, but ran down his neck, and drenched his coat.

He roared and bellowed, but the more he roared and bellowed the harder Catchpole pumped.

"I'm all right now," Grabham shrieked. "Leave off, will you? You're a' murdering of me."

"I'm acting the part of a friend," Catchpole declared, sending another copious stream over his half-drowned victim. "You'll thank me after I have rubbed you down a bit. There, I think it will do."

"It has nearly done for me," Grabham spluttered. "Rub me down! Why I am as wet as a flounder. How do you think I can try on a new uniform in this precious pickle?"

"There's a house hard by with a big fire in the kitchen," Catchpole replied. "I'll lock the door and dry your clothes while you run up and down."

Strange to say, Grabham did not seem at all grateful for this suggestion, but, on the contrary, he called Catchpole all sorts of wicked names, and gave him a back-hander which sent him spinning into the middle of the road.

Catchpole uttered a shriek of agony, and grasped his nose, while tears of agony flowed down his face.

"Villain, behold your work!" he cried. "Look upon my life's gore shed by your own hand!"

"I'll do it ag'in if you'll come a little nearer," said Grabham. "I'm sopped through and through, like a bit of lemon in a grog glass."

"I will not come any nearer," Catchpole declared. "Is this all the reward I am to have for making you sober? Could you go before Mr. Nabbitt with your eyes like burnt holes in a blanket?"

"If I can only get at you," said Mr. Grabham, wickedly, "your eyes won't look like anything, for I'll bung 'em up."

After a few minutes of gasping, wheezing, and coughing, Grabham calmed down, and consented to have his clothes dried.

This was soon done, for he was known to the landlord of the little public-house in Ivy Bridge-lane, in the Strand, a thoroughfare which still exists, although unknown to most Londoners.

A little after the time appointed they presented themselves at Bow-street, and were soon fitted with brand new uniforms.

Then Mr. Nabbitt beckoned to them in a strange and mysterious way.

"I have a few words to say to you in my private room," he said.

Catchpole and Grabham followed him, and as soon as the door was shut their superior officer folded his arms and bent his beetle brows.

"A very peculiar thing has happened," he said. "You may be aware that Ted Nickells, the keeper of the Chequers, was executed?"

"Yes, sir," Grabham responded; "and I am vain enough to flatter myself—"

"Never mind what you are vain enough to flatter yourself about," Nabbitt interposed. "Be kind enough to listen to me. From information received I have good reason to believe that Nickells was only half-hanged."

"Only half hanged?" Catchpole repeated, with his mouth open like a dying codfish. "Lor'! sir, it ain't possible. Surely you must be joking?"

"I am not givn to joking," Nabbitt roared. "How dare you say such a thing to me?"

Catchpole doubled up like an old-fashioned parasol, and Grabham glared at him as much as to say—

"Do you see what you have done?"

"I say," Nabbitt continued, "that Ted Nickells was only half-hanged, and that I believe him to be free at this very moment."

"Lor'! sir," said Grabham; "perhaps [illegible] wouldn't mind putting the case into our hands[illegible]"

"That is exactly what I am going to d[illegible]" Nabbitt replied. "Jackley, one of our cute[illegible] men, but who is too well known to undertake [illegible] job, thinks it very likely that Nickells' body w[illegible] taken for restoration to Buckler's-rents."

"Eh?" ejaculated Catchpole, tilting himself backwards on his heels.

A hollow sound, like the winding up of an eight day clock, came from Grabham's throat.

"What on earth is the matter with you?" Nabbitt demanded.

"Oh! nothing," said Catchpole, turning as white as a sheet. "Nothing at all, sir."

"You see, sir," said Grabham, "this news rather 'stonishing. It has come upon us sud[illegible] like."

"You will at once proceed to Buckler's-ren[illegible]" Mr. Nabbitt said, "and make all the nec[illegible] enquiries in the name of the law."

"Ye—e—s," Catchpole stuttered.

"There is a low character at Buckler's-rents named Muckrum, but almost as well known as Daddy," the head officer went on; "and it is just possible that he is hiding Ted Nickells. You follow me, I suppose?"

There was no need for him to ask such a question, simple as it was.

Both Catchpole and Grabham felt fit and ready to sink into the earth.

"I will give you a part of your pay now," Nabbitt resumed, "and you will start on your journey at once"

"Don't you think, sir," said Grabham, "that we had better take one or two other men with us?"

"What for?"

"There may be a row."

"But, surely, you are not afraid of that?" said Nabbitt.

"Oh! no," Grabham replied, affecting a boldness he did not feel. "We are ready to do anything in duty's cause."

"If you are successful in finding this villain Nickells and bringing him here," Nabbitt said, "you will receive twenty guineas a-piece, and perhaps get promotion. Let me think. You had half-a-crown a-piece. Here are five more shillings, so now start without delay."

Catchpole and Grabham staggered rather than walked out of the office.

When they got outside they held on to each other and groaned.

"Did you ever know the like of this?" Catchpole groaned.

"Never; it is too awful to think of!" Grabham replied. "It must be a dream. I ain't awake. Pinch me. Oh!—ah—h—h! That will do, thick-head!"

"I really think," Catchpole said, dismally, "that if I had received a whole week's pay I should cut and run. Must we—oh! must we go to Buckler's-rents?"

"We must," Grabham responded, striking an attitude of a stage martyr. "There ain't no help for it. But why despair? We are armed now in a double sense, and if we keep our heads about us we can make it warm for Daddy Muckrum."

"That is if he doesn't make it hot for us."

"Hot or cold, we must go," Grabham said. "Think of the twenty guineas, and keep up your pecker. Think how our names will get into the papers."

"Yes," Catchpole moaned—"yes, Grabham, our names will appear, but we shan't live to read 'em."

"What do you mean?"

"Why, that we shall be reported as missing, and at that time we shall be buried out of the way in some hole or corner, and our skeletons will never come to light until Buckler's-rents is levelled to the ground."

"That's a pleasant way to talk, certainly," Grabham said, trembling in his shoes. "You're a nice Job's comforter, you are."

"I can't help it; I must speak my mind. Ain't there no way of getting out of this job?"

"None that I can see."

"None!" said Catchpole, pleadingly. "Think again. You've got a head worth two of mine."

"I know it," Grabham replied, with conscious pride. "Anybody with half an eye could see that; but for once I am floored, and completely flabbergasted. Hold hard!"

"What is it?" demanded Catchpole, almost skipping out of his new shoes. "What—where? Is anything coming?"

"Yes."

"What is it, then?"

"A brilliant notion."

"Oh! Grabham," said Catchpole, with emotion. "If you can only show me a way of keeping outside Buckler's-rents, I'll be your slave until the day that I lay my head in the silent tomb."

"So you say."

"And I mean it."

"Well," said Grabham, "come round the corner and I'll unfold my plan. It's a risky one providing that it does not succeed, but if it does, we'll have a glass of punch at the Four Spies to-night, and drink our own jolly good healths."

## CHAPTER CXXXIII.

THE MIDNIGHT VOYAGE—THE GREY BROTHERHOOD—AN ATTEMPT TO RESCUE LANONI—THE RACK—SPRING-HEELED JACK APPEARS AT AN OPPORTUNE MOMENT.

LANONI had fallen asleep in her cavern prison.

She lay dreaming of wandering through the country under a light summer sun, as she had wandered many and many a time.

It was a fair vision of verdant meadows, fragrant flowers, and meandering brooks, laughing and leaping in their haste to reach the broad, shining river.

She thought that a lovely girl joined her and walked by her side.

Then the scene clouded.

A shadow fell upon the graceful girl's path.

It was the shadow of a young and handsome man, polite in discourse, lavish with compliments.

And then Lanoni thought that she was again alone, and watching this man and girl as they disappeared in the distance.

She tried to call out, she endeavoured to shriek a warning to the girl against the stranger, and in doing so she awoke.

As she did so, she flung out her arms and uttered a cry of despair.

In that moment the great sorrow of her life came back to her.

"Lillah, my child!" she gasped out—"Lillah, my child! Oh! my wronged child. Does the wrath of Heaven never fall upon the wicked who tread the earth?"

"Hush!" said a voice, so close to her ear that she felt the speaker's breath on her cheek.

"Who are you?" Lanoni demanded, starting up in alarm.

"Your friend."

"I have no friend here."

"Yes, you have; indeed you have."

It was a soft, silvery voice that spoke, and Lanoni, now being thoroughly awake, became convinced that Amy Corder was in the chamber.

"My poor child," she said, "you must not stop here. The brutal wretch who calls himself your father will kill you if you disobey his orders."

"I care not," Amy replied. "I am tired—oh! so tired—of life. See here. I have brought a shaded lamp with me. My father has drunk himself into a heavy slumber, and will not awake for some hours."

A sudden thought flashed in Lanoni's mind with the swiftness of lightning.

"This noble child has come to set me free," she mused. "But I will not accept my liberty at the price of her death."

But Lanoni was wrong.

"My father has hidden the keys," Amy Corder said, being seemingly aware of what was passing in Lanoni's mind, "and I fear that you must make up your mind to remain a prisoner. I have come to tell you something!"

"Well, that is good of you."

"You are to be removed from this place to-morrow at midnight," Amy said.

"Indeed; and you know where?"

"It is some place called the Recluse."

"Ha! a convent," Lanoni exclaimed, clasping her hands on her brow. "Oh! worse fate than death to be buried alive."

"Hush!" said Amy. "There are other men in these caves besides my father, though they have not shown themselves."

"And they are watchful?"

"Oh! yes," Amy replied. "Very watchful, but like my father they all made merry, because—"

"Why did they make merry, my child?"

"Because you were brought here," Amy continued. "They seem to look upon you as a great prisoner for whom a great price will be paid."

"No doubt," Lanoni returned, bitterly; "but how bitter will be the cost in the end. Have you more to tell me, child?"

"I want you to tell me now, despite any part I may play in what will take place, that you forgive me?" Amy said, placing her hands on Lanoni's arm.

"Freely; and I say it with all my heart. Are you, then, to go with me?"

"Yes; if I pretend to hate you."

"But your father caught me holding you in my arms," Lanoni said. "How will you, then, contrive to make him believe that your feelings towards me have altered?"

"I think that you may leave that to me," Amy said. "If questioned I shall say that you saw in me some resemblance of a child of your own."

Lanoni shaded her eyes with her hand and turned her head aside for a moment.

"What could have put such a thing in your head?" she demanded, after a pause.

"I am sure I don't know," the pretty little girl replied. "I must go now, and when you see me again you must treat me as a stranger. Promise."

Lanoni gave the required promise in a few kindly spoken words, and then Amy Corder tripped lightly out of the cavern.

The gipsy queen could sleep no more.

As she lay pondering on the events which had happened in so short a time she could hear the hoarse roar of the waves as they lashed the rock-bound shore with impotent fury.

She had no idea of the time, but she felt convinced that day was coming soon.

Every minute seemed an age to her.

But the longest night must end, and when she heard the sound of voices and heavy footsteps moving about she rose, and having dressed herself, walked into the outer apartment.

She had not been there long before Corder threw open the door and peered in.

"Oh! I see that you are an early bird," he said. "Did you sleep well?"

"It would not disturb your mind if I did not sleep at all," Lanoni retorted.

"Come, come," said Corder, "we may as well be friends as long as I have charge of you. Amy will bring your breakfast presently; but I warn you, as you value your life, not to speak to her."

"The warning is unnecessary," Lanoni replied. "I see in her a likeness to you, and that is more than sufficient to make me hate her."

An expression of satisfaction stole over Corder's face as these words were delivered, but he made no comment on them.

"There is a bell," he said, pointing to a silken rope dangling in a corner of the wall, "and when you feel inclined you may use it."

He strode across the floor, but turned back as he reached the door.

"You had better try to be cheerful and eat well," he said, "because there may be another surprise for you before many hours are over."

"Thank you for your kindness," Lanoni said, mockingly.

Corder had not left the cavern long before Lanoni rang the bell.

Amy appeared, silent and demure.

She spread a snow-white cloth on the table, and soon placed an appetising breakfast before the gipsy queen.

Not a word was said by either.

This was well, for Corder was watching them through a hole in the door.

Lanoni ate sparingly, but drank her share of the coffee, which was exceedingly good.

Amy stood behind her chair all the time as motionless as a statue.

She never once directed her eyes towards the door, although she knew that her father was there.

At last the ruffian, discovering that his suspicions were at fault, entered the room.

He pointed to the door, and Amy, in obedience to the signal, walked out of it.

Then Corder sat down, and folding his arms, looked steadily at Lanoni.

"You belong to a strange, vengeful race of people," he said, "and it is high time that your tribe was broken up."

Lanoni laughed scornfully, and then her face darkened with anger.

"Why have you come to tell me this?" she said. "I pray you leave me alone."

"The gipsies will have to find another queen," Corder resumed, in a mocking tone of voice "A nice quiet home has been prepared for you, and you must hold yourself in readiness to go to it to-night."

This was not such great news to Lanoni, but she feigned to start and look alarmed, for she saw that Corder was watching her features closely.

"I am in your hands," she said; "but my people will resent this insult, and take a rare revenge for it."

"If they find you they must be more clever than I think," Corder returned. "My daughter, the hateful child of a hateful father—ha! ha!—will be your companion until you are safe behind the walls of—"

"Why do you hesitate?" Lanoni demanded.

"Because I had very nearly made a slip of the tongue," Corder said. "I have told you all that you are to know, and so farewell."

Lanoni passed the rest of the day almost alone.

Amy visited her twice, in the same silent mysterious way, and vanished the instant she was no longer required.

It was growing late, when Corder entered the cavern with a wrapper of some heavy material hanging over his arm.

"If you will give me your word of honour not to struggle or cry out, I will not bind your hands?" he said.

"You have it."

"Then all I have to do is this," he said, throwing the wrapper over Lanoni's head and shoulders. "Now give me your hand, and I will lead you to the boat."

"A boat!" Lanoni thought. "Then I am to be taken by sea to my new place of imprisonment."

She did not hesitate, but gave Corder her hand and suffered him to lead her away.

Soon she felt that she was at sea.

But the boat did not go far.

It stopped alongside a larger vessel, and Lanoni was lifted on deck.

The rigging creaked, the sails spread gallantly to the wind, and the voyage commenced.

Presently the wrapper was removed from Lanoni's face.

The sudden rush of light almost blinded her; but as soon as she could discern objects plainly she saw that Amy was at her side.

"We are alone," the girl said. "See, here is a set of ivory tablets and a pencil. Write whatever instructions you may desire, and I will fulfil them."

"But you will remain with me?"

"Only for a few hours after we reach the Recluse," Amy Corder said. "I will then go where you will."

"But your life will pay for thus serving me?"

Amy shook her head.

"No," she replied. "I am not going back."

"Not going back?" Lanoni repeated, in astonishment. "Where, then, will you go?"

"I will stay with your people, if they will have me."

"Aye! that they will, and give you a royal welcome in my name," Lanoni said. "Heaven bless and reward you for this, child!"

She wrote a few words hastily, and then returned the tablets to Amy, who hid them away in the bosom of her dress.

"How long will this voyage last?" Lanoni asked.

"Only a few more hours," Amy replied. "You may come up on deck, if you choose, and I will point out the Recluse as soon as it appears in sight."

"Is it on the sea-coast, then?"

"Yes; on the top of a cliff, which can only be mounted from the beach."

"You seem to have been there before."

"Yes," Amy replied; "my father sent me there when I was quite a baby, and I was brought up by the nuns."

"Nuns?"

Lanoni's heart sank within her, for now she knew to a certainty that she was to be buried in a living tomb.

The ship sped on.

It was worked by five men, who took no more notice of Lanoni than if she had not been present.

At last a long line of dull brown appeared on the horizon.

It grew plainer, and presently Amy Corder pointed to what appeared to be a tower rising from the shore.

"The Recluse," she whispered. "Keep a good heart. I will read the tablets when I am alone, and obey what is written on them."

The strange-looking building grew more and more distinct every moment.

Lanoni could not help feeling a thrill of awe as she noted its strong dark walls and grated windows.

Suddenly the captain of the sailing vessel gave a word of command, and a boat was lowered.

Then, for the first time, he turned to Lanoni, and beckoned her to approach.

"You have behaved extremely well," he said. "Please step into the boat. We have signalled to the shore, and I see those who are to welcome you descending the cliff."

Lanoni saw them too.

Three nuns were descending the steep declivity with slow and measured steps.

The reached the beach ere the boat grated on the sand, and quietly but meaningly surrounded Lanoni as she stepped ashore, closely followed by Amy Corder.

The gipsy queen could not see the nuns' features, as they were hooded and veiled.

Like gaunt, black spectres of the night they retraced their footsteps to the base of the cliff, at which began a flight of rudely-hewn but broad stairs.

At last Lanoni lost all patience.

"Have you no tongues?" she cried. "Have done with this mummery, and act like women, if such you are!"

"Listen," said one of the nuns, in a solemn tone of voice. "You must learn to curb your passions here. We are but the sisters of obedience. Our Lady Superior will interview you presently, and you may converse freely with her, but not with us."

"Bah!" Lanoni exclaimed, contemptuously. "Lady Inferior, you know. Lead on, you mockeries of all that is just and good. I will follow you willingly, for the day is not far distant when your haunt shall be levelled to the ground."

Amy Corder gave the gipsy queen an appealing glance to be silent, and not another word was spoken until all stopped before a narrow door, only just wide enough to admit one person at a time.

One of the nuns advanced and tapped gently at the door.

It was opened immediately by a yellow-faced hag, who looked all the more ugly for wearing a white linen band round her head.

She said something to the nun which Lanoni could not understand, and then glanced in a supercilious manner at Lanoni, who swept past her with eyes flashing and cheeks burning with indignation.

A little way down a long, dim passage was a bare and comfortless room.

It had no furniture whatever, save two hard chairs and a solid table, on which stood materials for writing.

Lanoni was ushered into this room, and without being invited she sat down, and glared defiance at the nuns who were evidently observing her under the cover of their veils.

Presently a bell rang.

The nuns fell back and took up their places near the door.

An instant later a tall, commanding woman, wearing a long, black, flowing robe, swept into the room.

She returned the respectful salutations given by the nuns, gave Amy a nod of recognition, and then turned her large, dark eyes upon Lanoni.

"You know why you are brought here?" she said, sitting down, and taking up a pen in her hand.

"No."

"Then I will tell you," said the Lady Superior, for she it was. "Up to the present you have led a life unworthy of a Christian woman. One of our patrons has taken compassion on you and sent you here, that you may lead a quiet, peaceful, and repentant life."

"Are you thus instructed?" Lanoni demanded, clenching her hands.

"Yes."

"Look me in the face and repeat those words," Lanoni said, fiercely. "Woman, you lie—you lie basely! You know the real reason why Lord Mildendale has played the part of an unmanly villain, and sent me here to you—the willing instrument of his crime, if, indeed, you are nothing worse."

The Lady Superior did not change colour or betray the least emotion.

"You had better keep a curb on your tongue," she said, calmly. "We have a method of our own for taming refractory people."

"Indeed!"

"Yes; we place them in small dark cells, we feed them on low diet, and if that discipline is not sufficient, we use the lash."

"Shameless wretch!" Lanoni cried, starting to her feet. "Must I listen to such words as these?"

"They will be followed by the deeds I have spoken of if you persist in your unruly conduct," was the reply, spoken slowly and coldly. "In a few days you will get used to us and our ways. The choice of misery and happiness lies with you, and so you will find before long."

As she spoke she held up her hand, and one of the nuns advanced and placed her hand upon Lanoni's arm.

"Touch me not!" exclaimed the gipsy queen. "Take me where you will—do what you will, but touch me not."

"I will pay you another visit in the evening," the Lady Superior said, as Lanoni followed the nun to the door, "and I hope to find you in a better frame of mind."

"Oh! for a knife or a dagger," Lanoni hissed under her breath. "Oh! for some weapon to deal death to these monsters in human form."

The other two nuns followed Lanoni, and in a few minutes she found herself in a cell, the door of which was locked upon her.

And now the gipsy queen felt that she must rave and shriek to relieve her pent-up feelings.

She had borne much, and she became conscious that her fortitude was giving way.

"No, no," she said, running her fingers through her long, dark tresses. "I will bear this. I will mark each taunt and insult, and repay tenfold. If Amy keeps her word rescue must come, and come soon. Oh! to see this place consumed by flames. Oh! to hear the wretches who torture me in my helplessness cry for mercy."

Amy Corder did not come near her again, but Lanoni did not know that the boat was waiting on the beach for the child, and waiting in vain.

After a lapse of time some coarse food was brought to Lanoni by the attendant nun, who now wore her veil flowing down her back.

She was a young and not unpleasant-looking woman.

"What brought you to such a place as this?" Lanoni demanded. "Why deny yourself the fresh air and sunlight, which Heaven sent for your good?"

No answer was vouchsafed to these questions, but the nun's under lip quivered, and her eyes became moist.

"You pity me because you pity yourself," Lanoni said. "Tell me your story. Let me have at least one friend here."

The nun cast a frightened glance at the gipsy queen, and then rushed hurriedly from the cell.

"Poor wretch!" Lanoni said, "she is afraid to speak. What awful place is this? What nameless deeds have been perpetrated under its roof?"

Lanoni then fell into a reverie, from which she was disturbed by the entrance of the Lady Superior.

"To-morrow," she said, "you will exchange your clothes for such as the sisters wear, and at the same time you will enter upon your duties."

"I will do nothing," Lanoni said, in a firm, determined voice. "I have been brought here against my will, and I will not lift a hand to please you, or those over whom you rule."

"We shall see," the Lady Superior said. "Woman, you mistake this place. It is not a convent."

"What is it then?"

"A home for the weary and ill at ease."

"I do not understand you," Lanoni said.

"Wait, and you will."

. . . . . . .

The gipsies lay encamped, waiting for the return of their queen.

The light of the fires, roaring and crackling in the breeze, glowed alike upon the strangely-constructed tents and sallow faces of the men, women, and children.

What had become of Lanoni?

She had been absent two days, and not one of the tribe had heard a word concerning her actions or whereabouts.

Suddenly a man doing duty as sentry uttered a shrill warning cry, and the gipsies, starting from their recumbent attitudes about the fire, clamoured to know why the word of alarm had been given.

"I have taken a prisoner," the sentry said, laughing.

"Oh! please," said a plaintive voice, "I have come from Lanoni, and I want to see Namon Wallack."

"I am here," said a man of stalwart proportions. "What do you want with me, little girl? But, first of all, tell me your name?"

"Amy Corder."

"Well, and pray what does Amy Corder want with me?"

This question was soon answered.

Amy placed the tablets in Namon Wallack's hands, and as he read the characters written upon the slips of ivory the expression of his face grew awful to behold.

"Listen to this, children of the forest," he cried, in a voice of thunder. "Our queen is a prisoner in a place called the Recluse, at Hathwold, and this little girl is the bearer of the news."

A savage roar rent the air.

"Silence!" Namon Wallack shouted, holding up his hand; "we must have deeds, not words. Strike the tents, and follow me. I will go alone to the Recluse and demand the release of Lanoni. If that should be refused, I will return to you and tell you how to act."

As he finished speaking, he took Amy Corder up in his arms and kissed her affectionately.

"Our queen says that you wish to remain with us," he said; "and you shall. The softest bed and the daintiest food shall be your portion. Ha! who comes here? Who rides this way so late at night?"

"Ralph Ashton," cried a voice out of the darkness.

"You are welcome, Mr. Ashton," Namon Wallack said. "Who do you seek?"

"Lanoni."

In a few brief words Namon Wallack told Ralph what had happened, and he, without making any kind of a reply, put spurs to his horse and dashed away.

"I wonder what he means by that?" Namon Wallack growled. "He might have stayed to tell me what he thought of the situation."

But Ralph was gone, and no possible good

could come of reasoning out his seemingly unaccountable conduct.

The tents were struck, the fires extinguished, and then the whole band moved forward, with Namon Wallack at their head.

Day dawned, and found the journey only half completed.

The horses and mules required rest, and a halt of an hour's duration was made.

Then on again, until the rocky coast of Hathwold, and the grim building surmounting its highest point, appeared in view.

Again the band of gipsies halted, and this time in a wood.

Namon Wallack worked his way round to the beach, and then began to ascend the cliff leading to Lanoni's prison.

Namon Wallack was as bold and fearless as a lion.

He never dreamed for a moment that when it was known that Lanoni had been discovered that she would not be given up.

"Ha!" he said, as he stopped before the door through which the gipsy queen had passed. "A grim place this. Strong, and ugly, and forbidding. I begin to fear that I have set myself a rather troublesome task."

He knocked loudly at the door, and a little slide in it flew back.

"A woman was brought here yesterday," he said. "Her name is Lanoni, and I demand her release. I do not come alone, but I do not wish to threaten; nor do I wish to have recourse to violence. Release Lanoni, and I and my friends will go away in peace."

The wicket closed with a vicious snap, but it was presently opened again, and this was followed by the grating of locks and bolts.

The door then opened, and a figure shrouded in black stood before Namon Wallack.

"We have no secrets here," said a muffled voice, "neither do we know anything of the woman you speak of. Come in and see for yourself."

Suspecting nothing, Namon Wallack stepped forward.

In an instant the door was banged behind him, and he was seized by several pairs of strong hands.

A gag was thrust into his mouth, and a stout rope passed under his arms.

Wallack knew very well that no women could have done this, and, therefore, he was not at all surprised when he saw the faces of two brutal-looking men grinning into his.

The gipsy's nerve almost forsook him.

"You have come just in time to take part in one of our ceremonies," said the man nearest to him.

"Bring him hither," cried a gruff voice in the distance.

Namon Wallack was borne along a passage, and down a long flight of narrow steps.

Then he was placed on his feet, and the gag was removed from his mouth.

A spectral-like figure, draped from head to foot, approached him.

There were two small holes in the hood worn by this terrible-looking object, and Namon Wallack saw two fierce eyes glaring at him.

"Remove the gag," said the draped and hooded man.

"Have I been misled?" Wallack said. "Have I come to the wrong place? Is this not a recluse for women?"

"Recluse for women," said the spectral-like being, in a hollow tone of voice. "Who ever heard of women among the Grey Brotherhood?"

"Then let me go," Wallack said. "It may be that I have been deceived by a trick."

"You must pay the penalty for coming here," said the Grey Brother. "No man has ever dared to molest us yet without punishment. Bring him along, and we will show him how we treat those who foolishly venture through our doors."

But Namon Wallack was not going to give in without a struggle.

He shot out his long and muscular arms, and two of the Grey Brotherhood went down as if they had been shot.

Others appeared instantly on the scene, and Namon Wallack was dragged, shouting, fighting, and struggling into a dungeon, which was separated from another by a sliding panel.

As this was drawn aside a cry of terror came from Namon Wallack's lips, for confronting him was a rack in all its hideousness and awful meaning.

Two masked figures stood beside the devilish piece of mechanism, and Wallack, terror stricken and gasping, now flung up his hands in dismay.

"No—no!" he cried. "Not that! Anything but that!"

The hooded figure made a motion with his hand, and those who held Wallack tore his coat from his back, and bore him towards the rack.

Strong as the man was, he nearly swooned as the cords were passed tightly over his extended limbs, and a death-like sickness filled his heart.

The draped figure gave the signal.

The executioners seized the levers, but ere they could be drawn backwards, a crash, as if a thunder-bolt had fallen, startled all.

This crash was succeeded by another, and Spring-Heeled Jack, leaping as it were from the wall, and brandishing a bar of iron in his hand, rushed upon the draped men.

"Hold!" cried Spring-Heeled Jack. "Hold! monsters in human form."

## CHAPTER CXXXIV.

### MRS. CORCORAN IS VERY MUCH FRIGHTENED.

WE left Mrs. Corcoran endeavouring to escape from Sam Snatcher's unpleasant abode.

The only way out, if indeed there was a way at all, was by the cellar, and the old hag, having removed the piece of wood from between the bolt and the door, descended a step or two, and peered over the balustrade into the cellar.

The place was so dark that at first she could see nothing, so she went a little lower, swaying the leg of the chair in her hand, and ready to hit the first head that happened to come within reach of her arm.

But no head appeared, and at last Mrs. Corcoran's witch-like eyes became a little more accustomed to the dimness of the place.

In the centre of the cellar she saw something bulky lying upon a board supported by tressels.

This strange-looking object was covered with what appeared to be a dark carpet.

Mrs. Corcoran's curiosity was at once aroused, and, hopping down the rest of the stairs, she approached the object, and touched it with her hand.

It was neither hard nor soft.

It might be stolen plunder, or—

Mrs. Corcoran held her breath, as a sudden thought occurred to her.

She started from the object lying so still upon the board as if it had stung her.

What made her afraid?

What caused her to hide her face in her hands and totter back towards the staircase?

Surely there was nothing in the cellar to hurt her, for save the motionless object, it was perfectly empty?

Mrs. Corcoran had reached the bottom stair, when she rushed back, for the front door had been opened, and Sam Snatcher and his wife were walking through the hall.

For once in her life Mrs. Corcoran was very much frightened indeed.

Above, Sam Snatcher and his wife.

Below, that horrible-looking object on the table—ugh!

Mrs. Corcoran was rather at a loss to know what to do.

To run upstairs was to declare herself, and, perhaps, that meant death.

To remain where she was was too awful.

She knew what the object was upon the table.

It was a dead body, dragged by Sam Snatcher from the grave or from the river.

It was either a corpse ready for the surgeon's dissecting knife, or a hideous, bloated spectacle of what had once been a human being.

As we have said before, Mrs. Corcoran was very much frightened indeed, and she began to think how she should get out of her awful dilemma.

Leaning forward, with bated breath, she listened intently.

"Dick Sleuth is right," she heard Sam Snatcher say. "The old woman is no use to anybody now that she has done all that can be done. Let her die."

"Shall I go up and see whether she is asleep or awake?" his amiable spouse asked.

"No," Snatcher replied. "We will let her be until midnight, and then we can settle her hash comfortably. She isn't much of a price. I don't suppose that old Cutter will give more than a guinea for her carcase."

This was a nice thing for Mrs. Corcoran to hear with her own ears.

She pressed her temples and tweaked her own nose to convince herself that she was awake.

"Well, then," said the pure-minded Harriet Snatcher; "shall we go and see how the subject is getting on? It must be removed to-night, you know."

"Oh! there's time enough for that," her husband growled. "Come, let us taste what the contents of this bottle is like. When we have finished it, we'll pay a visit to the cellar."

This was quite enough—more than enough for our dear Mrs. Corcoran.

She made up her mind how to act quicker than it can be recorded.

Wholly bewildered, and half mad, she ran to the board, and bundled the object off it.

It fell with a hollow, ghastly thud, and the cover flying from it, revealed the shrouded corpse of a man.

The body had evidently been under the ground a number of days, and so awful was the spectacle that Mrs. Corcoran, used as she was to all kinds of horrors, shrank from it.

Presently the hag braced up her nerves and became calmer.

Then closing her eyes, she threw her arms round the corpse and began to drag it down in a slanting direction.

What was she going to do?

What new hideous thought born in her devilish brain set her such a task?

We shall see.

Very slowly and carefully Mrs. Corcoran performed the operation of removing the body.

At last the cold rigid feet touched the floor, and then Mrs. Corcoran, exerting all her strength, lowered the body at full length, and then began to roll it over and over into a corner of the cellar.

When she had accomplished this feat she gathered up armsful of shavings and rubbish, with which the cellar was littered, and strewed it over the body, so as to hide every portion of it.

This done, Mrs. Corcoran took her place upon the board supported by tressels, and drawing the covering over herself, lay still.

What she suffered no tongue can tell and no pen describe.

The sickly taint of the grave assailed her nostrils and sickened her heart.

She had no notion of how long she would have to remain there; but she made up her mind not to move until Sam Snatcher and his wife came down to look at the "subject."

Mrs. Corcoran had not long to wait.

Presently the door opened and heavy footsteps began to descend the stairs.

"The cart will be here at midnight," Sam Snatcher was saying, "and it can take the two bodies as well as one."

"Just so," his wife replied. "I'll make short work of the old woman as soon as we have made room for her here."

Mrs. Corcoran held her breath.

She felt inclined to shriek and yell, and it cost her a fearful effort to keep silence.

"Business is looking up," Sam Snatcher said, with a brutal laugh. "Well, a man ought to be paid well for such a work. Pah! How the old gentleman smells! We will have a look at him!"

Now was the moment that Mrs. Corcoran knew that she really carried her life in her hands.

If the idea she had conceived failed she could say good-bye to the world in right down earnest.

As Sam Snatcher took the covering in his hands, she started up, and, flinging open her arms, uttered a most unearthly shriek.

Sam Snatcher responded with another, and rushed wildly towards the staircase.

His wife followed him, and Mrs. Corcoran heard them dash along the passage and fling open the street door, as if they had received sudden warning that the house was falling down.

Sam Snatcher and his wife thought that the dead had come to life.

The cellar was so dimly lighted that they could not distinguish Mrs. Corcoran's features, and, under the circumstances just described, it is scarcely to be supposed that they would stay to inquire into particulars.

"Ho—ho!" laughed Mrs. Corcoran, as she scrambled off the board. "I thought I could scare them, and I have done it. Now we shall see—we shall see. I will pretend to know nothing of their intentions towards me. I will find my clothes, and then return to the Bull in Top Boots, and make myself nice and agreeable."

But Mrs. Corcoran seemed loth to leave the scene of her triumph.

"The fools!" she muttered. "If they had not

been drunk they must have discovered that somebody had been tampering with the board. What will not drink do? Well—well, I will not give it a bad name, because, perchance, it has saved my life."

The hag searched the cellar for hidden treasure, but finding none, went upstairs.

Now she was at perfect liberty to burst open doors, and make as much noise as she chose.

It was highly improbable that Sam Snatcher and his wife would return to the house again that day, if, indeed, they ever did.

Mrs. Corcoran found an iron bar behind the front door, and then commenced her attack on the locks of the different rooms.

At last she discovered her garments, and having arrayed herself in them, trotted nimbly down the stairs, and made her way to Blackfriars-stairs, without attracting any notice from the people she met on the way.

## CHAPTER CXXXV.

### SPRING-HEELED JACK'S REVENGE.

THE reader may have asked himself how the Grey Brotherhood came to be in possession of the Recluse, which but a few hours before was apparently occupied by a number of women.

The explanation is not very difficult.

Not far from the Recluse was another building, and a passage had been tunnelled from one place to another.

These men and women were nothing more or less than a gang of robbers, wolves in sheep's clothing, who lured hapless vessels to destruction by means of false lights, murdered and plundered, and made merry in secret on their unholy gains.

They also undertook to put any troublesome person out of the way for a consideration, and their agents were continually at work to discover where such people were to be found.

Furnished with plenty of money, they moved in good society, and using crafty means, soon became possessed of family secrets.

Once these "skeletons in the cupboard" became revealed to these wretches, they began to hint that they knew of a place where the lady or gentleman who stood in somebody's way could be taken to—a retreat out of which there was no escape—and if the bait took another victim was added to the list.

If the notion was treated indignantly, the "agent" vanished mysteriously, and never returned to the locality.

Nobody, of course, ever dreamed that such fiends were to be found within the walls of the Recluse at Hathwold, nor at the humble dwelling of the Grey Brotherhood, who went about with solemn faces, and gave alms to the poor and needy.

The sisters and brothers had changed places for the nonce, as was their custom when there was the slightest suspicion that any enquiries were likely to be made, and thus Namon Wallack found himself in such a perilous position.

The terror-stricken man could scarcely realise the appearance of Spring-Heeled Jack, nor could the hooded villain, who remained motionless and staring at the apparition until he received a terrific blow from the bar of iron, which sent him reeling and shrieking to the floor of the dungeon.

As he fell, the hood flew back, and revealed a most repulsive face of the lowest type.

The masked executioners had fled, leaving Namon Wallack secured to the rack; but Spring-Heeled Jack soon released him, and the gipsy, more dead than alive with fright, tottered to the wall, and leaned heavily against it.

Spring-Heeled Jack then turned his attention to the scoundrel he had felled like an ox in the shambles, and who now lay with closed eyes, pretending that he was dead.

"Such a ruse will not serve you," Spring-Heeled Jack cried, in an awful tone of voice. "Villain, your hour has come. Rise and meet your fate like a man, or I must slay you as you lie cringing there."

But the man made no movement, and Spring-Heeled Jack, losing all patience, raised him aloft and hurled him with terrible force against the wall.

A hollow groan followed the ghastly thud, the man's limbs twitched convulsively for a few moments, and then the end came.

"So much for one cur," Spring-Heeled Jack said. "Come, Namon, come; rouse yourself. You have no need to fear me. Rise, and hasten back to your people. Level this hellish den to the ground with fire, and let no villain escape, but spare the women. Unhappy creatures! it is possible that they are more to be pitied than blamed."

Namon Wallack passed his hand before his eyes, as if to collect his thoughts; and when he gazed at the spot where the strange creature had stood, he was no longer there.

But Namon could hear his voice and mocking laughter reverberating like thunder through the gloomy passages of the Recluse, and the gipsy, following the sound, reached the open air.

Snatching a whistle from his breast-pocket he blew a loud, shrill call upon it.

It was answered by a savage roar that rent the very air.

Again Namon Wallack sounded the whistle, and in a few moments the dusky forms of the gipsies appeared from the wood.

"Torches! Light torches!" Wallack gasped.

As he spoke he snatched a gun from the nearest man.

A figure draped in black had slipped by him, and was running away into the cover of the darkness.

Namon Wallack took aim and fired.

The bullet found its billet in the fugitive's back.

With a wild yell he sprang forward, falling with a crash upon his face, and a hoarse cry of triumph burst from Wallack's lips.

"Lanoni! Where is Lanoni?" demanded a chorus of voices. "Where is our queen?"

"This way!" Wallack thundered back. "Follow me quickly. There is not a moment to lose."

To their surprise Lanoni suddenly appeared in their midst.

"I have been set free by that mysterious being called Spring-Heeled Jack," she said. "He bade me come to you and lead you to this just work of destruction. Ha! look yonder."

As she extended her arm her followers saw a number of dusky figures creeping towards the edge of the cliff.

Half-a-dozen muskets and pistols rang out their death-dealing messages.

The fire was returned, and one of the gipsies fell.

"Ah! I am killed," he cried. "Avenge my death! Revenge! revenge!"

A score of men took up the cry, and, half

# SPRING-HEELED JACK,

## THE TERROR OF LONDON.

"HELP! I'M DONE FOR—I'M BEING CHOKED!" HE SHOUTED.

No. 38.

maddened with fury, bore down upon the wretches who were attempting to escape.

Then a terrible hand-to-hand encounter took place.

Shrieks, yells, and curses made the night hideous.

Clouds of dust arose as the gipsies took an awful revenge by hurling the members of the so-called Grey Brotherhood over the face of the cliff.

At last all was still, and Lanoni, looking like a savage prophetess, and brandishing a glowing torch over her head, led the way to the Recluse.

In less time than it takes to record the fact, flames were bursting through its narrow windows, and soon the place was one mass of living fire.

The sky grew red, and when at last the roof fell in, the glare lit up land and sea for miles around.

But Lanoni's work of retaliation was not yet complete.

There was the other building to demolish, and she, heading her excited people, moved hastily towards it.

It was evident that Lanoni had received some kind of warning from Spring-Heeled Jack, for, as the house was reached, she turned and spoke a few words to her people.

"There must be no bloodshed here," she said. "Make all the prisoners you can, but harm none."

There was no necessity for the warning.

The house had been deserted, and was as empty as a church on week days.

Again the torches were applied, and again fire did its work.

Then the gipsies moved away, and Lanoni entered a tent, and was met by Amy Corder, who flew into her arms, and embraced her affectionately.

"I owe you my liberty and life," Lanoni said. "In what manner can I repay you?"

Amy whispered something in Lanoni's ear.

"It shall be done, if possible," the gipsy queen replied. "Nay, it shall be. You have my word for it."

## CHAPTER CXXXVI.

### A SUPPER INTERRUPTED.

THERE was no way of getting out of it.

Go to Buckler's-rents Catchpole and Grabham must, and the only consolation afforded to them was that they were armed with the authority of the law.

They each had also a brace of pistols, and the promise of twenty guineas apiece if they discovered and captured Ted Nickells.

Still the constables were not happy.

Their late experiences of the place they were going to were of such a kind as to make them shrink from the undertaking with good reason.

"Well," Grabham growled out at last; "standing here won't mend matters. We had better move forward. For all we know Nabbitt may have sent somebody to watch our movements."

"I wish he had given the job to somebody else," Catchpole remarked, taking off his hat and wiping his perspiring brow. "It's like putting our heads into a wild lion's jaws to go to that place. But, I say, how about that idea of yours?"

Grabham shook his head.

"I've thought it over," he said, "and I am afraid it wouldn't do."

"What was it?"

"Why, to give each other black eyes, tear our uniforms, roll in the mud, and then go back to Bow-street, and say that after a deadly struggle, we were outnumbered."

"I can understand the tearing up and the rolling in the mud," Catchpole said, "but blow and jigger the black eye part of the business."

"But one wouldn't do without the other," Grabham returned. "What do you think Nabbitt would say if we went back without a scratch? He would tumble to our little game in a moment."

"I suppose he would," Catchpole observed. "There wasn't much in that idea."

"Will you think of a better one?" Grabham said, wrathfully.

"I can't."

"Then don't you grumble about me," said Grabham. "No; we must go, and the sooner we start the better. It is like having a tooth out, but it will be all right when it is over."

"Tooth out!" Catchpole repeated, "I feel as if I was going to have my head off."

Grabham made no reply, but moved gloomily forward.

His heart was knocking against his side, and though he tried to keep up a brave appearance, the ghastly whiteness of his face proclaimed the state of his feelings.

Very little was said during the rest of the journey, which was not hurried over.

At last the constables stood before the dark entry leading to Buckler's-rents.

"You go first," said Catchpole.

"If it's all the same to you," Grabham retorted, "we will go together. Get your pistols ready, and try not to look quite so much like a walking turnip."

"Well," said Catchpole, "you ain't very rosy, and you'd say so if you could see yourself in a looking-glass."

"It's my anxiety to catch these villains," Grabham replied, swelling out his chest. "Think of the reward, and let it brace you up."

Catchpole looked as if he required a deal of bracing up, and for that matter so did Grabham.

As they walked up the dark entry they took each other's arms most affectionately, and kept very close to each other when their footsteps found an echo in Buckler's-rents.

The place was very quiet.

Not a human being was to be seen, and the only living creature in sight was a half-starved cat, clawing at a heap of rubbish in the hope of finding something to eat.

"Strange!" said Grabham, as he cocked one of the pistols and held it in advance of him ready to fire at anything and anybody. "I should have thought that an alarm would have been raised at our appearance."

"Perhaps we are being watched!" Catchpole whispered. "They may take it in their heads to fire at us from the windows, and it strikes me forcibly that we form a nice pair of targets to be shot at."

But no such a thing happened.

Buckler's-rents was as silent as the grave, and, what was still more mysterious, some of the doors were wide open.

"Ah!" Grabham suddenly ejaculated.

Catchpole skipped into the air as if the earth had suddenly bounded up under his feet.

"How you startled me!" he gasped. "What's the matter?"

"I have it," Grabham replied. "I know now the cause of this silence. The beggars have bolted!"

"Then we are saved!" Catchpole cried, with an

expression of genuine thankfulness in his eyes. "We are saved!"

"For my part," said Grabham, smiting his chest, "I'm very sorry."

"I ain't," Catchpole remarked, emphatically. "I speak what I feels in my 'art. I'm as glad as if Nabbitt had given me the twenty guineas for doing nothing."

"That speech doesn't do you credit," Grabham returned, shaking his head reprovingly. "We are the members of a noble and useful force, and we ought to be glad when we are called upon to do our duty."

Catchpole smiled a doubtful kind of smile, which raised his comrade's ire.

"What are you grinning at now?" Grabham demanded.

"Oh! nothing—nothing."

"I'll know what it is," Grabham spluttered. "I'll not be grinned at like an ape for nothing."

"I was merely thinking that you didn't talk like that this morning," Catchpole said.

"What did I talk like?"

"Why, as if you didn't care any more for the job than me."

"If," said Mr. Grabham, turning up the cuffs of his coat-sleeves very slowly and deliberately, "if there is anything that I hate in the world, it is a mean liar. You are one, Catchpole. Now then, what have you to say to that?"

"I take it from whence it comes," Catchpole replied.

"Then take that!"

Catchpole took it—and it was Grabham's fist—so full upon the tip of his nose that he saw millions of stars, intermixed with all sorts of coloured lights.

It is a dangerous thing to afflict a man's nasal organ, more especially when he is off his guard, and so Grabham presently found.

With tears of anguish rushing from his eyes, and two small streams of blood trickling from his nose, Catchpole staggered back.

Recovering his balance, he glared at Grabham in a manner which that individual did not admire.

"You have shed my gore—my life's gore," Catchpole said. "You have hit me in an unmanly fashion upon the nose, and you must take the consequences."

Grabham pretended to laugh; but the sound was hollow and had no mirth in it.

"What are you going for to do?" he asked, as Catchpole suddenly flung off his coat and moistened the palms of his hands.

"I am going to wollop you," Catchpole replied, with unnatural calmness. "I am going to spoil the look of them features of yours, just in the same manner as you have damaged one of mine."

"Beware!" said Grabham. "Think twice before you act. Strike me once—only once, I say—and you make an enemy of me for life."

"Well," Catchpole returned, "if that ain't cool I should like to know what is! You pitch into me, and when I ask you to stand up like a man you talk of enemies. Ha! ha! Will you fight?"

"I will not," Grabham replied. "Where's the use of it? You riled my temper, or I shouldn't have dreamed of striking you. Come; let us shake hands?"

"No; I don't see it," Catchpole replied. "If you give, so you must take. I must give you one. Where will you have it?"

Grabham suddenly saw a way out of the difficulty.

"Look there!" he shrieked out.

"Look where?" Catchpole yelled, jerking on his coat again, and preparing to run. "What is it?"

"It's nothing," Grabham replied. "We are here quite alone, but I thought I would give you a kind of a turn. Say nothing more unfriendly, Catchpole, and I'll stand a supper to-night."

"Well, I suppose I must look over it," Catchpole growled; "but don't do it again, for if you do I shall go straight to business."

Grabham bit his under lip.

Catchpole was getting the upper hand of him, and that sort of thing would not do at any price.

"Do you know why I wouldn't fight?" he demanded, in a mysterious whisper.

"No."

"I had a friend once," Grabham said, brushing his hand hastily across his eyes, "and we fell out over a trivial matter. We fought, and—"

"You got a jolly good licking, I suppose?" Catchpole interposed.

"No," Grabham replied. "I killed him, poor fellow, and the memory of him flat on his back and staring at nothing haunts me now, and makes me careful how I use my strength."

Catchpole looked at Grabham, who was glaring straight ahead of him, as if he saw the ghost of his unfortunate friend.

"What did you do with the body?" Catchpole demanded, with a tremor in his voice.

"I—I buried it," Grabham gasped. "That is to say, I paid the funeral expenses, for I thought I couldn't do less."

Catchpole had never heard of this episode before, and conflicting emotions filled his mind.

For all he knew, Grabham might be a murderer, and if raised to fury, commit a similar crime.

"You shall stand the supper," he said; "and as for my nose, why, I daresay it will be all right before the morning."

"That's like your jolly old self to say so," Grabham replied. "Now, what do you think? Shall we search some of these houses?"

"No—no! We have been here, and that is quite enough."

"But we might find something worth taking away, don't you see?"

"We might take away more than we wanted with us," Catchpole rejoined, sagely. "I think we may think ourselves lucky and let matters stand as they are."

"Well, then," said Grabham, "we can go back to Nabbitt with clear consciences, and report that Buckler's-rents is empty."

"We can," Catchpole observed; "but I don't see why we should be in a hurry about returning to Bow-street. We've got a bit of money and may as well enjoy ourselves for the rest of the day."

Grabham fell in with this view; indeed, he would have fallen in with any view just then.

The worthy pair hastened out of the locality, and, selecting a public-house in a more peaceful clime, pledged each other in sundry flagons of nut-brown ale.

Catchpole forgot his injuries and became quite hilarious, and insisted upon spending money equally with Grabham.

The coins passed hands, and by the time that night was creeping slowly over London the constables had but one shilling left, and that was in Grabham's pocket.

"Hold hard!" he said; "we mustn't forget the

supper. A bit of something to eat will do us good."

"It will," replied Catchpole, whose eyes were wandering vaguely round the room. "I wonder what the landlord's got?"

The landlord, on being consulted, declared that his larder was cleared out with the exception of bread and cheese and a few herrings.

"Then," said Grabham, "we must put up with what we can get. "Here's sixpence for another quart of ale and sixpence for the wittles."

"I'm afraid that you'll have to cook the herrings yourself," the landlord remarked. "My people are all out, and I don't expect them back until very late."

"Don't trouble yourself on that score," Grabham replied. "Bring in the fish and a toasting-fork, and we shall be all right."

The landlord complied, and Grabham and Catchpole, having drawn their chairs nearer to the fire, proceeded to prepare supper and make themselves comfortable.

On one side of the fireplace was a tall screen, and for some reason or other neither of the constables had liked the look of it.

Both Catchpole and Grabham had peeped behind the screen several times, but saw nothing alarming.

"Ha! ha!" said Grabham, as he selected a herring and impaled it on the toasting-fork. "I wonder how our old friends are getting on."

"Which—what old friends?"

"Why, Sir Roland, Mrs. Corcoran, Jacob Butler—that lot, you know."

"I don't know, and I'm blessed if I care," Catchpole replied. "I think we are well quit of them. They won't tumble over us if they can help it; but there's another party who often troubles my mind."

"Who is that?"

"Why, Spring-Heeled Jack."

Grabham dropped toasting-fork and herring into the grate.

"I wish you wouldn't mention him," he said, as he resumed the cooking operations. "It appears to me that you could find something more cheerful to talk about."

"I wonder who he is?"

"Ah!" said Grabham, "I have often wondered the same thing. Perhaps he isn't flesh and blood, like ourselves."

"I'll be bound that he is," Catchpole returned; "and, what is more, he must be worth a heap of money. I should like to know where to find it."

"So should I, if I could make sure that Spring-Heeled Jack wasn't looking."

"Do you know," said Catchpole, who had grown pot-valiant under the influence of nut-brown ale, "I think you and I worried ourselves too much about this fellow. If we had tackled him boldly I think we might have brought him down."

"Perhaps we might and perhaps we mightn't," Grabham remarked, as he thrust the toasting-fork into anothing herring. "However, he hasn't troubled us of late, and I don't see why we should trouble ourselves about him."

At this moment something cold and unpleasant tickled Grabham's neck.

"That will do," he growled.

"What will do?" Catchpole demanded, in amazement. "Did you speak to me?"

"Yes, I did," Grabham replied; "and you're old enough to give over boyish larks."

"Boyish what?"

"Larks! Can't you hear? Don't I speak loud enough?"

"Well," said Catchpole, rubbing his chin thoughtfully, "I am aware that the ale is strong, and—"

"What's the ale got to do with my neck?" Grabham said, interrupting him. "You leave me alone, or— Ah! oh!"

Catchpole threw himself back in his chair, and jerked his knees up to his chin.

"What's the matter with you?" he gasped. "Are you mad?"

"No, I ain't," Grabham replied; "I'll swear that something got hold of me then. There must be somebody behind the screen."

In spite of the ruddy glow of the fire Catchpole went pale to his very lips.

"Some—somebody behind the screen?" he stammered. "Bah! it's all fancy. Look out; you're shrivelling that herring up to a cinder!"

The next instant Grabham gave vent to an awful yell.

"Help! I'm done for. I'm being choked!" he shouted.

Catchpole glanced upwards, and saw the cause of his friend's discomfiture.

A hideous face was peering over the screen, and a long, white arm, with a claw-like hand attached to it, had taken possession of Grabham's neck.

"Spring-Heeled Jack!" he roared, wildly. "Save yourself, Grabham, or you are a dead man!"

---

## CHAPTER CXXXVII.

### AN UGLY GIFT.

"Well," said the landlord of the Bull in Top Boots, "I suppose it is all over with Mrs. Corcoran by this time!"

He trimmed the lamp as he spoke, and set it on the table, so that the light fell upon Dick Sleuth's face.

"Yes," the other ruffian replied. "She served our purpose up to a certain extent, and I think you will agree with me that she is best out of the way."

"Odd that she should meet with Sam Snatcher, wasn't it?"

Dick Sleuth assented with a nod of his bullet-shaped head.

"It was not only odd but lucky," he said, after a pause. "Water couldn't drown her, and it seems almost a question whether—"

Tap—tap—tap! came at the door.

"Who the deuce is that?" the landlord queried. "I told the boys that I wanted to go to bed early, and wouldn't be disturbed any more to-night."

Tap—tap—tap!

"I suppose I had better go and see who it is," the landlord said.

"Yes, but you needn't leave me in the dark," Dick Sleuth said. "I have a nervous feeling creep over me sometimes—a beastly sensation that I am never alone, and that somebody is always looking over my shoulder."

"That's pleasant," the landlord remarked. "Well, then, you had better come with me."

Tap—tap—tap!

"Let us make haste then," said Dick Sleuth. "Whoever it is, the party is in a violent hurry. A messenger with some important business may have arrived."

"It can't be Sam Snatcher, can it?" the landlord queried.

"No; for he said that I was not to expect him before to-morrow," Dick Sleuth replied.

The landlord looked a little queer as he took the lamp in his hand and raised it above his head.

"I don't like these mysterious tappings," he said. "Some trap may be laid for us."

"If you don't recognise the voice, you need not open the door," said Dick Sleuth.

"That's true enough."

When they reached the door, the landlord shaded the lamp with his hand, so that no ray of light could pass through the key-hole.

"Who is there?" he demanded.

"Your own lovey-dovey."

It was the sweet, dulcet voice of Mrs. Corcoran.

The landlord staggered against Dick Sleuth, who uttered an oath as he fell against the wall.

"Let me in, deary," Mrs. Corcoran went on. "It is very cold standing out here, and, besides, I am hungry and thirsty—very thirsty."

"Sam Snatcher has failed," the landlord said, in a hoarse whisper. "What are we to do?"

"Why, open the door, and let the old witch in," Dick Sleuth responded, under his breath.

"All right, old woman," the landlord cried, assuming a cheery voice. "Curse the lock! How hard it is to turn!"

The key certainly made a great deal of noise, but it did its work at last, and as the door opened in walked Mrs. Corcoran.

She made a mock courtesy, and fell to mopping and mowing like a circus clown.

"Why, Dick," she said, holding out her hand, "I am so—so glad to see you. You can't tell how much obliged I am to you for saving my life."

"Oh! don't mention it," Sleuth returned, a little surlily. "Where have you been? Why didn't you come before."

"Because I could not," the hag replied. "A good-natured fellow rescued me, and took me home. He lived in a queer sort of place off Fleet-street, and his wife, bless her heart! was so good to me."

"Humph!" Dick growled. "Well, I must confess that you have had a very narrow escape. You seem to have more lives than a cat."

"I should have been here before," Mrs. Corcoran continued; "but I couldn't, for the simple reason that I wanted my clothes. The oddest thing happened. I had not been in the house more than two hours when I heard Mister—Mister Snatcher—that is his name—and his wife bolt out of the house as if chased by a fiend. I got up, thinking that I ought to go to, and so I broke open a door, found my clothes, and here I am."

The landlord of the Bull in Top Boots said nothing, but led the way to the back parlour.

Then he spoke, with his eyes fixed on Dick Sleuth, who was biting his finger nails nervously.

"There's the brandy bottle," he said. "Help yourself."

Mrs. Corcoran accepted the invitation, and helped herself so liberally that a groan escaped the landlord's lips.

"I feel better now," said Mrs. Corcoran, cheerfully, "my lovey-doveys. I am so glad to be among my friends again, and yet I feel that I should like to thank Mr. Snatcher and his good wife for their kindness."

Dick Sleuth heaved a deep sigh of relief.

"She doesn't know anything," he thought. "What a mercy she hasn't discovered the plot against us!"

Some more remarks passed.

The affairs of Bill Blarney were discussed, and then the landlord began to gape and yawn.

"You can sit up as long as you like," he said; "but I am going to bed."

"And so am I," said Dick Sleuth.

"And I, too, in a few minutes," Mrs. Corcoran chimed in. "You need not disturb yourselves on my account. I know where to find my room."

"I suppose I shall find the brandy bottle empty when I come down in the morning?" the landlord said, ironically.

"Very likely," Mrs. Corcoran replied, coolly. "There isn't much left."

The landlord was in the act of bouncing savagely out of the room, when something extraordinary took place.

It was not a tapping at the door now, but a crash, as if something huge and heavy had been hurled against it.

"What now?" Dick Sleuth roared, as he started to his feet. "Is the house coming down?"

The landlord was too much alarmed to make any reply, and Mrs. Corcoran made a dash for an open cupboard, and bolted herself in.

The crash was repeated, and with such effect that the house trembled to its foundation.

The landlord ran up the staircase, and throwing open a window, thrust out a pistol.

"Speak, or I fire!" he exclaimed. "Who are you to disturb an honest man at such a time?"

He received no verbal response, and for some time he could see nothing.

At last he discerned something bulky growing out of the gloom.

It was an odd-shaped object, and had been placed so as to lean at an angle against the door.

The inn-keeper was not a superstitious man, but a thrill of horror ran through his veins as he peered down at the object of which he could make nothing whatever.

"At first it looked like a box, then a fiddle-case, and then a huge, oblong, shapeless bundle, dark, dim, and motionless.

"Whatever it is it must not remain there," he said. "I must go down. Dick—Dick!"

"Hullo, there!" Sleuth shouted back. "Have you found out the meaning of the row?"

"No! Come up here!"

Dick Sleuth was soon at the window and peering out.

"Well," said the landlord, "what do you make out of the confounded thing?"

"Nothing."

"You and I are agreed upon that point," the landlord said. "What had we better do?"

"Take it in," Sleuth replied. "Hang me! if things are not coming to a pretty pass. Perhaps it is some plunder which our pals have had to leave in a hurry."

"But they would have asked for admittance."

"The traps may be close on their heels."

"That's true," the landlord said, running his fingers through his hair. "Well, follow me, and here's a loaded barker for you. Make it speak if you see a living creature. I care not whether he be friend or foe, he shall suffer for playing me such a fool's trick as this."

They went downstairs slowly and noiselessly.

As they reached the passage Mrs. Corcoran shot past them like a hare and disappeared.

"She's best out of the way, at any rate," said Dick Sleuth. "Now, steady—steady! You open the door, and, by Jupiter! if a strange man attempts to get in, in goes the lead and out goes his brains."

The landlord of the Bull in Top Boots was all of a tremble.

His hands shook so much as to be almost useless, and his teeth chattered in his head.

Something was pressing heavily against the door, and it pressed so hard that the landlord was compelled to use all his strength to prevent himself from reeling back into the passage.

"What the deuce is it?" he gasped. "It weighs half-a-ton."

"It's a box of some kind," Dick Sleuth replied. "Easy with it."

"Easy be hanged!" the landlord said. "I can hold it no longer."

As he spoke he let go his hold, and in tumbled a full-sized coffin.

Dick Sleuth and the inn-keeper clung to each other as the hideous object lay at their feet.

"What devil's trick is this?" the landlord gasped. "See! there are holes bored in it. What can it mean?"

"More than we can think or even dream of, perhaps," Dick Sleuth returned, hoarsely. "Shut the door."

This was done promptly, and then both men again glared at the coffin.

"There's something alive in it," Sleuth said; "but, hang me! if I care for the job of seeing what it is."

The light of the lamp which had been placed on the floor fell full upon the coffin, and a ghastly object it looked.

"I'll fetch an axe and burst the lid open," the landlord said, at last. "It is idle standing staring here, and gasping like a brace of fish out of water."

"I wouldn't care if I had the slightest clue to what it means," Dick Sleuth said; "but I have none. Shall I put a bullet through it first?"

The landlord felt inclined to assent to this arrangement, but on second thoughts he shook his head.

"No," he said; "we may be murdering some pal. Come, we must not act like children. If you're afraid to wait here, fetch the axe. You will find it in the cupboard in the room we came out of."

Dick Sleuth preferred going to staying alone with the coffin for a moment.

He soon returned with the axe, and then came the question who was to strike the blow and solve the seemingly impenetrable mystery.

"Give me the axe, if you are afraid," the landlord said, contemptuously. "I gave you the credit of having more nerve."

"I am not afraid," Dick Sleuth retorted; "but as you are the master of the house, I think you are the proper person to perform the work."

Crash!

The woodwork splintered, and the landlord forced up the fragments with his hands.

"It's a body?" he said, in a terrified whisper.

"Who's body?" Dick Sleuth demanded. "The light is behind me, and I cannot see plainly."

"Wait a moment. I have not got at the face yet."

Again the woodwork splintered, and then a cry came from the landlord's throat.

"Sir Roland Ashton, as I am a living man!" he yelled.

"What?"

"See for yourself," the landlord said. "And see this paper pinned upon his breast, '*With Spring-Heeled Jack's compliments.*'"

Both men rose to their feet and glared at the baronet's white, upturned face.

"Is he dead?" Dick Sleuth said, pressing his hand to his brow, and reeling as a sudden faintness came over him.

"I don't know, but I should say not," the landlord replied. "Be a man, and lend me a hand to help him out."

"I can't just yet; give me a moment; I have lost my breath," Sleuth said, shuddering.

The landlord grew impatient.

"Curse you for a weak-feeling fool!" he said. "If you will not help me get out of the house, and I will do the work alone."

He stooped down as he hissed out these words angrily, and placed his hand on the region of Sir Roland's heart.

"He lives, I tell you," he said. "We shall make profit out of this. What care I for Spring-Heeled Jack, or the whole pack of fiends he may belong to!"

Dick Sleuth now roused himself, and uniting his strength with that of the landlord, lifted the baronet's body clear of the coffin.

At that moment a hollow groan came from Sir Roland's lips.

He moved his hands feebly before his face, the muscles of which quivered, and then he opened his eyes and glared vacantly at the two men who were regarding him with so much interest.

"Well," said the landlord, grimly, "I have had a good many people come to me in all sorts of ways, but I never had one arrive boxed up in a coffin before. Where do you come from, and who sent you?"

"Water—water!" Sir Roland said, pleadingly.

"Give him some, with something else in it," Dick Sleuth said.

A glass of brandy and water was placed against the baronet's lips, and he drank it greedily.

"You ask me where I came from," he said, feebly. "I can hardly tell you. Ah! is he here?"

"He!" the landlord rejoined. "Of whom do you speak?"

"Spring-Heeled Jack."

"Oh! I forgot all about him," the landlord of the Bull in Top Boots said. "He sent a message with you."

"A message?"

"Yes—his compliments."

Sir Roland Ashton turned his weary, bloodshot eyes from the men to the coffin.

"The truth begins to dawn on me," he muttered. "Oh! what horrors I have suffered. He saved me, then, only to drug me and bring me here. Are you in his pay?"

"In his pay!" Dick Sleuth growled, through his set teeth. "I should like to have the chance of paying him a little back in his own coin."

"I know no more than I tell you," Sir Roland continued. "I have not the remotest idea of how I came to be placed in that detestable receptacle for the dead. If you are men with mercy in your hearts you will give me shelter."

"Wait a moment," the landlord returned. "I must discuss that with my friend."

He and Dick Sleuth moved a slight distance

away, and a conversation in a whisper ensued between them.

"Well, yes," the landlord said, "as you don't seem to be in a fit state to talk now you can remain here until the morning."

"Thanks, many thanks," Sir Roland said.

The baronet was so weak that he could scarcely stand, and Dick Sleuth, taking him into his arms as easily as he would have carried a baby, bore him into a room half-way up the landing and placed him on a bed.

"Is there anything you would like to have?" Sleuth asked; "if so, you had better say so now, as I am going to leave you."

"Nothing—nothing but rest," Sir Roland said.

He was asleep almost before Dick Sleuth had left the room and locked it.

The landlord was waiting outside.

"Shall we tell Mrs. Corcoran that he is here?" he said.

"No," Dick Sleuth replied. "It would be worse than madness to do so. There would be murder in the house in less than ten minutes."

"You think she would go for him?"

"Tooth and nail."

"Very well," said the landlord. "We must keep him a prisoner; but how are we to make profit out of him?"

"By using his name."

The landlord of the Bull in Top Boots rubbed the side of his nose and grinned.

"I am afraid that his name isn't worth much now," he said.

"But it may be," Dick Sleuth returned. "You ought to know by this time that a fool is born every day."

"Well—well," said the landlord, "I will leave it all to you. Your head was shaped in an artful mould."

Sleuth accepted the compliment with a laugh, and then, having removed the coffin to a back yard, and carefully covered it out of sight, they parted for the night.

Early in the morning, just as the landlord was taking down the shutters, and Dick Sleuth stood upon the doorstep rubbing his evil-looking eyes, Sam Snatcher peeped out of a court in the street.

For all the world he looked like some haunted animal which had successfully eluded the hounds, but expected them to be on its track again.

He had evidently passed a most uncomfortable night in the streets, and after having signalled to Dick Sleuth, he darted back to cover again.

Dick Sleuth walked across the road in an apparent heedless style; but the wary rogue was really on the watch for any suspicious-looking man who might be an officer in private clothes.

"Hullo! Snatcher," he said. "The coast is clear, and you may come out. What's been the matter?"

"Everything's been the matter," Snatcher replied. "The dead has come to life!"

"Do you mean Mrs. Corcoran? If so," said Sleuth, jerking his thumb over his shoulder, "she is here."

"No—no," Snatcher returned. "I mean the other body—the one that came from Harrow Churchyard and took me such a mortal trouble to get."

Dick Sleuth regarded the body-snatcher with a cynical grin.

"You ain't drunk," he said, "that's a certainty; but you may be mad."

"I'm neither one nor the other," Snatcher said. "What I have told you is nothing but the truth. Harriet and I went into the cellar, the body started up before our very eyes, and we bolted from the house."

"That bears out Mrs. Corcoran's statement to some degree," Dick Sleuth said, thoughtfully. "She found her clothes by breaking open a door, and came on here."

"Does she suspect anything?"

"Not in the least."

"Then I am safe as far as she is concerned," Sam Snatcher said.

"Yes; but what have you done with your wife?" Dick Sleuth demanded.

"Oh! she took refuge with a female friend," Sam Snatcher replied. "So the old hag is here? I wonder what she would think if she knew what a narrow escape she has had?"

"She wouldn't be over pleased, I daresay," Sleuth said. "You had better see her, for she is most anxious to thank you."

"But how can I account for leaving the house in such a violent hurry and turning up here?"

"Easily. Say that you received warning from a neighbour that the Bow-street runners were coming in force."

"That excuse will do as well as any, I suppose," Sam Snatcher said. "Well, I'm mortal glad that I am safe so far; but I must say farewell to my old quarters."

"No doubt about that," Dick Sleuth returned; "but there are plenty of others to be found. It is no use trying to hide anything from Mrs. Corcoran. She knows your business, the witch! and we must be patient and wait for a favourable opportunity to—"

He ceased speaking as one of the upper windows of the Bull in Top Boots opened rather noisily.

Looking up, he observed that Mrs. Corcoran was taking the morning air.

She looked very much like an old owl blinking in the sunlight, and the resemblance was increased when she cocked her head waggishly on one side, and favoured Dick Sleuth and Sam Snatcher with what she intended to be a friendly chuckle.

"Aha! old lady," Dick Sleuth sang out. "How do you find yourself this morning?"

"Pretty well, lovey-dovey," squeaked the old dame. "What a noise you were making after I went to bed last night. I thought you and our friend downstairs were having a fight."

"We know better than that," Dick Sleuth said, placing his hand before his face to hide an ugly frown.

"And there's my friend Snatcher—the dear, good man who saved my life," Mrs. Corcoran resumed. "If I didn't know that he was blessed with one of the best of wives, I should set my cap at him."

Sam Snatcher made no reply, but trying to look amiable, waved a salute with his hand.

"It makes me thankful to think that I have such friends," Mrs. Corcoran said. "One does me a good turn by pitching me into the river, and another pulls me out. I shall be down soon, and we'll all have breakfast together."

"Do you think she is laughing at us?" Sam Snatcher demanded, as Mrs. Corcoran closed the window and disappeared.

"You never can tell," Dick Sleuth replied. "At all events, she is harmless for the present, so come in."

True to her word, Mrs. Corcoran came down to breakfast and presided at the head of the table.

It was a ghoul-like meal, one drinking gin, another brandy, and all gnawing at their food like wolves.

Never had Mrs. Corcoran appeared so amiable before.

She cracked jokes with the company, and told dozens of anecdotes, and by such means entirely threw Sam Snatcher off his guard.

When the meal was over, she sidled up to Sam Snatcher, and placed her skinny hands upon his shoulders.

"I know something which you would give your ears to hear," she said.

"What is it?" he demanded, as a strange expression came over his face.

"Oh! now you are asking questions," she said. "It is a great secret, leading to business which only you can perform. There is an open space at the back of the house, and if you like to come with me I will whisper it in your ears."

"But why not here?"

"Because I do not choose," said Mrs. Corcoran.

Sam Snatcher shot an inquiring glance at Dick Sleuth, who formed "Go" with his mouth.

"All right!" he said. "I'll have another nip of brandy, and then follow you."

Little did the wretch dream that the journey he was about to make, though so short a one, would be his last on earth.

The yard spoken of by Mrs. Corcoran contained a number of tumble-down stables, and into one of these the hag marched.

"There are prying eyes and ears everywhere," she said. "Experience has taught me to be cautious. Come here!"

"You are right," Sam Snatcher said, as he approached her.

"I told you I knew what calling you followed," Mrs. Corcoran said, taking the unsuspecting man by the collar of his coat; "but I always like to act fair and above board to my friends. Sleuth has told me that you will have to shift your quarters, and that leaving the old one will be a loss to you."

"That's true," said Sam Snatcher.

"Then," Mrs. Corcoran returned, "I can tell you where to find a body this very day without the least trouble."

"Where?"

"Here!" Mrs. Corcoran yelled, thrusting a knife into the man's breast. "Here, you dog! Now go and dig your own carcase up and sell it to the doctor instead of mine!"

Sam Snatcher fell back as his life's blood gushed from the wound inflicted by the murderous weapon.

"Here, you hound!" Mrs. Corcoran shrieked, as she stabbed him again and again. "Take your reward. It was I who took the dead man's place in the cellar; it was I who overheard the plot against me, and the plot in which Dick Sleuth took such a pretty part. He shall follow you before long. Down, down, you cur!"

Sam Snatcher made a frantic effort to regain his feet, and to tear the knife from the hag's grasp.

Badly wounded as he was, he felt that he was not so fatally as yet, and, staggering forward, he threw his arms round Mrs. Corcoran, who, sweeping the hand armed with the knife, plunged it up to its handle through his lungs.

Then the death-cry came from Sam Snatcher's foaming lips.

He collapsed, and lay still at his murderess' feet.

"He would have done as much for me," Mrs. Corcoran said, grimly. "Now I will go and tell Dick Sleuth where to find his friend."

She stopped half-way to the back door of the Bull in Top Boots, remembering that she still carried the knife in her hand, and that her clothes were bedabbled with the blood of the murdered man.

She concealed one, but the other refused to be removed or hidden.

A cloud passed over the sun, as if to veil the glorious orb from shining upon so hideous a creature as Mrs. Corcoran, as now, upright as a dart, she stalked into the inn.

Dick Sleuth met her half-way in the passage, which was so dark that he could not see the blood upon her gown.

One glance at the beldame's face convinced him that something was the matter.

"Where is Sam Snatcher?" he demanded.

"He is waiting for you," she replied. "I have told him the secret, and you are to share it."

"I don't like the look of you," Dick Sleuth said, backing slowly. "There's something about your eyes that means mischief."

"Bah!" Mrs. Corcoran retorted. "Go to Sam Snatcher, and hear what he has to say."

She swept past Dick Sleuth, and left him uneasy in mind and full of vague apprehensions.

Walking a little way into the yard, he stopped and called Sam Snatcher by name.

Of course no reply came, and then he walked further, and began to peer here and there, with doubts and fears growing into his brain every moment.

At last he came upon the murdered man's body, and his very heart turned cold with horror.

Dick Sleuth uttered no cry, he spoke no word, but thrusting his hand into a pocket which contained a pistol, he walked slowly back to the house.

---

## CHAPTER CXXXVIII.

### BILL BLARNEY MAKES UP HIS MIND TO BE HIS OWN FRIEND.

WHILE all these events were transpiring, Bill Blarney fretted and fumed within the grim walls of Newgate.

To tell the truth, he had but little faith in Mrs. Corcoran, and the little he had was not of a kind calculated to inspire him with confidence.

The sudden attack he had made upon the hag caused the turnkeys to look after him sharper than ever.

The gaol delivery happened to be an exceptionally heavy one, and on the evening of the very same day that he had tried conclusions with Mrs. Corcoran a warder paid him a visit.

"Well, Blarney," he said, hanging a lantern upon a hook in the wall, "you seem determined to keep your old game up to the last. That old woman isn't your mother, you know. We have heard all about her since she went away, and she will do wise by not paying us another visit."

"Oh!" Bill Blarney growled. "Is that all you have come to tell me?"

"No."

"What then?"

"Why, I am going to give you a little society. You are to have company."

"I'd rather be alone," Bill Blarney said. "Who is it?"

"A fellow named Jem Basker," the warder

replied. "He would have been tried with Ted Nickells, only he was badly wounded by a man named Jacob Butler."

"I know the white-livered hound!" the ruffian hissed, savagely.

"Who is there that you don't know, Bill?" said the warder. "Well, whether you like it or not, Basker will have to share your cell, for we are as full as a bed-tick. I have come to shift you a little nearer to the door."

"I wish you could shift me out of it altogether," Bill Blarney observed. "If I had a few hundred shiners these walls would be as easy to pass through as paper."

"I don't think so," the warder returned. "You see, you are a special pet of the governor's, and he wouldn't part with you on any account."

At this moment another warder entered the cell, and the work of shifting Bill Blarney began.

The men knew what a hardened villain they had to deal with, and used every precaution against a surprise or an attack.

But Bill Blarney made no resistance whatsoever.

The game he had been playing at was a losing one, and only led to pains and penalties which might have been spared him had he remained quiet.

"Need I be fixed to the wall like a scarecrow?" he asked.

"Yes, until you go to bed," the warder replied; "and then our orders are to chain you down to it."

"Humph! I suppose I must put up with it," Bill Blarney growled.

"Yes; because there is no help for it," one of the warders said, as the other moved towards the door. "You have only yourself to thank."

"Oh! don't rant at me," Bill Blarney said, with an oath. "When is this—this what-do-ye-call-him?"

"Jem Basker."

"When is he coming?"

"In a very few minutes."

Bill Blarney kept his eyes on the cell door, and listened intently as each footstep sounded on the gloomy passage beyond.

At last there came a rattling of chains and a bumping sound, as if the warders were dragging something heavy along.

"It's a shame to treat me ill, and more than half dead as I am, like this," whined a voice, as the key grated noisily in the lock. "I shall never live to take my trial."

"So much the better for you," said a warder, as he half-led and half-pushed Jem Basker into the cell. "There's a friend for you. He can't come to you, but you can go to him."

Jem Basker said nothing, but looked ruefully at the irons dangling about his legs.

"If I do live to stand in the dock," he said, "I'll let the judge and jury know how I have been treated. Call this a Christian country? Bah! I'd rather live among a set of cannibals."

"There's no knowing what sort of creatures you may live among, if what the parson says at church is true. There, I will leave you for an hour, and then come in and make you comfortable for the night."

"Comfortable!"

Bang went the cell door.

The heavy footsteps of the warders died away, and Jem Basker stood erect, as if the irons were but feathers about his limbs.

"Why, Bill Blarney!" he said, running forward and grasping the scoundrel's hands. "It is many a long day since I saw you."

"And I'll be bound that you never expected to see me here."

"No," said Jem Basker; "but I thought it very probable that you might find your way here. So they have trussed you up pretty tight."

"As tight as a drumhead," Blarney growled.

"Ah! well," said Jem Basker, "people who take the most care often catch most cold."

"What do you mean by that?"

"Why, that I don't intend staying here any longer than I can help."

"You would be a fool if you would," said Bill Blarney; "but now that you are here, perhaps you'll tell me how you expect to get out?"

"Why, Bill," Jem Basker cried, "anybody to hear you talk would think that you had lost all heart. You did the trick yourself, you know."

Bill Blarney uttered a furious oath.

"Yes," he said; "but the warders would listen to reason then, but now—"

The ruffian's feelings overcame him, and after giving vent to a few more horrible curses, he hung his head sulkily.

"Oh! that's your game, is it?" said Jem Basker. "Well, I can play at it, too?"

"What do you mean?"

"That if you don't care to talk to me, you can do the other thing."

"What's the use of talking when it's all over with me?" Bill Blarney growled. "They don't mean to let me slip through their fingers this time."

"The more you take that view of the matter, the worse you will be," Jem Basker said. "I've gone through bigger troubles than this, and I have made up my mind to be out of this hole before this time to-morrow night."

He spoke so confidently that Bill Blarney stared at him in surprise.

"How will you manage it?" he asked.

"Wait and see," Basker replied; "the warders think themselves very clever, but they have a cunning dog to deal with."

Just then they were disturbed by the entrance of the two warders who brought the prisoners their suppers.

Bill Blarney devoured his share of the frugal fare, but Jem Basker thrust it contemptuously aside.

"If you won't eat it for your supper it will do for your breakfast," the warder said. "You have grown mighty particular all at once."

"Yes, because I have been robbed," Jem Basker said, wrathfully. "Before I was removed from the other wing of the prison I gave Tom, the warder, a crown-piece to fetch me something tasty, but deuce a bit did he bring me."

"We can't help what Tom did or what he didn't," said the warder. "Well, go to bed hungry if you like; it's no matter to us."

When the warders had secured Bill Blarney for the night and left the cell, Jem Basker threw himself upon the rude pallet prepared for him and began to chuckle.

"What's there here to make you laugh?" Bill Blarney demanded. "Stop that row, and let me go to sleep."

"I was laughing to think how oddly things come about," said Jem Basker.

"I suppose you mean it is odd that you and I should share the same cell?"

"Not exactly; but it so happens that I have occupied this cell before."

"You don't mean that?"

"I do."

"How long ago?"

"Less than two years," Jem Basker said. "I wore a beard then, and went under a different name. It was only a case of knocking an old woman down and robbing her of a few shillings, so the big-wig let me off with six months. The fellow who was tried before me stole a loaf of bread and got twelve."

"So you have been here before?" Bill Blarney observed. "Well, what of it?"

"More than you think," Jem Basker replied. "I tried to get out of this very cell, and I should have succeeded, but I was interrupted just as I was getting ready, and taken to another part of the prison."

"Oh! you were getting ready?" said Bill Blarney, becoming suddenly interested in what Jem Basker was saying. "What do you mean by that?"

"That I had buried a file and a crowbar, made of short joints, under the floor."

"But they must have been found long before this."

"That's a question to be decided in the morning," Jem Basker said. "I took good care to make the slab of stone just like the rest, and if the flooring hasn't been taken up the implements must be still there."

"A file and a crowbar ain't of much account," said Bill Blarney.

"Not unless you happen to know something of the place you are in," Jem Basker said. "You may not be aware that we are in a cell next to the street?"

"I was not aware of it."

"Then you know it now."

"You needn't fly into a temper," Bill Blarney said. "How on earth was I to know anything except that I have been caged up here and tortured almost out of my senses?"

"Well, I can't help that," said Jem Basker.

"I didn't say you could, but you might have some feeling for a fellow in distress."

"Perhaps I have more than you give me credit for," Jem Basker replied. "Well, let me resume. One night when I was here alone I went about tapping the walls for the want of something better to do, and—"

"Yes, go on."

"I thought I heard a sound in the passage outside."

"It was only the closing of a distant door."

"And," Jem Basker continued, lowering the tone of his voice, "I suddenly struck a portion that I thought sounded hollow. I struck at it again, and then felt sure of it. So, Bill, there's a hollow space between this cell and the outer wall."

"It would be a joyful thing for me to know, if I wasn't so chained hand and foot that I can scarcely turn on my side."

"The file will set you free, and the crowbar do the rest," Jem Basker said.

"I forgot to ask you how you got them."

"Ted Nickells—poor Ted Nickells—managed to smuggle them into the prison for me."

"All right," said Bill Blarney. "I understand. Now I think we had better go to sleep, for one of the warders may be sneaking about, and hear us talking."

When the dim light of early morning stole into the cell Jem Basker rose, and roused Bill Blarney by shaking him by the shoulders.

"What are you up to?" Bill said. "You know that I can't get up until those devils of warders come to me."

"I forgot that," Jem Basker returned; "but, never mind, I want to speak to you."

"Well, what is it?"

"Do you believe in dreams?"

"I ought to," Bill Blarney replied, grimly. "I have plenty of them, and they are ugly enough in all conscience."

"But I had a nice dream," said Jem Basker. "I thought that you and I were free, and cracking a lovely crib full of money and plate."

"I wish it may come true," Bill Blarney observed. "I'd give anything to be at my old work again."

"Hush!" Jem Basker whispered, "the warders are coming; when they have gone I'll see about the file and crowbar."

The warders did not stay longer than they could help.

They looked to the prisoners' irons, secured Bill Blarney as on the previous day, and finding everything satisfactory, were going away, when Jem Basker called them back.

"Get us a couple of bottles of wine, and keep the change," he said, tossing a guinea across the cell.

One of the warders caught the coin and spun it into the air.

"You live like a king, Jem," he said. "When do you want the wine?"

"In about an hour's time."

"All right; you shall have it, my noble pippin. Hadn't you better have something to eat? You had no supper last night, you know. It's just as well to eat while you drink."

"I'll think over it and let you know by the time that you have brought the wine."

The warder left the cell, and then Jem Basker, gathering up his irons so as to keep them as silent as possible, fell upon his hands and knees, and began to examine the floor minutely.

Bill Blarney watched him with bated breath and a hungering expression in his eyes, which told how anxious he was to know the result of the search.

"This was the slab, I think," he said, suddenly. "I marked it with my spoon. Yes, it is the same."

"And hasn't been touched?"

"No."

Bill Blarney's enormous mouth expanded almost from ear to ear in a triumphant and ferocious grin.

"You're a brick, Jem," he said; "that's what you are, and if I could get at you, I think I should hug you."

"Don't begin to jump for joy too soon," Jem Basker said. "When I said that the stone had not been disturbed, I meant that it was in the same place, and so it is, but—"

"Oh! lor'," Bill Blarney gasped; "don't dash all my hopes to the ground."

"I was about to remark that I hope the file and crowbar are in the same place too," Basker said. "Now let me think. I used to get this slab up by pressing my hand upon the marked corner and working it up and down. Yes, that's it. The stone begins to loosen, and we shall know our fates in a few moments."

Bill Blarney craned his neck forward, and so strained in his fetters that the veins upon his forehead grew black and as hard as whipcord.

"Do you see what you want?" he demanded, hoarsely.

"I—hush!—the fiends seize them! We are disturbed!"

Jem Basker thrust the slab into its place and sat upon it as the warder, who had been sent for the wine, entered with the bottles under his arm.

"Hullo!" he said, laughing. "Are you preparing for a picnic, Jem?"

Jem Basker made no reply.

He clutched his throat, and began to cough and sneeze violently.

"You had better get up," said the warder. "That floor is damp, and you will have rheumatism in your bones."

"According to what you told me," said Basker, speaking with an effort, "my bones won't trouble me long. I suppose I can sit where I like, so long as I don't break any of the prison rules?"

"Oh! yes; you needn't get crusty about it. Here's the wine. I fetched it at once, because I'm off duty until the afternoon."

"Put it on the floor," said Jem Basker. "Bill, we'll be merry as long as we can. We'll have a bottle each, and drink to our jolly ride to Tyburn!"

The warder, suspecting nothing, did as he was told, and left the prisoners to themselves.

"What an escape!" Basker said, pressing his hands to his temples. "By Jupiter! I thought it was all over."

"I never felt so bad in my life," Blarney said. "Knock off the neck of one of those bottles, and hand it here."

Nothing loth to oblige his friend and have a drink himself, Jem Basker complied, and soon the red wine was gushing down their throats.

"Now I feel ready for anything," Basker said, as he returned to the opposite corner of the cell.

"Don't be in a hurry," Bill Blarney gasped out, in an agony of fear. "That warder may think of something and come back again."

"Not he," Jem Basker replied. "He was in too much of a hurry to get off duty. Up—up comes the stone and here are the pretty little toys, Bill."

"Yes—yes," said Blarney; "but hide them again."

Jem Basker fondled the file and crowbar.

"They are our best friends," he said, "and we should not be in such a hurry to part with them, but, love them as I do, they must not get us into trouble."

He buried them in the hole, and replacing the slab, cut a few capers round Bill Blarney.

"We are as good as away," he said. "The cell wall will come down easy enough, and then all we have to do is to remove one block on the street side, which will enable us to pass through."

"But do you think the crowbar is strong enough?" Bill Blarney asked.

"It is strong enough for anything, if used properly," Basker replied. "As soon as it is dark, and we are left alone for the night, we will commence operations. Shall we have the other bottle of wine now?"

"No," Blarney replied. "I think we had better drink it just before we start working."

"Very well. I'll agree to anything, for I feel as happy as an alderman dreaming of turtle soup."

Dinner-time came and passed away.

It seemed a terrible long time to the hour when the warders made their last round, but it came at last.

The prisoners were left to themselves, one of the warders jocosely asking Jem Basker if he intended to give another wine-party on the morrow.

"Very likely," was the reply.

"That's lucky," said the warder, "for your trial takes place the day after to-morrow, and, from what I can hear, the counsel for the prosecution holds a hot brief against you."

"I don't doubt it for a moment," Jem Basker said, grinning; "but I hope the gentleman in the wig won't be too hard on me."

A sigh of relief came from his and Bill Blarney's lips when the rattling of bolts and grating of locks told them that in all probability they would not be disturbed until the morning.

The morning!

What would it bring forth to them?

Would it find them free, or in another and more secure cell, laden with still heavier fetters than they wore now?

The risk was great and the suspense almost beyond endurance.

Jem Basker had no ray of light to work by, which made the attempt still more hazardous.

The noise of an iron falling after it had been filed off would surely reach the ears of a warder, and then all their trouble and anxious care would end in dismal failure.

Raising the slab of stone slowly and noiselessly, Jem Basker felt about with his hand until it came in contact with the file.

"I am coming, Bill," he said. "Keep perfectly still, and if I happen to pinch you bear it without a murmur."

"I will," Blarney said.

A choking rattle in his throat told what hopes and fears were passing in his mind.

Jem Basker then commenced operations.

Thrusting a corner of the coarse sheet under one of the rings to which the irons were attached, so as to deaden the sound, he commenced filing swiftly but cautiously.

Presently he stopped.

"Lift your foot up, Bill," he said. "I think that will do for one. Steady—steady, or the whole lot will go clanking down on the floor."

Catching the fetter in his hand as Blarney moved, Jem Basker gave it a twist.

There was a slight snapping sound, and one of Bill Blarney's limbs was free.

The next ring was filed away in the same manner, but then the great difficulty had to be dealt with.

Bill Blarney wore about his waist a girdle of steel, fitted with two strong rings, through which a chain ran.

The chain was twisted round a post at the foot of the bed and padlocked.

Jem Basker did not attack the rings this time, but the chain, and the task proved the easier of the two.

The metal was softer, and gave way so readily that Jem Basker felt the file slip through before he thought he had half-finished.

He then drew the chain through the rings as quietly as possible, and piled the fetters in a heap gently on the floor.

This took at least ten minutes to accomplish, but it was done at last.

"Now, Bill," Basker said, "you may get up and perform upon me. I suppose you know what to do?"

"If I was as innocent as a baby about such matters," Blarney said, "I could not help profiting by such a lesson as I have just had."

# SPRING-HEELED JACK,

## THE TERROR OF LONDON.

"WHAT DOES MY NOBLE LORD REQUIRE?" SPRING-HEELED JACK DEMANDED.

In a few minutes Jem Barker had shaken off his irons, and stood in the centre of the cell stretching his aching arms above his head.

If the work had been hard, and the anxiety great, they had still greater trials to contend ith.

They were free, so far as concerned the fetters, it two thick walls lay between them and freedom.

The crowbar, which had lain hidden for so long time, was cunningly made in short pieces which rewed together.

It had been made by a master hand, and was of great strength.

Jem Basker now went round the wall tapping at it softly.

At last he stopped.

"Here we are!" he whispered. "Now, Bill, we must work with a will, for you know what it means to us."

"Shall I commence?" Blarney asked, as he wiped the clammy beads of perspiration from his brow.

"No; I'll do the first turn, and when I am tired you can go on."

Running his finger along the stonework, Jem Basker found the cemented part, and inserting the sharpened end of the crowbar into it, began to remove the loose stuff.

It made such a rattle on the floor that the hair of the prisoners stood on end.

"This will never do!" Bill Blarney gasped. "What on earth is to be done?"

"What fools we are not to have thought of the bedclothes," Jem Basker said. "Throw them down on the floor, close to the wall, and then there will be no noise at all."

Simple as the idea was, it was a good and effective one.

There was no rattle of cement now, and presently Jem Basker announced that the stone was rocking under the pressure of the crowbar, and was in a fit state to be removed.

"Catch hold of the corner, Bill," he said, "and pull it towards you."

Blarney did so, but so zealous was he to use his strength that he overdid it, and the huge block of stone came lumbering down.

## CHAPTER CXXXIX.

### NAMON WALLACK IS ENTRUSTED WITH A SACRED CHARGE.

LANONI and her tribe were moving eastward.

Most were to leave for a time to attend the fairs held at Norwich, Lynn, and Yarmouth.

Strange things were unpacked from the caravans and closely inspected, and stranger things were acted whenever the band halted in places where no other mortal eyes could see them.

Many of the younger members threw off their ragged clothes, and put on garments resplendent with fringe and tinsel.

The elder members touched up the caravan wheels with streaks of glaring paint; canvas pictures, with all the wonders of the world, were unravelled and revarnished, and almost every kind of musical instrument was brought to light.

They required no practising upon.

The showman's great idea is to make all the noise possible.

Tune and time are out of place with the country people, who want plenty for their money.

The Wild Man of the Woods rehearsed his part; the Queen of the May simpered and danced upon the green; and the bold, cruel-hearted baron glared fiercely upon the honest and intensely virtuous peasant.

Lanoni looked upon all these business-like preparations with a smiling face.

She was going into retirement for a time with a chosen few of her people, and her destination would remain a close secret.

Namon Wallack had a show of his own, containing a rather strange medley of curiosities.

A trained monkey, a learned pig, a fat boy, a thin man, and a calf blessed with two heads and ten legs, were a few of the wonders to be gaped at by a grinning crowd at the price of a penny a-head.

Who would have thought that this man, who had seen and encountered so much, would soon stand upon a rickety platform, and, dressed as a clown, set the grinning yokels roaring with laughter?

All was ready for the journey to the east, where the gipsies were almost sure of reaping a harvest.

The last night had come and was speeding away when Namon Wallack walked in thoughtful mood to his tent.

Nobody shared it, for, as yet, he had not chosen a wife, though many brown, bewitching eyes would have melted at a word of love from his lips.

Namon was renowned for his bravery, unselfishness, and honesty.

His word was law among the men, and the boys almost worshipped him.

There was nothing that came amiss to Namon Wallack.

He could swim like a duck, fetch fish out of a lake or pond as if by magic, and manufacture all sorts of useful articles out of trivial things such as most people would tread upon.

Namon Wallack entered his tent, and, shaking up his homely bed, threw himself down at full length.

But he could not sleep.

He was oppressed with a feeling that something was going to happen.

The sensation was a strange one, and he could not account for it.

It was not a sensation of fear, such as a man feels when he apprehends danger, but of awe—a chilling, creeping, uncanny notion that something unearthly was following him about.

Wallack, after a vain attempt to court the drowsy god, rose to his feet and stood at the door of his tent.

The stars shone brightly overhead, twinkling and peeping wistfully through the foliage of the trees, as if wondering at the strange sight beneath them.

The air was balmy, though cool, and all Nature lay resting peacefully.

As Namon Wallack looked through the forest glade he thought he saw two figures moving,

Quick as thought he went back to his tent, and, snatching up his gun, which was always kept loaded, returned to the open air.

Crouching down, he watched the spot where he thought he had seen the figures.

He might have been mistaken, for the branches, as they moved slowly to and fro, cast many strange shadows.

But Namon Wallack still watched, and presently he saw the figures again.

Grasping the gun tightly, he pressed his finger

upon the trigger, when, to his surprise, he heard his name called.

"I am Namon Wallack," he said. "What would you have with me? Speak out at once, for we allow no strangers here."

"I am no stranger to you," said the voice. "Put down that gun. Do you not see that I have brought a lad with me?"

"I see," Namon Wallack replied; "but I know not what he or you want here. Your business—quick! I am in no mood to be trifled with."

"I should have thought that you would have known the voice of Ralph Ashton," was the reply. "Why, Namon, if you had spoken to me at the bottom of a coal-pit, I should have recognised you in a moment."

"I am sure I beg your pardon," Namon said. "You are very welcome. Will you walk into my tent?"

"Yes; because I have something very serious to say to you—indeed, I may as well say that I am going to ask a favour of you."

"I shall be delighted to do anything to serve you," Namon Wallack said, as he led the way into the tent, and lit the naptha lamp; "but first allow me to ask you a question."

"Certainly, a dozen if you like."

"How was it, on the night when I told you of Lanoni's danger, that you galloped away on horseback without saying a word?"

"Shall I tell you?"

"If you please."

"It was I who told Spring-Heeled Jack of your danger, and sent him to you."

"A hundred thousand thanks!" Namon said, grasping Ralph's hand. "I shudder to think what I suffered at the hands of those wretches. Would that Spring-Heeled Jack had stayed to receive my thanks."

"He requires no thanks," Ralph replied. "Now to business. You see this boy?"

Namon Wallack turned his dark, penetrating eyes on a handsome, well-knit lad, who still retained Ralph Ashton's hand affectionately.

"Yes," said the gipsy.

"I call him Robin Gray," Ralph Ashton said, "and I wish you to call him the same."

"You wish me to call him the same?" Namon Wallack said, in astonishment. "I do not understand your meaning exactly."

"I wish you to take care of him," Ralph replied. "You will be travelling over many parts of the country, and the boy will be safer with you even than with me."

"I doubt it," Namon Wallack said, smiling; "but I am willing to take him if such be your wish."

"It is," said Ralph.

Then he turned to the boy.

"You will go with this man," he said, stroking the lad's head with his hand. "If you obey him you will find him kind and good."

"Oh! yes," Robin said. "I will do anything that you wish."

"Then that is settled," Ralph said.

He took out a well-filled purse, and began to count some gold into his hand.

"No—no," Namon said. "I do not want that."

"But I insist," Ralph replied. "This boy is under my protection, and his living must be paid for. You must make him useful, Namon. He is a likely lad, and I do not wish him to stand about idle."

Namon Wallack drew Ralph Ashton aside.

"I presume that there is some mystery about this boy's life?" the gipsy whispered.

"There is."

"May I enquire what it is?"

"Not at present."

"I will not press you upon the subject," Namon Wallack said; "but may I ask if Lanoni knows anything of this boy?"

"She does."

"Then I am satisfied," Namon said, "and I will put no more questions to you. Robin."

The boy crossed, unhesitatingly, over to him.

"Do you wish to come with me?" Namon asked.

"Yes, because Mr. Ashton wishes me to do so," Robin replied.

"Bravely spoken," Namon Wallack said. "You will find your life one of sweets and bitters—it may be more bitter than sweet; but you will be brave, and look hard times steadily in the face if they should come?"

"Yes."

"Then our interview is at an end," Ralph said. "I must away, and at once. Duty calls me miles from here."

Taking the boy up in his arms he kissed him on both cheeks, and then turned to Namon.

"You will let me hear from you often?" he said.

"Once a week."

"That will do, and if you should ever require a friend you know to whom to apply."

He was gone before another word could be spoken, and Namon Wallack was left alone with Robin Gray.

"You are tired, lad," the gipsy said, pointing to the bed. "Sleep!"

Robin's eyelids soon closed in slumber, and Namon Wallack sat watching him until the stars began to pale in the sky.

As the first ray of sunlight gilded the tree-tops Lanoni walked into the tent.

"I have come to say good-bye to you, Namon," she said, "and to thank you for the many good services you have done me."

Namon Wallack sank on one knee, and pressed his lips to the gipsy queen's hand.

"I beg that you will not mention my services," he said. "See here."

He pointed to the sleeping boy.

Lanoni started.

The colour flew into her cheeks, and then, fleeing swiftly, left her as pale as death.

"Who brought him here?"

"Ralph Ashton," Namon replied. "Has he deceived me? Did you not know that the boy was to be brought to me?"

"Yes; but not so soon—not so soon!" Lanoni said, pressing her hand on her heart.

"You are not well," Namon said, running forward to support her.

"It is nothing—nothing," Lanoni murmured. "Of late I have been subjected to this faintness, but it soon passes away."

At that moment the boy called Robin Gray awoke and opened his eyes.

He stared hard at Lanoni for a moment and then smiled a greeting.

"So," she said, caressing the boy as he rose, "Ralph Ashton has sent you to be a stroller?"

"I am to do what I am told," the boy replied.

"Your tongue could not have found a better answer," Lanoni said. "We may meet again and, perhaps, soon. For the present, good-bye, and may Heaven watch over you."

"Have you rested sufficiently?" Namon asked of Robin.

"Oh! yes, thank you; I feel quite refreshed," the boy replied. "Can I make myself useful in any way?"

"Do you understand anything about horses?"

Robin Gray shook his head.

"All that will come in time," Namon said. "Well, that yellow caravan before you is mine. Go inside and make it as tidy as you can."

Glad of anything to do, Robin ran off to obey.

He found himself in a curious house upon wheels.

It was divided into two compartments.

One for sleeping and one for living.

Robin Gray was delighted.

He had never seen anything like this before, and he set about his task in childish glee.

There were a good many things to dust and polish, and by the time he had finished the sun was well up.

As he came down the steps he almost ran against a very fairy of a little girl.

Both laughed, for Robin, to avoid a collision, had pitched himself down on his hands on the grass.

"I suppose I looked very stupid?" he said, as he picked himself up.

"I did not say so," the girl replied. "I have never seen you before."

"No; I only came early this morning."

"And are you going to stay with us?"

"I am going to travel with Namon Wallack," Robin replied.

"Well, it is all one and the same thing," the girl said. "I am going to travel too. Perhaps we shall see each other very often."

Robin Gray hoped so, but was too bashful to give effect to his thoughts in words.

"What is your name?" the girl asked.

"Robin Gray."

"Would you like to know mine?"

"Yes."

The girl laughed merrily as she went tripping away under the trees.

"That is a secret for the present," she said; "but I daresay you will know all about me soon. You may call me Jennie, if you like."

"Well," said Robin, "I shall like to call you Jennie. Won't you come back and shake hands?"

"Not now," the little fairy replied. "Lanoni is calling me. Good-bye, Robin Redbreast—I mean Robin Gray. Ha! ha! ha!"

---

## CHAPTER CXL.

### MRS. CORCORAN GOES HER WAY.

MRS. CORCORAN, after her terrible interview with Sam Snatcher, and after sending Dick Sleuth to find the body of his brother villain, walked boldly into the room behind the bar and confronted the landlord.

He saw in a moment that something had happened, and he started back as he gazed at the hag.

"What is this?" he cried. "There is blood on your dress!"

Mrs. Corcoran replied with a wild burst of hysterical laughter.

"Yes, it is blood," she said at length; "the blood of a dog. See, here is the knife that did the deed."

She cast the weapon down upon the floor.

It stuck quivering in the floor at the landlord's feet, as if trembling at the awful work it had accomplished.

A sickly green hue spread over the face of the landlord of the Bull in Top Boots.

"The blood of a dog!" he repeated, hoarsely. "There is no dog here."

"What else was Sam Snatcher?" Mrs. Corcoran demanded. "What else was he but a cold-blooded, cowardly dog, now? He is gone—"

"Gone—gone!" the landlord exclaimed. "What are you telling me—are you mad?"

"Yes, he is gone," Mrs. Corcoran rejoined. "I slew him before he had time to murder me. The villain has met with his just deserts."

Before the landlord of the Bull in Top Boots could say another word, Dick Sleuth stalked into the room.

His brow was dark with passion; his parted lips displayed his fang-like and blackened teeth, which he ground together in the intensity of his rage.

Dick Sleuth had the pistol in his hand, and his finger circled round the trigger.

The landlord, deeming what would happen, rushed in between Sleuth aud Mrs. Corcoran.

"Stand out of my way!" Sleuth said, in a tone of voice thick with passion. "Back! I will have the she-devil's life!"

"Don't be a fool, Dick," said the landlord, catching him by the wrist. "Listen to reason."

"Reason!" Dick Sleuth yelled. "I will listen to nothing. She has killed Sam Snatcher. He lies dead in one of the outhouses, and I will have her life."

The innkeeper tightened his grip upon Dick Sleuth's wrist, and held it down so that the muzzle of the pistol pointed to the floor.

Mrs. Corcoran folded her arms and looked calmly on the scene.

"If what you and she tell me be true," the landlord said, "more than enough blood has been shed for one day. Leave the room, old woman. Go where you will, and trouble us no longer."

Mrs. Corcoran stooped suddenly and snatched the knife from the floor.

"I will go when I please, and not until I please," she replied. "Let Dick Sleuth do his worst. His pistol may miss fire, or miss its aim. At all events its report will startle the people in the street; but this," she shrieked, "makes no noise, and never misses its aim."

The innkeeper and Dick Sleuth were struggling desperately now.

"Dick, Dick!—my old friend Dick!" the landlord gasped, "if you have no regard for yourself think of me. Naught but ill can come of this."

"I care not what comes of it," Sleuth cried. "Let go your hold, if you value your life. Curse you! Is this hag to live after what she has done?"

"No, no," the landlord replied; "but this is not the moment for your revenge."

"But it is for mine!" Mrs. Corcoran screeched. "Dick Sleuth, I will take the first chance."

As she spoke she leaned over the innkeeper's shoulder, and struck Dick Sleuth with the knife.

"Oh! I am stabbed," he cried. "Oh! I am wounded to death."

"Death and the devil!" roared the Bull in Top Boots. "This is too much."

Placing Dick Sleuth carefully on the floor, he turned round to grapple with Mrs. Corcoran.

But she was gone.

She had vanished as suddenly and mysteriously as if her shrivelled body had been composed of thin air.

The landlord smote his brow as he glanced round the room and then at the wounded man.

"Dick—Dick," he said, "you are not badly hurt. It is only a scratch, and you will be all right in a few days."

"Only a scratch!" Sleuth repeated, writhing and twisting in his agony. "Yes, yes—only a scratch, but a wide, wide one. Did you say that I should be all right in a few days? No, no; I have received my quietus. Oh! what is this? Is it death?"

He swooned from pain and loss of blood.

The landlord of the Bull in Top Boots thought that the man was dead.

He felt much relieved when Dick Sleuth opened his eyes again and stretched out his hand feebly.

"Don't leave me! Don't leave me for a moment!" he said.

"I was only going to fetch you some brandy," the landlord remarked.

"All the brandy in the world couldn't do me any good now," Sleuth said, in a faint tone of voice. "Ah! you have bound up my wound; but it is no use."

"Shall I send for a doctor?" demanded the landlord, who was almost frantic with terror and alarm.

"It would be waste of time," Sleuth replied, "for I should be gone before he could get here."

"Then what can I do?"

"Nothing—nothing! Sit by me. Take my hand. How dark it is! Has night come so soon?"

The landlord of the Bull in Top Boots cried like a child.

Tears had long been a stranger to him, as had been the better part of his nature.

"Don't go on like that, Dick," he said, in a trembling voice. "Let me fetch you something."

"No! Stay where you are," Sleuth replied, now panting. "If you leave me I will curse you with my dying breath. I have been a bad—bad man. I—"

"Not worse than the rest of us," the landlord interposed.

"Perhaps not," said Dick Sleuth; "but I am so bad that I am afraid to die."

At that moment a heavy sound came from overhead.

"Help! help! Let me out!" cried a voice. "Let me out. You have caught me in a trap, but I will rouse the neighbourhood. Let me out! Do you hear? Let me out!"

"That is Sir Roland Ashton," the landlord said, starting to his feet and tearing at his hair.

"Go to him—set him free—or the house will soon be full of people," Sleuth replied. "I don't want to get you into trouble. Bury me—you know where—promise that."

"Help! What oh! there. Help!" roared Sir Roland.

The landlord of the Bull in Top Boots dashed upstairs.

He had forgotten to take the key with him, but one kick sent the door flying open.

The next instant his iron hands were fixed upon Sir Roland Ashton's throat.

"Silence! or I will choke the life out of you," the landlord hissed. "Is it not enough that I should have a dead man on the premises, and another dying, without being troubled by you?"

He forced Sir Roland back, and hurling him on the bed, stood over him in a threatening attitude.

"What have I done to deserve this?" demanded the baronet, raising himself upon his elbow.

"What have I done that I should be plagued with such a villain as you?" the landlord retorted. "See, the door is open, but if you attempt to leave the house I will send you swiftly to another world. I must go downstairs now, but I will return presently."

With this the half-distracted man rushed back to Dick Sleuth.

A strange change had come over the dying man's face.

The hard, brutal lines had given way to a softer expression.

The dew of death had gathered upon his brow, and though his lips moved quickly, no sound came from them.

"What are you trying to tell me, Dick?" he said, placing his arm round Sleuth's neck. "Is there anything you wish to say?"

"You will not—not—let my body go to the doctors?"

"I swear I won't," the landlord said. "Surely you can't think so bad of me as that?"

"Men who lead such lives as we have led," Sleuth returned, forcing each word from his lips with an effort, "have no real friendship for each other. You know it as well as I."

The innkeeper bowed his head, and averted his eyes from those which were becoming glazed and filmy.

"But I always felt friendly towards you, Dick," he said.

"Yes, so long as money came and brandy flowed," Sleuth replied. "I don't blame you. I have made use of you and your house, but all that is over now—yes, over now."

His head fell back heavily, and for some moments he lay perfectly quiet.

The landlord of the Bull in Top Boots placed his hand upon Dick Sleuth's heart.

It was beating so feebly that he could scarcely feel its action.

The tide of Dick Sleuth's life was ebbing swiftly.

"Is there nothing more you wish to say?" the landlord asked, hoping to rouse the dying man.

"Yes."

"What is it?"

"Go back."

"Go back?" the landlord repeated. "I don't know what you mean."

"I mean go back from this life," Dick Sleuth said, in a voice hardly above a whisper. "It is too late for me, but not for you. Oh! the agony now and misery to come. Hold me—don't let me go—don't let me die! I cannot—I dare not—"

The room swam with the man watching this awful death scene, and, as a wild yell of despair burst from Dick Sleuth's lips—the last cry he ever uttered upon earth—the landlord sank, half-fainting, beside the dead body.

Recovering his self-control as quickly as possible, he dashed the beads of perspiration from his face and started to his feet.

Sir Roland Ashton stood in the doorway.

"Can I be of any help to you?" he asked, submissively.

"Any help to me!" the landlord returned, clutching at his cravat, for a lump had risen in his throat. "You see this man?"

"Yes."

"He is dead."

"There is no doubt about that," Sir Roland replied, calmly, "and I can see how he came by his death."

"He was foully murdered by a hag—a witch!" the landlord cried, flinging his arms wildly above his head. "This is the work of a she-devil; but she shall not walk the earth. I'll hunt her down, and for every moment of pain she gave the poor fellow she shall suffer a hundred. I swear it—I swear it by the heart that beats within me!"

Every word he uttered was full of energy and ferocity.

Sir Roland stood with his hand upon the door-post watching the enraged man.

"You see," the baronet said, "I have obeyed you. I have not left the house."

"You are welcome to go now, if you please," the landlord said. "Before night comes the Bull in Top Boots and I will have parted company. Henceforth I devote my money and my life to the object I have in view, and I will never rest until I have dragged Mrs. Corcoran down at my feet!"

"Mrs. Corcoran!" Sir Roland exclaimed. "Then this is her work?"

"Aye! it is her work," the landlord said; "but better for her if she had never been born. I tell you for every pang—"

"Repeated threats oft come to nothing," Sir Roland interposed. "I happen to know Mrs. Corcoran, and I owe her a grudge. Perhaps it was well that I came to you, though strangely. If you are bent upon revenge let me be your agent. I know this hag's haunts, and it is more than probable that she will go back to her old quarters, if so her capture will be an easy matter."

"Agreed!" said the landlord of the Bull in Top Boots. "But play me no tricks, or your life shall answer for it. My eyes will be always upon you."

"You have nothing to fear from me," Sir Roland Ashton replied. "I am so sorely in need of help myself that it is not probable that I shall turn from a friendly hand."

## CHAPTER CXLI.

### SPRING-HEELED JACK APPEARS AT BOW-STREET.

It must be confessed that both Catchpole and Grabham had more than ordinary reason to feel terrified, especially the latter, whose neck was so tightly clutched that he opened and shut his mouth as energetically as the handles of a pair of bellows when worked by a busy smith.

Catchpole, as a matter of course, made for the door, but his frantic terror was still further increased by finding his egress barred.

The door was locked—locked on the inside—and no doubt Spring-Heeled Jack had possessed himself of the key.

Catchpole opened his mouth to scream when Spring-Heeled Jack, dragging Grabham, as limp and lumpy as a dead cod-fish, after him, overtook Catchpole, and seizing him by the waistcoat, held him at arms' length with the level of the ceiling.

The wretched man thought that his last hour had come.

His brain whirled, and every object in the room became misty.

Then he experienced a sensation as if he had turned a number of complicated somersaults, in which his chin came in contact with his knees, and his heels with the back of his head.

Such, indeed, may have been the case, fc Spring-Heeled Jack, after whirling him round lik a mill-sail, deposited him flat on his back befo the fire.

Grabham was dimly conscious of what w taking place; but his thoughts were too muc occupied with his own safety to leave room t think or care what would become of Catchpole.

"What is to be done with such a pair of rasca as you?" Spring-Heeled Jack demanded, wi a grin in which comicality and anger were com bined. "Why should I not put an end to you base lives?"

"Because," said Catchpole, "because—well, don't know."

He stared in an idiotic fashion at the giganti figure towering over him, and the words he uttere were meaningless.

Grabham, however, contrived to keep his sens about him.

"Oh! if you please, sir," he moaned, "m good, dear sir, don't harm us. We have given u all our bad ways, and are trying to live honestly."

"You scheme, you plot, you do mean things t get money," Spring-Heeled Jack said. "Suc men as you are not worthy to guard the publi peace."

"Yes," Catchpole chimed in, vaguely; "I' all in pieces—I'm a wreck. Both my arms an legs are broken, and the top of my head is stov in."

Just then the landlord came to the door.

Finding it locked, he kicked and banged at i with all his might.

"What do you mean by taking possession of m house?" he bellowed. "Here! open this doo and clear out as soon as you like. I'll have n more of you."

"If you utter a word, it will be your last," Spring-Heeled Jack hissed, turning his glitterin eyes upon the half-petrified constables.

"Do you hear me?" the landlord roared "How long do you intend to keep me outside m own door?"

He screwed his eye into the key-hole, but h could see nothing.

But presently he heard something that chille the very marrow in his bones.

It was an awful laugh, such as he had neve heard before—a laugh that seemed to fill th whole house, and die away amid discordant echoes

The landlord rushed back to the parlour, i which he had left his cronies smoking long pipes drinking warm gin and water, and solemnl wagging their heads over some parish question.

"Why, bless my heart!" said a fat man, "wha is the matter with you, Jem Stubbs?"

Mr. Stubbs literally fell into an armchair, which fitted him to a nicety, and panted for breath.

The cronies drank up their gin and water in hurry, and put down their long pipes.

They thought that Jem Stubbs was going t have a fit, and in that case he might upset table glasses, and everything.

"Oh! oh! oh!" Mr. Stubbs gasped. "Isn' there a man among you? Won't somebody thum me on the back, and help me to get back m breath?"

Not only did somebody volunteer to perform this office, but all joined in it, and Jem Stubb soon cried—

"Hold! enough."

"Did—did you hear anything while I wa away?" Jem Stubbs gasped.

"Why, yes," said the fat man. "We heard a horrible row, but thought it came from the wild beasts in the Tower."

"It didn't come from the Tower," Jem Stubbs said; "it came from the devil. He has come for them constables I told you about, and he's got 'em safe and tight above our heads."

"Jem," said the fat man, "as clerk and overseer to this 'ere parish, I object to such language. You are drunk, Jem—you are beastly drunk, and you don't know what you are talking about."

"Gentlemen," thundered out a voice, "who will stand treat? Spring-Heeled Jack is desirous of drinking your healths."

The fat overseer made for the table, but a lean man, named Rue, and an undertaker by trade, had him by the leg in a moment.

Both fell, and an awful scramble took place on the floor.

Jem Stubbs and the rest of the cronies scampered about the room like scared rabbits when they see the red-eyed ferret on their track.

In the doorway, extending his arms from side to side, stood Spring-Heeled Jack.

"I'm sorry to disturb the harmony of so convivial a meeting," he said, "but I require something to drink. Shall I help myself from the bar?"

Jem Stubbs opened his mouth and clutched his waistcoat, as if he felt a sudden pain in that region.

"Do—do what you like," he gasped out at last. "Drink the lot, but leave us alone, please!"

Spring-Heeled Jack laughed so horribly, that the fat man, who was now sitting upon Mr. Rue, the undertaker, fell backwards, and produced a bump as big as a hen's egg on the back of his head.

The weird creature, however, did not go into the bar, but stalked out of the house, and, leaping upward, vanished into the darkness of the night.

"Who's drunk now?" Jem Stubbs demanded. "Do I know what I am talking about?"

"Mr. Spuffler," Rue groaned, "I'll thank you to take your feet out of my stomach."

Mr. Spuffler did so, and then all the cronies gathered together in one corner of the room.

"He hadn't the constables with him," Jem Stubbs said, at length. "What has he done with them, I wonder?"

Nobody ventured to make a guess.

Just then the clock struck the hour of midnight, and all the cronies said in a breath that it was time for them to be home and in bed.

"You don't mean to say that you are going to leave me here alone?" said Jem Stubbs. "My lad, Bob, has been asleep these three hours. Rue, Spuffler, and the rest of you, I call upon you to act like men."

"What can we do?" Mr. Rue asked.

"Why come with me upstairs, and see what has become of them constables," Jem Stubbs replied.

Rue and Spuffler shook their heads, and one and all began to glide along the wall towards the door.

"You're a lot of sneaks—a pack of cowards!" Jem Stubbs roared, snatching up the poker. "Keep out of my house for the future—d'ye hear? There'll be no more chalking up grog scores behind the door, and no more parties on my birthday, when you drink as much in one night as you pay for in a year."

But they turned a deaf ear to him, and soon Jem Stubbs was left alone in the room.

Then he began to reflect on his position.

"I don't see what I've got to be afraid of," he said. "I've lived well and honestly as the world goes. I've paid my debts and dues, and—and hang the devil!"

"Bravo!" cried a voice. "You speak like a true Briton, and are worth double the number of the cowardly rascals who have left you in the lurch. As you pass through the bar, you will find something on the counter. Good-night, and fear nothing from Spring-Heeled Jack."

"Well, I'm blessed if there was ever anything like this in the world before," Jem Stubbs gasped.

He rubbed the tip of his nose until it turned red-hot and looked high and low.

But he could see nothing.

"He said I had nothing to fear," Jem Stubbs muttered, "and I will take him at his word."

Very cautiously indeed, however, did Jem Stubbs advance towards the door.

He kept the poker well in advance of him; but he was in no way molested, and he gave a sigh of relief when he saw that the passage was clear and the street door open.

Glancing at the bar counter, Jem Stubbs saw a little pile of guineas.

At first he was afraid to touch them, for fear that they might sting him or turn hot in his hand, like golden gifts from mischievous goblins.

He pushed the guineas over with the end of the poker.

They fell with a pleasant ring upon the polished surface of the counter, and Jem Stubbs smiled.

"They are right enough," he said, "and I'll take 'em. Spring-Heeled Jack, whether you be man or fiend, I'm very much obliged to you. Now I'll go and see if I can find them blessed constables."

. . . . . .

It was just past midnight when Mr. Nabbitt, the ruling spirit at Bow-street, swaggered into the office.

"Jowl!" he cried.

"Yes, sir," replied a sleepy constable, waking up in a violent hurry.

"How dare you go to sleep when you are on duty?" Nabbitt demanded.

"I wasn't asleep, sir," Jowl declared. "I was only thinking with my eyes shut."

"But you sha'n't think, and you sha'n't shut your eyes here!" Nabbitt thundered. "You're public property, remember that. You belong to the Government—you're a walking machine. Do you hear?"

"Yes, sir," Jowl replied, meekly.

"Any charges since I have been away?" Nabbitt asked, as he seated himself at his desk.

"Only one."

"What was it?"

"A boy found half-starved and asleep up a court in the Strand."

"That's against the law," said Nabbitt, flourishing a quill pen full of ink. "People haven't a right to be half-starved. Why don't they starve right out and die?"

As Jowl could not find a ready answer to this question he said nothing at all, which was perhaps the wisest thing he could do.

"Sleeping up a court is a dangerous practice," Nabbitt went on. "People might fall over him. Fancy what would have happened if an alderman had tripped over that boy!"

Jowl groaned, and rolled his eyes up to the ceiling.

"I'll make a case of this before the magistrates," Nabbitt continued; "and if that boy doesn't get six months, I'm an ass."

"You're a what, sir?" Jowl asked.

"Nothing," Nabbitt returned, hastily. "Well, now then, for more important business. What message did Catchpole and Grabham leave for me?"

"They didn't leave no message, because they haven't been back," Jowl replied.

Mr. Nabbitt kicked out his legs so violently that he nearly fell off his stool.

"What!" he gasped; "not been back?"

"I haven't seen so much as their shadders," Jowl replied. "Perhaps they've got into some kind of a bother."

"I'll bother them," Nabbitt roared. "Look at the clock, and tell me what time it is?"

"Ten minutes past ten."

Mr. Nabbitt threw a heavy ruler at Jowl's head with such good aim that he was rewarded by a sound like a cracked basin.

"The clock has stopped, you villain," he said. "Wind up the clock, and put the hands at half-past twelve."

Jowl did so, and then stood rubbing his bumped head most ruefully before his superior officer.

"Get out of the office," said Nabbitt, "and don't let me see your face before noon to-morrow."

"It's time I went," Jowl growled, "considering that I have been on duty sixteen hours."

He fled, for Mr. Nabbitt clutched the heavy pewter inkstand in his hand, and went his way through the silent streets.

"So, oh! my merry masters," said Nabbitt, alluding to the absent constables, "I have caught you tripping again. This time you go to quod as sure as you are sinners. I'll make a note of your conduct now that the office is quiet."

The still hours of the morning were creeping on—the time when the hush of slumber lies so silently upon the earth, that the slighest creak or sound causes a watchful man to start.

Such trifles as pass unheeded when the sun is up and shining bravely become matters of importance when earth and sky seemed to have mingled together.

Then there are the homeless ones creeping noiselessly and spectre-like about the streets.

They look like the people of another sphere—the gaunt denizens of a world filled with everlasting care and trouble.

The watchman crying the hours has a ghastly voice, and sneaks back to his sentry-box, which is a yawning coffin in itself.

Talking of yawning, Mr. Nabbitt yawned, opening his heavy jaws to their utmost limits.

"When Skitts comes in," he said, rubbing his red eyes, "I'll look at the prisoner Jowl spoke about, and then have a nap in the armchair before the fire. I suppose that boy will ask for something to eat, but he won't get it. I hope Jowl wasn't fool enough to give him a rug. No, no; I think I know Jowl better than to believe he would do that."

Mr. Nabbitt then dipped a pen in the ink, and pored over the charge book.

He took it into his head to turn over some of the back leaves.

"What a strange history is written here!" he muttered. "'Joseph Hardy, aged sixteen, charged with stealing a coat and a loaf of bread.' Ah! I remember how he begged for mercy when he was hanged. I—"

Something touched Mr. Nabbitt's hair and tickled him.

"Bother the flies!" he said. "Let me see. 'Mary Ann Dexter, charged with stealing a roll of flannel'—to keep herself warm in the winter, she said. She was hanged too. She said good-bye to her baby-boy ten minutes before she was pinioned, and said that she felt sure she would meet him in Heaven. Bah!"

"Bah!"

It was certainly not an echo of Mr. Nabbitt's voice, and, starting violently, he looked up.

The green baize curtain running on a rod in front of the desk had been withdrawn, and Mr. Nabbitt saw an awful face within a few inches of his own.

It was the face of Spring-Heeled Jack.

Nabbitt neither moved nor spoke, for the simple reason that he was powerless to do either one or the other.

He could only gasp and pant with the knowledge that he was turning hot and cold, red and white, as swiftly as such changes could take place.

Terrified beyond description, his imagination became distorted.

The face seemed to grow as he looked at it until it filled up the entire aperture in front of the desk.

He would have given a year's pay for the power to shriek for help, but he could no nothing more than chatter his teeth within his head, and hold convulsively on to the edge of the desk.

"You have a boy here?" Spring-Heeled Jack said.

Mr. Nabbitt opened his mouth, but the action was wasted, for no sound whatever came from his throat.

"You have a boy here," Spring-Heeled Jack repeated. "My friend, I have come for him."

"Oh!" said Mr. Nabbitt, finding his tongue at last. "Oh! you have come for him. Who are you?"

"A very demon when I am put out," Spring-Heeled Jack replied. "If you want a taste of my temper you had better sit there staring at me like a frightened owl."

"It's against the regulations for anybody to see a prisoner here," said Mr. Nabbitt.

He had abandoned himself to his fate, and said what first came into his mind.

"I have no time to cut to waste," Spring-Heeled Jack returned, stretching out one of his long, muscular arms. "Where is the key of the cell in which the unhappy boy is imprisoned?"

"I have it, of course," Nabbitt replied. "Who do you think would keep the keys but me?"

The next instant Spring-Heeled Jack was on the other side of the desk, and in another he had Nabbitt flat upon his back and his knee on the officer's chest.

"The key—the key!" Spring-Heeled Jack cried. "Give it me, or by St. George I'll throttle you and throw your body into the Thames!"

Nabbitt almost fainted at the sight of the awful being now fully revealed to him.

"Spring-Heeled Jack!" he cried out.

"Aye! I am he indeed. Quick! Make your own choice—the key or death?"

"Let me raise myself up a little, and I will find it for you," Nabbitt groaned.

"Where is it?"

"In my pocket."

"Then I will help myself," said Spring-Heeled Jack.

No sooner said than done.

Spring-Heeled Jack rose and told the officer to follow his example.

"What more would you have of me?" Nabbitt demanded.

"Lead the way to the cell, and point it out to me."

As Nabbitt passed out of the office the idea entered his head that he would dash into the street and shriek for help.

But he had reckoned without his host.

Spring-Heeled Jack did not intend that he should do anything of the kind.

Suddenly Mr. Nabbitt felt the back of his coat-collar seized by a no light hand, and his face lengthened.

"There is no occasion to hold me," he said.

"But I would rather do so," Spring-Heeled Jack replied.

Nabbitt's heart was now beating violently against his side.

He had met his match at last.

"Here is the cell," he said.

"Then take the key and open it."

"No," said Nabbitt, hurriedly. "I made a mistake; it is the next cell."

"What, yet another ruse?" Spring-Heeled Jack said, shaking Nabbitt as a terrier shakes a rat. "Did you think I was going to march into the cell so that you might close the door upon me?"

"I never thought anything of the kind," Nabbitt said.

"You lie!" Spring-Heeled Jack hissed in his ear. "Beware of attempting to play me such a trick again!"

"Of course, I am compelled to put up with this," said Nabbitt, who was trembling between fear and rage.

"Of course. So this is the cell? You are quite sure you have not made a mistake this time?"

"Quite sure."

"Then open the door and go in first."

Nabbitt did so, and no sooner was he in the cell than Spring-Heeled Jack swung him round and struck him a terrific blow between the eyes.

The officer went down like an ox under a pole-axe.

"Lie there, you cowardly hound," said Spring-Heeled Jack. "When you recover your senses I hope that the lesson I have taught you to-day will do you good."

"Who is that?" a feeble voice cried. "What has happened? I am so cold and hungry."

"You shall have food and warmth presently, poor child!" Spring-Heeled Jack replied. "Do not fear me. My outward form may frighten you, but I have a better heart, thank Heaven! than the men who brought you here. Come with me."

Spring-Heeled Jack took the shivering, ragged form of a lad in his arms, and, stepping out of the cell, locked Nabbitt in.

Then, with a cry of triumph, the strange being leaped through the passage at a single bound, and passed into the silent, deserted street.

---

## CHAPTER CXLII.

### THE ROAD TO THE EAST—THE HALT OUTSIDE MILDENDALE.

THE leaves were turning sear and yellow when Robin Gray started on his journey with Namon Wallack.

The berries, black, red, and purple, clustered thickly upon the bushes; starlings, sparrows, and fieldfares flew about in flocks that darkened the air in search of suitable winter quarters.

The year had seen its best, and was slowly dying.

When the sun went down, it had none of its golden grandeur, but sank amid strange, ghastly autumnal mists, as if it, too, were putting on its shroud, and saying farewell to the world for ever.

Robin Gray noted all these things, and he began to wonder how the house on wheels and its occupants would get on when the snow lay thickly upon the roads, and that icy tyrant, the north wind, bellowed in its wrath.

The lad was of a dreamy nature, as his splendid dark eyes plainly told, but he found plenty to do, and he set about his work in a business-like fashion.

There were the pots and kettles to keep bright, the beds to make at night and stow away in the morning.

Behind Wallack's own van came another, also the property of the gipsy.

This contained the curiosities to be exhibited at the different fairs.

Namon often talked cheerfully to the boy.

He taught him many strange things—how fish could be lured to the surface of a pond by pounding up and casting certain berries into the water, how to imitate the cries of certain birds worth eating, and how to use a gun.

Sometimes Namon Wallack would sit silent and thoughtful for hours.

The lad never disturbed him, and when a spell of reverie was over Namon would start suddenly, smile, and begin to talk in a lively fashion.

The cavalcade had been on the road two days and a night.

On the third evening the gipsies halted on the border of a wood, and, after Namon Wallack had seen his horses fed and tethered, he returned to the caravan.

Robin Gray was busy with a needle and thread patching up a rent in his jacket.

Wallack looked strangely at the boy as he opened a tiny cupboard and took down a small bottle filled with a dark-coloured fluid.

"It is time that you left off work for to-day," he said. "How do you like your new life?"

"I am very happy," the boy replied.

"You always make the same reply," Wallack said, with a wistful glance at the youngster.

"What else can I say, when I am really happy?" Robin returned, smiling. "You would not have me say that I am miserable when I do not feel so?"

"No, no," said Namon; "but since you came to me, I have often wondered whether you thoroughly understand me."

"I think I do," Robin replied. "If at any time I appear not to do so, please put me right."

Namon put the bottle upon a little table and sat down.

"You still remember," he said, "that you promised Mr. Ashton to obey me in all things?"

"Yes," Robin said, colouring deeply. "Have I not done so?"

"You have," Namon Wallack replied; "but now a more trying ordeal is before you."

"What is it?" Robin Gray asked.

"Empty that bottle into a basin and rub your face, neck, arms, and hands with the liquid."

The command seemed so odd an one that Robin stared at his master in astonishment.

"What for?" he asked.

"To make you look like one of us," Namon Wallack replied. "Go to the door, look towards the west, and tell me what you see."

"I see an old house standing upon a hill, with dark, gloomy-looking woodlands creeping up to it," Robin said.

"Do you know what house it is?"

"No."

"What!" Namon Wallack said. "Have you never seen it before?"

Robin Gray shaded his eyes with his hand, and gazed at the mansion again.

"I seem to have some recollection of it," he said; "but it is more like the memory of a dream. Why have you called my attention to the place?"

"Because your enemy and mine lives there," Namon Wallack said, shooting an angry glance at the hill. "One of our people received a great wrong at the hands of its owner. He hates us as we hate him, and if he knew that we were here, he would seek to do us some injury."

"Indeed!" said Robin. "Is that the reason why you wish me to use that stuff?"

"It is," Wallack replied. "If he knew that we had a pale-faced lad with us, he would swear that we stole you, and you would be taken away from us."

Robin hesitated no longer.

Stripping to the waist, he rubbed the liquid thoroughly into his skin.

At first it made him smart and wince, but he did not cry out or utter a word, for Namon Wallack was watching him narrowly.

When the operation was over, Wallack raised the lid of one of the benches, and produced a mirror.

"Look at yourself, Robin," he said.

As the boy did so, he started back in surprise, for he could scarcely recognise his own features.

"It would take a clever man to tell who you are," Wallack said, smiling. "You are safe from prying eyes now."

"Who would care to pry after me?" Robin said. "Who cares for me but you and Mr. Ashton?"

"The world is wide and full of strange things," Namon Wallack said. "There is always somebody on land or sea coming to see us. Who can tell that the homeless wretch of to-night may find himself a lord to-morrow, and that the lord revelling at his table to-night may not be ready to beg a meal when the sun goes down again? But enough of this. Read to me, Robin. Read, read! You will find me a ready listener."

Robin Gray took down an old, well-thumbed book, full of strange, weird stories, freely translated from the German, and began to read.

Robin Gray knew that Namon Wallack had no ears for what passed from his lips.

The gipsy sat with his elbow upon his knee, and his chin upon his hand.

Robin came to the end of one of the stories.

"Shall I read more?" he asked.

"Eh? What?" Wallack demanded.

Robin Gray repeated the question.

"Yes—I mean no," said Namon, forcing a laugh to his lips. "That was a capital tale, wasn't it? Let me see, it was all about— Well, never mind; let us have supper and then to bed, for we shall have plenty to do in the morning."

There was a portion of a hare for the evening meal.

Wallack had brought the animal home after a walk in the morning while the dew still lay upon the grass.

How he had come by it he did not say, and Robin thought he had better not ask any questions on the subject.

Namon Wallack did all the cooking himself.

He was a cunning hand at the art, and though everything in the caravan was served in a humble style, it was tasty, and so appetising that Robin looked forward with pleasure to each meal.

Namon was silent and reserved during supper.

He strove to keep up a conversation, but lost the thread over and over again.

"It is no use," he said, throwing himself at full length upon one of the benches; "I can't talk; my head aches. When you have cleared away we will go to rest."

As he spoke a knock, sharp and distinct, came at the door.

Robin was in the act of answering the summons when Wallack called him back.

"I will go," he said. "It may be that one of our people has a private message for me."

On opening the door he was confronted by a man.

"Well?" said Namon.

"Come out," the man rejoined. "I have news for you."

Wallack left the caravan, closing the door carefully behind him, and he and the man walked a little way into the woods.

"You have news," said Wallack. "Is it good or bad?"

"That I will leave you to judge."

"Go on, and I will be as dumb as a mole while you speak," Namon Wallack said.

"Lord Mildendale," the man began, stretching out his arm towards the house on the hill, "has found us out. The bloodhounds roam loose in the park, and it will not be safe for any of us to approach the gates."

"I expected as much," Wallack said. "Is that all?"

"We may expect a visit from his lordship's hirelings."

"Let them come," said Namon Wallack, frowning. "We are not on Lord Mildendale's ground. Let them come and bring their hounds. Perchance I might make a mistake, and shoot a man instead of a dog."

"But the boy?" said the other gipsy. "He must not be allowed to roam about while we are in the neighbourhood."

"I have made provision for that."

"How?"

"By asking him to stain his skin, and he did so with scarcely a murmur."

"Good! Now I'll be off, for I, like the rest, am tired out."

"Isaac Day," Wallack said, placing his hands upon his friend's shoulders, "I want to exact a promise from your lips."

"I will perform it, if I can."

"If anything should happen to me," Wallack said, "I want you to look after the lad."

"But what on earth should happen to you?" said Day.

"I don't know," Wallack replied, looking up to the now starlit sky; "but I have had an odd presentiment that my days are numbered."

"Banish this nonsense from your mind," Isaac Day replied. "Of course your days are numbered, like the rest of mortals; but you will live to be a good old age. Bah! you talk of dying while your father and mother are still alive and hearty."

"But men have been removed suddenly from the face of the earth," Namon Wallack said.

"I'll listen to no more such talk as this," Isaac Day declared. "You have been working too hard with body and brain. Go to bed and sleep well. A good night's rest will put you right."

"But your promise?"

"I give it."

"Then I am satisfied," said Namon Wallack, turning away.

He did not go back to the caravan immediately, but roamed about the dark and silent woods.

One by one the lights of the gipsy encampment were extinguished, but that in his own van still burnt brightly.

"I must not let the boy sit up for me," he said. "I will go back and lie down, though no sleep comes to my eyes."

Robin Gray had left the lamp burning, but the boy was fast asleep.

"It is strange," he said, touching the lad's brow lightly with his hand, "that I should love this child almost as much as if he were my own—and I might have had children about my knee had it not been for—"

Namon Wallack stood still.

He thought he heard the tread of a footstep.

He listened for some minutes, but as there was no repetition of the sound, he extinguished the lamp, but not before he had secured the door—a thing he seldom did.

"What is this I fear?" he muttered. "Not thieves—no living man—none from the dead—what then? Why does my blood flow hot and fierce through my veins one instant, and then cold as ice the next? It may be an approaching illness. I have never felt like this until yonder poor lad was brought to me."

He sat down, with his heart growing heavier and heavier.

At last he sank back, and at length felt, to his great relief, that he was drifting slowly away into the mysterious land of dreams.

He slept, and slept soundly, his broad, manly chest heaving as he breathed.

On the other side lay Robin Gray, smiling, and dreaming pleasant dreams.

It was long past midnight, when a solitary man left the gates of Mildendale Park.

He had some altercation with the lodge-keeper, who did not wish him to go forth alone.

"Let me go with you, my lord," he said. "I have worked in your family, man and boy, for more than fifty years, and I cannot bear to think of your running into danger."

"There—there, go back to your fireside," said Lord Mildendale. "If I should require help, I know how to bring it to me. What have I to fear, armed as I am?"

"One bullet is as good as another, and sometimes better," the man replied, shaking his white locks. "My lord, I beg your pardon for daring to address you. The warning I have given comes from an old man who loved you when you were a child, and sorrowed in his heart when—"

"Hold!" Lord Mildendale cried. "Enough! Back, I say! I am going among these swarthy villains. They have not come here for nothing, and they shall tell me why they dog my footsteps, or I will force the truth from their lips."

Lord Mildendale strode away, clutching a brace of pistols with a nervous, anxious grasp.

"They have called me coward!" he said. "This night they shall prove their words. So, Namon Wallack, you are here? My spies have been faithful to me. But, hush! I must make no noise, for these cunning wretches would take my life did they know that I ventured out alone."

Lord Mildendale evidently had some great object in view which he wished to keep to himself, otherwise he would not have ventured forth at such an hour.

Striking into a path lined by tall, dark trees, he held his way.

A few dead leaves were falling and fluttered about his face.

The night wind sighed and moaned dismally, and from the distance came the voice of the river tearing madly along at full tide.

Lord Mildendale looked straight ahead, as if expecting to see a light which would lead him to the gipsy encampment.

But all was darkness—black, impenetrable darkness.

He walked carefully, touching the ground lightly with his feet, for a stumble, or the sharp snapping of a twig might betray him.

At last the road began to widen, and Lord Mildendale saw what appeared at first to be a cluster of glow-worms on the ground.

The light was dim and uncertain, but a thin wreath of smoke curling upwards told its own story.

His lordship had come upon one of the expiring fires at which the gipsies had cooked their food earlier in the evening.

The midnight prowler now hesitated, looking to the right and left, and holding a pistol in each hand.

Right before him, looming out of the night like a solid block, stood the caravan in which Namon Wallack and Robin Gray lay sleeping soundly.

Steady now!

Holding his breath, Lord Mildendale approached the little house on wheels, and creeping up the steps, listened intently.

He could hear no sound but the heavy breathing of the sleepers, and he was in the act of trying the door with his hand when something white suddenly appeared on the top of the caravan.

Before he could raise his eyes a voice spoke to him.

"What does the noble lord want here?" it said.

"Ha!" cried Lord Mildendale; "I am betrayed!"

Looking up, he saw Spring-Heeled Jack, who was upon his hands and knees on the roof, and gazing down with an expression of irony and contempt.

---

## CHAPTER CXLIII.

### TERROR OF THE PRISONERS—THE ESCAPE—DEATH OF JEM BASKER.

WHEN the block of stone fell with a heavy thud into the cell the terror of Bill Blarney and Jem Basker was so intense that they clung frantically to each other.

Perhaps the sound was not really so loud, but it startled them more than if a thunder-bolt had fallen at their feet.

For several moments—and each was an age of agony—neither of the prisoners spoke.

Streams of perspiration poured from their deadly cold faces.

# SPRING-HEELED JACK,

## THE TERROR OF LONDON.

"THERE'S A BEAM HALF-WAY DOWN," SAID SPRING-HEELED JACK. "MIND YOUR HEAD."

No. 40.

So quiet and motionless did they stand that they could hear their hearts beating.

Every moment they expected to hear the door fly open, and see the warders enter.

But, no; the man on guard at the end of the passage must either have been sound asleep, or absent from his post.

"All is well!" Jem Basker gasped out at length.

"Well," Bill Blarney growled, "you nearly settled our hash."

"Of course you had no hand in the muddle," Basker said, savagely; "but this is no time for squabbling. Up to now we are safe, and the best thing we can do is to make ourselves safer by getting out of this man-trap as quickly as we can. You did the trick by yourself once, and surely then two of us cannot fail?"

"Wait a minute," Bill Blarney returned, as he swept his hand across his face. "I am as limp as a sawdust doll, and as weak as a babe in arms."

"Come on!" Jem Basker said, desperately; "come on now, or I go alone. You will gather strength as you move. I tell you that there is not a moment to lose. Stay here, curse you! if you will, and die the death of a dog."

Bill Blarney stretched his arms over his head as if to brace himself up.

"I am ready," he said. "Lead on, and I will follow, though the devil himself blocked the way."

They were now in a cavity, which appeared to have been once the flue of a chimney, but had been partially blocked up.

Groping their way along, they were suddenly stopped by the outer wall.

Now they could hear the distant rumble of carts jolting through Newgate-street and down Snow-hill on their way to market.

"Only a few inches of stone lies between us and freedom," Jem Basker said; "but we must work hard, for this wall is much stronger than any other part of the building."

So saying, Jem Basker resumed his task, going through the similar operation of scraping away the cement, and then inserting the end of the crowbar into the crevice, and working it to and fro with all his strength.

When he was thoroughly worn out, Bill Blarney took his turn at the bar and wrenched it backwards and forwards, until the thews and sinews of his arm cracked under the exertion.

The stone, however, defied all efforts, and held its place as solid and rigid as a rock.

"It is no use," Bill Blarney said. "We couldn't do it if we stayed here for a month. We are fairly caught in a trap."

"Not yet," Jem Basker replied, with a terrible oath. "If I cannot leave the prison a free man, I will never return to it alive."

"I am with you then," Bill Blarney rejoined. "Better die fighting, than dragged to Tyburn in a cart."

Once more Jem Basker seized the crowbar, and worked at it with the strength of a giant.

"The stone moves," he said. "I'll swear I felt it move. Try for yourself, Bill, and tell me if I am not right?"

Blarney did so, and a hoarse whisper of delight came from his lips.

"There's no doubt about it," he said. "The stone moves and will soon give way."

They redoubled their exertions, and at last the block of stone gave way, and a ray of silvery light shone upon the ruffians.

It was the light of the moon, pure and beautiful, but Jem Basker cursed it like the scoundrel he was.

"If there is anybody about we shall be seen," he said. "There's a night house over the way, where the warders have a drink when they leave and go on duty, and it is just possible that some of the dogs may be there at this very moment."

"We must risk it," Bill Blarney responded. "Hark! I hear footsteps coming down the corridor leading to our cell."

"Then it is time to be off," Jem Basker said, clutching the stone. "Lend a hand here, Bill. We mustn't be afraid of making a noise now. Once in the street, nothing short of a greyhound will overtake me."

Both used their strength to remove the stone, and it fell with a crash from its position.

The warder, pacing the corridor, heard the sound and uttered a cry of alarm.

It so happened that he had not the key of the cell with him, but to rush back and snatch it from a hook in the wall was but the work of a moment.

Calling loudly for assistanee, he was joined by another man, and, as they rushed pell-mell into the cell, a glance told them what had happened.

In less than half-a-minute the prison was in a state of uproar.

Bells rang, doors opened and closed with a crash, and the turnkeys cursed and swore as they armed themselves for the pursuit.

So great was the noise that many of the prisoners thought that the building had taken fire, and clamoured to be let out of their cells.

On the side where the female criminals were locked up almost a panic took place.

The unhappy women shrieked, raved, and prayed, and their shrill cries, added to the hoarse bellowings of the sterner sex, made the air hideous.

The warders, however, paid no attention whatever to the wretched captives, but a party of them, headed by the governor, who was almost beside himself with rage, rushed into the street.

Bill Blarney and Jem Basker, however, had a good start, and made the best use of it.

They had hesitated for a moment to consult which way to go.

Little thinking what had taken place at the Bull in Top Boots, they decided to go there.

"Take care of yourself," said Jem Basker. "If we miss each other we shall meet again. Whoever reaches the Bull in Top Boots must make preparations to receive the other."

Away they went, dashing round the corner into Ludgate-hill, and up towards St. Paul's Churchyard.

Here they met with an unexpected check.

Some rollicking young men, more than half drunk, and ready for a fight, stood in their way.

"They're running a race," said one.

"Yes, a race!" Jem Basker yelled, grasping the idea; "out of my way!"

The midnight rollickers entered into the spirit of the thing and followed.

This was the very worst thing that could happen for Bill Blarney and Jem Basker.

The latter turned back and faced the reeling crew.

"Get you gone to your homes!" he panted. "Curse you! if you are seen we are lost."

"Ha! ha! ha!" laughed a gallant, who had lost his hat in some fray. "There is something wrong here. Didn't they turn round by the Old

Bailey? It strikes me that a couple of birds have escaped from Newgate."

Jem Basker's face grew blood-red with passion, but rattles were sounding, and whistles were blowing, so he could not wait to wreak his vengeance on the drunken gallant, as he would have liked to have done.

With a terrible oath he turned upon his heels, and started off with the speed of a hare in the track of Bill Blarney.

By this time Blarney was a good way ahead, but, he being the heavier of the two, Basker soon gained upon him.

Just then a gang of men from Newgate rushed up to the half-tipsy wine-bibbers, but paid no heed to them.

They saw the men they wanted in advance.

Some of the warders threw off their hats and coats to run the easier, and one, a tall, wiry fellow, with long legs, swept over the ground like a race-horse.

Jem Basker heard him coming, and doubled down a narrow way leading to the river.

His pursuer never lost sight of him for an instant.

"Surrender!" he shouted. "It is no use, you fool! I shall be on your back in a moment!"

Jem Basker replied with a yell of defiance, and, leaping over a pile of rotten timber, reached a river-side wharf.

The place was what is called a ship-breaker's yard, and filled with all kinds of lumber.

There were bolts, rings, chains, old rusty anchors, sheets of copper, and twisted masses of iron.

Basker snatched up a piece of chain to be used in case of emergency, but never stopping.

Dodging here and there like a pursued rat he made for the river.

If he could but reach it, he would laugh the warders to scorn, for he was an excellent swimmer, and had more than once during his career taken to the water for safety.

The black flowing river ran almost under his feet.

He saw it, and was making ready for a spring, when his foot caught in a ring secured to the wharf, and he fell heavily forward.

A yell of rage burst from the baffled villain's throat.

Still retaining the piece of chain, which was about two feet long, he started to his feet.

But now he was confronted by the swift-footed warder who had hunted him down so persistently.

Both men glared at each other, neither speaking.

The turnkey was wondering whether any of his mates were coming to his assistance, and Jem Basker was mentally weighing the man's strength.

"If you care to live and die in your bed," the fugitive said at length, "you had better go your way."

"Nonsense," the turnkey replied. "I tell you it is all over with you, Jem. Put that chain down, and come back with me quietly. I am armed, but I don't care to shoot you, because I like a game bird, and you are one and no mistake."

When the warder said that he was armed he did not speak the truth, for in his hurry to leave Newgate he had brought no kind of weapon whatever with him.

"If you were a cannon yourself, and loaded to the muzzle," Basker hissed, "I would not give myself up quietly. Don't think of it. If my time has come I may as well perish here as anywhere else."

They now braced themselves up for the struggle which they knew was at hand.

The warder stepped forward; Jem Basker retreated a step to give more effect to the blow with the chain, when two sharp reports rang through the air.

Unseen and unheard, two other warders had crept up amid the rubbish and litter of the yard, and fired simultaneously.

Jem Basker dropped the chain, and raised his arm slowly above his head, as a man roused from a sound sleep will do.

He turned half-round, took a step to the right, one to the left, and then collapsed like a house of cards.

"Curse you!" he shrieked out, "you have done for me at last."

"No doubt about that," said one of the warders, throwing down his still smoking pistol. "Make a litter, lads, and run him back to the stone jug, and let the doctor see him. He may not be mortally wounded."

"Not mortally wounded!" Jem Basker groaned, rolling heavily over, and drawing up his knees. "You hounds! you lie. I am shot through the spine. At—at least, I have robbed the hangman of his fee."

As the warders stooped down to raise him, he scratched and bit at them like a wild beast.

"Off! off!" he yelled. "Let me breathe my last under the sky, dark though it be. Where is Bill Blarney—have you taken him?"

"No," answered a warder.

"There's some comfort in that, at all events," said the wounded villain. "He may live to give you some trouble yet, and if—if I was sure that he would avenge my death on one of you—a life for a life—I should die the—the easier."

"Come—come, Jem," said the warder who had overtaken him first, "let us do all we can to make you comfortable. You are still now."

"Yes, so still," observed another turnkey, "that he will never move again. Jem Basker is dead!"

Yes, he was dead, and lay with his hands clenched, his teeth set, and an evil frown of dark malignity on his face.

It was agreed to leave him there for the present until the warders knew whether the rest of the the party had been successful in arresting Bill Blarney.

They soon found that such was not the case.

On the way back to the open street they met the governor and three men, but Bill Blarney was not among them.

They made their report of what had happened in as few words as possible, and a grim smile settled on the governor's face.

"At all events," he said, nodding approvingly, "there is one scoundrel less in the world. Blarney gave us the slip, but I am perfectly sure that he did not cross London-bridge."

"No, sir," said a warder. "If he had done so we must have overtaken him. He turned a little to the left, and dashed down towards the Monument."

"Well," the governor remarked, "we must let him rest for the present. To hunt for him to-night would be like looking for a needle in a bottle of hay. We can do no more now than take Jem Basker's body back to Newgate, where an inquest will be held upon it."

## CHAPTER CXLIV.

### OLD FRIENDS MEET AGAIN.

THE gentle-minded and amiable Mrs. Corcoran was never at a loss to take an advantage of an opportunity.

She had a very good idea of what would happen if she stayed in the presence of the landlord of the Bull in Top Boots after slaying Dick Sleuth in so treacherous a manner, and it therefore entered her mind to make herself scarce at the earliest possible moment.

That moment was when the innkeeper stooped over the murdered man.

Mrs. Corcoran hopped nimbly out of the room and into the street.

She then set off at a trot as if going upon an errand, and dived down the very first turning she came to.

This thoroughfare, like the rest of the locality, was not one to impress a stranger with its beauty.

It was evil-smelling and ugly.

Its inhabitants had acquired the custom of hanging bare-armed, and with dishevelled hair, half out of the windows, and greeting passers-by with fragments of flower-pots, or any kind of rubbish they could lay their hands upon.

Mrs. Corcoran came in for a full share of this playfulness, and she found herself running the gauntlet of cinders, brick-ends, bits of firewood, and sundry other missiles caught up in a heedless sportive moment.

But the hag troubled herself nothing about the fusilade buzzing and hissing around her ears.

She ran on through court after court until she came to a larger space.

Chance, and her tottering, aching feet, had taken her to Buckler's-rents.

It may as well be told at once that Mrs. Corcoran did not know where she had got to.

She knew nothing of Daddy Muckrum—in fact, she was, so to speak, in a strange land, and a stranger among strangers.

Mrs. Corcoran surveyed Buckler's-rents with her ferrety eyes.

She could see at a glance that it was not a place likely to be patronised by the aristocracy, or even by respectable people, for neither class care to have heaps of rotten vegetation before the doors, and dirty rags in lieu of polished glass windows.

The reader knows, by this time, that Mrs. Corcoran, though a very particular lady in some respects, had a knack of making herself at home and comfortable in any society her fate chanced to throw her.

After a moment's pause she knocked at the door of the house nearest to her, and was greeted with a curse by a scowling villain, who glared at her as the man-wolf was said to glare at his victims.

"What do you want?" he demanded. "If you are a beggar you have come to the wrong shop."

"I'm no beggar," Mrs. Corcoran replied. "If your wife is at home I should like to speak to her."

"Wife—wife!" exclaimed the man, running his fingers through his greasy, matted hair. "How do you think a poor, half-starved devil like me could keep a wife? I had one once, but she's been under the ground many a year—and a good job too for her and me."

"Really, this is very sad," Mrs. Corcoran said. "As I told you, I am not exactly a beggar, but I am very poor, and on the look-out for humble lodgings. I thought this was just the sort of place to get what I wanted."

The wreck of a man opened the door a little wider and stared Mrs. Corcoran out of countenance.

"Lodgings!" he said, taking in the whole of Buckler's-rents with a sweep of his arm. "Not a living creature would dare to give you a night's shelter for your weight in gold without Daddy Muckrum's permission. You must be known to him before that. Take my advice, old woman, and clear out."

"Oh! I see," returned Mrs. Corcoran, smirking and grinning. "This is something like the place I have come from."

"I don't understand."

"Well, people must live somehow," said Mrs. Corcoran, fencing cleverly. "Why should some folks have all the money and others none?"

"Oh! then you—"

"I have just made good my escape from the Bow-street runners," Mrs. Corcoran interposed, complacently, "and if you are one of the virtuous sort, all you have to do is to raise an alarm and have me retaken."

The man was now grinning.

"If you haven't told me a lie, I told you one at all events," he said, throwing the door wide open. "Come in, and you shall see the darling of my heart—Joan Spikes—Mrs. Spikes."

"What a nice name," Mrs. Corcoran observed. "It has such a genteel ring about it."

Mr. Spikes paid no heed to the compliment, but led the way into what he was pleased to call his parlour.

There were many thousands of pigstyes in the country cleaner and better appointed; and, used to all kinds of homely things and notions, the hag's heart sickened at the dreadful stench that invaded her nostrils.

"You see," said Mr. Spikes, making frantic and futile efforts to open the back window, "we can't afford to stand upon any kind of ceremony here."

"Oh! no; of course not," Mrs. Corcoran coughed. "Oh! dear me."

"What's the matter, old lady?" Spikes demanded.

"Don't you—don't you find this room just a little close—a little stuffy?"

"Well," Mr. Spikes replied, "people who are not used to it might, but we like it because there are no draughts unless we choose to let them in. Wait a minute, and I'll call the missus."

Mrs. Corcoran fondly wished that Mr. Spikes had let a draught in.

Indeed she would not have objected to a gale of wind.

"Joan!" Mr. Spikes roared.

A voice like a file rasped on a nutmeg-grater replied—

"What's up, Tim? Can't you let me be? I'm washin'."

Mrs. Corcoran felt grateful to hear this, although she had never evinced a strong affection for soap and cold water herself.

"Somebody—a woman wants to see you," Mr. Spikes bellowed at the top of his voice.

"Well, let her wait," screamed the lovable Joan. "I suppose she ain't a princess, or the Lady Mayoress?"

Mr. Spikes then returned to the odoriferous parlour.

"My wife has a playful way of her own," he

said; "but she's got a heart as can beat for another."

Mrs. Corcoran nodded her head.

"If you'll let me have a room as near to the roof as possible," she said, weighing a few silver coins carefully in her hand, "I'm your customer as far as a crown-piece goes."

"A crown-piece!" Spikes repeated, in a grumbling tone of voice. "It ain't much; but you had better hear what Joan says."

At that very moment Joan was on her way downstairs.

A gaunt, lop-sided, splay-footed, repulsive-featured woman stood before Mrs. Corcoran.

"Who's this?" Mrs. Spikes demanded, turning to her husband. "I never saw this woman before in my life. You must have been a fool to let her pass the threshold of the door!"

"Don't be hard on her," said Mr. Spikes. "We've seen troublesome times in our days. Let her speak for herself."

"Well," said Joan Spikes, turning almost fiercely upon Mrs. Corcoran, "tell me what brought you here, and tell me quick!"

"Misfortune, my dear," replied the hag, unmoved by this attack. "Misfortune brought me to crime—starvation dragged me to it. I happened to take a little money—only a little—that belonged to somebody else, and so I came here."

"Yes, I know," said Mrs. Spikes; "but who told you to come here—that's what I want to know?"

"Nobody," Mrs. Corcoran replied. "I went just where my legs took me, and so would you if an officer was after you!"

"So, you are a thief?" Mrs. Spikes returned, placing her arms akimbo; "you are rather too old to begin that game, I fancy. Well, that's nothing to me. We are not very particular about what people do, or what people don't. If you want my best room for a week, you'll have to pay a guinea for it, and I'll answer for getting Daddy Muckrum's permission for you to stay."

"A guinea?" Mrs. Corcoran gasped.

"And cheap, too," Mrs. Spikes retorted, "for you'll be safe here. We don't ask one price, and charge another at the end of the time. Money down is my motto."

"Well, there it is," said Mrs. Corcoran, placing the coin on an apology for a table. "And now I suppose I can see the room? I hope it is very near the roof."

"Why?"

"Because I like a little fresh air, deary," Mrs. Corcoran said.

Joan Spikes led the way to a miserable attic, the floor of which was half an inch deep with dirt.

"If you care to wash up the place," said Mrs. Spikes, "I'll lend you a pail and a scrubbing-brush."

"I'll let you know about that by-and-bye," Mrs. Gorcoran replied. "For the present I wish to be alone."

Mrs. Spikes closed the door, and Mrs. Corcoran, having locked it, and made sure that there were no chinks through which her landlady could see, counted out the balance of her money.

She had just five guineas left.

"Not much," said Mrs. Corcoran, leaning her peaked chin on her shrivelled hand. "It will soon be gone, and then—what then—what then?"

As may be imagined, the hag was thoroughly worn out, and it was only natural that she should desire to take a little rest after her sharp run from the Bull in Top Boots.

Mrs. Corcoran's eyes wandered towards the bedstead.

To say the very best of it, it was not a very pleasant-looking article of furniture, and Mrs. Corcoran did not like the look of the wall behind it.

Suspicious and wicked people see something odd in everything, and the hag, being perfectly aware of false walls, sliding panels, &c., took the trouble to examine her new quarters before lying down to rest.

Finding nothing to alarm her, Mrs. Corcoran fell into a state of repose, which cannot be called light and refreshing.

She kicked and jerked her body about in the most extraordinary fashion, and when she did awake it was with the idea that somebody had her by the throat.

Night had come, and it was quite dark—so dark that Mrs. Corcoran had to peer about before she could see where the window was situated.

She felt both hungry and thirsty, and, rising, she went silently down the stairs.

Mrs. Corcoran's usual way of moving about was like a cat creeping along after an unsuspecting sparrow, and in this instance she heard a conversation that interested her keenly.

Mr. and Mrs. Spikes, and a third person of the male gender, were talking.

"Hang me!" again said the stranger. "You're giving me such a description of her that I think she must be the same she-devil. I suppose there isn't a chance of having a look at her?"

"Not yet, Ted," Joan Spikes replied; "but you shall as soon as possible."

"Ted—Ted!" Mrs. Corcoran muttered to herself. "I wonder— no. How can it be him when he is dead and gone?"

"Do you think she would peach on you?" Mr. Spikes asked.

"There's no knowing what she might or mightn't do to serve her own ends," the man called Ted replied. "If she is the same witch, she has killed half-a-dozen people, and ruined double as many more."

"How I should like to get a look at you, my beauty!" Mrs. Corcoran muttered. "What shall I do? Go back, or declare myself boldly?"

The hag hesitated and rubbed her chin thoughtfully before doing one or the other.

Gazing at the door of the room from which the conversation issued, she saw a slight ray of light shining from the centre panel.

The door had evidently been split, perhaps by a blow from a brawny fist or poker.

Small as the aperture was, Mrs. Corcoran determined to make the most use of it.

No sooner had she applied one of her keen eyes to it than she started back and made her way to her room with the utmost expedition.

And there in the darkness sat Mrs. Corcoran, gasping, wheezing, holding her sides, and muttering.

"He died, and yet he is there!" she said. "The grave has given up its dead. I must be mad! If he is dead, how can he be here? And yet I heard his voice and saw his form. Let me think! What had I better do?"

It suddenly occurred to Mrs. Corcoran that the wisest course to pursue was to call for a light.

Going to the door, she lifted up her sweet voice, and Joan Spikes responded almost instantly.

She brought a long, ghastly dip with a rush wick which gave scarcely any light.

But it was better than nothing, and Mrs. Corcoran was thankful for it.

Joan Spikes lingered in the doorway, and did not seem in any hurry to depart.

It was evident that she wished to say something.

Mrs. Corcoran encouraged her.

"How long have you lived in this place, deary?" she asked.

"Ever since I was a child—as long as I can remember," Joan Spikes replied.

"You don't look much the worse for it," Mrs. Corcoran observed.

"Why should I?" the gentle Joan replied. "I have always lived well, at—"

"At other people's expense," Mrs. Corcoran interposed, with a snigger.

"So have you, it seems," Mrs. Spikes retorted. "Do you happen to know anything about the locality of Smithfield?"

"I know there is such a place," said Mrs. Corcoran, screwing up her mouth, and leering at her questioner. "Why do you ask me, love?"

"Because it will be as well for you to speak out," Mrs. Spikes replied. "Are you the woman who, with Bill Blarney, took a wounded gentleman to a house called the Chequers?"

"I am," said Mrs. Corcoran. And then she began to sigh and moan most dismally. "Poor Ted! poor Ted Nickells!" she continued. "I thought he was too clever to let the traps catch him after all his experienee. It nearly broke my heart when I heard that he came to so bad an end."

"Supposing he cheated the traps, after all?" said Mrs. Spikes. "Supposing that Ted Nickells is alive and well at this very moment—what would you say to that?"

"Why, the news would make me dance for joy," the hag replied. "But it can't be. I read of his execution in the paper, and, according to the account, poor Ted died awfully hard."

"Come with me," said Mrs. Spikes, in a tone of voice that admitted of no denial.

"Where—where to?" the hag stammered. "I hope you don't think that I had any hand in betraying poor, dear Ted?"

"Come with me," said Joan Spikes again, "and you shall see him with your own eyes."

Mrs. Corcoran flung up her arms, and feigned to be overcome with surprise.

Downstairs they went, and no sooner did Mrs. Corcoran see Ted Nickells than she opened her arms and made a rush at him.

"There, that will do," said the ruffian, warding her off with his arms. "Affection ain't much in my line, and if I wanted to be hugged by a woman I should choose a younger one than you."

Mrs. Corcoran sat down and forced a couple of crocodile tears from her eyes.

"Oh! what a happy meeting this is," she said. "Oh! the blessedness of it."

"Very," Ted Nickells said, dryly. "Now then, we may as well understand each other. If you tell a living soul that you have seen me I'll cut your throat."

"And welcome too," said Mrs. Corcoran. "You ought to know me better to think that I would do such a thing."

"This woman," said Ted Nickells, pointing at the hag, and turning to Spikes and his wife, "is as cunning as a fox and as wide awake as a weasel. She can give points in artfulness to the whole lot of you—yes, all Buckler's-rents. Keep her here, Spikes—keep her here until I am well out of the country."

At that moment a man dashed past the house at the top of his speed.

"Something's wrong!" Spikes said, starting to his feet. "Who can it be at this time of night—or, I should say, morning?"

"Go and see," his wife said.

Spikes seized a cudgel, Ted Nickells dived into a cupboard, and Joan, picking up a sharp-pointed table-knife, toyed meaningly with its handle as she gazed steadfastly at Mrs. Corcoran.

Spikes went to the door and looked carefully up and down.

He saw a man, hatless and breathless, and apparently half-dead with fatigue, leaning against a wall for support.

"Hullo!" Spikes roared out. "Who are you, and what do you want?"

"For mercy's sake," replied the stranger, "give me a drink of water, if you have nothing stronger. I am more dead than alive."

"I should know that voice," Spikes said. "Come here and let me have a look at you."

Seeing that no harm was to be apprehended from the miserable stranger, Spikes called to his wife, and that lady went to the door, taking care that Mrs. Corcoran went with her.

No sooner did Mrs. Corcoran look at the stranger than she flung up her arms, and fainted away in right down earnest.

Bill Blarney had found his way to Buckler's-rents, and thus three friends, who never thought of meeting again, were reunited.

---

## CHAPTER CXLV.

SPRING-HEELED JACK CREATES A SENSATION—THE CHASE ON THE ROOF—A NOVEL USE FOR A CHIMNEY.

SPRING-HEELED JACK seemed to be here, there, and everywhere at once.

Now news of his terrible presence came from the sea-coast, now from the country, and then all London rang with his exploits.

As a matter of course, his doings were somewhat exaggerated.

Rumour, like a snow-ball, gathers in size and strength as it goes onward, and the highest pitch was reached when a groggy old gentleman declared that he saw Spring-Heeled Jack take a leap to the top of St. Paul's, turn a somersault, and alight comfortably on the Monument.

This flight of a fertile imagination found many believers.

"And pray, why should not such be the case," observed Town Councillor Sniggers, as he sat in the Cock Tavern, near Temple-bar. "Didn't this—this—well, I don't know what to call him—jump from one side of the Thames to the other? Haven't we the watchman's word for it?"

"Yes," said Perkins, the hosier, moistening his clay with half-a-pint of warm brandy and water. "Well, things are coming to a pretty pass, I must say."

"A pretty pass!" Sniggers exclaimed, bringing his hand down heavily upon the table. "A pretty pass, did you say? It passes all human comprehension. Why doesn't the Lord Mayor call out the City watch in a body, and put an end to this wretch? When I'm out in the evening my wife hides up in a cupboard, and [illegible] be surprised if she died of fright."

The fat, stumpy, bald-headed waiter shuddered, and spilled some hot water over a gouty old gentleman's foot.

After the cursing on the part of the afflicted one had come to an end, the conversation was resumed.

"There's that affair at the Walnut Shades, kept by Stubbs," Sniggers went on. "Who can doubt the truth of it? Stubbs had two constables in his house—"

"Yes—yes," interposed Perkins; "we all know the story. It's—it's getting rather late. Don't you think we had better change the subject?"

"I was only about to observe," said Sniggers, "that the unhappy men were discovered, drugged and half-suffocated, in a cupboard."

"And early on the following morning," observed another man, "Mr. Nabbitt, of Bow-street, was brutally assaulted by Spring-Heeled Jack, and imprisoned in one of the cells."

"Lor' !" gasped the fat waiter, now anointing his own feet with hot water. "Lor' !"

"You speak when you are spoken to," said Sniggers. "Bilter, you must learn to know your place."

"Yes, sir," Bilter said, lurching against the table.

Just then who should walk into the far-famed hostelrie but Mr. Nabbitt himself.

He plumped himself into a chair, and snorted like a porpoise accidentally thrown ashore.

"Bring me some brandy and water," he said, glaring fiercely at the trembling waiter, "and be as quick about it as you can."

Bilter had a mortal horror of the chief constable, and bolted out of the room as if he had been shot out of a gun.

Mr. Nabbitt's eyes were still darkened by the blow he had received from Spring-Heeled Jack, and he cast a mute appeal round the room for sympathy.

"Well, Nabbitt," said Sniggers, "have you taken Spring-Heeled Jack into custody yet?"

"I have not, sir," Nabbitt replied; "but I have good reason to believe that he will be in my hands before many hours are over."

"That is good news," he said. "I suppose you are speaking from good information?"

Mr. Nabbitt laid two fingers on his lips, and shook his head knowingly.

"Sir," he said, "in my official capacity I beg to say that I must not, and do not intend to, divulge anything that may have happened to have come to me."

"Oh! of course not," Sniggers returned, hastily, but looking very savage.

"You, sir," Mr. Nabbitt went on—"I repeat—you, sir, as a town councillor for the Ward of Farringdon Within, do not produce the balance-sheet of expenditure to anybody who chooses to ask to see it?"

"No, no! certainly not," Mr. Sniggers replied. "You are quite right there. I do not."

"And in the same way," Nabbitt returned, "I say nothing of what may or may not come to my ears regarding Bow-street and its business."

Sniggers felt that he had been taken down, and by a man who had worked himself up from the humble position of a constable.

The thought was maddening, and he would have given more than a trifle to have been in the position to bundle Nabbitt neck and crop out of his situation.

Perkins, the hosier, rubbed the tip of his nose, and indulged in a sly grin as he looked into the fire.

"At all events, I will tell you this," said Nabbitt, as he gave Bilter sixpence for the brandy and nothing for himself, "I have made such preparations that if Spring-Heeled Jack was in London to-night, he could not escape alive! Indeed, gentlemen, nothing would give me greater pleasure than to tackle him alone."

Little did Nabbitt, the valiant, think how soon his wish was to be gratified.

"The cowardly villain attacked me in the rear," Nabbitt continued, after a pause, "and struck me with something like a poker—yes, I am almost sure it was a poker."

"What an awful liar you are!" said a voice so close to the chief constable that he started and turned pale.

"What?" he gasped, dropping his pipe and smashing it to atoms. "Who said that?"

"Who said what, sir?" demanded the unoffending but ever unlucky Bilter.

"Oh! it was you, was it?" Nabbitt roared. "How dare you?"

Poor Bilter rubbed the top of his shiny bald head and groaned inwardly.

"It seems to me that I comes in for everything," he said. "I ain't done nothin', and I ain't said nothin', and I'll take my alfred-david to it."

Mr. Nabbitt thought he must have been mistaken with regard to the voice, but here was a chance he could not help improving.

"Bilter," he said, "look me in the face. Don't turn your eyes away, but fix them on mine."

The unhappy waiter turned pale, and fully expected to be hauled off to the nearest lock-up.

"Do you know the nature of an oath?" the chief constable demanded.

"Why, yes, of course I do," Bilter replied, with a sinking motion in the region of his knees.

"Then tell me and tell these gentlemen what it is," said Nabbitt, shaking his forefinger at the wretched man. "No equivocation, no beating about the bush, no going this way or that; but answer me straightforward, according to the law of your country."

Bilter opened his mouth, but nothing more intelligible than a gasp came from it.

"What did I tell you long ago, gentlemen?" Nabbitt said, turning to the company. "This man is an ass—an ignorant ass. Put him in the witness-box and under cross-examination, and he would swear that his grandmother was his uncle."

This was a little too much, even for the meek, long-suffering Bilter.

"You'd swear to anything without being cross-examined at all," he blurted out.

"Did you intend that observation for me?" he asked.

"You made me say it," Bilter groaned; "you badgered and bullied me into it."

"He confesses it," Nabbitt cried, triumphantly, as he took a note-book from his pocket. "Gentlemen, it is just possible that I shall have to call you as witnesses. In all probability Bilter will be called upon to plead at the next sessions after the one now sitting."

Bilter looked as if he were going to fall on his knees, and in all probability he would have done so had not a loud peal of laughter rang through the room at that moment.

The noise was so strange and weird that the

entire company sat as if they had been struck dumb, motionless, and silly.

Before they could recover themselves, the landlord, accompanied by an ostler, whose eyes were standing out of his head like hat-pegs, rushed into the room.

"Nabbitt—Mr. Nabbitt!" the landlord said, in a kind of shriek. "I am glad that you are here—oh! you don't know how glad you are here.. There's Bill—my man Bill. Just listen to what he has to say!"

Bill did not look as if he were going to say anything more during his earthly career.

His face was perfectly green with terror, and his mouth opened and shut like a mechanical monkey in a fancy clock.

"Now, Bill," said Nabbitt, trying to look calm and collected, "what have you to say? Was it you who laughed in such a horrible fashion just now?"

"No! Oh—oh—no—o—o!"

"The man's had a fall or something," Nabbitt said. "He's half idiotic. If there's a pail of water handy, put it over him."

"I don't want a pail of water chucked over me," replied Bill, recovering himself somewhat. "I—I—I— Oh! lor', the spasms are comin' on again!"

"This is against the law," Nabbitt declared, in a tone of disgust. "Fancy a man like that giving evidence before a judge and jury. Bill, why don't you speak out like a man?"

"I'll try," the ostler replied, holding on to his waistcoat as if he were afraid that his body would fly out. "There's a—a—oh! lor', a-mussy—a great white thing a-sittin' on the top o' the stack o' chembleys!"

"The man's drunk," said Nabbitt, turning pale to the roots of his hair—"dead drunk!"

"I ain't!" Bill bellowed. "I ain't touched a drop since dinner. If you don't believe me, go and see for yourself."

"I have it!" cried Sniggers, skipping out of his chair. "It is Spring-Heeled Jack."

This announcement was more than sufficient to cause a general rush for the door.

Over to the other side of Fleet-street dashed the alarm party, and, sure enough, on the top of an ancient stack of chimneys sat Spring-Heeled Jack, cross-legged, his arms spread out, and his long hair flying in the wind.

"Hush!" said Nabbitt; "don't move, gentlemen, even if he jumps in among us. I call upon you in the name of the law to stand by me. Keep quiet and I'll bring him down."

Nabbitt thrust his hand into his back-pocket and brought forth a loaded pistol.

Bang!

Spring-Heeled Jack lurched forward, and fell quivering on the roof of the house.

"Hurrah!" said Nabbitt. "Didn't I tell you at I would settle his hash before long?"

"You did," Mr. Sniggers replied. "You have ne your duty well, and the country at large is ebted to you. Shall we get a ladder and help n to bring the body down?"

"Certainly not," Nabbitt replied. "I will take l the responsibility, and let me tell you that I am not to be interefered with at such a time as this. Let a ladder be brought, and I—I—do you hear me?—will see the body in the first instance, and then if you like you may come up and help me to bring it down."

This was smack in the face number two for the Town Councillor Sniggers, and, in modern parlance, he took a back seat.

The excitement was now intense.

The sound of the pistol brought a huge crowd to the spot, and the report that Spring-Heeled Jack had been captured spread like wild-fire.

Nabbitt was in his glory.

He punched at least a dozen men's heads for standing in his way, and elbowed everybody he came in contact with.

"The ladder—quick!" he roared. "The ladder, I say, or some of you will find yourselves laid by the heels in prison."

The ladder was soon brought, and the hero of the hour prepared to mount.

"Stand back, all of you!" he said, waving his hand pompously. "If any man attempts to follow me before I give the signal, I will rap him over the head with the butt-end of this pistol."

It never occurred to the jack-in-office to reload the weapon.

Up he went, watched by hundreds of eyes until he reached the roof.

As he commenced to crawl along it a grim smile of satisfaction stole across his face.

"There you are, my beauty," he said, touching Spring-Heeled Jack. "Ah! oh! ha! Help—help!"

Spring-Heeled Jack had risen suddenly and confronted Mr. Nabbitt.

The chief-constable's hair stood on end.

He reeled backwards, and would have fallen over the parapet had not Spring-Heeled Jack caught him by the throat.

"So," said the awful-looking being, "you thought you had shot me? You made a slight mistake, for your aim was wide of the mark; but I am going to shoot you."

"Oh! no. Oh, oh! Mercy!"

"Not with a pistol," Spring-Heeled Jack said. "I am going to shoot you down the chimney."

With these words he caught up Nabbitt, shrieking and struggling violently, and thrust him head first into the sooty abyss.

"There's a beam half-way down," Spring-Heeled Jack cried. "Mind your head."

Nabbitt went down amid a roar of rage and terror from the spectators.

"Gentlemen," said Spring-Heeled Jack, advancing to the parapet, "you had better see that the constable is not smoked like a ham. Good night!"

The next instant he had leaped to the adjoining house, then to the top of Temple-bar, and from thence over the houses fronting the Temple.

It was a sight awful enough to chill the heart of the boldest man.

Sniggers fainted dead away; Perkins roared "Fire!" and Bilter, who had clung to some iron railings, slid gently down, and, closing his eyes, favoured such as chose to listen with a long account of various sins committed in his life-time.

When the first paroxysm of terror and astonishment had passed away, a few of the boldest men rushed into the interior of the Cock Inn.

They had seen Mr. Nabbitt go down the chimney, but none had the slightest idea which fire-grate he would come out at.

Nabbitt answered this question himself by suddenly appearing head first into the coffee-room, black, ugly, and, if possible, more horrible-looking than Spring-Heeled Jack.

"I'm a dead man!" he said to the landlord,

who stooped over him. "Raise me up, and give me some brandy—neat."

"How much would you like?" demanded the landlord, who, in spite of all that had taken place, kept an eye on business matters.

"About a pint," Nabbitt groaned. "Oh! my head. Oh! my bones and body. I stuck half-way, and thought I never should have got down."

Then he swore a little, which seemed to have the effect of relieving his feelings.

"To think that I should be fool enough to be taken in in such a way!" he said. "If I had reloaded my pistol I could have shot the villain as he lay."

At this moment four men brought Sniggers in, giving him what police-constables pleasantly call "the frog's march."

Mr. Sniggers knew nothing about it, as he was still in an unconscious state; but when he came round, which he presently did, he groaned and moaned terribly.

"Who's been pulling my legs and arms out of joint?" he demanded. "Oh! hang it. I feel as if I had been on the rack."

"Please, sir," said a man, "we brought you in, and we want a couple of shillin's for the job."

"A couple of what?" Sniggers said, as he almost exploded with wrath.

"Shillin's, sir, and cheap at the price," the man said. "A hackney-coach might have gone over you, you know."

"If," Mr. Sniggers returned, "I had the strength to throw something heavy at your fat head, I would do it with all my heart. Bilter! Where's Bilter? Ah! here you are at last. Turn them people out, and if they won't go, run for a constable."

But Bilter was not in a fit condition to remove anybody or run anywhere.

His terror rather increased than diminished at the sight of Mr. Nabbitt, who was now being washed down.

At last something like order was restored.

The landlord, finding that his house contained a number of people who were desirous of drinking without paying, ejected half-a-dozen in as many seconds; and, having done this to the great relief of his feelings, he declared his intention of brewing a bowl of punch, which should be put down to Mr. Sniggers' account.

## CHAPTER CXLVI.

### THE STORY OF THE CONSTABLES' WOES—ON THE TRACK.

It was hinted in the foregoing chapter that Catchpole and Grabham had been discovered in a cupboard.

This was perfectly true; for, after hunting about a little, Mr. Stubbs, the worthy host of the Walnut Shades, came upon the wretched constables tied back to back, and, apparently, fast asleep.

Mr. Stubbs, though greatly alarmed at the appearance of Spring-Heeled Jack, could not help smiling as he gazed at Catchpole and Grabham.

"Why, bless my 'art!" he said, "they're trussed up as neat as fowls. But what's the matter with 'em? Here! Hi! wake up, will you?"

But neither of the constables stirred.

"Strikes me that they've been dosed with something," Stubbs said. "What shall I do to rouse 'em up? I can't have 'em here in this state."

Suddenly he remembered the wonderful power of a pin when applied to a fleshy portion of the human anatomy, and he at once proceeded to prove its effect.

Grabham opened one eye and gave vent to a faint "Oh!"

"He's coming round, at all events," said Mr. Stubbs; "a little more o' this kind o' physic will make another man of him."

Grabham howled lustily under the second application.

"Oh! don't," he gasped; "how can you be so unmanly? Wake up, Catchpole. Oh! I'm being stung to death!"

Catchpole woke up thoroughly at the first insertion of the pin in the calf of his leg, and then the landlord of the Walnut Shade cut the cords which had been so deftly tied and knotted by Spring-Heeled Jack.

"There now," said Stubbs, "you may thank me for saving your lives."

As the two constables sneaked out of the cupboard they looked in dismay at each other.

"Mister Stubbs," Grabham said, in a voice replete with emotion, "me and my mate are well aware that we took a drop too much, but we wants to know how we came into that blessed place."

"What! don't you know?" cried Stubbs. "Surely, you haven't forgotten Spring-Heeled Jack?"

"Oh! lor'," Grabham gasped. "It has all come back to me in a moment."

"So it has to me, worse luck," said Catchpole. "I just remember feeling something damp, which smelt awfully strong, being thrown upon my face, and I suppose it took my senses away."

"Is—is—is he here now?" demanded Grabham, with a nervous glance at the door.

"No," Stubbs replied, in a whisper; "but he paid a visit to the parlour, and all the customers ran bang out into the street. I was left all alone, but I faced the fiend, and all of a sudden—hey! presto!—he was gone, leaving nothing but a strong smell of sulphur behind him."

"Dear me!" said Grabham, "this is very extraordinary. At all events Spring-Heeled Jack didn't mean to kill us, or he could have done it easy. Well, Catchpole, my boy, I suppose we had better make our way back to Bow-street."

"What, at half-past two in the morning? Not I, for one; so don't think it."

"Well, what are you going to do?"

"Why, go home, and tumble into bed, like a sensible man."

"And I think I will, too," Grabham said. "Nabbitt will be a bit savage, but he will cool down when we call Mr. Stubbs as witness to what we have suffered."

So saying, the constables left the Walnut Shades, and did not revisit Bow-street until late in the afternoon, when they heard that Spring-Heeled Jack had favoured Mr. Nabbitt with some attention.

There was no end of bullying on Nabbitt's part, and for some time he refused to hear what Catchpole and Grabham had to say, but when their story was told Mr. Nabbitt smote his brow, and cried—

"This fellow is a demon indeed!"

On the same night Nabbitt met with his misfortune at the Cock Tavern, in Fleet-street.

Turning away from the official department, let us take a glance at Sir Roland Ashton and the landlord of the Bull in Top Boots.

The landlord had many aliases, and Sir Roland

having heard of him spoken as Joe Morth, called him by that name.

Sir Roland thought he might as well take Joe Morth into his confidence, and tell him everything he knew of Mrs. Corcoran.

Morth listened with a scowling face that deepened every moment.

"So," he said, "you've been as thick in the mud as she ha been in the mire. You're a nice sort of party to have anything to do with, I must say."

Sir Roland Ashton laughed at this speech as if it amused him intensely.

"Well," said he, "I thought I had better tell you the truth. We shall understand each other all the better."

"Humph! I suppose so," Morth replied, dubiously. "Well, I shall be satisfied if you can put me on Mrs. Corcoran's track."

"Which I will do in less time than you think," Sir Roland said.

"We must wait until night before we start," the landlord said, "for we have to bury Sam Snatcher and Dick Sleuth in the back premises. Poor Dick! I have lost a good friend in him."

The bodies were laid side by side and covered up. Morth then went back to the bar, and pouring out a tumbler of brandy, gulped it down his throat.

"I feel as miserable as if I were on the way to execution," he said.

At that moment a knock came at the door, which was securely locked and bolted.

Motioning Sir Roland Ashton to keep out of sight, Morth demanded who was there.

"It is I—Harriet Snatcher," said a shrill voice. "Where is my husband?"

"I don't know," Morth replied. "Don't come here. Keep out of the way; there is danger abroad."

"But where can Sam have got to?" said Mrs. Snatcher. "I have been half over London and am almost distracted. Won't you let me in?"

"No," the landlord responded; "I dare not. I am expecting the runners from Bow-street every moment."

Harriet Snatcher uttered a wailing cry and went back into the street.

She went back to look for the man she would never see again.

"Phew!" said Morth, wiping some beads of perspiration from his face as he went back to the parlour. "It is lucky that I did not let her in. My eyes would have told their own story. I would not look that woman in the face for a thousand pounds, though I had nothing to do with Snatcher's death."

Few people came to the Bull in Top Boots that day, and such as did come were compelled to seek another hostelry, for the door was never once unlocked.

When night came, Joe Morth and Sir Roland Ashton set about their ghastly task.

The bodies were buried in one grave, and the earth filled in.

As the work was completed the Borough Church clock struck the hour of midnight.

"It is time we started," Morth said. "Many days may pass away before I return to this house, and when I do Mrs. Corcoran shall be numbered with the dead."

Bidding Sir Roland Ashton remain where he was, the landlord made a journey into the lower regions of the house.

He was not away many minutes, and when he returned he carried a bag in his hand.

"Nothing can be done in the world without money," he said, "so we may as well take plenty of yellow-boys in case we want them."

Sir Roland's eyes glistened as Morth poured the gold out in a heap upon the table.

"I may as well tell you that at present I am without money," the baronet said.

The landlord pushed ten guineas across the table.

"You must make yourself satisfied with that," he observed. "So long as you are with me I will pay all expenses, so you will not stand in need of money. One more drink, and then we will start."

It was nearly one o'clock when Morth and the baronet, traversing through the Borough, reached London-bridge.

Not a soul was in sight, and no sound disturbed the stillness that hung over the sleeping city, save the rippling of the tide.

Keeping steadily on, they reached Fleet-street, and turning up Fetter-lane, reached the White Horse Inn.

In those days the White Horse was in its glory.

No less than half-a-dozen coaches started from its door, and morn, noon, and night the building presented an animated appearance.

It was an early coach that Morth and Sir Roland had come in search of.

"What time does the Magnet start?" Sir Roland asked of a tight-legged man, who, nibbling at a piece of hay, was leaning against one of the door-posts.

"Not before five," the man replied, "so you have plenty of time. A cold morning, sir."

"Very," said Sir Roland.

"Let us go into the house," Morth said; "I daresay we can manage to while away the time."

The bar was full of horsey-looking men, who were chatting about horses and nothing but horses.

In the coffee-room were several people waiting to meet friends, or to depart.

Sir Roland Ashton glanced at them one by one, as was his custom when he found himself in the presence of strangers.

There was one man that attracted his attention more than the rest.

He was apparently about fifty years of age, grizzled and bronzed, as if he had seen long service abroad.

His sharp, dark eyes twinkled when he spoke, and his voice had a trumpet-like ring in it.

"Waiter," he said, "poke the fire and bring me a newspaper. The latest, I mean; not one a fortnight old."

"Yes, sir," the waiter replied, and bustled off in a hurry.

"A cold morning for a drive outside a coach," the sharp-spoken gentleman said to Sir Roland.

"Yes," Sir Roland replied. "Are you tavelling?"

"I am—by the Magnet."

At that moment the waiter brought the paper, and the gentleman buried his head amongst its leaves.

"What is all this nonsense about Spring-Heeled Jack?" he said. "I'd Spring-Heeled-Jack him. By the living Jingo! I'd make him jump under fifty good lashes."

"I wish you could have your mind," said Morth,

who now thought it time to join in the conversation. "I have seen Spring-Heeled Jack."

"The deuce you have!" cried the gentleman, throwing down the paper. "What is he like?"

"Why, like Old Nick, only white instead of black," said Joe Morth.

"Oh! indeed," responded the gentleman. "Did you ever see Old Nick?"

Sir Roland edged up to Morth, and dug him in the ribs with his elbows, as a sign for him to be quiet.

"No," Morth then said, surlily; "but I have some idea what he is like."

"So I should think," the gentleman said, dryly.

This ended the conversation, and the rest of the time passed away in silence.

Day, cold and desolate, was just dawning when a cheery blast from a horn announced that the coach was at the door.

"Gentlemen for the Magnet will take their seats, please," said the guard of the coach, appearing at the door of the coffee-room. "We start in five minutes."

The Magnet, bound for the east, was lightly laden, for there was another coach at mid-day, and most people preferred travelling by it than getting up and dressing by candlelight.

The coach made its first stop at Romford, and went on, changing horses at the appointed stages, all day long.

And yet the journey was not yet completed.

At a quaint little town a fresh coachman and guard took charge of the Magnet; and after a couple of hours rest the weary passengers took their seats.

A strong wind was blowing, and it came laughing and roaring across the Fen country as if a legion of banshees were holding high revel and outdoing each other in dismal cries.

The light from the coach lamps drew forth all sorts of odd, fantastic shadows from the roads and banks, for now there was scarcely a tree to be seen.

The gentleman who had made enquiries about Spring-Heeled Jack at the White Horse, kept himself to himself, and never spoke to anyone save when he was spoken to, which was very seldom.

"Well," Morth whispered in Sir Roland's ear, "if this is the sort of place you expect to find Mrs. Corcoran in, all I can say is, that she is mightily fond of open country."

"Hush!" the baronet whispered back. "I am taking you to the place where she told me she was born. It struck me that she might take refuge there until she thinks over some fresh plan of action."

Morth only gave a grunt by way of reply, and, burying his head on his chest, fell asleep.

The road became still more desolate and lonesome, all the more so for its flatness.

As far as the eye could reach there was no hill worthy of the name, and there seemed to be no end of the long tracks of dreary, cheerless marsh lands.

It was past ten o'clock when a diversion took place.

Suddenly from behind a low stone wall three men leaped their horses, and turned and faced the coach.

Guard and driver knew what was the matter in an instant.

Shouting "Highwaymen! highwaymen!" at the top of their voices, they roused the passengers, who began to rave and curse, as suited them best.

"Gentlemen," said the leader of the highwaymen, who was closely masked, "all this noise is not the slightest use. We want your money, and mean to have it. If the guard or coachman move from their places, or attempt to find the blunderbuss, which, of course, is in the boot, it will be our painful duty to immediately blow their brains out."

Uttering a fearful oath, as he buttoned his coat up to the teeth, Joe Morth started to his feet.

The next instant he received a fearful blow on the side of the head, and went down like a leaden plummet into the road.

Who struck him, or by what means the blow was delivered, he had no notion whatever, and before he could recover from the effects of it one of the highwaymen dismounted and rifled him of everything he possessed.

Petrified with fright and astonishment, Sir Roland Ashton sat motionless on the coach, and when one of the masked men climbed up its side, he parted meekly with the ten guineas Morth had presented him with.

"Right, there! We've got all we want," said the leader of the highwaymen. "Away, boys!"

When the noise and confusion had somewhat abated, it was noticed that one of the passengers had disappeared.

This was the very man who had sat so silent during the whole journey.

"Curse him!" Morth said, wiping the mud and blood from his face. "Curse him! he was in this conspiracy. It must have been him who knocked me heels over head."

There seemed to be very little doubt of that now.

"Well," said the coachman, "you ought to think yourself lucky that you have escaped with your life."

"Ought to think myself lucky?" Morth growled. "If either you or the guard had had an ounce of pluck all this might have been averted."

"That's right," said the guard, "put the blame on our shoulders. Perhaps you will be good enough to say that we were in league with these fellows."

"I should not wonder if you were," Morth retorted, with another furious oath.

"It is well for you that you paid your fare at starting," said the guard, "or you would have to finish the journey on foot."

It was strange that nothing in the coach had been touched, and nobody relieved of their money save Morth and the baronet.

"It strikes me that we must have been watched," growled the landlord of the Bull in Top Boots. "Perhaps you will tell me what to do now, Sir Roland?"

"I am at a loss to know, unless we return to London," the baronet said.

"What would be the good of that?"

"I was thinking that you did not bring all your money with you."

"And you thought right," Morth said. "Bend down your head and listen to me."

Sir Roland did so, and Morth said—

"We have been robbed, and we must turn about and help ourselves. If there is a crib worth cracking in the neighbourhood we must see what it contains. Back to London? Bah! not I. There must be money or valuables even in such a place as this, and we will have them by hook or by crook."

# SPRING-HEELED JACK,

## THE TERROR OF LONDON.

"BACK—BACK!" YELLED THE HAG. "COME NOT NEAR ME."

No. 41.

## CHAPTER CXLVII.

### THE OLD CATHEDRAL CITY—THE FAIR—THE FIRE.

AT the moment that Lord Mildendale caught sight of Spring-Heeled Jack, and heard his voice, an awful feeling of helplessness came over him.

He trembled in every limb, and reeling backwards, stood glaring at the weird figure perched in so strange an attitude on the top of the caravan.

"What does my noble lord do here?" said Spring-Heeled Jack again. "Is it that he is anxious to know how the strollers live, or is there the spirit of mischief working in his mind?"

"These men are vagabonds—vile scoundrels—the scum of the earth!" Lord Mildendale gasped. "I was told that they were upon my land. Lucky it is for them that they are not."

"Beware!" Spring-Heeled Jack said, leaping to his feet, and drawing himself up to his full height. "Away! Back to your house of gloom and desolation, or the shadow of death will hover over it. Hark! Namon Wallack, your enemy, awakes."

Before Lord Mildendale could utter a word in reply Spring-Heeled Jack had vanished, and his lordship, hearing a hand upon the caravan door, darted in among the trees.

"Who goes there?" Namon Wallack cried, as he appeared. "Surely I heard the sound of voices. If there is a man about, let him speak, or it will go hard with him?"

By this time Robin Gray had huddled on a portion of his clothes, and stood at Namon Wallack's side.

"Go back, boy," the gipsy said. "If there is danger abroad you are not the one who ought to be exposed to it. Light the lantern—I will search the woods."

As Robin Gray turned to obey, the echoes of the woods were startled by a loud report.

Namon Wallack, uttering a heavy groan, fell forward upon his face.

"Help—help!" Robin cried, leaping from the caravan and kneeling down at the wounded man's side.

There was no occasion for the lad's shouts, for in an instant the encampment was alive with men, women, and children, shouting for vengeance.

"I am not much hurt!" Namon Wallack cried, raising himself upon his elbow. "The bullet struck me in the thigh. Search the woods, and if you find the villain hang him out of hand!"

Hither and thither ran the half-maddened gipsies, shouting to each other as they tore through brier and bramble.

The air grew red and lurid under the glare of torches, but they found no stranger, and at last the chase was reluctantly abandoned.

Namon Wallack's wound was bound up.

It was found that the bullet had glanced aside, and inflicted only a flesh wound, and, though the gipsies rejoiced at the safety of their favourite, their rage knew no bounds.

In their own minds they knew who had fired the shot, but that man's name never escaped from a single lip.

There would be a more opportune time to bring the would-be murderer to book, and the swarthy sons of the forest kept their own counsel.

Namon Wallack rested his wounded limbs all the next day, and Robin Gray nursed the gipsy with tenderness and care.

The march eastwards went steadily on, and when the first caravan rolled down the Newmarket road, and entered the good old city of Norwich by the gate dedicated to St. Giles, Namon Wallack was on his feet again, and little the worse for his adventure.

It was evening when the gipsies entered the city, followed by a crowd of youthful sightseers, who looked forward to the great Michaelmas fair with joy, and back at it with regret.

Seated on the box of Namon Wallack's dwelling-van, Robin Gray marked the splendid castle and the grand tapering spire of the cathedral, to which the quaintly-roofed houses seem to be creeping softly for rest.

The last lingering rays of the sun were playing about the sacred edifice, burnishing its gilded vane, while behind it the purple veil of twilight was rolling slowly down.

The fair was to be held in an open space, reserved on certain days for the sale of cattle; and already several shows—as yet closed caskets, so to speak, of marvel and mystery—had arrived, and taken up their stations.

The peace and quietude of the old city had a soothing effect upon Robin Gray.

It was a place to dream in, a place to wander about and picture the people of twice a hundred years ago pacing the quaint streets, and emerging from the arched entries.

Here, by the Close, hooded monk in the days gone by told his beads, as with bowed head he went his way on mission of mercy.

A little further on, by the river banks, mailed knight, in the name of King Edward VI., and sturdy peasant, under Robert Kett, the rebel, had battled fiercely, and back again in the open space before the great cathedral gates the blood of Puritan and Cavalier had reddened the ground.

Namon Wallack told Robin Gray all these things as they sat at supper—a well-earned meal—after some hours of earnest work.

The boy was delighted, and would willingly have listened throughout the night; but the following day promised to be a still more busy one, and soon the last sound of activity was heard.

A country fair of a hundred years ago was a very different thing to what it is nowadays.

Then there were no means of rushing country folk up to London and the great cities, at almost a nominal charge, to see sights, which have long since almost driven the travelling showman off the road.

The bold, fierce, bad baron has almost disappeared from the stage he so loved to tread.

He has played his little part and vanished from the scene, or given place, to a mere ghost of himself—a creature with thin legs and a squeaky voice.

The fair opened boldly enough.

Every thing that could possibly make a noise was brought into requisition.

Drums banged, trumpets blared, and cracked gongs rang out their unmelodious sounds.

The fat woman, the giant, the wild man of the woods, wonderfully painted and terrifically adorned with feathers, the snake-charmer *(sap engro)*, the trained pig, and the fortune-telling pony, had but little rest that day.

Every John had brought his Mary—he ruddy and smiling, she, good lass, gay with ribbons—to the fair, and for the time money seemed to be no object, even to the poorest peasant.

At last all was over.

The naphtha lamps were extinguished, the bold

baron drank with the man he had stabbed half-a-dozen times during the day, and the strollers, one and all, sat down with grateful hearts to eat and rest.

"A good day this," said Namon Wallack, rubbing his hands first, and then patting Robin Gray on the shoulder. "We have taken over twelve pounds."

"I am heartily glad to hear it," Robin replied, "but I am afraid I have not been much use."

"Why," Namon returned, "you played the most important part of all. You took the money."

Now that the toil of the day was over, the gipsies were in no hurry to retire to rest.

They went from show to show, asking their neighbours how they had fared, and if some drank a little too deeply, and sang a trifle too loud, good will prevailed.

It was past twelve when Robin Gray placed his head upon the pillow, and closed his eyes.

Namon Wallack soon followed his example, and by degrees silence asserted itself; and the moon, sailing grandly across a star-lit sky, looked down upon the white tents.

Robin Gray was suddenly awakened by hearing a sharp, cracking sound.

In an instant he reared himself up, and in another he gave utterance to a cry of alarm.

"Up—up!" he shouted; "the show is on fire. Oh! Heaven; this must be the work of some dastardly hand!"

## CHAPTER CXLVIII.

### MRS. CORCORAN IS PROVIDED FOR, BUT THINKS SHE CAN DO MUCH BETTER THAN RELY UPON HER FRIENDS.

BILL BLARNEY, hunted, out of breath, bruised and bleeding as he was, could not help grinning as he saw Mrs. Corcoran flop down at his feet, and to all appearance give up the ghost.

"Heart alive!" he cried. "Who would have thought of meeting that old hag here!"

"It seems to me," said Spikes, "that Buckler's-rents is getting a trifle too well-known. Who are you?"

"A bird just flown from gaol," Bill Blarney replied; "but I am not such a stranger to this place as you may think. Where is Daddy Muckrum?"

"He has gone to his country seat for a holiday," Spikes replied, grinning.

"Ha! I suppose he has found it necessary to keep out of the way?"

"That's just it," Spikes replied. "Well, as you know him you are welcome to come in; but you haven't told me your name yet."

"Bill Blarney."

A smothered cry came from the interior of the house, and Ted Nickells rushed to the door to greet his old friend.

"Now don't you go into a fit," said Ted Nickells. "It isn't my ghost that you see before you. Give me your hand, pal. I'm glad to see you. So you have given the stone jug the slip. Ha! ha! ha! Bravo! Well done you."

"Don't kick up such a row," said Bill Blarney, with a nervous glance over his shoulder. "The traps were thick and hot on my heels, I can tell you. Curse them, how I should like to catch one of them alone!"

"What about Jem Basker?" queried Ted Nickells, as he led the way into the house.

"I don't know," Bill Blarney replied. "He escaped with me; but I heard two pistol shots, and—"

"You fear the worst?"

"I do."

Mr. and Mrs. Spikes remained behind to look after Mrs. Corcoran.

They brought her in, as rigid and senseless as a log of wood.

"Throw some water over her," Ted Nickells said. "A pailful."

"Let her smell a brandy bottle," Bill Blarney remarked. "If that doesn't bring her round, nothing will."

Both remedies were applied, and after a deal of wheezing and sneezing Mrs. Corcoran opened her eyes, puckered up her features, and glared owl-like at the escaped felon.

"Is it really Bill—dear old Bill, for whom I worked so hard?"

"Oh! yes, it's Bill right enough," Blarney replied. "Well, I'll own that you put yourself out a little for my sake."

"Of course I did, lovey-dovey," Mrs. Corcoran said, as she reached out her hand for the brandy-bottle.

"None of that," Bill Blarney said, scowling; "and perhaps you will be good enough to leave a few drops of that liquor for other people."

"What a remarkable fund of humour Bill has!" Mrs. Corcoran cried. "It is quite delightful to hear him talk. There—there! I could cry for joy to see you back again."

"Don't cry, and don't laugh," Bill Blarney retorted, "for, hang me, if I know which is the worst of the two."

"There he goes again," said Mrs. Corcoran, rubbing her skinny hands. "That's just the way he used to go on at the Bull in Top Boots."

"How are they all getting on there?" Bill Blarney demanded.

"Why, you see," Mrs. Corcoran replied, "I don't know, because I have been there but very little of late."

"Where have you been, then?"

"Getting my lovey-dovey—"

Whizz went the now empty brandy-bottle a[t] Mrs. Corcoran's head.

It missed her by a hair's breadth, and smashe[d] into atoms against the wall.

"Come—come!" said Joan Spikes. "W[e] can't have that sort of game here. If you want [t]o make a fool of yourself, go and do it somewhere else."

"I'm sorry that I forgot myself," Blarney said, apologetically; "but why does she always speak to me in that way? It's enough to drive a man out of his senses and into a madhouse."

Peace having been proclaimed, the charming party began to talk over the past and to provide for the future.

Mrs. Corcoran knew that she was the subject of many sly glances, but she pretended not to see them.

At last the company broke up, it being arranged that Bill Blarney was to share Ted Nickell's room until more suitable accommodation could be provided for him.

When the house was still and quiet the two ruffians began to talk.

"Bill," Ted Nickells said, "that old hag, Corcoran, is in the way here."

"And in mine, too," Bill Blarney replied, brutally. "Curse her! Why doesn't she die?"

"And save somebody the trouble of shoving her out of the world," Nickells rejoined.

"The hangman will do that, perhaps," Blarney said; "but, no! Such a death is too good for her. I'll bet that at this very moment she is scheming or plotting, and wondering how she can make profit out of us."

"Did you watch her face when she spoke about the Bull in Top Boots?" Nickells demanded.

"No."

"Well, I did, and I am quite certain that she told a lie when she said that she had not been there lately."

"That can soon be proved."

"How?"

"By somebody going there and asking the question."

"But who's to go?" Nickells said.

"I thought you might."

"Bill," said Ted Nickells, "do you take me for a fool?"

"Oh! dear no," Bill Blarney replied.

"Then don't you say anything more about me going to the Bull in Top Boots, or anywhere else," Ted Nickells said. "I am only waiting for a supply of money to take me clean out of the country."

"It wouldn't be a bad idea for me to act upon, Blarney said.

"Well, think over it," Nickells replied. "America is a growing country, and I have heard that there is a fine field for— What's that?"

"What's what?" Bill Blarney demanded.

"I'll swear I heard somebody trip up against one of the stairs," Ted Nickells said, stretching out his hand for the tinder-box. "If that old hag is sneaking about, I'll make short work of her."

"The sound was nothing, perhaps," Blarney said; "very likely it was the wind rattling a door. Go to sleep, or you'll put our friends, the Spikes, in a passion."

"All right," Nickells replied. "The door is fast, so we can come to no harm without good warning. Look out, Mrs. Corcoran! I mean to provide for you before long. Yes; I mean to provide for you."

With these last words spoken drowsily the ruffian rolled over on his side, and, falling asleep, snored in such a tremendous fashion that Bill Blarney felt convinced that he would break a blood-vessel.

Upstairs, in her attic, sat Mrs. Corcoran, as wide awake as a rat in a granary.

"So," she muttered, "I have fallen into bad hands. What a blessing it is to have sharp ears!" She began to rock herself to and fro, and to chant, as if to invoke some familiar spirit. "Oh! oh!" she muttered. "Ted Nickells means to provide for me, does he?"

The hag then rose, and, walking to the window, looked out.

"I have just five guineas left," she said, "and if I do not make use of them pretty quickly they will fall into other hands. Oh! fool—fool, that I did not ask for more, when I had the chance."

Mrs. Corcoran was now perfectly well aware that Buckler's-rents would prove no longer a peaceful clime for her to reside in.

But with all the responsibilities on her head where was she to go to?

Whither could she go for safety?

Peace of mind she did not expect, and had not bargained for.

"I can't stop here, at any rate," she muttered, scowling, "and the sooner I am out of the place the better. Shall it be to-night or the morning?"

After a few moments reflection she determined to stay the night.

But not a wink of sleep did she get; indeed, she scarcely closed her eyes, and was not a little relieved when daylight stole in at the dirty window, as if ashamed of finding itself in such a place.

What miseries of mind had she suffered during that long dreary night!

With the blood of two men scarcely dry upon her hands, she had been haunted by their forms the live long hours, which had dragged themselve round so slowly as if they had determined to plunge the wicked wretch into everlasting darkness.

She went down, trying to looking cheerful, and having bargained with Joan Spikes for a breakfast, ate it with apparent relish.

But all the time she was on the watch for an opportunity to get away.

Yet, eyes as watchful as her own were upon her, and Mrs. Corcoran fretted and fumed in secret.

At last her chance came.

A hawker, with the suspicious look about him of being an officer in disguise, approached the house, and all save the hag made themselves extremely scarce.

Mrs. Corcoran bolted to the door, and opening it before she could be stopped, took to her heels.

The hawker only stared after her, and remarked in his mind that he had never seen an old woman run so fast in his life before.

Then he knocked at the door, but, of course, received no answer.

"A curious place, this," he muttered. "Never was down here before, and I don't think I shall come again."

Mrs. Corcoran, making good use of her time, travelled on until she came to the Borough-market, and, plunging into the scene of activity, wended her way down to the water-side and hailed a boat.

"Temple-stairs," she said to the waterman.

"All right, old lady," the man replied. "Step in. You're in a hurry, I see, for you are out of breath."

"No hurry—no hurry!" Mrs. Corcoran said. "It's dodging across the streets out of the way of the carts and waggons that's upset me."

The waterman put the boat in motion, and Mrs. Corcoran was landed safely at the foot of the Temple-stairs.

Surely the hag had some method in going there?

She had; for it suddenly occurred to her mind to return to Sam Snatcher's old quarters, and to search the place for hidden treasure.

"He never went back there, I'll be bound," she said; "and I know he'll never go again. No—no! But his wife. Would she venture? I think not; but what is the use of thinking? I'll go and see for myself."

Mrs. Corcoran's project was certainly a bold one.

A hundred things might occur to upset her designs and calculations; but necessity knows no law, and the hag had no alternative but to choose between going back to Sam Snatcher's old dwelling-place and the streets of London.

Keeping her lynx-like eyes well about her, Mrs. Corcoran dived into the then miserable and filthy neighbourhood lying between the river and Fleet-street.

Some squalid, half-naked children set up a yell at her appearance, but Mrs. Corcoran only scowled at them.

It was some time before she could find the house she wanted; but she did not dare to enter it, for she became conscious that she was being watched by a man, who lurked behind a door-post not far away.

"Confound the fellow!" Mrs. Corcoran gasped, under her breath. "He is evidently on the look-out. What shall I do?"

Mrs. Corcoran was scarcely ever at a loss how to act when a difficulty presented itself.

Singing, or rather croning, the snatch of a song, the wicked old woman advanced towards the man, and came to a standstill right before him.

The man, who wore a mangy fur cap upon his head, and a patched-up suit of ragged clothes upon his back, started back a step or two.

And not without reason.

Mrs. Corcoran, with her arms akimbo, wagged her head, and rolled her eyes at him in a ghoulish style.

"Well," said the fellow, at last, "you're a nice-looking old party, I must say. Are you often taken like this?"

"Yes," Mrs. Corcoran replied, "yes, I am, when I see an idle, loafing scoundrel skulking about, meddling with other people's business. My friend, I am sometimes taken worse, and then I scratch and bite."

"Oh!" said the man, who did not know what to make of Mrs. Corcoran. "Keep a civil tongue in your head. Perhaps I have more reason and right to be here than you think."

"Ho—ho!" cried the hag. "I'll be bound that Sam Snatcher didn't tell you to hang about here, though his wife might."

"Eh! do you know them?" the man demanded, changing colour.

"Do I know them?" Mrs. Corcoran rejoined; "why, you fool, I am their dearest friend."

"But I never saw you before."

"Who said you had?" Mrs. Corcoran retorted. "Just let me whisper a word in your ear, and I'll soon convince you that I know something about yonder house and what has been going on within its walls."

The man drew closer, but kept his arms raised as if in fear that the hag might pounce upon him.

"Has the body been removed from the cellar?" Mrs. Corcoran demanded, in a low tone of voice.

The evil-looking fellow was taken aback in the true sense of the word.

He recoiled from Mrs. Corcoran, and staggering against the wall of the house, stood there with a face livid and horrible.

"Ye—es," he stammered; "but—but how came you to know anything about it?"

"I know all about it, and a good many more which have found their way to the same place," Mrs. Corcoran replied. "Sam Snatcher and his wife Harriet have deemed it prudent to make themselves scarce, and—"

"Harriet Snatcher cannot find her husband anywhere, so she has gone to an old haunt in the country to see if she can find him," the ruffian interposed.

"That's old news to me," Mrs. Corcoran interposed. "She told me all that with her own lips, and sent me here to look after the house."

"I'll not believe it until she tells me so herself."

"But I will tell you something," Mrs. Corcoran remarked. "In less than an hour there will be a strong force of Bow-street runners, and if you are caught in this neighbourhood you'll find yourself laid by the heels in limbo."

"What about yourself?" the man asked.

"I am not suspected—not wanted, you know, up to the present," the hag said, leering cunningly at her questioner. "When the police arrive they will find that they have come upon a wild-goose chase. But do as you like—do as you like; but don't blame me if you march through these streets with a brace of darbies on your wrists."

The fellow looked up and down the street.

He was reluctant to go away; but if Mrs. Corcoran spoke the truth he had no wish to face Bow-street runners, to whom he was pretty well known.

"Well," he said, after a pause, "I suppose there is no help for it. I must go; but if you have lied the deepest mine under the earth will not hide you from my vengeance, as sure as my name is Luke Clye."

"Agreed," said Mrs. Corcoran. "You needn't fear that I shall run away from my trust."

So saying, Mrs. Corcoran, with many meaning winks and nods, hobbled towards the house.

"All danger will be passed before night-fall," she said; "you may come then."

"I mean to," Luke Clye replied, "and what is more, I shall expect to find you."

"You will," said the hag, and disappeared through the doorway.

Twice or thrice Luke Clye walked a little way up the street, but turned back as often.

"Hang me, if I can believe it!" he growled under his breath; "and yet this old beldame must be in the secret, or how would she know anything about Sam Snatcher's game. I'll not go further than Fadge's and ask his advice. If the runners are really coming this way he will be glad to be put on his guard."

"So," said Mrs. Corcoran, when she had passed through the hall, "all is well up to the present. Ha! ha! ha!"

The rumbling echoes of the house repeated the hag's wild laugh.

"There's a nasty, grave-like sound about this place," she muttered. "Perhaps, after all, there isn't a farthing in the place. What a fool I must have been not to ask Clye whether Harriet Snatcher had stayed any length of time."

She opened one door after the other, and her keen, searching eyes soon convinced her that no search had taken place.

Nothing had been touched, and Mrs. Corcoran proceeded to peer into cupboards, tap the walls, and turn over the frowsy beds.

Her efforts proved futile.

She could find nothing, and Mrs. Corcoran began to lose patience.

Her situation was a desperate one, for Luke Clye might repent of going away, and return with a few choice companions, who might take the law into their own hands, and put so sudden a stop to Mrs. Corcoran's operations that the continuance of them would be impossible.

There was only one apartment left unsearched now, and that was the cellar.

Mrs. Corcoran had reasons to feel a natural antipathy to this place.

Her experiences down in the dismal region were not such as to give her any amount of confidence, and as she stood upon the top stairs and peered down into the dirty, dimly-lighted den her courage almost forsook her.

The drip, drip of a leaky water-butt had an uncanny sound of its own, and when the rickety stairs creaked the sound created the reverse of a feeling of assurance.

Slowly, very slowly, Mrs. Corcoran descended the stairs.

She had not much to hope for now; but there was just a chance that some money might be hidden in the old chimney, in some chink of the wall, or even behind the leaky water-butt.

The hag reached the cellar floor at last.

A mouldy vault-like atmosphere pervaded the place.

Mrs. Corcoran shuddered in spite of herself.

It seemed to her that her nerves were giving way, for strange noises rang in her ears, and a mist gathered before her eyes.

Nevertheless, she approached the fire-gate.

The place had been once used as a kitchen, and Mrs. Corcoran came to the conclusion that no better hiding-place for ill-gotten gains could not be found than up the spacious flue.

She stooped down and was in the act of craning her neck up the aperture, when she dropped upon her hands and remained motionless.

"What's that?" she gasped. "I thought I heard somebody speak."

"Stop!" cried a voice.

Mrs. Corcoran started up erect, and then fell upon her knees and began to shriek.

"No—no!" she yelled, throwing up her arms. "Come not near me. Leave me to my fate!"

Emerging from a corner of the cellar, was a figure, hideous and ghastly.

Shrouded in white, with extended arms and features resembling Spring-Heeled Jack, it advanced, or rather stalked with noiseless steps.

"Witch!" said the terrific-looking creature, "I will not deal with you. Your plans have failed, and at this very moment the man you sought to deceive, has learned how you lied, and is returning."

Mrs. Corcoran had not lost power of speech.

Her tongue, dry and burning, clave to the roof of her mouth, and with a gurgling sound in her throat, she fell slowly back and swooned.

When she recovered consciousness she saw that Luke Clye was standing over her, and whetting a knife on the palm of his hand.

## CHAPTER CXLIV.

### THE ATTEMPTED MURDER—CRIBBED, CABINED, AND CONFINED.

WITHOUT money, without a hope of food or shelter, Sir Roland Ashton and Morth found themselves in a small town on the Lincolnshire coast.

Stay, Morth was not exactly without money.

He had a few copper coins in his waistcoat pocket. But he said nothing of them to Sir Roland Ashton.

"You have done a pretty thing by bringing me here," Morth growled, after delivering himself of the speech recorded in the last chapter.

"I?" said Sir Roland. "What had I to do with it?"

Morth raised his brawny arm as if to strike the baronet, but let it fall at his side.

"I should like to meet that man we met at the White Horse," he said, with a savage oath. "I don't think I should ask him many questions once I got my hands on his throat."

Sir Roland had his own notions about the mysterious individual alluded to.

He was more than half convinced that the man was either Ralph Ashton in disguise, or one of his agents, but he kept his own thoughts to himself, which, perhaps, was the wisest thing he could do under the circumstances.

The inn at which the coach had finally stopped was known as the Two-necked Swan, a huge rambling place, quite large enough to billet a regiment of soldiers.

"Well," said Morth, after a long pause, "the money is gone, and I suppose there is no help for it. I suppose you have none?"

"Not a farthing."

Morth gave vent to a horrible oath.

"I was an idiot not to start on the journey alone," he said. "Curse you! go your own way, and trouble me no more. A blight springs up in your very footsteps! I have often laughed at the idea of a man leading a haunted life, but I believe it now."

"It will be as well if you curb your temper and listen to reason," Sir Roland returned. "If you wish to part company with me I must go, but would such a course be of the slightest advantage to either of us?"

"I neither know nor care," Morth replied, savagely. "I only know that I am here in this miserable hole, with scarcely enough money to keep body and soul together for a couple of days."

"Then you have some money?"

"Yes; and I mean to keep it."

"Just so," said Sir Roland, calmly. "Listen. None of the passengers, save ourselves, were robbed. Some of them have gone chuckling into this very inn, where they evidently intend to put up for the night. Why shouldn't we do as we were done by and help ourselves?"

"I don't understand you!" Morth said, as he ground his teeth and stamped his feet in impotent rage.

"You are either a creature of strange impulses, or very dull of comprehension," Sir Roland said. "Not long ago you talked about breaking into the first house you came to, and now—"

"Stop your row," said Morth, interrupting him. "I see your drift now. You think that if we stop here, we may be able to fill our pockets and slip away before the people are about in the morning."

"Exactly so," said Sir Roland. "The man who occupied the box-seat had a well-lined pocket-book, and I noticed that the back of his watch was studded with diamonds."

"It is odd to hear a man of your birth and education speak in this way," Morth said.

"A man is bound to sink when his stomach grumbles at empty pockets," Sir Roland returned.

"There is something in that, and in what you have said," Morth remarked, musingly. "Let me see how much money I have."

On turning his pockets out, he discovered that he was in possession of eighteen shillings and a few coppers.

"This will be sufficient to ensure us an entry to the house," he said; "but if we have no luck to-night, what are we to do to-morrow?"

"That is a question I cannot answer."

"No; nor the man with the wisest head in the world," said Morth. "But come, we waste time. Let us go straight into the house, and book our room. I see that the coachman and guard are drinking at the tap, and, for all we know, they may be talking about us."

Passing through a cheerfully-lighted passage,

which led to a cosy-looking bar, with a plump landlady behind it, Morth asked, in as civil accents as he could summon to his lips, whether there was a spare double-bedded room in the house.

The landlady took down a slate from a nail, and ran her finger down a list.

"Yes," she replied, raising her eyes, and fixing them steadily upon Morth; "but—but—"

"But what?" Morth interposed. "We have money to pay, and I suppose that is all you want?"

"Well," said the landlady, "you will excuse me, but a most strange note was handed to me just before the coach came in. It told me to beware of two strangers, without luggage, who came from the Borough, and booked at the White Horse."

Morth mattered an oath under his breath, and Sir Roland could do no more than stare at the landlady in blank dismay.

"What foolery, what conspiracy is this?" Morth said. "Perhaps the messenger was one of the rascals who robbed us? It is evident we were followed and watched, although how the highwaymen contrived to get in front of the coach is more than I can tell."

"I am very sorry for you," the landlady said; "and I hope that when the rascals are caught that you will get your money."

"There's not much to hope for in that direction, madam," Sir Roland chimed in. "I am sure you will not leave us to hunt about for shelter on such a night as this. It has commenced to rain, and there is thunder in the clouds."

The landlady looked hesitatingly at the list.

"You shall have the room," she said. "Would you like to see it now?"

"If you please," said Morth.

The landlady rang a bell, and a girl, whose cap was gay with bright ribbons, appeared.

"Show these gentlemen up to No. 18," the landlady said.

The chambermaid illuminated a candle and conducted Sir Roland and Morth upstairs in silence.

The girl did not like the look of the two men, and the moment after she had opened the door and placed the candlestick on the dressing-table she vanished.

"That fool of a girl looked frightened," said Morth.

"All the better for us," Sir Roland replied, as he kicked off his boots. "Stay here a minute."

"What are you going to do?" Morth demanded, as the baronet moved towards the door.

"I am going to see whether it is likely that the rooms on either side of us will be occupied," Sir Roland replied.

Morth nodded his head, and sat down upon a chair.

Sir Roland was not absent more than ten minutes.

A strange smile played about his lips as he returned to the room.

"The very gentleman we were talking about will sleep next door," he said.

"How do you know?"

"By his luggage," Sir Roland replied. "I noticed him sort it out, and tell the boots to be careful how he carried it upstairs."

"So far, so well," Morth said, rubbing his hands. "This will be a ticklish job, I'm thinking."

"I've got through worse," Sir Roland returned, as he resumed his boots. "We shall be wise if we go downstairs, and join the people in the coffee-room."

"I will leave it all to you," Morth said; "but—"

"You are thinking about that note the landlady spoke of?"

"That is exactly what I was thinking about, and am thinking about now," Morth said.

"Bah! it is nothing," Sir Roland remarked, contemptuously. "I heed it not."

"It came from no friend."

"What then? We must be our own friends," said Sir Roland. "If we do not show ourselves again the landlady will be fretting and fuming her heart out, and fancying all kinds of things."

"Come, then," said Morth, rising and stretching his arms above his head. "I am as tired as a shepherd's dog; but I must shake it off. Lead the way. We will have a drink of brandy."

On entering the coffee-room they found but three other men there.

Two were of the farmer type, but the third—the man the scoundrels had their eyes upon—had the appearance of a man who had travelled far.

"I am truly sorry for you," he said, as Sir Roland Ashton and Morth sat down near the table. "I was just saying that if you would not mind, I should like you to accept the loan of a few guineas until you had time to recruit your purses."

"That is really and truly kind of you," Sir Roland said. "Most noble sir, we will borrow just a guinea apiece, and forward the amount on if you will be kind enough to furnish us with an address."

"I am John Fore, traveller for Messrs. Glint and Son, goldsmiths, Cheapside," said the gentleman, as he took out his purse. "There is no hurry to return the money, as I go to King's Lynn, and make my way back by Ely, Norwich, and Cambridge."

"A traveller for a firm of goldsmiths," Sir Roland thought. "If that be so, his samples must be in his trunks."

The same thought struck Morth, and his hand trembled as he took the guinea.

John Fore then began to talk freely.

He was in high spirits, evidently because he had lost nothing, and after his third glass of brandy and water, made stiff and strong, according to his own directions, he opened his heart.

"A man who travels with a couple of thousands of pounds' worth of jewellery had need to be careful in these times," he said. "Strange enough, I have never been attacked before until to-night."

"And then you lost nothing."

"Thank goodness for that," said John Fore. "We will have one more drink and then to bed. No—no! you shall pay for nothing, for you have suffered too much already."

Morth, who had been watching keenly the gentleman who was so lavish with his money and information, winked at Sir Roland.

The baronet returned the signal, and then changing the subject, began conversing about ordinary matters.

The two farmers took their hats and went to their respective rooms, and then John Fore, who had taken much more brandy and water, began to blink and nod drowsily.

"Let us get away upstairs," Sir Roland whispered. "He will fall asleep in his chair. Now is our time. We can help ourselves to what we think proper to take, and get clear away before the house closes."

"Yes, and have a hue and cry after us all over the country," Morth returned. "He's drunk, and will sleep soundly till a late hour in the morning."

"You are of opinion that it will be better to wait until he is in bed?" Sir Roland Ashton said.

"That is my idea," Morth replied. "A score of things might happen if we commence operations so early."

"Well, I will be ruled by your advice," Sir Roland said. "Let us call the landlady's atten- to Mr Fore's state. The boots will have a nice job to get him upstairs."

"Go and tell the landlady then," Moth returned. "She will think that—"

"We are honest men," Sir Roland interposed, with a short laugh.

At that moment John Fore opened his eyes and stared about him in a dazed, confused style.

"Who laughed?" he hiccuped. "That's right, keep it up. Order in some more brandy. I'll pay for it."

"No—no, good sir," said Sir Roland. "We are going to bed, and you had better do the same. Pray let us assist you upstairs?"

"I don't require any assistance," Fore said, with a solemn glare that made him look intensely ridiculous. "I know how to take care of myself and my property too."

"No doubt about it," Moth observed. "Well, there is no harm done. We thank you kindly for your good company, and wish you good-night."

John Fore's lips moved, but no sound came from them.

As he sank back in his chair, his head lurched forward, and in another instant he was sound asleep.

The landlady of the Two-necked Swan took Sir Roland Ashton's communication with very good grace.

She thanked him, and promised that Mr. Fore should be attended to immediately.

"I have told him over and over again when he has been this way that he ought not to drink so much," she said. "His head is weak, and he cannot stand it."

"Oh! by-the-way, madam," Sir Roland said, "I should like to see the handwriting of the note you spoke of."

"Never mind that," the landlady returned. "I came to the conclusion that it was some silly hoax to scare me, and put the paper in the fire. Dear! dear! Where can my husband be? I don't like the idea of him being on these roads after dark."

"So she has a husband," Sir Roland muttered to himself. "That is rather unfortunate, for he might be a troublesome customer to deal with in case of an accident."

In less than another minute Morth and Sir Roland were in the room they had paid for.

"Blow out the candle, and get into bed with your clothes on," Morth said. "If the boots sees a light under the door when he passes he may think proper to mention it downstairs."

"But how are we to light the candle again?" Sir Roland asked.

Morth drew the curtains aside and pointed to the sky.

The full moon was rising, and dispersing the heavy clouds.

"See there!" he said. "In an hour, or perhaps less, it will be bright as day. The storm has rolled away to the north, and we shall not be troubled with it any more to-night."

"But supposing that you are wrong, and the sky is obscured by heavy clouds?"

Morth remained silent for a moment.

"Well, shade the light," he said.

"What a head you have!" Sir Roland remarked, laughing. "I will place the candle in this cupboard, and shut the door."

"Right you are!" said Morth, as he threw himself on the bed, and drew the counterpane up to his neck. "Hark! Here comes our valuable friend."

The boots was a strong man, but it was evident that he had all his work cut out to keep John Fore on his legs.

"Steady, sir, steady!" he said. "Keep up! Now, then, that's right!"

Sir Roland's bed was close to the wall, and he placed his ear against it.

There was a deal of stumbling and scrambling to get John Fore into bed, but it was accomplished at last.

The boots was a practical man, and experience had taught him to think little or nothing of such episodes as he had just witnessed.

"I'll blow out the candle," he thought, "and the next question is whether I ought to lock him in. Well, I'll ask the guv'nor about that when he comes home. If I take it upon myself I may be wrong."

As the boots blew out one light he saw another streaming through a chink in the wall.

The valuable assistant at the Two-necked Swan rejoiced in the name of Jemmy Stocks, and he stood still and glared at the strange phenomenon with his hair almost on end, and his mind filled with conflicting emotions.

At last he plucked up courage to investigate the matter, and then, in an instant, the mystery was solved.

That part of the wall through which the light was streaming was but mere match boarding, and really the back of the cupboard in which Sir Roland had so artfully concealed the candle.

The paper with which John Fore's room was decorated had cracked and given way in several places, and thus it was that Jemmy Stocks was momentarily alarmed.

"There's something wrong here," he muttered, as he withdrew his eye from the crevice. "What's the game o' them two fellers in the next room? It can't be to set fire to the house. It's—it's—"

A feeling of horror overcame Jemmy Stocks as his eyes wandered from the sleeping man to his trunks, which were placed near the bedside.

"It's robbery," Stocks gasped, under his breath. "They've planted the light there so that I mightn't catch a glimpse of it, or peep through the key-hole of their room and see what they were about. What shall I do? Rouse the house now, or wait—"

"Jem—Jem!" roared a voice from below, "are you going to stay there all night?"

"Good luck, that's master!" said Jemmy Stocks. "Coming, sir, coming."

The landlord was soon acquainted with what Jemmy Stocks had seen, as also was the landlady, who at once manifested strong inclinations to scream.

But her husband checked her with a motion of his hand.

"Silence, Martha," he said, sternly. "This is not a matter which can be brought to a proper conclusion by kicking up a row. Jem, just run round to the parish constable's house and rouse him up. I'll get my pistols ready meanwhile, and if those rascals really mean mischief they will find that they have met with their match."

Jemmy Stocks was off like a shot out of a gun, and presently returned with a red-haired gentleman, wearing a shovel-shaped hat, and bearing a staff tipped with a crown.

When the constable—for such the new arrival was—had heard everybody's version of the affair he put on a grave look, and ran his fingers through his hair.

"Shut up the house, and pretend to go to bed as usual," he said. "You and Stocks can creep out on the landing and watch. I will remain here."

"But what is to become of me?" the landlady demanded.

"You can't do better than go to your own room and remain there," said the parish constable. "There isn't much to fear, as we are three to two, and well armed.

The officer's advice was adopted without delay.

Humming and whistling carelessly, the landlord closed his house, and soon silence and darkness reigned supreme.

Little dreaming that they were in any way suspected, Sir Roland Ashton and Joe Morth waited such a time as they might reasonably suppose that the inmates of the Two-necked Swan would take to get to sleep.

Sir Roland Ashton was the first to stir.

"Is it time to act yet, do you think?" he asked, softly.

"I don't see the use of waiting any longer," Morth replied. "The sooner the job is over the better I shall like it."

"And I."

"Fetch out the light," said Joe Morth. "I can't bear this darkness. I feel like a black-beetle in a cellar."

As Sir Roland removed the candle from the cupboard, and set it gently down upon a chair, Joe Morth took a sheathed knife from the inside pocket of his coat, and examined the blade carefully.

"I hadn't time to get this out when the highwayman attacked me," he said, "or I would have let daylight through his ribs."

"Perhaps it is well that you did not try the experiment," Sir Roland remarked.

"Why?"

"Because the knife might not have been in your possession by this time or you able to use it."

"I don't want to use it now, if I can help it," Joe Morth replied, surlily.

"Oh! of course not," Sir Roland said, hastily; "but it is just as well to be prepared. Our friend in the next room might wake up suddenly, and it would be extremely awkward if he had time to cry out."

"Our friend, indeed!" Morth ejaculated. "I don't how it is, but it goes against my grain to do this."

"You are not chicken-hearted, I hope," Sir Roland Ashton said, with a touch of contempt in his voice.

"Chicken-hearted — no!" Morth replied, hoarsely. "But the man treated us well. He lent us money when we wanted it, he paid for everything we drank, and—"

"Played the part of a fool," Sir Roland interposed. "I hope and trust that he will not wake to disturb us. When he finds his trunks the lighter, he will become a wiser man."

Joe Morth passed his hand swiftly across his brow, and grunted out some unintelligible reply.

"Well," he said, at last, "if it must be done, let it be done quickly. Hist! what was that?"

"I heard nothing."

"But I thought I did."

"What was it like?"

"I scarcely know," Morth said. "It did not resemble a footstep, but was more like the closing of a door."

"It was the wind, no doubt," Sir Roland said; "but I will see. If I am questioned I will find a ready excuse, fear not."

"Don't take the candle," Joe Morth said; "the passage must be bright with moonlight by this time."

"You don't care to remain here without a light," Sir Roland said, turning and glancing back at Morth over his shoulder.

"I confess I do not. I've got a nasty creepy feeling all over me, for which I cannot account in any way."

"I am afraid that the brandy, instead of bracing you up, has let you down," Sir Roland said.

"There—there! Take the light, and do as you please," Morth rejoined. "Perhaps the noise I heard was nothing to be alarmed at."

But to show how bold and courageous he was, Sir Roland refused to take the light.

As Morth had predicted, the passage was one flood of pure silver light, which streamed through a window at the further end.

Sir Roland knew that if anybody was about that he was sure to see a lengthened black shadow.

"All is well," he said, turning back into the room. "Are you ready?"

"Yes."

"Then follow me."

Morth braced up his shoulders, and thrust the knife behind his back, as he trod softly at Sir Roland Ashton's heels.

The terrible moment was at hand.

They entered the room in which the man they intended to rob and murder, if he offered any resistance, was sleeping and snoring heavily.

John Fore lay with his head pillowed on his arm, all unconscious of the danger that surrounded him.

Sir Roland Ashton pointed in silence to the trunks which were piled one upon the other, and Morth, lifting the first one that came to hand, placed it lightly on the floor.

The trunk was an old-fashioned one, bound with strong straps, and secured with a hasp lock.

The straps yielded easily enough, but not so the lock.

Morth pressed the hasp this way and that, but in vain.

"Give me the knife, and let me try," Sir Roland whispered. "Stand over the sleeping man, and if he moves seize him by the throat, and give him no time to cry out."

Morth trembled a little as he placed the weapon in Sir Roland's hand, and made ready to pounce, hawk-like, upon John Fore should he show the slightest sign of returning consciousness.

Sir Roland Ashton, though anxious to possess himself of the treasure, lost none of his usual caution.

"We are wrong to stay here at all," he said. "Let us carry the trunk into our own room and help ourselves at leisure."

At that moment John Fore uttered a guttural sound and changed his position.

He was in the act of rolling over upon his side, when Morth, exerting all his strength, clutched him by the throat, and so pressed him down.

John Fore tried to shriek for help, and struggled violently.

He was a strong man, and Morth discovered he had met his match.

"Strike him — strike him!" Morth said, hoarsely. "Quick. He will slip through my fingers!"

Sir Roland started to his feet, and raised the knife in his clenched hand.

The blade glinted and gleamed for a moment in the air, but before it could descend Sir Roland's wrist was seized by a strong hand, and a stunning blow on the back of the head sent him reeling to the floor.

The landlord of the Two-necked Swan, Jemmy Stocks, and the constable had glided noiselessly into the room, and saved John Fore's life.

It was Jemmy Stocks who had given Sir Roland his quietus, and the landlord and the constable now threw themselves upon Morth.

A short but terrible struggle took place, Morth rolling over and over, scratching, biting, and kicking at his assailants like a wild beast.

But John Fore had now recovered sufficiently to lend his aid, and before Joe Morth could do much harm he was handcuffed and dragged into a corner of the room.

"That's all right," said the parish constable. "Perhaps it was well that I came upstairs after all. What a precious pair of beauties we have caught. . Lift that other fellow up."

"Come—come," said Jemmy Stocks, touching Sir Roland with his foot, "you are more frightened than hurt, you know. Shamming won't do in this establishment."

Sir Roland raised himself upon his elbow and glared at the scene before him.

He could scarcely realise what had happened, but another kick from Jemmy Stocks fully convinced him that he had been caught in his own trap.

"Here's another pair of handcuffs," said the parish constable. "Click them over his wrists and bring him along. The sooner this pair of scoundrels are between four strong walls the better."

In less than ten minutes Sir Roland Ashton and Joe Morth occupied separate cells in the Roundhouse, with the prospect of having to appear before the magistrate in two days' time, and then charged with robbery and attempted murder.

## CHAPTER CL

A SEARCH FOR A VILLAIN—WHO GOES THERE?—A CHALLENGE—RALPH ASHTON GETS INTO TROUBLE.

ROBIN GRAY'S cries not only roused Namon Wallack, but the whole of the strollers, who, after a hard day's work, had sunk into profound slumber.

Dragging on some of his clothes, Namon Wallack rushed from the caravan which had been placed at the back of the tent, and he saw in a moment that it would be impossible to save it.

More than one-half of the inflammable material was on fire, and the flames, fanned by the wind, were hissing and curling like gigantic serpents into the air.

"Strike your tents, and remove your caravans!" he shouted to the bewildered men and women, who were rushing hither and thither. "Save your own property! Mine must perish! Up, men, and work with a will! This is the handiwork of a coward and a villain."

The gipsies, throwing aside their bewilderment and terror, now began to exert themselves.

In a short time the well-ordered fair was a chaotic heap of stalls, piles of canvas, timber, and every conceivable lumber.

The men raved, and the women wrung their hands as their children clung to their gowns.

Scores of buckets full of water were brought into requisition and flung upon Namon Wallack's tent; but in spite of all efforts it was reduced to tinder, which went floating away in flakes over the sleeping city.

When all was over the beadle, who had stopped to dress himself carefully in his cocked hat and gown, and two feeble watchmen, at afrantic trot, came up with the parish engine.

The beadle asked a hundred questions, and fell over everybody he came in contact with, and insisted upon playing upon the wreck.

Namon Wallack offered no objection by word or deed.

He stood, with folded arms and compressed lips, gazing on the scene.

Presently, looking down, and seeing Robin Gray standing at his side, he patted the boy's curly head kindly.

"It is not that I fear we shall not recover from this misfortune," Namon said, "but it may occur again and again, unless the perpetrator of this outrage is rendered powerless to do more mischief."

"Who do you suspect it to be?" Robin Gray demanded, in trembling accents.

"Ask me no more questions on that score," Namon Wallack replied. "I—I—well—well," he muttered, aside, "it is no fault of his, poor lad!"

Suddenly he turned on his heel, and walked away abruptly.

"I do not understand this," Robin Gray said, pressing his hand to his brow. "What does it mean? Wherever I go I seem to take misfortune with me."

He started as a light hand touched him on the arm, and he saw the fairy-like little girl to whom he had spoken in the wood just before the journey to Norwich began.

"You are to come with me," said Amy Corder.

"Where to?" the boy demanded, vaguely.

"To shelter and rest," Amy replied. "Namon Wallack sent me to you. He has left the fair for a time, but you may expect to see him again in the morning."

"I almost wish that I was dead," Robin said, as tears welled into his eyes.

"Hush—hush! It is wicked to talk in that way."

"I know it is," Robin replied, "but I cannot help it. Though I know not why, yet I am convinced that all this wreck and ruin has been caused by me."

"What nonsense!" Amy Carder said. "How can that be possible? It may have been a pure accident. Come with me. You are more upset even than the rest of us, for you were in more danger."

She took him by the hand, and he followed her

submissively to a caravan which had been prepared for his reception.

. . . . . . .

Namon Wallack's show had scarcely caught fire when a man, extinguishing a torch by striking it on the toe of his boot, flung the instrument of his dastardly deed into the air, and took to flight.

Running at full speed from the fair, he darted through the upper part of King street, and did not stop until he was well within the shadow of the houses flanking the Cathedral Close.

Here he paused a moment for breath, and then went skulking along down Bishop-street, and so on, until he paused before the hospital endowed by Edward VI. for the shelter of worthy citizens who had failed in business, or whose health compelled them to give up work.

Above the tower of the old church attached to this home for the weak and helpless, the clouds seemed to be drifting the waning moon along.

No sound disturbed the stillness of the air of that peaceful, solemn place save the echo of the fugitive's footsteps.

More than once he stopped, fancying that he was being followed, and gripped the handle of his sword.

Straight ahead of him was a bridge crossing the river, and beyond that a steep hill leading to a wild and open heath.

It was to this heath that the man was making, but he received a check at the foot of the bridge.

A man, wearing a slouched hat, and a cloak that hung to his heels, suddenly stepped from an old archway and accosted him by name.

"Lord Mildendale," he said, "I would have a word with you."

"I am no lord, but a peaceful, humble citizen," was the reply. "Trifle not with me, but let me pass."

"Do not add falsehood to your crime of this night," the stranger said. "You must answer to me for this deed."

"Who are you?" Lord Mildendale cried, throwing his camlet cloak quickly over his shoulder and drawing his sword.

"I am the man who would fain have been your friend, but am now your foe. I am known as Ralph Ashton."

"Hah!" Lord Mildendale exclaimed, starting. "What then? You spoke of crime and unlawful deeds. What dare you accuse me of?"

"Of attempting to burn in his bed the man you have already wronged so deeply."

"I'll fling the lie in your teeth!" Lord Mildendale hissed. "Here's at you, liar and dog!"

Hat and cloak fell from Ralph Ashton as if by magic, and in a moment he stood, sword in hand, on guard.

The light of the moon played upon the keen, bright blade, held by so steady and skilful a hand.

"Pooh!" Lord Mildendale said, sneeringly, as he stepped back; "I'll not fight with you, for if it be that you are related to Sir Roland Ashton the blood of a villain must flow in your veins."

"Mark me well," Ralph replied. "The man you speak of is allied to me, but I own him not. I am no villain, but the bane and curse of villains. You were seen to-night creeping, like a snake in the grass, to accomplish the vile task you had set your heart upon."

"Indeed!" Lord Mildendale said, scornfully. "Tell me the name of the man who saw me."

"Spring-Heeled Jack!"

"Again you lie."

Ralph Ashton snapped the fingers of his disengaged hand, and made an impatient motion with his sword.

"My lord," he said, "this denial will avail you nothing. Spring-Heeled Jack sent me hither, and you must answer to me for your deed."

"This is but an attempt to frighten me out of ransom," Lord Mildendale replied; "but I'll have none of you or the demon you follow. Again, I say, let me pass, and begone ere I summon assistance."

"This is worthy of you," Ralph Ashton said, still blocking the way; "but, by the Heaven above us, you shall not leave this place until you have answered to me man to man, and sword to sword. Come, defend yourself."

At that moment Lord Mildendale saw the glimmer of lanterns.

He concluded that some of the City Watch were going their rounds, and he stood still, trifling with the handle of his sword until the men drew nearer.

"Ralph Ashton," he said, "if such be your name, you have made mistake for once. I call upon you to surrender in the name of the law, and I call upon these guardians of the peace to take you into custody. What ho, there! Help! Thieves! Murder!"

"Thieves—thieves!" shouted the watchmen, in response.

Before Ralph Ashton could recover from his astonishment, or it may be before he choosed to take any action, the men came up at a run, and seized him by the arms.

"I give that man into your custody," Lord Mildendale. "He has stopped me on the king's highway, and threatened me with death."

"What a craven wretch you are," Ralph Ashton said. "It is well that my sword did not touch you, for the very steel would have turned upon me in anger."

"Come—come!" said one of the watch, "we want no speeches. You hear what the gentleman says, and you must come with us to Bridewell."

"I will follow you," Lord Mildendale said, "and repeat the charge."

Ralph Ashton said no more, but marched between the watchmen with head erect and his face calm and passive.

His captors led him to a strong flint-fronted building in the heart of the city, and thrust him into a cell.

Day was just dawning when Lord Mildendale roused the sleepy-headed porter of the Angel Hotel, and demanded a bed.

"Secure me a suite of rooms to-morrow," his lordship said, "for I find I must remain here to prosecute a scoundrel. Forsooth, things are coming to a pretty pass in your good old city."

In the morning Ralph Ashton was visited by a warder.

"You can have anything you like, if you choose to pay for it," the man said, surlily; "and I put it to you because you don't look like a man who has been used to such fare as we give our prisoners."

Ralph Ashton smiled, and shook his head faintly.

"I thank you, my friend," he said, taking a guinea from his purse; "get me some light refreshment and keep the change."

"I shouldn't mind having a few more like you

# SPRING-HEELED JACK,

## THE TERROR OF LONDON.

"SEEK YOUR PRISONER ELSEWHERE," SAID SPRING-HEELED JACK, MOCKINGLY.

No. 42.

here," the man said, grinning, as he moved towards the door.

"Stay!" said Ralph Ashton; "another word with you. When shall I be called upon to answer this charge?"

"To-morrow," the warder replied.

"May I send for somebody?"

"Your legal adviser?"

"No."

"Who, then?"

"A friend."

"I am not so sure about that," the warder said. "It is against the rules to admit strangers."

"But," said Ralph Ashton, "you can manage it for me if you care to do so. Here is another guinea, and it is yours if you will do me a slight favour."

"Well, well," said the warder, "what am I to do? You see I am in charge here alone, and it would be my ruin if you were to escape during my absence."

"Rest assured on that account," Ralph Ashton replied. "No such intention is mine. I want you to make your way quickly to the fair—"

"To the fair?" the warder interposed. "What do you want me to go there for?"

"Listen; and do not interrupt me," Ralph Ashton continued. "Do as I tell you, and when you have found a man named Namon Wallack, whose show was burnt down last night, tell him what has happened to me, and bring him hither."

"I'll do it," the warder said.

Before he went out, he cast a searching glance round the cell, and took the precaution of doubly locking the door as he stepped outside.

In less than half an hour Ralph heard the sound of footsteps.

"The warder has not failed me," he said. "He has brought Namon Wallack back with him."

Another moment and the gipsy and Ralph were shaking hands.

## CHAPTER CLI.

### MRS. CORCORAN LOSES AN ENEMY.

"I WAS born to deal with a set of fools, I suppose," said Nabbitt, as he glared at Catchpole and Grabham. "Do you mean to say that you two could not have taken this Spring-Heeled Jack when you were in the same room with him?"

"Which, sir, I would beg to make a remark—" Catchpole began, when his superior officer interrupted him.

"Silence!" Nabbitt roared. "How dare you speak to me without leave? I don't believe that you went to Buckler's-rents at all, and, to prove what I say, you shall go there with me, and—"

Here Grabham became very weak in the knees, and gave vent to a most heartrending groan.

"If you make that noise again I will knock your head off your shoulders!" Nabbitt declared. "You shall go to Buckler's-rents with me and two other officers, for I am determined to rout out that hornets' nest."

Catchpole looked as if he had been suddenly seized with a very bad complaint.

"I am not a coward, if you are," Nabbitt continued. "I will show you how to deal with a nest of scoundrels, so just prepare yourselves to act like men or you'll find yourselves out in the cold again."

So saying, Mr. Nabbitt bounced off his stool, and made a great show of loading a brace of pistols.

Having done this, he unsheathed an enormous cutlass and sharpened it on the hearthstone.

"There!" said he, with evident satisfaction. "Now I'll show them what's o'clock. If I had had this little tickler with me when I tackled Spring-Heeled Jack alone and single-handed—alone and single-handed, mind you—the villain would have been hung out of the way by this time."

Catchpole happened to cough behind his hand, and this action, though perfectly accidental, incensed Mr. Nabbitt.

"Dare you dispute what I say?" he cried, in high dudgeon. "You thick-headed fool! what do you mean by mocking me?"

"I—I mock you!" Catchpole gasped; "bless your heart, sir, I wouldn't go for to think of doing such a thing."

"Mind you don't!" Nabbitt growled. "Now just attend to me, and take care that you don't make a mistake about what I say. It is now three o'clock, and by five it will be getting dusk. We will start then so as to reach Buckler's-rents at dark."

"Oh!" Catchpole gasped.

"What now?" Nabbitt yelled.

"I can't help it," Catchpole said. "It's spasms, and comes on when least expected."

"If they come on when you are out with me to-day," said Nabbitt, scowling ferociously, "I'll treat you as an enemy and shoot you when—when you ain't looking."

"Are we to stay here until the time of starting, sir?" Grabham asked, meekly.

"You are," Nabbitt replied. "Surely you don't think that I'm such a fool as to let you go out of my sight now? Sit down, and when I am ready to go I will see that you are properly armed."

A bench ran alongside the wall, and Catchpole and Grabham sat down upon it.

"Ain't this awful?" Grabham whispered.

"It's enough to friz the marrer in a man's bones," Catchpole replied. "I've got a what-d'ye-call-it sort of a curious feeling that one of us, if not both, will be left behind to-night."

"Don't talk like that," Grabham said. "Nabbitt takes so kindly to his idea that I mean to let him have the glory of it. If I see any danger I shall dodge behind him and let him say what he likes."

At this moment something hurtled through the air, and struck the wall with a loud crash.

It was only an inkstand thrown by Mr. Nabbitt, but it startled the constables almost out of their senses.

"If I hear another word from either of you," Nabbitt said, "I'll send a naked cutlass after you. Confound it! how am I to go through these charge-sheets with you jabbering like a pair of monkeys?"

Catchpole and Grabham were silent after this, and having nothing else to do they both went to sleep.

Meanwhile, let us take a look at Buckler's-rents, in which such stirring scenes will presently take place.

Great was the rage and astonishment when it was found that Mrs. Corcoran had said farewell to Mr. Spikes' pleasant home.

Joan Spikes threw off the flimsy mask of civility she had worn, and cursed like a trooper.

Bill Blarney and Ted Nickells followed suit, and for more than an hour Mr. Spikes walked up and down in a state of frenzy.

"This is a pretty business," he said. "Who can tell but that old woman may call in at the first police-station, and blow the gaff on us?"

"She won't do that," Bill Blarney said. "She has as great a dislike to the law as Old Nick has to holy water."

"Well, then, why kick up all this rumpus?" demanded Spikes. "What else is there to fear? Surely you ain't afraid of an old hag like that?"

"You don't know her," said Bill Blarney. "She'll find some hole and corner to sit and use her brain to plot against us in many ways. Hang me, if I believe she is mortal!"

"What then is she?" Spikes demanded.

"A witch."

"She's ugly enough to be anything," Spikes responded. "But a witch! Bah You surely don't believe that the beldame is possessed of any power but that which is earthly?"

"I don't know so much about that," Bill Blarney said. "I have known her to do things and get out of such difficulties as would make the strongest of us to quake it."

"If I only had her here," Joan Spikes cried; "if I only had her here for a few minutes!"

"What would you do, dear?" her amiable husband asked.

"I would poison her, and when she was in throes of agony I would strike and kick her until she howled for mercy."

This speech was applauded to the echo, and then a dismal silence fell upon the select assembly.

"For my part," Ted Nickells observed, at last, "I don't like the look of things at all, and I wish that I was on my way across the sea. Daddy Muckrum has been the very deuce of a time away."

"Leave Daddy alone to do the trick in a proper manner," Spikes said. "He is not keeping away for nothing."

The day was drawing to a close, when that villainous old wretch, Daddy Muckrum, hobbled into Buckler's-rents.

He glanced to the right and left, keeping in a straight line with the entry that led to the street.

Perhaps he did this in case that a sudden alarm might be given; but whatever his notions were, he held his way direct across the court, though his own house stood in a corner.

Then he stopped to listen.

"All's still, and all's well," he mumbled. "Dear boys and girls! they respect old Daddy too much to play any tricks. If they did—"

He clawed the air with his hooked fingers as he glanced up at the darkened windows of his house.

Suddenly he turned and made for the abode of Mr. Spikes and his friend.

Daddy Muckrum placed his hand upon the door as if he expected it to yield, but as it did not do so, he rubbed the side of his nose.

"This either means danger, or a stranger," he muttered, under his breath. "No! It can't be danger, for Spikes would have been on the look-out to warn me. All fast and close. I wonder who you have got in tow now? Ah! my pretty dears, I am afraid that I must disturb you."

A knock from his knuckles produced a sound from within as if somebody had suddenly bolted into a room and closed the door with all haste.

"Who's there?" presently demanded the shrill voice of Joan Spikes.

"The very best friend you ever had in your life, you jade!"

"What, Daddy?"

"The same old Daddy—the same old true and faithful Daddy!"

The door flew open, and Joan Spikes almost embraced the dirty, villainous old wretch.

"Why all this bolting and locking up?" he demanded, as he stepped inside.

"Because things ain't so comfortable as they might be," Joan Spikes replied.

She explained what she meant in a few more words, and Daddy Muckrum, opening his vilely-shaped mouth, made a noise something like that produced by a caged tiger when annoyed.

"Well, it can't be helped now," he said, after he had relieved his feelings in this way; "but you shouldn't have given her the chance to get away."

"I couldn't help it, and I confess that she was too clever for me."

"Why Joan, it is odd to hear you talk like that," said Daddy Muckrum. "But let me see your husband and Ted Nickells. I can't say that I have very good news for Ted."

"Haven't you brought the money?" Joan Spikes said.

"No," Daddy Muckrum replied. "He must wait a week for it."

"Why?"

"For the simple reason that his friends haven't got it to spare."

Joan Spikes said no more, but opened the door that led into the parlour.

"Why, what is this?" said Daddy Muckrum. "No light—nobody here."

"The rest are in the cellar," Joan returned, with a grim smile. "Sit down, and I will call them."

In response to her voice the three skulking ruffians came tumbling up the stairs in a great haste.

A lamp and a bottle of brandy were placed on the table, and then Daddy Muckrum at once proceeded to business.

Ted Nickells' face fell to a doleful length when he heard that he must abide in Buckler's-rents for at least a week, and Bill Blarney shifted his feet about uneasily.

"Look here, Daddy," Nickells said, "every moment here is like an age to me. Why can't you advance the money? You know it is safe enough."

"That may be," Daddy Muckrum replied, nodding his head waggishly; "but you know the old saying about a bird in hand being worth two in the bush. I can't do it, and that's flat."

Ted Nickells growled out something unpleasant under his breath.

"Curse you!" Daddy Muckrum said, bringing his hand down heavily upon the table. "Haven't I done enough for you? If you don't think so, manage your own affairs, you—you half-hung dog!"

"Come—come!" said Joan Spikes. "Don't get out of temper with him, Daddy. Any man in his position would be anxious and fidgety."

"Perhaps so," Daddy replied; "but I hate base ingratitude."

Ted Nickells stretched his hand across the table, and commenced speaking in a whining voice.

"If I have offended you, Daddy, I am very sorry," he said. "How can I help being in a miserable state of mind? Whenever I sit still a minute I fancy that somebody is looking over my shoulder. When I sleep I feel the touch of the hangman and the tightening of that horrible rope. I—"

"There—there! I want to hear no more," said Daddy Muckrum. "A week will soon pass away. You are safer here than in any other place in London, so make your mind easy."

"Spikes tells me," Bill Blarney said, folding his arms and leaning them upon the table, "that two officers came here not long ago."

"Yes. Ha! ha! ha!" laughed Daddy Muckrum. "But banish them from your mind. They brought two flash notes from the Bull in Top Boots. That reminds me; I passed through the Borough and noticed that the house was closed."

"Closed?"

"Shut up," said Daddy Muckrum.

"Then there must be something wrong," Bill Blarney said. "We seem to be getting wedged in on all sides."

"Silence!" Joan Spikes said, holding up her hands. "If my ears do not deceive me, I hear the tramping of heavy boots coming down the entry."

Bill Blarney blew out the light, and was about to make for the cellar, when Spikes grabbed him by the shoulder.

"Sit still," he said. "If the traps are about we must make no noise."

A stream of perspiration flowed down Bill Blarney's brow, and trickled off his nose in drops.

The footsteps that Joan Spikes had heard now sounded louder.

"Hist!" she said; "they are talking now. Daddy—Daddy! They want you particularly."

The old fence trembled in every limb.

His face grew so white that it became almost luminous in the dark.

"What is to be done?" he gasped. "Can't you hide me anywhere?"

"Silence!" Spikes said. "This will ruin all. Let them go to your house, Daddy; they will find nothing there, and go away as wise as they came."

They were silent after this, but more than one heart beat audibly as the heavily-booted constables crossed Buckler's-rents.

Nabbitt, as a matter of course, led the way, with a drawn cutlass in his hand.

"Pah!" he said, turning up his nose. "What a stench! Hang me, if this place isn't enough to give a man a fever. Grabham!"

"Yes, sir?" replied that official, starting as from a dream.

"Point out the house in which you say you and Catchpole were molested."

Grabham did so.

"Ah!" said Nabbitt. "The place is in darkness; but that may only be a ruse to throw us off our guard. Get your pistols ready, Grabham, and go back to the entry. Stop any man who attempts to pass you, and shoot him if he resists your authority."

The wretched Grabham tried to put on a cool, brave demeanour, but it was a dismal failure.

"Am I—am I," he faltered, "to be left alone?"

"Do you want the whole force with you?" Nabbitt rejoined. "Do as I tell you, or—"

He waved the blade of the cutlass so close to Grabham's nose that the unhappy man stepped back in such a hurry that he floored the constable nearest to him like a ninepin.

"Confound you all!" Nabbitt said. "You make noise enough to wake the dead."

"The back of my head is busted in," groaned the afflicted constable, as he picked himself up.

"Serve you right!" Nabbitt said. "You're drunk—beastly drunk—or you would be more steady on your feet."

Meanwhile Grabham, with his heart rising into his throat, was tottering back towards the entry.

"Now," said Nabbitt, "we will just see if Muckrum is at home. Stand ready for a scrimmage, men, for if there should be a fight we may have some nasty customers to deal with. Come to the front, Catchpole. How dare you dodge behind Parker?"

Nabbitt, seeing that his men were in something like orderly array, stepped up to Daddy Muckrum's house, and hammered and kicked vigorously at the door.

"Open in the name of the king!" he shouted. "Open in the name of the law, or I'll pull the place down about your ears!"

There was no response to this summons, for the simple reason that the house was as empty as a church at midnight.

"I'll have these rats out of their holes," Nabbitt said. "Break down the door!"

This was more easily said than done.

The door was of stout oak, and furnished with a ponderous lock, which refused to yield.

Catchpole almost put his shoulder out of joint in his exertions, and when he was exhausted another officer took his place.

But all in vain.

"This is strange," said Nabbitt, looking round at the old houses. "It is odd that there seems to be nobody about. Can the whole lot have bolted?"

"The door won't give way," Parker said. "It seems to have more than one lock, but where the other is, is more than I can tell."

"If the door has a hundred locks I'll have it down!" said Nabbitt, with an oath. "Stand aside, and I'll try what a charge of powder will do."

The chief constable took a large pistol from his pocket, and, placing it within a few inches of the lock, fired.

The effect was startling.

Not only did the door give way, but also Nabbitt.

He reeled backwards among his men, and dropped the pistol as if it had stung him.

"I thought my hand was blown off," he growled; "but it is only a little singed. Now turn on your lanterns, men, and we'll rake out every corner of this den."

The startled wretches huddling together in Spikes' house had no notion of what was going on now.

They heard the crash of woodwork following the report of the pistol, and they came to the conclusion that some of the inhabitants of Buckler's-rents were in custody.

"This is too awful to bear," Ted Nickells groaned, as he mopped his heated face. "I can't stand it. If I stay here I shall lose my senses and yell like a madman. I must make a run for it if the attempt costs my life."

"And so will I," Bill Blarney said. "The traps are in earnest this time and no mistake."

"If you will go, you must," Spikes said. "I'll open the door for you. Daddy!"

"Oh! lor'; don't turn me out," Muckrum gasped. "My legs are too old and weak to run."

"I don't want you to run," Spikes replied.

"I want you to get down into the cellar and keep yourself quiet, no matter what may happen."

The old villain shuffled down into his hiding-place, and Spikes, drawing the bolts softly, suddenly opened the door.

Ted Nickells and Bill Blarney glided out.

To all appearances the coast was clear, for Nabbitt and his men were ransacking Muckrum's house at that time.

But the ruffians reckoned without their host.

They had no notion that Grabham had been planted at the mouth of the narrow entry, and before they were aware of his presence they came suddenly upon him.

"Aha! Ha! ha! ha!" cried Grabham, bursting into a wild shriek of hysterical laughter. "Hi! I say. Stand! or by the piper that played before Moses you are dead men."

Bill Blarney aimed a furious blow at the constable.

His brawny fist missed its aim, and caused Blarney to swerve so suddenly that he reeled and fell.

Grabham made a rush towards him, and Ted Nickells, taking advantage of the opportunity, rushed pell-mell up the entry.

It was so narrow that his shoulders almost grazed the walls; and Grabham, suddenly leaving Blarney to scamper away on his hands and knees into the darkness, fired at the fugitive.

It was almost impossible to miss him, and Ted Nickells, with a shriek that awoke a hundred strange echoes, leaped forward and fell upon his face.

"Hooray!" Grabham roared. "I've brought one down, and t'other ain't far off. Mr. Nabbitt—Catchpole—everybody—come here! Help—help—help!"

## CHAPTER CLII.

### MRS. CORCORAN GETS THE SACK.

MRS. CORCORAN looked vaguely at Luke Clye, and then at the glittering dagger he held in his hand.

Her mind was so confused that she had not the slightest notion where she was, what had happened, or why Luke Clye was paying her such unpleasant attentions.

"Well, deary?" she murmured. "Is it Bill? No; it isn't Bill. Who are you?"

"You'll find out presently," Clye growled. "Get up, you she-dragon, and tell me what you mean by telling me lies?"

"Lies!" Mrs. Corcoran repeated. "Lies did you say, lovey-dovey? I'll tell you anything, if you will put that knife down."

"I'll put it down into your back," Clye returned, brutally. "Don't give me any of your humbug. I've seen Harriet Snatcher, and she had no more idea that you were coming here than the man in the moon."

Mrs. Corcoran now fully appreciated the danger she was in.

"What!" she cried, as she regained her feet, "not know that I was coming here? Where is Harriet Snatcher? Let her tell me that to my face!"

"You'll see her quite soon enough for your liking," said Luke Clye, grinning. "I must be a born fool not to scent out your reason for coming here. So you thought to find something worth taking away, did you?"

"What is there worth taking away here?" Mrs. Corcoran rejoined. "Look round the place and ask yourself the question."

Luke Clye muttered something under his breath which Mrs. Corcoran could not hear.

"Perhaps I was mistaken, after all," the hag said. "Mrs. Snatcher—I have always thought of her as dear Mrs. Snatcher—told me that I was welcome, and so—"

"Shut up!" Luke Clye interposed.

Knife in hand, he moved backwards towards the staircase, and sat down on the bottom step.

Mrs. Corcoran felt that she must do something definite or resign herself to her fate.

"Ha!" she muttered; "I have just five guineas left, and I must purchase my freedom of this fellow as cheaply as possible."

As the hag dived her hand into her pocket a change came over her face.

Not a single coin could she find.

"You have robbed me," she said, confronting Luke Clye. "You cowardly cur! you stole my money while I lay senseless at your feet."

"That's a lie!" Clye replied; "but if it were true it wouldn't matter, for money won't be much use to you long."

"What do you mean?"

"You ought to know."

"You mean that you will murder me?"

"Put it in that way, if you like," said Luke Clye. "All I'll tell you is this. I am to watch you until Harriet Snatcher and a few friends come back, and if you try to get away or make a noise, I shall quiet you with this."

Mrs. Corcoran winced before the glittering blade of the knife which Clye flashed to and fro.

"No—no!" said Mrs. Corcoran. "Think a moment. I am old enough to be your mother—"

"My great-grandmother, you mean," said Clye, with a hoarse laugh.

"You had a mother once," continued Mrs. Corcoran, wringing her hands, "and as you would have saved her in a moment of peril, so let me go now."

Luke Clye was not in any way affected by this appeal.

"Did you ever have any children?" he asked.

"Yes, one; a bright-eyed, charming boy—very much like you."

"Then he must have been a beauty!" said Clye, thrusting a piece of tobacco into his mouth. "Was he hung or transported?"

"Oh! cruel, cruel to talk to me in that way!" Mrs. Corcoran groaned. "Will nothing move you? Is your heart made of stone?"

"As I never saw it, I don't know," Luke Clye returned; "but I know that when I was starving about the streets it used to feel as heavy as lead."

Mrs. Corcoran now began to run about very much like a rat in a trap.

She trotted up and down moaning, sometimes casting her eyes up to the dirt-begrimed grating which admitted a feeble ray of light, and then by degrees she hobbled nearer to Clye.

"Keep off," he cried. "I know your game. I've been put on my guard against you. You want the knife, and you'll get it in a way you least expect, if you come another inch nearer."

He had risen to his feet now, and thrown back his arm ready to strike.

Mrs. Corcoran retired, and crouched down in a corner.

Her shrivelled, puckered-up face was appalling in its hideousness.

It was made all the more ghastly by her red eyes,

which flashed deep down in her head like two jets of living fire.

"I wish they would come and get it over," Clye growled, under his breath. "I wouldn't take on such another job as this for all the money in the Bank of England. Now then, old lady, rouse yourself up and say something. Wouldn't you like me to run round to the Temple for a lawyer?"

"A lawyer! What have I to do with lawyers?" Mrs. Corcoran demanded, with a snarl.

"I thought you would like to make your will," Clye said.

"I have some property," the hag said, looking keenly at him; "but where it is I alone know. The secret shall die with me if my life is taken by foul means. Yes; I have some gold—a pleasant, merry, ringing thing is gold."

"It is," Clye said. "Now, supposing I let you go free, would you reward me handsomely?"

"Oh! yes—yes."

"How much would you give me?"

"A hundred guineas."

"Thank'ee," said Luke Clye; "but I'm fly. It won't do, I tell you. Here you are, and here you must stay. Hullo! They come at last, and I am jolly glad of it."

Mrs. Corcoran shrank back aghast as footsteps sounded in the upper part of the house.

"I will give you a hundred guineas for my freedom, I tell you," she said, in a hoarse whisper. "It is not too late. Give me the knife and I will fight my way out."

"I don't think so," Clye returned. "You might, but what would become of me? My life is as good as yours, and worth much more at present."

"Where is she?" cried the voice of Harriet Snatcher. "Let me get near her!"

"Steady—steady!" said a burly fellow, who was following closely upon the enraged woman's heels. "Screaming and making a noise won't mend matters. Oh! here's Clye at his post."

"And precious pleased I shall be to get away from it," Clye said. "I never spent such a miserable time in my life. There she is, Fadge—there she is!"

Harriet Snatcher made a tigress-like spring at Mrs. Corcoran, but Fadge seized her by the arm and forced her back.

"Don't play the part of a fool!" he said, fling-down something that looked like a sack upon the floor. "You have brought me here to do the business, and you had better leave it all to me."

"Well, well," Harriet Snatcher said, "that is common sense."

"Of course it is," Fadge returned. "Put what questions you want to ask her, but don't be long about it."

"Where is my husband?" Harriet Snatcher said, extending her arm towards Mrs. Corcoran. "He went to the Bull in Top Boots and saw you there. Where is he? How comes it that the house is closed?"

Mrs. Corcoran's lips moved convulsively, but no audible sound came from them.

"Answer me, you fiend, or I will force the words from your throat," Harriet Snatcher yelled.

Mrs. Corcoran looked at her questioner, but her eyes had a far-away expression.

"It is no use," said Fadge, stepping forward. "If she has made up her mind to be obstinate, a falling mountain would not move her."

As he spoke he struck Mrs. Corcoran with a heavy life-preserver, and she went down at his feet like an ox in the shambles.

"That's settled," said the horrible villain. "Now, Clye, lend a hand here, to put her in the sack. As soon as it is dark we will give her a swim down the Thames."

## CHAPTER CLIII.

### THE APPARITION IN THE CELL.

NAMON WALLACK did not remain with Ralph Ashton more than a quarter of an hour.

What passed between them in conversation the warder of Norwich Bridewell did not trouble him-himself about, but walked up and down the passage to convince the prisoner and his visitor that he was not listening.

There was an odd expression on Namon Wallack's face when he left the lock-up.

He stopped in the door-way, and rubbed his eyes like a man waking from a heavy sleep.

"I will be there," he said. "I will see how this villain bears himself before the sword of Justice. Justice, indeed! How long will you be blind? Snatch the bandage from your eyes."

He did not go back to the fair, where the gipsies were packing up their goods, with the view of making another move, but wandered through the narrow streets until he came to a bridge over-looking the river.

Here he paused, and leaning his arms upon the rail, fell into a reverie.

Hundreds of people passed him unnoticed; but at last he moved on aimlessly, peering into the quaint shop windows, turning into courts which had no thoroughfare, and back again like one who is half-demented.

Presently he stopped, and listened to a conversation between a constable and a tradesman.

"Oh! yes, Mr. Nickem; it will be a hanging job," the constable said. "The magistrates will sit in an hour's time, and if you care to hear the case, I'll manage to find a place for you."

"I can't come," Mr. Nickem replied; "but I daresay there will be a full report of it in the paper."

"That there certainly will," said the constable. "Dear me! I shouldn't have thought it, would you?"

"Excuse my rudeness," said Namon Wallack. "Is there to be any particular case tried before the magistrates to day?"

"You must be a stranger to Norwich not to have heard of it," the constable returned.

"I am a showman," Namon Wallack returned. "I am here, there, and everywhere in a week."

"Haven't you heard that a real live lord was attacked at the foot of Bishop's-bridge?" demanded the constable. "Aye! and would have lost his life, only two of our men rushed up and seized the assassin in the very nick of time."

"You don't say so?"

"But I do," said the constable, "and I mean it, too. But I mustn't stay to talk to you; I must go to the court, for there will be an awful rush to get a glance at the prisoner."

"I have an hour to spare," said Namon, taking a crown-piece out of his pocket, and slipping it into the constable's hand, "so if you like you can pass me through before the mob gets too thick."

"Certainly," the constable replied. "Really, you showmen are very good fellows, but I suppose that is because you earn plenty of money."

"Are all people with plenty of money good?" Namon Wallack demanded.

"No," said the constable. "There's old

Spiffen, our head magistrate. He's as cold as ice, as hard as a flint, and wouldn't give a piece of bread to a hungry child, and goes hard against the prisoners when he has the gout, I can tell you."

Namon Wallack's dark face became darker still.

"I suppose so," he said, thoughtfully. "Justices' justice is a strange thing. I was once present when a labouring man was sentenced to a month's imprisonment for stealing a wisp of hay to remove the mud from his boots."

"Oh! that's nothing," chuckled the constable. "Spiffen had a case before him of an old woman who crawled under a haystack to sleep. She got six months and ten stripes from the Bridewell beadle's cane."

"What?" Namon Wallack cried, starting.

"Oh! it's quite true," said the constable, cheerfully. "Spiffen was present when the thrashing took place, and seemed to enjoy himself immensely."

"What became of the woman?" Namon Wallack asked, clutching at his throat as if something was choking him.

"She died before her time was up," the constable replied. "She said that every blow cut into her heart and broke it."

"And this man will sit to day?"

"Of course he will, and I have good reason to know that he is in a precious bad temper."

This conversation beguiled the time until they reached the door of the court-house.

A huge crowd had collected about it, and the javelin men, sturdy fellows, armed with steel-tipped staves as long as themselves, found it hard work to keep the people back.

"My name is Joltier," the constable whispered to Namon Wallack, "and if anybody questions you as to how you got into the court say that you are my cousin."

The gipsy nodded, and then Mr. Joltier led him to a side door and passed him through.

A few lawyers and their clerks had already assembled, and were chatting gaily among themselves, but their voices were lost in the din that took place when the public were admitted.

In less than a minute the court was crammed, and the doors were again closed.

"Order! order!" roared two energetic ushers.

The magistrates filed in, with Spiffen at their head.

He was a small, weazened-up little man, with a red-tipped nose, and curious little eyes, which were almost hidden under heavy, bushy eyebrows.

As he came in, he glared viciously round the court, and acknowledged the clerk's salute with a bad grace.

"I shouldn't care to argue with him in a wood on a dark night," Namon Wallack thought.

The usual cases were soon got through.

A few drunken boobies paid their fines, a man cursed the magistrate when a term of imprisonment stared him in the face, and an unhappy girl, sentenced to six months for purloining a loaf of bread, was dragged shrieking to the cells, declaring that nothing but starvation drove her to commit the crime.

Now all necks were craned forward, and every eye and ear on the alert.

Namon Wallack felt his heart beat against his side as Ralph Ashton, handcuffed and closely guarded, was placed in the dock.

A moment later Lord Mildendale appeared.

He was accommodated with a chair near to the magistrates, and Spiffen, sinking his austere expression under a fawning smile, absolutely beamed upon his lordship.

"Let the case proceed," said Spiffen, "and if I hear a sound from the public I will have the court cleared."

"What is your name?" demanded the magistrate's clerk of the prisoner.

"Ralph Ashton."

"Where do you live?"

"I refuse to answer."

"What—what does he say?" wheezed Spiffen, with his hand to his ear.

"He refuses to say where he resides, your worship."

"Pooh — pooh! — nonsense!" said Spiffen, waspishly. "Now, prisoner, you waste time. Where do you live?"

"I refuse to answer."

The chief magistrate leaned back in his chair, and rubbed the tip of his red nose.

"Well," he gasped out, after a pause, "if you are ashamed to say where you live, tell us what brought you to this city?"

"Again I must decline to reply."

"Then all we have to do is to proceed," Spiffen said. "But, stay. Prisoner, are you defended by any legal gentleman?"

"No; and I do not intend to be so."

Spiffen waved his hand towards the clerk, who said—

"Prisoner, you are charged with stopping Lord Mildendale and attempting to rob him on the king's highway, against the peace of his majesty and his subjects. What have you to say in answer to the charge?"

"Nothing!"

"Nothing?"

"I do not intend to trouble myself about it one way or the other," Ralph Ashton said, smiling.

"It seems to me that the case is as good as proved," Spiffen said, "but we must have Lord Mildendale's evidence for the depositions."

As his lordship stood up, so did Namon Wallack.

As Lord Mildendale caught sight of the stalwart gipsy's stern, but calm, face his own went deadly white.

He brushed one hand hastily across his features, and clutched the rail of the witness-box with the other.

"I am not well," he muttered. "A sudden faintness has come over me. Give me, I pray, a glass of water!"

"A glass of water for his lordship," Spiffen roared. "Bless my heart, what a dreadful thing!"

"There is a man in court—" Lord Mildendale began. "I cannot go on. Take me away. I am not well—not well."

The usher caught his lordship as he reeled half-fainting into his arms.

"The case is remanded," Spiffen said. "Take the prisoner away and bring him up again to-morrow. My carriage is at the door, and at Lord Mildendale's service. Convey him to my house, I will follow."

As his lordship was supported out of court a disappointed murmur came from the spectators.

They considered that they had been cheated out of a pleasant entertainment, and waxed exceedingly wrath.

"There must be something wrong," said a man, whose ribs had suffered in the crush. "I begin to pity the prisoner."

"So do I," said another. "Perhaps Lord Mildendale is the worst of the two."

"He looked as if he saw a ghost!" exclaimed a third. "Here comes the prisoner. Stand back—stand back!"

Ralph Ashton was taken back to the Bridewell as quickly as possible, and having paid for a substantial meal, eat it heartily.

Another guinea gained him a second visit from Namon Wallack, and again the gipsy departed with that dream-like expression in his eyes.

He was longer in the cell than before, and the warder remarked to himself that the gipsy walked less stiffly than when he came in.

Evening came, and the quaint old city lay almost hushed to repose.

The curfew bell from St. Peter's Tower, which has been rung from its institution down to the present day, boomed out its notes.

The sound floated mournfully along, the autumn wind catching it up and bearing it far and wide.

The warder of the Bridewell sat in a chair just inside the open door.

He was more than half-asleep, for his head was nodding and rolling to and fro.

Suddenly he started up.

"I must get the prisoner's supper ready," he said. "He asked me for a light. That's against the rules and regulations, I know; but he has treated me so well that I can't refuse him."

The custodian of the ancient and strongly built place took down a lantern from an iron hook, and trimming the wick of a candle carefully lit it.

"All's well," he said, as he passed the doors of the cells and tried them with his hand. "I should like to know something of the history of this Ralph Ashton. He seems to be a perfect gentleman, and—"

The warder ceased speaking.

He heard the the sound of singing emanating from the cell in which Ralph Ashton was imprisoned.

And yet the voice had a strange ring in it, and the warder coming to a standstill, ran his fingers through his hair in a perplexed manner.

"We are merry to-night," he said, as he inserted the key in the lock and threw open the door. "Ha! murder! mercy!"

He flung up the lantern and recoiled as if he had been shot.

On the bench, right before him, sat Spring-Heeled Jack, his legs crossed, and one arm extended towards the warder.

"Ha! ha! ha!" laughed the strange creature. "Do you seek your prisoner—if so, seek him elsewhere. If you would keep your life, lay no hand upon me, nor attempt to bar my way."

There was no need for this warning.

The warder bolted, gasping and shrieking, but got no further than the doorway.

His legs tottered beneath him, and he fell writhing and raving in a fit.

## CHAPTER CLIV.

### LYNCH LAW.

The Two-necked Swan, in which Sir Roland Ashton and Morth had been so neatly trapped, stood in the centre of an oddly-built town, bearing as odd a name—Cockleton.

It was an out-of-the-way, primitive place, its people keeping up old styles, and speaking in a manner which would have puzzled a stranger.

For instance, the wick of a candle was called a "snaist," and the latch of a door a "snack," and a jug a "gutch."

Life went very easy at Cockleton.

Its humdrum people worked, ate, and slumbered with monotonous regularity, and so little excitement was there at most times that, when it was known that Sir Roland Ashton and Joe Morth had been taken red-handed, the wiseacres shook their heads and declared the report to be a London lie.

It is not for us to discuss whether a falsehood from town is of greater iniquity than one emanating from any lesser place, but the people of Cockleton thought so, and that was enough for them.

The sexton, a great authority on most matters, and who hobbled about on two oak sticks with crooked handles, was consulted.

"It's quite true," he said. "I've not only heard the story at the Two-necked Swan, but I have seen the constable."

Then all Cockleton went mad.

What?

They have a brace of such villains breathing the same air as themselves?

Never!

Labourers left the fields, staid old clerks their desks, and portly tradesmen their counters.

How it came about will never be exactly known, but when somebody suggested that they should march to the round-house and lynch the prisoners, the good men of Cockleton seized upon the idea, and marched shoulder to shoulder, in silence, with set teeth, and clenched hands.

Puddy and Jakes, the two constables of Cockleton, who, as a rule, had nothing else to do but to walk about, begged and prayed of the men to go quietly back to their homes.

But they appealed to deaf ears, and could do no more than follow in the rear.

When the round-house came in sight a change came over the demeanour of the men.

They began to hoot and yell out the names of the prisoners.

"Hang the villains!" shouted a short, fat man, who in his ordinary life would have gone out of his way to avoid crushing an insect in his path. "Hang 'em, I say! We don't want to wait for the assizes in any such thing!"

"No—no!" bellowed a butcher. "That's right—we'll hang 'em out of the way!"

Both Sir Roland Ashton and Joe Morth heard these unpleasant remarks.

Loth as they had been to enter the round-house, they now clung hopefully to its shelter.

Puddy and Jakes now ran to the head of the crowd, and, by waving their arms, held them in check for a moment.

"You don't know what you're a-doin' of!" Puddy cried. "If you touch that round-house it will be an act against the king and its constitution. If you kill the prisoners it will be murder in the eyes of the law."

But the blood of the Cockletonians was up.

Tinker, tailor, blacksmith, butcher, baker, and tanner surged onwards, completely upsetting Puddy and Jakes.

"It's useless!" Jakes gasped, as he picked himself up and rubbed the back of his head. "They must have their own way. We have done our best, and can do no more."

"I ain't a-goin' to try, for one," Puddy remarked. "But, bless my heart alive! the world must be coming to an end. Was there ever such a sight since the day that Cockleton was named?"

The crowd, mustering about a hundred and fifty strong, stopped before the round-house.

"Down with the door!" yelled a dozen voices.

"We must have a battering-ram, or it will never give way," shrieked a practical individual. "A ladder, or a scaffold-pole will do."

The last-named article was dragged from a builder's yard, and half-a-dozen of the strongest men ran full tilt with it against the door.

Nothing weaker than the door of a castle keep could have withstood that shock.

Wood splintered into atoms, and iron shivered like glass.

There was a rather dangerous rush over the fragments; but what were scratches and bruises to the men of Cockleton now?

"Here's a cell!" shouted the butcher. "Let us break it open!"

No sooner said than done, and Joe Morth, a mere heap of quivering clothes, was dragged out.

They did not strike or buffet him, as he expected, but, twisting a rope round his legs and arms, placed him on the floor.

"Now for the other!" roared the butcher, who was the leading spirit in the fray.

Crash!

The other cell door gave way.

They found Sir Roland Ashton on his knees in an attitude of supplication.

"Listen to reason," he faltered; "be just and fair. Every man is innocent until he is found guilty. The law of your country says so, and to rouse it is a criminal offence."

"What?" said the butcher, whose face looked red-hot, after the exertions he had undergone; "what! do you mean to say that there is the slightest doubt about your guilt?"

"That is for a jury of my countrymen to decide," Sir Roland replied.

"Just so," the butcher responded. "That is exactly what we are going to do, and if you are found guilty you shall hang as surely as I believe you to be a villain. Bring him out, and place him by his brother rascal. Where shall we hold the trial?"

"On One Tree-hill," said somebody.

"No better place could be found," the butcher replied. "We must be quick, or Puddy and Jakes will have time to ride over to Lincoln."

The prisoners were hurried along without delay.

Of the two Joe Morth looked very much the worse.

Sir Roland Ashton now assumed a calm, defiant demeanour.

"In a calmer moment your common sense will tell you that you are doing wrong," he said.

But in his heart he expected no mercy from the men of Cockleton.

And yet he hoped to get out of the scrape as he had got out of many similar ones.

One Tree-hill was not far away, and as soon as it was reached the butcher was chosen as foreman of the jury; and a mild-looking man, wearing a pair of horned rimmed spectacles, which gave him an owlish appearance, was elected as the judge.

But now a difficulty stood in the way, and a very serious one it proved to be.

Angry and determined as the men were, they could not convict the prisoners without evidence, and they had no witnesses to call.

It now struck several of the crowd that they had made fools of themselves.

While they were debating John Fore came running up the hill.

His appearance was greeted with a burst of applause.

"Mercy on me!" he cried, "have you lost your senses? Confusion take you for a pack of idiots! Get away as quick as you can. A regiment of soldiers on their way to Lincoln have just entered the town, and the constables have called upon them to quell the riot."

"They can't do it," said the butcher. "There must be the magistrate present."

"Just so," said John Fore. "There is one, and he will be here soon. Bring those rascals back to the round-house, and then go on your knees and beg for mercy."

The crowd began to melt away.

The news that John Fore had brought caused many to wish that they had no hand in the matter, and very few cared to stay to take the prisoners back to Cockleton.

Joe Morth and Sir Roland Ashton watched the scene with anxious eyes.

Hope again animated their breasts, but it fled when John Fore took a brace of pistols from his pocket.

"I have brought these in case there should be any nonsense," he said; "so if none of you will stay I will take the prisoners back alone."

"Then do it!" said the butcher, dashing down his hat. "This is a nice reward for all our trouble!"

"Come, come!" said John Fore, "don't fly into a temper. That will do no good. This matter will be smoothed over with a few fines, if you act like sensible men, and here I give you my word of honour to pay them."

There was a little comfort in this, and some of the men cheered and volnnteered to return with the prisoners, but the majority slunk away abashed and terrified.

Of course, there was no end of a bother in Cockleton about the affair.

Puddy argued that the people had committed high treason, and wondered how many would be hung, drawn, and quartered for the dreadful offence of breaking into the round-house.

That place having been rendered useless, the question was where to stow Sir Roland Ashton and Joe Morth in safety.

At last it was decided to take them to the Two-necked Swan until the round-house was restored; but the landlord shook his head.

"No, thank'ee," he said. "I've had quite enough of the scoundrels, and, besides, if I was ever so much inclined the other way, my wife wouldn't get a wink of sleep while they were in the house."

"Well," said Jakes, "something must be done with them. We can't walk them about the town like performing bears."

"Steady!" said the host of the Two-necked Swan, "an idea strikes me. There's a strong coach-house at the end of the yard, and you may make what use of it you like."

The constables thanked the landlord, and then turned their attention to the prisoners, who had listened in silence to the arrangements made for them.

"We shall give them the slip yet," Sir Roland whispered to Morth.

"But not if you keep jabbering about it," Morth

returned, savagely. "These fellows are as sharp as needles. If you want to say anything, wait until we are alone."

## CHAPTER CLV.

### WHEN THE TIDE WAS UP AND HIGH.

A FEW lights were glimmering fitfully from the mast-heads of vessels moored below London-bridge, when a boat, containing two men, shot from under the shadow of a water-gate at the lower end of Milford-lane.

The men were Luke Clye and Fadge, and at the bottom of the boat was a huge, shapeless bundle.

This bundle was nothing more nor less than Mrs. Corcoran, enclosed in the sack which Fadge had provided for her reception.

"Phew!" Luke Clye said. "I turn hot and cold by turns. Haven't we gone far enough?"

"You attend to the steering and shut up!" Fadge growled. "Don't you think that I know what I am about?"

"Yes," Clye returned; "but—but the figure of that old woman haunts me. I can scarcely believe that she is dead."

"She's as dead as a doornail," Fadge replied. "If I didn't think so I'd— What are you staring at now?"

"I thought I saw the sack move," Luke Clye gasped.

"You're enough to drive a man off his head!" Fadge said, tugging savagely at the oars. "Here's Blackfriars-bridge, and here we will get rid of what troubles you. Hang on to that ring, and slip a cord through it. That's right. Now, then, lend a hand here. Good-bye, old lady!"

Splash!

In went Mrs. Corcoran, sack and all.

"She's gone," Luke Clye said, rubbing his hands gleefully. "She'll never come back again."

"Unless her ghost haunts us," Fadge replied, laughing.

Luke Clye shuddered.

"Don't talk like that," he said. "It gives me the creeps to think of such a thing. Where's she gone, I wonder?"

"To the devil."

"I don't mean that," Clye said. "I was wondering whether she would sink or float. I have heard say that a witch never sinks."

"Bother your talk," Fadge growled. "We'll pull ashore, and while we have something to warm us, we'll drink to Mrs. Corcoran's journey."

The body of that wretched woman was whirled round and round by the tide, bumped against piles, the hulls of barges, and the slimy sides of wharves, and then sent spinning into the middle of the stream.

A boat containing some noisy sailors put off from the shore and made its way towards a vessel lying at anchor on the Surrey side.

One of the rollicking tars suddenly espied the sack, and snatched up a boat-hook.

"Here's a prize," he said. "What on earth can it be? It's as heavy as lead."

"Let it go," said another man. "It's some bundle of rubbish, no doubt. Let us get on board, or we shall have the captain shoving some of us in irons."

But the man, having once hooked Mrs. Corcoran, was loth to let her go again.

"Rubbish or no rubbish, I'll see what it is," he said. "How do you know that it is not some valuable plunder which had to be pitched into the river in a hurry? Easy! Steady—steady!"

The sack and it ugly burden was lifted into the boat.

"Why, hang me if there ain't a human body in it!" the sailor cried, as he cut the string at the mouth of the sack. "Pull for the shore again. This is a case of murder!"

The men were thoroughly alarmed, and the boat went back quick enough.

The stentorian cries of the sailors soon brought a number of people to the water side.

A sleepy watchman roused from a comfortable nap in his sentry-box cursed Mrs. Corcoran.

"An old woman in a sack?" he said, snarling at the man who had brought the news. "Why couldn't they let her be?"

"But the woman has been murdered!" the man gasped.

"How do you know that?" the watchman demanded. "Did you see it done?"

"No, I didn't."

"Then don't talk about what you know nothing," the watchman growled, as he picked up his lantern. "Ugh! what a beastly night to turn out."

When he arrived at the spot where Mrs. Corcoran's body lay he became a little more interested in the proceedings.

"First and foremost," he said, "that sack must be taken great care of. After that, the next thing to be done is to carry the body to the dead-house. Where's the man who found the woman?"

"Here!" said the sailor, stepping forward.

"What's your name?"

"Tom Bunk."

"Well, Tom Bunk, my fine fellow," said the watchman, "you will have to attend at the inquest, which, of course, will be held according to law."

Tom Bunk shook his head and hitched up his slacks.

"Inkwitches ain't much in my way," he said. "If I'd ha' known the old woman was a dead 'un she might ha' gone with the tide."

The watchman knocked up the beadle, and just as St. Paul's clock was booming out the hour of midnight the remains of gentle, amiable Mrs. Corcoran were deposited in the nearest dead house.

The watchman went back to his sentry box, and the beadle went to bed and slept all the sounder for being called up to perform such an unpleasant task.

When the morning came, and the parish beadle had had his sleep out and a comfortable breakfast, it suddenly occurred to him that he ought to put himself in communication with the coroner.

"I'll have a look at the body first," he said, as he put on his cocked hat and sallied forth. "I was too tired last night to make notes of her description."

The dead-house stood near to one of the old city churches, and was far from a pleasant place to gaze upon.

But the beadle was used to it, and he whistled softly as he unlocked the door, and pushed it slowly open with his foot.

"Now then, old gal," he said. "Let's take—"

The beadle said no more.

He turned and fled as if a mad bull was at his heels.

Away he went, helter-skelter, paying no attention to the shouts of the wondering people.

Perhaps it was a marvellous thing to see a beadle, more especially a fat beadle, run.

The usual number of boys, of course, appeared on the scene.

"Mumps, the beadle, is mad!" one youth cried. "Stop him! He's running down to the river to drown himself. I heard him say so."

"Stop him—stop him!" roared the people, taking up the cry. "Mumps is mad!"

If Mr. Mumps heard the shouts of his friendly pursuers he did not heed them.

He lost his hat, his cloak floated out at full length, and his eyes stood out like hat pegs, as his fat legs bounded over the ground.

Mr. Mumps had not gone quite mad, and he had not the remotest notion of committing suicide.

His great idea was to get home as quickly as possible, and when he did reach there he bounced into the house like a cannon ball.

It took a great deal to frighten Mrs. Mumps; but when she saw her husband's red and terrified face, and heard the clamouring of people in the street, she fully made up her mind that a revolution had broken out, and that the ring-leaders were thirsting for the blood of Mr. Mumps.

But she was a practical woman, and before saying a word to the beadle she locked and bolted the door.

Mumps was in his armchair, puffing and blowing like a porpoise among a shoal of herrings.

"Now then, Mumps," his spouse said, "perhaps you will tell me the meaning of this?"

"Oh! horror—horror!" Mr. Mumps groaned. "It can't be real."

"What can't be real? Is the king dead?"

"Wus—much wus than that," gasped Mumps. "Oh! Ugh! Ah!"

Mrs. Mumps, thinking that her husband was going to faint, applied the safe and wholesome remedy of thumping him on the back.

"That will do," he said. "Maria, go to the door and ask the crowd to go away."

"But why did they follow you? What made you run, Jeremiah?"

"I will tell you," he said, in a tragic whisper. "The dead has come to life again!"

Mrs. Mumps felt a cold thrill run through her frame.

"Oh! my, Jeremiah," she said. "Don't talk like that, or I shall think that you have lost your senses."

"Go to the dead house," he said, hoarsely, "and see for yourself; I left the key in the door. The woman as was dead last night is alive this morning. Go to the deadhouse, Maria. I can't —I daren't!"

Mrs. Mumps put on her bonnet and shawl and walked abroad.

Most of the people had left, and Mrs. Mumps, having boxed the ears of several juveniles, cleared a path for herself.

Mrs. Mumps did not hesitate or falter until she reached the dead house.

Sure enough the door was open, and the key in the door.

The beadle's wife approached the place boldly, and looked in.

It was empty.

There were the horrible slabs on which the bodies were laid, but nothing else.

Mrs. Mumps turned a little pale, as she locked the door and put the key in her pocket.

"What horrible mystery is this?" she said. "The woman was found floating down the river in a sack. Perhaps she wasn't dead after all?"

Mrs. Mumps flattered herself that this was a brilliant idea, and repeated it to her beloved Jeremiah.

But Mr. Mumps shook his head.

"She was dead, right enough," he said. "What I saw didn't belong to this earth. I see them eyes, that hooked nose, that—oh! dash it, give me a drink of brandy, or I shall bust."

---

## CHAPTER CLVI.

### JUSTICE SPIFFEN RECEIVES A SHOCK TO HIS NERVES.

The turnkey of Norwich Bridewell was found by a passer-by, who at once raised an alarm.

For some time the man could do nothing but stare vacantly.

Speech and sense seemed to have completely left him.

One thing, however, was certain.

Ralph Ashton had broken out of prison, for there was the empty cell and the open door to prove that fact.

Later at night the warder rallied a little, and requested that he might see a magistrate as soon as possible.

It so happened that one was already on the way to Bridewell.

The news of Ralph Ashton's escape spread like wild-fire through the city, and, as a matter of course, soon came to the ears of Mr. Spiffen, the chief magistrate.

That worthy was dining with Lord Mildendale, who had consented to be his guest, when a footman brought the tidings.

"What?" Spiffen yelled, bouncing ont of his chair. "It can't be true!"

"But it is, sir," the footman replied. "Mr. Jorum, the sheriff's officer, was sent to tell you. He is waiting below now, if you would like to see him."

"My hat and cane," Spiffen said. "Order the carriage to be brought round. I am very sorry that this should have happened, Lord Mildendale. Will you come with me to the Bridewell?"

"No; I think not," his lordship said, nervously. "Of course, if it is imperative, I must go. I shall be very anxious to know how the rascal escaped."

"But we will have him again," Spiffen said. "I will have every inch of the country scoured. Yes, my lord; the scoundrel shall be hunted down, even if we have to employ bloodhounds to do it."

The chief magistrate lived just two miles out of the city, on the Cromer-road.

"Drive as fast as you can," Spiffen said to the coachman as he bustled into his carriage. "Don't stop for anything or anybody."

The coachman obeyed his master's injunctions by lashing the horses into a mad gallop, and the first mile of the journey was accomplished in a few minutes.

But the horses came to a standstill so violently that Mr. Spiffen was shot from one side of the carriage to the other, and then deposited on the floor.

Half-dazed, and not a little bruised, he flung the door open and jumped into the road.

"What has happened?" he demanded.

"I don't know what it was, sir," the coachman replied. "It's a mercy that we didn't go into the ditch. Look at the horses, sir!"

# SPRING-HEELED JACK,

## THE TERROR OF LONDON.

"I HOPE YOU CAN SWIM," SAID SPRING-HEELED JACK, "FOR DOWN YOU MUST GO."

No. 43.

Mr. Spiffen did look at the horses, and he was horrified to see that they were covered with foam and trembling in every limb.

"But there must be some cause for this?" he said.

"Well, sir, there was," the coachman replied. "Something white seemed to dart down from the trees, and dance right before the horses' heads. I shall lead them the rest of the way, for I shouldn't like to be answerable for the consequences if they were to bolt again."

Spiffen began to rave and swear.

He didn't care for twenty thousand white things, and he commanded the driver to remount the box-seat and drive on.

The man grumbled audibly, but had no alternative left but to obey.

"My neck is nothing to him," he said, as he took the reins. "If I broke it in his service I wonder how much he would give my widow and children? Not a penny, I'll be bound, the mean hunks."

Spiffen, the chief magistrate, linked himself with Ralph Ashton, though he could not tell how.

He hated him, and the young man's escape cut him to the quick.

Twenty other prisoners might have got away without rousing his interest to such an extent, and sitting there in his carriage he fretted and fumed because the coachman did not drive faster.

The night was very dark, and a heavy mist floated from the meadows across the road, and was at times so dense that the horses could go not faster than a foot-pace.

Just as the lights of the city appeared the coachman heard something fall with a thud on the roof of the carriage.

Before he could turn to see what it was a strong arm encircled his waist, and he was sent spinning over a hedge.

The man was more frightened than hurt, but he did not go back to the carriage.

One glance of Spring-Heeled Jack, who had now taken the reins, was quite sufficient for him.

He took to his heels, fully believing that the arch-fiend had come for his master.

Mr. Spiffen, all unconscious that anything had happened, let down the window.

"John—John!" he bellowed; "confound your thick head! Drive on, or, hang me, if I don't discharge you!"

He nearly boiled over with fury, when, instead of obeying orders, the driver brought the horses to a standstill.

## CHAPTER CLVII.

### OLD QUARTERS—AN UNEXPECTED ARRIVAL.

The reader has doubtless arrived at the conclusion ere this that Mrs. Corcoran's cat-like tenacity of life had once more stood her in good stead.

When she came to her senses in the deadhouse her first notion was that she had found her way into Newgate.

The place, with its barred window and cold, bare walls, was very much like a prison cell.

But Mrs. Corcoran very soon became convinced to the contrary.

A terrible pain shot through her head at intervals.

She was drenched to the skin and chilled to the bone.

Mrs. Corcoran lay still, with her eyes closed, collecting her scattered thoughts.

By degrees the truth came back to her mind, so far up to the moment that Fadge had struck her down.

From that time, of course, Mrs. Corcoran was ignorant of what happened.

Shivering with cold and the heat of fever alternately, the hag slid off the slate slab, and hobbled around the deadhouse.

She tried the door, which was locked.

Then she peeped through the iron grating, and saw a few men plodding on their way to work.

Mrs. Corcoran opened her mouth to shout for help, but she closed it again.

"No—no," she muttered; "that would be the worst thing I could do under the circumstances. Those who brought me here think that I am dead. Who were they? My enemies, perchance, or it may be that some friendly hand snatched me from the jaws of death. At all events, I had better wait."

Mrs. Corcoran had not to wait long.

Day had already dawned, and the hag, unobserved by the people, who passed in greater numbers as the light strengthened, watched every face and form, until she saw Mr. Mumps turn round a corner into the street.

"Ha!" she muttered, "the parish beadle. He is coming this way to pay me a visit, I'll be bound. Now may my old tact stand me in good need. But how cold—how weak I am!"

Shuddering and moaning as she gathered her dripping garments about her, Mrs. Corcoran stepped back and seated herself upon the slab.

As Mr. Mumps opened the door, she extended her arms, and made so horrible a sound in her throat, that the beadle, as has been already recorded, bolted for his life.

The hag chuckled as she tottered towards the open door.

No time was to be lost, and gliding into the street, she mingled with the crowd.

In those days, beggars, hideous and uncouth in appearance, were so common that the better class of people paid no more attention to them than to give them as wide a berth as possible.

Thus it was that Mrs. Corcoran escaped notice.

"What an escape!" she gasped. "A night in the deadhouse. Ugh! My heart grows sick at the thought."

Diving down a number of narrow turnings, she stopped at last, and overcome with faintness, sank down upon a doorstep.

As she did so, a well-dressed gentleman stopped and looked at her.

"Why, what's the matter here?" he said. "My good woman, you seem to be in a very bad plight."

The kind tone in which she was addressed caused Mrs. Corcoran to wince, and she did not much relish the idea of being called a good woman, for she knew that she was nothing of the kind.

"Charity, good sir?" she said. "I crave your charity. I am starving!"

"So are a great many more, I regret to say," the gentleman returned. "But your wretched dress clings about you as if—"

"Yes, yes," Mrs. Corcoran said, interrupting him hastily. "I went down to the riverside last night, hoping to pick up something I might sell for a few pence, and I slipped into the water."

Mrs. Corcoran's heart beat with quite a new emotion as the gentlemen took his purse from his pocket.

The emotion was a stranger to the hag, for it was one of gratitude, and grimy tears gushed from her eyes.

"Here is a guinea for you," the gentleman said. "I wish I could give you more, for your fate seems to be a very hard one indeed."

Mrs. Corcoran poured out a torrent of thanks, amid which the gentleman walked away.

"Once more in luck," the hag said, as she pressed the shining coin to her thin, bloodless lips, "but not enough, not half enough. Perhaps if I had whined and moaned, as I know how, I might have got more."

The witch felt a little stronger now, and remembering that it would be advisable for her to get further away from the locality, she struggled on until she found herself near the Borough-market.

Here was the usual scene of confusion salesmen shouting, porters jostling—and cursing each other roundly, as they staggered under loads which might have astonished Hercules.

A hundred carts blocked up the road, and Mrs. Corcoran, as she dodged hither and thither, found herself in imminent danger of either being crushed between wheels or trampled down by the hoofs of restive horses, who, being fresh from the country, had no relish for the noisy streets of London.

The hag now began to attract attention.

One man asked her whether she had fallen out of the moon, another inquired why she had left her broomstick behind, and a third declared that she smelt strongly of brimstone and sulphur.

To these and other remarks of a similar character Mrs. Corcoran paid no heed whatever, but, selecting a cheap eating-house, she entered it and requested to be served with some food and tea.

The proprietor of the establishment, which was greasy and dirty, said he had no objection whatever, providing that Mrs. Corcoran convinced him that she was in a position to pay for the viands.

The moment that the guinea was produced the proprietor became all smiles and affability, and in a few minutes he placed before the almost famished hag a dish of ham and eggs, and a huge cup of a strange concoction supposed to be tea.

The bacon was rancid, the eggs a little "gone," but Mrs. Corcoran was too hungry to turn up her nose at such trifles.

"Perhaps you can tell me something about this locality?" she said, as the man gave her the change out of the guinea. "Do you happen to know a house called the Bull in Top Boots?"

"Rather," said the proprietor of the eating-house, tapping the side of his nose with his forefinger; "but the house is closed for some reason best known to the landlord."

"I am sorry for that," Mrs. Corcoran replied. "I expected to meet a friend there."

"Well, you can see for yourself. Keep straight on, and you will see the sign on the left-hand side."

"Thank'ee," said Mrs. Corcoran. "I daresay I shall find the house very well, but if it is shut up I don't see that there is much use in going to it."

"Perhaps it is lucky for you that the house is closed."

"Why?" demanded the hag, starting in spite of herself.

"Well," said the man, "the Bull in Top Boots bears a bad character. All sorts of strange things have taken place between its walls, so people say, and only yesterday I heard that the landlord had bolted because he was wanted by the police."

"Oh! indeed," said the hag, grinning. "Well, it's no business of mine or yours. Perhaps I shall meet my friend outside. Good-day."

"I've seen a great many ugly old women in my time," the eating-house keeper muttered as the door closed behind Mrs. Corcoran, "but you are the ugliest. If I had the time to spare, hang me! if I wouldn't see what your little game is."

When Mrs. Corcoran reached the open street she began to reflect.

"So," she thought, "Morth is gone, and in a hurry, too, it appears. Good! If I could but find my way into the house I should have shelter and time to form some plan for the future."

The idea seemed a feasible one, and the hag hobbled and tottered on until she stood before the inn.

A glance told her that the door and windows had been made secure and fast.

"There's more than one way to kill and cook a goose," the hag muttered. "I know my way into the back premises, but—"

Mrs. Corcoran shuddered from head to foot as she thought of the men she hurried out of the world, and she asked herself the question whether she dare enter the house now.

"Why not?" she continued. "I failed at Snatcher's house, but here I am certain to find something worth taking away. What have I to fear? Let weak-minded fools believe that the earth gives up its dead. Bah! I crack my finger and thumb at such nonsense."

The back gates leading to the stabling were down a dark, narrow lane, and Mrs. Corcoran, after looking wistfully about her, walked carelessly by the gates, and tried them with her hand as she passed.

They were fastened on the inside, but seemed inclined to yield, and the hag, waiting until two or three wretched-looking people had gone by, renewed her efforts.

She shook the gates until she heard the rusty bolt with which they were secured creak.

The bolt gave way suddenly, and Mrs. Corcoran slipped into the yard.

Her first precaution was to refasten the gates, and then she darted across the yard, and entered one of the stables.

"Ah! dear me," she gasped, "I think I must be getting old at last. There was a time when I could have sent the bolt flying without half the trouble I have just taken."

She crouched down upon some damp straw, with which the floor of the stable was littered, and moaned as she rocked herself to and fro.

"I must have a change of clothes, or I shall perish with the ague or some similar complaint."

After waiting a few minutes, Mrs. Corcoran, gliding along in the shadow of the buildings, reached the door through which she had passed after stabbing Sam Snatcher.

This, as she had fully expected, was locked; but there was a small window close at hand just large enough to allow the hag to crawl through.

Nothwithstanding all Morth's cunning, he had left this little window open, and Mrs. Corcoran, summoning all her streugth, made a spring, and fell flat upon the boards of the passage beyond.

The noise occasioned by her fall was considerable.

It so startled her that she held her breath and listened, for so strange were the echoes of the rambling old house that she made almost certain that she heard somebody stumbling up the cellar stairs.

But silence soon reigned again, and the witch-like old woman crept stealthily into the parlour.

How still the place was now!

There was something uncanny about the dreary aspect of the place, and Mrs. Corcoran glanced nervously over her shoulder and almost feared to move.

But presently she did so, going from room to room, marking the signs of a hurried flight, but never dreaming that Morth's sole object in leaving his house was to find her.

Search where she would, Mrs. Corcoran could find no articles of female attire; but there were plenty of men's garments, and at last she made up her mind to attire herself in some of these.

She did so as quickly as possible, and then chuckled at the marvellous change in her appearance.

"Why have I never thought of this before?" she said. "Who would know me? I look quite a venerable old man. Ha! ha!"

Strange enough the hag did most certainly look.

The disguise was perfect, and Mrs. Corcoran, with an old hat pulled down over one eye, looked more hideous than ever.

Then she went on with the search, selecting such things as she could sell, and dispose easily of.

In less than an hour she had made up a large bundle, and then sat down to wait until darkness came.

For hours she sat patiently, never moving, and at last the day waned slowly away, and the oil lamps began to flicker in the street.

It was a rainy evening, and such people who were abroad made haste home, and at last the street became silent.

Mrs. Corcoran grasped the bundle, and flinging it over her shoulder crossed the room and stood upon the landing.

But only for a moment.

Suppressing a cry of terror, she darted back into the room, for by the dim light flickering through a window she had seen a man creeping up the stairs in a stooping, dejected attitude.

She heard his heavy breathing, she heard his muttered curses, and a fear that sent her blood tingling through her veins took possession of her, and left her bereft of speech and strength.

## CHAPTER CLVIII.

### JUSTICE IS FOILED.

Sir Roland Ashton and Joe Morth were duly locked up in the coach-house of the Two-necked Swan, at Cockleton, and a man planted outside to keep guard over them.

The coach-house was not a pleasant lodging.

A mouldy aroma pervaded it, and as nothing had been prepared for the prisoners to lie down upon they had to content themselves with the bare earth.

The man outside did not seem to relish his task, for he grumbled audibly as he paced up and down.

"Confound 'em!" he said. "It would have been a good job if they had been hung out of hand. What's the use of keeping such wretches, when everybody knows them to be guilty. Humph! I am to have eight hours of this precious work, so I may as well make myself as comfortable as possible."

This he did by pouring half the contents of a flask of brandy down his throat, and then lighting a pipe.

Tramp—tramp!

Up and down he went, smoking vigorously and shrugging his shoulders as the cold wind sought him out and reminded him of its strength.

After a time he emptied the flask and began to feel a little drowsy.

Drawing his coat-collar about his ears, he planted his back against the coach-house door and tried to make out what the prisoners were about

"They are quiet enough," he said, under his breath. "Perhaps they have gone to sleep, and I'd give a trifle to do the same. It's odd that they, with the gallows before them, can take matters so easy. If I was in their place I should be tearing my hair and wishing myself well out of the world."

But Sir Roland Ashton and Joe Morth were not quite so inactive as the man thought.

Lying close together, they conversed in whispers.

"We may have a chance, if we keep quiet," Sir Roland said. "I have noticed something which has escaped your eyes."

"What is that?"

"The wall nearest to me is old and crumbling," Sir Roland replied. "A good kick would send the bricks and plaster flying."

"A good kick!" Morth repeated. "Are you mad to think of such a thing?"

"Not quite," Sir Roland returned; "but we may be able to remove the rubbish without making a noise."

"And fall into that fellow's hands who is outside, and well armed, I'll be bound."

"Listen!" said Sir Roland.

The sentinel was snoring loudly.

Joe Morth's eyes lit up with the light of hope.

"If he would only keep on for an hour or so," he said, "we might have reason to laugh in our sleeves. Well, he is off sound enough just now, at all events."

"If I had a hundred guineas I would give them freely for the loan of an iron bar," Sir Roland remarked. "Let us see if we can find something which will answer the same purpose."

"Oh! yes," said Joe Morth. "I shouldn't be at all astonished if they have left us a basket packed with burglar's implements."

"You throw cold water on everything I say," Sir Roland Ashton returned, sullenly. "At all events, we can but try. Down on your hands and knees, and crawl about. You may come upon something you least expect in such a place as this."

"Right you are," said Morth; "there can't be any harm done, at all events. Steady—steady! or we shall bang our heads together in this dark hole."

Just then the man on guard woke up with a start.

"Hullo!" he cried out, "did either of you blackguards speak."

"Yes," Morth replied.

"Well, what do you want?"

"A drink of something to warm us, if it can be had for love or money."

"Ha—ha!" said the man, laughing. "You'll get a lot for love, I'm thinking, and if you have any money, you can keep it. Do you think I am such a fool as to budge an inch away from this door?"

"Who wants you to do so?" said Sir Roland, now joining in the conversation. "Can't you call another, and send him into the inn. If the law is just, it is not cruel. The cold of this horrible place is chilling the very marrow in our bones."

"I don't suppose it is quite as warm as a furnace," the constable replied, grinning to himself. "Well, I'll see what can be done. Shove half-a-crown under the door, and I'll call the first man I see cross the yard."

"You'll want a drink yourself, of course," Morth said, as he produced the coin; "so you ay as well keep the change, and do as you like ith it."

The constable waited until he espied an ostler.

"Jim!" he called out.

"Well," the man replied, "what's up? Do you want any help?"

"No; but I want you to fill my flask, and get a quartern of brandy for the prisoners," the constable replied. "I think they may have it, as they are in deucedly uncomfortable quarters."

"I'd let them go without it, if I were you," said the ostler, with a growl; "or I'd know whether I was doing right."

"I shouldn't be doing right if the rascals died before the morning for want of nourishment," the constable returned. "I'll take this upon myself, so cut along, and be as quick as you can, there's a good fellow."

Jim the ostler went his way reluctantly enough, and returned in about five minutes.

"There's the stuff," he said. "May it do you good; but as for theirs, may it choke 'em!"

Having delivered himself of this amiable speech, the ostler departed.

The aperture between the ground and the door was sufficiently large to admit of a small flat bottle being passed under it, and the constable, having carefully ascertained which vessel contained the most liquor, passed the one holding the lesser quantity into Joe Morth's hand.

Morth made sure of his share of the brandy, and then passed what was left to Sir Roland.

The constable again refreshed himself, and flattered himself that he felt all the better for it.

"Good stuff this," he said. "It warms the very cockles of a fellow's heart. I really believe that I could drink half-a-gallon of it without feeling the least harm."

Sir Roland overheard what the man said, and nudged Joe Morth with his elbow.

"If we only keep quiet, he will go off as sound as a roach again," he whispered.

"I hope he will not be long about it," Morth muttered, under his breath, "Hah! That drop of brandy has done me good, and I feel ready for anything."

"Did you find anything on the floor?" Sir Roland asked.

"Yes."

"What is it?"

"A portion of an old wheel-tyre."

"That's splendid," Sir Roland remarked. "It will not only do the work of a crowbar, but do splendidly as a weapon, should we be molested."

"Let us get out of this crib first, and then talk afterwards," Morth returned. "Confound that fellow! I believe he has made up his mind to keep awake. Listen to him! He is singing now."

The constable was gurgling out a ditty in a hoarse voice, but he stopped soon to take another pull at the bottle.

"I must be careful or the stuff won't last out," he muttered; "and it's very plain to me that I shall get no more to-night."

But the temptation was too strong for him to resist it.

After a short mental struggle, in which the flesh got the better of the mind, he emptied the flask to the last drop and again took up his station against the coach-house door.

The moaning wind sang a lullaby to him, and soon his head began to nod and roll from side to side, until his chin sank upon his breast.

He now began to snore like a litter of pigs, and Joe Morth commenced his attack upon the wall.

It was an easy task, for both bricks and plaster were almost as soft as putty.

In a few minutes a rush of air told the prisoners that an aperture had been made.

"Hark!" Joe Morth said, holding up his hand. "Don't let us make any mistake. We must be sure that the fellow outside is still sleeping."

"Nothing less than a pistol shot could wake him," Sir Roland replied. "He is making more noise than the wind."

"Then out we go," said Joe Morth, as he placed his hands under the loosened bricks.

Down they came with such a run that the villain's heart thumped against his side.

But the constable slumbered on.

Joe Morth, having done the work, claimed the right of leaving the coach-house first.

To this Sir Roland Ashton could offer no objection, but so impatient was he to get into the open air that in crawling over the mass of rubbish he scattered some of it noisily with his feet.

Joe Morth heard the clatter, and, springing up, took to his heels, leaving Sir Roland Ashton to take care of himself.

He threw down the portion of wheel-tyre, so that he might run all the faster, and the baronet clutched it, just as the drunken constable woke up and came running round to see what was the matter.

Sir Roland, crouching down, drew back, and gradually drew himself erect.

"I could have sworn I heard something as it the wall had given way," the constable muttered, "but perhaps it was only my fancy after all. I'll have a look, though, to see that all is safe."

A dark lantern hung suspended from his belt, and he was in the act of drawing back the slide, when Sir Roland, leaping forward, struck him a fearful blow over the head with the piece of rusty iron.

The unfortunate man uttered one cry of agony, and then fell in a huddled, quivering heap upon the ground.

The cry was not very loud, but sufficiently so to attract the attention of Jim the ostler, who had just finished his work, and was closing the doors.

"Hullo!" he cried. "Is anything the matter?"

"No;" Sir Roland replied, mimicking the unconscious constable's voice. "I was only driving away some noisy cats—drat 'em! Good-night!"

"Good night," the ostler replied, "and I wish you well out of your job. It's one that I shouldn't care about, I can tell you."

He went his way whistling, and, reaching home, tumbled into bed, and dreamed that Sir Roland Ashton and Joe Morth had quarrelled and strangled each other.

Meanwhile, Sir Roland Ashton was not permitting the grass to grow under his feet.

As soon as the sound of the ostler's footsteps had died away he slipped across the yard and, climbing over a low hedge, found himself in a narrow lane.

In what direction Joe Morth had gone Sir Roland had not the least notion, and in his anxiety to leave the premises of the Two-necked Swan well behind him he did not much care.

Walking on the grass, which grew in ridges on each side, he reached the end of the lane, and then began to look about him.

No light shone from the windows of the scattered houses, and this was a relief to Sir Roland, as it told him that the simple folk had gone to bed, and were, doubtless, fast asleep.

A strange sense of loneliness came over the baronet.

Even Joe Morth had deserted him, and, bad as he was, his company would have been better than traversing the dismal roads alone, which, for all he knew, might be guarded.

He determined to leave the roads and take to the fields, and was in the act of mounting a gate when the figure of a man sprang from a ditch.

"Is that you, Morth?" Sir Roland demanded.

"Yes," was the reply. "Ah! what a start you gave me. I took you for a constable."

"A constable might have taken me for all you cared," Sir Roland hissed.

"You lie!" Morth retorted. "Well, what if he did? My life is as good as yours. It was you who brought me into all this trouble."

"It was I who showed you the way how to get out of it," Sir Roland replied.

A short spell of silence then ensued.

"I think we had better understand each other," Joe Morth said, at length. "I am tired of your company, and wish to go my own way."

"Indeed!"

"Yes."

"And pray what are your intentions?" Sir Roland demanded. "Are you going back to London?"

"That is my business," Joe Morth returned. "Whichever way I choose to go I don't want your company."

"You have changed your mind suddenly," said Sir Roland. "What if I happen to be of a different opinion—what if I say that I will not leave you?"

Joe Morth burst into a hoarse roar of laughter.

"You had better not try that on," he said. "I have the strength of a giant, and when I once get my fingers on a man's throat I do not let go in a hurry."

"I take that as a threat," Sir Roland replied; "but I heed it not. We sink or swim together. I would not leave you now if you had the strength of twenty giants."

"Beware of me," Morth said. "I have done enough in my life without wishing to spill more blood. Beware how you trifle with me before my temper gets the better of my resolution."

"It is you who must beware of me," Sir Roland replied. "It is you who would trifle with me, but I will not permit it. Come to my terms or you shall never see another day dawn."

These words roused Morth's fury.

He had no notion that Sir Roland had possessed himself of the piece of wheel-tyre, but he became convinced of the fact as he sprang forward to grapple with him.

A stunning blow in the face sent him reeling back.

"Ah! coward," he yelled. "Dog! why did I not see through this from the first?"

"Because," said Sir Roland, as he followed him up, and dealt him another and a still heavier blow—"because you were a fool! It must have come to this sooner or later, so die now!"

With the blood streaming from the jagged wounds inflicted by the rusty iron, Joe Morth covered his face with his hands and tried to regain his feet.

But Sir Roland beat him down, and spurned Morth as he sank moaning upon his back.

Then all was still.

"He is dead," Sir Roland said. "He brought his own fate upon his head. Ah! a thought strikes me. The balance of silver must be still in his pocket. It is not much, but it is better than nothing."

Stooping down, he robbed the apparently lifeless body of his companion in crime, and then, with the brand of Cain indented deeper than ever upon his brow, Sir Roland dashed away like a madman across the darkened fields.

## CHAPTER CLIV.

### MR. SPIFFEN IS ASKED WHETHER HE CAN SWIM.

As may be better imagined than described, the terror of Spiffen, the chief magistrate, was intense when he found that he and his carriage were in the power of Spring-Heeled Jack.

It is contended that a man endures only a few moments of real agony in his lifetime, and it is certain that Spiffen was in the full possession of one of them just then.

His hair rose bolt upright on his head, a deathlike perspiration poured down his face, and his knees knocked together.

But there was rage in his heart, as well as abject fear.

That he, who was usually a source of fear—he, who small culprits whimpered at, and strong men turned pale when he administered justice—save the mark!—should be kidnapped on the open road, a short distance from his own house, was incomprehensible to him.

"It must be a dream!" he gasped. "It can't be real!"

But he found that there was a deal of reality in his situation as the carriage dashed along, and more so when it suddenly came to a standstill, and Spring-Heeled Jack hauled him out in the most unceremonious manner.

"Man, demon, or whatever you are, have mercy on me!" Spiffen groaned. "My good fellow, you have no idea of what you are doing."

"I think I do," Spring-Heeled Jack replied, with so ferocious a grin that Spiffen almost fainted. "It is you who send children and the starving to prison; it is you who sentence shrinking women to be flogged. Ho—ho! I know you, and now I claim you as a prize."

The magistrate sank on his knees, and grovelled so low that his very nose came in contact with the earth.

"What have I done to you?" he whined. "You must have mistaken me for some other man."

"It would be impossible for me to mistake you for a man," Spring-Heeled Jack returned, contemptuously. "Get up, or I will trample you under my feet!"

"I will do anything in reason to oblige you," Spiffen replied; "but you are going too far. You may not be aware of the pains and penalties attached to such an outrage as this. When you strike at me you strike at the mighty machine of the law."

Again Spring-Heeled Jack laughed.

"Listen," he said, hissing the words into Spiffen's ear. "I have something to show you, so follow me quietly, or as sure as you are as helpless as a mouse in the talons of a cat, I will twist your neck and fling you upon some dung-hill."

Mr. Spiffen grasped his throat and stared at the terrific creature in the same manner as a rabbit, petrified with fright, stares at a snake's fascinating eyes.

"Perhaps," he said, in a maudlin tone of voice —"perhaps this is a joke. I know that some young fellows when out on the spree like to have a bit of fun, but—"

"Silence!" said Spring-Heeled Jack, interrupting him. "Silence! Come with me. Not a word, now, or it will be your last."

More dead than alive, Spiffen suffered himself to be led away.

His feet did not seem to touch the ground, but trod upon air.

Spring-Heeled Jack danced him hither and thither, and up and down, until his head grew giddy, and his heart sick.

A dull, red mist gathered before his eyes, and a sound like the beating of a drum rang in his ears.

In this way they crossed several fields, and at last Mr. Spiffen found that he had been brought to a standstill upon a bridge.

"We have reached our destination at last," Spring-Heeled Jack said. "It is here where you and I must part."

"Part?"

"Yes. Do I not speak sufficiently plain? I said that we must part here, and I mean't what I said!"

There was something peculiar in Spring-Heeled Jack's tone of voice.

It thrilled Spiffen through and through, and he would have grovelled on the ground again if Spring-Heeled Jack had not held him up by sheer force.

"You speak plain enough," the wretched man said, with a groan, "but I don't understand you exactly. Of course, if you wish to say good-night, why, we will do it at once, and I promise you, on the honour of a gentleman, and a justice of the peace, that you shall hear no more of this matter."

"I must, and shall," Spring-Heeled Jack replied. "It strikes me, that it is you who will hear no more about the affair."

The awful truth flashed into Spiffen's brain.

"No, no, no!" he shrieked, wildly. "Don't murder me! Give me another chance. I will endeavour to be a kinder and a better man. At least, I have never done you any wrong, so spare me."

"You speak, you appeal to deaf ears," the weird creature said. "Long ago you deserved what you must suffer now. The cries of helpless women under the lash have not been uttered in vain. Vengeance is at hand. The hour of retribution has come, and unless you can save yourself by your own efforts you must die."

As Spring-Heeled Jack spoke he lifted Spiffen clear over the parapet of the bridge and suspended him between air and water.

"I hope you can swim, for down you must go."

Spiffen closed his eyes as he heard these words.

He kicked out with his dangling legs, and a horrible gurgling came from his throat as he felt Spring-Heeled Jack's hold relax.

Down, down, down he went.

There was a splash, a short, choking cry, and then all was still.

Spring-Heeled Jack leaped upon the parapet, and extending his arms, suddenly rose into the air and vanished.

* * * * * *

Lord Mildendale sat waiting for Mr. Spiffen's return.

He was anxious to know what had really taken place, and fretted and fumed at the bare notion of Ralph Ashton's escape.

"I can scarcely believe in the truth of the report," he said; "but if it be fact, it is shameful."

Glancing at a handsome clock, he noticed that the hour of midnight was approaching.

"It seems strange that my newly-found friend has not returned," he murmured. "Perhaps the rascal who attacked me has been chased and captured. And yet—"

Lord Mildendale turned his head as he thought he heard a slight sound outside the window.

"How full of odd fancies I am to-night," he said. "It was but the wind, and perhaps the pattering of rain, for the sky promised a wild night."

At this moment a servant tapped at the door.

"Come in," said Lord Mildendale.

A footman with frightened eyes and lengthened face entered the room.

"Something has happened I see," said Lord Mildendale, as he rose from his chair. "What it it?"

"A most terrible thing, my lord," the man stammered. "Mr. Spiffen's carriage has been attacked."

"Attacked!"

"It is only too true, my lord," the footman replied. "The coachman managed to escape with his life, and he has only just arrived with the news."

"Let me see him at once," Lord Mildendale said, striding across the room. "There is no time to lose."

The coachman made his appearance, but it was some time before he could give a coherent account of what had happened.

All he really knew was that he had been hurled from the box by a demoniac figure, and that he had left Mr. Spiffen to get out of the muddle as well as he could.

Without speaking, Lord Mildendale stood glaring vacantly at the man.

"It must have been the fiend known as Spring-Heeled Jack," he said.

"Oh! lor'," said the coachman, with a groan. "If that be so we are lost. For the love of mercy, let me have a drop of brandy, or I shall fall into a fit."

"You may help yourself," Lord Mildendale replied; "and when you have drunk your fill, see that a horse is brought round to the door, and be careful that loaded pistols are placed in the holsters."

"You—you are going out, my lord?"

"Yes; I am going to find your master. I happen to know something of this Spring-Heeled Jack and his freaks, and I will bring him down with a bullet if he crosses my path."

In a few minutes Lord Mildendale was galloping along at a furious rate.

Furnished with a few particulars, he took the direction which had been taken by Justice Spiffen, when he thought he was going to reach Norwich so comfortably.

On went Lord Mildendale, spurring his horse until the tortured animal dashed along at a maddened pace.

The road was deserted, and Lord Mildendale reached the first gate without meeting with a single creature.

Leaping from the saddle, he roused the porter, who had been dreaming before a cheery fire composed of logs of wood.

He was a white-haired, tottering old man, and had passed more than half-a-century in the strange, ghostly rooms above the arch which spanned the roadway.

Holding a lantern above his head, so that it shed a glow of light upon Lord Mildendale's face, he said—

"You must give an account of yourself, good sir. No strangers are admitted into the City after midnight, unless they have business, or good reason to do so."

"I have not come to enter the city," Lord Mildendale replied; "but to enquire whether or not you have seen or heard anything of Mr. Spiffen, the chief magistrate."

The porter of the gate shook his head.

"Nay, sir," he replied. "A messenger was sent post haste to him a short time ago."

"Is it possible that he may have passed through another gate on foot?"

"Very possible; for there are several other entrances to the City."

"I have heard that Mr. Spiffen has been stopped," Lord Mildendale said, after a pause. "Perhaps, after all, I had better enter the City and rouse the watch."

"I can do so at once, without further trouble," the old man said.

"By what means?"

"I have a bell here," said the porter, "which is never rung, save in case of serious alarm or fire."

"Then ring the bell at once," Lord Mildendale returned. "I have travelled the same way that Mr. Spiffen came, and it seems that he got so far that the light from your windows was visible; but I can find no trace of him."

The porter of the gate pressed his hand to his wrinkled brow.

"Now that I come to think of it," he said, "I thought I heard a strange sound some time ago, but I put it down to the wind, which often moans and sighs about here like a living creature in pain."

Lord Mildendale climbed into the saddle again, and waved his hand impatiently.

"Let me pass," he said; "something tells me that Mr. Spiffen must have reached the interior o the City by some means. Ring the bell—rouse the citizens, for if one criminal has escaped let the perpetrator of this outrage be secured without delay."

With the notes of the alarm bell ringing in his ears Lord Mildendale galloped down the old-fashioned street.

The clatter of the horse's hoofs, and the sound of his voice startled the people almost as much as the clanging of the bell.

Windows and doors flew open as if by magic.

A dozen voices enquired what was the matter.

"Up—up!" Lord Mildendale shouted. "Your chief magistrate has been robbed, and perhaps murdered."

Some of the men who heard this announcement did not seem to be very much affected by it, and not a few closed their windows and went to bed again.

Onward went his lordship to the Bridewell, where he hoped to hear some news of the missing magistrate, but he was only met by a man with a vacant stare on his face.

"Dolt!" hissed Lord Mildendale, when he had told the news, "have you no tongue in your head?"

"Aye, my lord," the warder replied; "and in times gone by it used to wag as freely as any man's. But such strange things have come to our old City that methinks it would be better to be silent."

"What do you fear?"

"The demon who can burst open these strong doors, and set prisoners free."

"Fool! coward!" Lord Mildendale said. "If you are frightened by such wretched trickery, it were as well if a man with a stouter heart took your place."

"Willingly," the warder replied. "But keep a civil tongue in your head, my lord, for you are not yet my master with the right to bully me."

Lord Mildendale made a cut at the warder's head with his riding-whip, as he set his spurs into his horse's flanks.

"A curse upon all such dolts!" he muttered. "Which way am I to turn for news now? 'Sdeath! it would seem that I have come upon a wild-goose-chase."

Presently he saw a crowd of people approaching.

Some were shouting in tones of alarm, while others, apparently finding something to be mirthful about, were laughing boisterously.

The crowd was headed by two men with torches, and Lord Mildendale, drawing nearer, beheld as strange a sight as ever met man's eyes.

## CHAPTER CLX.

### BUCKLER'S RENTS HAS A BAD TIME OF IT—A FIGHT TO THE BITTER END.

STARTLED by Grabham's shouts, Nabbitt and his followers quitted Daddy Muckrum's house with all speed.

"He's dead—he's dead! Dead as a door-nail!" Grabham yelled, capering about as the chief constable and the others came up.

"Who's dead, you fat-headed lump of destruction?" Nabbitt demanded.

"Ted Nickells!" Grabham replied; a little crestfallen at the doubtful compliments showered upon him by his superior officer. "He won't want hanging again. You'll find his body up the passage, and t'other one ain't far off."

Mr. Nabbitt was rather exasperated at Grabham's success.

"Who is the other one you are talking about?" he asked.

"Bill Blarney!"

"Then he may as well give himself up," said Nabbitt; "as he can't leave this hornet's-nest with his life. I'd sooner take the responsibility of burning Buckler's-rents down than let him escape. Now, constables, direct your lanterns to the roof-tops, and shoot anybody you may see crawling along them."

"We'll do it, sir," said Catchpole, who had become so suddenly valiant that he looked nearly double his size. "Didn't I tell you that Grabham and me would settle the business properly?"

"Your business will be settled if you don't keep your tongue still," Nabbitt growled. "Look after the fugitives, while Grabham and I take a glance at the dead man."

Ted Nickells was lying at full length as prone and senseless as a log of wood.

To all appearances he was dead; but as Nabbitt threw his arms round him a heavy groan came from his lips, and he moved slightly.

"I don't think he will rob the hangman of his proper due yet," Nabbitt said, brutally; "but be that as it may, the law compels us to do the best we can for him now."

"You may do your worst or best now," Nickells said, as a choking sob rose in his throat, "but you cannot save me. Curse you all! If I had been spared a few days I would have given you the slip and laughed at you all; but it was not to be—not to be."

"Come—come!" said Nabbitt, in a softened tone of voice. "If your time has come this is not the proper frame of mind to die in."

"Would you have me whine and snivel?"

As Ted Nickells spoke he twisted himself over and glared at Nabbitt with an awful expression of face.

"If you only knew how I hate you, and hate you all, you would let me be," he said, gaspingly. "I tell you, you can do nothing. I am booked! Born bad, I must die bad! Let those who brought me up to the life I have led look to it. Ah! this must be death at last."

His body stretched out at full length, and his head fell back.

"He's gone at last," Nabbitt said. "Let him lie where he is. We will go back. Ugh! I little reckoned upon such a night's work as this; but justice must be dealt out to all villains.

Now that the excitement was partly over, Grabham felt as if his back had been converted into an icicle.

"Mercy on me!" said he, catching his breath, "how bad I do feel. Upon my word, I'd rather that somebody else had fired the shot. The last glance that he gave me with his eyes will haunt me for months."

"Pooh—pooh!" said Nabbitt, sneeringly, but trembling, nevertheless, for the very same reason. "When you have gone through half what I have experienced you will pay but little attention to such a trifle as this."

While all this was going on, Mr. Spikes' house was a most uncomfortable place to dwell in.

Daddy Muckrum, half-dead with fright, was crouching in the cellar, and Spikes, armed with a short bar of iron, stood with his back against the door, with his breath coming short and thick, and his heart beating like a clock.

The woman was the coolest of the three.

Harriett Spikes never lost her head.

"Come away from there," she said to her husband; "we must go upon another tack."

"What do you mean?" he demanded, hoarsely.

"I mean that you had better walk into the room and light the lamp."

"Light the lamp!" he repeated. "That would be the very thing to bring the constables here."

"Well, let them come," said Mrs. Spikes. "We can't keep them out if we play the parts of fools. I have a notion that I can throw them off the scent. Light the lamp, I say, and leave the rest to me."

"You forget the old man in the cellar," Spikes said.

"I forget nothing," she replied; "but I shall so far forget myself presently as to take that bar of iron away from you, and hit you over the head with it."

Growling out something under his breath that two could play at that sort of game, Spikes returned to the room and illuminated the lamp.

"What now?" he demanded.

"Sit down and wait," the beauteous Harriet said, compressing her lips, and folding her arms. "If the constables come to the door, I will answer it."

Mr. Spikes could not be otherwise than proud of possessing such a wife, though he had often assaulted her to the extent of black eyes, and she had playfully retaliated with a flat iron, or any harmless little thing she happened to place her hands upon.

They could hear the constables hurrying up and down, and all around Buckler's-rents, searching for Bill Blarney, and they could also hear the officers cursing because they could not find the man they wanted.

Presently the door leading to the cellar was pushed open, and the head and shoulders of Daddy Muckrum appeared.

"It is no use," he gasped. "I can't stay there in the dark any longer. The place seems to be full of ghosts. I'll swear that something cold and death-like touched me on the face just now."

"Fiddle-sticks!" Harriet Spikes ejaculated. "Go back, or you life is not worth the price of a rush candle."

"I can't go back—I won't go back!" Daddy Muckrum said, with a groan. "It's like being buried in a grave."

We have said before that Harriet Spikes was a practical woman, and one of few words.

Without saying any more, she stalked across room, and seizing the livid-faced old man by the collar, pitched him headlong down the stairs.

Daddy Muckrum did not expect this unceremonious treatment, and he howled dismally as he fell all of a heap on the floor.

Nabbitt happened to be standing at that moment on the little grating used for lighting and ventilating the cellar.

He heard the sound, and pricked up his ears.

"Hallo!" he muttered; "there is something wrong here. I'll see what is the matter."

"Beckoning to two constables to follow him closely, he knocked in an authoritative fashion at the door of Spikes' house.

"At last!" said Harriet. "Let them knock again."

"I wish the house would fall upon them!" Spikes returned, with an oath. "It strikes me that there will be a pretty kettle of fish to fry presently."

"There would be, if I were so faint-hearted as you are," she replied.

Bang—bang!

"They are impatient," Mrs. Spikes said, grinning. "I think it is time for me to go now. Sit you still."

This injunction was perfectly unnecessary.

Spikes sat as motionless as a statue, clinging almost frantically to his chair.

"Well, gentlemen," said Mrs. Spikes, as she presented herself at the door, "what may you please to want?"

"Entrance, in the name of the law," Nabbitt replied, flourishing his staff of office in the woman's face.

"Oh! certainly," Mrs. Spikes replied. "We

are only poor humble working people, and have nothing to fear. Will you walk in?"

Mr. Nabbitt was rather staggered at meeting with so ready an invitation to inspect the premises; but he was not quite thrown off his guard, as he was up to many tricks played by thieves and bad characters when driven into a corner.

By the time that he and the two other constables had entered the so-called parlour Mr. Spikes had recovered his self-control somewhat.

"Why, bless me!" he said, in well-feigned surprise, "what is all this fuss about? Pray tell us? When we heard the pistol shots we thought that the place had been attacked by a band of villains."

"No doubt you felt very much alarmed," Nabbitt returned, sneeringly. "Well, my friend, since you are so innocent you will have no objection to have the premises searched; so we will commence with the cellar, if you please."

Spikes shot a terrified glance at his wife, which plainly said—

"What on earth are to do now?"

Harriett remained as motionless and stolid, as if Nabbitt's words had not affected her in the least.

"Objection!" she said, speaking for her husband, "what objection should we have? Spikes, get out the stone bottle and some glasses. I am sure these gentlemen must be thirsty after such hard work as they have undergone."

But Nabbitt was not of the kind of bird to be caught with such chaff.

"No, no," he said; "we will drink after we have searched the house. I suppose the stone bottle and its contents were not supplied by Daddy Muckrum—eh?

"Whoever supplied them was paid in honest coin," Harriet Spikes retorted, "and that is as much as you can say with respect to your dealings."

Nabbitt winced a little, but, suddenly drawing himself up to his full height, he pointed to the cellar.

"Search that place," he said. "I will remain here."

"Stay!" said Spikes, starting to his feet. "I have always understood that an Englishman's house is his castle. Before you search mine I call upon you to produce your warrant."

"I require no warrant," Nabbitt replied. "I am the chief officer of Bow-street, and will take all the consequences of my actions."

"Oh! let them go," cried the woman. "What does it matter to us?"

As the constables dived into the cellar she gave a signal with her hand to her husband.

Spikes snatched up a chair, and brought it down with a crash upon Nabbitt's head, and at the same moment the woman locked the cellar on the outside.

Stunned by the blow, Nabbitt reeled into the corner of the room, and fell heavily.

Spikes threw himself upon the fallen man, and, clutching him by the throat, hissed in his ear—

"Better that you had never been born than to come here to-night, for I will have your life."

Nabbitt tried to shake off the grip, and to get his right arm free.

But it was wedged down behind his back, and thus rendered useless.

"Help! help!" he cried, hoarsely, as he kicked his heels upon the floor. "Murder!"

"Aye; murder it is, and shall be," Spikes said. "You shall pay for your cleverness."

"Finish him quickly," said the fiendish woman; "and we will get away. It will take those fellows downstairs fully ten minutes to break down the door. Listen! Here they come upstairs. Be quick—quick, I say!"

Nabbitt now felt that unless he made a superhuman effort that his last moment was at hand.

He made the effort, and so far succeeded as to able to free both arms and fling them round Spikes' waist.

Then commenced a fierce and horrible struggle.

Both were strong men, and, as they rolled over and over, cursing and yelling, blood flew like water.

Mrs. Spikes now flew to her husband's aid, and, snatching up the bar of iron, which had been placed against the wall, she poised it in the air.

Nabbitt saw it quivering in the wretch's cruel, vengeful hands, and, closing his eyes, breathed out a plea for mercy.

---

## CHAPTER CLXI.

### THE STRANGE OCCUPANTS OF THE DESERTED INN.

Mrs. Corcoran backed slowly towards the window, and, having reached it, turned and looked down.

There was nothing between her and the street, and to leap from such a height might result in death, and broken limbs almost to a certainty.

"Who can this man be?" she muttered. "It is very evident that I cannot get out of this room without passing him just now. Ah! Here is a cupboard."

She darted in and closed the door as the stumbling, uncertain steps of the stranger reached the landing.

"I thought I could have found my way blindfolded all over the place," he muttered, as he entered the room. "How cold and deserted it is; but much better than Buckler's-rents, which, at present, is a little too lively for my liking.'

It was Bill Blarney who spoke.

He had all the appearance of a hunted animal upon him, and though now in comparative safety he walked as gingerly as if the floor had turned red-hot under his feet.

"My curse on them all!" he hissed. "What a narrow escape. It is a wonder that I did not get the bullet instead of Ted Nickells."

An awful thing now happened to Mrs, Corcoran.

She felt an uncontrollable desire to sneeze, and held her nose and mouth to keep it back.

The result was a terrific snort, and Bill Blarney, starting back, tripped over the bundle which the hag had prepared to take away, and measured his length upon the floor.

"What's that? Who's there?" he gasped out, as he scrambled to his feet.

Mrs. Corcoran was too wise to make any kind of reply, and held her breath until she grew purple in the face.

"I suppose it was one of those odd night sounds which cannot be accounted for," Blarney said at length. "Rats, perhaps. This old house is a perfect hunting ground for such vermin."

He shuffled his feet noisily to drive the imaginary rats away, and then walked within a short distance and peered down into the silent, deserted street.

"It's enough to make a man melancholy to think how this place has changed," he said. "Where are the old faces, the merry nights, the flowing bowl? All gone! If I was a sentimental chap I should snivel."

He then thought of the bundle he had tripped over, and crossing the room, inspected it narrowly.

"Joe must have been in a mighty hurry to get away," he muttered. "I suppose he was surprised as he was packing up. Well, I will borrow these things of him."

This was an alarming announcement to Mrs. Corcoran, and the time had been when she would have pounced down upon Bill Blarney as he stooped greedily over the bundle, and reminded him of the sharpness of her nails.

But she was weaker now, and felt compelled to resort to strategy in lieu of farce.

"It's an ill wind that blows nobody good," Blarney continued. "Here's enough to fetch a few pounds at any fence's, and perhaps I can find some skipper willing to take me across the channel without asking too many questions."

He then began to pace up and down, speaking aloud.

"If I could have foreseen what was going to happen," he said, "I would have given that hag Corcoran her quietus. I wonder where she is?"

Mrs. Corcoran could not help grinning and chuckling to herself.

"I wonder if he would have a fit if I was to jump out of the cupboard suddenly?" she thought. "Oh! dear. What is the fellow going to do now?'

Bill Blarney had thrown himself upon the floor, and in such an attitude that his burly form was so stretched across the cupboard that it was a sheer impossibility to open it without rousing him.

He had evidently made up his mind to go to sleep, which was exactly what Mrs. Corcoran did not want him to do.

She thought the matter over, and then determined upon a bold resolve.

As soon as Bill Blarney began to breathe heavily, and snore, she made a squeaking noise like a rat.

Blarney uttered an oath, and struck out with his hands.

He thought that the famished, red-eyed brutes had run over his body.

"I wish they were all at the bottom of the sea,' he growled. "Well—well, I ought not to grumble at them, perhaps, for I feel very much like a rat myself."

"I wish you were," Mrs. Corcoran thought, "and that I had my heel upon your neck."

Overcome by fatigue, Bill Blarney began to slumber heavily again.

His repose was not of that light and refreshing character which blesses the pillow of a man at peace with the world.

He spoke and muttered in his sleep, and turned and writhed as horrible dreams filled his imagination.

Mrs. Corcoran was on the horns of a delemma.

The squeaking like a rat had failed, but she felt imperature to do something to drive Bill Blarney away.

"Death! death! death!" she suddenly said, in a sepulchral tone of voice.

Bill Blarney started to his feet and clutched at his clammy brow.

"This is worse than all," he cried, wildly. "I will leave this place. It is haunted by the spirits of the dead."

Mrs. Corcoran breathed more freely, but reaction set in when she saw Bill Blarney snatch up the bundle and make for the door.

As he sped down the stairs she glided to the landing, and leaning over the balustrade uttered one word.

"Stop!"

Bill Blarney uttered a cry of terror.

His feet slipped from under him, and hurling the bundle aside, he completed the rest of the descent upon his back.

Mrs. Corcoran did not dart back into the room again, as was her intention.

Bill Blarney lay perfectly still, and the hag thought that the fall had stunned him.

"Now to get away," she muttered. "How surprised he will be when he comes round to find the bundle gone."

There could be very little doubt about that; but Mrs. Corcoran was reckoning without her host.

The ruffian was neither stunned nor senseless.

He was sitting up bewildered, and alarmed more at the sound of the voice than the fall, and his terror increased as he heard Mrs. Corcoran descending the staircase.

Bill Blarney now braced himself up to resist any attack.

Getting noiselessly upon his feet he flattened himself against the wall, and, as Mrs. Corcoran sneaked passed him, he dealt her such a blow with his fist that the amiable old lady turned a complete somersault.

She flew into the well-known parlour, scattering chairs and tables in her involuntary flight.

"I should like to see who it is," Bill Blarney said. "If it is a friend he should have been more careful than to run in my way in the dark. If an enemy woe to him."

The scoundrel suddenly remembered where Morth used to keep the steel and tinder-box, and, groping his way behind the bar, he secured both.

He listened, but not a sound disturbed the stillness of the street.

"I have nothing to fear after all, even if the light shines through the chinks in the shutters," he said; "for what is more natural than that Joe Morth should return sooner or later."

To get a light was the work of some difficulty, but at last Bill Blarney accomplished it.

In spite of his argument that the neighbours might naturally conclude that Joe Morth had returned to his dwelling, the sudden glare frightened him, and he shaded the light carefully with his hand.

With fear in his heart, and trembling in every limb, he stole into the back room.

Mrs. Corcoran, in her novel attire, lay under one of the overturned chairs, and Bill Blarney looked at her with an odd expression of doubt and wonder.

"I don't know him," he muttered, naturally taking the hag for a withered up old man. "Perhaps Joe Morth put him in to take care of the house while he was away. If so, I've done a nice thing, certainly."

Bill Blarney drew nearer and scrutinised the hag's features more attentively.

He recognised her then, and a hoarse cry of savage delight sprang from his lips.

"Old Mother Corcoran, by all that is wonderful!" he said. Ha! ha! ha! So the same notion of coming back here entered her brain as it did mine. Well, my dear, I'll leave you to come round the best you can. If you awake and recognise me, something unpleasant is sure to happen."

# SPRING-HEELED JACK,

## THE TERROR OF LONDON.

"TAKE A SWORD, IF YOU HAVE THE COURAGE OF A GENTLEMAN," SAID SPRING-HEELED JACK.

No. 44.

## CHAPTER CLXII.

### THE USE OF A HORSEWHIP—THE FIRST FALL OF SNOW.

LORD MILDENDALE rubbed his eyes as if to convince himself of the reality of what he saw.

In the centre of the crowd was the figure of a fat but extremely washed-out man, and that man was no other than the great Mr. Spiffen.

"Oh! my lord," he gasped, "look at me!"

Look at him!

Lord Mildendale could do nothing else, and in speechless wonder.

"No wonder you can't speak," Spiffen spluttered. "I have passed through an awful time, and if it hadn't been for these two watermen, who heard me shout for help, I should have been floating down the tide on the way to Yarmouth by this time."

"No doubt about that, sir," said one of the watermen, stepping forward and touching his hat.

"You shall be rewarded," Spiffen gasped. "Yes, I will pay you well as soon as I can get my hand in my pocket, but I am in a dreadful state of stickiness just now."

For once he spoke the truth.

He was one mass of mud and weeds.

"How did this happen?" demanded Lord Mildendale, forcing the words from his lips. "Tell me how you got into the water?"

"I was set upon and attacked by at least a dozen ruffians disguised as demons," Spiffen replied. "I defended my life as long as possible, but what could I do against such fearful odds? Is my coachman dead?"

"No."

"Oh!" said Mr. Spiffen, drawing down the corners of his mouth, "I had some hope that the cowardly villain might have met with his deserts. Well—well, get me some kind of conveyance, and I will go home. Good people, I thank you—yes, I thank you very much for your kind attention to me."

"Beg pardon, your honour," said the waterman; "but it seems as how you have forgotten me and my mate."

"Oh! dear me, no," Mr. Spiffen replied. "I think I can get at my pocket now. Ah! yes, here is a shilling a-piece for you."

The man looked at the coins, turned them over between his finger and thumb, and having bit them as if to test their goodness, flung them down at the feet of the liberal justice of the peace.

"Keep your money," said the waterman, "and if you ever fall into the water again, may you holler to your last gasp, and never get out."

Lord Mildendale could not help feeling a little disgusted at Mr. Spiffen's conduct.

"Come—come!" he said. "Don't let us have any ill words at such a moment as this. Here are two guineas, so now go without any more bother."

"It's a waste of money," Spiffen declared. "These fellows will only get drunk and appear before me to-morrow."

"Hush—hush!" said Lord Mildendale, who did not like the angry attitude of the people. "Let them do as they like. Here comes a man with a cart, and perhaps he will drive you to your home for a small consideration. For my own part I shall return to the Angel Inn.

After some haggling the man consented to drive Spiffen to his residence, and after promising to call early in the morning, Lord Mildendale stalked off, glad to get away from the scene.

The people of the Angel Inn, which then stood at the farther end of Tombland, were astonished, and not over glad to see him.

They were not accustomed to being roused up in the small hours of the morning; but they could make but few complaints to so important a personage as Lord Mildendale, who, after seeing that the horse he had ridden was properly stabled, went to bed.

He rose again almost as soon as daylight, for the few hours he spent in bed were restless and miserable ones.

His appetite had failed him, and thinking that a walk might bring it back he walked into the City.

The old houses, and still older churches, seemed to frown upon him as he passed.

The morning was raw and cold, and the hand of winter lay upon the slowly moving clouds.

Lord Mildendale shrugged his shoulders, and mentally remarked that snow would fall ere long.

As he turned the corner of a narrow street he saw a man walking with hasty strides towards him.

At first Lord Mildendale did not recognise this individual, but when he did, and saw that the man was no other than Namon Wallack, the colour fled from his cheeks, and left them blanched and livid.

Namon Wallack carried a horsewhip, mounted on a short stock, under his arm.

"Well met, my lord," he said. "Of all men in the world I have sought you most. I have a few words to say to you."

"I will have none with you," Lord Mildendale replied. "Out of my path, fellow!"

"Your path!" said the gipsy, curling his lips with scorn. "I have yet to learn why you should claim the king's highway as your own."

"You misconstrue the meaning of my words," Lord Mildendale returned. "I wish to have nothing to say to you."

"But you shall," cried Namon Wallack. "By the Heaven above us you shall not leave me until I have had a full explanation from your lips."

"What would you have me explain?"

"What would I have you explain?" said Namon Wallack, in a voice hoarse with passion. "Dare you ask me such a question? Who was it that came skulking to my caravan with murder in his heart—who followed me here and set fire to my show?"

"Dare you say that my hands did the deed?" Lord Mildendale thundered.

"I dare, because it is the truth."

"The lie in your teeth!"

"Take it back, and with the present of my contempt," Namon Wallack retorted. "Listen! Nay, start not back, for you shall listen. Tell me that you never heard of a woman named Lanoni, and lie again?"

"I have heard of her—a vagabond queen of a vagabond people."

"I take your answer for what it is worth," Namon Wallack said. "What she has suffered at your hands is already known to us, for Corder's child is under our protection."

"Well," said Lord Mildendale, "if you know so much, why trouble me with so many questions?"

"I spoke of Lanoni," Wallack returned; "and now I will come to her daughter, who listened to your poisoned lies. You married her, and she bore you a child—a boy. Where is your wife? Where is your son? Nay, I will ask you more.

Where is the fiend in the shape of a woman you hired to slay the wife you swore to love and cherish?"

Lord Mildendale stepped back and smote his brow.

For a moment he looked as if he were going to swoon, but recovered himself as quickly.

"You talk like a madman," he said.

"I talk like the man you wronged years ago," hissed Namon Wallack. "You destroyed my heart's best hopes. You robbed me by fraud and lying of the woman who would have made me happy, and not content with this, you seek to ruin me. Nay, you seek my life."

"Your life? You seem to value it highly."

"As you doubtless do your honour."

"Again, I say, let me pass," Lord Mildendale said. "You see that I wear a sword at my side, therefore tempt me not to use it."

"My weapon against yours," Namon Wallack said.

He swung the whip round and brought it heavily over Lord Mildendale's shoulders.

Stung to the quick, Lord Mildendale laid his hand upon his sword.

Before he could use it the lash of the whip curled about his face.

Blow followed blow, and Lord Mildendale, maddened with pain, slipped and fell.

"Curse you!" he cried, shielding his head with his arms, "you shall suffer for this."

"And you shall never know a moment's peace until you have made full atonement for your mis-spent life," Namon Wallack replied, as he twisted the lash of the whip round his hand. "There are marks upon your face, my lord, which will not wear off in a hurry; go, show them to your friends, and tell them they were inflicted by me."

So saying, he walked haughtily away, leaving Lord Mildendale almost beside himself with pain and fury.

He was unconscious that several people had gathered round him, and paid no heed whatever to their enquiries, but walked back to the Angel Inn like a man in a dream.

His appearance created no end of gossip among the servants; but he pushed them rudely aside when they pointed to the blood upon his face, and asked what they could do for him.

"Nothing," he said, savagely. "It is a mere accident, nothing more. I will go to my room, and let no one interrupt me unless I ring."

In about an hour, Lord Mildendale made his appearance again.

He had endeavoured to remove the traces left upon his features by the whip; but they remained red and swoollen momentoes of what he had undergone.

Lord Mildendale breakfasted, or rather went through the farce of eating a meal; and having paid his bill, departed for Mr. Spiffen's residence.

He took a roundabout way to escape observation; and, striking as quickly as posible through the City, turned into a road from which some shady lanes flanked by woodlands, branched off in all directions.

The air had grown colder and colder, and snow was falling heavily.

It was the first snow of the season, and so early had it come, that poor people, to whom luxury and plentiful fuel were strangers, shook their heads, and groaned at the prospect of a long winter.

Lord Mildendale now began to repent that he had come on foot.

The spot was a lonely one, and there was an appearance about it which he did not like.

He had almost made up his mind to turn back towards the City, when he heard himself called by name.

At first he could hardly believe his ears; but a repetition of the voice convinced him of its reality.

"Who calls?" he shouted.

"I do."

His lordship drew his sword as Spring-Heeled Jack appeared, as if from the very snow-covered earth.

But the next instant a blade flashed like a streak of lightning before his eyes, and his own went hurtling up into the air.

Spring-Heeled Jack caught the sword as it descended, and placing it lengthwise with his, approached the dumbfounded nobleman.

"I did not seek to take an advantage of you," Spring-Heeled Jack said, "and I am sorry that you did of me. Now we are on equal terms, and if you have the courage of a gentleman you will take a sword, I care not which; but I think that you will find my rapier the better of the two."

"I'll not fight with you," Lord Mildendale said, starting back. "Come to me as a man, and, if you have cause to quarrel with me I will give you satisfaction."

"As you did to the gipsy this morning," Spring-Heeled Jack said, sneeringly. "I was there to see, and, oh! it was a glorious sight. It was well done and richly deserved."

"Give me my sword and leave me," Lord Mildendale said. "I know that you are mortal, but with some gift or secret unknown to mortals."

"Ha! ha! ha!" laughed Spring-Heeled Jack.

The woods rang again with the wild, unearthly sound.

"If I am mortal I have but the strength and cunning of a man," he said. "Come, take a sword, and use it like a gentleman."

"I will not face you in combat," Lord Mildendale said. "Go back to the fiend who sent you to curse the world."

"I will go," Spring-Heeled Jack said, "and perchance I may send you a man who has just cause to cross his sword with yours. Here, take your weapon."

Spring-Heeled Jack vanished like a figure in a dream as Lord Mildendale stooped to pick up his sword.

"This is too horrible!" his lordship gasped. "He is not mortal, but an avenging spirit."

He hastened to quit the lonely path, but yet another obstacle appeared in his way.

He had not gone very far before he beheld Ralph Ashton emerge from behind a giant oak, and confront him face to face.

## CHAPTER CLXIII.

### SIR ROLAND ASHTON TRAVELS EASTWARD.

GUILTY men are ever unhappy.

The petty thief trembles at the sight of a constable, the burglar trembles as he parts with his ill-gotten gains, and the murderer at large knows no rest.

The spectre of his victim haunts him, and the gibbet dances before his eyes morn, noon, and night.

Men have gone on for years in this way, until they have thought themselves safe from all save the pangs of conscience, but blood cries aloud, and the day comes when the prison door closes to be-opened for a wretch condemned to pay the dread penalty of the law.

Sir Roland Ashton believed in what some people are pleased to call fate, but he was continually cursing it when things went wrong with him.

It was so pitch dark that, as he fled, he could see no object until he was close upon it.

He tripped and stumbled over all sorts of things that happened to be in his way, and more than once he came down heavily.

But he must go on.

There was no rest for him.

He thought of Joe Morth's body lying so still under the pall of night.

Day would come, and when the truth was known every man round about Cockleton would be up in arms. Through brake and bramble, over holly-hedge, across ploughed fields, the earth clogging his feet, he went, torn and bleeding, and never stopping until the black curtain was rent with a seam of greyish hue.

Then Sir Roland Ashton came to a standstill.

He was knee-deep in wet grass, and found that he was standing on the banks of a sluggish river.

It was bitterly cold, and the white-capped clouds, sweeping down earthwards in ragged masses, promised a storm.

The day came on apace, and the fugitive gazed across the dreary landscape.

As far as the eye could reach no human habitation was in sight.

Here, a gaunt mill, creaking and groaning, there, a slimy sluice-gate, through which the pent-up water oozed and gurgled; but no shelter, not even a herdsman's hut, though there were hundreds of cattle grazing on the marshes.

Sir Roland Ashton turned his face to the east, but strength had almost failed him now.

His body ached and burned, as if he had been thrashed with a cudgel, and a singing noise rang in his ears.

"If I could but see a house," he said, with a groan. "Oh! to lay my head down under some roof."

He kept on until he felt fit to drop; but he exercised all his will, for now peeping through the mist were the chimneys and roof-tops of a distant town.

Again he stopped to rest and to reflect,

He gazed down at his attire, and saw what a change had come over his personal appearance in a few hours.

He looked for all the world like a beggar; but this fact did not trouble him, but rather encouraged him to enter the town boldly.

The river path now grew wider, and a few boats and barges lay moored to huge wooden posts of immense strength, and driven deep into the earth.

Sir Roland paused, and he looked down upon the deck of a small vessel.

A man, whistling and singing, was mopping the deck right merrily, and seemed to enjoy the task, in spite of the rawness of the morning.

"Hullo!" he said, as he caught sight of Sir Roland, "you are in a nice pickle. Been sleeping out all night, I suppose."

"Not the first time by many," Sir Roland replied, with a weary sigh.

"Well, that's hard lines," said the sailor, as he twisted the mop handle, and sent the water flying in a circle.

"It strikes me you haven't chosen a nice part of the country. These marshes are full of fever and ague. Ugh!"

"I know them," Sir Roland said, shuddering. "What town is that in the distance, my friend?"

"Lincoln."

"Thank you," Sir Roland said. "I will make my way there as quickly as possible."

"Come back!" the sailor shouted. "I suppose you can drink some hot coffee?"

"Yes, and feel grateful for it."

"Then run down that ladder, and I will get you a canful out of the galley."

As Sir Roland reached the deck, the ruddy and bronzed sailor looked at him strangely.

"What is that upon your coat-sleeve?" he said, pointing to a dark stain.

Sir Roland started in spite of himself.

"It is blood!" the sailor said, suspiciously.

"And my own," Sir Roland returned. "I lost my way, and fell several times."

"That may be so," the sailor replied; "but—but— Well, to cut matters short, I don't want you here, and won't have you here. Go on shore again."

"As you will," Sir Roland replied. "But why this change in you?"

"Well, to tell you the truth," said the sailor, "I don't care to harbour a man who comes to me with blood bespattered all over his clothes."

"But I have explained the circumstance."

"Not to my satisfaction," the sailor said, pointing to the ladder. "You had better go before I detain you and hand you over to a constable."

Sir Roland Ashton parted his lips and showed his teeth as he climbed up the ladder.

He went his way without saying a word, thinking it wiser to do so, though his heart was filled with rage and malice.

He now deemed that it would be unsafe for him to stay at Lincoln longer than to purchase a few necessaries to keep body and soul together.

Wherever he went he was received with suspicion, and he felt much relieved when he had left the good old city behind him.

Eating of the food he had purchased, he tottered wearily down the road, examining the mile-stones carefully, for of all places he wished to avoid now was the path that led to London.

He passed the whole of that day walking and resting at intervals.

It seemed to the baronet, though it might have been fancy, that the poorest of men he met on the road avoided him.

Even the very tramps appeared to give him a wide berth, and once an old crone, bent nearly double with age, pointed a shrivelled finger at him, and gave vent to a loud, mocking laugh.

The sun was setting with a yellow glare and amid a bank of heavy clouds when Sir Roland Ashton stopped before a cottage.

He chose it on account of its poverty-stricken appearance, and argued with himself that its inmates would be only too glad to shelter him for the night in consideration of a shilling or even a lesser coin.

Sir Roland knocked at the door, and waited patiently until somebody, moving very slowly, shuffled down the passage.

At last an old man appeared, and, shading his eyes with his hand, said—

"Ah! a stranger. I thought it was Tom at first, but I might have known that it was too early for the waggon."

"The waggon?" Sir Roland said. "If one passes here pray tell me whither it is bound."

"My son has charge of the team," the old man said, stretching out his arm to the east. "Well, what may you require?"

"I had some idea of asking whether you could accommodate me with a lodging," Sir Roland replied; "but as I wish to get along the road as quickly as possible, I will endeavour to make a bargain with your son."

"Come in, then," said the old man, holding open the door. "I expect that my son will be here in about an hour's time, and you are welcome to rest in the meanwhile."

The cottage was poorly but neatly furnished, and Sir Roland, having partaken of some tea which the occupier offered him, felt almost cheerful, and made himself extremely agreeable.

At last came the sound of heavy wheels rumbling in the distance, and presently the old man, snatching up a candle from the table, ran to the door.

"Halloa! father," cried a cheery voice. "Here you are as usual. Glad that you look so well. You see that I am punctual to the moment?"

"You always are, Tom," the old man replied. "Got a full load this time?"

"Pretty well, but not a single passenger. The fast coaches are the things for people nowadays."

"Break-neck things them coaches," the waggoner's father replied. "I should be sorry to trust my old bones on one. Well, Tom, a man is here, and wants to travel with you."

"I must be careful who I take up," Tom replied. "There's been a dreadful scene of murder and robbery."

"You don't say so! Where?"

"At Cockleton."

"Bless my heart! Tell me all about it," said the old man, trembling with excitement.

"Why, all I know about the affair can be told in a very few words," the sturdy team-man replied. "It seems that two rascals attempted to commit a robbery at the Two-necked Swan—"

"Ah! I knew the house forty years ago—"

"Don't interrupt, father," said the younger man. "Well, let me see where I had got to. Oh! I know. The rascals were locked up, but they escaped, and one murdered the other."

"We live in sad—sad times," the old man said, wringing his hands. "Somehow, I wish you were not going on the road to-night."

"Bah!" ejaculated the son, as he stretched out his strong arms. "I should just like to meet with the scoundrel. I'd break nearly every bone in his body, and then hand him over to justice."

Sir Roland Ashton overheard this conversation with a hundred conflicting emotions rushing through his heart and brain.

One thing was very certain. He must get away from the locality as quickly as possible.

Perhaps, after all, the waggoner had not received any description of him, and Sir Roland, walking boldly up to the open door, accosted the waggoner, and joined freely in the conversation.

"I heard something about what you have just told your good father," he said, "but I paid little attention to it."

"It's true enough," the team-man said; "for I passed through Cockleton about noon and found the place in a terrible state of excitement. Stay! did I say that one of the rascals had murdered the other? I should have said he attempted to murder him."

Sir Roland made no reply, but he found much food for thought in the last words.

"So you are the man who wants a lift?" said Tom, after a pause.

"Yes, as far as Lynn, if you can take me on reasonable terms."

"Well," said the waggoner, "as you seem to be as poor as most of us, I will take you there for three shillings."

"When will you reach the town?"

"Some time to-morrow. I can't be certain to an hour or two, as the bulk of my packages will be left on the way."

"I agree," said Sir Roland. "I did not ask you the question because I am in a hurry, but out of curiosity's sake."

In less than an hour Sir Roland Ashton was on his way to Lynn.

Snug and warm, and half-buried in the straw at the bottom of the waggon, he fell asleep.

He awoke on hearing a confused sound as of half-a-dozen people talking at once.

"I have only one man here," he heard the waggoner say, "and you can have a look at him if you like. Whoa! Magic—stand still, Thunder! One moment, gentlemen, and I will show you the way with the lantern."

## CHAPTER CLIV.

### DADDY MUCKRUM RUNS THE LENGTH OF HIS TETHER.

THE constables in the cellar had just pounced upon Daddy Muckrum, who fell half-fainting and shrieking in a corner, when they heard the scuffle and the cries for help above their heads.

Leaving their prisoner handcuffed and comparatively secure, they bounded up the stairs, but only to find the door locked.

It was when they began to batter and kick at the panels that Mrs. Spikes stood over Nabbitt with the iron bar.

A moment's reflection caused her to stay the impending blow.

"Let him go, and bolt for your life," she whispered to her husband. "He is too much exhausted to follow us."

Spikes took his wife's advice, and, leaping to his feet, rushed towards the door.

But here he was met by the barrel of a pistol for the constables outside had heard something o. the uproar, and were now hastening to the rescue.

The weapon exploded in Spikes' face, and, with a yell of agony that rung through the house, he fell with a crash.

Catchpole and another man dashed into the room, and, scarcely deigning to notice the woman, raised Nabbitt from the floor, and then released the men from the cellar.

"Thank you," he said, as he wiped away the foam which had gathered on his lips. "I shall remember this in my list for promotions. If either of you have anything to drink let me have it, for mercy's sake."

"I have a small flask with me," Catchpole said, feebly. "I know it is against orders, but—"

Nabbitt snatched it from his hand, and emptied its contents down his throat.

Then he turned to where Mrs. Spikes stood, defiant and still holding the bar of iron in her hand.

"Secure that virago," he said. "She tried to murder me."

"I saved your life," she said, backing against

the wall. "Don't touch me, or one life at least will answer for it."

Catchpole, to show his bravery, made a rush at the woman, but received such a swinging bang on the head for his pains that he whirled round and flopped down on the floor like a lopsided teetotum.

But Nabbitt was not to be denied of his prey, and Mrs. Spikes was soon secured and handcuffed.

"Do your worst now," she said, stolidly. "I have had my day. You have killed a man worth ten times your number, and I care not when the the end comes."

"Phew!" said Nabbitt. "This is about the warmest work I have ever experienced."

He seemed so overjoyed with his timely rescue, that he actually shook hands with Catchpole, and called him a good fellow.

"Any news from outside?" Nabbitt asked, turning to the other constable.

"No; all is quiet, sir."

"Well," the chief constable returned, "I think we have done quite enough for to-night. Take care of that woman, and that—that—old villain," he added, pointing to Daddy Muckrum who had been dragged from the cellar, and was huddled up in a corner. "I will follow presently."

"You must call my carriage," Mrs. Spikes said, smiling grimly.

"What do you mean?" demanded Catchpole. "Here, come along, and don't let us have any of your nonsense."

"You shall either take me in a hackney coach or carry me," Mrs. Spikes returned, "for not an inch will I budge of my own free will."

Daddy Muckrum seemed to be of the same opinion, or perhaps he was powerless to move, for when a constable jerked him to his feet, he went down like a lump of lead again.

"To put an end to all this bother," said Nabbitt, "call a hackney couch. The expense will not be much, and perhaps that will be the better way of getting the prisoners to Bow-street."

After some trouble and delay a hackney coach was found.

The driver was three-parts drunk, but he pulled himself together when he saw who required his services.

The journey to Bow-street was not a particularly delightful one.

The vehicle jolted and bumped to an alarming extent.

Mrs. Spikes laughed hoarsely, and raved at intervals; and Daddy Muckrum whined, cursed, pleaded, and prayed in a breath.

But at last the police station was reached, and the prisoners were bundled unceremoniously into the office.

The charges were entered in the usual way, and Catchpole touched Mrs. Spikes on the shoulder as a gentle intimation that he was going to lock her up.

A great change had now come over her.

The hard lines in her face had softened and her eyes swam with tears.

"You will let me see my husband's dead body before it is buried?" she said. "I am sure you will not deny me that."

"I don't know anything about it," Catchpole replied; "but it strikes me that you will have to make a representation to the Home Secretary. But where's the good of looking at him now that he is dead and gone, I should like to know? Come along. I have something else to do, besides talking to you."

As the ponderous door of the cell closed behind the wretched woman, she sat down and buried her face in her hands.

Some slight relic of the better part of her nature still remained in her, and she began to think of what might have been, but could never be now.

Like all such miserable creatures fallen so lowly in crime, she had been good and innocent once.

She thought of those days with a bitterness that racked her heart and brain.

It was too late now.

The man she had loved in her strange way was dead, and there was no prospect before her but the gallows.

She knew she was a doomed woman, that her last act would only harden the stern hand of the law, but it was hard to die so shameful a death, and she sat pondering on it until her aching eyes closed in fitful slumber.

Mr. Nabbitt did not appear to be in any particular hurry about returning to Bow-street.

Perhaps he called upon a few convivial friends, to narrate to them, with a few additions, the adventures of the eventful night.

At all events, it was four o'clock in the morning when he entered the office.

His gait was rather unsteady, and his eyes shone with a peculiar light.

"Prisoners all right?" he asked.

"As trivets," Catchpole replied. "May I go off duty now, sir?"

"Go off duty?" Nabbitt repeated, glaring at him. "Of course not. How dare you think of such a thing, much more speak about it?"

Catchpole groaned.

"He's in another of his beastly tempers," he said, to himself. "My eye! ain't he been keeping up his spirits. I should like to be suffering from half his complaint."

"Cashpole," said Nabbitt, with a hiccup between his words, "did you notice anything p'culiar about the sky?"

"No, sir."

"That shows that you are not a—hic—a man of obser—hic—vation. There are two moons."

"Two what?" demanded Catchpole, aghast.

"Two moons, you—hic—ass."

"Oh! yes," said Catchpole. "Now I come to think about it there was two; but if there was forty I shouldn't trouble my head about them."

With this philosophical remark Catchpole turned his head aside to take a sly drink from the bottle which he had taken great pains to replenish.

Nabbitt was down on him like a cartload of bricks.

"Cashpole," he said, trying to look solemn out of one eye, "I was just about to enter you for promotion, but after that—that—never mind what—I can't find a word for it just now—I'll report you for being drunk; and so you are—silly drunk, and—"

Down went Nabbitt's head upon his arms, and he began to snore vehemently.

"I'll let him be," Catchpole thought. "He will forget all about it by the morning. Just to while away the time I'll go and have a look at the prisoners."

Taking a bunch of keys in his hand Catchpole went into that part of the building where the cells were situated.

They were built in a double row, one side being for male and the other for female captives.

"They're quiet enough, at all events," he muttered. "Well, that shows their good sense, for what's the good of kicking up a row when nothing can be got by it."

In each of the cell doors was a small iron wicket, opening by a catch-latch outside.

"Now then, Daddy," said Catchpole, grinning. "I'll have a look at you to begin with."

He opened the wicket as noiselessly as possible, and turned the light of his lantern into the cell.

Daddy Muckrum was stretched at full length upon the bench.

His face was downwards, and apparently resting upon his manacled hands.

"Turn on your side, old fellow," said Catchpole. "You'll find sleeping that way much more comfortable. If you want the cramp or the nightmare you had better keep as you are."

But Daddy Muckrum did not move or speak.

"I suppose he knows best," he said; but, hang me! if there isn't something peculiar about him. Perhaps I had better go and rouse him up."

Catchpole grumbled at the trouble, but finally entered the cell.

He shook Daddy Muckrum roughly by the shoulder, but awakened no response from him.

"Why—why," the constable gasped, "he's run the length of his tether at last. As sure as I am a sinner, he is dead!"

There could be very little doubt about it, and Catchpole, running out of the cell, endeavoured to rouse Mr. Nabbitt.

"It's all right," mumbled the chief constable. "Wake me at nine. I've got a headache."

"But, sir—but—please attend to me," Catchpole stammered. "One of the prisoners is dead—Muckrum is dead. Please to say what I am to do."

Mr. Nabbitt started up and fixed a pair of glassy eyes upon the frightened constable.

"Dead—dead! Who's dead?" he gasped, in a tone of voice implying that his tongue was as dry as a lime-kiln.

"Muckrum, sir."

Mr. Nabbitt nearly fell off his stool, and only saved himself by clutching at the edge of the desk.

"Dead—dead!" he repeated. "Who killed him? Speak, you villain, or I will knock your head off your shoulders."

"Nobody killed him," Catchpole replied, backing precipitately. "I found him dead in his cell, and I suppose that he died a natural death."

Mr. Nabbitt could come to no other conclusion when he viewed the body.

"Well, he's better off than he would have been," he remarked. "Close the door, and come back with me. No good can be done by staying here, and looking at such a horrible corpse."

## CHAPTER CLV.

### CONTAINS A SHORT ACCOUNT OF A DUEL.

LORD MILDENDALE'S chest heaved as he and Ralph Ashton stood face to face.

Ralph's face had more of sorrow than of anger in its expression, and for a moment he stood looking at the nobleman without speaking.

"My lord," he said, at last, "we meet again, and in a place where you least expected."

"I grant you the truth of that speech," Lord Mildendale replied. "What would you have with me, gaol-bird? Do you surrender?"

"Surrender!"

Ralph Ashton laughed.

"I know the wretch you are in league with," Lord Mildendale said. "I know now who released you from prison."

"Indeed!" Ralph Ashton said. "Pray, who was it?"

"The perdition-born scoundrel known as Spring Heeled Jack!"

"I should imagine, by the way you speak, that you have had an interview with him."

"You know I have."

"I know! Most noble lord, you give me the credit of double sight."

"I give you the credit of being even a baser villain than the wretch who tempted me to fight him in this wood but a few minutes back," Lord Mildendale replied.

"Tempted you to fight?" said Ralph Ashton. "But surely you did not play the part of a coward?"

Lord Mildendale bit his under-lip.

"It matters nothing to you what sort of part I played," he hissed. "I will hold no parley with you, felon that you are. In less than an hour the officers of justice shall be upon your track."

Lord Mildendale took a few strides forward, but Ralph Ashton barred the way with his outstretched arm.

"My lord," he said, quietly, "since you would not fight Spring-Heeled Jack, you must fight me. You have insulted me—you have called me felon, when you know full well that I am nothing of the kind. Now, by the Heaven above us! you shall answer to me. Defend yourself, or I will run my sword through your body!"

## CHAPTER CLVI.

### AT BAY.

BILL BLARNEY approached the window by which he and Mrs. Corcoran had entered the Bull in Top-Boots, with the intention of departing from the place as quickly as possible.

Once he turned back into the room, muttering—

"Shall I kill her?"

Then it struck him that the hag might be dead already, or would probably die, from the effects of the blow he had dealt her, and he turned away, thinking that he had better let matters remain as they were.

Just as he reached the window, a disc of light flashed upon it.

Bill Blarney staggered back as if he had been struck by a bullet.

He knew that the light came from a lantern such as the officers of the law carried, and his heart thumped violently against his side.

The ruffian crouched down and listened.

He could hear no sound whatever, and then a hundred superstitious fears began to haunt his mind.

Bill Blarney began to think that the spirit c some murdered victim had returned to the scen of crime.

But all such notions were entirely upset.

Somebody sneezed.

"You are at it again, you ass!" growled a voice. "What is the use of us prowling about here in list slippers, if you keep on playing tunes with your nasal organ?"

"I couldn't help it, indeed, I couldn't!"

"Catchpole and Grabham by all that's horrible and unlucky," Bill Blarney growled, as he crouched still lower down against the wall.

"Put the slide over that light," Grabham said. "You're flashing it all over the neighbourhood, as if you wanted everybody to see us."

"Well," Catchpole replied, "what if they did. We're on a lawful errand, ain't we?"

"Lawful! Ha! ha!" Grabham said, laughing. "I don't think that we said anything about coming here to Mr. Nabbitt, did we?"

"Hang him!" said Catchpole, savagely. "He kept me up the whole of last night, and had the cheek to tell me that if I had looked after Daddy Muckrum he would be alive now."

"So Daddy is dead," Bill Blarney gasped, as large beads of cold perspiration started to his brow. "I almost wish I was."

"It strikes me that we are only wasting time," Grabham remarked. "If we are to have a look round the house, now or never is the time. I wonder what Joe Morth would think if he could see us!"

"It ain't what he'd think, but what he'd say and do," Catchpole remarked. "I shouldn't much care to see him shove his head through that window."

"Nor I," said Grabham; "and yet I've got an idea that we shall be sure to find somebody in the house."

"If I thought so," Catchpole returned, "I'd take jolly good care to keep outside it. Bah! who do you think would be fool enough to come here? Shall I give you a leg up, Grabham?"

"No. I'd rather do it for you. You are always behind when the least danger is to be feared, and in front when there is anything to share."

"If I stay here," Bill Blarney muttered, "the fat, over-fed hounds will fall on me. What is to be done?"

A sudden thought struck him.

Removing his boots, he slipped back into the so-called parlour, and, raising Mrs. Corcoran in his arms, returned to the window, and placed the unconscious lady directly under it.

Bill Blarney could not help grinning and chuckling to himself as he did this.

"She shall have the full benefit of their weight," he said. "Whoever comes in first will be almost certain to kick against her, and then there will be no end of a row. It will give me time to find some place of concealment."

He darted back into the darkness as Catchpole replied to Grabham.

"All right," he said. "I don't mind going in first so long as you follow me quickly."

"Which, of course, I will do," Grabham replied. "Now then, up you go. Lor'! how heavy you are, to be sure. Hold on to the window-sill, or I shall let you go."

"I never was a good hand at climbing," said Catchpole, who was puffing and blowing. "I shall be mortally savage if we don't find something after all this trouble. Oh—oh! All right; I shall be through in a second."

Mr. Catchpole found more than he expected.

His feet came in contact with Mrs. Corcoran with no light pressure, and had the effect of restoring her to consciousness.

"Who's that?" she cried out.

Catchpole's hair stood on end, for Mrs. Corcoran had now seized him by the legs, and was holding on to him like grim death.

"What's the matter?" demanded Grabham, from the outside.

"I—I don't exactly know," Catchpole gasped, "but something has got hold of me."

Grabham had a good deal of agility in his composition when he chose to make use of it.

He made a spring at the window, and, making sure his hold, climbed through.

A shriek now came from Mrs. Corcoran's lips.

She saw her peril now, for she recognised the voices of the constables, and, relaxing her hold, made a dash for the staircase and vanished in the upper regions of the house.

Just as she did so Grabham removed the dark slide of his lantern, and flashed the light along the passage.

"Did you hear that shriek?" said Catchpole, whose features were as white as a turnip.

"Hear it?" Grabham returned. "Do you think I am stone deaf? But where is the party as made it?"

"Grabham," Catchpole said, trembling so violently that he leaned against the wall for support, "I don't—don't think it was a human being that laid hold of me, and gave that horrid shriek."

"What was it then?"

"Some wild animal," Catchpole replied. "I felt its claws stick into my legs."

"Why don't you say it was the devil, and have done with it at once," Grabham growled.

This was an idea which had not occurred to Mr. Catchpole, and he was not at all loth to adopt it.

"Perhaps it was," he said, in a hushed tone of voice. "This is just the sort of place he might come to to look after some of his friends."

"You're going a little wrong in the upper story, my friend," said Grabham, tapping Catchpole smartly over the head with the lantern. "That noise was either made by a woman or a madman. Come, follow me, and we will soon see who it was."

"I'd rather not," Catchpole said. "I'm good for a tuzzle with a man I can grapple with, but I can't agree to fight with mad coves or women as howl like wild wolves."

"You're a miserable coward," Grabham replied, contemptuously. "Well, I will go alone, and if I find anything I will keep it. Joe Morth must have left a lot of treasure knocking about."

"Hold hard a minute," Catchpole cried, "my lantern has gone out."

"So much the better," Grabham replied, grinning. "If you wait for me in the dark you may have another visit from the party who took such a fancy to you before."

Catchpole smiled an oily kind of smile.

"Of course, when I said I was afraid I was only joking," he remarked. "I did it to see how you wonld take it. I'll go with you, my dear old pal."

"Dear old pal be blowed," Grabham growled. "You'd leave me in the lurch quick enough if you had the chance."

"No—no. You can't think so bad of me as that."

"I think that you are bad enough to do anything mean and sneaking."

"And has it come to this?" moaned Catchpole, rolling up his eyes. "Did my ears deceive me?"

"No, they didn't."

"This is hard—very hard!" Catchpole said, shaking his head mournfully.

"You'll find my fist harder, if you don't shut up," Grabham returned.

"I know it; I have felt it before," Catchpole-observed. "I will not leave you, Grabham, and I forgive any unkind words which you may have said to me."

"Jigger your forgiveness!" said Grabham. "Who wants it? I don't, I'm sure. Well, come along. We will run our eyes over the place, and we can soon tell whether it will pay us to stay. Hullo! what's this?"

"It looks like a bundle."

"It is a bundle," Grabham replied. "Dash my buttons! we've hit upon a prize. I was right when I said that we should find somebody here."

Bill Blarney had leaped over the bar and taken refuge under the counter.

As he heard Grabham speak he suppressed a hoarse cry of rage and dismay that rose unbidden into his throat.

"I shall be nabbed as sure as eggs are eggs," he said. "Curse these dogs! Why did they want to come prowling about here at such a time? Oh! that I had a weapon to defend myself with; I would show them that there is life and pluck left in me yet."

The scoundrel glared savagely into the darkness, and moved his hands about in the hope of coming upon a cudgel or a bar of iron.

But he could find nothing, and there was no other alternative for him but to wait the course of events.

"Shall we search the upper or lower part of the house first?" Catchpole said.

"Oh! the lower by all means," Grabham replied. "Just hold the lantern while I see if my pistols are ready for use."

Catchpole took the lantern, but his hands tembled so violently that he let it fall, and as a matter of course, the light was extinguished.

Grabham made a blow in the darkness at the head of his careless companion.

"Why—why do I suffer myself to be tormented by an idiot?" he gasped. "A nice thing this. If there should be any of the old gang here they could pounce on us, and give us pepper before we knew what was the matter."

"I couldn't help it," Catchpole whined. "Oh! lor', what shall we do? I feel as if I could sink through the floor."

"I wish Spring-Heeled Jack would fly away with you," said Grabham, grinding his teeth furiously. "Here's a nice mess! No light, and the certainty that there is somebody in the house. There is nothing to be done. We must go back and make ourselves scarce as quickly as possible."

Catchpole entered into the spirit of this idea with all his heart.

He was feeling his way by the wall when he heard a most peculiar sound.

It was like the snort of a man who had held his breath until he could hold it no longer, and he was certain that it did not come from Grabham.

"Get your pistols ready," he said. "There is somebody coming behind us."

Grabham darted forward, and coming in contact with a sharp angle of the wall, not only floored himself, but knocked Catchpole down into the bargain.

Grabham was first upon his feet.

All sorts of strange and highly-coloured lights danced before his eyes, and it seemed to him that he had been struck by a brick.

"What was it? Who did it?" he howled, as he snatched a pistol from his belt. "Keep your head down; I'm going to fire."

This warning was perfectly unnecessary. Catchpole lay spread out upon the floor as flat as a turtle, and he had not the slightest intention of moving so long as there was the least danger of his being molested.

Bang!

Grabham thought he saw a human form by the flash that came from the pistol.

"Surrender to the law," he cried. "Get up, Catchpole. Sound an alarm in the street? I must and will know who is here."

Catchpole got up, and by way of sounding an alarm, screamed out "Fire!" at the top of his voice.

This so incensed his brother officer that he drew another pistol with the full intention of blowing Catchpole's brains out, but remembering that he had no other weapon to defend himself with, he postponed the interesting operation.

Mr. Grabham had caught sight of Bill Blarney.

The hunted ruffian, taking advantage of the fact that the constables had no light to guide them, darted from his hiding-place and made for the staircase.

His intention was to reach the roof, and then get clear away by means of the adjoining houses.

"Hold hard!" said Catchpole; "I think we can get a light, after all. I have a phosphorus match in my pocket."

"Why didn't you say so before?"

"Because I didn't know it."

"If I had such a head as yours I would sell it for firewood," growled Grabham. "Here, give me the match. If you try to ignite it, you'll be sure to make a muddle of the job."

The so-called phosphorus match had just been invented, and Grabham, after rubbing it first on his cord smalls and then on the wall, produced a fitful bluish light.

"Here you are!" he said, excitedly. "Open the lantern. Now, then, make haste, you idiot! or I shall burn my fingers."

Great was the joy of the constables when their lanterns were relighted.

"That fellow went upstairs," Grabham cried, excitedly; "and if we don't have the darbies upon his wrists in less than ten minutes it will be no fault of mine."

"Nor of mine," Catchpole squeaked, feebly.

Grabham led the way, with a loaded pistol in his hand.

They ran into the different rooms, flashing their lanterns high and low.

For some time the search seemed as if it would prove fruitless, but Catchpole suddenly saw something move amid a heap of rubbish in a corner.

"Look there!" he said, clutching Grabham's arm.

"It's a man!" Grabham yelled. "Have him out!"

Mrs. Corcoran came out accordingly, and after she had been shaken up until her few remaining teeth chattered, and had been knocked on the head until she was half silly, she was kindly requested to give an account of herself.

The constables took her to be a man, and addressed her as one.

"Now, then, old fellow," said Grabham, "just tell us how you got here, and what is your little game."

"I'm poor and homeless," said Mrs. Corcoran, assuming the whining tone of a beggar, "so I crept in here for shelter. I didn't think I should be doing any harm—indeed, I didn't."

"No harm in tying up bundles of rich clothing and trinkets which have been torn from the backs of murdered men—eh?" thundered Grabham, in a tone of virtuous indignation. "Catchpole, fit him with a pair of handcuffs. We'll soon see if he wasn't up to any harm."

"No—no!" cried Mrs. Corcoran, shrinking back.

"But I say yes."

"Hush!" said Mrs. Corcoran, holding up her hand. "If you are merciful to me I will tell you something you will be glad to know."

"Well, what is it?"

"There's a man in this house who you have been looking for a long time."

"What is his name?" Grabham demanded. "Tell us no lies or it will be the worse for you."

"His name is Bill Blarney," Mrs. Corcoran replied. "He passed through this room not a minute before you came in."

These words completely staggered the constables.

"If this is the truth," said Grabham, "you shall have your liberty, but if you have lied you shall pass the rest of your days in prison."

"It is the truth," Mrs. Corcoran declared. "Listen! Don't you hear? He is forcing open the trap-door that leads to the roof at this very moment."

Leaving Mrs. Corcoran to do as she pleased, the constables dashed forward and just caught a glimpse of Bill Blarney's disappearing legs.

Grabham pressed his finger on the trigger.

The pistol missed fire, and the constable uttering a curse on the mischance, scrambled up to the roof, and shouted to Catchpole to follow him.

But Bill Blarney had got a fair start, and made the best use of it.

The tiles were old and greasy.

They cracked and slipped under his feet as he sped along, hotly pursued by the constables.

Presently the ruffian received an unexpected check.

He came to an opening where a court divided the houses, and halted, panting and glaring like a tiger.

He dodged behind a ruinous stack of chimneys, and dislodging some of the bricks, hurled them with terrible force at the constables.

Grabham threw himself down flat, and proceeded to refill the powder-pan of his pistol, while Catchpole, with bricks flying over and around his head in the most uncomfortable fashion, danced about screaming for help.

Bill Blarney was losing strength.

He knew that he could not hold out much longer, and finding that he inflicted no harm with the missiles, for his aim was at fault, he determined to reserve his waning energy for one last effort.

"I'll surrender quietly if only one of you will advance," he said. "Grabham, I give myself up to you; but if Catchpole comes within my reach I will brain him."

"Very well," Grabham replied; "but play me no tricks. I have a pistol here, and if you lift a hand against me I will send a bullet into your skull."

Bill Blarney folded his arms as a sign of his submission, and with a cry of exultation Grabham leaped forward to capture his prisoner.

As he did so, Blarney unfolded his arms, and throwing them round Grabham's body, hissed in his ears—

"If I must die, so shall you!"

"Help!" Grabham yelled, "Knock him on the head Catchpole. Quick, or it will be too late. Heaven! I am falling."

Bill Blarney lifted the unhappy constable clean off his feet; and, as they fell with a crash, they went rolling over and over down the sloping roof.

---

## CHAPTER CLVII.

### THE ADVENTURES OF SIR ROLAND ASHTON CONTINUED.

Sir Roland Ashton heard what the waggoner said, and filled with a terror which has no name, he slipped out at the back of the vehicle, and ran for his life.

Strangely enough, the men in search of him neither saw nor heard him, which may perhaps be accounted for by the fact that they were too intent upon the front part of the waggon to think of anything else,

"You will find him inside," the waggoner said, handing the lantern to a man; "but I don't think you will say that he is the party you are looking for."

"Perhaps he is, and perhaps he isn't," said the constable. "Hi—hi! there. Get up, and let us have a look at you. Why, hang it! there is nobody here."

"Nobody!" exclaimed the waggoner. "That's all nonsense. Turn the straw over, and you'll find him right enough."

"If I turned the straw over, burnt it, and the waggon as well," the constable said, "I should find no man here. Come and see for yourself."

The team-man tilted his hat on to the back of his head, and ran his fingers through his hair.

"Where can he have got to?" he said, with an expression of blank amazement upon his face.

"That's what we should like to know—if he was ever here at all?" said another constable.

"Ever here at all!" the waggoner repeated. "Why, I had a look at him not ten minutes ago, and he seemed to be sound asleep."

"Perhaps," said the first constable, sarcastically, "he slept so soundly that he vanished altogether into the land of dreams. I suppose you are not having a lark with us—trying to put us on the wrong scent, or anything of that sort?"

"No—no," replied the waggoner, beginning to tremble. "Why, my father saw him start with me, and we all three spoke about the murder at Cockleton."

There was truth in every word the young fellow said, and the constables could not disbelieve him.

"Well," said he who acted as leader, "he can't be far away, that's one comfort. Good-night, waggoner, and keep your eyes open. If you should see anybody skulking about by the roadside for a mile or so, use this whistle."

"I will," the team-man replied. "But, hang me! if I can get over this. It's more like a dream than anything else. I'll loiter about for a time in case you should require my assistance."

"Oh! no; you will do better by going on," the constable said. "We are quite strong enough to cope with the murderous hound or of half-a-dozen like him."

In the blinding darkness, and with the voices of the baffled pursuers still ringing in his ears, Sir Roland Ashton held on his course.

He became a little more cautious how he moved

along, for the road he had taken by chance was full of holes and ruts.

Here and there the gnarled roots of trees spread themselves right across the path, and Sir Roland slipping, tripping, and stumbling, checked his pace.

He came to the conclusion that he must have dived into some narrow lane.

"So much the better," he muttered; "but I could wish for just one ray of light to guide me. This place is as black as the bottomless pit."

Then he stopped to listen, stooping down and placing his ear close to the ground.

He heard the waggon-wheels as they went rumbling on their way, and for a time they drowned all other sounds.

But at last they grew fainter, and then Sir Roland distinguished the measured beat of horses trotting.

"Not my way," he said. "They are not coming my way. Ha—ha! You will have some trouble to catch me yet my very clever friends."

He felt that he could afford to rest awhile now, and so he determined to do until day dawned and showed him the nature of the locality he was in.

Leaping a ditch, he crawled through a hedge and lay down beside it.

He had not been long in this attitude when he heard the sound of voices, and the footsteps of men creeping stealthily along.

The guilty man's heart beat audibly.

Sir Roland's first impulse was to start to his feet and fly.

But second thoughts convinced him that to pursue such a course would be little short of madness.

If he kept still, the men might not suspect his presence and pass.

"I am glad we came round this way," he heard a gruff voice say. "The traps are out to-night, and no mistake. I suppose they are on the alert about this affair at Cockleton."

"That's about it," replied another. "They say that the deed was committed by a gentleman of quality."

"Ha—ha! rare quality, I'll be bound. Something like ourselves, Jack."

"You are inclined to be merry, Phil Merrick," said the man called Jack. "If half what is said is true the fellow must have some pluck, and be as slippery as an eel to get away when the whole county is up in arms against him."

"Just so, and I should like to see him."

"To get the reward, Jack Starr?"

"Bah! no."

"What for, then?"

"Why, see how useful such a man as he would be to us," Jack Starr replied. "We've done a fair week's work in the neighbourhood, so we had better go at once and try our luck in some other part."

This conversation set Sir Roland Ashton thinking.

"Shall I declare myself?" he asked himself. "Shall I take the risk of speaking to them?"

It was now or never, as the men were gliding away in the distance.

"Hullo!" he cried out. "A word or two with you, my friends."

Click—click went the triggers of a brace of pistols.

"You have nothing to fear from me," Sir Roland said. "I am a poor, hunted wretch, without home or shelter."

"Hunted, did you say?" Jack Starr growled.

"Yes. The officers are after me."

"What for?"

"I will tell you if we should become better acquainted," Sir Roland replied. "I heard what you said as you were passing along."

"Hah! you are the man wanted at Cockleton."

"I never said so," Sir Roland returned; "but this I will tell you. I want employment—I care not what—I must live, and will dare anything for the means of living."

"Come here," said Phil Merrick, "and we will have a look at you."

"Your eyes will have to be good to see me in this darkness."

"I have a lantern," Merrick replied. "Stand still. We are not the men to be trifled with, and if you move without orders down you go."

Sir Roland Ashton advanced a few steps and then stood perfectly still.

A light flashed upon him.

"Well, I must say that you are in a pretty pickle, whoever you may be," Jack Starr said. "You have the appearance of a man who has seen better days."

"I have," Sir Roland replied.

"Come," said Jack Starr, "if we are to be of any use to you, you must tell us who you are and what brought you here."

"You will not betray me?"

"Betray you—we!" Jack Starr cried. "The last place we should think of going to is a police-office. Let that fact comfort you, and so speak out plainly."

Sir Roland did so, and as he went on telling his horrible story, Phil Merrick and Jack Starr glanced at each other.

The latter was the first to speak after Sir Roland had completed his narrative.

"See here," he said, "it would not be safe for all parties for you to travel with us. We are bound for Norwich, and hope to reach the City to-morrow night. Do you know anything about the place?"

"Positively nothing, beyond hearsay."

"So much the better," said Starr, "for that proves beyond doubt that you are not known there. You want money, and, see, we will trust you as far as a couple of guineas go. Make your way to Norwich, and when there, ask for the Cow and Cucumber, on St. Andrew's-hill. You will find us there."

Sir Roland began to pour out his thanks, but Jack Starr stopped him.

"Enough," he said. "We don't want your thanks. We will find work for you."

The two men walked swiftly away, and as Sir Roland Ashton turned his face to the east he saw that the day had began to dawn.

Which way should he go now?

He had money in his pocket, but who would give him food and shelter?

"Bad news travels fast, it is said," he muttered; "but surely it must take time in such an out-of-the-way place as this. I will risk calling at the first house I see, whether it be mansion or hovel."

Having thus resolved, Sir Roland kept on until the sun rose above the hills and dispersed the clouds.

But the air was still bitterly cold, and the wretched man shivered as he stood alone—yes; alone in the world, with no real friendly hand to grasp his own.

# SPRING-HEELED JACK,

## THE TERROR OF LONDON.

"LET GO YOUR HOLD, OR YOU PERISH !" CRIED SPRING-HEELED JACK.

No. 45.

## CHAPTER CLVIII.

### THE DUEL INTERRUPTED.

RALPH ASHTON'S eyes flashed fire as he challenged Lord Mildendale.

"Yes," he cried, "defend yourself, or I will run my sword through your body."

"That would be murder—a worthy deed for you to commit," his lordship replied. "I'll not cross swords with you. I am a gentleman, and only fight with my equals."

"Your equals!" Ralph Ashton said, as he tapped the point of his rapier impatiently on the ground. "Find them if you can. Show me the dastard who is cowardly enough to endeavour to burn innocent people in their beds, and I will proclaim him to all the world as your equal. Bring to me the man who tires of a woman's love, and then employs an assassin to slay her in cold blood, and he shall be your peer."

Lord Mildendale's face became truly awful in expression.

Death-like, and trembling between rage and fear, he stood glaring at Ralph Ashton.

"I call you coward," Ralph said. "I tell you to your teeth that you are a monster. Lord Mildendale, can nothing move you, base villain that you are?"

"Death and the devil!" Lord Mildendale hissed, between his teeth. "How came this fellow acquainted with the history of my life?"

Ralph Ashton overheard the words, and laughed aloud.

"By means such as you wot not of," he said. "I know the lonely, miserable man, who night after night has sat wretched amid his luxury and splend , with fear gnawing at his heart, and quaking at every sound. I know the miserable wretch who dares scarcely to walk abroad on his own estate alone, for fear that an avenging bullet may strike into his body. I know—"

"Hold, curse you!" Lord Mildendale interposed. "Since you know so much, make the best or worst of it, as it may suit you. If you would save your neck, go while there is yet time. How you escaped from prison I know not, nor care to know. For my own part you are welcome to go where you will, so long as you do not cross my path. Out of it now! I have other and better business to do than to play the fool here."

"My lord," said Ralph Ashton, "you will find that it is no fool's game that I intend to play at. Here is my sword, and you shall not pass it without endangering your body. I have sworn it, and I will keep my oath."

Lord Mildendale looked first to the right and then to the left.

There was not a creature in sight, and the helplessness of his situation sent a thrill to his heart's core.

The snow was still falling, spreading its white mantle upon the face of the earth, and, save when one or the other spoke, deep silence reigned in the woods.

"How now, my lord?" Ralph Ashton cried; "are you ready?"

Suddenly Lord Mildendale laid his hand upon his sword and snatched it from its sheath.

With a face burning with passion, he lunged at Ralph; but ineffectually, for the blow was neatly parried.

"It is seldom that I am caught napping," Ralph said, smiling; "but I am glad, my lord, that I have roused you to something like activity. Now we stand upon an equal footing. Come. Soh—soh! Let us get on, for time flies."

The fight then commenced in earnest.

Cool, firm, and determined, watching every movement on the part of his adversary, stood Ralph Ashton.

At first Lord Mildendale rushed with mad impetuosity into the fray.

But, finding that he failed not only to break down Ralph's guard, but endangered his own life, he used more discretion, and reserved his strength.

Both men were excellent swordsmen, and several thrusts were given on each side without inflicting a wound.

And yet Lord Mildendale knew that he had met with more than his match.

He exerted all his skill.

He tried every trick he knew in the art of fencing, but nothing availed him.

At last his temper got the mastery of him again.

"Curse you!" he cried. "How long is this to last?"

"Until I kill you," Ralph Ashton replied. "My lord, I warn you not throw away a chance."

Just as Ralph Ashton spoke a shrill whistle was heard in the wood, and two men, dressed as gamekeepers, appeared in sight.

Lord Mildendale recoiled a few paces, and his eyes gleamed with exultation.

"What ho, there!" he cried. "Seize this miscreant, and I will reward you well. This is he who escaped from prison. At him, my men—bring him down!"

The men hesitated, as if they did not know what to make of the scene presented to their eyes.

But presently one of them recognised Lord Mildendale, and, raising his gun, brought it to bear upon Ralph Ashton.

The trigger was drawn, but it missed fire, but the other man was armed, and he was in the act of taking aim at Ralph, when he dodged among the trees and was lost to sight.

"Follow him!" Lord Mildendale cried, in a voice of thunder. "I will pay twenty guineas for his capture."

"Right you are, my lord," said one of the keepers. "We will have him safe enough. Come along, Tom. Put a fresh priming in the pan and make sure of your game this time."

"Miserable cowards, all of you!" cried the voice of Ralph Ashton. "I defy you!"

He ran on through the snow, keeping well within the cover of the trees.

He was fully aware that his footmarks would make the chase an easy one unless he exerted himself to the utmost.

Trained in every sport in his youth, Ralph could run like a hare, and he soon left his plodding pursuers far behind.

But there was still danger on every hand.

The wood rang with the shouts of Lord Mildendale and the keepers, and it was just possible that other men might appear on the scene.

With his drawn sword in his hand, Ralph Ashton ran on, and, leaping over a hedge, found that he was facing the open heath.

As far as the eye could reach there was nothing but the dazzling whiteness of the snow, thickly covering hill and dale.

"Fool that I was to leave my pistols behind," Ralph muttered. "If I have to pay for my folly I shall only have myself to blame."

He stopped a moment to listen.

It seemed to him that his pursuers had either lost the track or had given up the pursuit, for he could hear nothing of them.

Ralph had some idea of returning to the woods, but he abandoned it, and determined to cross the open heath at any risk.

Beyond it, in a dim, misty line, in relief against the grey, snow-laden sky, he could see the Sprowston-woods, which would take him to a wild and unfrequented locality called Rackheath.

There he could lie concealed until night came.

His progress was now slow and painful, for the snow had drifted in parts, and more than once he found himself up to his waist, and struggling for his life.

"Lord Mildendale!" he hissed, as he scrambled along, "we shall meet again. Ah! why did I—but no matter. Next time I shall be wiser. Experience is often bought dearly, and this will be a lesson to me."

Just as Ralph Ashton felt so weary and overcome that it seemed impossible for him to drag his weary limbs another hundred yards, he saw a thin wreath of smoke curling up into the air.

Ralph gazed at it in wonder, for no sign of a habitation met his eyes.

There was nothing but snow.

Snow to the right of him, snow to the left of him, snow everywhere.

The wind came with pitiless blasts, numbing his limbs, and turning his face blue with deadly cold.

But there was the smoke, growing more and more distinct, and at last Ralph Ashton saw a little round hillock, with here and there a patch of black upon it.

"It cannot be a shepherd's hut," he said, musingly, "for here there are no flocks to watch. It must be a gipsy's tent. If so, I am safe."

As he drew nearer to the object he saw others of a similar description, but smaller.

Ralph tottered on, increasing his speed as well as he could, and, just as he was within a few yards of the tent, a huge, shaggy dog rushed out furiously at him.

"Back—back! you cur!" Ralph cried, in alarm.

"Down, Demon—down!" cried a woman's voice.

Lanoni, the gipsy queen, came to the door of the tent, and Ralph Ashton, giving vent to a cry of joy, fell forward upon his face in the snow.

For a moment he lost consciousness, but recovering himself as quickly, he sprang to his feet and grasped Lanoni's hand.

"In the name of all that is wonderful, what may this mean?" she cried.

"I am pursued."

"You pursued?" Lanoni said, elevating her beautifully-arched eyebrows in astonishment. "You pursued, Ralph Ashton?"

"Yes, yes," he said, hastily. "I know the cause of your surprise; but ask me no questions now. Hide me—hide me!"

Lanoni pointed to the tent and followed Ralph Ashton into it.

"Have you seen Namon Wallack?" he asked, as he sank down panting and almost breathless.

"No."

"Then you do not know that I have been in prison and only lately escaped from it?"

"How should I?" Lanoni replied. "I arrived here last night, just in time to escape from the storm. Ah! you marvel at seeing me here? I have much to tell you. Hist! What is that?"

Lanoni took an instrument, shaped something like a whistle, from a fold in her dress, and made a peculiar sound upon it.

In an instant the door of the tent was darkened by the form of a man.

"Seth," she said, "go to yonder hill, and should you see anybody, return quickly and tell me."

The man made a sign of obedience, and departed without saying a word.

He was not long away, and Lanoni glanced at him inquiringly.

"Well?" she said.

"Three men are approaching," he said.

"Enough, you may go."

Lanoni gathered up a number of furs and rugs, and threw them down at Ralph Ashton's feet.

"Cover yourself with these, and leave the rest to me," she said.

"How like a coward I feel!" Ralph Ashton said. "Lanoni, give me a brace of pistols, and I will render a good account of myself."

"No—no!" she replied; "that would be madness, and ruin all. Do as I desire, or it had been better that you never came to my tent."

Ralph ground his teeth with rage as he enveloped himself among the pile of furs and rugs, and lay still.

Lanoni then piled more logs of wood upon the fire, the smoke of which escaped through a hole in the roof of the tent, and calmly awaited the coming of the strangers.

Nor had she long to wait, for the two keepers, with Lord Mildendale bringing up the rear, soon presented themselves before her.

"Why have you come here with weapons of war in your hands?" she demanded, rising, and drawing herself up to her full height. "Ha! Lord Mildendale, you are indeed welcome. I little expected to meet you in such a place as this."

Lord Mildendale started back as he recognised the gipsy queen.

"This woman," he said, pointing at her with a trembling hand, "is the recognised leader of a desperate gang. It is she who conspired against my life, and when foiled in that, declared that I caused her abduction."

Lanoni gazed scornfully at his lordship.

"I conspire!" she said, laughing contemptuously. "Go to! The lie is upon your white, bloodless lips. What want you here? Tell me quickly, for here, on this common land, I am mistress of my own home, and will protect it with my life."

The keepers did not like her determined attitude, and they began to whisper among themselves.

"It comes to this," said one of them, "a prisoner who escaped from Norwich Bridewell is at large and near at hand."

"Find him then," said Lanoni.

"That's what we are trying to do," the man replied, "and we don't think we shall have to look very far. We have tracked him here, and we rather fancy that if we looked in this tent we should find him."

"Indeed!" said Lanoni, smiling. "You have evidently mistaken your vocation, my men. It is said that most of the constables are useless, and there is a chance for you to distinguish yourselves in that direction. But why should I waste words with you? Show me your authority for coming there, or begone, lest you should raise the passions of my kind."

The keepers looked at Lord Mildendale for instructions.

"I will take all the consequences upon myself," he said. "Search the tent."

Lanoni clapped her hands.

A dozen men appeared as suddenly as if they had sprung from the earth and surrounded her.

"Friends," Lanoni said, calmly, "these men are here with the intention of entering my tent without leave or permission. Shall it be said that either you or I consented to such indignity?"

"No, no!" shouted the gipsies.

A dozen knives flashed in the air, and as many pistol-barrels gleamed ominously before the eyes of the terrified keepers.

They recoiled, and at last retreated as fast as their legs could carry them, and, hissing out maledictions on the heads of the gipsies, Lord Mildendale followed in their wake.

## CHAPTER CLIX.

### A FEARFUL LEAP.

THE downward progress of Bill Blarney and Grabham received a sudden check.

They reached the parapet, and, in spite of their combined weights thudding against it with terrific force, the stonework held good.

Bill Blarney and Grabham now lay in the gutter, and amid the filth that had accumulated there for years.

Both were so out of breath and terrified that for some seconds neither moved, but Blarney roused himself as he head Catchpole scrambling down the roof.

He knew what would happen unless he made an effort.

Once more the gibbet danced before his eyes, and, striking Grabham full in the face, he released himself from his grasp and leaped to his feet.

Catchpole discharged a pistol at the ruffian, but the aim was wild and uncertain, and the bullet whistled harmlessly over Blarney's head.

This saved his life so far, but what was he to do?

Grabham lay groaning in the gutter, and making frantic attempts to extricate himself.

Catchpole was reloading the pistol, and Bill Blarney knew that he could not get back to the stack of chimneys without running a great risk.

He glanced down into the street.

The height between him and the ground made him giddy, and caused his brain to reel.

He could not make up his mind what to do.

There was not a moment to be lost or thrown away in useless reflection.

Just then a waggon, laden with vegetables on its way to market, turned a corner, and with a yell of defiance, Bill Blarney hurled himself over the parapet.

This bold act sickened Catchpole's heart.

"He's gone, Grabham," he gasped. "He has cheated the hangman, and will never trouble us again."

"And a good job too," Grabham groaned, as he crawled up the roof on his hands and knees. "We shall find him crushed like a spider under a cart-wheel down below."

But such, however, was not the case.

Bill Blarney, trusting to a hope that he might alight on the top of the waggon, went down like a plummet, and alighted among the vegetables with such force that they flew into the air like water.

The fall knocked the breath out of the villain's body.

He thought that both his legs were broken; but finding that some strength was left in them yet, he scrambled down and dropped into the street before the man who was leading the horses could recover from his astonishment.

He was country bred, and though he had seen many astonishing things connected with the vegetable world, he had never seen a waggon-load of cabbages come to life and fly into the air of their own accord, as he thought.

"Dang it!" he said, as he sat down flat. "Be the devil among the things? Why—why— Lor' a-mussy! Help! oh—oh!—murder! I'm a sinner, but my time ain't come yet."

He had no more notion of what had really taken place than the man in the moon.

He heard the crash, he saw the cabbages fly, and that was all.

Meanwhile, Bill Blarney was dragging his almost breathless body and aching limbs up a narrow court.

Reeling and tottering, but not daring to groan, though his agonies were almost past endurance, he stumbled against a door.

It yielded to his weight, and he fell headlong into a darkened passage.

Bill Blarney uttered a gasping cry.

He thought that all was over now, for if the people of the house were not dead asleep they must have heard the sound occasioned by his fall.

He listened, but heard no sound of voices or any indication that his presence had been made known.

Having satisfied himself of this, he rose slowly and painfully to his feet, and, closing the door, bolted it at the top and bottom.

"So far so good," he muttered. "I wonder what sort of place this is? What would I not give for a light."

He dare not move a step for fear of falling into a cellar or down a staircase, and therefore he concluded that it would be better for him to remain perfectly still until the light of day should guide him.

Meanwhile, Catchpole and Grabham were making their way down through the Bull in Top Boots with all speed.

In their own minds they felt perfectly assured that they would find the mangled remains of Bill Blarney in the street.

When they reached it, and beheld the half-dazed waggoner, who was groping about on all fours collecting the scattering cabbages, they shouted to him.

"Where is he?" Catchpole demanded.

"He? Who?" the waggoner rejoined. "I don't know what you mean."

"Where's the man—or what is left of him—who jumped off the roof?"

"It strikes me," said Catchpole, "that I am talking to a fool."

"Very likely," the man replied. "I might be anything after what happened just now."

"What do you mean?"

"I mean that the devil, or something like him, came crashing down on the top of my waggon and did all this mischief."

Catchpole and Grabham now glared at each other in blank dismay.

"Blarney must have fallen on the waggon," said Grabham.

"Yes, that's all very well, but where is he?"

This was a question more easily put than answered.

"Did you see the man?" Grabham asked of the waggoner.

"How should I? I was leading my horses, and the shock to my nerves knocked me silly."

"Here's a precious go," said Grabham. "Blarney gone! Why, the fellow must have more lives than a cat."

"It ain't possible that a man could have leaped from such a height without injuring himself," Catchpole returned. "Just look up and tell me how you would like to attempt it yourself."

"It's a fearful thing to think of," Grabham replied, as he flashed his lantern to and fro. "At any rate, he ain't here, and so there's an end of the matter. All we have to do is find him."

"Just so. But how are you going to do that?"

"He can't be far away," replied Grabham. "He has crawled somewhere for shelter. Come, follow me, Catchpole, and it will be a singular thing if Bill Blarney is not laid by the heels in Bow-street before a couple of hours have passed over his head."

The two valiant constables then set about their task.

They hunted high and low, but not the slightest trace of Bill Blarney could they find, and at last they came to a standstill to consult again.

"Of all the rum things this is the rummest," said Grabham, tilting his hat on to the back of his head and pulling his hair. "Catchpole, look at me. I'm disfigured for life."

"He certainly hit you hard."

"Hard! He hit me like a sledge-hammer. I thought my skull was fractured."

"Never mind," said Catchpole. "When we have collared him, you can pay him with interest."

"But I do mind," Grabham said, with a deep groan. "How do you think I can appear among my pals as I meet every evening with such a nose as this? It's as big as a turnip, and seems to be all over my face."

Mr. Grabham, having indulged in a few more groans, kicked Catchpole, because he thought he heard him laugh.

Catchpole denied the impeachment, and gave Grabham such a dig in the waistcoat that he sat down with startling suddenness upon a doorstep.

"Oh!" he yelled. "You shall suffer for this, my boy."

"Then what did you kick me for?" demanded Catchpole, rubbing his shin.

"Because you are a wiper."

"You're another!"

"I ain't in a fit state to have it out with you just now," Grabham moaned. "Wait until I am better, and then I'll settle accounts with you."

The doorstep on which Grabham reposed in anything but an elegant attitude was the one through which Bill Blarney had fallen.

Little did the constables think that the ruffian was so near to them, and could hear every word that they said.

Bill Blarney could not help chuckling at the state of things going on within arm's reach of him.

"If they would only pitch into each other a little more," he muttered, under his breath, "they would give up looking for me and go home."

Vain hope.

The constables did not intend to leave the locality, for they had both made up their minds that it was impossible for Bill Blarney to hav. left it.

He might be hiding in some out-of-the-way corner which had escaped their notice; and after a little more jangling, in which both indulged in all sorts of horrible threats, they became calmer, and began to talk in a business-like manner.

"It may be," said Grabham, "that he has made for the river."

"Not he," Catchpole replied. "If so he must come back. The tide is up and flooding the arches, and it's a thousand guineas to a gooseberry that Blarney would not attempt to cross one of the bridges."

"Only give me a chance, and see what I would do," the ruffian growled.

"This is a nice sheltered place," Grabham continued; "and I don't think we can do better than to stay where we are."

"I'm agreeable to anything, so long as you keep your feet to yourself," Catchpole said.

"And the same with your fists."

"What's the use of going on that tack again?" said Catchpole. "Anybody would think that we were a couple of dogs squabbling over a bone."

Grabham muttered something under his breath, and then lapsed into silence.

"They may stay here all night," Blarney gasped. "What will become of me if the people of the house come down before they go away?"

His face became damp with perspiration, and his heart beat violently at the bare thought of such a thing.

"I must do something, or all is lost," he mused, clutching at his throat.

There was a choking sensation in that region—a kind of lump which had risen—giving him an almost uncontrollable desire to shout and rave.

"Am I going mad?" he said. "Shall I lose my senses, and let these bloodhounds know where I am by my cries? No—no! anything but that."

He was lying at full length, and turning his face towards the door, the draught of air rushing under cooled him, and helped him to reflect in a calmer mood.

"Curse them!" he muttered. "Will no kind fate drive them away, and leave me to go free? Now they are at it again, calling each other everything they can lay their tongues to. How I wish they would murder each other!"

No doubt he did, and probably he would have liked the chance of doing it himself.

Catchpole and Grabham had no notion of taking each other's lives.

They were too fond of each other's company in time of danger to do that, and, though they often quarrelled, they were really on the very best of terms.

More than an hour passed away, but there they remained.

Suddenly Catchpole began to complain of the cold.

"Let us walk about a bit," he said. "What do you say to a turn through the market and back again?"

"Anything for a quiet life," Grabham remarked.

Bill Blarney clasped his hands in gratitude.

It was a wonder that such a villain as he could be grateful for anything, but in this instance he felt a sensation of relief such as he had seldom experienced.

How gladly he listened to the sound of the constables' footsteps, as they rattled noisily over the flagstones of the court, and then died away in the road beyond.

It was music, sweet music, to his ears, and he drank it in greedily.

Presently he thought he heard the sound of a bell.

Boom—boom!

It could not be the tolling of a death-knell at such a time in the morning.

What could it mean?"

In those days, when a fire broke out in any part of London the people were roused to activity by the ringing of bells.

"Yes," said Bill Blarney, "it must be a fire, and duty will call those confounded constables to it. May it blaze! Curse them! may they perish in the flames."

He waited a few more minutes, and then began to unfasten the bolts.

What a noise they made!

How they creaked and groaned, as if anxious to attract the attention of the people in the house to the hunted villain.

Just as Bill Blarney had succeeded in unfastening the top bolt, he heard someone trying the handle of the door.

Overcome with rage and horror, Bill Blarney staggered back.

"What devil's fate is mine?" he hissed, between his teeth. "Is it possible that this door should have been left undone purposely?"

"Well, I never!" said a voice in the court. "Mother Griggs has locked me out, and after I paid a week in advance, too."

A thought flashed into Bill Blarney's mind.

Chance had brought him to one of those low, common lodging-houses, where porters engaged in the market paid a few pence for the accommodation of sleeping under a roof.

"Who's there?" Bill Blarney demanded, softly, through the keyhole.

"Who ain't there—that's the question."

The voice was youthful, and Bill Blarney, finding that he had only a boy to deal with, put on a bold demeanour.

After a moment's reflection he opened the door, and saw a weedy-looking boy standing before him.

"You live here, I suppose?" he said.

"Don't I just?" the precocious youth replied. "Did Mother Griggs tell you to lock the door?"

"Well, not quite," Bill Blarney replied, cautiously.

"What did you want to go for and do it then?" said the boy. "It would have been a nice thing if I had to sleep out in the cold, wouldn't it? If I was bigger I'd punch your head, as sure as my name is Lobbs."

"I am a stranger here, and unacquainted with the rules of the house," Bill Blarney returned. "There—there! it is no use making a fuss. There is no harm done after all, and you can go to bed as soon as you like."

Grumbling and growling, Master Lobbs felt his way up a dark, tortuous staircase, and no sooner was he well out of the way than Bill Blarney darted into the passage of the court.

He met with no obstacle, and turning his face towards the south, he dashed down the Borough High-street.

He now felt comparatively safe.

The street was full of early workers and vehicles of every description, all bound towards the market.

"So," he muttered, as he pushed and jostled his way along, "I have given the traps the slip once more; but how long will this game of hide-and-seek last?"

He came upon a stall set out temptingly with cups and saucers, and plates piled with bread-and-butter.

Fain would he have stopped to quench his thirst and satisfy his hunger, but he dared not do so.

He peered into every face suspiciously, and thought that every man cast a meaning glance at him.

How long and miserable the night was!

It seemed as if it would never come to an end.

At last the houses became fewer in number, but Bill Blarney kept on until he reached the old-fashioned village of Dulwich.

Then, to all intents and purposes, he had reached the open country, for Dulwich in those days was as out-of-the-way a place as could be found within fifty miles from London.

"Here I am safe, at any rate, until daylight," Bill Blarney muttered, as he threw himself down under a hedge; "and then—what then? I have no money and nowhere to go. I'll have the first, at any rate, before long. Lor'! what a treat it would be to see an old gentleman with a well-filled purse pass this way just now."

---

## CHAPTER CLX.

### MRS. CORCORAN LAUGHS IN HER SLEEVE.

Mrs. Corcoran lost not a moment in making herself scarce from the Bull in Top Boots.

She did not stay to ascertain whether the constables succeeded in capturing Bill Blarney.

The hag was too crafty for that, and, leaving the premises, made her way towards London-bridge.

She now began to tire of London, and began to sigh for the seclusion and safety of the open country.

It was not that she was an admirer of nature or of lovely sunsets, but she thirsted to reach some quiet place, where perhaps she could win the heart of some charitable person, and make profit out of it.

Suddenly the idea struck her that the best thing she could do was to make her way to her native place.

"Who would know me at Cockleton?" she thought. "Not a soul, though I daresay I should remember a good many faces. Let me think. What could I do there?" I am disguised as a man, but I am getting much too feeble to work as one. Work—bah! But let me think."

She fell into a train of thought as to the best way to get to Cockleton.

The place was a long distance away, and, though she knew that an early coach started from the White Horse, in Fetter-lane, she almost feared to go there in her novel attire.

Mrs. Corcoran glanced down at the garments, which did not fit her so badly after all.

"I'll go," she said, as she thrust some of her lank back-hair under the three-cornered hat. "Perhaps they will take a little less fare because I am poor."

Trudging on, Mrs. Corcoran reached the coach-office, and, after a sharp argument with the clerk, booked an outside seat.

People laughed as they looked at her, and thought that she was the oddest old man they had ever seen.

It would be tedious to record the story of the

journey, as it was of an uneventful kind in every respect, save that Mrs. Corcoran was not amiably received by her fellow-passengers.

At last she stood at the door of the Two-necked Swan, worn and weary after a long and miserable journey.

Her money had dwindled down to a guinea and a-half, but she deemed that sum quite sufficient for the time being.

"My memory is good," she said, "and, as I happen to know a few secrets of the people in these parts, I will make use of them."

"Now then, old chap," said an ostler, "out of my way or I shall knock you down, or the horses will, and that will be the same thing."

"Oh!" Mrs. Corcoran said, "perhaps you can tell me what I want to know."

"I'll try, at any rate."

"Well, then," Mrs. Corcoran said, "you see that I am a poor old man, and I want humble lodgings."

The ostler shook his head.

"I don't think you'll find anybody to take you in after what has happened in this 'ere place," he said.

"Indeed!"

"Yes, indeed; so take my advice and try further on."

Mrs. Corcoran became interested in what the man said without exactly knowing why.

"What has happened?"

"Robbery and attempted murder."

"Here?" queried Mrs. Corcoran, pointing to the inn.

"Wait till I have put the horses up, and if you will stand a drink I will tell you all about it."

"That's right—" She was going to say "lovey-dovey," but checked herself just in time. "Ill wait for you."

The ostler was not long away, and Mrs. Corcoran, blinking and winking over a glass of warm brandy and water, heard the story of Sir Roland and Joe Morth.

The expression of her face did not change, nor did she display emotion of any kind.

"Is the poor fellow—the wounded man—still here?" she asked.

"Poor fellow be jiggered!" growled the ostler, as he pushed his glass across the counter to be refilled. "I should like to have the hanging of him."

"So would I," Mrs. Corcoran remarked, and meant what she said. "Well, is he here?"

"Yes, he is still at Cockleton, being looked after," the ostler replied. "As soon as he is well enough to be brought to justice he will be sent to Lincoln to wait for the assizes."

"And I suppose he is in prison now?" said Mrs. Corcoran.

"Well, not exactly," the man returned. "The doctor said that the round-house would kill him, so they took him to a little cottage at the end of High-street, and there he is, in charge of a constable."

"Thank you," said Mrs. Corcoran. "It is a wonderful story, and one that I shall not forget in a hurry. Let me see. You paid for the last drink. Suppose we have one more, and then part?"

"You ain't much to look at," the ostler said; "but you seem to be a nice old chap, after all, although—no offence, mind you—you are as ugly as sin; so, if you like, I'll rig you up a room in my house, and charge you reasonably for it."

Nothing could have suited Mrs. Corcoran better.

"You mustn't charge me much," she said; "for I am almost as poor as a church mouse. Will four shillings for the week suit you?"

"Make it five."

"I said four."

"Then let four be the figure," said the ostler, who had grown generous over the repeated glasses of brandy. "I detest the man who will stand and haggle all night over a shilling. But, by-the-way, you haven't told me what you have come to Cockleton for."

Mrs. Corcoran winked artfully at the ostler.

"Though I am hard up just at present," she said, "it is just likely that I shall come into a tremendous fortune."

"Lor'! you don't say so," gasped the ostler, open mouthed.

"I do, and mean it, too. I have come down to inspect the parish register with regard to the birth of an eccentric woman named—named Corcoran."

"Oh! I have heard of her," said the ostler, "and the people here say that she was a regular bad 'un."

"That might be," the hag replied, wincing a little, "but she made money, and I'll make it fly if I can get hold of it."

The ostler laughed and then became lavishly generous.

He insisted upon Mrs. Corcoran having some more brandy, and she did not say No.

She laughed in her sleeve, for, though the liquid was making the ostler drunk very quickly, it had no visible effect on her.

At last, when the man began to reel and tumble about, she thought that it was time to go.

"All ri'," hiccupped the ostler. "Hold on to me a bit—everything is going round."

Mrs. Corcoran was enjoying herself immensely, but then she began to wonder whether the ostler was a married man, and what his wife would say to him bringing home a stranger in such a state.

"Hold up," said Mrs. Corcoran. "You will be better as soon as you reach the open air."

"Better!" repeated the ostler. "Why, I never felt better in all my life."

Mrs. Corcoran had all she could do to keep the drunken fool on his legs.

The ostler dragged her from one side of the road to the other, until they both lost their balance, and fell floundering into a ditch.

Mrs. Corcoran was the first to get up, and she began to think that it would be best to leave the ostler to get home as well as he could.

And this she probably would have done had not the man pulled himself together with an effort.

"Curse the drink!" he said. "I'll never touch another drop as long as I live."

"So I have often said," Mrs. Corcoran remarked; "but as soon as I got better I went at it again."

"It's lucky that my wife is away on a visit to her friends," the ostler said, as he swayed to and fro. "There would have been a pretty bobbery if she had been at home, and you would have gone without your bed."

The ostler's house was not far away, and Mrs. Corcoran, having been shown her room—a small, but clean, attic—was soon fast asleep.

Early in the morning she was up and scheming as usual.

"What brought Sir Roland Ashton and Joe

Morth here?" she muttered. "I remember once telling Sir Roland that this was my native place. Ha! They came here after me. Now, the next question is, shall I try to get an interview with Joe Morth, or keep out of his sight? I must not be in a hurry, but think well over it."

Presently she heard the ostler moving about below, and went down to see how he fared.

"I'm mortally bad," he said, in answer to Mrs. Corcoran's question. "I feel as if I had been at sea the whole night."

"Well, I can't say that you have a particularly rosy appearance," Mrs. Corcoran said. "Let us go somewhere and have a couple of hairs out of the dog that bit us."

"A couple of what?"

"A drop of brandy, to pull us round."

"Not for worlds!" the ostler said, shuddering. "You can do as you like, but I'll take nothing but tea."

Mrs. Corcoran then began to question the man about Joe Morth.

"There's no telling when he may be removed," the ostler said. "I heard that he was getting along all right. Strange to say, when the fever was upon him he raved about the very woman you spoke of last night."

"Mrs. Corcoran?"

"Yes, and swore that he would murder her."

"How very kind of him!" Mrs. Corcoran said. "But he won't have the chance now."

"Not if she is dead."

"But if she were alive it would be one and the same thing," said Mrs. Corcoran, a little nervously. "I suppose he will be hanged?"

"As sure as he has a neck between his head and his body."

This was very comforting to Mrs. Corcoran, and she could not conceal her exultation.

Having paid a few pence for her breakfast, she wandered out into the open air.

Without much difficulty she discovered the cottage in which Joe Morth lay wounded and a prisoner.

A constable, smoking a short, black pipe, stood at the door, and he gave Mrs. Corcoran a glance that boded her no good.

"What are you hanging about here for?" he demanded. "There is nothing to see, so take yourself off."

"Don't be uncivil," croaked the hag. "You will grow old if you live long enough."

"If I thought I should be anything like you," the constable said, growling out his words, "I'd die at once. Come, cut it. I won't have you standing staring about here, and there's an end of it."

As Mrs. Corcoran slouched away a thought flashed into her brain.

"They are going to remove Joe Morth to-day," she mused. "I must keep a sharp look-out. Oh! to see him weak and bandaged. Oh! to know that he is going to certain death while I am free."

True to her word, Mrs. Corcoran kept a sharp look-out, and about eleven o'clock a closed vehicle drove up to the cottage.

As a matter of course, a crowd collected round the door.

It was but a small concourse of people, principally composed of boys, female gossips, and idlers.

The constable on duty used his baton pretty freely upon every head he could reach, but this had not the effect of driving away the sight-seers, who would have rather suffered the agonies of the Inquisition than be deprived of a view of such a celebrated criminal as Joe Morth.

At last there came a lumbering, bumping sound on the stairs.

Every neck was craned forward.

The door opened, and there stood Joe Morth between two constables.

The once stalwart landlord of the Bull in Top Boots was but a shadow of his former self.

His face was pinched, and his clothes hung loosely about him.

He groaned at every step he took, and glared with his sunken eyes at the curious crowd.

"Curse you all!" he hissed. "Could you not let me go quietly on my last journey?"

At this moment a wild burst of discordant laughter came from where the people were thickest.

Joe Morth started, and clung to the constable nearest to him.

"She is here," he gasped. "I should know her voice from a million. Give me but a moment! Give me but the chance of getting my hands upon her throat, and then you may do with me what you will."

But the constables hurried him into the vehicle, and the driver gathered up the reins.

As the horses moved away there came another burst of laughter, and Joe Morth, thrusting his fingers into his ears, grovelled in a fit at the feet of the constables.

## CHAPTER CLXI.

### THE SCENE AT LYNN MART.

THE night after Ralph Ashton had claimed Lanoni's protection, there was not a tent to be seen on the heath, nor a stroller's show or caravan within the walls of Norwich.

Whither they had gone nobody knew, and, after the events recorded in previous chapters, Lord Mildendale and Mr. Spiffen, the chief magistrate, were heartily glad to see their backs.

Lord Mildendale soon took his leave of the city, promising to return at an hour's notice if Ralph Ashton should be recaptured.

He did not return to his home, however, for in common parlance he had other fish to fry.

One or two words dropped from Namon Wallack's lips set him thinking deeply.

It was evident that the gipsy was in possession of certain information concerning his lordship which would be very unpleasant to him if it went forth to the world, and Lord Mildendale, still smarting under the indignity he had received at Namon Wallack's hands, determined to follow up the clue at any cost or risk.

Whilst his lordship was thus engaged, Namon Wallack and Robin Gray were on their way to the ancient town of Lynn.

The gipsy's loss had been replaced by another show.

"I don't think they will burn this one down, Robin," Namon Wallack said, "for we will watch it night and day."

"It was an evil hand that did the deed," the boy said. "It has made me so miserable, because, as I said before, I seem to be connected with it in some way without knowing why."

"You must try to banish such thoughts rom your mind," Namon Wallack replied. "All we have to think about now is doing good business, and as for our enemies, we shall soon be able to snap our fingers at them."

The journey to Lynn was a tedious one, as the snow lay thickly upon the ground, and continued to fall heavily at intervals.

The winter was an early and very severe one.

King Frost held the earth in his icy fetters, and the sufferings of the gipsies were considerable, for when the bitter, strong wind came roaring across hill and dale, it found out the smallest crevices, and filled the caravan with particles of hoar frost, which lodged themselves upon everything, and refused to be driven out.

At last the journey came to an end, and the cavalcade of houses upon wheels bumped and rumbled through the narrow streets.

They were received, as in most places, by goggle-eyed, admiring boys and girls, who, with no money to spend, feasted their eyes upon what could be seen for nothing.

The journey had taken three long, dreary days, and the worn-out strollers rested another day before they commenced operations.

The only man who did not rest, nor seemed to require any, was Namon Wallack.

He was ever on the alert, and when sheer fatigue compelled him to throw himself down for an hour or two, another man took his place.

And yet there seemed to be no alteration in him.

He was a little quiet at times, but seemed to be as hale and hearty as ever.

Early the next morning every hand and muscle were at work, and by noontide Lynn Mart, as the festival was called, was in full swing.

Robin Gray had been supplied with an acrobat's dress, which lent an additional charm to the boy's graceful limbs.

He had picked up many things from the strollers, and was now able to exhort the people to pay their money and see such wonders as the world never saw before.

The rustics, nothing loth, drew out their pennies, and, whilst marvelling at the most simple things, went away and dreamed of them.

Moving among the laughing crowds was an old, grey-bearded man.

He did not seem to pay much attention to the shows or the stalls, but kept wandering to and fro, never murmuring when he was rudely jostled and pushed hither and thither by the unceremonious rustics.

Nevertheless, he seemed to be looking for somebody, and as he caught sight of Robin Gray a perceptible change came over his face.

"It is time for me to go now," he muttered. "Ha! how perfect is my disguise. I was almost afraid that these keen-eyed gipsies would have found me out."

The disguised man was no other than Lord Mildendale.

Having marked the spot where Namon Wallack's show stood, he left the fair, and, striking into a narrow way, where the trodden snow lay brown and slushy, he entered a public-house.

The place did not boast of a bar.

It was more like a kitchen, and, with the exception of a few benches, a table, and two or three beer-barrels, it was utterly devoid of all signs of comfort.

A shrewish-looking woman, appearing from a back room, greeted Lord Mildendale.

"You are too early," she said. "Maglitch has not arrived yet."

"Then I will sit down and wait," his lordship said. "Have you no licence to sell anything but beer?"

"No."

Lord Mildendale shrugged his shoulders.

"I suppose I must put up with that," he said.

"You might put up with worse," the landlady replied, sharply.

"True—true! Well, bring me some of your best."

As Lord Mildendale spoke, a tall, evil-looking fellow walked into the room.

"Ah! Maglitch," said Lord Mildendale, rising, "I am glad to see you. I have news—great news."

Maglitch made no reply until a flagon of ale was placed before him, and he had partaken of a long, deep draught.

"Mind you," he said, "if there is any mistake about the matter the whole blame must fall upon your shoulders."

"That is already understood."

"I have been thinking that it would have been better to have made an application to the magistrate," he said.

"Bah!" said Lord Mildendale, contemptuously. "That would have ruined all. I call you as a constable, I point out the boy, and declare that he was stolen by the gipsies. You exert your authority and hand the lad over to me, and take ten guineas for your pains. What is easier?"

"It sounds easy enough," Maglitch replied; "but there is another difficulty to be got over."

"What is it?"

"Supposing that I succeed in handing the boy over to you, how will you get him away?" demanded Maglitch.

"I shall have a carriage waiting for his immediate reception."

"I don't think your plan will answer—the gipsies may follow you."

"You and your men must prevent them."

"There has been nothing said about paying my men," Maglitch said. "I thought I was to receive ten guineas for my own trouble."

"Well," Lord Mildendale returned, "supposing that I add five more. Will that satisfy you?"

"I will try to make it do," Maglitch replied; "but it is none too much for such a risky job."

"What time do you think it will be best to make the attempt?" Lord Mildendale enquired.

Maglitch leaned his chin upon his hand and thought the matter out in silence.

"The crowd will be greater in the evening," he said, after a pause. "There will be more confusion. The gipsies will be busiest, and less likely to take notice of anything unusual."

"You are a sharp man, Maglitch, and I had better leave it all to you."

"You may trust to me," replied Maglitch.

"Need I be on the spot?" Lord Mildendale asked.

"Well, of course, you will not be far away."

"Certainly not; but I need not be near when the—"

"When the what?"

"I was going to say when the struggle takes place," Lord Mildendale said.

"I don't think there will be much of a struggle," Maglitch replied. "My only doubt is about the legality of the affair. Mind, I hold you to your word. If I am discharged from the force, you must find me as good a situation, if not a better one."

"You may rely upon me."

"Then consider it done," Maglitch said. "At nine o'clock I will capture the boy, and by a quarter past he shall be in your hands."

Lord Mildendale opened his purse and placed some money on the table.

"The moment that your work is done," he said, "you shall have the rest."

"I am content. And now good-day. You had better remain here, my lord, because you could not be in a safer place."

Maglitch then took his leave, jingling the money in his pocket, and thinking what a capital day's work he had done.

"Lucky for me that I fell in with that fellow," Lord Mildendale said to himself. "What will not gold do? How many crimes has it to answer for? How many ruined lives, and ruined homes? Men have gone mad in their greed for it; and but to the few it brings true peace and enjoyment."

The day passed slowly away—much too slowly for Lord Mildendale.

At last night fell, and then he wandered forth into the town.

A huge glare of light in the sky showed him where the mart was, but he had no intention of going there just yet.

Seeking a quiet street he turned into an archway, under which stood a pair of horses already harnessed to a carriage.

A man stood at the horses' heads, and Lord Mildendale spoke to him.

"Nine o'clock," he said.

"All right, your honour," the man replied "you will find me and my mate punctual to the moment."

"Good!" said Lord Mildendale. "There is nothing like dealing with men of business."

Leaving the archway, his lordship paced the narrowest streets until he heard a church clock chime half-past eight.

Then he began to grow impatient.

Something might go wrong.

How galling it would be if he were foiled, after all, and what little peace the gipsies would give him then!

"No—no!" he said. "All must be well. If I walk slowly I shall arrive at the place where I promised to meet Maglitch and the boy just in time."

As he neared the mart and its scene of rollicking confusion, his heart almost failed him.

He still wore the disguise he had assumed, and meant to keep it until he was fairly on the way to Mildendale.

A quarter to nine!

Nine o'clock!

Lord Mildendale, crouching under the shadow of a high wall, stood and listened, as an assassin might have listened for the footsteps of his victim.

Just about that time, Maglitch, with the men he had enlisted into his service, entered the mart, and strolled about for some time as if they were ordinary sightseers.

They, however, kept close together, and the focus their eyes rested upon was Namon Wallack's show.

Robin Gray was not visible, and Maglitch's face began to fall.

"Perhaps they have suspected something, and smuggled the boy away!" Maglitch thought. "These swarthy gentry are as cunning as foxes, and as sharp-eyed as weasels."

Presently the people began to pour out of the show at the conclusion of one of the performances.

"Hear what they say!" Namon Wallack cried, rushing to the edge of the platform. "They will tell you that they never saw anything half so wonderful for ten times the money."

At that moment Robin Gray appeared, and began to lend his voice to the general din.

"Stand back," Maglitch whispered to his two men. "Keep your distance, but be ready to do my bidding at the moment I call upon you."

Pushing his way through the crowd, he walked up the steps with an authoritative swagger.

"A word with you," he said, addressing Namon Wallack.

"A dozen, if you like," the gipsy replied; "but you must be quick. I am up to my neck in business, and don't want to throw away a chance."

"Is that boy your son?" Maglitch demanded, pointing to Robin Gray.

"No."

"Who is he, then?"

"That is his business and mine."

"Just remember that you are talking to a constable," said Maglitch, throwing out his chest.

"What then?"

"Why, you had better keep a civil tongue in your head."

"My tongue is my own, and I shall use it as I like," Wallack retorted.

"And so will I use my authority," Maglitch replied. "I have every reason to believe that you stole that boy, or, at any rate, have no right to keep him here, so he must come with me."

Namon Wallack stepped back a pace and raised his sledge-hammer-like fists.

"Beware!" Maglitch cried; "I am not alone. If you so much as lay a hand upon me, I will have you dragged to prison."

To tell the truth, Namon Wallack was completely staggered.

"There must be some mistake," he said, hoarsely. "The boy came to me of his own free will. Let him speak for himself."

"He can do that at a more suitable time," Maglitch replied; "but at present I have not time to hear what he has to say."

Dashing forward, Maglitch seized the boy.

At the same moment there was a sound like a thunder-clap, and Spring-Heeled Jack laid his hands upon the astonished constable.

"Let go your hold, or you perish!" cried the weird creature. "Arrant fool you must be to come here on such a mission."

One of Namon Wallack's men came darting through the curtains which separated the show from the platform, and dashing down the ladder, stopped the other two constables just as they were coming up.

Spring-Heeled Jack released Robin Gray from the grasp of Maglitch, and then, striking him full in the face, took a leap clean over the heads of the people and vanished.

Spring-Heeled Jack had taken Robin Gray with him, and the terrified boy was more dead than alive.

---

## CHAPTER CLXII

### THE COW AND CUCUMBER.

LIKE most places then, as now, the good old city of Norwich had its plague spots. It had its houses of low repute, its thieves' dens, and places even more objectionable.

The number of constables were but few, and villains of all descriptions prowled about the ancient streets at night, playing havoc among the respectable portion of the community.

Most of the citizens took good care to keep within doors after nightfall, especially those who lived in the more remote quarters.

It was dark.

The curfew-bell was tolling from the steeple of St. Peter's Mancroft Church, and there was silence in the streets, save when the echoes were awakened by the footsteps of some pedestrian hurrying homewards.

With bent head, and battling against wind and snow, a man reached the foot of St. Andrew's-hill.

He was evidently a stranger to the locality, for as he came to a standstill he looked wistfully about him, as if uncertain which direction to take.

Presently he began to ascend the hill, which at that part was darkened by the wall of St. Andrew's Church.

He cast his eyes to the right and left, and then stopped again.

"I can see no sign of an inn or place of entertainment," he said, under his breath. "Surely those fellows have not deceived me? No—no. They could have no object in doing that, as they gave me money to get here."

Sir Roland Ashton, for he it was, was sorely perplexed.

There was not a soul in sight, and as far as he could see, there was no light in any of the windows of the ancient houses around him.

After wandering up and down for some time, he heard the sound of approaching footsteps.

"Hullo! there," he cried out.

"What now?" demanded a rough voice. "This place is not so dark that I cannot see. What would you? Speak if you are a friend, but keep well out of my path if you are a foe."

"I am a friend, and yet a stranger among strangers," Sir Roland replied. "It may be that I have lost my way, for I cannot find the house I seek."

"Who lives there?"

"I know not."

"Well, then, what is the house called?"

"The Cow and Cucumber."

"Enter the court you are standing near, and you will find it."

The man went grumbling down the hill, for he was not at all fond of encountering men who used the Cow and Cucumber as a place of rest and refreshment.

The entry pointed out to Sir Roland was as black as pitch.

He groped his way up to it, touching the walls with his hands.

Presently he saw a ruddy glow of light shining through a crimson curtain, completely covering the glass portion of a door.

"This must be the place I seek," he said. "At all events, I can do no harm by asking."

At that moment a loud burst of merriment came to his ears.

Then followed a hoarse, grating voice roaring a ribald song, and Sir Roland, hesitating no longer, opened the door and passed into the inn.

"Hullo! there," demanded a brawny fellow, blocking the way in the passage. "This is what we call a private night, and no strangers are admitted."

"And yet I think you will admit me when I tell you that Phil Merrick and Jack Starr told me that I should find them here," Sir Roland said.

"If you know them you are welcome," the fellow returned. "Tell me your name, and I will take it into them."

"Roland Ashton."

"Any relation to Ralph Ashton?"

"What know you of him?" demanded Sir Roland, starting violently.

"That does not matter. I asked you a question. Answer it."

"Well, I am a blood relation of Ralph Ashton, but little did I expect to hear his name mentioned here."

"This world is full of surprises, my friend," said the man, placing his hands upon Sir Roland's shoulders. "Well, since you have told me your name, I will tell you mine. I am Jos Townshend, and I am proud to say that I am the landlord of this house."

Sir Roland could not help thinking that, as far as he could see, there was little to be proud of.

"You have quickened my curiosity," he said. "Tell me how it was that you mentioned Ralph Ashton's name? Is he in Norwich?"

"Oh! you'll hear all about it soon enough," said Jos Townshend. "I'll just let the boys know that you are here, and you'll soon find yourself among jovial company."

Sir Roland had not long to wait.

He heard the landlord give some kind of signal at a door at the further end of a passage.

The door was immediately opened, and as quickly reopened for Jos Townshend.

"You are wanted," he said. "Follow me."

When Sir Roland Ashton entered the room everything was dim and hazy to his eyes.

He could distinguish no object clearly, for the place reeked with tobacco smoke and the fumes of a long array of glasses upon a table covered with coarse, green baize.

"Welcome," said Phil Merrick, handing Sir Roland a chair. "Jack Starr and I began to think that you would never come. But now you are here make yourself comfortable."

Jack Starr now approached Sir Roland, and whispered in his ear.

"Pay no attention to whatever you may see or hear," he said.

Sir Roland nodded and smiled.

It was not the first time that he had been in such company, but he could not help confessing that he never saw a more villainous lot of men in all his life.

There were some who looked as if they had been scarred, bruised, and beaten from the day of their birth.

There were men with lowering brows, hard, cruel lips, and receding chins—certain marks of criminal type.

They smoked and drank uproariously, apparently paying but little heed to Sir Roland, who did not feel at all comfortable.

The select assembly of men were evidently bent on getting drunk, and Sir Roland knew from experience that one or the other would be sure to raise a quarrel at the slightest pretence.

Nor was he wrong; for when Jack Starr, who was in the chair, rose to his feet and said that he wished to introduce a new pal, a brawny ruffian, wearing a patch over one of his eyes, brought his fist heavily down upon the table and demanded, with an oath, why Sir Roland's probable arrival had not been announced before.

# SPRING-HEELED JACK,

## THE TERROR OF LONDON.

"IT IS OVER," SPRING-HEELED JACK SAID, AS HE TURNED AWAY.

No. 46.

"That's my business, Endicott," Jack Starr said. "Sit still and be quiet, can't you?"

"I shall do as I like about that," Endicott replied, scowling. "Who are you to order me about, I should like to know?"

"You will find out to your cost, if you are not careful," said Jack Starr, his eyes glittering with a baneful light.

"I have a right to speak as well as you, and I'll have my say," roared Endicott. "Who is this fellow you picked up on the road? How are we to know that he isn't a spy?"

"My friend," said Phil Merrick, tapping the drunken wretch on the shoulder, "if you do not pay attention to the chair, you'll find yourself in an awkward predicament before you can wink the only useful eye you have left."

"Who will do it?"

"I will."

This was enough for Endicott.

Kicking over his chair as he rose to his feet, he snatched a knife from a sheath, and made a furious stab at Phil Merrick.

The glittering blade missed him by a hair's breadth, and Endicott fell forward and struck his head heavily against the table.

In a moment Phil Merrick was upon him, and wrenching the knife from the ruffian's grasp, he poised it in the air and was about to plunge it into Endicott's back, when the landlord interposed.

Seizing Merrick's wrist, he held it as if it had been suddenly twisted into a vice.

"Come—come!" he said; "you ought to know better, Phil. Endicott is so drunk that he can't see a hole in a ladder. Have done with this, or I shall have to interfere and settle both of you."

"I'll talk to him when he is sober," Merrick growled, as he threw himself sulkily into a chair.

"I am sorry that this has happened," Sir Roland Ashton said, as he wiped his pale face. "If it is the wish of the company at large, I will retire."

"But it isn't," Jack Starr said. "Keep your seat. Endicott is asleep now, and he will know nothing about what has happened when he wakes. Boys, you see before you the man who is wanted for that job at Cockleton."

The ruffians cast admiring glances at Sir Roland, and several stretched out their hands towards him.

"I introduce him to you as one of us," Jack Starr continued, "and the best thing we can do is to administer the oath to him at once."

"Hear—hear!" cried Phil Merrick. "There is plenty to be done, and the sooner we have his services the better."

The oath administered to Sir Roland Ashton was a fearful one, and he shuddered as he took it.

When all was over a flagon of wine was pressed to his lips and he drained it to the dregs.

Scarcely had he done so, when the floor seemed to reel under his feet and he fell into a kind of stupor, and knew no more until he awoke and found that the light of day was streaming through a small window facing him.

The light at the best was a feeble one.

Sir Roland could see that the snow was falling so fast and thick that it seemed as if a lace curtain had been drawn between heaven and earth.

The wind moaned and sighed dismally down the huge chimney, and scattered the white ashes of an expired wood fire.

Sir Roland glanced round the bare, whitewashed walls of the room, at the carpetless floor, and at the miserable bed he was lying upon.

Soon the events of the previous evening became fixed upon his brain.

But where was he now?

Was he still at the Cow and Cucumber, or had he been removed from that delectable establishment?

With aching head and trembling limbs he walked to the window, and saw nothing but a wilderness of blackened walls and chimney-pots, made dim and indistinct in the falling snow.

Then he tried the door and found that it was locked.

Sir Roland's face flushed with anger.

"This must be altered," he muttered. "I will not be treated like a prisoner. I have already suffered too much of that sort of thing not to know the consequence of it."

The air was bitterly cold, and Sir Roland glanced round for his clothes.

They had been removed.

"This is too bad," he said, with an oath. "I will tell Merrick and Starr that I am not to be trifled with in this sort of way. Whatever I may be, I am not their slave yet."

Sir Roland had no alternative before him but to go to bed again, and, drawing the blankets over his shivering form, he tried to fall asleep.

But finding this impossible, he lay awake listening for some sound to denote that the people of the house were moving about.

For a long time no such sound came to his ears.

At last he heard a dull thud, as if somebody had jumped or fallen out of bed.

Then there was a deal of coughing and wheezing, and after a few minutes Sir Roland heard footsteps approaching.

A key grated in the lock, the door opened, and Jos Townshend, blear-eyed, frowsy, and gibbering with the effects of the previous night's debauch, stood in the doorway.

"Well, my tulip," he demanded, "how do you feel after the little excitement?"

"What does this mean?" Sir Roland demanded. "Why am I imprisoned here? Why have my clothes been removed?"

"For safety's sake, that's all," replied Jos Townshend, grinning. "You might have walked in your sleep, you know, and done yourself an injury."

"This is mere trifling," Sir Roland said, angrily. "I did not come here to be drugged, and then shut up like a rat in a trap."

"Of course you didn't," Jos Townshend said, in an exasperating tone of voice. "That's the proper way to look at it."

"Well, then," Sir Roland returned, "I'll thank you to bring my clothes, so that I may get up and dress."

Jos Townshend shook his head.

"It can't be done," he said.

"Why not?"

"Because I haven't got them."

"Who has, then?" demanded Sir Roland, almost beside himself with rage.

"Perhaps Phil Merrick or Jack Starr may know something about the matter," Townshend replied. "I don't."

"Where are they?"

"Asleep, I suppose."

Sir Roland Ashton clenched his fists and ground his teeth.

"I came up to ask you whether you would like anything to eat," Jos Townshend said.

"To eat?—no. You can bring me something to drink, if you like."

"Very well," said Townshend, placing his hand upon the key and turning away.

"Hold!" Sir Roland cried. "You are not going to lock me in again?"

"I must obey orders," Jos Townshend replied, coolly. "Now, don't put yourself into a temper, as that will only upset you and do no good."

Bang went the door.

"I did not bargain for this," Sir Roland thought. "These fellows do not trust me evidently, but I will be even with them yet."

In a few minutes Jos Townshend returned with a glass of liquor in his hand.

With a grim smile upon his face he watched Sir Roland as he drank it greedily.

"I suppose that was not drugged?" the baronet said.

"Oh! no," Jos Townshend replied. "Jack Starr is getting up, and he will be with you directly."

In about a quarter of an hour Jack Starr made his appearance.

"Here are your clothes," he said, pitching a bundle down on the floor. "Now you can get up as soon as you like, and have breakfast with me and Phil Merrick."

"I want to know—" Sir Roland began.

Jack Starr checked the baronet with a meaning motion of his hand.

"The best thing that you can do is to ask no questions," he said, "and abide patiently with what has been done. No man ever did himself a service by kicking against a brick wall. Come, get up, and we will have a long talk."

Sir Roland complied sulkily enough, but he became a little more cheerful when he entered a room in which a bright fire was burning, and saw a table laden with a substantial meal.

"There," said Jack Starr, "you see we mean well. Now I will tell you why we locked you in and took your clothes away."

"That is the very thing I should like to know."

"To show you that you were entirely in our power."

"That's just it," chimed in Phil Merrick, toying with the handle of his knife. "You see, you are almost a stranger to us, and, although you took the oath, you might have taken a sudden scare as well, if we had not been cautious; and we are always cautious—very."

"So it seems," said Sir Roland, smiling in spite of himself. "You need not doubt me. A man in my position is not likely to run away from his friends."

"Now, then, to business," said Jack Starr.

"That's the style," observed Phil Merrick, still toying with his knife. "We had a merry night, and we must make up for it as quickly as possible."

"From information I have received," Jack Starr continued, "the high sheriff will give a ball to-morrow night, and all the swells of the city and county will be there. Of course, most of the people will arrive in carriages, and as some will come from a long distance there would not be much difficulty in stopping one of the most valuable, if not two."

"I see," said Sir Roland, "you want me to turn highwayman?"

"Call it what name you like," Jack Starr replied, sneeringly; "but I can't see that you have any reason to grumble. The man who knocks another on the head in a wood might find the change to his advantage, and think it a little more respectable line of business."

"Go on," said Sir Roland, wincing; "I will listen to you without saying another word."

"Which will show your common sense," said Phil Merrick, tossing the knife in the air and catching it adroitly.

"Among the invited guests are Sir Henry Levarre and his two daughters," Jack Starr continued. "The ladies are renowned for their beauty, but what will please us better is the jewels which will be worn by them. I have every reason to believe that the gems would fetch five thousand pounds, even in such a market as we should have to take them to."

"What a haul it would be!" Phil Merrick observed.

"Yes; but let me get on," said Jack Starr. "Sir Henry Levarre lives at Wymondham, and the road, for the most part, is a lonely and unfrequented one, especially after nightfall."

"Black as pitch, and with only a house here and there," said Phil Merrick.

"Now, then," Jack Starr continued, "if you go with us, and if we succeed, you shall share equally with us, and then, if you like, you can leave us and get out of the country. We have chosen you because we think you are a bold man, and one who will not stick at trifles."

"You mean—"

"We mean," said Phil Merrick, interrupting him, and slashing the knife in the air, "that if Sir Henry Levarre and his daughters will not listen to reason they must listen to something else."

Sir Roland nodded his head.

"I understand you perfectly well," he said; "but in what manner do you make the attack? On foot?"

"No," Jack Starr replied; "I have arranged for three good horses, masks, and suitable dresses.'

"I agree," Sir Roland said. "You will not find me wanting in courage. You said that the ladies were lovely?"

"Lovely in the extreme."

"Why not hold one, if not both, in ransom?" said Sir Roland, laughing. "No doubt Sir Henry would be glad to pay handsomely for the restoration of his darlings."

"That's a matter for consideration," said Jack Starr. "But don't let us be too ambitious, or we may lose all."

## CHAPTER CLXIII.

### THE HIDDEN TREASURE.

As soon as the light of day began to show itself Bill Blarney continued his journey, and by eight o'clock he had reached the village of Carshalton.

The morning was as cold and raw as a morning could be, and the ruffian, with his head huddled into his shoulders, looked wistfully into the faces of the people who passed him, wondering if they would bestow a few pence for charity's sake upon him.

But Blarney had not a face calculated to impress even the softest-hearted favourably, and he received nothing in response to his mumbled supplications.

Thirst and hunger made him bolder.

He began to threaten, and by such means extracted a shilling out of a nervous old lady's purse.

With this he purchased a draught of beer and some provisions, and once more leaving all signs of human habitation behind him, struck out into the fields and woods.

His plight was a miserable one at the best.

He dare not show himself in a town, for fear that a description of him should have been sent from London, and he skulked about all day with his hands in his pockets, and his eyes directed towards the ground.

Once he was challenged by a shepherd, who warned him off a track of pasture-ground, and threatened to send for the village constable if he did not use his legs pretty quickly.

Bill Blarney felt a horrible desire to throttle the man.

But the sight of a huge dog at the shepherd's heels convinced him that any such attempt would only bring its own punishment.

"All right, my friend," he said. "I didn't know that I was doing any harm. I suppose you don't think that I want to carry the land away with me?"

"You look as if you would carry anything, as long as it came handy," the shepherd replied.

The glance that Bill Blarney gave out of the corners of his eyes at the man was not a pleasant one.

But he said no more, and turned away towards the road.

"That's an ugly brute of a fellow," the shepherd muttered, as he watched the ruffian's receding form, "and he's after no good, I'll be bound. I think I had better speak to the constable about him, or there may be some mischief to answer for."

Bill Blarney cursed and swore in the savage bitterness of his heart, as he made his way out of the neighbourhood as quickly as possible.

"I wish I had been born a dog, or some animal," he growled. "No homeless cur ever put up with what I have. I used to think that I might have been better if I had been treated with more kindness. Bah! men make war against me, and I will make war against them."

He devoured the fragments of the meal he had purchased in the morning, and spent his last penny at a roadside inn.

Here he found some labourers, and listened to their conversation, half fearing to hear something about himself.

But his name was not mentioned, and it was with a sensation of relief that the villain went his way.

After wandering about in an idle, listless manner for some time, Bill Blarney discovered that he was on the high road for Canterbury.

It occurred to him that Canterbury was a quiet, humdrum town, and one in which he would be less likely to be sought for.

It was on the way to the sea-coast, too, and Blarney entertained some hope that he might be able to stow himself away on some ocean-bound vessel, and get clear of the country which he now hated with all the strength of his evil heart.

Towards Canterbury, then, he bent his weary footsteps, and kept plodding on until the sun went down with a yellow glare into the western sky.

As the shades of night fell upon the landscape, so the cold increased.

"I must have shelter," he said. "I shall perish like a starved bird in the open air."

Here and there he passed a farmhouse with smoking chimneys, cosily-lighted rooms, and every evidence of comfort.

Like most rascals who meet with their deserts, he felt a hatred for the inmates of those homes, simply because he could not change places with them.

Onward he went, until darkness set in and silence reigned, save when a watchful dog uttered a warning bark at the approach of his footsteps.

Presently he stopped and leaned heavily upon a gate.

He felt so exhausted that he could go no further, and great drops of clammy perspiration rolled down his face.

Recovering himself somewhat, he looked over the gate, and saw that it opened upon a garden-path leading to a cottage.

There was no light in any of the windows, but presently he saw a faint glimmer flashing fitfully to and fro at the back part of the premises.

Bill Blarney took his arms from the gate and crouched down by the side of the adjoining hedge.

Soon the light grew stronger, and Bill Blarney saw a man, old, white-headed, and tottering, creep round to the front of the house.

Over his shoulder he carried a spade, which he clung to as if his life depended upon it.

"I wonder what the meaning of this is?" Bill Blarney muttered, under his breath. "Hang it! he is coming this way."

Noiselessly he darted across the road, and, stealing through a gap in the hedge, lay quiet.

"All is still," the old man muttered. "There is nobody about. Now to look at my hard savings—my idol—my god! People say that men cannot take gold out of the world with them, but how sweet it is to have it for a lifetime!"

Pausing in his speech as he swung the lantern to and fro, the old man passed his hand across his wrinkled brow.

"I dreamt last night that it was gone," he said, "and I cannot rest until I have seen it shimmering before my eyes. Yes—yes; I must feast my eyesight upon it, and then, and not until then, I shall be satisfied."

Bill Blarney could not hear a word uttered by the old man, but he guessed his object.

The ruffian's chest heaved, and his eyes glared like living coals.

"This is a slice of luck I did not expect," he muttered, grinning. "I'll let him take his time. Oh! yes, he shall have plenty of time."

After waiting a few minutes by the gate the old man retraced his footsteps slowly and painfully to the rear of the house.

Bill Blarney followed, but not by the way of the garden-path.

He climbed into the next field, and glided slowly along, as silently as a snake, and soon got a view of the old man and what he was doing.

He was hard at work at the base of a fir-tree, shovelling up the earth, and groaning under the exertion.

The hole deepened rapidly, and presently the spade rang upon something hard and metallic.

Stooping down, the old man drew out a box bound with iron clasps, and, placing it under his arm, made for the cottage.

Bill Blarney could not follow him.

He was spell-bound by what he had seen, and it was a relief to him when the miser was gone, for he could now give vent to his pent-up breath.

"I could attack him in the cottage," he thought; "but no! He would scream and shriek, and how am I to know that there is not some house within call? I will wait, for he will be certain to bury the treasure again."

For more than two hours Bill Blarney waited, scarcely moving.

Sometimes he fancied that he could hear the chinking of the gold as the miser counted it out, and his mouth watered at the bare idea of plunging his hands into the shining metal.

"Will he never come?" he said. "Or must I risk a struggle in the cottage? I have no weapon—nothing that I could silence him with quickly. Ah!"

The cottage door creaked upon its hinges, and as the old man emerged into the open air a huge grey owl flew round about his head.

It was an evil omen, but the miser heeded it not.

"All is safe," he mumbled. "Every piece good and sound. Ah! how many poor people would give half their lives to possess a tithe of it. Bah! let the poor take care of themselves."

Approaching the hole under the fir-tree, the old man replaced the box and filled in the earth carefully.

Reluctantly and very slowly he went back to the cottage.

Bill Blarney listened to the rattling of bolts and a chain as the house was secured.

"I must not be in a hurry," he said. "Misers seldom go to the expense of a light. Darkness costs them nothing, and they like it. He may be watching from the window at this very moment, for all I know. I'll wait—I'll wait until I think the hour of midnight has struck."

The ruffian remained where he was until his limbs grew cramped, and the excitement of his feelings nearly drove him mad.

At last he made a move towards the fir-tree, but how was he to dig up the earth which the miser had so carefully flattened down?

It was impossible to do so with his hands he knew full well.

But what other implement could he find?

To go blundering about in the dark in search of something suitable for the purpose was to run the risk of discovery, while, on the other hand, he did not intend to leave the spot without making an effort to rescue the hidden treasure.

He summoned up sufficient courage to go to the cottage door and listen for some minutes.

All was silent, and Bill Blarney could come to no other conclusion than that the old man had retired to rest.

As Bill Blarney was moving away one of his knees struck against something hard.

He reached out his hand, and, to his great joy, it grasped a bar of rusty iron.

All impatient to lose no time, Blarney went to work with a will, stopping every now and then to rest and listen.

He was not molested, and slaved on until he came to the iron-bound box.

As he raised it to the surface of the earth he could scarcely suppress a cry of exultation; but he controlled his feelings until he had put quite a mile between himself and the cottage.

The box was a heavy one, but not quite so heavy as Bill Blarney had expected.

"I mustn't grumble," he chuckled. "Supposing there is only a hundred pounds—say fifty—that will be quite sufficient to set me on my legs in fine style."

Then he began to reflect that it would not be safe for him to carry the box about.

"When I have opened it I'll fling it in a pond," he said, "and then, heigho! for the life of a gentleman as long as the shiners last."

He stopped at the first roadside pond he came to, and tested its depth by throwing in a stone.

"This will do," he muttered. "Now, then, to open the box."

He struck it against a post, and the iron bands, which were old and rusty, snapped almost immediately.

"Ha—ha—ha!" he laughed.

But the expression of his face changed as he wrenched open the box.

Instead of the gold which he hoped to feast his greedy eyes upon, he saw nothing but a number of worthless roadside stones and some dead leaves.

At first he could not believe in their reality, but suddenly the truth burst upon him.

"Oh! fool—fool," he cried. "I have been duped! I see it all now. The old man is as poor as a church mouse; but mad—stark, staring mad!"

---

## CHAPTER CLXIV.

### LEFT FOR DEAD.

LORD MILDENDALE waited, and waited in vain, for the return of Maglitch.

Half an hour passed away, and his lordship grew more and more impatient.

He knew that something must have happened, but he had not the courage to make his way into the Mart and ascertain how matters stood.

"Curses on the fellow!" he hissed, between his set teeth. "If he has failed, it will be my ruin."

But in spite of all his apprehensions, he could not tear himself away from the spot.

Suddenly he saw a man approaching him, and assuming a careless demeanour, Lord Mildendale walked to and fro humming a tune, and looking about him as if he was waiting for somebody.

His lordship started as he heard his name uttered by the stranger.

"I am he," Lord Mildendale said; "but I know you not. What do you require of me?"

"Merely to deliver a letter into your hands."

"Who is it from?"

"From Constable Maglitch," the man replied. "He told me not to wait for an answer, so your humble servant will wish your lordship Good-night."

Lord Mildendale tore the paper open.

"*All is well*," he read, "*but for reasons, which I will explain, I have thought it better not to meet you at the place appointed. Come to the woods near Castle Rising, and there you will find me.*"

"Good!" said Lord Mildendale, his face beaming with exultation. "I had begun to fear that all was lost. Well done, Maglitch; you have earned your money, and, perchance, I may reward you with a few extra guineas."

For fear that he might lose the letter he tore it into atoms, and scattered them before the wind.

"I will go at once," he said. "But, stay. Maglitch's instructions are vague. Shall I go on foot, or— Yes, on foot it shall be, as Maglitch must have procured another conveyance."

After a sharp walk he reached the border of the wood and looked about him.

The darkness was impenetrable, and the silence profound.

Suddenly a ray of light appeared in the sky.

The rising moon burst through the clouds and enabled Lord Mildendale to see something of the locality he was in.

The gaunt, leafless trees tossed their bare arms to the night wind as if in pain, and a feeling of superstitious awe crept into Lord Mildendale's heart.

He could see nothing and hear nothing of Maglitch, and he fretted and fumed at his absence.

Lord Mildendale began to ask himself if it could be possible that a trick had been played upon him.

But he abandoned that idea almost as soon as it had flashed into his brain.

"Bah!" he muttered; "I must not give way to foolish weakness. He will come if I only wait with patience."

The time went on, each moment an hour and each minute an age to Lord Mildendale.

How silent and mysterious the wood seemed, in spite of the wind, and the creaking and the groaning of the tortured trees!

"Perhaps the boy has fainted," muttered Lord Mildendale, "and Maglitch has decided not to bring him to me until he has recovered. Ha! What was that? I thought I heard a voice!"

"Hi—hi!" somebody called out. "This way—this way."

Lord Mildendale followed the sound, which, being repeated, led him into the deepest part of the wood.

Then silence reigned again, and he stopped, with the old feeling of terror stronger upon him.

"What is this?" he said, gripping the handle of his sword. "Have I been lured into this lonely place by some spectre? Maglitch—Maglitch, if you are near, answer me."

"He is not here, but I am!"

Lord Mildendale uttered a cry as Spring-Heeled Jack, who seemed to fall from the clouds, dropped at his feet.

"How now, my lord?" he said. "You do not look quite so well since our last merry meeting."

"Impostor!—base mockery in the garb of a fiend!" Lord Mildendale cried, "who sent you here? How comes it that you thwart my every purpose! What have I done to you that you should dog my footsteps?"

"Nothing, my lord, nothing," Spring-Heeled Jack replied, bowing low; "and yet I am here."

"Beware!" said his lordship. "There are constables approaching."

"I should not fear them were they a hundred strong," Spring-Heeled Jack returned; "but they will not come hither, take my word for it."

"You seem to be aware of their movements?"

"I am."

Lord Mildendale bit his under-lip until a thin stream of blood ran down to his chin.

"Yes," Spring-Heeled Jack continued, "I am aware of their movements. One—Maglitch—is moaning over a well-deserved blow, the other two are spending the money they had from you."

"From me!"

"Dare you deny it?"

Trembling in every limb, but forcing a calm expression upon his face, Lord Mildendale turned upon his heel.

"You must not go—you cannot go," Spring-Heeled Jack said, catching him by the shoulders and drawing him back.

"Who will stop me?'

"I will."

"For what purpose?"

"That I will tell you when I have forced you to listen to me," Spring-Heeled Jack replied. "Hear me patiently, for hear me you must and shall."

Lord Mildendale, finding that escape was impossible, folded his arms and compressed his lips.

"If I ask you a question I will answer it for you," Spring-Heeled Jack said, "and, when I have finished speaking, the rest shall be done quickly."

"The rest?"

"Aye! the rest," Spring-Heeled Jack repeated. "But listen, for my time grows short. I must return to succour and comfort your terrified and almost heart-broken son."

Lord Mildendale started as if stung by a serpent.

"My son!" he said, with a face so ghastly white that even Spring-Heeled Jack recoiled a pace before it.

"Your son—yes," the strange creature replied. "If he were not so why have you followed him since the hour that you thought that you had a clue to his whereabouts?"

"If he is my son," said Lord Mildendale, "by what right is he kept from me?"

"By the right of a natural law, which tells honest men that an unnatural parent is not a fit guardian for his children."

"See here," Spring-Heeled Jack said, as his height seemed to increase as he spoke. "Has your object been kind in seeking him? To your teeth I tell you no. As you sought to slay the mother, so you seek to slay her child. Oh! is it possible that such men as you are allowed to walk the earth in the sight of Heaven?

"Shall I tell you why you have done this in the blackness of your heart? Shall I tell you why that, after mourning, more out of fear than grief, for your last wife, you desire to be wholly free of her and her blood?"

"I care not what you tell me, or what you say."

"You lie!" Spring-Heeled Jack cried. "Your ghastly face betrays the fear that gnaws at your heart. Two years after Nana—Lanoni's daughter—was supposed to perish at the hands of a hag you employed to do the deed, you married again in France."

"I deny it," Lord Mildendale said, hoarsely.

"Of what avail is your denial, when I have every proof of my assertions?" Spring-Heeled Jack replied, leaning his back against a tree, and pointing mockingly at his lordship. "For ten years you have kept your second wife secretly in France, but she knows now the story of your perfidy, and is on her way for England."

"Devil!" Lord Mildendale yelled. "Give me the name of the man who has poisoned her ears!"

"Spring-Heeled Jack, who is very much at your service."

Lord Mildendale staggered back and smote his brow with his open hand.

"Oh! I am undone indeed."

"Undone!" Spring-Heeled Jack cried. "Is it in your power to undo what you have done? Can you restore happiness to Nana, who now lies pining and dying? Can you remove from her mother's heart the deadly feelings of vengeance, planted and nurtured there by you? Can you now say, 'Give me back my wife, my son, and let me implore their forgiveness,' when there is another who claims to take their place?"

"Why did you not tell me this when we met before?" Lord Mildendale said. "Fiend! You have kept this to yourself so that you might bring down all this misery upon my head with one fell swoop."

"I kept what I thought to be your secret, because I did not think that your heart was so hardened as to prevent a ray of repentance to enter it," Spring-Heeled Jack returned. "I had no notion that you had married again until a short time back. How I found it out it matters not. This very night Jannette Mildendale, as she calls herself, reached England, and travels to your home. She was never your wife; but 'ere day-break she will have good reason to fancy herself a widow."

"Your words are strange, and I do not comprehend them."

"My sword shall speak for me, then," said Spring-Heeled Jack, drawing a gleaming rapier. "Your son shall never know that he possessed so base a father. He shall never own your name, or share your ruined fortune. That may go to the wretched woman you have deceived. I have done. Come—come! my lord, we shall not part on such easy terms as we did last time."

As Spring-Heeled Jack spoke, he pressed the point of his rapier against Lord Mildendale's breast.

"A word," his lordship said.

"I'll hear no more," Spring-Heeled Jack replied. "Cross your sword with mine, or I will slay you as I would a rabid dog."

"If you fall, so, something tells me, will your knowledge," Lord Mildendale shouted. "So here's at you. Down—down to the depths of that perdition which cast you up to blight my life!"

He made so furious an onslaught that after two or three thrusts he lost his balance.

Then came a gasping, gurgling cry, and Spring-Heeled Jack stood, with his rapier dripping with blood, over the prostrate form of Lord Mildendale.

"It is over," Spring-Heeled Jack said, and turned away with the dirge-like wind singing in his ears.

## CHAPTER CLXV.

### THE EXECUTION OF JOE MORTH—WHAT HE SAW ON THE SCAFFOLD.

THE Lincoln Assizes were close at hand, and Joe Morth was duly arraigned before a judge and jury of his countrymen.

The facts of the case were so clear that only a few witnesses were called, and the jury returned a verdict of guilty without leaving the box.

Joe Morth clung to the rail of the dock as the verdict was delivered by the foreman.

The clerk then put the formal question to him as to whether he had anything to say why sentence of death should not be passed on him,

"I should waste words," he said, gloomily; "and yet I have a few words to say, my lord. At my house in the Borough, called the Bull in Top Boots, there is some property—'

"You stand convicted of robbery and attempted murder," the judge interposed; "and, therefore, such property as you may have will be confiscated by the Crown."

"I took no man's life, and, therefore, do not deserve death," Joe Morth said, as a ghastly hue overspread his face. "Attempted murder! You will murder me, indeed!"

"I sit here to administer the law as I find it," the judge replied. "It n ay be altered ere very many years have passed, out with that I have nothing to do. By that law, you have forfeited your life, and it only remains with me to pass sentence upon you."

"But I have more to say," Morth cried, clasping his hands. "I implore your lordship to let me speak. I was dragged into this position by a designing villain—the man who struck me down, like a coward—Sir Roland Ashton."

"The same law that deals with you will deal with him," his lordship replied. "Enough; I will hear no more."

The ushers proclaimed silence, and the judge proceeded to pass sentence.

Joe Morth listened to it like a man in a dream. To be hanged by his neck until he was dead!

He stared round the court with lack-lustre eyes, and then, as a warder touched him on the shoulder, he walked away with a vague notion that the sea of faces crowding the court were still before him.

As he passed through a long corridor, his brutal nature gained the ascendancy.

"I suppose," he said, snarling like a beast, "after all this, you will give me something to eat?"

Hardened as his warders were to all kinds of miserable scenes, and the sayings and doings of desperate men, they could not but help feeling disgusted and horrified at such words coming from the lips of a wretch who stood on the threshold of the grave.

"Something to eat," said one of the men. "I should think that you have not much appetite."

"And why not?" demanded Joe Morth, affecting a boldness which, perhaps, he did not feel. "A man can only die once, and why should I cringe and whine now that I know my fate?"

"Oh! well," said the warder, "there is no accounting for taste. For my own part, I should think of something else besides gorging and swilling."

As the man spoke he opened the door of a cell and thrust the wretch into it.

"As you will have to remain here for an hour or so," the warder said, speaking through a barred wicket, "you shall have your dinner."

"Why shall I have to wait so long?"

"To give the people time to disperse," the warder replied. "They are most anxious to get hold of you."

"I wish I was free and had a few of my old pals at my back," Morth replied. "I'd precious soon see whether they would care about tackling me."

One of the warders went over to a neighbouring public-house, in order to procure a meal, but when the landlord heard who it was for he refused to provide it.

"Not I!" he said. "If I had my mind, the dog should die by starvation."

Joe Morth was not only doomed to go dinnerless, but the people refused to disperse.

They lingered about with that morbid feeling which will keep idlers about for whole days and nights, with no other hope but to catch sight of a notorious criminal.

In vain the constables declared that Joe Morth had been removed by a back-way.

The crowd refused to believe it, and hung doggedly about until night set in.

Then there was no other alternative but to remove Joe Morth to Lincoln Gaol.

In those days there were no police-vans, or other contrivances for the removal of prisoners, and, as the officers had no instructions to order a carriage, they decided upon escorting Morth through the streets.

Forming as strong a body as possible round him, they brought him out.

A yell of execration rent the air.

"Down with him!" roared the people. "Down with him! Why weren't we allowed to hang him before without all this trouble?"

Warders and constables had fairly to fight their way through the surging mob.

Joe Morth's evil face underwent as many changes as there are colours in the rainbow.

To see the rabble trying to get at him was to suffer pangs worse than those of death itself.

"Oh! for one of the old days, when my hands were free and grasped a knife or pistol," he hissed, as the warders dragged him unceremoniously along. "I would give a good account of myself to some of these white-livered curs!"

At last the constables were reinforced just as Lincoln Gaol came in sight, and the people were driven back.

But they did not forget to throw mud, stones, and every conceivable missiles upon Morth, who howled and snarled like a wild beast.

It was a great relief to him when the ponderous prison doors closed upon his bruised and beaten body.

"Curse you all!" he growled, turning to the warders. "You were as much in this as the howling mob. They took good care not to hit you."

"Hold your tongue," said the leader of the warders, "or you'll go to bed hungry and thirsty to-night, I can tell you."

Though handcuffed and heavily-ironed beyond escape, Morth wrenched and tore at his fetters as if he had taken leave of his senses.

"Take me where you will," he hissed, "and do what you like. In three days it will be all over. At least I have the consolation of knowing that I have given you no end of trouble, and I'd die happy if I thought I could take one or two of you with me."

At this moment the governor of the gaol came bustling into the lobby.

He did not speak to Joe Morth for some moments, but eyed him up and down as if receiving him in custody gave him no great amount of pleasure.

"You will be taken to the condemned cell," he said at last, "and you will have the privilege of sending for me at any time you choose, and also for the chaplain of the gaol."

"I shall see quite enough of you on Monday morning, I'm thinking," Morth said, grinning. "All I ask is to be left alone. If you want to do me a favour, let me have a few sheets of paper and an inkstand."

"Everything you write must pass through my hands," the governor said.

"Then I have nothing more to say, and want nothing."

The governor of Lincoln Gaol made a sign with his hand.

Clank—clank! went a new set of chains which a warder took down from hooks driven into the wall.

"Oh! I see," said Morth, sneeringly. "You are afraid that I shall yet give you the slip."

"We will take as much possible care that you do not," the governor replied. "Ring the bell for the smith."

Joe Morth folded his arms and leaned his back against the wall as the smith came, bringing with him a basket of tools and a small anvil.

The warders surrounded the condemned man as the new set of manacles were fitted to his limbs, and when the task was completed, and each rivet tested, Morth was led to his last abode on earth.

When alone, a reaction of feeling came upon him.

All his hardened boldness fled in a moment, and he began to whimper that the iron cut into his flesh, and, finding that no attention whatever was paid to him on this score, he roared and yelled that Sir Roland Ashton ought to be with him.

"Hold your tongue, will you?" the warder said. "Do you want to wake all the prisoners up?"

"I know of secrets well worth the hearing," Morth said. "If time is given me, I can tell the authorities where the worst criminals in London are to be found."

The dastard nature of the vile wretch was creeping out at last.

"It is not for me to make any assertion," the warder replied; "but I think you may take my word that not a single hour will be given you. Keep your tongue still and go to sleep."

"Sleep!" echoed Joe Morth. "Who could go to sleep in such a hole as this?"

"Many have done so," said the warder, growling.

He closed the wicket with a bang and continued his dreary walk up and down the corridor.

Morth rested his brow upon his manacled hands and tried to think calmly.

Though he had heard the solemn words of the judge telling him to prepare for the worst, he could not believe that he had been brought there to die.

He lived again in the past.

He went back to the time when money flew about as freely as the vile liquor sold at the Bull in Top Boots.

And he had brought himself to this position through a feeling of revenge.

"Fool—fool!" he groaned. "Why could I not let fate deal with the old hag? I must have been mad."

Then his thoughts reverted to Sir Roland Ashton, and he ground his teeth with rage.

"He struck me, like the cur he is!" Morth muttered; "and he is free, while I am here caged like a rat."

Again he dashed at the door, kicking and beating at it, and demanding to know whether he was to be left there to starve.

No notice was taken of him for more than half an hour, but at the expiration of that time two warders entered the cell, and placed a plentiful meal before him.

"Of course you will remove these handcuffs?" Joe Morth said.

"Of course we shall do nothing of the kind," a warder replied.

"How am I to get at the food?"

"The best way you can. You'll manage it very well, I have no doubt; but, if you can't, why you will have to go hungry, so there is an end of the matter."

The cell door was no sooner closed than a malicious grin stole over the convict's face.

"If they had been green enough to take off the handcuffs," he said, "I would have left one of them at least a memento. Well, I will eat and drink, and it may be that I shall sleep."

And Joe Morth did sleep.

He dreamed horribly all the night through, and often called out aloud, but did not unclose his eyes until day had dawned.

He was then visited by the chaplain of the prison, but repulsed him rudely.

The good man bore Morth's insults meekly, and exchanged kind words for coarse ones, and at last the stony heart of the villain melted, and he listened attentively to what was said to him.

That day he passed wretchedly enough.

He often made enquiries as to whether Sir Roland Ashton or Mrs. Corcoran had been taken, and when replied to in the negative he flew into paroxysms of rage fearful to behold.

Night came again, and with it the most dismal thoughts.

He had only a few more hours to live.

When the grey dawn began to steal along the prison walls the sound of labour would break upon his ears.

An awful task would be in operation—the construction of the scaffold upon which he was to die.

To be hanged like a dog, to be strangled in the full view of a surging mob!

His brain seemed to catch fire as he pictured the scene that was to come.

His imagination became so haunted that every thought became a reality.

He heard the tolling of the bell; he heard the prison doors close upon him for ever; he saw the mob, and shrank as they hailed him with a howl of savage delight; he saw the executioner, and felt the dread touch of the rope about his neck, and then—

Joe Morth sprang to his feet, jangling his irons noisily.

"I must have been dreaming," he gasped. "Oh! what a dream. It cannot be as bad as that. Mercy—mercy! Let me die now."

Suddenly an idea that had never occurred to him flashed through his brain.

Die he must; but there was one way of preventing death by so violent means as that which threatened him—self-destruction!

"If I could but open a vein," he muttered, "I should bleed slowly to death, and they would find, when they came for me in the morning, that I had cheated them. But how is it to be done?"

His wrists were so closely held together that he could scarcely move them, but he had sharp teeth.

With an awful determination, he set his teeth into his flesh, and the blood began to flow.

"I have done it," he said; "and now to sleep—a long—long sleep."

Scarcely had he uttered the last word when the door opened, and the governor of Lincoln Gaol entered the cell.

Morth staggered back, and a cry scarcely human sprang from his lips.

"What's this?" the governor demanded, as a warder, who had accompanied him, turned the light of a lantern on the convict. "This man has opened a vein in his arm. Ring up the doctor. Quick! There is not a moment to lose."

"May a blight fall upon one and all of you!" Morth hissed, as he crouched snarling and wolf-like into a corner. "Why could you not let me die in peace?"

The doctor was soon on the spot, and in a dreadful bad temper at being dragged from his bed at such a time.

He pronounced the wound of no consequence, and having bound up the prisoner's arm, went yawning and grumbling back to his room again.

The governor now ordered two warders to remain with Morth, and to keep a strict watch upon him.

Morth now became quiet—almost to passiveness.

He seldom spoke, even when spoken to; but at the first sound of a hammer striking upon those awful black beams he started up.

"What's that?" he cried.

"Oh! nothing," said a warder.

"You lie!" Morth yelled. "They are making the scaffold. Oh! cruel—cruel!"

The men drew closer to him, fearing that he would dash his head against the stone wall, or attempt some other desperate act; but the villain, after raving for a few minutes, lapsed into a kind of torpor, from which he did not recover until the prison clock chimed a quarter to eight.

Then the chapel bell began to toll forth its sonorous notes.

The door opened, and a dismal procession filed in. The sheriff first, then the governor, with a double row of warders at his heels, and, lastly, the executioner, with the dread instruments of his horrible calling flung lightly over his arm.

Joe Morth listened like a man in a dream as the warrant was read over to him; and it was not until he was pinioned, and his irons struck off, that he seemed to realise the fact that his last moment was at hand.

Rousing and steadying himself, he asked for a drink of brandy.

It was brought to him and pressed against his white and bloodless lips.

"Not half enough," he said, groaning. "Give me more; for mercy's sake, give me more!"

The sheriff exchanged glances with the governor, and they made a move forward.

The booming of the bell mingled with the sound of the chaplain's tremulous voice, and both were drowned as the prison doors were opened and Morth stood upon the scaffold, in full view of an ocean of the upturned faces of the people who had come to see him die.

The sun was shining brightly, rendering the snow-covered roofs of the houses brilliant and beautiful.

Joe Morth cast a glance at the scene upon which his eyes were to close so soon, and then came the end.

As his quivering body dangled from the blackened beam, a wild shriek rose high above the cries of the mob, and a little, shrivelled-up old man fell into the arms of one of the crowd.

It was not a man, but Mrs. Corcoran, who had come to see the last moments of the landlord of the Bull in Top Boots.

---

## CHAPTER CLXVI.

### HEMMED IN—THE BARN—THE FIRE.

We left Bill Blarney with his treasure of dried leaves and common stones picked up by the roadside, but carefully washed and polished.

"This must be a ruse," he muttered, as he spurned the worthless rubbish with his feet. "The old man must have money. Perhaps he knew that I was lurking about and removed the gold when indoors. All is dark and still. Shall I go back and attack him in his den?"

Blarney was almost beside him elf with rage, and he could not make up his mind what to do.

"I must have money," he muttered, as he clutched despairingly at his hair. "Aye! and I will have it, for be what I may I was not born to starve."

He was in the act of retracing his footsteps, when he heard a slight sound just ahead of him.

Bill Blarney stood perfectly still, for the sound might have been caused by a bird stirring in a bush, or a rabbit scuttling through the grass.

But presently the noise increased, and he made sure that a human being was approaching.

Bill Blarney held his breath, for the man seemed to be creeping stealthily along the grass with which the road was bordered, as if to avoid being heard.

"Who the deuce can this be?" Blarney thought. "The fellow is no good, I'll be bound. He may be one of my kidney, and if so I'll chum up to him if only company's sake."

"Hullo!" he cried out. "Who goes there?"

The sound of footsteps ceased, but the challenge was not answered.

Bill Blarney tried to peer through the darkness, but all was so black around him that he could scarcely see an inch before his nose.

"Come," he cried; "can't you speak? Haven't you a tongue in your head?"

"Yes; but why on earth are you prowling about here at such a time?"

"Well, that's cool, at any rate," said Bill Blarney. "Supposing I have no home, what else can I do but to prowl about?"

"People ain't allowed to prowl about," said the voice.

"Then what are you doing here?"

"Why, it so happens that I am a constable, and I shall call upon you to give an account of yourself."

The last word had been scarcely uttered when Bill Blarney discovered that a light had been thrown upon his face.

He stood still and tried to look unperturbed, though his heart sank and his blood ran cold.

As yet he could not see the constable, for the light occupied the whole of his vision.

"Well," he said, "what do you make of me?"

"No good."

"Ha! ha! ha!" laughed Bill Blarney. "If you are a constable you are a joker, and fun don't often run in men of your stamp."

The officer shut the slide of the dark lantern, and striding up to Bill Blarney touched him on the shoulder.

"You will have to walk a little way with me, my lad," he said. "Several robberies have been committed in the neighbourhood of late, and I am always on the look-out for suspicious characters."

"You take me for one, then?" said Bill Blarney, as his heart thumped against his side.

"That remains to be seen. I have a duty to perform, and I mean to do it," the constable replied. "Last year a pack of vagabonds robbed poor old Byson of his money and drove him mad. People say that he now goes about in the dead of night burying all sorts of worthless rubbish, which he thinks is gold."

The secret was out now with a vengeance, and for some moments Bill Blarney could not speak.

"My friend," he said, at length, "you will waste time by taking me to the lock-up. I am only a poor miserable wretch, on the look-out for work to help me to reach Canterbury, where have friends."

"I am a native of the place, and know every body in it," the constable returned. "What your name, and the names of the people you ar going to?"

"Smith."

"A very common name indeed," said the con stable sneeringly. "What may the Smiths o Canterbury be by trade?"

"Tanners."

"That's enough," said the constable, gruffly "There's no tanner of that name in the whol length and breadth of Canterbury. Come along and come quietly, or it will be the worse for you."

Bill Blarney saw that the game was up, and tha he must either surrender quietly to the constabl or do something desperate to effect his escape.

He chose the latter course, and put his whol brain into thinking how he should get rid of th constable's unwelcome company.

"Of course, if I must go with you, I must," h said; "but it is jolly hard that because a man i weary and almost tired to death that he is take for a thief and treated like one."

"If you can give a better account of yourself, the constable returned, "I'll go bail that you sha fare well."

"That's a bargain," said Bill Blarney. "Yo need not hold me. I will walk quietly along b your side."

This threw the country constable off his guard and he relaxed his hold on Blarney's arm.

The moment he had done so he had ever cause to repent it.

Blarney dashed his brawny left fist into the con stable's face, and followed it up with so terrific blow with his right, that the man went heels ove head into a ditch before he could utter a cry.

The ruffian did not stop to see what injuries hi victim had sustained, but took to his heels.

His first thought was to leave the road, an having climbed over a gate, he began scramblin through a copse.

But here he discovered that he had fallen into trap which he little expected.

The undergrowth was so dense that it entangle his feet and so impeded his progress that he coul scarce move a yard without falling.

He went down heavily at least a dozen times.

The faster he tried to run, the less speed h made.

Uttering a horrible curse as his head came i contact with the branch of a tree which hun across his path, he dashed the drops of the thick clotted blood from his brow, and pressed on i spite of all difficulties.

Every moment he expected to hear some soun indicative of the constable pursuing him, and h strained every nerve and muscle to such an exten that his heart and brain seemed to turn red-hc and fit to burst.

On he went—now up, now down, sometime erect, and at others crawling along upon his hand and knees, bruised, torn, beaten, and bleedin profusely.

Suddenly he felt that his strength was failin him.

He closed his eyes, and, feeling that he coul hold out no longer, almost fainted.

"Hi—hi! Help! Stop thief! Murder Help—help!"

The constable had now regained his feet and hi senses, and was shouting at the top of his voice.

Each sound came to Bill Blarney's ears like a death-knell.

"I cannot be in a safer place than this," he mused. "I don't know how large this copse is, and, if I leave it, it will be all over with me, as the light of those accursed dark lanterns show a long way."

He lay as quiet as possible, but in spite of all he could do he breathed heavily.

So heavily, indeed, that the sound frightened him, and he almost choked himself to keep back the gurgling noise.

Presently he heard tottering footsteps moving about outside the copse.

"I'll give the scoundrel something for this," the constable growled. "I must have been an ass to trust him. I'll be bound that he is a prisoner worth catching, and he'll be clever indeed if he escapes after I have once laid hands on him."

Suddenly Bill Blarney saw a ray of light flitting in and out among the trees.

"It's all over with me," he gasped. "That thick-skulled wretch will pounce down upon me like a hawk, and what chance have I, in my condition, to resist him?"

But Bill Blarney's time had not come yet.

Chance decreed that the constable did not venture far into the copse.

Perhaps he did not care to do so, thinking that the ruffian might have armed himself with a stick, and be lurking behind a tree.

The constable walked on a few yards, and just as Bill Blarney was congratulating himself on the fact that he had another chance of escape, the man came back again.

"I'd give a year of my life to have my hands upon his throat," he muttered under his breath. "If he stops here until daylight people will pass and come to his assistance. Will he never go? He must, or I shall go stark, staring mad."

The constable, however, had no notion of waiting in so lonely a place until day dawned.

There was a station and a lock-up, to which he was attached, not far away, and after listening awhile, and hearing nothing to arouse his suspicions, he thought he had better consult his superior officer as to the best course to pursue.

The blows he had received left him still in a rather confused state of mind, and lent rather erratic movements to his legs.

Rage was in the constable's heart, and as soon as he came within sight of the station, he braced himself up to make his story as good as possible.

"Ah!" said the inspector, when he had listened attentively to the end. "This may be the very man who is wanted in London. While you were on duty, Stokes, a messenger arrived by the nearest way with a description of a fellow named William Blarney. Did you notice the customer who tackled you very attentively?"

"Yes, sir," Stokes replied; "I had a good look at him."

"Well?" queried the inspector, glancing down at a sheet of paper lying upon his desk. "Go on."

"About five feet nine high, rather flat nose, dull, dark eyes, scar over the right one, broad, thin mouth, straggling moustache, one end being longer than the other."

"That's enough," said the inspector. "You have painted the rascal's portrait to a nicety. William Blarney it is, and we must have him by hook or by crook, just to show these cute London people that we are up to a move or two."

"Yes, sir," said Stokes. "What shall I do now?"

"Go round and rouse up all the day constables, and tell them to block all the roads," the inspector replied. "Two horse-patrols will be here presently, and I will instruct them how to act."

Constable Stokes was off like a shot out of a gun.

"I only wish I may have the taking care of him when we get him in the lock-up," he muttered. "His gruel shall be thin enough, I'll warrant him."

Two or three other constables lived close handy, and though they grumbled and growled in no measured or polite tones, they turned out immediately and joined Stokes, whose blood was up and eager for the fray.

The two mounted patrols arrived in due course, and took up positions on roads such as Bill Blarney might be likely to choose.

It was scarcely likely that Bill Blarney would make his way to Canterbury now, if, indeed, he had ever intended to go there at all.

Nor was it probable that he would retrace his footsteps towards London.

Thus the officials came to the conclusion that he would hide in some hole or corner in the neighbourhood until the efforts to capture him were relaxed.

The hunted wretch still lay concealed in the copse.

But as day began to dawn he became frightened, and creeping to the border, looked out.

Scarcely a hundred yards from him were some outhouses, which belonged to what is called an "off" farm.

That is to say, where no dwelling-house is attached, but where the buildings are handy for storage.

"Anywhere is better than this shivering place," Bill Blarney said. "There are beams, and rafters, and false ceilings in those buildings where I can hide. And, what is better, if I am attacked, I shall be almost sure to find some weapon to defend myself with."

Summoning up all his courage, he made a rush for the nearest building, which happened to be a barn of fair dimensions.

The door was only secured by an iron hook, which could be replaced on the inside in consequence of a hole which had been made in the woodwork.

Bill Blarney breathed a sigh of relief as he reached the interior and looked about him.

One side of the barn was piled high with trusses of hay and straw, affording every means of shelter.

In a corner stood an old-fashioned hay-cutting machine with its wheel of knives, and the ruffian made haste to secure one of the sharpest.

"Now they may come," he hissed. "Yes, curse them, they may come; but the first man who comes within the length of my arm had better make his will quickly."

He then proceeded to climb to the very top of the trusses, and looking down, he saw that there was a space between him and the wall through which he could lower himself, in a case of emergency, by clinging to the hay-bands.

"How warm and comfortable it is here," he said, as he stretched himself at full length. "I'm as safe as if I was behind a stone fortress, so here goes for a good, long snooze."

# SPRING-HEELED JACK,

## THE TERROR OF LONDON.

"YOUR TIME HAS COME AT LAST, BILL BLARNEY," SAID SPRING-HEELED JACK.

No. 47.

It did not take him long to get to sleep, for his head ached after what he had undergone; but Blarney's rest was of short duration.

"Whoy, look 'ere!" roared a rustic voice. "Somebody's been 'ere a-smashin' up t' hay machine! Run, Jem, run, and tell measter afore he gets out of t' seven-acre field."

The man ran off as fast as his legs would carry him to tell the farmer of the mischief that had been done in the barn.

The agriculturist was a fat man, and given to bursts of violent temper, and he swore that if he caught the fellow who had destroyed the hay cutting machine, he would not only flog him, but eat him into the bargain.

The noise of the farmer and his labourers talking in the barn awoke Bill Blarney.

"See, here are his footprints on the chaff," the farmer said, "and it strikes me that he's up among the straw now. One of you run for a constable, and we'll soon ferret the rascal out."

There was no reason to go for an officer of the law, for at that very moment Stokes and two other constables appeared.

"Ah!" cried Stokes, when the report had been made to him, "I smell a rat. I expect that Bill Blarney, the greatest rogue that ever escaped the gallows, is your visitor. If I get hold of him, he may make sure of the rope."

"May I?" Bill Blarney hissed between his teeth. "If you come within reach of my arm I'll cut your head from your shoulders."

For better security Bill Blarney began to lower himself down the aperture between the wall and the trusses of hay.

This, to all appearance, was not a difficult task, but the ruffian's feet happened to slip, and he went down heels over head.

As he reached the floor with a thud, a savage oath sprang to his lips.

"We have him now," cried Stokes. "Follow me, lads."

The constables scrambled up the hay, but the farmer and his men held back and kept very near the door.

"Stand back!" Blarney cried, as he caught sight of the officers. "I am armed and will sell my life dearly."

"What's the use of talking such nonsense?" Stokes said. "You've got to surrender, so you may as well do it quietly."

As he spoke, he took a pistol from his belt, and levelled it at Bill Blarney's head.

"Hold up your hands, or I fire!" cried the constable, sternly.

Blarney snatched up the hay-knife, which had fallen at his feet, and hurled it with all his strength at the officer.

It is just possible that Stokes had no intention of firing, but as the blade whizzed past his head he pulled the trigger.

There was the usual flash and report, but Bill Blarney stood unharmed.

But something else had been done.

The discharge set the hay on fire, and before any remedy could be applied, a huge flame shot up towards the roof of the barn.

The constables forgot all about Bill Blarney in a moment, and thought of nobody and nothing but themselves.

Down they came with all speed, and ran to where the farmer, open-mouthed and aghast, was standing.

"Curse you!" he yelled, as soon as he could speak. "If these buildings are destroyed I am a ruined man."

"If I were you," said Stokes, "I should think of doing something instead of swearing at us. Where do you keep the buckets? There's a pond not far off."

"There isn't a bucket to be found within a mile," the farmer replied.

"Then Bill Blarney will be burned."

"So will my barn," gasped the farmer.

The place was so full of smoke that they were compelled to retreat into the open air.

"Help—help!" Bill Blarney shrieked. "Do not leave me to die such a horrible death as this! Help! Save me! Mercy! If you have a grain of pity in your hearts do not leave me here."

## CHAPTER CLXVII.

### SIR ROLAND ASHTON TURNS HIGHWAYMAN.

A DULL, stormy afternoon had passed away, and given place to gloomy, sullen night.

It seemed as if the darkness had lulled the elements to rest, for not a sound disturbed the stillness.

The streets of the city of Norwich were covered with snow, and people kept within their homes, save the linkmen who had been engaged to attend the sheriff's ball.

Not a carriage had as yet arrived; but it was early as yet, and the linkmen, huddling together, cursed the bitter cold, which nipped their noses with icy tweezers, and penetrated to their very bones.

"This would be a fine night for a cracksman's business," said one, with a hoarse laugh. "I'll go bail that the watchmen will take care to keep well within their boxes."

"Who blames 'em?" queried another. "If this wasn't a good paying job, I'd throw it up, and roll into bed as soon as I could get home."

"Halloa!" cried a third. "Here comes somebody. He can't be a guest, for he is on horseback and alone."

"Perhaps he is a highwayman," observed the man who had first spoken. "Jem, flash the light of your torch in his face, and have a look at him."

As the man addressed did so, the horse shied and reared violently, and Jem caught a stinging cut from the whip across his head and shoulders for his pains.

"How dare you?" said the equestrian. "How dare you stop a gentleman on a peaceful and lawful errand? Your mad act might have resulted in my death."

Jem mumbled out an apology as he rubbed his head and returned to his companions, who were grinning hugely at his misfortune.

"Well, what was he like?" one asked.

"I hadn't time to see," Jem replied, ruefully; "but there's plenty of time for you to do so. He is riding very slowly, and you can easily overtake him."

But the linkmen declined, and the horseman rode on his way as coolly as if nothing had happened.

Though cool in demeanour he did not feel so in heart.

"Phew!" he muttered; "I thought I had been pounced upon by a posse of constables."

It was Sir Roland Ashton who spoke.

He was handsomely attired, and nobly mounted on a spirited horse.

"If Merrick and Starr do not meet me at the appointed place," he said, "I shall not attempt the work. I do not like it, rich as the prize promises to be."

Then he began to meditate upon the fact that he was riding a horse which he could sell for a considerable amount of money; but he also remembered that, for all he knew, the eyes of the villains who had hired him might be upon him at that very moment.

Sir Roland had been well instructed with regard to the way he was to take.

He passed through a toll-gate, and about a mile further on came to four cross-roads.

Here he drew rein, and began to look about him.

Presently he heard a sound like the hooting of an owl.

"That is the signal," he said. "They are coming this way."

Phil Merrick and Jack Starr, advancing quickly on foot, saluted Sir Roland.

Take a nip of something to keep yourself warm," said Jack Starr, handing the baronet a flask.

"Thanks, I am grateful for it," Sir Roland replied. "Ah! I feel better now. Why did you not let me bring some on the road?"

"Because you might have muddled your head," said Phil Merrick, as he held out his hand for the flask. "How long have you been here?"

"Not five minutes."

"Then you have not seen or heard anything?"

"Not set eyes on a living creature or heard a sound."

"It would be an awful sell if Sir Henry Levarre and his daughters kept at home," Phil Merrick said.

"I shouldn't wonder at that," Jack Starr returned. "I should have to be mighty fond of dancing to leave my fireside to come out on such a night as this."

"Unless you could make something out of it," said Phil Merrick.

"Just so," Starr replied. "But enough of this kind of talk. We have some business to settle yet, and the sooner we get over it the better. Now, Merrick, just you instruct Sir Roland for the last time, so that he can't make any mistake."

"I will," said Merrick. "We came round by Hethersett and left our horses there, thinking we had better come on foot. You, Sir Roland, will stop the carriage by shooting the coachman and footman, and we will be at each door before Sir Henry and his daughters have time to know what has happened."

Sir Roland Ashton rubbed his chin thoughtfully.

He now began to suspect the men.

"If I do the shooting part, I run the most danger," he said. "How am I to know—"

He ceased speaking, and Phil Merrick turned upon him with an oath.

"Come, out with it," he said. "How are you to know what?"

"I was thinking," said Sir Roland, "that the coachman and footman might be armed, and if I missed one or the other, I should stand a good chance of getting a bullet through my brain."

"You were not thinking of anything of the kind," said Merrick. "You thought that if we got the jewels that you would not get your share."

"I assure you," Sir Roland began, when Merrick silenced him.

"I don't want any of your assurances," he said. "Do the work you have promised to perform and leave the rest to me, or it will be the worse for you, my friend."

"Here, cease this jangling," said Jack Starr. "I thought I heard something like the cracking of a whip. Pull your horse under those trees and hold your tongue."

Sir Roland's face grew dark with suppressed passion as he obeyed.

"If they attempt to cheat me I will be the death of them," he muttered, under his breath. "They thought themselves very clever when they gave me two loaded pistols and no more ammunition, but I took the precaution to purloin another brace of barkers from Jos Townshend's house."

Phil Merrick and Jack Starr took up their places directly opposite Sir Roland, so that they could watch his every movement.

Jack Starr was not mistaken.

The cracking of the whip sounded loud and distinct on the still air, but the snow muffled the wheels.

At last Sir Roland Ashton saw a faint flash of light.

"The carriage is not far away," he said, softly; "I can see the lamps."

"Wait until we tell you to advance, and then do so boldly," Merrick replied.

On came the carriage, the lamps dancing, and glimmering, and casting all sorts of fantastic shadows along the road.

The coachman was driving very carefully, and the footman on the box beside him kept a sharp look-out.

"Now," said Merrick, "gallop straight at them, and make sure of your aim."

Sir Roland Ashton set his teeth as he put spurs to his horse.

"Hold, there!" he cried. "Stop your horses—there is a fallen tree in the way."

The coachman, thrown off his guard for a moment, pulled the horses back on their haunches.

As he did so Sir Roland Ashton fired point-blank at the unfortunate man's head.

The reins fell from his hands.

He threw up his arms, and, uttering a yell of agony, rolled headlong from the box.

"You coward—you devil in the form of a man!" shouted the footman.

He said no more, for a second bullet sent him reeling after the coachman, and Sir Roland Ashton, drawing his sword, cut the traces, and allowed the half-maddened horses to gallop away.

While this was going on, Merrick and Starr had masked their faces and rushed to the doors of the carriage.

Sir Henry Levarre, a handsome gentleman in the prime of life, sat facing his two lovely daughters, who, as a matter of course, began to scream the moment that they heard the report of the pistols.

"By Jove! we are attacked," Sir Henry cried. "Sit still, girls, and try to be brave, for there may not be anything to be alarmed about, after all."

Dashing down one of the windows, he thrust his head out and beheld the hideously-masked face of Phil Merrick.

"It's no use making a fuss, Sir Henry," the ruffian said. "This job has been well planned, so you may as well give in quietly to save trouble."

"What do you want, you audacious scoundrel?" Sir Henry Levarre demanded.

"All the cash you have about you, and the jewels your daughters are wearing."

"You shall have neither," Sir Henry declared. "Be off, you hang-dog. Neither your ugly looks nor the pistol you hold in your hand will frighten me."

At that moment Jack Starr opened the other door and seized one of the young ladies violently by the wrist.

Her frenzied cry for help caused her father to turn round, and Merrick, seizing him by the collar of his coat, dragged him half through the window.

"You had better consent to our proposals," Merrick hissed in Sir Henry Levarre's ear; "or not one of you shall leave this place alive."

"I consent," Sir Henry gasped. "Let go your hold, you are choking me."

Phil Merrick grinned under his mask as he thrust Sir Henry back into the carriage.

"Make haste!" he said. "Me and my mate don't want to stand about here in the cold all night."

Sir Roland came riding up to take his share of the plunder, and his eyes gleamed as the pale-faced ladies removed their necklaces and other articles of jewellery.

"Now for your purse," said Jack Starr. "We've made a good haul, but you will not feel it. That's right. Now, boys, let us away. We had better part."

"Yes," said Sir Roland; "but before we do so, I suggest that we share the plunder."

"Oh! that will be a matter for after consideration," Merrick said, sneeringly. "What could you do if we told you you were not to have a farthing?"

"This," said Sir Roland.

He drew the pistols which he held in reserve and covered both the ruffians' heads.

Phil Merrick and Jack Starr started as if they had been shot in right down earnest.

It is said that when thieves fall out honest men get their due.

If it does not always happen, it did so in this instance.

Sir Henry Levarre, seeing how matters stood, seized upon his own pistols, and before either Merrick or Starr could speak a word both men were grovelling on the ground and tearing up the snow in handfuls.

Sir Roland's horse saved its rider from a similar fate.

The animal leaped forward and dashed away at a furious gallop.

Sir Roland was too much astonished to do anything but keep his balance in the saddle, and this was a matter of no little difficulty, as the horse seemed bent upon throwing him.

Foaming at the lips with rage and disappointment, Sir Roland was borne away mile after mile, until the horse grew tired and stopped of its own accord.

"So this is the end of the venture which was to make me rich," he hissed, through his foam-flecked lips. "Foiled again! But I am well served for joining in such an expedition."

He began to reflect on what he should do next.

He had no money of any account, and if he attempted to sell the horse, questions which he would find hard to answer might be asked.

Appearances, at all events, were with him.

He was handsomely dressed, and could easily get credit at an inn, and this he thought would be the best thing he could possibly do.

He was unknown in the neighbourhood, and some time would elapse before the officers of the district were upon his track, even if they came at all.

Sir Roland argued that Sir Henry Levarre would be satisfied with his revenge upon the robbers, and not trouble his head any more about the matter.

He rode on, keeping to the broad path until some houses loomed out of the darkness.

He chose the first one offering entertainment, and, ordering supper as soon as he had seen his horse stabled, sat down to chat with the landlord over a bottle of wine.

"That's a fine horse of yours, sir," the landlord said.

"Yes," Sir Roland replied; "but he is not quite up to my weight, and I think of parting with him."

"Indeed! Well, I have been asked to look out for just such a horse. What may you want for him?"

"Fifty guineas."

"Say forty, and the bargain's struck."

A thrill of delight shot into Sir Roland's heart, but he was too artful to appear to be in a hurry to accept the offer.

"We will talk about it in the morning," he said, raising his glass of wine to the light. "Here's your very good health."

"And yours, sir," the landlord replied. "All right; I did not know that you intended to stay all night, so we can talk the matter over in the morning, as you say; but I will not advance a single shilling on my offer, so you may make up your mind to that."

## CHAPTER CLXVIII.

### ROBIN GRAY'S NEW QUARTERS—A STRANGE ARRIVAL.

ROBIN GRAY fainted when he was borne away by Spring-Heeled Jack.

When he opened his eyes he discovered that he was tucked up in a warm bed, in a place that seemed to be neither cave nor room, but a mixture of both.

On each side there were evidences of comfort, but the apartment had no window, and was lighted by a handsome lamp, which hung suspended from the ceiling.

Robin's brain was so confused that he could not collect his thoughts, nor was he aware that anybody was near him until he heard a sound like a deep-drawn breath.

He then saw a shadow on the wall, and following it with his eyes, beheld a man, who sat near a wood fire.

"I beg your pardon," Robin said, "but would you mind telling me where I am and how I came here?"

The man started up immediately and approached the bed with noiseless footsteps.

"I am glad to find you better," he said.

"Have I been ill?" Robin demanded. "Really, I do not remember anything about it."

"Well, not very," the man said, kindly, as he poured a cooling fluid into a glass and held it to the boy's lips. "You have had a slight shock to your nerves. Surely you remember something about it?"

"No," Robin replied. "I have no recollection

of anything. All is vague and indistinct. I want to go back to Namon Wallack. Take me back to him, as he is my best friend."

"You are in good hands here," the man said. "I am known by the name of Lorrimer; but my real name is Henry Banks. I know Namon Wallack very well, and he is aware that you are here."

"Then why does he not come to see me?"

"All in good time," Harry Banks said. "Come—come! I will try to refresh your memory. Don't you remember anything that happened at the Mart?"

In an instant everything flashed back into the lad's brain.

"Yes—yes," he said, eagerly, "I do remember. The strange creature they call Spring-Heeled Jack saved me. He did so once before, and yet I only see him for a moment. He never comes back to let me thank him."

Harry Banks smiled quietly as he looked at the lad.

"Never mind about Spring-Heeled Jack just now," he said. "I daresay you will know all about him one of these days. All you have to do is to keep quiet and make yourself as happy as possible."

"As happy as possible," the boy said, sighing. "How can I be happy when such strange things take place daily?"

"Hush—hush!" said Harry Banks. "No good can come of such talk; indeed, I will not permit it."

"Forgive me if I have offended you," Robin returned. "Though young, I feel as if a great number of years have passed over my head. I would not care if I could read this mystery. But I will be obedient and patient."

"That's right," said Harry Banks, cheerfully. "I am waiting for instructions to return you to your friends, and it may be that you will have to go some distance as soon as you are able to bear the journey."

"What is that?" demanded Robin Gray, raising himself upon his elbow. "Surely I heard a low moaning, like somebody in dreadful pain?"

"It was but the wind," Harry Banks replied. "It is a bitter night, and the snow falls fast and thick."

"But listen," the boy returned. "That was not the wind. There—there it is again."

An anxious expression stole over Harry Banks' face.

He heard the sound now, and it perplexed him not a little.

"I must see to this," he murmured. "It is certainly a human voice."

Leaving the room, he ascended a flight of steps, at the end of which was a trap-door.

This flew open under the pressure of a spring, and Harry Banks, hastening along a narrow passage until he came to a door, stood and listened.

Outside he could hear the branches of the trees crashing against each other as the storm-wind swept pass.

Then came that cry of woe.

"Help—help! Let me in! I am dying!"

"What am I to do?" Harry Banks said. "My instructions are to open the door to nobody; but here is a creature in dire distress. Stay! How am I to know that this is not a ruse to gain admittance?"

After a moment's reflection he brought his mouth down level with the keyhole and spoke.

"Who is there?" he demanded.

"A dying man," was the reply. "Oh! give me shelter for mercy's sake."

"Your name?"

"Lord Mildendale."

Harry Banks drew himself up to his full height and pressed his hand upon his brow.

"Lord Mildendale!" he gasped. "Great Heaven! how strangely things come about. I will admit him at all risks."

Harry Banks opened the door, and discovered Lord Mildendale near it.

His lordship was in an almost fainting condition.

The hue of death was upon his face, and a stream of blood flowed from under a handkerchief he held tightly to his side.

Harry Banks took him in his arms, and lifted him easily and tenderly.

"Who has done this?" Banks demanded. "How did this come about?"

Lord Mildendale's lips quivered and strove to speak, but for some moments he was incapable of doing so.

"My fate is well deserved," he gasped out at last. "This is the work of Spring-Heeled Jack. My head swims, and all is darkness. Lay me down, and let me rest."

Harry Banks carried the dying man into a room, and, having placed him on a couch, applied some brandy to his lips.

The spirit revived Lord Mildendale.

He opened his eyes and stared wildly about him.

"I wish I had a few more hours to live," he said, moving his hands feebly to and fro. "I have much to tell; but it may be told after my death. Oh! Heaven, that I could ask forgiveness of my son—the poor lad I have wronged so deeply!"

"He goes by the name of Robin Gray," said Harry Banks, quietly.

These words seemed to endow Lord Mildendale with new life.

"Ha!" he cried, "how do you know that? Has the secret been sent forth to the world?"

"Not so," Banks replied. "Robin Gray is in this very house."

"Let me see him," Lord Mildendale said; "I must see him."

"No, no," said Harry Banks; "it would be madness. He suspects nothing, he does not even know your name; and if the truth were known to him, it would condemn him to a life of unhappiness."

"Yes—yes," Lord Mildendale returned. "Perhaps you are right. But let me think. My brain is in a whirl, and my heart is torn with pain. Tell him, then, that there was a man who sought to wrong him. Ask him to forgive that man."

"I will," Harry Banks said. "And I am sure he will do so from the very bottom of his boyish heart."

"I am content," Lord Mildendale murmured.

After this he remained quiet, but breathing heavily for some minutes.

"Nana!" he cried, suddenly starting up—"Nana!"

This was the last word that he uttered.

Sinking slowly back upon Harry Banks' arm, he passed away.

There was something in the expression of those glazed and fixed eyes which seemed to tell that though the body was dead the spirit had not yet fled.

Harry Banks trembled from head to foot.

He felt afraid to remain in the room, and moving slowly away, closed the door of the chamber of death and locked it.

Scarcely had he done so when he heard a sound at the trap door.

"Let me out—let me out!" cried the voice of Robin Gray. "I have had a terrible dream of men slaying each other in a wood."

"Oh! what a task is mine," Harry Banks said.

And then he started, for he heard another voice behind him.

"I will complete it."

Turning sharply, he saw Ralph Ashton.

"How thankful I am that you have come," Banks said. "The events of this night are enough to madden a man."

"Leave the rest to me," Ralph Ashton replied. "The carriage is at the door, and the boy must be removed forthwith."

As Harry Banks moved away, Ralph Ashton opened the trap-door and Robin Gray sprang out.

Ralph caught him in his arms, and smoothing back his hair, endeavoured to calm him with a few kind words.

But the boy sobbed as if his young heart would break.

"I cannot rest," he said; "my life is a misery to me. I wish I was dead!"

"Hush—hush!" Ralph replied. "The time of trouble is drawing to an end, and there is a good time coming. Listen, Robin. Spring-Heeled Jack has sent me to you, and I am going to take you back to those young ladies who took such an interest in you when you first fell into my hands."

"I want to see Namon Wallack. Will he be there?" Robin asked.

"Yes," Ralph replied, "and the little girl, Amy, too."

"Then I am content," Robin replied, as he clung to his benefactor. "Take me anywhere—anywhere from this place. There seems to be a huge black shadow following me about, and it frightens me."

## CHAPTER CLXIX.

### MRS. CORCORAN SAYS GOOD-BYE.

Mrs. Corcoran did not remain long in a fainting state. Recovering herself quickly, she wrested herself from the man who had caught her, and fled from the scene.

Though she had come to see Joe Morth die she dare not look at his body as it hung dangling from the scaffold.

Pushing her way through the crowd, she made her way back to her lodgings, and found the door closed against her. A new terror came over her.

Had she been tracked and discovered?

The hag hardly knew what to make of the state of affairs, and she knocked and kicked wildly at the door.

While thus engaged, one of the upper windows of the cottage flew open, and a small parcel came flying out.

Mrs. Corcoran picked it up, and, having opened it, discovered the precise amount of money she had paid to the ostler.

This was still more mysterious, but a few words scribbled on the paper announced that the ostler's wife had come home and refused to open the door.

"I can't make this out," the hag muttered. "Something must have happened during my absence. Perchance that demon Spring-Heeled Jack has been here, or sent one of his messengers. If so, I had better make myself scarce."

Just then a man, wearing a cloak down to his heels, passed, and looked sharply into Mrs. Corcoran's face.

She recoiled andt urned pale, for she thought that she had seen the features somewhere, though for the life of her she could not recall the time and place to mind.

The man walked a few paces, and then turned again.

Mrs. Corcoran shrank back at his approach, and put out her hands, as if to ward off a blow.

"Go!" he said. "This is no place for you. The people at the cottage know who and what you are."

Mrs. Corcoran heard these words as if they had been drummed into her ears, but she made no reply.

She turned and hobbled down the road, with her heart heavy and cold, and a strange conviction upon her that she was already dead.

A mist gathered before her eyes, rendering everything indistinct and uncertain.

She went on and on, passing through Cockleton and into the open country, with the words of the mysterious stranger buzzing and ringing in her ears.

For some hours her tottering feet bore her up, and even when the sun went down Mrs. Corcoran was still pursuing her aimless journey.

Nature at last gave way, and she sank moaning by the roadside.

But she was given no rest.

The air seemed full of strange sounds and voices, and in them she heard the story of her detestable life repeated.

Mrs. Corcoran was going mad.

The cunning brain that had worked so much mischief had become unhinged at last.

As the darkness increased she began to mumble and rave.

She talked to all sorts of imaginary people, and then suddenly springing up, she repeated her words uttered when she foully murdered Lady Ashton.

"There," she yelled—"there, she won't trouble you again, Sir Roland. Ha! ha! my lady, you would have me turned out of the house. Poor old Mother Corcoran was to go forth homeless! Ah! you were a kind, merciful lady, you were. But I was more so. I have found you a home from which you will never rise until the end of the world—the grave! Ha! ha! ha!"

She ceased speaking, and seemed to be listening to some words uttered by Sir Roland at that awful time.

"Remorse!" she cried. "Ho! ho! ho! I like that. Have you no remorse? Who ordered me to kill her? You—you talk to me of remorse, and I reply that when such men as you are to be found, such women as I will be always ready at hand to carry out your plans. Who is the worst? The head that plans the deed, or the hand that carries it out?"

Again she was silent, and then her voice rang out awakening the echoes far and near.

"I will not be silent, Sir Roland. Henceforth I would have you to know that I am your equal. I have heard it said that in some eastern country, many, many years ago, that if a man murdered his wife, the body was chained to the murderer, who had to drag it about with him until the loathsome thing caused him to die with terror or gave him some pestilence from which he died. You will bury this body; but you will drag about with you the ghost—the true corpse—remorse."

A sudden paroxysm then seized the wretched creature.

She flung herself down upon the ground and filled the air with her yells and screams.

"Avaunt!" she cried. "Why have you come to haunt me? Back, all of you! I did one good deed, at least. When Lord Mildendale sought me out and put gold into my hand I did not kill Diana. I bid her flee. No—no; I could not do the deed. She was too beautiful."

"Hullo! What is this?" cried a voice. "What's the matter, old chap?"

A yeoman passing on his way homeward had nearly fallen over the hag.

"You are another of them. And yet I know you not," the hag said, as she rose. "Let me see your face. No—no. If you died a cruel death, it was not by my hand."

"What are you talking about?" the yeoman demanded, stepping back. "What do you take me for?"

"A ghost, a restless spirit from the grave. See, there are numbers of them; but they leave you and crowd about me."

The yeoman knew what was the matter now.

He did not bargain to parley with a madman, as he took Mrs. Corcoran to be, and, giving the hag as wide a berth as possible, he walked swiftly away.

Mrs. Corcoran staggered along in the opposite direction.

At times she thrust her fingers into her ears as if to drown the awful voices.

Her lips were white and her throat parched.

A spring bubbled up at her feet, but she fled from it as if it was poison, and began making hideous, cat-like sounds, and to claw the air as if fighting with the shapes that haunted her.

She stopped as she came to a house, from which a light was shining.

"At last," she said. "Here I shall find rest. This is Lilac Cottage. Ha! ha! Now I shall see Daisy Leigh—pretty Daisy Leigh—sweet Daisy Leigh!"

The hag began to caper and dance about as if a fiend had taken possession of her.

Her reason had entirely fled, otherwise she would have remembered that Lilac Cottage had been burnt to the ground long ago.

The owner of the house, hearing a noise outside, opened the door to see what was the matter, and shut it as quickly.

If an apparition had suddenly appeared he could not have been more astonished and alarmed.

"Why, wife," he said, turning to a buxom woman who sat in the chimney-corner, "there's a man outside like an ugly jack-in-the-box come to life!"

The woman turned pale as she heard the hideous din Mrs. Corcoran was making.

"Get down your gun, Bill," she cried, "and shoot him if he won't go away."

The man's hands trembled as he took down the weapon from over the fire-place.

"Now, then," he said, as he opened the door again, "take yourself off; we don't want any such antics here."

"Sir Roland," the hag cried, extending her shrivelled arm, "I know you, in spite of your disguise. I have come to stay with you, and you shall not cast me out. Fool that you were to think that you had got rid of me!"

"Well, I never!" gasped the cottager. "Hang me, if he isn't talking about the very villain that tried to commit the robbery at the Two-necked Swan, and then struck down his pal, Joe Morth."

"Joe Morth—Joe Morth!" exclaimed Mrs. Corcoran. "He is dead and gone. I saw him die, Sir Roland. Come, stand back, and let me pass. I am not to be duped by such idle excuses."

As she saw the gun and heard the click of the trigger, a gleam of reason came back to her brain.

Then, with a shriek like a Banshee bewailing the dead, she rushed away, leaving the cottager cold and terror-stricken.

"If the night wasn't so dark," he stammered, "I'd—I'd fetch the village constable. Mary, my dear, throw some fresh logs on the fire, for my flesh is creeping all over my body."

The wind was now roaring boisterously, and snow, mingled with sleet, fell fast.

Into the howling night went the demented hag.

Her hair blew out to the wind like snakes, and she answered the bellowing gale by throwing up her arms and screaming a chorus.

Like a fearful spirit chased by a legion of demons she sped on, never stopping, for now a strength which was not her own urged her onwards.

Presently another sound mingled with the storm.

It was the crashing, the roaring, and the churning of a cataract.

But Mrs. Corcoran heard it not.

She reached the brink—she stepped over it.

Then, as she fell from rock to rock, clawing savagely at objects that gave way, she uttered a prolonged yell.

The water swept with irresistible force over her, and bore her away as lightly as a straw.

It toyed with her, it whirled her round and round, striking her against the bank, and then hurrying her into mid-stream, as if it had taken upon itself to avenge the wrongs of many a victim.

The icy coldness of the water brought Mrs. Corcoran to her senses.

She knew where she was and that death was at hand.

Nothing short of a miracle could save her now.

In that moment of supreme agony she recalled to mind how many remarkable escapes she had had during her extraordinary career, and she did not lose all hope.

Throwing out her arms, she clutched an overhanging branch, and, though a slender one, it enabled her to keep her head above water.

"Help—help!" she cried. "I will not die! I am not fit to die."

She thought she saw a white, yet shadowy, form loom up from the bank.

"Save me!" she gasped. "Take me where you will. Let justice deal with me. I have led a sinful life, and have much to tell. If you are human, stretch out a hand to me."

The figure, if, indeed, there had been one, vanished.

"Lost—lost!" the hag cried. "My strength is failing me. I die—I perish!"

The branch was slipping from her frozen fingers.

But Mrs. Corcoran hung on until she could do so no longer, and then, crying out again that she was not fit for death, fell back into the turbulent water.

With an angry roar it seized upon its prey, but sported with it no longer.

Twice Mrs. Corcoran rose and made an ineffectual attempt to clutch at the shore.

The third time her hands only appeared, and then the river went on its way, as if rejoicing at what it had done.

When morning came, a miller, clearing away the weeds and rubbish which had been washed into the dam, came upon all that remained of Mrs. Corcoran.

Her body was carried to a dead house—there was no escape now—and after an inquest had been held, the corpse was thrust into a pauper's grave.

## CHAPTER CLXX.

### SIR ROLAND ASHTON FINDS THAT HORSE-DEALING IS NOT IN HIS LINE.

Sir Roland Ashton did not sleep well that night, and he was heartily glad when the light of day crept slowly across the wall of his chamber.

He thought he heard voices talking below, and on going to the window, saw that the horse he had ridden had been brought out, and that the landlord and another man were inspecting it.

Sir Roland Ashton rubbed his hands gleefully.

"Mine host's customer has arrived sooner than expected," he said. "So much the better. As soon as I get the money in my pocket I will take myself off, and then— What then? France is the place for me; but before I go I will leave my mark—I will leave Ralph Ashton and those girls he thinks so secure something to remember me by."

After waiting about an hour, he went downstairs in a jaunty fashion.

"Well, landlord," he said, as that individual appeared, "have you thought over what we talked about?"

"Well, yes," said the landlord, looking at him in a peculiar way. "To tell you the truth, I have thought a good deal about it."

"So have I," Sir Roland returned; "and I cannot help thinking that you are a little hard upon me. The horse is worth more money than I asked for him—nearly double the amount."

"Very likely," said the innkeeper, dryly; "but buying and selling are two very different things, you know."

"Just so," Sir Roland responded. "Well, I don't want to haggle about the matter, I'll take the money."

"Certainly; but you must wait until after breakfast, as I find that I have not quite enough in the house."

Sir Roland Ashton began to chafe and fume.

"Come—come!" he said. "I want to get away, and, therefore, I don't intend that a guinea or two shall stand between us."

"You are very generous, my good sir," the landlord replied, "but it so happens that I find that I have only just half the amount. I have sent my man for the remainder, and told him to make haste."

"How long do you think he will be?"

"Oh! about an hour—perhaps a little longer."

Sir Roland, finding that he had no alternative but to wait, ordered breakfast and sat down.

The room into which he was shown had two large windows.

One faced the road, and the other a yard with outhouses and stabling, where farmers on their way to and from market put up their carts and horses.

Sir Roland Ashton lacked appetite, but he made a show of eating the meal placed before him.

He noticed that the landlord seemed to hang about the door a great deal more than was absolutely necessary, and it suddenly dawned into the baronet's brain that something was wrong.

More than an hour—in point of fact, nearly two—passed away, and the man who had been sent for the money did not return.

"Confusion take him!" Sir Roland muttered. "I wish I was behind him with my sword. He would travel quicker, I'll be bound."

As Sir Roland ceased speaking, the window looking out upon the back premises became darkened for a moment.

The baronet turned his head quickly, but he could see nothing.

"My brain is either full of fancies," he said, "or I am being watched. I should be in a nice predicament if the landlord thinks I have not come by the horse by fair means."

He rose and went to the door and opened it suddenly.

The landlord was in the passage, apparently intent upon an old-fashioned eight-day clock, which had stopped.

"Now, my friend," said Sir Roland, "has that man of yours returned?"

"Just come back."

"Then we can settle the business without any further delay."

"Why, that was what I was thinking myself," said the innkeeper, in an exasperating tone of voice. "Of course we can, and so we will after I have oiled these wheels, and then I shall have time to count out the money."

Sir Roland cursed the clock and the man attending to it.

How much longer was he to be kept waiting?

A hundred things might happen unless he got away before people were about and full of the news about Sir Henry Levarre.

The landlord went on leisurely with his work, and it was evident that he was not a man to be hurried under any circumstances.

"I suppose it was your man who looked at me through the back window?" Sir Roland said.

The innkeeper raised his head, and the same peculiar look he had previously favoured the baronet with stole across his face.

"No, honoured sir," he said, after a pause, "it was not my man."

"Who was it, then?"

"I don't know."

"Some rude person, perhaps."

"Very likely," said the landlord. "It must have been a rude person who would stare at a gentleman when he is at breakfast."

The baronet did not know what to make of this reply, nor of the man who uttered it.

Presently the landlord replaced the feather in the oil-bottle, and drew a long breath.

"Are you ready now?" Sir Roland demanded.

"Yes—quite ready."

"Will you bring the money to me?"

"I would rather that you walked into my bar-parlour," the landlord replied. "I always transact all my private business there."

"Very good. I will follow you."

"After you, sir," said the innkeeper. "You will find the door straight ahead down the passage."

Sir Roland winced a little.

He thought more than ever that something was wrong, but he determined to put a bold face on the matter.

"It seems to me," he said, "that you are not very willing to complete the bargain. If that is the case, say so at once, and I will take the horse away."

"I do not wish the horse to be taken away," the landlord said, quietly. "Indeed, I have locked the stable-door, and the key is in my pocket. See, here it is!"

But, instead of the key, the innkeeper drew a pistol from his pocket.

"Move hand or foot, and you are a dead man!" he cried. "Hi! there. I have got the rascal safe."

Two constables rushed pell-mell out of the bar-parlour.

Sir Roland Ashton yelled out a horrible oath as he struck up the landlord's arm.

The pistol exploded in the air, and the baronet, drawing his sword, slashed right and left as he dashed down the passage.

He was followed by the crash of fire-arms, and two bullets whistled so close to him that one grazed his right ear, and brought another cry to his lips.

Out into the open air he rushed, hotly pursued by the constables.

He ran across the road, and leaping a hedge, saw a boy leading a horse which he had just caught, and was taking it through a gate at the other end of the field.

"Stop, you dog!" Sir Roland yelled. "Bring that horse to me, or I will run you through the body."

The boy did not bring the horse, but he became transfixed with terror.

Sir Roland thrust him aside, and leaping upon the horse's back, seized its mane, and spurred the animal with the point of his sword.

The startled horse, though a heavy and usually slow-going one, bounded away at what may be called a thumping gallop, and plunging heavily along across two or three fields, soon put a considerable distance between Sir Roland and his pursuers.

The baronet knew that the horse would be of no service to him on the road, and flinging himself from its back, he ran towards a wood.

Doubling and turning like a hare, so as to baffle and confuse the constables, the baronet suddenly espied a tree so thickly covered with ivy, that it hung in huge clusters more than sufficient to hide the body of an ordinary man.

This seemed to him to be the most likely haven of refuge he could fly to. Exerting all his strength, he climbed to the thickest part, and, entwining his limbs among the roots, pulled a mass of the evergreen over his head and shoulders, and listened with bated breath for any sound indicative of the approach of the officers.

Nor had he to wait long.

Shouting and bellowing, the constables came up, with the landlord and some field labourers who had left their work to join in the chase.

A halt was made so near the tree in which Sir Roland lay concealed, that he could observe every movement made by the men, and hear every word they uttered.

"He can't be far away," said one of the constables, panting and blowing for breath. "We shall have him right enough if we surround this bit of wood. Now then, lads, don't stand there staring at us, but make yourselves useful. I'll guarantee that you shall be paid, whether you catch the rascal or not."

This was not very cheerful intelligence to Sir Roland.

The slightest thing might betray him, and a mortal dread came upon him when the labourers having departed, the two constables sat down under the ivy-covered tree.

"This is a rum start, and no mistake," said one of the constables. "Why, they say he is the very man who has been searched for all over the eastern counties!"

"If we should be so lucky as to click the darbies over his wrist, it would be a good thing for us," the other remarked. "I say, Tom."

"What now?"

"I've got an idea."

"An idea never caught a thief yet," said Tom. "Ideas ain't much in my line, Peter. I suppose my head is too thick to let 'em in."

"If I had said that," Peter remarked, "you would have wanted to have known what I meant by it."

"Never mind. What is that idea of yours?"

"Why," Tom replied, "I once read something about King Charles—him as they call the Merry Monarch—hiding up in an oak-tree. Supposing the man we are looking for is up in this ivy above our heads?"

"That won't do for me," said Tom. "Well, if he is, I'll fetch him down jolly soon."

Sir Roland Ashton groaned under his breath as he heard this, and shrank back so suddenly that it is a wonder he did not reveal his presence.

Tom drew a pistol from his belt, and looked up at the tree.

"What are you going to do?" demanded his companion.

"Why, fire, of course!"

"Yes, of course, and fire at nothing, as far as you can see," gasped Peter. "You would bring all the yokels running this way fit to break their necks, and give the man plenty of time to get away. Talk about ideas—that's a nice one, at all events."

"I never thought of that," said Tom. "You are right, my boy. What shall we do—move further on or stay here?"

"Wait a minute," Peter replied. "I've got an idea that I should like to climb the tree just to satisfy myself; but perhaps I should find nothing in it but a lot of old birds' nests."

"That's just about what you would find."

"Then we'll take a walk round, and keep our eyes open."

Sir Roland Ashton felt as much relieved as a man reprieved from the scaffold.

"I am safe here," he thought. "They may muddle about for hours, even until nightfall, but no longer."

For a long time he could hear the tramping of feet, sometimes near him, and sometimes afar off.

Securely hidden in his leafy hiding-place, he grew drowsy, and felt inclined to fall asleep.

But this would have been fatal to him, and he kept himself awake and listened to the monotonous tread of the men, and the sound of their voices as they called to each other.

At last they began to tire of the job.

The constables began to think at last that the fugitive must have made his way through the wood before they arrived, and finally came to the conclusion that they were wasting time.

At last all was still.

Profound silence reigned in the wood; but Sir

Roland remained in his leafy perch long after darkness set in.

He dare not move, fearing that he might be pounced upon, and more than once he fancied he saw a ray of light, such as comes from a lantern, flash to and fro.

At last he became convinced that this was not the case, and began the descent.

His limbs had become so cramped that he groaned as he moved them, and when his feet touched the ground, he still crouched close to the tree, as if half-repenting that he had left its friendly shelter.

Shelter!

There was none for him.

Where could he go, now that the whole country was up in arms against him?

Where was there a man or woman who would not raise a cry of alarm at his approach?

There was nothing for him but to skulk along until he was free of the neighbourhood.

Even if he succeeded in doing so, he knew that a description of himself would be circulated about; and he lowered his aching head into his hands and tried to think of some project likely to serve him in his extremity.

But none came to his rescue.

He could see nothing before him but capture, and a death such as a man of any feeling would hesitate to deal to a dog.

For several minutes he did not seem to have the strength to move, but at length he began to drag his legs heavily and wearily over the ground.

If there had been a single constable about, Sir Roland Ashton would have stood no chance in resisting arrest; but the minions of the law had departed and nine-tenths of the villagers were safe within their homes.

People who have passed through a wood when the darkness can be almost felt know something of the doubt and alarm attached to such a journey.

There seems to be danger where there is none whatever.

The wind has a different sound, the rain patters mournfully, every gnarled root becomes a spectre, and inanimate objects seem to take a short lease of life.

But to such a man as Sir Roland, with blood upon his hands, an outcast and a hunted wretch, these terrors became increased a hundred-fold.

The wood seemed to have no end, and to grow blacker and blacker at every step.

The very silence of the dismal place seemed to have a voice of its own, and the twinkling stars, peeping down whenever there was a break in the trees, appeared to be following and watching him.

At last Sir Roland came to the borders of the wood.

Beyond lay a long stretch of flat earth, broken here and there by rugged hedges and clumps of trees.

There was no hill worthy of the name, and the baronet could see for miles.

Shrugging his shoulders as the bitter frost, refusing to be denied, found its way through his clothing, he kept straight on, carefully avoiding all habitations, for, though they were the abodes of peace to the law-abiding people, danger for the baronet lurked in every one of them.

What was to become of him he did not know and hardly cared.

He almost wished that he had surrendered himself to the constables, and trusted to telling a plausible tale to get out of the difficulty.

Phil Merrick and Jack Starr were either dead or desperately wounded, and he might have said that he purchased the horse from them a few minutes before they attacked Sir Henry Levarre, and was riding up to his rescue when he settled the difficulty.

But what about the man who shot the coachman and footman?

He would have been quite a different individual to Sir Roland.

Even if the story had not been believed, it would have given him an opportunity to get away and mature some fresh plan; but the chance was gone for ever.

These and a hundred other thoughts flitted through his brain as he stood gazing across the snow-covered landscape, which was being made gradually brilliant by the rising moon.

The stars paled before the superior light of the bright orb, and Sir Roland's shadow became, as it were, a thing of life mocking his actions.

The silence was suddenly broken by a strange sound.

It was one of loud, mocking laughter, and the baronet, pressing his hand to his heart, fell back step by step.

He knew to whom that voice belonged and who was coming.

It was Spring-Heeled Jack, and he came leaping with gigantic strides that gave him the appearance of literally flying in the air.

"Back! foul fiend," exclaimed Sir Roland. "Touch me not!"

"Ha! ha! ha!" laughed Spring-Heeled Jack. "You have escaped most eyes, but you could not escape mine. I have travelled many, many miles to see you. Sir Roland, we meet again, and I swear, by all that I hold good and holy, that there will be but one more parting."

"Well, take my life," Sir Roland said. "I am so weak and weary that I may be accounted as one who is defenceless."

"Nay," Spring-Heeled Jack replied. "I will not take your life, for through you I desire to know much. You have parted with money and property, but there are things you have not parted with."

"What are they?"

"The papers which relate to Ralph Ashton."

Sir Roland made a clutch at his breast-pocket.

In an instant Spring-Heeled Jack's hand of iron was upon the baronet's wrist.

"That trick will not do for me, Sir Roland," he said. "I felt almost convinced, but not quite sure, that you had never lost hold on those papers, and I take them now."

Forgetting that he was a criminal, searched all over the country for, Sir Roland shouted for help.

"Silence, you dog! or I will leave your body to stiffen under this freezing sky," Spring-Heeled Jack hissed, as he seized the baronet by the throat.

"Your object is to murder me," Sir Roland said, gurgling out the words. "The papers are useless. I—I—"

Spring-Heeled Jack stopped his speech by pressing him down to the ground.

Sir Roland lay as still as if the hand of death had smitten him, but a quivering of his eyelids showed that he still lived.

"Not yet," Spring-Heeled Jack said. "The hour of retribution is fast approaching, but it has not yet arrived. It may be to-morrow or the next day, but I must know more before I rid the world of so base a villain."

As he ceased speaking he uttered a peculiar cry, and two men appeared from behind a clump of bushes.

"Away with him !" Spring-Heeled Jack cried. "The officers of the law have failed to bring him down, but I will deal with him. You have my instructions. Watch him well, and see that he is never left alone for a moment."

## CHAPTER CLXXI.

### CHERTSEY ABBEY—THE RIVER—BILL BLARNEY MEETS WITH HIS DESERTS.

THE barn in which Bill Blarney had voluntarily imprisoned himself burned fiercely, and the ruffian ran to and fro the narrow space between the ignited hay and the wall like a rat in a trap.

Naturally enough, he thought that he was lost; but he could not resign himself in any way to such an ending to his earthly career.

A portion of the woodwork at the upper part of the barn was already alight, and as Bill Blarney heard it crackle, and saw it crumble up like paper, it occurred to him that one or two of the planks, which were nailed to strong supports and beams, might be removed without much difficulty.

At all events, he would try to do so.

Anything was better than risking such an awful death as that by burning, and thrusting his fingers through a crevice, he tore at a plank with the strength of a madman.

At first it refused to yield, and Blarney, discovering that he was pulling at the centre of the plank, groped his way through the smoke to the end, and redoubled his efforts.

They were rewarded at last.

The wood rent and splintered, and a draught of fresh air drove back the smoke for a moment.

Bill Blarney had now an easy task before him.

Another plank gave way, and blinded and half-suffocated with the smoke, he crawled into the open air.

He was not observed by the frantic farmer and the constables, who were on the other side of the barn, and he crept away until he came to a cluster of trees, where he sank down exhausted and so racked with pain, that he bit his tongue to keep back a yell of agony.

People were running in all directions towards the scene of the catastrophe, and so intent were all upon it, that not one noticed the villain as he lay writhing on the ground.

There was no lack of willing hands.

But they could do nothing, and so the rustics made a kind of holiday of the affair, and stood staring and gaping as the flames rushed furiously upwards.

Bill Blarney regained his feet, and seeing that nobody was likely to trouble about him, he stole away and retraced his footsteps on the London road.

He had not gone far before he was challenged by a mounted officer, who was galloping on his way to the fire.

"Hold, there!" cried the officer, drawing his sword. "No man must pass along these roads unless he can give a good account of himself."

"I should think my appearance would vouch for that," said Bill Blarney, growling. "Look at my blistered face; look at my scorched hands, and call me a fool for trying to play the part of a hero by entering a barn on fire."

"Trying to play the part of a hero?" the officer repeated. "Explain yourself."

"Idiot that I am!" Bill Blarney replied, "when I heard that a hunted wretch had taken refuge in the barn and set fire to it accidentally, I must attempt to rescue him, and you see what I have got by it."

"It must be Bill Blarney—the man I am looking for," the officer said.

"I think that was the name I heard mentioned," the scoundrel said. "But let me pass on, unless you want me to go mad with this miserable pain. I must have my burns attended to at once, or I shall wear the scars to the day of my death."

Little suspecting who he was talking to, the officer put spurs to his horse and galloped away; but what a man on horseback can do in the way of quenching a fire was perhaps only known to himself.

Bill Blarney was certainly badly burnt, and he did not exaggerate in the least when he said that the pain was maddening.

A stream running across the road, invited him to bathe his smarting hands and face; but he avoided it, knowing that the pain would be intensified.

Some hours' march, during which he bore the most frightful agonies, brought him to an out-of-the-way village, where he found a man skilled in the use of herbs.

Bill Blarney told his story, and excited so much pity that the village sage not only bound up his wounds, but begged him to remain at his home for a time.

Nothing loth, the villain rested and ate his fill; but, fearing that he might be searched for, took his departure just before nightfall.

But he did not depart penniless, for the people, hearing of his misfortune, made a small subscription and pressed it upon him.

Bill Blarney's luck seemed to be in the ascendant, for just as he was moving away a pedlar, who travelled the country with all sorts of things in a cart, offered to give him a lift back to London by a roundabout way.

"I shall touch Croydon, Epsom, and then make my way to Chertsey," he said. "You will get to London as quickly in my cart, and I sha'n't begrudge you a meal or two. I know what misery is, and can feel for another."

Bill Blarney thanked the pedlar and closed with his offer at once, but he winced a little when, as soon as they were fairly upon the road, the vendor of odds and ends began to talk about himself.

"They say that the rascal cannot get away," the pedlar said, "and the sooner he is hung the better."

"So say I," Bill Blarney returned, almost choking himself in the endeavour to get the words out.

"It comes to this," the pedlar continued; "if a man is ever so hard up he can always find enough to do to earn him a crust, without sneaking about with murder in his heart, and his fingers itching to do some brutal deed."

"Yes—yes," said Bill Blarney; "you are quite right."

"It seems an odd thing to me," the pedlar remarked, "that such rascals as this Bill Blarney never think of it, and try to turn over a new leaf; but I suppose they are born bad, and if so, I suppose they will die bad."

# SPRING-HEELED JACK,

## THE TERROR OF LONDON.

"HERE LIES SIR ROLAND, AND HERE ENDS MY PART AS SPRING-HEELED JACK."

No. 48.

Bill Blarney fidgeted about, and seemed very anxious to change the subject.

He took an intense interest in everything that the cart contained, and asked a hundred questions, all of which the pedlar answered good-humouredly.

For two whole days the cart went on from village to village.

The pedlar rattled the plates, jingled the knives, and sounded the basins, and had so many pleasant things to say that he invariably drew a small sum of money from the pockets of the smiling rustics.

Bill Blarney seldom left the cart, and when he did so it was with an amount of reluctance that did not fail to meet the pedlar's observation.

He began to suspect the ruffian, and took the precaution to keep the pockets which held his daily takings tightly buttoned up.

At last the cart rolled into the pretty little market town of Chertsey.

The pedlar pulled up at the corner of the Addlestone-road, and motioned to Bill Blarney to alight.

"We must part here," he said, "and we should have parted before, only I didn't wish to break my word to you."

"Well," said Bill Blarney, in a surly tone of voice, "I don't see what I have done to deserve such a speech from your lips."

"It isn't what you have done," the pedlar replied, shortening his whip so as to hold it useful at any moment; "but it is what I think you would do, if you had the chance."

"Oh!" said Blarney; "what is that?"

"Anything you could lay your hands upon rather than work."

"Such words as those have caused many an ugly blow from my fist," Bill Blarney said, with a savage oath.

"Very likely," the pedlar replied; "and if you think it worth your while, you can try it on now. I've got a notion in my head about you, but I am not going to take the trouble to carry it out."

"Come, speak out," said the ruffian; "you may as well have your say out."

"I believe that you are Bill Blarney," the pedlar replied. "I did not think so when I took you up, but when you removed the bandages from your face, it struck me that I had come across the man who is wanted so particularly."

"Ha! ha! ha!" laughed the scoundrel. "If you think so, why don't you run for a constable, and give me in charge? I'll wait here for you!"

"Yes; until I was out of sight, and then you would make good use of your legs," the pedlar said; "but I am not going to take the trouble. Sheer off before I lose my temper. As far as the lift I have given you, you are welcome to it; but, hang me! if you should turn out to be the rascal I take you to be, I'll have the cart emptied and washed out, before I touch another thing in it."

With these words he drove slowly away, leaving Bill Blarney standing in the middle of the road, speechless with alarm and amazement.

"Well," he said, "I have heard that there is nothing like speaking your mind, and I've had a bit of his with a vengeance."

The ruffian's alarm became less, and presently entirely abated.

He felt that the pedlar would keep his word when he said that he would not trouble himself about him, and for this, at least, Bill Blarney had every reason to feel grateful.

Walking into Chertsey town, he entered the Swan Inn, then a sleepy, ramshackle old place, with sufficient stabling in the rear to have accommodated the horses of a full regiment of cavalry.

Bill Blarney called for some ale, and drank it in a hurry, for he thought that the landlord was watching him narrowly.

"I'm blowed if I can move about anywhere without being worried," he growled, as he returned to the street. "I'll have a walk round, and see where I can put up for the night."

On the outskirts of the town were a number of pleasant little cottages, inhabited by poor, but contented folk.

One after another refused to let Bill Blarney a lodging on any terms, and he was growing tired of making so many applications, when his eyes were attracted towards a handsome villa, whose grounds swept down to the river's bank.

"That must be a jolly crib to live in during the summer months," he thought; "and not very hard to crack at any time."

Bill Blarney seemed to enjoy this little joke of his own making immensely.

"If I had a pal I could depend on, I would risk it to-night," he muttered. "The snow would muffle our footsteps, and— Eh! is my head going wrong, or do I see Daisy Leigh and Con stance Marfield?"

The ruffian had only just time to hide himself to escape the notice of the two lovely girls.

"It's like old times to get a glance at 'em," Bill Blarney said, grinning. "So Ralph Ashton has been shifting them about from place to place for safety's sake, I suppose. Very clever of him, no doubt. I wonder if I can turn this discovery to my profit. I must think it over."

He had crouched down under the garden-wall, and recognised the rather painful fact that he would have to remain there until the ladies thought proper to retire into the house.

They were talking as they walked to and fro, their dainty feet scarcely disturbing the snow, bright and crisp with the frost.

"How peaceful we have been here!" Daisy Leigh said. "And Ralph—good, kind Ralph—has told us that his journeys will soon be over for good and all. Ah! Constance, you blush. Your cheeks are the tell-tales of the love you bear for him.

"I do not think that I am alone with regard to the tender passion," Constance said, smiling. "What was it that Ralph said about your lover—the Prince Charming of the old fairy story, you know, who will soon ride this way to take you away?"

"It seems to me that he has taken a long time about the journey," Daisy returned, laughing. "But let us be serious now. How grave Ralph is since he brought Robin Gray back to us!"

"Ha!" Bill Blarney muttered. "I know something of that boy. Look to yourselves, all of you!"

"Yes," Constance Marfield replied. "Something has happened, I am sure, which he deems necessary to keep from us. I shall be glad when he is back again, for he said that he fondly hoped that he would never part with me again."

"Won't he?" Bill Blarney growled. "We will see about that. If Ralph Ashton—how I hate him!—does not come back to-night you may say good-bye to him for ever."

"Come," said Daisy Leigh, "let us go indoors again, for the air is piercing cold, and I think you will agree with me that there is no better place than a cheerful fire-side on such a day as this."

"Agreed without argument," said Constance, laughing. "You shall sing to me, Daisy. Your voice grows sweeter every day."

"Base flatterer," said Daisy, in a bantering tone of voice, "you know that it is your own voice that improves."

"Which I take it that you think I was fishing for compliments."

These were the last words that Bill Blarney heard before the door closed upon the happy girls.

They were more than sufficient, however, to fill his evil heart with rage and envy.

"Cherry-lipped, rosy-cheeked dolls that you are," he said, shaking his fist in the direction of the house. "You may warble now like a pair of nightingales, but it will be a different song that you will sing to-night."

So saying the ruffian skulked away, and chance directed his footsteps towards Chertsey Abbey.

A grim and grey old place it was.

In times gone by cowled monks had chanted their prayers and counted their beads.

Within the reach of the shadow of the sturdy building ran, and still runs, a stream from Penton Hook to Chertsey weir.

It is said that the monks, finding a rivulet, widened and deepened it to their advantage, for the sleepy chub, carp, and tench, revelling in the still waters, took up their abode there in thousands, and, consequently, fell an easy prey to the recluses, who, like other men, have appetites, and the desire to satisfy them.

Chertsey Abbey had long been uninhabited, even at the time when Bill Blarney paid it a visit.

He stood looking wistfully at the crumbling walls, and suddenly it struck him that he might pass the night there without fear of being molested.

He pushed open an old gate, swinging and creaking on its rusty hinges, and approached a door so old and worm-eaten that when he shook it, some of the iron bolts with which it was studded, fell rattling at his feet.

If Bill Blarney's conscience had been free, and his nature a poetic one, he would have been delighted at the interior of the abbey.

Here was the chapel, there the cells, and here lay winding passages which had echoed to the sound of tuneful voices a thousand times.

"This will do," he muttered. "I'll buy something to eat and drink first, and then take up my quarters until midnight."

This resolution Bill Blarney soon put into execution, and having furnished himself with some provisions, a dark lantern, and the means of getting a light, he returned to the ruin.

"If ever a place was haunted, this ought to be," he muttered. "But if there are such things as ghosts they cannot hurt anybody, for what are they after all but thin air? Ha! ha!"

"Ha! ha!"

Bill Blarney started, and felt his flesh creep upon his bones.

"What beastly echoes these old places have!" he said, under his breath. "I must not speak aloud again."

And yet he could hardly convince himself that the voice he heard was his own; but hearing nothing more, he became convinced that it was only an echo.

He commenced eating and drinking wolfishly, and as he conveyed the food to his mouth by the aid of a clasp-knife, his brain was busy.

He was thinking how he could gain admittance to Ralph Ashton's villa.

"It would be easy enough if I had the proper implements," he muttered; "but where there's a will there's a way, and I'll have a try. I'll frighten those puny-faced girls out of their ready cash and jewels, and then I'll make a clean bolt out of the country."

He felt inclined to laugh again, but the memory of the echo he had awakened kept him silent.

"Now, in this old place there is plenty of hidden treasure, I'll be bound, if I only knew where to find it," he said. "The old monks were artful customers, and—"

"They were," said a voice close to his ear.

Bill Blarney started to his feet and struck out madly with the knife, but the blade came in contact with nothing but the air.

"Phew! Who was that?" he gasped, as his face grew damp and his limbs limp with fear. "I don't like this place, and I'll clear out of it. It may be my fancy, but I'd rather indulge it in the open air."

As Bill Blarney strode towards the door he thought he heard the sound of soft footsteps following him.

"Who's there?" he cried. "If you are a man, show yourself!"

There was no reply, and as Bill Blarney reached the door he turned back for a moment, and flashed the light of the lantern into the interior of the building.

There was nothing to be seen, save the grim relics of the past, and the ruffian began to think, that perhaps, after all, he was doing wrong in quitting so snug a hiding-place.

"Who should know that I am here?" he said. "Why, there isn't one man in a hundred who would care to stay here after dark for a minute Ah!"

As the ruffian uttered the exclamation he dropped knife and lantern, and staggered back from the abbey, for he had seen the face of Spring-Heeled Jack peering at him from behind a column.

There was no mistake about it.

He knew the stern but grinning features too well, and with a hoarse cry he flew, dashing up the snow.

As he crossed a rustic bridge he heard Spring-Heeled Jack thundering after him.

The mocking laugh that had often rang in Bill Blarney's ears had now a vengeful and determined ring, and the villain fled on with the swiftness of the wind.

He made for the river bank, and seeing a boat moored to the side was about to enter it, when Spring-Heeled Jack, who seemed to be aware of Blarney's intentions, overtook him.

"Your time has come at last," Spring-Heeled Jack yelled. "Die, you dog—die!"

Bill Blarney turned just in time to see that a pistol was levelled at his head.

He never saw the flash, or heard the report.

A bullet penetrated his brain, and stretched him dead upon the snow.

"The task of many a weary year is almost co pleted," Spring-Heeled Jack said, as he hurled pistol into the river. "Never again will I firearm against man. My sword shall do rest!"

---

## CHAPTER CLXXII.

CORDER PAYS A VISIT TO MILDENDALE HALL AND DEMANDS HIS PRICE—MY LADY KNOWS THE TRUTH.

THE gathering shadows of twilight were hovering about the turrets of Mildendale Hall when Jannette, the wife of Lord Mildendale, arrived.

She was a pretty little French woman, with bright, sparkling eyes and delicately-chiselled features.

She spoke the English language well, and having learnt from her maid the names of some of the principal servants, sent for Lord Mildendale's valet, and asked him how it was that her husband was not at home to meet her.

The man could not give a satisfactory reply.

His lordship, he said, had often been away of late, and never left word when he might be expected to return.

Lady Mildendale, as we must call her, shrugged her shoulders, and looked wistfully at the fire.

"Enough," she said; and dismissed the man with a wave of her hand.

"Would your ladyship please to partake of any refreshment?" the maid asked.

"You may bring me a cup of chocolate, and then retire."

The maid did as she was requested, and having drawn a screen round her mistress, glided softly out of the room.

Lady Mildendale left the beverage untouched.

"When I proposed to come to England, it did not seem to please his lordship," she said, musingly. "But why should he be so anxious to keep me away? Is there some mystery? No, no; I must not get excited. My physician warned me that I had a weak heart, and it would be folly to run a great risk when there may be nothing wrong."

She heard the door open and close, and pushing the screen aside, saw that her maid had entered the room.

"What is it, Joan?" her ladyship demanded. "Did you not understand that I wished to be left alone?"

"Yes, my lady," Joan replied; "but I have come to tell you that there is a man below who says that he brings you a message from Lord Mildendale."

"I will see him," Lady Mildendale replied. "Admit him to my presence without delay."

The girl courtesied, and presently returned with a man, who pulled a lock of coal-black hair as he saw Lady Mildendale.

"What have you come to tell me?" she said.

"Something that no ears but your own must hear, my lady."

"Indeed!" said Lady Mildendale, elevating her arched eyebrows. "Joan, retire. Now," said her ladyship, "perhaps you will tell me your name?"

"Corder."

"And you have brought me a message from Lord Mildendale. I am all anxiety to hear it."

"Well, my lady," said Corder, plucking at a fur cap he held in his hand, "it doesn't exactly come from his lordship, but it concerns him, so—"

"Hold!" Lady Mildendale interposed, as she stretched out her hand towards the bell-rope. "I will hear no more from you. Your presence is an insult to me."

"Ring that bell, my lady," said Corder coolly, "and I will say that which will make your ears and cheeks burn with shame."

"Speak, then."

"I will, if your ladyship will allo[w me]. May I sit down?"

"Yes; but keep your distance fro[m me]."

Corder scowled, and bit his underlip.

"You treat me as you would a dog," he said; "but I will bear that. I have done many a stroke of business for Lord Mildendale. He thinks that I was killed in a fight with some gipsies; but I didn't trouble to contradict him as long as the money lasted, and he paid me well."

"You speak in riddles," Lady Mildendale said. "I do not comprehend the meaning of a word you say."

"You will presently," Corder returned, grinning behind his hand. "I have never said or done anything in a hurry, and I ain't going to begin now."

Lady Mildendale stamped her foot impatiently, and her face grew white, in spite of the glow of the fire.

"I was saying that as long as the money lasted, I didn't care; but now that it is gone, I do," Corder continued. "It is money I want, and money I must have."

"From whom do you expect to get it?"

"From you, my lady."

"From me!" exclaimed Lady Mildendale. "From me, did you say?"

Her full rich mouth parted, displaying a double row of white, pearly teeth, and Corder saw in a moment that he had a dangerous woman to deal with.

"Yes," he said; "and I don't think that you will hesitate to pay me well, when I tell you that I am in the possession of a secret which, if kept, will enable you to keep your position here, or bring you to misery."

Lady Mildendale rose from her chair.

"Enable me to keep my position here?" she said, hoarsely.

"Yes, as Lord Mildendale's wife."

"As Lord Mildendale's wife. Am I not his wife?"

"No."

"Not his wife!" cried Lady Mildendale, clutching at her heart. "How—I— Speak plainly?"

"Well," said Corder, gruffly, "I may as well speak out plainly. Lord Mildendale married just over fourteen years ago, and his wife is still alive."

He put out his hands, thinking that the Frenchwoman was going to spring at him; but she, after glaring at him for a moment, sank into her chair, and buried her face in her hands.

"If what you tell me is true, what a heartless villain Lord Mildendale is, and how wretched a woman am I!" she sobbed.

"It certainly ain't a very comfortable state of things," Corder said. "But, my lady, I wouldn't take on so much about it, if I were you. He married a gipsy, according to the gipsy laws, so—"

"He is her husband in the sight of Heaven," Lady Mildendale cried. "Enough! I will leave this place. I will never look in the false wretch's face. I will return to my own country, and end my days in a convent. Joan—Joan!"

"Hush—hush!" said Corder. "Think twice before you do anything rash."

"Stand back!" the infuriated woman cried. "I have tried to live a good and pure life, and, before Heaven, it is so still, and shall be. I will renounce all claim here for once and for ever. It is I who will tell the secret to the world, and it shall judge between Lord Mildendale and me."

Corder's repulsive face fell.

He had thought to put money in his pocket, and now that he found how great a mistake he had made, he changed his tactics.

"Look 'ere," he said, brutally. "I am not to be trifled with like this. I have travelled many a score of miles to tell you what I knew, and I will be paid for it."

"Out of my path, you detestable hound!" the unhappy woman cried. "Touch me not, or I will raise the house with my cries for help."

The thwarted villain ran to the door and placed his back against it.

Then drawing a pistol, he fixed his eyes full of evil intent upon the noble-hearted lady.

"Listen to me," he said. "If my secret is worth nothing to you, I came here thinking it might be. Do with it as you choose, act as you will, I care not, but I will have my price, or I will kill you."

Lady Mildendale advanced fearlessly towards him, and then stopped.

Again she clutched at her heart, and a death-like pallor spread over her features.

"Oh! this faintness," she gasped. "I was warned, but it is too late. Heaven have mercy upon me, I am dying!"

Terror-stricken at what he had done, Corder replaced the pistol in his pocket, and ran forward to catch the woman.

She warded him off feebly with her hands, and then fell in a dead faint at his feet.

"She may be dead," Corder said. "What shall I do—call for assistance, or—"

"There is no need to do that, for assistance is at hand," said a voice."

Corder uttered a yell as Lanoni, the gipsy queen, appeared from behind the screen.

"You cowardly villain!" she cried. "This is as much your work as if you had shot or stabbed this unhappy woman. Keep your hands from your coat pockets, for I know what you have there, and I have come prepared to deal with you."

"How did you gain admittance to the Hall?" Corder demanded.

"By the right that I am the mother of the true Lady Mildendale."

Lanoni pounced upon him as she spoke, and such was her strength, that she brought him down upon his knees.

"Death you deserve, and death shall be the reward of your iniquities!" she cried. "Your brawny frame, and muscles of iron, will avail you nothing now. Had you the strength of twenty men, I would hold you with this hand, and with this thus do I avenge the insults and cruelties you showered upon me."

"Hold your hand one moment," Corder cried, as the blade of a dagger gleamed before his eyes. "I have heard that the child Amy left me for you. She—"

"I know her history," Lanoni replied. "She was washed ashore from a wreck which you and your dastardly gang lured on to destruction by false lights and beacons. Her parents were saved, and in a few days she will be restored to them. Say no more of earthly things, for in another minute you die."

Corder made an ineffectual attempt to get at the pistol in his pocket, but his right arm rested on Lanoni's, and she did not give him time to carry out his purpose.

She buried the knife in his body, and left him writhing upon the floor.

"This I promised him on the night that I was in his custody."

"Come away!" said a voice, apparently proceeding from behind the screen. "This is an accursed house, and not until it is levelled to the ground and its site tilled by the plough shall its rightful owner take possession of the land."

## CHAPTER CLXXIII.

### SIR ROLAND IS TOLD TO PREPARE FOR THE WORST.

"So," said Sir Roland, "it is all a dream—but what a dream!"

He raised himself upon his elbow and stared vacantly round the handsomely-furnished apartment in which he found himself.

At the side of the couch on which he was reclining stood a small table, and upon it a decanter, apparently half-full of wine.

"This must be the sitting-room of the Cow and Cucumber," he said; "but, no. The truth dawns upon me. I remember the appearance of Spring-Heeled Jack—I feel his fingers of steel upon my throat. The papers—the papers."

With trembling fingers he searched in his breast pocket.

It was empty.

With a moan and a suppressed curse Sir Roland Ashton turned upon his side.

"Lost—lost!" he said. "The secret I have kept so long, and which I thought would die with me, will be made known. Fool that I was not to burn the papers!"

"I should have been the greater fool to let you do so," said a voice.

Sir Roland had scarcely time to utter an exclamation of rage before Ralph Ashton stood before him.

"My bitterest curse light upon your head!" Sir Roland said, springing up, and seizing the neck of the decanter. "By all that is unholy I will have your life!"

"My life!" Ralph replied, drawing his sword, and speaking calmly and deliberately. "You had better look to your own. Don't lose your temper, or attempt to do anything foolish, or you may have less time to live upon this earth even than I intended to grant you."

"You grant me!" Sir Roland hectored. "By what right?"

Ralph Ashton silenced him with a loud, ringing laugh.

Sir Roland's face turned pale, and then flushed red to the roots of his hair.

"I have heard that laugh before, but not from your lips," he said. "Are you—"

"I am the only son of Sir Guy Ashton, as you know, and when you—coward—villain—murderer—forger—as you dubbed me falsely, but which I now accuse you of being in good truth—are dead I shall gain my own."

Sir Roland bit his underlip and remained silent for a space.

"This is not the first time that you have thought you held me in your power," he said, "and I will thwart you yet."

"We shall see," Ralph replied, calmly. "Let me tell you a little story. When Sir Guy Ashton died, his only son mysteriously disappeared. He was spirited away, and placed in the hands of a distant relation, who was foolish and wicked enough to take a bribe from you."

"It is a lie!" Sir Roland gasped. "What proofs have you?"

"The proofs Caleb Masters, your secretary, robbed me of when I came to Ashton Hall a mere lad. The proofs, Sir Roland, which Spring-Heeled Jack took from you only last night. See, here are the papers, and I am grateful to you for preserving them in such good order."

Sir Roland hissed out an awful imprecation through his closed teeth.

"You had better drink a glass of wine," Ralph said, "as you have to listen to a good many things yet, and some will not sound very pleasant to your ears."

"As a boy you were an exquisite liar, and you have improved in the art."

Ralph Ashton inclined his head and made Sir Roland a mock bow.

"There are some men who see themselves in others," he said. "Think not to move me to senseless anger by such words. I have come here to perform a duty, and neither taunt nor insult shall deter me from it.

"From the moment that you hired the ruffian Ned Wilmot to murder Herbert Leigh and drove me from the place of my birth your conscience began to speak.

"Knowing that no farthing was your own and that you had no claim to an inch of land, you squandered both.

"You flung money about like water and mortgaged the estates, and having done that, and finding that even such a man as Gedge Foote would not lend you a shilling, you, and a fellow villain, named Bill Blarney, foully murdered him."

"You seem to be well acquainted with the movements of my past life," Sir Roland said, sneeringly.

"There I give you the credit of speaking the truth," Ralph returned. "Morn, noon, and night, either I or one of my agents have had you in sight."

Sir Roland started again, and though he exerted all his self-control, he trembled in every limb.

"Herbert Leigh, my father's cousin, was murdered by your direction, because a part of the estates would eventually come to him. I presume that you will admit that?"

"I admit nothing," Sir Roland replied, hoarsely, and gnashing his teeth furiously.

"Well, then, you know it now," Ralph said. "He lent my father money; but all is gone—stolen and squandered by you.

"But his daughter, Daisy, found a friend in the being who rescued her from your toils—the very being who has thwarted you in every way and brought you here to listen to the story of your base life—Spring-Heeled Jack!"

Sir Roland closed his eyes as if he was half-afraid the weird creature would start up at his feet.

"The opportunities you have had to reform and lead a better life have been flung away," Ralph Ashton went on. "All the associates of your base crimes are dead and gone—Mrs. Corcoran, Bill Blarney, Joe Morth, and a score of others have paid the penalty, and you are the last."

"The last?" Sir Roland repeated.

"Yes; and let my words ring a death-knell in your ears," Ralph Ashton said. "But I will again refer to Daisy Leigh. The money you thought to rob Gedge Foote of is hers—the gift of Spring-Heeled Jack. It was not two thousand pounds, as you supposed, but twenty, and she and the lover of her choice, Harry Banks, will live as man and wife to apply the gold to better purposes than it was intended."

This was too much for Sir Roland to hear.

Leaping to his feet, he made a rush at Ralph, but recoiled as the point of the young man's rapier touched his breast.

"I have no wish to kill you yet unless you force me to do so," Ralph said. "Go back! Sit down and make your peace, if you can. We shall meet again—once more."

So saying, he turned upon his heel and left the room.

The next instant Harry Banks and Palmer appeared.

Sir Roland started as if he had been stung as they approached.

"You don't seem comfortable," Harry Banks said. "I am the bearer of a message to you."

"Curse you and your message!" Sir Roland said, growling.

"A man who stands on the brink of the grave, as you do, should find better words," Banks said. "Well, I will deliver the message whether you like it or not. It comes jointly from Constance and Daisy. They send you their forgiveness."

"Indeed," Sir Roland returned. "I never asked for it, nor do I need it."

Then came a pause, which was broken by Sir Roland.

"I am your prisoner, and you are my warder," he said.

"Yes."

"Where am I?"

"It is strange that you should have forgotten this room, considering that you have been in it hundreds of times," Harry Banks replied; "but since it may have been a little altered in appearance I will tell you. This is the inner library of Ashton Hall."

"Ashton Hall!" Sir Roland cried.

"Yes," Banks returned. "A sum of money has been paid down, and the rightful owner is in possession of the place."

"I will not believe it," Sir Roland raved. "It is a lie to deceive me."

"You will find out too soon that I have spoken nothing but the truth," Harry Banks said. "This is indeed Ashton Hall, and if I choosed I could convince you of it in a moment."

"How?"

"By opening yonder doors and showing you the picture gallery."

"Do so then," said Sir Roland, with a sudden gleam in his eyes.

"That would be going in direct opposition to my instructions, which I do not intend to do," Harry Banks said.

Here Palmer rose, and striding heavily across the room tried the doors with his hand.

"All is safe," he said.

"Speak no more to me," Sir Roland said; "I wish to be occupied with my thoughts."

## CHAPTER CLXXIV.

### NANA.

In an easy chair of a room, looking out upon as pleasant a scene as the wintry weather afforded, sat a dark-eyed and dark-haired woman about thirty-five years of age.

She was ill, as her pale face and the pillows against which she rested testified.

On a footstool at her feet sat Daisy Leigh.

She held the sick woman's hand and looked up into her eyes.

"Nana," Daisy said, "you are better to-day. When I came into the room suddenly quite a colour sprang into your face."

"I was dreaming," Nana said; "and you startled me."

"Dreaming?"

"Yes; a pleasant dream," Nana replied. "I thought that I nursed my child upon my knee again."

"I have often wondered if your son lives," Daisy said; "he should be a fine lad."

Daisy's voice trembled, and she looked towards the door as if she expected to see somebody there.

"Hush!" Nana said. "Such words, even kindly meant, as I know them to be, only bring trouble to my poor weary brain."

She was very beautiful still, in spite of the deep lines upon her face, and as she spoke her eyes sparkled with a light which told how lustrous and beautiful they once had been.

"You must forgive me," Daisy continued, nervously; "but sometimes I cannot help thinking that there is yet a happy time for you."

"Not here—not here!" Nana said. "I have suffered too much to trust in that. My hopes are no longer fixed on this earth. Has my mother called to-day?"

"No; but she will come."

"How I wish she would!" Nana said. "Was it fancy, or did I hear the sound of a boy's musical voice singing?"

"You did," Daisy replied. "He was singing a song taught him by Namon Wallack."

"Poor Namon—poor Namon!" Nana murmured. "How he loved me! Oh! that I had never thrown that love aside like a soiled glove."

"As I said of you, so I say of him," Daisy said. "There may be happier times in store. Heaven grant that it may be so."

"Tap! tap! tap!" came very gently at the door.

"Come in!" said Daisy.

The door opened, and Namon Wallack stood face to face with Nana.

He had not seen her for many a year—not since her mother sent her to Spain, which happened soon after Lord Mildendale's villainy was brought to light.

"Nana," he said, keeping his eyes fixed upon the ground, "I know that I have taken a great liberty, but when I knew that you were under Ralph Ashton's roof I could not keep away."

"And why should you?" Nana said. "I am too weak to rise, but here is my hand, Namon. It is I who should shrink and feel ashamed to see you. Say to me, Nana, I forgive you, and a great weight will be lifted from my heart."

Not only did Namon Wallack take her hand, but he fell on his knees at her side.

"Nay!" he said. "Why should you trouble yourself about the past? It cannot be recalled, so bid it begone from your memory. You have not seen Lanoni to-day?"

"No."

"Indeed!" Namon said, evasively, and glancing at Daisy Leigh, "I thought she would have come early to bring you the news."

"News — what news?" Nana demanded. "Namon, I see by the expression of your eyes that you have something to tell me. Whether it be for good or for evil, let me hear it?"

"If I thought you would be brave I would, but—"

"There is some of the old blood in me yet," Nana interposed, proudly. "I have borne bodily pain, and I can hear the word which would bring me more affliction without fincing."

"Nana," briefly then said Namon Wallack, "your husband has ceased to exist."

Nana closed her eyes for a moment, and a gasping cry welled up from her heart.

"I have killed her!" Namon wailed.

"No—no," Nana said. "Dead! How did he die? Tell me quickly."

"He was killed in a duel."

"With whom?"

"It is not known precisely," Namon Wallack replied, with another sharp and meaning glance at Daisy Leigh. "I—I— Well, Nana, a lad was placed in my care by Ralph Ashton. For some reason of his own, Lord Mildendale employed a set of rascals to take the boy from me; but there came upon the scene another being, called Spring-Heeled Jack, who restored the boy to Ralph Ashton. It is supposed that Spring-Heeled Jack must have met Lord Mildendale and killed him."

Nana remained silent for some minutes, seemingly fully occupied with her thoughts.

"Dead!" she said at last. "Dead, and not a word from him."

"It is better as it is," Namon said. "He lived sufficient time to utter a few words. He asked your forgiveness, and his son's, who—who—"

"Yes?"

"Was so cruelly taken away from you."

"Taken away for ever."

"Not so," Namon cried. "Now Heaven give you strength to bear this joy. Your son lives! He is in the very house. Robin—Robin! Fly to your mother's arms. Her poor, weary heart is yearning for your embrace."

Smiling all over her pretty face, Constance led Robin in.

We will not dwell upon the meeting of mother and son so long parted, but pass on to another scene, and bid farewell to two characters who have from time to time played an important part in our story.

---

## CHAPTER CLXXV.

### CATCHPOLE AND GRABHAM RETIRE INTO PRIVATE LIFE.

HAVING failed to capture Bill Blarney on that eventful night, Catchpole and Grabham went back to Bow-street with a long story to Nabbitt, to the effect that though they had failed, they hoped for better luck at some future time.

Mr. Nabbitt fairly squinted in his rage as he glared at the unhappy constables.

"Perhaps you will tell me what you were doing at the Bull in Top Boots?" he demanded.

"Well, you see, sir," Grabham replied, "we thought as how Bill Blarney might have sneaked back to his old quarters."

"Why did you not acquaint me with your suspicions?" Nabbitt thundered. "How dare you do anything without orders—eh? What do you mean by it? How did you get into the house?"

"Through a window," gasped Catchpole.

"And, pray, who told you to crawl through a window?"

"Nobody."

"Oh—oh!" cried Nabbitt. "This looks very suspicious. I will send a description of Blarney round to the out-lying stations, and then think what is the best thing to do with you. It strikes me that I ought to put you under lock and key without delay."

"Mercy!" Grabham groaned. "We thought that we were doing everything for the best."

"So we did," Catchpole chimed in. "I'll take my dying oath of it."

"It's my firm opinion," said Mr. Nabbitt, shaking a fat forefinger at the trembling constables, "that you thought you would find plenty to drink or something worth taking away at the Bull in Top Boots."

"Oh! sir," moaned Catchpole, "how can you go for to say sich a thing?"

"It's jolly hard to be treated like this after what we have done and what we have suffered in the force," Grabham said. "I wish I was out of it."

"Then take your wish, you good-for-nothing, interfering scoundrel!" Nabbitt roared. "If it hadn't been for your muddling Bill Blarney would have been here long ago, and that jumping fiend Spring-Heeled Jack, too."

"I ain't going without my money," said Grabham, bridling up. "There was a reward for Ted Nickells and Jem Basker, and I'll have my share of it, or know the reason why."

"Hear—hear, old boy!" cried Catchpole, becoming suddenly valiant. "I'm with you in that."

Mr. Nabbitt swelled out with indignation until he appeared to be double his size.

"I discharge you both!" he blurted out, "and let that suffice for the present. If you don't go I'll have you before the magistrate in the morning, and committed to prison for gross insubordination."

"Can't be done if we are out of the force," said Grabham, grinning. "I accept my discharge, and sha'n't look to you for justice The Home Office issued the reward, and will pay me fairly enough, I know."

"And now," said Catchpole, shaking his fist so close to Mr. Nabbitt's nose that he shrank back to prevent an unpleasant collision; "just hear a word from me. You're a jumped-up Jack-in-office, that's what you are—a jumped-up Jack-in-office! A feller who stands and looks on while other people do all the work. Lor'! I'd give something for the pleasure of pulling your fat nose, that I would! I'd make you howl, and skip, and dance!"

Nabbitt skipped and danced off his stool, and, armed with a ruler weighing about a pound, made such a sudden rush at Catchpole that he had no time to get out of the way.

Catchpole succeeded in wrenching the ruler out of the inspector's grasp, and then in an instant they were locked together in a wild and fierce embrace.

They rattled about all over the floor in a truly exhilarating fashion, planting blows here, there, and, in fact, anywhere.

Of course Grabham went to the rescue of his bosom friend Catchpole!

Alas! he did nothing of the kind, but hastened into the street, arguing that the conflict had nothing to do with him and he was best out of it.

In about five minutes Catchpole staggered out with all the signs of a sound thrashing upon him.

Both eyes were swollen to an alarming extent, his lips appeared to have been converted into sausages, and there was no skin to speak of upon his nose.

"I let him have it," he said, forgetting his own injuries in the excitement of the moment. "He's a-layin' in the fender, grinning like a monkey at the ceiling."

"Perhaps he won't get over it?" Grabham suggested.

"If he don't it won't be my fault," Catchpole said. "He set on me first. You saw that, and can prove it."

"The fact is," Grabham returned. "I didn't see much of the affair. I thought I heard somebody holler fire outside, so I thought it my duty to see if it was true."

What Catchpole would have said it is impossible to guess, but at that moment his battered features claimed all his attention.

"It seems to me," he said, as tears of agony rushed into his eyes, "that I haven't had it all my own way."

"I thought so too, but didn't like to say so," Grabham remarked. "But come along, a bit of raw beef will soon put you to rights. Nabbitt will keep quiet over this affair and say nothing about his share of the walloping."

"I wish he had kept the whole of it!" Catchpole said, as he wiped his nose with the greatest tenderness. "My face seems to be all over alike—a red-hot jelly, with a dab of cold putty here and there."

"Bear it," said Grabham. "The pain will soon be over."

. . . . . . .

Some days elapsed before the valiant officers presented themselves at Bow-street again, and then they were sent for to receive twenty guineas a-piece for services rendered at Buckler's-rents.

What became of them after that nobody knows, and probably nobody cared, and so we let them go with all their faults and follies.

## CHAPTER CLXXVI.

### THE BROKEN SWORD.

SIR ROLAND fell into a slumber, and slept the sleep of a man who, when he awakes, knows that he must stand face to face with death.

What strange dreams came to him as he lay there, closely watched by the two stern and silent men.

He murmured out incoherent words, and his fingers twitched convulsively.

He was living his life over again.

Back to the scenes of his youth his imagination took him—back to the evil companions he had chosen it took him, bringing each one and each crime committed by him and them with vivid force before his eyes.

And yet he knew that he was dreaming; for, though asleep, he remembered that Ralph Ashton had told him that they were dead, and he was the only one living.

Living but to die before the years allotted to him had been fulfilled!

One by one the shadowy forms passed before him.

Mrs. Corcoran mocked and gibed at him, Bill Blarney cursed him, and the whole tribe of spectres had something to say, or some act to perform to remind him of the miserable past.

But amid all there was one form he could not make out, or understand why it should come to him.

It was a black figure, shrouded from head to foot.

Silent and motionless it stood, its head inclined as if peering through its sable garb at the sleeping man.

Suddenly the folds melted away, and Sir Roland saw a grizzly skeleton standing before him.

The bones were entirely fleshless, but eyes, bright and awful eyes, glittered and rattled in the sockets of the skull.

The unhappy man awoke with a start and a shriek.

"No—no!" he cried; "not yet. Back, gaunt and fearful apparition. Ha! Then it was not a reality, but a dream!"

He turned his head to Harry Banks as he spoke, and seemed to be much relieved to find that he was not alone.

"What time is it?" he asked.

"Five."

"The afternoon or the morning?" demanded Sir Roland. "I know nothing as to how the time goes. Day and night are all the same to me now."

"It is the morning," Harry Banks replied; "and yonder doors will be opened to you as the clock strikes eight."

"Then I am to go free?" Sir Roland said, as a ray of hope darted into his head. "Ralph Ashton has relented—he has forgiven me! I did not expect this from him of all men."

"I say no more than that you will be allowed to pass from this room into the next unattended."

"There is no new misery for me?" Sir Roland said, groaning. "Some fresh plot to harrow up my feelings?"

"There is no plot," Harry Banks said; "and as for misery, who have you to blame for it but yourself?"

"Let the justice of my country deal with me," Sir Roland returned, as he rose and paced the room with nervous and unsteady steps; "I demand a fair trial. I have much to say, and there are many things I wish to put in their proper light."

"Fear not," Harry Banks replied. "The trial you will have to undergo will be fair, and ought to be to your taste. Silence, now, for I will say no more."

As Sir Roland resumed his seat, his eyes fell upon the decanter of wine.

"May I drink?" he asked.

"Yes; but I should advise you to be careful of how you do so."

Sir Roland merely emptied the decanter, and lay down again.

The wine warmed his blood, and though his brain was tortured by a hundred conflicting emotions, he slumbered again.

When he awoke he was alone.

A dim light that "counterfeited a gloom" was struggling through the curtains.

The cold, wintry morn had dawned.

"Alone!" Sir Roland said, as he went to the window.

Snow was still falling, and the landscape looked enchanting in its white apparel.

As his eyes wandered across the park he remembered every tree and every object.

The place was never his own, and never could be; but he might have participated in its pleasures, and grasped the hand of Ralph Ashton as a friend.

All such notions were hopelessly gone for ever, and tears, blinding, unbidden tears, softened the heart of the hardened man for a moment.

There was no escape from the window, as a row of spiked bars prevented it.

They seemed to have been lately put up, for the steel of which they were made was bright and devoid of rust.

Sir Roland turned back into the room.

"I must have more wine," he said. "I feel that a crisis is at hand, and I must nerve myself for whatever may happen."

The decanter and glasses had been removed, and a sword lay in their place.

"What is this?" Sir Roland cried, in astonishment. "Surely this must have been left here by mistake."

He took the sword in his hand, and tried its suppleness by thrusting the point into the floor and bending it to and fro.

There was no mistake about the quality of the metal.

It was as lithe and limber as a cane, and bent from hilt to point.

Sir Roland tested the edge and point on his thumb, and found the blade perfect in every respect.

Then a new sensation came over him.

He felt more assured now that he had the means of defending his life in his hand; but suddenly he dropped the sword as if it had stung him, for on the groove, close to the hilt, he read these words—

"*The first and last present from Ralph Ashton.*"

"Curse him!" he hissed. "It may be that I shall return the gift."

"I accept the challenge in his name," cried a voice.

The folding doors, leading into the picture-gallery, flew open, and Spring-Heeled Jack appeared.

"What have I to do with you," Sir Roland cried, recoiling, "or you with me?"

"Much," Spring-Heeled Jack replied, sternly. "Pick up that sword, Sir Roland, and follow me."

"I refuse," Sir Roland replied.

"Beware!" Spring-Heeled Jack said. "If you refuse, you will compel me to use force, which I should be loth to do in such an hour as this."

Sir Roland's face went blue with terror as he stooped and recovered the weapon.

"You have some other name than that you are known to the world by?"

"I have."

"Reveal it to me."

"It shall be revealed to you as the turret clock chimes a quarter past eight," Spring-Heeled Jack replied. "Come with me."

"I am helpless here, and must obey," Sir Roland said. "Lead on, and I will follow you."

The terrible features of Spring-Heeled Jack relaxed into a smile.

"I will repeat a well-worn adage to you," he said. "'An old bird is not to be caught with chaff.' I do not forget that you have a sword in your hand, nor that you would use it if I turned my back upon you for a moment. It is you who must go first. I will direct you, and tell you when to stop."

Sir Roland's face lengthened.

Spring-Heeled Jack had rightly guessed his intentions.

"Would that I had had the opportunity of killing you long ago," Sir Roland hissed. "Such an act would have saved me very much trouble and misery."

"I grant you the trouble," Spring-Heeled Jack retorted; "for you would have remained the undisputed master of Ashton Hall."

Sir Roland started as he gazed at the weird creature.

Spring-Heeled Jack's peculiar dress had sometimes been red, and at others white, but now it assumed a dull, black hue, as if some other garb was worn under it.

His frame had a more bulky appearance, and Sir Roland noticed that he did not seem to be so tall by several inches.

Again Spring-Heeled Jack smiled as he beheld Sir Roland's discomfiture, but there was more of sadness than of mirth in the expression.

The false baronet, swinging the sword in his hand, marched through the picture-gallery until he came to a room from which most of the furniture had been cleared.

"Halt!" cried Spring-Heeled Jack. "It is here that you must atone for the past, Sir Roland."

"Atone to whom?"

"To outraged Heaven and to me!"

"Ralph Ashton told me that I had to answer to him."

At that moment came a metallic sound.

Spring-Heeled Jack's appearance began to alter.

His dress, as it were, crumpled up, and fell loosely upon the floor, and Ralph Ashton stood face to face with his deadly foe."

"Ah!" gasped Sir Roland, "the secret is out at last. I had often expected that you were the villain who has been the terror of London and the whole country."

"I took this character when I was young, not to plunder and kill the helpless and weak, as you have done," Ralph Ashton said, as he drew a sword that hung at his side. "I assumed it to help them, and to punish their wicked persecutors. In that I have prospered beyond my fondest expectations. I have succeeded in bringing you here for the last time, as I swore I would do."

In spite of the position in which he stood the false baronet could not help feeling a little curious.

He gazed in wonder at the skin-like dress, which though now harmless and inactive, had something demoniac in its appearance.

The ghastly headpiece still seemed to mock and gibe, and its huge mouth gaped even wider than of yore.

"You wish to understand why they gave me such power?" Ralph Ashton said. "I will presently make that known to many who are interested, but to you it must ever remain a mystery."

"For ever?"

"Unless you rise from the grave in the spirit and hear what I say," Ralph Ashton said. "Now, listen to me, and these words will be the last you will hear from my lips. My vow is nearly accomplished, but I have not brought you here to take a mean advantage. It was I who ordered the sword to be put within your reach and—"

"For that I thank you," said the false baronet, interrupting him.

Ralph Ashton made an impatient movement with his hand.

"Silence!" he said. "I hurl your thanks, as I have hurled your threats, back into your teeth. Once I left you for dead, and more than once we have met in open combat. I have always treated you fairly, and have met with attemped treachery. And now, by Heaven! base villain, I swear that one or the other must cease to live. I have right on my side, and fear nothing. Draw coward, and prepare yourself for the worst."

Sir Roland's face grew livid.

"This has come upon me too suddenly," he said. "Give me an hour to reflect, and then I will fight you."

"I will not give you another instant," Ralph Ashton replied.

"But hear me—"

"Not another word," Ralph thundered. "You seek extra time to commit some act of treachery."

"Come, then," Sir Roland cried, as a fierce light darted into his eyes. "A man can die but once."

Their swords and eyes met at the same moment.

It was to be a duel to the death.

Both had fully made up their minds to that, and several swift passes were exchanged, in which Ralph Ashton received a slight wound in the arm.

"You fight well," Ralph said. "You have had your wish in part, for you have drawn my blood."

The fight commenced again.

Sir Roland tried to beat down Ralph Ashton's guard; but failing in that, he delivered a series of thrusts so rapidly that the younger man had to exert all his knowledge in the art of fencing to keep him off.

But Ralph was the cooler of the two, and the self-control he put upon himself prevailed in the end.

Suddenly he whipped his rapier round Sir Roland's.

Then came the snapping sound of a broken blade, and the death-yell of the false baronet as he fell, stabbed through the heart, at Ralph's feet.

"Here lies Sir Roland," Ralph said, "and here ends my part as Spring-Heeled Jack."

## CHAPTER CLXXVII.

### AN EXPLANATION—FAREWELL.

WE have followed Ralph Ashton, as a persecuted gentleman and as Spring-Heeled Jack, through a series of extraordinary adventures, and, after a few words of explanation, we shall reluctantly bid adieu to the reader.

The hideous dresses in which Ralph Ashton personated so extraordinary a character were marvels of mechanism.

They had been the labour of many months, and he had worked at them in secret through many a long night.

The dresses were two in number, and composed of chamois leather—one dyed a blood-red colour, and the other bleached snow-white.

From the hips to the ankles ran steel bars, so joined as to work freely with the limbs, and these were attached to a number of springs forming the soles and toes of the false feet, upon which Ralph's own rested.

When stooping for a leap the steel bars gave tremendous force to the springs, pressing them down and sending him forward with a bound which astonished and alarmed everybody with whom he came in contact.

Ralph Ashton practised for a long time before he ventured to make his appearance in public, and by degrees he learned to moderate his leaps according to the circumstances needed and to walk like an ordinary individual.

For a year and a day after Sir Roland's death Ralph kept the dresses locked in a chest.

One morning—it was the morning of his wedding-day—he rose, and drawing the ghastly objects from their resting-place, made a fire of them.

"Constance must not know yet," he said. "It will be time enough to tell her when we are man and wife, and have settled down."

A mighty concourse of people lined the road and filled the old church at Barnet to see Ralph Ashton married to Constance; and when the ceremony was over, Ralph had to shake so many outstretched hands that his own fairly ached.

He had found a rich reward in the blushing bride that clung lovingly to his arm, and Ralph experienced not a little pleasure when he heard the rustic folk shouting with glee that the real owner of Ashton Hall was about to live in their midst.

There was no end to the rejoicings—fireworks in the park after Ralph and his wife had departed for Paris to spend the honeymoon; a huge bonfire on the village green, and every man, woman, and child, in their very best holiday attire, made merry long after their wonted time to be abroad.

One thing was certain.

There was a tremendous quantity of sound old ale quaffed, and stacks of good English beef eaten during the day and evening, and there is a rumour to the effect that the band engaged to amuse the rustics left off playing for four hours, and fell asleep in consequence of an excess of good things.

But when they woke up refreshed how they played, and how the people danced.

A few days after Harry Banks and Daisy Leigh were quietly married, and remained at Ashton Hall, where they stayed until Ralph Ashton and his bonny wife returned.

Harry Banks, though a rich man, thanks to the kindness of Ralph Ashton, did not care to lead an idle life, so he leased a theatre in London, and was eminently successful in the venture; but Daisy never put foot upon the boards again, and her husband, after a time, began to think that some quieter occupation would be more suitable to him, so he bought a farm near Barnet, and, having thrown his heart into his new profession, flourished famously.

Palmer retired from the scene with a good round sum of money, and took his departure for South America, where fortune smiled upon him as well as brought him a good wife.

Strange, dark-featured men and women often paid a visit to Ashton Hall, for Ralph never forgot those who were kind to him, and the gipsies were ever welcome.

Nana did not die.

She grew better by degrees, and she and her son Robin went abroad for some time.

During that time her claims to the Mildendale estates were made good, Ralph Ashton taking the case up, and succeeding so well that in less than a year he sent for Lady Mildendale and her son.

Meanwhile, the old hall at Mildendale had been pulled down and another built.

Nana and Robin never knew by whose hand Lord Mildendale fell.

One day, in the early springtime, Namon Wallack went to Mildendale Hall, by invitation.

He was met there by Ralph Ashton, his wife, and several other friends, and at eventide, when he stood hand in hand with our hero, there was a happy glow upon his face.

"I can almost guess what has happened," Ralph said. "You have spoken to Nana, and you will one day come to this place, not as a friend or a guest, but to claim Nana as your wife."

"I hardly know what to say to that," Namon replied. "I did not speak to her of our old love, but I read in her eyes that she was glad to see me, and her hand trembled, as it trembled in days gone by, when she bade me Good-night."

"And she will be your wife in good time," Ralph replied. "I have thought so all through the time of trouble which has now passed away."

Time flew on, and ere the snow of another winter had begun to fall Nana confessed that the love she once bore to Naman Wallack had found a fresh place in her heart, and they were married when the Christmas bells were flinging their glad tidings in musical cadence far and wide.

Robin went to school and soon forged ahead along the stony path of knowledge, and at the age of eighteen he went to college, and remained there until he came of age, when he took the title which was his own by birth.

He then fell in love with and married the daughter of a rich gentleman in Berkshire, but his mother and his step-father remained at Mildendale Hall, and a happy family soon filled the place and made it bright with infants' prattle and childish laughter.

Ralph Ashton and his wife were blessed with a family, as were also Mr. and Mrs. Banks, and when all met, as they did on every Christmas day, Ashton Hall was as full as it could fairly be.

One Christmas Eve Sir Ralph and Lady Constance were waiting the arrival of the guests.

"Ralph," said Constance, "I have had something on my mind which I have often wished to ask you about. It is nothing much; only a suspicion. It is a long time since we have heard anything of Spring-Heeled Jack."

"You will never hear of him again. You suspect—"

"That you played the character."

"Well," said Sir Ralph, "I have some suspicion of that myself. But Spring-Heeled Jack is dead, and I am alive. Let him rest. He played his part so well that you and I, sitting by this fireside, owe him some thanks."

"I owe all to you, Ralph, my love," Constance replied. "Yes; even my life."

"See—see!" Ralph exclaimed, starting up. "Here comes Lord Mildendale's four-in-hand across the park. Let us greet our friends at the door, and wish them a merry Christmas, long lives, and lasting happiness."

THE END.

www.ingramcontent.com/pod-product-compliance
Lightning Source LLC
Chambersburg PA
CBHW080942020726
47505CB00009B/2119